I0763277

The Novels of Henry Fielding

By

Henry Fielding

Cover Photograph: Evan Leeson

ISBN: 978-1-78139-475-5

Contents

THE HISTORY OF TOM JONES, A FOUNDLING

BOOK I.

BOOK II.

BOOK III.

BOOK IV.

BOOK V.

BOOK VI.

BOOK VII.

BOOK VIII.

BOOK XII.

BOOK XIII.

BOOK XIV.

BOOK XV.

BOOK XVI.

BOOK XVII.

BOOK XVIII.

THE HISTORY OF THE ADVENTURES OF JOSEPH ANDREWS AND HIS FRIEND MR ABRAHAM ADAMS

BOOK III.

BOOK IV.

AN APOLOGY FOR THE LIFE OF MRS. SHAMELA ANDREWS.

THE HISTORY OF TOM JONES, A FOUNDLING

By Henry Fielding

To the Honourable
GEORGE LYTTLETON, ESQ;

One of the Lords Commissioners of the Treasury.

Sir,

Notwithstanding your constant refusal, when I have asked leave to prefix your name to this dedication, I must still insist on my right to desire your protection of this work.

To you, Sir, it is owing that this history was ever begun. It was by your desire that I first thought of such a composition. So many years have since past, that you may have, perhaps, forgotten this circumstance: but your desires are to me in the nature of commands; and the impression of them is never to be erased from my memory.

Again, Sir, without your assistance this history had never been completed. Be not startled at the assertion. I do not intend to draw on you the suspicion of being a romance writer. I mean no more than that I partly owe to you my existence during great part of the time which I have employed in composing it: another matter which it may be necessary to remind you of; since there are certain actions of which you are apt to be extremely forgetful; but of these I hope I shall always have a better memory than yourself.

Lastly, It is owing to you that the history appears what it now is. If there be in this work, as some have been pleased to say, a stronger picture of a truly benevolent mind than is to be found in any other, who that knows you, and a particular acquaintance of yours, will doubt whence that benevolence hath been copied? The world will not, I believe, make me the compliment of thinking I took it from myself. I care not: this they shall own, that the two persons from whom I have taken it, that is to say, two of the best and worthiest men in the world, are strongly and zealously my friends. I might be contented with this, and yet my vanity will add a third to the number; and him one of the greatest and noblest, not only in his rank, but in every public and private virtue. But here, whilst my gratitude for the princely benefactions of the Duke of Bedford bursts from my heart, you must forgive my reminding you that it was you who first recommended me to the notice of my benefactor.

And what are your objections to the allowance of the honour which I have solicited? Why, you have commended the book so warmly, that you should be ashamed of reading your name before the dedication. Indeed, sir, if the book itself doth not make you ashamed of your commendations, nothing that I can here write will, or ought. I am not to give up my right to your protection and patronage, because you have commended my book: for though I acknowledge so many obligations to you, I do not add this to the **number**; in which friendship, I am convinced, hath so little share: since that can neither biass your judgment, nor pervert your integrity. An enemy may at any time obtain your commendation by only deserving it; and the utmost which the faults of your friends can hope for, is your silence; or, perhaps, if too severely accused, your gentle palliation.

In short, sir, I suspect, that your dislike of public praise is your true objection to granting my request. I have observed that you have, in common with my two other friends, an unwillingness to hear the least mention of your own virtues; that, as a great poet says of one of you, (he might justly have said it of all three), you

Do good by stealth, and blush to find it fame.

If men of this disposition are as careful to shun applause, as others are to escape censure, how just must be your apprehension of your character falling into my hands; since what would not a man have reason to dread, if attacked by an author who had received from him injuries equal to my obligations to you!

And will not this dread of censure increase in proportion to the matter which a man is conscious of having afforded for it? If his whole life, for instance, should have been one continued subject of satire, he may well tremble when an incensed satirist takes him in hand. Now, sir, if we apply this to your modest aversion to panegyric, how reasonable will your fears of me appear!

Yet surely you might have gratified my ambition, from this single confidence, that I shall always prefer the indulgence of your inclinations to the satisfaction of my own. A very strong instance of which I shall give you in this address, in which I am determined to follow the example of all other dedicators, and will consider not what my patron really deserves to have written, but what he will be best pleased to read.

Without further preface then, I here present you with the labours of some years of my life. What merit these labours have is already known to yourself. If, from your favourable judgment, I have conceived some esteem for them, it cannot be imputed to vanity; since I should have agreed as implicitly to your opinion, had it been given in favour of any other man's production. Negatively, at least, I may be allowed to say, that had I been sensible of any great demerit in the work, you are the last person to whose protection I would have ventured to recommend it.

From the name of my patron, indeed, I hope my reader will be convinced, at his very entrance on this work, that he will find in the whole course of it nothing prejudicial to the cause of religion and virtue, nothing inconsistent with the strictest rules of decency, nor which can offend even the chastest eye in the perusal. On the contrary, I declare, that to recommend goodness and innocence hath been my sincere endeavour in this history. This honest purpose you have been pleased to think I have attained: and to say the truth, it is likeliest to be attained in books of this kind; for an example is a kind of picture, in which virtue becomes, as it were, an object of sight, and strikes us with an idea of that loveliness, which Plato asserts there is in her naked charms.

Besides displaying that beauty of virtue which may attract the admiration of mankind, I have attempted to engage a stronger motive to human action in her favour, by convincing men, that their true interest directs them to a pursuit of her. For this purpose I have shown that no acquisitions of guilt can compensate the loss of that solid inward comfort of mind, which is the sure companion of innocence and virtue; nor can in the least balance the evil of that horror and anxiety which, in their room, guilt introduces into our bosoms. And again, that as these acquisitions are in themselves generally worthless, so are the means to attain them not only base and infamous, but at best incertain, and always full of danger. Lastly, I have endeavoured strongly to inculcate, that virtue and innocence can scarce ever be injured but by indiscretion; and that it is this alone which often betrays them into the snares that deceit and villainy spread for them. A moral which I have the more industriously laboured, as the teaching it is, of all others, the likeliest to be attended with success; since, I believe, it is much easier to make good men wise, than to make bad men good.

For these purposes I have employed all the wit and humour of which I am master in the following history; wherein I have endeavoured to laugh mankind out of their favourite follies and vices. How far I have succeeded in this good attempt, I shall submit to the candid reader, with only two requests: First, that he will not expect to find perfection in this work; and Secondly, that he will excuse some parts of it, if they fall short of that little merit which I hope may appear in others.

I will detain you, sir, no longer. Indeed I have run into a preface, while I professed to write a dedication. But how can it be otherwise? I dare not praise you; and the only means I know of to avoid it, when you are in my thoughts, are either to be entirely silent, or to turn my thoughts to some other subject.

Pardon, therefore, what I have said in this epistle, not only without your consent, but absolutely against it; and give me at least leave, in this public manner, to declare that I am, with the highest respect and gratitude,—

Sir,
Your most obliged,
Obedient, humble servant,
HENRY FIELDING.

BOOK I.

CONTAINING AS MUCH OF THE BIRTH OF THE FOUNDLING AS IS NECESSARY OR PROPER TO ACQUAINT THE READER WITH IN THE BEGINNING OF THIS HISTORY.

CHAPTER I.

The introduction to the work, or bill of fare to the feast.

An author ought to consider himself, not as a gentleman who gives a private or eleemosynary treat, but rather as one who keeps a public ordinary, at which all persons are welcome for their money. In the former case, it is well known that the entertainer provides what fare he pleases; and though this should be very indifferent, and utterly disagreeable to the taste of his company, they must not find any fault; nay, on the contrary, good breeding forces them outwardly to approve and to commend whatever is set before them. Now the contrary of this happens to the master of an ordinary. Men who pay for what they eat will insist on gratifying their palates, however nice and whimsical these may prove; and if everything is not agreeable to their taste, will challenge a right to censure, to abuse, and to d—n their dinner without controul.

To prevent, therefore, giving offence to their customers by any such disappointment, it hath been usual with the honest and well-meaning host to provide a bill of fare which all persons may peruse at their first entrance into the house; and having thence acquainted themselves with the entertainment which they may expect, may either stay and regale with what is provided for them, or may depart to some other ordinary better accommodated to their taste.

As we do not disdain to borrow wit or wisdom from any man who is capable of lending us either, we have condescended to take a hint from these honest victuallers, and shall prefix not only a general bill of fare to our whole entertainment, but shall likewise give the reader particular bills to every course which is to be served up in this and the ensuing volumes.

The provision, then, which we have here made is no other than *Human Nature*. Nor do I fear that my sensible reader, though most luxurious in his taste, will start, cavil, or be offended, because I have named but one article. The tortoise—as the alderman of Bristol, well learned in eating, knows by much experience—besides the delicious calipash and calipee, contains many different kinds of food; nor can the learned reader be ignorant, that in human nature, though here collected under one general name, is such prodigious variety, that a cook will have sooner gone through all the several species of animal and vegetable food in the world, than an author will be able to exhaust so extensive a subject.

An objection may perhaps be apprehended from the more delicate, that this dish is too common and vulgar; for what else is the subject of all the romances, novels, plays, and poems, with which the stalls abound? Many exquisite viands might be rejected by the epicure, if it was a sufficient cause for his contemning of them as common and vulgar, that something was to be found in the most paltry alleys under the same name. In reality, true nature is as difficult to be met with in authors, as the Bayonne ham, or Bologna sausage, is to be found in the shops.

But the whole, to continue the same metaphor, consists in the cookery of the author; for, as Mr Pope tells us—

"True wit is nature to advantage drest;
What oft was thought, but ne'er so well exprest."

The same animal which hath the honour to have some part of his flesh eaten at the table of a duke, may perhaps be degraded in another part, and some of his limbs gibbeted, as it were, in the vilest stall in town. Where, then, lies the difference between the food of the nobleman and the porter, if both are at dinner on the same ox or calf, but in the seasoning, the dressing, the garnishing, and the setting forth? Hence the one provokes and incites the most languid appetite, and the other turns and palls that which is the sharpest and keenest.

In like manner, the excellence of the mental entertainment consists less in the subject than in the author's skill in well dressing it up. How pleased, therefore, will the reader be to find that we have, in the following work, adhered closely to one of the highest principles of the best cook which the present age, or perhaps that of Heliogabalus, hath produced. This great man, as is well known to all lovers of polite eating, begins at first by setting plain things before his hungry guests, rising afterwards by degrees as their stomachs may be supposed to decrease, to the very quintessence of sauce and spices. In like manner, we shall represent human nature at first to the keen appetite of our reader, in that more plain and simple manner in which it is found in the country, and shall hereafter hash and ragoo it with all the high French and Italian seasoning of affectation and vice which courts and cities afford. By these means, we doubt not but our reader may be rendered desirous to read on for ever, as the great person just above-mentioned is supposed to have made some persons eat.

Having premised thus much, we will now detain those who like our bill of fare no longer from their diet, and shall proceed directly to serve up the first course of our history for their entertainment.

CHAPTER II.

A short description of squire Allworthy, and a fuller account of Miss Bridget Allworthy, his sister.

In that part of the western division of this kingdom which is commonly called Somersetshire, there lately lived, and perhaps lives still, a gentleman whose name was Allworthy, and who might well be called the favourite of both nature and fortune; for both of these seem to have contended which should bless and enrich him most. In this contention, nature may seem to some to have come off victorious, as she bestowed on him many gifts, while fortune had only one gift in her power; but in pouring forth this, she was so very profuse, that others perhaps may think this single endowment to have been more than equivalent to all the various blessings which he enjoyed from nature. From the former of these, he derived an agreeable person, a sound constitution, a solid understanding, and a benevolent heart; by the latter, he was decreed to the inheritance of one of the largest estates in the county.

This gentleman had in his youth married a very worthy and beautiful woman, of whom he had been extremely fond: by her he had three children, all of whom died in their infancy. He had likewise had the misfortune of burying this beloved wife herself, about five years before the time in which this history chuses to set out. This loss, however great, he bore like a man of sense and constancy, though it must be confest he would often talk a little whimsically on this head; for he sometimes said he looked on himself as still married, and considered his wife as only gone a little before him, a journey which he should most certainly, sooner or later, take after her; and that he had not the least doubt of meeting her again in a place where he should never part with her more—sentiments for which his sense was arraigned by one part of his neighbours, his religion by a second, and his sincerity by a third.

He now lived, for the most part, retired in the country, with one sister, for whom he had a very tender affection. This lady was now somewhat past the age of thirty, an aera at which, in the opinion of the malicious, the title of old maid may with no impropriety be assumed. She was of that species of women whom you commend rather for good qualities than beauty, and who are generally called, by their own sex, very good sort of women—as good a sort of woman, madam, as you would wish to know. Indeed, she was so far from regretting want of beauty, that she never mentioned that perfection, if it can be called one, without contempt;

and would often thank God she was not as handsome as Miss Such-a-one, whom perhaps beauty had led into errors which she might have otherwise avoided. Miss Bridget Allworthy (for that was the name of this lady) very rightly conceived the charms of person in a woman to be no better than snares for herself, as well as for others; and yet so discreet was she in her conduct, that her prudence was as much on the guard as if she had all the snares to apprehend which were ever laid for her whole sex. Indeed, I have observed, though it may seem unaccountable to the reader, that this guard of prudence, like the trained bands, is always readiest to go on duty where there is the least danger. It often basely and cowardly deserts those paragons for whom the men are all wishing, sighing, dying, and spreading, every net in their power; and constantly attends at the heels of that higher order of women for whom the other sex have a more distant and awful respect, and whom (from despair, I suppose, of success) they never venture to attack.

Reader, I think proper, before we proceed any farther together, to acquaint thee that I intend to digress, through this whole history, as often as I see occasion, of which I am myself a better judge than any pitiful critic whatever; and here I must desire all those critics to mind their own business, and not to intermeddle with affairs or works which no ways concern them; for till they produce the authority by which they are constituted judges, I shall not plead to their jurisdiction.

CHAPTER III.

An odd accident which befel Mr Allworthy at his return home. The decent behaviour of Mrs Deborah Wilkins, with some proper animadversions on bastards.

I have told my reader, in the preceding chapter, that Mr Allworthy inherited a large fortune; that he had a good heart, and no family. Hence, doubtless, it will be concluded by many that he lived like an honest man, owed no one a shilling, took nothing but what was his own, kept a good house, entertained his neighbours with a hearty welcome at his table, and was charitable to the poor, i.e. to those who had rather beg than work, by giving them the offals from it; that he died immensely rich and built an hospital.

And true it is that he did many of these things; but had he done nothing more I should have left him to have recorded his own merit on some fair freestone over the door of that hospital. Matters of a much more extraordinary kind are to be the subject of this history, or I should grossly mis-spend my time in writing so voluminous a work; and you, my sagacious friend, might with equal profit and pleasure travel through some pages which certain droll authors have been facetiously pleased to call *The History of England*.

Mr Allworthy had been absent a full quarter of a year in London, on some very particular business, though I know not what it was; but judge of its importance by its having detained him so long from home, whence he had not been absent a month at a time during the space of many years. He came to his house very late in the evening, and after a short supper with his sister, retired much fatigued to his chamber. Here, having spent some minutes on his knees—a custom which he never broke through on any account—he was preparing to step into bed, when, upon opening the cloathes, to his great surprize he beheld an infant, wrapt up in some coarse linen, in a sweet and profound sleep, between his sheets. He stood some time lost in astonishment at this sight; but, as good nature had always the ascendant in his mind, he soon began to be touched with sentiments of compassion for the little wretch before him. He then rang his bell, and ordered an elderly woman-servant to rise immediately, and come to him; and in the meantime was so eager in contemplating the beauty of innocence, appearing in those lively colours with which infancy and sleep always display it, that his thoughts were too much engaged to reflect that he was in his shirt when the matron came in. She had indeed given her master sufficient time to dress himself; for out of respect to him, and regard to decency, she had spent many minutes in adjusting her hair at the looking-glass, notwithstanding all the hurry in which she had been summoned by the servant, and though her master, for aught she knew, lay expiring in an apoplexy, or in some other fit.

It will not be wondered at that a creature who had so strict a regard to decency in her own person, should be shocked at the least deviation from it in another. She therefore no sooner opened the door, and saw her master standing by the bedside in his shirt, with a candle in his hand, than she started back in a most terrible fright, and might perhaps have swooned away, had he not now recollected his being undrest, and put an end to her terrors by desiring her to stay without the door till he had thrown some cloathes over his back, and was become incapable of shocking the pure eyes of Mrs Deborah Wilkins, who, though in the fifty-second year of her age, vowed she had never beheld a man without his coat. Sneerers and prophane wits may perhaps laugh at her first fright; yet my graver reader, when he considers the time of night, the summons from her bed, and the situation in which she found her master, will highly justify and applaud her conduct, unless the prudence which must be supposed to attend maidens at that period of life at which Mrs Deborah had arrived, should a little lessen his admiration.

When Mrs Deborah returned into the room, and was acquainted by her master with the finding the little infant, her consternation was rather greater than his had been; nor could she refrain from crying out, with great horror of accent as well as look, "My good sir! what's to be done?" Mr Allworthy answered, she must take care of the child that evening, and in the morning he would give orders to provide it a nurse. "Yes, sir," says she; "and I hope your worship will send out your warrant to take up the hussy its mother, for she must be one of the neighbourhood; and I should be glad to see her committed to Bridewell, and whipt at the cart's tail. Indeed, such wicked sluts cannot be too severely punished. I'll warrant 'tis not her first, by her impudence in laying it to your worship." "In laying it to me, Deborah!" answered Allworthy: "I can't think she hath any such design. I suppose she hath only taken this method to provide for her child; and truly I am glad she hath not done worse." "I don't know what is worse," cries Deborah, "than for such wicked strumpets to lay their sins at honest men's doors; and though your worship knows your own innocence, yet the world is censorious; and it hath been many an honest man's hap to pass for the father of children he never begot; and if your worship should provide for the child, it may make the people the apter to believe; besides, why should your worship provide for what the parish is obliged to maintain? For my own part, if it was an honest man's child, indeed—but for my own part, it goes against me to touch these misbegotten wretches, whom I don't look upon as my fellow-creatures. Faugh! how it stinks! It doth not smell like a Christian. If I might be so bold to give my advice, I would have it put in a basket, and sent out and laid at the churchwarden's door. It is a good night, only a little rainy and windy; and if it was well wrapt up, and put in a warm basket, it is two to one but it lives till it is found in the morning. But if it should not, we have discharged our duty in taking proper care of it; and it is, perhaps, better for such creatures to die in a state of innocence, than to grow up and imitate their mothers; for nothing better can be expected of them."

There were some strokes in this speech which perhaps would have offended Mr Allworthy, had he strictly attended to it; but he had now got one of his fingers into the infant's hand, which, by its gentle pressure, seeming to implore his assistance, had certainly out-pleaded the eloquence of Mrs Deborah, had it been ten times greater than it was. He now gave Mrs Deborah positive orders to take the child to her own bed, and to call up a maid-servant to provide it pap, and other things, against it waked. He likewise ordered that proper cloathes should be procured for it early in the morning, and that it should be brought to himself as soon as he was stirring.

Such was the discernment of Mrs Wilkins, and such the respect she bore her master, under whom she enjoyed a most excellent place, that her scruples gave way to his peremptory commands; and she took the child under her arms, without any apparent disgust at the illegality of its birth; and declaring it was a sweet little infant, walked off with it to her own chamber.

Allworthy here betook himself to those pleasing slumbers which a heart that hungers after goodness is apt to enjoy when thoroughly satisfied. As these are possibly sweeter than what are occasioned by any other hearty meal, I should take more pains to display them to the reader, if I knew any air to recommend him to for the procuring such an appetite.

CHAPTER IV.

The reader's neck brought into danger by a description; his escape; and the great condescension of Miss Bridget Allworthy.

The Gothic stile of building could produce nothing nobler than Mr Allworthy's house. There was an air of grandeur in it that struck you with awe, and rivalled the beauties of the best Grecian architecture; and it was as commodious within as venerable without.

It stood on the south-east side of a hill, but nearer the bottom than the top of it, so as to be sheltered from the north-east by a grove of old oaks which rose above it in a gradual ascent of near half a mile, and yet high enough to enjoy a most charming prospect of the valley beneath.

In the midst of the grove was a fine lawn, sloping down towards the house, near the summit of which rose a plentiful spring, gushing out of a rock covered with firs, and forming a constant cascade of about thirty feet, not carried down a regular flight of steps, but tumbling in a natural fall over the broken and mossy stones till it came to the bottom of the rock, then running off in a pebly channel, that with many lesser falls winded along, till it fell into a lake at the foot of the hill, about a quarter of a mile below the house on the south side, and which was seen from every room in the front. Out of this lake, which filled the center of a beautiful plain, embellished with groups of beeches and elms, and fed with sheep, issued a river, that for several miles was seen to meander through an amazing variety of meadows and woods till it emptied itself into the sea, with a large arm of which, and an island beyond it, the prospect was closed.

On the right of this valley opened another of less extent, adorned with several villages, and terminated by one of the towers of an old ruined abby, grown over with ivy, and part of the front, which remained still entire.

The left-hand scene presented the view of a very fine park, composed of very unequal ground, and agreeably varied with all the diversity that hills, lawns, wood, and water, laid out with admirable taste, but owing less to art than to nature, could give. Beyond this, the country gradually rose into a ridge of wild mountains, the tops of which were above the clouds.

It was now the middle of May, and the morning was remarkably serene, when Mr Allworthy walked forth on the terrace, where the dawn opened every minute that lovely prospect we have before described to his eye; and now having sent forth streams of light, which ascended the blue firmament before him, as harbingers preceding his pomp, in the full blaze of his majesty rose the sun, than which one object alone in this lower creation could be more glorious, and that Mr Allworthy himself presented—a human being replete with benevolence, meditating in what manner he might render himself most acceptable to his Creator, by doing most good to his creatures.

Reader, take care. I have unadvisedly led thee to the top of as high a hill as Mr Allworthy's, and how to get thee down without breaking thy neck, I do not well know. However, let us e'en venture to slide down together; for Miss Bridget rings her bell, and Mr Allworthy is summoned to breakfast, where I must attend, and, if you please, shall be glad of your company.

The usual compliments having past between Mr Allworthy and Miss Bridget, and the tea being poured out, he summoned Mrs Wilkins, and told his sister he had a present for her, for which she thanked him—imagining, I suppose, it had been a gown, or some ornament for her person. Indeed, he very often made her such presents; and she, in complacence to him, spent much time in adorning herself. I say in complacence to him, because she always exprest the greatest contempt for dress, and for those ladies who made it their study.

But if such was her expectation, how was she disappointed when Mrs Wilkins, according to the order she had received from her master, produced the little infant? Great surprizes, as hath been observed, are apt to be silent; and so was Miss Bridget, till her brother began, and told her the whole story, which, as the reader knows it already, we shall not repeat.

Miss Bridget had always exprest so great a regard for what the ladies are pleased to call virtue, and had herself maintained such a severity of character, that it was expected, especially by Wilkins, that she would have vented much bitterness on this occasion, and would have voted for sending the child, as a kind of noxious animal, immediately out of the house; but, on the contrary, she rather took the good-natured side of the question, intimated some compassion for the helpless little creature, and commended her brother's charity in what he had done.

Perhaps the reader may account for this behaviour from her condescension to Mr Allworthy, when we have informed him that the good man had ended his narrative with owning a resolution to take care of the child, and to breed him up as his own; for, to acknowledge the truth, she was always ready to oblige her brother, and very seldom, if ever, contradicted his sentiments. She would, indeed, sometimes make a few observations, as that men were headstrong, and must have their own way, and would wish she had been blest with an independent fortune; but these were always vented in a low voice, and at the most amounted only to what is called muttering.

However, what she withheld from the infant, she bestowed with the utmost profuseness on the poor unknown mother, whom she called an impudent slut, a wanton hussy, an audacious harlot, a wicked jade, a FIXME(replacing -- with —)-->vile strumpet, with every other appellation with which the tongue of virtue never fails to lash those who bring a disgrace on the sex. -- A consultation was now entered into how to proceed in order to discover the mother. A scrutiny was first made into the characters of the female servants of the house, who were all acquitted by Mrs Wilkins, and with apparent merit; for she had collected them herself, and perhaps it would be difficult to find such another set of scarecrows.

The next step was to examine among the inhabitants of the parish; and this was referred to Mrs Wilkins, who was to enquire with all imaginable diligence, and to make her report in the afternoon.

Matters being thus settled, Mr Allworthy withdrew to his study, as was his custom, and left the child to his sister, who, at his desire, had undertaken the care of it.

CHAPTER V.

Containing a few common matters, with a very uncommon observation upon them.

When her master was departed, Mrs Deborah stood silent, expecting her cue from Miss Bridget; for as to what had past before her master, the prudent housekeeper by no means relied upon it, as she had often known the sentiments of the lady in her brother's absence to differ greatly from those which she had expressed in his presence. Miss Bridget did not, however, suffer her to continue long in this doubtful situation; for having looked some time earnestly at the child, as it lay asleep in the lap of Mrs Deborah, the good lady could not forbear giving it a hearty kiss, at the same time declaring herself wonderfully pleased with its beauty and innocence. Mrs Deborah no sooner observed this than she fell to squeezing and kissing, with as great raptures as sometimes inspire the sage dame of forty and five towards a youthful and vigorous bridegroom, crying out, in a shrill voice, "O, the dear little creature!—The dear, sweet, pretty creature! Well, I vow it is as fine a boy as ever was seen!"

These exclamations continued till they were interrupted by the lady, who now proceeded to execute the commission given her by her brother, and gave orders for providing all necessaries for the child, appointing a very good room in the house for his nursery. Her orders were indeed so liberal, that, had it been a child of her own, she could not have exceeded them; but, lest the virtuous reader may condemn her for showing too great regard to a base-born infant, to which all charity is condemned by law as irreligious, we think proper to observe that she concluded the whole with saying, "Since it was her brother's whim to adopt the little brat, she supposed little master must be treated with great tenderness. For her part, she could not help thinking it was an encouragement to vice; but that she knew too much of the obstinacy of mankind to oppose any of their ridiculous humours."

With reflections of this nature she usually, as has been hinted, accompanied every act of compliance with her brother's inclinations; and surely nothing could more contribute to heighten the merit of this compliance than a declaration that she knew, at the same time, the folly and unreasonableness of those inclinations to which she submitted. Tacit obedience implies no force upon the will, and consequently may be easily, and without any pains, preserved; but when a wife, a child, a relation, or a friend, performs what we desire, with grumbling and reluctance, with expressions of dislike and dissatisfaction, the manifest difficulty which they undergo must greatly enhance the obligation.

As this is one of those deep observations which very few readers can be supposed capable of making themselves, I have thought proper to lend them my assistance; but this is a favour rarely to be expected in the course of my work. Indeed, I shall seldom or never so indulge him, unless in such instances as this, where nothing but the inspiration with which we writers are gifted, can possibly enable any one to make the discovery.

CHAPTER VI.

Mrs Deborah is introduced into the parish with a simile. A short account of Jenny Jones, with the difficulties and discouragements which may attend young women in the pursuit of learning.

Mrs Deborah, having disposed of the child according to the will of her master, now prepared to visit those habitations which were supposed to conceal its mother.

Not otherwise than when a kite, tremendous bird, is beheld by the feathered generation soaring aloft, and hovering over their heads, the amorous dove, and every innocent little bird, spread wide the alarm, and fly trembling to their hiding-places. He proudly beats the air, conscious of his dignity, and meditates intended mischief.

So when the approach of Mrs Deborah was proclaimed through the street, all the inhabitants ran trembling into their houses, each matron dreading lest the visit should fall to her lot. She with stately steps proudly advances over the field: aloft she bears her towering head, filled with conceit of her own pre-eminence, and schemes to effect her intended discovery.

The sagacious reader will not from this simile imagine these poor people had any apprehension of the design with which Mrs Wilkins was now coming towards them; but as the great beauty of the simile may possibly sleep these hundred years, till some future commentator shall take this work in hand, I think proper to lend the reader a little assistance in this place.

It is my intention, therefore, to signify, that, as it is the nature of a kite to devour little birds, so is it the nature of such persons as Mrs Wilkins to insult and tyrannize over little people. This being indeed the means which they use to recompense to themselves their extreme servility and condescension to their superiors; for nothing can be more reasonable, than that slaves and flatterers should exact the same taxes on all below them, which they themselves pay to all above them.

Whenever Mrs Deborah had occasion to exert any extraordinary condescension to Mrs Bridget, and by that means had a little soured her natural disposition, it was usual with her to walk forth among these people, in order to refine her temper, by venting, and, as it were, purging off all ill humours; on which account she was by no means a welcome visitant: to say the truth, she was universally dreaded and hated by them all.

On her arrival in this place, she went immediately to the habitation of an elderly matron; to whom, as this matron had the good fortune to resemble herself in the comeliness of her person, as well as in her age, she had generally been more favourable than to any of the rest. To this woman she imparted what had happened, and the design upon which she was come thither that morning. These two began presently to scrutinize the characters of the several young girls who lived in any of those houses, and at last fixed their strongest suspicion on one Jenny Jones, who, they both agreed, was the likeliest person to have committed this fact.

This Jenny Jones was no very comely girl, either in her face or person; but nature had somewhat compensated the want of beauty with what is generally more esteemed by those ladies whose judgment is arrived at years of perfect maturity, for she had given her a very uncommon share of understanding. This gift Jenny had a good deal improved by erudition. She had lived several years a servant with a schoolmaster, who, discovering a great quickness of parts in the girl, and an extraordinary desire of learning—for every leisure hour she was always found reading in the books of the scholars—had the good-nature, or folly—just as the reader pleases to call it—to instruct her so far, that she obtained a competent skill in the Latin language, and was, perhaps, as good a scholar as most of the young men of quality of the age. This advantage, however, like most others of an extraordinary kind, was attended with some small inconveniences: for as it is not to be wondered at, that a young woman so well accomplished should have little relish for the society of those whom fortune had made her equals, but whom education had rendered so much her inferiors; so is it matter of no greater astonishment, that this superiority in Jenny, together with that behaviour which is its certain consequence, should produce among the rest some little envy and ill-will towards her; and these had, perhaps, secretly burnt in the bosoms of her neighbours ever since her return from her service.

Their envy did not, however, display itself openly, till poor Jenny, to the surprize of everybody, and to the vexation of all the young women in these parts, had publickly shone forth on a Sunday in a new silk gown, with a laced cap, and other proper appendages to these.

The flame, which had before lain in embryo, now burst forth. Jenny had, by her learning, increased her own pride, which none of her neighbours were kind enough to feed with the honour she seemed to demand; and now, instead of respect and adoration, she gained nothing but hatred and abuse by her finery. The whole parish declared she could not come honestly by such things; and parents, instead of wishing their daughters the same, felicitated themselves that their children had them not.

Hence, perhaps, it was, that the good woman first mentioned the name of this poor girl to Mrs Wilkins; but there was another circumstance that confirmed the latter in her suspicion; for Jenny had lately been often at Mr Allworthy's house. She had officiated as nurse to Miss Bridget, in a violent fit of illness, and had sat up many nights with that lady; besides which, she had been seen there the very day before Mr Allworthy's return, by Mrs Wilkins herself, though that sagacious person had not at first conceived any suspicion of her on that account: for, as she herself said, "She had always esteemed Jenny as a very sober girl (though indeed she knew very little of her), and had rather suspected some of those wanton trollops, who gave themselves airs, because, forsooth, they thought themselves handsome."

Jenny was now summoned to appear in person before Mrs Deborah, which she immediately did. When Mrs Deborah, putting on the gravity of a judge, with somewhat more than his austerity, began an oration with the words, "You audacious strumpet!" in which she proceeded rather to pass sentence on the prisoner than to accuse her.

Though Mrs Deborah was fully satisfied of the guilt of Jenny, from the reasons above shewn, it is possible Mr Allworthy might have required some stronger evidence to have convicted her; but she saved her accusers any such trouble, by freely confessing the whole fact with which she was charged.

This confession, though delivered rather in terms of contrition, as it appeared, did not at all mollify Mrs Deborah, who now pronounced a second judgment against her, in more opprobrious language than before; nor had it any better success with the bystanders, who were now grown very numerous. Many of them cried out, "They thought what madam's silk gown would end in;" others spoke sarcastically of her learning. Not a single female was present but found some means of expressing her abhorrence of poor Jenny, who bore all very patiently, except the malice of one woman, who reflected upon her person, and tossing up her nose, said, "The man must have a good stomach who would give silk gowns for such sort of trumpery!" Jenny replied to this with a bitterness which might have surprized a judicious person, who had observed the tranquillity with which she bore all the affronts to her chastity; but her patience was perhaps tired out, for this is a virtue which is very apt to be fatigued by exercise.

Mrs Deborah having succeeded beyond her hopes in her inquiry, returned with much triumph, and, at the appointed hour, made a faithful report to Mr Allworthy, who was much surprized at the relation; for he had heard of the extraordinary parts and improvements of this girl, whom he intended to have given in marriage, together with a small living, to a neighbouring curate. His concern, therefore, on this occasion, was at least equal to the satisfaction which appeared in Mrs Deborah, and to many readers may seem much more reasonable.

Miss Bridget blessed herself, and said, "For her part, she should never hereafter entertain a good opinion of any woman." For Jenny before this had the happiness of being much in her good graces also.

The prudent housekeeper was again dispatched to bring the unhappy culprit before Mr Allworthy, in order, not as it was hoped by some, and expected by all, to be sent to the house of correction, but to receive wholesome admonition and reproof; which those who relish that kind of instructive writing may peruse in the next chapter.

CHAPTER VII.

Containing such grave matter, that the reader cannot laugh once through the whole chapter, unless peradventure he should laugh at the author.

When Jenny appeared, Mr Allworthy took her into his study, and spoke to her as follows: "You know, child, it is in my power as a magistrate, to punish you very rigorously for what you have done; and you will, perhaps, be the more apt to fear I should execute that power, because you have in a manner laid your sins at my door.

"But, perhaps, this is one reason which hath determined me to act in a milder manner with you: for, as no private resentment should ever influence a magistrate, I will be so far from considering your having deposited the infant in my house as an aggravation of your offence, that I will suppose, in your favour, this to have proceeded from a natural affection to your child, since you might have some hopes to see it thus better provided for than was in the power of yourself, or its wicked father, to provide for it. I should indeed have been highly offended with you had you exposed the little wretch in the manner of some inhuman mothers, who seem no less to have abandoned their humanity, than to have parted with their chastity. It is the other part of your offence, therefore, upon which I intend to admonish you, I mean the violation of your chastity;—a crime, however lightly it may be treated by debauched persons, very heinous in itself, and very dreadful in its consequences.

"The heinous nature of this offence must be sufficiently apparent to every Christian, inasmuch as it is committed in defiance of the laws of our religion, and of the express commands of Him who founded that religion.

"And here its consequences may well be argued to be dreadful; for what can be more so, than to incur the divine displeasure, by the breach of the divine commands; and that in an instance against which the highest vengeance is specifically denounced?

"But these things, though too little, I am afraid, regarded, are so plain, that mankind, however they may want to be reminded, can never need information on this head. A hint, therefore, to awaken your sense of this matter, shall suffice; for I would inspire you with repentance, and not drive you to desperation.

"There are other consequences, not indeed so dreadful or replete with horror as this; and yet such, as, if attentively considered, must, one would think, deter all of your sex at least from the commission of this crime.

"For by it you are rendered infamous, and driven, like lepers of old, out of society; at least, from the society of all but wicked and reprobate persons; for no others will associate with you.

"If you have fortunes, you are hereby rendered incapable of enjoying them; if you have none, you are disabled from acquiring any, nay almost of procuring your sustenance; for no persons of character will receive you into their houses. Thus you are often driven by necessity itself into a state of shame and misery, which unavoidably ends in the destruction of both body and soul.

"Can any pleasure compensate these evils? Can any temptation have sophistry and delusion strong enough to persuade you to so simple a bargain? Or can any carnal appetite so overpower your reason, or so totally lay it asleep, as to prevent your flying with affright and terror from a crime which carries such punishment always with it?

"How base and mean must that woman be, how void of that dignity of mind, and decent pride, without which we are not worthy the name of human creatures, who can bear to level herself with the lowest animal, and to sacrifice all that is great and noble in her, all her heavenly part, to an appetite which she hath in common with the vilest branch of the creation! For no woman, sure, will plead the passion of love for an excuse. This would be to own herself the mere tool and bubble of the man. Love, however barbarously we may corrupt and pervert its meaning, as it is a laudable, is a rational passion, and can never be violent but when reciprocal; for though the Scripture bids us love our enemies, it means not with that fervent love which we naturally bear towards our friends; much less that we should sacrifice to them our lives, and what ought to be dearer to us, our innocence. Now in what light, but that of an enemy, can a reasonable woman regard the man who solicits her to entail on herself all the misery I have described to you, and who would purchase to himself a short, trivial, contemptible pleasure, so greatly at her expense! For, by the laws of custom, the whole shame, with all its dreadful consequences, falls intirely upon her. Can love, which always seeks the good of its object, attempt to betray a woman into a bargain where she is so greatly to be the loser? If such corrupter, therefore, should have the impudence to pretend a real affection for her, ought not the woman to regard him not only as an enemy, but as the worst of all enemies, a false, designing, treacherous, pretended friend, who intends not only to debauch her body, but her understanding at the same time?"

Here Jenny expressing great concern, Allworthy paused a moment, and then proceeded: "I have talked thus to you, child, not to insult you for what is past and irrevocable, but to caution and strengthen you for the future. Nor should I have taken this trouble, but from some opinion of your good sense, notwithstanding the dreadful slip you have made; and from some hopes of your hearty repentance, which are founded on the openness and sincerity of your confession. If these do not deceive me, I will take care to convey you from this scene of your shame, where you shall, by being unknown, avoid the punishment which, as I have said, is allotted to your crime in this world; and I hope, by repentance, you will avoid the much heavier sentence denounced against it in the other. Be a good girl the rest of your days, and want shall be no motive to your going astray; and, believe me, there is more pleasure, even in this world, in an innocent and virtuous life, than in one debauched and vicious.

"As to your child, let no thoughts concerning it molest you; I will provide for it in a better manner than you can ever hope. And now nothing remains but that you inform me who was the wicked man that seduced you; for my anger against him will be much greater than you have experienced on this occasion."

Jenny now lifted her eyes from the ground, and with a modest look and decent voice thus began:—

"To know you, sir, and not love your goodness, would be an argument of total want of sense or goodness in any one. In me it would amount to the highest ingratitude, not to feel, in the most sensible manner, the great degree of goodness you have been pleased to exert on this occasion. As to my concern for what is past, I know you will spare my blushes the repetition. My future conduct will much better declare my sentiments than any professions I can now make. I beg leave to assure you, sir, that I take your advice much kinder than your generous offer with which you concluded it; for, as you are pleased to say, sir, it is an instance of your opinion of my understanding."—Here her tears flowing apace, she stopped a few moments, and then proceeded thus:—"Indeed, sir, your kindness overcomes me; but I will endeavour to deserve this good opinion: for if I have the understanding you are so kindly pleased to allow me, such advice cannot be thrown away upon me. I thank you, sir, heartily, for your intended kindness to my poor helpless child: he is innocent, and I hope will live to be grateful for all the favours you shall show him. But now, sir, I must on my knees entreat you not to persist in asking me to declare the father of my infant. I promise you faithfully you shall one day know; but I am under the most solemn ties and engagements of honour, as well as the most religious vows and protestations, to conceal his name at this time. And I know you too well, to think you would desire I should sacrifice either my honour or my religion."

Mr Allworthy, whom the least mention of those sacred words was sufficient to stagger, hesitated a moment before he replied, and then told her, she had done wrong to enter into such engagements to a villain; but since she had, he could not insist on her breaking them. He said, it was not from a motive of vain curiosity he had inquired, but in order to punish the fellow; at least, that he might not ignorantly confer favours on the undeserving.

As to these points, Jenny satisfied him by the most solemn assurances, that the man was entirely out of his reach; and was neither subject to his power, nor in any probability of becoming an object of his goodness.

The ingenuity of this behaviour had gained Jenny so much credit with this worthy man, that he easily believed what she told him; for as she had disdained to excuse herself by a lie, and had hazarded his further displeasure in her present situation, rather than she would forfeit her honour or integrity by betraying another, he had but little apprehensions that she would be guilty of falsehood towards himself.

He therefore dismissed her with assurances that he would very soon remove her out of the reach of that obloquy she had incurred; concluding with some additional documents, in which he recommended repentance, saying, "Consider, child, there is one still to reconcile yourself to, whose favour is of much greater importance to you than mine."

CHAPTER VIII.

A dialogue between Mesdames Bridget and Deborah; containing more amusement, but less instruction, than the former.

When Mr Allworthy had retired to his study with Jenny Jones, as hath been seen, Mrs Bridget, with the good housekeeper, had betaken themselves to a post next adjoining to the said study; whence, through the conveyance of a keyhole, they sucked in at their ears the instructive lecture delivered by Mr Allworthy, together with the answers of Jenny, and indeed every other particular which passed in the last chapter.

This hole in her brother's study-door was indeed as well known to Mrs Bridget, and had been as frequently applied to by her, as the famous hole in the wall was by Thisbe of old. This served to many good purposes. For by such means Mrs Bridget became often acquainted with her brother's inclinations, without giving him the trouble of repeating them to her. It is true, some inconveniences attended this intercourse, and she had sometimes reason to cry out with Thisbe, in Shakspeare, "O, wicked, wicked wall!" For as Mr Allworthy was a justice of peace, certain things occurred in examinations concerning bastards, and such like, which are apt to give great offence to the chaste ears of virgins, especially when they approach the age of forty, as was the case of Mrs Bridget. However, she had, on such occasions, the advantage of concealing her blushes from the eyes of men; and *De non apparentibus, et non existentibus eadem est ratio*—in English, "When a woman is not seen to blush, she doth not blush at all."

Both the good women kept strict silence during the whole scene between Mr Allworthy and the girl; but as soon as it was ended, and that gentleman was out of hearing, Mrs Deborah could not help exclaiming against the clemency of her master, and especially against his suffering her to conceal the father of the child, which she swore she would have out of her before the sun set.

At these words Mrs Bridget discomposed her features with a smile (a thing very unusual to her). Not that I would have my reader imagine, that this was one of those wanton smiles which Homer would have you conceive came from Venus, when he calls her the laughter-loving goddess; nor was it one of those smiles which Lady Seraphina shoots from the stage-box, and which Venus would quit her immortality to be able to equal. No, this was rather one of those smiles which might be supposed to have come from the dimpled cheeks of the august Tisiphone, or from one of the misses, her sisters.

With such a smile then, and with a voice sweet as the evening breeze of Boreas in the pleasant month of November, Mrs Bridget gently reproved the curiosity of Mrs Deborah; a vice with which it seems the latter was too much tainted, and which the former inveighed against with great bitterness, adding, "That, among all her faults, she thanked Heaven her enemies could not accuse her of prying into the affairs of other people."

She then proceeded to commend the honour and spirit with which Jenny had acted. She said, she could not help agreeing with her brother, that there was some merit in the sincerity of her confession, and in her integrity to her lover: that she had always thought her a very good girl, and doubted not but she had been seduced by some rascal, who had been infinitely more to blame than herself, and very probably had prevailed with her by a promise of marriage, or some other treacherous proceeding.

This behaviour of Mrs Bridget greatly surprised Mrs Deborah; for this well-bred woman seldom opened her lips, either to her master or his sister, till she had first sounded their inclinations, with which her sentiments were always consonant. Here, however, she thought she might have launched forth with safety; and the sagacious reader will not perhaps accuse her of want of sufficient forecast in so doing, but will rather admire with what wonderful celerity she tacked about, when she found herself steering a wrong course.

"Nay, madam," said this able woman, and truly great politician, "I must own I cannot help admiring the girl's spirit, as well as your ladyship. And, as your ladyship says, if she was deceived by some wicked man, the poor wretch is to be pitied. And to be sure, as your ladyship says, the girl hath always appeared like a good, honest, plain girl, and not vain of her face, forsooth, as some wanton husseys in the neighbourhood are."

"You say true, Deborah," said Miss Bridget. "If the girl had been one of those vain trollops, of which we have too many in the parish, I should have condemned my brother for his lenity towards her. I saw two farmers' daughters at church, the other day, with bare necks. I protest they shocked me. If wenches will hang out lures for fellows, it is no matter what they suffer. I detest such creatures; and it would be much better for them that their faces had been seamed with the small-pox; but I must confess, I never saw any of this wanton behaviour in poor Jenny: some artful villain, I am convinced, hath betrayed, nay perhaps forced her; and I pity the poor wretch with all my heart."

Mrs Deborah approved all these sentiments, and the dialogue concluded with a general and bitter invective against beauty, and with many compassionate considerations for all honest plain girls who are deluded by the wicked arts of deceitful men.

CHAPTER IX.

Containing matters which will surprize the reader.

Jenny returned home well pleased with the reception she had met with from Mr Allworthy, whose indulgence to her she industriously made public; partly perhaps as a sacrifice to her own pride, and partly from the more prudent motive of reconciling her neighbours to her, and silencing their clamours.

But though this latter view, if she indeed had it, may appear reasonable enough, yet the event did not answer her expectation; for when she was convened before the justice, and it was universally apprehended that the house of correction would have been her fate, though some of the young women cryed out "It was good enough for her," and diverted themselves with the thoughts of her beating hemp in a silk gown; yet there were many others who began to pity her condition: but when it was known in what manner Mr Allworthy had behaved, the tide turned against her. One said, "I'll assure you, madam hath had good luck." A second cryed, "See what it is to be a favourite!" A third, "Ay, this comes of her learning." Every person made some malicious comment or other on the occasion, and reflected on the partiality of the justice.

The behaviour of these people may appear impolitic and ungrateful to the reader, who considers the power and benevolence of Mr Allworthy. But as to his power, he never used it; and as to his benevolence, he exerted so much, that he had thereby disobliged all his neighbours; for it is a secret well known to great men, that, by conferring an obligation, they do not always procure a friend, but are certain of creating many enemies.

Jenny was, however, by the care and goodness of Mr Allworthy, soon removed out of the reach of reproach; when malice being no longer able to vent its rage on her, began to seek another object of its bitterness, and this was no less than Mr Allworthy, himself; for a whisper soon went abroad, that he himself was the father of the foundling child.

This supposition so well reconciled his conduct to the general opinion, that it met with universal assent; and the outcry against his lenity soon began to take another turn, and was changed into an invective against his cruelty to the poor girl. Very grave and good women exclaimed against men who begot children, and then disowned them. Nor were there wanting some, who, after the departure of Jenny, insinuated that she was spirited away with a design too black to be mentioned, and who gave frequent hints that a legal inquiry ought to be made into the whole matter, and that some people should be forced to produce the girl.

These calumnies might have probably produced ill consequences, at the least might have occasioned some trouble, to a person of a more doubtful and suspicious character than Mr Allworthy was blessed with; but in his case they had no such effect; and, being heartily despised by him, they served only to afford an innocent amusement to the good gossips of the neighbourhood.

But as we cannot possibly divine what complection our reader may be of, and as it will be some time before he will hear any more of Jenny, we think proper to give him a very early intimation, that Mr Allworthy was, and will hereafter appear to be, absolutely innocent of any criminal intention whatever. He had indeed committed no other than an error in politics, by tempering justice with mercy, and by refusing to gratify the good-natured disposition of the mob,[1] with an object for their compassion to work on in the person of poor Jenny, whom, in order to pity, they desired to have seen sacrificed to ruin and infamy, by a shameful correction in Bridewell.

So far from complying with this their inclination, by which all hopes of reformation would have been abolished, and even the gate shut against her if her own inclinations should ever hereafter lead her to chuse the road of virtue, Mr Allworthy rather chose to encourage the girl to return thither by the only possible means; for too true I am afraid it is, that many women have become abandoned, and have sunk to the last degree of vice, by being unable to retrieve the first slip. This will be, I am afraid, always the case while they remain among their former acquaintance; it was therefore wisely done by Mr Allworthy, to remove Jenny to a place where she might enjoy the pleasure of reputation, after having tasted the ill consequences of losing it.

To this place therefore, wherever it was, we will wish her a good journey, and for the present take leave of her, and of the little foundling her child, having matters of much higher importance to communicate to the reader.

---

[1] Whenever this word occurs in our writings, it intends persons without virtue or sense, in all stations; and many of the highest rank are often meant by it.

CHAPTER X.

The hospitality of Allworthy; with a short sketch of the characters of two brothers, a doctor and a captain, who were entertained by that gentleman.

Neither Mr Allworthy's house, nor his heart, were shut against any part of mankind, but they were both more particularly open to men of merit. To say the truth, this was the only house in the kingdom where you was sure to gain a dinner by deserving it.

Above all others, men of genius and learning shared the principal place in his favour; and in these he had much discernment: for though he had missed the advantage of a learned education, yet, being blest with vast natural abilities, he had so well profited by a vigorous though late application to letters, and by much conversation with men of eminence in this way, that he was himself a very competent judge in most kinds of literature.

It is no wonder that in an age when this kind of merit is so little in fashion, and so slenderly provided for, persons possessed of it should very eagerly flock to a place where they were sure of being received with great complaisance; indeed, where they might enjoy almost the same advantages of a liberal fortune as if they were entitled to it in their own right; for Mr Allworthy was not one of those generous persons who are ready most bountifully to bestow meat, drink, and lodging on men of wit and learning, for which they expect no other return but entertainment, instruction, flattery, and subserviency; in a word, that such persons should be enrolled in the number of domestics, without wearing their master's cloathes, or receiving wages.

On the contrary, every person in this house was perfect master of his own time: and as he might at his pleasure satisfy all his appetites within the restrictions only of law, virtue, and religion; so he might, if his health required, or his inclination prompted him to temperance, or even to abstinence, absent himself from any meals, or retire from them, whenever he was so disposed, without even a sollicitation to the contrary: for, indeed, such sollicitations from superiors always savour very strongly of commands. But all here were free from such impertinence, not only those whose company is in all other places esteemed a favour from their equality of fortune, but even those whose indigent circumstances make such an eleemosynary abode convenient to them, and who are therefore less welcome to a great man's table because they stand in need of it.

Among others of this kind was Dr Blifil, a gentleman who had the misfortune of losing the advantage of great talents by the obstinacy of a father, who would breed him to a profession he disliked. In obedience to this obstinacy the doctor had in his youth been obliged to study physic, or rather to say he studied it; for in reality books of this kind were almost the only ones with which he was unacquainted; and unfortunately for him, the doctor was master of almost every other science but that by which he was to get his bread; the consequence of which was, that the doctor at the age of forty had no bread to eat.

Such a person as this was certain to find a welcome at Mr Allworthy's table, to whom misfortunes were ever a recommendation, when they were derived from the folly or villany of others, and not of the unfortunate person himself. Besides this negative merit, the doctor had one positive recommendation;—this was a great appearance of religion. Whether his religion was real, or consisted only in appearance, I shall not presume to say, as I am not possessed of any touchstone which can distinguish the true from the false.

If this part of his character pleased Mr Allworthy, it delighted Miss Bridget. She engaged him in many religious controversies; on which occasions she constantly expressed great satisfaction in the doctor's knowledge, and not much less in the compliments which he frequently bestowed on her own. To say the truth, she had read much English divinity, and had puzzled more than one of the neighbouring curates. Indeed, her conversation was so pure, her looks so sage, and her whole deportment so grave and solemn, that she seemed to deserve the name of saint equally with her namesake, or with any other female in the Roman kalendar.

As sympathies of all kinds are apt to beget love, so experience teaches us that none have a more direct tendency this way than those of a religious kind between persons of different sexes. The doctor found himself so agreeable to Miss Bridget, that he now began to lament an unfortunate accident which had happened to him about ten years before; namely, his marriage with another woman, who was not only still alive, but, what was worse, known to be so by Mr Allworthy. This was a fatal bar to that happiness which he otherwise saw sufficient probability of obtaining with this young lady; for as to criminal indulgences, he certainly never thought of them. This was owing either to his religion, as is most probable, or to the purity of his passion, which was fixed on those things which matrimony only, and not criminal correspondence, could put him in possession of, or could give him any title to.

He had not long ruminated on these matters, before it occurred to his memory that he had a brother who was under no such unhappy incapacity. This brother he made no doubt would succeed; for he discerned, as he thought, an inclination to marriage in the lady; and the reader perhaps, when he hears the brother's qualifications, will not blame the confidence which he entertained of his success.

This gentleman was about thirty-five years of age. He was of a middle size, and what is called well-built. He had a scar on his forehead, which did not so much injure his beauty as it denoted his valour (for he was a half-pay officer). He had good teeth, and something affable, when he pleased, in his smile; though naturally his countenance, as well as his air and voice, had much of roughness in it: yet he could at any time deposit this, and appear all gentleness and good-humour. He was not ungenteel, nor entirely devoid of wit, and in his youth had abounded in sprightliness, which, though he had lately put on a more serious character, he could, when he pleased, resume.

He had, as well as the doctor, an academic education; for his father had, with the same paternal authority we have mentioned before, decreed him for holy orders; but as the old gentleman died before he was ordained, he chose the church military, and preferred the king's commission to the bishop's.

He had purchased the post of lieutenant of dragoons, and afterwards came to be a captain; but having quarrelled with his colonel, was by his interest obliged to sell; from which time he had entirely rusticated himself, had betaken himself to studying the Scriptures, and was not a little suspected of an inclination to methodism.

It seemed, therefore, not unlikely that such a person should succeed with a lady of so saint-like a disposition, and whose inclinations were no otherwise engaged than to the marriage state in general; but why the doctor, who certainly had no great friendship for his brother, should for his sake think of making so ill a return to the hospitality of Allworthy, is a matter not so easy to be accounted for.

Is it that some natures delight in evil, as others are thought to delight in virtue? Or is there a pleasure in being accessory to a theft when we cannot commit it ourselves? Or lastly (which experience seems to make probable), have we a satisfaction in aggrandizing our families, even though we have not the least love or respect for them?

Whether any of these motives operated on the doctor, we will not determine; but so the fact was. He sent for his brother, and easily found means to introduce him at Allworthy's as a person who intended only a short visit to himself.

The captain had not been in the house a week before the doctor had reason to felicitate himself on his discernment. The captain was indeed as great a master of the art of love as Ovid was formerly. He had besides received proper hints from his brother, which he failed not to improve to the best advantage.

CHAPTER XI.

Containing many rules, and some examples, concerning falling in love: descriptions of beauty, and other more prudential inducements to matrimony.

It hath been observed, by wise men or women, I forget which, that all persons are doomed to be in love once in their lives. No particular season is, as I remember, assigned for this; but the age at which Miss Bridget was arrived, seems to me as proper a period as any to be fixed on for this purpose: it often, indeed, happens much earlier; but when it doth not, I have observed it seldom or never fails about this time. Moreover, we may remark that at this season love is of a more serious and steady nature than what sometimes shows itself in the younger parts of life. The love of girls is uncertain, capricious, and so foolish that we cannot always discover what the young lady would be at; nay, it may almost be doubted whether she always knows this herself.

Now we are never at a loss to discern this in women about forty; for as such grave, serious, and experienced ladies well know their own meaning, so it is always very easy for a man of the least sagacity to discover it with the utmost certainty.

Miss Bridget is an example of all these observations. She had not been many times in the captain's company before she was seized with this passion. Nor did she go pining and moping about the house, like a puny, foolish girl, ignorant of her distemper: she felt, she knew, and she enjoyed, the pleasing sensation, of which, as she was certain it was not only innocent but laudable, she was neither afraid nor ashamed.

And to say the truth, there is, in all points, great difference between the reasonable passion which women at this age conceive towards men, and the idle and childish liking of a girl to a boy, which is often fixed on the outside only, and on things of little value and no duration; as on cherry-cheeks, small, lily-white hands, sloe-black eyes, flowing locks, downy chins, dapper shapes; nay, sometimes on charms more worthless than these, and less the party's own; such are the outward ornaments of the person, for which men are beholden to the taylor, the laceman, the periwig-maker, the hatter, and the milliner, and not to nature. Such a passion girls may well be ashamed, as they generally are, to own either to themselves or others.

The love of Miss Bridget was of another kind. The captain owed nothing to any of these fop-makers in his dress, nor was his person much more beholden to nature. Both his dress and person were such as, had they appeared in an assembly or a drawing-room, would have been the contempt and ridicule of all the fine ladies there. The former of these was indeed neat, but plain, coarse, ill-fancied, and out of fashion. As for the latter, we have expressly described it above. So far was the skin on his cheeks from being cherry-coloured, that you could not discern what the natural colour of his cheeks was, they being totally overgrown by a black beard, which ascended to his eyes. His shape and limbs were indeed exactly proportioned, but so large that they denoted the strength rather of a ploughman than any other. His shoulders were broad beyond all size, and the calves of his legs larger than those of a common chairman. In short, his whole person wanted all that elegance and beauty which is the very reverse of clumsy strength, and which so agreeably sets off most of our fine gentlemen; being partly owing to the high blood of their ancestors, viz., blood made of rich sauces and generous wines, and partly to an early town education.

Though Miss Bridget was a woman of the greatest delicacy of taste, yet such were the charms of the captain's conversation, that she totally overlooked the defects of his person. She imagined, and perhaps very wisely, that she should enjoy more agreeable minutes with the captain than with a much prettier fellow; and forewent the consideration of pleasing her eyes, in order to procure herself much more solid satisfaction.

The captain no sooner perceived the passion of Miss Bridget, in which discovery he was very quick-sighted, than he faithfully returned it. The lady, no more than her lover, was remarkable for beauty. I would attempt to draw her picture, but that is done already by a more able master, Mr Hogarth himself, to whom she sat many years ago, and hath been lately exhibited by that gentleman in his print of a winter's morning, of which she was no improper emblem, and may be seen walking (for walk she doth in the print) to Covent Garden church, with a starved foot-boy behind carrying her prayer-book.

The captain likewise very wisely preferred the more solid enjoyments he expected with this lady, to the fleeting charms of person. He was one of those wise men who regard beauty in the other sex as a very worthless and superficial qualification; or, to speak more truly, who rather chuse to possess every convenience of life with an ugly woman, than a handsome one without any of those conveniences. And having a very good appetite, and but little nicety, he fancied he should play his part very well at the matrimonial banquet, without the sauce of beauty.

To deal plainly with the reader, the captain, ever since his arrival, at least from the moment his brother had proposed the match to him, long before he had discovered any flattering symptoms in Miss Bridget, had been greatly enamoured; that is to say, of Mr Allworthy's house and gardens, and of his lands, tenements, and hereditaments; of all which the captain was so passionately fond, that he would most probably have contracted marriage with them, had he been obliged to have taken the witch of Endor into the bargain.

As Mr Allworthy, therefore, had declared to the doctor that he never intended to take a second wife, as his sister was his nearest relation, and as the doctor had fished out that his intentions were to make any child of hers his heir, which indeed the law, without his interposition, would have done for him; the doctor and his brother thought it an act of benevolence to give being to a human creature, who would be so plentifully provided with the most essential means of happiness. The whole thoughts, therefore, of both the brothers were how to engage the affections of this amiable lady.

But fortune, who is a tender parent, and often doth more for her favourite offspring than either they deserve or wish, had been so industrious for the captain, that whilst he was laying schemes to execute his purpose, the lady conceived the same desires with himself, and was on her side contriving how to give the captain proper encouragement, without appearing too forward; for she was a strict observer of all rules of decorum. In this, however, she easily succeeded; for as the captain was always on the look-out, no glance, gesture, or word escaped him.

The satisfaction which the captain received from the kind behaviour of Miss Bridget, was not a little abated by his apprehensions of Mr Allworthy; for, notwithstanding his disinterested professions, the captain imagined he would, when he came to act, follow the example of the rest of the world, and refuse his consent to a match so disadvantageous, in point of interest, to his sister. From what oracle he received this opinion, I shall leave the reader to determine: but however he came by it, it strangely perplexed him how to regulate his conduct so as at once to convey his affection to the lady, and to conceal it from her brother. He at length resolved to take all private opportunities of making his addresses; but in the presence of Mr Allworthy to be as reserved and as much upon his guard as was possible; and this conduct was highly approved by the brother.

He soon found means to make his addresses, in express terms, to his mistress, from whom he received an answer in the proper form, viz.: the answer which was first made some thousands of years ago, and which hath been handed down by tradition from mother to daughter ever since. If I was to translate this into Latin, I should render it by these two words, *Nolo Episcopari*: a phrase likewise of immemorial use on another occasion.

The captain, however he came by his knowledge, perfectly well understood the lady, and very soon after repeated his application with more warmth and earnestness than before, and was again, according to due form, rejected; but as he had increased in the eagerness of his desires, so the lady, with the same propriety, decreased in the violence of her refusal.

Not to tire the reader, by leading him through every scene of this courtship (which, though in the opinion of a certain great author, it is the pleasantest scene of life to the actor, is, perhaps, as dull and tiresome as any whatever to the audience), the captain made his advances in form, the citadel was defended in form, and at length, in proper form, surrendered at discretion.

During this whole time, which filled the space of near a month, the captain preserved great distance of behaviour to his lady in the presence of the brother; and the more he succeeded with her in private, the more reserved was he in public. And as for the lady, she had no sooner secured her lover than she behaved to him before company with the highest degree of indifference; so that Mr Allworthy must have had the insight of the devil (or perhaps some of his worse qualities) to have entertained the least suspicion of what was going forward.

CHAPTER XII.

Containing what the reader may, perhaps, expect to find in it.

In all bargains, whether to fight or to marry, or concerning any other such business, little previous ceremony is required to bring the matter to an issue when both parties are really in earnest. This was the case at present, and in less than a month the captain and his lady were man and wife.

The great concern now was to break the matter to Mr Allworthy; and this was undertaken by the doctor.

One day, then, as Allworthy was walking in his garden, the doctor came to him, and, with great gravity of aspect, and all the concern which he could possibly affect in his countenance, said, "I am come, sir, to impart an affair to you of the utmost consequence; but how shall I mention to you what it almost distracts me to think of!" He then launched forth into the most bitter invectives both against men and women; accusing the former of having no attachment but to their interest, and the latter of being so addicted to vicious inclinations that they could never be safely trusted with one of the other sex. "Could I," said he, "sir, have suspected that a lady of such prudence, such judgment, such learning, should indulge so indiscreet a passion! or could I have imagined that my brother—why do I call him so? he is no longer a brother of mine——"

"Indeed but he is," said Allworthy, "and a brother of mine too."

"Bless me, sir!" said the doctor, "do you know the shocking affair?"

"Look'ee, Mr Blifil," answered the good man, "it hath been my constant maxim in life to make the best of all matters which happen. My sister, though many years younger than I, is at least old enough to be at the age of discretion. Had he imposed on a child, I should have been more averse to have forgiven him; but a woman upwards of thirty must certainly be supposed to know what will make her most happy. She hath married a gentleman, though perhaps not quite her equal in fortune; and if he hath any perfections in her eye which can make up that deficiency, I see no reason why I should object to her choice of her own happiness; which I, no more than herself, imagine to consist only in immense wealth. I might, perhaps, from the many declarations I have made of complying with almost any proposal, have expected to have been consulted on this occasion; but these matters are of a very delicate nature, and the scruples of modesty, perhaps, are not to be overcome. As to your brother, I have really no anger against him at all. He hath no obligations to me, nor do I think he was under any necessity of asking my consent, since the woman is, as I have said, *sui juris*, and of a proper age to be entirely answerable only, to herself for her conduct."

The doctor accused Mr Allworthy of too great lenity, repeated his accusations against his brother, and declared that he should never more be brought either to see, or to own him for his relation. He then launched forth into a panegyric on Allworthy's goodness; into the highest encomiums on his friendship; and concluded by saying, he should never forgive his brother for having put the place which he bore in that friendship to a hazard.

Allworthy thus answered: "Had I conceived any displeasure against your brother, I should never have carried that resentment to the innocent: but I assure you I have no such displeasure. Your brother appears to me to be a man of sense and honour. I do not disapprove the taste of my sister; nor will I doubt but that she is equally the object of his inclinations. I have always thought love the only foundation of happiness in a married state, as it can only produce that high and tender friendship which should always be the cement of this union; and, in my opinion, all those marriages which are contracted from other motives are greatly criminal; they are a profanation of a most holy ceremony, and generally end in disquiet and misery: for surely we may call it a profanation to convert this most sacred institution into a wicked sacrifice to lust or avarice: and what better can be said of those matches to which men are induced merely by the consideration of a beautiful person, or a great fortune?

"To deny that beauty is an agreeable object to the eye, and even worthy some admiration, would be false and foolish. Beautiful is an epithet often used in Scripture, and always mentioned with honour. It was my own fortune to marry a woman whom the world thought handsome, and I can truly say I liked her the better on that account. But to make this the sole consideration of marriage, to lust after it so violently as to overlook all imperfections for its sake, or to require it so absolutely as to reject and disdain religion, virtue, and sense, which are qualities in their nature of much higher perfection, only because an elegance of person is wanting: this is surely inconsistent, either with a wise man or a good Christian. And it is, perhaps, being too charitable to conclude that such persons mean anything more by their marriage than to please their carnal appetites; for the satisfaction of which, we are taught, it was not ordained.

"In the next place, with respect to fortune. Worldly prudence, perhaps, exacts some consideration on this head; nor will I absolutely and altogether condemn it. As the world is constituted, the demands of a married state, and the care of posterity, require some little regard to what we call circumstances. Yet this provision is greatly increased, beyond what is really necessary, by folly and vanity, which create abundantly more wants than nature. Equipage for the wife, and large fortunes for the children, are by custom enrolled in the list of necessaries; and to procure these, everything truly solid and sweet, and virtuous and religious, are neglected and overlooked.

"And this in many degrees; the last and greatest of which seems scarce distinguishable from madness;—I mean where persons of immense fortunes contract themselves to those who are, and must be, disagreeable to them—to fools and knaves—in order to increase an estate already larger even than the demands of their pleasures. Surely such persons, if they will not be thought mad, must own, either that they are incapable of tasting the sweets of the tenderest friendship, or that they sacrifice the greatest happiness of which they are capable to the vain, uncertain, and senseless laws of vulgar opinion, which owe as well their force as their foundation to folly."

Here Allworthy concluded his sermon, to which Blifil had listened with the profoundest attention, though it cost him some pains to prevent now and then a small discomposure of his muscles. He now praised every period of what he had heard with the warmth of a young divine, who hath the honour to dine with a bishop the same day in which his lordship hath mounted the pulpit.

CHAPTER XIII.

Which concludes the first book; with an instance of ingratitude, which, we hope, will appear unnatural.

The reader, from what hath been said, may imagine that the reconciliation (if indeed it could be so called) was only matter of form; we shall therefore pass it over, and hasten to what must surely be thought matter of substance.

The doctor had acquainted his brother with what had past between Mr Allworthy and him; and added with a smile, "I promise you I paid you off; nay, I absolutely desired the good gentleman not to forgive you: for you know after he had made a declaration in your favour, I might with safety venture on such a request with a person of his temper; and I was willing, as well for your sake as for my own, to prevent the least possibility of a suspicion."

Captain Blifil took not the least notice of this, at that time; but he afterwards made a very notable use of it.

One of the maxims which the devil, in a late visit upon earth, left to his disciples, is, when once you are got up, to kick the stool from under you. In plain English, when you have made your fortune by the good offices of a friend, you are advised to discard him as soon as you can.

Whether the captain acted by this maxim, I will not positively determine: so far we may confidently say, that his actions may be fairly derived from this diabolical principle; and indeed it is difficult to assign any other motive to them: for no sooner was he possessed of Miss Bridget, and reconciled to Allworthy, than he began to show a coldness to his brother which increased daily; till at length it grew into rudeness, and became very visible to every one.

The doctor remonstrated to him privately concerning this behaviour, but could obtain no other satisfaction than the following plain declaration: "If you dislike anything in my brother's house, sir, you know you are at liberty to quit it." This strange, cruel, and almost unaccountable ingratitude in the captain, absolutely broke the poor doctor's heart; for ingratitude never so thoroughly pierces the human breast as when it proceeds from those in whose behalf we have been guilty of transgressions. Reflections on great and good actions, however they are received or returned by those in whose favour they are performed, always administer some comfort to us; but what consolation shall we receive under so biting a calamity as the ungrateful behaviour of our friend, when our wounded conscience at the same time flies in our face, and upbraids us with having spotted it in the service of one so worthless!

Mr Allworthy himself spoke to the captain in his brother's behalf, and desired to know what offence the doctor had committed; when the hard-hearted villain had the baseness to say that he should never forgive him for the injury which he had endeavoured to do him in his favour; which, he said, he had pumped out of him, and was such a cruelty that it ought not to be forgiven.

Allworthy spoke in very high terms upon this declaration, which, he said, became not a human creature. He expressed, indeed, so much resentment against an unforgiving temper, that the captain at last pretended to be convinced by his arguments, and outwardly professed to be reconciled.

As for the bride, she was now in her honeymoon, and so passionately fond of her new husband that he never appeared to her to be in the wrong; and his displeasure against any person was a sufficient reason for her dislike to the same.

The captain, at Mr Allworthy's instance, was outwardly, as we have said, reconciled to his brother; yet the same rancour remained in his heart; and he found so many opportunities of giving him private hints of this, that the house at last grew insupportable to the poor doctor; and he chose rather to submit to any inconveniences which he might encounter in the world, than longer to bear these cruel and ungrateful insults from a brother for whom he had done so much.

He once intended to acquaint Allworthy with the whole; but he could not bring himself to submit to the confession, by which he must take to his share so great a portion of guilt. Besides, by how much the worse man he represented his brother to be, so much the greater would his own offence appear to Allworthy, and so much the greater, he had reason to imagine, would be his resentment.

He feigned, therefore, some excuse of business for his departure, and promised to return soon again; and took leave of his brother with so well-dissembled content, that, as the captain played his part to the same perfection, Allworthy remained well satisfied with the truth of the reconciliation.

The doctor went directly to London, where he died soon after of a broken heart; a distemper which kills many more than is generally imagined, and would have a fair title to a place in the bill of mortality, did it not differ in one instance from all other diseases—viz., that no physician can cure it.

Now, upon the most diligent enquiry into the former lives of these two brothers, I find, besides the cursed and hellish maxim of policy above mentioned, another reason for the captain's conduct: the captain, besides what we have before said of him, was a man of great pride and fierceness, and had always treated his brother, who was of a different complexion, and greatly deficient in both these qualities, with the utmost air of superiority. The doctor, however, had much the larger share of learning, and was by many reputed to have the better understanding. This the captain knew, and could not bear; for though envy is at best a very malignant passion, yet is its bitterness greatly heightened by mixing with contempt towards the same object; and very much afraid I am, that whenever an obligation is joined to these two, indignation and not gratitude will be the product of all three.

BOOK II.

CONTAINING SCENES OF MATRIMONIAL FELICITY IN DIFFERENT DEGREES OF LIFE; AND VARIOUS OTHER TRANSACTIONS DURING THE FIRST TWO YEARS AFTER THE MARRIAGE BETWEEN CAPTAIN BLIFIL AND MISS BRIDGET ALLWORTHY.

CHAPTER I.

Showing what kind of a history this is; what it is like, and what it is not like.

Though we have properly enough entitled this our work, a history, and not a life; nor an apology for a life, as is more in fashion; yet we intend in it rather to pursue the method of those writers, who profess to disclose the revolutions of countries, than to imitate the painful and voluminous historian, who, to preserve the regularity of his series, thinks himself obliged to fill up as much paper with the detail of months and years in which nothing remarkable happened, as he employs upon those notable aeras when the greatest scenes have been transacted on the human stage.

Such histories as these do, in reality, very much resemble a newspaper, which consists of just the same number of words, whether there be any news in it or not. They may likewise be compared to a stage coach, which performs constantly the same course, empty as well as full. The writer, indeed, seems to think himself obliged to keep even pace with time, whose amanuensis he is; and, like his master, travels as slowly through centuries of monkish dulness, when the world seems to have been asleep, as through that bright and busy age so nobly distinguished by the excellent Latin poet—

Ad confligendum venientibus undique poenis,
Omnia cum belli trepido concussa tumultu
Horrida contremuere sub altis aetheris auris;
In dubioque fuit sub utrorum regna cadendum
Omnibus humanis esset, terraque marique.

Of which we wish we could give our readers a more adequate translation than that by Mr Creech—

When dreadful Carthage frighted Rome with arms,
And all the world was shook with fierce alarms;
Whilst undecided yet, which part should fall,
Which nation rise the glorious lord of all.

Now it is our purpose, in the ensuing pages, to pursue a contrary method. When any extraordinary scene presents itself (as we trust will often be the case), we shall spare no pains nor paper to open it at large to our reader; but if whole years should pass without producing anything worthy his notice, we shall not be afraid of a chasm in our history; but shall hasten on to matters of consequence, and leave such periods of time totally unobserved.

These are indeed to be considered as blanks in the grand lottery of time. We therefore, who are the registers of that lottery, shall imitate those sagacious persons who deal in that which is drawn at Guildhall, and who never trouble the public with the many blanks they dispose of; but when a great prize happens to be drawn, the newspapers are presently filled with it, and the world is sure to be informed at whose office it was sold: indeed, commonly two or three different offices lay claim to the honour of having disposed of it; by which, I suppose, the adventurers are given to understand that certain brokers are in the secrets of Fortune, and indeed of her cabinet council.

My reader then is not to be surprized, if, in the course of this work, he shall find some chapters very short, and others altogether as long; some that contain only the time of a single day, and others that comprise years; in a word, if my history sometimes seems to stand still, and sometimes to fly. For all which I shall not look on myself as accountable to any court of critical jurisdiction whatever: for as I am, in reality, the founder of a new province of writing, so I am at liberty to make what laws I please therein. And these laws, my readers, whom I consider as my subjects, are bound to believe in and to obey; with which that they may readily and cheerfully comply, I do hereby assure them that I shall principally regard their ease and advantage in all such institutions: for I do not, like a *jure divino* tyrant, imagine that they are my slaves, or my commodity. I am, indeed, set over them for their own good only, and was created for their use, and not they for mine. Nor do I doubt, while I make their interest the great rule of my writings, they will unanimously concur in supporting my dignity, and in rendering me all the honour I shall deserve or desire.

CHAPTER II.

Religious cautions against showing too much favour to bastards; and a great discovery made by Mrs Deborah Wilkins.

Eight months after the celebration of the nuptials between Captain Blifil and Miss Bridget Allworthy, a young lady of great beauty, merit, and fortune, was Miss Bridget, by reason of a fright, delivered of a fine boy. The child was indeed to all appearances perfect; but the midwife discovered it was born a month before its full time.

Though the birth of an heir by his beloved sister was a circumstance of great joy to Mr Allworthy, yet it did not alienate his affections from the little foundling, to whom he had been godfather, had given his own name of Thomas, and whom he had hitherto seldom failed of visiting, at least once a day, in his nursery.

He told his sister, if she pleased, the new-born infant should be bred up together with little Tommy; to which she consented, though with some little reluctance: for she had truly a great complacence for her brother; and hence she had always behaved towards the foundling with rather more kindness than ladies of rigid virtue can sometimes bring themselves to show to these children, who, however innocent, may be truly called the living monuments of incontinence.

The captain could not so easily bring himself to bear what he condemned as a fault in Mr Allworthy. He gave him frequent hints, that to adopt the fruits of sin, was to give countenance to it. He quoted several texts (for he was well read in Scripture), such as, *He visits the sins of the fathers upon the children; and the fathers have eaten sour grapes, and the children's teeth are set on edge*,&c. Whence he argued the legality of punishing the crime of the parent on the bastard. He said, "Though the law did not positively allow the destroying such base-born children, yet it held them to be the children of nobody; that the Church considered them as the children of nobody; and that at the best, they ought to be brought up to the lowest and vilest offices of the commonwealth."

Mr Allworthy answered to all this, and much more, which the captain had urged on this subject, "That, however guilty the parents might be, the children were certainly innocent: that as to the texts he had quoted, the former of them was a particular denunciation against the Jews, for the sin of idolatry, of relinquishing and hating their heavenly King; and the latter was parabolically spoken, and rather intended to denote the certain and necessary consequences of sin, than any express judgment against it. But to represent the Almighty as avenging the sins of the guilty on the innocent, was indecent, if not blasphemous, as it was to represent him acting against the first principles of natural justice, and against the original notions of right and wrong, which he himself had implanted in our minds; by which we were to judge not only in all matters which were not revealed, but even of the truth of revelation itself. He said he knew many held the same principles with the captain on this head; but he was himself firmly convinced to the contrary, and would provide in the same manner for this poor infant, as if a legitimate child had had fortune to have been found in the same place."

While the captain was taking all opportunities to press these and such like arguments, to remove the little foundling from Mr Allworthy's, of whose fondness for him he began to be jealous, Mrs Deborah had made a discovery, which, in its event, threatened at least to prove more fatal to poor Tommy than all the reasonings of the captain.

Whether the insatiable curiosity of this good woman had carried her on to that business, or whether she did it to confirm herself in the good graces of Mrs Blifil, who, notwithstanding her outward behaviour to the foundling, frequently abused the infant in private, and her brother too, for his fondness to it, I will not determine; but she had now, as she conceived, fully detected the father of the foundling.

Now, as this was a discovery of great consequence, it may be necessary to trace it from the fountain-head. We shall therefore very minutely lay open those previous matters by which it was produced; and for that purpose we shall be obliged to reveal all the secrets of a little family with which my reader is at present entirely unacquainted; and of which the oeconomy was so rare and extraordinary, that I fear it will shock the utmost credulity of many married persons.

CHAPTER III.

The description of a domestic government founded upon rules directly contrary to those of Aristotle.

My reader may please to remember he hath been informed that Jenny Jones had lived some years with a certain schoolmaster, who had, at her earnest desire, instructed her in Latin, in which, to do justice to her genius, she had so improved herself, that she was become a better scholar than her master.

Indeed, though this poor man had undertaken a profession to which learning must be allowed necessary, this was the least of his commendations. He was one of the best-natured fellows in the world, and was, at the same time, master of so much pleasantry and humour, that he was reputed the wit of the country; and all the neighbouring gentlemen were so desirous of his company, that as denying was not his talent, he spent much time at their houses, which he might, with more emolument, have spent in his school.

It may be imagined that a gentleman so qualified and so disposed, was in no danger of becoming formidable to the learned seminaries of Eton or Westminster. To speak plainly, his scholars were divided into two classes: in the upper of which was a young gentleman, the son of a neighbouring squire, who, at the age of seventeen, was just entered into his Syntaxis; and in the lower was a second son of the same gentleman, who, together with seven parish-boys, was learning to read and write.

The stipend arising hence would hardly have indulged the schoolmaster in the luxuries of life, had he not added to this office those of clerk and barber, and had not Mr Allworthy added to the whole an annuity of ten pounds, which the poor man received every Christmas, and with which he was enabled to cheer his heart during that sacred festival.

Among his other treasures, the pedagogue had a wife, whom he had married out of Mr Allworthy's kitchen for her fortune, viz., twenty pounds, which she had there amassed.

This woman was not very amiable in her person. Whether she sat to my friend Hogarth, or no, I will not determine; but she exactly resembled the young woman who is pouring out her mistress's tea in the third picture of the Harlot's Progress. She was, besides, a profest follower of that noble sect founded by Xantippe of old; by means of which she became more formidable in the school than her husband; for, to confess the truth, he was never master there, or anywhere else, in her presence.

Though her countenance did not denote much natural sweetness of temper, yet this was, perhaps, somewhat soured by a circumstance which generally poisons matrimonial felicity; for children are rightly called the pledges of love; and her husband, though they had been married nine years, had given her no such pledges; a default for which he had no excuse, either from age or health, being not yet thirty years old, and what they call a jolly brisk young man.

Hence arose another evil, which produced no little uneasiness to the poor pedagogue, of whom she maintained so constant a jealousy, that he durst hardly speak to one woman in the parish; for the least degree of civility, or even correspondence, with any female, was sure to bring his wife upon her back, and his own.

In order to guard herself against matrimonial injuries in her own house, as she kept one maid-servant, she always took care to chuse her out of that order of females whose faces are taken as a kind of security for their virtue; of which number Jenny Jones, as the reader hath been before informed, was one.

As the face of this young woman might be called pretty good security of the before-mentioned kind, and as her behaviour had been always extremely modest, which is the certain consequence of understanding in women; she had passed above four years at Mr Partridge's (for that was the schoolmaster's name) without creating the least suspicion in her mistress. Nay, she had been treated with uncommon kindness, and her mistress had permitted Mr Partridge to give her those instructions which have been before commemorated.

But it is with jealousy as with the gout: when such distempers are in the blood, there is never any security against their breaking out; and that often on the slightest occasions, and when least suspected.

Thus it happened to Mrs Partridge, who had submitted four years to her husband's teaching this young woman, and had suffered her often to neglect her work, in order to pursue her learning. For, passing by one day, as the girl was reading, and her master leaning over her, the girl, I know not for what reason, suddenly started up from her chair: and this was the first time that suspicion ever entered into the head of her mistress. This did not, however, at that time discover itself, but lay lurking in her mind, like a concealed enemy, who waits for a reinforcement of additional strength before he openly declares himself and proceeds upon hostile operations: and such additional strength soon arrived to corroborate her suspicion; for not long after, the husband and wife being at dinner, the master said to his maid, *Da mihi aliquid potum:* upon which the poor girl smiled, perhaps at the badness of the Latin, and, when her mistress cast her eyes on her, blushed, possibly with a consciousness of having laughed at her master. Mrs Partridge, upon this, immediately fell into a fury, and discharged the trencher on which she was eating, at the head of poor Jenny, crying out, "You impudent whore, do you play tricks with my husband before my face?" and at the same instant rose from her chair with a knife in her hand, with which, most probably, she would have executed very tragical vengeance, had not the girl taken the advantage of being nearer the door than her mistress, and avoided her fury by running away: for, as to the poor husband, whether surprize had rendered him motionless, or fear (which is full as probable) had restrained him from venturing at any opposition, he sat staring and trembling in his chair; nor did he once offer to move or speak, till his wife, returning from the pursuit of Jenny, made some defensive measures necessary for his own preservation; and he likewise was obliged to retreat, after the example of the maid.

This good woman was, no more than Othello, of a disposition

To make a life of jealousy
And follow still the changes of the moon
With fresh suspicions—

With her, as well as him,

—To be once in doubt,
Was once to be resolvd—

she therefore ordered Jenny immediately to pack up her alls and begone, for that she was determined she should not sleep that night within her walls.

Mr Partridge had profited too much by experience to interpose in a matter of this nature. He therefore had recourse to his usual receipt of patience, for, though he was not a great adept in Latin, he remembered, and well understood, the advice contained in these words

—Leve fit quod bene fertur onus

in English:

A burden becomes lightest when it is well borne—

which he had always in his mouth; and of which, to say the truth, he had often occasion to experience the truth.

Jenny offered to make protestations of her innocence; but the tempest was too strong for her to be heard. She then betook herself to the business of packing, for which a small quantity of brown paper sufficed, and, having received her small pittance of wages, she returned home.

The schoolmaster and his consort passed their time unpleasantly enough that evening, but something or other happened before the next morning, which a little abated the fury of Mrs Partridge; and she at length admitted her husband to make his excuses: to which she gave the readier belief, as he had, instead of desiring her to recall Jenny, professed a satisfaction in her being dismissed, saying, she was grown of little use as a servant, spending all her time in reading, and was become, moreover, very pert and obstinate; for, indeed, she and her master had lately had frequent disputes in literature; in which, as hath been said, she was become greatly his superior. This, however, he would by no means allow; and as he called her persisting in the right, obstinacy, he began to hate her with no small inveteracy.

CHAPTER IV.

Containing one of the most bloody battles, or rather duels, that were ever recorded in domestic history.

For the reasons mentioned in the preceding chapter, and from some other matrimonial concessions, well known to most husbands, and which, like the secrets of freemasonry, should be divulged to none who are not members of that honourable fraternity, Mrs Partridge was pretty well satisfied that she had condemned her husband without cause, and endeavoured by acts of kindness to make him amends for her false suspicion. Her passions were indeed equally violent, whichever way they inclined; for as she could be extremely angry, so could she be altogether as fond.

But though these passions ordinarily succeed each other, and scarce twenty-four hours ever passed in which the pedagogue was not, in some degree, the object of both; yet, on extraordinary occasions, when the passion of anger had raged very high, the remission was usually longer: and so was the case at present; for she continued longer in a state of affability, after this fit of jealousy was ended, than her husband had ever known before: and, had it not been for some little exercises, which all the followers of Xantippe are obliged to perform daily, Mr Partridge would have enjoyed a perfect serenity of several months.

Perfect calms at sea are always suspected by the experienced mariner to be the forerunners of a storm, and I know some persons, who, without being generally the devotees of superstition, are apt to apprehend that great and unusual peace or tranquillity will be attended with its opposite. For which reason the antients used, on such occasions, to sacrifice to the goddess Nemesis, a deity who was thought by them to look with an invidious eye on human felicity, and to have a peculiar delight in overturning it.

As we are very far from believing in any such heathen goddess, or from encouraging any superstition, so we wish Mr John Fr——, or some other such philosopher, would bestir himself a little, in order to find out the real cause of this sudden transition from good to bad fortune, which hath been so often remarked, and of which we shall proceed to give an instance; for it is our province to relate facts, and we shall leave causes to persons of much higher genius.

Mankind have always taken great delight in knowing and descanting on the actions of others. Hence there have been, in all ages and nations, certain places set apart for public rendezvous, where the curious might meet and satisfy their mutual curiosity. Among these, the barbers' shops have justly borne the pre-eminence. Among the Greeks, barbers' news was a proverbial expression; and Horace, in one of his epistles, makes honourable mention of the Roman barbers in the same light.

Those of England are known to be no wise inferior to their Greek or Roman predecessors. You there see foreign affairs discussed in a manner little inferior to that with which they are handled in the coffee-houses; and domestic occurrences are much more largely and freely treated in the former than in the latter. But this serves only for the men. Now, whereas the females of this country, especially those of the lower order, do associate themselves much more than those of other nations, our polity would be highly deficient, if they had not some place set apart likewise for the indulgence of their curiosity, seeing they are in this no way inferior to the other half of the species.

In enjoying, therefore, such place of rendezvous, the British fair ought to esteem themselves more happy than any of their foreign sisters; as I do not remember either to have read in history, or to have seen in my travels, anything of the like kind.

This place then is no other than the chandler's shop, the known seat of all the news; or, as it is vulgarly called, gossiping, in every parish in England.

Mrs Partridge being one day at this assembly of females, was asked by one of her neighbours, if she had heard no news lately of Jenny Jones? To which she answered in the negative. Upon this the other replied, with a smile, That the parish was very much obliged to her for having turned Jenny away as she did.

Mrs Partridge, whose jealousy, as the reader well knows, was long since cured, and who had no other quarrel to her maid, answered boldly, She did not know any obligation the parish had to her on that account; for she believed Jenny had scarce left her equal behind her.

"No, truly," said the gossip, "I hope not, though I fancy we have sluts enow too. Then you have not heard, it seems, that she hath been brought to bed of two bastards? but as they are not born here, my husband and the other overseer says we shall not be obliged to keep them."

"Two bastards!" answered Mrs Partridge hastily: "you surprize me! I don't know whether we must keep them; but I am sure they must have been begotten here, for the wench hath not been nine months gone away."

Nothing can be so quick and sudden as the operations of the mind, especially when hope, or fear, or jealousy, to which the two others are but journeymen, set it to work. It occurred instantly to her, that Jenny had scarce ever been out of her own house while she lived with her. The leaning over the chair, the sudden starting up, the Latin, the smile, and many other things, rushed upon her all at once. The satisfaction her husband expressed in the departure of Jenny, appeared now to be only dissembled; again, in the same instant, to be real; but yet to confirm her jealousy, proceeding from satiety, and a hundred other bad causes. In a word, she was convinced of her husband's guilt, and immediately left the assembly in confusion.

As fair Grimalkin, who, though the youngest of the feline family, degenerates not in ferocity from the elder branches of her house, and though inferior in strength, is equal in fierceness to the noble tiger himself, when a little mouse, whom it hath long tormented in sport, escapes from her clutches for a while, frets, scolds, growls, swears; but if the trunk, or box, behind which the mouse lay hid be again removed, she flies like lightning on her prey, and, with envenomed wrath, bites, scratches, mumbles, and tears the little animal.

Not with less fury did Mrs Partridge fly on the poor pedagogue. Her tongue, teeth, and hands, fell all upon him at once. His wig was in an instant torn from his head, his shirt from his back, and from his face descended five streams of blood, denoting the number of claws with which nature had unhappily armed the enemy.

Mr Partridge acted for some time on the defensive only; indeed he attempted only to guard his face with his hands; but as he found that his antagonist abated nothing of her rage, he thought he might, at least, endeavour to disarm her, or rather to confine her arms; in doing which her cap fell off in the struggle, and her hair being too short to reach her shoulders, erected itself on her head; her stays likewise, which were laced through one single hole at the bottom, burst open; and her breasts, which were much more redundant than her hair, hung down below her middle; her face was likewise marked with the blood of her husband: her teeth gnashed with rage; and fire, such as sparkles from a smith's forge, darted from her eyes. So that, altogether, this Amazonian heroine might have been an object of terror to a much bolder man than Mr Partridge.

He had, at length, the good fortune, by getting possession of her arms, to render those weapons which she wore at the ends of her fingers useless; which she no sooner perceived, than the softness of her sex prevailed over her rage, and she presently dissolved in tears, which soon after concluded in a fit.

That small share of sense which Mr Partridge had hitherto preserved through this scene of fury, of the cause of which he was hitherto ignorant, now utterly abandoned him. He ran instantly into the street, hallowing out that his wife was in the agonies of death, and beseeching the neighbours to fly with the utmost haste to her assistance. Several good women obeyed his summons, who entering his house, and applying the usual remedies on such occasions, Mrs Partridge was at length, to the great joy of her husband, brought to herself.

As soon as she had a little recollected her spirits, and somewhat composed herself with a cordial, she began to inform the company of the manifold injuries she had received from her husband; who, she said, was not contented to injure her in her bed; but, upon her upbraiding him with it, had treated her in the cruelest manner imaginable; had tore her cap and hair from her head, and her stays from her body, giving her, at the same time, several blows, the marks of which she should carry to the grave.

The poor man, who bore on his face many more visible marks of the indignation of his wife, stood in silent astonishment at this accusation; which the reader will, I believe, bear witness for him, had greatly exceeded the truth; for indeed he had not struck her once; and this silence being interpreted to be a confession of the charge by the whole court, they all began at once, *una voce*, to rebuke and revile him, repeating often, that none but a coward ever struck a woman.

Mr Partridge bore all this patiently; but when his wife appealed to the blood on her face, as an evidence of his barbarity, he could not help laying claim to his own blood, for so it really was; as he thought it very unnatural, that this should rise up (as we are taught that of a murdered person often doth) in vengeance against him.

To this the women made no other answer, than that it was a pity it had not come from his heart, instead of his face; all declaring, that, if their husbands should lift their hands against them, they would have their hearts' bloods out of their bodies.

After much admonition for what was past, and much good advice to Mr Partridge for his future behaviour, the company at length departed, and left the husband and wife to a personal conference together, in which Mr Partridge soon learned the cause of all his sufferings.

CHAPTER V.

Containing much matter to exercise the judgment and reflection of the reader.

I believe it is a true observation, that few secrets are divulged to one person only; but certainly, it would be next to a miracle that a fact of this kind should be known to a whole parish, and not transpire any farther.

And, indeed, a very few days had past, before the country, to use a common phrase, rung of the schoolmaster of Little Baddington; who was said to have beaten his wife in the most cruel manner. Nay, in some places it was reported he had murdered her; in others, that he had broke her arms; in others, her legs: in short, there was scarce an injury which can be done to a human creature, but what Mrs Partridge was somewhere or other affirmed to have received from her husband.

The cause of this quarrel was likewise variously reported; for as some people said that Mrs Partridge had caught her husband in bed with his maid, so many other reasons, of a very different kind, went abroad. Nay, some transferred the guilt to the wife, and the jealousy to the husband.

Mrs Wilkins had long ago heard of this quarrel; but, as a different cause from the true one had reached her ears, she thought proper to conceal it; and the rather, perhaps, as the blame was universally laid on Mr Partridge; and his wife, when she was servant to Mr Allworthy, had in something offended Mrs Wilkins, who was not of a very forgiving temper.

But Mrs Wilkins, whose eyes could see objects at a distance, and who could very well look forward a few years into futurity, had perceived a strong likelihood of Captain Blifil's being hereafter her master; and as she plainly discerned that the captain bore no great goodwill to the little foundling, she fancied it would be rendering him an agreeable service, if she could make any discoveries that might lessen the affection which Mr Allworthy seemed to have contracted for this child, and which gave visible uneasiness to the captain, who could not entirely conceal it even before Allworthy himself; though his wife, who acted her part much better in public, frequently recommended to him her own example, of conniving at the folly of her brother, which, she said, she at least as well perceived, and as much resented, as any other possibly could.

Mrs Wilkins having therefore, by accident, gotten a true scent of the above story,—though long after it had happened, failed not to satisfy herself thoroughly of all the particulars; and then acquainted the captain, that she had at last discovered the true father of the little bastard, which she was sorry, she said, to see her master lose his reputation in the country, by taking so much notice of.

The captain chid her for the conclusion of her speech, as an improper assurance in judging of her master's actions: for if his honour, or his understanding, would have suffered the captain to make an alliance with Mrs Wilkins, his pride would by no means have admitted it. And to say the truth, there is no conduct less politic, than to enter into any confederacy with your friend's servants against their master: for by these means you afterwards become the slave of these very servants; by whom you are constantly liable to be betrayed. And this consideration, perhaps it was, which prevented Captain Blifil from being more explicit with Mrs Wilkins, or from encouraging the abuse which she had bestowed on Allworthy.

But though he declared no satisfaction to Mrs Wilkins at this discovery, he enjoyed not a little from it in his own mind, and resolved to make the best use of it he was able.

He kept this matter a long time concealed within his own breast, in hopes that Mr Allworthy might hear it from some other person; but Mrs Wilkins, whether she resented the captain's behaviour, or whether his cunning was beyond her, and she feared the discovery might displease him, never afterwards opened her lips about the matter.

I have thought it somewhat strange, upon reflection, that the housekeeper never acquainted Mrs Blifil with this news, as women are more inclined to communicate all pieces of intelligence to their own sex, than to ours. The only way, as it appears to me, of solving this difficulty, is, by imputing it to that distance which was now grown between the lady and the housekeeper: whether this arose from a jealousy in Mrs Blifil, that Wilkins showed too great a respect to the foundling; for while she was endeavouring to ruin the little infant, in order to ingratiate herself with the captain, she was every day more and more commending it before Allworthy, as his fondness for it every day increased. This, notwithstanding all the care she took at other times to express the direct contrary to Mrs Blifil, perhaps offended that delicate lady, who certainly now hated Mrs Wilkins; and though she did not, or possibly could not, absolutely remove her from her place, she found, however, the means of making her life very uneasy. This Mrs Wilkins, at length, so resented, that she very openly showed all manner of respect and fondness to little Tommy, in opposition to Mrs Blifil.

The captain, therefore, finding the story in danger of perishing, at last took an opportunity to reveal it himself.

He was one day engaged with Mr Allworthy in a discourse on charity: in which the captain, with great learning, proved to Mr Allworthy, that the word charity in Scripture nowhere means beneficence or generosity.

"The Christian religion," he said, "was instituted for much nobler purposes, than to enforce a lesson which many heathen philosophers had taught us long before, and which, though it might perhaps be called a moral virtue, savoured but little of that sublime, Christian-like disposition, that vast elevation of thought, in purity approaching to angelic perfection, to be attained, expressed, and felt only by grace. Those," he said, "came nearer to the Scripture meaning, who understood by it candour, or the forming of a benevolent opinion of our brethren, and passing a favourable judgment on their actions; a virtue much higher, and more extensive in its nature, than a pitiful distribution of alms, which, though we would never so much prejudice, or even ruin our families, could never reach many; whereas charity, in the other and truer sense, might be extended to all mankind."

He said, "Considering who the disciples were, it would be absurd to conceive the doctrine of generosity, or giving alms, to have been preached to them. And, as we could not well imagine this doctrine should be preached by its Divine Author to men who could not practise it, much less should we think it understood so by those who can practise it, and do not.

"But though," continued he, "there is, I am afraid, little merit in these benefactions, there would, I must confess, be much pleasure in them to a good mind, if it was not abated by one consideration. I mean, that we are liable to be imposed upon, and to confer our choicest favours often on the undeserving, as you must own was your case in your bounty to that worthless fellow Partridge: for two or three such examples must greatly lessen the inward satisfaction which a good man would otherwise find in generosity; nay, may even make him timorous in bestowing, lest he should be guilty of supporting vice, and encouraging the wicked; a crime of a very black dye, and for which it will by no means be a sufficient excuse, that we have not actually intended such an encouragement; unless we have used the utmost caution in chusing the objects of our beneficence. A consideration which, I make no doubt, hath greatly checked the liberality of many a worthy and pious man."

Mr Allworthy answered, "He could not dispute with the captain in the Greek language, and therefore could say nothing as to the true sense of the word which is translated charity; but that he had always thought it was interpreted to consist in action, and that giving alms constituted at least one branch of that virtue.

"As to the meritorious part," he said, "he readily agreed with the captain; for where could be the merit of barely discharging a duty? which," he said, "let the word charity have what construction it would, it sufficiently appeared to be from the whole tenor of the New Testament. And as he thought it an indispensable duty, enjoined both by the Christian law, and by the law of nature itself; so was it withal so pleasant, that if any duty could be said to be its own reward, or to pay us while we are discharging it, it was this.

"To confess the truth," said he, "there is one degree of generosity (of charity I would have called it), which seems to have some show of merit, and that is, where, from a principle of benevolence and Christian love, we bestow on another what we really want ourselves; where, in order to lessen the distresses of another, we condescend to share some part of them, by giving what even our own necessities cannot well spare. This is, I think, meritorious; but to relieve our brethren only with our superfluities; to be charitable (I must use the word) rather at the expense of our coffers than ourselves; to save several families from misery rather than hang up an extraordinary picture in our houses or gratify any other idle ridiculous vanity—this seems to be only being human creatures. Nay, I will venture to go farther, it is being in some degree epicures: for what could the greatest epicure wish rather than to eat with many mouths instead of one? which I think may be predicated of any one who knows that the bread of many is owing to his own largesses.

"As to the apprehension of bestowing bounty on such as may hereafter prove unworthy objects, because many have proved such; surely it can never deter a good man from generosity. I do not think a few or many examples of ingratitude can justify a man's hardening his heart against the distresses of his fellow-creatures; nor do I believe it can ever have such effect on a truly benevolent mind. Nothing less than a persuasion of universal depravity can lock up the charity of a good man; and this persuasion must lead him, I think, either into atheism, or enthusiasm; but surely it is unfair to argue such universal depravity from a few vicious individuals; nor was this, I believe, ever done by a man, who, upon searching his own mind, found one certain exception to the general rule." He then concluded by asking, "who that Partridge was, whom he had called a worthless fellow?"

"I mean," said the captain, "Partridge the barber, the schoolmaster, what do you call him? Partridge, the father of the little child which you found in your bed."

Mr Allworthy exprest great surprize at this account, and the captain as great at his ignorance of it; for he said he had known it above a month: and at length recollected with much difficulty that he was told it by Mrs Wilkins.

Upon this, Wilkins was immediately summoned; who having confirmed what the captain had said, was by Mr Allworthy, by and with the captain's advice, dispatched to Little Baddington, to inform herself of the truth of the fact: for the captain exprest great dislike at all hasty proceedings in criminal matters, and said he would by no means have Mr Allworthy take any resolution either to the prejudice of the child or its father, before he was satisfied that the latter was guilty; for though he had privately satisfied himself of this from one of Partridge's neighbours, yet he was too generous to give any such evidence to Mr Allworthy.

CHAPTER VI.

The trial of Partridge, the schoolmaster, for incontinency; the evidence of his wife; a short reflection on the wisdom of our law; with other grave matters, which those will like best who understand

them most.

It may be wondered that a story so well known, and which had furnished so much matter of conversation, should never have been mentioned to Mr Allworthy himself, who was perhaps the only person in that country who had never heard of it.

To account in some measure for this to the reader, I think proper to inform him, that there was no one in the kingdom less interested in opposing that doctrine concerning the meaning of the word charity, which hath been seen in the preceding chapter, than our good man. Indeed, he was equally intitled to this virtue in either sense; for as no man was ever more sensible of the wants, or more ready to relieve the distresses of others, so none could be more tender of their characters, or slower to believe anything to their disadvantage.

Scandal, therefore, never found any access to his table; for as it hath been long since observed that you may know a man by his companions, so I will venture to say, that, by attending to the conversation at a great man's table, you may satisfy yourself of his religion, his politics, his taste, and indeed of his entire disposition: for though a few odd fellows will utter their own sentiments in all places, yet much the greater part of mankind have enough of the courtier to accommodate their conversation to the taste and inclination of their superiors.

But to return to Mrs Wilkins, who, having executed her commission with great dispatch, though at fifteen miles distance, brought back such a confirmation of the schoolmaster's guilt, that Mr Allworthy determined to send for the criminal, and examine him *viva voce*. Mr Partridge, therefore, was summoned to attend, in order to his defence (if he could make any) against this accusation.

At the time appointed, before Mr Allworthy himself, at Paradise-hall, came as well the said Partridge, with Anne, his wife, as Mrs Wilkins his accuser.

And now Mr Allworthy being seated in the chair of justice, Mr Partridge was brought before him. Having heard his accusation from the mouth of Mrs Wilkins, he pleaded not guilty, making many vehement protestations of his innocence.

Mrs Partridge was then examined, who, after a modest apology for being obliged to speak the truth against her husband, related all the circumstances with which the reader hath already been acquainted; and at last concluded with her husband's confession of his guilt.

Whether she had forgiven him or no, I will not venture to determine; but it is certain she was an unwilling witness in this cause; and it is probable from certain other reasons, would never have been brought to depose as she did, had not Mrs Wilkins, with great art, fished all out of her at her own house, and had she not indeed made promises, in Mr Allworthy's name, that the punishment of her husband should not be such as might anywise affect his family.

Partridge still persisted in asserting his innocence, though he admitted he had made the above-mentioned confession; which he however endeavoured to account for, by protesting that he was forced into it by the continued importunity she used: who vowed, that, as she was sure of his guilt, she would never leave tormenting him till he had owned it; and faithfully promised, that, in such case, she would never mention it to him more. Hence, he said, he had been induced falsely to confess himself guilty, though he was innocent; and that he believed he should have confest a murder from the same motive.

Mrs Partridge could not bear this imputation with patience; and having no other remedy in the present place but tears, she called forth a plentiful assistance from them, and then addressing herself to Mr Allworthy, she said (or rather cried), "May it please your worship, there never was any poor woman so injured as I am by that base man; for this is not the only instance of his falsehood to me. No, may it please your worship, he hath injured my bed many's the good time and often. I could have put up with his drunkenness and neglect of his business, if he had not broke one of the sacred commandments. Besides, if it had been out of doors I had not mattered it so much; but with my own servant, in my own house, under my own roof, to defile my own chaste bed, which to be sure he hath, with his beastly stinking whores. Yes, you villain, you have defiled my own bed, you have; and then you have charged me with bullocking you into owning the truth. It is very likely, an't please your worship, that I should bullock him? I have marks enow about my body to show of his cruelty to me. If you had been a man, you villain, you would have scorned to injure a woman in that manner. But you an't half a man, you know it. Nor have you been half a husband to me. You need run after whores, you need, when I'm sure—And since he provokes me, I am ready, an't please your worship, to take my bodily oath that I found them a-bed together. What, you have forgot, I suppose, when you beat me into a fit, and made the blood run down my forehead, because I only civilly taxed you with adultery! but I can prove it by all my neighbours. You have almost broke my heart, you have, you have."

Here Mr Allworthy interrupted, and begged her to be pacified, promising her that she should have justice; then turning to Partridge, who stood aghast, one half of his wits being hurried away by surprize and the other half by fear, he said he was sorry to see there was so wicked a man in the world. He assured him that his prevaricating and lying backward and forward was a great aggravation of his guilt; for which the only atonement he could make was by confession and repentance. He exhorted him, therefore, to begin by immediately confessing the fact, and not to persist in denying what was so plainly proved against him even by his own wife.

Here, reader, I beg your patience a moment, while I make a just compliment to the great wisdom and sagacity of our law, which refuses to admit the evidence of a wife for or against her husband. This, says a certain learned author, who, I believe, was never quoted before in any but a law-book, would be the means of creating an eternal dissension between them. It would, indeed, be the means of much perjury, and of much whipping, fining, imprisoning, transporting, and hanging.

Partridge stood a while silent, till, being bid to speak, he said he had already spoken the truth, and appealed to Heaven for his innocence, and lastly to the girl herself, whom he desired his worship immediately to send for; for he was ignorant, or at least pretended to be so, that she had left that part of the country.

Mr Allworthy, whose natural love of justice, joined to his coolness of temper, made him always a most patient magistrate in hearing all the witnesses which an accused person could produce in his defence, agreed to defer his final determination of this matter till the arrival of Jenny, for whom he immediately dispatched a messenger; and then having recommended peace between Partridge and his wife (though he addressed himself chiefly to the wrong person), he appointed them to attend again the third day; for he had sent Jenny a whole day's journey from his own house.

At the appointed time the parties all assembled, when the messenger returning brought word, that Jenny was not to be found; for that she had left her habitation a few days before, in company with a recruiting officer.

Mr Allworthy then declared that the evidence of such a slut as she appeared to be would have deserved no credit; but he said he could not help thinking that, had she been present, and would have declared the truth, she must have confirmed what so many circumstances, together with his own confession, and the declaration of his wife that she had caught her husband in the fact, did sufficiently prove. He therefore once more exhorted Partridge to confess; but he still avowing his innocence, Mr Allworthy declared himself satisfied of his guilt, and that he was too bad a man to receive any encouragement from him. He therefore deprived him of his annuity, and recommended repentance to him on account of another world, and industry to maintain himself and his wife in this.

There were not, perhaps, many more unhappy persons than poor Partridge. He had lost the best part of his income by the evidence of his wife, and yet was daily upbraided by her for having, among other things, been the occasion of depriving her of that benefit; but such was his fortune, and he was obliged to submit to it.

Though I called him poor Partridge in the last paragraph, I would have the reader rather impute that epithet to the compassion in my temper than conceive it to be any declaration of his innocence. Whether he was innocent or not will perhaps appear hereafter; but if the historic muse hath entrusted me with any secrets, I will by no means be guilty of discovering them till she shall give me leave.

Here therefore the reader must suspend his curiosity. Certain it is that, whatever was the truth of the case, there was evidence more than sufficient to convict him before Allworthy; indeed, much less would have satisfied a bench of justices on an order of bastardy; and yet, notwithstanding the positiveness of Mrs Partridge, who would have taken the sacrament upon the matter, there is a possibility that the schoolmaster was entirely innocent: for though it appeared clear on comparing the time when Jenny departed from Little Baddington with that of her delivery that she had there conceived this infant, yet it by no means followed of necessity that Partridge must have been its father; for, to omit other particulars, there was in the same house a lad near eighteen, between whom and Jenny there had subsisted sufficient intimacy to found a reasonable suspicion; and yet, so blind is jealousy, this circumstance never once entered into the head of the enraged wife.

Whether Partridge repented or not, according to Mr Allworthy's advice, is not so apparent. Certain it is that his wife repented heartily of the evidence she had given against him: especially when she found Mrs Deborah had deceived her, and refused to make any application to Mr Allworthy on her behalf. She had, however, somewhat better success with Mrs Blifil, who was, as the reader must have perceived, a much better-tempered woman, and very kindly undertook to solicit her brother to restore the annuity; in which, though good-nature might have some share, yet a stronger and more natural motive will appear in the next chapter.

These solicitations were nevertheless unsuccessful: for though Mr Allworthy did not think, with some late writers, that mercy consists only in punishing offenders; yet he was as far from thinking that it is proper to this excellent quality to pardon great criminals wantonly, without any reason whatever. Any doubtfulness of the fact, or any circumstance of mitigation, was never disregarded: but the petitions of an offender, or the intercessions of others, did not in the least affect him. In a word, he never pardoned because the offender himself, or his friends, were unwilling that he should be punished.

Partridge and his wife were therefore both obliged to submit to their fate; which was indeed severe enough: for so far was he from doubling his industry on the account of his lessened income, that he did in a manner abandon himself to despair; and as he was by nature indolent, that vice now increased upon him, by which means he lost the little school he had; so that neither his wife nor himself would have had any bread to eat, had not the charity of some good Christian interposed, and provided them with what was just sufficient for their sustenance.

As this support was conveyed to them by an unknown hand, they imagined, and so, I doubt not, will the reader, that Mr Allworthy himself was their secret benefactor; who, though he would not openly encourage vice, could yet privately relieve the distresses of the vicious themselves, when these became too exquisite and disproportionate to their demerit. In which light their wretchedness appeared now to Fortune herself; for she at length took pity on this miserable couple, and considerably lessened the wretched state of Partridge, by putting a final end to that of his wife, who soon after caught the small-pox, and died.

The justice which Mr Allworthy had executed on Partridge at first met with universal approbation; but no sooner had he felt its consequences, than his neighbours began to relent, and to compassionate his case; and presently after, to blame that as rigour and severity which they before called justice. They now exclaimed against punishing in cold blood, and sang forth the praises of mercy and forgiveness.

These cries were considerably increased by the death of Mrs Partridge, which, though owing to the distemper above mentioned, which is no consequence of poverty or distress, many were not ashamed to impute to Mr Allworthy's severity, or, as they now termed it, cruelty.

Partridge having now lost his wife, his school, and his annuity, and the unknown person having now discontinued the last-mentioned charity, resolved to change the scene, and left the country, where he was in danger of starving, with the universal compassion of all his neighbours.

CHAPTER VII.

A short sketch of that felicity which prudent couples may extract from hatred: with a short apology for those people who overlook imperfections in their friends.

Though the captain had effectually demolished poor Partridge, yet had he not reaped the harvest he hoped for, which was to turn the foundling out of Mr Allworthy's house.

On the contrary, that gentleman grew every day fonder of little Tommy, as if he intended to counterbalance his severity to the father with extraordinary fondness and affection towards the son.

This a good deal soured the captain's temper, as did all the other daily instances of Mr Allworthy's generosity; for he looked on all such largesses to be diminutions of his own wealth.

In this, we have said, he did not agree with his wife; nor, indeed, in anything else: for though an affection placed on the understanding is, by many wise persons, thought more durable than that which is founded on beauty, yet it happened otherwise in the present case. Nay, the understandings of this couple were their principal bone of contention, and one great cause of many quarrels, which from time to time arose between them; and which at last ended, on the side of the lady, in a sovereign contempt for her husband; and on the husband's, in an utter abhorrence of his wife.

As these had both exercised their talents chiefly in the study of divinity, this was, from their first acquaintance, the most common topic of conversation between them. The captain, like a well-bred man, had, before marriage, always given up his opinion to that of the lady; and this, not in the clumsy awkward manner of a conceited blockhead, who, while he civilly yields to a superior in an argument, is desirous of being still known to think himself in the right. The captain, on the contrary, though one of the proudest fellows in the world, so absolutely yielded the victory to his antagonist, that she, who had not the least doubt of his sincerity, retired always from the dispute with an admiration of her own understanding and a love for his.

But though this complacence to one whom the captain thoroughly despised, was not so uneasy to him as it would have been had any hopes of preferment made it necessary to show the same submission to a Hoadley, or to some other of great reputation in the science, yet even this cost him too much to be endured without some motive. Matrimony, therefore, having removed all such motives, he grew weary of this condescension, and began to treat the opinions of his wife with that haughtiness and insolence, which none but those who deserve some contempt themselves can bestow, and those only who deserve no contempt can bear.

When the first torrent of tenderness was over, and when, in the calm and long interval between the fits, reason began to open the eyes of the lady, and she saw this alteration of behaviour in the captain, who at length answered all her arguments only with pish and pshaw, she was far from enduring the indignity with a tame submission. Indeed, it at first so highly provoked her, that it might have produced some tragical event, had it not taken a more harmless turn, by filling her with the utmost contempt for her husband's understanding, which somewhat qualified her hatred towards him; though of this likewise she had a pretty moderate share.

The captain's hatred to her was of a purer kind: for as to any imperfections in her knowledge or understanding, he no more despised her for them, than for her not being six feet high. In his opinion of the female sex, he exceeded the moroseness of Aristotle himself: he looked on a woman as on an animal of domestic use, of somewhat higher consideration than a cat, since her offices were of rather more importance; but the difference between these two was, in his estimation, so small, that, in his marriage contracted with Mr Allworthy's lands and tenements, it would have been pretty equal which of them he had taken into the bargain. And yet so tender was his pride, that it felt the contempt which his wife now began to express towards him; and this, added to the surfeit he had before taken of her love, created in him a degree of disgust and abhorrence, perhaps hardly to be exceeded.

One situation only of the married state is excluded from pleasure: and that is, a state of indifference: but as many of my readers, I hope, know what an exquisite delight there is in conveying pleasure to a beloved object, so some few, I am afraid, may have experienced the satisfaction of tormenting one we hate. It is, I apprehend, to come at this latter pleasure, that we see both sexes often give up that ease in marriage which they might otherwise possess, though their mate was never so disagreeable to them. Hence the wife often puts on fits of love and jealousy, nay, even denies herself any pleasure, to disturb and prevent those of her husband; and he again, in return, puts frequent restraints on himself, and stays at home in company which he dislikes, in order to confine his wife to what she equally detests. Hence, too, must flow those tears which a widow sometimes so plentifully sheds over the ashes of a husband with whom she led a life of constant disquiet and turbulency, and whom now she can never hope to torment any more.

But if ever any couple enjoyed this pleasure, it was at present experienced by the captain and his lady. It was always a sufficient reason to either of them to be obstinate in any opinion, that the other had previously asserted the contrary. If the one proposed any amusement, the other constantly objected to it: they never loved or hated, commended or abused, the same person. And for this reason, as the captain looked with an evil eye on the little foundling, his wife began now to caress it almost equally with her own child.

The reader will be apt to conceive, that this behaviour between the husband and wife did not greatly contribute to Mr Allworthy's repose, as it tended so little to that serene happiness which he had designed for all three from this alliance; but the truth is, though he might be a little disappointed in his sanguine expectations, yet he was far from being acquainted with the whole matter; for, as the captain was, from certain obvious reasons, much on his guard before him, the lady was obliged, for fear of her brother's displeasure, to pursue the same conduct. In fact, it is possible for a third person to be very intimate, nay even to live long in the same house, with a married couple, who have any tolerable discretion, and not even guess at the sour sentiments which they bear to each other: for though the whole day may be sometimes too short for hatred, as well as for love; yet the many hours which they naturally spend together, apart from all observers, furnish people of tolerable moderation with such ample opportunity for the enjoyment of either passion, that, if they love, they can support being a few hours in company without toying, or if they hate, without spitting in each other's faces.

It is possible, however, that Mr Allworthy saw enough to render him a little uneasy; for we are not always to conclude, that a wise man is not hurt, because he doth not cry out and lament himself, like those of a childish or effeminate temper. But indeed it is possible he might see some faults in the captain without any uneasiness at all; for men of true wisdom and goodness are contented to take persons and things as they are, without complaining of their imperfections, or attempting to amend them. They can see a fault in a friend, a relation, or an acquaintance, without ever mentioning it to the parties themselves, or to any others; and this often without lessening their affection. Indeed, unless great discernment be tempered with this overlooking disposition, we ought never to contract friendship but with a degree of folly which we can deceive; for I hope my friends will pardon me when I declare, I know none of them without a fault; and I should be sorry if I could imagine I had any friend who could not see mine. Forgiveness of this kind we give and demand in turn. It is an exercise of friendship, and perhaps none of the least pleasant. And this forgiveness we must bestow, without desire of amendment. There is, perhaps, no surer mark of folly, than an attempt to correct the natural infirmities of those we love. The finest composition of human nature, as well as the finest china, may have a flaw in it; and this, I am afraid, in either case, is equally incurable; though, nevertheless, the pattern may remain of the highest value.

Upon the whole, then, Mr Allworthy certainly saw some imperfections in the captain; but as this was a very artful man, and eternally upon his guard before him, these appeared to him no more than blemishes in a good character, which his goodness made him overlook, and his wisdom prevented him from discovering to the captain himself. Very different would have been his sentiments had he discovered the whole; which perhaps would in time have been the case, had the husband and wife long continued this kind of behaviour to each other; but this kind Fortune took effectual means to prevent, by forcing the captain to do that which rendered him again dear to his wife, and restored all her tenderness and affection towards him.

CHAPTER VIII.

A receipt to regain the lost affections of a wife, which hath never been known to fail in the most desperate cases.

The captain was made large amends for the unpleasant minutes which he passed in the conversation of his wife (and which were as few as he could contrive to make them), by the pleasant meditations he enjoyed when alone.

These meditations were entirely employed on Mr Allworthy's fortune; for, first, he exercised much thought in calculating, as well as he could, the exact value of the whole: which calculations he often saw occasion to alter in his own favour: and, secondly and chiefly, he pleased himself with intended alterations in the house and gardens, and in projecting many other schemes, as well for the improvement of the estate as of the grandeur of the place: for this purpose he applied himself to the studies of architecture and gardening, and read over many books on both these subjects; for these sciences, indeed, employed his whole time, and formed his only amusement. He at last completed a most excellent plan: and very sorry we are, that it is not in our power to present it to our reader, since even the luxury of the present age, I believe, would hardly match it. It had, indeed, in a superlative degree, the two principal ingredients which serve to recommend all great and noble designs of this nature; for it required an immoderate expense to execute, and a vast length of time to bring it to any sort of perfection. The former of these, the immense wealth of which the captain supposed Mr Allworthy possessed, and which he thought himself sure of inheriting, promised very effectually to supply; and the latter, the soundness of his own constitution, and his time of life, which was only what is called middle-age, removed all apprehension of his not living to accomplish.

Nothing was wanting to enable him to enter upon the immediate execution of this plan, but the death of Mr Allworthy; in calculating which he had employed much of his own algebra, besides purchasing every book extant that treats of the value of lives, reversions, &c. From all which he satisfied himself, that as he had every day a chance of this happening, so had he more than an even chance of its happening within a few years.

But while the captain was one day busied in deep contemplations of this kind, one of the most unlucky as well as unseasonable accidents happened to him. The utmost malice of Fortune could, indeed, have contrived nothing so cruel, so mal-a-propos, so absolutely destructive to all his schemes. In short, not to keep the reader in long suspense, just at the very instant when his heart was exulting in meditations on the happiness which would accrue to him by Mr Allworthy's death, he himself—died of an apoplexy.

This unfortunately befel the captain as he was taking his evening walk by himself, so that nobody was present to lend him any assistance, if indeed, any assistance could have preserved him. He took, therefore, measure of that proportion of soil which was now become adequate to all his future purposes, and he lay dead on the ground, a great (though not a living) example of the truth of that observation of Horace:

Tu secanda marmora
Locas sub ipsum funus; et sepulchri
Immemor, struis domos.

Which sentiment I shall thus give to the English reader: "You provide the noblest materials for building, when a pickaxe and a spade are only necessary: and build houses of five hundred by a hundred feet, forgetting that of six by two."

CHAPTER IX.

A proof of the infallibility of the foregoing receipt, in the lamentations of the widow; with other suitable decorations of death, such as physicians, &c., and an epitaph in the true stile.

Mr Allworthy, his sister, and another lady, were assembled at the accustomed hour in the supper-room, where, having waited a considerable time longer than usual, Mr Allworthy first declared he began to grow uneasy at the captain's stay (for he was always most punctual at his meals); and gave orders that the bell should be rung without the doors, and especially towards those walks which the captain was wont to use.

All these summons proving ineffectual (for the captain had, by perverse accident, betaken himself to a new walk that evening), Mrs Blifil declared she was seriously frightened. Upon which the other lady, who was one of her most intimate acquaintance, and who well knew the true state of her affections, endeavoured all she could to pacify her, telling her—To be sure she could not help being uneasy; but that she should hope the best. That, perhaps the sweetness of the evening had inticed the captain to go farther than his usual walk: or he might be detained at some neighbour's. Mrs Blifil answered, No; she was sure some accident had befallen him; for that he would never stay out without sending her word, as he must know how uneasy it would make her. The other lady, having no other arguments to use, betook herself to the entreaties usual on such occasions, and begged her not to frighten herself, for it might be of very ill consequence to her own health; and, filling out a very large glass of wine, advised, and at last prevailed with her to drink it.

Mr Allworthy now returned into the parlour; for he had been himself in search after the captain. His countenance sufficiently showed the consternation he was under, which, indeed, had a good deal deprived him of speech; but as grief operates variously on different minds, so the same apprehension which depressed his voice, elevated that of Mrs Blifil. She now began to bewail herself in very bitter terms, and floods of tears accompanied her lamentations; which the lady, her companion, declared she could not blame, but at the same time dissuaded her from indulging; attempting to moderate the grief of her friend by philosophical observations on the many disappointments to which human life is daily subject, which, she said, was a sufficient consideration to fortify our minds against any accidents, how sudden or terrible soever. She said her brother's example ought to teach her patience, who, though indeed he could not be supposed as much concerned as herself, yet was, doubtless, very uneasy, though his resignation to the Divine will had restrained his grief within due bounds.

"Mention not my brother," said Mrs Blifil; "I alone am the object of your pity. What are the terrors of friendship to what a wife feels on these occasions? Oh, he is lost! Somebody hath murdered him—I shall never see him more!"—Here a torrent of tears had the same consequence with what the suppression had occasioned to Mr Allworthy, and she remained silent.

At this interval a servant came running in, out of breath, and cried out, The captain was found; and, before he could proceed farther, he was followed by two more, bearing the dead body between them.

Here the curious reader may observe another diversity in the operations of grief: for as Mr Allworthy had been before silent, from the same cause which had made his sister vociferous; so did the present sight, which drew tears from the gentleman, put an entire stop to those of the lady; who first gave a violent scream, and presently after fell into a fit.

The room was soon full of servants, some of whom, with the lady visitant, were employed in care of the wife; and others, with Mr Allworthy, assisted in carrying off the captain to a warm bed; where every method was tried, in order to restore him to life.

And glad should we be, could we inform the reader that both these bodies had been attended with equal success; for those who undertook the care of the lady succeeded so well, that, after the fit had continued a decent time, she again revived, to their great satisfaction: but as to the captain, all experiments of bleeding, chafing, dropping, &c., proved ineffectual. Death, that inexorable judge, had passed sentence on him, and refused to grant him a reprieve, though two doctors who arrived, and were fee'd at one and the same instant, were his counsel.

These two doctors, whom, to avoid any malicious applications, we shall distinguish by the names of Dr Y. and Dr Z., having felt his pulse; to wit, Dr Y. his right arm, and Dr Z. his left; both agreed that he was absolutely dead; but as to the distemper, or cause of his death, they differed; Dr Y. holding that he died of an apoplexy, and Dr Z. of an epilepsy.

Hence arose a dispute between the learned men, in which each delivered the reasons of their several opinions. These were of such equal force, that they served both to confirm either doctor in his own sentiments, and made not the least impression on his adversary.

To say the truth, every physician almost hath his favourite disease, to which he ascribes all the victories obtained over human nature. The gout, the rheumatism, the stone, the gravel, and the consumption, have all their several patrons in the faculty; and none more than the nervous fever, or the fever on the spirits. And here we may account for those disagreements in opinion, concerning the cause of a patient's death, which sometimes occur, between the most learned of the college; and which have greatly surprized that part of the world who have been ignorant of the fact we have above asserted.

The reader may perhaps be surprized, that, instead of endeavouring to revive the patient, the learned gentlemen should fall immediately into a dispute on the occasion of his death; but in reality all such experiments had been made before their arrival: for the captain was put into a warm bed, had his veins scarified, his forehead chafed, and all sorts of strong drops applied to his lips and nostrils.

The physicians, therefore, finding themselves anticipated in everything they ordered, were at a loss how to apply that portion of time which it is usual and decent to remain for their fee, and were therefore necessitated to find some subject or other for discourse; and what could more naturally present itself than that before mentioned?

Our doctors were about to take their leave, when Mr Allworthy, having given over the captain, and acquiesced in the Divine will, began to enquire after his sister, whom he desired them to visit before their departure.

This lady was now recovered of her fit, and, to use the common phrase, as well as could be expected for one in her condition. The doctors, therefore, all previous ceremonies being complied with, as this was a new patient, attended, according to desire, and laid hold on each of her hands, as they had before done on those of the corpse.

The case of the lady was in the other extreme from that of her husband: for as he was past all the assistance of physic, so in reality she required none.

There is nothing more unjust than the vulgar opinion, by which physicians are misrepresented, as friends to death. On the contrary, I believe, if the number of those who recover by physic could be opposed to that of the martyrs to it, the former would rather exceed the latter. Nay, some are so cautious on this head, that, to avoid a possibility of killing the patient, they abstain from all methods of curing, and prescribe nothing but what can neither do good nor harm. I have heard some of these, with great gravity, deliver it as a maxim, "That Nature should be left to do her own work, while the physician stands by as it were to clap her on the back, and encourage her when she doth well."

So little then did our doctors delight in death, that they discharged the corpse after a single fee; but they were not so disgusted with their living patient; concerning whose case they immediately agreed, and fell to prescribing with great diligence.

Whether, as the lady had at first persuaded her physicians to believe her ill, they had now, in return, persuaded her to believe herself so, I will not determine; but she continued a whole month with all the decorations of sickness. During this time she was visited by physicians, attended by nurses, and received constant messages from her acquaintance to enquire after her health.

At length the decent time for sickness and immoderate grief being expired, the doctors were discharged, and the lady began to see company; being altered only from what she was before, by that colour of sadness in which she had dressed her person and countenance.

The captain was now interred, and might, perhaps, have already made a large progress towards oblivion, had not the friendship of Mr Allworthy taken care to preserve his memory, by the following epitaph, which was written by a man of as great genius as integrity, and one who perfectly well knew the captain.

HERE LIES,
IN EXPECTATION OF A JOYFUL RISING,
THE BODY OF

CAPTAIN JOHN BLIFIL.

LONDON
HAD THE HONOUR OF HIS BIRTH,
OXFORD
OF HIS EDUCATION.

HIS PARTS
WERE AN HONOUR TO HIS PROFESSION
AND TO HIS COUNTRY:
HIS LIFE, TO HIS RELIGION
AND HUMAN NATURE.
HE WAS A DUTIFUL SON,
A TENDER HUSBAND,
AN AFFECTIONATE FATHER,
A MOST KIND BROTHER,
A SINCERE FRIEND,
A DEVOUT CHRISTIAN,
AND A GOOD MAN.

HIS INCONSOLABLE WIDOW
HATH ERECTED THIS STONE,
THE MONUMENT OF
HIS VIRTUES
AND OF HER AFFECTION.

BOOK III.

CONTAINING THE MOST MEMORABLE TRANSACTIONS WHICH PASSED IN THE FAMILY OF MR ALLWORTHY, FROM THE TIME WHEN TOMMY JONES ARRIVED AT THE AGE OF FOURTEEN, TILL HE ATTAINED THE AGE OF NINETEEN. IN THIS BOOK
THE READER MAY PICK UP SOME HINTS CONCERNING THE EDUCATION OF CHILDREN.

CHAPTER I.

Containing little or nothing.

The reader will be pleased to remember, that, at the beginning of the second book of this history, we gave him a hint of our intention to pass over several large periods of time, in which nothing happened worthy of being recorded in a chronicle of this kind.

In so doing, we do not only consult our own dignity and ease, but the good and advantage of the reader: for besides that by these means we prevent him from throwing away his time, in reading without either pleasure or emolument, we give him, at all such seasons, an opportunity of employing that wonderful sagacity, of which he is master, by filling up these vacant spaces of time with his own conjectures; for which purpose we have taken care to qualify him in the preceding pages.

For instance, what reader but knows that Mr Allworthy felt, at first, for the loss of his friend, those emotions of grief, which on such occasions enter into all men whose hearts are not composed of flint, or their heads of as solid materials? Again, what reader doth not know that philosophy and religion in time moderated, and at last extinguished, this grief? The former of these teaching the folly and vanity of it, and the latter correcting it as unlawful, and at the same time assuaging it, by raising future hopes and assurances, which enable a strong and religious mind to take leave of a friend, on his deathbed, with little less indifference than if he was preparing for a long journey; and, indeed, with little less hope of seeing him again.

Nor can the judicious reader be at a greater loss on account of Mrs Bridget Blifil, who, he may be assured, conducted herself through the whole season in which grief is to make its appearance on the outside of the body, with the strictest regard to all the rules of custom and decency, suiting the alterations of her countenance to the several alterations of her habit: for as this changed from weeds to black, from black to grey, from grey to white, so did her countenance change from dismal to sorrowful, from sorrowful to sad, and from sad to serious, till the day came in which she was allowed to return to her former serenity.

We have mentioned these two, as examples only of the task which may be imposed on readers of the lowest class. Much higher and harder exercises of judgment and penetration may reasonably be expected from the upper graduates in criticism. Many notable discoveries will, I doubt not, be made by such, of the transactions which happened in the family of our worthy man, during all the years which we have thought proper to pass over: for though nothing worthy of a place in this history occurred within that period, yet did several incidents happen of equal importance with those reported by the daily and weekly historians of the age; in reading which great numbers of persons consume a considerable part of their time, very little, I am afraid, to their emolument. Now, in the conjectures here proposed, some of the most excellent faculties of the mind may be employed to much advantage, since it is a more useful capacity to be able to foretel the actions of men, in any circumstance, from their characters, than to judge of their characters from their actions. The former, I own, requires the greater penetration; but may be accomplished by true sagacity with no less certainty than the latter.

As we are sensible that much the greatest part of our readers are very eminently possessed of this quality, we have left them a space of twelve years to exert it in; and shall now bring forth our heroe, at about fourteen years of age, not questioning that many have been long impatient to be introduced to his acquaintance.

CHAPTER II.

The heroe of this great history appears with very bad omens. A little tale of so LOW a kind that some may think it not worth their notice. A word or two concerning a squire, and more relating to a gamekeeper and a schoolmaster.

As we determined, when we first sat down to write this history, to flatter no man, but to guide our pen throughout by the directions of truth, we are obliged to bring our heroe on the stage in a much more disadvantageous manner than we could wish; and to declare honestly, even at his first appearance, that it was the universal opinion of all Mr Allworthy's family that he was certainly born to be hanged.

Indeed, I am sorry to say there was too much reason for this conjecture; the lad having from his earliest years discovered a propensity to many vices, and especially to one which hath as direct a tendency as any other to that fate which we have just now observed to have been prophetically denounced against him: he had been already convicted of three robberies, viz., of robbing an orchard, of stealing a duck out of a farmer's yard, and of picking Master Blifil's pocket of a ball.

The vices of this young man were, moreover, heightened by the disadvantageous light in which they appeared when opposed to the virtues of Master Blifil, his companion; a youth of so different a cast from little Jones, that not only the family but all the neighbourhood resounded his praises. He was, indeed, a lad of a remarkable disposition; sober, discreet, and pious beyond his age; qualities which gained him the love of every one who knew him: while Tom Jones was universally disliked; and many expressed their wonder that Mr Allworthy would suffer such a lad to be educated with his nephew, lest the morals of the latter should be corrupted by his example.

An incident which happened about this time will set the characters of these two lads more fairly before the discerning reader than is in the power of the longest dissertation.

Tom Jones, who, bad as he is, must serve for the heroe of this history, had only one friend among all the servants of the family; for as to Mrs Wilkins, she had long since given him up, and was perfectly reconciled to her mistress. This friend was the gamekeeper, a fellow of a loose kind of disposition, and who was thought not to entertain much stricter notions concerning the difference of *meum* and *tuum* than the young gentleman himself. And hence this friendship gave occasion to many sarcastical remarks among the domestics, most of which were either proverbs before, or at least are become so now; and, indeed, the wit of them all may be comprised in that short Latin proverb, "*Noscitur a socio;*" which, I think, is thus expressed in English, "You may know him by the company he keeps."

To say the truth, some of that atrocious wickedness in Jones, of which we have just mentioned three examples, might perhaps be derived from the encouragement he had received from this fellow, who, in two or three instances, had been what the law calls an accessary after the fact: for the whole duck, and great part of the apples, were converted to the use of the gamekeeper and his family; though, as Jones alone was discovered, the poor lad bore not only the whole smart, but the whole blame; both which fell again to his lot on the following occasion.

Contiguous to Mr Allworthy's estate was the manor of one of those gentlemen who are called preservers of the game. This species of men, from the great severity with which they revenge the death of a hare or partridge, might be thought to cultivate the same superstition with the Bannians in India; many of whom, we are told, dedicate their whole lives to the preservation and protection of certain animals; was it not that our English Bannians, while they preserve them from other enemies, will most unmercifully slaughter whole horse-loads themselves; so that they stand clearly acquitted of any such heathenish superstition.

I have, indeed, a much better opinion of this kind of men than is entertained by some, as I take them to answer the order of Nature, and the good purposes for which they were ordained, in a more ample manner than many others. Now, as Horace tells us that there are a set of human beings

Fruges consumere nati,

"Born to consume the fruits of the earth;" so I make no manner of doubt but that there are others

Feras consumere nati,

"Born to consume the beasts of the field;" or, as it is commonly called, the game; and none, I believe, will deny but that those squires fulfil this end of their creation.

Little Jones went one day a shooting with the gamekeeper; when happening to spring a covey of partridges near the border of that manor over which Fortune, to fulfil the wise purposes of Nature, had planted one of the game consumers, the birds flew into it, and were marked (as it is called) by the two sportsmen, in some furze bushes, about two or three hundred paces beyond Mr Allworthy's dominions.

Mr Allworthy had given the fellow strict orders, on pain of forfeiting his place, never to trespass on any of his neighbours; no more on those who were less rigid in this matter than on the lord of this manor. With regard to others, indeed, these orders had not been always very scrupulously kept; but as the disposition of the gentleman with whom the partridges had taken sanctuary was well known, the gamekeeper had never yet attempted to invade his territories. Nor had he done it now, had not the younger sportsman, who was excessively eager to pursue the flying game, over-persuaded him; but Jones being very importunate, the other, who was himself keen enough after the sport, yielded to his persuasions, entered the manor, and shot one of the partridges.

The gentleman himself was at that time on horse-back, at a little distance from them; and hearing the gun go off, he immediately made towards the place, and discovered poor Tom; for the gamekeeper had leapt into the thickest part of the furze-brake, where he had happily concealed himself.

The gentleman having searched the lad, and found the partridge upon him, denounced great vengeance, swearing he would acquaint Mr Allworthy. He was as good as his word: for he rode immediately to his house, and complained of the trespass on his manor in as high terms and as bitter language as if his house had been broken open, and the most valuable furniture stole out of it. He added, that some other person was in his company, though he could not discover him; for that two guns had been discharged almost in the same instant. And, says he, "We have found only this partridge, but the Lord knows what mischief they have done."

At his return home, Tom was presently convened before Mr Allworthy. He owned the fact, and alledged no other excuse but what was really true, viz., that the covey was originally sprung in Mr Allworthy's own manor.

Tom was then interrogated who was with him, which Mr Allworthy declared he was resolved to know, acquainting the culprit with the circumstance of the two guns, which had been deposed by the squire and both his servants; but Tom stoutly persisted in asserting that he was alone; yet, to say the truth, he hesitated a little at first, which would have confirmed Mr Allworthy's belief, had what the squire and his servants said wanted any further confirmation.

The gamekeeper, being a suspected person, was now sent for, and the question put to him; but he, relying on the promise which Tom had made him, to take all upon himself, very resolutely denied being in company with the young gentleman, or indeed having seen him the whole afternoon.

Mr Allworthy then turned towards Tom, with more than usual anger in his countenance, and advised him to confess who was with him; repeating, that he was resolved to know. The lad, however, still maintained his resolution, and was dismissed with much wrath by Mr Allworthy, who told him he should have to the next morning to consider of it, when he should be questioned by another person, and in another manner.

Poor Jones spent a very melancholy night; and the more so, as he was without his usual companion; for Master Blifil was gone abroad on a visit with his mother. Fear of the punishment he was to suffer was on this occasion his least evil; his chief anxiety being, lest his constancy should fail him, and he should be brought to betray the gamekeeper, whose ruin he knew must now be the consequence.

Nor did the gamekeeper pass his time much better. He had the same apprehensions with the youth; for whose honour he had likewise a much tenderer regard than for his skin.

In the morning, when Tom attended the reverend Mr Thwackum, the person to whom Mr Allworthy had committed the instruction of the two boys, he had the same questions put to him by that gentleman which he had been asked the evening before, to which he returned the same answers. The consequence of this was, so severe a whipping, that it possibly fell little short of the torture with which confessions are in some countries extorted from criminals.

Tom bore his punishment with great resolution; and though his master asked him, between every stroke, whether he would not confess, he was contented to be flead rather than betray his friend, or break the promise he had made.

The gamekeeper was now relieved from his anxiety, and Mr Allworthy himself began to be concerned at Tom's sufferings: for besides that Mr Thwackum, being highly enraged that he was not able to make the boy say what he himself pleased, had carried his severity much beyond the good man's intention, this latter began now to suspect that the squire had been mistaken; which his extreme eagerness and anger seemed to make probable; and as for what the servants had said in confirmation of their master's account, he laid no great stress upon that. Now, as cruelty and injustice were two ideas of which Mr Allworthy could by no means support the consciousness a single moment, he sent for Tom, and after many kind and friendly exhortations, said, "I am convinced, my dear child, that my suspicions have wronged you; I am sorry that you have been so severely punished on this account." And at last gave him a little horse to make him amends; again repeating his sorrow for what had past.

Tom's guilt now flew in his face more than any severity could make it. He could more easily bear the lashes of Thwackum, than the generosity of Allworthy. The tears burst from his eyes, and he fell upon his knees, crying, "Oh, sir, you are too good to me. Indeed you are. Indeed I don't deserve it." And at that very instant, from the fulness of his heart, had almost betrayed the secret; but the good genius of the gamekeeper suggested to him what might be the consequence to the poor fellow, and this consideration sealed his lips.

Thwackum did all he could to persuade Allworthy from showing any compassion or kindness to the boy, saying, "He had persisted in an untruth;" and gave some hints, that a second whipping might probably bring the matter to light.

But Mr Allworthy absolutely refused to consent to the experiment. He said, the boy had suffered enough already for concealing the truth, even if he was guilty, seeing that he could have no motive but a mistaken point of honour for so doing.

"Honour!" cryed Thwackum, with some warmth, "mere stubbornness and obstinacy! Can honour teach any one to tell a lie, or can any honour exist independent of religion?"

This discourse happened at table when dinner was just ended; and there were present Mr Allworthy, Mr Thwackum, and a third gentleman, who now entered into the debate, and whom, before we proceed any further, we shall briefly introduce to our reader's acquaintance.

CHAPTER III.

The character of Mr Square the philosopher, and of Mr Thwackum the divine; with a dispute concerning——

The name of this gentleman, who had then resided some time at Mr Allworthy's house, was Mr Square. His natural parts were not of the first rate, but he had greatly improved them by a learned education. He was deeply read in the antients, and a profest master of all the works of Plato and Aristotle. Upon which great models he had principally formed himself; sometimes according with the opinion of the one, and sometimes with that of the other. In morals he was a profest Platonist, and in religion he inclined to be an Aristotelian.

But though he had, as we have said, formed his morals on the Platonic model, yet he perfectly agreed with the opinion of Aristotle, in considering that great man rather in the quality of a philosopher or a speculatist, than as a legislator. This sentiment he carried a great way; indeed, so far, as to regard all virtue as matter of theory only. This, it is true, he never affirmed, as I have heard, to any one; and yet upon the least attention to his conduct, I cannot help thinking it was his real opinion, as it will perfectly reconcile some contradictions which might otherwise appear in his character.

This gentleman and Mr Thwackum scarce ever met without a disputation; for their tenets were indeed diametrically opposite to each other. Square held human nature to be the perfection of all virtue, and that vice was a deviation from our nature, in the same manner as deformity of body is. Thwackum, on the contrary, maintained that the human mind, since the fall, was nothing but a sink of iniquity, till purified and redeemed by grace. In one point only they agreed, which was, in all their discourses on morality never to mention the word goodness. The favourite phrase of the former, was the natural beauty of virtue; that of the latter, was the divine power of grace. The former measured all actions by the unalterable rule of right, and the eternal fitness of things; the latter decided all matters by authority; but in doing this, he always used the scriptures and their commentators, as the lawyer doth his Coke upon Lyttleton, where the comment is of equal authority with the text.

After this short introduction, the reader will be pleased to remember, that the parson had concluded his speech with a triumphant question, to which he had apprehended no answer; viz., Can any honour exist independent on religion?

To this Square answered; that it was impossible to discourse philosophically concerning words, till their meaning was first established: that there were scarce any two words of a more vague and uncertain signification, than the two he had mentioned; for that there were almost as many different opinions concerning honour, as concerning religion. "But," says he, "if by honour you mean the true natural beauty of virtue, I will maintain it may exist independent of any religion whatever. Nay," added he, "you yourself will allow it may exist independent of all but one: so will a Mahometan, a Jew, and all the maintainers of all the different sects in the world."

Thwackum replied, this was arguing with the usual malice of all the enemies to the true Church. He said, he doubted not but that all the infidels and hereticks in the world would, if they could, confine honour to their own absurd errors and damnable deceptions; "but honour," says he, "is not therefore manifold, because there are many absurd opinions about it; nor is religion manifold, because there are various sects and heresies in the world. When I mention religion, I mean the Christian religion; and not only the Christian religion, but the Protestant religion; and not only the Protestant religion, but the Church of England. And when I mention honour, I mean that mode of Divine grace which is not only consistent with, but dependent upon, this religion; and is consistent with and dependent upon no other. Now to say that the honour I here mean, and which was, I thought, all the honour I could be supposed to mean, will uphold, much less dictate an untruth, is to assert an absurdity too shocking to be conceived."

"I purposely avoided," says Square, "drawing a conclusion which I thought evident from what I have said; but if you perceived it, I am sure you have not attempted to answer it. However, to drop the article of religion, I think it is plain, from what you have said, that we have different ideas of honour; or why do we not agree in the same terms of its explanation? I have asserted, that true honour and true virtue are almost synonymous terms, and they are both founded on the unalterable rule of right, and the eternal fitness of things; to which an untruth being absolutely repugnant and contrary, it is certain that true honour cannot support an untruth. In this, therefore, I think we are agreed; but that this honour can be said to be founded on religion, to which it is antecedent, if by religion be meant any positive law—"

"I agree," answered Thwackum, with great warmth, "with a man who asserts honour to be antecedent to religion! Mr Allworthy, did I agree—?"

He was proceeding when Mr Allworthy interposed, telling them very coldly, they had both mistaken his meaning; for that he had said nothing of true honour.—It is possible, however, he would not have easily quieted the disputants, who were growing equally warm, had not another matter now fallen out, which put a final end to the conversation at present.

CHAPTER IV.

Containing a necessary apology for the author; and a childish incident, which perhaps requires an apology likewise.

Before I proceed farther, I shall beg leave to obviate some misconstructions into which the zeal of some few readers may lead them; for I would not willingly give offence to any, especially to men who are warm in the cause of virtue or religion.

I hope, therefore, no man will, by the grossest misunderstanding or perversion of my meaning, misrepresent me, as endeavouring to cast any ridicule on the greatest perfections of human nature; and which do, indeed, alone purify and ennoble the heart of man, and raise him above the brute creation. This, reader, I will venture to say (and by how much the better man you are yourself, by so much the more will you be inclined to believe me), that I would rather have buried the sentiments of these two persons in eternal oblivion, than have done any injury to either of these glorious causes.

On the contrary, it is with a view to their service, that I have taken upon me to record the lives and actions of two of their false and pretended champions. A treacherous friend is the most dangerous enemy; and I will say boldly, that both religion and virtue have received more real discredit from hypocrites than the wittiest profligates or infidels could ever cast upon them: nay, farther, as these two, in their purity, are rightly called the bands of civil society, and are indeed the greatest of blessings; so when poisoned and corrupted with fraud, pretence, and affectation, they have become the worst of civil curses, and have enabled men to perpetrate the most cruel mischiefs to their own species.

Indeed, I doubt not but this ridicule will in general be allowed: my chief apprehension is, as many true and just sentiments often came from the mouths of these persons, lest the whole should be taken together, and I should be conceived to ridicule all alike. Now the reader will be pleased to consider, that, as neither of these men were fools, they could not be supposed to have holden none but wrong principles, and to have uttered nothing but absurdities; what injustice, therefore, must I have done to their characters, had I selected only what was bad! And how horribly wretched and maimed must their arguments have appeared!

Upon the whole, it is not religion or virtue, but the want of them, which is here exposed. Had not Thwackum too much neglected virtue, and Square, religion, in the composition of their several systems, and had not both utterly discarded all natural goodness of heart, they had never been represented as the objects of derision in this history; in which we will now proceed.

This matter then, which put an end to the debate mentioned in the last chapter, was no other than a quarrel between Master Blifil and Tom Jones, the consequence of which had been a bloody nose to the former; for though Master Blifil, notwithstanding he was the younger, was in size above the other's match, yet Tom was much his superior at the noble art of boxing.

Tom, however, cautiously avoided all engagements with that youth; for besides that Tommy Jones was an inoffensive lad amidst all his roguery, and really loved Blifil, Mr Thwackum being always the second of the latter, would have been sufficient to deter him.

But well says a certain author, No man is wise at all hours; it is therefore no wonder that a boy is not so. A difference arising at play between the two lads, Master Blifil called Tom a beggarly bastard. Upon which the latter, who was somewhat passionate in his disposition, immediately caused that phenomenon in the face of the former, which we have above remembered.

Master Blifil now, with his blood running from his nose, and the tears galloping after from his eyes, appeared before his uncle and the tremendous Thwackum. In which court an indictment of assault, battery, and wounding, was instantly preferred against Tom; who in his excuse only pleaded the provocation, which was indeed all the matter that Master Blifil had omitted.

It is indeed possible that this circumstance might have escaped his memory; for, in his reply, he positively insisted, that he had made use of no such appellation; adding, "Heaven forbid such naughty words should ever come out of his mouth!"

Tom, though against all form of law, rejoined in affirmance of the words. Upon which Master Blifil said, "It is no wonder. Those who will tell one fib, will hardly stick at another. If I had told my master such a wicked fib as you have done, I should be ashamed to show my face."

"What fib, child?" cries Thwackum pretty eagerly.

"Why, he told you that nobody was with him a shooting when he killed the partridge; but he knows" (here he burst into a flood of tears), "yes, he knows, for he confessed it to me, that Black George the gamekeeper was there. Nay, he said—yes you did—deny it if you can, that you would not have confest the truth, though master had cut you to pieces."

At this the fire flashed from Thwackum's eyes, and he cried out in triumph—"Oh! ho! this is your mistaken notion of honour! This is the boy who was not to be whipped again!" But Mr Allworthy, with a more gentle aspect, turned towards the lad, and said, "Is this true, child? How came you to persist so obstinately in a falsehood?"

Tom said, "He scorned a lie as much as any one: but he thought his honour engaged him to act as he did; for he had promised the poor fellow to conceal him: which," he said, "he thought himself farther obliged to, as the gamekeeper had begged him not to go into the gentleman's manor, and had at last gone himself, in compliance with his persuasions." He said, "This was the whole truth of the matter, and he would take his oath of it;" and concluded with very passionately begging Mr Allworthy "to have compassion on the poor fellow's family, especially as he himself only had been guilty, and the other had been very difficultly prevailed on to do what he did. Indeed, sir," said he, "it could hardly be called a lie that I told; for the poor fellow was entirely innocent of the whole matter. I should have gone alone after the birds; nay, I did go at first, and he only followed me to prevent more mischief. Do, pray, sir, let me be punished; take my little horse away again; but pray, sir, forgive poor George."

Mr Allworthy hesitated a few moments, and then dismissed the boys, advising them to live more friendly and peaceably together.

CHAPTER V.

The opinions of the divine and the philosopher concerning the two boys; with some reasons for their opinions, and other matters.

It is probable, that by disclosing this secret, which had been communicated in the utmost confidence to him, young Blifil preserved his companion from a good lashing; for the offence of the bloody nose would have been of itself sufficient cause for Thwackum to have proceeded to correction; but now this was totally absorbed in the consideration of the other matter; and with regard to this, Mr Allworthy declared privately, he thought the boy deserved reward rather than punishment, so that Thwackum's hand was withheld by a general pardon.

Thwackum, whose meditations were full of birch, exclaimed against this weak, and, as he said he would venture to call it, wicked lenity. To remit the punishment of such crimes was, he said, to encourage them. He enlarged much on the correction of children, and quoted many texts from Solomon, and others; which being to be found in so many other books, shall not be found here. He then applied himself to the vice of lying, on which head he was altogether as learned as he had been on the other.

Square said, he had been endeavouring to reconcile the behaviour of Tom with his idea of perfect virtue, but could not. He owned there was something which at first sight appeared like fortitude in the action; but as fortitude was a virtue, and falsehood a vice, they could by no means agree or unite together. He added, that as this was in some measure to confound virtue and vice, it might be worth Mr Thwackum's consideration, whether a larger castigation might not be laid on upon the account.

As both these learned men concurred in censuring Jones, so were they no less unanimous in applauding Master Blifil. To bring truth to light, was by the parson asserted to be the duty of every religious man; and by the philosopher this was declared to be highly conformable with the rule of right, and the eternal and unalterable fitness of things.

All this, however, weighed very little with Mr Allworthy. He could not be prevailed on to sign the warrant for the execution of Jones. There was something within his own breast with which the invincible fidelity which that youth had preserved, corresponded much better than it had done with the religion of Thwackum, or with the virtue of Square. He therefore strictly ordered the former of these gentlemen to abstain from laying violent hands on Tom for what had past. The pedagogue was obliged to obey those orders; but not without great reluctance, and frequent mutterings that the boy would be certainly spoiled.

Towards the gamekeeper the good man behaved with more severity. He presently summoned that poor fellow before him, and after many bitter remonstrances, paid him his wages, and dismist him from his service; for Mr Allworthy rightly observed, that there was a great difference between being guilty of a falsehood to excuse yourself, and to excuse another. He likewise urged, as the principal motive to his inflexible severity against this man, that he had basely suffered Tom Jones to undergo so heavy a punishment for his sake, whereas he ought to have prevented it by making the discovery himself.

When this story became public, many people differed from Square and Thwackum, in judging the conduct of the two lads on the occasion. Master Blifil was generally called a sneaking rascal, a poor-spirited wretch, with other epithets of the like kind; whilst Tom was honoured with the appellations of a brave lad, a jolly dog, and an honest fellow. Indeed, his behaviour to Black George much ingratiated him with all the servants; for though that fellow was before universally disliked, yet he was no sooner turned away than he was as universally pitied; and the friendship and gallantry of Tom Jones was celebrated by them all with the highest applause; and they condemned Master Blifil as openly as they durst, without incurring the danger of offending his mother. For all this, however, poor Tom smarted in the flesh; for though Thwackum had been inhibited to exercise his arm on the foregoing account, yet, as the proverb says, It is easy to find a stick, &c. So was it easy to find a rod; and, indeed, the not being able to find one was the only thing which could have kept Thwackum any long time from chastising poor Jones.

Had the bare delight in the sport been the only inducement to the pedagogue, it is probable Master Blifil would likewise have had his share; but though Mr Allworthy had given him frequent orders to make no difference between the lads, yet was Thwackum altogether as kind and gentle to this youth, as he was harsh, nay even barbarous, to the other. To say the truth, Blifil had greatly gained his master's affections; partly by the profound respect he always showed his person, but much more by the decent reverence with which he received his doctrine; for he had got by heart, and frequently repeated, his phrases, and maintained all his master's religious principles with a zeal which was surprizing in one so young, and which greatly endeared him to the worthy preceptor.

Tom Jones, on the other hand, was not only deficient in outward tokens of respect, often forgetting to pull off his hat, or to bow at his master's approach; but was altogether as unmindful both of his master's precepts and example. He was indeed a thoughtless, giddy youth, with little sobriety in his manners, and less in his countenance; and would often very impudently and indecently laugh at his companion for his serious behaviour.

Mr Square had the same reason for his preference of the former lad; for Tom Jones showed no more regard to the learned discourses which this gentleman would sometimes throw away upon him, than to those of Thwackum. He once ventured to make a jest of the rule of right; and at another time said, he believed there was no rule in the world capable of making such a man as his father (for so Mr Allworthy suffered himself to be called).

Master Blifil, on the contrary, had address enough at sixteen to recommend himself at one and the same time to both these opposites. With one he was all religion, with the other he was all virtue. And when both were present, he was profoundly silent, which both interpreted in his favour and in their own.

Nor was Blifil contented with flattering both these gentlemen to their faces; he took frequent occasions of praising them behind their backs to Allworthy; before whom, when they two were alone, and his uncle commended any religious or virtuous sentiment (for many such came constantly from him) he seldom failed to ascribe it to the good instructions he had received from either Thwackum or Square; for he knew his uncle repeated all such compliments to the persons for whose use they were meant; and he found by experience the great impressions which they made on the philosopher, as well as on the divine: for, to say the truth, there is no kind of flattery so irresistible as this, at second hand.

The young gentleman, moreover, soon perceived how extremely grateful all those panegyrics on his instructors were to Mr Allworthy himself, as they so loudly resounded the praise of that singular plan of education which he had laid down; for this worthy man having observed the imperfect institution of our public schools, and the many vices which boys were there liable to learn, had resolved to educate his nephew, as well as the other lad, whom he had in a manner adopted, in his own house; where he thought their morals would escape all that danger of being corrupted to which they would be unavoidably exposed in any public school or university.

Having, therefore, determined to commit these boys to the tuition of a private tutor, Mr Thwackum was recommended to him for that office, by a very particular friend, of whose understanding Mr Allworthy had a great opinion, and in whose integrity he placed much confidence. This Thwackum was fellow of a college, where he almost entirely resided; and had a great reputation for learning, religion, and sobriety of manners. And these were doubtless the qualifications by which Mr Allworthy's friend had been induced to recommend him; though indeed this friend had some obligations to Thwackum's family, who were the most considerable persons in a borough which that gentleman represented in parliament.

Thwackum, at his first arrival, was extremely agreeable to Allworthy; and indeed he perfectly answered the character which had been given of him. Upon longer acquaintance, however, and more intimate conversation, this worthy man saw infirmities in the tutor, which he could have wished him to have been without; though as those seemed greatly overbalanced by his good qualities, they did not incline Mr Allworthy to part with him: nor would they indeed have justified such a proceeding; for the reader is greatly mistaken, if he conceives that Thwackum appeared to Mr Allworthy in the same light as he doth to him in this history; and he is as much deceived, if he imagines that the most intimate acquaintance which he himself could have had with that divine, would have informed him of those things which we, from our inspiration, are enabled to open and discover. Of readers who, from such conceits as these, condemn the wisdom or penetration of Mr Allworthy, I shall not scruple to say, that they make a very bad and ungrateful use of that knowledge which we have communicated to them.

These apparent errors in the doctrine of Thwackum served greatly to palliate the contrary errors in that of Square, which our good man no less saw and condemned. He thought, indeed, that the different exuberancies of these gentlemen would correct their different imperfections; and that from both, especially with his assistance, the two lads would derive sufficient precepts of true religion and virtue. If the event happened contrary to his expectations, this possibly proceeded from some fault in the plan itself; which the reader hath my leave to discover, if he can: for we do not pretend to introduce any infallible characters into this history; where we hope nothing will be found which hath never yet been seen in human nature.

To return therefore: the reader will not, I think, wonder that the different behaviour of the two lads above commemorated, produced the different effects of which he hath already seen some instance; and besides this, there was another reason for the conduct of the philosopher and the pedagogue; but this being matter of great importance, we shall reveal it in the next chapter.

CHAPTER VI.

Containing a better reason still for the before-mentioned opinions.

It is to be known then, that those two learned personages, who have lately made a considerable figure on the theatre of this history, had, from their first arrival at Mr Allworthy's house, taken so great an affection, the one to his virtue, the other to his religion, that they had meditated the closest alliance with him.

For this purpose they had cast their eyes on that fair widow, whom, though we have not for some time made any mention of her, the reader, we trust, hath not forgot. Mrs Blifil was indeed the object to which they both aspired.

It may seem remarkable, that, of four persons whom we have commemorated at Mr Allworthy's house, three of them should fix their inclinations on a lady who was never greatly celebrated for her beauty, and who was, moreover, now a little descended into the vale of years; but in reality bosom friends, and intimate acquaintance, have a kind of natural propensity to particular females at the house of a friend—viz., to his grandmother, mother, sister, daughter, aunt, niece, or cousin, when they are rich; and to his wife, sister, daughter, niece, cousin, mistress, or servant-maid, if they should be handsome.

We would not, however, have our reader imagine, that persons of such characters as were supported by Thwackum and Square, would undertake a matter of this kind, which hath been a little censured by some rigid moralists, before they had thoroughly examined it, and considered whether it was (as Shakespear phrases it) "Stuff o' th' conscience," or no. Thwackum was encouraged to the undertaking by reflecting that to covet your neighbour's sister is nowhere forbidden: and he knew it was a rule in the construction of all laws, that "*Expressum facit cessare tacitum.*" The sense of which is, "When a lawgiver sets down plainly his whole meaning, we are prevented from making him mean what we please ourselves." As some instances of women, therefore, are mentioned in the divine law, which forbids us to covet our neighbour's goods, and that of a sister omitted, he concluded it to be lawful. And as to Square, who was in his person what is called a jolly fellow, or a widow's man, he easily reconciled his choice to the eternal fitness of things.

Now, as both of these gentlemen were industrious in taking every opportunity of recommending themselves to the widow, they apprehended one certain method was, by giving her son the constant preference to the other lad; and as they conceived the kindness and affection which Mr Allworthy showed the latter, must be highly disagreeable to her, they doubted not but the laying hold on all occasions to degrade and vilify him, would be highly pleasing to her; who, as she hated the boy, must love all those who did him any hurt. In this Thwackum had the advantage; for while Square could only scarify the poor lad's reputation, he could flea his skin; and, indeed, he considered every lash he gave him as a compliment paid to his mistress; so that he could, with the utmost propriety, repeat this old flogging line, *"Castigo te non quod odio habeam, sed quod* AMEM. I chastise thee not out of hatred, but out of love." And this, indeed, he often had in his mouth, or rather, according to the old phrase, never more properly applied, at his fingers' ends.

For this reason, principally, the two gentlemen concurred, as we have seen above, in their opinion concerning the two lads; this being, indeed, almost the only instance of their concurring on any point; for, beside the difference of their principles, they had both long ago strongly suspected each other's design, and hated one another with no little degree of inveteracy.

This mutual animosity was a good deal increased by their alternate successes; for Mrs Blifil knew what they would be at long before they imagined it; or, indeed, intended she should: for they proceeded with great caution, lest she should be offended, and acquaint Mr Allworthy. But they had no reason for any such fear; she was well enough pleased with a passion, of which she intended none should have any fruits but herself. And the only fruits she designed for herself were, flattery and courtship; for which purpose she soothed them by turns, and a long time equally. She was, indeed, rather inclined to favour the parson's principles; but Square's person was more agreeable to her eye, for he was a comely man; whereas the pedagogue did in countenance very nearly resemble that gentleman, who, in the Harlot's Progress, is seen correcting the ladies in Bridewell.

Whether Mrs Blifil had been surfeited with the sweets of marriage, or disgusted by its bitters, or from what other cause it proceeded, I will not determine; but she could never be brought to listen to any second proposals. However, she at last conversed with Square with such a degree of intimacy that malicious tongues began to whisper things of her, to which, as well for the sake of the lady, as that they were highly disagreeable to the rule of right and the fitness of things, we will give no credit, and therefore shall not blot our paper with them. The pedagogue, 'tis certain, whipped on, without getting a step nearer to his journey's end.

Indeed he had committed a great error, and that Square discovered much sooner than himself. Mrs Blifil (as, perhaps, the reader may have formerly guessed) was not over and above pleased with the behaviour of her husband; nay, to be honest, she absolutely hated him, till his death at last a little reconciled him to her affections. It will not be therefore greatly wondered at, if she had not the most violent regard to the offspring she had by him. And, in fact, she had so little of this regard, that in his infancy she seldom saw her son, or took any notice of him; and hence she acquiesced, after a little reluctance, in all the favours which Mr Allworthy showered on the foundling; whom the good man called his own boy, and in all things put on an entire equality with Master Blifil. This acquiescence in

Mrs Blifil was considered by the neighbours, and by the family, as a mark of her condescension to her brother's humour, and she was imagined by all others, as well as Thwackum and Square, to hate the foundling in her heart; nay, the more civility she showed him, the more they conceived she detested him, and the surer schemes she was laying for his ruin: for as they thought it her interest to hate him, it was very difficult for her to persuade them she did not.

Thwackum was the more confirmed in his opinion, as she had more than once slily caused him to whip Tom Jones, when Mr Allworthy, who was an enemy to this exercise, was abroad; whereas she had never given any such orders concerning young Blifil. And this had likewise imposed upon Square. In reality, though she certainly hated her own son—of which, however monstrous it appears, I am assured she is not a singular instance—she appeared, notwithstanding all her outward compliance, to be in her heart sufficiently displeased with all the favour shown by Mr Allworthy to the foundling. She frequently complained of this behind her brother's back, and very sharply censured him for it, both to Thwackum and Square; nay, she would throw it in the teeth of Allworthy himself, when a little quarrel, or miff, as it is vulgarly called, arose between them.

However, when Tom grew up, and gave tokens of that gallantry of temper which greatly recommends men to women, this disinclination which she had discovered to him when a child, by degrees abated, and at last she so evidently demonstrated her affection to him to be much stronger than what she bore her own son, that it was impossible to mistake her any longer. She was so desirous of often seeing him, and discovered such satisfaction and delight in his company, that before he was eighteen years old he was become a rival to both Square and Thwackum; and what is worse, the whole country began to talk as loudly of her inclination to Tom, as they had before done of that which she had shown to Square: on which account the philosopher conceived the most implacable hatred for our poor heroe.

CHAPTER VII.

In which the author himself makes his appearance on the stage.

Though Mr Allworthy was not of himself hasty to see things in a disadvantageous light, and was a stranger to the public voice, which seldom reaches to a brother or a husband, though it rings in the ears of all the neighbourhood; yet was this affection of Mrs Blifil to Tom, and the preference which she too visibly gave him to her own son, of the utmost disadvantage to that youth.

For such was the compassion which inhabited Mr Allworthy's mind, that nothing but the steel of justice could ever subdue it. To be unfortunate in any respect was sufficient, if there was no demerit to counterpoise it, to turn the scale of that good man's pity, and to engage his friendship and his benefaction.

When therefore he plainly saw Master Blifil was absolutely detested (for that he was) by his own mother, he began, on that account only, to look with an eye of compassion upon him; and what the effects of compassion are, in good and benevolent minds, I need not here explain to most of my readers.

Hcnccforward hc saw cvcry appcarancc of virtuc in thc youth through the magnifying end, and viewed all his faults with the glass inverted, so that they became scarce perceptible. And this perhaps the amiable temper of pity may make commendable; but the next step the weakness of human nature alone must excuse; for he no sooner perceived that preference which Mrs Blifil gave to Tom, than that poor youth (however innocent) began to sink in his affections as he rose in hers. This, it is true, would of itself alone never have been able to eradicate Jones from his bosom; but it was greatly injurious to him, and prepared Mr Allworthy's mind for those impressions which afterwards produced the mighty events that will be contained hereafter in this history; and to which, it must be confest, the unfortunate lad, by his own wantonness, wildness, and want of caution, too much contributed.

In recording some instances of these, we shall, if rightly understood, afford a very useful lesson to those well-disposed youths who shall hereafter be our readers; for they may here find, that goodness of heart, and openness of temper, though these may give them great comfort within, and administer to an honest pride in their own minds, will by no means, alas! do their business in the world. Prudence and circumspection are necessary even to the best of men. They are indeed, as it were, a guard to Virtue, without which she can never be safe. It is not enough that your designs, nay, that your actions, are intrinsically good; you must take care they shall appear so. If your inside be never so beautiful, you must preserve a fair outside also. This must be constantly looked to, or malice and envy will take care to blacken it so, that the sagacity and goodness of an Allworthy will not be able to see through it, and to discern the beauties within. Let this, my young readers, be your constant maxim, that no man can be good enough to enable him to neglect the rules of prudence; nor will Virtue herself look beautiful, unless she be bedecked with the outward ornaments of decency and decorum. And this precept, my worthy disciples, if you read with due attention, you will, I hope, find sufficiently enforced by examples in the following pages.

I ask pardon for this short appearance, by way of chorus, on the stage. It is in reality for my own sake, that, while I am discovering the rocks on which innocence and goodness often split, I may not be misunderstood to recommend the very means to my worthy readers, by which I intend to show them they will be undone. And this, as I could not prevail on any of my actors to speak, I myself was obliged to declare.

CHAPTER VIII.

A childish incident, in which, however, is seen a good-natured disposition in Tom Jones.

The reader may remember that Mr Allworthy gave Tom Jones a little horse, as a kind of smart-money for the punishment which he imagined he had suffered innocently.

This horse Tom kept above half a year, and then rode him to a neighbouring fair, and sold him.

At his return, being questioned by Thwackum what he had done with the money for which the horse was sold, he frankly declared he would not tell him.

"Oho!" says Thwackum, "you will not! then I will have it out of your br—h;" that being the place to which he always applied for information on every doubtful occasion.

Tom was now mounted on the back of a footman, and everything prepared for execution, when Mr Allworthy, entering the room, gave the criminal a reprieve, and took him with him into another apartment; where, being alone with Tom, he put the same question to him which Thwackum had before asked him.

Tom answered, he could in duty refuse him nothing; but as for that tyrannical rascal, he would never make him any other answer than with a cudgel, with which he hoped soon to be able to pay him for all his barbarities.

Mr Allworthy very severely reprimanded the lad for his indecent and disrespectful expressions concerning his master; but much more for his avowing an intention of revenge. He threatened him with the entire loss of his favour, if he ever heard such another word from his mouth; for, he said, he would never support or befriend a reprobate. By these and the like declarations, he extorted some compunction from Tom, in which that youth was not over-sincere; for he really meditated some return for all the smarting favours he had received at the hands of the pedagogue. He was, however, brought by Mr Allworthy to express a concern for his resentment against Thwackum; and then the good man, after some wholesome admonition, permitted him to proceed, which he did as follows:—

"Indeed, my dear sir, I love and honour you more than all the world: I know the great obligations I have to you, and should detest myself if I thought my heart was capable of ingratitude. Could the little horse you gave me speak, I am sure he could tell you how fond I was of your present; for I had more pleasure in feeding him than in riding him. Indeed, sir, it went to my heart to part with him; nor would I have sold him upon any other account in the world than what I did. You yourself, sir, I am convinced, in my case, would have done the same: for none ever so sensibly felt the misfortunes of others. What would you feel, dear sir, if you thought yourself the occasion of them? Indeed, sir, there never was any misery like theirs."

"Like whose, child?" says Allworthy: "What do you mean?"

"Oh, sir!" answered Tom, "your poor gamekeeper, with all his large family, ever since your discarding him, have been perishing with all the miseries of cold and hunger: I could not bear to see these poor wretches naked and starving, and at the same time know myself to have been the occasion of all their sufferings. I could not bear it, sir; upon my soul, I could not." [Here the tears ran down his cheeks, and he thus proceeded.] "It was to save them from absolute destruction I parted with your dear present, notwithstanding all the value I had for it: I sold the horse for them, and they have every farthing of the money."

Mr Allworthy now stood silent for some moments, and before he spoke the tears started from his eyes. He at length dismissed Tom with a gentle rebuke, advising him for the future to apply to him in cases of distress, rather than to use extraordinary means of relieving them himself.

This affair was afterwards the subject of much debate between Thwackum and Square. Thwackum held, that this was flying in Mr Allworthy's face, who had intended to punish the fellow for his disobedience. He said, in some instances, what the world called charity appeared to him to be opposing the will of the Almighty, which had marked some particular persons for destruction; and that this was in like manner acting in opposition to Mr Allworthy; concluding, as usual, with a hearty recommendation of birch.

Square argued strongly on the other side, in opposition perhaps to Thwackum, or in compliance with Mr Allworthy, who seemed very much to approve what Jones had done. As to what he urged on this occasion, as I am convinced most of my readers will be much abler advocates for poor Jones, it would be impertinent to relate it. Indeed it was not difficult to reconcile to the rule of right an action which it would have been impossible to deduce from the rule of wrong.

CHAPTER IX.

Containing an incident of a more heinous kind, with the comments of Thwackum and Square.

It hath been observed by some man of much greater reputation for wisdom than myself, that misfortunes seldom come single. An instance of this may, I believe, be seen in those gentlemen who have the misfortune to have any of their rogueries detected; for here discovery seldom stops till the whole is come out. Thus it happened to poor Tom; who was no sooner pardoned for selling the horse, than he was discovered to have some time before sold a fine Bible which Mr Allworthy gave him, the money arising from which sale he had disposed of in the same manner. This Bible Master Blifil had purchased, though he had already such another of his own, partly out of respect for the book, and partly out of friendship to Tom, being unwilling that the Bible should be sold out of the family at half-price. He therefore deposited the said half-price himself; for he was a very prudent lad, and so careful of his money, that he had laid up almost every penny which he had received from Mr Allworthy.

Some people have been noted to be able to read in no book but their own. On the contrary, from the time when Master Blifil was first possessed of this Bible, he never used any other. Nay, he was seen reading in it much oftener than he had before been in his own. Now, as he frequently asked Thwackum to explain difficult passages to him, that gentleman unfortunately took notice of Tom's name, which was written in many parts of the book. This brought on an inquiry, which obliged Master Blifil to discover the whole matter.

Thwackum was resolved a crime of this kind, which he called sacrilege, should not go unpunished. He therefore proceeded immediately to castigation: and not contented with that he acquainted Mr Allworthy, at their next meeting, with this monstrous crime, as it appeared to him: inveighing against Tom in the most bitter terms, and likening him to the buyers and sellers who were driven out of the temple.

Square saw this matter in a very different light. He said, he could not perceive any higher crime in selling one book than in selling another. That to sell Bibles was strictly lawful by all laws both Divine and human, and consequently there was no unfitness in it. He told Thwackum, that his great concern on this occasion brought to his mind the story of a very devout woman, who, out of pure regard to religion, stole Tillotson's Sermons from a lady of her acquaintance.

This story caused a vast quantity of blood to rush into the parson's face, which of itself was none of the palest; and he was going to reply with great warmth and anger, had not Mrs Blifil, who was present at this debate, interposed. That lady declared herself absolutely of Mr Square's side. She argued, indeed, very learnedly in support of his opinion; and concluded with saying, if Tom had been guilty of any fault, she must confess her own son appeared to be equally culpable; for that she could see no difference between the buyer and the seller; both of whom were alike to be driven out of the temple.

Mrs Blifil having declared her opinion, put an end to the debate. Square's triumph would almost have stopt his words, had he needed them; and Thwackum, who, for reasons before-mentioned, durst not venture at disobliging the lady, was almost choaked with indignation. As to Mr Allworthy, he said, since the boy had been already punished he would not deliver his sentiments on the occasion; and whether he was or was not angry with the lad, I must leave to the reader's own conjecture.

Soon after this, an action was brought against the gamekeeper by Squire Western (the gentleman in whose manor the partridge was killed), for depredations of the like kind. This was a most unfortunate circumstance for the fellow, as it not only of itself threatened his ruin, but actually prevented Mr Allworthy from restoring him to his favour: for as that gentleman was walking out one evening with Master Blifil and young Jones, the latter slily drew him to the habitation of Black George; where the family of that poor wretch, namely, his wife and children, were found in all the misery with which cold, hunger, and nakedness, can affect human creatures: for as to the money they had received from Jones, former debts had consumed almost the whole.

Such a scene as this could not fail of affecting the heart of Mr Allworthy. He immediately gave the mother a couple of guineas, with which he bid her cloath her children. The poor woman burst into tears at this goodness, and while she was thanking him, could not refrain from expressing her gratitude to Tom; who had, she said, long preserved both her and hers from starving. "We have not," says she, "had a morsel to eat, nor have these poor children had a rag to put on, but what his goodness hath bestowed on us." For, indeed, besides the horse and the Bible, Tom had sacrificed a night-gown, and other things, to the use of this distressed family.

On their return home, Tom made use of all his eloquence to display the wretchedness of these people, and the penitence of Black George himself; and in this he succeeded so well, that Mr Allworthy said, he thought the man had suffered enough for what was past; that he would forgive him, and think of some means of providing for him and his family.

Jones was so delighted with this news, that, though it was dark when they returned home, he could not help going back a mile, in a shower of rain, to acquaint the poor woman with the glad tidings; but, like other hasty divulgers of news, he only brought on himself the trouble of contradicting it: for the ill fortune of Black George made use of the very opportunity of his friend's absence to overturn all again.

CHAPTER X.

In which Master Blifil and Jones appear in different lights.

Master Blifil fell very short of his companion in the amiable quality of mercy; but he as greatly exceeded him in one of a much higher kind, namely, in justice: in which he followed both the precepts and example of Thwackum and Square; for though they would both make frequent use of the word mercy, yet it was plain that in reality Square held it to be inconsistent with the rule of right; and Thwackum was for doing justice, and leaving mercy to heaven. The two gentlemen did indeed somewhat differ in opinion concerning the objects of this sublime virtue; by which Thwackum would probably have destroyed one half of mankind, and Square the other half.

Master Blifil then, though he had kept silence in the presence of Jones, yet, when he had better considered the matter, could by no means endure the thought of suffering his uncle to confer favours on the undeserving. He therefore resolved immediately to acquaint him with the fact which we have above slightly hinted to the readers. The truth of which was as follows:

The gamekeeper, about a year after he was dismissed from Mr Allworthy's service, and before Tom's selling the horse, being in want of bread, either to fill his own mouth or those of his family, as he passed through a field belonging to Mr Western espied a hare sitting in her form. This hare he had basely and barbarously knocked on the head, against the laws of the land, and no less against the laws of sportsmen.

The higgler to whom the hare was sold, being unfortunately taken many months after with a quantity of game upon him, was obliged to make his peace with the squire, by becoming evidence against some poacher. And now Black George was pitched upon by him, as being a person already obnoxious to Mr Western, and one of no good fame in the country. He was, besides, the best sacrifice the higgler could make, as he had supplied him with no game since; and by this means the witness had an opportunity of screening his better customers: for the squire, being charmed with the power of punishing Black George, whom a single transgression was sufficient to ruin, made no further enquiry.

Had this fact been truly laid before Mr Allworthy, it might probably have done the gamekeeper very little mischief. But there is no zeal blinder than that which is inspired with the love of justice against offenders. Master Blifil had forgot the distance of the time. He varied likewise in the manner of the fact: and by the hasty addition of the single letter S he considerably altered the story; for he said that George had wired hares. These alterations might probably have been set right, had not Master Blifil unluckily insisted on a promise of secrecy from Mr Allworthy before he revealed the matter to him; but by that means the poor gamekeeper was condemned without having an opportunity to defend himself: for as the fact of killing the hare, and of the action brought, were certainly true, Mr Allworthy had no doubt concerning the rest.

Short-lived then was the joy of these poor people; for Mr Allworthy the next morning declared he had fresh reason, without assigning it, for his anger, and strictly forbad Tom to mention George any more: though as for his family, he said he would endeavour to keep them from starving; but as to the fellow himself, he would leave him to the laws, which nothing could keep him from breaking.

Tom could by no means divine what had incensed Mr Allworthy, for of Master Blifil he had not the least suspicion. However, as his friendship was to be tired out by no disappointments, he now determined to try another method of preserving the poor gamekeeper from ruin.

Jones was lately grown very intimate with Mr Western. He had so greatly recommended himself to that gentleman, by leaping over five-barred gates, and by other acts of sportsmanship, that the squire had declared Tom would certainly make a great man if he had but sufficient encouragement. He often wished he had himself a son with such parts; and one day very solemnly asserted at a drinking bout, that Tom should hunt a pack of hounds for a thousand pound of his money, with any huntsman in the whole country.

By such kind of talents he had so ingratiated himself with the squire, that he was a most welcome guest at his table, and a favourite companion in his sport: everything which the squire held most dear, to wit, his guns, dogs, and horses, were now as much at the command of Jones, as if they had been his own. He resolved therefore to make use of this favour on behalf of his friend Black George, whom he hoped to introduce into Mr Western's family, in the same capacity in which he had before served Mr Allworthy.

The reader, if he considers that this fellow was already obnoxious to Mr Western, and if he considers farther the weighty business by which that gentleman's displeasure had been incurred, will perhaps condemn this as a foolish and desperate undertaking; but if he should totally condemn young Jones on that account, he will greatly applaud him for strengthening himself with all imaginable interest on so arduous an occasion.

For this purpose, then, Tom applied to Mr Western's daughter, a young lady of about seventeen years of age, whom her father, next after those necessary implements of sport just before mentioned, loved and esteemed above all the world. Now, as she had some influence on the squire, so Tom had some little influence on her. But this being the intended heroine of this work, a lady with whom we ourselves are greatly in love, and with whom many of our readers will probably be in love too, before we part, it is by no means proper she should make her appearance at the end of a book.

BOOK IV.

CONTAINING THE TIME OF A YEAR.

CHAPTER I.

Containing five pages of paper.

As truth distinguishes our writings from those idle romances which are filled with monsters, the productions, not of nature, but of distempered brains; and which have been therefore recommended by an eminent critic to the sole use of the pastry-cook; so, on the other hand, we would avoid any resemblance to that kind of history which a celebrated poet seems to think is no less calculated for the emolument of the brewer, as the reading it should be always attended with a tankard of good ale—

> While—history with her comrade ale,
> Soothes the sad series of her serious tale

For as this is the liquor of modern historians, nay, perhaps their muse, if we may believe the opinion of Butler, who attributes inspiration to ale, it ought likewise to be the potation of their readers, since every book ought to be read with the same spirit and in the same manner as it is writ. Thus the famous author of Hurlothrumbo told a learned bishop, that the reason his lordship could not taste the excellence of his piece was, that he did not read it with a fiddle in his hand; which instrument he himself had always had in his own, when he composed it.

That our work, therefore, might be in no danger of being likened to the labours of these historians, we have taken every occasion of interspersing through the whole sundry similes, descriptions, and other kind of poetical embellishments. These are, indeed, designed to supply the place of the said ale, and to refresh the mind, whenever those slumbers, which in a long work are apt to invade the reader as well as the writer, shall begin to creep upon him. Without interruptions of this kind, the best narrative of plain matter of fact must overpower every reader; for nothing but the ever lasting watchfulness, which Homer has ascribed only to Jove himself, can be proof against a newspaper of many volumes.

We shall leave to the reader to determine with what judgment we have chosen the several occasions for inserting those ornamental parts of our work. Surely it will be allowed that none could be more proper than the present, where we are about to introduce a considerable character on the scene; no less, indeed, than the heroine of this heroic, historical, prosaic poem. Here, therefore, we have thought proper to prepare the mind of the reader for her reception, by filling it with every pleasing image which we can draw from the face of nature. And for this method we plead many precedents. First, this is an art well known to, and much practised by, our tragick poets, who seldom fail to prepare their audience for the reception of their principal characters.

Thus the heroe is always introduced with a flourish of drums and trumpets, in order to rouse a martial spirit in the audience, and to accommodate their ears to bombast and fustian, which Mr Locke's blind man would not have grossly erred in likening to the sound of a trumpet. Again, when lovers are coming forth, soft music often conducts them on the stage, either to soothe the audience with the softness of the tender passion, or to lull and prepare them for that gentle slumber in which they will most probably be composed by the ensuing scene.

And not only the poets, but the masters of these poets, the managers of playhouses, seem to be in this secret; for, besides the aforesaid kettle-drums, &c., which denote the heroe's approach, he is generally ushered on the stage by a large troop of half a dozen scene-shifters; and how necessary these are imagined to his appearance, may be concluded from the following theatrical story:—

King Pyrrhus was at dinner at an ale-house bordering on the theatre, when he was summoned to go on the stage. The heroe, being unwilling to quit his shoulder of mutton, and as unwilling to draw on himself the indignation of Mr Wilks (his brother-manager) for making the audience wait, had bribed these his harbingers to be out of the way. While Mr Wilks, therefore, was thundering out, "Where are the carpenters to walk on before King Pyrrhus?" that monarch very quietly eat his mutton, and the audience, however impatient, were obliged to entertain themselves with music in his absence.

To be plain, I much question whether the politician, who hath generally a good nose, hath not scented out somewhat of the utility of this practice. I am convinced that awful magistrate my lord-mayor contracts a good deal of that reverence which attends him through the year, by the several pageants which precede his pomp. Nay, I must confess, that even I myself, who am not remarkably liable to be captivated with show, have yielded not a little to the impressions of much preceding state. When I have seen a man strutting in a procession, after others whose business was only to walk before him, I have conceived a higher notion of his dignity than I have felt on seeing him in a common situation. But there is one instance, which comes exactly up to my purpose. This is the custom of sending on a basket-woman, who is to precede the pomp at a coronation, and to strew the stage with flowers, before the great personages begin their procession. The antients would certainly have invoked the goddess Flora for this purpose, and it would have been no difficulty for their priests, or politicians to have persuaded the people of the real presence of the deity, though a plain mortal had personated her and performed her office. But we have no such design of imposing on our reader; and therefore those who object to the heathen theology, may, if they please, change our goddess into the above-mentioned basket-woman. Our intention, in short, is to introduce our heroine with the utmost solemnity in our power, with an elevation of stile, and all other circumstances proper to raise the veneration of our reader.—Indeed we would, for certain causes, advise those of our male readers who have any hearts, to read no farther, were we not well assured, that how amiable soever the picture of our heroine will appear, as it is really a copy from nature, many of our fair countrywomen will be found worthy to satisfy any passion, and to answer any idea of female perfection which our pencil will be able to raise.

And now, without any further preface, we proceed to our next chapter.

CHAPTER II.

A short hint of what we can do in the sublime, and a description of Miss Sophia Western.

Hushed be every ruder breath. May the heathen ruler of the winds confine in iron chains the boisterous limbs of noisy Boreas, and the sharp-pointed nose of bitter-biting Eurus. Do thou, sweet Zephyrus, rising from thy fragrant bed, mount the western sky, and lead on those delicious gales, the charms of which call forth the lovely Flora from her chamber, perfumed with pearly dews, when on the 1st of June, her birth-day, the blooming maid, in loose attire, gently trips it over the verdant mead, where every flower rises to do her homage, till the whole field becomes enamelled, and colours contend with sweets which shall ravish her most.

So charming may she now appear! and you the feathered choristers of nature, whose sweetest notes not even Handel can excell, tune your melodious throats to celebrate her appearance. From love proceeds your music, and to love it returns. Awaken therefore that gentle passion in every swain: for lo! adorned with all the charms in which nature can array her; bedecked with beauty, youth, sprightliness, innocence, modesty, and tenderness, breathing sweetness from her rosy lips, and darting brightness from her sparkling eyes, the lovely Sophia comes!

Reader, perhaps thou hast seen the statue of the *Venus de Medicis*. Perhaps, too, thou hast seen the gallery of beauties at Hampton Court. Thou may'st remember each bright Churchill of the galaxy, and all the toasts of the Kit-cat. Or, if their reign was before thy times, at least thou hast seen their daughters, the no less dazzling beauties of the present age; whose names, should we here insert, we apprehend they would fill the whole volume.

Now if thou hast seen all these, be not afraid of the rude answer which Lord Rochester once gave to a man who had seen many things. No. If thou hast seen all these without knowing what beauty is, thou hast no eyes; if without feeling its power, thou hast no heart.

Yet is it possible, my friend, that thou mayest have seen all these without being able to form an exact idea of Sophia; for she did not exactly resemble any of them. She was most like the picture of Lady Ranelagh: and, I have heard, more still to the famous dutchess of Mazarine; but most of all she resembled one whose image never can depart from my breast, and whom, if thou dost remember, thou hast then, my friend, an adequate idea of Sophia.

But lest this should not have been thy fortune, we will endeavour with our utmost skill to describe this paragon, though we are sensible that our highest abilities are very inadequate to the task.

Sophia, then, the only daughter of Mr Western, was a middle-sized woman; but rather inclining to tall. Her shape was not only exact, but extremely delicate: and the nice proportion of her arms promised the truest symmetry in her limbs. Her hair, which was black, was so luxuriant, that it reached her middle, before she cut it to comply with the modern fashion; and it was now curled so gracefully in her neck, that few could believe it to be her own. If envy could find any part of the face which demanded less commendation than the rest, it might possibly think her forehead might have been higher without prejudice to her. Her eyebrows were full, even, and arched beyond the power of art to imitate. Her black eyes had a lustre in them, which all her softness could not extinguish. Her nose was exactly regular, and her mouth, in which were two rows of ivory, exactly answered Sir John Suckling's description in those lines:—

> Her lips were red, and one was thin,
> Compar'd to that was next her chin.
> Some bee had stung it newly.

Her cheeks were of the oval kind; and in her right she had a dimple, which the least smile discovered. Her chin had certainly its share in forming the beauty of her face; but it was difficult to say it was either large or small, though perhaps it was rather of the former kind. Her complexion had rather more of the lily than of the rose; but when exercise or modesty increased her natural colour, no vermilion could equal it. Then one might indeed cry out with the celebrated Dr Donne:

> —Her pure and eloquent blood
> Spoke in her cheeks, and so distinctly wrought
> That one might almost say her body thought.

Her neck was long and finely turned: and here, if I was not afraid of offending her delicacy, I might justly say, the highest beauties of the famous *Venus de Medicis* were outdone. Here was whiteness which no lilies, ivory, nor alabaster could match. The finest cambric might indeed be supposed from envy to cover that bosom which was much whiter than itself.—It was indeed,

> *Nitor splendens Pario marmore purius.*

A gloss shining beyond the purest brightness of Parian marble.

Such was the outside of Sophia; nor was this beautiful frame disgraced by an inhabitant unworthy of it. Her mind was every way equal to her person; nay, the latter borrowed some charms from the former; for when she smiled, the sweetness of her temper diffused that glory over her countenance which no regularity of features can give. But as there are no perfections of the mind which do not discover themselves in that perfect intimacy to which we intend to introduce our reader with this charming young creature, so it is needless to mention them here: nay, it is a kind of tacit affront to our reader's understanding, and may also rob him of that pleasure which he will receive in forming his own judgment of her character.

It may, however, be proper to say, that whatever mental accomplishments she had derived from nature, they were somewhat improved and cultivated by art: for she had been educated under the care of an aunt, who was a lady of great discretion, and was thoroughly acquainted with the world, having lived in her youth about the court, whence she had retired some years since into the country. By her conversation and instructions, Sophia was perfectly well bred, though perhaps she wanted a little of that ease in her behaviour which is to be acquired only by habit, and living within what is called the polite circle. But this, to say the truth, is often too dearly purchased; and though it hath charms so inexpressible, that the French, perhaps, among other qualities, mean to express this, when they declare they know not what it is; yet its absence is well compensated by innocence; nor can good sense and a natural gentility ever stand in need of it.

CHAPTER III.

Wherein the history goes back to commemorate a trifling incident that happened some years since; but which, trifling as it was, had some future consequences.

The amiable Sophia was now in her eighteenth year, when she is introduced into this history. Her father, as hath been said, was fonder of her than of any other human creature. To her, therefore, Tom Jones applied, in order to engage her interest on the behalf of his friend the gamekeeper.

But before we proceed to this business, a short recapitulation of some previous matters may be necessary.

Though the different tempers of Mr Allworthy and of Mr Western did not admit of a very intimate correspondence, yet they lived upon what is called a decent footing together; by which means the young people of both families had been acquainted from their infancy; and as they were all near of the same age, had been frequent playmates together.

The gaiety of Tom's temper suited better with Sophia, than the grave and sober disposition of Master Blifil. And the preference which she gave the former of these, would often appear so plainly, that a lad of a more passionate turn than Master Blifil was, might have shown some displeasure at it.

As he did not, however, outwardly express any such disgust, it would be an ill office in us to pay a visit to the inmost recesses of his mind, as some scandalous people search into the most secret affairs of their friends, and often pry into their closets and cupboards, only to discover their poverty and meanness to the world.

However, as persons who suspect they have given others cause of offence, are apt to conclude they are offended; so Sophia imputed an action of Master Blifil to his anger, which the superior sagacity of Thwackum and Square discerned to have arisen from a much better principle.

Tom Jones, when very young, had presented Sophia with a little bird, which he had taken from the nest, had nursed up, and taught to sing.

Of this bird, Sophia, then about thirteen years old, was so extremely fond, that her chief business was to feed and tend it, and her chief pleasure to play with it. By these means little Tommy, for so the bird was called, was become so tame, that it would feed out of the hand of its mistress, would perch upon the finger, and lie contented in her bosom, where it seemed almost sensible of its own happiness;

though she always kept a small string about its leg, nor would ever trust it with the liberty of flying away.

One day, when Mr Allworthy and his whole family dined at Mr Western's, Master Blifil, being in the garden with little Sophia, and observing the extreme fondness that she showed for her little bird, desired her to trust it for a moment in his hands. Sophia presently complied with the young gentleman's request, and after some previous caution, delivered him her bird; of which he was no sooner in possession, than he slipt the string from its leg and tossed it into the air.

The foolish animal no sooner perceived itself at liberty, than forgetting all the favours it had received from Sophia, it flew directly from her, and perched on a bough at some distance.

Sophia, seeing her bird gone, screamed out so loud, that Tom Jones, who was at a little distance, immediately ran to her assistance.

He was no sooner informed of what had happened, than he cursed Blifil for a pitiful malicious rascal; and then immediately stripping off his coat he applied himself to climbing the tree to which the bird escaped.

Tom had almost recovered his little namesake, when the branch on which it was perched, and that hung over a canal, broke, and the poor lad plumped over head and ears into the water.

Sophia's concern now changed its object. And as she apprehended the boy's life was in danger, she screamed ten times louder than before; and indeed Master Blifil himself now seconded her with all the vociferation in his power.

The company, who were sitting in a room next the garden, were instantly alarmed, and came all forth; but just as they reached the canal, Tom (for the water was luckily pretty shallow in that part) arrived safely on shore.

Thwackum fell violently on poor Tom, who stood dropping and shivering before him, when Mr Allworthy desired him to have patience; and turning to Master Blifil, said, "Pray, child, what is the reason of all this disturbance?"

Master Blifil answered, "Indeed, uncle, I am very sorry for what I have done; I have been unhappily the occasion of it all. I had Miss Sophia's bird in my hand, and thinking the poor creature languished for liberty, I own I could not forbear giving it what it desired; for I always thought there was something very cruel in confining anything. It seemed to be against the law of nature, by which everything hath a right to liberty; nay, it is even unchristian, for it is not doing what we would be done by; but if I had imagined Miss Sophia would have been so much concerned at it, I am sure I never would have done it; nay, if I had known what would have happened to the bird itself: for when Master Jones, who climbed up that tree after it, fell into the water, the bird took a second flight, and presently a nasty hawk carried it away."

Poor Sophia, who now first heard of her little Tommy's fate (for her concern for Jones had prevented her perceiving it when it happened), shed a shower of tears. These Mr Allworthy endeavoured to assuage, promising her a much finer bird: but she declared she would never have another. Her father chid her for crying so for a foolish bird; but could not help telling young Blifil, if he was a son of his, his backside should be well flead.

Sophia now returned to her chamber, the two young gentlemen were sent home, and the rest of the company returned to their bottle; where a conversation ensued on the subject of the bird, so curious, that we think it deserves a chapter by itself.

CHAPTER IV.

Containing such very deep and grave matters, that some readers, perhaps, may not relish it.

Square had no sooner lighted his pipe, than, addressing himself to Allworthy, he thus began: "Sir, I cannot help congratulating you on your nephew; who, at an age when few lads have any ideas but of sensible objects, is arrived at a capacity of distinguishing right from wrong. To confine anything, seems to me against the law of nature, by which everything hath a right to liberty. These were his words; and the impression they have made on me is never to be eradicated. Can any man have a higher notion of the rule of right, and the eternal fitness of things? I cannot help promising myself, from such a dawn, that the meridian of this youth will be equal to that of either the elder or the younger Brutus."

Here Thwackum hastily interrupted, and spilling some of his wine, and swallowing the rest with great eagerness, answered, "From another expression he made use of, I hope he will resemble much better men. The law of nature is a jargon of words, which means nothing. I know not of any such law, nor of any right which can be derived from it. To do as we would be done by, is indeed a Christian motive, as the boy well expressed himself; and I am glad to find my instructions have borne such good fruit."

"If vanity was a thing fit," says Square, "I might indulge some on the same occasion; for whence only he can have learnt his notions of right or wrong, I think is pretty apparent. If there be no law of nature, there is no right nor wrong."

"How!" says the parson, "do you then banish revelation? Am I talking with a deist or an atheist?"

"Drink about," says Western. "Pox of your laws of nature! I don't know what you mean, either of you, by right and wrong. To take away my girl's bird was wrong, in my opinion; and my neighbour Allworthy may do as he pleases; but to encourage boys in such practices, is to breed them up to the gallows."

Allworthy answered, "That he was sorry for what his nephew had done, but could not consent to punish him, as he acted rather from a generous than unworthy motive." He said, "If the boy had stolen the bird, none would have been more ready to vote for a severe chastisement than himself; but it was plain that was not his design:" and, indeed, it was as apparent to him, that he could have no other view but what he had himself avowed. (For as to that malicious purpose which Sophia suspected, it never once entered into the head of Mr Allworthy.) He at length concluded with again blaming the action as inconsiderate, and which, he said, was pardonable only in a child.

Square had delivered his opinion so openly, that if he was now silent, he must submit to have his judgment censured. He said, therefore, with some warmth, "That Mr Allworthy had too much respect to the dirty consideration of property. That in passing our judgments on great and mighty actions, all private regards should be laid aside; for by adhering to those narrow rules, the younger Brutus had been condemned of ingratitude, and the elder of parricide."

"And if they had been hanged too for those crimes," cried Thwackum, "they would have had no more than their deserts. A couple of heathenish villains! Heaven be praised we have no Brutuses now-a-days! I wish, Mr Square, you would desist from filling the minds of my pupils with such antichristian stuff; for the consequence must be, while they are under my care, its being well scourged out of them again. There is your disciple Tom almost spoiled already. I overheard him the other day disputing with Master Blifil that there was no merit in faith without works. I know that is one of your tenets, and I suppose he had it from you."

"Don't accuse me of spoiling him," says Square. "Who taught him to laugh at whatever is virtuous and decent, and fit and right in the nature of things? He is your own scholar, and I disclaim him. No, no, Master Blifil is my boy. Young as he is, that lad's notions of moral rectitude I defy you ever to eradicate."

Thwackum put on a contemptuous sneer at this, and replied, "Ay, ay, I will venture him with you. He is too well grounded for all your philosophical cant to hurt. No, no, I have taken care to instil such principles into him—"

"And I have instilled principles into him too," cries Square. "What but the sublime idea of virtue could inspire a human mind with the generous thought of giving liberty? And I repeat to you again, if it was a fit thing to be proud, I might claim the honour of having infused that idea."—

"And if pride was not forbidden," said Thwackum, "I might boast of having taught him that duty which he himself assigned as his motive."

"So between you both," says the squire, "the young gentleman hath been taught to rob my daughter of her bird. I find I must take care of my partridge-mew. I shall have some virtuous religious man or other set all my partridges at liberty." Then slapping a gentleman of the law, who was present, on the back, he cried out, "What say you to this, Mr Counsellor? Is not this against law?"

The lawyer with great gravity delivered himself as follows:—

"If the case be put of a partridge, there can be no doubt but an action would lie; for though this be *ferae naturae*, yet being reclaimed, property vests: but being the case of a singing bird, though reclaimed, as it is a thing of base nature, it must be considered as *nullius in bonis*. In this case, therefore, I conceive the plaintiff must be non-suited; and I should disadvise the bringing any such action."

"Well," says the squire, "if it be *nullus bonus*, let us drink about, and talk a little of the state of the nation, or some such discourse that we all understand; for I am sure I don't understand a word of this. It may be learning and sense for aught I know: but you shall never persuade me into it. Pox! you have neither of you mentioned a word of that poor lad who deserves to be commended: to venture breaking his neck to oblige my girl was a generous-spirited action: I have learning enough to see that. D—n me, here's Tom's health! I shall love the boy for it the longest day I have to live."

Thus was the debate interrupted; but it would probably have been soon resumed, had not Mr Allworthy presently called for his coach, and carried off the two combatants.

Such was the conclusion of this adventure of the bird, and of the dialogue occasioned by it; which we could not help recounting to our reader, though it happened some years before that stage or period of time at which our history is now arrived.

CHAPTER V.

Containing matter accommodated to every taste.

"Parva leves capiunt animos—Small things affect light minds," was the sentiment of a great master of the passion of love. And certain it is, that from this day Sophia began to have some little kindness for Tom Jones, and no little aversion for his companion.

Many accidents from time to time improved both these passions in her breast; which, without our recounting, the reader may well conclude, from what we have before hinted of the different tempers of these lads, and how much the one suited with her own inclinations more than the other. To say the truth, Sophia, when very young, discerned that Tom, though an idle, thoughtless, rattling rascal, was nobody's enemy but his own; and that Master Blifil, though a prudent, discreet, sober young gentleman, was at the same time strongly attached to the interest only of one single person; and who that single person was the reader will be able to divine without any assistance of ours.

These two characters are not always received in the world with the different regard which seems severally due to either; and which one would imagine mankind, from self-interest, should show towards them. But perhaps there may be a political reason for it: in finding one of a truly benevolent disposition, men may very reasonably suppose they have found a treasure, and be desirous of keeping it, like all other good things, to themselves. Hence they may imagine, that to trumpet forth the praises of such a person, would, in the vulgar phrase, be crying Roast-meat, and calling in partakers of what they intend to apply solely to their own use. If this reason does not satisfy the reader, I know no other means of accounting for the little respect which I have commonly seen paid to a character which really does great honour to human nature, and is productive of the highest good to society. But it was otherwise with Sophia. She honoured Tom Jones, and scorned Master Blifil, almost as soon as she knew the meaning of those two words.

Sophia had been absent upwards of three years with her aunt; during all which time she had seldom seen either of these young gentlemen. She dined, however, once, together with her aunt, at Mr Allworthy's. This was a few days after the adventure of the partridge, before commemorated. Sophia heard the whole story at table, where she said nothing: nor indeed could her aunt get many words from her as she returned home; but her maid, when undressing her, happening to say, "Well, miss, I suppose you have seen young Master Blifil to-day?" she answered with much passion, "I hate the name of Master Blifil, as I do whatever is base and treacherous: and I wonder Mr Allworthy would suffer that old barbarous schoolmaster to punish a poor boy so cruelly for what was only the effect of his good-nature." She then recounted the story to her maid, and concluded with saying, "Don't you think he is a boy of noble spirit?"

This young lady was now returned to her father; who gave her the command of his house, and placed her at the upper end of his table, where Tom (who for his great love of hunting was become a great favourite of the squire) often dined. Young men of open, generous dispositions are naturally inclined to gallantry, which, if they have good understandings, as was in reality Tom's case, exerts itself in an obliging complacent behaviour to all women in general. This greatly distinguished Tom from the boisterous brutality of mere country squires on the one hand, and from the solemn and somewhat sullen deportment of Master Blifil on the other; and he began now, at twenty, to have the name of a pretty fellow among all the women in the neighbourhood.

Tom behaved to Sophia with no particularity, unless perhaps by showing her a higher respect than he paid to any other. This distinction her beauty, fortune, sense, and amiable carriage, seemed to demand; but as to design upon her person he had none; for which we shall at present suffer the reader to condemn him of stupidity; but perhaps we shall be able indifferently well to account for it hereafter.

Sophia, with the highest degree of innocence and modesty, had a remarkable sprightliness in her temper. This was so greatly increased whenever she was in company with Tom, that had he not been very young and thoughtless, he must have observed it: or had not Mr Western's thoughts been generally either in the field, the stable, or the dog-kennel, it might have perhaps created some jealousy in him: but so far was the good gentleman from entertaining any such suspicions, that he gave Tom every opportunity with his daughter which any lover could have wished; and this Tom innocently improved to better advantage, by following only the dictates of his natural gallantry and good-nature, than he might perhaps have done had he had the deepest designs on the young lady.

But indeed it can occasion little wonder that this matter escaped the observation of others, since poor Sophia herself never remarked it; and her heart was irretrievably lost before she suspected it was in danger.

Matters were in this situation, when Tom, one afternoon, finding Sophia alone, began, after a short apology, with a very serious face, to acquaint her that he had a favour to ask of her which he hoped her goodness would comply with.

Though neither the young man's behaviour, nor indeed his manner of opening this business, were such as could give her any just cause of suspecting he intended to make love to her; yet whether Nature whispered something into her ear, or from what cause it arose I will not determine; certain it is, some idea of that kind must have intruded itself; for her colour forsook her cheeks, her limbs trembled, and her tongue would have faltered, had Tom stopped for an answer; but he soon relieved her from her perplexity, by proceeding to inform her of his request;

which was to solicit her interest on behalf of the gamekeeper, whose own ruin, and that of a large family, must be, he said, the consequence of Mr Western's pursuing his action against him.

Sophia presently recovered her confusion, and, with a smile full of sweetness, said, "Is this the mighty favour you asked with so much gravity? I will do it with all my heart. I really pity the poor fellow, and no longer ago than yesterday sent a small matter to his wife." This small matter was one of her gowns, some linen, and ten shillings in money, of which Tom had heard, and it had, in reality, put this solicitation into his head.

Our youth, now, emboldened with his success, resolved to push the matter farther, and ventured even to beg her recommendation of him to her father's service; protesting that he thought him one of the honestest fellows in the country, and extremely well qualified for the place of a gamekeeper, which luckily then happened to be vacant.

Sophia answered, "Well, I will undertake this too; but I cannot promise you as much success as in the former part, which I assure you I will not quit my father without obtaining. However, I will do what I can for the poor fellow; for I sincerely look upon him and his family as objects of great compassion. And now, Mr Jones, I must ask you a favour."

"A favour, madam!" cries Tom: "if you knew the pleasure you have given me in the hopes of receiving a command from you, you would think by mentioning it you did confer the greatest favour on me; for by this dear hand I would sacrifice my life to oblige you."

He then snatched her hand, and eagerly kissed it, which was the first time his lips had ever touched her. The blood, which before had forsaken her cheeks, now made her sufficient amends, by rushing all over her face and neck with such violence, that they became all of a scarlet colour. She now first felt a sensation to which she had been before a stranger, and which, when she had leisure to reflect on it, began to acquaint her with some secrets, which the reader, if he doth not already guess them, will know in due time.

Sophia, as soon as she could speak (which was not instantly), informed him that the favour she had to desire of him was, not to lead her father through so many dangers in hunting; for that, from what she had heard, she was terribly frightened every time they went out together, and expected some day or other to see her father brought home with broken limbs. She therefore begged him, for her sake, to be more cautious; and as he well knew Mr Western would follow him, not to ride so madly, nor to take those dangerous leaps for the future.

Tom promised faithfully to obey her commands; and after thanking her for her kind compliance with his request, took his leave, and departed highly charmed with his success.

Poor Sophia was charmed too, but in a very different way. Her sensations, however, the reader's heart (if he or she have any) will better represent than I can, if I had as many mouths as ever poet wished for, to eat, I suppose, those many dainties with which he was so plentifully provided.

It was Mr Western's custom every afternoon, as soon as he was drunk, to hear his daughter play on the harpsichord; for he was a great lover of music, and perhaps, had he lived in town, might have passed for a connoisseur; for he always excepted against the finest compositions of Mr Handel. He never relished any music but what was light and airy; and indeed his most favourite tunes were Old Sir Simon the King, St George he was for England, Bobbing Joan, and some others.

His daughter, though she was a perfect mistress of music, and would never willingly have played any but Handel's, was so devoted to her father's pleasure, that she learnt all those tunes to oblige him. However, she would now and then endeavour to lead him into her own taste; and when he required the repetition of his ballads, would answer with a "Nay, dear sir;" and would often beg him to suffer her to play something else.

This evening, however, when the gentleman was retired from his bottle, she played all his favourites three times over without any solicitation. This so pleased the good squire, that he started from his couch, gave his daughter a kiss, and swore her hand was greatly improved. She took this opportunity to execute her promise to Tom; in which she succeeded so well, that the squire declared, if she would give him t'other bout of Old Sir Simon, he would give the gamekeeper his deputation the next morning. Sir Simon was played again and again, till the charms of the music soothed Mr Western to sleep. In the morning Sophia did not fail to remind him of his engagement; and his attorney was immediately sent for, ordered to stop any further proceedings in the action, and to make out the deputation.

Tom's success in this affair soon began to ring over the country, and various were the censures passed upon it; some greatly applauding it as an act of good nature; others sneering, and saying, "No wonder that one idle fellow should love another." Young Blifil was greatly enraged at it. He had long hated Black George in the same proportion as Jones delighted in him; not from any offence which he had ever received, but from his great love to religion and virtue;—for Black George had the reputation of a loose kind of a fellow. Blifil therefore represented this as flying in Mr Allworthy's face; and declared, with great concern, that it was impossible to find any other motive for doing good to such a wretch.

Thwackum and Square likewise sung to the same tune. They were now (especially the latter) become greatly jealous of young Jones with the widow; for he now approached the age of twenty, was really a fine young fellow, and that lady, by her encouragements to him, seemed daily more and more to think him so.

Allworthy was not, however, moved with their malice. He declared himself very well satisfied with what Jones had done. He said the perseverance and integrity of his friendship was highly commendable, and he wished he could see more frequent instances of that virtue.

But Fortune, who seldom greatly relishes such sparks as my friend Tom, perhaps because they do not pay more ardent addresses to her, gave now a very different turn to all his actions, and showed them to Mr Allworthy in a light far less agreeable than that gentleman's goodness had hitherto seen them in.

CHAPTER VI.

An apology for the insensibility of Mr Jones to all the charms of the lovely Sophia; in which possibly we may, in a considerable degree, lower his character in the estimation of those men of wit and

gallantry who approve the heroes in most of our modern comedies.

There are two sorts of people, who, I am afraid, have already conceived some contempt for my heroe, on account of his behaviour to Sophia. The former of these will blame his prudence in neglecting an opportunity to possess himself of Mr Western's fortune; and the latter will no less despise him for his backwardness to so fine a girl, who seemed ready to fly into his arms, if he would open them to receive her.

Now, though I shall not perhaps be able absolutely to acquit him of either of these charges (for want of prudence admits of no excuse; and what I shall produce against the latter charge will, I apprehend, be scarce satisfactory); yet, as evidence may sometimes be offered in mitigation, I shall set forth the plain matter of fact, and leave the whole to the reader's determination.

Mr Jones had somewhat about him, which, though I think writers are not thoroughly agreed in its name, doth certainly inhabit some human breasts; whose use is not so properly to distinguish right from wrong, as to prompt and incite them to the former, and to restrain and withhold them from the latter.

This somewhat may be indeed resembled to the famous trunk-maker in the playhouse; for, whenever the person who is possessed of it doth what is right, no ravished or friendly spectator is so eager or so loud in his applause: on the contrary, when he doth wrong, no critic is so apt to hiss and explode him.

To give a higher idea of the principle I mean, as well as one more familiar to the present age; it may be considered as sitting on its throne in the mind, like the Lord High Chancellor of this kingdom in his court; where it presides, governs, directs, judges, acquits, and condemns according to merit and justice, with a knowledge which nothing escapes, a penetration which nothing can deceive, and an integrity which nothing can corrupt.

This active principle may perhaps be said to constitute the most essential barrier between us and our neighbours the brutes; for if there be some in the human shape who are not under any such dominion, I choose rather to consider them as deserters from us to our neighbours; among whom they will have the fate of deserters, and not be placed in the first rank.

BOOK IV. CHAPTER VI.

Our heroe, whether he derived it from Thwackum or Square I will not determine, was very strongly under the guidance of this principle; for though he did not always act rightly, yet he never did otherwise without feeling and suffering for it. It was this which taught him, that to repay the civilities and little friendships of hospitality by robbing the house where you have received them, is to be the basest and meanest of thieves. He did not think the baseness of this offence lessened by the height of the injury committed; on the contrary, if to steal another's plate deserved death and infamy, it seemed to him difficult to assign a punishment adequate to the robbing a man of his whole fortune, and of his child into the bargain.

This principle, therefore, prevented him from any thought of making his fortune by such means (for this, as I have said, is an active principle, and doth not content itself with knowledge or belief only). Had he been greatly enamoured of Sophia, he possibly might have thought otherwise; but give me leave to say, there is great difference between running away with a man's daughter from the motive of love, and doing the same thing from the motive of theft.

Now, though this young gentleman was not insensible of the charms of Sophia; though he greatly liked her beauty, and esteemed all her other qualifications, she had made, however, no deep impression on his heart; for which, as it renders him liable to the charge of stupidity, or at least of want of taste, we shall now proceed to account.

The truth then is, his heart was in the possession of another woman. Here I question not but the reader will be surprized at our long taciturnity as to this matter; and quite at a loss to divine who this woman was, since we have hitherto not dropt a hint of any one likely to be a rival to Sophia; for as to Mrs Blifil, though we have been obliged to mention some suspicions of her affection for Tom, we have not hitherto given the least latitude for imagining that he had any for her; and, indeed, I am sorry to say it, but the youth of both sexes are too apt to be deficient in their gratitude for that regard with which persons more advanced in years are sometimes so kind to honour them.

That the reader may be no longer in suspense, he will be pleased to remember, that we have often mentioned the family of George Seagrim (commonly called Black George, the gamekeeper), which consisted at present of a wife and five children.

The second of these children was a daughter, whose name was Molly, and who was esteemed one of the handsomest girls in the whole country.

Congreve well says there is in true beauty something which vulgar souls cannot admire; so can no dirt or rags hide this something from those souls which are not of the vulgar stamp.

The beauty of this girl made, however, no impression on Tom, till she grew towards the age of sixteen, when Tom, who was near three years older, began first to cast the eyes of affection upon her. And this affection he had fixed on the girl long before he could bring himself to attempt the possession of her person: for though his constitution urged him greatly to this, his principles no less forcibly restrained him. To debauch a young woman, however low her condition was, appeared to him a very heinous crime; and the good-will he bore the father, with the compassion he had for his family, very strongly corroborated all such sober reflections; so that he once resolved to get the better of his inclinations, and he actually abstained three whole months without ever going to Seagrim's house, or seeing his daughter.

Now, though Molly was, as we have said, generally thought a very fine girl, and in reality she was so, yet her beauty was not of the most amiable kind. It had, indeed, very little of feminine in it, and would have become a man at least as well as a woman; for, to say the truth, youth and florid health had a very considerable share in the composition.

Nor was her mind more effeminate than her person. As this was tall and robust, so was that bold and forward. So little had she of modesty, that Jones had more regard for her virtue than she herself. And as most probably she liked Tom as well as he liked her, so when she perceived his backwardness she herself grew proportionably forward; and when she saw he had entirely deserted the house, she found means of throwing herself in his way, and behaved in such a manner that the youth must have had very much or very little of the heroe if her endeavours had proved unsuccessful. In a word, she soon triumphed over all the virtuous resolutions of Jones; for though she behaved at last with all decent reluctance, yet I rather chuse to attribute the triumph to her, since, in fact, it was her design which succeeded.

In the conduct of this matter, I say, Molly so well played her part, that Jones attributed the conquest entirely to himself, and considered the young woman as one who had yielded to the violent attacks of his passion. He likewise imputed her yielding to the ungovernable force of her love towards him; and this the reader will allow to have been a very natural and probable supposition, as we have more than once mentioned the uncommon comeliness of his person: and, indeed, he was one of the handsomest young fellows in the world.

As there are some minds whose affections, like Master Blifil's, are solely placed on one single person, whose interest and indulgence alone they consider on every occasion; regarding the good and ill of all others as merely indifferent, any farther than as they contribute to the pleasure or advantage of that person: so there is a different temper of mind which borrows a degree of virtue even from self-love. Such can never receive any kind of satisfaction from another, without loving the creature to whom that satisfaction is owing, and without making its well-being in some sort necessary to their own ease.

Of this latter species was our heroe. He considered this poor girl as one whose happiness or misery he had caused to be dependent on himself. Her beauty was still the object of desire, though greater beauty, or a fresher object, might have been more so; but the little abatement which fruition had occasioned to this was highly overbalanced by the considerations of the affection which she visibly bore him, and of the situation into which he had brought her. The former of these created gratitude, the latter compassion; and both, together with his desire for her person, raised in him a passion which might, without any great violence to the word, be called love; though, perhaps, it was at first not very judiciously placed.

This, then, was the true reason of that insensibility which he had shown to the charms of Sophia, and that behaviour in her which might have been reasonably enough interpreted as an encouragement to his addresses; for as he could not think of abandoning his Molly, poor and destitute as she was, so no more could he entertain a notion of betraying such a creature as Sophia. And surely, had he given the least encouragement to any passion for that young lady, he must have been absolutely guilty of one or other of those crimes; either of which would, in my opinion, have very justly subjected him to that fate, which, at his first introduction into this history, I mentioned to have been generally predicted as his certain destiny.

CHAPTER VII.

Being the shortest chapter in this book.

Her mother first perceived the alteration in the shape of Molly; and in order to hide it from her neighbours, she foolishly clothed her in that sack which Sophia had sent her; though, indeed, that young lady had little apprehension that the poor woman would have been weak enough to let any of her daughters wear it in that form.

Molly was charmed with the first opportunity she ever had of showing her beauty to advantage; for though she could very well bear to contemplate herself in the glass, even when dressed in rags; and though she had in that dress conquered the heart of Jones, and perhaps of some others; yet she thought the addition of finery would much improve her charms, and extend her conquests.

Molly, therefore, having dressed herself out in this sack, with a new laced cap, and some other ornaments which Tom had given her, repairs to church with her fan in her hand the very next Sunday. The great are deceived if they imagine they have appropriated ambition and vanity to themselves. These noble qualities flourish as notably in a country church and churchyard as in the drawing-room, or in the closet. Schemes have indeed been laid in the vestry which would hardly disgrace the conclave. Here is a ministry, and here is an opposition. Here are plots and circumventions, parties and factions, equal to those which are to be found in courts.

Nor are the women here less practised in the highest feminine arts than their fair superiors in quality and fortune. Here are prudes and coquettes. Here are dressing and ogling, falsehood, envy, malice, scandal; in short, everything which is common to the most splendid assembly, or politest circle. Let those of high life, therefore, no longer despise the ignorance of their inferiors; nor the vulgar any longer rail at the vices of their betters.

Molly had seated herself some time before she was known by her neighbours. And then a whisper ran through the whole congregation, "Who is she?" but when she was discovered, such sneering, gigling, tittering, and laughing ensued among the women, that Mr Allworthy was obliged to exert his authority to preserve any decency among them.

CHAPTER VIII.

A battle sung by the muse in the Homerican style, and which none but the classical reader can taste.

Mr Western had an estate in this parish; and as his house stood at little greater distance from this church than from his own, he very often came to Divine Service here; and both he and the charming Sophia happened to be present at this time.

Sophia was much pleased with the beauty of the girl, whom she pitied for her simplicity in having dressed herself in that manner, as she saw the envy which it had occasioned among her equals. She no sooner came home than she sent for the gamekeeper, and ordered him to bring his daughter to her; saying she would provide for her in the family, and might possibly place the girl about her own person, when her own maid, who was now going away, had left her.

Poor Seagrim was thunderstruck at this; for he was no stranger to the fault in the shape of his daughter. He answered, in a stammering voice, "That he was afraid Molly would be too awkward to wait on her ladyship, as she had never been at service." "No matter for that," says Sophia; "she will soon improve. I am pleased with the girl, and am resolved to try her."

Black George now repaired to his wife, on whose prudent counsel he depended to extricate him out of this dilemma; but when he came thither he found his house in some confusion. So great envy had this sack occasioned, that when Mr Allworthy and the other gentry were gone from church, the rage, which had hitherto been confined, burst into an uproar; and, having vented itself at first in opprobrious words, laughs, hisses, and gestures, betook itself at last to certain missile weapons; which, though from their plastic nature they threatened neither the loss of life or of limb, were however sufficiently dreadful to a well-dressed lady. Molly had too much spirit to bear this treatment tamely. Having therefore—but hold, as we are diffident of our own abilities, let us here invite a superior power to our assistance.

Ye Muses, then, whoever ye are, who love to sing battles, and principally thou who whilom didst recount the slaughter in those fields where Hudibras and Trulla fought, if thou wert not starved with thy friend Butler, assist me on this great occasion. All things are not in the power of all.

As a vast herd of cows in a rich farmer's yard, if, while they are milked, they hear their calves at a distance, lamenting the robbery which is then committing, roar and bellow; so roared forth the Somersetshire mob an hallaloo, made up of almost as many squalls, screams, and other different sounds as there were persons, or indeed passions among them: some were inspired by rage, others alarmed by fear, and others had nothing in their heads but the love of fun; but chiefly Envy, the sister of Satan, and his constant companion, rushed among the crowd, and blew up the fury of the women; who no sooner came up to Molly than they pelted her with dirt and rubbish.

Molly, having endeavoured in vain to make a handsome retreat, faced about; and laying hold of ragged Bess, who advanced in the front of the enemy, she at one blow felled her to the ground. The whole army of the enemy (though near a hundred in number), seeing the fate of their general, gave back many paces, and retired behind a new-dug grave; for the churchyard was the field of battle, where there was to be a funeral that very evening. Molly pursued her victory, and catching up a skull which lay on the side of the grave, discharged it with such fury, that having hit a taylor on the head, the two skulls sent equally forth a hollow sound at their meeting, and the taylor took presently measure of his length on the ground, where the skulls lay side by side, and it was doubtful which was the more valuable of the two. Molly then taking a thigh-bone in her hand, fell in among the flying ranks, and dealing her blows with great liberality on either side, overthrew the carcass of many a mighty heroe and heroine.

Recount, O Muse, the names of those who fell on this fatal day. First, Jemmy Tweedle felt on his hinder head the direful bone. Him the pleasant banks of sweetly-winding Stour had nourished, where he first learnt the vocal art, with which, wandering up and down at wakes and fairs, he cheered the rural nymphs and swains, when upon the green they interweaved the sprightly dance; while he himself stood fiddling and jumping to his own music. How little now avails his fiddle! He thumps the verdant floor with his carcass. Next, old Echepole, the sowgelder, received a blow in his forehead from our Amazonian heroine, and immediately fell to the ground. He was a swinging fat fellow, and fell with almost as much noise as a house. His tobacco-box dropped at the same time from his pocket, which Molly took up as lawful spoils. Then Kate of the Mill tumbled unfortunately over a tombstone, which catching hold of her ungartered stocking inverted the order of nature, and gave her heels the superiority to her head. Betty Pippin, with young Roger her lover, fell both to the ground; where, oh perverse fate! she salutes the earth, and he the sky. Tom Freckle, the smith's son, was the next victim to her rage. He was an ingenious workman, and made excellent pattens; nay, the very patten with which he was knocked down was his own workmanship. Had he been at that time singing psalms in the church, he would have avoided a broken head. Miss Crow, the daughter of a farmer; John Giddish, himself a farmer; Nan Slouch, Esther Codling, Will Spray, Tom Bennet; the three Misses Potter, whose father keeps the sign of the Red Lion; Betty Chambermaid, Jack Ostler, and many others of inferior note, lay rolling among the graves.

Not that the strenuous arm of Molly reached all these; for many of them in their flight overthrew each other.

But now Fortune, fearing she had acted out of character, and had inclined too long to the same side, especially as it was the right side, hastily turned about: for now Goody Brown—whom Zekiel Brown caressed in his arms; nor he alone, but half the parish besides; so famous was she in the fields of Venus, nor indeed less in those of Mars. The trophies of both these her husband always bore about on his head and face; for if ever human head did by its horns display the amorous glories of a wife, Zekiel's did; nor did his well-scratched face less denote her talents (or rather talons) of a different kind.

No longer bore this Amazon the shameful flight of her party. She stopt short, and, calling aloud to all who fled, spoke as follows: "Ye Somersetshire men, or rather ye Somersetshire women, are ye not ashamed thus to fly from a single woman? But if no other will oppose her, I myself and Joan Top here will have the honour of the victory." Having thus said, she flew at Molly Seagrim, and easily wrenched the thigh-bone from her hand, at the same time clawing off her cap from her head. Then laying hold of the hair of Molly with her left hand, she attacked her so furiously in the face with the right, that the blood soon began to trickle from her nose. Molly was not idle this while. She soon removed the clout from the head of Goody Brown, and then fastening on her hair with one hand, with the other she caused another bloody stream to issue forth from the nostrils of the enemy.

When each of the combatants had borne off sufficient spoils of hair from the head of her antagonist, the next rage was against the garments. In this attack they exerted so much violence, that in a very few minutes they were both naked to the middle.

It is lucky for the women that the seat of fistycuff war is not the same with them as among men; but though they may seem a little to deviate from their sex, when they go forth to battle, yet I have observed, they never so far forget, as to assail the bosoms of each other; where a few blows would be fatal to most of them. This, I know, some derive from their being of a more bloody inclination than the males. On which account they apply to the nose, as to the part whence blood may most easily be drawn; but this seems a far-fetched as well as ill-natured supposition.

Goody Brown had great advantage of Molly in this particular; for the former had indeed no breasts, her bosom (if it may be so called), as well in colour as in many other properties, exactly resembling an antient piece of parchment, upon which any one might have drummed a considerable while without doing her any great damage.

Molly, beside her present unhappy condition, was differently formed in those parts, and might, perhaps, have tempted the envy of Brown to give her a fatal blow, had not the lucky arrival of Tom Jones at this instant put an immediate end to the bloody scene.

This accident was luckily owing to Mr Square; for he, Master Blifil, and Jones, had mounted their horses, after church, to take the air, and had ridden about a quarter of a mile, when Square, changing his mind (not idly, but for a reason which we shall unfold as soon as we have leisure), desired the young gentlemen to ride with him another way than they had at first purposed. This motion being complied with, brought them of necessity back again to the churchyard.

Master Blifil, who rode first, seeing such a mob assembled, and two women in the posture in which we left the combatants, stopt his horse to enquire what was the matter. A country fellow, scratching his head, answered him: "I don't know, measter, un't I; an't please your honour, here hath been a vight, I think, between Goody Brown and Moll Seagrim."

"Who, who?" cries Tom; but without waiting for an answer, having discovered the features of his Molly through all the discomposure in which they now were, he hastily alighted, turned his horse loose, and, leaping over the wall, ran to her. She now first bursting into tears, told him how barbarously she had been treated. Upon which, forgetting the sex of Goody Brown, or perhaps not knowing it in his rage—for, in reality, she had no feminine appearance but a petticoat, which he might not observe—he gave her a lash or two with his horsewhip; and then flying at the mob, who were all accused by Moll, he dealt his blows so profusely on all sides, that unless I would again invoke the muse (which the good-natured reader may think a little too hard upon her, as she hath so lately been violently sweated), it would be impossible for me to recount the horse-whipping of that day.

Having scoured the whole coast of the enemy, as well as any of Homer's heroes ever did, or as Don Quixote or any knight-errant in the world could have done, he returned to Molly, whom he found in a condition which must give both me and my reader pain, was it to be described here. Tom raved like a madman, beat his breast, tore his hair, stamped on the ground, and vowed the utmost vengeance on all who had been concerned. He then pulled off his coat, and buttoned it round her, put his hat upon her head, wiped the blood from her face as well as he could with his handkerchief, and called out to the servant to ride as fast as possible for a side-saddle, or a pillion, that he might carry her safe home.

Master Blifil objected to the sending away the servant, as they had only one with them; but as Square seconded the order of Jones, he was obliged to comply.

The servant returned in a very short time with the pillion, and Molly, having collected her rags as well as she could, was placed behind him. In which manner she was carried home, Square, Blifil, and Jones attending.

Here Jones having received his coat, given her a sly kiss, and whispered her, that he would return in the evening, quitted his Molly, and rode on after his companions.

CHAPTER IX.

Containing matter of no very peaceable colour.

Molly had no sooner apparelled herself in her accustomed rags, than her sisters began to fall violently upon her, particularly her eldest sister, who told her she was well enough served. "How had she the assurance to wear a gown which young Madam Western had given to mother! If one of us was to wear it, I think," says she, "I myself have the best right; but I warrant you think it belongs to your beauty. I suppose you think yourself more handsomer than any of us."—"Hand her down the bit of glass from over the cupboard," cries another; "I'd wash the blood from my face before I talked of my beauty."—"You'd better have minded what the parson says," cries the eldest, "and not a harkened after men voke."—"Indeed, child, and so she had," says the mother, sobbing: "she hath brought a disgrace upon us all. She's the vurst of the vamily that ever was a whore."

"You need not upbraid me with that, mother," cries Molly; "you yourself was brought-to-bed of sister there, within a week after you was married."

"Yes, hussy," answered the enraged mother, "so I was, and what was the mighty matter of that? I was made an honest woman then; and if you was to be made an honest woman, I should not be angry; but you must have to doing with a gentleman, you nasty slut; you will have a bastard, hussy, you will; and that I defy any one to say of me."

In this situation Black George found his family, when he came home for the purpose before mentioned. As his wife and three daughters were all of them talking together, and most of them crying, it was some time before he could get an opportunity of being heard; but as soon as such an interval occurred, he acquainted the company with what Sophia had said to him.

Goody Seagrim then began to revile her daughter afresh. "Here," says she, "you have brought us into a fine quandary indeed. What will madam say to that big belly? Oh that ever I should live to see this day!"

Molly answered with great spirit, "And what is this mighty place which you have got for me, father?" (for he had not well understood the phrase used by Sophia of being about her person). "I suppose it is to be under the cook; but I shan't wash dishes for anybody. My gentleman will provide better for me. See what he hath given me this afternoon. He hath promised I shall never want money; and you shan't want money neither, mother, if you will hold your tongue, and know when you are well." And so saying, she pulled out several guineas, and gave her mother one of them.

The good woman no sooner felt the gold within her palm, than her temper began (such is the efficacy of that panacea) to be mollified. "Why, husband," says she, "would any but such a blockhead as you not have enquired what place this was before he had accepted it? Perhaps, as Molly says, it may be in the kitchen; and truly I don't care my daughter should be a scullion wench; for, poor as I am, I am a gentlewoman. And thof I was obliged, as my father, who was a clergyman, died worse than nothing, and so could not give me a shilling of *potion*, to undervalue myself by marrying a poor man; yet I would have you to know, I have a spirit above all them things. Marry come up! it would better become Madam Western to look at home, and remember who her own grandfather was. Some of my family, for aught I know, might ride in their coaches, when the grandfathers of some voke walked a-voot. I warrant she fancies she did a mighty matter, when she sent us that old gownd; some of my family would not have picked up such rags in the street; but poor people are always trampled upon.—The parish need not have been in such a fluster with Molly. You might have told them, child, your grandmother wore better things new out of the shop."

"Well, but consider," cried George, "what answer shall I make to madam?"

"I don't know what answer," says she; "you are always bringing your family into one quandary or other. Do you remember when you shot the partridge, the occasion of all our misfortunes? Did not I advise you never to go into Squire Western's manor? Did not I tell you many a good year ago what would come of it? But you would have your own headstrong ways; yes, you would, you villain."

Black George was, in the main, a peaceable kind of fellow, and nothing choleric nor rash; yet did he bear about him something of what the antients called the irascible, and which his wife, if she had been endowed with much wisdom, would have feared. He had long experienced, that when the storm grew very high, arguments were but wind, which served rather to increase, than to abate it. He was therefore seldom unprovided with a small switch, a remedy of wonderful force, as he had often essayed, and which the word villain served as a hint for his applying.

No sooner, therefore, had this symptom appeared, than he had immediate recourse to the said remedy, which though, as it is usual in all very efficacious medicines, it at first seemed to heighten and inflame the disease, soon produced a total calm, and restored the patient to perfect ease and tranquillity.

This is, however, a kind of horse-medicine, which requires a very robust constitution to digest, and is therefore proper only for the vulgar, unless in one single instance, viz., where superiority of birth breaks out; in which case, we should not think it very improperly applied by any husband whatever, if the application was not in itself so base, that, like certain applications of the physical kind which need not be mentioned, it so much degrades and contaminates the hand employed in it, that no gentleman should endure the thought of anything so low and detestable.

The whole family were soon reduced to a state of perfect quiet; for the virtue of this medicine, like that of electricity, is often communicated through one person to many others, who are not touched by the instrument. To say the truth, as they both operate by friction, it may be doubted whether there is not something analogous between them, of which Mr Freke would do well to enquire, before he publishes the next edition of his book.

A council was now called, in which, after many debates, Molly still persisting that she would not go to service, it was at length resolved, that Goody Seagrim herself should wait on Miss Western, and endeavour to procure the place for her eldest daughter, who declared great readiness to accept it: but Fortune, who seems to have been an enemy of this little family, afterwards put a stop to her promotion.

CHAPTER X.

A story told by Mr Supple, the curate. The penetration of Squire Western. His great love for his daughter, and the return to it made by her.

The next morning Tom Jones hunted with Mr Western, and was at his return invited by that gentleman to dinner.

The lovely Sophia shone forth that day with more gaiety and sprightliness than usual. Her battery was certainly levelled at our heroe; though, I believe, she herself scarce yet knew her own intention; but if she had any design of charming him, she now succeeded.

Mr Supple, the curate of Mr Allworthy's parish, made one of the company. He was a good-natured worthy man; but chiefly remarkable for his great taciturnity at table, though his mouth was never shut at it. In short, he had one of the best appetites in the world. However, the cloth was no sooner taken away, than he always made sufficient amends for his silence: for he was a very hearty fellow; and his conversation was often entertaining, never offensive.

At his first arrival, which was immediately before the entrance of the roast-beef, he had given an intimation that he had brought some news with him, and was beginning to tell, that he came that moment from Mr Allworthy's, when the sight of the roast-beef struck him dumb, permitting him only to say grace, and to declare he must pay his respect to the baronet, for so he called the sirloin.

When dinner was over, being reminded by Sophia of his news, he began as follows: "I believe, lady, your ladyship observed a young woman at church yesterday at even-song, who was drest in one of your outlandish garments; I think I have seen your ladyship in such a one. However, in the country, such dresses are

Rara avis in terris, nigroque simillima cygno.

That is, madam, as much as to say, 'A rare bird upon the earth, and very like a black swan.' The verse is in Juvenal. But to return to what I was relating. I was saying such garments are rare sights in the country; and perchance, too, it was thought the more rare, respect being had to the person who wore it, who, they tell me, is the daughter of Black George, your worship's gamekeeper, whose sufferings, I should have opined, might have taught him more wit, than to dress forth his wenches in such gaudy apparel. She created so much confusion in the congregation, that if Squire Allworthy had not silenced it, it would have interrupted the service: for I was once about to stop in the middle of the first lesson. Howbeit, nevertheless, after prayer was over, and I was departed home, this occasioned a battle in the churchyard, where, amongst other mischief, the head of a travelling fidler was very much broken. This morning the fidler came to Squire Allworthy for a warrant, and the wench was brought before him. The squire was inclined to have compounded matters; when, lo! on a sudden the wench appeared (I ask your ladyship's pardon) to be, as it were, at the eve of bringing forth a bastard. The squire demanded of her who was the father? But she pertinaciously refused to make any response. So that he was about to make her mittimus to Bridewell when I departed."

"And is a wench having a bastard all your news, doctor?" cries Western; "I thought it might have been some public matter, something about the nation."

"I am afraid it is too common, indeed," answered the parson; "but I thought the whole story altogether deserved commemorating. As to national matters, your worship knows them best. My concerns extend no farther than my own parish."

"Why, ay," says the squire, "I believe I do know a little of that matter, as you say. But, come, Tommy, drink about; the bottle stands with you."

Tom begged to be excused, for that he had particular business; and getting up from table, escaped the clutches of the squire, who was rising to stop him, and went off with very little ceremony.

The squire gave him a good curse at his departure; and then turning to the parson, he cried out, "I smoke it: I smoke it. Tom is certainly the father of this bastard. Zooks, parson, you remember how he recommended the veather o' her to me. D—n un, what a sly b—ch 'tis. Ay, ay, as sure as two-pence, Tom is the veather of the bastard."

"I should be very sorry for that," says the parson.

"Why sorry," cries the squire: "Where is the mighty matter o't? What, I suppose dost pretend that thee hast never got a bastard? Pox! more good luck's thine? for I warrant hast a done a *therefore* many's the good time and often."

"Your worship is pleased to be jocular," answered the parson; "but I do not only animadvert on the sinfulness of the action—though that surely is to be greatly deprecated—but I fear his unrighteousness may injure him with Mr Allworthy. And truly I must say, though he hath the character of being a little wild, I never saw any harm in the young man; nor can I say I have heard any, save what your worship now mentions. I wish, indeed, he was a little more regular in his responses at church; but altogether he seems

Ingenui vultus puer ingenuique pudoris.

That is a classical line, young lady; and, being rendered into English, is, `a lad of an ingenuous countenance, and of an ingenuous modesty;' for this was a virtue in great repute both among the Latins and Greeks. I must say, the young gentleman (for so I think I may call him, notwithstanding his birth) appears to me a very modest, civil lad, and I should be sorry that he should do himself any injury in Squire Allworthy's opinion."

"Poogh!" says the squire: "Injury, with Allworthy! Why, Allworthy loves a wench himself. Doth not all the country know whose son Tom is? You must talk to another person in that manner. I remember Allworthy at college."

"I thought," said the parson, "he had never been at the university."

"Yes, yes, he was," says the squire: "and many a wench have we two had together. As arrant a whore-master as any within five miles o'un. No, no. It will do'n no harm with he, assure yourself; nor with anybody else. Ask Sophy there—You have not the worse opinion of a young fellow for getting a bastard, have you, girl? No, no, the women will like un the better for't."

This was a cruel question to poor Sophia. She had observed Tom's colour change at the parson's story; and that, with his hasty and abrupt departure, gave her sufficient reason to think her father's suspicion not groundless. Her heart now at once discovered the great secret to her which it had been so long disclosing by little and little; and she found herself highly interested in this matter. In such a situation, her father's malapert question rushing suddenly upon her, produced some symptoms which might have alarmed a suspicious heart; but, to do the squire justice, that was not his fault. When she rose therefore from her chair, and told him a hint from him was always sufficient to make her withdraw, he suffered her to leave the room, and then with great gravity of countenance remarked, "That it was better to see a daughter over-modest than over-forward;"—a sentiment which was highly applauded by the parson.

There now ensued between the squire and the parson a most excellent political discourse, framed out of newspapers and political pamphlets; in which they made a libation of four bottles of wine to the good of their country: and then, the squire being fast asleep, the parson lighted his pipe, mounted his horse, and rode home.

When the squire had finished his half-hour's nap, he summoned his daughter to her harpsichord; but she begged to be excused that evening, on account of a violent head-ache. This remission was presently granted; for indeed she seldom had occasion to ask him twice, as he loved her with such ardent affection, that, by gratifying her, he commonly conveyed the highest gratification to himself. She was really, what he frequently called her, his little darling, and she well deserved to be so; for she returned all his affection in the most ample manner. She had preserved the most inviolable duty to him in all things; and this her love made not only easy, but so delightful, that when one of her companions laughed at her for placing so much merit in such scrupulous obedience, as that young lady called it, Sophia answered, "You mistake me, madam, if you think I value myself upon this account; for besides that I am barely discharging my duty, I am likewise pleasing myself. I can truly say I have no delight equal to that of contributing to my father's happiness; and if I value myself, my dear, it is on having this power, and not on executing it."

This was a satisfaction, however, which poor Sophia was incapable of tasting this evening. She therefore not only desired to be excused from her attendance at the harpsichord, but likewise begged that he would suffer her to absent herself from supper. To this request likewise the squire agreed, though not without some reluctance; for he scarce ever permitted her to be out of his sight, unless when he was engaged with his horses, dogs, or bottle. Nevertheless he yielded to the desire of his daughter, though the poor man was at the same time obliged to avoid his own company (if I may so express myself), by sending for a neighbouring farmer to sit with him.

CHAPTER XI.

The narrow escape of Molly Seagrim, with some observations for which we have been forced to dive pretty deep into nature.

Tom Jones had ridden one of Mr Western's horses that morning in the chase; so that having no horse of his own in the squire's stable, he was obliged to go home on foot: this he did so expeditiously that he ran upwards of three miles within the half-hour.

Just as he arrived at Mr Allworthy's outward gate, he met the constable and company with Molly in their possession, whom they were conducting to that house where the inferior sort of people may learn one good lesson, viz., respect and deference to their superiors; since it must show them the wide distinction Fortune intends between those persons who are to be corrected for their faults, and those who are not; which lesson if they do not learn, I am afraid they very rarely learn any other good lesson, or improve their morals, at the house of correction.

A lawyer may perhaps think Mr Allworthy exceeded his authority a little in this instance. And, to say the truth, I question, as here was no regular information before him, whether his conduct was strictly regular. However, as his intention was truly upright, he ought to be excused in *foro conscientiae*; since so many arbitrary acts are daily committed by magistrates who have not this excuse to plead for themselves.

Tom was no sooner informed by the constable whither they were proceeding (indeed he pretty well guessed it of himself), than he caught Molly in his arms, and embracing her tenderly before them all, swore he would murder the first man who offered to lay hold of her. He bid her dry her eyes and be comforted; for, wherever she went, he would accompany her. Then turning to the constable, who stood trembling with his hat off, he desired him, in a very mild voice, to return with him for a moment only to his father (for so he now called Allworthy); for he durst, he said, be assured, that, when he had alledged what he had to say in her favour, the girl would be discharged.

The constable, who, I make no doubt, would have surrendered his prisoner had Tom demanded her, very readily consented to this request. So back they all went into Mr Allworthy's hall; where Tom desired them to stay till his return, and then went himself in pursuit of the good man. As soon as he was found, Tom threw himself at his feet, and having begged a patient hearing, confessed himself to be the father of the child of which Molly was then big. He entreated him to have compassion on the poor girl, and to consider, if there was any guilt in the case, it lay principally at his door.

"If there is any guilt in the case!" answered Allworthy warmly: "Are you then so profligate and abandoned a libertine to doubt whether the breaking the laws of God and man, the corrupting and ruining a poor girl be guilt? I own, indeed, it doth lie principally upon you; and so heavy it is, that you ought to expect it should crush you."

"Whatever may be my fate," says Tom, "let me succeed in my intercessions for the poor girl. I confess I have corrupted her! but whether she shall be ruined, depends on you. For Heaven's sake, sir, revoke your warrant, and do not send her to a place which must unavoidably prove her destruction."

Allworthy bid him immediately call a servant. Tom answered there was no occasion; for he had luckily met them at the gate, and relying upon his goodness, had brought them all back into his hall, where they now waited his final resolution, which upon his knees he besought him might be in favour of the girl; that she might be permitted to go home to her parents, and not be exposed to a greater degree of shame and scorn than must necessarily fall upon her. "I know," said he, "that is too much. I know I am the wicked occasion of it. I will endeavour to make amends, if possible; and if you shall have hereafter the goodness to forgive me, I hope I shall deserve it."

Allworthy hesitated some time, and at last said, "Well, I will discharge my mittimus.—You may send the constable to me." He was instantly called, discharged, and so was the girl.

It will be believed that Mr Allworthy failed not to read Tom a very severe lecture on this occasion; but it is unnecessary to insert it here, as we have faithfully transcribed what he said to Jenny Jones in the first book, most of which may be applied to the men, equally with the women. So sensible an effect had these reproofs on the young man, who was no hardened sinner, that he retired to his own room, where he passed the evening alone, in much melancholy contemplation.

Allworthy was sufficiently offended by this transgression of Jones; for notwithstanding the assertions of Mr Western, it is certain this worthy man had never indulged himself in any loose pleasures with women, and greatly condemned the vice of incontinence in others. Indeed, there is much reason to imagine that there was not the least truth in what Mr Western affirmed, especially as he laid the scene of those impurities at the university, where Mr Allworthy had never been. In fact, the good squire was a little too apt to indulge that kind of pleasantry which is generally called rhodomontade: but which may, with as much propriety, be expressed by a much shorter word; and perhaps we too often supply the use of this little monosyllable by others; since very much of what frequently passes in the world for wit and humour, should, in the strictest purity of language, receive that short appellation, which, in conformity to the well-bred laws of custom, I here suppress.

But whatever detestation Mr Allworthy had to this or to any other vice, he was not so blinded by it but that he could discern any virtue in the guilty person, as clearly indeed as if there had been no mixture of vice in the same character. While he was angry therefore with the incontinence of Jones, he was no less pleased with the honour and honesty of his self-accusation. He began now to form in his mind the same opinion of this young fellow, which, we hope, our reader may have conceived. And in balancing his faults with his perfections, the latter seemed rather to preponderate.

It was to no purpose, therefore, that Thwackum, who was immediately charged by Mr Blifil with the story, unbended all his rancour against poor Tom. Allworthy gave a patient hearing to their invectives, and then answered coldly: "That young men of Tom's complexion were too generally addicted to this vice; but he believed that youth was sincerely affected with what he had said to him on the occasion, and he hoped he would not transgress again." So that, as the days of whipping were at an end, the tutor had no other vent but his own mouth for his gall, the usual poor resource of impotent revenge.

But Square, who was a less violent, was a much more artful man; and as he hated Jones more perhaps than Thwackum himself did, so he contrived to do him more mischief in the mind of Mr Allworthy.

The reader must remember the several little incidents of the partridge, the horse, and the Bible, which were recounted in the second book. By all which Jones had rather improved than injured the affection which Mr Allworthy was inclined to entertain for him. The same, I believe, must have happened to him with every other person who hath any idea of friendship, generosity, and greatness of spirit, that is to say, who hath any traces of goodness in his mind.

Square himself was not unacquainted with the true impression which those several instances of goodness had made on the excellent heart of Allworthy; for the philosopher very well knew what virtue was, though he was not always perhaps steady in its pursuit; but as for Thwackum, from what reason I will not determine, no such thoughts ever entered into his head: he saw Jones in a bad light, and he imagined Allworthy saw him in the same, but that he was resolved, from pride and stubbornness of spirit, not to give up the boy whom he had once cherished; since by so doing, he must tacitly acknowledge that his former opinion of him had been wrong.

Square therefore embraced this opportunity of injuring Jones in the tenderest part, by giving a very bad turn to all these before-mentioned occurrences. "I am sorry, sir," said he, "to own I have been deceived as well as yourself. I could not, I confess, help being pleased with what I ascribed to the motive of friendship, though it was carried to an excess, and all excess is faulty and vicious: but in this I made allowance for youth. Little did I suspect that the sacrifice of truth, which we both imagined to have been made to friendship, was in reality a prostitution of it to a depraved and debauched appetite. You now plainly see whence all the seeming generosity of this young man to the family of the gamekeeper proceeded. He supported the father in order to corrupt the daughter, and preserved the family from starving, to bring one of them to shame and ruin. This is friendship! this is generosity! As Sir Richard Steele says, `Gluttons who give high prices for delicacies, are very worthy to be called generous.' In short I am resolved, from this instance, never to give way to the weakness of human nature more, nor to think anything virtue which doth not exactly quadrate with the unerring rule of right."

The goodness of Allworthy had prevented those considerations from occurring to himself; yet were they too plausible to be absolutely and hastily rejected, when laid before his eyes by another. Indeed what Square had said sunk very deeply into his mind, and the uneasiness which it there created was very visible to the other; though the good man would not acknowledge this, but made a very slight answer, and forcibly drove off the discourse to some other subject. It was well perhaps for poor Tom, that no such suggestions had been made before he was pardoned; for they certainly stamped in the mind of Allworthy the first bad impression concerning Jones.

CHAPTER XII.

Containing much clearer matters; but which flowed from the same fountain with those in the preceding chapter.

The reader will be pleased, I believe, to return with me to Sophia. She passed the night, after we saw her last, in no very agreeable manner. Sleep befriended her but little, and dreams less. In the morning, when Mrs Honour, her maid, attended her at the usual hour, she was found already up and drest.

Persons who live two or three miles' distance in the country are considered as next-door neighbours, and transactions at the one house fly with incredible celerity to the other. Mrs Honour, therefore, had heard the whole story of Molly's shame; which she, being of a very communicative temper, had no sooner entered the apartment of her mistress, than she began to relate in the following manner:—

"La, ma'am, what doth your la'ship think? the girl that your la'ship saw at church on Sunday, whom you thought so handsome; though you would not have thought her so handsome neither, if you had seen her nearer, but to be sure she hath been carried before the justice for being big with child. She seemed to me to look like a confident slut: and to be sure she hath laid the child to young Mr Jones. And all the parish says Mr Allworthy is so angry with young Mr Jones, that he won't see him. To be sure, one can't help pitying the poor young man, and yet he doth not deserve much pity neither, for demeaning himself with such kind of trumpery. Yet he is so pretty a gentleman, I should be sorry to have him turned out of doors. I dares to swear the wench was as willing as he; for she was always a forward kind of body. And when wenches are so coming, young men are not so much to be blamed neither; for to be sure they do no more than what is natural. Indeed it is beneath them to meddle with such dirty draggle-tails; and whatever happens to them, it is good enough for them. And yet, to be sure, the vile baggages are most in fault. I wishes, with all my heart, they were well to be whipped at the cart's tail; for it is pity they should be the ruin of a pretty young gentleman; and nobody can deny but that Mr Jones is one of the most handsomest young men that ever——"

She was running on thus, when Sophia, with a more peevish voice than she had ever spoken to her in before, cried, "Prithee, why dost thou trouble me with all this stuff? What concern have I in what Mr Jones doth? I suppose you are all alike. And you seem to me to be angry it was not your own case."

"I, ma'am!" answered Mrs Honour, "I am sorry your ladyship should have such an opinion of me. I am sure nobody can say any such thing of me. All the young fellows in the world may go to the divil for me. Because I said he was a handsome man? Everybody says it as well as I. To be sure, I never thought as it was any harm to say a young man was handsome; but to be sure I shall never think him so any more now; for handsome is that handsome does. A beggar wench!—"

"Stop thy torrent of impertinence," cries Sophia, "and see whether my father wants me at breakfast."

Mrs Honour then flung out of the room, muttering much to herself, of which "Marry come up, I assure you," was all that could be plainly distinguished.

Whether Mrs Honour really deserved that suspicion, of which her mistress gave her a hint, is a matter which we cannot indulge our reader's curiosity by resolving. We will, however, make him amends in disclosing what passed in the mind of Sophia.

The reader will be pleased to recollect, that a secret affection for Mr Jones had insensibly stolen into the bosom of this young lady. That it had there grown to a pretty great height before she herself had discovered it. When she first began to perceive its symptoms, the sensations were so sweet and pleasing, that she had not resolution sufficient to check or repel them; and thus she went on cherishing a passion of which she never once considered the consequences.

This incident relating to Molly first opened her eyes. She now first perceived the weakness of which she had been guilty; and though it caused the utmost perturbation in her mind, yet it had the effect of other nauseous physic, and for the time expelled her distemper. Its operation indeed was most wonderfully quick; and in the short interval, while her maid was absent, so entirely removed all symptoms, that when Mrs Honour returned with a summons from her father, she was become perfectly easy, and had brought herself to a thorough indifference for Mr Jones.

The diseases of the mind do in almost every particular imitate those of the body. For which reason, we hope, that learned faculty, for whom we have so profound a respect, will pardon us the violent hands we have been necessitated to lay on several words and phrases, which of right belong to them, and without which our descriptions must have been often unintelligible.

Now there is no one circumstance in which the distempers of the mind bear a more exact analogy to those which are called bodily, than that aptness which both have to a relapse. This is plain in the violent diseases of ambition and avarice. I have known ambition, when cured at court by frequent disappointments (which are the only physic for it), to break out again in a contest for foreman of the grand jury at an assizes; and have heard of a man who had so far conquered avarice, as to give away many a sixpence, that comforted himself, at last, on his deathbed, by making a crafty and advantageous bargain concerning his ensuing funeral, with an undertaker who had married his only child.

In the affair of love, which, out of strict conformity with the Stoic philosophy, we shall here treat as a disease, this proneness to relapse is no less conspicuous.

Thus it happened to poor Sophia; upon whom, the very next time she saw young Jones, all the former symptoms returned, and from that time cold and hot fits alternately seized her heart.

The situation of this young lady was now very different from what it had ever been before. That passion which had formerly been so exquisitely delicious, became now a scorpion in her bosom. She resisted it therefore with her utmost force, and summoned every argument her reason (which was surprisingly strong for her age) could suggest, to subdue and expel it. In this she so far succeeded, that she began to hope from time and absence a perfect cure. She resolved therefore to avoid Tom Jones as much as possible; for which purpose she began to conceive a design of visiting her aunt, to which she made no doubt of obtaining her father's consent.

But Fortune, who had other designs in her head, put an immediate stop to any such proceeding, by introducing an accident, which will be related in the next chapter.

CHAPTER XIII.

A dreadful accident which befel Sophia. The gallant behaviour of Jones, and the more dreadful consequence of that behaviour to the young lady; with a short digression in favour of the female sex. —

Mr Western grew every day fonder and fonder of Sophia, insomuch that his beloved dogs themselves almost gave place to her in his affections; but as he could not prevail on himself to abandon these, he contrived very cunningly to enjoy their company, together with that of his daughter, by insisting on her riding a hunting with him.

Sophia, to whom her father's word was a law, readily complied with his desires, though she had not the least delight in a sport, which was of too rough and masculine a nature to suit with her disposition. She had however another motive, beside her obedience, to accompany the old gentleman in the chase; for by her presence she hoped in some measure to restrain his impetuosity, and to prevent him from so frequently exposing his neck to the utmost hazard.

The strongest objection was that which would have formerly been an inducement to her, namely, the frequent meeting with young Jones, whom she had determined to avoid; but as the end of the hunting season now approached, she hoped, by a short absence with her aunt, to reason herself entirely out of her unfortunate passion; and had not any doubt of being able to meet him in the field the subsequent season without the least danger.

On the second day of her hunting, as she was returning from the chase, and was arrived within a little distance from Mr Western's house, her horse, whose mettlesome spirit required a better rider, fell suddenly to prancing and capering in such a manner that she was in the most imminent peril of falling. Tom Jones, who was at a little distance behind, saw this, and immediately galloped up to her assistance. As soon as he came up, he leapt from his own horse, and caught hold of hers by the bridle. The unruly beast presently reared himself an end on his hind legs, and threw his lovely burthen from his back, and Jones caught her in his arms.

She was so affected with the fright, that she was not immediately able to satisfy Jones, who was very sollicitous to know whether she had received any hurt. She soon after, however, recovered her spirits, assured him she was safe, and thanked him for the care he had taken of her. Jones answered, "If I have preserved you, madam, I am sufficiently repaid; for I promise you, I would have secured you from the least harm at the expense of a much greater misfortune to myself than I have suffered on this occasion."

"What misfortune?" replied Sophia eagerly; "I hope you have come to no mischief?"

"Be not concerned, madam," answered Jones. "Heaven be praised you have escaped so well, considering the danger you was in. If I have broke my arm, I consider it as a trifle, in comparison of what I feared upon your account."

Sophia then screamed out, "Broke your arm! Heaven forbid."

"I am afraid I have, madam," says Jones: "but I beg you will suffer me first to take care of you. I have a right hand yet at your service, to help you into the next field, whence we have but a very little walk to your father's house."

Sophia seeing his left arm dangling by his side, while he was using the other to lead her, no longer doubted of the truth. She now grew much paler than her fears for herself had made her before. All her limbs were seized with a trembling, insomuch that Jones could scarce support her; and as her thoughts were in no less agitation, she could not refrain from giving Jones a look so full of tenderness, that it almost argued a stronger sensation in her mind, than even gratitude and pity united can raise in the gentlest female bosom, without the assistance of a third more powerful passion.

Mr Western, who was advanced at some distance when this accident happened, was now returned, as were the rest of the horsemen. Sophia immediately acquainted them with what had befallen Jones, and begged them to take care of him. Upon which Western, who had been much alarmed by meeting his daughter's horse without its rider, and was now overjoyed to find her unhurt, cried out, "I am glad it is no worse. If Tom hath broken his arm, we will get a joiner to mend un again."

The squire alighted from his horse, and proceeded to his house on foot, with his daughter and Jones. An impartial spectator, who had met them on the way, would, on viewing their several countenances, have concluded Sophia alone to have been the object of compassion: for as to Jones, he exulted in having probably saved the life of the young lady, at the price only of a broken bone; and Mr Western, though he was not unconcerned at the accident which had befallen Jones, was, however, delighted in a much higher degree with the fortunate escape of his daughter.

The generosity of Sophia's temper construed this behaviour of Jones into great bravery; and it made a deep impression on her heart: for certain it is, that there is no one quality which so generally recommends men to women as this; proceeding, if we believe the common opinion, from that natural timidity of the sex, which is, says Mr Osborne, "so great, that a woman is the most cowardly of all the creatures God ever made;"—a sentiment more remarkable for its bluntness than for its truth. Aristotle, in his Politics, doth them, I believe, more justice, when he says, "The modesty and fortitude of men differ from those virtues in women; for the fortitude which becomes a woman, would be cowardice in a man; and the modesty which becomes a man, would be pertness in a woman." Nor is there, perhaps, more of truth in the opinion of those who derive the partiality which women are inclined to show to the brave, from this excess of their fear. Mr Bayle (I think, in his article of Helen) imputes this, and with greater probability, to their violent love of glory; for the truth of which, we have the authority of him who of all others saw farthest into human nature, and who introduces the heroine of his Odyssey, the great pattern of matrimonial love and constancy, assigning the glory of her husband as the only source of her affection towards him.[1]

However this be, certain it is that the accident operated very strongly on Sophia; and, indeed, after much enquiry into the matter, I am inclined to believe, that, at this very time, the charming Sophia made no less impression on the heart of Jones; to say truth, he had for some time become sensible of the irresistible power of her charms.

---

[1] The English reader will not find this in the poem; for the sentiment is entirely left out in the translation.

CHAPTER XIV.

The arrival of a surgeon.—His operations, and a long dialogue between Sophia and her maid.

When they arrived at Mr Western's hall, Sophia, who had tottered along with much difficulty, sunk down in her chair; but by the assistance of hartshorn and water, she was prevented from fainting away, and had pretty well recovered her spirits, when the surgeon who was sent for to Jones appeared. Mr Western, who imputed these symptoms in his daughter to her fall, advised her to be presently blooded by way of prevention. In this opinion he was seconded by the surgeon, who gave so many reasons for bleeding, and quoted so many cases where persons had miscarried for want of it, that the squire became very importunate, and indeed insisted peremptorily that his daughter should be blooded.

Sophia soon yielded to the commands of her father, though entirely contrary to her own inclinations, for she suspected, I believe, less danger from the fright, than either the squire or the surgeon. She then stretched out her beautiful arm, and the operator began to prepare for his work.

While the servants were busied in providing materials, the surgeon, who imputed the backwardness which had appeared in Sophia to her fears, began to comfort her with assurances that there was not the least danger; for no accident, he said, could ever happen in bleeding, but from the monstrous ignorance of pretenders to surgery, which he pretty plainly insinuated was not at present to be apprehended. Sophia declared she was not under the least apprehension; adding, "If you open an artery, I promise you I'll forgive you." "Will you?" cries Western: "D—n me, if I will. If he does thee the least mischief, d—n me if I don't ha' the heart's blood o'un out." The surgeon assented to bleed her upon these conditions, and then proceeded to his operation, which he performed with as much dexterity as he had promised; and with as much quickness: for he took but little blood from her, saying, it was much safer to bleed again and again, than to take away too much at once.

Sophia, when her arm was bound up, retired: for she was not willing (nor was it, perhaps, strictly decent) to be present at the operation on Jones. Indeed, one objection which she had to bleeding (though she did not make it) was the delay which it would occasion to setting the broken bone. For Western, when Sophia was concerned, had no consideration but for her; and as for Jones himself, he "sat like patience on a monument smiling at grief." To say the truth, when he saw the blood springing from the lovely arm of Sophia, he scarce thought of what had happened to himself.

The surgeon now ordered his patient to be stript to his shirt, and then entirely baring the arm, he began to stretch and examine it, in such a manner that the tortures he put him to caused Jones to make several wry faces; which the surgeon observing, greatly wondered at, crying, "What is the matter, sir? I am sure it is impossible I should hurt you." And then holding forth the broken arm, he began a long and very learned lecture of anatomy, in which simple and double fractures were most accurately considered; and the several ways in which Jones might have broken his arm were discussed, with proper annotations showing how many of these would have been better, and how many worse than the present case.

Having at length finished his laboured harangue, with which the audience, though it had greatly raised their attention and admiration, were not much edified, as they really understood not a single syllable of all he had said, he proceeded to business, which he was more expeditious in finishing, than he had been in beginning.

Jones was then ordered into a bed, which Mr Western compelled him to accept at his own house, and sentence of water-gruel was passed upon him.

Among the good company which had attended in the hall during the bone-setting, Mrs Honour was one; who being summoned to her mistress as soon as it was over, and asked by her how the young gentleman did, presently launched into extravagant praises on the magnanimity, as she called it, of his behaviour, which, she said, "was so charming in so pretty a creature." She then burst forth into much warmer encomiums on the beauty of his person; enumerating many particulars, and ending with the whiteness of his skin.

This discourse had an effect on Sophia's countenance, which would not perhaps have escaped the observance of the sagacious waiting-woman, had she once looked her mistress in the face, all the time she was speaking: but as a looking-glass, which was most commodiously placed opposite to her, gave her an opportunity of surveying those features, in which, of all others, she took most delight; so she had not once removed her eyes from that amiable object during her whole speech.

Mrs Honour was so intirely wrapped up in the subject on which she exercised her tongue, and the object before her eyes, that she gave her mistress time to conquer her confusion; which having done, she smiled on her maid, and told her, "she was certainly in love with this young fellow."—"I in love, madam!" answers she: "upon my word, ma'am, I assure you, ma'am, upon my soul, ma'am, I am not."—"Why, if you was," cries her mistress, "I see no reason that you should be ashamed of it; for he is certainly a pretty fellow."—"Yes, ma'am," answered the other, "that he is, the most handsomest man I ever saw in my life. Yes, to be sure, that he is, and, as your ladyship says, I don't know why I should be ashamed of loving him, though he is my betters. To be sure, gentlefolks are but flesh and blood no more than us servants. Besides, as for Mr Jones, thof Squire Allworthy hath made a gentleman of him, he was not so good as myself by birth: for thof I am a poor body, I am an honest person's child, and my father and mother were married, which is more than some people can say, as high as they hold their heads. Marry, come up! I assure you, my dirty cousin! thof his skin be so white, and to be sure it is the most whitest that ever was seen, I am a Christian as well as he, and nobody can say that I am base born: my grandfather was a clergyman,[1] and would have been very angry, I believe, to have thought any of his family should have taken up with Molly Seagrim's dirty leavings."

Perhaps Sophia might have suffered her maid to run on in this manner, from wanting sufficient spirits to stop her tongue, which the reader may probably conjecture was no very easy task; for certainly there were some passages in her speech which were far from being agreeable to the lady. However, she now checked the torrent, as there seemed no end of its flowing. "I wonder," says she, "at your assurance in daring to talk thus of one of my father's friends. As to the wench, I order you never to mention her name to me. And with regard to the young gentleman's birth, those who can say nothing more to his disadvantage, may as well be silent on that head, as I desire you will be for the future."

"I am sorry I have offended your ladyship," answered Mrs Honour. "I am sure I hate Molly Seagrim as much as your ladyship can; and as for abusing Squire Jones, I can call all the servants in the house to witness, that whenever any talk hath been about bastards, I have always taken his part; for which of you, says I to the footmen, would not be a bastard, if he could, to be made a gentleman of? And, says I, I am sure he is a very fine gentleman; and he hath one of the whitest hands in the world; for to be sure so he hath: and, says I, one of the sweetest temperedest, best naturedest men in the world he is; and, says I, all the servants and neighbours all round the country loves him. And, to be sure, I could tell your ladyship something, but that I am afraid it would offend you."—"What could you tell me, Honour?" says Sophia. "Nay, ma'am, to be sure he meant nothing by it, therefore I would not have your ladyship be offended."—"Prithee tell me," says Sophia; "I will know it this instant."—"Why, ma'am," answered Mrs Honour, "he came into the room one day last week when I was at work, and there lay your ladyship's muff on a chair, and to be sure he put his hands into it; that very muff your ladyship gave me but yesterday. La! says I, Mr Jones, you will stretch my lady's muff, and spoil it: but he still kept his hands in it: and then he kissed it—to be sure I hardly ever saw such a kiss in my life as he gave it."—"I suppose he did not know it was mine," replied Sophia. "Your ladyship shall hear, ma'am. He kissed it again and again, and said it was the prettiest muff in the world. La! sir, says I, you have seen it a hundred times. Yes, Mrs Honour, cried he; but who can

---

[1] This is the second person of low condition whom we have recorded in this history to have sprung from the clergy. It is to be hoped such instances will, in future ages, when some provision is made for the families of the inferior clergy, appear stranger than they can be thought at present.

see anything beautiful in the presence of your lady but herself?—Nay, that's not all neither; but I hope your ladyship won't be offended, for to be sure he meant nothing. One day, as your ladyship was playing on the harpsichord to my master, Mr Jones was sitting in the next room, and methought he looked melancholy. La! says I, Mr Jones, what's the matter? a penny for your thoughts, says I. Why, hussy, says he, starting up from a dream, what can I be thinking of, when that angel your mistress is playing? And then squeezing me by the hand, Oh! Mrs Honour, says he, how happy will that man be!—and then he sighed. Upon my troth, his breath is as sweet as a nosegay.—But to be sure he meant no harm by it. So I hope your ladyship will not mention a word; for he gave me a crown never to mention it, and made me swear upon a book, but I believe, indeed, it was not the Bible."

Till something of a more beautiful red than vermilion be found out, I shall say nothing of Sophia's colour on this occasion. "Ho—nour," says she, "I—if you will not mention this any more to me—nor to anybody else, I will not betray you—I mean, I will not be angry; but I am afraid of your tongue. Why, my girl, will you give it such liberties?"—"Nay, ma'am," answered she, "to be sure, I would sooner cut out my tongue than offend your ladyship. To be sure I shall never mention a word that your ladyship would not have me."—"Why, I would not have you mention this any more," said Sophia, "for it may come to my father's ears, and he would be angry with Mr Jones; though I really believe, as you say, he meant nothing. I should be very angry myself, if I imagined—"—"Nay, ma'am," says Honour, "I protest I believe he meant nothing. I thought he talked as if he was out of his senses; nay, he said he believed he was beside himself when he had spoken the words. Ay, sir, says I, I believe so too. Yes, says he, Honour.—But I ask your ladyship's pardon; I could tear my tongue out for offending you." "Go on," says Sophia; "you may mention anything you have not told me before."—"Yes, Honour, says he (this was some time afterwards, when he gave me the crown), I am neither such a coxcomb, or such a villain, as to think of her in any other delight but as my goddess; as such I will always worship and adore her while I have breath.—This was all, ma'am, I will be sworn, to the best of my remembrance. I was in a passion with him myself, till I found he meant no harm."—"Indeed, Honour," says Sophia, "I believe you have a real affection for me. I was provoked the other day when I gave you warning; but if you have a desire to stay with me, you shall."—"To be sure, ma'am," answered Mrs Honour, "I shall never desire to part with your ladyship. To be sure, I almost cried my eyes out when you gave me warning. It would be very ungrateful in me to desire to leave your ladyship; because as why, I should never get so good a place again. I am sure I would live and die with your ladyship; for, as poor Mr Jones said, happy is the man——"

Here the dinner bell interrupted a conversation which had wrought such an effect on Sophia, that she was, perhaps, more obliged to her bleeding in the morning, than she, at the time, had apprehended she should be. As to the present situation of her mind, I shall adhere to a rule of Horace, by not attempting to describe it, from despair of success. Most of my readers will suggest it easily to themselves; and the few who cannot, would not understand the picture, or at least would deny it to be natural, if ever so well drawn.

BOOK V.

CONTAINING A PORTION OF TIME SOMEWHAT LONGER THAN HALF A YEAR.

CHAPTER I.

Of the SERIOUS in writing, and for what purpose it is introduced.

Peradventure there may be no parts in this prodigious work which will give the reader less pleasure in the perusing, than those which have given the author the greatest pains in composing. Among these probably may be reckoned those initial essays which we have prefixed to the historical matter contained in every book; and which we have determined to be essentially necessary to this kind of writing, of which we have set ourselves at the head.

For this our determination we do not hold ourselves strictly bound to assign any reason; it being abundantly sufficient that we have laid it down as a rule necessary to be observed in all prosai-comi-epic writing. Who ever demanded the reasons of that nice unity of time or place which is now established to be so essential to dramatic poetry? What critic hath been ever asked, why a play may not contain two days as well as one? Or why the audience (provided they travel, like electors, without any expense) may not be wafted fifty miles as well as five? Hath any commentator well accounted for the limitation which an antient critic hath set to the drama, which he will have contain neither more nor less than five acts? Or hath any one living attempted to explain what the modern judges of our theatres mean by that word *low*; by which they have happily succeeded in banishing all humour from the stage, and have made the theatre as dull as a drawing-room! Upon all these occasions the world seems to have embraced a maxim of our law, viz., *cuicunque in arte sua perito credendum est:* for it seems perhaps difficult to conceive that any one should have had enough of impudence to lay down dogmatical rules in any art or science without the least foundation. In such cases, therefore, we are apt to conclude there are sound and good reasons at the bottom, though we are unfortunately not able to see so far.

Now, in reality, the world have paid too great a compliment to critics, and have imagined them men of much greater profundity than they really are. From this complacence, the critics have been emboldened to assume a dictatorial power, and have so far succeeded, that they are now become the masters, and have the assurance to give laws to those authors from whose predecessors they originally received them.

The critic, rightly considered, is no more than the clerk, whose office it is to transcribe the rules and laws laid down by those great judges whose vast strength of genius hath placed them in the light of legislators, in the several sciences over which they presided. This office was all which the critics of old aspired to; nor did they ever dare to advance a sentence, without supporting it by the authority of the judge from whence it was borrowed.

But in process of time, and in ages of ignorance, the clerk began to invade the power and assume the dignity of his master. The laws of writing were no longer founded on the practice of the author, but on the dictates of the critic. The clerk became the legislator, and those very peremptorily gave laws whose business it was, at first, only to transcribe them.

Hence arose an obvious, and perhaps an unavoidable error; for these critics being men of shallow capacities, very easily mistook mere form for substance. They acted as a judge would, who should adhere to the lifeless letter of law, and reject the spirit. Little circumstances, which were perhaps accidental in a great author, were by these critics considered to constitute his chief merit, and transmitted as essentials to be observed by all his successors. To these encroachments, time and ignorance, the two great supporters of imposture, gave authority; and thus many rules for good writing have been established, which have not the least foundation in truth or nature; and which commonly serve for no other purpose than to curb and restrain genius, in the same manner as it would have restrained the dancing-master, had the many excellent treatises on that art laid it down as an essential rule that every man must dance in chains.

To avoid, therefore, all imputation of laying down a rule for posterity, founded only on the authority of *ipse dixit*—for which, to say the truth, we have not the profoundest veneration—we shall here waive the privilege above contended for, and proceed to lay before the reader the reasons which have induced us to intersperse these several digressive essays in the course of this work.

And here we shall of necessity be led to open a new vein of knowledge, which if it hath been discovered, hath not, to our remembrance, been wrought on by any antient or modern writer. This vein is no other than that of contrast, which runs through all the works of the creation, and may probably have a large share in constituting in us the idea of all beauty, as well natural as artificial: for what demonstrates the beauty and excellence of anything but its reverse? Thus the beauty of day, and that of summer, is set off by the horrors of night and winter. And, I believe, if it was possible for a man to have seen only the two former, he would have a very imperfect idea of their beauty.

But to avoid too serious an air; can it be doubted, but that the finest woman in the world would lose all benefit of her charms in the eye of a man who had never seen one of another cast? The ladies themselves seem so sensible of this, that they are all industrious to procure foils: nay, they will become foils to themselves; for I have observed (at Bath particularly) that they endeavour to appear as ugly as possible in the morning, in order to set off that beauty which they intend to show you in the evening.

Most artists have this secret in practice, though some, perhaps, have not much studied the theory. The jeweller knows that the finest brilliant requires a foil; and the painter, by the contrast of his figures, often acquires great applause.

A great genius among us will illustrate this matter fully. I cannot, indeed, range him under any general head of common artists, as he hath a title to be placed among those

Inventas qui vitam excoluere per artes.
Who by invented arts have life improved.

I mean here the inventor of that most exquisite entertainment, called the English Pantomime.

This entertainment consisted of two parts, which the inventor distinguished by the names of the serious and the comic. The serious exhibited a certain number of heathen gods and heroes, who were certainly the worst and dullest company into which an audience was ever introduced; and (which was a secret known to few) were actually intended so to be, in order to contrast the comic part of the entertainment, and to display the tricks of harlequin to the better advantage.

This was, perhaps, no very civil use of such personages: but the contrivance was, nevertheless, ingenious enough, and had its effect. And this will now plainly appear, if, instead of serious and comic, we supply the words duller and dullest; for the comic was certainly duller than anything before shown on the stage, and could be set off only by that superlative degree of dulness which composed the serious. So intolerably serious, indeed, were these gods and heroes, that harlequin (though the English gentleman of that name is not at all related to the French family, for he is of a much more serious disposition) was always welcome on the stage, as he relieved the audience from worse company.

Judicious writers have always practised this art of contrast with great success. I have been surprized that Horace should cavil at this art in Homer; but indeed he contradicts himself in the very next line:

Indignor quandoque bonus dormitat Homerus;
Verum opere in longo fas est obrepere somnum.

I grieve if e'er great Homer chance to sleep,
Yet slumbers on long works have right to creep.

For we are not here to understand, as perhaps some have, that an author actually falls asleep while he is writing. It is true, that readers are too apt to be so overtaken; but if the work was as long as any of Oldmixon, the author himself is too well entertained to be subject to the least drowsiness. He is, as Mr Pope observes,

Sleepless himself to give his readers sleep.

To say the truth, these soporific parts are so many scenes of serious artfully interwoven, in order to contrast and set off the rest; and this is the true meaning of a late facetious writer, who told the public that whenever he was dull they might be assured there was a design in it.

In this light, then, or rather in this darkness, I would have the reader to consider these initial essays. And after this warning, if he shall be of opinion that he can find enough of serious in other parts of this history, he may pass over these, in which we profess to be laboriously dull, and begin the following books at the second chapter.

CHAPTER II.

In which Mr Jones receives many friendly visits during his confinement; with some fine touches of the passion of love, scarce visible to the naked eye.

Tom Jones had many visitors during his confinement, though some, perhaps, were not very agreeable to him. Mr Allworthy saw him almost every day; but though he pitied Tom's sufferings, and greatly approved the gallant behaviour which had occasioned them; yet he thought this was a favourable opportunity to bring him to a sober sense of his indiscreet conduct; and that wholesome advice for that purpose could never be applied at a more proper season than at the present, when the mind was softened by pain and sickness, and alarmed by danger; and when its attention was unembarrassed with those turbulent passions which engage us in the pursuit of pleasure.

At all seasons, therefore, when the good man was alone with the youth, especially when the latter was totally at ease, he took occasion to remind him of his former miscarriages, but in the mildest and tenderest manner, and only in order to introduce the caution which he prescribed for his future behaviour; "on which alone," he assured him, "would depend his own felicity, and the kindness which he might yet promise himself to receive at the hands of his father by adoption, unless he should hereafter forfeit his good opinion: for as to what had past," he said, "it should be all forgiven and forgotten. He therefore advised him to make a good use of this accident, that so in the end it might prove a visitation for his own good."

Thwackum was likewise pretty assiduous in his visits; and he too considered a sick-bed to be a convenient scene for lectures. His stile, however, was more severe than Mr Allworthy's: he told his pupil, "That he ought to look on his broken limb as a judgment from heaven on his sins. That it would become him to be daily on his knees, pouring forth thanksgivings that he had broken his arm only, and not his neck; which latter," he said, "was very probably reserved for some future occasion, and that, perhaps, not very remote. For his part," he said, "he had often wondered some judgment had not overtaken him before; but it might be perceived by this, that Divine punishments, though slow, are always sure." Hence likewise he advised him, "to foresee, with equal certainty, the greater evils which were yet behind, and which were as sure as this of overtaking him in his state of reprobacy. These are," said he, "to be averted only by such a thorough and sincere repentance as is not to be expected or hoped for from one so abandoned in his youth, and whose mind, I am afraid, is totally corrupted. It is my duty, however, to exhort you to this repentance, though I too well know all exhortations will be vain and fruitless. But *liberavi animam meam.* I can accuse my own conscience of no neglect; though it is at the same time with the utmost concern I see you travelling on to certain misery in this world, and to as certain damnation in the next."

Square talked in a very different strain; he said, "Such accidents as a broken bone were below the consideration of a wise man. That it was abundantly sufficient to reconcile the mind to any of these mischances, to reflect that they are liable to befal the wisest of mankind, and are undoubtedly for the good of the whole." He said, "It was a mere abuse of words to call those things evils, in which there was no moral unfitness: that pain, which was the worst consequence of such accidents, was the most contemptible thing in the world;" with more of the like sentences, extracted out of the second book of Tully's Tusculan questions, and from the great Lord Shaftesbury. In pronouncing these he was one day so eager, that he unfortunately bit his tongue; and in such a manner, that it not only put an end to his discourse, but created much emotion in him, and caused him to mutter an oath or two: but what was worst of all, this accident gave Thwackum, who was present, and who held all such doctrine to be heathenish and atheistical, an opportunity to clap a judgment on his back. Now this was done with so malicious a sneer, that it totally unhinged (if I may so say) the temper of the philosopher, which the bite of his tongue had somewhat ruffled; and as he was disabled from venting his wrath at his lips, he had possibly found a more violent method of revenging himself, had not the surgeon, who was then luckily in the room, contrary to his own interest, interposed and preserved the peace.

Mr Blifil visited his friend Jones but seldom, and never alone. This worthy young man, however, professed much regard for him, and as great concern at his misfortune; but cautiously avoided any intimacy, lest, as he frequently hinted, it might contaminate the sobriety of his own character: for which purpose he had constantly in his mouth that proverb in which Solomon speaks against evil communication. Not that he was so bitter as Thwackum; for he always expressed some hopes of Tom's reformation; "which," he said, "the unparalleled goodness shown by his uncle on this occasion, must certainly effect in one not absolutely abandoned:" but concluded, "if Mr Jones ever offends hereafter, I shall not be able to say a syllable in his favour."

As to Squire Western, he was seldom out of the sick-room, unless when he was engaged either in the field or over his bottle. Nay, he would sometimes retire hither to take his beer, and it was not without difficulty that he was prevented from forcing Jones to take his beer too: for no quack ever held his nostrum to be a more general panacea than he did this; which, he said, had more virtue in it than was in all the physic in an apothecary's shop. He was, however, by much entreaty, prevailed on to forbear the application of this medicine; but from serenading his patient every hunting morning with the horn under his window, it was impossible to withhold him; nor did he ever lay aside that hallow, with which he entered into all companies, when he visited Jones, without any regard to the sick person's being at that time either awake or asleep.

This boisterous behaviour, as it meant no harm, so happily it effected none, and was abundantly compensated to Jones, as soon as he was able to sit up, by the company of Sophia, whom the squire then brought to visit him; nor was it, indeed, long before Jones was able to attend her to the harpsichord, where she would kindly condescend, for hours together, to charm him with the most delicious music, unless when the squire thought proper to interrupt her, by insisting on Old Sir Simon, or some other of his favourite pieces.

Notwithstanding the nicest guard which Sophia endeavoured to set on her behaviour, she could not avoid letting some appearances now and then slip forth: for love may again be likened to a disease in this, that when it is denied a vent in one part, it will certainly break out in another. What her lips, therefore, concealed, her eyes, her blushes, and many little involuntary actions, betrayed.

One day, when Sophia was playing on the harpsichord, and Jones was attending, the squire came into the room, crying, "There, Tom, I have had a battle for thee below-stairs with thick parson Thwackum. He hath been a telling Allworthy, before my face, that the broken bone was a judgment upon thee. D—n it, says I, how can that be? Did he not come by it in defence of a young woman? A judgment indeed! Pox, if he never doth anything worse, he will go to heaven sooner than all the parsons in the country. He hath more reason to glory in it than to be ashamed of it."—"Indeed, sir," says Jones, "I have no reason for either; but if it preserved Miss Western, I shall always think it the happiest accident of my life."—"And to gu," said the squire, "to zet Allworthy against thee vor it! D—n un, if the parson had unt his petticuoats on, I should have lent un o flick; for I love thee dearly, my boy, and d—n me if there is anything in my power which I won't do for thee. Sha't take thy choice of all the horses in my stable to-morrow morning, except only the Chevalier and Miss Slouch." Jones thanked him, but declined accepting the offer. "Nay," added the squire, "sha't ha the sorrel mare that Sophy rode. She cost me fifty guineas, and comes six years old this grass." "If she had cost me a thousand," cries Jones passionately, "I would have given her to the dogs." "Pooh! pooh!" answered Western; "what! because she broke thy arm? Shouldst forget and forgive. I thought hadst been more a man than to bear malice against a dumb creature."—Here Sophia interposed, and put an end to the conversation, by desiring her father's leave to play to him; a request which he never refused.

The countenance of Sophia had undergone more than one change during the foregoing speeches; and probably she imputed the passionate resentment which Jones had expressed against the mare, to a different motive from that from which her father had derived it. Her spirits were at this time in a visible flutter; and she played so intolerably ill, that had not Western soon fallen asleep, he must have remarked it. Jones, however, who was sufficiently awake, and was not without an ear any more than without eyes, made some observations; which being joined to all which the reader may remember to have passed formerly, gave him pretty strong assurances, when he came to reflect on the whole, that all was not well in the tender bosom of Sophia; an opinion which many young gentlemen will, I doubt not, extremely wonder at his not having been well confirmed in long ago. To confess the truth, he had rather too much diffidence in himself, and was not forward enough in seeing the advances of a young lady; a misfortune which can be cured only by that early town education, which is at present so generally in fashion.

When these thoughts had fully taken possession of Jones, they occasioned a perturbation in his mind, which, in a constitution less pure and firm than his, might have been, at such a season, attended with very dangerous consequences. He was truly sensible of the great worth of Sophia. He extremely liked her person, no less admired her accomplishments, and tenderly loved her goodness. In reality, as he had never once entertained any thought of possessing her, nor had ever given the least voluntary indulgence to his inclinations, he had a much stronger passion for her than he himself was acquainted with. His heart now brought forth the full secret, at the same time that it assured him the adorable object returned his affection.

CHAPTER III.

Which all who have no heart will think to contain much ado about nothing.

The reader will perhaps imagine the sensations which now arose in Jones to have been so sweet and delicious, that they would rather tend to produce a chearful serenity in the mind, than any of those dangerous effects which we have mentioned; but in fact, sensations of this kind, however delicious, are, at their first recognition, of a very tumultuous nature, and have very little of the opiate in them. They were, moreover, in the present case, embittered with certain circumstances, which being mixed with sweeter ingredients, tended altogether to compose a draught that might be termed bitter-sweet; than which, as nothing can be more disagreeable to the palate, so nothing, in the metaphorical sense, can be so injurious to the mind.

For first, though he had sufficient foundation to flatter himself in what he had observed in Sophia, he was not yet free from doubt of misconstruing compassion, or at best, esteem, into a warmer regard. He was far from a sanguine assurance that Sophia had any such affection towards him, as might promise his inclinations that harvest, which, if they were encouraged and nursed, they would finally grow up to require. Besides, if he could hope to find no bar to his happiness from the daughter, he thought himself certain of meeting an effectual bar in the father; who, though he was a country squire in his diversions, was perfectly a man of the world in whatever regarded his fortune; had the most violent affection for his only daughter, and had often signified, in his cups, the pleasure he proposed in seeing her married to one of the richest men in the county. Jones was not so vain and senseless a coxcomb as to expect, from any regard which Western had professed for him, that he would ever be induced to lay aside these views of advancing his daughter. He well knew that fortune is generally the principal, if not the sole, consideration, which operates on the best of parents in these matters: for friendship makes us warmly espouse the interest of others; but it is very cold to the gratification of their passions. Indeed, to feel the happiness which may result from this, it is necessary we should possess the passion ourselves. As he had therefore no hopes of obtaining her father's consent; so he thought to endeavour to succeed without it, and by such means to frustrate the great point of Mr Western's life, was to make a very ill use of his hospitality, and a very ungrateful return to the many little favours received (however roughly) at his hands. If he saw such a consequence with horror and disdain, how much more was he shocked with what regarded Mr Allworthy; to whom, as he had more than filial obligations, so had he for him more than filial piety! He knew the nature of that good man to be so averse to any baseness or treachery, that the least attempt of such a kind would make the sight of the guilty person for ever odious to his eyes, and his name a detestable sound in his ears. The appearance of such unsurmountable difficulties was sufficient to have inspired him with despair, however ardent his wishes had been; but even these were contruoled by compassion for another woman. The idea of lovely Molly now intruded itself before him. He had sworn eternal constancy in her arms, and she had as often vowed never to out-live his deserting her. He now saw her in all the most shocking postures of death; nay, he considered all the miseries of prostitution to which she would be liable, and of which he would be doubly the occasion; first by seducing, and then by deserting her; for he well knew the hatred which all her neighbours, and even her own sisters, bore her, and how ready they would all be to tear her to pieces. Indeed, he had exposed her to more envy than shame, or rather to the latter by means of the former: for many women abused her for being a whore, while they envied her her lover, and her finery, and would have been themselves glad to have purchased these at the same rate. The ruin, therefore, of the poor girl must, he foresaw, unavoidably attend his deserting her; and this thought stung him to the soul. Poverty and distress seemed to him to give none a right of aggravating those misfortunes. The meanness of her condition did not represent her misery as of little consequence in his eyes, nor did it appear to justify, or even to palliate, his guilt, in bringing that misery upon her. But why do I mention justification? His own heart would not suffer him to destroy a human creature who, he thought, loved him, and had to that love sacrificed her innocence. His own good heart pleaded her cause; not as a cold venal advocate, but as one interested in the event, and which must itself deeply share in all the agonies its owner brought on another.

When this powerful advocate had sufficiently raised the pity of Jones, by painting poor Molly in all the circumstances of wretchedness; it artfully called in the assistance of another passion, and represented the girl in all the amiable colours of youth, health, and beauty; as one greatly the object of desire, and much more so, at least to a good mind, from being, at the same time, the object of compassion.

Amidst these thoughts, poor Jones passed a long sleepless night, and in the morning the result of the whole was to abide by Molly, and to think no more of Sophia.

In this virtuous resolution he continued all the next day till the evening, cherishing the idea of Molly, and driving Sophia from his thoughts; but in the fatal evening, a very trifling accident set all his passions again on float, and worked so total a change in his mind, that we think it decent to communicate it in a fresh chapter.

CHAPTER IV.

A little chapter, in which is contained a little incident.

Among other visitants, who paid their compliments to the young gentleman in his confinement, Mrs Honour was one. The reader, perhaps, when he reflects on some expressions which have formerly dropt from her, may conceive that she herself had a very particular affection for Mr Jones; but, in reality, it was no such thing. Tom was a handsome young fellow; and for that species of men Mrs Honour had some regard; but this was perfectly indiscriminate; for having being crossed in the love which she bore a certain nobleman's footman, who had basely deserted her after a promise of marriage, she had so securely kept together the broken remains of her heart, that no man had ever since been able to possess himself of any single fragment. She viewed all handsome men with that equal regard and benevolence which a sober and virtuous mind bears to all the good. She might indeed be called a lover of men, as Socrates was a lover of mankind, preferring one to another for corporeal, as he for mental qualifications; but never carrying this preference so far as to cause any perturbation in the philosophical serenity of her temper.

The day after Mr Jones had that conflict with himself which we have seen in the preceding chapter, Mrs Honour came into his room, and finding him alone, began in the following manner:—"La, sir, where do you think I have been? I warrants you, you would not guess in fifty years; but if you did guess, to be sure I must not tell you neither."—"Nay, if it be something which you must not tell me," said Jones, "I shall have the curiosity to enquire, and I know you will not be so barbarous to refuse me."—"I don't know," cries she, "why I should refuse you neither, for that matter; for to be sure you won't mention it any more. And for that matter, if you knew where I have been, unless you knew what I have been about, it would not signify much. Nay, I don't see why it should be kept a secret for my part; for to be sure she is the best lady in the world." Upon this, Jones began to beg earnestly to be let into this secret, and faithfully promised not to divulge it. She then proceeded thus:—"Why, you must know, sir, my young lady sent me to enquire after Molly Seagrim, and to see whether the wench wanted anything; to be sure, I did not care to go, methinks; but servants must do what they are ordered.—How could you undervalue yourself so, Mr Jones?—So my lady bid me go and carry her some linen, and other things. She is too good. If such forward sluts were sent to Bridewell, it would be better for them. I told my lady, says I, madam, your la'ship is encouraging idleness."—"And was my Sophia so good?" says Jones. "My Sophia! I assure you, marry come up," answered Honour. "And yet if you knew all—indeed, if I was as Mr Jones, I should look a little higher than such trumpery as Molly Seagrim." "What do you mean by these words," replied Jones, "if I knew all?" "I mean what I mean," says Honour. "Don't you remember putting your hands in my lady's muff once? I vow I could almost find in my heart to tell, if I was certain my lady would never come to the hearing on't." Jones then made several solemn protestations. And Honour proceeded—"Then to be sure, my lady gave me that muff; and afterwards, upon hearing what you had done"—"Then you told her what I had done?" interrupted Jones. "If I did, sir," answered she, "you need not be angry with me. Many's the man would have given his head to have had my lady told, if they had known,—for, to be sure, the biggest lord in the land might be proud—but, I protest, I have a great mind not to tell you." Jones fell to entreaties, and soon prevailed on her to go on thus. "You must know then, sir, that my lady had given this muff to me; but about a day or two after I had told her the story, she quarrels with her new muff, and to be sure it is the prettiest that ever was seen. Honour, says she, this is an odious muff; it is too big for me, I can't wear it: till I can get another, you must let me have my old one again, and you may have this in the room on't—for she's a good lady, and scorns to give a thing and take a thing, I promise you that. So to be sure I fetched it her back again, and, I believe, she hath worn it upon her arm almost ever since, and I warrants hath given it many a kiss when nobody hath seen her."

Here the conversation was interrupted by Mr Western himself, who came to summon Jones to the harpsichord; whither the poor young fellow went all pale and trembling. This Western observed, but, on seeing Mrs Honour, imputed it to a wrong cause; and having given Jones a hearty curse between jest and earnest, he bid him beat abroad, and not poach up the game in his warren.

Sophia looked this evening with more than usual beauty, and we may believe it was no small addition to her charms, in the eye of Mr Jones, that she now happened to have on her right arm this very muff.

She was playing one of her father's favourite tunes, and he was leaning on her chair, when the muff fell over her fingers, and put her out. This so disconcerted the squire, that he snatched the muff from her, and with a hearty curse threw it into the fire. Sophia instantly started up, and with the utmost eagerness recovered it from the flames.

Though this incident will probably appear of little consequence to many of our readers; yet, trifling as it was, it had so violent an effect on poor Jones, that we thought it our duty to relate it. In reality, there are many little circumstances too often omitted by injudicious historians, from which events of the utmost importance arise. The world may indeed be considered as a vast machine, in which the great wheels are originally set in motion by those which are very minute, and almost imperceptible to any but the strongest eyes.

Thus, not all the charms of the incomparable Sophia; not all the dazzling brightness, and languishing softness of her eyes; the harmony of her voice, and of her person; not all her wit, good-humour, greatness of mind, or sweetness of disposition, had been able so absolutely to conquer and enslave the heart of poor Jones, as this little incident of the muff. Thus the poet sweetly sings of Troy—

—Captique dolis lachrymisque coacti
Quos neque Tydides, nec Larissaeus Achilles,
Non anni domuere decem, non mille Carinae.

What Diomede or Thetis' greater son,
A thousand ships, nor ten years' siege had done
False tears and fawning words the city won.

The citadel of Jones was now taken by surprize. All those considerations of honour and prudence which our heroe had lately with so much military wisdom placed as guards over the avenues of his heart, ran away from their posts, and the god of love marched in, in triumph.

CHAPTER V.

A very long chapter, containing a very great incident.

But though this victorious deity easily expelled his avowed enemies from the heart of Jones, he found it more difficult to supplant the garrison which he himself had placed there. To lay aside all allegory, the concern for what must become of poor Molly greatly disturbed and perplexed the mind of the worthy youth. The superior merit of Sophia totally eclipsed, or rather extinguished, all the beauties of the poor girl; but compassion instead of contempt succeeded to love. He was convinced the girl had placed all her affections, and all her prospect of future happiness, in him only. For this he had, he knew, given sufficient occasion, by the utmost profusion of tenderness towards her: a tenderness which he had taken every means to persuade her he would always maintain. She, on her side, had assured him of her firm belief in his promise, and had with the most solemn vows declared, that on his fulfilling or breaking these promises, it depended, whether she should be the happiest or most miserable of womankind. And to be the author of this highest degree of misery to a human being, was a thought on which he could not bear to ruminate a single moment. He considered this poor girl as having sacrificed to him everything in her little power; as having been at her own expense the object of his pleasure; as sighing and languishing for him even at that very instant. Shall then, says he, my recovery, for which she hath so ardently wished; shall my presence, which she hath so eagerly expected, instead of giving her that joy with which she hath flattered herself, cast her at once down into misery and despair? Can I be such a villain? Here, when the genius of poor Molly seemed triumphant, the love of Sophia towards him, which now appeared no longer dubious, rushed upon his mind, and bore away every obstacle before it.

At length it occurred to him, that he might possibly be able to make Molly amends another way; namely, by giving her a sum of money. This, nevertheless, he almost despaired of her accepting, when he recollected the frequent and vehement assurances he had received from her, that the world put in balance with him would make her no amends for his loss. However, her extreme poverty, and chiefly her egregious vanity (somewhat of which hath been already hinted to the reader), gave him some little hope, that, notwithstanding all her avowed tenderness, she might in time be brought to content herself with a fortune superior to her expectation, and which might indulge her vanity, by setting her above all her equals. He resolved therefore to take the first opportunity of making a proposal of this kind.

One day, accordingly, when his arm was so well recovered that he could walk easily with it slung in a sash, he stole forth, at a season when the squire was engaged in his field exercises, and visited his fair one. Her mother and sisters, whom he found taking their tea, informed him first that Molly was not at home; but afterwards the eldest sister acquainted him, with a malicious smile, that she was above stairs a-bed. Tom had no objection to this situation of his mistress, and immediately ascended the ladder which led towards her bed-chamber; but when he came to the top, he, to his great surprize, found the door fast; nor could he for some time obtain any answer from within; for Molly, as she herself afterwards informed him, was fast asleep.

The extremes of grief and joy have been remarked to produce very similar effects; and when either of these rushes on us by surprize, it is apt to create such a total perturbation and confusion, that we are often thereby deprived of the use of all our faculties. It cannot therefore be wondered at, that the unexpected sight of Mr Jones should so strongly operate on the mind of Molly, and should overwhelm her with such confusion, that for some minutes she was unable to express the great raptures, with which the reader will suppose she was affected on this occasion. As for Jones, he was so entirely possessed, and as it were enchanted, by the presence of his beloved object, that he for a while forgot Sophia, and consequently the principal purpose of his visit.

This, however, soon recurred to his memory; and after the first transports of their meeting were over, he found means by degrees to introduce a discourse on the fatal consequences which must attend their amour, if Mr Allworthy, who had strictly forbidden him ever seeing her more, should discover that he still carried on this commerce. Such a discovery, which his enemies gave him reason to think would be unavoidable, must, he said, end in his ruin, and consequently in hers. Since therefore their hard fates had determined that they must separate, he advised her to bear it with resolution, and swore he would never omit any opportunity, through the course of his life, of showing her the sincerity of his affection, by providing for her in a manner beyond her utmost expectation, or even beyond her wishes, if ever that should be in his power; concluding at last, that she might soon find some man who would marry her, and who would make her much happier than she could be by leading a disreputable life with him.

Molly remained a few moments in silence, and then bursting into a flood of tears, she began to upbraid him in the following words: "And this is your love for me, to forsake me in this manner, now you have ruined me! How often, when I have told you that all men are false and perjury alike, and grow tired of us as soon as ever they have had their wicked wills of us, how often have you sworn you would never forsake me! And can you be such a perjury man after all? What signifies all the riches in the world to me without you, now you have gained my heart, so you have—you have—? Why do you mention another man to me? I can never love any other man as long as I live. All other men are nothing to me. If the greatest squire in all the country would come a suiting to me to-morrow, I would not give my company to him. No, I shall always hate and despise the whole sex for your sake."—

She was proceeding thus, when an accident put a stop to her tongue, before it had run out half its career. The room, or rather garret, in which Molly lay, being up one pair of stairs, that is to say, at the top of the house, was of a sloping figure, resembling the great Delta of the Greeks. The English reader may perhaps form a better idea of it, by being told that it was impossible to stand upright anywhere but in the middle. Now, as this room wanted the conveniency of a closet, Molly had, to supply that defect, nailed up an old rug against the rafters of the house, which enclosed a little hole where her best apparel, such as the remains of that sack which we have formerly mentioned, some caps, and other things with which she had lately provided herself, were hung up and secured from the dust.

This enclosed place exactly fronted the foot of the bed, to which, indeed, the rug hung so near, that it served in a manner to supply the want of curtains. Now, whether Molly, in the agonies of her rage, pushed this rug with her feet; or Jones might touch it; or whether the pin or nail gave way of its own accord, I am not certain; but as Molly pronounced those last words, which are recorded above, the wicked rug got loose from its fastening, and discovered everything hid behind it; where among other female utensils appeared—(with shame I write it, and with sorrow will it be read)—the philosopher Square, in a posture (for the place would not near admit his standing upright) as ridiculous as can possibly be conceived.

The posture, indeed, in which he stood, was not greatly unlike that of a soldier who is tied neck and heels; or rather resembling the attitude in which we often see fellows in the public streets of London, who are not suffering but deserving punishment by so standing. He had a nightcap belonging to Molly on his head, and his two large eyes, the moment the rug fell, stared directly at Jones; so that when the idea of philosophy was added to the figure now discovered, it would have been very difficult for any spectator to have refrained from immoderate laughter.

I question not but the surprize of the reader will be here equal to that of Jones; as the suspicions which must arise from the appearance of this wise and grave man in such a place, may seem so inconsistent with that character which he hath, doubtless, maintained hitherto, in the opinion of every one.

But to confess the truth, this inconsistency is rather imaginary than real. Philosophers are composed of flesh and blood as well as other human creatures; and however sublimated and refined the theory of these may be, a little practical frailty is as incident to them as to other mortals. It is, indeed, in theory only, and not in practice, as we have before hinted, that consists the difference: for though such great beings think much better and more wisely, they always act exactly like other men. They know very well how to subdue all appetites and passions, and to despise both pain and pleasure; and this knowledge affords much delightful contemplation, and is easily acquired; but the practice would be vexatious and troublesome; and, therefore, the same wisdom which teaches them to know this, teaches them to avoid carrying it into execution.

Mr Square happened to be at church on that Sunday, when, as the reader may be pleased to remember, the appearance of Molly in her sack had caused all that disturbance. Here he first observed her, and was so pleased with her beauty, that he prevailed with the young gentlemen to change their intended ride that evening, that he might pass by the habitation of Molly, and by that means might obtain a second chance of seeing her. This reason, however, as he did not at that time mention to any, so neither did we think proper to communicate it then to the reader.

Among other particulars which constituted the unfitness of things in Mr Square's opinion, danger and difficulty were two. The difficulty therefore which he apprehended there might be in corrupting this young wench, and the danger which would accrue to his character on the discovery, were such strong dissuasives, that it is probable he at first intended to have contented himself with the pleasing ideas which the sight of beauty furnishes us with. These the gravest men, after a full meal of serious meditation, often allow themselves by way of dessert: for which purpose, certain books and pictures find their way into the most private recesses of their study, and a certain liquorish part of natural philosophy is often the principal subject of their conversation.

But when the philosopher heard, a day or two afterwards, that the fortress of virtue had already been subdued, he began to give a larger scope to his desires. His appetite was not of that squeamish kind which cannot feed on a dainty because another hath tasted it. In short, he liked the girl the better for the want of that chastity, which, if she had possessed it, must have been a bar to his pleasures; he pursued and obtained her.

The reader will be mistaken, if he thinks Molly gave Square the preference to her younger lover: on the contrary, had she been confined to the choice of one only, Tom Jones would undoubtedly have been, of the two, the victorious person. Nor was it solely the consideration that two are better than one (though this had its proper weight) to which Mr Square owed his success: the absence of Jones during his confinement was an unlucky circumstance; and in that interval some well-chosen presents from the philosopher so softened and unguarded the girl's heart, that a favourable opportunity became irresistible, and Square triumphed over the poor remains of virtue which subsisted in the bosom of Molly.

It was now about a fortnight since this conquest, when Jones paid the abovementioned visit to his mistress, at a time when she and Square were in bed together. This was the true reason why the mother denied her as we have seen; for as the old woman shared in the profits arising from the iniquity of her daughter, she encouraged and protected her in it to the utmost of her power; but such was the envy and hatred which the elder sister bore towards Molly, that, notwithstanding she had some part of the booty, she would willingly have parted with this to ruin her sister and spoil her trade. Hence she had acquainted Jones with her being abovestairs in bed, in hopes that he might have caught her in Square's arms. This, however, Molly found means to prevent, as the door was fastened; which gave her an opportunity of conveying her lover behind that rug or blanket where he now was unhappily discovered.

Square no sooner made his appearance than Molly flung herself back in her bed, cried out she was undone, and abandoned herself to despair. This poor girl, who was yet but a novice in her business, had not arrived to that perfection of assurance which helps off a town lady in any extremity; and either prompts her with an excuse, or else inspires her to brazen out the matter with her husband, who, from love of quiet, or out of fear of his reputation—and sometimes, perhaps, from fear of the gallant, who, like Mr Constant in the play, wears a sword—is glad to shut his eyes, and content to put his horns in his pocket. Molly, on the contrary, was silenced by this evidence, and very fairly gave up a cause which she had hitherto maintained with so many tears, and with such solemn and vehement protestations of the purest love and constancy.

As to the gentleman behind the arras, he was not in much less consternation. He stood for a while motionless, and seemed equally at a loss what to say, or whither to direct his eyes. Jones, though perhaps the most astonished of the three, first found his tongue; and being immediately recovered from those uneasy sensations which Molly by her upbraidings had occasioned, he burst into a loud laughter, and then saluting Mr Square, advanced to take him by the hand, and to relieve him from his place of confinement.

Square being now arrived in the middle of the room, in which part only he could stand upright, looked at Jones with a very grave countenance, and said to him, "Well, sir, I see you enjoy this mighty discovery, and, I dare swear, take great delight in the thoughts of exposing me; but if you will consider the matter fairly, you will find you are yourself only to blame. I am not guilty of corrupting innocence. I have done nothing for which that part of the world which judges of matters by the rule of right, will condemn me. Fitness is governed by the nature of things, and not by customs, forms, or municipal laws. Nothing is indeed unfit which is not unnatural."—"Well reasoned, old boy," answered Jones; "but why dost thou think that I should desire to expose thee? I promise thee, I was never better pleased with thee in my life; and unless thou hast a mind to discover it thyself, this affair may remain a profound secret for me."—"Nay, Mr Jones," replied Square, "I would not be thought to undervalue reputation. Good fame is a species of the Kalon, and it is by no means fitting to neglect it. Besides, to murder one's own reputation is a kind of suicide, a detestable and odious vice. If you think proper, therefore, to conceal any infirmity of mine (for such I may have, since no man is perfectly perfect), I promise you I will not betray myself. Things may be fitting to be done, which are not fitting to be boasted of; for by the perverse judgment of the world, that often becomes the subject of censure, which is, in truth, not only innocent but laudable."—"Right!" cries Jones: "what can be more innocent than the indulgence of a natural appetite? or what more laudable than the propagation of our species?"—"To be serious with you," answered Square, "I profess they always appeared so to me."—"And yet," said Jones, "you was of a different opinion when my affair with this girl was first discovered."—"Why, I must confess," says Square, "as the matter was misrepresented to me, by that parson Thwackum, I might condemn the corruption of innocence: it was that, sir, it was that—and that—: for you must know, Mr Jones, in the consideration of fitness, very minute circumstances, sir, very minute circumstances cause great alteration."—"Well," cries Jones, "be that as it will, it shall be your own fault, as I have promised you, if you ever hear any more of this adventure. Behave kindly to the girl, and I will never open my lips concerning the matter to any one. And, Molly, do you be faithful to your friend, and I will not only forgive your infidelity to me, but will do you all the service I can." So saying, he took a hasty leave, and, slipping down the ladder, retired with much expedition.

Square was rejoiced to find this adventure was likely to have no worse conclusion; and as for Molly, being recovered from her confusion, she began at first to upbraid Square with having been the occasion of her loss of Jones; but that gentleman soon found the means of mitigating her anger, partly by caresses, and partly by a small nostrum from his purse, of wonderful and approved efficacy in purging off the ill humours of the mind, and in restoring it to a good temper.

She then poured forth a vast profusion of tenderness towards her new lover; turned all she had said to Jones, and Jones himself, into ridicule; and vowed, though he once had the possession of her person, that none but Square had ever been master of her heart.

CHAPTER VI.

By comparing which with the former, the reader may possibly correct some abuse which he hath formerly been guilty of in the application of the word love.

The infidelity of Molly, which Jones had now discovered, would, perhaps, have vindicated a much greater degree of resentment than he expressed on the occasion; and if he had abandoned her directly from that moment, very few, I believe, would have blamed him.

Certain, however, it is, that he saw her in the light of compassion; and though his love to her was not of that kind which could give him any great uneasiness at her inconstancy, yet was he not a little shocked on reflecting that he had himself originally corrupted her innocence; for to this corruption he imputed all the vice into which she appeared now so likely to plunge herself.

This consideration gave him no little uneasiness, till Betty, the elder sister, was so kind, some time afterwards, entirely to cure him by a hint, that one Will Barnes, and not himself, had been the first seducer of Molly; and that the little child, which he had hitherto so certainly concluded to be his own, might very probably have an equal title, at least, to claim Barnes for its father.

Jones eagerly pursued this scent when he had first received it; and in a very short time was sufficiently assured that the girl had told him truth, not only by the confession of the fellow, but at last by that of Molly herself.

This Will Barnes was a country gallant, and had acquired as many trophies of this kind as any ensign or attorney's clerk in the kingdom. He had, indeed, reduced several women to a state of utter profligacy, had broke the hearts of some, and had the honour of occasioning the violent death of one poor girl, who had either drowned herself, or, what was rather more probable, had been drowned by him.

Among other of his conquests, this fellow had triumphed over the heart of Betty Seagrim. He had made love to her long before Molly was grown to be a fit object of that pastime; but had afterwards deserted her, and applied to her sister, with whom he had almost immediate success. Now Will had, in reality, the sole possession of Molly's affection, while Jones and Square were almost equally sacrifices to her interest and to her pride.

Hence had grown that implacable hatred which we have before seen raging in the mind of Betty; though we did not think it necessary to assign this cause sooner, as envy itself alone was adequate to all the effects we have mentioned.

Jones was become perfectly easy by possession of this secret with regard to Molly; but as to Sophia, he was far from being in a state of tranquillity; nay, indeed, he was under the most violent perturbation; his heart was now, if I may use the metaphor, entirely evacuated, and Sophia took absolute possession of it. He loved her with an unbounded passion, and plainly saw the tender sentiments she had for him; yet could not this assurance lessen his despair of obtaining the consent of her father, nor the horrors which attended his pursuit of her by any base or treacherous method.

The injury which he must thus do to Mr Western, and the concern which would accrue to Mr Allworthy, were circumstances that tormented him all day, and haunted him on his pillow at night. His life was a constant struggle between honour and inclination, which alternately triumphed over each other in his mind. He often resolved, in the absence of Sophia, to leave her father's house, and to see her no more; and as often, in her presence, forgot all those resolutions, and determined to pursue her at the hazard of his life, and at the forfeiture of what was much dearer to him.

This conflict began soon to produce very strong and visible effects: for he lost all his usual sprightliness and gaiety of temper, and became not only melancholy when alone, but dejected and absent in company; nay, if ever he put on a forced mirth, to comply with Mr Western's humour, the constraint appeared so plain, that he seemed to have been giving the strongest evidence of what he endeavoured to conceal by such ostentation.

It may, perhaps, be a question, whether the art which he used to conceal his passion, or the means which honest nature employed to reveal it, betrayed him most: for while art made him more than ever reserved to Sophia, and forbad him to address any of his discourse to her, nay, to avoid meeting her eyes, with the utmost caution; nature was no less busy in counterplotting him. Hence, at the approach of the young lady, he grew pale; and if this was sudden, started. If his eyes accidentally met hers, the blood rushed into his cheeks, and his countenance became all over scarlet. If common civility ever obliged him to speak to her, as to drink her health at table, his tongue was sure to falter. If he touched her, his hand, nay his whole frame, trembled. And if any discourse tended, however remotely, to raise the idea of love, an involuntary sigh seldom failed to steal from his bosom. Most of which accidents nature was wonderfully industrious to throw daily in his way.

All these symptoms escaped the notice of the squire: but not so of Sophia. She soon perceived these agitations of mind in Jones, and was at no loss to discover the cause; for indeed she recognized it in her own breast. And this recognition is, I suppose, that sympathy which hath been so often noted in lovers, and which will sufficiently account for her being so much quicker-sighted than her father.

But, to say the truth, there is a more simple and plain method of accounting for that prodigious superiority of penetration which we must observe in some men over the rest of the human species, and one which will serve not only in the case of lovers, but of all others. From whence is it that the knave is generally so quick-sighted to those symptoms and operations of knavery, which often dupe an honest man of a much better understanding? There surely is no general sympathy among knaves; nor have they, like freemasons, any common sign of communication. In reality, it is only because they have the same thing in their heads, and their thoughts are turned the same way. Thus, that Sophia saw, and that Western did not see, the plain symptoms of love in Jones can be no wonder, when we consider that the idea of love never entered into the head of the father, whereas the daughter, at present, thought of nothing else.

When Sophia was well satisfied of the violent passion which tormented poor Jones, and no less certain that she herself was its object, she had not the least difficulty in discovering the true cause of his present behaviour. This highly endeared him to her, and raised in her mind two of the best affections which any lover can wish to raise in a mistress—these were, esteem and pity—for sure the most outrageously rigid among her sex will excuse her pitying a man whom she saw miserable on her own account; nor can they blame her for esteeming one who visibly, from the most honourable motives, endeavoured to smother a flame in his own bosom, which, like the famous Spartan theft, was preying upon and consuming his very vitals. Thus his backwardness, his shunning her, his coldness, and his silence, were the forwardest, the most diligent, the warmest, and most eloquent advocates; and wrought so violently on her sensible and tender heart, that she soon felt for him all those gentle sensations which are consistent with a virtuous and elevated female mind. In short, all which esteem, gratitude, and pity, can inspire in such towards an agreeable man—indeed, all which the nicest delicacy can allow. In a word, she was in love with him to distraction.

One day this young couple accidentally met in the garden, at the end of the two walks which were both bounded by that canal in which Jones had formerly risqued drowning to retrieve the little bird that Sophia had there lost.

This place had been of late much frequented by Sophia. Here she used to ruminate, with a mixture of pain and pleasure, on an incident which, however trifling in itself, had possibly sown the first seeds of that affection which was now arrived to such maturity in her heart.

Here then this young couple met. They were almost close together before either of them knew anything of the other's approach. A bystander would have discovered sufficient marks of confusion in the countenance of each; but they felt too much themselves to make any observation. As soon as Jones had a little recovered his first surprize, he accosted the young lady with some of the ordinary forms of salutation, which she in the same manner returned; and their conversation began, as usual, on the delicious beauty of the morning. Hence they past to the beauty of the place, on which Jones launched forth very high encomiums. When they came to the tree whence he had formerly tumbled into the canal, Sophia could not help reminding him of that accident, and said, "I fancy, Mr Jones, you have some little shuddering when you see that water."—"I assure you, madam," answered Jones, "the concern you felt at the loss of your little bird will always appear to me the highest circumstance in that adventure. Poor little Tommy! there is the branch he stood upon. How could the little wretch have the folly to fly away from that state of happiness in which I had the honour to place him? His fate was a just punishment for his ingratitude."—"Upon my word, Mr Jones," said she, "your gallantry very narrowly escaped as severe a fate. Sure the remembrance must affect you."—"Indeed, madam," answered he, "if I have any reason to reflect with sorrow on it, it is, perhaps, that the water had not been a little deeper, by which I might have escaped many bitter heart-aches that Fortune seems to have in store for me."—"Fie, Mr Jones!" replied Sophia; "I am sure you cannot be in earnest now. This affected contempt of life is only an excess of your complacence to me. You would endeavour to lessen the obligation of having twice ventured it for my sake. Beware the third time." She spoke these last words with a smile, and a softness inexpressible. Jones answered with a sigh, "He feared it was already too late for caution:" and then looking tenderly and stedfastly on her, he cried, "Oh, Miss Western! can you desire me to live? Can you wish me so ill?" Sophia, looking down on the ground, answered with some hesitation, "Indeed, Mr Jones, I do not wish you ill."—"Oh, I know too well that heavenly temper," cries Jones, "that divine goodness, which is beyond every other charm."—"Nay, now," answered she, "I understand you not. I can stay no longer."—"I—I would not be understood!" cries he; "nay, I can't be understood. I know not what I say. Meeting you here so unexpectedly, I have been unguarded: for Heaven's sake pardon me, if I have said anything to offend you. I did not mean it. Indeed, I would rather have died—nay, the very thought would kill me."—"You surprize me," answered she. "How can you possibly think you have offended me?"—"Fear, madam," says he, "easily runs into madness; and there is no degree of fear like that which I feel of offending you. How can I speak then? Nay, don't look angrily at me: one frown will destroy me. I mean nothing. Blame my eyes, or blame those beauties. What am I saying? Pardon me if I have said too much. My heart overflowed. I have struggled with my love to the utmost, and have endeavoured to conceal a fever which preys on my vitals, and will, I hope, soon make it impossible for me ever to offend you more."

Mr Jones now fell a trembling as if he had been shaken with the fit of an ague. Sophia, who was in a situation not very different from his, answered in these words: "Mr Jones, I will not affect to misunderstand you; indeed, I understand you too well; but, for Heaven's sake, if you have any affection for me, let me make the best of my way into the house. I wish I may be able to support myself thither."

Jones, who was hardly able to support himself, offered her his arm, which she condescended to accept, but begged he would not mention a word more to her of this nature at present. He promised he would not; insisting only on her forgiveness of what love, without the leave of his will, had forced from him: this, she told him, he knew how to obtain by his future behaviour; and thus this young pair tottered and trembled along, the lover not once daring to squeeze the hand of his mistress, though it was locked in his.

Sophia immediately retired to her chamber, where Mrs Honour and the hartshorn were summoned to her assistance. As to poor Jones, the only relief to his distempered mind was an unwelcome piece of news, which, as it opens a scene of different nature from those in which the reader hath lately been conversant, will be communicated to him in the next chapter.

CHAPTER VII.

In which Mr Allworthy appears on a sick-bed.

Mr Western was become so fond of Jones that he was unwilling to part with him, though his arm had been long since cured; and Jones, either from the love of sport, or from some other reason, was easily persuaded to continue at his house, which he did sometimes for a fortnight together without paying a single visit at Mr Allworthy's; nay, without ever hearing from thence.

Mr Allworthy had been for some days indisposed with a cold, which had been attended with a little fever. This he had, however, neglected; as it was usual with him to do all manner of disorders which did not confine him to his bed, or prevent his several faculties from performing their ordinary functions;—a conduct which we would by no means be thought to approve or recommend to imitation; for surely the gentlemen of the Aesculapian art are in the right in advising, that the moment the disease has entered at one door, the physician should be introduced at the other: what else is meant by that old adage, *Venienti occurrite morbo?* "Oppose a distemper at its first approach." Thus the doctor and the disease meet in fair and equal conflict; whereas, by giving time to the latter, we often suffer him to fortify and entrench himself, like a French army; so that the learned gentleman finds it very difficult, and sometimes impossible, to come at the enemy. Nay, sometimes by gaining time the disease applies to the French military politics, and corrupts nature over to his side, and then all the powers of physic must arrive too late. Agreeable to these observations was, I remember, the complaint of the great Doctor Misaubin, who used very pathetically to lament the late applications which were made to his skill, saying, "Bygar, me believe my pation take me for de undertaker, for dey never send for me till de physicion have kill dem."

Mr Allworthy's distemper, by means of this neglect, gained such ground, that, when the increase of his fever obliged him to send for assistance, the doctor at his first arrival shook his head, wished he had been sent for sooner, and intimated that he thought him in very imminent danger. Mr Allworthy, who had settled all his affairs in this world, and was as well prepared as it is possible for human nature to be for the other, received this information with the utmost calmness and unconcern. He could, indeed, whenever he laid himself down to rest, say with Cato in the tragical poem—

Let guilt or fear

Disturb man's rest: Cato knows neither of them;
Indifferent in his choice to sleep or die.

In reality, he could say this with ten times more reason and confidence than Cato, or any other proud fellow among the antient or modern heroes; for he was not only devoid of fear, but might be considered as a faithful labourer, when at the end of harvest he is summoned to receive his reward at the hands of a bountiful master.

The good man gave immediate orders for all his family to be summoned round him. None of these were then abroad, but Mrs Blifil, who had been some time in London, and Mr Jones, whom the reader hath just parted from at Mr Western's, and who received this summons just as Sophia had left him.

The news of Mr Allworthy's danger (for the servant told him he was dying) drove all thoughts of love out of his head. He hurried instantly into the chariot which was sent for him, and ordered the coachman to drive with all imaginable haste; nor did the idea of Sophia, I believe, once occur to him on the way.

And now the whole family, namely, Mr Blifil, Mr Jones, Mr Thwackum, Mr Square, and some of the servants (for such were Mr Allworthy's orders) being all assembled round his bed, the good man sat up in it, and was beginning to speak, when Blifil fell to blubbering, and began to express very loud and bitter lamentations. Upon this Mr Allworthy shook him by the hand, and said, "Do not sorrow thus, my dear nephew, at the most ordinary of all human occurrences. When misfortunes befal our friends we are justly grieved; for those are accidents which might often have been avoided, and which may seem to render the lot of one man more peculiarly unhappy than that of others; but death is certainly unavoidable, and is that common lot in which alone the fortunes of all men agree: nor is the time when this happens to us very material. If the wisest of men hath compared life to a span, surely we may be allowed to consider it as a day. It is my fate to leave it in the evening; but those who are taken away earlier have only lost a few hours, at the best little worth lamenting, and much oftener hours of labour and fatigue, of pain and sorrow. One of the Roman poets, I remember, likens our leaving life to our departure from a feast;—a thought which hath often occurred to me when I have seen men struggling to protract an entertainment, and to enjoy the company of their friends a few moments longer. Alas! how short is the most protracted of such enjoyments! how immaterial the difference between him who retires the soonest, and him who stays the latest! This is seeing life in the best view, and this unwillingness to quit our friends is the most amiable motive from which we can derive the fear of death; and yet the longest enjoyment which we can hope for of this kind is of so trivial a duration, that it is to a wise man truly contemptible. Few men, I own, think in this manner; for, indeed, few men think of death till they are in its jaws. However gigantic and terrible an object this may appear when it approaches them, they are nevertheless incapable of seeing it at any distance; nay, though they have been ever so much alarmed and frightened when they have apprehended themselves in danger of dying, they are no sooner cleared from this apprehension than even the fears of it are erased from their minds. But, alas! he who escapes from death is not pardoned; he is only reprieved, and reprieved to a short day.

"Grieve, therefore, no more, my dear child, on this occasion: an event which may happen every hour; which every element, nay, almost every particle of matter that surrounds us is capable of producing, and which must and will most unavoidably reach us all at last, ought neither to occasion our surprize nor our lamentation.

"My physician having acquainted me (which I take very kindly of him) that I am in danger of leaving you all very shortly, I have determined to say a few words to you at this our parting, before my distemper, which I find grows very fast upon me, puts it out of my power.

"But I shall waste my strength too much. I intended to speak concerning my will, which, though I have settled long ago, I think proper to mention such heads of it as concern any of you, that I may have the comfort of perceiving you are all satisfied with the provision I have there made for you.

"Nephew Blifil, I leave you the heir to my whole estate, except only £500 a-year, which is to revert to you after the death of your mother, and except one other estate of £500 a-year, and the sum of £6000, which I have bestowed in the following manner:

"The estate of £500 a-year I have given to you, Mr Jones: and as I know the inconvenience which attends the want of ready money, I have added £1000 in specie. In this I know not whether I have exceeded or fallen short of your expectation. Perhaps you will think I have given you too little, and the world will be as ready to condemn me for giving you too much; but the latter censure I despise; and as to the former, unless you should entertain that common error which I have often heard in my life pleaded as an excuse for a total want of charity, namely, that instead of raising gratitude by voluntary acts of bounty, we are apt to raise demands, which of all others are the most boundless and most difficult to satisfy.—Pardon me the bare mention of this; I will not suspect any such thing."

Jones flung himself at his benefactor's feet, and taking eagerly hold of his hand, assured him his goodness to him, both now and all other times, had so infinitely exceeded not only his merit but his hopes, that no words could express his sense of it. "And I assure you, sir," said he, "your present generosity hath left me no other concern than for the present melancholy occasion. Oh, my friend, my father!" Here his words choaked him, and he turned away to hide a tear which was starting from his eyes.

Allworthy then gently squeezed his hand, and proceeded thus: "I am convinced, my child, that you have much goodness, generosity, and honour, in your temper: if you will add prudence and religion to these, you must be happy; for the three former qualities, I admit, make you worthy of happiness, but they are the latter only which will put you in possession of it.

"One thousand pound I have given to you, Mr Thwackum; a sum I am convinced which greatly exceeds your desires, as well as your wants. However, you will receive it as a memorial of my friendship; and whatever superfluities may redound to you, that piety which you so rigidly maintain will instruct you how to dispose of them.

"A like sum, Mr Square, I have bequeathed to you. This, I hope, will enable you to pursue your profession with better success than hitherto. I have often observed with concern, that distress is more apt to excite contempt than commiseration, especially among men of business, with whom poverty is understood to indicate want of ability. But the little I have been able to leave you will extricate you from those difficulties with which you have formerly struggled; and then I doubt not but you will meet with sufficient prosperity to supply what a man of your philosophical temper will require.

"I find myself growing faint, so I shall refer you to my will for my disposition of the residue. My servants will there find some tokens to remember me by; and there are a few charities which, I trust, my executors will see faithfully performed. Bless you all. I am setting out a little before you."—

Here a footman came hastily into the room, and said there was an attorney from Salisbury who had a particular message, which he said he must communicate to Mr Allworthy himself: that he seemed in a violent hurry, and protested he had so much business to do, that, if he could cut himself into four quarters, all would not be sufficient.

"Go, child," said Allworthy to Blifil, "see what the gentleman wants. I am not able to do any business now, nor can he have any with me, in which you are not at present more concerned than myself. Besides, I really am—I am incapable of seeing any one at present, or of any longer attention." He then saluted them all, saying, perhaps he should be able to see them again, but he should be now glad to compose himself a little, finding that he had too much exhausted his spirits in discourse.

Some of the company shed tears at their parting; and even the philosopher Square wiped his eyes, albeit unused to the melting mood. As to Mrs Wilkins, she dropt her pearls as fast as the Arabian trees their medicinal gums; for this was a ceremonial which that gentlewoman never omitted on a proper occasion.

After this Mr Allworthy again laid himself down on his pillow, and endeavoured to compose himself to rest.

CHAPTER VIII.

Containing matter rather natural than pleasing.

Besides grief for her master, there was another source for that briny stream which so plentifully rose above the two mountainous cheek-bones of the housekeeper. She was no sooner retired, than she began to mutter to herself in the following pleasant strain: "Sure master might have made some difference, methinks, between me and the other servants. I suppose he hath left me mourning; but, i'fackins! if that be all, the devil shall wear it for him, for me. I'd have his worship know I am no beggar. I have saved five hundred pound in his service, and after all to be used in this manner.—It is a fine encouragement to servants to be honest; and to be sure, if I have taken a little something now and then, others have taken ten times as much; and now we are all put in a lump together. If so be that it be so, the legacy may go to the devil with him that gave it. No, I won't give it up neither, because that will please some folks. No, I'll buy the gayest gown I can get, and dance over the old curmudgeon's grave in it. This is my reward for taking his part so often, when all the country have cried shame of him, for breeding up his bastard in that manner; but he is going now where he must pay for all. It would have become him better to have repented of his sins on his deathbed, than to glory in them, and give away his estate out of his own family to a misbegotten child. Found in his bed, forsooth! a pretty story! ay, ay, those that hide know where to find. Lord forgive him! I warrant he hath many more bastards to answer for, if the truth was known. One comfort is, they will all be known where he is a going now.—`The servants will find some token to remember me by.' Those were the very words; I shall never forget them, if I was to live a thousand years. Ay, ay, I shall remember you for huddling me among the servants. One would have thought he might have mentioned my name as well as that of Square; but he is a gentleman forsooth, though he had not cloths on his back when he came hither first. Marry come up with such gentlemen! though he hath lived here this many years, I don't believe there is arrow a servant in the house ever saw the colour of his money. The devil shall wait upon such a gentleman for me." Much more of the like kind she muttered to herself; but this taste shall suffice to the reader.

Neither Thwackum nor Square were much better satisfied with their legacies. Though they breathed not their resentment so loud, yet from the discontent which appeared in their countenances, as well as from the following dialogue, we collect that no great pleasure reigned in their minds.

About an hour after they had left the sick-room, Square met Thwackum in the hall and accosted him thus: "Well, sir, have you heard any news of your friend since we parted from him?"—"If you mean Mr Allworthy," answered Thwackum, "I think you might rather give him the appellation of your friend; for he seems to me to have deserved that title."—"The title is as good on your side," replied Square, "for his bounty, such as it is, hath been equal to both."—"I should not have mentioned it first," cries Thwackum, "but since you begin, I must inform you I am of a different opinion. There is a wide distinction between voluntary favours and rewards. The duty I have done in his family, and the care I have taken in the education of his two boys, are services for which some men might have expected a greater return. I would not have you imagine I am therefore dissatisfied; for St Paul hath taught me to be content with the little I have. Had the modicum been less, I should have known my duty. But though the Scriptures obliges me to remain contented, it doth not enjoin me to shut my eyes to my own merit, nor restrain me from seeing when I am injured by an unjust comparison."—"Since you provoke me," returned Square, "that injury is done to me; nor did I ever imagine Mr Allworthy had held my friendship so light, as to put me in balance with one who received his wages. I know to what it is owing; it proceeds from those narrow principles which you have been so long endeavouring to infuse into him, in contempt of everything which is great and noble. The beauty and loveliness of friendship is too strong for dim eyes, nor can it be perceived by any other medium than that unerring rule of right, which you have so often endeavoured to ridicule, that you have perverted your friend's understanding."—"I wish," cries Thwackum, in a rage, "I wish, for the sake of his soul, your damnable doctrines have not perverted his faith. It is to this I impute his present behaviour, so unbecoming a Christian. Who but an atheist could think of leaving the world without having first made up his account? without confessing his sins, and receiving that absolution which he knew he had one in the house duly authorized to give him? He will feel the want of these necessaries when it is too late, when he is arrived at that place where there is wailing and gnashing of teeth. It is then he will find in what mighty stead that heathen goddess, that virtue, which you and all other deists of the age adore, will stand him. He will then summon his priest, when there is none to be found, and will lament the want of that absolution, without which no sinner can be safe."—"If it be so material," says Square, "why don't you present it him of your own accord?" "It hath no virtue," cries Thwackum, "but to those who have sufficient grace to require it. But why do I talk thus to a heathen and an unbeliever? It is you that taught him this lesson, for which you have been well rewarded in this world, as I doubt not your disciple will soon be in the other."—"I know not what you mean by reward," said Square; "but if you hint at that pitiful memorial of our friendship, which he hath thought fit to bequeath me, I despise it; and nothing but the unfortunate situation of my circumstances should prevail on me to accept it."

The physician now arrived, and began to inquire of the two disputants, how we all did above-stairs? "In a miserable way," answered Thwackum. "It is no more than I expected," cries the doctor: "but pray what symptoms have appeared since I left you?"—"No good ones, I am afraid," replied Thwackum: "after what past at our departure, I think there were little hopes." The bodily physician, perhaps, misunderstood the curer of souls; and before they came to an explanation, Mr Blifil came to them with a most melancholy countenance, and acquainted them that he brought sad news, that his mother was dead at Salisbury; that she had been seized on the road home with the gout in her head and stomach, which had carried her off in a few hours. "Good-lack-a-day!" says the doctor. "One cannot answer for events; but I wish I had been at hand, to have been called in. The gout is a distemper which it is difficult to treat; yet I have been remarkably successful in it." Thwackum and Square both condoled with Mr Blifil for the loss of his mother, which the one advised him to bear like a man, and the other like a Christian. The young gentleman said he knew very well we were all mortal, and he would endeavour to submit to his loss as well as he could. That he could not, however, help complaining a little against the peculiar severity of his fate, which brought the news of so great a calamity to him by surprize, and that at a time when he hourly expected the severest blow he was capable of feeling from the malice of fortune. He said, the present occasion would put to the test those excellent rudiments which he had learnt from Mr Thwackum and Mr Square; and it would be entirely owing to them, if he was enabled to survive such misfortunes.

It was now debated whether Mr Allworthy should be informed of the death of his sister. This the doctor violently opposed; in which, I believe, the whole college would agree with him: but Mr Blifil said, he had received such positive and repeated orders from his uncle, never to keep any secret from him for fear of the disquietude which it might give him, that he durst not think of disobedience, whatever might be the consequence. He said, for his part, considering the religious and philosophic temper of his uncle, he could not agree with the doctor in his apprehensions. He was therefore resolved to communicate it to him: for if his uncle recovered (as he heartily prayed he might) he knew he would never forgive an endeavour to keep a secret of this kind from him.

The physician was forced to submit to these resolutions, which the two other learned gentlemen very highly commended. So together moved Mr Blifil and the doctor toward the sick-room; where the physician first entered, and approached the bed, in order to feel his patient's pulse, which he had no sooner done, than he declared he was much better; that the last application had succeeded to a miracle, and had brought the fever to intermit: so that, he said, there appeared now to be as little danger as he had before apprehended there were hopes.

To say the truth, Mr Allworthy's situation had never been so bad as the great caution of the doctor had represented it: but as a wise general never despises his enemy, however inferior that enemy's force may be, so neither doth a wise physician ever despise a distemper, however inconsiderable. As the former preserves the same strict discipline, places the same guards, and employs the same scouts, though the enemy be never so weak; so the latter maintains the same gravity of countenance, and shakes his head with the same significant air, let the distemper be never so trifling. And both, among many other good ones, may assign this solid reason for their conduct, that by these means the greater glory redounds to them if they gain the victory, and the less disgrace if by any unlucky accident they should happen to be conquered.

Mr Allworthy had no sooner lifted up his eyes, and thanked Heaven for these hopes of his recovery, than Mr Blifil drew near, with a very dejected aspect, and having applied his handkerchief to his eye, either to wipe away his tears, or to do as Ovid somewhere expresses himself on another occasion

Si nullus erit, tamen excute nullum,

If there be none, then wipe away that none,

he communicated to his uncle what the reader hath been just before acquainted with.

Allworthy received the news with concern, with patience, and with resignation. He dropt a tender tear, then composed his countenance, and at last cried, "The Lord's will be done in everything."

He now enquired for the messenger; but Blifil told him it had been impossible to detain him a moment; for he appeared by the great hurry he was in to have some business of importance on his hands; that he complained of being hurried and driven and torn out of his life, and repeated many times, that if he could divide himself into four quarters, he knew how to dispose of every one.

Allworthy then desired Blifil to take care of the funeral. He said, he would have his sister deposited in his own chapel; and as to the particulars, he left them to his own discretion, only mentioning the person whom he would have employed on this occasion.

CHAPTER IX.

Which, among other things, may serve as a comment on that saying of Aeschines, that "drunkenness shows the mind of a man, as a mirrour reflects his person."

The reader may perhaps wonder at hearing nothing of Mr Jones in the last chapter. In fact, his behaviour was so different from that of the persons there mentioned, that we chose not to confound his name with theirs.

When the good man had ended his speech, Jones was the last who deserted the room. Thence he retired to his own apartment, to give vent to his concern; but the restlessness of his mind would not suffer him to remain long there; he slipped softly therefore to Allworthy's chamber-door, where he listened a considerable time without hearing any kind of motion within, unless a violent snoring, which at last his fears misrepresented as groans. This so alarmed him, that he could not forbear entering the room; where he found the good man in the bed, in a sweet composed sleep, and his nurse snoring in the above mentioned hearty manner, at the bed's feet. He immediately took the only method of silencing this thorough bass, whose music he feared might disturb Mr Allworthy; and then sitting down by the nurse, he remained motionless till Blifil and the doctor came in together and waked the sick man, in order that the doctor might feel his pulse, and that the other might communicate to him that piece of news, which, had Jones been apprized of it, would have had great difficulty of finding its way to Mr Allworthy's ear at such a season.

When he first heard Blifil tell his uncle this story, Jones could hardly contain the wrath which kindled in him at the other's indiscretion, especially as the doctor shook his head, and declared his unwillingness to have the matter mentioned to his patient. But as his passion did not so far deprive him of all use of his understanding, as to hide from him the consequences which any violent expression towards Blifil might have on the sick, this apprehension stilled his rage at the present; and he grew afterwards so satisfied with finding that this news had, in fact, produced no mischief, that he suffered his anger to die in his own bosom, without ever mentioning it to Blifil.

The physician dined that day at Mr Allworthy's; and having after dinner visited his patient, he returned to the company, and told them, that he had now the satisfaction to say, with assurance, that his patient was out of all danger: that he had brought his fever to a perfect intermission, and doubted not by throwing in the bark to prevent its return.

This account so pleased Jones, and threw him into such immoderate excess of rapture, that he might be truly said to be drunk with joy—an intoxication which greatly forwards the effects of wine; and as he was very free too with the bottle on this occasion (for he drank many bumpers to the doctor's health, as well as to other toasts) he became very soon literally drunk.

Jones had naturally violent animal spirits: these being set on float and augmented by the spirit of wine, produced most extravagant effects. He kissed the doctor, and embraced him with the most passionate endearments; swearing that next to Mr Allworthy himself, he loved him of all men living. "Doctor," added he, "you deserve a statue to be erected to you at the public expense, for having preserved a man, who is not only the darling of all good men who know him, but a blessing to society, the glory of his country, and an honour to human nature. D—n me if I don't love him better than my own soul."

"More shame for you," cries Thwackum. "Though I think you have reason to love him, for he hath provided very well for you. And perhaps it might have been better for some folks that he had not lived to see just reason of revoking his gift."

Jones now looking on Thwackum with inconceivable disdain, answered, "And doth thy mean soul imagine that any such considerations could weigh with me? No, let the earth open and swallow her own dirt (if I had millions of acres I would say it) rather than swallow up my dear glorious friend."

Quis desiderio sit pudor aut modus
Tam chari capitis?[1]

The doctor now interposed, and prevented the effects of a wrath which was kindling between Jones and Thwackum; after which the former gave a loose to mirth, sang two or three amorous songs, and fell into every frantic disorder which unbridled joy is apt to inspire; but so far was he from any disposition to quarrel, that he was ten times better humoured, if possible, than when he was sober.

To say truth, nothing is more erroneous than the common observation, that men who are ill-natured and quarrelsome when they are drunk, are very worthy persons when they are sober: for drink, in reality, doth not reverse nature, or create passions in men which did not exist in them before. It takes away the guard of reason, and consequently forces us to produce those symptoms, which many, when sober, have art enough to conceal. It heightens and inflames our passions (generally indeed that passion which is uppermost in our mind), so that the angry temper, the amorous, the generous, the good-humoured, the avaricious, and all other dispositions of men, are in their cups heightened and exposed.

---

[1] "What modesty or measure can set bounds to our desire of so dear a friend?" The word desiderium here cannot be easily translated. It includes our desire of enjoying our friend again, and the grief which attends that desire.

And yet as no nation produces so many drunken quarrels, especially among the lower people, as England (for indeed, with them, to drink and to fight together are almost synonymous terms), I would not, methinks, have it thence concluded, that the English are the worst-natured people alive. Perhaps the love of glory only is at the bottom of this; so that the fair conclusion seems to be, that our countrymen have more of that love, and more of bravery, than any other plebeians. And this the rather, as there is seldom anything ungenerous, unfair, or ill-natured, exercised on these occasions: nay, it is common for the combatants to express good-will for each other even at the time of the conflict; and as their drunken mirth generally ends in a battle, so do most of their battles end in friendship.

But to return to our history. Though Jones had shown no design of giving offence, yet Mr Blifil was highly offended at a behaviour which was so inconsistent with the sober and prudent reserve of his own temper. He bore it too with the greater impatience, as it appeared to him very indecent at this season; "When," as he said, "the house was a house of mourning, on the account of his dear mother; and if it had pleased Heaven to give him some prospect of Mr Allworthy's recovery, it would become them better to express the exultations of their hearts in thanksgiving, than in drunkenness and riots; which were properer methods to encrease the Divine wrath, than to avert it." Thwackum, who had swallowed more liquor than Jones, but without any ill effect on his brain, seconded the pious harangue of Blifil; but Square, for reasons which the reader may probably guess, was totally silent.

Wine had not so totally overpowered Jones, as to prevent his recollecting Mr Blifil's loss, the moment it was mentioned. As no person, therefore, was more ready to confess and condemn his own errors, he offered to shake Mr Blifil by the hand, and begged his pardon, saying, "His excessive joy for Mr Allworthy's recovery had driven every other thought out of his mind."

Blifil scornfully rejected his hand; and with much indignation answered, "It was little to be wondered at, if tragical spectacles made no impression on the blind; but, for his part, he had the misfortune to know who his parents were, and consequently must be affected with their loss."

Jones, who, notwithstanding his good humour, had some mixture of the irascible in his constitution, leaped hastily from his chair, and catching hold of Blifil's collar, cried out, "D—n you for a rascal, do you insult me with the misfortune of my birth?" He accompanied these words with such rough actions, that they soon got the better of Mr Blifil's peaceful temper; and a scuffle immediately ensued, which might have produced mischief, had it not been prevented by the interposition of Thwackum and the physician; for the philosophy of Square rendered him superior to all emotions, and he very calmly smoaked his pipe, as was his custom in all broils, unless when he apprehended some danger of having it broke in his mouth.

The combatants being now prevented from executing present vengeance on each other, betook themselves to the common resources of disappointed rage, and vented their wrath in threats and defiance. In this kind of conflict, Fortune, which, in the personal attack, seemed to incline to Jones, was now altogether as favourable to his enemy.

A truce, nevertheless, was at length agreed on, by the mediation of the neutral parties, and the whole company again sat down at the table; where Jones being prevailed on to ask pardon, and Blifil to give it, peace was restored, and everything seemed *in statu quo*.

But though the quarrel was, in all appearance, perfectly reconciled, the good humour which had been interrupted by it, was by no means restored. All merriment was now at an end, and the subsequent discourse consisted only of grave relations of matters of fact, and of as grave observations upon them; a species of conversation, in which, though there is much of dignity and instruction, there is but little entertainment. As we presume therefore to convey only this last to the reader, we shall pass by whatever was said, till the rest of the company having by degrees dropped off, left only Square and the physician together; at which time the conversation was a little heightened by some comments on what had happened between the two young gentlemen; both of whom the doctor declared to be no better than scoundrels; to which appellation the philosopher, very sagaciously shaking his head, agreed.

CHAPTER X.

Showing the truth of many observations of Ovid, and of other more grave writers, who have proved beyond contradiction, that wine is often the forerunner of incontinency.

Jones retired from the company, in which we have seen him engaged, into the fields, where he intended to cool himself by a walk in the open air before he attended Mr Allworthy. There, whilst he renewed those meditations on his dear Sophia, which the dangerous illness of his friend and benefactor had for some time interrupted, an accident happened, which with sorrow we relate, and with sorrow doubtless will it be read; however, that historic truth to which we profess so inviolable an attachment, obliges us to communicate it to posterity.

It was now a pleasant evening in the latter end of June, when our heroe was walking in a most delicious grove, where the gentle breezes fanning the leaves, together with the sweet trilling of a murmuring stream, and the melodious notes of nightingales, formed altogether the most enchanting harmony. In this scene, so sweetly accommodated to love, he meditated on his dear Sophia. While his wanton fancy roamed unbounded over all her beauties, and his lively imagination painted the charming maid in various ravishing forms, his warm heart melted with tenderness; and at length, throwing himself on the ground, by the side of a gently murmuring brook, he broke forth into the following ejaculation:

"O Sophia, would Heaven give thee to my arms, how blest would be my condition! Curst be that fortune which sets a distance between us. Was I but possessed of thee, one only suit of rags thy whole estate, is there a man on earth whom I would envy! How contemptible would the brightest Circassian beauty, drest in all the jewels of the Indies, appear to my eyes! But why do I mention another woman? Could I think my eyes capable of looking at any other with tenderness, these hands should tear them from my head. No, my Sophia, if cruel fortune separates us for ever, my soul shall doat on thee alone. The chastest constancy will I ever preserve to thy image. Though I should never have possession of thy charming person, still shalt thou alone have possession of my thoughts, my love, my soul. Oh! my fond heart is so wrapt in that tender bosom, that the brightest beauties would for me have no charms, nor would a hermit be colder in their embraces. Sophia, Sophia alone shall be mine. What raptures are in that name! I will engrave it on every tree."

At these words he started up, and beheld—not his Sophia—no, nor a Circassian maid richly and elegantly attired for the grand Signior's seraglio. No; without a gown, in a shift that was somewhat of the coarsest, and none of the cleanest, bedewed likewise with some odoriferous effluvia, the produce of the day's labour, with a pitchfork in her hand, Molly Seagrim approached. Our hero had his penknife in his hand, which he had drawn for the before-mentioned purpose of carving on the bark; when the girl coming near him, cryed out with a smile, "You don't intend to kill me, squire, I hope!"—"Why should you think I would kill you?" answered Jones. "Nay," replied she, "after your cruel usage of me when I saw you last, killing me would, perhaps, be too great kindness for me to expect."

Here ensued a parley, which, as I do not think myself obliged to relate it, I shall omit. It is sufficient that it lasted a full quarter of an hour, at the conclusion of which they retired into the thickest part of the grove.

Some of my readers may be inclined to think this event unnatural. However, the fact is true; and perhaps may be sufficiently accounted for by suggesting, that Jones probably thought one woman better than none, and Molly as probably imagined two men to be better than one. Besides the before-mentioned motive assigned to the present behaviour of Jones, the reader will be likewise pleased to recollect in his favour, that he was not at this time perfect master of that wonderful power of reason, which so well enables grave and wise men to subdue their unruly passions, and to decline any of these prohibited amusements. Wine now had totally subdued this power in Jones. He was, indeed, in a condition, in which, if reason had interposed, though only to advise, she might have received the answer which one Cleostratus gave many years ago to a silly fellow, who asked him, if he was not ashamed to be drunk? "Are not you," said Cleostratus, "ashamed to admonish a drunken man?"—To say the truth, in a court of justice drunkenness must not be an excuse, yet in a court of conscience it is greatly so; and therefore Aristotle, who commends the laws of Pittacus, by which drunken men received double punishment for their crimes, allows there is more of policy than justice in that law. Now, if there are any transgressions pardonable from drunkenness, they are certainly such as Mr Jones was at present guilty of; on which head I could pour forth a vast profusion of learning, if I imagined it would either entertain my reader, or teach him anything more than he knows already. For his sake therefore I shall keep my learning to myself, and return to my history.

It hath been observed, that Fortune seldom doth things by halves. To say truth, there is no end to her freaks whenever she is disposed to gratify or displease. No sooner had our heroe retired with his Dido, but

> *Speluncam* Blifil *dux et divinus eandem*
> *Deveniunt—*

the parson and the young squire, who were taking a serious walk, arrived at the stile which leads into the grove, and the latter caught a view of the lovers just as they were sinking out of sight.

Blifil knew Jones very well, though he was at above a hundred yards' distance, and he was as positive to the sex of his companion, though not to the individual person. He started, blessed himself, and uttered a very solemn ejaculation.

Thwackum expressed some surprize at these sudden emotions, and asked the reason of them. To which Blifil answered, "He was certain he had seen a fellow and wench retire together among the bushes, which he doubted not was with some wicked purpose." As to the name of Jones, he thought proper to conceal it, and why he did so must be left to the judgment of the sagacious reader; for we never chuse to assign motives to the actions of men, when there is any possibility of our being mistaken.

The parson, who was not only strictly chaste in his own person, but a great enemy to the opposite vice in all others, fired at this information. He desired Mr Blifil to conduct him immediately to the place, which as he approached he breathed forth vengeance mixed with lamentations; nor did he refrain from casting some oblique reflections on Mr Allworthy; insinuating that the wickedness of the country was principally owing to the encouragement he had given to vice, by having exerted such kindness to a bastard, and by having mitigated that just and wholesome rigour of the law which allots a very severe punishment to loose wenches.

The way through which our hunters were to pass in pursuit of their game was so beset with briars, that it greatly obstructed their walk, and caused besides such a rustling, that Jones had sufficient warning of their arrival before they could surprize him; nay, indeed, so incapable was Thwackum of concealing his indignation, and such vengeance did he mutter forth every step he took, that this alone must have abundantly satisfied Jones that he was (to use the language of sportsmen) found sitting.

CHAPTER XI.

In which a simile in Mr Pope's period of a mile introduces as bloody a battle as can possibly be fought without the assistance of steel or cold iron.

As in the season of *rutting* (an uncouth phrase, by which the vulgar denote that gentle dalliance, which in the well-wooded[1] forest of Hampshire, passes between lovers of the ferine kind), if, while the lofty-crested stag meditates the amorous sport, a couple of puppies, or any other beasts of hostile note, should wander so near the temple of Venus Ferina that the fair hind should shrink from the place, touched with that somewhat, either of fear or frolic, of nicety or skittishness, with which nature hath bedecked all females, or hath at least instructed them how to put it on; lest, through the indelicacy of males, the Samean mysteries should be pryed into by unhallowed eyes: for, at the celebration of these rites, the female priestess cries out with her in Virgil (who was then, probably, hard at work on such celebration),

—Procul, o procul este, profani;
Proclamat vates, totoque absistite luco.

—Far hence be souls profane,
The sibyl cry'd, and from the grove abstain.—DRYDEN.

If, I say, while these sacred rites, which are in common to *genus omne animantium,* are in agitation between the stag and his mistress, any hostile beasts should venture too near, on the first hint given by the frighted hind, fierce and tremendous rushes forth the stag to the entrance of the thicket; there stands he centinel over his love, stamps the ground with his foot, and with his horns brandished aloft in air, proudly provokes the apprehended foe to combat.

Thus, and more terrible, when he perceived the enemy's approach, leaped forth our heroe. Many a step advanced he forwards, in order to conceal the trembling hind, and, if possible, to secure her retreat. And now Thwackum, having first

---

[1] This is an ambiguous phrase, and may mean either a forest well cloathed with wood, or well stript of it.

darted some livid lightning from his fiery eyes, began to thunder forth, "Fie upon it! Fie upon it! Mr Jones. Is it possible you should be the person?"—"You see," answered Jones, "it is possible I should be here."—"And who," said Thwackum, "is that wicked slut with you?"—"If I have any wicked slut with me," cries Jones, "it is possible I shall not let you know who she is."—"I command you to tell me immediately," says Thwackum: "and I would not have you imagine, young man, that your age, though it hath somewhat abridged the purpose of tuition, hath totally taken away the authority of the master. The relation of the master and scholar is indelible; as, indeed, all other relations are; for they all derive their original from heaven. I would have you think yourself, therefore, as much obliged to obey me now, as when I taught you your first rudiments."—"I believe you would," cries Jones; "but that will not happen, unless you had the same birchen argument to convince me."—"Then I must tell you plainly," said Thwackum, "I am resolved to discover the wicked wretch."—"And I must tell you plainly," returned Jones, "I am resolved you shall not." Thwackum then offered to advance, and Jones laid hold of his arms; which Mr Blifil endeavoured to rescue, declaring, "he would not see his old master insulted."

Jones now finding himself engaged with two, thought it necessary to rid himself of one of his antagonists as soon as possible. He therefore applied to the weakest first; and, letting the parson go, he directed a blow at the young squire's breast, which luckily taking place, reduced him to measure his length on the ground.

Thwackum was so intent on the discovery, that, the moment he found himself at liberty, he stept forward directly into the fern, without any great consideration of what might in the meantime befal his friend; but he had advanced a very few paces into the thicket, before Jones, having defeated Blifil, overtook the parson, and dragged him backward by the skirt of his coat.

This parson had been a champion in his youth, and had won much honour by his fist, both at school and at the university. He had now indeed, for a great number of years, declined the practice of that noble art; yet was his courage full as strong as his faith, and his body no less strong than either. He was moreover, as the reader may perhaps have conceived, somewhat irascible in his nature. When he looked back, therefore, and saw his friend stretched out on the ground, and found himself at the same time so roughly handled by one who had formerly been only passive in all conflicts between them (a circumstance which highly aggravated the whole), his patience at length gave way; he threw himself into a posture of offence; and collecting all his force, attacked Jones in the front with as much impetuosity as he had formerly attacked him in the rear.

Our heroe received the enemy's attack with the most undaunted intrepidity, and his bosom resounded with the blow. This he presently returned with no less violence, aiming likewise at the parson's breast; but he dexterously drove down the fist of Jones, so that it reached only his belly, where two pounds of beef and as many of pudding were then deposited, and whence consequently no hollow sound could proceed. Many lusty blows, much more pleasant as well as easy to have seen, than to read or describe, were given on both sides: at last a violent fall, in which Jones had thrown his knees into Thwackum's breast, so weakened the latter, that victory had been no longer dubious, had not Blifil, who had now recovered his strength, again renewed the fight, and by engaging with Jones, given the parson a moment's time to shake his ears, and to regain his breath.

And now both together attacked our heroe, whose blows did not retain that force with which they had fallen at first, so weakened was he by his combat with Thwackum; for though the pedagogue chose rather to play *solos* on the human instrument, and had been lately used to those only, yet he still retained enough of his antient knowledge to perform his part very well in a *duet*.

The victory, according to modern custom, was like to be decided by numbers, when, on a sudden, a fourth pair of fists appeared in the battle, and immediately paid their compliments to the parson; and the owner of them at the same time crying out, "Are not you ashamed, and be d—n'd to you, to fall two of you upon one?"

The battle, which was of the kind that for distinction's sake is called royal, now raged with the utmost violence during a few minutes; till Blifil being a second time laid sprawling by Jones, Thwackum condescended to apply for quarter to his new antagonist, who was now found to be Mr Western himself; for in the heat of the action none of the combatants had recognized him.

In fact, that honest squire, happening, in his afternoon's walk with some company, to pass through the field where the bloody battle was fought, and having concluded, from seeing three men engaged, that two of them must be on a side, he hastened from his companions, and with more gallantry than policy, espoused the cause of the weaker party. By which generous proceeding he very probably prevented Mr Jones from becoming a victim to the wrath of Thwackum, and to the pious friendship which Blifil bore his old master; for, besides the disadvantage of such odds, Jones had not yet sufficiently recovered the former strength of his broken arm. This reinforcement, however, soon put an end to the action, and Jones with his ally obtained the victory.

CHAPTER XII.

In which is seen a more moving spectacle than all the blood in the bodies of Thwackum and Blifil, and of twenty other such, is capable of producing.

The rest of Mr Western's company were now come up, being just at the instant when the action was over. These were the honest clergyman, whom we have formerly seen at Mr Western's table; Mrs Western, the aunt of Sophia; and lastly, the lovely Sophia herself.

At this time, the following was the aspect of the bloody field. In one place lay on the ground, all pale, and almost breathless, the vanquished Blifil. Near him stood the conqueror Jones, almost covered with blood, part of which was naturally his own, and part had been lately the property of the Reverend Mr Thwackum. In a third place stood the said Thwackum, like King Porus, sullenly submitting to the conqueror. The last figure in the piece was Western the Great, most gloriously forbearing the vanquished foe.

Blifil, in whom there was little sign of life, was at first the principal object of the concern of every one, and particularly of Mrs Western, who had drawn from her pocket a bottle of hartshorn, and was herself about to apply it to his nostrils, when on a sudden the attention of the whole company was diverted from poor Blifil, whose spirit, if it had any such design, might have now taken an opportunity of stealing off to the other world, without any ceremony.

For now a more melancholy and a more lovely object lay motionless before them. This was no other than the charming Sophia herself, who, from the sight of blood, or from fear for her father, or from some other reason, had fallen down in a swoon, before any one could get to her assistance.

Mrs Western first saw her and screamed. Immediately two or three voices cried out, "Miss Western is dead." Hartshorn, water, every remedy was called for, almost at one and the same instant.

The reader may remember, that in our description of this grove we mentioned a murmuring brook, which brook did not come there, as such gentle streams flow through vulgar romances, with no other purpose than to murmur. No! Fortune had decreed to ennoble this little brook with a higher honour than any of those which wash the plains of Arcadia ever deserved.

Jones was rubbing Blifil's temples, for he began to fear he had given him a blow too much, when the words, Miss Western and Dead, rushed at once on his ear. He started up, left Blifil to his fate, and flew to Sophia, whom, while all the rest were running against each other, backward and forward, looking for water in the dry paths, he caught up in his arms, and then ran away with her over the field to the rivulet above mentioned; where, plunging himself into the water, he contrived to besprinkle her face, head, and neck very plentifully.

Happy was it for Sophia that the same confusion which prevented her other friends from serving her, prevented them likewise from obstructing Jones. He had carried her half ways before they knew what he was doing, and he had actually restored her to life before they reached the waterside. She stretched out her arms, opened her eyes, and cried, "Oh! heavens!" just as her father, aunt, and the parson came up.

Jones, who had hitherto held this lovely burthen in his arms, now relinquished his hold; but gave her at the same instant a tender caress, which, had her senses been then perfectly restored, could not have escaped her observation. As she expressed, therefore, no displeasure at this freedom, we suppose she was not sufficiently recovered from her swoon at the time.

This tragical scene was now converted into a sudden scene of joy. In this our heroe was certainly the principal character; for as he probably felt more ecstatic delight in having saved Sophia than she herself received from being saved, so neither were the congratulations paid to her equal to what were conferred on Jones, especially by Mr Western himself, who, after having once or twice embraced his daughter, fell to hugging and kissing Jones. He called him the preserver of Sophia, and declared there was nothing, except her, or his estate, which he would not give him; but upon recollection, he afterwards excepted his fox-hounds, the Chevalier, and Miss Slouch (for so he called his favourite mare).

All fears for Sophia being now removed, Jones became the object of the squire's consideration.—"Come, my lad," says Western, "d'off thy quoat and wash thy feace; for att in a devilish pickle, I promise thee. Come, come, wash thyself, and shat go huome with me; and we'l zee to vind thee another quoat."

Jones immediately complied, threw off his coat, went down to the water, and washed both his face and bosom; for the latter was as much exposed and as bloody as the former. But though the water could clear off the blood, it could not remove the black and blue marks which Thwackum had imprinted on both his face and breast, and which, being discerned by Sophia, drew from her a sigh and a look full of inexpressible tenderness.

Jones received this full in his eyes, and it had infinitely a stronger effect on him than all the contusions which he had received before. An effect, however, widely different; for so soft and balmy was it, that, had all his former blows been stabs, it would for some minutes have prevented his feeling their smart.

The company now moved backwards, and soon arrived where Thwackum had got Mr Blifil again on his legs. Here we cannot suppress a pious wish, that all quarrels were to be decided by those weapons only with which Nature, knowing what is proper for us, hath supplied us; and that cold iron was to be used in digging no bowels but those of the earth. Then would war, the pastime of monarchs, be almost inoffensive, and battles between great armies might be fought at the particular desire of several ladies of quality; who, together with the kings themselves, might be actual spectators of the conflict. Then might the field be this moment well strewed with human carcasses, and the next, the dead men, or infinitely the greatest part of them, might get up, like Mr Bayes's troops, and march off either at the sound of a drum or fiddle, as should be previously agreed on.

I would avoid, if possible, treating this matter ludicrously, lest grave men and politicians, whom I know to be offended at a jest, may cry pish at it; but, in reality, might not a battle be as well decided by the greater number of broken heads, bloody noses, and black eyes, as by the greater heaps of mangled and murdered human bodies? Might not towns be contended for in the same manner? Indeed, this may be thought too detrimental a scheme to the French interest, since they would thus lose the advantage they have over other nations in the superiority of their engineers; but when I consider the gallantry and generosity of that people, I am persuaded they would never decline putting themselves upon a par with their adversary; or, as the phrase is, making themselves his match.

But such reformations are rather to be wished than hoped for: I shall content myself, therefore, with this short hint, and return to my narrative.

Western began now to inquire into the original rise of this quarrel. To which neither Blifil nor Jones gave any answer; but Thwackum said surlily, "I believe the cause is not far off; if you beat the bushes well you may find her."—"Find her?" replied Western: "what! have you been fighting for a wench?"—"Ask the gentleman in his waistcoat there," said Thwackum: "he best knows." "Nay then," cries Western, "it is a wench certainly.—Ah, Tom, Tom, thou art a liquorish dog. But come, gentlemen, be all friends, and go home with me, and make final peace over a bottle." "I ask your pardon, sir," says Thwackum: "it is no such slight matter for a man of my character to be thus injuriously treated, and buffeted by a boy, only because I would have done my duty, in endeavouring to detect and bring to justice a wanton harlot; but, indeed, the principal fault lies in Mr Allworthy and yourself; for if you put the laws in execution, as you ought to do, you will soon rid the country of these vermin."

"I would as soon rid the country of foxes," cries Western. "I think we ought to encourage the recruiting those numbers which we are every day losing in the war.—But where is she? Prithee, Tom, show me." He then began to beat about, in the same language and in the same manner as if he had been beating for a hare; and at last cried out, "Soho! Puss is not far off. Here's her form, upon my soul; I believe I may cry stole away." And indeed so he might; for he had now discovered the place whence the poor girl had, at the beginning of the fray, stolen away, upon as many feet as a hare generally uses in travelling.

Sophia now desired her father to return home; saying she found herself very faint, and apprehended a relapse. The squire immediately complied with his daughter's request (for he was the fondest of parents). He earnestly endeavoured to prevail with the whole company to go and sup with him: but Blifil and Thwackum absolutely refused; the former saying, there were more reasons than he could then mention, why he must decline this honour; and the latter declaring (perhaps rightly) that it was not proper for a person of his function to be seen at any place in his present condition.

Jones was incapable of refusing the pleasure of being with his Sophia; so on he marched with Squire Western and his ladies, the parson bringing up the rear. This had, indeed, offered to tarry with his brother Thwackum, professing his regard for the cloth would not permit him to depart; but Thwackum would not accept the favour, and, with no great civility, pushed him after Mr Western.

Thus ended this bloody fray; and thus shall end the fifth book of this history.

BOOK VI.

CONTAINING ABOUT THREE WEEKS.

CHAPTER I.

Of love.

In our last book we have been obliged to deal pretty much with the passion of love; and in our succeeding book shall be forced to handle this subject still more largely. It may not therefore in this place be improper to apply ourselves to the examination of that modern doctrine, by which certain philosophers, among many other wonderful discoveries, pretend to have found out, that there is no such passion in the human breast.

Whether these philosophers be the same with that surprising sect, who are honourably mentioned by the late Dr Swift, as having, by the mere force of genius alone, without the least assistance of any kind of learning, or even reading, discovered that profound and invaluable secret that there is no God; or whether they are not rather the same with those who some years since very much alarmed the world, by showing that there were no such things as virtue or goodness really existing in human nature, and who deduced our best actions from pride, I will not here presume to determine. In reality, I am inclined to suspect, that all these several finders of truth, are the very identical men who are by others called the finders of gold. The method used in both these searches after truth and after gold, being indeed one and the same, viz., the searching, rummaging, and examining into a nasty place; indeed, in the former instances, into the nastiest of all places, A BAD MIND.

But though in this particular, and perhaps in their success, the truth-finder and the gold-finder may very properly be compared together; yet in modesty, surely, there can be no comparison between the two; for who ever heard of a gold-finder that had the impudence or folly to assert, from the ill success of his search, that there was no such thing as gold in the world? whereas the truth-finder, having raked out that jakes, his own mind, and being there capable of tracing no ray of divinity, nor anything virtuous or good, or lovely, or loving, very fairly, honestly, and logically concludes that no such things exist in the whole creation.

To avoid, however, all contention, if possible, with these philosophers, if they will be called so; and to show our own disposition to accommodate matters peaceably between us, we shall here make them some concessions, which may possibly put an end to the dispute.

First, we will grant that many minds, and perhaps those of the philosophers, are entirely free from the least traces of such a passion.

Secondly, that what is commonly called love, namely, the desire of satisfying a voracious appetite with a certain quantity of delicate white human flesh, is by no means that passion for which I here contend. This is indeed more properly hunger; and as no glutton is ashamed to apply the word love to his appetite, and to say he LOVES such and such dishes; so may the lover of this kind, with equal propriety, say, he HUNGERS after such and such women.

Thirdly, I will grant, which I believe will be a most acceptable concession, that this love for which I am an advocate, though it satisfies itself in a much more delicate manner, doth nevertheless seek its own satisfaction as much as the grossest of all our appetites.

And, lastly, that this love, when it operates towards one of a different sex, is very apt, towards its complete gratification, to call in the aid of that hunger which I have mentioned above; and which it is so far from abating, that it heightens all its delights to a degree scarce imaginable by those who have never been susceptible of any other emotions than what have proceeded from appetite alone.

In return to all these concessions, I desire of the philosophers to grant, that there is in some (I believe in many) human breasts a kind and benevolent disposition, which is gratified by contributing to the happiness of others. That in this gratification alone, as in friendship, in parental and filial affection, as indeed in general philanthropy, there is a great and exquisite delight. That if we will not call such disposition love, we have no name for it. That though the pleasures arising from such pure love may be heightened and sweetened by the assistance of amorous desires, yet the former can subsist alone, nor are they destroyed by the intervention of the latter. Lastly, that esteem and gratitude are the proper motives to love, as youth and beauty are to desire, and, therefore, though such desire may naturally cease, when age or sickness overtakes its object; yet these can have no effect on love, nor ever shake or remove, from a good mind, that sensation or passion which hath gratitude and esteem for its basis.

To deny the existence of a passion of which we often see manifest instances, seems to be very strange and absurd; and can indeed proceed only from that self-admonition which we have mentioned above: but how unfair is this! Doth the man who recognizes in his own heart no traces of avarice or ambition, conclude, therefore, that there are no such passions in human nature? Why will we not modestly observe the same rule in judging of the good, as well as the evil of others? Or why, in any case, will we, as Shakespear phrases it, "put the world in our own person?"

Predominant vanity is, I am afraid, too much concerned here. This is one instance of that adulation which we bestow on our own minds, and this almost universally. For there is scarce any man, how much soever he may despise the character of a flatterer, but will condescend in the meanest manner to flatter himself.

To those therefore I apply for the truth of the above observations, whose own minds can bear testimony to what I have advanced.

Examine your heart, my good reader, and resolve whether you do believe these matters with me. If you do, you may now proceed to their exemplification in the following pages: if you do not, you have, I assure you, already read more than you have understood; and it would be wiser to pursue your business, or your pleasures (such as they are), than to throw away any more of your time in reading what you can neither taste nor comprehend. To treat of the effects of love to you, must be as absurd as to discourse on colours to a man born blind; since possibly your idea of love may be as absurd as that which we are told such blind man once entertained of the colour scarlet; that colour seemed to him to be very much like the sound of a trumpet: and love probably may, in your opinion, very greatly resemble a dish of soup, or a surloin of roast-beef.

CHAPTER II.

The character of Mrs Western. Her great learning and knowledge of the world, and an instance of the deep penetration which she derived from those advantages.

The reader hath seen Mr Western, his sister, and daughter, with young Jones, and the parson, going together to Mr Western's house, where the greater part of the company spent the evening with much joy and festivity. Sophia was indeed the only grave person; for as to Jones, though love had now gotten entire possession of his heart, yet the pleasing reflection on Mr Allworthy's recovery, and the presence of his mistress, joined to some tender looks which she now and then could not refrain from giving him, so elevated our heroe, that he joined the mirth of the other three, who were perhaps as good-humoured people as any in the world.

Sophia retained the same gravity of countenance the next morning at breakfast; whence she retired likewise earlier than usual, leaving her father and aunt together. The squire took no notice of this change in his daughter's disposition. To say the truth, though he was somewhat of a politician, and had been twice a candidate in the country interest at an election, he was a man of no great observation. His sister was a lady of a different turn. She had lived about the court, and had seen the world. Hence she had acquired all that knowledge which the said world usually communicates; and was a perfect mistress of manners, customs, ceremonies, and fashions. Nor did her erudition stop here. She had considerably improved her mind by study; she had not only read all the modern plays, operas, oratorios, poems, and romances—in all which she was a critic; but had gone through Rapin's History of England, Eachard's Roman History, and many French *Mémoires pour servir à l'Histoire*: to these she had added most of the political pamphlets and journals published within the last twenty years. From which she had attained a very competent skill in politics, and could discourse very learnedly on the affairs of Europe. She was, moreover, excellently well skilled in the doctrine of amour, and knew better than anybody who and who were together; a knowledge which she the more easily attained, as her pursuit of it was never diverted by any affairs of her own; for either she had no inclinations, or they had never been solicited; which last is indeed very probable; for her masculine person, which was near six foot high, added to her manner and learning, possibly prevented the other sex from regarding her, notwithstanding her petticoats, in the light of a woman. However, as she had considered the matter scientifically, she perfectly well knew, though she had never practised them, all the arts which fine ladies use when they desire to give encouragement, or to conceal liking, with all the long appendage of smiles, ogles, glances, &c., as they are at present practised in the beau-monde. To sum the whole, no species of disguise or affectation had escaped her notice; but as to the plain simple workings of honest nature, as she had never seen any such, she could know but little of them.

By means of this wonderful sagacity, Mrs Western had now, as she thought, made a discovery of something in the mind of Sophia. The first hint of this she took from the behaviour of the young lady in the field of battle; and the suspicion which she then conceived, was greatly corroborated by some observations which she had made that evening and the next morning. However, being greatly cautious to avoid being found in a mistake, she carried the secret a whole fortnight in her bosom, giving only some oblique hints, by simpering, winks, nods, and now and then dropping an obscure word, which indeed sufficiently alarmed Sophia, but did not at all affect her brother.

Being at length, however, thoroughly satisfied of the truth of her observation, she took an opportunity, one morning, when she was alone with her brother, to interrupt one of his whistles in the following manner:—

"Pray, brother, have you not observed something very extraordinary in my niece lately?"—"No, not I," answered Western; "is anything the matter with the girl?"—"I think there is," replied she; "and something of much consequence too."—"Why, she doth not complain of anything," cries Western; "and she hath had the small-pox."—"Brother," returned she, "girls are liable to other distempers besides the small-pox, and sometimes possibly to much worse." Here Western interrupted her with much earnestness, and begged her, if anything ailed his daughter, to acquaint him immediately; adding, "she knew he loved her more than his own soul, and that he would send to the world's end for the best physician to her." "Nay, nay," answered she, smiling, "the distemper is not so terrible; but I believe, brother, you are convinced I know the world, and I promise you I was never more deceived in my life, if my niece be not most desperately in love."—"How! in love!" cries Western, in a passion; "in love, without acquainting me! I'll disinherit her; I'll turn her out of doors, stark naked, without a farthing. Is all my kindness vor 'ur, and vondness o'ur come to this, to fall in love without asking me leave?"—"But you will not," answered Mrs Western, "turn this daughter, whom you love better than your own soul, out of doors, before you know whether you shall approve her choice. Suppose she should have fixed on the very person whom you yourself would wish, I hope you would not be angry then?"—"No, no," cries Western, "that would make a difference. If she marries the man I would ha' her, she may love whom she pleases, I shan't trouble my head about that." "That is spoken," answered the sister, "like a sensible man; but I believe the very person she hath chosen would be the very person you would choose for her. I will disclaim all knowledge of the world, if it is not so; and I believe, brother, you will allow I have some."—"Why, lookee, sister," said Western, "I do believe you have as much as any woman; and to be sure those are women's matters. You know I don't love to hear you talk about politics; they belong to us, and petticoats should not meddle: but come, who is the man?"—"Marry!" said she, "you may find him out yourself if you please. You, who are so great a politician, can be at no great loss. The judgment which can penetrate into the cabinets of princes, and discover the secret springs which move the great state wheels in all the political machines of Europe, must surely, with very little difficulty, find out what passes in the rude uninformed mind of a girl."—"Sister," cries the squire, "I have often warn'd you not to talk the court gibberish to me. I tell you, I don't understand the lingo: but I can read a journal, or the *London Evening Post.* Perhaps, indeed, there may be now and tan a verse which I can't make much of, because half the letters are left out; yet I know very well what is meant by that, and that our affairs don't go so well as they should do, because of bribery and corruption."—"I pity your country ignorance from my heart," cries the lady.—"Do you?" answered Western; "and I pity your town learning; I had rather be anything than a courtier, and a Presbyterian, and a Hanoverian too, as some people, I believe, are."—"If you mean me," answered she, "you know I am a woman, brother; and it signifies nothing what I am. Besides—"—"I do know you are a woman," cries the squire, "and it's well for thee that art one; if hadst been a man, I promise thee I had lent thee a flick long ago."—"Ay, there," said she, "in that flick lies all your fancied superiority. Your bodies, and not your brains, are stronger than ours. Believe me, it is well for you that you are able to beat us; or, such is the superiority of our understanding, we should make all of you what the brave, and wise, and witty, and polite are already—our slaves."—"I am glad I know your mind," answered the squire. "But we'll talk more of this matter another time. At present, do tell me what man is it you mean about my daughter?"—"Hold a moment," said she, "while I digest that sovereign contempt I have for your sex; or else I ought to be angry too with you. There—I have made a shift to gulp it down. And now, good politic sir, what think you of Mr Blifil? Did she not faint away on seeing him lie breathless on the ground? Did she not, after he was recovered, turn pale again the moment we came up to that part of the field where he stood? And pray what else should be the occasion of all her melancholy that night at supper, the next morning, and indeed ever since?"—"'Fore George!" cries the squire, "now you mind me on't, I remember it all. It is certainly so, and I am glad on't with all my heart. I knew Sophy was a good girl, and would not fall in love to make me angry. I was never more rejoiced in my life; for nothing can lie so handy together as our two estates. I had this matter in my head some time ago: for certainly the two estates are in a manner joined together in matrimony already, and it would be a thousand pities to part them. It is true, indeed, there be larger estates in the kingdom, but not in this county, and I had rather bate something, than marry my daughter among strangers and foreigners. Besides, most o' zuch great estates be in the hands of lords, and I heate the very name of *themmun.* Well but, sister, what would you advise me to do; for I tell you women know these matters better than we do?"—"Oh, your humble servant, sir," answered the lady: "we are obliged to you for allowing us a capacity in anything. Since you are pleased, then, most politic sir, to ask my advice, I think you may propose the match to Allworthy yourself. There is no indecorum in the proposal's coming from the parent of either side. King Alcinous, in Mr Pope's Odyssey, offers his daughter to Ulysses. I need not caution so politic a person not to say that your daughter is in love; that would indeed be against all rules."—"Well," said the squire, "I will propose it; but I shall certainly lend un a flick, if he should refuse me." "Fear not," cries Mrs Western; "the match is too advantageous to be refused." "I don't know that," answered the squire: "Allworthy is a queer b—ch, and money hath no effect o'un." "Brother," said the lady, "your politics astonish me. Are you really to be imposed on by professions? Do you think Mr Allworthy hath more contempt for money than other men because he professes more? Such credulity would better become one of us weak women, than that wise sex which heaven hath formed for politicians. Indeed, brother, you would make a fine plenipo to negotiate with the French. They would soon persuade you, that they take towns out of mere defensive principles." "Sister," answered the squire, with much scorn, "let your friends at court answer for the towns taken; as you are a woman, I shall lay no blame upon you; for I suppose they are wiser than to trust women with secrets." He accompanied this with so sarcastical a laugh, that Mrs Western could bear no longer. She had been all this time fretted in a tender part (for she was indeed very deeply skilled in these matters, and very violent in them), and therefore, burst forth in a rage, declared her brother to be both a clown and a blockhead, and that she would stay no longer in his house.

The squire, though perhaps he had never read Machiavel, was, however, in many points, a perfect politician. He strongly held all those wise tenets, which are so well inculcated in that Politico-Peripatetic school of Exchange-alley. He knew the just value and only use of money, viz., to lay it up. He was likewise well skilled in the exact value of reversions, expectations, &c., and had often considered the amount of his sister's fortune, and the chance which he or his posterity had of inheriting it. This he was infinitely too wise to sacrifice to a trifling resentment. When he found, therefore, he had carried matters too far, he began to think of reconciling them; which was no very difficult task, as the lady had great affection for her brother, and still greater for her niece; and though too susceptible of an affront offered to her skill in politics, on which she much valued herself, was a woman of a very extraordinary good and sweet disposition.

Having first, therefore, laid violent hands on the horses, for whose escape from the stable no place but the window was left open, he next applied himself to his sister; softened and soothed her, by unsaying all he had said, and by assertions directly contrary to those which had incensed her. Lastly, he summoned the eloquence of Sophia to his assistance, who, besides a most graceful and winning address, had the advantage of being heard with great favour and partiality by her aunt.

The result of the whole was a kind smile from Mrs Western, who said, "Brother, you are absolutely a perfect Croat; but as those have their use in the army of the empress queen, so you likewise have some good in you. I will therefore once more sign a treaty of peace with you, and see that you do not infringe it on your side; at least, as you are so excellent a politician, I may expect you will keep your leagues, like the French, till your interest calls upon you to break them."

CHAPTER III.

Containing two defiances to the critics.

The squire having settled matters with his sister, as we have seen in the last chapter, was so greatly impatient to communicate the proposal to Allworthy, that Mrs Western had the utmost difficulty to prevent him from visiting that gentleman in his sickness, for this purpose.

Mr Allworthy had been engaged to dine with Mr Western at the time when he was taken ill. He was therefore no sooner discharged out of the custody of physic, but he thought (as was usual with him on all occasions, both the highest and the lowest) of fulfilling his engagement.

In the interval between the time of the dialogue in the last chapter, and this day of public entertainment, Sophia had, from certain obscure hints thrown out by her aunt, collected some apprehension that the sagacious lady suspected her passion for Jones. She now resolved to take this opportunity of wiping out all such suspicion, and for that purpose to put an entire constraint on her behaviour.

First, she endeavoured to conceal a throbbing melancholy heart with the utmost sprightliness in her countenance, and the highest gaiety in her manner. Secondly, she addressed her whole discourse to Mr Blifil, and took not the least notice of poor Jones the whole day.

The squire was so delighted with this conduct of his daughter, that he scarce eat any dinner, and spent almost his whole time in watching opportunities of conveying signs of his approbation by winks and nods to his sister; who was not at first altogether so pleased with what she saw as was her brother.

In short, Sophia so greatly overacted her part, that her aunt was at first staggered, and began to suspect some affectation in her niece; but as she was herself a woman of great art, so she soon attributed this to extreme art in Sophia. She remembered the many hints she had given her niece concerning her being in love, and imagined the young lady had taken this way to rally her out of her opinion, by an overacted civility: a notion that was greatly corroborated by the excessive gaiety with which the whole was accompanied. We cannot here avoid remarking, that this conjecture would have been better founded had Sophia lived ten years in the air of Grosvenor Square, where young ladies do learn a wonderful knack of rallying and playing with that passion, which is a mighty serious thing in woods and groves an hundred miles distant from London.

To say the truth, in discovering the deceit of others, it matters much that our own art be wound up, if I may use the expression, in the same key with theirs: for very artful men sometimes miscarry by fancying others wiser, or, in other words, greater knaves, than they really are. As this observation is pretty deep, I will illustrate it by the following short story. Three countrymen were pursuing a Wiltshire thief through Brentford. The simplest of them seeing "The Wiltshire House," written under a sign, advised his companions to enter it, for there most probably they would find their countryman. The second, who was wiser, laughed at this simplicity; but the third, who was wiser still, answered, "Let us go in, however, for he may think we should not suspect him of going amongst his own countrymen." They accordingly went in and searched the house, and by that means missed overtaking the thief, who was at that time but a little way before them; and who, as they all knew, but had never once reflected, could not read.

The reader will pardon a digression in which so invaluable a secret is communicated, since every gamester will agree how necessary it is to know exactly the play of another, in order to countermine him. This will, moreover, afford a reason why the wiser man, as is often seen, is the bubble of the weaker, and why many simple and innocent characters are so generally misunderstood and misrepresented; but what is most material, this will account for the deceit which Sophia put on her politic aunt.

Dinner being ended, and the company retired into the garden, Mr Western, who was thoroughly convinced of the certainty of what his sister had told him, took Mr Allworthy aside, and very bluntly proposed a match between Sophia and young Mr Blifil.

Mr Allworthy was not one of those men whose hearts flutter at any unexpected and sudden tidings of worldly profit. His mind was, indeed, tempered with that philosophy which becomes a man and a Christian. He affected no absolute superiority to all pleasure and pain, to all joy and grief; but was not at the same time to be discomposed and ruffled by every accidental blast, by every smile or frown of fortune. He received, therefore, Mr Western's proposal without any visible emotion, or without any alteration of countenance. He said the alliance was such as he sincerely wished; then launched forth into a very just encomium on the young lady's merit; acknowledged the offer to be advantageous in point of fortune; and after thanking Mr Western for the good opinion he had professed of his nephew, concluded, that if the young people liked each other, he should be very desirous to complete the affair.

Western was a little disappointed at Mr Allworthy's answer, which was not so warm as he expected. He treated the doubt whether the young people might like one another with great contempt, saying, "That parents were the best judges of proper matches for their children: that for his part he should insist on the most resigned obedience from his daughter: and if any young fellow could refuse such a bed-fellow, he was his humble servant, and hoped there was no harm done."

Allworthy endeavoured to soften this resentment by many eulogiums on Sophia, declaring he had no doubt but that Mr Blifil would very gladly receive the offer; but all was ineffectual; he could obtain no other answer from the squire but—"I say no more—I humbly hope there's no harm done—that's all." Which words he repeated at least a hundred times before they parted.

Allworthy was too well acquainted with his neighbour to be offended at this behaviour; and though he was so averse to the rigour which some parents exercise on their children in the article of marriage, that he had resolved never to force his nephew's inclinations, he was nevertheless much pleased with the prospect of this union; for the whole country resounded the praises of Sophia, and he had himself greatly admired the uncommon endowments of both her mind and person.

To which I believe we may add, the consideration of her vast fortune, which, though he was too sober to be intoxicated with it, he was too sensible to despise.

And here, in defiance of all the barking critics in the world, I must and will introduce a digression concerning true wisdom, of which Mr Allworthy was in reality as great a pattern as he was of goodness.

True wisdom then, notwithstanding all which Mr Hogarth's poor poet may have writ against riches, and in spite of all which any rich well-fed divine may have preached against pleasure, consists not in the contempt of either of these. A man may have as much wisdom in the possession of an affluent fortune, as any beggar in the streets; or may enjoy a handsome wife or a hearty friend, and still remain as wise as any sour popish recluse, who buries all his social faculties, and starves his belly while he well lashes his back.

To say truth, the wisest man is the likeliest to possess all worldly blessings in an eminent degree; for as that moderation which wisdom prescribes is the surest way to useful wealth, so can it alone qualify us to taste many pleasures. The wise man gratifies every appetite and every passion, while the fool sacrifices all the rest to pall and satiate one.

It may be objected, that very wise men have been notoriously avaricious. I answer, Not wise in that instance. It may likewise be said, That the wisest men have been in their youth immoderately fond of pleasure. I answer, They were not wise then.

Wisdom, in short, whose lessons have been represented as so hard to learn by those who never were at her school, only teaches us to extend a simple maxim universally known and followed even in the lowest life, a little farther than that life carries it. And this is, not to buy at too dear a price.

Now, whoever takes this maxim abroad with him into the grand market of the world, and constantly applies it to honours, to riches, to pleasures, and to every other commodity which that market affords, is, I will venture to affirm, a wise man, and must be so acknowledged in the worldly sense of the word; for he makes the best of bargains, since in reality he purchases everything at the price only of a little trouble, and carries home all the good things I have mentioned, while he keeps his health, his innocence, and his reputation, the common prices which are paid for them by others, entire and to himself.

From this moderation, likewise, he learns two other lessons, which complete his character. First, never to be intoxicated when he hath made the best bargain, nor dejected when the market is empty, or when its commodities are too dear for his purchase.

But I must remember on what subject I am writing, and not trespass too far on the patience of a good-natured critic. Here, therefore, I put an end to the chapter.

CHAPTER IV.

Containing sundry curious matters.

As soon as Mr Allworthy returned home, he took Mr Blifil apart, and after some preface, communicated to him the proposal which had been made by Mr Western, and at the same time informed him how agreeable this match would be to himself.

The charms of Sophia had not made the least impression on Blifil; not that his heart was pre-engaged; neither was he totally insensible of beauty, or had any aversion to women; but his appetites were by nature so moderate, that he was able, by philosophy, or by study, or by some other method, easily to subdue them: and as to that passion which we have treated of in the first chapter of this book, he had not the least tincture of it in his whole composition.

But though he was so entirely free from that mixed passion, of which we there treated, and of which the virtues and beauty of Sophia formed so notable an object; yet was he altogether as well furnished with some other passions, that promised themselves very full gratification in the young lady's fortune. Such were avarice and ambition, which divided the dominion of his mind between them. He had more than once considered the possession of this fortune as a very desirable thing, and had entertained some distant views concerning it; but his own youth, and that of the young lady, and indeed principally a reflection that Mr Western might marry again, and have more children, had restrained him from too hasty or eager a pursuit.

This last and most material objection was now in great measure removed, as the proposal came from Mr Western himself. Blifil, therefore, after a very short hesitation, answered Mr Allworthy, that matrimony was a subject on which he had not yet thought; but that he was so sensible of his friendly and fatherly care, that he should in all things submit himself to his pleasure.

Allworthy was naturally a man of spirit, and his present gravity arose from true wisdom and philosophy, not from any original phlegm in his disposition; for he had possessed much fire in his youth, and had married a beautiful woman for love. He was not therefore greatly pleased with this cold answer of his nephew; nor could he help launching forth into the praises of Sophia, and expressing some wonder that the heart of a young man could be impregnable to the force of such charms, unless it was guarded by some prior affection.

Blifil assured him he had no such guard; and then proceeded to discourse so wisely and religiously on love and marriage, that he would have stopt the mouth of a parent much less devoutly inclined than was his uncle. In the end, the good man was satisfied that his nephew, far from having any objections to Sophia, had that esteem for her, which in sober and virtuous minds is the sure foundation of friendship and love. And as he doubted not but the lover would, in a little time, become altogether as agreeable to his mistress, he foresaw great happiness arising to all parties by so proper and desirable an union. With Mr Blifil's consent therefore he wrote the next morning to Mr Western, acquainting him that his nephew had very thankfully and gladly received the proposal, and would be ready to wait on the young lady, whenever she should be pleased to accept his visit.

Western was much pleased with this letter, and immediately returned an answer; in which, without having mentioned a word to his daughter, he appointed that very afternoon for opening the scene of courtship.

As soon as he had dispatched this messenger, he went in quest of his sister, whom he found reading and expounding the *Gazette* to parson Supple. To this exposition he was obliged to attend near a quarter of an hour, though with great violence to his natural impetuosity, before he was suffered to speak. At length, however, he found an opportunity of acquainting the lady, that he had business of great consequence to impart to her; to which she answered, "Brother, I am entirely at your service. Things look so well in the north, that I was never in a better humour."

The parson then withdrawing, Western acquainted her with all which had passed, and desired her to communicate the affair to Sophia, which she readily and chearfully undertook; though perhaps her brother was a little obliged to that agreeable northern aspect which had so delighted her, that he heard no comment on his proceedings; for they were certainly somewhat too hasty and violent.

CHAPTER V.

In which is related what passed between Sophia and her aunt.

Sophia was in her chamber, reading, when her aunt came in. The moment she saw Mrs Western, she shut the book with so much eagerness, that the good lady could not forbear asking her, What book that was which she seemed so much afraid of showing? "Upon my word, madam," answered Sophia, "it is a book which I am neither ashamed nor afraid to own I have read. It is the production of a young lady of fashion, whose good understanding, I think, doth honour to her sex, and whose good heart is an honour to human nature." Mrs Western then took up the book, and immediately after threw it down, saying—"Yes, the author is of a very good family; but she is not much among people one knows. I have never read it; for the best judges say, there is not much in it."—"I dare not, madam, set up my own opinion," says Sophia, "against the best judges, but there appears to me a great deal of human nature in it; and in many parts so much true tenderness and delicacy, that it hath cost me many a tear."—"Ay, and do you love to cry then?" says the aunt. "I love a tender sensation," answered the niece, "and would pay the price of a tear for it at any time."—"Well, but show me," said the aunt, "what was you reading when I came in; there was something very tender in that, I believe, and very loving too. You blush, my dear Sophia. Ah! child, you should read books which would teach you a little hypocrisy, which would instruct you how to hide your thoughts a little better."—"I hope, madam," answered Sophia, "I have no thoughts which I ought to be ashamed of discovering."—"Ashamed! no," cries the aunt, "I don't think you have any thoughts which you ought to be ashamed of; and yet, child, you blushed just now when I mentioned the word loving. Dear Sophy, be assured you have not one thought which I am not well acquainted with; as well, child, as the French are with our motions, long before we put them in execution. Did you think, child, because you have been able to impose upon your father, that you could impose upon me? Do you imagine I did not know the reason of your overacting all that friendship for Mr Blifil yesterday? I have seen a little too much of the world, to be so deceived. Nay, nay, do not blush again. I tell you it is a passion you need not be ashamed of. It is a passion I myself approve, and have already brought your father into the approbation of it. Indeed, I solely consider your inclination; for I would always have that gratified, if possible, though one may sacrifice higher prospects. Come, I have news which will delight your very soul. Make me your confident, and I will undertake you shall be happy to the very extent of your wishes." "La, madam," says Sophia, looking more foolishly than ever she did in her life, "I know not what to say—why, madam, should you suspect?"—"Nay, no dishonesty," returned Mrs Western. "Consider, you are speaking to one of your own sex, to an aunt, and I hope you are convinced you speak to a friend. Consider, you are only revealing to me what I know already, and what I plainly saw yesterday, through that most artful of all disguises, which you had put on, and which must have deceived any one who had not perfectly known the world. Lastly, consider it is a passion which I highly approve." "La, madam," says Sophia, "you come upon one so unawares, and on a sudden. To be sure, madam, I am not blind—and certainly, if it be a fault to see all human perfections assembled together—but is it possible my father and you, madam, can see with my eyes?" "I tell you," answered the aunt, "we do entirely approve; and this very afternoon your father hath appointed for you to receive your lover." "My father, this afternoon!" cries Sophia, with the blood starting from her face.—"Yes, child," said the aunt, "this afternoon. You know the impetuosity of my brother's temper. I acquainted him with the passion which I first discovered in you that evening when you fainted away in the field. I saw it in your fainting. I saw it immediately upon your recovery. I saw it that evening at supper, and the next morning at breakfast (you know, child, I have seen the world). Well, I no sooner acquainted my brother, but he immediately wanted to propose it to Allworthy. He proposed it yesterday, Allworthy consented (as to be sure he must with joy), and this afternoon, I tell you, you are to put on all your best airs." "This afternoon!" cries Sophia. "Dear aunt, you frighten me out of my senses." "O, my dear," said the aunt, "you will soon come to yourself again; for he is a charming young fellow, that's the truth on't." "Nay, I will own," says Sophia, "I know none with such perfections. So brave, and yet so gentle; so witty, yet so inoffensive; so humane, so civil, so genteel, so handsome! What signifies his being base born, when compared with such qualifications as these?" "Base born? What do you mean?" said the aunt, "Mr Blifil base born!" Sophia turned instantly pale at this name, and faintly repeated it. Upon which the aunt cried, "Mr Blifil—ay, Mr Blifil, of whom else have we been talking?" "Good heavens," answered Sophia, ready to sink, "of Mr Jones, I thought; I am sure I know no other who deserves—" "I protest," cries the aunt, "you frighten me in your turn. Is it Mr Jones, and not Mr Blifil, who is the object of your affection?" "Mr Blifil!" repeated Sophia. "Sure it is impossible you can be in earnest; if you are, I am the most miserable woman alive." Mrs Western now stood a few moments silent, while sparks of fiery rage flashed from her eyes. At length, collecting all her force of voice, she thundered forth in the following articulate sounds:

"And is it possible you can think of disgracing your family by allying yourself to a bastard? Can the blood of the Westerns submit to such contamination? If you have not sense sufficient to restrain such monstrous inclinations, I thought the pride of our family would have prevented you from giving the least encouragement to so base an affection; much less did I imagine you would ever have had the assurance to own it to my face."

"Madam," answered Sophia, trembling, "what I have said you have extorted from me. I do not remember to have ever mentioned the name of Mr Jones with approbation to any one before; nor should I now had I not conceived he had your approbation. Whatever were my thoughts of that poor, unhappy young man, I intended to have carried them with me to my grave—to that grave where only now, I find, I am to seek repose." Here she sunk down in her chair, drowned in her tears, and, in all the moving silence of unutterable grief, presented a spectacle which must have affected almost the hardest heart.

All this tender sorrow, however, raised no compassion in her aunt. On the contrary, she now fell into the most violent rage.—"And I would rather," she cried, in a most vehement voice, "follow you to your grave, than I would see you disgrace yourself and your family by such a match. O Heavens! could I have ever suspected that I should live to hear a niece of mine declare a passion for such a fellow? You are the first—yes, Miss Western, you are the first of your name who ever entertained so grovelling a thought. A family so noted for the prudence of its women"—here she ran on a full quarter of an hour, till, having exhausted her breath rather than her rage, she concluded with threatening to go immediately and acquaint her brother.

Sophia then threw herself at her feet, and laying hold of her hands, begged her with tears to conceal what she had drawn from her; urging the violence of her father's temper, and protesting that no inclinations of hers should ever prevail with her to do anything which might offend him.

Mrs Western stood a moment looking at her, and then, having recollected herself, said, "That on one consideration only she would keep the secret from her brother; and this was, that Sophia should promise to entertain Mr Blifil that very afternoon as her lover, and to regard him as the person who was to be her husband."

Poor Sophia was too much in her aunt's power to deny her anything positively; she was obliged to promise that she would see Mr Blifil, and be as civil to him as possible; but begged her aunt that the match might not be hurried on. She said, "Mr Blifil was by no means agreeable to her, and she hoped her father would be prevailed on not to make her the most wretched of women."

Mrs Western assured her, "That the match was entirely agreed upon, and that nothing could or should prevent it. I must own," said she, "I looked on it as on a matter of indifference; nay, perhaps, had some scruples about it before, which were actually got over by my thinking it highly agreeable to your own inclinations; but now I regard it as the most eligible thing in the world: nor shall there be, if I can prevent it, a moment of time lost on the occasion."

Sophia replied, "Delay at least, madam, I may expect from both your goodness and my father's. Surely you will give me time to endeavour to get the better of so strong a disinclination as I have at present to this person."

The aunt answered, "She knew too much of the world to be so deceived; that as she was sensible another man had her affections, she should persuade Mr Western to hasten the match as much as possible. It would be bad politics, indeed," added she, "to protract a siege when the enemy's army is at hand, and in danger of relieving it. No, no, Sophy," said she, "as I am convinced you have a violent passion which you can never satisfy with honour, I will do all I can to put your honour out of the care of your family: for when you are married those matters will belong only to the consideration of your husband. I hope, child, you will always have prudence enough to act as becomes you; but if you should not, marriage hath saved many a woman from ruin."

Sophia well understood what her aunt meant; but did not think proper to make her an answer. However, she took a resolution to see Mr Blifil, and to behave to him as civilly as she could, for on that condition only she obtained a promise from her aunt to keep secret the liking which her ill fortune, rather than any scheme of Mrs Western, had unhappily drawn from her.

CHAPTER VI.

Containing a dialogue between Sophia and Mrs Honour, which may a little relieve those tender affections which the foregoing scene may have raised in the mind of a good-natured reader.

Mrs Western having obtained that promise from her niece which we have seen in the last chapter, withdrew; and presently after arrived Mrs Honour. She was at work in a neighbouring apartment, and had been summoned to the keyhole by some vociferation in the preceding dialogue, where she had continued during the remaining part of it. At her entry into the room, she found Sophia standing motionless, with the tears trickling from her eyes. Upon which she immediately ordered a proper quantity of tears into her own eyes, and then began, "O Gemini, my dear lady, what is the matter?"—"Nothing," cries Sophia. "Nothing! O dear Madam!" answers Honour, "you must not tell me that, when your ladyship is in this taking, and when there hath been such a preamble between your ladyship and Madam Western."—"Don't teaze me," cries Sophia; "I tell you nothing is the matter. Good heavens! why was I born?"—"Nay, madam," says Mrs Honour, "you shall never persuade me that your la'ship can lament yourself so for nothing. To be sure I am but a servant; but to be sure I have been always faithful to your la'ship, and to be sure I would serve your la'ship with my life."—"My dear Honour," says Sophia, "'tis not in thy power to be of any service to me. I am irretrievably undone."—"Heaven forbid!" answered the waiting-woman; "but if I can't be of any service to you, pray tell me, madam—it will be some comfort to me to know—pray, dear ma'am, tell me what's the matter."—"My father," cries Sophia, "is going to marry me to a man I both despise and hate."—"O dear, ma'am," answered the other, "who is this wicked man? for to be sure he is very bad, or your la'ship would not despise him."—"His name is poison to my tongue," replied Sophia: "thou wilt know it too soon." Indeed, to confess the truth, she knew it already, and therefore was not very inquisitive as to that point. She then proceeded thus: "I don't pretend to give your la'ship advice, whereof your la'ship knows much better than I can pretend to, being but a servant; but, i-fackins! no father in England should marry me against my consent. And, to be sure, the 'squire is so good, that if he did but know your la'ship despises and hates the young man, to be sure he would not desire you to marry him. And if your la'ship would but give me leave to tell my master so. To be sure, it would be more properer to come from your own mouth; but as your la'ship doth not care to foul your tongue with his nasty name—"—"You are mistaken, Honour," says Sophia; "my father was determined before he ever thought fit to mention it to me."—"More shame for him," cries Honour: "you are to go to bed to him, and not master: and thof a man may be a very proper man, yet every woman mayn't think him handsome alike. I am sure my master would never act in this manner of his own head. I wish some people would trouble themselves only with what belongs to them; they would not, I believe, like to be served so, if it was their own case; for though I am a maid, I can easily believe as how all men are not equally agreeable. And what signifies your la'ship having so great a fortune, if you can't please yourself with the man you think most handsomest? Well, I say nothing; but to be sure it is a pity some folks had not been better born; nay, as for that matter, I should not mind it myself; but then there is not so much money; and what of that? your la'ship hath money enough for both; and where can your la'ship bestow your fortune better? for to be sure every one must allow that he is the most handsomest, charmingest, finest, tallest, properest man in the world."—"What do you mean by running on in this manner to me?" cries Sophia, with a very grave countenance. "Have I ever given any encouragement for these liberties?"—"Nay, ma'am, I ask pardon; I meant no harm," answered she; "but to be sure the poor gentleman hath run in my head ever since I saw him this morning. To be sure, if your la'ship had but seen him just now, you must have pitied him. Poor gentleman! I wishes some misfortune hath not happened to him; for he hath been walking about with his arms across, and looking so melancholy, all this morning: I vow and protest it made me almost cry to see him."—"To see whom?" says Sophia. "Poor Mr Jones," answered Honour. "See him! why, where did you see him?" cries Sophia. "By the canal, ma'am," says Honour. "There he hath been walking all this morning, and at last there he laid himself down: I believe he lies there still. To be sure, if it had not been for my modesty, being a maid, as I am, I should have gone and spoke to him. Do, ma'am, let me go and see, only for a fancy, whether he is there still."—"Pugh!" says Sophia. "There! no, no: what should he do there? He is gone before this time, to be sure. Besides, why—what—why should you go to see? besides, I want you for something else. Go, fetch me my hat and gloves. I shall walk with my aunt in the grove before dinner." Honour did immediately as she was bid, and Sophia put her hat on; when, looking in the glass, she fancied the ribbon with which her hat was tied did not become her, and so sent her maid back again for a ribbon of a different colour; and then giving Mrs Honour repeated charges not to leave her work on any account, as she said it was in violent haste, and must be finished that very day, she muttered something more about going to the grove, and then sallied out the contrary way, and walked, as fast as her tender trembling limbs could carry her, directly towards the canal.

Jones had been there as Mrs Honour had told her; he had indeed spent two hours there that morning in melancholy contemplation on his Sophia, and had gone out from the garden at one door the moment she entered it at another. So that those unlucky minutes which had been spent in changing the ribbons, had prevented the lovers from meeting at this time;—a most unfortunate accident, from which my fair readers will not fail to draw a very wholesome lesson. And here I strictly forbid all male critics to intermeddle with a circumstance which I have recounted only for the sake of the ladies, and upon which they only are at liberty to comment.

CHAPTER VII.

A picture of formal courtship in miniature, as it always ought to be drawn, and a scene of a tenderer kind painted at full length.

It was well remarked by one (and perhaps by more), that misfortunes do not come single. This wise maxim was now verified by Sophia, who was not only disappointed of seeing the man she loved, but had the vexation of being obliged to dress herself out, in order to receive a visit from the man she hated.

That afternoon Mr Western, for the first time, acquainted his daughter with his intention; telling her, he knew very well that she had heard it before from her aunt. Sophia looked very grave upon this, nor could she prevent a few pearls from stealing into her eyes. "Come, come," says Western, "none of your maidenish airs; I know all; I assure you sister hath told me all."

"Is it possible," says Sophia, "that my aunt can have betrayed me already?"—"Ay, ay," says Western; "betrayed you! ay. Why, you betrayed yourself yesterday at dinner. You showed your fancy very plainly, I think. But you young girls never know what you would be at. So you cry because I am going to marry you to the man you are in love with! Your mother, I remember, whimpered and whined just in the same manner; but it was all over within twenty-four hours after we were married: Mr Blifil is a brisk young man, and will soon put an end to your squeamishness. Come, chear up, chear up; I expect un every minute."

Sophia was now convinced that her aunt had behaved honourably to her: and she determined to go through that disagreeable afternoon with as much resolution as possible, and without giving the least suspicion in the world to her father.

Mr Blifil soon arrived; and Mr Western soon after withdrawing, left the young couple together.

Here a long silence of near a quarter of an hour ensued; for the gentleman who was to begin the conversation had all the unbecoming modesty which consists in bashfulness. He often attempted to speak, and as often suppressed his words just at the very point of utterance. At last out they broke in a torrent of far-fetched and high-strained compliments, which were answered on her side by downcast looks, half bows, and civil monosyllables. Blifil, from his inexperience in the ways of women, and from his conceit of himself, took this behaviour for a modest assent to his courtship; and when, to shorten a scene which she could no longer support, Sophia rose up and left the room, he imputed that, too, merely to bashfulness, and comforted himself that he should soon have enough of her company.

He was indeed perfectly well satisfied with his prospect of success; for as to that entire and absolute possession of the heart of his mistress which romantic lovers require, the very idea of it never entered his head. Her fortune and her person were the sole objects of his wishes, of which he made no doubt soon to obtain the absolute property; as Mr Western's mind was so earnestly bent on the match; and as he well knew the strict obedience which Sophia was always ready to pay to her father's will, and the greater still which her father would exact, if there was occasion. This authority, therefore, together with the charms which he fancied in his own person and conversation, could not fail, he thought, of succeeding with a young lady, whose inclinations were, he doubted not, entirely disengaged.

Of Jones he certainly had not even the least jealousy; and I have often thought it wonderful that he had not. Perhaps he imagined the character which Jones bore all over the country (how justly, let the reader determine), of being one of the wildest fellows in England, might render him odious to a lady of the most exemplary modesty. Perhaps his suspicions might be laid asleep by the behaviour of Sophia, and of Jones himself, when they were all in company together. Lastly, and indeed principally, he was well assured there was not another self in the case. He fancied that he knew Jones to the bottom, and had in reality a great contempt for his understanding, for not being more attached to his own interest. He had no apprehension that Jones was in love with Sophia; and as for any lucrative motives, he imagined they would sway very little with so silly a fellow. Blifil, moreover, thought the affair of Molly Seagrim still went on, and indeed believed it would end in marriage; for Jones really loved him from his childhood, and had kept no secret from him, till his behaviour on the sickness of Mr Allworthy had entirely alienated his heart; and it was by means of the quarrel which had ensued on this occasion, and which was not yet reconciled, that Mr Blifil knew nothing of the alteration which had happened in the affection which Jones had formerly borne towards Molly.

From these reasons, therefore, Mr Blifil saw no bar to his success with Sophia. He concluded her behaviour was like that of all other young ladies on a first visit from a lover, and it had indeed entirely answered his expectations.

Mr Western took care to way-lay the lover at his exit from his mistress. He found him so elevated with his success, so enamoured with his daughter, and so satisfied with her reception of him, that the old gentleman began to caper and dance about his hall, and by many other antic actions to express the extravagance of his joy; for he had not the least command over any of his passions; and that which had at any time the ascendant in his mind hurried him to the wildest excesses.

As soon as Blifil was departed, which was not till after many hearty kisses and embraces bestowed on him by Western, the good squire went instantly in quest of his daughter, whom he no sooner found than he poured forth the most extravagant raptures, bidding her chuse what clothes and jewels she pleased; and declaring that he had no other use for fortune but to make her happy. He then caressed her again and again with the utmost profusion of fondness, called her by the most endearing names, and protested she was his only joy on earth.

Sophia perceiving her father in this fit of affection, which she did not absolutely know the reason of (for fits of fondness were not unusual to him, though this was rather more violent than ordinary), thought she should never have a better opportunity of disclosing herself than at present, as far at least as regarded Mr Blifil; and she too well foresaw the necessity which she should soon be under of coming to a full explanation. After having thanked the squire, therefore, for all his professions of kindness, she added, with a look full of inexpressible softness, "And is it possible my papa can be so good to place all his joy in his Sophy's happiness?" which Western having confirmed by a great oath, and a kiss; she then laid hold of his hand, and, falling on her knees, after many warm and passionate declarations of affection and duty, she begged him "not to make her the most miserable creature on earth by forcing her to marry a man whom she detested. This I entreat of you, dear sir," said she, "for your sake, as well as my own, since you are so very kind to tell me your happiness depends on mine."—"How! what!" says Western, staring wildly. "Oh! sir," continued she, "not only your poor Sophy's happiness; her very life, her being, depends upon your granting her request. I cannot live with Mr Blifil. To force me into this marriage would be killing me."—"You can't live with Mr Blifil?" says Western. "No, upon my soul I can't," answered Sophia. "Then die and be d—d," cries he, spurning her from him. "Oh! sir," cries Sophia, catching hold of the skirt of his coat, "take pity on me, I beseech you. Don't look and say such cruel—Can you be unmoved while you see your Sophy in this dreadful condition? Can the best of fathers break my heart? Will he kill me by the most painful, cruel, lingering death?"—"Pooh! pooh!" cries the squire; "all stuff and nonsense; all maidenish tricks. Kill you, indeed! Will marriage kill you?"—"Oh! sir," answered Sophia, "such a marriage is worse than death. He is not even indifferent; I hate and detest him."—"If you detest un never so much," cries Western, "you shall ha'un." This he bound by an oath too shocking to repeat; and after many violent asseverations, concluded in these words: "I am resolved upon the match, and unless you consent to it I will not give you a groat, not a single farthing; no, though I saw you expiring with famine in the street, I would not relieve you with a morsel of bread. This is my fixed resolution, and so I leave you to consider on it." He then broke from her with such violence, that her face dashed against the floor; and he burst directly out of the room, leaving poor Sophia prostrate on the ground.

When Western came into the hall, he there found Jones; who seeing his friend looking wild, pale, and almost breathless, could not forbear enquiring the reason of all these melancholy appearances. Upon which the squire immediately acquainted him with the whole matter, concluding with bitter denunciations against Sophia, and very pathetic lamentations of the misery of all fathers who are so unfortunate to have daughters.

Jones, to whom all the resolutions which had been taken in favour of Blifil were yet a secret, was at first almost struck dead with this relation; but recovering his spirits a little, mere despair, as he afterwards said, inspired him to mention a matter to Mr Western, which seemed to require more impudence than a human forehead was ever gifted with. He desired leave to go to Sophia, that he might endeavour to obtain her concurrence with her father's inclinations.

If the squire had been as quicksighted as he was remarkable for the contrary, passion might at present very well have blinded him. He thanked Jones for offering to undertake the office, and said, "Go, go, prithee, try what canst do;" and then swore many execrable oaths that he would turn her out of doors unless she consented to the match.

CHAPTER VIII.

The meeting between Jones and Sophia.

Jones departed instantly in quest of Sophia, whom he found just risen from the ground, where her father had left her, with the tears trickling from her eyes, and the blood running from her lips. He presently ran to her, and with a voice full at once of tenderness and terrour, cried, "O my Sophia, what means this dreadful sight?" She looked softly at him for a moment before she spoke, and then said, "Mr Jones, for Heaven's sake how came you here?—Leave me, I beseech you, this moment."—"Do not," says he, "impose so harsh a command upon me—my heart bleeds faster than those lips. O Sophia, how easily could I drain my veins to preserve one drop of that dear blood."—"I have too many obligations to you already," answered she, "for sure you meant them such." Here she looked at him tenderly almost a minute, and then bursting into an agony, cried, "Oh, Mr Jones, why did you save my life? my death would have been happier for us both."—"Happier for us both!" cried he. "Could racks or wheels kill me so painfully as Sophia's—I cannot bear the dreadful sound. Do I live but for her?" Both his voice and looks were full of inexpressible tenderness when he spoke these words; and at the same time he laid gently hold on her hand, which she did not withdraw from him; to say the truth, she hardly knew what she did or suffered. A few moments now passed in silence between these lovers, while his eyes were eagerly fixed on Sophia, and hers declining towards the ground: at last she recovered strength enough to desire him again to leave her, for that her certain ruin would be the consequence of their being found together; adding, "Oh, Mr Jones, you know not, you know not what hath passed this cruel afternoon."—"I know all, my Sophia," answered he; "your cruel father hath told me all, and he himself hath sent me hither to you."—"My father sent you to me!" replied she: "sure you dream."—"Would to Heaven," cries he, "it was but a dream! Oh, Sophia, your father hath sent me to you, to be an advocate for my odious rival, to solicit you in his favour. I took any means to get access to you. O speak to me, Sophia! comfort my bleeding heart. Sure no one ever loved, ever doated like me. Do not unkindly withhold this dear, this soft, this gentle hand—one moment, perhaps, tears you for ever from me—nothing less than this cruel occasion could, I believe, have ever conquered the respect and awe with which you have inspired me." She stood a moment silent, and covered with confusion; then lifting up her eyes gently towards him, she cried, "What would Mr Jones have me say?"—"O do but promise," cries he, "that you never will give yourself to Blifil."—"Name not," answered she, "the detested sound. Be assured I never will give him what is in my power to withhold from him."—"Now then," cries he, "while you are so perfectly kind, go a little farther, and add that I may hope."—"Alas!" says she, "Mr Jones, whither will you drive me? What hope have I to bestow? You know my father's intentions."—"But I know," answered he, "your compliance with them cannot be compelled."—"What," says she, "must be the dreadful consequence of my disobedience? My own ruin is my least concern. I cannot bear the thoughts of being the cause of my father's misery."—"He is himself the cause," cries Jones, "by exacting a power over you which Nature hath not given him. Think on the misery which I am to suffer if I am to lose you, and see on which side pity will turn the balance."—"Think of it!" replied she: "can you imagine I do not feel the ruin which I must bring on you, should I comply with your desire? It is that thought which gives me resolution to bid you fly from me for ever, and avoid your own destruction."—"I fear no destruction," cries he, "but the loss of Sophia. If you would save me from the most bitter agonies, recall that cruel sentence. Indeed, I can never part with you, indeed I cannot."

The lovers now stood both silent and trembling, Sophia being unable to withdraw her hand from Jones, and he almost as unable to hold it; when the scene, which I believe some of my readers will think had lasted long enough, was interrupted by one of so different a nature, that we shall reserve the relation of it for a different chapter.

CHAPTER IX.

Being of a much more tempestuous kind than the former.

Before we proceed with what now happened to our lovers, it may be proper to recount what had past in the hall during their tender interview.

Soon after Jones had left Mr Western in the manner above mentioned, his sister came to him, and was presently informed of all that had passed between her brother and Sophia relating to Blifil.

This behaviour in her niece the good lady construed to be an absolute breach of the condition on which she had engaged to keep her love for Mr Jones a secret. She considered herself, therefore, at full liberty to reveal all she knew to the squire, which she immediately did in the most explicit terms, and without any ceremony or preface.

The idea of a marriage between Jones and his daughter, had never once entered into the squire's head, either in the warmest minutes of his affection towards that young man, or from suspicion, or on any other occasion. He did indeed consider a parity of fortune and circumstances to be physically as necessary an ingredient in marriage, as difference of sexes, or any other essential; and had no more apprehension of his daughter's falling in love with a poor man, than with any animal of a different species.

He became, therefore, like one thunderstruck at his sister's relation. He was, at first, incapable of making any answer, having been almost deprived of his breath by the violence of the surprize. This, however, soon returned, and, as is usual in other cases after an intermission, with redoubled force and fury.

The first use he made of the power of speech, after his recovery from the sudden effects of his astonishment, was to discharge a round volley of oaths and imprecations. After which he proceeded hastily to the apartment where he expected to find the lovers, and murmured, or rather indeed roared forth, intentions of revenge every step he went.

As when two doves, or two wood-pigeons, or as when Strephon and Phyllis (for that comes nearest to the mark) are retired into some pleasant solitary grove, to enjoy the delightful conversation of Love, that bashful boy, who cannot speak in public, and is never a good companion to more than two at a time; here, while every object is serene, should hoarse thunder burst suddenly through the shattered clouds, and rumbling roll along the sky, the frightened maid starts from the mossy bank or verdant turf, the pale livery of death succeeds the red regimentals in which Love had before drest her cheeks, fear shakes her whole frame, and her lover scarce supports her trembling tottering limbs.

Or as when two gentlemen, strangers to the wondrous wit of the place, are cracking a bottle together at some inn or tavern at Salisbury, if the great Dowdy, who acts the part of a madman as well as some of his setters-on do that of a fool, should rattle his chains, and dreadfully hum forth the grumbling catch along the gallery; the frighted strangers stand aghast; scared at the horrid sound, they seek some place of shelter from the approaching danger; and if the well-barred windows did admit their exit, would venture their necks to escape the threatening fury now coming upon them.

So trembled poor Sophia, so turned she pale at the noise of her father, who, in a voice most dreadful to hear, came on swearing, cursing, and vowing the destruction of Jones. To say the truth, I believe the youth himself would, from some prudent considerations, have preferred another place of abode at this time, had his terror on Sophia's account given him liberty to reflect a moment on what any otherways concerned himself, than as his love made him partake whatever affected her.

And now the squire, having burst open the door, beheld an object which instantly suspended all his fury against Jones; this was the ghastly appearance of Sophia, who had fainted away in her lover's arms. This tragical sight Mr Western no sooner beheld, than all his rage forsook him; he roared for help with his utmost violence; ran first to his daughter, then back to the door calling for water, and then back again to Sophia, never considering in whose arms she then was, nor perhaps once recollecting that there was such a person in the world as Jones; for indeed I believe the present circumstances of his daughter were now the sole consideration which employed his thoughts.

Mrs Western and a great number of servants soon came to the assistance of Sophia with water, cordials, and everything necessary on those occasions. These were applied with such success, that Sophia in a very few minutes began to recover, and all the symptoms of life to return. Upon which she was presently led off by her own maid and Mrs Western: nor did that good lady depart without leaving some wholesome admonitions with her brother, on the dreadful effects of his passion, or, as she pleased to call it, madness.

The squire, perhaps, did not understand this good advice, as it was delivered in obscure hints, shrugs, and notes of admiration: at least, if he did understand it, he profited very little by it; for no sooner was he cured of his immediate fears for his daughter, than he relapsed into his former frenzy, which must have produced an immediate battle with Jones, had not parson Supple, who was a very strong man, been present, and by mere force restrained the squire from acts of hostility.

The moment Sophia was departed, Jones advanced in a very suppliant manner to Mr Western, whom the parson held in his arms, and begged him to be pacified; for that, while he continued in such a passion, it would be impossible to give him any satisfaction.

"I wull have satisfaction o' thee," answered the squire; "so doff thy clothes. *At unt* half a man, and I'll lick thee as well as wast ever licked in thy life." He then bespattered the youth with abundance of that language which passes between country gentlemen who embrace opposite sides of the question; with frequent applications to him to salute that part which is generally introduced into all controversies that arise among the lower orders of the English gentry at horse-races, cock-matches, and other public places. Allusions to this part are likewise often made for the sake of the jest. And here, I believe, the wit is generally misunderstood. In reality, it lies in desiring another to kiss your a— for having just before threatened to kick his; for I have observed very accurately, that no one ever desires you to kick that which belongs to himself, nor offers to kiss this part in another.

It may likewise seem surprizing that in the many thousand kind invitations of this sort, which every one who hath conversed with country gentlemen must have heard, no one, I believe, hath ever seen a single instance where the desire hath been complied with;—a great instance of their want of politeness; for in town nothing can be more common than for the finest gentlemen to perform this ceremony every day to their superiors, without having that favour once requested of them.

To all such wit, Jones very calmly answered, "Sir, this usage may perhaps cancel every other obligation you have conferred on me; but there is one you can never cancel; nor will I be provoked by your abuse to lift my hand against the father of Sophia."

At these words the squire grew still more outrageous than before; so that the parson begged Jones to retire; saying, "You behold, sir, how he waxeth wrath at your abode here; therefore let me pray you not to tarry any longer. His anger is too much kindled for you to commune with him at present. You had better, therefore, conclude your visit, and refer what matters you have to urge in your behalf to some other opportunity."

Jones accepted this advice with thanks, and immediately departed. The squire now regained the liberty of his hands, and so much temper as to express some satisfaction in the restraint which had been laid upon him; declaring that he should certainly have beat his brains out; and adding, "It would have vexed one confoundedly to have been hanged for such a rascal."

The parson now began to triumph in the success of his peace-making endeavours, and proceeded to read a lecture against anger, which might perhaps rather have tended to raise than to quiet that passion in some hasty minds. This lecture he enriched with many valuable quotations from the antients, particularly from Seneca; who hath indeed so well handled this passion, that none but a very angry man can read him without great pleasure and profit. The doctor concluded this harangue with the famous story of Alexander and Clitus; but as I find that entered in my common-place under title Drunkenness, I shall not insert it here.

The squire took no notice of this story, nor perhaps of anything he said; for he interrupted him before he had finished, by calling for a tankard of beer; observing (which is perhaps as true as any observation on this fever of the mind) that anger makes a man dry.

No sooner had the squire swallowed a large draught than he renewed the discourse on Jones, and declared a resolution of going the next morning early to acquaint Mr Allworthy. His friend would have dissuaded him from this, from the mere motive of good-nature; but his dissuasion had no other effect than to produce a large volley of oaths and curses, which greatly shocked the pious ears of Supple; but he did not dare to remonstrate against a privilege which the squire claimed as a freeborn Englishman. To say truth, the parson submitted to please his palate at the squire's table, at the expense of suffering now and then this violence to his ears. He contented himself with thinking he did not promote this evil practice, and that the squire would not swear an oath the less, if he never entered within his gates. However, though he was not guilty of ill manners by rebuking a gentleman in his own house, he paid him off obliquely in the pulpit: which had not, indeed, the good effect of working a reformation in the squire himself; yet it so far operated on his conscience, that he put the laws very severely in execution against others, and the magistrate was the only person in the parish who could swear with impunity.

CHAPTER X.

In which Mr Western visits Mr Allworthy.

Mr Allworthy was now retired from breakfast with his nephew, well satisfied with the report of the young gentleman's successful visit to Sophia (for he greatly desired the match, more on account of the young lady's character than of her riches), when Mr Western broke abruptly in upon them, and without any ceremony began as follows:—

"There, you have done a fine piece of work truly! You have brought up your bastard to a fine purpose; not that I believe you have had any hand in it neither, that is, as a man may say, designedly: but there is a fine kettle-of-fish made on't up at our house." "What can be the matter, Mr Western?" said Allworthy. "O, matter enow of all conscience: my daughter hath fallen in love with your bastard, that's all; but I won't ge her a hapeny, not the twentieth part of a brass varden. I always thought what would come o' breeding up a bastard like a gentleman, and letting un come about to vok's houses. It's well vor un I could not get at un: I'd a lick'd un; I'd a spoil'd his caterwauling; I'd a taught the son of a whore to meddle with meat for his master. He shan't ever have a morsel of meat of mine, or a varden to buy it: if she will ha un, one smock shall be her portion. I'd sooner ge my esteate to the zinking fund, that it may be sent to Hanover to corrupt our nation with." "I am heartily sorry," cries Allworthy. "Pox o' your sorrow," says Western; "it will do me abundance of good when I have lost my only child, my poor Sophy, that was the joy of my heart, and all the hope and comfort of my age; but I am resolved I will turn her out o' doors; she shall beg, and starve, and rot in the streets. Not one hapeny, not a hapeny shall she ever hae o' mine. The son of a bitch was always good at finding a hare sitting, an be rotted to'n: I little thought what puss he was looking after; but it shall be the worst he ever vound in his life. She shall be no better than carrion: the skin o'er is all he shall ha, and zu you may tell un." "I am in amazement," cries Allworthy, "at what you tell me, after what passed between my nephew and the young lady no longer ago than yesterday." "Yes, sir," answered Western, "it was after what passed between your nephew and she that the whole matter came out. Mr Blifil there was no sooner gone than the son of a whore came lurching about the house. Little did I think when I used to love him for a sportsman that he was all the while a poaching after my daughter." "Why truly," says Allworthy, "I could wish you had not given him so many opportunities with her; and you will do me the justice to acknowledge that I have always been averse to his staying so much at your house, though I own I had no suspicion of this kind." "Why, zounds," cries Western, "who could have thought it? What the devil had she to do wi'n? He did not come there a courting to her; he came there a hunting with me." "But was it possible," says Allworthy, "that you should never discern any symptoms of love between them, when you have seen them so often together?" "Never in my life, as I hope to be saved," cries Western: "I never so much as zeed him kiss her in all my life; and so far from courting her, he used rather to be more silent when she was in company than at any other time; and as for the girl, she was always less civil to'n than to any young man that came to the house. As to that matter, I am not more easy to be deceived than another; I would not have you think I am, neighbour." Allworthy could scarce refrain laughter at this; but he resolved to do a violence to himself; for he perfectly well knew mankind, and had too much good-breeding and good-nature to offend the squire in his present circumstances. He then asked Western what he would have him do upon this occasion. To which the other answered, "That he would have him keep the rascal away from his house, and that he would go and lock up the wench; for he was resolved to make her marry Mr Blifil in spite of her teeth." He then shook Blifil by the hand, and swore he would have no other son-in-law. Presently after which he took his leave; saying his house was in such disorder that it was necessary for him to make haste home, to take care his daughter did not give him the slip; and as for Jones, he swore if he caught him at his house, he would qualify him to run for the geldings' plate.

When Allworthy and Blifil were again left together, a long silence ensued between them; all which interval the young gentleman filled up with sighs, which proceeded partly from disappointment, but more from hatred; for the success of Jones was much more grievous to him than the loss of Sophia.

At length his uncle asked him what he was determined to do, and he answered in the following words:—"Alas! sir, can it be a question what step a lover will take, when reason and passion point different ways? I am afraid it is too certain he will, in that dilemma, always follow the latter. Reason dictates to me, to quit all thoughts of a woman who places her affections on another; my passion bids me hope she may in time change her inclinations in my favour. Here, however, I conceive an objection may be raised, which, if it could not fully be answered, would totally deter me from any further pursuit. I mean the injustice of endeavouring to supplant another in a heart of which he seems already in possession; but the determined resolution of Mr Western shows that, in this case, I shall, by so doing, promote the happiness of every party; not only that of the parent, who will thus be preserved from the highest degree of misery, but of both the others, who must be undone by this match. The lady, I am sure, will be undone in every sense; for, besides the loss of most part of her own fortune, she will be not only married to a beggar, but the little fortune which her father cannot withhold from her will be squandered on that wench with whom I know he yet converses. Nay, that is a trifle; for I know him to be one of the worst men in the world; for had my dear uncle known what I have hitherto endeavoured to conceal, he must have long since abandoned so profligate a wretch." "How!" said Allworthy; "hath he done anything worse than I already know? Tell me, I beseech you?" "No," replied Blifil; "it is now past, and perhaps he may have repented of it." "I command you, on your duty," said Allworthy, "to tell me what you mean." "You know, sir," says Blifil, "I never disobeyed you; but I am sorry I mentioned it, since it may now look like revenge, whereas, I thank Heaven, no such motive ever entered my heart; and if you oblige me to discover it, I must be his petitioner to you for your forgiveness." "I will have no conditions," answered Allworthy; "I think I have shown tenderness enough towards him, and more perhaps than you ought to thank me for." "More, indeed, I fear, than he deserved," cries Blifil; "for in the very day of your utmost danger, when myself and all the family were in tears, he filled the house with riot and debauchery. He drank, and sung, and roared; and when I gave him a gentle hint of the indecency of his actions, he fell into a violent passion, swore many oaths, called me rascal, and struck me." "How!" cries Allworthy; "did he dare to strike you?" "I am sure," cries Blifil, "I have forgiven him that long ago. I wish I could so easily forget his ingratitude to the best of benefactors; and yet even that I hope you will forgive him, since he must have certainly been possessed with the devil: for that very evening, as Mr Thwackum and myself were taking the air in the fields, and exulting in the good symptoms which then first began to discover themselves, we unluckily saw him engaged with a wench in a manner not fit to be mentioned. Mr Thwackum, with more boldness than prudence, advanced to rebuke him, when (I am sorry to say it) he fell upon the worthy man, and beat him so outrageously that I wish he may have yet recovered the bruises. Nor was I without my share of the effects of his malice, while I endeavoured to protect my tutor; but that I have long forgiven; nay, I prevailed with Mr Thwackum to forgive him too, and not to inform you of a secret which I feared might be fatal to him. And now, sir, since I have unadvisedly dropped a hint of this matter, and your commands have obliged me to discover the whole, let me intercede with you for him." "O child!" said Allworthy, "I know not whether I should blame or applaud your goodness, in concealing such villany a moment: but where is Mr Thwackum? Not that I want any confirmation of what you say; but I will examine all the evidence of this matter, to justify to the world the example I am resolved to make of such a monster."

Thwackum was now sent for, and presently appeared. He corroborated every circumstance which the other had deposed; nay, he produced the record upon his breast, where the handwriting of Mr Jones remained very legible in black and blue. He concluded with declaring to Mr Allworthy, that he should have long since informed him of this matter, had not Mr Blifil, by the most earnest interpositions, prevented him. "He is," says he, "an excellent youth: though such forgiveness of enemies is carrying the matter too far."

In reality, Blifil had taken some pains to prevail with the parson, and to prevent the discovery at that time; for which he had many reasons. He knew that the minds of men are apt to be softened and relaxed from their usual severity by sickness. Besides, he imagined that if the story was told when the fact was so recent, and the physician about the house, who might have unravelled the real truth, he should never be able to give it the malicious turn which he intended. Again, he resolved to hoard up this business, till the indiscretion of Jones should afford some additional complaints; for he thought the joint weight of many facts falling upon him together, would be the most likely to crush him; and he watched, therefore, some such opportunity as that with which fortune had now kindly presented him. Lastly, by prevailing with Thwackum to conceal the matter for a time, he knew he should confirm an opinion of his friendship to Jones, which he had greatly laboured to establish in Mr Allworthy.

CHAPTER XI.

A short chapter; but which contains sufficient matter to affect the good-natured reader.

It was Mr Allworthy's custom never to punish any one, not even to turn away a servant, in a passion. He resolved therefore to delay passing sentence on Jones till the afternoon.

The poor young man attended at dinner, as usual; but his heart was too much loaded to suffer him to eat. His grief too was a good deal aggravated by the unkind looks of Mr Allworthy; whence he concluded that Western had discovered the whole affair between him and Sophia; but as to Mr Blifil's story, he had not the least apprehension; for of much the greater part he was entirely innocent; and for the residue, as he had forgiven and forgotten it himself, so he suspected no remembrance on the other side. When dinner was over, and the servants departed, Mr Allworthy began to harangue. He set forth, in a long speech, the many iniquities of which Jones had been guilty, particularly those which this day had brought to light; and concluded by telling him, "That unless he could clear himself of the charge, he was resolved to banish him his sight for ever."

Many disadvantages attended poor Jones in making his defence; nay, indeed, he hardly knew his accusation; for as Mr Allworthy, in recounting the drunkenness, &c., while he lay ill, out of modesty sunk everything that related particularly to himself, which indeed principally constituted the crime; Jones could not deny the charge. His heart was, besides, almost broken already; and his spirits were so sunk, that he could say nothing for himself; but acknowledged the whole, and, like a criminal in despair, threw himself upon mercy; concluding, "That though he must own himself guilty of many follies and inadvertencies, he hoped he had done nothing to deserve what would be to him the greatest punishment in the world."

Allworthy answered, "That he had forgiven him too often already, in compassion to his youth, and in hopes of his amendment: that he now found he was an abandoned reprobate, and such as it would be criminal in any one to support and encourage. Nay," said Mr Allworthy to him, "your audacious attempt to steal away the young lady, calls upon me to justify my own character in punishing you. The world who have already censured the regard I have shown for you may think, with some colour at least of justice, that I connive at so base and barbarous an action—an action of which you must have known my abhorrence: and which, had you had any concern for my ease and honour, as well as for my friendship, you would never have thought of undertaking. Fie upon it, young man! indeed there is scarce any punishment equal to your crimes, and I can scarce think myself justifiable in what I am now going to bestow on you. However, as I have educated you like a child of my own, I will not turn you naked into the world. When you open this paper, therefore, you will find something which may enable you, with industry, to get an honest livelihood; but if you employ it to worse purposes, I shall not think myself obliged to supply you farther, being resolved, from this day forward, to converse no more with you on any account. I cannot avoid saying, there is no part of your conduct which I resent more than your ill-treatment of that good young man (meaning Blifil) who hath behaved with so much tenderness and honour towards you."

These last words were a dose almost too bitter to be swallowed. A flood of tears now gushed from the eyes of Jones, and every faculty of speech and motion seemed to have deserted him. It was some time before he was able to obey Allworthy's peremptory commands of departing; which he at length did, having first kissed his hands with a passion difficult to be affected, and as difficult to be described.

The reader must be very weak, if, when he considers the light in which Jones then appeared to Mr Allworthy, he should blame the rigour of his sentence. And yet all the neighbourhood, either from this weakness, or from some worse motive, condemned this justice and severity as the highest cruelty. Nay, the very persons who had before censured the good man for the kindness and tenderness shown to a bastard (his own, according to the general opinion), now cried out as loudly against turning his own child out of doors. The women especially were unanimous in taking the part of Jones, and raised more stories on the occasion than I have room, in this chapter, to set down.

One thing must not be omitted, that, in their censures on this occasion, none ever mentioned the sum contained in the paper which Allworthy gave Jones, which was no less than five hundred pounds; but all agreed that he was sent away penniless, and some said naked, from the house of his inhuman father.

CHAPTER XII.

Containing love-letters, &c.

Jones was commanded to leave the house immediately, and told, that his clothes and everything else should be sent to him whithersoever he should order them.

He accordingly set out, and walked above a mile, not regarding, and indeed scarce knowing, whither he went. At length a little brook obstructing his passage, he threw himself down by the side of it; nor could he help muttering with some little indignation, "Sure my father will not deny me this place to rest in!"

Here he presently fell into the most violent agonies, tearing his hair from his head, and using most other actions which generally accompany fits of madness, rage, and despair.

When he had in this manner vented the first emotions of passion, he began to come a little to himself. His grief now took another turn, and discharged itself in a gentler way, till he became at last cool enough to reason with his passion, and to consider what steps were proper to be taken in his deplorable condition.

And now the great doubt was, how to act with regard to Sophia. The thoughts of leaving her almost rent his heart asunder; but the consideration of reducing her to ruin and beggary still racked him, if possible, more; and if the violent desire of possessing her person could have induced him to listen one moment to this alternative, still he was by no means certain of her resolution to indulge his wishes at so high an expense. The resentment of Mr Allworthy, and the injury he must do to his quiet, argued strongly against this latter; and lastly, the apparent impossibility of his success, even if he would sacrifice all these considerations to it, came to his assistance; and thus honour at last backed with despair, with gratitude to his benefactor, and with real love to his mistress, got the better of burning desire, and he resolved rather to quit Sophia, than pursue her to her ruin.

It is difficult for any who have not felt it, to conceive the glowing warmth which filled his breast on the first contemplation of this victory over his passion. Pride flattered him so agreeably, that his mind perhaps enjoyed perfect happiness; but this was only momentary: Sophia soon returned to his imagination, and allayed the joy of his triumph with no less bitter pangs than a good-natured general must feel, when he surveys the bleeding heaps, at the price of whose blood he hath purchased his laurels; for thousands of tender ideas lay murdered before our conqueror.

Being resolved, however, to pursue the paths of this giant honour, as the gigantic poet Lee calls it, he determined to write a farewel letter to Sophia; and accordingly proceeded to a house not far off, where, being furnished with proper materials, he wrote as follows:—

> "MADAM,
>
> "When you reflect on the situation in which I write, I am sure your good-nature will pardon any inconsistency or absurdity which my letter contains; for everything here flows from a heart so full, that no language can express its dictates.
>
> "I have resolved, madam, to obey your commands, in flying for ever from your dear, your lovely sight. Cruel indeed those commands are; but it is a cruelty which proceeds from fortune, not from my Sophia. Fortune hath made it necessary, necessary to your preservation, to forget there ever was such a wretch as I am.
>
> "Believe me, I would not hint all my sufferings to you, if I imagined they could possibly escape your ears. I know the goodness and tenderness of your heart, and would avoid giving you any of those pains which you always feel for the miserable. O let nothing, which you shall hear of my hard fortune, cause a moment's concern; for, after the loss of you, everything is to me a trifle.
>
> "O Sophia! it is hard to leave you; it is harder still to desire you to forget me; yet the sincerest love obliges me to both. Pardon my conceiving that any remembrance of me can give you disquiet; but if I am so gloriously wretched, sacrifice me every way to your relief. Think I never loved you; or think truly how little I deserve you; and learn to scorn me for a presumption which can never be too severely punished.—I am unable to say more.—May guardian angels protect you for ever!"

He was now searching his pockets for his wax, but found none, nor indeed anything else, therein; for in truth he had, in his frantic disposition, tossed everything from him, and amongst the rest, his pocket-book, which he had received from Mr Allworthy, which he had never opened, and which now first occurred to his memory.

The house supplied him with a wafer for his present purpose, with which, having sealed his letter, he returned hastily towards the brook side, in order to search for the things which he had there lost. In his way he met his old friend Black George, who heartily condoled with him on his misfortune; for this had already reached his ears, and indeed those of all the neighbourhood.

Jones acquainted the gamekeeper with his loss, and he as readily went back with him to the brook, where they searched every tuft of grass in the meadow, as well where Jones had not been as where he had been; but all to no purpose, for they found nothing; for, indeed, though the things were then in the meadow, they omitted to search the only place where they were deposited; to wit, in the pockets of the said George; for he had just before found them, and being luckily apprized of their value, had very carefully put them up for his own use.

The gamekeeper having exerted as much diligence in quest of the lost goods, as if he had hoped to find them, desired Mr Jones to recollect if he had been in no other place: "For sure," said he, "if you had lost them here so lately, the things must have been here still; for this is a very unlikely place for any one to pass by." And indeed it was by great accident that he himself had passed through that field, in order to lay wires for hares, with which he was to supply a poulterer at Bath the next morning.

Jones now gave over all hopes of recovering his loss, and almost all thoughts concerning it, and turning to Black George, asked him earnestly if he would do him the greatest favour in the world?

George answered with some hesitation, "Sir, you know you may command me whatever is in my power, and I heartily wish it was in my power to do you any service." In fact, the question staggered him; for he had, by selling game, amassed a pretty good sum of money in Mr Western's service, and was afraid that Jones wanted to borrow some small matter of him; but he was presently relieved from his anxiety, by being desired to convey a letter to Sophia, which with great pleasure he promised to do. And indeed I believe there are few favours which he would not have gladly conferred on Mr Jones; for he bore as much gratitude towards him as he could, and was as honest as men who love money better than any other thing in the universe, generally are.

Mrs Honour was agreed by both to be the proper means by which this letter should pass to Sophia. They then separated; the gamekeeper returned home to Mr Western's, and Jones walked to an alehouse at half a mile's distance, to wait for his messenger's return.

George no sooner came home to his master's house than he met with Mrs Honour; to whom, having first sounded her with a few previous questions, he delivered the letter for her mistress, and received at the same time another from her, for Mr Jones; which Honour told him she had carried all that day in her bosom, and began to despair of finding any means of delivering it.

The gamekeeper returned hastily and joyfully to Jones, who, having received Sophia's letter from him, instantly withdrew, and eagerly breaking it open, read as follows:—

> "SIR,
>
> "It is impossible to express what I have felt since I saw you. Your submitting, on my account, to such cruel insults from my father, lays me under an obligation I shall ever own. As you know his temper, I beg you will, for my sake, avoid him. I wish I had any comfort to send you; but believe this, that nothing but the last violence shall ever give my hand or heart where you would be sorry to see them bestowed."

Jones read this letter a hundred times over, and kissed it a hundred times as often. His passion now brought all tender desires back into his mind. He repented that he had writ to Sophia in the manner we have seen above; but he repented more that he had made use of the interval of his messenger's absence to write and dispatch a letter to Mr Allworthy, in which he had faithfully promised and bound himself to quit all thoughts of his love. However, when his cool reflections returned, he plainly perceived that his case was neither mended nor altered by Sophia's billet, unless to give him some little glimpse of hope, from her constancy, of some favourable accident hereafter. He therefore resumed his resolution, and taking leave of Black George, set forward to a town about five miles distant, whither he had desired Mr Allworthy, unless he pleased to revoke his sentence, to send his things after him.

CHAPTER XIII.

The behaviour of Sophia on the present occasion; which none of her sex will blame, who are capable of behaving in the same manner. And the discussion of a knotty point in the court of conscience.

Sophia had passed the last twenty-four hours in no very desirable manner. During a large part of them she had been entertained by her aunt with lectures of prudence, recommending to her the example of the polite world, where love (so the good lady said) is at present entirely laughed at, and where women consider matrimony, as men do offices of public trust, only as the means of making their fortunes, and of advancing themselves in the world. In commenting on which text Mrs Western had displayed her eloquence during several hours.

These sagacious lectures, though little suited either to the taste or inclination of Sophia, were, however, less irksome to her than her own thoughts, that formed the entertainment of the night, during which she never once closed her eyes.

But though she could neither sleep nor rest in her bed, yet, having no avocation from it, she was found there by her father at his return from Allworthy's, which was not till past ten o'clock in the morning. He went directly up to her apartment, opened the door, and seeing she was not up, cried, "Oh! you are safe then, and I am resolved to keep you so." He then locked the door, and delivered the key to Honour, having first given her the strictest charge, with great promises of rewards for her fidelity, and most dreadful menaces of punishment in case she should betray her trust.

Honour's orders were, not to suffer her mistress to come out of her room without the authority of the squire himself, and to admit none to her but him and her aunt; but she was herself to attend her with whatever Sophia pleased, except only pen, ink, and paper, of which she was forbidden the use.

The squire ordered his daughter to dress herself and attend him at dinner; which she obeyed; and having sat the usual time, was again conducted to her prison.

In the evening the gaoler Honour brought her the letter which she received from the gamekeeper. Sophia read it very attentively twice or thrice over, and then threw herself upon the bed, and burst into a flood of tears. Mrs Honour expressed great astonishment at this behaviour in her mistress; nor could she forbear very eagerly begging to know the cause of this passion. Sophia made her no answer for some time, and then, starting suddenly up, caught her maid by the hand,

and cried, "O Honour! I am undone." "Marry forbid," cries Honour: "I wish the letter had been burnt before I had brought it to your la'ship. I'm sure I thought it would have comforted your la'ship, or I would have seen it at the devil before I would have touched it." "Honour," says Sophia, "you are a good girl, and it is vain to attempt concealing longer my weakness from you; I have thrown away my heart on a man who hath forsaken me." "And is Mr Jones," answered the maid, "such a perfidy man?" "He hath taken his leave of me," says Sophia, "for ever in that letter. Nay, he hath desired me to forget him. Could he have desired that if he had loved me? Could he have borne such a thought? Could he have written such a word?" "No, certainly, ma'am," cries Honour; "and to be sure, if the best man in England was to desire me to forget him, I'd take him at his word. Marry, come up! I am sure your la'ship hath done him too much honour ever to think on him;—a young lady who may take her choice of all the young men in the country. And to be sure, if I may be so presumptuous as to offer my poor opinion, there is young Mr Blifil, who, besides that he is come of honest parents, and will be one of the greatest squires all hereabouts, he is to be sure, in my poor opinion, a more handsomer and a more politer man by half; and besides, he is a young gentleman of a sober character, and who may defy any of the neighbours to say black is his eye; he follows no dirty trollops, nor can any bastards be laid at his door. Forget him, indeed! I thank Heaven I myself am not so much at my last prayers as to suffer any man to bid me forget him twice. If the best he that wears a head was for to go for to offer to say such an affronting word to me, I would never give him my company afterwards, if there was another young man in the kingdom. And as I was a saying, to be sure, there is young Mr Blifil." "Name not his detested name," cries Sophia. "Nay, ma'am," says Honour, "if your la'ship doth not like him, there be more jolly handsome young men that would court your la'ship, if they had but the least encouragement. I don't believe there is arrow young gentleman in this county, or in the next to it, that if your la'ship was but to look as if you had a mind to him, would not come about to make his offers directly." "What a wretch dost thou imagine me," cries Sophia, "by affronting my ears with such stuff! I detest all mankind." "Nay, to be sure, ma'am," answered Honour, "your la'ship hath had enough to give you a surfeit of them. To be used ill by such a poor, beggarly, bastardly fellow."—"Hold your blasphemous tongue," cries Sophia: "how dare you mention his name with disrespect before me? He use me ill? No, his poor bleeding heart suffered more when he writ the cruel words than mine from reading them. O! he is all heroic virtue and angelic goodness. I am ashamed of the weakness of my own passion, for blaming what I ought to admire. O, Honour! it is my good only which he consults. To my interest he sacrifices both himself and me. The apprehension of ruining me hath driven him to despair." "I am very glad," says Honour, "to hear your la'ship takes that into your consideration; for to be sure, it must be nothing less than ruin to give your mind to one that is turned out of doors, and is not worth a farthing in the world." "Turned out of doors!" cries Sophia hastily: "how! what dost thou mean?" "Why, to be sure, ma'am, my master no sooner told Squire Allworthy about Mr Jones having offered to make love to your la'ship than the squire stripped him stark naked, and turned him out of doors!" "Ha!" says Sophia, "I have been the cursed, wretched cause of his destruction! Turned naked out of doors! Here, Honour, take all the money I have; take the rings from my fingers. Here, my watch: carry him all. Go find him immediately." "For Heaven's sake, ma'am," answered Mrs Honour, "do but consider, if my master should miss any of these things, I should be made to answer for them. Therefore let me beg your la'ship not to part with your watch and jewels. Besides, the money, I think, is enough of all conscience; and as for that, my master can never know anything of the matter." "Here, then," cries Sophia, "take every farthing I am worth, find him out immediately, and give it him. Go, go, lose not a moment."

Mrs Honour departed according to orders, and finding Black George belowstairs, delivered him the purse, which contained sixteen guineas, being, indeed, the whole stock of Sophia; for though her father was very liberal to her, she was much too generous to be rich.

Black George having received the purse, set forward towards the alehouse; but in the way a thought occurred to him, whether he should not detain this money likewise. His conscience, however, immediately started at this suggestion, and began to upbraid him with ingratitude to his benefactor. To this his avarice answered, That his conscience should have considered the matter before, when he deprived poor Jones of his £500. That having quietly acquiesced in what was of so much greater importance, it was absurd, if not downright hypocrisy, to affect any qualms at this trifle. In return to which, Conscience, like a good lawyer, attempted to distinguish between an absolute breach of trust, as here, where the goods were delivered, and a bare concealment of what was found, as in the former case. Avarice presently treated this with ridicule, called it a distinction without a difference, and absolutely insisted that when once all pretensions of honour and virtue were given up in any one instance, that there was no precedent for resorting to them upon a second occasion. In short, poor Conscience had certainly been defeated in the argument, had not Fear stept in to her assistance, and very strenuously urged that the real distinction between the two actions, did not lie in the different degrees of honour but of safety: for that the secreting the £500 was a matter of very little hazard; whereas the detaining the sixteen guineas was liable to the utmost danger of discovery.

By this friendly aid of Fear, Conscience obtained a compleat victory in the mind of Black George, and, after making him a few compliments on his honesty, forced him to deliver the money to Jones.

CHAPTER XIV.

A short chapter, containing a short dialogue between Squire Western and his sister.

Mrs Western had been engaged abroad all that day. The squire met her at her return home; and when she enquired after Sophia, he acquainted her that he had secured her safe enough. "She is locked up in chamber," cries he, "and Honour keeps the key." As his looks were full of prodigious wisdom and sagacity when he gave his sister this information, it is probable he expected much applause from her for what he had done; but how was he disappointed when, with a most disdainful aspect, she cried, "Sure, brother, you are the weakest of all men. Why will you not confide in me for the management of my niece? Why will you interpose? You have now undone all that I have been spending my breath in order to bring about. While I have been endeavouring to fill her mind with maxims of prudence, you have been provoking her to reject them. English women, brother, I thank heaven, are no slaves. We are not to be locked up like the Spanish and Italian wives. We have as good a right to liberty as yourselves. We are to be convinced by reason and persuasion only, and not governed by force. I have seen the world, brother, and know what arguments to make use of; and if your folly had not prevented me, should have prevailed with her to form her conduct by those rules of prudence and discretion which I formerly taught her." "To be sure," said the squire, "I am always in the wrong." "Brother," answered the lady, "you are not in the wrong, unless when you meddle with matters beyond your knowledge. You must agree that I have seen most of the world; and happy had it been for my niece if she had not been taken from under my care. It is by living at home with you that she hath learnt romantic notions of love and nonsense." "You don't imagine, I hope," cries the squire, "that I have taught her any such things." "Your ignorance, brother," returned she, "as the great Milton says, almost subdues my patience."[1] "D—n Milton!" answered the squire: "if he had the impudence to say so to my face, I'd lend him a douse, thof he was never so great a man. Patience! An you come to that, sister, I have more occasion of patience, to be used like an overgrown schoolboy, as I am by you. Do you think no one hath any understanding,

---

[1] The reader may, perhaps, subdue his own patience, if he searches for this in Milton.

unless he hath been about at court. Pox! the world is come to a fine pass indeed, if we are all fools, except a parcel of round-heads and Hanover rats. Pox! I hope the times are a coming when we shall make fools of them, and every man shall enjoy his own. That's all, sister; and every man shall enjoy his own. I hope to zee it, sister, before the Hanover rats have eat up all our corn, and left us nothing but turneps to feed upon."—"I protest, brother," cries she, "you are now got beyond my understanding. Your jargon of turneps and Hanover rats is to me perfectly unintelligible."—"I believe," cries he, "you don't care to hear o'em; but the country interest may succeed one day or other for all that."—"I wish," answered the lady, "you would think a little of your daughter's interest; for, believe me, she is in greater danger than the nation."—"Just now," said he, "you chid me for thinking on her, and would ha' her left to you."—"And if you will promise to interpose no more," answered she, "I will, out of my regard to my niece, undertake the charge."—"Well, do then," said the squire, "for you know I always agreed, that women are the properest to manage women."

Mrs Western then departed, muttering something with an air of disdain, concerning women and management of the nation. She immediately repaired to Sophia's apartment, who was now, after a day's confinement, released again from her captivity.

BOOK VII.

CONTAINING THREE DAYS.

CHAPTER I.

A comparison between the world and the stage.

The world hath been often compared to the theatre; and many grave writers, as well as the poets, have considered human life as a great drama, resembling, in almost every particular, those scenical representations which Thespis is first reported to have invented, and which have been since received with so much approbation and delight in all polite countries.

This thought hath been carried so far, and is become so general, that some words proper to the theatre, and which were at first metaphorically applied to the world, are now indiscriminately and literally spoken of both; thus stage and scene are by common use grown as familiar to us, when we speak of life in general, as when we confine ourselves to dramatic performances: and when transactions behind the curtain are mentioned, St James's is more likely to occur to our thoughts than Drury-lane.

It may seem easy enough to account for all this, by reflecting that the theatrical stage is nothing more than a representation, or, as Aristotle calls it, an imitation of what really exists; and hence, perhaps, we might fairly pay a very high compliment to those who by their writings or actions have been so capable of imitating life, as to have their pictures in a manner confounded with, or mistaken for, the originals.

But, in reality, we are not so fond of paying compliments to these people, whom we use as children frequently do the instruments of their amusement; and have much more pleasure in hissing and buffeting them, than in admiring their excellence. There are many other reasons which have induced us to see this analogy between the world and the stage.

Some have considered the larger part of mankind in the light of actors, as personating characters no more their own, and to which in fact they have no better title, than the player hath to be in earnest thought the king or emperor whom he represents. Thus the hypocrite may be said to be a player; and indeed the Greeks called them both by one and the same name.

The brevity of life hath likewise given occasion to this comparison. So the immortal Shakespear—

—Life's a poor player,
That struts and frets his hour upon the stage,
And then is heard no more.

For which hackneyed quotation I will make the reader amends by a very noble one, which few, I believe, have read. It is taken from a poem called the Deity, published about nine years ago, and long since buried in oblivion; a proof that good books, no more than good men, do always survive the bad.

From Thee[1] all human actions take their springs,
The rise of empires and the fall of kings!
See the vast Theatre of Time display'd,
While o'er the scene succeeding heroes tread!
With pomp the shining images succeed,
What leaders triumph, and what monarchs bleed!
Perform the parts thy providence assign'd,
Their pride, their passions, to thy ends inclin'd:
Awhile they glitter in the face of day,
Then at thy nod the phantoms pass away;
No traces left of all the busy scene,
But that remembrance says—*The things have been!*

In all these, however, and in every other similitude of life to the theatre, the resemblance hath been always taken from the stage only. None, as I remember, have at all considered the audience at this great drama.

But as Nature often exhibits some of her best performances to a very full house, so will the behaviour of her spectators no less admit the above-mentioned comparison than that of her actors. In this vast theatre of time are seated the friend and the critic; here are claps and shouts, hisses and groans; in short, everything which was ever seen or heard at the Theatre-Royal.

Let us examine this in one example; for instance, in the behaviour of the great audience on that scene which Nature was pleased to exhibit in the twelfth chapter of the preceding book, where she introduced Black George running away with the £500 from his friend and benefactor.

Those who sat in the world's upper gallery treated that incident, I am well convinced, with their usual vociferation; and every term of scurrilous reproach was most probably vented on that occasion.

If we had descended to the next order of spectators, we should have found an equal degree of abhorrence, though less of noise and scurrility; yet here the good women gave Black George to the devil, and many of them expected every minute that the cloven-footed gentleman would fetch his own.

---

[1] The Deity.

The pit, as usual, was no doubt divided; those who delight in heroic virtue and perfect character objected to the producing such instances of villany, without punishing them very severely for the sake of example. Some of the author's friends cryed, "Look'e, gentlemen, the man is a villain, but it is nature for all that." And all the young critics of the age, the clerks, apprentices, &c., called it low, and fell a groaning.

As for the boxes, they behaved with their accustomed politeness. Most of them were attending to something else. Some of those few who regarded the scene at all, declared he was a bad kind of man; while others refused to give their opinion, till they had heard that of the best judges.

Now we, who are admitted behind the scenes of this great theatre of Nature (and no author ought to write anything besides dictionaries and spelling-books who hath not this privilege), can censure the action, without conceiving any absolute detestation of the person, whom perhaps Nature may not have designed to act an ill part in all her dramas; for in this instance life most exactly resembles the stage, since it is often the same person who represents the villain and the heroe; and he who engages your admiration to-day will probably attract your contempt to-morrow. As Garrick, whom I regard in tragedy to be the greatest genius the world hath ever produced, sometimes condescends to play the fool; so did Scipio the Great, and Laelius the Wise, according to Horace, many years ago; nay, Cicero reports them to have been "incredibly childish." These, it is true, played the fool, like my friend Garrick, in jest only; but several eminent characters have, in numberless instances of their lives, played the fool egregiously in earnest; so far as to render it a matter of some doubt whether their wisdom or folly was predominant; or whether they were better intitled to the applause or censure, the admiration or contempt, the love or hatred, of mankind.

Those persons, indeed, who have passed any time behind the scenes of this great theatre, and are thoroughly acquainted not only with the several disguises which are there put on, but also with the fantastic and capricious behaviour of the Passions, who are the managers and directors of this theatre (for as to Reason, the patentee, he is known to be a very idle fellow and seldom to exert himself), may most probably have learned to understand the famous *nil admirari* of Horace, or in the English phrase, to stare at nothing.

A single bad act no more constitutes a villain in life, than a single bad part on the stage. The passions, like the managers of a playhouse, often force men upon parts without consulting their judgment, and sometimes without any regard to their talents. Thus the man, as well as the player, may condemn what he himself acts; nay, it is common to see vice sit as awkwardly on some men, as the character of Iago would on the honest face of Mr William Mills.

Upon the whole, then, the man of candour and of true understanding is never hasty to condemn. He can censure an imperfection, or even a vice, without rage against the guilty party. In a word, they are the same folly, the same childishness, the same ill-breeding, and the same ill-nature, which raise all the clamours and uproars both in life and on the stage. The worst of men generally have the words rogue and villain most in their mouths, as the lowest of all wretches are the aptest to cry out low in the pit.

CHAPTER II.

Containing a conversation which Mr Jones had with himself.

Jones received his effects from Mr Allworthy's early in the morning, with the following answer to his letter:—

> "SIR,
>
> "I am commanded by my uncle to acquaint you, that as he did not proceed to those measures he had taken with you, without the greatest deliberation, and after the fullest evidence of your unworthiness, so will it be always out of your power to cause the least alteration in his resolution. He expresses great surprize at your presumption in saying you have resigned all pretensions to a young lady, to whom it is impossible you should ever have had any, her birth and fortune having made her so infinitely your superior. Lastly, I am commanded to tell you, that the only instance of your compliance with my uncle's inclinations which he requires, is, your immediately quitting this country. I cannot conclude this without offering you my advice, as a Christian, that you would seriously think of amending your life. That you may be assisted with grace so to do, will be always the prayer of
>
> "Your humble servant,
>
> "W. BLIFIL."

Many contending passions were raised in our heroe's mind by this letter; but the tender prevailed at last over the indignant and irascible, and a flood of tears came seasonably to his assistance, and possibly prevented his misfortunes from either turning his head, or bursting his heart.

He grew, however, soon ashamed of indulging this remedy; and starting up, he cried, "Well, then, I will give Mr Allworthy the only instance he requires of my obedience. I will go this moment—but whither?—why, let Fortune direct; since there is no other who thinks it of any consequence what becomes of this wretched person, it shall be a matter of equal indifference to myself. Shall I alone regard what no other—Ha! have I not reason to think there is another?—one whose value is above that of the whole world!—I may, I must imagine my Sophia is not indifferent to what becomes of me. Shall I then leave this only friend—and such a friend? Shall I not stay with her?—Where—how can I stay with her? Have I any hopes of ever seeing her, though she was as desirous as myself, without exposing her to the wrath of her father, and to what purpose? Can I think of soliciting such a creature to consent to her own ruin? Shall I indulge any passion of mine at such a price? Shall I lurk about this country like a thief, with such intentions?—No, I disdain, I detest the thought. Farewel, Sophia; farewel, most lovely, most beloved—" Here passion stopped his mouth, and found a vent at his eyes.

And now having taken a resolution to leave the country, he began to debate with himself whither he should go. The world, as Milton phrases it, lay all before him; and Jones, no more than Adam, had any man to whom he might resort for comfort or assistance. All his acquaintance were the acquaintance of Mr Allworthy; and he had no reason to expect any countenance from them, as that gentlegentleman had withdrawn his favour from him. Men of great and good characters should indeed be very cautious how they discard their dependents; for the consequence to the unhappy sufferer is being discarded by all others.

What course of life to pursue, or to what business to apply himself, was a second consideration: and here the prospect was all a melancholy void. Every profession, and every trade, required length of time, and what was worse, money; for matters are so constituted, that "nothing out of nothing" is not a truer maxim in physics than in politics; and every man who is greatly destitute of money, is on that account entirely excluded from all means of acquiring it.

At last the Ocean, that hospitable friend to the wretched, opened her capacious arms to receive him; and he instantly resolved to accept her kind invitation. To express myself less figuratively, he determined to go to sea.

This thought indeed no sooner suggested itself, than he eagerly embraced it; and having presently hired horses, he set out for Bristol to put it in execution.

But before we attend him on this expedition, we shall resort awhile to Mr Western's, and see what further happened to the charming Sophia.

CHAPTER III.

Containing several dialogues.

The morning in which Mr Jones departed, Mrs Western summoned Sophia into her apartment; and having first acquainted her that she had obtained her liberty of her father, she proceeded to read her a long lecture on the subject of matrimony; which she treated not as a romantic scheme of happiness arising from love, as it hath been described by the poets; nor did she mention any of those purposes for which we are taught by divines to regard it as instituted by sacred authority; she considered it rather as a fund in which prudent women deposit their fortunes to the best advantage, in order to receive a larger interest for them than they could have elsewhere.

When Mrs Western had finished, Sophia answered, "That she was very incapable of arguing with a lady of her aunt's superior knowledge and experience, especially on a subject which she had so very little considered, as this of matrimony."

"Argue with me, child!" replied the other; "I do not indeed expect it. I should have seen the world to very little purpose truly, if I am to argue with one of your years. I have taken this trouble, in order to instruct you. The antient philosophers, such as Socrates, Alcibiades, and others, did not use to argue with their scholars. You are to consider me, child, as Socrates, not asking your opinion, but only informing you of mine." From which last words the reader may possibly imagine, that this lady had read no more of the philosophy of Socrates, than she had of that of Alcibiades; and indeed we cannot resolve his curiosity as to this point.

"Madam," cries Sophia, "I have never presumed to controvert any opinion of yours; and this subject, as I said, I have never yet thought of, and perhaps never may."

"Indeed, Sophy," replied the aunt, "this dissimulation with me is very foolish. The French shall as soon persuade me that they take foreign towns in defence only of their own country, as you can impose on me to believe you have never yet thought seriously of matrimony. How can you, child, affect to deny that you have considered of contracting an alliance, when you so well know I am acquainted with the party with whom you desire to contract it?—an alliance as unnatural, and contrary to your interest, as a separate league with the French would be to the interest of the Dutch! But however, if you have not hitherto considered of this matter, I promise you it is now high time, for my brother is resolved immediately to conclude the treaty with Mr Blifil; and indeed I am a sort of guarantee in the affair, and have promised your concurrence."

"Indeed, madam," cries Sophia, "this is the only instance in which I must disobey both yourself and my father. For this is a match which requires very little consideration in me to refuse."

"If I was not as great a philosopher as Socrates himself," returned Mrs Western, "you would overcome my patience. What objection can you have to the young gentleman?"

"A very solid objection, in my opinion," says Sophia—"I hate him."

"Will you never learn a proper use of words?" answered the aunt. "Indeed, child, you should consult Bailey's Dictionary. It is impossible you should hate a man from whom you have received no injury. By hatred, therefore, you mean no more than dislike, which is no sufficient objection against your marrying of him. I have known many couples, who have entirely disliked each other, lead very comfortable genteel lives. Believe me, child, I know these things better than you. You will allow me, I think, to have seen the world, in which I have not an acquaintance who would not rather be thought to dislike her husband than to like him. The contrary is such out-of-fashion romantic nonsense, that the very imagination of it is shocking."

"Indeed, madam," replied Sophia, "I shall never marry a man I dislike. If I promise my father never to consent to any marriage contrary to his inclinations, I think I may hope he will never force me into that state contrary to my own."

"Inclinations!" cries the aunt, with some warmth. "Inclinations! I am astonished at your assurance. A young woman of your age, and unmarried, to talk of inclinations! But whatever your inclinations may be, my brother is resolved; nay, since you talk of inclinations, I shall advise him to hasten the treaty. Inclinations!"

Sophia then flung herself upon her knees, and tears began to trickle from her shining eyes. She entreated her aunt, "to have mercy upon her, and not to resent so cruelly her unwillingness to make herself miserable;" often urging, "that she alone was concerned, and that her happiness only was at stake."

As a bailiff, when well authorized by his writ, having possessed himself of the person of some unhappy debtor, views all his tears without concern; in vain the wretched captive attempts to raise compassion; in vain the tender wife bereft of her companion, the little prattling boy, or frighted girl, are mentioned as inducements to reluctance. The noble bumtrap, blind and deaf to every circumstance of distress, greatly rises above all the motives to humanity, and into the hands of the gaoler resolves to deliver his miserable prey.

Not less blind to the tears, or less deaf to every entreaty of Sophia was the politic aunt, nor less determined was she to deliver over the trembling maid into the arms of the gaoler Blifil. She answered with great impetuosity, "So far, madam, from your being concerned alone, your concern is the least, or surely the least important. It is the honour of your family which is concerned in this alliance; you are only the instrument. Do you conceive, mistress, that in an intermarriage between kingdoms, as when a daughter of France is married into Spain, the princess herself is alone considered in the match? No! it is a match between two kingdoms, rather than between two persons. The same happens in great families such as ours. The alliance between the families is the principal matter. You ought to have a greater regard for the honour of your family than for your own person; and if the example of a princess cannot inspire you with these noble thoughts, you cannot surely complain at being used no worse than all princesses are used."

"I hope, madam," cries Sophia, with a little elevation of voice, "I shall never do anything to dishonour my family; but as for Mr Blifil, whatever may be the consequence, I am resolved against him, and no force shall prevail in his favour."

Western, who had been within hearing during the greater part of the preceding dialogue, had now exhausted all his patience; he therefore entered the room in a violent passion, crying, "D—n me then if shatunt ha'un, d—n me if shatunt, that's all—that's all; d—n me if shatunt."

Mrs Western had collected a sufficient quantity of wrath for the use of Sophia; but she now transferred it all to the squire. "Brother," said she, "it is astonishing that you will interfere in a matter which you had totally left to my negotiation. Regard to my family hath made me take upon myself to be the mediating power, in order to rectify those mistakes in policy which you have committed in your daughter's education. For, brother, it is you—it is your preposterous conduct which hath eradicated all the seeds that I had formerly sown in her tender mind. It is you yourself who have taught her disobedience."—"Blood!" cries the squire, foaming at the mouth, "you are enough to conquer the patience of the devil! Have I ever taught my daughter disobedience?—Here she stands; speak honestly, girl, did ever I bid you be disobedient to me? Have not I done everything to humour and to gratify you, and to make you obedient to me? And very obedient to me she was when a little child, before you took her in hand and spoiled her, by filling her head with a pack of court notions. Why—why—why—did I not overhear you telling her she must behave like a princess? You have made a Whig of the girl; and how should her father, or anybody else, expect any obedience from her?"—"Brother," answered Mrs Western, with an air of great disdain, "I cannot express the contempt I have for your politics of all kinds; but I will appeal likewise to the young lady herself, whether I have ever taught her any principles of disobedience. On the contrary, niece, have I not endeavoured to inspire you with a true idea of the several relations in which a human creature stands in society? Have I not taken infinite pains to show you, that the law of nature hath enjoined a duty on children to their parents? Have I not told you what Plato says on that subject?—a subject on which you was so notoriously ignorant when you came first under my care, that I verily believe you did not know the relation between a daughter and a father."—"'Tis a lie," answered Western. "The girl is no such fool, as to live to eleven years old without knowing that she was her father's relation."—"O! more than Gothic ignorance," answered the lady. "And as for your manners, brother, I must tell you, they deserve a cane."—"Why then you may gi' it me, if you think you are able," cries the squire; "nay, I suppose your niece there will be ready enough to help you."—"Brother," said Mrs Western, "though I despise you beyond expression, yet I shall endure your insolence no longer; so I desire my coach may be got ready immediately, for I am resolved to leave your house this very morning."—"And a good riddance too," answered he; "I can bear your insolence no longer, an you come to that. Blood! it is almost enough of itself to make my daughter undervalue my sense, when she hears you telling me every minute you despise me."—"It is impossible, it is impossible," cries the aunt; "no one can undervalue such a boor."—"Boar," answered the squire, "I am no boar; no, nor ass; no, nor rat neither, madam. Remember that—I am no rat. I am a true Englishman, and not of your Hanover breed, that have eat up the nation."—"Thou art one of those wise men," cries she, "whose nonsensical principles have undone the nation; by weakening the hands of our government at home, and by discouraging our friends and encouraging our enemies abroad."—"Ho! are you come back to your politics?" cries the squire: "as for those I despise them as much as I do a f—t." Which last words he accompanied and graced with the very action, which, of all others, was the most proper to it. And whether it was this word or the contempt exprest for her politics, which most affected Mrs Western, I will not determine; but she flew into the most violent rage, uttered phrases improper to be here related, and instantly burst out of the house. Nor did her brother or her niece think proper either to stop or to follow her; for the one was so much possessed by concern, and the other by anger, that they were rendered almost motionless.

The squire, however, sent after his sister the same holloa which attends the departure of a hare, when she is first started before the hounds. He was indeed a great master of this kind of vociferation, and had a holla proper for most occasions in life.

Women who, like Mrs Western, know the world, and have applied themselves to philosophy and politics, would have immediately availed themselves of the present disposition of Mr Western's mind, by throwing in a few artful compliments to his understanding at the expense of his absent adversary; but poor Sophia was all simplicity. By which word we do not intend to insinuate to the reader, that she was silly, which is generally understood as a synonymous term with simple; for she was indeed a most sensible girl, and her understanding was of the first rate; but she wanted all that useful art which females convert to so many good purposes in life, and which, as it rather arises from the heart than from the head, is often the property of the silliest of women.

CHAPTER IV.

A picture of a country gentlewoman taken from the life.

Mr Western having finished his holla, and taken a little breath, began to lament, in very pathetic terms, the unfortunate condition of men, who are, says he, "always whipt in by the humours of some d—n'd b— or other. I think I was hard run enough by your mother for one man; but after giving her a dodge, here's another b— follows me upon the foil; but curse my jacket if I will be run down in this manner by any o'um."

Sophia never had a single dispute with her father, till this unlucky affair of Blifil, on any account, except in defence of her mother, whom she had loved most tenderly, though she lost her in the eleventh year of her age. The squire, to whom that poor woman had been a faithful upper-servant all the time of their marriage, had returned that behaviour by making what the world calls a good husband. He very seldom swore at her (perhaps not above once a week) and never beat her; she had not the least occasion for jealousy, and was perfect mistress of her time; for she was never interrupted by her husband, who was engaged all the morning in his field exercises, and all the evening with bottle companions. She scarce indeed ever saw him but at meals; where she had the pleasure of carving those dishes which she had before attended at the dressing. From these meals she retired about five minutes after the other servants, having only stayed to drink "the king over the water." Such were, it seems, Mr Western's orders; for it was a maxim with him, that women should come in with the first dish, and go out after the first glass. Obedience to these orders was perhaps no difficult task; for the conversation (if it may be called so) was seldom such as could entertain a lady. It consisted chiefly of hallowing, singing, relations of sporting adventures, b—d—y, and abuse of women, and of the government.

These, however, were the only seasons when Mr Western saw his wife; for when he repaired to her bed, he was generally so drunk that he could not see; and in the sporting season he always rose from her before it was light. Thus was she perfect mistress of her time, and had besides a coach and four usually at her command; though unhappily, indeed, the badness of the neighbourhood, and of the roads, made this of little use; for none who had set much value on their necks would have passed through the one, or who had set any value on their hours, would have visited the other. Now to deal honestly with the reader, she did not make all the return expected to so much indulgence; for she had been married against her will by a fond father, the match having been rather advantageous on her side; for the squire's estate was upward of £3000 a year, and her fortune no more than a bare £8000. Hence perhaps she had contracted a little gloominess of temper, for she was rather a good servant than a good wife; nor had she always the gratitude to return the extraordinary degree of roaring mirth, with which the squire received her, even with a good-humoured smile. She would, moreover, sometimes interfere with matters which did not concern her, as the violent drinking of her husband, which in the gentlest terms she would take some of the few opportunities he gave her of remonstrating against. And once in her life she very earnestly entreated him to carry her for two months to London, which he peremptorily denied; nay, was angry with his wife for the request ever after, being well assured that all the husbands in London are cuckolds.

For this last, and many other good reasons, Western at length heartily hated his wife; and as he never concealed this hatred before her death, so he never forgot it afterwards; but when anything in the least soured him, as a bad scenting day, or a distemper among his hounds, or any other such misfortune, he constantly vented his spleen by invectives against the deceased, saying, "If my wife was alive now, she would be glad of this."

These invectives he was especially desirous of throwing forth before Sophia; for as he loved her more than he did any other, so he was really jealous that she had loved her mother better than him. And this jealousy Sophia seldom failed of heightening on these occasions; for he was not contented with violating her ears with the abuse of her mother, but endeavoured to force an explicit approbation of all this abuse; with which desire he never could prevail upon her by any promise or threats to comply.

Hence some of my readers will, perhaps, wonder that the squire had not hated Sophia as much as he had hated her mother; but I must inform them, that hatred is not the effect of love, even through the medium of jealousy. It is, indeed, very possible for jealous persons to kill the objects of their jealousy, but not to hate them. Which sentiment being a pretty hard morsel, and bearing something of the air of a paradox, we shall leave the reader to chew the cud upon it to the end of the chapter.

CHAPTER V.

The generous behaviour of Sophia towards her aunt.

Sophia kept silence during the foregoing speech of her father, nor did she once answer otherwise than with a sigh; but as he understood none of the language, or, as he called it, lingo of the eyes, so he was not satisfied without some further approbation of his sentiments, which he now demanded of his daughter; telling her, in the usual way, "he expected she was ready to take the part of everybody against him, as she had always done that of the b— her mother." Sophia remaining still silent, he cryed out, "What, art dumb? why dost unt speak? Was not thy mother a d—d b— to me? answer me that. What, I suppose you despise your father too, and don't think him good enough to speak to?"

"For Heaven's sake, sir," answered Sophia, "do not give so cruel a turn to my silence. I am sure I would sooner die than be guilty of any disrespect towards you; but how can I venture to speak, when every word must either offend my dear papa, or convict me of the blackest ingratitude as well as impiety to the memory of the best of mothers; for such, I am certain, my mamma was always to me?"

"And your aunt, I suppose, is the best of sisters too!" replied the squire. "Will you be so kind as to allow that she is a b—? I may fairly insist upon that, I think?"

"Indeed, sir," says Sophia, "I have great obligations to my aunt. She hath been a second mother to me."

"And a second wife to me too," returned Western; "so you will take her part too! You won't confess that she hath acted the part of the vilest sister in the world?"

"Upon my word, sir," cries Sophia, "I must belie my heart wickedly if I did. I know my aunt and you differ very much in your ways of thinking; but I have heard her a thousand times express the greatest affection for you; and I am convinced, so far from her being the worst sister in the world, there are very few who love a brother better."

"The English of all which is," answered the squire, "that I am in the wrong. Ay, certainly. Ay, to be sure the woman is in the right, and the man in the wrong always."

"Pardon me, sir," cries Sophia. "I do not say so."

"What don't you say?" answered the father: "you have the impudence to say she's in the right: doth it not follow then of course that I am in the wrong? And perhaps I am in the wrong to suffer such a Presbyterian Hanoverian b— to come into my house. She may 'dite me of a plot for anything I know, and give my estate to the government."

"So far, sir, from injuring you or your estate," says Sophia, "if my aunt had died yesterday, I am convinced she would have left you her whole fortune."

Whether Sophia intended it or no, I shall not presume to assert; but certain it is, these last words penetrated very deep into the ears of her father, and produced a much more sensible effect than all she had said before. He received the sound with much the same action as a man receives a bullet in his head. He started, staggered, and turned pale. After which he remained silent above a minute, and then began in the following hesitating manner: "Yesterday! she would have left me her esteate yesterday! would she? Why yesterday, of all the days in the year? I suppose if she dies to-morrow, she will leave it to somebody else, and perhaps out of the vamily."—"My aunt, sir," cries Sophia, "hath very violent passions, and I can't answer what she may do under their influence."

"You can't!" returned the father: "and pray who hath been the occasion of putting her into those violent passions? Nay, who hath actually put her into them? Was not you and she hard at it before I came into the room? Besides, was not all our quarrel about you? I have not quarrelled with sister this many years but upon your account; and now you would throw the whole blame upon me, as thof I should be the occasion of her leaving the esteate out o' the vamily. I could have expected no better indeed; this is like the return you make to all the rest of my fondness."

"I beseech you then," cries Sophia, "upon my knees I beseech you, if I have been the unhappy occasion of this difference, that you will endeavour to make it up with my aunt, and not suffer her to leave your house in this violent rage of anger: she is a very good-natured woman, and a few civil words will satisfy her. Let me entreat you, sir."

"So I must go and ask pardon for your fault, must I?" answered Western. "You have lost the hare, and I must draw every way to find her again? Indeed, if I was certain"—Here he stopt, and Sophia throwing in more entreaties, at length prevailed upon him; so that after venting two or three bitter sarcastical expressions against his daughter, he departed as fast as he could to recover his sister, before her equipage could be gotten ready.

Sophia then returned to her chamber of mourning, where she indulged herself (if the phrase may be allowed me) in all the luxury of tender grief. She read over more than once the letter which she had received from Jones; her muff too was used on this occasion; and she bathed both these, as well as herself, with her tears. In this situation the friendly Mrs Honour exerted her utmost abilities to comfort her afflicted mistress. She ran over the names of many young gentlemen: and having greatly commended their parts and persons, assured Sophia that she might take her choice of any. These methods must have certainly been used with some success in disorders of the like kind, or so skilful a practitioner as Mrs Honour would never have ventured to apply them; nay, I have heard that the college of chambermaids hold them to be as sovereign remedies as any in the female dispensary; but whether it was that Sophia's disease differed inwardly from those cases with which it agreed in external symptoms, I will not assert; but, in fact, the good waiting-woman did more harm than good, and at last so incensed her mistress (which was no easy matter) that with an angry voice she dismissed her from her presence.

CHAPTER VI.

Containing great variety of matter.

The squire overtook his sister just as she was stepping into the coach, and partly by force, and partly by solicitations, prevailed upon her to order her horses back into their quarters. He succeeded in this attempt without much difficulty; for the lady was, as we have already hinted, of a most placable disposition, and greatly loved her brother, though she despised his parts, or rather his little knowledge of the world.

Poor Sophia, who had first set on foot this reconciliation, was now made the sacrifice to it. They both concurred in their censures on her conduct; jointly declared war against her, and directly proceeded to counsel, how to carry it on in the most vigorous manner. For this purpose, Mrs Western proposed not only an immediate conclusion of the treaty with Allworthy, but as immediately to carry it into execution; saying, "That there was no other way to succeed with her niece, but by violent methods, which she was convinced Sophia had not sufficient resolution to resist. By violent," says she, "I mean rather, hasty measures; for as to confinement or absolute force, no such things must or can be attempted. Our plan must be concerted for a surprize, and not for a storm."

These matters were resolved on, when Mr Blifil came to pay a visit to his mistress. The squire no sooner heard of his arrival, than he stept aside, by his sister's advice, to give his daughter orders for the proper reception of her lover: which he did with the most bitter execrations and denunciations of judgment on her refusal.

The impetuosity of the squire bore down all before him; and Sophia, as her aunt very wisely foresaw, was not able to resist him. She agreed, therefore, to see Blifil, though she had scarce spirits or strength sufficient to utter her assent. Indeed, to give a peremptory denial to a father whom she so tenderly loved, was no easy task. Had this circumstance been out of the case, much less resolution than what she was really mistress of, would, perhaps, have served her; but it is no unusual thing to ascribe those actions entirely to fear, which are in a great measure produced by love.

In pursuance, therefore, of her father's peremptory command, Sophia now admitted Mr Blifil's visit. Scenes like this, when painted at large, afford, as we have observed, very little entertainment to the reader. Here, therefore, we shall strictly adhere to a rule of Horace; by which writers are directed to pass over all those matters which they despair of placing in a shining light;—a rule, we conceive, of excellent use as well to the historian as to the poet; and which, if followed, must at least have this good effect, that many a great evil (for so all great books are called) would thus be reduced to a small one.

It is possible the great art used by Blifil at this interview would have prevailed on Sophia to have made another man in his circumstances her confident, and to have revealed the whole secret of her heart to him; but she had contracted so ill an opinion of this young gentleman, that she was resolved to place no confidence in him; for simplicity, when set on its guard, is often a match for cunning. Her behaviour to him, therefore, was entirely forced, and indeed such as is generally prescribed to virgins upon the second formal visit from one who is appointed for their husband.

But though Blifil declared himself to the squire perfectly satisfied with his reception; yet that gentleman, who, in company with his sister, had overheard all, was not so well pleased. He resolved, in pursuance of the advice of the sage lady, to push matters as forward as possible; and addressing himself to his intended son-in-law in the hunting phrase, he cried, after a loud holla, "Follow her, boy, follow her; run in, run in; that's it, honeys. Dead, dead, dead. Never be bashful, nor stand shall I, shall I? Allworthy and I can finish all matters between us this afternoon, and let us ha' the wedding to-morrow."

Blifil having conveyed the utmost satisfaction into his countenance, answered, "As there is nothing, sir, in this world which I so eagerly desire as an alliance with your family, except my union with the most amiable and deserving Sophia, you may easily imagine how impatient I must be to see myself in possession of my two highest wishes. If I have not therefore importuned you on this head, you will impute it only to my fear of offending the lady, by endeavouring to hurry on so blessed an event faster than a strict compliance with all the rules of decency and decorum will permit. But if, by your interest, sir, she might be induced to dispense with any formalities—"

"Formalities! with a pox!" answered the squire. "Pooh, all stuff and nonsense! I tell thee, she shall ha' thee to-morrow: you will know the world better hereafter, when you come to my age. Women never gi' their consent, man, if they can help it, 'tis not the fashion. If I had stayed for her mother's consent, I might have been a batchelor to this day.—To her, to her, co to her, that's it, you jolly dog. I tell thee shat ha' her to-morrow morning."

Blifil suffered himself to be overpowered by the forcible rhetoric of the squire; and it being agreed that Western should close with Allworthy that very afternoon, the lover departed home, having first earnestly begged that no violence might be offered to the lady by this haste, in the same manner as a popish inquisitor begs the lay power to do no violence to the heretic delivered over to it, and against whom the church hath passed sentence.

And, to say the truth, Blifil had passed sentence against Sophia; for, however pleased he had declared himself to Western with his reception, he was by no means satisfied, unless it was that he was convinced of the hatred and scorn of his mistress: and this had produced no less reciprocal hatred and scorn in him. It may, perhaps, be asked, Why then did he not put an immediate end to all further courtship? I answer, for that very reason, as well as for several others equally good, which we shall now proceed to open to the reader.

Though Mr Blifil was not of the complexion of Jones, nor ready to eat every woman he saw; yet he was far from being destitute of that appetite which is said to be the common property of all animals. With this, he had likewise that distinguishing taste, which serves to direct men in their choice of the object or food of their several appetites; and this taught him to consider Sophia as a most delicious morsel, indeed to regard her with the same desires which an ortolan inspires into the soul of an epicure. Now the agonies which affected the mind of Sophia, rather augmented than impaired her beauty; for her tears added brightness to her eyes, and her breasts rose higher with her sighs. Indeed, no one hath seen beauty in its highest lustre who hath never seen it in distress. Blifil therefore looked on this human ortolan with greater desire than when he viewed her last; nor was his desire at all lessened by the aversion which he discovered in her to himself. On the contrary, this served rather to heighten the pleasure he proposed in rifling her charms, as it added triumph to lust; nay, he had some further views, from obtaining the absolute possession of her person, which we detest too much even to mention; and revenge itself was not without its share in the gratifications which he promised himself. The rivalling poor Jones, and supplanting him in her affections, added another spur to his pursuit, and promised another additional rapture to his enjoyment.

Besides all these views, which to some scrupulous persons may seem to savour too much of malevolence, he had one prospect, which few readers will regard with any great abhorrence. And this was the estate of Mr Western; which was all to be settled on his daughter and her issue; for so extravagant was the affection of that fond parent, that, provided his child would but consent to be miserable with the husband he chose, he cared not at what price he purchased him.

For these reasons Mr Blifil was so desirous of the match that he intended to deceive Sophia, by pretending love to her; and to deceive her father and his own uncle, by pretending he was beloved by her. In doing this he availed himself of the piety of Thwackum, who held, that if the end proposed was religious (as surely matrimony is), it mattered not how wicked were the means. As to other occasions, he used to apply the philosophy of Square, which taught, that the end was immaterial, so that the means were fair and consistent with moral rectitude. To say truth, there were few occurrences in life on which he could not draw advantage from the precepts of one or other of those great masters.

Little deceit was indeed necessary to be practised on Mr Western; who thought the inclinations of his daughter of as little consequence as Blifil himself conceived them to be; but as the sentiments of Mr Allworthy were of a very different kind, so it was absolutely necessary to impose on him. In this, however, Blifil was so well assisted by Western, that he succeeded without difficulty; for as Mr Allworthy had been assured by her father that Sophia had a proper affection for Blifil, and that all which he had suspected concerning Jones was entirely false,

Blifil had nothing more to do than to confirm these assertions; which he did with such equivocations, that he preserved a salvo for his conscience; and had the satisfaction of conveying a lie to his uncle, without the guilt of telling one. When he was examined touching the inclinations of Sophia by Allworthy, who said, "He would on no account be accessary to forcing a young lady into a marriage contrary to her own will;" he answered, "That the real sentiments of young ladies were very difficult to be understood; that her behaviour to him was full as forward as he wished it, and that if he could believe her father, she had all the affection for him which any lover could desire. As for Jones," said he, "whom I am loth to call villain, though his behaviour to you, sir, sufficiently justifies the appellation, his own vanity, or perhaps some wicked views, might make him boast of a falsehood; for if there had been any reality in Miss Western's love to him, the greatness of her fortune would never have suffered him to desert her, as you are well informed he hath. Lastly, sir, I promise you I would not myself, for any consideration, no, not for the whole world, consent to marry this young lady, if I was not persuaded she had all the passion for me which I desire she should have."

This excellent method of conveying a falsehood with the heart only, without making the tongue guilty of an untruth, by the means of equivocation and imposture, hath quieted the conscience of many a notable deceiver; and yet, when we consider that it is Omniscience on which these endeavour to impose, it may possibly seem capable of affording only a very superficial comfort; and that this artful and refined distinction between communicating a lie, and telling one, is hardly worth the pains it costs them.

Allworthy was pretty well satisfied with what Mr Western and Mr Blifil told him: and the treaty was now, at the end of two days, concluded. Nothing then remained previous to the office of the priest, but the office of the lawyers, which threatened to take up so much time, that Western offered to bind himself by all manner of covenants, rather than defer the happiness of the young couple. Indeed, he was so very earnest and pressing, that an indifferent person might have concluded he was more a principal in this match than he really was; but this eagerness was natural to him on all occasions: and he conducted every scheme he undertook in such a manner, as if the success of that alone was sufficient to constitute the whole happiness of his life.

The joint importunities of both father and son-in-law would probably have prevailed on Mr Allworthy, who brooked but ill any delay of giving happiness to others, had not Sophia herself prevented it, and taken measures to put a final end to the whole treaty, and to rob both church and law of those taxes which these wise bodies have thought proper to receive from the propagation of the human species in a lawful manner. Of which in the next chapter.

CHAPTER VII.

A strange resolution of Sophia, and a more strange stratagem of Mrs Honour.

Though Mrs Honour was principally attached to her own interest, she was not without some little attachment to Sophia. To say truth, it was very difficult for any one to know that young lady without loving her. She no sooner therefore heard a piece of news, which she imagined to be of great importance to her mistress, than, quite forgetting the anger which she had conceived two days before, at her unpleasant dismission from Sophia's presence, she ran hastily to inform her of the news.

The beginning of her discourse was as abrupt as her entrance into the room. "O dear ma'am!" says she, "what doth your la'ship think? To be sure I am frightened out of my wits; and yet I thought it my duty to tell your la'ship, though perhaps it may make you angry, for we servants don't always know what will make our ladies angry; for, to be sure, everything is always laid to the charge of a servant. When our ladies are out of humour, to be sure we must be scolded; and to be sure I should not wonder if your la'ship should be out of humour; nay, it must surprize you certainly, ay, and shock you too."—"Good Honour, let me know it without any longer preface," says Sophia; "there are few things, I promise you, which will surprize, and fewer which will shock me."—"Dear ma'am," answered Honour, "to be sure, I overheard my master talking to parson Supple about getting a licence this very afternoon; and to be sure I heard him say, your la'ship should be married to-morrow morning." Sophia turned pale at these words, and repeated eagerly, "To-morrow morning!"—"Yes, ma'am," replied the trusty waiting-woman, "I will take my oath I heard my master say so."—"Honour," says Sophia, "you have both surprized and shocked me to such a degree that I have scarce any breath or spirits left. What is to be done in my dreadful situation?"—"I wish I was able to advise your la'ship," says she. "Do advise me," cries Sophia; "pray, dear Honour, advise me. Think what you would attempt if it was your own case."—"Indeed, ma'am," cries Honour, "I wish your la'ship and I could change situations; that is, I mean without hurting your la'ship; for to be sure I don't wish you so bad as to be a servant; but because that if so be it was my case, I should find no manner of difficulty in it; for, in my poor opinion, young Squire Blifil is a charming, sweet, handsome man."—"Don't mention such stuff," cries Sophia. "Such stuff!" repeated Honour; "why, there. Well, to be sure, what's one man's meat is another man's poison, and the same is altogether as true of women."—"Honour," says Sophia, "rather than submit to be the wife of that contemptible wretch, I would plunge a dagger into my heart."—"O lud! ma'am!" answered the other, "I am sure you frighten me out of my wits now. Let me beseech your la'ship not to suffer such wicked thoughts to come into your head. O lud! to be sure I tremble every inch of me. Dear ma'am, consider, that to be denied Christian burial, and to have your corpse buried in the highway, and a stake drove through you, as farmer Halfpenny was served at Ox Cross; and, to be sure, his ghost hath walked there ever since, for several people have seen him. To be sure it can be nothing but the devil which can put such wicked thoughts into the head of anybody; for certainly it is less wicked to hurt all the world than one's own dear self; and so I have heard said by more parsons than one. If your la'ship hath such a violent aversion, and hates the young gentleman so very bad, that you can't bear to think of going into bed to him; for to be sure there may be such antipathies in nature, and one had lieverer touch a toad than the flesh of some people."—

Sophia had been too much wrapt in contemplation to pay any great attention to the foregoing excellent discourse of her maid; interrupting her therefore, without making any answer to it, she said, "Honour, I am come to a resolution. I am determined to leave my father's house this very night; and if you have the friendship for me which you have often professed, you will keep me company."—"That I will, ma'am, to the world's end," answered Honour; "but I beg your la'ship to consider the consequence before you undertake any rash action. Where can your la'ship possibly go?"—"There is," replied Sophia, "a lady of quality in London, a relation of mine, who spent several months with my aunt in the country; during all which time she treated me with great kindness, and expressed so much pleasure in my company, that she earnestly desired my aunt to suffer me to go with her to London. As she is a woman of very great note, I shall easily find her out, and I make no doubt of being very well and kindly received by her."—"I would not have your la'ship too confident of that," cries Honour; "for the first lady I lived with used to invite people very earnestly to her house; but if she heard afterwards they were coming, she used to get out of the way. Besides, though this lady would be very glad to see your la'ship, as to be sure anybody would be glad to see your la'ship, yet when she hears your la'ship is run away from my master—" "You are mistaken, Honour," says Sophia: "she looks upon the authority of a father in a much lower light than I do; for she pressed me violently to go to London with her, and when I refused to go without my father's consent, she laughed me to scorn, called me silly country girl, and said, I should make a pure loving wife, since I could be so dutiful a daughter. So I have no doubt but she will both receive me and protect me too, till my father, finding me out of his power, can be brought to some reason."

"Well, but, ma'am," answered Honour, "how doth your la'ship think of making your escape? Where will you get any horses or conveyance? For as for your own horse, as all the servants know a little how matters stand between my master and your la'ship, Robin will be hanged before he will suffer it to go out of the stable without my master's express orders." "I intend to escape," said Sophia, "by walking out of the doors when they are open. I thank Heaven my legs are very able to carry me. They have supported me many a long evening"—"Yes, to be sure," cries Honour, "I will follow your la'ship through the world; but your la'ship had almost as good be alone: for I should not be able to defend you, if any robbers, or other villains, should meet with you. Nay, I should be in as horrible a fright as your la'ship; for to be certain, they would ravish us both. Besides, ma'am, consider how cold the nights are now; we shall be frozen to death."—"A good brisk pace," answered Sophia, "will preserve us from the cold; and if you cannot defend me from a villain, Honour, I will defend you; for I will take a pistol with me. There are two always charged in the hall."—"Dear ma'am, you frighten me more and more," cries Honour: "sure your la'ship would not venture to fire it off! I had rather run any chance than your la'ship should do that."—"Why so?" says Sophia, smiling; "would not you, Honour, fire a pistol at any one who should attack your virtue?"—"To be sure, ma'am," cries Honour, "one's virtue is a dear thing, especially to us poor servants; for it is our livelihood, as a body may say: yet I mortally hate fire-arms; for so many accidents happen by them."—"Well, well," says Sophia, "I believe I may ensure your virtue at a very cheap rate, without carrying any arms with us; for I intend to take horses at the very first town we come to, and we shall hardly be attacked in our way thither. Look'ee, Honour, I am resolved to go; and if you will attend me, I promise you I will reward you to the very utmost of my power."

This last argument had a stronger effect on Honour than all the preceding. And since she saw her mistress so determined, she desisted from any further dissuasions. They then entered into a debate on ways and means of executing their project. Here a very stubborn difficulty occurred, and this was the removal of their effects, which was much more easily got over by the mistress than by the maid; for when a lady hath once taken a resolution to run to a lover, or to run from him, all obstacles are considered as trifles. But Honour was inspired by no such motive; she had no raptures to expect, nor any terrors to shun; and besides the real value of her clothes, in which consisted a great part of her fortune, she had a capricious fondness for several gowns, and other things; either because they became her, or because they were given her by such a particular person; because she had bought them lately, or because she had had them long; or for some other reasons equally good; so that she could not endure the thoughts of leaving the poor things behind her exposed to the mercy of Western, who, she doubted not, would in his rage make them suffer martyrdom.

The ingenious Mrs Honour having applied all her oratory to dissuade her mistress from her purpose, when she found her positively determined, at last started the following expedient to remove her clothes, viz., to get herself turned out of doors that very evening. Sophia highly approved this method, but doubted how it might be brought about. "O, ma'am," cries Honour, "your la'ship may trust that to me; we servants very well know how to obtain this favour of our masters and mistresses; though sometimes, indeed, where they owe us more wages than they can readily pay, they will put up with all our affronts, and will hardly take any warning we can give them; but the squire is none of those; and since your la'ship is resolved upon setting out to-night, I warrant I get discharged this afternoon." It was then resolved that she should pack up some linen and a night-gown for Sophia, with her own things; and as for all her other clothes, the young lady abandoned them with no more remorse than the sailor feels when he throws over the goods of others, in order to save his own life.

CHAPTER VIII.

Containing scenes of altercation, of no very uncommon kind.

Mrs Honour had scarce sooner parted from her young lady, than something (for I would not, like the old woman in Quevedo, injure the devil by any false accusation, and possibly he might have no hand in it)—but something, I say, suggested itself to her, that by sacrificing Sophia and all her secrets to Mr Western, she might probably make her fortune. Many considerations urged this discovery. The fair prospect of a handsome reward for so great and acceptable a service to the squire, tempted her avarice; and again, the danger of the enterprize she had undertaken; the uncertainty of its success; night, cold, robbers, ravishers, all alarmed her fears. So forcibly did all these operate upon her, that she was almost determined to go directly to the squire, and to lay open the whole affair. She was, however, too upright a judge to decree on one side, before she had heard the other. And here, first, a journey to London appeared very strongly in support of Sophia. She eagerly longed to see a place in which she fancied charms short only of those which a raptured saint imagines in heaven. In the next place, as she knew Sophia to have much more generosity than her master, so her fidelity promised her a greater reward than she could gain by treachery. She then cross-examined all the articles which had raised her fears on the other side, and found, on fairly sifting the matter, that there was very little in them. And now both scales being reduced to a pretty even balance, her love to her mistress being thrown into the scale of her integrity, made that rather preponderate, when a circumstance struck upon her imagination which might have had a dangerous effect, had its whole weight been fairly put into the other scale. This was the length of time which must intervene before Sophia would be able to fulfil her promises; for though she was intitled to her mother's fortune at the death of her father, and to the sum of £3000 left her by an uncle when she came of age; yet these were distant days, and many accidents might prevent the intended generosity of the young lady; whereas the rewards she might expect from Mr Western were immediate. But while she was pursuing this thought the good genius of Sophia, or that which presided over the integrity of Mrs Honour, or perhaps mere chance, sent an accident in her way, which at once preserved her fidelity, and even facilitated the intended business.

Mrs Western's maid claimed great superiority over Mrs Honour on several accounts. First, her birth was higher; for her great-grandmother by the mother's side was a cousin, not far removed, to an Irish peer. Secondly, her wages were greater.

And lastly, she had been at London, and had of consequence seen more of the world. She had always behaved, therefore, to Mrs Honour with that reserve, and had always exacted of her those marks of distinction, which every order of females preserves and requires in conversation with those of an inferior order. Now as Honour did not at all times agree with this doctrine, but would frequently break in upon the respect which the other demanded, Mrs Western's maid was not at all pleased with her company; indeed, she earnestly longed to return home to the house of her mistress, where she domineered at will over all the other servants. She had been greatly, therefore, disappointed in the morning, when Mrs Western had changed her mind on the very point of departure; and had been in what is vulgarly called a glouting humour ever since.

In this humour, which was none of the sweetest, she came into the room where Honour was debating with herself in the manner we have above related. Honour no sooner saw her, than she addressed her in the following obliging phrase: "Soh, madam, I find we are to have the pleasure of your company longer, which I was afraid the quarrel between my master and your lady would have robbed us of."—"I don't know, madam," answered the other, "what you mean by we and us. I assure you I do not look on any of the servants in this house to be proper company for me. I am company, I hope, for their betters every day in the week. I do not speak on your account, Mrs Honour; for you are a civilized young woman; and when you have seen a little more of the world, I should not be ashamed to walk with you in St James's Park."—"Hoity toity!" cries Honour, "madam is in her airs, I protest. Mrs Honour, forsooth! sure, madam, you might call me by my sir-name; for though my lady calls me Honour, I have a sir-name as well as other folks. Ashamed to walk with me, quotha! marry, as good as yourself, I hope."—"Since you make such a return to my civility," said the other, "I must acquaint you, Mrs Honour, that you are not so good as me. In the country, indeed, one is obliged to take up with all kind of trumpery; but in town I visit none but the women of women of quality. Indeed, Mrs Honour, there is some difference, I hope, between you and me."—"I hope so too," answered Honour: "there is some difference in our ages, and—I think in our persons." Upon speaking which last words, she strutted by Mrs Western's maid with the most provoking air of contempt; turning up her nose, tossing her head, and violently brushing the hoop of her competitor with her own. The other lady put on one of her most malicious sneers, and said, "Creature! you are below my anger; and it is beneath me to give ill words to such an audacious saucy trollop; but, hussy, I must tell you, your breeding shows the meanness of your birth as well as of your education; and both very properly qualify you to be the mean serving-woman of a country girl."—"Don't abuse my lady," cries Honour: "I won't take that of you; she's as much better than yours as she is younger, and ten thousand times more handsomer."

Here ill luck, or rather good luck, sent Mrs Western to see her maid in tears, which began to flow plentifully at her approach; and of which being asked the reason by her mistress, she presently acquainted her that her tears were occasioned by the rude treatment of that creature there—meaning Honour. "And, madam," continued she, "I could have despised all she said to me; but she hath had the audacity to affront your ladyship, and to call you ugly—Yes, madam, she called you ugly old cat to my face. I could not bear to hear your ladyship called ugly."—"Why do you repeat her impudence so often?" said Mrs Western. And then turning to Mrs Honour, she asked her "How she had the assurance to mention her name with disrespect?"—"Disrespect, madam!" answered Honour; "I never mentioned your name at all: I said somebody was not as handsome as my mistress, and to be sure you know that as well as I."—"Hussy," replied the lady, "I will make such a saucy trollop as yourself know that I am not a proper subject of your discourse. And if my brother doth not discharge you this moment, I will never sleep in his house again. I will find him out, and have you discharged this moment."—"Discharged!" cries Honour; "and suppose I am: there are more places in the world than one. Thank Heaven, good servants need not want places; and if you turn away all who do not think you handsome, you will want servants very soon; let me tell you that."

Mrs Western spoke, or rather thundered, in answer; but as she was hardly articulate, we cannot be very certain of the identical words; we shall therefore omit inserting a speech which at best would not greatly redound to her honour. She then departed in search of her brother, with a countenance so full of rage, that she resembled one of the furies rather than a human creature.

The two chambermaids being again left alone, began a second bout at altercation, which soon produced a combat of a more active kind. In this the victory belonged to the lady of inferior rank, but not without some loss of blood, of hair, and of lawn and muslin.

CHAPTER IX.

The wise demeanour of Mr Western in the character of a magistrate. A hint to justices of peace, concerning the necessary qualifications of a clerk; with extraordinary instances of paternal madness and

filial affection.

Logicians sometimes prove too much by an argument, and politicians often overreach themselves in a scheme. Thus had it like to have happened to Mrs Honour, who, instead of recovering the rest of her clothes, had like to have stopped even those she had on her back from escaping; for the squire no sooner heard of her having abused his sister, than he swore twenty oaths he would send her to Bridewell.

Mrs Western was a very good-natured woman, and ordinarily of a forgiving temper. She had lately remitted the trespass of a stage-coachman, who had overturned her post-chaise into a ditch; nay, she had even broken the law, in refusing to prosecute a highwayman who had robbed her, not only of a sum of money, but of her ear-rings; at the same time d—ning her, and saying, "Such handsome b—s as you don't want jewels to set them off, and be d—n'd to you." But now, so uncertain are our tempers, and so much do we at different times differ from ourselves, she would hear of no mitigation; nor could all the affected penitence of Honour, nor all the entreaties of Sophia for her own servant, prevail with her to desist from earnestly desiring her brother to execute justiceship (for it was indeed a syllable more than justice) on the wench.

But luckily the clerk had a qualification, which no clerk to a justice of peace ought ever to be without, namely, some understanding in the law of this realm. He therefore whispered in the ear of the justice that he would exceed his authority by committing the girl to Bridewell, as there had been no attempt to break the peace; "for I am afraid, sir," says he, "you cannot legally commit any one to Bridewell only for ill-breeding."

In matters of high importance, particularly in cases relating to the game, the justice was not always attentive to these admonitions of his clerk; for, indeed, in executing the laws under that head, many justices of peace suppose they have a large discretionary power, by virtue of which, under the notion of searching for and taking away engines for the destruction of the game, they often commit trespasses, and sometimes felony, at their pleasure.

But this offence was not of quite so high a nature, nor so dangerous to the society. Here, therefore, the justice behaved with some attention to the advice of his clerk; for, in fact, he had already had two informations exhibited against him in the King's Bench, and had no curiosity to try a third.

The squire, therefore, putting on a most wise and significant countenance, after a preface of several hums and hahs, told his sister, that upon more mature deliberation, he was of opinion, that "as there was no breaking up of the peace, such as the law," says he, "calls breaking open a door, or breaking a hedge, or breaking a head, or any such sort of breaking, the matter did not amount to a felonious kind of a thing, nor trespasses, nor damages, and, therefore, there was no punishment in the law for it."

Mrs Western said, "she knew the law much better; that she had known servants very severely punished for affronting their masters;" and then named a certain justice of the peace in London, "who," she said, "would commit a servant to Bridewell at any time when a master or mistress desired it."

"Like enough," cries the squire; "it may be so in London; but the law is different in the country." Here followed a very learned dispute between the brother and sister concerning the law, which we would insert, if we imagined many of our readers could understand it. This was, however, at length referred by both parties to the clerk, who decided it in favour of the magistrate; and Mrs Western was, in the end, obliged to content herself with the satisfaction of having Honour turned away; to which Sophia herself very readily and cheerfully consented.

Thus Fortune, after having diverted herself, according to custom, with two or three frolicks, at last disposed all matters to the advantage of our heroine; who indeed succeeded admirably well in her deceit, considering it was the first she had ever practised. And, to say the truth, I have often concluded, that the honest part of mankind would be much too hard for the knavish, if they could bring themselves to incur the guilt, or thought it worth their while to take the trouble.

Honour acted her part to the utmost perfection. She no sooner saw herself secure from all danger of Bridewell, a word which had raised most horrible ideas in her mind, than she resumed those airs which her terrors before had a little abated; and laid down her place, with as much affectation of content, and indeed of contempt, as was ever practised at the resignation of places of much greater importance. If the reader pleases, therefore, we chuse rather to say she resigned—which hath, indeed, been always held a synonymous expression with being turned out, or turned away.

Mr Western ordered her to be very expeditious in packing; for his sister declared she would not sleep another night under the same roof with so impudent a slut. To work therefore she went, and that so earnestly, that everything was ready early in the evening; when, having received her wages, away packed bag and baggage, to the great satisfaction of every one, but of none more than of Sophia; who, having appointed her maid to meet her at a certain place not far from the house, exactly at the dreadful and ghostly hour of twelve, began to prepare for her own departure.

But first she was obliged to give two painful audiences, the one to her aunt, and the other to her father. In these Mrs Western herself began to talk to her in a more peremptory stile than before: but her father treated her in so violent and outrageous a manner, that he frightened her into an affected compliance with his will; which so highly pleased the good squire, that he changed his frowns into smiles, and his menaces into promises: he vowed his whole soul was wrapt in hers; that her consent (for so he construed the words, "You know, sir, I must not, nor can, refuse to obey any absolute command of yours") had made him the happiest of mankind. He then gave her a large bank-bill to dispose of in any trinkets she pleased, and kissed and embraced her in the fondest manner, while tears of joy trickled from those eyes which a few moments before had darted fire and rage against the dear object of all his affection.

Instances of this behaviour in parents are so common, that the reader, I doubt not, will be very little astonished at the whole conduct of Mr Western. If he should, I own I am not able to account for it; since that he loved his daughter most tenderly, is, I think, beyond dispute. So indeed have many others, who have rendered their children most completely miserable by the same conduct; which, though it is almost universal in parents, hath always appeared to me to be the most unaccountable of all the absurdities which ever entered into the brain of that strange prodigious creature man.

The latter part of Mr Western's behaviour had so strong an effect on the tender heart of Sophia, that it suggested a thought to her, which not all the sophistry of her politic aunt, nor all the menaces of her father, had ever once brought into her head. She reverenced her father so piously, and loved him so passionately, that she had scarce ever felt more pleasing sensations, than what arose from the share she frequently had of contributing to his amusement, and sometimes, perhaps, to higher gratifications; for he never could contain the delight of hearing her commended, which he had the satisfaction of hearing almost every day of her life. The idea, therefore, of the immense happiness she should convey to her father by her consent to this match, made a strong impression on her mind. Again, the extreme piety of such an act of obedience worked very forcibly, as she had a very deep sense of religion. Lastly, when she reflected how much she herself was to suffer, being indeed to become little less than a sacrifice, or a martyr, to filial love and duty, she felt an agreeable tickling in a certain little passion, which though it bears no immediate affinity either to religion or virtue, is often so kind as to lend great assistance in executing the purposes of both.

Sophia was charmed with the contemplation of so heroic an action, and began to compliment herself with much premature flattery, when Cupid, who lay hid in her muff, suddenly crept out, and like Punchinello in a puppet-show, kicked all out before him. In truth (for we scorn to deceive our reader, or to vindicate the character of our heroine by ascribing her actions to supernatural impulse) the thoughts of her beloved Jones, and some hopes (however distant) in which he was very particularly concerned, immediately destroyed all which filial love, piety, and pride had, with their joint endeavours, been labouring to bring about.

But before we proceed any farther with Sophia, we must now look back to Mr Jones.

CHAPTER X.

Containing several matters, natural enough perhaps, but low.

The reader will be pleased to remember, that we left Mr Jones, in the beginning of this book, on his road to Bristol; being determined to seek his fortune at sea, or rather, indeed, to fly away from his fortune on shore.

It happened (a thing not very unusual), that the guide who undertook to conduct him on his way, was unluckily unacquainted with the road; so that having missed his right track, and being ashamed to ask information, he rambled about backwards and forwards till night came on, and it began to grow dark. Jones suspecting what had happened, acquainted the guide with his apprehensions; but he insisted on it, that they were in the right road, and added, it would be very strange if he should not know the road to Bristol; though, in reality, it would have been much stranger if he had known it, having never past through it in his life before.

Jones had not such implicit faith in his guide, but that on their arrival at a village he inquired of the first fellow he saw, whether they were in the road to Bristol. "Whence did you come?" cries the fellow. "No matter," says Jones, a little hastily; "I want to know if this be the road to Bristol?"—"The road to Bristol!" cries the fellow, scratching his head: "why, measter, I believe you will hardly get to Bristol this way to-night."—"Prithee, friend, then," answered Jones, "do tell us which is the way."—"Why, measter," cries the fellow, "you must be come out of your road the Lord knows whither; for thick way goeth to Glocester."—"Well, and which way goes to Bristol?" said Jones. "Why, you be going away from Bristol," answered the fellow. "Then," said Jones, "we must go back again?"—"Ay, you must," said the fellow. "Well, and when we come back to the top of the hill, which way must we take?"—"Why, you must keep the strait road."—"But I remember there are two roads, one to the right and the other to the left."—"Why, you must keep the right-hand road, and then gu strait vorwards; only remember to turn vurst to your right, and then to your left again, and then to your right, and that brings you to the squire's; and then you must keep strait vorwards, and turn to the left."

Another fellow now came up, and asked which way the gentlemen were going; of which being informed by Jones, he first scratched his head, and then leaning upon a pole he had in his hand, began to tell him, "That he must keep the right-hand road for about a mile, or a mile and a half, or such a matter, and then he must turn short to the left, which would bring him round by Measter Jin Bearnes's."—"But which is Mr John Bearnes's?" says Jones. "O Lord!" cries the fellow, "why, don't you know Measter Jin Bearnes? Whence then did you come?"

These two fellows had almost conquered the patience of Jones, when a plain well-looking man (who was indeed a Quaker) accosted him thus: "Friend, I perceive thou hast lost thy way; and if thou wilt take my advice, thou wilt not attempt to find it to-night. It is almost dark, and the road is difficult to hit; besides, there have been several robberies committed lately between this and Bristol. Here is a very creditable good house just by, where thou may'st find good entertainment for thyself and thy cattle till morning." Jones, after a little persuasion, agreed to stay in this place till the morning, and was conducted by his friend to the public-house.

The landlord, who was a very civil fellow, told Jones, "He hoped he would excuse the badness of his accommodation; for that his wife was gone from home, and had locked up almost everything, and carried the keys along with her." Indeed the fact was, that a favourite daughter of hers was just married, and gone that morning home with her husband; and that she and her mother together had almost stript the poor man of all his goods, as well as money; for though he had several children, this daughter only, who was the mother's favourite, was the object of her consideration; and to the humour of this one child she would with pleasure have sacrificed all the rest, and her husband into the bargain.

Though Jones was very unfit for any kind of company, and would have preferred being alone, yet he could not resist the importunities of the honest Quaker; who was the more desirous of sitting with him, from having remarked the melancholy which appeared both in his countenance and behaviour; and which the poor Quaker thought his conversation might in some measure relieve.

After they had past some time together, in such a manner that my honest friend might have thought himself at one of his silent meetings, the Quaker began to be moved by some spirit or other, probably that of curiosity, and said, "Friend, I perceive some sad disaster hath befallen thee; but pray be of comfort. Perhaps thou hast lost a friend. If so, thou must consider we are all mortal. And why shouldst thou grieve, when thou knowest thy grief will do thy friend no good? We are all born to affliction. I myself have my sorrows as well as thee, and most probably greater sorrows. Though I have a clear estate of £100 a year, which is as much as I want, and I have a conscience, I thank the Lord, void of offence; my constitution is sound and strong, and there is no man can demand a debt of me, nor accuse me of an injury; yet, friend, I should be concerned to think thee as miserable as myself."

Here the Quaker ended with a deep sigh; and Jones presently answered, "I am very sorry, sir, for your unhappiness, whatever is the occasion of it."—"Ah! friend," replied the Quaker, "one only daughter is the occasion; one who was my greatest delight upon earth, and who within this week is run away from me, and is married against my consent. I had provided her a proper match, a sober man and one of substance; but she, forsooth, would chuse for herself, and away she is gone with a young fellow not worth a groat. If she had been dead, as I suppose thy friend is, I should have been happy."—"That is very strange, sir," said Jones.

"Why, would it not be better for her to be dead, than to be a beggar?" replied the Quaker: "for, as I told you, the fellow is not worth a groat; and surely she cannot expect that I shall ever give her a shilling. No, as she hath married for love, let her live on love if she can; let her carry her love to market, and see whether any one will change it into silver, or even into halfpence."—"You know your own concerns best, sir," said Jones. "It must have been," continued the Quaker, "a long premeditated scheme to cheat me: for they have known one another from their infancy; and I always preached to her against love, and told her a thousand times over it was all folly and wickedness. Nay, the cunning slut pretended to hearken to me, and to despise all wantonness of the flesh; and yet at last broke out at a window two pair of stairs: for I began, indeed, a little to suspect her, and had locked her up carefully, intending the very next morning to have married her up to my liking. But she disappointed me within a few hours, and escaped away to the lover of her own chusing; who lost no time, for they were married and bedded and all within an hour. But it shall be the worst hour's work for them both that ever they did; for they may starve, or beg, or steal together, for me. I will never give either of them a farthing." Here Jones starting up cried, "I really must be excused: I wish you would leave me."—"Come, come, friend," said the Quaker, "don't give way to concern. You see there are other people miserable besides yourself."—"I see there are madmen, and fools, and villains in the world," cries Jones. "But let me give you a piece of advice: send for your daughter and son-in-law home, and don't be yourself the only cause of misery to one you pretend to love."—"Send for her and her husband home!" cries the Quaker loudly; "I would sooner send for the two greatest enemies I have in the world!"—"Well, go home yourself, or where you please," said Jones, "for I will sit no longer in such company."—"Nay, friend," answered the Quaker, "I scorn to impose my company on any one." He then offered to pull money from his pocket, but Jones pushed him with some violence out of the room.

The subject of the Quaker's discourse had so deeply affected Jones, that he stared very wildly all the time he was speaking. This the Quaker had observed, and this, added to the rest of his behaviour, inspired honest Broadbrim with a conceit, that his companion was in reality out of his senses. Instead of resenting the affront, therefore, the Quaker was moved with compassion for his unhappy circumstances; and having communicated his opinion to the landlord, he desired him to take great care of his guest, and to treat him with the highest civility.

"Indeed," says the landlord, "I shall use no such civility towards him; for it seems, for all his laced waistcoat there, he is no more a gentleman than myself, but a poor parish bastard, bred up at a great squire's about thirty miles off, and now turned out of doors (not for any good to be sure). I shall get him out of my house as soon as possible. If I do lose my reckoning, the first loss is always the best. It is not above a year ago that I lost a silver spoon."

"What dost thou talk of a parish bastard, Robin?" answered the Quaker. "Thou must certainly be mistaken in thy man."

"Not at all," replied Robin; "the guide, who knows him very well, told it me." For, indeed, the guide had no sooner taken his place at the kitchen fire, than he acquainted the whole company with all he knew or had ever heard concerning Jones.

The Quaker was no sooner assured by this fellow of the birth and low fortune of Jones, than all compassion for him vanished; and the honest plain man went home fired with no less indignation than a duke would have felt at receiving an affront from such a person.

The landlord himself conceived an equal disdain for his guest; so that when Jones rung the bell in order to retire to bed, he was acquainted that he could have no bed there. Besides disdain of the mean condition of his guest, Robin entertained violent suspicion of his intentions, which were, he supposed, to watch some favourable opportunity of robbing the house. In reality, he might have been very well eased of these apprehensions, by the prudent precautions of his wife and daughter, who had already removed everything which was not fixed to the freehold; but he was by nature suspicious, and had been more particularly so since the loss of his spoon. In short, the dread of being robbed totally absorbed the comfortable consideration that he had nothing to lose.

Jones being assured that he could have no bed, very contentedly betook himself to a great chair made with rushes, when sleep, which had lately shunned his company in much better apartments, generously paid him a visit in his humble cell.

As for the landlord, he was prevented by his fears from retiring to rest. He returned therefore to the kitchen fire, whence he could survey the only door which opened into the parlour, or rather hole, where Jones was seated; and as for the window to that room, it was impossible for any creature larger than a cat to have made his escape through it.

CHAPTER XI.

The adventure of a company of soldiers.

The landlord having taken his seat directly opposite to the door of the parlour, determined to keep guard there the whole night. The guide and another fellow remained long on duty with him, though they neither knew his suspicions, nor had any of their own. The true cause of their watching did, indeed, at length, put an end to it; for this was no other than the strength and goodness of the beer, of which having tippled a very large quantity, they grew at first very noisy and vociferous, and afterwards fell both asleep.

But it was not in the power of liquor to compose the fears of Robin. He continued still waking in his chair, with his eyes fixed stedfastly on the door which led into the apartment of Mr Jones, till a violent thundering at his outward gate called him from his seat, and obliged him to open it; which he had no sooner done, than his kitchen was immediately full of gentlemen in red coats, who all rushed upon him in as tumultuous a manner as if they intended to take his little castle by storm.

The landlord was now forced from his post to furnish his numerous guests with beer, which they called for with great eagerness; and upon his second or third return from the cellar, he saw Mr Jones standing before the fire in the midst of the soldiers; for it may easily be believed, that the arrival of so much good company should put an end to any sleep, unless that from which we are to be awakened only by the last trumpet.

The company having now pretty well satisfied their thirst, nothing remained but to pay the reckoning, a circumstance often productive of much mischief and discontent among the inferior rank of gentry, who are apt to find great difficulty in assessing the sum, with exact regard to distributive justice, which directs that every man shall pay according to the quantity which he drinks. This difficulty occurred upon the present occasion; and it was the greater, as some gentlemen had, in their extreme hurry, marched off, after their first draught, and had entirely forgot to contribute anything towards the said reckoning.

A violent dispute now arose, in which every word may be said to have been deposed upon oath; for the oaths were at least equal to all the other words spoken. In this controversy the whole company spoke together, and every man seemed wholly bent to extenuate the sum which fell to his share; so that the most probable conclusion which could be foreseen was, that a large portion of the reckoning would fall to the landlord's share to pay, or (what is much the same thing) would remain unpaid.

All this while Mr Jones was engaged in conversation with the serjeant; for that officer was entirely unconcerned in the present dispute, being privileged by immemorial custom from all contribution.

The dispute now grew so very warm that it seemed to draw towards a military decision, when Jones, stepping forward, silenced all their clamours at once, by declaring that he would pay the whole reckoning, which indeed amounted to no more than three shillings and fourpence.

This declaration procured Jones the thanks and applause of the whole company. The terms honourable, noble, and worthy gentleman, resounded through the room; nay, my landlord himself began to have a better opinion of him, and almost to disbelieve the account which the guide had given.

The serjeant had informed Mr Jones that they were marching against the rebels, and expected to be commanded by the glorious Duke of Cumberland. By which the reader may perceive (a circumstance which we have not thought necessary to communicate before) that this was the very time when the late rebellion was at the highest; and indeed the banditti were now marched into England, intending, as it was thought, to fight the king's forces, and to attempt pushing forward to the metropolis.

Jones had some heroic ingredients in his composition, and was a hearty well-wisher to the glorious cause of liberty, and of the Protestant religion. It is no wonder, therefore, that in circumstances which would have warranted a much more romantic and wild undertaking, it should occur to him to serve as a volunteer in this expedition.

Our commanding officer had said all in his power to encourage and promote this good disposition, from the first moment he had been acquainted with it. He now proclaimed the noble resolution aloud, which was received with great pleasure by the whole company, who all cried out, "God bless King George and your honour;" and then added, with many oaths, "We will stand by you both to the last drops of our blood."

The gentleman who had been all night tippling at the alehouse, was prevailed on by some arguments which a corporal had put into his hands, to undertake the same expedition. And now the portmanteau belonging to Mr Jones being put up in the baggage-cart, the forces were about to move forwards; when the guide, stepping up to Jones, said, "Sir, I hope you will consider that the horses have been kept out all night, and we have travelled a great ways out of our way." Jones was surprized at the impudence of this demand, and acquainted the soldiers with the merits of his cause, who were all unanimous in condemning the guide for his endeavours to put upon a gentleman. Some said, he ought to be tied neck and heels; others that he deserved to run the gantlope; and the serjeant shook his cane at him, and wished he had him under his command, swearing heartily he would make an example of him.

Jones contented himself however with a negative punishment, and walked off with his new comrades, leaving the guide to the poor revenge of cursing and reviling him; in which latter the landlord joined, saying, "Ay, ay, he is a pure one, I warrant you. A pretty gentleman, indeed, to go for a soldier! He shall wear a laced wastecoat truly. It is an old proverb and a true one, all is not gold that glisters. I am glad my house is well rid of him."

All that day the serjeant and the young soldier marched together; and the former, who was an arch fellow, told the latter many entertaining stories of his campaigns, though in reality he had never made any; for he was but lately come into the service, and had, by his own dexterity, so well ingratiated himself with his officers, that he had promoted himself to a halberd; chiefly indeed by his merit in recruiting, in which he was most excellently well skilled.

Much mirth and festivity passed among the soldiers during their march. In which the many occurrences that had passed at their last quarters were remembered, and every one, with great freedom, made what jokes he pleased on his officers, some of which were of the coarser kind, and very near bordering on scandal. This brought to our heroe's mind the custom which he had read of among the Greeks and Romans, of indulging, on certain festivals and solemn occasions, the liberty to slaves, of using an uncontrouled freedom of speech towards their masters.

Our little army, which consisted of two companies of foot, were now arrived at the place where they were to halt that evening. The serjeant then acquainted his lieutenant, who was the commanding officer, that they had picked up two fellows in that day's march, one of which, he said, was as fine a man as ever he saw (meaning the tippler), for that he was near six feet, well proportioned, and strongly limbed; and the other (meaning Jones) would do well enough for the rear rank.

The new soldiers were now produced before the officer, who having examined the six-feet man, he being first produced, came next to survey Jones: at the first sight of whom, the lieutenant could not help showing some surprize; for besides that he was very well dressed, and was naturally genteel, he had a remarkable air of dignity in his look, which is rarely seen among the vulgar, and is indeed not inseparably annexed to the features of their superiors.

"Sir," said the lieutenant, "my serjeant informed me that you are desirous of enlisting in the company I have at present under my command; if so, sir, we shall very gladly receive a gentleman who promises to do much honour to the company by bearing arms in it."

Jones answered: "That he had not mentioned anything of enlisting himself; that he was most zealously attached to the glorious cause for which they were going to fight, and was very desirous of serving as a volunteer;" concluding with some compliments to the lieutenant, and expressing the great satisfaction he should have in being under his command.

The lieutenant returned his civility, commended his resolution, shook him by the hand, and invited him to dine with himself and the rest of the officers.

CHAPTER XII.

The adventure of a company of officers.

The lieutenant, whom we mentioned in the preceding chapter, and who commanded this party, was now near sixty years of age. He had entered very young into the army, and had served in the capacity of an ensign at the battle of Tannieres; here he had received two wounds, and had so well distinguished himself, that he was by the Duke of Marlborough advanced to be a lieutenant, immediately after that battle.

In this commission he had continued ever since, viz., near forty years; during which time he had seen vast numbers preferred over his head, and had now the mortification to be commanded by boys, whose fathers were at nurse when he first entered into the service.

Nor was this ill success in his profession solely owing to his having no friends among the men in power. He had the misfortune to incur the displeasure of his colonel, who for many years continued in the command of this regiment. Nor did he owe the implacable ill-will which this man bore him to any neglect or deficiency as an officer, nor indeed to any fault in himself; but solely to the indiscretion of his wife, who was a very beautiful woman, and who, though she was remarkably fond of her husband, would not purchase his preferment at the expense of certain favours which the colonel required of her.

The poor lieutenant was more peculiarly unhappy in this, that while he felt the effects of the enmity of his colonel, he neither knew, nor suspected, that he really bore him any; for he could not suspect an ill-will for which he was not conscious of giving any cause; and his wife, fearing what her husband's nice regard to his honour might have occasioned, contented herself with preserving her virtue without enjoying the triumphs of her conquest.

This unfortunate officer (for so I think he may be called) had many good qualities besides his merit in his profession; for he was a religious, honest, good-natured man; and had behaved so well in his command, that he was highly esteemed and beloved not only by the soldiers of his own company, but by the whole regiment.

The other officers who marched with him were a French lieutenant, who had been long enough out of France to forget his own language, but not long enough in England to learn ours, so that he really spoke no language at all, and could barely make himself understood on the most ordinary occasions. There were likewise two ensigns, both very young fellows; one of whom had been bred under an attorney, and the other was son to the wife of a nobleman's butler.

As soon as dinner was ended, Jones informed the company of the merriment which had passed among the soldiers upon their march; "and yet," says he, "notwithstanding all their vociferation, I dare swear they will behave more like Grecians than Trojans when they come to the enemy."—"Grecians and Trojans!" says one of the ensigns, "who the devil are they? I have heard of all the troops in Europe, but never of any such as these."

"Don't pretend to more ignorance than you have, Mr Northerton," said the worthy lieutenant. "I suppose you have heard of the Greeks and Trojans, though perhaps you never read Pope's Homer; who, I remember, now the gentleman mentions it, compares the march of the Trojans to the cackling of geese, and greatly commends the silence of the Grecians. And upon my honour there is great justice in the cadet's observation."

"Begar, me remember dem ver well," said the French lieutenant: "me ave read them at school in dans Madam Daciere, des Greek, des Trojan, dey fight for von woman—ouy, ouy, me ave read all dat."

"D—n Homo with all my heart," says Northerton; "I have the marks of him on my a— yet. There's Thomas, of our regiment, always carries a Homo in his pocket; d—n me, if ever I come at it, if I don't burn it. And there's Corderius, another d—n'd son of a whore, that hath got me many a flogging."

"Then you have been at school, Mr Northerton?" said the lieutenant.

"Ay, d—n me, have I," answered he; "the devil take my father for sending me thither! The old put wanted to make a parson of me, but d—n me, thinks I to myself, I'll nick you there, old cull; the devil a smack of your nonsense shall you ever get into me. There's Jemmy Oliver, of our regiment, he narrowly escaped being a pimp too, and that would have been a thousand pities; for d—n me if he is not one of the prettiest fellows in the whole world; but he went farther than I with the old cull, for Jimmey can neither write nor read."

"You give your friend a very good character," said the lieutenant, "and a very deserved one, I dare say. But prithee, Northerton, leave off that foolish as well as wicked custom of swearing; for you are deceived, I promise you, if you think there is wit or politeness in it. I wish, too, you would take my advice, and desist from abusing the clergy. Scandalous names, and reflections cast on any body of men, must be always unjustifiable; but especially so, when thrown on so sacred a function; for to abuse the body is to abuse the function itself; and I leave to you to judge how inconsistent such behaviour is in men who are going to fight in defence of the Protestant religion."

Mr Adderly, which was the name of the other ensign, had sat hitherto kicking his heels and humming a tune, without seeming to listen to the discourse; he now answered, "*O, Monsieur, on ne parle pas de la religion dans la guerre*."—"Well said, Jack," cries Northerton: "if *la religion* was the only matter, the parsons should fight their own battles for me."

"I don't know, gentlemen," said Jones, "what may be your opinion; but I think no man can engage in a nobler cause than that of his religion; and I have observed, in the little I have read of history, that no soldiers have fought so bravely as those who have been inspired with a religious zeal: for my own part, though I love my king and country, I hope, as well as any man in it, yet the Protestant interest is no small motive to my becoming a volunteer in the cause."

Northerton now winked on Adderly, and whispered to him slily, "Smoke the prig, Adderly, smoke him." Then turning to Jones, said to him, "I am very glad, sir, you have chosen our regiment to be a volunteer in; for if our parson should at any time take a cup too much, I find you can supply his place. I presume, sir, you have been at the university; may I crave the favour to know what college?"

"Sir," answered Jones, "so far from having been at the university, I have even had the advantage of yourself, for I was never at school."

"I presumed," cries the ensign, "only upon the information of your great learning."—"Oh! sir," answered Jones, "it is as possible for a man to know something without having been at school, as it is to have been at school and to know nothing."

"Well said, young volunteer," cries the lieutenant. "Upon my word, Northerton, you had better let him alone; for he will be too hard for you."

Northerton did not very well relish the sarcasm of Jones; but he thought the provocation was scarce sufficient to justify a blow, or a rascal, or scoundrel, which were the only repartees that suggested themselves. He was, therefore, silent at present; but resolved to take the first opportunity of returning the jest by abuse.

It now came to the turn of Mr Jones to give a toast, as it is called; who could not refrain from mentioning his dear Sophia. This he did the more readily, as he imagined it utterly impossible that any one present should guess the person he meant.

But the lieutenant, who was the toast-master, was not contented with Sophia only. He said, he must have her sir-name; upon which Jones hesitated a little, and presently after named Miss Sophia Western. Ensign Northerton declared he would not drink her health in the same round with his own toast, unless somebody would vouch for her. "I knew one Sophy Western," says he, "that was lain with by half the young fellows at Bath; and perhaps this is the same woman." Jones very solemnly assured him of the contrary; asserting that the young lady he named was one of great fashion and fortune. "Ay, ay," says the ensign, "and so she is: d—n me, it is the same woman; and I'll hold half a dozen of Burgundy, Tom French of our regiment brings her into company with us at any tavern in Bridges-street." He then proceeded to describe her person exactly (for he had seen her with her aunt), and concluded with saying, "that her father had a great estate in Somersetshire."

The tenderness of lovers can ill brook the least jesting with the names of their mistresses. However, Jones, though he had enough of the lover and of the heroe too in his disposition, did not resent these slanders as hastily as, perhaps, he ought to have done. To say the truth, having seen but little of this kind of wit, he did not readily understand it, and for a long time imagined Mr Northerton had really mistaken his charmer for some other. But now, turning to the ensign with a stern aspect, he said, "Pray, sir, chuse some other subject for your wit; for I promise you I will bear no jesting with this lady's character." "Jesting!" cries the other, "d—n me if ever I was more in earnest in my life. Tom French of our regiment had both her and her aunt at Bath." "Then I must tell you in earnest," cries Jones, "that you are one of the most impudent rascals upon earth."

He had no sooner spoken these words, than the ensign, together with a volley of curses, discharged a bottle full at the head of Jones, which hitting him a little above the right temple, brought him instantly to the ground.

The conqueror perceiving the enemy to lie motionless before him, and blood beginning to flow pretty plentifully from his wound, began now to think of quitting the field of battle, where no more honour was to be gotten; but the lieutenant interposed, by stepping before the door, and thus cut off his retreat.

Northerton was very importunate with the lieutenant for his liberty; urging the ill consequences of his stay, asking him, what he could have done less? "Zounds!" says he, "I was but in jest with the fellow. I never heard any harm of Miss Western in my life." "Have not you?" said the lieutenant; "then you richly deserve to be hanged, as well for making such jests, as for using such a weapon: you are my prisoner, sir; nor shall you stir from hence till a proper guard comes to secure you."

Such an ascendant had our lieutenant over this ensign, that all that fervency of courage which had levelled our poor heroe with the floor, would scarce have animated the said ensign to have drawn his sword against the lieutenant, had he then had one dangling at his side: but all the swords being hung up in the room, were, at the very beginning of the fray, secured by the French officer. So that Mr Northerton was obliged to attend the final issue of this affair.

The French gentleman and Mr Adderly, at the desire of their commanding officer, had raised up the body of Jones, but as they could perceive but little (if any) sign of life in him, they again let him fall, Adderly damning him for having blooded his wastecoat; and the Frenchman declaring, "Begar, me no tush the Engliseman de mort: me have heard de Englise ley, law, what you call, hang up de man dat tush him last."

When the good lieutenant applied himself to the door, he applied himself likewise to the bell; and the drawer immediately attending, he dispatched him for a file of musqueteers and a surgeon. These commands, together with the drawer's report of what he had himself seen, not only produced the soldiers, but presently drew up the landlord of the house, his wife, and servants, and, indeed, every one else who happened at that time to be in the inn.

To describe every particular, and to relate the whole conversation of the ensuing scene, is not within my power, unless I had forty pens, and could, at once, write with them all together, as the company now spoke. The reader must, therefore, content himself with the most remarkable incidents, and perhaps he may very well excuse the rest.

The first thing done was securing the body of Northerton, who being delivered into the custody of six men with a corporal at their head, was by them conducted from a place which he was very willing to leave, but it was unluckily to a place whither he was very unwilling to go. To say the truth, so whimsical are the desires of ambition, the very moment this youth had attained the above-mentioned honour, he would have been well contented to have retired to some corner of the world, where the fame of it should never have reached his ears.

It surprizes us, and so perhaps, it may the reader, that the lieutenant, a worthy and good man, should have applied his chief care, rather to secure the offender, than to preserve the life of the wounded person. We mention this observation, not with any view of pretending to account for so odd a behaviour, but lest some critic should hereafter plume himself on discovering it. We would have these gentlemen know we can see what is odd in characters as well as themselves, but it is our business to relate facts as they are; which, when we have done, it is the part of the learned and sagacious reader to consult that original book of nature, whence every passage in our work is transcribed, though we quote not always the particular page for its authority.

The company which now arrived were of a different disposition. They suspended their curiosity concerning the person of the ensign, till they should see him hereafter in a more engaging attitude. At present, their whole concern and attention were employed about the bloody object on the floor; which being placed upright in a chair, soon began to discover some symptoms of life and motion. These were no sooner perceived by the company (for Jones was at first generally concluded to be dead) than they all fell at once to prescribing for him (for as none of the physical order was present, every one there took that office upon him).

Bleeding was the unanimous voice of the whole room; but unluckily there was no operator at hand; every one then cried, "Call the barber;" but none stirred a step. Several cordials was likewise prescribed in the same ineffective manner; till the landlord ordered up a tankard of strong beer, with a toast, which he said was the best cordial in England.

The person principally assistant on this occasion, indeed the only one who did any service, or seemed likely to do any, was the landlady: she cut off some of her hair, and applied it to the wound to stop the blood; she fell to chafing the youth's temples with her hand; and having exprest great contempt for her husband's prescription of beer, she despatched one of her maids to her own closet for a bottle of brandy, of which, as soon as it was brought, she prevailed on Jones, who was just returned to his senses, to drink a very large and plentiful draught.

Soon afterwards arrived the surgeon, who having viewed the wound, having shaken his head, and blamed everything which was done, ordered his patient instantly to bed; in which place we think proper to leave him some time to his repose, and shall here, therefore, put an end to this chapter.

CHAPTER XIII.

Containing the great address of the landlady, the great learning of a surgeon, and the solid skill in casuistry of the worthy lieutenant.

When the wounded man was carried to his bed, and the house began again to clear up from the hurry which this accident had occasioned, the landlady thus addressed the commanding officer: "I am afraid, sir," said she, "this young man did not behave himself as well as he should do to your honours; and if he had been killed, I suppose he had but his desarts: to be sure, when gentlemen admit inferior parsons into their company, they oft to keep their distance; but, as my first husband used to say, few of 'em know how to do it. For my own part, I am sure I should not have suffered any fellows to *include* themselves into gentlemen's company; but I thoft he had been an officer himself, till the serjeant told me he was but a recruit."

"Landlady," answered the lieutenant, "you mistake the whole matter. The young man behaved himself extremely well, and is, I believe, a much better gentleman than the ensign who abused him. If the young fellow dies, the man who struck him will have most reason to be sorry for it: for the regiment will get rid of a very troublesome fellow, who is a scandal to the army; and if he escapes from the hands of justice, blame me, madam, that's all."

"Ay! ay! good lack-a-day!" said the landlady; "who could have thoft it? Ay, ay, ay, I am satisfied your honour will see justice done; and to be sure it oft to be to every one. Gentlemen oft not to kill poor folks without answering for it. A poor man hath a soul to be saved, as well as his betters."

"Indeed, madam," said the lieutenant, "you do the volunteer wrong: I dare swear he is more of a gentleman than the officer."

"Ay!" cries the landlady; "why, look you there, now: well, my first husband was a wise man; he used to say, you can't always know the inside by the outside. Nay, that might have been well enough too; for I never *saw'd* him till he was all over blood. Who would have thoft it? mayhap, some young gentleman crossed in love. Good lack-a-day, if he should die, what a concern it will be to his parents! why, sure the devil must possess the wicked wretch to do such an act. To be sure, he is a scandal to the army, as your honour says; for most of the gentlemen of the army that ever I saw, are quite different sort of people, and look as if they would scorn to spill any Christian blood as much as any men: I mean, that is, in a civil way, as my first husband used to say. To be sure, when they come into the wars, there must be bloodshed: but that they are not to be blamed for. The more of our enemies they kill there, the better: and I wish, with all my heart, they could kill every mother's son of them."

"O fie, madam!" said the lieutenant, smiling; "*all* is rather too bloody-minded a wish."

"Not at all, sir," answered she; "I am not at all bloody-minded, only to our enemies; and there is no harm in that. To be sure it is natural for us to wish our enemies dead, that the wars may be at an end, and our taxes be lowered; for it is a dreadful thing to pay as we do. Why now, there is above forty shillings for window-lights, and yet we have stopt up all we could; we have almost blinded the house, I am sure. Says I to the exciseman, says I, I think you oft to favour us; I am sure we are very good friends to the government: and so we are for sartain, for we pay a mint of money to 'um. And yet I often think to myself the government doth not imagine itself more obliged to us, than to those that don't pay 'um a farthing. Ay, ay, it is the way of the world."

She was proceeding in this manner when the surgeon entered the room. The lieutenant immediately asked how his patient did. But he resolved him only by saying, "Better, I believe, than he would have been by this time, if I had not been called; and even as it is, perhaps it would have been lucky if I could have been called sooner."—"I hope, sir," said the lieutenant, "the skull is not fractured."—"Hum," cries the surgeon: "fractures are not always the most dangerous symptoms. Contusions and lacerations are often attended with worse phaenomena, and with more fatal consequences, than fractures. People who know nothing of the matter conclude, if the skull is not fractured, all is well; whereas, I had rather see a man's skull broke all to pieces, than some contusions I have met with."—"I hope," says the lieutenant, "there are no such symptoms here."—"Symptoms," answered the surgeon, "are not always regular nor constant. I have known very unfavourable symptoms in the morning change to favourable ones at noon, and return to unfavourable again at night. Of wounds, indeed, it is rightly and truly said, *Nemo repente fuit turpissimus*. I was once, I remember, called to a patient who had received a violent contusion in his tibia, by which the exterior cutis was lacerated, so that there was a profuse sanguinary discharge; and the interior membranes were so divellicated, that the os or bone very plainly appeared through the aperture of the vulnus or wound. Some febrile symptoms intervening at the same time (for the pulse was exuberant and indicated much phlebotomy), I apprehended an immediate mortification. To prevent which, I presently made a large orifice in the vein of the left arm, whence I drew twenty ounces of blood; which I expected to have found extremely sizy and glutinous, or indeed coagulated, as it is in pleuretic complaints; but, to my surprize, it appeared rosy and florid, and its consistency differed little from the blood of those in perfect health. I then applied a fomentation to the part, which highly answered the intention; and after three or four times dressing, the wound began to discharge a thick pus or matter, by which means the cohesion—But perhaps I do not make myself perfectly well understood?"—"No, really," answered the lieutenant, "I cannot say I understand a syllable."—"Well, sir," said the surgeon, "then I shall not tire your patience; in short, within six weeks my patient was able to walk upon his legs as perfectly as he could have done before he received the contusion."—"I wish, sir," said the lieutenant, "you would be so kind only to inform me, whether the wound this young gentleman hath had the misfortune to receive, is likely to prove mortal."—"Sir," answered the surgeon, "to say whether a wound will prove mortal or not at first dressing, would be very weak and foolish presumption: we are all mortal, and symptoms often occur in a cure which the greatest of our profession could never foresee."—"But do you think him in danger?" says the other.—"In danger! ay, surely," cries the doctor: "who is there among us, who, in the most perfect health, can be said not to be in danger? Can a man, therefore, with so bad a wound as this be said to be out of danger? All I can say at present is, that it is well I was called as I was, and perhaps it would have been better if I had been called sooner. I will see him again early in the morning; and in the meantime let him be kept extremely quiet, and drink liberally of water-gruel."—"Won't you allow him sack-whey?" said the landlady.—"Ay, ay, sack-whey," cries the doctor, "if you will, provided it be very small."—"And a little chicken broth too?" added she.—"Yes, yes, chicken broth," said the doctor, "is very good."—"Mayn't I make him some jellies too?" said the landlady.—"Ay, ay," answered the doctor, "jellies are very good for wounds, for they promote cohesion." And indeed it was lucky she had not named soup or high sauces, for the doctor would have complied, rather than have lost the custom of the house.

The doctor was no sooner gone, than the landlady began to trumpet forth his fame to the lieutenant, who had not, from their short acquaintance, conceived quite so favourable an opinion of his physical abilities as the good woman, and all the neighbourhood, entertained (and perhaps very rightly); for though I am afraid the doctor was a little of a coxcomb, he might be nevertheless very much of a surgeon.

The lieutenant having collected from the learned discourse of the surgeon that Mr Jones was in great danger, gave orders for keeping Mr Northerton under a very strict guard, designing in the morning to attend him to a justice of peace, and to commit the conducting the troops to Gloucester to the French lieutenant, who, though he could neither read, write, nor speak any language, was, however, a good officer.

In the evening, our commander sent a message to Mr Jones, that if a visit would not be troublesome, he would wait on him. This civility was very kindly and thankfully received by Jones, and the lieutenant accordingly went up to his room, where he found the wounded man much better than he expected; nay, Jones assured his friend, that if he had not received express orders to the contrary from the surgeon, he should have got up long ago; for he appeared to himself to be as well as ever, and felt no other inconvenience from his wound but an extreme soreness on that side of his head.

"I should be very glad," quoth the lieutenant, "if you was as well as you fancy yourself, for then you could be able to do yourself justice immediately; for when a matter can't be made up, as in case of a blow, the sooner you take him out the better; but I am afraid you think yourself better than you are, and he would have too much advantage over you."

"I'll try, however," answered Jones, "if you please, and will be so kind to lend me a sword, for I have none here of my own."

"My sword is heartily at your service, my dear boy," cries the lieutenant, kissing him; "you are a brave lad, and I love your spirit; but I fear your strength; for such a blow, and so much loss of blood, must have very much weakened you; and though you feel no want of strength in your bed, yet you most probably would after a thrust or two. I can't consent to your taking him out tonight; but I hope you will be able to come up with us before we get many days' march advance; and I give you my honour you shall have satisfaction, or the man who hath injured you shan't stay in our regiment."

"I wish," said Jones, "it was possible to decide this matter to-night: now you have mentioned it to me, I shall not be able to rest."

"Oh, never think of it," returned the other: "a few days will make no difference. The wounds of honour are not like those in your body: they suffer nothing by the delay of cure. It will be altogether as well for you to receive satisfaction a week hence as now."

"But suppose," says Jones, "I should grow worse, and die of the consequences of my present wound?"

"Then your honour," answered the lieutenant, "will require no reparation at all. I myself will do justice to your character, and testify to the world your intention to have acted properly, if you had recovered."

"Still," replied Jones, "I am concerned at the delay. I am almost afraid to mention it to you who are a soldier; but though I have been a very wild young fellow, still in my most serious moments, and at the bottom, I am really a Christian."

"So am I too, I assure you," said the officer; "and so zealous a one, that I was pleased with you at dinner for taking up the cause of your religion; and I am a little offended with you now, young gentleman, that you should express a fear of declaring your faith before any one."

"But how terrible must it be," cries Jones, "to any one who is really a Christian, to cherish malice in his breast, in opposition to the command of Him who hath expressly forbid it? How can I bear to do this on a sick-bed? Or how shall I make up my account, with such an article as this in my bosom against me?"

"Why, I believe there is such a command," cries the lieutenant; "but a man of honour can't keep it. And you must be a man of honour, if you will be in the army. I remember I once put the case to our chaplain over a bowl of punch, and he confessed there was much difficulty in it; but he said, he hoped there might be a latitude granted to soldiers in this one instance; and to be sure it is our duty to hope so; for who would bear to live without his honour? No, no, my dear boy, be a good Christian as long as you live; but be a man of honour too, and never put up an affront; not all the books, nor all the parsons in the world, shall ever persuade me to that. I love my religion very well, but I love my honour more. There must be some mistake in the wording the text, or in the translation, or in the understanding it, or somewhere or other. But however that be, a man must run the risque, for he must preserve his honour. So compose yourself to-night, and I promise you you shall have an opportunity of doing yourself justice." Here he gave Jones a hearty buss, shook him by the hand, and took his leave.

But though the lieutenant's reasoning was very satisfactory to himself, it was not entirely so to his friend. Jones therefore, having revolved this matter much in his thoughts, at last came to a resolution, which the reader will find in the next chapter.

CHAPTER XIV.

A most dreadful chapter indeed; and which few readers ought to venture upon in an evening, especially when alone.

Jones swallowed a large mess of chicken, or rather cock, broth, with a very good appetite, as indeed he would have done the cock it was made of, with a pound of bacon into the bargain; and now, finding in himself no deficiency of either health or spirit, he resolved to get up and seek his enemy.

But first he sent for the serjeant, who was his first acquaintance among these military gentlemen. Unluckily that worthy officer having, in a literal sense, taken his fill of liquor, had been some time retired to his bolster, where he was snoring so loud that it was not easy to convey a noise in at his ears capable of drowning that which issued from his nostrils.

However, as Jones persisted in his desire of seeing him, a vociferous drawer at length found means to disturb his slumbers, and to acquaint him with the message. Of which the serjeant was no sooner made sensible, than he arose from his bed, and having his clothes already on, immediately attended. Jones did not think fit to acquaint the serjeant with his design; though he might have done it with great safety, for the halberdier was himself a man of honour, and had killed his man. He would therefore have faithfully kept this secret, or indeed any other which no reward was published for discovering. But as Jones knew not those virtues in so short an acquaintance, his caution was perhaps prudent and commendable enough.

He began therefore by acquainting the serjeant, that as he was now entered into the army, he was ashamed of being without what was perhaps the most necessary implement of a soldier; namely, a sword; adding, that he should be infinitely obliged to him, if he could procure one. "For which," says he, "I will give you any reasonable price; nor do I insist upon its being silver-hilted; only a good blade, and such as may become a soldier's thigh."

The serjeant, who well knew what had happened, and had heard that Jones was in a very dangerous condition, immediately concluded, from such a message, at such a time of night, and from a man in such a situation, that he was light-headed. Now as he had his wit (to use that word in its common signification) always ready, he bethought himself of making his advantage of this humour in the sick man. "Sir," says he, "I believe I can fit you. I have a most excellent piece of stuff by me. It is not indeed silver-hilted, which, as you say, doth not become a soldier;

but the handle is decent enough, and the blade one of the best in Europe. It is a blade that—a blade that—in short, I will fetch it you this instant, and you shall see it and handle it. I am glad to see your honour so well with all my heart."

Being instantly returned with the sword, he delivered it to Jones, who took it and drew it; and then told the serjeant it would do very well, and bid him name his price.

The serjeant now began to harangue in praise of his goods. He said (nay he swore very heartily), "that the blade was taken from a French officer, of very high rank, at the battle of Dettingen. I took it myself," says he, "from his side, after I had knocked him o' the head. The hilt was a golden one. That I sold to one of our fine gentlemen; for there are some of them, an't please your honour, who value the hilt of a sword more than the blade."

Here the other stopped him, and begged him to name a price. The serjeant, who thought Jones absolutely out of his senses, and very near his end, was afraid lest he should injure his family by asking too little. However, after a moment's hesitation, he contented himself with naming twenty guineas, and swore he would not sell it for less to his own brother.

"Twenty guineas!" says Jones, in the utmost surprize: "sure you think I am mad, or that I never saw a sword in my life. Twenty guineas, indeed! I did not imagine you would endeavour to impose upon me. Here, take the sword—No, now I think on't, I will keep it myself, and show it your officer in the morning, acquainting him, at the same time, what a price you asked me for it."

The serjeant, as we have said, had always his wit (*in sensu praedicto*) about him, and now plainly saw that Jones was not in the condition he had apprehended him to be; he now, therefore, counterfeited as great surprize as the other had shown, and said, "I am certain, sir, I have not asked you so much out of the way. Besides, you are to consider, it is the only sword I have, and I must run the risque of my officer's displeasure, by going without one myself. And truly, putting all this together, I don't think twenty shillings was so much out of the way."

"Twenty shillings!" cries Jones; "why, you just now asked me twenty guineas."—"How!" cries the serjeant, "sure your honour must have mistaken me: or else I mistook myself—and indeed I am but half awake. Twenty guineas, indeed! no wonder your honour flew into such a passion. I say twenty guineas too. No, no, I mean twenty shillings, I assure you. And when your honour comes to consider everything, I hope you will not think that so extravagant a price. It is indeed true, you may buy a weapon which looks as well for less money. But——"

Here Jones interrupted him, saying, "I will be so far from making any words with you, that I will give you a shilling more than your demand." He then gave him a guinea, bid him return to his bed, and wished him a good march; adding, he hoped to overtake them before the division reached Worcester.

The serjeant very civilly took his leave, fully satisfied with his merchandize, and not a little pleased with his dexterous recovery from that false step into which his opinion of the sick man's light-headedness had betrayed him.

As soon as the serjeant was departed, Jones rose from his bed, and dressed himself entirely, putting on even his coat, which, as its colour was white, showed very visibly the streams of blood which had flowed down it; and now, having grasped his new-purchased sword in his hand, he was going to issue forth, when the thought of what he was about to undertake laid suddenly hold of him, and he began to reflect that in a few minutes he might possibly deprive a human being of life, or might lose his own. "Very well," said he, "and in what cause do I venture my life? Why, in that of my honour. And who is this human being? A rascal who hath injured and insulted me without provocation. But is not revenge forbidden by Heaven? Yes, but it is enjoined by the world. Well, but shall I obey the world in opposition to the express commands of Heaven? Shall I incur the Divine displeasure rather than be called—ha—coward—scoundrel?—I'll think no more; I am resolved, and must fight him."

The clock had now struck twelve, and every one in the house were in their beds, except the centinel who stood to guard Northerton, when Jones softly opening his door, issued forth in pursuit of his enemy, of whose place of confinement he had received a perfect description from the drawer. It is not easy to conceive a much more tremendous figure than he now exhibited. He had on, as we have said, a light-coloured coat, covered with streams of blood. His face, which missed that very blood, as well as twenty ounces more drawn from him by the surgeon, was pallid. Round his head was a quantity of bandage, not unlike a turban. In the right hand he carried a sword, and in the left a candle. So that the bloody Banquo was not worthy to be compared to him. In fact, I believe a more dreadful apparition was never raised in a church-yard, nor in the imagination of any good people met in a winter evening over a Christmas fire in Somersetshire.

When the centinel first saw our heroe approach, his hair began gently to lift up his grenadier cap; and in the same instant his knees fell to blows with each other. Presently his whole body was seized with worse than an ague fit. He then fired his piece, and fell flat on his face.

Whether fear or courage was the occasion of his firing, or whether he took aim at the object of his terror, I cannot say. If he did, however, he had the good fortune to miss his man.

Jones seeing the fellow fall, guessed the cause of his fright, at which he could not forbear smiling, not in the least reflecting on the danger from which he had just escaped. He then passed by the fellow, who still continued in the posture in which he fell, and entered the room where Northerton, as he had heard, was confined. Here, in a solitary situation, he found—an empty quart pot standing on the table, on which some beer being spilt, it looked as if the room had lately been inhabited; but at present it was entirely vacant.

Jones then apprehended it might lead to some other apartment; but upon searching all round it, he could perceive no other door than that at which he entered, and where the centinel had been posted. He then proceeded to call Northerton several times by his name; but no one answered; nor did this serve to any other purpose than to confirm the centinel in his terrors, who was now convinced that the volunteer was dead of his wounds, and that his ghost was come in search of the murderer: he now lay in all the agonies of horror; and I wish, with all my heart, some of those actors who are hereafter to represent a man frighted out of his wits had seen him, that they might be taught to copy nature, instead of performing several antic tricks and gestures, for the entertainment and applause of the galleries.

Perceiving the bird was flown, at least despairing to find him, and rightly apprehending that the report of the firelock would alarm the whole house, our heroe now blew out his candle, and gently stole back again to his chamber, and to his bed; whither he would not have been able to have gotten undiscovered, had any other person been on the same staircase, save only one gentleman who was confined to his bed by the gout; for before he could reach the door to his chamber, the hall where the centinel had been posted was half full of people, some in their shirts, and others not half drest, all very earnestly enquiring of each other what was the matter.

The soldier was now found lying in the same place and posture in which we just now left him. Several immediately applied themselves to raise him, and some concluded him dead; but they presently saw their mistake, for he not only struggled with those who laid their hands on him, but fell a roaring like a bull. In reality, he imagined so many spirits or devils were handling him; for his imagination being possessed with the horror of an apparition, converted every object he saw or felt into nothing but ghosts and spectres.

At length he was overpowered by numbers, and got upon his legs; when candles being brought, and seeing two or three of his comrades present, he came a little to himself; but when they asked him what was the matter? he answered, "I am a dead man, that's all, I am a dead man, I can't recover it, I have seen him." "What hast thou seen, Jack?" says one of the soldiers. "Why, I have seen the young volunteer that was killed yesterday." He then imprecated the most heavy curses on himself, if he had not seen the volunteer, all over blood, vomiting fire out of his mouth and nostrils, pass by him into the chamber where Ensign Northerton was, and then seizing the ensign by the throat, fly away with him in a clap of thunder.

This relation met with a gracious reception from the audience. All the women present believed it firmly, and prayed Heaven to defend them from murder. Amongst the men too, many had faith in the story; but others turned it into derision and ridicule; and a serjeant who was present answered very coolly, "Young man, you will hear more of this, for going to sleep and dreaming on your post."

The soldier replied, "You may punish me if you please; but I was as broad awake as I am now; and the devil carry me away, as he hath the ensign, if I did not see the dead man, as I tell you, with eyes as big and as fiery as two large flambeaux."

The commander of the forces, and the commander of the house, were now both arrived; for the former being awake at the time, and hearing the centinel fire his piece, thought it his duty to rise immediately, though he had no great apprehensions of any mischief; whereas the apprehensions of the latter were much greater, lest her spoons and tankards should be upon the march, without having received any such orders from her.

Our poor centinel, to whom the sight of this officer was not much more welcome than the apparition, as he thought it, which he had seen before, again related the dreadful story, and with many additions of blood and fire; but he had the misfortune to gain no credit with either of the last-mentioned persons: for the officer, though a very religious man, was free from all terrors of this kind; besides, having so lately left Jones in the condition we have seen, he had no suspicion of his being dead. As for the landlady, though not over religious, she had no kind of aversion to the doctrine of spirits; but there was a circumstance in the tale which she well knew to be false, as we shall inform the reader presently.

But whether Northerton was carried away in thunder or fire, or in whatever other manner he was gone, it was now certain that his body was no longer in custody. Upon this occasion the lieutenant formed a conclusion not very different from what the serjeant is just mentioned to have made before, and immediately ordered the centinel to be taken prisoner. So that, by a strange reverse of fortune (though not very uncommon in a military life), the guard became the guarded.

CHAPTER XV.

The conclusion of the foregoing adventure.

Besides the suspicion of sleep, the lieutenant harboured another and worse doubt against the poor centinel, and this was, that of treachery; for as he believed not one syllable of the apparition, so he imagined the whole to be an invention formed only to impose upon him, and that the fellow had in reality been bribed by Northerton to let him escape. And this he imagined the rather, as the fright appeared to him the more unnatural in one who had the character of as brave and bold a man as any in the regiment, having been in several actions, having received several wounds, and, in a word, having behaved himself always like a good and valiant soldier.

That the reader, therefore, may not conceive the least ill opinion of such a person, we shall not delay a moment in rescuing his character from the imputation of this guilt.

Mr Northerton then, as we have before observed, was fully satisfied with the glory which he had obtained from this action. He had perhaps seen, or heard, or guessed, that envy is apt to attend fame. Not that I would here insinuate that he was heathenishly inclined to believe in or to worship the goddess Nemesis; for, in fact, I am convinced he never heard of her name. He was, besides, of an active disposition, and had a great antipathy to those close quarters in the castle of Gloucester, for which a justice of peace might possibly give him a billet. Nor was he moreover free from some uneasy meditations on a certain wooden edifice, which I forbear to name, in conformity to the opinion of mankind, who, I think, rather ought to honour than to be ashamed of this building, as it is, or at least might be made, of more benefit to society than almost any other public erection. In a word, to hint at no more reasons for his conduct, Mr Northerton was desirous of departing that evening, and nothing remained for him but to contrive the quomodo, which appeared to be a matter of some difficulty.

Now this young gentleman, though somewhat crooked in his morals, was perfectly straight in his person, which was extremely strong and well made. His face too was accounted handsome by the generality of women, for it was broad and ruddy, with tolerably good teeth. Such charms did not fail making an impression on my landlady, who had no little relish for this kind of beauty. She had, indeed, a real compassion for the young man; and hearing from the surgeon that affairs were like to go ill with the volunteer, she suspected they might hereafter wear no benign aspect with the ensign. Having obtained, therefore, leave to make him a visit, and finding him in a very melancholy mood, which she considerably heightened by telling him there were scarce any hopes of the volunteer's life, she proceeded to throw forth some hints, which the other readily and eagerly taking up, they soon came to a right understanding; and it was at length agreed that the ensign should, at a certain signal, ascend the chimney, which communicating very soon with that of the kitchen, he might there again let himself down; for which she would give him an opportunity by keeping the coast clear.

But lest our readers, of a different complexion, should take this occasion of too hastily condemning all compassion as a folly, and pernicious to society, we think proper to mention another particular which might possibly have some little share in this action. The ensign happened to be at this time possessed of the sum of fifty pounds, which did indeed belong to the whole company; for the captain having quarrelled with his lieutenant, had entrusted the payment of his company to the ensign. This money, however, he thought proper to deposit in my landlady's hand, possibly by way of bail or security that he would hereafter appear and answer to the charge against him; but whatever were the conditions, certain it is, that she had the money and the ensign his liberty.

The reader may perhaps expect, from the compassionate temper of this good woman, that when she saw the poor centinel taken prisoner for a fact of which she knew him innocent, she should immediately have interposed in his behalf; but whether it was that she had already exhausted all her compassion in the above-mentioned instance, or that the features of this fellow, though not very different from those of the ensign, could not raise it, I will not determine; but, far from being an advocate for the present prisoner, she urged his guilt to his officer, declaring, with uplifted eyes and hands, that she would not have had any concern in the escape of a murderer for all the world.

Everything was now once more quiet, and most of the company returned again to their beds; but the landlady, either from the natural activity of her disposition, or from her fear for her plate, having no propensity to sleep, prevailed with the officers, as they were to march within little more than an hour, to spend that time with her over a bowl of punch.

Jones had lain awake all this while, and had heard great part of the hurry and bustle that had passed, of which he had now some curiosity to know the particulars. He therefore applied to his bell, which he rung at least twenty times without any effect: for my landlady was in such high mirth with her company, that no clapper could be heard there but her own; and the drawer and chambermaid, who were sitting together in the kitchen (for neither durst he sit up nor she lie in bed alone), the more they heard the bell ring the more they were frightened, and as it were nailed down in their places.

At last, at a lucky interval of chat, the sound reached the ears of our good landlady, who presently sent forth her summons, which both her servants instantly obeyed. "Joe," says the mistress, "don't you hear the gentleman's bell ring? Why don't you go up?"—"It is not my business," answered the drawer, "to wait upon the chambers—it is Betty Chambermaid's."—"If you come to that," answered the maid, "it is not my business to wait upon gentlemen. I have done it indeed sometimes; but the devil fetch me if ever I do again, since you make your preambles about it." The bell still ringing violently, their mistress fell into a passion, and swore, if the drawer did not go up immediately, she would turn him away that very morning. "If you do, madam," says he, "I can't help it. I won't do another servant's business." She then applied herself to the maid, and endeavoured to prevail by gentle means; but all in vain: Betty was as inflexible as Joe. Both insisted it was not their business, and they would not do it.

The lieutenant then fell a laughing, and said, "Come, I will put an end to this contention;" and then turning to the servants, commended them for their resolution in not giving up the point; but added, he was sure, if one would consent to go the other would. To which proposal they both agreed in an instant, and accordingly went up very lovingly and close together. When they were gone, the lieutenant appeased the wrath of the landlady, by satisfying her why they were both so unwilling to go alone.

They returned soon after, and acquainted their mistress, that the sick gentleman was so far from being dead, that he spoke as heartily as if he was well; and that he gave his service to the captain, and should be very glad of the favour of seeing him before he marched.

The good lieutenant immediately complied with his desires, and sitting down by his bed-side, acquainted him with the scene which had happened below, concluding with his intentions to make an example of the centinel.

Upon this Jones related to him the whole truth, and earnestly begged him not to punish the poor soldier, "who, I am confident," says he, "is as innocent of the ensign's escape, as he is of forging any lie, or of endeavouring to impose on you."

The lieutenant hesitated a few moments, and then answered: "Why, as you have cleared the fellow of one part of the charge, so it will be impossible to prove the other, because he was not the only centinel. But I have a good mind to punish the rascal for being a coward. Yet who knows what effect the terror of such an apprehension may have? and, to say the truth, he hath always behaved well against an enemy. Come, it is a good thing to see any sign of religion in these fellows; so I promise you he shall be set at liberty when we march. But hark, the general beats. My dear boy, give me another buss. Don't discompose nor hurry yourself; but remember the Christian doctrine of patience, and I warrant you will soon be able to do yourself justice, and to take an honourable revenge on the fellow who hath injured you." The lieutenant then departed, and Jones endeavoured to compose himself to rest.

BOOK VIII.

CONTAINING ABOUT TWO DAYS.

CHAPTER I.

A wonderful long chapter concerning the marvellous; being much the longest of all our introductory chapters.

As we are now entering upon a book in which the course of our history will oblige us to relate some matters of a more strange and surprizing kind than any which have hitherto occurred, it may not be amiss, in the prolegomenous or introductory chapter, to say something of that species of writing which is called the marvellous. To this we shall, as well for the sake of ourselves as of others, endeavour to set some certain bounds, and indeed nothing can be more necessary, as critics[1] of different complexions are here apt to run into very different extremes; for while some are, with M. Dacier, ready to allow, that the same thing which is impossible may be yet probable,[2] others have so little historic or poetic faith, that they believe nothing to be either possible or probable, the like to which hath not occurred to their own observation.

First, then, I think it may very reasonably be required of every writer, that he keeps within the bounds of possibility; and still remembers that what it is not possible for man to perform, it is scarce possible for man to believe he did perform. This conviction perhaps gave birth to many stories of the antient heathen deities (for most of them are of poetical original). The poet, being desirous to indulge a wanton and extravagant imagination, took refuge in that power, of the extent of which his readers were no judges, or rather which they imagined to be infinite, and consequently they could not be shocked at any prodigies related of it. This hath been strongly urged in defence of Homer's miracles; and it is perhaps a defence; not, as Mr Pope would have it, because Ulysses told a set of foolish lies to the Phaeacians, who were a very dull nation; but because the poet himself wrote to heathens, to whom poetical fables were articles of faith. For my own part, I must confess, so compassionate is my temper, I wish Polypheme had confined himself to his milk diet, and preserved his eye; nor could Ulysses be much more concerned than myself, when his companions were turned into swine by Circe,

---

[1] By this word here, and in most other parts of our work, we mean every reader in the world.

[2] It is happy for M. Dacier that he was not an Irishman.

who showed, I think, afterwards, too much regard for man's flesh to be supposed capable of converting it into bacon. I wish, likewise, with all my heart, that Homer could have known the rule prescribed by Horace, to introduce supernatural agents as seldom as possible. We should not then have seen his gods coming on trivial errands, and often behaving themselves so as not only to forfeit all title to respect, but to become the objects of scorn and derision. A conduct which must have shocked the credulity of a pious and sagacious heathen; and which could never have been defended, unless by agreeing with a supposition to which I have been sometimes almost inclined, that this most glorious poet, as he certainly was, had an intent to burlesque the superstitious faith of his own age and country.

But I have rested too long on a doctrine which can be of no use to a Christian writer; for as he cannot introduce into his works any of that heavenly host which make a part of his creed, so it is horrid puerility to search the heathen theology for any of those deities who have been long since dethroned from their immortality. Lord Shaftesbury observes, that nothing is more cold than the invocation of a muse by a modern; he might have added, that nothing can be more absurd. A modern may with much more elegance invoke a ballad, as some have thought Homer did, or a mug of ale, with the author of Hudibras; which latter may perhaps have inspired much more poetry, as well as prose, than all the liquors of Hippocrene or Helicon.

The only supernatural agents which can in any manner be allowed to us moderns, are ghosts; but of these I would advise an author to be extremely sparing. These are indeed, like arsenic, and other dangerous drugs in physic, to be used with the utmost caution; nor would I advise the introduction of them at all in those works, or by those authors, to which, or to whom, a horse-laugh in the reader would be any great prejudice or mortification.

As for elves and fairies, and other such mummery, I purposely omit the mention of them, as I should be very unwilling to confine within any bounds those surprizing imaginations, for whose vast capacity the limits of human nature are too narrow; whose works are to be considered as a new creation; and who have consequently just right to do what they will with their own.

Man therefore is the highest subject (unless on very extraordinary occasions indeed) which presents itself to the pen of our historian, or of our poet; and, in relating his actions, great care is to be taken that we do not exceed the capacity of the agent we describe.

Nor is possibility alone sufficient to justify us; we must keep likewise within the rules of probability. It is, I think, the opinion of Aristotle; or if not, it is the opinion of some wise man, whose authority will be as weighty when it is as old, "That it is no excuse for a poet who relates what is incredible, that the thing related is really matter of fact." This may perhaps be allowed true with regard to poetry, but it may be thought impracticable to extend it to the historian; for he is obliged to record matters as he finds them, though they may be of so extraordinary a nature as will require no small degree of historical faith to swallow them. Such was the successless armament of Xerxes described by Herodotus, or the successful expedition of Alexander related by Arrian. Such of later years was the victory of Agincourt obtained by Harry the Fifth, or that of Narva won by Charles the Twelfth of Sweden. All which instances, the more we reflect on them, appear still the more astonishing.

Such facts, however, as they occur in the thread of the story, nay, indeed, as they constitute the essential parts of it, the historian is not only justifiable in recording as they really happened, but indeed would be unpardonable should he omit or alter them. But there are other facts not of such consequence nor so necessary, which, though ever so well attested, may nevertheless be sacrificed to oblivion in complacence to the scepticism of a reader. Such is that memorable story of the ghost of George Villiers, which might with more propriety have been made a present of to Dr Drelincourt, to have kept the ghost of Mrs Veale company, at the head of his Discourse upon Death, than have been introduced into so solemn a work as the History of the Rebellion.

To say the truth, if the historian will confine himself to what really happened, and utterly reject any circumstance, which, though never so well attested, he must be well assured is false, he will sometimes fall into the marvellous, but never into the incredible. He will often raise the wonder and surprize of his reader, but never that incredulous hatred mentioned by Horace. It is by falling into fiction, therefore, that we generally offend against this rule, of deserting probability, which the historian seldom, if ever, quits, till he forsakes his character and commences a writer of romance. In this, however, those historians who relate public transactions, have the advantage of us who confine ourselves to scenes of private life. The credit of the former is by common notoriety supported for a long time; and public records, with the concurrent testimony of many authors, bear evidence to their truth in future ages. Thus a Trajan and an Antoninus, a Nero and a Caligula, have all met with the belief of posterity; and no one doubts but that men so very good, and so very bad, were once the masters of mankind.

But we who deal in private character, who search into the most retired recesses, and draw forth examples of virtue and vice from holes and corners of the world, are in a more dangerous situation. As we have no public notoriety, no concurrent testimony, no records to support and corroborate what we deliver, it becomes us to keep within the limits not only of possibility, but of probability too; and this more especially in painting what is greatly good and amiable. Knavery and folly, though never so exorbitant, will more easily meet with assent; for ill-nature adds great support and strength to faith.

Thus we may, perhaps, with little danger, relate the history of Fisher; who having long owed his bread to the generosity of Mr Derby, and having one morning received a considerable bounty from his hands, yet, in order to possess himself of what remained in his friend's scrutore, concealed himself in a public office of the Temple, through which there was a passage into Mr Derby's chambers. Here he overheard Mr Derby for many hours solacing himself at an entertainment which he that evening gave his friends, and to which Fisher had been invited. During all this time, no tender, no grateful reflections arose to restrain his purpose; but when the poor gentleman had let his company out through the office, Fisher came suddenly from his lurking-place, and walking softly behind his friend into his chamber, discharged a pistol-ball into his head. This may be believed when the bones of Fisher are as rotten as his heart. Nay, perhaps, it will be credited, that the villain went two days afterwards with some young ladies to the play of Hamlet; and with an unaltered countenance heard one of the ladies, who little suspected how near she was to the person, cry out, "Good God! if the man that murdered Mr Derby was now present!" manifesting in this a more seared and callous conscience than even Nero himself; of whom we are told by Suetonius, "that the consciousness of his guilt, after the death of his mother, became immediately intolerable, and so continued; nor could all the congratulations of the soldiers, of the senate, and the people, allay the horrors of his conscience."

But now, on the other hand, should I tell my reader, that I had known a man whose penetrating genius had enabled him to raise a large fortune in a way where no beginning was chaulked out to him; that he had done this with the most perfect preservation of his integrity, and not only without the least injustice or injury to any one individual person, but with the highest advantage to trade, and a vast increase of the public revenue; that he had expended one part of the income of this fortune in discovering a taste superior to most, by works where the highest dignity was united with the purest simplicity, and another part in displaying a degree of goodness superior to all men, by acts of charity to objects whose only recommendations were their merits, or their wants; that he was most industrious in searching after merit in distress, most eager to relieve it, and then as careful (perhaps too careful) to conceal what he had done; that his house, his furniture, his gardens, his table, his private hospitality, and his public beneficence, all denoted the mind from which they flowed, and were all intrinsically rich and noble, without tinsel, or external ostentation; that he filled every relation in life with the most adequate virtue; that he was most piously religious to his Creator, most zealously loyal to his sovereign; a most tender husband to his wife, a kind relation, a munificent patron, a warm and firm friend, a knowing and a chearful companion, indulgent to his servants, hospitable to his neighbours, charitable to the poor, and benevolent to all mankind. Should I add to these the epithets of wise, brave, elegant, and indeed every other amiable epithet in our language, I might surely say,

—Quis credet? nemo Hercule! nemo;
Vel duo, vel nemo;

and yet I know a man who is all I have here described. But a single instance (and I really know not such another) is not sufficient to justify us, while we are writing to thousands who never heard of the person, nor of anything like him. Such *rarae aves* should be remitted to the epitaph writer, or to some poet who may condescend to hitch him in a distich, or to slide him into a rhime with an air of carelessness and neglect, without giving any offence to the reader.

In the last place, the actions should be such as may not only be within the compass of human agency, and which human agents may probably be supposed to do; but they should be likely for the very actors and characters themselves to have performed; for what may be only wonderful and surprizing in one man, may become improbable, or indeed impossible, when related of another.

This last requisite is what the dramatic critics call conversation of character; and it requires a very extraordinary degree of judgment, and a most exact knowledge of human nature.

It is admirably remarked by a most excellent writer, that zeal can no more hurry a man to act in direct opposition to itself, than a rapid stream can carry a boat against its own current. I will venture to say, that for a man to act in direct contradiction to the dictates of his nature, is, if not impossible, as improbable and as miraculous as anything which can well be conceived. Should the best parts of the story of M. Antoninus be ascribed to Nero, or should the worst incidents of Nero's life be imputed to Antoninus, what would be more shocking to belief than either instance? whereas both these being related of their proper agent, constitute the truly marvellous.

Our modern authors of comedy have fallen almost universally into the error here hinted at; their heroes generally are notorious rogues, and their heroines abandoned jades, during the first four acts; but in the fifth, the former become very worthy gentlemen, and the latter women of virtue and discretion: nor is the writer often so kind as to give himself the least trouble to reconcile or account for this monstrous change and incongruity. There is, indeed, no other reason to be assigned for it, than because the play is drawing to a conclusion; as if it was no less natural in a rogue to repent in the last act of a play, than in the last of his life; which we perceive to be generally the case at Tyburn, a place which might indeed close the scene of some comedies with much propriety, as the heroes in these are most commonly eminent for those very talents which not only bring men to the gallows, but enable them to make an heroic figure when they are there.

Within these few restrictions, I think, every writer may be permitted to deal as much in the wonderful as he pleases; nay, if he thus keeps within the rules of credibility, the more he can surprize the reader the more he will engage his attention, and the more he will charm him. As a genius of the highest rank observes in his fifth chapter of the Bathos, "The great art of all poetry is to mix truth with fiction, in order to join the credible with the surprizing."

For though every good author will confine himself within the bounds of probability, it is by no means necessary that his characters, or his incidents, should be trite, common, or vulgar; such as happen in every street, or in every house, or which may be met with in the home articles of a newspaper. Nor must he be inhibited from showing many persons and things, which may possibly have never fallen within the knowledge of great part of his readers. If the writer strictly observes the rules above-mentioned, he hath discharged his part; and is then intitled to some faith from his reader, who is indeed guilty of critical infidelity if he disbelieves him.

For want of a portion of such faith, I remember the character of a young lady of quality, which was condemned on the stage for being unnatural, by the unanimous voice of a very large assembly of clerks and apprentices; though it had the previous suffrages of many ladies of the first rank; one of whom, very eminent for her understanding, declared it was the picture of half the young people of her acquaintance.

CHAPTER II.

In which the landlady pays a visit to Mr Jones.

When Jones had taken leave of his friend the lieutenant, he endeavoured to close his eyes, but all in vain; his spirits were too lively and wakeful to be lulled to sleep. So having amused, or rather tormented, himself with the thoughts of his Sophia till it was open daylight, he called for some tea; upon which occasion my landlady herself vouchsafed to pay him a visit.

This was indeed the first time she had seen him, or at least had taken any notice of him; but as the lieutenant had assured her that he was certainly some young gentleman of fashion, she now determined to show him all the respect in her power; for, to speak truly, this was one of those houses where gentlemen, to use the language of advertisements, meet with civil treatment for their money.

She had no sooner begun to make his tea, than she likewise began to discourse:—"La! sir," said she, "I think it is great pity that such a pretty young gentleman should under-value himself so, as to go about with these soldier fellows. They call themselves gentlemen, I warrant you; but, as my first husband used to say, they should remember it is we that pay them. And to be sure it is very hard upon us to be obliged to pay them, and to keep 'um too, as we publicans are. I had twenty of 'um last night, besides officers: nay, for matter o' that, I had rather have the soldiers than officers: for nothing is ever good enough for those sparks; and I am sure, if you was to see the bills; la! sir, it is nothing. I have had less trouble, I warrant you, with a good squire's family, where we take forty or fifty shillings of a night, besides horses. And yet I warrants me, there is narrow a one of those officer fellows but looks upon himself to be as good as arrow a squire of £500 a year. To be sure it doth me good to hear their men run about after 'um, crying your honour, and your honour. Marry come up with such honour, and an ordinary at a shilling a head. Then there's such swearing among 'um, to be sure it frightens me out o' my wits: I thinks nothing can ever prosper with such wicked people. And here one of 'um has used you in so barbarous a manner. I thought indeed how well the rest would secure him; they all hang together; for if you had been in danger of death, which I am glad to see you are not, it would have been all as one to such wicked people. They would have let the murderer go. Laud have mercy upon 'um; I would not have such a sin to answer for, for the whole world. But though you are likely, with the blessing, to recover, there is laa for him yet; and if you will employ lawyer Small, I darest be sworn he'll make the fellow fly the country for him; though perhaps he'll have fled the country before; for it is here to-day and gone to-morrow with such chaps. I hope, however, you will learn more wit for the future, and return back to your friends; I warrant they are all miserable for your loss; and if they was but to know what had happened—La, my seeming! I would not for the world they should. Come, come, we know very well what all the matter is; but if one won't, another will; so pretty a gentleman need never want a lady. I am sure, if I was you, I would see the finest she that ever wore a head hanged, before I would go for a soldier for her.—Nay, don't blush so" (for indeed he did to a violent degree). "Why, you thought, sir, I knew nothing of the matter, I warrant you, about Madam Sophia."—"How," says Jones, starting up, "do you know my Sophia?"—"Do I! ay marry," cries the landlady; "many's the time hath she lain in this house."—"With her aunt, I suppose," says Jones. "Why, there it is now," cries the landlady. "Ay, ay, ay, I know the old lady very well. And a sweet young creature is Madam Sophia, that's the truth on't."—"A sweet creature," cries Jones; "O heavens!"

> Angels are painted fair to look like her.
> There's in her all that we believe of heav'n,
> Amazing brightness, purity, and truth,
> Eternal joy and everlasting love.

"And could I ever have imagined that you had known my Sophia!"—"I wish," says the landlady, "you knew half so much of her. What would you have given to have sat by her bed-side? What a delicious neck she hath! Her lovely limbs have stretched themselves in that very bed you now lie in."—"Here!" cries Jones: "hath Sophia ever laid here?"—"Ay, ay, here; there, in that very bed," says the landlady; "where I wish you had her this moment; and she may wish so too for anything I know to the contrary, for she hath mentioned your name to me."—"Ha!" cries he; "did she ever mention her poor Jones? You flatter me now: I can never believe so much."—"Why, then," answered she, "as I hope to be saved, and may the devil fetch me if I speak a syllable more than the truth, I have heard her mention Mr Jones; but in a civil and modest way, I confess; yet I could perceive she thought a great deal more than she said."—"O my dear woman!" cries Jones, "her thoughts of me I shall never be worthy of. Oh, she is all gentleness, kindness, goodness! Why was such a rascal as I born, ever to give her soft bosom a moment's uneasiness? Why am I cursed? I, who would undergo all the plagues and miseries which any daemon ever invented for mankind, to procure her any good; nay, torture itself could not be misery to me, did I but know that she was happy."—"Why, look you there now," says the landlady; "I told her you was a constant lovier."—"But pray, madam, tell me when or where you knew anything of me; for I never was here before, nor do I remember ever to have seen you."—"Nor is it possible you should," answered she; "for you was a little thing when I had you in my lap at the squire's."—"How, the squire's?" says Jones: "what, do you know that great and good Mr Allworthy then?"—"Yes, marry, do I," says she: "who in the country doth not?"—"The fame of his goodness indeed," answered Jones, "must have extended farther than this; but heaven only can know him—can know that benevolence which it copied from itself, and sent upon earth as its own pattern. Mankind are as ignorant of such divine goodness, as they are unworthy of it; but none so unworthy of it as myself. I, who was raised by him to such a height; taken in, as you must well know, a poor base-born child, adopted by him, and treated as his own son, to dare by my follies to disoblige him, to draw his vengeance upon me. Yes, I deserve it all; for I will never be so ungrateful as ever to think he hath done an act of injustice by me. No, I deserve to be turned out of doors, as I am. And now, madam," says he, "I believe you will not blame me for turning soldier, especially with such a fortune as this in my pocket." At which words he shook a purse, which had but very little in it, and which still appeared to the landlady to have less.

My good landlady was (according to vulgar phrase) struck all of a heap by this relation. She answered coldly, "That to be sure people were the best judges what was most proper for their circumstances. But hark," says she, "I think I hear somebody call. Coming! coming! the devil's in all our volk; nobody hath any ears. I must go down-stairs; if you want any more breakfast the maid will come up. Coming!" At which words, without taking any leave, she flung out of the room; for the lower sort of people are very tenacious of respect; and though they are contented to give this gratis to persons of quality, yet they never confer it on those of their own order without taking care to be well paid for their pains.

CHAPTER III.

In which the surgeon makes his second appearance.

Before we proceed any farther, that the reader may not be mistaken in imagining the landlady knew more than she did, nor surprized that she knew so much, it may be necessary to inform him that the lieutenant had acquainted her that the name of Sophia had been the occasion of the quarrel; and as for the rest of her knowledge, the sagacious reader will observe how she came by it in the preceding scene. Great curiosity was indeed mixed with her virtues; and she never willingly suffered any one to depart from her house, without enquiring as much as possible into their names, families, and fortunes.

She was no sooner gone than Jones, instead of animadverting on her behaviour, reflected that he was in the same bed which he was informed had held his dear Sophia. This occasioned a thousand fond and tender thoughts, which we would dwell longer upon, did we not consider that such kind of lovers will make a very inconsiderable part of our readers. In this situation the surgeon found him, when he came to dress his wound. The doctor perceiving, upon examination, that his pulse was disordered, and hearing that he had not slept, declared that he was in great danger; for he apprehended a fever was coming on, which he would have prevented by bleeding, but Jones would not submit, declaring he would lose no more blood; "and, doctor," says he, "if you will be so kind only to dress my head, I have no doubt of being well in a day or two."

"I wish," answered the surgeon, "I could assure your being well in a month or two. Well, indeed! No, no, people are not so soon well of such contusions; but, sir, I am not at this time of day to be instructed in my operations by a patient, and I insist on making a revulsion before I dress you."

Jones persisted obstinately in his refusal, and the doctor at last yielded; telling him at the same time that he would not be answerable for the ill consequence, and hoped he would do him the justice to acknowledge that he had given him a contrary advice; which the patient promised he would.

The doctor retired into the kitchen, where, addressing himself to the landlady, he complained bitterly of the undutiful behaviour of his patient, who would not be blooded, though he was in a fever.

"It is an eating fever then," says the landlady; "for he hath devoured two swinging buttered toasts this morning for breakfast."

"Very likely," says the doctor: "I have known people eat in a fever; and it is very easily accounted for; because the acidity occasioned by the febrile matter may stimulate the nerves of the diaphragm, and thereby occasion a craving which will not be easily distinguishable from a natural appetite; but the aliment will not be concreted, nor assimilated into chyle, and so will corrode the vascular orifices, and thus will aggravate the febrific symptoms. Indeed, I think the gentleman in a very dangerous way, and, if he is not blooded, I am afraid will die."

"Every man must die some time or other," answered the good woman; "it is no business of mine. I hope, doctor, you would not have me hold him while you bleed him. But, hark'ee, a word in your ear; I would advise you, before you proceed too far, to take care who is to be your paymaster."

"Paymaster!" said the doctor, staring; "why, I've a gentleman under my hands, have I not?"

"I imagined so as well as you," said the landlady; "but, as my first husband used to say, everything is not what it looks to be. He is an arrant scrub, I assure you. However, take no notice that I mentioned anything to you of the matter; but I think people in business oft always to let one another know such things."

"And have I suffered such a fellow as this," cries the doctor, in a passion, "to instruct me? Shall I hear my practice insulted by one who will not pay me? I am glad I have made this discovery in time. I will see now whether he will be blooded or no." He then immediately went upstairs, and flinging open the door of the chamber with much violence, awaked poor Jones from a very sound nap, into which he was fallen, and, what was still worse, from a delicious dream concerning Sophia.

"Will you be blooded or no?" cries the doctor, in a rage. "I have told you my resolution already," answered Jones, "and I wish with all my heart you had taken my answer; for you have awaked me out of the sweetest sleep which I ever had in my life."

"Ay, ay," cries the doctor; "many a man hath dozed away his life. Sleep is not always good, no more than food; but remember, I demand of you for the last time, will you be blooded?"—"I answer you for the last time," said Jones, "I will not."—"Then I wash my hands of you," cries the doctor; "and I desire you to pay me for the trouble I have had already. Two journeys at 5s. each, two dressings at 5s. more, and half a crown for phlebotomy."—"I hope," said Jones, "you don't intend to leave me in this condition."—"Indeed but I shall," said the other. "Then," said Jones, "you have used me rascally, and I will not pay you a farthing."—"Very well," cries the doctor; "the first loss is the best. What a pox did my landlady mean by sending for me to such vagabonds!" At which words he flung out of the room, and his patient turning himself about soon recovered his sleep; but his dream was unfortunately gone.

CHAPTER IV.

In which is introduced one of the pleasantest barbers that was ever recorded in history, the barber of Bagdad, or he in Don Quixote, not excepted.

The clock had now struck five when Jones awaked from a nap of seven hours, so much refreshed, and in such perfect health and spirits, that he resolved to get up and dress himself; for which purpose he unlocked his portmanteau, and took out clean linen, and a suit of cloaths; but first he slipt on a frock, and went down into the kitchen to bespeak something that might pacify certain tumults he found rising within his stomach.

Meeting the landlady, he accosted her with great civility, and asked, "What he could have for dinner?"—"For dinner!" says she; "it is an odd time a day to think about dinner. There is nothing drest in the house, and the fire is almost out."—"Well, but," says he, "I must have something to eat, and it is almost indifferent to me what; for, to tell you the truth, I was never more hungry in my life."—"Then," says she, "I believe there is a piece of cold buttock and carrot, which will fit you."—"Nothing better," answered Jones; "but I should be obliged to you, if you would let it be fried." To which the landlady consented, and said, smiling, "she was glad to see him so well recovered;" for the sweetness of our heroe's temper was almost irresistible; besides, she was really no ill-humoured woman at the bottom; but she loved money so much, that she hated everything which had the semblance of poverty.

Jones now returned in order to dress himself, while his dinner was preparing, and was, according to his orders, attended by the barber.

This barber, who went by the name of Little Benjamin, was a fellow of great oddity and humour, which had frequently let him into small inconveniencies, such as slaps in the face, kicks in the breech, broken bones, &c. For every one doth not understand a jest; and those who do are often displeased with being themselves the subjects of it. This vice was, however, incurable in him; and though he had often smarted for it, yet if ever he conceived a joke, he was certain to be delivered of it, without the least respect of persons, time, or place.

He had a great many other particularities in his character, which I shall not mention, as the reader will himself very easily perceive them, on his farther acquaintance with this extraordinary person.

Jones being impatient to be drest, for a reason which may be easily imagined, thought the shaver was very tedious in preparing his suds, and begged him to make haste; to which the other answered with much gravity, for he never discomposed his muscles on any account, "*Festina lente*, is a proverb which I learned long before I ever touched a razor."—"I find, friend, you are a scholar," replied Jones. "A poor one," said the barber, "*non omnia possumus omnes.*"—"Again!" said Jones; "I fancy you are good at capping verses."—"Excuse me, sir," said the barber, "*non tanto me dignor honore*." And then proceeding to his operation, "Sir," said he, "since I have dealt in suds, I could never discover more than two reasons for shaving; the one is to get a beard, and the other to get rid of one. I conjecture, sir, it may not be long since you shaved from the former of these motives. Upon my word, you have had good success; for one may say of your beard, that it is *tondenti gravior*."—"I conjecture," says Jones, "that thou art a very comical fellow."—"You mistake me widely, sir," said the barber: "I am too much addicted to the study of philosophy; *hinc illae lacrymae*, sir; that's my misfortune. Too much learning hath been my ruin."—"Indeed," says Jones, "I confess, friend, you have more learning than generally belongs to your trade; but I can't see how it can have injured you."—"Alas! sir," answered the shaver, "my father disinherited me for it. He was a dancing-master; and because I could read before I could dance, he took an aversion to me, and left every farthing among his other children.—Will you please to have your temples—O la! I ask your pardon, I fancy there is *hiatus in manuscriptis*. I heard you was going to the wars; but I find it was a mistake."—"Why do you conclude so?" says Jones. "Sure, sir," answered the barber, "you are too wise a man to carry a broken head thither; for that would be carrying coals to Newcastle."

"Upon my word," cries Jones, "thou art a very odd fellow, and I like thy humour extremely; I shall be very glad if thou wilt come to me after dinner, and drink a glass with me; I long to be better acquainted with thee."

"O dear sir!" said the barber, "I can do you twenty times as great a favour, if you will accept of it."—"What is that, my friend?" cries Jones. "Why, I will drink a bottle with you if you please; for I dearly love good-nature; and as you have found me out to be a comical fellow, so I have no skill in physiognomy, if you are not one of the best-natured gentlemen in the universe." Jones now walked downstairs neatly drest, and perhaps the fair Adonis was not a lovelier figure; and yet he had no charms for my landlady; for as that good woman did not resemble Venus at all in her person, so neither did she in her taste. Happy had it been for Nanny the chambermaid, if she had seen with the eyes of her mistress, for that poor girl fell so violently in love with Jones in five minutes, that her passion afterwards cost her many a sigh. This Nanny was extremely pretty, and altogether as coy; for she had refused a drawer, and one or two young farmers in the neighbourhood, but the bright eyes of our heroe thawed all her ice in a moment.

When Jones returned to the kitchen, his cloth was not yet laid; nor indeed was there any occasion it should, his dinner remaining *in statu quo*, as did the fire which was to dress it. This disappointment might have put many a philosophical temper into a passion; but it had no such effect on Jones. He only gave the landlady a gentle rebuke, saying, "Since it was so difficult to get it heated he would eat the beef cold." But now the good woman, whether moved by compassion, or by shame, or by whatever other motive, I cannot tell, first gave her servants a round scold for disobeying the orders which she had never given, and then bidding the drawer lay a napkin in the Sun, she set about the matter in good earnest, and soon accomplished it.

This Sun, into which Jones was now conducted, was truly named, as *lucus a non lucendo*; for it was an apartment into which the sun had scarce ever looked. It was indeed the worst room in the house; and happy was it for Jones that it was so. However, he was now too hungry to find any fault; but having once satisfied his appetite, he ordered the drawer to carry a bottle of wine into a better room, and expressed some resentment at having been shown into a dungeon.

The drawer having obeyed his commands, he was, after some time, attended by the barber, who would not indeed have suffered him to wait so long for his company had he not been listening in the kitchen to the landlady, who was entertaining a circle that she had gathered round her with the history of poor Jones, part of which she had extracted from his own lips, and the other part was her own ingenious composition; for she said "he was a poor parish boy, taken into the house of Squire Allworthy, where he was bred up as an apprentice, and now turned out of doors for his misdeeds, particularly for making love to his young mistress, and probably for robbing the house; for how else should he come by the little money he hath; and this," says she, "is your gentleman, forsooth!"—"A servant of Squire Allworthy!" says the barber; "what's his name?"—"Why he told me his name was Jones," says she: "perhaps he goes by a wrong name. Nay, and he told me, too, that the squire had maintained him as his own son, thof he had quarrelled with him now."—"And if his name be Jones, he told you the truth," said the barber; "for I have relations who live in that country; nay, and some people say he is his son."—"Why doth he not go by the name of his father?"—"I can't tell that," said the barber; "many people's sons don't go by the name of their father."—"Nay," said the landlady, "if I thought he was a gentleman's son, thof he was a bye-blow, I should behave to him in another guess manner; for many of these bye-blows come to be great men, and, as my poor first husband used to say, never affront any customer that's a gentleman."

CHAPTER V.

A dialogue between Mr Jones and the barber.

This conversation passed partly while Jones was at dinner in his dungeon, and partly while he was expecting the barber in the parlour. And, as soon as it was ended, Mr Benjamin, as we have said, attended him, and was very kindly desired to sit down. Jones then filling out a glass of wine, drank his health by the appellation of *doctissime tonsorum*. "*Ago tibi gratias, domine*" said the barber; and then looking very steadfastly at Jones, he said, with great gravity, and with a seeming surprize, as if he had recollected a face he had seen before, "Sir, may I crave the favour to know if your name is not Jones?" To which the other answered, "That it was."—"*Proh deum atque hominum fidem*!" says the barber; "how strangely things come to pass! Mr Jones, I am your most obedient servant. I find you do not know me, which indeed is no wonder, since you never saw me but once, and then you was very young. Pray, sir, how doth the good Squire Allworthy? how doth *ille optimus omnium patronus*?"—"I find," said Jones, "you do indeed know me; but I have not the like happiness of recollecting you."—"I do not wonder at that," cries Benjamin; "but I am surprized I did not know you sooner, for you are not in the least altered. And pray, sir, may I, without offence, enquire whither you are travelling this way?"—"Fill the glass, Mr Barber," said Jones, "and ask no more questions."—"Nay, sir," answered Benjamin, "I would not be troublesome; and I hope you don't think me a man of an impertinent curiosity, for that is a vice which nobody can lay to my charge; but I ask pardon; for when a gentleman of your figure travels without his servants, we may suppose him to be, as we say, *in casu incognito*, and perhaps I ought not to have mentioned your name."—"I own," says Jones, "I did not expect to have been so well known in this country as I find I am; yet, for particular reasons, I shall be obliged to you if you will not mention my name to any other person till I am gone from hence."—"*Pauca verba*," answered the barber;" and I wish no other here knew you but myself; for some people have tongues; but I promise you I can keep a secret. My enemies will allow me that virtue."—"And yet that is not the characteristic of your profession, Mr Barber," answered Jones. "Alas! sir," replied Benjamin, "*Non si male nunc et olim sic erit*. I was not born nor bred a barber, I assure you. I have spent most of my time among gentlemen, and though I say it, I understand something of gentility. And if you had thought me as worthy of your confidence as you have some other people, I should have shown you I could have kept a secret better. I should not have degraded your name in a public kitchen; for indeed, sir, some people have not used you well; for besides making a public proclamation of what you told them of a quarrel between yourself and Squire Allworthy, they added lies of their own, things which I knew to be lies."—"You surprize me greatly," cries Jones. "Upon my word, sir," answered Benjamin, "I tell the truth, and I need not tell you my landlady was the person. I am sure it moved me to hear the story, and I hope it is all false; for I have a great respect for you, I do assure you I have, and have had ever since the good-nature you showed to Black George, which was talked of all over the country, and I received more than one letter about it. Indeed, it made you beloved by everybody. You will pardon me, therefore; for it was real concern at what I heard made me ask many questions; for I have no impertinent curiosity about me: but I love good-nature and thence became *amoris abundantia erga te*."

Every profession of friendship easily gains credit with the miserable; it is no wonder therefore, if Jones, who, besides his being miserable, was extremely open-hearted, very readily believed all the professions of Benjamin, and received him into his bosom. The scraps of Latin, some of which Benjamin applied properly enough, though it did not savour of profound literature, seemed yet to indicate something superior to a common barber; and so indeed did his whole behaviour. Jones therefore believed the truth of what he had said, as to his original and education; and at length, after much entreaty, he said, "Since you have heard, my friend, so much of my affairs, and seem so desirous to know the truth, if you will have patience to hear it, I will inform you of the whole."—"Patience!" cries Benjamin, "that I will, if the chapter was never so long; and I am very much obliged to you for the honour you do me."

Jones now began, and related the whole history, forgetting only a circumstance or two, namely, everything which passed on that day in which he had fought with Thwackum; and ended with his resolution to go to sea, till the rebellion in the North had made him change his purpose, and had brought him to the place where he then was.

Little Benjamin, who had been all attention, never once interrupted the narrative; but when it was ended he could not help observing, that there must be surely something more invented by his enemies, and told Mr Allworthy against him, or so good a man would never have dismissed one he had loved so tenderly, in such a manner. To which Jones answered, "He doubted not but such villanous arts had been made use of to destroy him."

And surely it was scarce possible for any one to have avoided making the same remark with the barber, who had not indeed heard from Jones one single circumstance upon which he was condemned; for his actions were not now placed in those injurious lights in which they had been misrepresented to Allworthy; nor could he mention those many false accusations which had been from time to time preferred against him to Allworthy: for with none of these he was himself acquainted. He had likewise, as we have observed, omitted many material facts in his present relation. Upon the whole, indeed, everything now appeared in such favourable colours to Jones, that malice itself would have found it no easy matter to fix any blame upon him.

Not that Jones desired to conceal or to disguise the truth; nay, he would have been more unwilling to have suffered any censure to fall on Mr Allworthy for punishing him, than on his own actions for deserving it; but, in reality, so it happened, and so it always will happen; for let a man be never so honest, the account of his own conduct will, in spite of himself, be so very favourable, that his vices will come purified through his lips, and, like foul liquors well strained, will leave all their foulness behind. For though the facts themselves may appear, yet so different will be the motives, circumstances, and consequences, when a man tells his own story, and when his enemy tells it, that we scarce can recognise the facts to be one and the same.

Though the barber had drank down this story with greedy ears, he was not yet satisfied. There was a circumstance behind which his curiosity, cold as it was, most eagerly longed for. Jones had mentioned the fact of his amour, and of his being the rival of Blifil, but had cautiously concealed the name of the young lady. The barber, therefore, after some hesitation, and many hums and hahs, at last begged leave to crave the name of the lady, who appeared to be the principal cause of all this mischief. Jones paused a moment, and then said, "Since I have trusted you with so much, and since, I am afraid, her name is become too publick already on this occasion, I will not conceal it from you. Her name is Sophia Western."

"*Proh deum atque hominum fidem*! Squire Western hath a daughter grown a woman!"—"Ay, and such a woman," cries Jones, "that the world cannot match. No eye ever saw anything so beautiful; but that is her least excellence. Such sense! such goodness! Oh, I could praise her for ever, and yet should omit half her virtues!"—"Mr Western a daughter grown up!" cries the barber: "I remember the father a boy; well, *Tempus edax rerum*."

The wine being now at an end, the barber pressed very eagerly to be his bottle; but Jones absolutely refused, saying, "He had already drank more than he ought: and that he now chose to retire to his room, where he wished he could procure himself a book."—"A book!" cries Benjamin; "what book would you have? Latin or English? I have some curious books in both languages; such as *Erasmi Colloquia, Ovid de Tristibus, Gradus ad Parnassum;* and in English I have several of the best books, though some of them are a little torn; but I have a great part of Stowe's Chronicle; the sixth volume of Pope's Homer; the third volume of the Spectator; the second volume of Echard's Roman History; the Craftsman; Robinson Crusoe; Thomas a Kempis; and two volumes of Tom Brown's Works."

"Those last," cries Jones, "are books I never saw, so if you please lend me one of those volumes." The barber assured him he would be highly entertained, for he looked upon the author to have been one of the greatest wits that ever the nation produced. He then stepped to his house, which was hard by, and immediately returned; after which, the barber having received very strict injunctions of secrecy from Jones, and having sworn inviolably to maintain it, they separated; the barber went home, and Jones retired to his chamber.

CHAPTER VI.

In which more of the talents of Mr Benjamin will appear, as well as who this extraordinary person was.

In the morning Jones grew a little uneasy at the desertion of his surgeon, as he apprehended some inconvenience, or even danger, might attend the not dressing his wound; he enquired of the drawer, what other surgeons were to be met with in that neighbourhood. The drawer told him, there was one not far off; but he had known him often refuse to be concerned after another had been sent before him; "but, sir," says he, "if you will take my advice, there is not a man in the kingdom can do your business better than the barber who was with you last night. We look upon him to be one of the ablest men at a cut in all this neighbourhood. For though he hath not been her above three months, he hath done several great cures."

The drawer was presently dispatched for Little Benjamin, who being acquainted in what capacity he was wanted, prepared himself accordingly, and attended; but with so different an air and aspect from that which he wore when his basin was under his arm, that he could scarce be known to be the same person.

"So, tonsor," says Jones, "I find you have more trades than one; how came you not to inform me of this last night?"—"A surgeon," answered Benjamin, with great gravity, "is a profession, not a trade. The reason why I did not acquaint you last night that I professed this art, was, that I then concluded you was under the hands of another gentleman, and I never love to interfere with my brethren in their business. *Ars omnibus communis*. But now, sir, if you please, I will inspect your head, and when I see into your skull, I will give my opinion of your case."

Jones had no great faith in this new professor; however, he suffered him to open the bandage and to look at his wound; which as soon as he had done, Benjamin began to groan and shake his head violently. Upon which Jones, in a peevish manner, bid him not play the fool, but tell him in what condition he found him. "Shall I answer you as a surgeon, or a friend?" said Benjamin. "As a friend, and seriously," said Jones. "Why then, upon my soul," cries Benjamin, "it would require a great deal of art to keep you from being well after a very few dressings; and if you will suffer me to apply some salve of mine, I will answer for the success." Jones gave his consent, and the plaister was applied accordingly.

"There, sir," cries Benjamin: "now I will, if you please, resume my former self; but a man is obliged to keep up some dignity in his countenance whilst he is performing these operations, or the world will not submit to be handled by him. You can't imagine, sir, of how much consequence a grave aspect is to a grave character. A barber may make you laugh, but a surgeon ought rather to make you cry."

"Mr Barber, or Mr Surgeon, or Mr Barber-surgeon," said Jones. "O dear sir!" answered Benjamin, interrupting him, "*Infandum, regina, jubes renovare dolorem.* You recall to my mind that cruel separation of the united fraternities, so much to the prejudice of both bodies, as all separations must be, according to the old adage, *Vis unita fortior*; which to be sure there are not wanting some of one or of the other fraternity who are able to construe. What a blow was this to me, who unite both in my own person!" "Well, by whatever name you please to be called," continued Jones, "you certainly are one of the oddest, most comical fellows I ever met with, and must have something very surprizing in your story, which you must confess I have a right to hear."—"I do confess it," answered Benjamin, "and will very readily acquaint you with it, when you have sufficient leisure, for I promise you it will require a good deal of time." Jones told him, he could never be more at leisure than at present. "Well, then," said Benjamin, "I will obey you; but first I will fasten the door, that none may interrupt us." He did so, and then advancing with a solemn air to Jones, said: "I must begin by telling you, sir, that you yourself have been the greatest enemy I ever had." Jones was a little startled at this sudden declaration. "I your enemy, sir!" says he, with much amazement, and some sternness in his look. "Nay, be not angry," said Benjamin, "for I promise you I am not. You are perfectly innocent of having intended me any wrong; for you was then an infant: but I shall, I believe, unriddle all this the moment I mention my name. Did you never hear, sir, of one Partridge, who had the honour of being reputed your father, and the misfortune of being ruined by that honour?" "I have, indeed, heard of that Partridge," says Jones, "and have always believed myself to be his son." "Well, sir," answered Benjamin, "I am that Partridge; but I here absolve you from all filial duty, for I do assure you, you are no son of mine." "How!" replied Jones, "and is it possible that a false suspicion should have drawn all the ill consequences upon you, with which I am too well acquainted?" "It is possible," cries Benjamin, "for it is so: but though it is natural enough for men to hate even the innocent causes of their sufferings, yet I am of a different temper. I have loved you ever since I heard of your behaviour to Black George, as I told you; and I am convinced, from this extraordinary meeting, that you are born to make me amends for all I have suffered on that account. Besides, I dreamt, the night before I saw you, that I stumbled over a stool without hurting myself; which plainly showed me something good was towards me: and last night I dreamt again, that I rode behind you on a milk-white mare, which is a very excellent dream, and betokens much good fortune, which I am resolved to pursue unless you have the cruelty to deny me."

"I should be very glad, Mr Partridge," answered Jones, "to have it in my power to make you amends for your sufferings on my account, though at present I see no likelihood of it; however, I assure you I will deny you nothing which is in my power to grant."

"It is in your power sure enough," replied Benjamin; "for I desire nothing more than leave to attend you in this expedition. Nay, I have so entirely set my heart upon it, that if you should refuse me, you will kill both a barber and a surgeon in one breath."

Jones answered, smiling, that he should be very sorry to be the occasion of so much mischief to the public. He then advanced many prudential reasons, in order to dissuade Benjamin (whom we shall hereafter call Partridge) from his purpose; but all were in vain. Partridge relied strongly on his dream of the milk-white mare. "Besides, sir," says he, "I promise you I have as good an inclination to the cause as any man can possibly have; and go I will, whether you admit me to go in your company or not."

Jones, who was as much pleased with Partridge as Partridge could be with him, and who had not consulted his own inclination but the good of the other in desiring him to stay behind, when he found his friend so resolute, at last gave his consent; but then recollecting himself, he said, "Perhaps, Mr Partridge, you think I shall be able to support you, but I really am not;" and then taking out his purse, he told out nine guineas, which he declared were his whole fortune.

Partridge answered, "That his dependence was only on his future favour; for he was thoroughly convinced he would shortly have enough in his power. At present, sir," said he, "I believe I am rather the richer man of the two; but all I have is at your service, and at your disposal. I insist upon your taking the whole, and I beg only to attend you in the quality of your servant; *Nil desperandum est Teucro duce et auspice Teucro*": but to this generous proposal concerning the money, Jones would by no means submit.

It was resolved to set out the next morning, when a difficulty arose concerning the baggage; for the portmanteau of Mr Jones was too large to be carried without a horse.

"If I may presume to give my advice," says Partridge, "this portmanteau, with everything in it, except a few shirts, should be left behind. Those I shall be easily able to carry for you, and the rest of your cloaths will remain very safe locked up in my house."

This method was no sooner proposed than agreed to; and then the barber departed, in order to prepare everything for his intended expedition.

CHAPTER VII.

Containing better reasons than any which have yet appeared for the conduct of Partridge; an apology for the weakness of Jones; and some further anecdotes concerning my landlady.

Though Partridge was one of the most superstitious of men, he would hardly perhaps have desired to accompany Jones on his expedition merely from the omens of the joint-stool and white mare, if his prospect had been no better than to have shared the plunder gained in the field of battle. In fact, when Partridge came to ruminate on the relation he had heard from Jones, he could not reconcile to himself that Mr Allworthy should turn his son (for so he most firmly believed him to be) out of doors, for any reason which he had heard assigned. He concluded, therefore, that the whole was a fiction, and that Jones, of whom he had often from his correspondents heard the wildest character, had in reality run away from his father. It came into his head, therefore, that if he could prevail with the young gentleman to return back to his father, he should by that means render a service to Allworthy, which would obliterate all his former anger; nay, indeed, he conceived that very anger was counterfeited, and that Allworthy had sacrificed him to his own reputation. And this suspicion indeed he well accounted for, from the tender behaviour of that excellent man to the foundling child; from his great severity to Partridge, who, knowing himself to be innocent, could not conceive that any other should think him guilty; lastly, from the allowance which he had privately received long after the annuity had been publickly taken from him, and which he looked upon as a kind of smart-money, or rather by way of atonement for injustice; for it is very uncommon, I believe, for men to ascribe the benefactions they receive to pure charity, when they can possibly impute them to any other motive. If he could by any means therefore persuade the young gentleman to return home, he doubted not but that he should again be received into the favour of Allworthy, and well rewarded for his pains; nay, and should be again restored to his native country; a restoration which Ulysses himself never wished more heartily than poor Partridge.

As for Jones, he was well satisfied with the truth of what the other had asserted, and believed that Partridge had no other inducements but love to him, and zeal for the cause; a blameable want of caution and diffidence in the veracity of others, in which he was highly worthy of censure. To say the truth, there are but two ways by which men become possessed of this excellent quality. The one is from long experience, and the other is from nature; which last, I presume, is often meant by genius, or great natural parts; and it is infinitely the better of the two, not only as we are masters of it much earlier in life, but as it is much more infallible and conclusive; for a man who hath been imposed on by ever so many, may still hope to find others more honest; whereas he who receives certain necessary admonitions from within, that this is impossible, must have very little understanding indeed, if he ever renders himself liable to be once deceived. As Jones had not this gift from nature, he was too young to have gained it by experience; for at the diffident wisdom which is to be acquired this way, we seldom arrive till very late in life; which is perhaps the reason why some old men are apt to despise the understandings of all those who are a little younger than themselves.

Jones spent most part of the day in the company of a new acquaintance. This was no other than the landlord of the house, or rather the husband of the landlady. He had but lately made his descent downstairs, after a long fit of the gout, in which distemper he was generally confined to his room during one half of the year; and during the rest, he walked about the house, smoaked his pipe, and drank his bottle with his friends, without concerning himself in the least with any kind of business. He had been bred, as they call it, a gentleman; that is, bred up to do nothing; and had spent a very small fortune, which he inherited from an industrious farmer his uncle, in hunting, horse-racing, and cock-fighting, and had been married by my landlady for certain purposes, which he had long since desisted from answering; for which she hated him heartily. But as he was a surly kind of fellow, so she contented herself with frequently upbraiding him by disadvantageous comparisons with her first husband, whose praise she had eternally in her mouth; and as she was for the most part mistress of the profit, so she was satisfied to take upon herself the care and government of the family, and, after a long successless struggle, to suffer her husband to be master of himself.

In the evening, when Jones retired to his room, a small dispute arose between this fond couple concerning him:—"What," says the wife, "you have been tippling with the gentleman, I see?"—"Yes," answered the husband, "we have cracked a bottle together, and a very gentlemanlike man he is, and hath a very pretty notion of horse-flesh. Indeed, he is young, and hath not seen much of the world; for I believe he hath been at very few horse-races."—"Oho! he is one of your order, is he?" replies the landlady: "he must be a gentleman to be sure, if he is a horse-racer. The devil fetch such gentry! I am sure I wish I had never seen any of them. I have reason to love horse-racers truly!"—"That you have," says the husband; "for I was one, you know."—"Yes," answered she, "you are a pure one indeed. As my first husband used to say, I may put all the good I have ever got by you in my eyes, and see never the worse."—"D—n your first husband!" cries he. "Don't d—n a better man than yourself," answered the wife: "if he had been alive, you durst not have done it."—"Then you think," says he, "I have not so much courage as yourself; for you have d—n'd him often in my hearing."—"If I did," says she, "I have repented of it many's the good time and oft. And if he was so good to forgive me a word spoken in haste or so, it doth not become such a one as you to twitter me. He was a husband to me, he was; and if ever I did make use of an ill word or so in a passion, I never called him rascal; I should have told a lie, if I had called him rascal." Much more she said, but not in his hearing; for having lighted his pipe, he staggered off as fast as he could. We shall therefore transcribe no more of her speech, as it approached still nearer and nearer to a subject too indelicate to find any place in this history.

Early in the morning Partridge appeared at the bedside of Jones, ready equipped for the journey, with his knapsack at his back. This was his own workmanship; for besides his other trades, he was no indifferent taylor. He had already put up his whole stock of linen in it, consisting of four shirts, to which he now added eight for Mr Jones; and then packing up the portmanteau, he was departing with it towards his own house, but was stopt in his way by the landlady, who refused to suffer any removals till after the payment of the reckoning.

The landlady was, as we have said, absolute governess in these regions; it was therefore necessary to comply with her rules; so the bill was presently writ out, which amounted to a much larger sum than might have been expected, from the entertainment which Jones had met with. But here we are obliged to disclose some maxims, which publicans hold to be the grand mysteries of their trade. The first is, If they have anything good in their house (which indeed very seldom happens) to produce it only to persons who travel with great equipages. 2dly, To charge the same for the very worst provisions, as if they were the best. And lastly, If any of their guests call but for little, to make them pay a double price for everything they have; so that the amount by the head may be much the same.

The bill being made and discharged, Jones set forward with Partridge, carrying his knapsack; nor did the landlady condescend to wish him a good journey; for this was, it seems, an inn frequented by people of fashion; and I know not whence it is, but all those who get their livelihood by people of fashion, contract as much insolence to the rest of mankind, as if they really belonged to that rank themselves.

CHAPTER VIII.

Jones arrives at Gloucester, and goes to the Bell; the character of that house, and of a petty-fogger which he there meets with.

Mr Jones and Partridge, or Little Benjamin (which epithet of Little was perhaps given him ironically, he being in reality near six feet high), having left their last quarters in the manner before described, travelled on to Gloucester without meeting any adventure worth relating.

Being arrived here, they chose for their house of entertainment the sign of the Bell, an excellent house indeed, and which I do most seriously recommend to every reader who shall visit this antient city. The master of it is brother to the great preacher Whitefield; but is absolutely untainted with the pernicious principles of Methodism, or of any other heretical sect. He is indeed a very honest plain man, and, in my opinion, not likely to create any disturbance either in church or state. His wife hath, I believe, had much pretension to beauty, and is still a very fine woman. Her person and deportment might have made a shining figure in the politest assemblies; but though she must be conscious of this and many other perfections, she seems perfectly contented with, and resigned to, that state of life to which she is called; and this resignation is entirely owing to the prudence and wisdom of her temper; for she is at present as free from any Methodistical notions as her husband: I say at present; for she freely confesses that her brother's documents made at first some impression upon her, and that she had put herself to the expense of a long hood, in order to attend the extraordinary emotions of the Spirit; but having found, during an experiment of three weeks, no emotions, she says, worth a farthing, she very wisely laid by her hood, and abandoned the sect. To be concise, she is a very friendly good-natured woman; and so industrious to oblige, that the guests must be of a very morose disposition who are not extremely well satisfied in her house.

Mrs Whitefield happened to be in the yard when Jones and his attendant marched in. Her sagacity soon discovered in the air of our heroe something which distinguished him from the vulgar. She ordered her servants, therefore, immediately to show him into a room, and presently afterwards invited him to dinner with herself; which invitation he very thankfully accepted; for indeed much less agreeable company than that of Mrs Whitefield, and a much worse entertainment than she had provided, would have been welcome after so long fasting and so long a walk.

Besides Mr Jones and the good governess of the mansion, there sat down at table an attorney of Salisbury, indeed the very same who had brought the news of Mrs Blifil's death to Mr Allworthy, and whose name, which I think we did not before mention, was Dowling: there was likewise present another person, who stiled himself a lawyer, and who lived somewhere near Linlinch, in Somersetshire. This fellow, I say, stiled himself a lawyer, but was indeed a most vile petty-fogger, without sense or knowledge of any kind; one of those who may be termed train-bearers to the law; a sort of supernumeraries in the profession, who are the hackneys of attorneys, and will ride more miles for half-a-crown than a postboy.

During the time of dinner, the Somersetshire lawyer recollected the face of Jones, which he had seen at Mr Allworthy's; for he had often visited in that gentleman's kitchen. He therefore took occasion to enquire after the good family there with that familiarity which would have become an intimate friend or acquaintance of Mr Allworthy; and indeed he did all in his power to insinuate himself to be such, though he had never had the honour of speaking to any person in that family higher than the butler. Jones answered all his questions with much civility, though he never remembered to have seen the petty-fogger before; and though he concluded, from the outward appearance and behaviour of the man, that he usurped a freedom with his betters, to which he was by no means intitled.

As the conversation of fellows of this kind is of all others the most detestable to men of any sense, the cloth was no sooner removed than Mr Jones withdrew, and a little barbarously left poor Mrs Whitefield to do a penance, which I have often heard Mr Timothy Harris, and other publicans of good taste, lament, as the severest lot annexed to their calling, namely, that of being obliged to keep company with their guests.

Jones had no sooner quitted the room, than the petty-fogger, in a whispering tone, asked Mrs Whitefield, "If she knew who that fine spark was?" She answered, "She had never seen the gentleman before."—"The gentleman, indeed!" replied the petty-fogger; "a pretty gentleman, truly! Why, he's the bastard of a fellow who was hanged for horse-stealing. He was dropt at Squire Allworthy's door, where one of the servants found him in a box so full of rain-water, that he would certainly have been drowned, had he not been reserved for another fate."—"Ay, ay, you need not mention it, I protest: we understand what that fate is very well," cries Dowling, with a most facetious grin.—"Well," continued the other, "the squire ordered him to be taken in; for he is a timbersome man everybody knows, and was afraid of drawing himself into a scrape; and there the bastard was bred up, and fed, and cloathified all to the world like any gentleman; and there he got one of the servant-maids with child, and persuaded her to swear it to the squire himself; and afterwards he broke the arm of one Mr Thwackum a clergyman, only because he reprimanded him for following whores; and afterwards he snapt a pistol at Mr Blifil behind his back; and once, when Squire Allworthy was sick, he got a drum, and beat it all over the house to prevent him from sleeping; and twenty other pranks he hath played, for all which, about four or five days ago, just before I left the country, the squire stripped him stark naked, and turned him out of doors."

"And very justly too, I protest," cries Dowling; "I would turn my own son out of doors, if he was guilty of half as much. And pray what is the name of this pretty gentleman?"

"The name o' un?" answered Petty-fogger; "why, he is called Thomas Jones."

"Jones!" answered Dowling a little eagerly; "what, Mr Jones that lived at Mr Allworthy's? was that the gentleman that dined with us?"—"The very same," said the other. "I have heard of the gentleman," cries Dowling, "often; but I never heard any ill character of him."—"And I am sure," says Mrs Whitefield, "if half what this gentleman hath said be true, Mr Jones hath the most deceitful countenance I ever saw; for sure his looks promise something very different; and I must say, for the little I have seen of him, he is as civil a well-bred man as you would wish to converse with."

Petty-fogger calling to mind that he had not been sworn, as he usually was, before he gave his evidence, now bound what he had declared with so many oaths and imprecations that the landlady's ears were shocked, and she put a stop to his swearing, by assuring him of her belief. Upon which he said, "I hope, madam, you imagine I would scorn to tell such things of any man, unless I knew them to be true. What interest have I in taking away the reputation of a man who never injured me? I promise you every syllable of what I have said is fact, and the whole country knows it."

As Mrs Whitefield had no reason to suspect that the petty-fogger had any motive or temptation to abuse Jones, the reader cannot blame her for believing what he so confidently affirmed with many oaths. She accordingly gave up her skill in physiognomy, and hence-forwards conceived so ill an opinion of her guest, that she heartily wished him out of her house.

This dislike was now farther increased by a report which Mr Whitefield made from the kitchen, where Partridge had informed the company, "That though he carried the knapsack, and contented himself with staying among servants, while Tom Jones (as he called him) was regaling in the parlour, he was not his servant, but only a friend and companion, and as good a gentleman as Mr Jones himself."

Dowling sat all this while silent, biting his fingers, making faces, grinning, and looking wonderfully arch; at last he opened his lips, and protested that the gentleman looked like another sort of man. He then called for his bill with the utmost haste, declared he must be at Hereford that evening, lamented his great hurry of business, and wished he could divide himself into twenty pieces, in order to be at once in twenty places.

The petty-fogger now likewise departed, and then Jones desired the favour of Mrs Whitefield's company to drink tea with him; but she refused, and with a manner so different from that with which she had received him at dinner, that it a little surprized him. And now he soon perceived her behaviour totally changed; for instead of that natural affability which we have before celebrated, she wore a constrained severity on her countenance, which was so disagreeable to Mr Jones, that he resolved, however late, to quit the house that evening.

He did indeed account somewhat unfairly for this sudden change; for besides some hard and unjust surmises concerning female fickleness and mutability, he began to suspect that he owed this want of civility to his want of horses; a sort of animals which, as they dirty no sheets, are thought in inns to pay better for their beds than their riders, and are therefore considered as the more desirable company; but Mrs Whitefield, to do her justice, had a much more liberal way of thinking. She was perfectly well-bred, and could be very civil to a gentleman, though he walked on foot. In reality, she looked on our heroe as a sorry scoundrel, and therefore treated him as such, for which not even Jones himself, had he known as much as the reader, could have blamed her; nay, on the contrary, he must have approved her conduct, and have esteemed her the more for the disrespect shown towards himself. This is indeed a most aggravating circumstance, which attends depriving men unjustly of their reputation; for a man who is conscious of having an ill character, cannot justly be angry with those who neglect and slight him; but ought rather to despise such as affect his conversation, unless where a perfect intimacy must have convinced them that their friend's character hath been falsely and injuriously aspersed.

This was not, however, the case of Jones; for as he was a perfect stranger to the truth, so he was with good reason offended at the treatment he received. He therefore paid his reckoning and departed, highly against the will of Mr Partridge, who having remonstrated much against it to no purpose, at last condescended to take up his knapsack and to attend his friend.

CHAPTER IX.

Containing several dialogues between Jones and Partridge, concerning love, cold, hunger, and other matters; with the lucky and narrow escape of Partridge, as he was on the very brink of making a fatal

discovery to his friend.

The shadows began now to descend larger from the high mountains; the feathered creation had betaken themselves to their rest. Now the highest order of mortals were sitting down to their dinners, and the lowest order to their suppers. In a word, the clock struck five just as Mr Jones took his leave of Gloucester; an hour at which (as it was now mid-winter) the dirty fingers of Night would have drawn her sable curtain over the universe, had not the moon forbid her, who now, with a face as broad and as red as those of some jolly mortals, who, like her, turn night into day, began to rise from her bed, where she had slumbered away the day, in order to sit up all night. Jones had not travelled far before he paid his compliments to that beautiful planet, and, turning to his companion, asked him if he had ever beheld so delicious an evening? Partridge making no ready answer to his question, he proceeded to comment on the beauty of the moon, and repeated some passages from Milton, who hath certainly excelled all other poets in his description of the heavenly luminaries. He then told Partridge the story from the Spectator, of two lovers who had agreed to entertain themselves when they were at a great distance from each other, by repairing, at a certain fixed hour, to look at the moon; thus pleasing themselves with the thought that they were both employed in contemplating the same object at the same time. "Those lovers," added he, "must have had souls truly capable of feeling all the tenderness of the sublimest of all human passions."—"Very probably," cries Partridge: "but I envy them more, if they had bodies incapable of feeling cold; for I am almost frozen to death, and am very much afraid I shall lose a piece of my nose before we get to another house of entertainment. Nay, truly, we may well expect some judgment should happen to us for our folly in running away so by night from one of the most excellent inns I ever set my foot into. I am sure I never saw more good things in my life, and the greatest lord in the land cannot live better in his own house than he may there. And to forsake such a house, and go a rambling about the country, the Lord knows whither, *per devia rura viarum*, I say nothing for my part; but some people might not have charity enough to conclude we were in our sober senses."—"Fie upon it, Mr Partridge!" says Jones, "have a better heart; consider you are going to face an enemy; and are you afraid of facing a little cold? I wish, indeed, we had a guide to advise which of these roads we should take."—"May I be so bold," says Partridge, "to offer my advice? *Interdum stultus opportuna loquitur*"—"Why, which of them," cries Jones, "would you recommend?"—"Truly neither of them," answered Partridge. "The only road we can be certain of finding, is the road we came. A good hearty pace will bring us back to Gloucester in an hour; but if we go forward, the Lord Harry knows when we shall arrive at any place; for I see at least fifty miles before me, and no house in all the way."—"You see, indeed, a very fair prospect," says Jones, "which receives great additional beauty from the extreme lustre of the moon. However, I will keep the left-hand track, as that seems to lead directly to those hills, which we were informed lie not far from Worcester. And here, if you are inclined to quit me, you may, and return back again; but for my part, I am resolved to go forward."

"It is unkind in you, sir," says Partridge, "to suspect me of any such intention. What I have advised hath been as much on your account as on my own: but since you are determined to go on, I am as much determined to follow. *I prae sequar te*."

They now travelled some miles without speaking to each other, during which suspense of discourse Jones often sighed, and Benjamin groaned as bitterly, though from a very different reason. At length Jones made a full stop, and turning about, cries, "Who knows, Partridge, but the loveliest creature in the universe may have her eyes now fixed on that very moon which I behold at this instant?" "Very likely, sir," answered Partridge; "and if my eyes were fixed on a good surloin of roast beef, the devil might take the moon and her horns into the bargain." "Did ever Tramontane make such an answer?" cries Jones. "Prithee, Partridge, wast thou ever susceptible of love in thy life, or hath time worn away all the traces of it from thy memory?" "Alack-a-day!" cries Partridge, "well would it have been for me if I had never known what love was. *Infandum regina jubes renovare dolorem*. I am sure I have tasted all the tenderness, and sublimities, and bitternesses of the passion." "Was your mistress unkind, then?" says Jones. "Very unkind, indeed, sir," answered Partridge; "for she married me, and made one of the most confounded wives in the world. However, heaven be praised, she's gone; and if I believed she was in the moon, according to a book I once read, which teaches that to be the receptacle of departed spirits, I would never look at it for fear of seeing her; but I wish, sir, that the moon was a looking-glass for your sake, and that Miss Sophia Western was now placed before it." "My dear Partridge," cries Jones, "what a thought was there! A thought which I am certain could never have entered into any mind but that of a lover. O Partridge! could I hope once again to see that face; but, alas! all those golden dreams are vanished for ever, and my only refuge from future misery is to forget the object of all my former happiness." "And do you really despair of ever seeing Miss Western again?" answered Partridge; "if you will follow my advice I will engage you shall not only see her but have her in your arms." "Ha! do not awaken a thought of that nature," cries Jones: "I have struggled sufficiently to conquer all such wishes already." "Nay," answered Partridge, "if you do not wish to have your mistress in your arms you are a most extraordinary lover indeed." "Well, well," says Jones, "let us avoid this subject; but pray what is your advice?" "To give it you in the military phrase, then," says Partridge, "as we are soldiers, `To the right about.' Let us return the way we came; we may yet reach Gloucester to-night, though late; whereas, if we proceed, we are likely, for aught I see, to ramble about for ever without coming either to house or home." "I have already told you my resolution is to go on," answered Jones; "but I would have you go back. I am obliged to you for your company hither; and I beg you to accept a guinea as a small instance of my gratitude. Nay, it would be cruel in me to suffer you to go any farther; for, to deal plainly with you, my chief end and desire is a glorious death in the service of my king and country." "As for your money," replied Partridge, "I beg, sir, you will put it up; I will receive none of you at this time; for at present I am, I believe, the richer man of the two. And as your resolution is to go on, so mine is to follow you if you do. Nay, now my presence appears absolutely necessary to take care of you, since your intentions are so desperate; for I promise you my views are much more prudent; as you are resolved to fall in battle if you can, so I am resolved as firmly to come to no hurt if I can help it. And, indeed, I have the comfort to think there will be but little danger; for a popish priest told me the other day the business would soon be over, and he believed without a battle." "A popish priest!" cries Jones, "I have heard is not always to be believed when he speaks in behalf of his religion." "Yes, but so far," answered the other, "from speaking in behalf of his religion, he assured me the Catholicks did not expect to be any gainers by the change; for that Prince Charles was as good a Protestant as any in England; and that nothing but regard to right made him and the rest of the popish party to be Jacobites."—"I believe him to be as much a Protestant as I believe he hath any right," says Jones; "and I make no doubt of our success, but not without a battle. So that I am not so sanguine as your friend the popish priest." "Nay, to be sure, sir," answered Partridge, "all the prophecies I have ever read speak of a great deal of blood to be spilt in the quarrel, and the miller with three thumbs, who is now alive, is to hold the horses of three kings, up to his knees in blood. Lord, have mercy upon us all, and send better times!" "With what stuff and nonsense hast thou filled thy head!" answered Jones: "this too, I suppose, comes from the popish priest. Monsters and prodigies are the proper arguments to support monstrous and absurd doctrines. The cause of King George is the cause of liberty and true religion. In other words, it is the cause of common sense, my boy, and I warrant you will succeed, though Briarius himself was to rise again with his hundred thumbs, and to turn miller." Partridge made no reply to this. He was, indeed, cast into the utmost confusion by this declaration of Jones. For, to inform the reader of a secret, which he had no proper opportunity of revealing before, Partridge was in truth a Jacobite, and had concluded that Jones was of the same party, and was now proceeding to join the rebels. An opinion which was not without foundation. For the tall, long-sided dame, mentioned by Hudibras—that many-eyed, many-tongued, many-mouthed, many-eared monster of Virgil, had related the story of the quarrel between Jones and the officer, with the usual regard to truth. She had, indeed, changed the name of Sophia into that of the Pretender, and had reported, that drinking his health was the cause for which Jones was knocked down. This Partridge had heard, and most firmly believed. 'Tis no wonder, therefore, that he had thence entertained the above-mentioned opinion of Jones; and which he had almost discovered to him before he found out his own mistake. And at this the reader will be the less inclined to wonder, if he pleases to recollect the doubtful phrase in which Jones first communicated his resolution to Mr Partridge; and, indeed, had the words been less ambiguous, Partridge might very well have construed them as he did; being persuaded as he was that the whole nation were of the same inclination in their hearts; nor did it stagger him that Jones had travelled in the company of soldiers; for he had the same opinion of the army which he had of the rest of the people.

But however well affected he might be to James or Charles, he was still much more attached to Little Benjamin than to either; for which reason he no sooner discovered the principles of his fellow-traveller than he thought proper to conceal and outwardly give up his own to the man on whom he depended for the making his fortune, since he by no means believed the affairs of Jones to be so desperate as they really were with Mr Allworthy; for as he had kept a constant correspondence with some of his neighbours since he left that country, he had heard much, indeed more than was true, of the great affection Mr Allworthy bore this young man, who, as Partridge had been instructed, was to be that gentleman's heir, and whom, as we have said, he did not in the least doubt to be his son.

He imagined therefore that whatever quarrel was between them, it would be certainly made up at the return of Mr Jones; an event from which he promised great advantages, if he could take this opportunity of ingratiating himself with that young gentleman; and if he could by any means be instrumental in procuring his return, he doubted not, as we have before said, but it would as highly advance him in the favour of Mr Allworthy.

We have already observed, that he was a very good-natured fellow, and he hath himself declared the violent attachment he had to the person and character of Jones; but possibly the views which I have just before mentioned, might likewise have some little share in prompting him to undertake this expedition, at least in urging him to continue it, after he had discovered that his master and himself, like some prudent fathers and sons, though they travelled together in great friendship, had embraced opposite parties. I am led into this conjecture, by having remarked, that though love, friendship, esteem, and such like, have very powerful operations in the human mind; interest, however, is an ingredient seldom omitted by wise men, when they would work others to their own purposes. This is indeed a most excellent medicine, and, like Ward's pill, flies at once to the particular part of the body on which you desire to operate, whether it be the tongue, the hand, or any other member, where it scarce ever fails of immediately producing the desired effect.

CHAPTER X.

In which our travellers meet with a very extraordinary adventure.

Just as Jones and his friend came to the end of their dialogue in the preceding chapter, they arrived at the bottom of a very steep hill. Here Jones stopt short, and directing his eyes upwards, stood for a while silent. At length he called to his companion, and said, "Partridge, I wish I was at the top of this hill; it must certainly afford a most charming prospect, especially by this light; for the solemn gloom which the moon casts on all objects, is beyond expression beautiful, especially to an imagination which is desirous of cultivating melancholy ideas."—"Very probably," answered Partridge; "but if the top of the hill be properest to produce melancholy thoughts, I suppose the bottom is the likeliest to produce merry ones, and these I take to be much the better of the two. I protest you have made my blood run cold with the very mentioning the top of that mountain; which seems to me to be one of the highest in the world. No, no, if we look for anything, let it be for a place under ground, to screen ourselves from the frost."—"Do so," said Jones; "let it be but within hearing of this place, and I will hallow to you at my return back."—"Surely, sir, you are not mad," said Partridge.—"Indeed, I am," answered Jones, "if ascending this hill be madness; but as you complain so much of the cold already, I would have you stay below. I will certainly return to you within an hour."—"Pardon me, sir," cries Partridge; "I have determined to follow you wherever you go." Indeed he was now afraid to stay behind; for though he was coward enough in all respects, yet his chief fear was that of ghosts, with which the present time of night, and the wildness of the place, extremely well suited.

At this instant Partridge espied a glimmering light through some trees, which seemed very near to them. He immediately cried out in a rapture, "Oh, sir! Heaven hath at last heard my prayers, and hath brought us to a house; perhaps it may be an inn. Let me beseech you, sir, if you have any compassion either for me or yourself, do not despise the goodness of Providence, but let us go directly to yon light. Whether it be a public-house or no, I am sure if they be Christians that dwell there, they will not refuse a little house-room to persons in our miserable condition." Jones at length yielded to the earnest supplications of Partridge, and both together made directly towards the place whence the light issued.

They soon arrived at the door of this house, or cottage, for it might be called either, without much impropriety. Here Jones knocked several times without receiving any answer from within; at which Partridge, whose head was full of nothing but of ghosts, devils, witches, and such like, began to tremble, crying, "Lord, have mercy upon us! surely the people must be all dead. I can see no light neither now, and yet I am certain I saw a candle burning but a moment before.—Well! I have heard of such things."—"What hast thou heard of?" said Jones. "The people are either fast asleep, or probably, as this is a lonely place, are afraid to open their door." He then began to vociferate pretty loudly, and at last an old woman, opening an upper casement, asked, Who they were, and what they wanted? Jones answered, They were travellers who had lost their way, and having seen a light in the window, had been led thither in hopes of finding some fire to warm themselves. "Whoever you are," cries the woman, "you have no business here; nor shall I open the door to any one at this time of night." Partridge, whom the sound of a human voice had recovered from his fright, fell to the most earnest supplications to be admitted for a few minutes to the fire, saying, he was almost dead with the cold; to which fear had indeed contributed equally with the frost. He assured her that the gentleman who spoke to her was one of the greatest squires in the country; and made use of every argument, save one, which Jones afterwards effectually added; and this was, the promise of half-a-crown;—a bribe too great to be resisted by such a person, especially as the genteel appearance of Jones, which the light of the moon plainly discovered to her, together with his affable behaviour, had entirely subdued those apprehensions of thieves which she had at first conceived. She agreed, therefore, at last, to let them in; where Partridge, to his infinite joy, found a good fire ready for his reception.

The poor fellow, however, had no sooner warmed himself, than those thoughts which were always uppermost in his mind, began a little to disturb his brain. There was no article of his creed in which he had a stronger faith than he had in witchcraft, nor can the reader conceive a figure more adapted to inspire this idea, than the old woman who now stood before him. She answered exactly to that picture drawn by Otway in his Orphan. Indeed, if this woman had lived in the reign of James the First, her appearance alone would have hanged her, almost without any evidence.

Many circumstances likewise conspired to confirm Partridge in his opinion. Her living, as he then imagined, by herself in so lonely a place; and in a house, the outside of which seemed much too good for her, but its inside was furnished in the most neat and elegant manner. To say the truth, Jones himself was not a little surprized at what he saw; for, besides the extraordinary neatness of the room, it was adorned with a great number of nicknacks and curiosities, which might have engaged the attention of a virtuoso.

While Jones was admiring these things, and Partridge sat trembling with the firm belief that he was in the house of a witch, the old woman said, "I hope, gentlemen, you will make what haste you can; for I expect my master presently, and I would not for double the money he should find you here."—"Then you have a master?" cried Jones. "Indeed, you will excuse me, good woman, but I was surprized to see all those fine things in your house."—"Ah, sir," said she, "if the twentieth part of these things were mine, I should think myself a rich woman. But pray, sir, do not stay much longer, for I look for him in every minute."—"Why, sure he would not be angry with you," said Jones, "for doing a common act of charity?"—"Alack-a-day, sir!" said she, "he is a strange man, not at all like other people. He keeps no company with anybody, and seldom walks out but by night, for he doth not care to be seen; and all the country people are as much afraid of meeting him; for his dress is enough to frighten those who are not used to it. They call him, the Man of the Hill (for there he walks by night), and the country people are not, I believe, more afraid of the devil himself. He would be terribly angry if he found you here."—"Pray, sir," says Partridge, "don't let us offend the gentleman; I am ready to walk, and was never warmer in my life. Do pray, sir, let us go. Here are pistols over the chimney: who knows whether they be charged or no, or what he may do with them?"—"Fear nothing, Partridge," cries Jones; "I will secure thee from danger."—"Nay, for matter o' that, he never doth any mischief," said the woman; "but to be sure it is necessary he should keep some arms for his own safety; for his house hath been beset more than once; and it is not many nights ago that we thought we heard thieves about it: for my own part, I have often wondered that he is not murdered by some villain or other, as he walks out by himself at such hours; but then, as I said, the people are afraid of him; and besides, they think, I suppose, he hath nothing about him worth taking."—"I should imagine, by this collection of rarities," cries Jones, "that your master had been a traveller."—"Yes, sir," answered she, "he hath been a very great one: there be few gentlemen that know more of all matters than he. I fancy he hath been crost in love, or whatever it is I know not; but I have lived with him above these thirty years, and in all that time he hath hardly spoke to six living people." She then again solicited their departure, in which she was backed by Partridge; but Jones purposely protracted the time, for his curiosity was greatly raised to see this extraordinary person. Though the old woman, therefore, concluded every one of her answers with desiring him to be gone, and Partridge proceeded so far as to pull him by the sleeve, he still continued to invent new questions, till the old woman, with an affrighted countenance, declared she heard her master's signal; and at the same instant more than one voice was heard without the door, crying, "D—n your blood, show us your money this instant. Your money, you villain, or we will blow your brains about your ears."

"O, good heaven!" cries the old woman, "some villains, to be sure, have attacked my master. O la! what shall I do? what shall I do?"—"How!" cries Jones, "how!—Are these pistols loaded?"—"O, good sir, there is nothing in them, indeed. O pray don't murder us, gentlemen!" (for in reality she now had the same opinion of those within as she had of those without). Jones made her no answer; but snatching an old broad sword which hung in the room, he instantly sallied out, where he found the old gentleman struggling with two ruffians, and begging for mercy. Jones asked no questions, but fell so briskly to work with his broad sword, that the fellows immediately quitted their hold; and without offering to attack our heroe, betook themselves to their heels and made their escape; for he did not attempt to pursue them, being contented with having delivered the old gentleman; and indeed he concluded he had pretty well done their business, for both of them, as they ran off, cried out with bitter oaths that they were dead men.

Jones presently ran to lift up the old gentleman, who had been thrown down in the scuffle, expressing at the same time great concern lest he should have received any harm from the villains. The old man stared a moment at Jones, and then cried, "No, sir, no, I have very little harm, I thank you. Lord have mercy upon me!"—"I see, sir," said Jones, "you are not free from apprehensions even of those who have had the happiness to be your deliverers; nor can I blame any suspicions which you may have; but indeed you have no real occasion for any; here are none but your friends present. Having mist our way this cold night, we took the liberty of warming ourselves at your fire, whence we were just departing when we heard you call for assistance, which, I must say, Providence alone seems to have sent you."—"Providence, indeed," cries the old gentleman, "if it be so."—"So it is, I assure you," cries Jones. "Here is your own sword, sir; I have used it in your defence, and I now return it into your hand." The old man having received the sword, which was stained with the blood of his enemies, looked stedfastly at Jones during some moments, and then with a sigh cried out, "You will pardon me, young gentleman; I was not always of a suspicious temper, nor am I a friend to ingratitude."

"Be thankful then," cries Jones, "to that Providence to which you owe your deliverance: as to my part, I have only discharged the common duties of humanity, and what I would have done for any fellow-creature in your situation."—"Let me look at you a little longer," cries the old gentleman. "You are a human creature then? Well, perhaps you are. Come pray walk into my little hutt. You have been my deliverer indeed."

The old woman was distracted between the fears which she had of her master, and for him; and Partridge was, if possible, in a greater fright. The former of these, however, when she heard her master speak kindly to Jones, and perceived what had happened, came again to herself; but Partridge no sooner saw the gentleman, than the strangeness of his dress infused greater terrors into that poor fellow than he had before felt, either from the strange description which he had heard, or from the uproar which had happened at the door.

To say the truth, it was an appearance which might have affected a more constant mind than that of Mr Partridge. This person was of the tallest size, with a long beard as white as snow. His body was cloathed with the skin of an ass, made something into the form of a coat. He wore likewise boots on his legs, and a cap on his head, both composed of the skin of some other animals.

As soon as the old gentleman came into his house, the old woman began her congratulations on his happy escape from the ruffians. "Yes," cried he, "I have escaped, indeed, thanks to my preserver."—"O the blessing on him!" answered she: "he is a good gentleman, I warrant him. I was afraid your worship would have been angry with me for letting him in; and to be certain I should not have done it, had not I seen by the moon-light, that he was a gentleman, and almost frozen to death. And to be certain it must have been some good angel that sent him hither, and tempted me to do it."

"I am afraid, sir," said the old gentleman to Jones, "that I have nothing in this house which you can either eat or drink, unless you will accept a dram of brandy; of which I can give you some most excellent, and which I have had by me these thirty years." Jones declined this offer in a very civil and proper speech, and then the other asked him, "Whither he was travelling when he mist his way?" saying, "I must own myself surprized to see such a person as you appear to be, journeying on foot at this time of night. I suppose, sir, you are a gentleman of these parts; for you do not look like one who is used to travel far without horses?"

"Appearances," cried Jones, "are often deceitful; men sometimes look what they are not. I assure you I am not of this country; and whither I am travelling, in reality I scarce know myself."

"Whoever you are, or whithersoever you are going," answered the old man, "I have obligations to you which I can never return."

"I once more," replied Jones, "affirm that you have none; for there can be no merit in having hazarded that in your service on which I set no value; and nothing is so contemptible in my eyes as life."

"I am sorry, young gentleman," answered the stranger, "that you have any reason to be so unhappy at your years."

"Indeed I am, sir," answered Jones, "the most unhappy of mankind."— "Perhaps you have had a friend, or a mistress?" replied the other. "How could you," cries Jones, "mention two words sufficient to drive me to distraction?"— "Either of them are enough to drive any man to distraction," answered the old man. "I enquire no farther, sir; perhaps my curiosity hath led me too far already."

"Indeed, sir," cries Jones, "I cannot censure a passion which I feel at this instant in the highest degree. You will pardon me when I assure you, that everything which I have seen or heard since I first entered this house hath conspired to raise the greatest curiosity in me. Something very extraordinary must have determined you to this course of life, and I have reason to fear your own history is not without misfortunes."

Here the old gentleman again sighed, and remained silent for some minutes: at last, looking earnestly on Jones, he said, "I have read that a good countenance is a letter of recommendation; if so, none ever can be more strongly recommended than yourself. If I did not feel some yearnings towards you from another consideration, I must be the most ungrateful monster upon earth; and I am really concerned it is no otherwise in my power than by words to convince you of my gratitude."

Jones, after a moment's hesitation, answered, "That it was in his power by words to gratify him extremely. I have confest a curiosity," said he, "sir; need I say how much obliged I should be to you, if you would condescend to gratify it? Will you suffer me therefore to beg, unless any consideration restrains you, that you would be pleased to acquaint me what motives have induced you thus to withdraw from the society of mankind, and to betake yourself to a course of life to which it sufficiently appears you were not born?"

"I scarce think myself at liberty to refuse you anything after what hath happened," replied the old man. "If you desire therefore to hear the story of an unhappy man, I will relate it to you. Indeed you judge rightly, in thinking there is commonly something extraordinary in the fortunes of those who fly from society; for however it may seem a paradox, or even a contradiction, certain it is, that great philanthropy chiefly inclines us to avoid and detest mankind; not on account so much of their private and selfish vices, but for those of a relative kind; such as envy, malice, treachery, cruelty, with every other species of malevolence. These are the vices which true philanthropy abhors, and which rather than see and converse with, she avoids society itself. However, without a compliment to you, you do not appear to me one of those whom I should shun or detest; nay, I must say, in what little hath dropt from you, there appears some parity in our fortunes: I hope, however, yours will conclude more successfully."

Here some compliments passed between our heroe and his host, and then the latter was going to begin his history, when Partridge interrupted him. His apprehensions had now pretty well left him, but some effects of his terrors remained; he therefore reminded the gentleman of that excellent brandy which he had mentioned. This was presently brought, and Partridge swallowed a large bumper.

The gentleman then, without any farther preface, began as you may read in the next chapter.

CHAPTER XI.

In which the Man of the Hill begins to relate his history.

"I was born in a village of Somersetshire, called Mark, in the year 1657. My father was one of those whom they call gentlemen farmers. He had a little estate of about £300 a year of his own, and rented another estate of near the same value. He was prudent and industrious, and so good a husbandman, that he might have led a very easy and comfortable life, had not an arrant vixen of a wife soured his domestic quiet. But though this circumstance perhaps made him miserable, it did not make him poor; for he confined her almost entirely at home, and rather chose to bear eternal upbraidings in his own house, than to injure his fortune by indulging her in the extravagancies she desired abroad.

"By this Xanthippe" (so was the wife of Socrates called, said Partridge)—"by this Xanthippe he had two sons, of which I was the younger. He designed to give us both good education; but my elder brother, who, unhappily for him, was the favourite of my mother, utterly neglected his learning; insomuch that, after having been five or six years at school with little or no improvement, my father, being told by his master that it would be to no purpose to keep him longer there, at last complied with my mother in taking him home from the hands of that tyrant, as she called his master; though indeed he gave the lad much less correction than his idleness deserved, but much more, it seems, than the young gentleman liked, who constantly complained to his mother of his severe treatment, and she as constantly gave him a hearing."

"Yes, yes," cries Partridge, "I have seen such mothers; I have been abused myself by them, and very unjustly; such parents deserve correction as much as their children."

Jones chid the pedagogue for his interruption, and then the stranger proceeded.

"My brother now, at the age of fifteen, bade adieu to all learning, and to everything else but to his dog and gun; with which latter he became so expert, that, though perhaps you may think it incredible, he could not only hit a standing mark with great certainty, but hath actually shot a crow as it was flying in the air. He was likewise excellent at finding a hare sitting, and was soon reputed one of the best sportsmen in the country; a reputation which both he and his mother enjoyed as much as if he had been thought the finest scholar.

"The situation of my brother made me at first think my lot the harder, in being continued at school: but I soon changed my opinion; for as I advanced pretty fast in learning, my labours became easy, and my exercise so delightful, that holidays were my most unpleasant time; for my mother, who never loved me, now apprehending that I had the greater share of my father's affection, and finding, or at least thinking, that I was more taken notice of by some gentlemen of learning, and particularly by the parson of the parish, than my brother, she now hated my sight, and made home so disagreeable to me, that what is called by school-boys Black Monday, was to me the whitest in the whole year.

"Having at length gone through the school at Taunton, I was thence removed to Exeter College in Oxford, where I remained four years; at the end of which an accident took me off entirely from my studies; and hence, I may truly date the rise of all which happened to me afterwards in life.

"There was at the same college with myself one Sir George Gresham, a young fellow who was intitled to a very considerable fortune, which he was not, by the will of his father, to come into full possession of till he arrived at the age of twenty-five. However, the liberality of his guardians gave him little cause to regret the abundant caution of his father; for they allowed him five hundred pounds a year while he remained at the university, where he kept his horses and his whore, and lived as wicked and as profligate a life as he could have done had he been never so entirely master of his fortune; for besides the five hundred a year which he received from his guardians, he found means to spend a thousand more. He was above the age of twenty-one, and had no difficulty in gaining what credit he pleased.

"This young fellow, among many other tolerable bad qualities, had one very diabolical. He had a great delight in destroying and ruining the youth of inferior fortune, by drawing them into expenses which they could not afford so well as himself; and the better, and worthier, and soberer any young man was, the greater pleasure and triumph had he in his destruction. Thus acting the character which is recorded of the devil, and going about seeking whom he might devour.

"It was my misfortune to fall into an acquaintance and intimacy with this gentleman. My reputation of diligence in my studies made me a desirable object of his mischievous intention; and my own inclination made it sufficiently easy for him to effect his purpose; for though I had applied myself with much industry to books, in which I took great delight, there were other pleasures in which I was capable of taking much greater; for I was high-mettled, had a violent flow of animal spirits, was a little ambitious, and extremely amorous.

"I had not long contracted an intimacy with Sir George before I became a partaker of all his pleasures; and when I was once entered on that scene, neither my inclination nor my spirit would suffer me to play an under part. I was second to none of the company in any acts of debauchery; nay, I soon distinguished myself so notably in all riots and disorders, that my name generally stood first in the roll of delinquents; and instead of being lamented as the unfortunate pupil of Sir George, I was now accused as the person who had misled and debauched that hopeful young gentleman; for though he was the ringleader and promoter of all the mischief, he was never so considered. I fell at last under the censure of the vice-chancellor, and very narrowly escaped expulsion.

"You will easily believe, sir, that such a life as I am now describing must be incompatible with my further progress in learning; and that in proportion as I addicted myself more and more to loose pleasure, I must grow more and more remiss in application to my studies. This was truly the consequence; but this was not all. My expenses now greatly exceeded not only my former income, but those additions which I extorted from my poor generous father, on pretences of sums being necessary for preparing for my approaching degree of batchelor of arts. These demands, however, grew at last so frequent and exorbitant, that my father by slow degrees opened his ears to the accounts which he received from many quarters of my present behaviour, and which my mother failed not to echo very faithfully and loudly; adding, `Ay, this is the fine gentleman, the scholar who doth so much honour to his family, and is to be the making of it. I thought what all this learning would come to. He is to be the ruin of us all, I find, after his elder brother hath been denied necessaries for his sake, to perfect his education forsooth, for which he was to pay us such interest: I thought what the interest would come to,' with much more of the same kind; but I have, I believe, satisfied you with this taste.

"My father, therefore, began now to return remonstrances instead of money to my demands, which brought my affairs perhaps a little sooner to a crisis; but had he remitted me his whole income, you will imagine it could have sufficed a very short time to support one who kept pace with the expenses of Sir George Gresham.

"It is more than possible that the distress I was now in for money, and the impracticability of going on in this manner, might have restored me at once to my senses and to my studies, had I opened my eyes before I became involved in debts from which I saw no hopes of ever extricating myself. This was indeed the great art of Sir George, and by which he accomplished the ruin of many, whom he afterwards laughed at as fools and coxcombs, for vying, as he called it, with a man of his fortune. To bring this about, he would now and then advance a little money himself, in order to support the credit of the unfortunate youth with other people; till, by means of that very credit, he was irretrievably undone.

"My mind being by these means grown as desperate as my fortune, there was scarce a wickedness which I did not meditate, in order for my relief. Self-murder itself became the subject of my serious deliberation; and I had certainly resolved on it, had not a more shameful, though perhaps less sinful, thought expelled it from my head."—Here he hesitated a moment, and then cried out, "I protest, so many years have not washed away the shame of this act, and I shall blush while I relate it." Jones desired him to pass over anything that might give him pain in the relation; but Partridge eagerly cried out, "Oh, pray, sir, let us hear this; I had rather hear this than all the rest; as I hope to be saved, I will never mention a word of it." Jones was going to rebuke him, but the stranger prevented it by proceeding thus: "I had a chum, a very prudent, frugal young lad, who, though he had no very large allowance, had by his parsimony heaped up upwards of forty guineas, which I knew he kept in his escritore. I took therefore an opportunity of purloining his key from his breeches-pocket, while he was asleep, and thus made myself master of all his riches: after which I again conveyed his key into his pocket, and counterfeiting sleep—though I never once closed my eyes, lay in bed till after he arose and went to prayers—an exercise to which I had long been unaccustomed.

"Timorous thieves, by extreme caution, often subject themselves to discoveries, which those of a bolder kind escape. Thus it happened to me; for had I boldly broke open his escritore, I had, perhaps, escaped even his suspicion; but as it was plain that the person who robbed him had possessed himself of his key, he had no doubt, when he first missed his money, but that his chum was certainly the thief. Now as he was of a fearful disposition, and much my inferior in strength, and I believe in courage, he did not dare to confront me with my guilt, for fear of worse bodily consequences which might happen to him. He repaired therefore immediately to the vice-chancellor, and upon swearing to the robbery, and to the circumstances of it, very easily obtained a warrant against one who had now so bad a character through the whole university.

"Luckily for me, I lay out of the college the next evening; for that day I attended a young lady in a chaise to Witney, where we staid all night, and in our return, the next morning, to Oxford, I met one of my cronies, who acquainted me with sufficient news concerning myself to make me turn my horse another way."

"Pray, sir, did he mention anything of the warrant?" said Partridge. But Jones begged the gentleman to proceed without regarding any impertinent questions; which he did as follows:—

"Having now abandoned all thoughts of returning to Oxford, the next thing which offered itself was a journey to London. I imparted this intention to my female companion, who at first remonstrated against it; but upon producing my wealth, she immediately consented. We then struck across the country, into the great Cirencester road, and made such haste, that we spent the next evening, save one, in London.

"When you consider the place where I now was, and the company with whom I was, you will, I fancy, conceive that a very short time brought me to an end of that sum of which I had so iniquitously possessed myself.

"I was now reduced to a much higher degree of distress than before: the necessaries of life began to be numbered among my wants; and what made my case still the more grievous was, that my paramour, of whom I was now grown immoderately fond, shared the same distresses with myself. To see a woman you love in distress; to be unable to relieve her, and at the same time to reflect that you have brought her into this situation, is perhaps a curse of which no imagination can represent the horrors to those who have not felt it."—"I believe it from my soul," cries Jones, "and I pity you from the bottom of my heart:" he then took two or three disorderly turns about the room, and at last begged pardon, and flung himself into his chair, crying, "I thank Heaven, I have escaped that!"

"This circumstance," continued the gentleman, "so severely aggravated the horrors of my present situation, that they became absolutely intolerable. I could with less pain endure the raging in my own natural unsatisfied appetites, even hunger or thirst, than I could submit to leave ungratified the most whimsical desires of a woman on whom I so extravagantly doated, that, though I knew she had been the mistress of half my acquaintance, I firmly intended to marry her. But the good creature was unwilling to consent to an action which the world might think so much to my disadvantage. And as, possibly, she compassionated the daily anxieties which she must have perceived me suffer on her account, she resolved to put an end to my distress. She soon, indeed, found means to relieve me from my troublesome and perplexed situation; for while I was distracted with various inventions to supply her with pleasures, she very kindly—betrayed me to one of her former lovers at Oxford, by whose care and diligence I was immediately apprehended and committed to gaol.

"Here I first began seriously to reflect on the miscarriages of my former life; on the errors I had been guilty of; on the misfortunes which I had brought on myself; and on the grief which I must have occasioned to one of the best of fathers. When I added to all these the perfidy of my mistress, such was the horror of my mind, that life, instead of being longer desirable, grew the object of my abhorrence; and I could have gladly embraced death as my dearest friend, if it had offered itself to my choice unattended by shame.

"The time of the assizes soon came, and I was removed by habeas corpus to Oxford, where I expected certain conviction and condemnation; but, to my great surprize, none appeared against me, and I was, at the end of the sessions, discharged for want of prosecution. In short, my chum had left Oxford, and whether from indolence, or from what other motive I am ignorant, had declined concerning himself any farther in the affair."

"Perhaps," cries Partridge, "he did not care to have your blood upon his hands; and he was in the right on't. If any person was to be hanged upon my evidence, I should never be able to lie alone afterwards, for fear of seeing his ghost."

"I shall shortly doubt, Partridge," says Jones, "whether thou art more brave or wise."—"You may laugh at me, sir, if you please," answered Partridge; "but if you will hear a very short story which I can tell, and which is most certainly true, perhaps you may change your opinion. In the parish where I was born—" Here Jones would have silenced him; but the stranger interceded that he might be permitted to tell his story, and in the meantime promised to recollect the remainder of his own.

Partridge then proceeded thus: "In the parish where I was born, there lived a farmer whose name was Bridle, and he had a son named Francis, a good hopeful young fellow: I was at the grammar-school with him, where I remember he was got into Ovid's Epistles, and he could construe you three lines together sometimes without looking into a dictionary. Besides all this, he was a very good lad, never missed church o' Sundays, and was reckoned one of the best psalm-singers in the whole parish. He would indeed now and then take a cup too much, and that was the only fault he had."—"Well, but come to the ghost," cries Jones. "Never fear, sir; I shall come to him soon enough," answered Partridge. "You must know, then, that farmer Bridle lost a mare, a sorrel one, to the best of my remembrance; and so it fell out that this young Francis shortly afterward being at a fair at Hindon, and as I think it was on—, I can't remember the day; and being as he was, what should he happen to meet but a man upon his father's mare. Frank called out presently, Stop thief; and it being in the middle of the fair, it was impossible, you know, for the man to make his escape. So they apprehended him and carried him before the justice: I remember it was Justice Willoughby, of Noyle, a very worthy good gentleman; and he committed him to prison, and bound Frank in a recognisance, I think they call it—a hard word compounded of *re* and *cognosco*; but it differs in its meaning from the use of the simple, as many other compounds do. Well, at last down came my Lord Justice Page to hold the assizes; and so the fellow was had up, and Frank was had up for a witness. To be sure, I shall never forget the face of the judge, when he began to ask him what he had to say against the prisoner. He made poor Frank tremble and shake in his shoes. `Well you, fellow,' says my lord, `what have you to say? Don't stand humming and hawing, but speak out.' But, however, he soon turned altogether as civil to Frank, and began to thunder at the fellow; and when he asked him if he had anything to say for himself, the fellow said, he had found the horse. `Ay!' answered the judge, `thou art a lucky fellow: I have travelled the circuit these forty years, and never found a horse in my life: but I'll tell thee what, friend, thou wast more lucky than thou didst know of; for thou didst not only find a horse, but a halter too, I promise thee.' To be sure, I shall never forget the word. Upon which everybody fell a laughing, as how could they help it? Nay, and twenty other jests he made, which I can't remember now. There was something about his skill in horse-flesh which made all the folks laugh. To be certain, the judge must have been a very brave man, as well as a man of much learning. It is indeed charming sport to hear trials upon life and death. One thing I own I thought a little hard, that the prisoner's counsel was not suffered to speak for him, though he desired only to be heard one very short word, but my lord would not hearken to him, though he suffered a counsellor to talk against him for above half-an-hour. I thought it hard, I own, that there should be so many of them; my lord, and the court, and the jury, and the counsellors, and the witnesses, all upon one poor man, and he too in chains. Well, the fellow was hanged, as to be sure it could be no otherwise, and poor Frank could never be easy about it. He never was in the dark alone, but he fancied he saw the fellow's spirit."—"Well, and is this thy story?" cries Jones. "No, no," answered Partridge. "O Lord have mercy upon me! I am just now coming to the matter; for one night, coming from the alehouse, in a long, narrow, dark lane, there he ran directly up against him; and the spirit was all in white, and fell upon Frank; and Frank, who was a sturdy lad, fell upon the spirit again, and there they had a tussel together, and poor Frank was dreadfully beat: indeed he made a shift at last to crawl home; but what with the beating, and what with the fright, he lay ill above a fortnight; and all this is most certainly true, and the whole parish will bear witness to it."

The stranger smiled at this story, and Jones burst into a loud fit of laughter; upon which Partridge cried, "Ay, you may laugh, sir; and so did some others, particularly a squire, who is thought to be no better than an atheist; who, forsooth, because there was a calf with a white face found dead in the same lane the next morning, would fain have it that the battle was between Frank and that, as if a calf would set upon a man. Besides, Frank told me he knew it to be a spirit, and could swear to him in any court in Christendom; and he had not drank above a quart or two or such a matter of liquor, at the time. Lud have mercy upon us, and keep us all from dipping our hands in blood, I say!"

"Well, sir," said Jones to the stranger, "Mr Partridge hath finished his story, and I hope will give you no future interruption, if you will be so kind to proceed." He then resumed his narration; but as he hath taken breath for a while, we think proper to give it to our reader, and shall therefore put an end to this chapter.

CHAPTER XII.

In which the Man of the Hill continues his history.

"I had now regained my liberty," said the stranger; "but I had lost my reputation; for there is a wide difference between the case of a man who is barely acquitted of a crime in a court of justice, and of him who is acquitted in his own heart, and in the opinion of the people. I was conscious of my guilt, and ashamed to look any one in the face; so resolved to leave Oxford the next morning, before the daylight discovered me to the eyes of any beholders.

"When I had got clear of the city, it first entered into my head to return home to my father, and endeavour to obtain his forgiveness; but as I had no reason to doubt his knowledge of all which had past, and as I was well assured of his great aversion to all acts of dishonesty, I could entertain no hopes of being received by him, especially since I was too certain of all the good offices in the power of my mother; nay, had my father's pardon been as sure, as I conceived his resentment to be, I yet question whether I could have had the assurance to behold him, or whether I could, upon any terms, have submitted to live and converse with those who, I was convinced, knew me to have been guilty of so base an action.

"I hastened therefore back to London, the best retirement of either grief or shame, unless for persons of a very public character; for here you have the advantage of solitude without its disadvantage, since you may be alone and in company at the same time; and while you walk or sit unobserved, noise, hurry, and a constant succession of objects, entertain the mind, and prevent the spirits from preying on themselves, or rather on grief or shame, which are the most unwholesome diet in the world; and on which (though there are many who never taste either but in public) there are some who can feed very plentifully and very fatally when alone.

"But as there is scarce any human good without its concomitant evil, so there are people who find an inconvenience in this unobserving temper of mankind; I mean persons who have no money; for as you are not put out of countenance, so neither are you cloathed or fed by those who do not know you. And a man may be as easily starved in Leadenhall-market as in the deserts of Arabia.

"It was at present my fortune to be destitute of that great evil, as it is apprehended to be by several writers, who I suppose were overburthened with it, namely, money."—"With submission, sir," said Partridge, "I do not remember any writers who have called it *malorum*; but *irritamenta malorum. Effodiuntur opes, irritamenta malorum*"—"Well, sir," continued the stranger, "whether it be an evil, or only the cause of evil, I was entirely void of it, and at the same time of friends, and, as I thought, of acquaintance; when one evening, as I was passing through the Inner Temple, very hungry, and very miserable, I heard a voice on a sudden hailing me with great familiarity by my Christian name; and upon turning about, I presently recollected the person who so saluted me to have been my fellow-collegiate; one who had left the university above a year, and long before any of my misfortunes had befallen me. This gentleman, whose name was Watson, shook me heartily by the hand; and expressing great joy at meeting me, proposed our immediately drinking a bottle together. I first declined the proposal, and pretended business, but as he was very earnest and pressing, hunger at last overcame my pride, and I fairly confessed to him I had no money in my pocket; yet not without framing a lie for an excuse, and imputing it to my having changed my breeches that morning. Mr Watson answered, `I thought, Jack, you and I had been too old acquaintance for you to mention such a matter.' He then took me by the arm, and was pulling me along; but I gave him very little trouble, for my own inclinations pulled me much stronger than he could do.

"We then went into the Friars, which you know is the scene of all mirth and jollity. Here, when we arrived at the tavern, Mr Watson applied himself to the drawer only, without taking the least notice of the cook; for he had no suspicion but that I had dined long since. However, as the case was really otherwise, I forged another falsehood, and told my companion I had been at the further end of the city on business of consequence, and had snapt up a mutton-chop in haste; so that I was again hungry, and wished he would add a beef-steak to his bottle."—"Some people," cries Partridge, "ought to have good memories; or did you find just money enough in your breeches to pay for the mutton-chop?"—"Your observation is right," answered the stranger, "and I believe such blunders are inseparable from all dealing in untruth.—But to proceed—I began now to feel myself extremely happy. The meat and wine soon revived my spirits to a high pitch, and I enjoyed much pleasure in the conversation of my old acquaintance, the rather as I thought him entirely ignorant of what had happened at the university since his leaving it.

"But he did not suffer me to remain long in this agreeable delusion; for taking a bumper in one hand, and holding me by the other, `Here, my boy,' cries he, `here's wishing you joy of your being so honourably acquitted of that affair laid to your charge.' I was thunderstruck with confusion at those words, which Watson observing, proceeded thus: `Nay, never be ashamed, man; thou hast been acquitted, and no one now dares call thee guilty; but, prithee, do tell me, who am thy friend—I hope thou didst really rob him? for rat me if it was not a meritorious action to strip such a sneaking, pitiful rascal; and instead of the two hundred guineas, I wish you had taken as many thousand. Come, come, my boy, don't be shy of confessing to me: you are not now brought before one of the pimps. D—n me if I don't honour you for it; for, as I hope for salvation, I would have made no manner of scruple of doing the same thing.'

"This declaration a little relieved my abashment; and as wine had now somewhat opened my heart, I very freely acknowledged the robbery, but acquainted him that he had been misinformed as to the sum taken, which was little more than a fifth part of what he had mentioned.

"`I am sorry for it with all my heart,' quoth he, `and I wish thee better success another time. Though, if you will take my advice, you shall have no occasion to run any such risque. Here,' said he, taking some dice out of his pocket, `here's the stuff. Here are the implements; here are the little doctors which cure the distempers of the purse. Follow but my counsel, and I will show you a way to empty the pocket of a queer cull without any danger of the nubbing cheat.'"

"Nubbing cheat!" cries Partridge: "pray, sir, what is that?"

"Why that, sir," says the stranger, "is a cant phrase for the gallows; for as gamesters differ little from highwaymen in their morals, so do they very much resemble them in their language.

"We had now each drank our bottle, when Mr Watson said, the board was sitting, and that he must attend, earnestly pressing me at the same time to go with him and try my fortune. I answered he knew that was at present out of my power, as I had informed him of the emptiness of my pocket. To say the truth, I doubted not from his many strong expressions of friendship, but that he would offer to lend me a small sum for that purpose, but he answered, `Never mind that, man; e'en boldly run a levant' [Partridge was going to inquire the meaning of that word, but Jones stopped his mouth]: `but be circumspect as to the man. I will tip you the proper person, which may be necessary, as you do not know the town, nor can distinguish a rum cull from a queer one."

"The bill was now brought, when Watson paid his share, and was departing. I reminded him, not without blushing, of my having no money. He answered, `That signifies nothing; score it behind the door, or make a bold brush and take no notice.—Or—stay,' says he; `I will go down-stairs first, and then do you take up my money, and score the whole reckoning at the bar, and I will wait for you at the corner.' I expressed some dislike at this, and hinted my expectations that he would have deposited the whole; but he swore he had not another sixpence in his pocket.

"He then went down, and I was prevailed on to take up the money and follow him, which I did close enough to hear him tell the drawer the reckoning was upon the table. The drawer past by me up-stairs; but I made such haste into the street, that I heard nothing of his disappointment, nor did I mention a syllable at the bar, according to my instructions.

"We now went directly to the gaming-table, where Mr Watson, to my surprize, pulled out a large sum of money and placed it before him, as did many others; all of them, no doubt, considering their own heaps as so many decoy birds, which were to intice and draw over the heaps of their neighbours.

"Here it would be tedious to relate all the freaks which Fortune, or rather the dice, played in this her temple. Mountains of gold were in a few moments reduced to nothing at one part of the table, and rose as suddenly in another. The rich grew in a moment poor, and the poor as suddenly became rich; so that it seemed a philosopher could nowhere have so well instructed his pupils in the contempt of riches, at least he could nowhere have better inculcated the incertainty of their duration.

"For my own part, after having considerably improved my small estate, I at last entirely demolished it. Mr Watson too, after much variety of luck, rose from the table in some heat, and declared he had lost a cool hundred, and would play no longer. Then coming up to me, he asked me to return with him to the tavern; but I positively refused, saying, I would not bring myself a second time into such a dilemma, and especially as he had lost all his money and was now in my own condition. `Pooh!' says he, `I have just borrowed a couple of guineas of a friend, and one of them is at your service.' He immediately put one of them into my hand, and I no longer resisted his inclination.

"I was at first a little shocked at returning to the same house whence we had departed in so unhandsome a manner; but when the drawer, with very civil address, told us, `he believed we had forgot to pay our reckoning,' I became perfectly easy, and very readily gave him a guinea, bid him pay himself, and acquiesced in the unjust charge which had been laid on my memory.

"Mr Watson now bespoke the most extravagant supper he could well think of; and though he had contented himself with simple claret before, nothing now but the most precious Burgundy would serve his purpose.

"Our company was soon encreased by the addition of several gentlemen from the gaming-table; most of whom, as I afterwards found, came not to the tavern to drink, but in the way of business; for the true gamesters pretended to be ill, and refused their glass, while they plied heartily two young fellows, who were to be afterwards pillaged, as indeed they were without mercy. Of this plunder I had the good fortune to be a sharer, though I was not yet let into the secret.

"There was one remarkable accident attended this tavern play; for the money by degrees totally disappeared; so that though at the beginning the table was half covered with gold, yet before the play ended, which it did not till the next day, being Sunday, at noon, there was scarce a single guinea to be seen on the table; and this was the stranger as every person present, except myself, declared he had lost; and what was become of the money, unless the devil himself carried it away, is difficult to determine."

"Most certainly he did," says Partridge, "for evil spirits can carry away anything without being seen, though there were never so many folk in the room; and I should not have been surprized if he had carried away all the company of a set of wicked wretches, who were at play in sermon time. And I could tell you a true story, if I would, where the devil took a man out of bed from another man's wife, and carried him away through the keyhole of the door. I've seen the very house where it was done, and nobody hath lived in it these thirty years."

Though Jones was a little offended by the impertinence of Partridge, he could not however avoid smiling at his simplicity. The stranger did the same, and then proceeded with his story, as will be seen in the next chapter.

CHAPTER XIII.

In which the foregoing story is farther continued.

"My fellow-collegiate had now entered me in a new scene of life. I soon became acquainted with the whole fraternity of sharpers, and was let into their secrets; I mean, into the knowledge of those gross cheats which are proper to impose upon the raw and unexperienced; for there are some tricks of a finer kind, which are known only to a few of the gang, who are at the head of their profession; a degree of honour beyond my expectation; for drink, to which I was immoderately addicted, and the natural warmth of my passions, prevented me from arriving at any great success in an art which requires as much coolness as the most austere school of philosophy.

"Mr Watson, with whom I now lived in the closest amity, had unluckily the former failing to a very great excess; so that instead of making a fortune by his profession, as some others did, he was alternately rich and poor, and was often obliged to surrender to his cooler friends, over a bottle which they never tasted, that plunder that he had taken from culls at the public table.

"However, we both made a shift to pick up an uncomfortable livelihood; and for two years I continued of the calling; during which time I tasted all the varieties of fortune, sometimes flourishing in affluence, and at others being obliged to struggle with almost incredible difficulties. To-day wallowing in luxury, and to-morrow reduced to the coarsest and most homely fare. My fine clothes being often on my back in the evening, and at the pawn-shop the next morning.

"One night, as I was returning pennyless from the gaming-table, I observed a very great disturbance, and a large mob gathered together in the street. As I was in no danger from pickpockets, I ventured into the croud, where upon enquiry I found that a man had been robbed and very ill used by some ruffians. The wounded man appeared very bloody, and seemed scarce able to support himself on his legs. As I had not therefore been deprived of my humanity by my present life and conversation, though they had left me very little of either honesty or shame, I immediately offered my assistance to the unhappy person, who thankfully accepted it, and, putting himself under my conduct, begged me to convey him to some tavern, where he might send for a surgeon, being, as he said, faint with loss of blood. He seemed indeed highly pleased at finding one who appeared in the dress of a gentleman; for as to all the rest of the company present, their outside was such that he could not wisely place any confidence in them.

"I took the poor man by the arm, and led him to the tavern where we kept our rendezvous, as it happened to be the nearest at hand. A surgeon happening luckily to be in the house, immediately attended, and applied himself to dressing his wounds, which I had the pleasure to hear were not likely to be mortal.

"The surgeon having very expeditiously and dextrously finished his business, began to enquire in what part of the town the wounded man lodged; who answered, `That he was come to town that very morning; that his horse was at an inn in Piccadilly, and that he had no other lodging, and very little or no acquaintance in town.'

"This surgeon, whose name I have forgot, though I remember it began with an R, had the first character in his profession, and was serjeant-surgeon to the king. He had moreover many good qualities, and was a very generous good-natured man, and ready to do any service to his fellow-creatures. He offered his patient the use of his chariot to carry him to his inn, and at the same time whispered in his ear, `That if he wanted any money, he would furnish him.'

"The poor man was not now capable of returning thanks for this generous offer; for having had his eyes for some time stedfastly on me, he threw himself back in his chair, crying, `Oh, my son! my son!' and then fainted away.

"Many of the people present imagined this accident had happened through his loss of blood; but I, who at the same time began to recollect the features of my father, was now confirmed in my suspicion, and satisfied that it was he himself who appeared before me. I presently ran to him, raised him in my arms, and kissed his cold lips with the utmost eagerness. Here I must draw a curtain over a scene which I cannot describe; for though I did not lose my being, as my father for a while did, my senses were however so overpowered with affright and surprize, that I am a stranger to what passed during some minutes, and indeed till my father had again recovered from his swoon, and I found myself in his arms, both tenderly embracing each other, while the tears trickled a-pace down the cheeks of each of us.

"Most of those present seemed affected by this scene, which we, who might be considered as the actors in it, were desirous of removing from the eyes of all spectators as fast as we could; my father therefore accepted the kind offer of the surgeon's chariot, and I attended him in it to his inn.

"When we were alone together, he gently upbraided me with having neglected to write to him during so long a time, but entirely omitted the mention of that crime which had occasioned it. He then informed me of my mother's death, and insisted on my returning home with him, saying, `That he had long suffered the greatest anxiety on my account; that he knew not whether he had most feared my death or wished it, since he had so many more dreadful apprehensions for me. At last, he said, a neighbouring gentleman, who had just recovered a son from the same place, informed him where I was; and that to reclaim me from this course of life was the sole cause of his journey to London.' He thanked Heaven he had succeeded so far as to find me out by means of an accident which had like to have proved fatal to him; and had the pleasure to think he partly owed his preservation to my humanity, with which he profest himself to be more delighted than he should have been with my filial piety, if I had known that the object of all my care was my own father.

"Vice had not so depraved my heart as to excite in it an insensibility of so much paternal affection, though so unworthily bestowed. I presently promised to obey his commands in my return home with him, as soon as he was able to travel, which indeed he was in a very few days, by the assistance of that excellent surgeon who had undertaken his cure.

"The day preceding my father's journey (before which time I scarce ever left him), I went to take my leave of some of my most intimate acquaintance, particularly of Mr Watson, who dissuaded me from burying myself, as he called it, out of a simple compliance with the fond desires of a foolish old fellow. Such sollicitations, however, had no effect, and I once more saw my own home. My father now greatly sollicited me to think of marriage; but my inclinations were utterly averse to any such thoughts. I had tasted of love already, and perhaps you know the extravagant excesses of that most tender and most violent passion."—Here the old gentleman paused, and looked earnestly at Jones; whose countenance, within a minute's space, displayed the extremities of both red and white. Upon which the old man, without making any observations, renewed his narrative.

"Being now provided with all the necessaries of life, I betook myself once again to study, and that with a more inordinate application than I had ever done formerly. The books which now employed my time solely were those, as well antient as modern, which treat of true philosophy, a word which is by many thought to be the subject only of farce and ridicule. I now read over the works of Aristotle and Plato, with the rest of those inestimable treasures which antient Greece had bequeathed to the world.

"These authors, though they instructed me in no science by which men may promise to themselves to acquire the least riches or worldly power, taught me, however, the art of despising the highest acquisitions of both. They elevate the mind, and steel and harden it against the capricious invasions of fortune. They not only instruct in the knowledge of Wisdom, but confirm men in her habits, and demonstrate plainly, that this must be our guide, if we propose ever to arrive at the greatest worldly happiness, or to defend ourselves, with any tolerable security, against the misery which everywhere surrounds and invests us.

"To this I added another study, compared to which, all the philosophy taught by the wisest heathens is little better than a dream, and is indeed as full of vanity as the silliest jester ever pleased to represent it. This is that Divine wisdom which is alone to be found in the Holy Scriptures; for they impart to us the knowledge and assurance of things much more worthy our attention than all which this world can offer to our acceptance; of things which Heaven itself hath condescended to reveal to us, and to the smallest knowledge of which the highest human wit unassisted could never ascend. I began now to think all the time I had spent with the best heathen writers was little more than labour lost: for, however pleasant and delightful their lessons may be, or however adequate to the right regulation of our conduct with respect to this world only; yet, when compared with the glory revealed in Scripture, their highest documents will appear as trifling, and of as little consequence, as the rules by which children regulate their childish little games and pastime. True it is, that philosophy makes us wiser, but Christianity makes us better men. Philosophy elevates and steels the mind, Christianity softens and sweetens it. The former makes us the objects of human admiration, the latter of Divine love. That insures us a temporal, but this an eternal happiness.—But I am afraid I tire you with my rhapsody."

"Not at all," cries Partridge; "Lud forbid we should be tired with good things!"

"I had spent," continued the stranger, "about four years in the most delightful manner to myself, totally given up to contemplation, and entirely unembarrassed with the affairs of the world, when I lost the best of fathers, and one whom I so entirely loved, that my grief at his loss exceeds all description. I now abandoned my books, and gave myself up for a whole month to the effects of melancholy and despair. Time, however, the best physician of the mind, at length brought me relief."—"Ay, ay; *Tempus edax rerum*" said Partridge.—"I then," continued the stranger, "betook myself again to my former studies, which I may say perfected my cure; for philosophy and religion may be called the exercises of the mind, and when this is disordered, they are as wholesome as exercise can be to a distempered body. They do indeed produce similar effects with exercise; for they strengthen and confirm the mind, till man becomes, in the noble strain of Horace—

Fortis, et in seipso totus teres atque rotundus,
Externi ne quid valeat per laeve morari;
In quem manca ruit semper Fortuna."[1]

Here Jones smiled at some conceit which intruded itself into his imagination; but the stranger, I believe, perceived it not, and proceeded thus:—

"My circumstances were now greatly altered by the death of that best of men; for my brother, who was now become master of the house, differed so widely from me in his inclinations, and our pursuits in life had been so very various, that we were the worst of company to each other: but what made our living together still more disagreeable, was the little harmony which could subsist between the few who resorted to me, and the numerous train of sportsmen who often attended my brother from the field to the table; for such fellows, besides the noise and nonsense with which they persecute the ears of sober men, endeavour always to attack them with affront and contempt. This was so much the case, that neither I myself, nor my friends, could ever sit down to a meal with them without being

---

[1] Firm in himself, who on himself relies,
Polish'd and round, who runs his proper course
And breaks misfortunes with superior force.—MR FRANCIS.

treated with derision, because we were unacquainted with the phrases of sportsmen. For men of true learning, and almost universal knowledge, always compassionate the ignorance of others; but fellows who excel in some little, low, contemptible art, are always certain to despise those who are unacquainted with that art.

"In short, we soon separated, and I went, by the advice of a physician, to drink the Bath waters; for my violent affliction, added to a sedentary life, had thrown me into a kind of paralytic disorder, for which those waters are accounted an almost *certain* cure. The second day after my arrival, as I was walking by the river, the sun shone so intensely hot (though it was early in the year), that I retired to the shelter of some willows, and sat down by the river side. Here I had not been seated long before I heard a person on the other side of the willows sighing and bemoaning himself bitterly. On a sudden, having uttered a most impious oath, he cried, `I am resolved to bear it no longer,' and directly threw himself into the water. I immediately started, and ran towards the place, calling at the same time as loudly as I could for assistance. An angler happened luckily to be a-fishing a little below me, though some very high sedge had hid him from my sight. He immediately came up, and both of us together, not without some hazard of our lives, drew the body to the shore. At first we perceived no sign of life remaining; but having held the body up by the heels (for we soon had assistance enough), it discharged a vast quantity of water at the mouth, and at length began to discover some symptoms of breathing, and a little afterwards to move both its hands and its legs.

"An apothecary, who happened to be present among others, advised that the body, which seemed now to have pretty well emptied itself of water, and which began to have many convulsive motions, should be directly taken up, and carried into a warm bed. This was accordingly performed, the apothecary and myself attending.

"As we were going towards an inn, for we knew not the man's lodgings, luckily a woman met us, who, after some violent screaming, told us that the gentleman lodged at her house.

"When I had seen the man safely deposited there, I left him to the care of the apothecary; who, I suppose, used all the right methods with him, for the next morning I heard he had perfectly recovered his senses.

"I then went to visit him, intending to search out, as well as I could, the cause of his having attempted so desperate an act, and to prevent, as far as I was able, his pursuing such wicked intentions for the future. I was no sooner admitted into his chamber, than we both instantly knew each other; for who should this person be but my good friend Mr Watson! Here I will not trouble you with what past at our first interview; for I would avoid prolixity as much as possible."—"Pray let us hear all," cries Partridge; "I want mightily to know what brought him to Bath."

"You shall hear everything material," answered the stranger; and then proceeded to relate what we shall proceed to write, after we have given a short breathing time to both ourselves and the reader.

CHAPTER XIV.

In which the Man of the Hill concludes his history.

"Mr Watson," continued the stranger, "very freely acquainted me, that the unhappy situation of his circumstances, occasioned by a tide of ill luck, had in a manner forced him to a resolution of destroying himself.

"I now began to argue very seriously with him, in opposition to this heathenish, or indeed diabolical, principle of the lawfulness of self-murder; and said everything which occurred to me on the subject; but, to my great concern, it seemed to have very little effect on him. He seemed not at all to repent of what he had done, and gave me reason to fear he would soon make a second attempt of the like horrible kind.

"When I had finished my discourse, instead of endeavouring to answer my arguments, he looked me stedfastly in the face, and with a smile said, `You are strangely altered, my good friend, since I remember you. I question whether any of our bishops could make a better argument against suicide than you have entertained me with; but unless you can find somebody who will lend me a cool hundred, I must either hang, or drown, or starve; and, in my opinion, the last death is the most terrible of the three.'

"I answered him very gravely that I was indeed altered since I had seen him last. That I had found leisure to look into my follies and to repent of them. I then advised him to pursue the same steps; and at last concluded with an assurance that I myself would lend him a hundred pound, if it would be of any service to his affairs, and he would not put it into the power of a die to deprive him of it.

"Mr Watson, who seemed almost composed in slumber by the former part of my discourse, was roused by the latter. He seized my hand eagerly, gave me a thousand thanks, and declared I was a friend indeed; adding that he hoped I had a better opinion of him than to imagine he had profited so little by experience, as to put any confidence in those damned dice which had so often deceived him. `No, no,' cries he; `let me but once handsomely be set up again, and if ever Fortune makes a broken merchant of me afterwards, I will forgive her.'

"I very well understood the language of setting up, and broken merchant. I therefore said to him, with a very grave face, Mr Watson, you must endeavour to find out some business or employment, by which you may procure yourself a livelihood; and I promise you, could I see any probability of being repaid hereafter, I would advance a much larger sum than what you have mentioned, to equip you in any fair and honourable calling; but as to gaming, besides the baseness and wickedness of making it a profession, you are really, to my own knowledge, unfit for it, and it will end in your certain ruin.

"`Why now, that's strange,' answered he; `neither you, nor any of my friends, would ever allow me to know anything of the matter, and yet I believe I *am* as good a hand at every game as any of you all; and I heartily wish I was to play with you only for your whole fortune: I should desire no better sport, and I would let you name your game into the bargain: but come, my dear boy, have you the hundred in your pocket?"

"I answered I had only a bill for £50, which I delivered him, and promised to bring him the rest next morning; and after giving him a little more advice, took my leave.

"I was indeed better than my word; for I returned to him that very afternoon. When I entered the room, I found him sitting up in his bed at cards with a notorious gamester. This sight, you will imagine, shocked me not a little; to which I may add the mortification of seeing my bill delivered by him to his antagonist, and thirty guineas only given in exchange for it.

"The other gamester presently quitted the room, and then Watson declared he was ashamed to see me; `but,' says he, `I find luck runs so damnably against me, that I will resolve to leave off play for ever. I have thought of the kind proposal you made me ever since, and I promise you there shall be no fault in me, if I do not put it in execution.'

"Though I had no great faith in his promises, I produced him the remainder of the hundred in consequence of my own; for which he gave me a note, which was all I ever expected to see in return for my money.

"We were prevented from any further discourse at present by the arrival of the apothecary; who, with much joy in his countenance, and without even asking his patient how he did, proclaimed there was great news arrived in a letter to himself, which he said would shortly be public, `That the Duke of Monmouth was landed in the west with a vast army of Dutch; and that another vast fleet hovered over the coast of Norfolk, and was to make a descent there, in order to favour the duke's enterprize with a diversion on that side.'

"This apothecary was one of the greatest politicians of his time. He was more delighted with the most paultry packet, than with the best patient, and the highest joy he was capable of, he received from having a piece of news in his possession an hour or two sooner than any other person in the town. His advices, however, were seldom authentic; for he would swallow almost anything as a truth—a humour which many made use of to impose upon him.

"Thus it happened with what he at present communicated; for it was known within a short time afterwards that the duke was really landed, but that his army consisted only of a few attendants; and as to the diversion in Norfolk, it was entirely false.

"The apothecary staid no longer in the room than while he acquainted us with his news; and then, without saying a syllable to his patient on any other subject, departed to spread his advices all over the town.

"Events of this nature in the public are generally apt to eclipse all private concerns. Our discourse therefore now became entirely political.[1] For my own part, I

---

[1] The rest of this paragraph and the two following paragraphs in the first edition were as follows:

"For my own part, I had been for some time very seriously affected with the danger to which the Protestant religion was so visibly exposed, that nothing but the immediate interposition of Providence seemed capable of preserving it; for King James had indeed declared war against the Protestant cause. He had brought known papists into the army and attempted to bring them into the Church and into the University. Popish priests swarmed through the nation, appeared publicly in their habits, and boasted that they should shortly walk in procession through the streets. Our own clergy were forbid to preach against popery, and bishops were ordered to supend those who did; and to do the business at once an illegal ecclesiastical commission was erected, little inferior to an inquisition, of which, probably, it was intended to be the ringleader. Thus, as our duty to the king can never be called more than our second duty, he had discharged us from this by making it incompatible with our preserving the first, which is surely to heaven. Besides this, he had dissolved his subjects from their allegiance by breaking his Coronation Oath, to which their allegiance is annexed; for he had imprisoned bishops because they would not give up their religion, and turned out judges because they would not absolutely surrender the law into his hands; nay, he seized this himself, and when he claimed a dispensing power, he declared himself, in fact, as absolute as any tyrant ever was or can be. I have recapitulated these matters in full lest some of them should have been omitted in history; and I think nothing less than such provocations as I have here mentioned, nothing less than certain and imminent danger to their religion and liberties, can justify or even mitigate the dreadful sin of rebellion in any people."

"I promise you, sir," says Jones, "all these facts, and more, I have read in history, but I will tell you a fact which is not yet recorded and of which I suppose you are ignorant. There is actually now a rebellion on foot in this kingdom in favour of the son of that very King James, a professed papist, more bigoted, if possible, than his father, and this carried on by Protestants against a king who hath never in one single instance made the least invasion on our liberties."

"Prodigious indeed!" answered the stranger. "You tell me what would be incredible of a nation which did not deserve the character that Virgil gives of a woman, varium et mutabile semper. Surely this is to be unworthy of the care which Providence seems to have taken of us in the preservation of our religion against the powerful designs and constant machinations of Popery, a preservation so strange and unaccountable that I almost think we may appeal to it as to a miracle for the proof of its holiness. Prodigious indeed! A Protestant rebellion in favour of a popish prince! The folly of mankind is as wonderful as their knavery—But to conclude my story: I resolved to take arms in defence of my had been for some time very seriously affected with the danger to which the Protestant religion was so visibly exposed under a Popish prince, and thought the apprehension of it alone sufficient to justify that insurrection; for no real security can ever be found against the persecuting spirit of Popery, when armed with power, except the depriving it of that power, as woeful experience presently showed. You know how King James behaved after getting the better of this attempt; how little he valued either his royal word, or coronation oath, or the liberties and rights of his people. But all had not the sense to foresee this at first; and therefore the Duke of Monmouth was weakly supported; yet all could feel when the evil came upon them; and therefore all united, at last, to drive out that king, against whose exclusion a great party among us had so warmly contended during the reign of his brother, and for whom they now fought with such zeal and affection."

"What you say," interrupted Jones, "is very true; and it has often struck me, as the most wonderful thing I ever read of in history, that so soon after this convincing experience which brought our whole nation to join so unanimously in expelling King James, for the preservation of our religion and liberties, there should be a party among us mad enough to desire the placing his family again on the throne." "You are not in earnest!" answered the old man; "there can be no such party. As bad an opinion as I have of mankind, I cannot believe them infatuated to such a degree. There may be some hot-headed Papists led by their priests to engage in this desperate cause, and think it a holy war; but that Protestants, that are members of the Church of England, should be such apostates, such *felos de se*, I cannot believe it; no, no, young man, unacquainted as I am with what has past in the world for these last thirty years, I cannot be so imposed upon as to credit so foolish a tale; but I see you have a mind to sport with my ignorance."—"Can it be possible," replied Jones, "that you have lived so much out of the world as not to know that during that time there have been two rebellions in favour of the son of King James, one of which is now actually raging in the very heart of the kingdom." At these words the old gentleman started up, and in a most solemn tone of voice, conjured Jones by his Maker to tell him if what he said was really true; which the other as solemnly affirming, he walked several turns about the room in a profound silence, then cried, then laughed, and at last fell down on his knees, and blessed God, in a loud thanksgiving prayer, for having delivered him from all society with human nature, which could be capable of such monstrous extravagances. After which, being reminded by Jones that he had broke off his story, he resumed it again in this manner:—

---

country, of my religion, and my liberty, and Mr. Watson joined in the same resolution. We soon provided ourselves with an necessaries and joined the Duke at Bridgewater."

"The unfortunate event of this enterprise you are perhaps better acquainted with than myself. I escaped together with Mr. Watson from the battle at Sedgemore,...

"As mankind, in the days I was speaking of, was not yet arrived at that pitch of madness which I find they are capable of now, and which, to be sure, I have only escaped by living alone, and at a distance from the contagion, there was a considerable rising in favour of Monmouth; and my principles strongly inclining me to take the same part, I determined to join him; and Mr Watson, from different motives concurring in the same resolution (for the spirit of a gamester will carry a man as far upon such an occasion as the spirit of patriotism), we soon provided ourselves with all necessaries, and went to the duke at Bridgewater.

"The unfortunate event of this enterprize, you are, I conclude, as well acquainted with as myself. I escaped, together with Mr Watson, from the battle at Sedgemore, in which action I received a slight wound. We rode near forty miles together on the Exeter road, and then abandoning our horses, scrambled as well as we could through the fields and bye-roads, till we arrived at a little wild hut on a common, where a poor old woman took all the care of us she could, and dressed my wound with salve, which quickly healed it."

"Pray, sir, where was the wound?" says Partridge. The stranger satisfied him it was in his arm, and then continued his narrative. "Here, sir," said he, "Mr Watson left me the next morning, in order, as he pretended, to get us some provision from the town of Collumpton; but—can I relate it, or can you believe it?—this Mr Watson, this friend, this base, barbarous, treacherous villain, betrayed me to a party of horse belonging to King James, and at his return delivered me into their hands.

"The soldiers, being six in number, had now seized me, and were conducting me to Taunton gaol; but neither my present situation, nor the apprehensions of what might happen to me, were half so irksome to my mind as the company of my false friend, who, having surrendered himself, was likewise considered as a prisoner, though he was better treated, as being to make his peace at my expense. He at first endeavoured to excuse his treachery; but when he received nothing but scorn and upbraiding from me, he soon changed his note, abused me as the most atrocious and malicious rebel, and laid all his own guilt to my charge, who, as he declared, had solicited, and even threatened him, to make him take up arms against his gracious as well as lawful sovereign.

"This false evidence (for in reality he had been much the forwarder of the two) stung me to the quick, and raised an indignation scarce conceivable by those who have not felt it. However, fortune at length took pity on me; for as we were got a little beyond Wellington, in a narrow lane, my guards received a false alarm, that near fifty of the enemy were at hand; upon which they shifted for themselves, and left me and my betrayer to do the same. That villain immediately ran from me, and I am glad he did, or I should have certainly endeavoured, though I had no arms, to have executed vengeance on his baseness.

"I was now once more at liberty; and immediately withdrawing from the highway into the fields, I travelled on, scarce knowing which way I went, and making it my chief care to avoid all public roads and all towns—nay, even the most homely houses; for I imagined every human creature whom I saw desirous of betraying me.

"At last, after rambling several days about the country, during which the fields afforded me the same bed and the same food which nature bestows on our savage brothers of the creation, I at length arrived at this place, where the solitude and wildness of the country invited me to fix my abode. The first person with whom I took up my habitation was the mother of this old woman, with whom I remained concealed till the news of the glorious revolution put an end to all my apprehensions of danger, and gave me an opportunity of once more visiting my own home, and of enquiring a little into my affairs, which I soon settled as agreeably to my brother as to myself; having resigned everything to him, for which he paid me the sum of a thousand pounds, and settled on me an annuity for life.

"His behaviour in this last instance, as in all others, was selfish and ungenerous. I could not look on him as my friend, nor indeed did he desire that I should; so I presently took my leave of him, as well as of my other acquaintance; and from that day to this, my history is little better than a blank."

"And is it possible, sir," said Jones, "that you can have resided here from that day to this?"—"O no, sir," answered the gentleman; "I have been a great traveller, and there are few parts of Europe with which I am not acquainted." "I have not, sir," cried Jones, "the assurance to ask it of you now; indeed it would be cruel, after so much breath as you have already spent: but you will give me leave to wish for some further opportunity of hearing the excellent observations which a man of your sense and knowledge of the world must have made in so long a course of travels."—"Indeed, young gentleman," answered the stranger, "I will endeavour to satisfy your curiosity on this head likewise, as far as I am able." Jones attempted fresh apologies, but was prevented; and while he and Partridge sat with greedy and impatient ears, the stranger proceeded as in the next chapter.

CHAPTER XV.

A brief history of Europe; and a curious discourse between Mr Jones and the Man of the Hill.

"In Italy the landlords are very silent. In France they are more talkative, but yet civil. In Germany and Holland they are generally very impertinent. And as for their honesty, I believe it is pretty equal in all those countries. The *laquais à louange* are sure to lose no opportunity of cheating you; and as for the postilions, I think they are pretty much alike all the world over. These, sir, are the observations on men which I made in my travels; for these were the only men I ever conversed with. My design, when I went abroad, was to divert myself by seeing the wondrous variety of prospects, beasts, birds, fishes, insects, and vegetables, with which God has been pleased to enrich the several parts of this globe; a variety which, as it must give great pleasure to a contemplative beholder, so doth it admirably display the power, and wisdom, and goodness of the Creator. Indeed, to say the truth, there is but one work in his whole creation that doth him any dishonour, and with that I have long since avoided holding any conversation."

"You will pardon me," cries Jones; "but I have always imagined that there is in this very work you mention as great variety as in all the rest; for, besides the difference of inclination, customs and climates have, I am told, introduced the utmost diversity into human nature."

"Very little indeed," answered the other: "those who travel in order to acquaint themselves with the different manners of men might spare themselves much pains by going to a carnival at Venice; for there they will see at once all which they can discover in the several courts of Europe. The same hypocrisy, the same fraud; in short, the same follies and vices dressed in different habits. In Spain, these are equipped with much gravity; and in Italy, with vast splendor. In France, a knave is dressed like a fop; and in the northern countries, like a sloven. But human nature is everywhere the same, everywhere the object of detestation and scorn.

"As for my own part, I past through all these nations as you perhaps may have done through a croud at a shew-jostling to get by them, holding my nose with one hand, and defending my pockets with the other, without speaking a word to any of them, while I was pressing on to see what I wanted to see; which, however entertaining it might be in itself, scarce made me amends for the trouble the company gave me."

"Did not you find some of the nations among which you travelled less troublesome to you than others?" said Jones. "O yes," replied the old man: "the Turks were much more tolerable to me than the Christians; for they are men of profound taciturnity, and never disturb a stranger with questions. Now and then indeed they bestow a short curse upon him, or spit in his face as he walks the streets, but then they have done with him; and a man may live an age in their country without hearing a dozen words from them. But of all the people I ever saw, heaven defend me from the French! With their damned prate and civilities, and doing the honour of their nation to strangers (as they are pleased to call it), but indeed setting forth their own vanity; they are so troublesome, that I had infinitely rather pass my life with the Hottentots than set my foot in Paris again. They are a nasty people, but their nastiness is mostly without; whereas, in France, and some other nations that I won't name, it is all within, and makes them stink much more to my reason than that of Hottentots does to my nose.

"Thus, sir, I have ended the history of my life; for as to all that series of years during which I have lived retired here, it affords no variety to entertain you, and may be almost considered as one day.[1] The retirement has been so compleat, that I could hardly have enjoyed a more absolute solitude in the deserts of the Thebais than here in the midst of this populous kingdom. As I have no estate, I am plagued with no tenants or stewards: my annuity is paid me pretty regularly, as indeed it ought to be; for it is much less than what I might have expected in return for what I gave up. Visits I admit none; and the old woman who keeps my house knows that her place entirely depends upon her saving me all the trouble of buying the things that I want, keeping off all sollicitation or business from me, and holding her tongue whenever I am within hearing. As my walks are all by night, I am pretty secure in this wild unfrequented place from meeting any company. Some few persons I have met by chance, and sent them home heartily frighted, as from the oddness of my dress and figure they took me for a ghost or a hobgoblin. But what has happened to-night shows that even here I cannot be safe from the villany of men; for without your assistance I had not only been robbed, but very probably murdered."

Jones thanked the stranger for the trouble he had taken in relating his story, and then expressed some wonder how he could possibly endure a life of such solitude; "in which," says he, "you may well complain of the want of variety. Indeed I am astonished how you have filled up, or rather killed, so much of your time."

"I am not at all surprized," answered the other, "that to one whose affections and thoughts are fixed on the world my hours should appear to have wanted employment in this place: but there is one single act, for which the whole life of man is infinitely too short: what time can suffice for the contemplation and worship of that glorious, immortal, and eternal Being, among the works of whose stupendous creation not only this globe, but even those numberless luminaries which we may

[1] the rest of this paragraph is omitted in the third edition

here behold spangling all the sky, though they should many of them be suns lighting different systems of worlds, may possibly appear but as a few atoms opposed to the whole earth which we inhabit? Can a man who by divine meditations is admitted as it were into the conversation of this ineffable, incomprehensible Majesty, think days, or years, or ages, too long for the continuance of so ravishing an honour? Shall the trifling amusements, the palling pleasures, the silly business of the world, roll away our hours too swiftly from us; and shall the pace of time seem sluggish to a mind exercised in studies so high, so important, and so glorious? As no time is sufficient, so no place is improper, for this great concern. On what object can we cast our eyes which may not inspire us with ideas of his power, of his wisdom, and of his goodness? It is not necessary that the rising sun should dart his fiery glories over the eastern horizon; nor that the boisterous winds should rush from their caverns, and shake the lofty forest; nor that the opening clouds should pour their deluges on the plains: it is not necessary, I say, that any of these should proclaim his majesty: there is not an insect, not a vegetable, of so low an order in the creation as not to be honoured with bearing marks of the attributes of its great Creator; marks not only of his power, but of his wisdom and goodness. Man alone, the king of this globe, the last and greatest work of the Supreme Being, below the sun; man alone hath basely dishonoured his own nature; and by dishonesty, cruelty, ingratitude, and treachery, hath called his Maker's goodness in question, by puzzling us to account how a benevolent being should form so foolish and so vile an animal. Yet this is the being from whose conversation you think, I suppose, that I have been unfortunately restrained, and without whose blessed society, life, in your opinion, must be tedious and insipid."

"In the former part of what you said," replied Jones, "I most heartily and readily concur; but I believe, as well as hope, that the abhorrence which you express for mankind in the conclusion, is much too general. Indeed, you here fall into an error, which in my little experience I have observed to be a very common one, by taking the character of mankind from the worst and basest among them; whereas, indeed, as an excellent writer observes, nothing should be esteemed as characteristical of a species, but what is to be found among the best and most perfect individuals of that species. This error, I believe, is generally committed by those who from want of proper caution in the choice of their friends and acquaintance, have suffered injuries from bad and worthless men; two or three instances of which are very unjustly charged on all human nature."

"I think I had experience enough of it," answered the other: "my first mistress and my first friend betrayed me in the basest manner, and in matters which threatened to be of the worst of consequences—even to bring me to a shameful death."

"But you will pardon me," cries Jones, "if I desire you to reflect who that mistress and who that friend were. What better, my good sir, could be expected in love derived from the stews, or in friendship first produced and nourished at the gaming-table? To take the characters of women from the former instance, or of men from the latter, would be as unjust as to assert that air is a nauseous and unwholesome element, because we find it so in a jakes. I have lived but a short time in the world, and yet have known men worthy of the highest friendship, and women of the highest love."

"Alas! young man," answered the stranger, "you have lived, you confess, but a very short time in the world: I was somewhat older than you when I was of the same opinion."

"You might have remained so still," replies Jones, "if you had not been unfortunate, I will venture to say incautious, in the placing your affections. If there was, indeed, much more wickedness in the world than there is, it would not prove such general assertions against human nature, since much of this arrives by mere accident, and many a man who commits evil is not totally bad and corrupt in his heart. In truth, none seem to have any title to assert human nature to be necessarily and universally evil, but those whose own minds afford them one instance of this natural depravity; which is not, I am convinced, your case."

"And such," said the stranger, "will be always the most backward to assert any such thing. Knaves will no more endeavour to persuade us of the baseness of mankind, than a highwayman will inform you that there are thieves on the road. This would, indeed, be a method to put you on your guard, and to defeat their own purposes. For which reason, though knaves, as I remember, are very apt to abuse particular persons, yet they never cast any reflection on human nature in general." The old gentleman spoke this so warmly, that as Jones despaired of making a convert, and was unwilling to offend, he returned no answer.

The day now began to send forth its first streams of light, when Jones made an apology to the stranger for having staid so long, and perhaps detained him from his rest. The stranger answered, "He never wanted rest less than at present; for that day and night were indifferent seasons to him; and that he commonly made use of the former for the time of his repose and of the latter for his walks and lucubrations. However," said he, "it is now a most lovely morning, and if you can bear any longer to be without your own rest or food, I will gladly entertain you with the sight of some very fine prospects which I believe you have not yet seen."

Jones very readily embraced this offer, and they immediately set forward together from the cottage. As for Partridge, he had fallen into a profound repose just as the stranger had finished his story; for his curiosity was satisfied, and the subsequent discourse was not forcible enough in its operation to conjure down the charms of sleep. Jones therefore left him to enjoy his nap; and as the reader may perhaps be at this season glad of the same favour, we will here put an end to the eighth book of our history.

BOOK IX.

CONTAINING TWELVE HOURS.

CHAPTER I.

Of those who lawfully may, and of those who may not, write such histories as this.

Among other good uses for which I have thought proper to institute these several introductory chapters, I have considered them as a kind of mark or stamp, which may hereafter enable a very indifferent reader to distinguish what is true and genuine in this historic kind of writing, from what is false and counterfeit. Indeed, it seems likely that some such mark may shortly become necessary, since the favourable reception which two or three authors have lately procured for their works of this nature from the public, will probably serve as an encouragement to many others to undertake the like. Thus a swarm of foolish novels and monstrous romances will be produced, either to the great impoverishing of booksellers, or to the great loss of time and depravation of morals in the reader; nay, often to the spreading of scandal and calumny, and to the prejudice of the characters of many worthy and honest people.

I question not but the ingenious author of the Spectator was principally induced to prefix Greek and Latin mottos to every paper, from the same consideration of guarding against the pursuit of those scribblers, who having no talents of a writer but what is taught by the writing-master, are yet nowise afraid nor ashamed to assume the same titles with the greatest genius, than their good brother in the fable was of braying in the lion's skin.

By the device therefore of his motto, it became impracticable for any man to presume to imitate the Spectators, without understanding at least one sentence in the learned languages. In the same manner I have now secured myself from the imitation of those who are utterly incapable of any degree of reflection, and whose learning is not equal to an essay.

I would not be here understood to insinuate, that the greatest merit of such historical productions can ever lie in these introductory chapters; but, in fact, those parts which contain mere narrative only, afford much more encouragement to the pen of an imitator, than those which are composed of observation and reflection. Here I mean such imitators as Rowe was of Shakespear, or as Horace hints some of the Romans were of Cato, by bare feet and sour faces.

To invent good stories, and to tell them well, are possibly very rare talents, and yet I have observed few persons who have scrupled to aim at both: and if we examine the romances and novels with which the world abounds, I think we may fairly conclude, that most of the authors would not have attempted to show their teeth (if the expression may be allowed me) in any other way of writing; nor could indeed have strung together a dozen sentences on any other subject whatever.

Scribimus indocti doctique passim,[1]

may be more truly said of the historian and biographer, than of any other species of writing; for all the arts and sciences (even criticism itself) require some little degree of learning and knowledge. Poetry, indeed, may perhaps be thought an exception; but then it demands numbers, or something like numbers: whereas, to the composition of novels and romances, nothing is necessary but paper, pens, and ink, with the manual capacity of using them. This, I conceive, their productions show to be the opinion of the authors themselves: and this must be the opinion of their readers, if indeed there be any such.

Hence we are to derive that universal contempt which the world, who always denominate the whole from the majority, have cast on all historical writers who do not draw their materials from records. And it is the apprehension of this contempt that hath made us so cautiously avoid the term romance, a name with which we might otherwise have been well enough contented. Though, as we have good authority for all our characters, no less indeed than the vast authentic doomsday-book of nature, as is elsewhere hinted, our labours have sufficient title to the name of history. Certainly they deserve some distinction from those works, which one of the wittiest of men regarded only as proceeding from a *pruritus*, or indeed rather from a looseness of the brain.

But besides the dishonour which is thus cast on one of the most useful as well as entertaining of all kinds of writing, there is just reason to apprehend, that by encouraging such authors we shall propagate much dishonour of another kind; I mean to the characters of many good and valuable members of society; for the dullest writers, no more than the dullest companions, are always inoffensive. They have both enough of language to be indecent and abusive. And surely if the opinion just above cited be true, we cannot wonder that works so nastily derived should be nasty themselves, or have a tendency to make others so.

To prevent therefore, for the future, such intemperate abuses of leisure, of letters, and of the liberty of the press, especially as the world seems at present to be more than usually threatened with them, I shall here venture to mention some qualifications, every one of which are in a pretty high degree necessary to this order of historians.

The first is, genius, without a full vein of which no study, says Horace, can avail us. By genius I would understand that power or rather those powers of the mind, which are capable of penetrating into all things within our reach and

---

[1] —Each desperate blockhead dares to write:
Verse is the trade of every living wight.—FRANCIS.

knowledge, and of distinguishing their essential differences. These are no other than invention and judgment; and they are both called by the collective name of genius, as they are of those gifts of nature which we bring with us into the world. Concerning each of which many seem to have fallen into very great errors; for by invention, I believe, is generally understood a creative faculty, which would indeed prove most romance writers to have the highest pretensions to it; whereas by invention is really meant no more (and so the word signifies) than discovery, or finding out; or to explain it at large, a quick and sagacious penetration into the true essence of all the objects of our contemplation. This, I think, can rarely exist without the concomitancy of judgment; for how we can be said to have discovered the true essence of two things, without discerning their difference, seems to me hard to conceive. Now this last is the undisputed province of judgment, and yet some few men of wit have agreed with all the dull fellows in the world in representing these two to have been seldom or never the property of one and the same person.

But though they should be so, they are not sufficient for our purpose, without a good share of learning; for which I could again cite the authority of Horace, and of many others, if any was necessary to prove that tools are of no service to a workman, when they are not sharpened by art, or when he wants rules to direct him in his work, or hath no matter to work upon. All these uses are supplied by learning; for nature can only furnish us with capacity; or, as I have chose to illustrate it, with the tools of our profession; learning must fit them for use, must direct them in it, and, lastly, must contribute part at least of the materials. A competent knowledge of history and of the belles-lettres is here absolutely necessary; and without this share of knowledge at least, to affect the character of an historian, is as vain as to endeavour at building a house without timber or mortar, or brick or stone. Homer and Milton, who, though they added the ornament of numbers to their works, were both historians of our order, were masters of all the learning of their times.

Again, there is another sort of knowledge, beyond the power of learning to bestow, and this is to be had by conversation. So necessary is this to the understanding the characters of men, that none are more ignorant of them than those learned pedants whose lives have been entirely consumed in colleges, and among books; for however exquisitely human nature may have been described by writers, the true practical system can be learnt only in the world. Indeed the like happens in every other kind of knowledge. Neither physic nor law are to be practically known from books. Nay, the farmer, the planter, the gardener, must perfect by experience what he hath acquired the rudiments of by reading. How accurately soever the ingenious Mr Miller may have described the plant, he himself would advise his disciple to see it in the garden. As we must perceive, that after the nicest strokes of a Shakespear or a Jonson, of a Wycherly or an Otway, some touches of nature will escape the reader, which the judicious action of a Garrick, of a Cibber, or a Clive,[1] can convey to him; so, on the real stage, the character shows himself in a stronger and bolder light than he can be described. And if this be the case in those fine and nervous descriptions which great authors themselves have taken from life, how much more strongly will it hold when the writer himself takes his lines not from nature, but from books? Such characters are only the faint copy of a copy, and can have neither the justness nor spirit of an original.

Now this conversation in our historian must be universal, that is, with all ranks and degrees of men; for the knowledge of what is called high life will not instruct him in low; nor, *e converso*, will his being acquainted with the inferior part of mankind teach him the manners of the superior. And though it may be thought that the knowledge of either may sufficiently enable him to describe at least that in which he hath been conversant, yet he will even here fall greatly short of perfection; for the follies of either rank do in reality illustrate each other. For instance, the affectation of high life appears more glaring and ridiculous from the simplicity of the low; and again, the rudeness and barbarity of this latter, strikes with much stronger ideas of absurdity, when contrasted with, and opposed to, the politeness which controuls the former. Besides, to say the truth, the manners of our historian will be improved by both these conversations; for in the one he will easily find examples of plainness, honesty, and sincerity; in the other of refinement, elegance, and a liberality of spirit; which last quality I myself have scarce ever seen in men of low birth and education.

Nor will all the qualities I have hitherto given my historian avail him, unless he have what is generally meant by a good heart, and be capable of feeling. The author who will make me weep, says Horace, must first weep himself. In reality, no man can paint a distress well which he doth not feel while he is painting it; nor do I doubt, but that the most pathetic and affecting scenes have been writ with tears. In the same manner it is with the ridiculous. I am convinced I never make my reader laugh heartily but where I have laughed before him; unless it should happen at any time, that instead of laughing with me he should be inclined to laugh at me. Perhaps this may have been the case at some passages in this chapter, from which apprehension I will here put an end to it.

---

[1] There is a peculiar propriety in mentioning this great actor, and these two most justly celebrated actresses, in this place, as they have all formed themselves on the study of nature only, and not on the imitation of their predecessors. Hence they have been able to excel all who have gone before them; a degree of merit which the servile herd of imitators can never possibly arrive at.

CHAPTER II.

Containing a very surprizing adventure indeed, which Mr Jones met with in his walk with the Man of the Hill.

Aurora now first opened her casement, *Anglice* the day began to break, when Jones walked forth in company with the stranger, and mounted Mazard Hill; of which they had no sooner gained the summit than one of the most noble prospects in the world presented itself to their view, and which we would likewise present to the reader, but for two reasons: first, we despair of making those who have seen this prospect admire our description; secondly, we very much doubt whether those who have not seen it would understand it.

Jones stood for some minutes fixed in one posture, and directing his eyes towards the south; upon which the old gentleman asked, What he was looking at with so much attention? "Alas! sir," answered he with a sigh, "I was endeavouring to trace out my own journey hither. Good heavens! what a distance is Gloucester from us! What a vast track of land must be between me and my own home!"—"Ay, ay, young gentleman," cries the other, "and by your sighing, from what you love better than your own home, or I am mistaken. I perceive now the object of your contemplation is not within your sight, and yet I fancy you have a pleasure in looking that way." Jones answered with a smile, "I find, old friend, you have not yet forgot the sensations of your youth. I own my thoughts were employed as you have guessed."

They now walked to that part of the hill which looks to the north-west, and which hangs over a vast and extensive wood. Here they were no sooner arrived than they heard at a distance the most violent screams of a woman, proceeding from the wood below them. Jones listened a moment, and then, without saying a word to his companion (for indeed the occasion seemed sufficiently pressing), ran, or rather slid, down the hill, and, without the least apprehension or concern for his own safety, made directly to the thicket, whence the sound had issued.

He had not entered far into the wood before he beheld a most shocking sight indeed, a woman stript half naked, under the hands of a ruffian, who had put his garter round her neck, and was endeavouring to draw her up to a tree. Jones asked no questions at this interval, but fell instantly upon the villain, and made such good use of his trusty oaken stick that he laid him sprawling on the ground before he could defend himself, indeed almost before he knew he was attacked; nor did he cease the prosecution of his blows till the woman herself begged him to forbear, saying, she believed he had sufficiently done his business.

The poor wretch then fell upon her knees to Jones, and gave him a thousand thanks for her deliverance. He presently lifted her up, and told her he was highly pleased with the extraordinary accident which had sent him thither for her relief, where it was so improbable she should find any; adding, that Heaven seemed to have designed him as the happy instrument of her protection. "Nay," answered she, "I could almost conceive you to be some good angel; and, to say the truth, you look more like an angel than a man in my eye." Indeed he was a charming figure; and if a very fine person, and a most comely set of features, adorned with youth, health, strength, freshness, spirit, and good-nature, can make a man resemble an angel, he certainly had that resemblance.

The redeemed captive had not altogether so much of the human-angelic species: she seemed to be at least of the middle age, nor had her face much appearance of beauty; but her cloaths being torn from all the upper part of her body, her breasts, which were well formed and extremely white, attracted the eyes of her deliverer, and for a few moments they stood silent, and gazing at each other; till the ruffian on the ground beginning to move, Jones took the garter which had been intended for another purpose, and bound both his hands behind him. And now, on contemplating his face, he discovered, greatly to his surprize, and perhaps not a little to his satisfaction, this very person to be no other than ensign Northerton. Nor had the ensign forgotten his former antagonist, whom he knew the moment he came to himself. His surprize was equal to that of Jones; but I conceive his pleasure was rather less on this occasion.

Jones helped Northerton upon his legs, and then looking him stedfastly in the face, "I fancy, sir," said he, "you did not expect to meet me any more in this world, and I confess I had as little expectation to find you here. However, fortune, I see, hath brought us once more together, and hath given me satisfaction for the injury I have received, even without my own knowledge."

"It is very much like a man of honour, indeed," answered Northerton, "to take satisfaction by knocking a man down behind his back. Neither am I capable of giving you satisfaction here, as I have no sword; but if you dare behave like a gentleman, let us go where I can furnish myself with one, and I will do by you as a man of honour ought."

"Doth it become such a villain as you are," cries Jones, "to contaminate the name of honour by assuming it? But I shall waste no time in discourse with you. Justice requires satisfaction of you now, and shall have it." Then turning to the woman, he asked her, if she was near her home; or if not, whether she was acquainted with any house in the neighbourhood, where she might procure herself some decent cloaths, in order to proceed to a justice of the peace.

She answered she was an entire stranger in that part of the world. Jones then recollecting himself, said, he had a friend near who would direct them; indeed, he wondered at his not following; but, in fact, the good Man of the Hill, when our heroe departed, sat himself down on the brow, where, though he had a gun in his hand, he with great patience and unconcern had attended the issue.

Jones then stepping without the wood, perceived the old man sitting as we have just described him; he presently exerted his utmost agility, and with surprizing expedition ascended the hill.

The old man advised him to carry the woman to Upton, which, he said, was the nearest town, and there he would be sure of furnishing her with all manner of conveniencies. Jones having received his direction to the place, took his leave of the Man of the Hill, and, desiring him to direct Partridge the same way, returned hastily to the wood.

Our heroe, at his departure to make this enquiry of his friend, had considered, that as the ruffian's hands were tied behind him, he was incapable of executing any wicked purposes on the poor woman. Besides, he knew he should not be beyond the reach of her voice, and could return soon enough to prevent any mischief. He had moreover declared to the villain, that if he attempted the least insult, he would be himself immediately the executioner of vengeance on him. But Jones unluckily forgot, that though the hands of Northerton were tied, his legs were at liberty; nor did he lay the least injunction on the prisoner that he should not make what use of these he pleased. Northerton therefore having given no parole of that kind, thought he might without any breach of honour depart; not being obliged, as he imagined, by any rules, to wait for a formal discharge. He therefore took up his legs, which were at liberty, and walked off through the wood, which favoured his retreat; nor did the woman, whose eyes were perhaps rather turned toward her deliverer, once think of his escape, or give herself any concern or trouble to prevent it.

Jones therefore, at his return, found the woman alone. He would have spent some time in searching for Northerton, but she would not permit him; earnestly entreating that he would accompany her to the town whither they had been directed. "As to the fellow's escape," said she, "it gives me no uneasiness; for philosophy and Christianity both preach up forgiveness of injuries. But for you, sir, I am concerned at the trouble I give you; nay, indeed, my nakedness may well make me ashamed to look you in the face; and if it was not for the sake of your protection, I should wish to go alone."

Jones offered her his coat; but, I know not for what reason, she absolutely refused the most earnest solicitations to accept it. He then begged her to forget both the causes of her confusion. "With regard to the former," says he, "I have done no more than my duty in protecting you; and as for the latter, I will entirely remove it, by walking before you all the way; for I would not have my eyes offend you, and I could not answer for my power of resisting the attractive charms of so much beauty."

Thus our heroe and the redeemed lady walked in the same manner as Orpheus and Eurydice marched heretofore; but though I cannot believe that Jones was designedly tempted by his fair one to look behind him, yet as she frequently wanted his assistance to help her over stiles, and had besides many trips and other accidents, he was often obliged to turn about. However, he had better fortune than what attended poor Orpheus, for he brought his companion, or rather follower, safe into the famous town of Upton.

CHAPTER III.

The arrival of Mr Jones with his lady at the inn; with a very full description of the battle of Upton.

Though the reader, we doubt not, is very eager to know who this lady was, and how she fell into the hands of Mr Northerton, we must beg him to suspend his curiosity for a short time, as we are obliged, for some very good reasons which hereafter perhaps he may guess, to delay his satisfaction a little longer.

Mr Jones and his fair companion no sooner entered the town, than they went directly to that inn which in their eyes presented the fairest appearance to the street. Here Jones, having ordered a servant to show a room above stairs, was ascending, when the dishevelled fair, hastily following, was laid hold on by the master of the house, who cried, "Heyday, where is that beggar wench going? Stay below stairs, I desire you." But Jones at that instant thundered from above, "Let the lady come up," in so authoritative a voice, that the good man instantly withdrew his hands, and the lady made the best of her way to the chamber.

Here Jones wished her joy of her safe arrival, and then departed, in order, as he promised, to send the landlady up with some cloaths. The poor woman thanked him heartily for all his kindness, and said, she hoped she should see him again soon, to thank him a thousand times more. During this short conversation, she covered her white bosom as well as she could possibly with her arms; for Jones could not avoid stealing a sly peep or two, though he took all imaginable care to avoid giving any offence.

Our travellers had happened to take up their residence at a house of exceeding good repute, whither Irish ladies of strict virtue, and many northern lasses of the same predicament, were accustomed to resort in their way to Bath. The landlady therefore would by no means have admitted any conversation of a disreputable kind to pass under her roof. Indeed, so foul and contagious are all such proceedings, that they contaminate the very innocent scenes where they are committed, and give the name of a bad house, or of a house of ill repute, to all those where they are suffered to be carried on.

Not that I would intimate that such strict chastity as was preserved in the temple of Vesta can possibly be maintained at a public inn. My good landlady did not hope for such a blessing, nor would any of the ladies I have spoken of, or indeed any others of the most rigid note, have expected or insisted on any such thing. But to exclude all vulgar concubinage, and to drive all whores in rags from within the walls, is within the power of every one. This my landlady very strictly adhered to, and this her virtuous guests, who did not travel in rags, would very reasonably have expected of her.

Now it required no very blameable degree of suspicion to imagine that Mr Jones and his ragged companion had certain purposes in their intention, which, though tolerated in some Christian countries, connived at in others, and practised in all, are however as expressly forbidden as murder, or any other horrid vice, by that religion which is universally believed in those countries. The landlady, therefore, had no sooner received an intimation of the entrance of the above-said persons than she began to meditate the most expeditious means for their expulsion. In order to this, she had provided herself with a long and deadly instrument, with which, in times of peace, the chambermaid was wont to demolish the labours of the industrious spider. In vulgar phrase, she had taken up the broomstick, and was just about to sally from the kitchen, when Jones accosted her with a demand of a gown and other vestments, to cover the half-naked woman upstairs.

Nothing can be more provoking to the human temper, nor more dangerous to that cardinal virtue, patience, than solicitations of extraordinary offices of kindness on behalf of those very persons with whom we are highly incensed. For this reason Shakespear hath artfully introduced his Desdemona soliciting favours for Cassio of her husband, as the means of inflaming, not only his jealousy, but his rage, to the highest pitch of madness; and we find the unfortunate Moor less able to command his passion on this occasion, than even when he beheld his valued present to his wife in the hands of his supposed rival. In fact, we regard these efforts as insults on our understanding, and to such the pride of man is very difficultly brought to submit.

My landlady, though a very good-tempered woman, had, I suppose, some of this pride in her composition, for Jones had scarce ended his request, when she fell upon him with a certain weapon, which, though it be neither long, nor sharp, nor hard, nor indeed threatens from its appearance with either death or wound, hath been however held in great dread and abhorrence by many wise men—nay, by many brave ones; insomuch, that some who have dared to look into the mouth of a loaded cannon, have not dared to look into a mouth where this weapon was brandished; and rather than run the hazard of its execution, have contented themselves with making a most pitiful and sneaking figure in the eyes of all their acquaintance.

To confess the truth, I am afraid Mr Jones was one of these; for though he was attacked and violently belaboured with the aforesaid weapon, he could not be provoked to make any resistance; but in a most cowardly manner applied, with many entreaties, to his antagonist to desist from pursuing her blows; in plain English, he only begged her with the utmost earnestness to hear him; but before he could obtain his request, my landlord himself entered into the fray, and embraced that side of the cause which seemed to stand very little in need of assistance.

There are a sort of heroes who are supposed to be determined in their chusing or avoiding a conflict by the character and behaviour of the person whom they are to engage. These are said to know their men, and Jones, I believe, knew his woman; for though he had been so submissive to her, he was no sooner attacked by her husband, than he demonstrated an immediate spirit of resentment, and enjoined him silence under a very severe penalty; no less than that, I think, of being converted into fuel for his own fire.

The husband, with great indignation, but with a mixture of pity, answered, "You must pray first to be made able. I believe I am a better man than yourself; ay, every way, that I am;" and presently proceeded to discharge half-a-dozen whores at the lady above stairs, the last of which had scarce issued from his lips, when a swinging blow from the cudgel that Jones carried in his hand assaulted him over the shoulders.

It is a question whether the landlord or the landlady was the most expeditious in returning this blow. My landlord, whose hands were empty, fell to with his fist, and the good wife, uplifting her broom and aiming at the head of Jones, had probably put an immediate end to the fray, and to Jones likewise, had not the descent of this broom been prevented—not by the miraculous intervention of any heathen deity, but by a very natural though fortunate accident, viz., by the arrival of Partridge; who entered the house at that instant (for fear had caused him to run every step from the hill), and who, seeing the danger which threatened his master or companion (which you chuse to call him), prevented so sad a catastrophe, by catching hold of the landlady's arm, as it was brandished aloft in the air.

The landlady soon perceived the impediment which prevented her blow; and being unable to rescue her arm from the hands of Partridge, she let fall the broom; and then leaving Jones to the discipline of her husband, she fell with the utmost fury on that poor fellow, who had already given some intimation of himself, by crying, "Zounds! do you intend to kill my friend?"

Partridge, though not much addicted to battle, would not however stand still when his friend was attacked; nor was he much displeased with that part of the combat which fell to his share; he therefore returned my landlady's blows as soon as he received them: and now the fight was obstinately maintained on all parts, and it seemed doubtful to which side Fortune would incline, when the naked lady, who had listened at the top of the stairs to the dialogue which preceded the engagement, descended suddenly from above, and without weighing the unfair inequality of two to one, fell upon the poor woman who was boxing with Partridge; nor did that great champion desist, but rather redoubled his fury, when he found fresh succours were arrived to his assistance.

Victory must now have fallen to the side of the travellers (for the bravest troops must yield to numbers) had not Susan the chambermaid come luckily to support her mistress. This Susan was as two-handed a wench (according to the phrase) as any in the country, and would, I believe, have beat the famed Thalestris herself, or any of her subject Amazons; for her form was robust and man-like, and every way made for such encounters. As her hands and arms were formed to give blows with great mischief to an enemy, so was her face as well contrived to receive blows without any great injury to herself, her nose being already flat to her face; her lips were so large, that no swelling could be perceived in them, and moreover they were so hard, that a fist could hardly make any impression on them. Lastly, her cheek-bones stood out, as if nature had intended them for two bastions to defend her eyes in those encounters for which she seemed so well calculated, and to which she was most wonderfully well inclined.

This fair creature entering the field of battle, immediately filed to that wing where her mistress maintained so unequal a fight with one of either sex. Here she presently challenged Partridge to single combat. He accepted the challenge, and a most desperate fight began between them.

Now the dogs of war being let loose, began to lick their bloody lips; now Victory, with golden wings, hung hovering in the air; now Fortune, taking her scales from her shelf, began to weigh the fates of Tom Jones, his female companion, and Partridge, against the landlord, his wife, and maid; all which hung in exact balance before her; when a good-natured accident put suddenly an end to the bloody fray, with which half of the combatants had already sufficiently feasted. This accident was the arrival of a coach and four; upon which my landlord and landlady immediately desisted from fighting, and at their entreaty obtained the same favour of their antagonists: but Susan was not so kind to Partridge; for that Amazonian fair having overthrown and bestrid her enemy, was now cuffing him lustily with both her hands, without any regard to his request of a cessation of arms, or to those loud exclamations of murder which he roared forth.

No sooner, however, had Jones quitted the landlord, than he flew to the rescue of his defeated companion, from whom he with much difficulty drew off the enraged chambermaid: but Partridge was not immediately sensible of his deliverance, for he still lay flat on the floor, guarding his face with his hands; nor did he cease roaring till Jones had forced him to look up, and to perceive that the battle was at an end.

The landlord, who had no visible hurt, and the landlady, hiding her well-scratched face with her handkerchief, ran both hastily to the door to attend the coach, from which a young lady and her maid now alighted. These the landlady presently ushered into that room where Mr Jones had at first deposited his fair prize, as it was the best apartment in the house. Hither they were obliged to pass through the field of battle, which they did with the utmost haste, covering their faces with their handkerchiefs, as desirous to avoid the notice of any one. Indeed their caution was quite unnecessary; for the poor unfortunate Helen, the fatal cause of all the bloodshed, was entirely taken up in endeavouring to conceal her own face, and Jones was no less occupied in rescuing Partridge from the fury of Susan; which being happily effected, the poor fellow immediately departed to the pump to wash his face, and to stop that bloody torrent which Susan had plentifully set a-flowing from his nostrils.

CHAPTER IV.

In which the arrival of a man of war puts a final end to hostilities, and causes the conclusion of a firm and lasting peace between all parties.

A serjeant and a file of musqueteers, with a deserter in their custody, arrived about this time. The serjeant presently enquired for the principal magistrate of the town, and was informed by my landlord, that he himself was vested in that office. He then demanded his billets, together with a mug of beer, and complaining it was cold, spread himself before the kitchen fire.

Mr Jones was at this time comforting the poor distressed lady, who sat down at a table in the kitchen, and leaning her head upon her arm, was bemoaning her misfortunes; but lest my fair readers should be in pain concerning a particular circumstance, I think proper here to acquaint them, that before she had quitted the room above stairs, she had so well covered herself with a pillowbeer which she there found, that her regard to decency was not in the least violated by the presence of so many men as were now in the room.

One of the soldiers now went up to the serjeant, and whispered something in his ear; upon which he stedfastly fixed his eyes on the lady, and having looked at her for near a minute, he came up to her, saying, "I ask pardon, madam; but I am certain I am not deceived; you can be no other person than Captain Waters's lady?"

The poor woman, who in her present distress had very little regarded the face of any person present, no sooner looked at the serjeant than she presently recollected him, and calling him by his name, answered, "That she was indeed the unhappy person he imagined her to be;" but added, "I wonder any one should know me in this disguise." To which the serjeant replied, "He was very much surprized to see her ladyship in such a dress, and was afraid some accident had happened to her."—"An accident hath happened to me, indeed," says she, "and I am highly obliged to this gentleman" (pointing to Jones) "that it was not a fatal one, or that I am now living to mention it."—"Whatever the gentleman hath done," cries the serjeant, "I am sure the captain will make him amends for it; and if I can be of any service, your ladyship may command me, and I shall think myself very happy to have it in my power to serve your ladyship; and so indeed may any one, for I know the captain will well reward them for it."

The landlady, who heard from the stairs all that past between the serjeant and Mrs Waters, came hastily down, and running directly up to her, began to ask pardon for the offences she had committed, begging that all might be imputed to ignorance of her quality: for, "Lud! madam," says she, "how should I have imagimagined that a lady of your fashion would appear in such a dress? I am sure, madam, if I had once suspected that your ladyship was your ladyship, I would sooner have burnt my tongue out, than have said what I have said; and I hope your ladyship will accept of a gown, till you can get your own cloaths."

"Prithee, woman," says Mrs Waters, "cease your impertinence: how can you imagine I should concern myself about anything which comes from the lips of such low creatures as yourself? But I am surprized at your assurance in thinking, after what is past, that I will condescend to put on any of your dirty things. I would have you know, creature, I have a spirit above that."

Here Jones interfered, and begged Mrs Waters to forgive the landlady, and to accept her gown: "for I must confess," cries he, "our appearance was a little suspicious when first we came in; and I am well assured all this good woman did was, as she professed, out of regard to the reputation of her house."

"Yes, upon my truly was it," says she: "the gentleman speaks very much like a gentleman, and I see very plainly is so; and to be certain the house is well known to be a house of as good reputation as any on the road, and though I say it, is frequented by gentry of the best quality, both Irish and English. I defy anybody to say black is my eye, for that matter. And, as I was saying, if I had known your ladyship to be your ladyship, I would as soon have burnt my fingers as have affronted your ladyship; but truly where gentry come and spend their money, I am not willing that they should be scandalized by a set of poor shabby vermin, that, wherever they go, leave more lice than money behind them; such folks never raise my compassion, for to be certain it is foolish to have any for them; and if our justices did as they ought, they would be all whipt out of the kingdom, for to be certain it is what is most fitting for them. But as for your ladyship, I am heartily sorry your ladyship hath had a misfortune, and if your ladyship will do me the honour to wear my cloaths till you can get some of your ladyship's own, to be certain the best I have is at your ladyship's service."

Whether cold, shame, or the persuasions of Mr Jones prevailed most on Mrs Waters, I will not determine, but she suffered herself to be pacified by this speech of my landlady, and retired with that good woman, in order to apparel herself in a decent manner.

My landlord was likewise beginning his oration to Jones, but was presently interrupted by that generous youth, who shook him heartily by the hand, and assured him of entire forgiveness, saying, "If you are satisfied, my worthy friend, I promise you I am;" and indeed, in one sense, the landlord had the better reason to be satisfied; for he had received a bellyfull of drubbing, whereas Jones had scarce felt a single blow.

Partridge, who had been all this time washing his bloody nose at the pump, returned into the kitchen at the instant when his master and the landlord were shaking hands with each other. As he was of a peaceable disposition, he was pleased with those symptoms of reconciliation; and though his face bore some marks of Susan's fist, and many more of her nails, he rather chose to be contented with his fortune in the last battle than to endeavour at bettering it in another.

The heroic Susan was likewise well contented with her victory, though it had cost her a black eye, which Partridge had given her at the first onset. Between these two, therefore, a league was struck, and those hands which had been the instruments of war became now the mediators of peace.

Matters were thus restored to a perfect calm; at which the serjeant, though it may seem so contrary to the principles of his profession, testified his approbation. "Why now, that's friendly," said he; "d—n me, I hate to see two people bear ill-will to one another after they have had a tussel. The only way when friends quarrel is to see it out fairly in a friendly manner, as a man may call it, either with a fist, or sword, or pistol, according as they like, and then let it be all over; for my own part, d—n me if ever I love my friend better than when I am fighting with him! To bear malice is more like a Frenchman than an Englishman."

He then proposed a libation as a necessary part of the ceremony at all treaties of this kind. Perhaps the reader may here conclude that he was well versed in antient history; but this, though highly probable, as he cited no authority to support the custom, I will not affirm with any confidence. Most likely indeed it is, that he founded his opinion on very good authority, since he confirmed it with many violent oaths.

Jones no sooner heard the proposal than, immediately agreeing with the learned serjeant, he ordered a bowl, or rather a large mug, filled with the liquor used on these occasions, to be brought in, and then began the ceremony himself. He placed his right hand in that of the landlord, and, seizing the bowl with his left, uttered the usual words, and then made his libation. After which, the same was observed by all present. Indeed, there is very little need of being particular in describing the whole form, as it differed so little from those libations of which so much is recorded in antient authors and their modern transcribers. The principal difference lay in two instances; for, first, the present company poured the liquor only down their throats; and, secondly, the serjeant, who officiated as priest, drank the last; but he preserved, I believe, the antient form, in swallowing much the largest draught of the whole company, and in being the only person present who contributed nothing towards the libation besides his good offices in assisting at the performance.

The good people now ranged themselves round the kitchen fire, where good humour seemed to maintain an absolute dominion; and Partridge not only forgot his shameful defeat, but converted hunger into thirst, and soon became extremely facetious. We must however quit this agreeable assembly for a while, and attend Mr Jones to Mrs Waters's apartment, where the dinner which he had bespoke was now on the table. Indeed, it took no long time in preparing, having been all drest three days before, and required nothing more from the cook than to warm it over again.

CHAPTER V.

An apology for all heroes who have good stomachs, with a description of a battle of the amorous kind.

Heroes, notwithstanding the high ideas which, by the means of flatterers, they may entertain of themselves, or the world may conceive of them, have certainly more of mortal than divine about them. However elevated their minds may be, their bodies at least (which is much the major part of most) are liable to the worst infirmities, and subject to the vilest offices of human nature. Among these latter, the act of eating, which hath by several wise men been considered as extremely mean and derogatory from the philosophic dignity, must be in some measure performed by the greatest prince, heroe, or philosopher upon earth; nay, sometimes Nature hath been so frolicsome as to exact of these dignified characters a much more exorbitant share of this office than she hath obliged those of the lowest order to perform.

To say the truth, as no known inhabitant of this globe is really more than man, so none need be ashamed of submitting to what the necessities of man demand; but when those great personages I have just mentioned condescend to aim at confining such low offices to themselves—as when, by hoarding or destroying, they seem desirous to prevent any others from eating—then they surely become very low and despicable.

Now, after this short preface, we think it no disparagement to our heroe to mention the immoderate ardour with which he laid about him at this season. Indeed, it may be doubted whether Ulysses, who by the way seems to have had the best stomach of all the heroes in that eating poem of the Odyssey, ever made a better meal. Three pounds at least of that flesh which formerly had contributed to the composition of an ox was now honoured with becoming part of the individual Mr Jones.

This particular we thought ourselves obliged to mention, as it may account for our heroe's temporary neglect of his fair companion, who eat but very little, and was indeed employed in considerations of a very different nature, which passed unobserved by Jones, till he had entirely satisfied that appetite which a fast of twenty-four hours had procured him; but his dinner was no sooner ended than his attention to other matters revived; with these matters therefore we shall now proceed to acquaint the reader.

Mr Jones, of whose personal accomplishments we have hitherto said very little, was, in reality, one of the handsomest young fellows in the world. His face, besides being the picture of health, had in it the most apparent marks of sweetness and good-nature. These qualities were indeed so characteristical in his countenance, that, while the spirit and sensibility in his eyes, though they must have been perceived by an accurate observer, might have escaped the notice of the less discerning, so strongly was this good-nature painted in his look, that it was remarked by almost every one who saw him.

It was, perhaps, as much owing to this as to a very fine complexion that his face had a delicacy in it almost inexpressible, and which might have given him an air rather too effeminate, had it not been joined to a most masculine person and mien: which latter had as much in them of the Hercules as the former had of the Adonis. He was besides active, genteel, gay, and good-humoured; and had a flow of animal spirits which enlivened every conversation where he was present.

When the reader hath duly reflected on these many charms which all centered in our heroe, and considers at the same time the fresh obligations which Mrs Waters had to him, it will be a mark more of prudery than candour to entertain a bad opinion of her because she conceived a very good opinion of him.

But, whatever censures may be passed upon her, it is my business to relate matters of fact with veracity. Mrs Waters had, in truth, not only a good opinion of our heroe, but a very great affection for him. To speak out boldly at once, she was in love, according to the present universally-received sense of that phrase, by which love is applied indiscriminately to the desirable objects of all our passions, appetites, and senses, and is understood to be that preference which we give to one kind of food rather than to another.

But though the love to these several objects may possibly be one and the same in all cases, its operations however must be allowed to be different; for, how much soever we may be in love with an excellent surloin of beef, or bottle of Burgundy; with a damask rose, or Cremona fiddle; yet do we never smile, nor ogle, nor dress, nor flatter, nor endeavour by any other arts or tricks to gain the affection of the said beef, &c. Sigh indeed we sometimes may; but it is generally in the absence, not in the presence, of the beloved object. For otherwise we might possibly complain of their ingratitude and deafness, with the same reason as Pasiphae doth of her bull, whom she endeavoured to engage by all the coquetry practised with good success in the drawing-room on the much more sensible as well as tender hearts of the fine gentlemen there.

The contrary happens in that love which operates between persons of the same species, but of different sexes. Here we are no sooner in love than it becomes our principal care to engage the affection of the object beloved. For what other purpose indeed are our youth instructed in all the arts of rendering themselves agreeable? If it was not with a view to this love, I question whether any of those trades which deal in setting off and adorning the human person would procure a livelihood. Nay, those great polishers of our manners, who are by some thought to teach what principally distinguishes us from the brute creation, even dancing-masters themselves, might possibly find no place in society. In short, all the graces which young ladies and young gentlemen too learn from others, and the many improvements which, by the help of a looking-glass, they add of their own, are in reality those very *spicula et faces amoris* so often mentioned by Ovid; or, as they are sometimes called in our own language, the whole artillery of love.

Now Mrs Waters and our heroe had no sooner sat down together than the former began to play this artillery upon the latter. But here, as we are about to attempt a description hitherto unassayed either in prose or verse, we think proper to invoke the assistance of certain aërial beings, who will, we doubt not, come kindly to our aid on this occasion.

"Say then, ye Graces! you that inhabit the heavenly mansions of Seraphina's countenance; for you are truly divine, are always in her presence, and well know all the arts of charming; say, what were the weapons now used to captivate the heart of Mr Jones."

"First, from two lovely blue eyes, whose bright orbs flashed lightning at their discharge, flew forth two pointed ogles; but, happily for our heroe, hit only a vast piece of beef which he was then conveying into his plate, and harmless spent their force. The fair warrior perceived their miscarriage, and immediately from her fair bosom drew forth a deadly sigh. A sigh which none could have heard unmoved, and which was sufficient at once to have swept off a dozen beaus; so soft, so sweet, so tender, that the insinuating air must have found its subtle way to the heart of our heroe, had it not luckily been driven from his ears by the coarse bubbling of some bottled ale, which at that time he was pouring forth. Many other weapons did she assay; but the god of eating (if there be any such deity, for I do not confidently assert it) preserved his votary; or perhaps it may not be *dignus vindice nodus*, and the present security of Jones may be accounted for by natural means; for as love frequently preserves from the attacks of hunger, so may hunger possibly, in some cases, defend us against love.

"The fair one, enraged at her frequent disappointments, determined on a short cessation of arms. Which interval she employed in making ready every engine of amorous warfare for the renewing of the attack when dinner should be over.

"No sooner then was the cloth removed than she again began her operations. First, having planted her right eye sidewise against Mr Jones, she shot from its corner a most penetrating glance; which, though great part of its force was spent before it reached our heroe, did not vent itself absolutely without effect. This the fair one perceiving, hastily withdrew her eyes, and levelled them downwards, as if she was concerned for what she had done; though by this means she designed only to draw him from his guard, and indeed to open his eyes, through which she intended to surprize his heart. And now, gently lifting up those two bright orbs which had already begun to make an impression on poor Jones, she discharged a volley of small charms at once from her whole countenance in a smile. Not a smile of mirth, nor of joy; but a smile of affection, which most ladies have always ready at their command, and which serves them to show at once their good-humour, their pretty dimples, and their white teeth.

"This smile our heroe received full in his eyes, and was immediately staggered with its force. He then began to see the designs of the enemy, and indeed to feel their success. A parley now was set on foot between the parties; during which the artful fair so slily and imperceptibly carried on her attack, that she had almost subdued the heart of our heroe before she again repaired to acts of hostility. To confess the truth, I am afraid Mr Jones maintained a kind of Dutch defence, and treacherously delivered up the garrison, without duly weighing his allegiance to the fair Sophia. In short, no sooner had the amorous parley ended and the lady had unmasked the royal battery, by carelessly letting her handkerchief drop from her neck, than the heart of Mr Jones was entirely taken, and the fair conqueror enjoyed the usual fruits of her victory."

Here the Graces think proper to end their description, and here we think proper to end the chapter.

CHAPTER VI.

A friendly conversation in the kitchen, which had a very common, though not very friendly, conclusion.

While our lovers were entertaining themselves in the manner which is partly described in the foregoing chapter, they were likewise furnishing out an entertainment for their good friends in the kitchen. And this in a double sense, by affording them matter for their conversation, and, at the same time, drink to enliven their spirits.

There were now assembled round the kitchen fire, besides my landlord and landlady, who occasionally went backward and forward, Mr Partridge, the serjeant, and the coachman who drove the young lady and her maid.

Partridge having acquainted the company with what he had learnt from the Man of the Hill concerning the situation in which Mrs Waters had been found by Jones, the serjeant proceeded to that part of her history which was known to him. He said she was the wife of Mr Waters, who was a captain in their regiment, and had often been with him at quarters. "Some folks," says he, "used indeed to doubt whether they were lawfully married in a church or no. But, for my part, that's no business of mine: I must own, if I was put to my corporal oath, I believe she is little better than one of us; and I fancy the captain may go to heaven when the sun shines upon a rainy day. But if he does, that is neither here nor there; for he won't want company. And the lady, to give the devil his due, is a very good sort of lady, and loves the cloth, and is always desirous to do strict justice to it; for she hath begged off many a poor soldier, and, by her good-will, would never have any of them punished. But yet, to be sure, Ensign Northerton and she were very well acquainted together at our last quarters; that is the very right and truth of the matter. But the captain he knows nothing about it; and as long as there is enough for him too, what does it signify? He loves her not a bit the worse, and I am certain would run any man through the body that was to abuse her; therefore I won't abuse her, for my part. I only repeat what other folks say; and, to be certain, what everybody says, there must be some truth in."—"Ay, ay, a great deal of truth, I warrant you," cries Partridge; "*Veritas odium parit*"—"All a parcel of scandalous stuff," answered the mistress of the house. "I am sure, now she is drest, she looks like a very good sort of lady, and she behaves herself like one; for she gave me a guinea for the use of my cloaths."—"A very good lady indeed!" cries the landlord; "and if you had not been a little too hasty, you would not have quarrelled with her as you did at first."—"You need mention that with my truly!" answered she: "if it had not been for your nonsense, nothing had happened. You must be meddling with what did not belong to you, and throw in your fool's discourse."—"Well, well," answered he; "what's past cannot be mended, so there's an end of the matter."—"Yes," cries she, "for this once; but will it be mended ever the more hereafter? This is not the first time I have suffered for your numscull's pate. I wish you would always hold your tongue in the house, and meddle only in matters without doors, which concern you. Don't you remember what happened about seven years ago?"—"Nay, my dear," returned he, "don't rip up old stories. Come, come, all's well, and I am sorry for what I have done." The landlady was going to reply, but was prevented by the peace-making serjeant, sorely to the displeasure of Partridge, who was a great lover of what is called fun, and a great promoter of those harmless quarrels which tend rather to the production of comical than tragical incidents.

The serjeant asked Partridge whither he and his master were travelling? "None of your magisters," answered Partridge; "I am no man's servant, I assure you; for, though I have had misfortunes in the world, I write gentleman after my name; and, as poor and simple as I may appear now, I have taught grammar-school in my time; *sed hei mihi! non sum quod fui*."—"No offence, I hope, sir," said the serjeant; "where, then, if I may venture to be so bold, may you and your friend be travelling?"—"You have now denominated us right," says Partridge. "*Amici sumus*. And I promise you my friend is one of the greatest gentlemen in the kingdom" (at which words both landlord and landlady pricked up their ears). "He is the heir of Squire Allworthy."—"What, the squire who doth so much good all over the country?" cries my landlady. "Even he," answered Partridge.—"Then I warrant," says she, "he'll have a swinging great estate hereafter."—"Most certainly," answered Partridge.—"Well," replied the landlady, "I thought the first moment I saw him he looked like a good sort of gentleman; but my husband here, to be sure, is wiser than anybody."—"I own, my dear," cries he, "it was a mistake."—"A mistake, indeed!" answered she; "but when did you ever know me to make such mistakes?"—"But how comes it, sir," cries the landlord, "that such a great gentleman walks about the country afoot?"—"I don't know," returned Partridge; "great gentlemen have humours sometimes. He hath now a dozen horses and servants at Gloucester; and nothing would serve him, but last night, it being very hot weather, he must cool himself with a walk to yon high hill, whither I likewise walked with him to bear him company; but if ever you catch me there again: for I was never so frightened in all my life. We met with the strangest man there."—"I'll be hanged," cries the landlord, "if it was not the Man of the Hill, as they call him; if indeed he be a man; but I know several people who believe it is the devil that lives there."—"Nay, nay, like enough," says Partridge; "and now you put me in the head of it, I verily and sincerely believe it was the devil, though I could not perceive his cloven foot: but perhaps he might have the power given him to hide that, since evil spirits can appear in what shapes they please."—"And pray, sir," says the serjeant, "no offence, I hope; but pray what sort of a gentleman is the devil? For I have heard some of our officers say there is no such person; and that it is only a trick of the parsons, to prevent their being broke; for, if it was publickly known that there was no devil, the parsons would be of no more use than we are in time of peace."—"Those officers," says Partridge, "are very great scholars, I suppose."—"Not much of schollards neither," answered the serjeant; "they have not half your learning, sir, I believe; and, to be sure, I thought there must be a devil, notwithstanding what they said, though one of them was a captain; for methought, thinks I to myself, if there be no devil, how can wicked people be sent to him? and I have read all that upon a book."—"Some of your officers," quoth the landlord, "will find there is a devil, to their shame, I believe. I don't question but he'll pay off some old scores upon my account. Here was one quartered upon me half a year, who had the conscience to take up one of my best beds, though he hardly spent a shilling a day in the house, and suffered his men to roast cabbages at the kitchen fire, because I would not give them a dinner on a Sunday. Every good Christian must desire there should be a devil for the punishment of such wretches."—"Harkee, landlord," said the serjeant, "don't abuse the cloth, for I won't take it."—"D—n the cloth!" answered the landlord, "I have suffered enough by them."—"Bear witness, gentlemen," says the serjeant, "he curses the king, and that's high treason."—"I curse the king! you villain," said the landlord. "Yes, you did," cries the serjeant; "you cursed the cloth, and that's cursing the king. It's all one and the same; for every man who curses the cloth would curse the king if he durst; so for matter o' that, it's all one and the same thing."—"Excuse me there, Mr Serjeant," quoth Partridge, "that's a *non sequitur*."—"None of your outlandish linguo," answered the serjeant, leaping from his seat; "I will not sit still and hear the cloth abused."—"You mistake me, friend," cries Partridge. "I did not mean to abuse the cloth; I only said your conclusion was a *non sequitur*.[1]"—"You are another," cries the serjeant," an you come to that. No more a *sequitur* than yourself. You are a pack of rascals, and I'll prove it; for I will fight the best man of you all for twenty pound." This challenge effectually silenced Partridge, whose stomach for drubbing did not so soon return after the hearty meal which he had lately been treated with; but the coachman, whose bones were less sore, and whose appetite for fighting was somewhat sharper, did not so easily brook the affront, of which he conceived some part at least fell to his share. He started therefore from his seat, and, advancing to the serjeant, swore he looked on himself to be as good a man as any in the army, and offered to box for a guinea. The military man accepted the combat, but refused the wager; upon which both immediately stript and engaged, till the driver of horses was so well mauled by the leader of men, that he was obliged to exhaust his small remainder of breath in begging for quarter.

---

[1] This word, which the serjeant unhappily mistook for an affront, is a term in logic, and means that the conclusion does not follow from the premises.

The young lady was now desirous to depart, and had given orders for her coach to be prepared; but all in vain, for the coachman was disabled from performing his office for that evening. An antient heathen would perhaps have imimputed this disability to the god of drink, no less than to the god of war; for, in reality, both the combatants had sacrificed as well to the former deity as to the latter. To speak plainly, they were both dead drunk, nor was Partridge in a much better situation. As for my landlord, drinking was his trade; and the liquor had no more effect on him than it had on any other vessel in his house.

The mistress of the inn, being summoned to attend Mr Jones and his companion at their tea, gave a full relation of the latter part of the foregoing scene; and at the same time expressed great concern for the young lady, "who," she said, "was under the utmost uneasiness at being prevented from pursuing her journey. She is a sweet pretty creature," added she, "and I am certain I have seen her face before. I fancy she is in love, and running away from her friends. Who knows but some young gentleman or other may be expecting her, with a heart as heavy as her own?"

Jones fetched a heavy sigh at those words; of which, though Mrs Waters observed it, she took no notice while the landlady continued in the room; but, after the departure of that good woman, she could not forbear giving our heroe certain hints on her suspecting some very dangerous rival in his affections. The aukward behaviour of Mr Jones on this occasion convinced her of the truth, without his giving her a direct answer to any of her questions; but she was not nice enough in her amours to be greatly concerned at the discovery. The beauty of Jones highly charmed her eye; but as she could not see his heart, she gave herself no concern about it. She could feast heartily at the table of love, without reflecting that some other already had been, or hereafter might be, feasted with the same repast. A sentiment which, if it deals but little in refinement, deals, however, much in substance; and is less capricious, and perhaps less ill-natured and selfish, than the desires of those females who can be contented enough to abstain from the possession of their lovers, provided they are sufficiently satisfied that no one else possesses them.

CHAPTER VII.

Containing a fuller account of Mrs Waters, and by what means she came into that distressful situation from which she was rescued by Jones.

Though Nature hath by no means mixed up an equal share either of curiosity or vanity in every human composition, there is perhaps no individual to whom she hath not allotted such a proportion of both as requires much arts, and pains too, to subdue and keep under;—a conquest, however, absolutely necessary to every one who would in any degree deserve the characters of wisdom or good breeding.

As Jones, therefore, might very justly be called a well-bred man, he had stifled all that curiosity which the extraordinary manner in which he had found Mrs Waters must be supposed to have occasioned. He had, indeed, at first thrown out some few hints to the lady; but, when he perceived her industriously avoiding any explanation, he was contented to remain in ignorance, the rather as he was not without suspicion that there were some circumstances which must have raised her blushes, had she related the whole truth.

Now since it is possible that some of our readers may not so easily acquiesce under the same ignorance, and as we are very desirous to satisfy them all, we have taken uncommon pains to inform ourselves of the real fact, with the relation of which we shall conclude this book.

This lady, then, had lived some years with one Captain Waters, who was a captain in the same regiment to which Mr Northerton belonged. She past for that gentleman's wife, and went by his name; and yet, as the serjeant said, there were some doubts concerning the reality of their marriage, which we shall not at present take upon us to resolve.

Mrs Waters, I am sorry to say it, had for some time contracted an intimacy with the above-mentioned ensign, which did no great credit to her reputation. That she had a remarkable fondness for that young fellow is most certain; but whether she indulged this to any very criminal lengths is not so extremely clear, unless we will suppose that women never grant every favour to a man but one, without granting him that one also.

The division of the regiment to which Captain Waters belonged had two days preceded the march of that company to which Mr Northerton was the ensign; so that the former had reached Worcester the very day after the unfortunate re-encounter between Jones and Northerton which we have before recorded.

Now, it had been agreed between Mrs Waters and the captain that she would accompany him in his march as far as Worcester, where they were to take their leave of each other, and she was thence to return to Bath, where she was to stay till the end of the winter's campaign against the rebels.

With this agreement Mr Northerton was made acquainted. To say the truth, the lady had made him an assignation at this very place, and promised to stay at Worcester till his division came thither; with what view, and for what purpose, must be left to the reader's divination; for, though we are obliged to relate facts, we are not obliged to do a violence to our nature by any comments to the disadvantage of the loveliest part of the creation.

Northerton no sooner obtained a release from his captivity, as we have seen, than he hasted away to overtake Mrs Waters; which, as he was a very active nimble fellow, he did at the last-mentioned city, some few hours after Captain Waters had left her. At his first arrival he made no scruple of acquainting her with the unfortunate accident; which he made appear very unfortunate indeed, for he totally extracted every particle of what could be called fault, at least in a court of honour, though he left some circumstances which might be questionable in a court of law.

Women, to their glory be it spoken, are more generally capable of that violent and apparently disinterested passion of love, which seeks only the good of its object, than men. Mrs Waters, therefore, was no sooner apprized of the danger to which her lover was exposed, than she lost every consideration besides that of his safety; and this being a matter equally agreeable to the gentleman, it became the immediate subject of debate between them.

After much consultation on this matter, it was at length agreed that the ensign should go across the country to Hereford, whence he might find some conveyance to one of the sea-ports in Wales, and thence might make his escape abroad. In all which expedition Mrs Waters declared she would bear him company; and for which she was able to furnish him with money, a very material article to Mr Northerton, she having then in her pocket three bank-notes to the amount of £90, besides some cash, and a diamond ring of pretty considerable value on her finger. All which she, with the utmost confidence, revealed to this wicked man, little suspecting she should by these means inspire him with a design of robbing her. Now, as they must, by taking horses from Worcester, have furnished any pursuers with the means of hereafter discovering their route, the ensign proposed, and the lady presently agreed, to make their first stage on foot; for which purpose the hardness of the frost was very seasonable.

The main part of the lady's baggage was already at Bath, and she had nothing with her at present besides a very small quantity of linen, which the gallant undertook to carry in his own pockets. All things, therefore, being settled in the evening, they arose early the next morning, and at five o'clock departed from Worcester, it being then above two hours before day, but the moon, which was then at the full, gave them all the light she was capable of affording.

Mrs Waters was not of that delicate race of women who are obliged to the invention of vehicles for the capacity of removing themselves from one place to another, and with whom consequently a coach is reckoned among the necessaries of life. Her limbs were indeed full of strength and agility, and, as her mind was no less animated with spirit, she was perfectly able to keep pace with her nimble lover.

Having travelled on for some miles in a high road, which Northerton said he was informed led to Hereford, they came at the break of day to the side of a large wood, where he suddenly stopped, and, affecting to meditate a moment with himself, expressed some apprehensions from travelling any longer in so public a way. Upon which he easily persuaded his fair companion to strike with him into a path which seemed to lead directly through the wood, and which at length brought them both to the bottom of Mazard Hill.

Whether the execrable scheme which he now attempted to execute was the effect of previous deliberation, or whether it now first came into his head, I cannot determine. But being arrived in this lonely place, where it was very improbable he should meet with any interruption, he suddenly slipped his garter from his leg, and, laying violent hands on the poor woman, endeavoured to perpetrate that dreadful and detestable fact which we have before commemorated, and which the providential appearance of Jones did so fortunately prevent.

Happy was it for Mrs Waters that she was not of the weakest order of females; for no sooner did she perceive, by his tying a knot in his garter, and by his declarations, what his hellish intentions were, than she stood stoutly to her defence, and so strongly struggled with her enemy, screaming all the while for assistance, that she delayed the execution of the villain's purpose several minutes, by which means Mr Jones came to her relief at that very instant when her strength failed and she was totally overpowered, and delivered her from the ruffian's hands, with no other loss than that of her cloaths, which were torn from her back, and of the diamond ring, which during the contention either dropped from her finger, or was wrenched from it by Northerton.

Thus, reader, we have given thee the fruits of a very painful enquiry which for thy satisfaction we have made into this matter. And here we have opened to thee a scene of folly as well as villany, which we could scarce have believed a human creature capable of being guilty of, had we not remembered that this fellow was at that time firmly persuaded that he had already committed a murder, and had forfeited his life to the law. As he concluded therefore that his only safety lay in flight, he thought the possessing himself of this poor woman's money and ring would make him amends for the additional burthen he was to lay on his conscience.

And here, reader, we must strictly caution thee that thou dost not take any occasion, from the misbehaviour of such a wretch as this, to reflect on so worthy and honourable a body of men as are the officers of our army in general. Thou wilt be pleased to consider that this fellow, as we have already informed thee, had neither the birth nor education of a gentleman, nor was a proper person to be enrolled among the number of such. If, therefore, his baseness can justly reflect on any besides himself, it must be only on those who gave him his commission.

BOOK X.

IN WHICH THE HISTORY GOES FORWARD ABOUT TWELVE HOURS.

CHAPTER I.

Containing instructions very necessary to be perused by modern critics.

Reader, it is impossible we should know what sort of person thou wilt be; for, perhaps, thou may'st be as learned in human nature as Shakespear himself was, and, perhaps, thou may'st be no wiser than some of his editors. Now, lest this latter should be the case, we think proper, before we go any farther together, to give thee a few wholesome admonitions; that thou may'st not as grossly misunderstand and misrepresent us, as some of the said editors have misunderstood and misrepresented their author.

First, then, we warn thee not too hastily to condemn any of the incidents in this our history as impertinent and foreign to our main design, because thou dost not immediately conceive in what manner such incident may conduce to that design. This work may, indeed, be considered as a great creation of our own; and for a little reptile of a critic to presume to find fault with any of its parts, without knowing the manner in which the whole is connected, and before he comes to the final catastrophe, is a most presumptuous absurdity. The allusion and metaphor we have here made use of, we must acknowledge to be infinitely too great for our occasion; but there is, indeed, no other, which is at all adequate to express the difference between an author of the first rate and a critic of the lowest.

Another caution we would give thee, my good reptile, is, that thou dost not find out too near a resemblance between certain characters here introduced; as, for instance, between the landlady who appears in the seventh book and her in the ninth. Thou art to know, friend, that there are certain characteristics in which most individuals of every profession and occupation agree. To be able to preserve these characteristics, and at the same time to diversify their operations, is one talent of a good writer. Again, to mark the nice distinction between two persons actuated by the same vice or folly is another; and, as this last talent is found in very few writers, so is the true discernment of it found in as few readers; though, I believe, the observation of this forms a very principal pleasure in those who are capable of the discovery; every person, for instance, can distinguish between Sir Epicure Mammon and Sir Fopling Flutter; but to note the difference between Sir Fopling Flutter and Sir Courtly Nice requires a more exquisite judgment: for want of which, vulgar spectators of plays very often do great injustice in the theatre; where I have sometimes known a poet in danger of being convicted as a thief, upon much worse evidence than the resemblance of hands hath been held to be in the law. In reality, I apprehend every amorous widow on the stage would run the hazard of being condemned as a servile imitation of Dido, but that happily very few of our play-house critics understand enough of Latin to read Virgil.

In the next place, we must admonish thee, my worthy friend (for, perhaps, thy heart may be better than thy head), not to condemn a character as a bad one, because it is not perfectly a good one. If thou dost delight in these models of perfection, there are books enow written to gratify thy taste; but, as we have not, in the course of our conversation, ever happened to meet with any such person, we have not chosen to introduce any such here. To say the truth, I a little question whether mere man ever arrived at this consummate degree of excellence, as well as whether there hath ever existed a monster bad enough to verify that

——nulla virtute redemptum
A vitiis——[1]

in Juvenal; nor do I, indeed, conceive the good purposes served by inserting characters of such angelic perfection, or such diabolical depravity, in any work of invention; since, from contemplating either, the mind of man is more likely to be overwhelmed with sorrow and shame than to draw any good uses from such patterns; for in the former instance he may be both concerned and ashamed to see a pattern of excellence in his nature, which he may reasonably despair of ever arriving at; and in contemplating the latter he may be no less affected with those uneasy sensations, at seeing the nature of which he is a partaker degraded into so odious and detestable a creature.

In fact, if there be enough of goodness in a character to engage the admiration and affection of a well-disposed mind, though there should appear some of those little blemishes *quas humana parum cavit natura,* they will raise our compassion rather than our abhorrence. Indeed, nothing can be of more moral use than the imperfections which are seen in examples of this kind; since such form a kind of surprize, more apt to affect and dwell upon our minds than the faults of very vicious and wicked persons. The foibles and vices of men, in whom there is great mixture of good, become more glaring objects from the virtues which contrast them and shew their deformity; and when we find such vices attended with their evil consequence to our favourite characters, we are not only taught to shun them for our own sake, but to hate them for the mischiefs they have already brought on those we love.

And now, my friend, having given you these few admonitions, we will, if you please, once more set forward with our history.

---

[1] Whose vices are not allayed with a single virtue

CHAPTER II.

Containing the arrival of an Irish gentleman, with very extraordinary adventures which ensued at the inn.

Now the little trembling hare, which the dread of all her numerous enemies, and chiefly of that cunning, cruel, carnivorous animal, man, had confined all the day to her lurking-place, sports wantonly o'er the lawns; now on some hollow tree the owl, shrill chorister of the night, hoots forth notes which might charm the ears of some modern connoisseurs in music; now, in the imagination of the half-drunk clown, as he staggers through the churchyard, or rather charnelyard, to his home, fear paints the bloody hobgoblin; now thieves and ruffians are awake, and honest watchmen fast asleep; in plain English, it was now midnight; and the company at the inn, as well those who have been already mentioned in this history, as some others who arrived in the evening, were all in bed. Only Susan Chambermaid was now stirring, she being obliged to wash the kitchen before she retired to the arms of the fond expecting hostler.

In this posture were affairs at the inn when a gentleman arrived there post. He immediately alighted from his horse, and, coming up to Susan, enquired of her, in a very abrupt and confused manner, being almost out of breath with eagerness, Whether there was any lady in the house? The hour of night, and the behaviour of the man, who stared very wildly all the time, a little surprized Susan, so that she hesitated before she made any answer; upon which the gentleman, with redoubled eagerness, begged her to give him a true information, saying, He had lost his wife, and was come in pursuit of her. "Upon my shoul," cries he, "I have been near catching her already in two or three places, if I had not found her gone just as I came up with her. If she be in the house, do carry me up in the dark and show her to me; and if she be gone away before me, do tell me which way I shall go after her to meet her, and, upon my shoul, I will make you the richest poor woman in the nation." He then pulled out a handful of guineas, a sight which would have bribed persons of much greater consequence than this poor wench to much worse purposes.

Susan, from the account she had received of Mrs Waters, made not the least doubt but that she was the very identical stray whom the right owner pursued. As she concluded, therefore, with great appearance of reason, that she never could get money in an honester way than by restoring a wife to her husband, she made no scruple of assuring the gentleman that the lady he wanted was then in the house; and was presently afterwards prevailed upon (by very liberal promises, and some earnest paid into her hands) to conduct him to the bedchamber of Mrs Waters.

It hath been a custom long established in the polite world, and that upon very solid and substantial reasons, that a husband shall never enter his wife's apartment without first knocking at the door. The many excellent uses of this custom need scarce be hinted to a reader who hath any knowledge of the world; for by this means the lady hath time to adjust herself, or to remove any disagreeable object out of the way; for there are some situations in which nice and delicate women would not be discovered by their husbands.

To say the truth, there are several ceremonies instituted among the polished part of mankind, which, though they may, to coarser judgments, appear as matters of mere form, are found to have much of substance in them, by the more discerning; and lucky would it have been had the custom above mentioned been observed by our gentleman in the present instance. Knock, indeed, he did at the door, but not with one of those gentle raps which is usual on such occasions. On the contrary, when he found the door locked, he flew at it with such violence, that the lock immediately gave way, the door burst open, and he fell headlong into the room.

He had no sooner recovered his legs than forth from the bed, upon his legs likewise, appeared—with shame and sorrow are we obliged to proceed—our heroe himself, who, with a menacing voice, demanded of the gentleman who he was, and what he meant by daring to burst open his chamber in that outrageous manner.

The gentleman at first thought he had committed a mistake, and was going to ask pardon and retreat, when, on a sudden, as the moon shone very bright, he cast his eyes on stays, gowns, petticoats, caps, ribbons, stockings, garters, shoes, clogs, &c., all which lay in a disordered manner on the floor. All these, operating on the natural jealousy of his temper, so enraged him, that he lost all power of speech; and, without returning any answer to Jones, he endeavoured to approach the bed.

Jones immediately interposing, a fierce contention arose, which soon proceeded to blows on both sides. And now Mrs Waters (for we must confess she was in the same bed), being, I suppose, awakened from her sleep, and seeing two men fighting in her bedchamber, began to scream in the most violent manner, crying out murder! robbery! and more frequently rape! which last, some, perhaps, may wonder she should mention, who do not consider that these words of exclamation are used by ladies in a fright, as fa, la, la, ra, da, &c., are in music, only as the vehicles of sound, and without any fixed ideas.

Next to the lady's chamber was deposited the body of an Irish gentleman who arrived too late at the inn to have been mentioned before. This gentleman was one of those whom the Irish call a calabalaro, or cavalier. He was a younger brother of a good family, and, having no fortune at home, was obliged to look abroad in order to get one; for which purpose he was proceeding to the Bath, to try his luck with cards and the women.

This young fellow lay in bed reading one of Mrs Behn's novels; for he had been instructed by a friend that he would find no more effectual method of recommending himself to the ladies than the improving his understanding, and filling his mind with good literature. He no sooner, therefore, heard the violent uproar in the next room, than he leapt from his bolster, and, taking his sword in one hand, and the candle which burnt by him in the other, he went directly to Mrs Waters's chamber.

If the sight of another man in his shirt at first added some shock to the decency of the lady, it made her presently amends by considerably abating her fears; for no sooner had the calabalaro entered the room than he cried out, "Mr Fitzpatrick, what the devil is the maning of this?" Upon which the other immediately answered, "O, Mr Maclachlan! I am rejoiced you are here.—This villain hath debauched my wife, and is got into bed with her."—"What wife?" cries Maclachlan; "do not I know Mrs Fitzpatrick very well, and don't I see that the lady, whom the gentleman who stands here in his shirt is lying in bed with, is none of her?"

Fitzpatrick, now perceiving, as well by the glimpse he had of the lady, as by her voice, which might have been distinguished at a greater distance than he now stood from her, that he had made a very unfortunate mistake, began to ask many pardons of the lady; and then, turning to Jones, he said, "I would have you take notice I do not ask your pardon, for you have bate me; for which I am resolved to have your blood in the morning."

Jones treated this menace with much contempt; and Mr Maclachlan answered, "Indeed, Mr Fitzpatrick, you may be ashamed of your own self, to disturb people at this time of night; if all the people in the inn were not asleep, you would have awakened them as you have me. The gentleman has served you very rightly. Upon my conscience, though I have no wife, if you had treated her so, I would have cut your throat."

Jones was so confounded with his fears for his lady's reputation, that he knew neither what to say or do; but the invention of women is, as hath been observed, much readier than that of men. She recollected that there was a communication between her chamber and that of Mr Jones; relying, therefore, on his honour and her own assurance, she answered, "I know not what you mean, villains! I am wife to none of you. Help! Rape! Murder! Rape!"—And now, the landlady coming into the room, Mrs Waters fell upon her with the utmost virulence, saying, "She thought herself in a sober inn, and not in a bawdy-house; but that a set of villains had broke into her room, with an intent upon her honour, if not upon her life; and both, she said, were equally dear to her."

The landlady now began to roar as loudly as the poor woman in bed had done before. She cried, "She was undone, and that the reputation of her house, which was never blown upon before, was utterly destroyed." Then, turning to the men, she cried, "What, in the devil's name, is the reason of all this disturbance in the lady's room?" Fitzpatrick, hanging down his head, repeated, "That he had committed a mistake, for which he heartily asked pardon," and then retired with his countryman. Jones, who was too ingenious to have missed the hint given him by his fair one, boldly asserted, "That he had run to her assistance upon hearing the door broke open, with what design he could not conceive, unless of robbing the lady; which, if they intended, he said, he had the good fortune to prevent." "I never had a robbery committed in my house since I have kept it," cries the landlady; "I would have you to know, sir, I harbour no highwaymen here; I scorn the word, thof I say it. None but honest, good gentlefolks, are welcome to my house; and, I thank good luck, I have always had enow of such customers; indeed as many as I could entertain. Here hath been my lord—," and then she repeated over a catalogue of names and titles, many of which we might, perhaps, be guilty of a breach of privilege by inserting.

Jones, after much patience, at length interrupted her, by making an apology to Mrs Waters, for having appeared before her in his shirt, assuring her "That nothing but a concern for her safety could have prevailed on him to do it." The reader may inform himself of her answer, and, indeed, of her whole behaviour to the end of the scene, by considering the situation which she affected, it being that of a modest lady, who was awakened out of her sleep by three strange men in her chamber. This was the part which she undertook to perform; and, indeed, she executed it so well, that none of our theatrical actresses could exceed her, in any of their performances, either on or off the stage.

And hence, I think, we may very fairly draw an argument, to prove how extremely natural virtue is to the fair sex; for, though there is not, perhaps, one in ten thousand who is capable of making a good actress, and even among these we rarely see two who are equally able to personate the same character, yet this of virtue they can all admirably well put on; and as well those individuals who have it not, as those who possess it, can all act it to the utmost degree of perfection.

When the men were all departed, Mrs Waters, recovering from her fear, recovered likewise from her anger, and spoke in much gentler accents to the landlady, who did not so readily quit her concern for the reputation of the house, in favour of which she began again to number the many great persons who had slept under her roof; but the lady stopt her short, and having absolutely acquitted her of having had any share in the past disturbance, begged to be left to her repose, which, she said, she hoped to enjoy unmolested during the remainder of the night. Upon which the landlady, after much civility and many courtsies, took her leave.

CHAPTER III.

A dialogue between the landlady and Susan the chamber-maid, proper to be read by all inn-keepers and their servants; with the arrival, and affable behaviour of a beautiful young lady; which may teach

persons of condition how they may acquire the love of the whole world.

The landlady, remembering that Susan had been the only person out of bed when the door was burst open, resorted presently to her, to enquire into the first occasion of the disturbance, as well as who the strange gentleman was, and when and how he arrived.

Susan related the whole story which the reader knows already, varying the truth only in some circumstances, as she saw convenient, and totally concealing the money which she had received. But whereas her mistress had, in the preface to her enquiry, spoken much in compassion for the fright which the lady had been in concerning any intended depredations on her virtue, Susan could not help endeavouring to quiet the concern which her mistress seemed to be under on that account, by swearing heartily she saw Jones leap out from her bed.

The landlady fell into a violent rage at these words. "A likely story, truly," cried she, "that a woman should cry out, and endeavour to expose herself, if that was the case! I desire to know what better proof any lady can give of her virtue than her crying out, which, I believe, twenty people can witness for her she did? I beg, madam, you would spread no such scandal of any of my guests; for it will not only reflect on them, but upon the house; and I am sure no vagabonds, nor wicked beggarly people, come here."

"Well," says Susan, "then I must not believe my own eyes." "No, indeed, must you not always," answered her mistress; "I would not have believed my own eyes against such good gentlefolks. I have not had a better supper ordered this half-year than they ordered last night; and so easy and good-humoured were they, that they found no fault with my Worcestershire perry, which I sold them for champagne; and to be sure it is as well tasted and as wholesome as the best champagne in the kingdom, otherwise I would scorn to give it 'em; and they drank me two bottles. No, no, I will never believe any harm of such sober good sort of people."

Susan being thus silenced, her mistress proceeded to other matters. "And so you tell me," continued she, "that the strange gentleman came post, and there is a footman without with the horses; why, then, he is certainly some of your great gentlefolks too. Why did not you ask him whether he'd have any supper? I think he is in the other gentleman's room; go up and ask whether he called. Perhaps he'll order something when he finds anybody stirring in the house to dress it. Now don't commit any of your usual blunders, by telling him the fire's out, and the fowls alive. And if he should order mutton, don't blab out that we have none. The butcher, I know, killed a sheep just before I went to bed, and he never refuses to cut it up warm when I desire it. Go, remember there's all sorts of mutton and fowls; go, open the door with, Gentlemen, d'ye call? and if they say nothing, ask what his honour will be pleased to have for supper? Don't forget his honour. Go; if you don't mind all these matters better, you'll never come to anything."

Susan departed, and soon returned with an account that the two gentlemen were got both into the same bed. "Two gentlemen," says the landlady, "in the same bed! that's impossible; they are two arrant scrubs, I warrant them; and I believe young Squire Allworthy guessed right, that the fellow intended to rob her ladyship; for, if he had broke open the lady's door with any of the wicked designs of a gentleman, he would never have sneaked away to another room to save the expense of a supper and a bed to himself. They are certainly thieves, and their searching after a wife is nothing but a pretence."

In these censures my landlady did Mr Fitzpatrick great injustice; for he was really born a gentleman, though not worth a groat; and though, perhaps, he had some few blemishes in his heart as well as in his head, yet being a sneaking or a niggardly fellow was not one of them. In reality, he was so generous a man, that, whereas he had received a very handsome fortune with his wife, he had now spent every penny of it, except some little pittance which was settled upon her; and, in order to possess himself of this, he had used her with such cruelty, that, together with his jealousy, which was of the bitterest kind, it had forced the poor woman to run away from him.

This gentleman then being well tired with his long journey from Chester in one day, with which, and some good dry blows he had received in the scuffle, his bones were so sore, that, added to the soreness of his mind, it had quite deprived him of any appetite for eating. And being now so violently disappointed in the woman whom, at the maid's instance, he had mistaken for his wife, it never once entered into his head that she might nevertheless be in the house, though he had erred in the first person he had attacked. He therefore yielded to the dissuasions of his friend from searching any farther after her that night, and accepted the kind offer of part of his bed.

The footman and post-boy were in a different disposition. They were more ready to order than the landlady was to provide; however, after being pretty well satisfied by them of the real truth of the case, and that Mr Fitzpatrick was no thief, she was at length prevailed on to set some cold meat before them, which they were devouring with great greediness, when Partridge came into the kitchen. He had been first awaked by the hurry which we have before seen; and while he was endeavouring to compose himself again on his pillow, a screech-owl had given him such a serenade at his window, that he leapt in a most horrible affright from his bed, and, huddling on his cloaths with great expedition, ran down to the protection of the company, whom he heard talking below in the kitchen.

His arrival detained my landlady from returning to her rest; for she was just about to leave the other two guests to the care of Susan; but the friend of young Squire Allworthy was not to be so neglected, especially as he called for a pint of wine to be mulled. She immediately obeyed, by putting the same quantity of perry to the fire; for this readily answered to the name of every kind of wine.

The Irish footman was retired to bed, and the post-boy was going to follow; but Partridge invited him to stay and partake of his wine, which the lad very thankfully accepted. The schoolmaster was indeed afraid to return to bed by himself; and as he did not know how soon he might lose the company of my landlady, he was resolved to secure that of the boy, in whose presence he apprehended no danger from the devil or any of his adherents.

And now arrived another post-boy at the gate; upon which Susan, being ordered out, returned, introducing two young women in riding habits, one of which was so very richly laced, that Partridge and the post-boy instantly started from their chairs, and my landlady fell to her courtsies, and her ladyships, with great eagerness.

The lady in the rich habit said, with a smile of great condescension, "If you will give me leave, madam, I will warm myself a few minutes at your kitchen fire, for it is really very cold; but I must insist on disturbing no one from his seat." This was spoken on account of Partridge, who had retreated to the other end of the room, struck with the utmost awe and astonishment at the splendor of the lady's dress. Indeed, she had a much better title to respect than this; for she was one of the most beautiful creatures in the world.

The lady earnestly desired Partridge to return to his seat; but could not prevail. She then pulled off her gloves, and displayed to the fire two hands, which had every property of snow in them, except that of melting. Her companion, who was indeed her maid, likewise pulled off her gloves, and discovered what bore an exact resemblance, in cold and colour, to a piece of frozen beef.

"I wish, madam," quoth the latter, "your ladyship would not think of going any farther to-night. I am terribly afraid your ladyship will not be able to bear the fatigue."

"Why sure," cries the landlady, "her ladyship's honour can never intend it. O, bless me! farther to-night, indeed! let me beseech your ladyship not to think on't——But, to be sure, your ladyship can't. What will your honour be pleased to have for supper? I have mutton of all kinds, and some nice chicken."

"I think, madam," said the lady, "it would be rather breakfast than supper; but I can't eat anything; and, if I stay, shall only lie down for an hour or two. However, if you please, madam, you may get me a little sack whey, made very small and thin."

"Yes, madam," cries the mistress of the house, "I have some excellent white wine."—"You have no sack, then?" says the lady. "Yes, an't please your honour, I have; I may challenge the country for that—but let me beg your ladyship to eat something."

"Upon my word, I can't eat a morsel," answered the lady; "and I shall be much obliged to you if you will please to get my apartment ready as soon as possible; for I am resolved to be on horseback again in three hours."

"Why, Susan," cries the landlady, "is there a fire lit yet in the Wild-goose? I am sorry, madam, all my best rooms are full. Several people of the first quality are now in bed. Here's a great young squire, and many other great gentlefolks of quality." Susan answered, "That the Irish gentlemen were got into the Wild-goose."

"Was ever anything like it?" says the mistress; "why the devil would you not keep some of the best rooms for the quality, when you know scarce a day passes without some calling here?——If they be gentlemen, I am certain, when they know it is for her ladyship, they will get up again."

"Not upon my account," says the lady; "I will have no person disturbed for me. If you have a room that is commonly decent, it will serve me very well, though it be never so plain. I beg, madam, you will not give yourself so much trouble on my account." "O, madam!" cries the other, "I have several very good rooms for that matter, but none good enough for your honour's ladyship. However, as you are so condescending to take up with the best I have, do, Susan, get a fire in the Rose this minute. Will your ladyship be pleased to go up now, or stay till the fire is lighted?" "I think I have sufficiently warmed myself," answered the lady; "so, if you please, I will go now; I am afraid I have kept people, and particularly that gentleman (meaning Partridge), too long in the cold already. Indeed, I cannot bear to think of keeping any person from the fire this dreadful weather."—She then departed with her maid, the landlady marching with two lighted candles before her.

When that good woman returned, the conversation in the kitchen was all upon the charms of the young lady. There is indeed in perfect beauty a power which none almost can withstand; for my landlady, though she was not pleased at the negative given to the supper, declared she had never seen so lovely a creature. Partridge ran out into the most extravagant encomiums on her face, though he could not refrain from paying some compliments to the gold lace on her habit; the post-boy sung forth the praises of her goodness, which were likewise echoed by the other post-boy, who was now come in. "She's a true good lady, I warrant her," says he; "for she hath mercy upon dumb creatures; for she asked me every now and tan upon the journey, if I did not think she should hurt the horses by riding too fast? and when she came in she charged me to give them as much corn as ever they would eat."

Such charms are there in affability, and so sure is it to attract the praises of all kinds of people. It may indeed be compared to the celebrated Mrs Hussey.[1] It is

[1] A celebrated mantua-maker in the Strand, famous for setting off the shapes of women.

equally sure to set off every female perfection to the highest advantage, and to palliate and conceal every defect. A short reflection, which we could not forbear making in this place, where my reader hath seen the loveliness of an affable deportment; and truth will now oblige us to contrast it, by showing the reverse.

CHAPTER IV.

Containing infallible nostrums for procuring universal disesteem and hatred.

The lady had no sooner laid herself on her pillow than the waiting-woman returned to the kitchen to regale with some of those dainties which her mistress had refused.

The company, at her entrance, shewed her the same respect which they had before paid to her mistress, by rising; but she forgot to imitate her, by desiring them to sit down again. Indeed, it was scarce possible they should have done so, for she placed her chair in such a posture as to occupy almost the whole fire. She then ordered a chicken to be broiled that instant, declaring, if it was not ready in a quarter of an hour, she would not stay for it. Now, though the said chicken was then at roost in the stable, and required the several ceremonies of catching, killing, and picking, before it was brought to the gridiron, my landlady would nevertheless have undertaken to do all within the time; but the guest, being unfortunately admitted behind the scenes, must have been witness to the *fourberie*; the poor woman was therefore obliged to confess that she had none in the house; "but, madam," said she, "I can get any kind of mutton in an instant from the butcher's."

"Do you think, then," answered the waiting-gentlewoman, "that I have the stomach of a horse, to eat mutton at this time of night? Sure you people that keep inns imagine your betters are like yourselves. Indeed, I expected to get nothing at this wretched place. I wonder my lady would stop at it. I suppose none but tradesmen and grasiers ever call here." The landlady fired at this indignity offered to her house; however, she suppressed her temper, and contented herself with saying, "Very good quality frequented it, she thanked heaven!" "Don't tell me," cries the other, "of quality! I believe I know more of people of quality than such as you.—But, prithee, without troubling me with any of your impertinence, do tell me what I can have for supper; for, though I cannot eat horse-flesh, I am really hungry." "Why, truly, madam," answered the landlady, "you could not take me again at such a disadvantage; for I must confess I have nothing in the house, unless a cold piece of beef, which indeed a gentleman's footman and the post-boy have almost cleared to the bone." "Woman," said Mrs Abigail (so for shortness we will call her), "I entreat you not to make me sick. If I had fasted a month, I could not eat what had been touched by the fingers of such fellows. Is there nothing neat or decent to be had in this horrid place?" "What think you of some eggs and bacon, madam?" said the landlady. "Are your eggs new laid? are you certain they were laid to-day? and let me have the bacon cut very nice and thin; for I can't endure anything that's gross.—Prithee try if you can do a little tolerably for once, and don't think you have a farmer's wife, or some of those creatures, in the house."—The landlady began then to handle her knife; but the other stopt her, saying, "Good woman, I must insist upon your first washing your hands; for I am extremely nice, and have been always used from my cradle to have everything in the most elegant manner."

The landlady, who governed herself with much difficulty, began now the necessary preparations; for as to Susan, she was utterly rejected, and with such disdain, that the poor wench was as hard put to it to restrain her hands from violence as her mistress had been to hold her tongue. This indeed Susan did not entirely; for, though she literally kept it within her teeth, yet there it muttered many "marry-come-ups, as good flesh and blood as yourself;" with other such indignant phrases.

While the supper was preparing, Mrs Abigail began to lament she had not ordered a fire in the parlour; but, she said, that was now too late. "However," said she, "I have novelty to recommend a kitchen; for I do not believe I ever eat in one before." Then, turning to the post-boys, she asked them, "Why they were not in the stable with their horses? If I must eat my hard fare here, madam," cries she to the landlady, "I beg the kitchen may be kept clear, that I may not be surrounded with all the blackguards in town: as for you, sir," says she to Partridge, "you look somewhat like a gentleman, and may sit still if you please; I don't desire to disturb anybody but mob."

"Yes, yes, madam," cries Partridge, "I am a gentleman, I do assure you, and I am not so easily to be disturbed. *Non semper vox casualis est verbo nominativus.*" This Latin she took to be some affront, and answered, "You may be a gentleman, sir; but you don't show yourself as one to talk Latin to a woman." Partridge made a gentle reply, and concluded with more Latin; upon which she tossed up her nose, and contented herself by abusing him with the name of a great scholar.

The supper being now on the table, Mrs Abigail eat very heartily for so delicate a person; and, while a second course of the same was by her order preparing, she said, "And so, madam, you tell me your house is frequented by people of great quality?"

The landlady answered in the affirmative, saying, "There were a great many very good quality and gentlefolks in it now. There's young Squire Allworthy, as that gentleman there knows."

"And pray who is this young gentleman of quality, this young Squire Allworthy?" said Abigail.

"Who should he be," answered Partridge, "but the son and heir of the great Squire Allworthy, of Somersetshire!"

"Upon my word," said she, "you tell me strange news; for I know Mr Allworthy of Somersetshire very well, and I know he hath no son alive."

The landlady pricked up her ears at this, and Partridge looked a little confounded. However, after a short hesitation, he answered, "Indeed, madam, it is true, everybody doth not know him to be Squire Allworthy's son; for he was never married to his mother; but his son he certainly is, and will be his heir too, as certainly as his name is Jones." At that word, Abigail let drop the bacon which she was conveying to her mouth, and cried out, "You surprize me, sir! Is it possible Mr Jones should be now in the house?" "*Quare non?*" answered Partridge, "it is possible, and it is certain."

Abigail now made haste to finish the remainder of her meal, and then repaired back to her mistress, when the conversation passed which may be read in the next chapter.

CHAPTER V.

Showing who the amiable lady, and her unamiable maid, were.

As in the month of June, the damask rose, which chance hath planted among the lilies, with their candid hue mixes his vermilion; or as some playsome heifer in the pleasant month of May diffuses her odoriferous breath over the flowery meadows; or as, in the blooming month of April, the gentle, constant dove, perched on some fair bough, sits meditating on her mate; so, looking a hundred charms and breathing as many sweets, her thoughts being fixed on her Tommy, with a heart as good and innocent as her face was beautiful, Sophia (for it was she herself) lay reclining her lovely head on her hand, when her maid entered the room, and, running directly to the bed, cried, "Madam—madam—who doth your ladyship think is in the house?" Sophia, starting up, cried, "I hope my father hath not overtaken us." "No, madam, it is one worth a hundred fathers; Mr Jones himself is here at this very instant." "Mr Jones!" says Sophia, "it is impossible! I cannot be so fortunate." Her maid averred the fact, and was presently detached by her mistress to order him to be called; for she said she was resolved to see him immediately.

Mrs Honour had no sooner left the kitchen in the manner we have before seen than the landlady fell severely upon her. The poor woman had indeed been loading her heart with foul language for some time, and now it scoured out of her mouth, as filth doth from a mud-cart, when the board which confines it is removed. Partridge likewise shovelled in his share of calumny, and (what may surprize the reader) not only bespattered the maid, but attempted to sully the lily-white character of Sophia herself. "Never a barrel the better herring," cries he, "*Noscitur a socio*, is a true saying. It must be confessed, indeed, that the lady in the fine garments is the civiller of the two; but I warrant neither of them are a bit better than they should be. A couple of Bath trulls, I'll answer for them; your quality don't ride about at this time o' night without servants." "Sbodlikins, and that's true," cries the landlady, "you have certainly hit upon the very matter; for quality don't come into a house without bespeaking a supper, whether they eat or no."

While they were thus discoursing, Mrs Honour returned and discharged her commission, by bidding the landlady immediately wake Mr Jones, and tell him a lady wanted to speak with him. The landlady referred her to Partridge, saying, "he was the squire's friend: but, for her part, she never called men-folks, especially gentlemen," and then walked sullenly out of the kitchen. Honour applied herself to Partridge; but he refused, "for my friend," cries he, "went to bed very late, and he would be very angry to be disturbed so soon." Mrs Honour insisted still to have him called, saying, "she was sure, instead of being angry, that he would be to the highest degree delighted when he knew the occasion." "Another time, perhaps, he might," cries Partridge; "but *non omnia possumus omnes*. One woman is enough at once for a reasonable man." "What do you mean by one woman, fellow?" cries Honour. "None of your fellow," answered Partridge. He then proceeded to inform her plainly that Jones was in bed with a wench, and made use of an expression too indelicate to be here inserted; which so enraged Mrs Honour, that she called him jackanapes, and returned in a violent hurry to her mistress, whom she acquainted with the success of her errand, and with the account she had received; which, if possible, she exaggerated, being as angry with Jones as if he had pronounced all the words that came from the mouth of Partridge. She discharged a torrent of abuse on the master, and advised her mistress to quit all thoughts of a man who had never shown himself deserving of her. She then ripped up the story of Molly Seagrim, and gave the most malicious turn to his formerly quitting Sophia herself; which, I must confess, the present incident not a little countenanced.

The spirits of Sophia were too much dissipated by concern to enable her to stop the torrent of her maid. At last, however, she interrupted her, saying, "I never can believe this; some villain hath belied him. You say you had it from his friend; but surely it is not the office of a friend to betray such secrets." "I suppose," cries Honour, "the fellow is his pimp; for I never saw so ill-looked a villain. Besides, such profligate rakes as Mr Jones are never ashamed of these matters."

To say the truth, this behaviour of Partridge was a little inexcusable; but he had not slept off the effect of the dose which he swallowed the evening before; which had, in the morning, received the addition of above a pint of wine, or indeed rather of malt spirits; for the perry was by no means pure. Now, that part of his head which Nature designed for the reservoir of drink being very shallow, a small quantity of liquor overflowed it, and opened the sluices of his heart; so that all the secrets there deposited run out. These sluices were indeed, naturally, very ill-secured. To give the best-natured turn we can to his disposition, he was a very honest man; for, as he was the most inquisitive of mortals, and eternally prying into the secrets of others, so he very faithfully paid them by communicating, in return, everything within his knowledge.

While Sophia, tormented with anxiety, knew not what to believe, nor what resolution to take, Susan arrived with the sack-whey. Mrs Honour immediately advised her mistress, in a whisper, to pump this wench, who probably could inform her of the truth. Sophia approved it, and began as follows: "Come hither, child; now answer me truly what I am going to ask you, and I promise you I will very well reward you. Is there a young gentleman in this house, a handsome young gentleman, that——." Here Sophia blushed and was confounded. "A young gentleman," cries Honour, "that came hither in company with that saucy rascal who is now in the kitchen?" Susan answered, "There was."—"Do you know anything of any lady?" continues Sophia, "any lady? I don't ask you whether she is handsome or no; perhaps she is not; that's nothing to the purpose; but do you know of any lady?" "La, madam," cries Honour, "you will make a very bad examiner. Hark'ee, child," says she, "is not that very young gentleman now in bed with some nasty trull or other?" Here Susan smiled, and was silent. "Answer the question, child," says Sophia, "and here's a guinea for you."—"A guinea! madam," cries Susan; "la, what's a guinea? If my mistress should know it I shall certainly lose my place that very instant." "Here's another for you," says Sophia, "and I promise you faithfully your mistress shall never know it." Susan, after a very short hesitation, took the money, and told the whole story, concluding with saying, "If you have any great curiosity, madam, I can steal softly into his room, and see whether he be in his own bed or no." She accordingly did this by Sophia's desire, and returned with an answer in the negative.

Sophia now trembled and turned pale. Mrs Honour begged her to be comforted, and not to think any more of so worthless a fellow. "Why there," says Susan, "I hope, madam, your ladyship won't be offended; but pray, madam, is not your ladyship's name Madam Sophia Western?" "How is it possible you should know me?" answered Sophia. "Why that man, that the gentlewoman spoke of, who is in the kitchen, told about you last night. But I hope your ladyship is not angry with me." "Indeed, child," said she, "I am not; pray tell me all, and I promise you I'll reward you." "Why, madam," continued Susan, "that man told us all in the kitchen that Madam Sophia Western—indeed I don't know how to bring it out."—Here she stopt, till, having received encouragement from Sophia, and being vehemently pressed by Mrs Honour, she proceeded thus:—"He told us, madam, though to be sure it is all a lie, that your ladyship was dying for love of the young squire, and that he was going to the wars to get rid of you. I thought to myself then he was a false-hearted wretch; but, now, to see such a fine, rich, beautiful lady as you be, forsaken for such an ordinary woman; for to be sure so she is, and another man's wife into the bargain. It is such a strange unnatural thing, in a manner."

Sophia gave her a third guinea, and, telling her she would certainly be her friend if she mentioned nothing of what had passed, nor informed any one who she was, dismissed the girl, with orders to the post-boy to get the horses ready immediately.

Being now left alone with her maid, she told her trusty waiting-woman, "That she never was more easy than at present. I am now convinced," said she, "he is not only a villain, but a low despicable wretch. I can forgive all rather than his exposing my name in so barbarous a manner. That renders him the object of my contempt. Yes, Honour, I am now easy; I am indeed; I am very easy;" and then she burst into a violent flood of tears.

After a short interval spent by Sophia, chiefly in crying, and assuring her maid that she was perfectly easy, Susan arrived with an account that the horses were ready, when a very extraordinary thought suggested itself to our young heroine, by which Mr Jones would be acquainted with her having been at the inn, in a way which, if any sparks of affection for her remained in him, would be at least some punishment for his faults.

The reader will be pleased to remember a little muff, which hath had the honour of being more than once remembered already in this history. This muff, ever since the departure of Mr Jones, had been the constant companion of Sophia by day, and her bedfellow by night; and this muff she had at this very instant upon her arm; whence she took it off with great indignation, and, having writ her name with her pencil upon a piece of paper which she pinned to it, she bribed the maid to convey it into the empty bed of Mr Jones, in which, if he did not find it, she charged her to take some method of conveying it before his eyes in the morning.

Then, having paid for what Mrs Honour had eaten, in which bill was included an account for what she herself might have eaten, she mounted her horse, and, once more assuring her companion that she was perfectly easy, continued her journey.

CHAPTER VI.

Containing, among other things, the ingenuity of Partridge, the madness of Jones, and the folly of Fitzpatrick.

It was now past five in the morning, and other company began to rise and come to the kitchen, among whom were the serjeant and the coachman, who, being thoroughly reconciled, made a libation, or, in the English phrase, drank a hearty cup together.

In this drinking nothing more remarkable happened than the behaviour of Partridge, who, when the serjeant drank a health to King George, repeated only the word King; nor could he be brought to utter more; for though he was going to fight against his own cause, yet he could not be prevailed upon to drink against it.

Mr Jones, being now returned to his own bed (but from whence he returned we must beg to be excused from relating), summoned Partridge from this agreeable company, who, after a ceremonious preface, having obtained leave to offer his advice, delivered himself as follows:—

"It is, sir, an old saying, and a true one, that a wise man may sometimes learn counsel from a fool; I wish, therefore, I might be so bold as to offer you my advice, which is to return home again, and leave these *horrida bella*, these bloody wars, to fellows who are contented to swallow gunpowder, because they have nothing else to eat. Now, everybody knows your honour wants for nothing at home; when that's the case, why should any man travel abroad?"

"Partridge," cries Jones, "thou art certainly a coward; I wish, therefore, thou wouldst return home thyself, and trouble me no more."

"I ask your honour's pardon," cries Partridge; "I spoke on your account more than my own; for as to me, Heaven knows my circumstances are bad enough, and I am so far from being afraid, that I value a pistol, or a blunderbuss, or any such thing, no more than a pop-gun. Every man must die once, and what signifies the manner how? besides, perhaps I may come off with the loss only of an arm or a leg. I assure you, sir, I was never less afraid in my life; and so, if your honour is resolved to go on, I am resolved to follow you. But, in that case, I wish I might give my opinion. To be sure, it is a scandalous way of travelling, for a great gentleman like you to walk afoot. Now here are two or three good horses in the stable, which the landlord will certainly make no scruple of trusting you with; but, if he should, I can easily contrive to take them; and, let the worst come to the worst, the king would certainly pardon you, as you are going to fight in his cause."

Now, as the honesty of Partridge was equal to his understanding, and both dealt only in small matters, he would never have attempted a roguery of this kind, had he not imagined it altogether safe; for he was one of those who have more consideration of the gallows than of the fitness of things; but, in reality, he thought he might have committed this felony without any danger; for, besides that he doubted not but the name of Mr Allworthy would sufficiently quiet the landlord, he conceived they should be altogether safe, whatever turn affairs might take; as Jones, he imagined, would have friends enough on one side, and as his friends would as well secure him on the other.

When Mr Jones found that Partridge was in earnest in this proposal, he very severely rebuked him, and that in such bitter terms, that the other attempted to laugh it off, and presently turned the discourse to other matters; saying, he believed they were then in a bawdy house, and that he had with much ado prevented two wenches from disturbing his honour in the middle of the night. "Heyday!" says he, "I believe they got into your chamber whether I would or no; for here lies the muff of one of them on the ground." Indeed, as Jones returned to his bed in the dark, he had never perceived the muff on the quilt, and, in leaping into his bed, he had tumbled it on the floor. This Partridge now took up, and was going to put into his pocket, when Jones desired to see it. The muff was so very remarkable, that our heroe might possibly have recollected it without the information annexed. But his memory was not put to that hard office; for at the same instant he saw and read the words Sophia Western upon the paper which was pinned to it. His looks now grew frantic in a moment, and he eagerly cried out, "Oh Heavens! how came this muff here?" "I know no more than your honour," cried Partridge; "but I saw it upon the arm of one of the women who would have disturbed you, if I would have suffered them." "Where are they?" cries Jones, jumping out of bed, and laying hold of his cloaths. "Many miles off, I believe, by this time," said Partridge. And now Jones, upon further enquiry, was sufficiently assured that the bearer of this muff was no other than the lovely Sophia herself.

The behaviour of Jones on this occasion, his thoughts, his looks, his words, his actions, were such as beggar all description. After many bitter execrations on Partridge, and not fewer on himself, he ordered the poor fellow, who was frightened out of his wits, to run down and hire him horses at any rate; and a very few minutes afterwards, having shuffled on his clothes, he hastened down-stairs to execute the orders himself, which he had just before given.

But before we proceed to what passed on his arrival in the kitchen, it will be necessary to recur to what had there happened since Partridge had first left it on his master's summons.

The serjeant was just marched off with his party, when the two Irish gentlemen arose, and came downstairs; both complaining that they had been so often waked by the noises in the inn, that they had never once been able to close their eyes all night.

The coach which had brought the young lady and her maid, and which, perhaps, the reader may have hitherto concluded was her own, was, indeed, a returned coach belonging to Mr King, of Bath, one of the worthiest and honestest men that ever dealt in horse-flesh, and whose coaches we heartily recommend to all our readers who travel that road. By which means they may, perhaps, have the pleasure of riding in the very coach, and being driven by the very coachman, that is recorded in this history.

The coachman, having but two passengers, and hearing Mr Maclachlan was going to Bath, offered to carry him thither at a very moderate price. He was induced to this by the report of the hostler, who said that the horse which Mr Maclachlan had hired from Worcester would be much more pleased with returning to his friends there than to prosecute a long journey; for that the said horse was rather a two-legged than a four-legged animal.

Mr Maclachlan immediately closed with the proposal of the coachman, and, at the same time, persuaded his friend Fitzpatrick to accept of the fourth place in the coach. This conveyance the soreness of his bones made more agreeable to him than a horse; and, being well assured of meeting with his wife at Bath, he thought a little delay would be of no consequence.

Maclachlan, who was much the sharper man of the two, no sooner heard that this lady came from Chester, with the other circumstances which he learned from the hostler, than it came into his head that she might possibly be his friend's wife; and presently acquainted him with this suspicion, which had never once occurred to Fitzpatrick himself. To say the truth, he was one of those compositions which nature makes up in too great a hurry, and forgets to put any brains into their head.

Now it happens to this sort of men, as to bad hounds, who never hit off a fault themselves; but no sooner doth a dog of sagacity open his mouth than they immediately do the same, and, without the guidance of any scent, run directly forwards as fast as they are able. In the same manner, the very moment Mr Maclachlan had mentioned his apprehension, Mr Fitzpatrick instantly concurred, and flew directly up-stairs, to surprize his wife, before he knew where she was; and unluckily (as Fortune loves to play tricks with those gentlemen who put themselves entirely under her conduct) ran his head against several doors and posts to no purpose. Much kinder was she to me, when she suggested that simile of the hounds, just before inserted; since the poor wife may, on these occasions, be so justly compared to a hunted hare. Like that little wretched animal, she pricks up her ears to listen after the voice of her pursuer; like her, flies away trembling when she hears it; and, like her, is generally overtaken and destroyed in the end.

This was not however the case at present; for after a long fruitless search, Mr Fitzpatrick returned to the kitchen, where, as if this had been a real chace, entered a gentleman hallowing as hunters do when the hounds are at a fault. He was just alighted from his horse, and had many attendants at his heels.

Here, reader, it may be necessary to acquaint thee with some matters, which, if thou dost know already, thou art wiser than I take thee to be. And this information thou shalt receive in the next chapter.

CHAPTER VII.

In which are concluded the adventures that happened at the inn at Upton.

In the first place, then, this gentleman just arrived was no other person than Squire Western himself, who was come hither in pursuit of his daughter; and, had he fortunately been two hours earlier, he had not only found her, but his niece into the bargain; for such was the wife of Mr Fitzpatrick, who had run away with her five years before, out of the custody of that sage lady, Madam Western.

Now this lady had departed from the inn much about the same time with Sophia; for, having been waked by the voice of her husband, she had sent up for the landlady, and being by her apprized of the matter, had bribed the good woman, at an extravagant price, to furnish her with horses for her escape. Such prevalence had money in this family; and though the mistress would have turned away her maid for a corrupt hussy, if she had known as much as the reader, yet she was no more proof against corruption herself than poor Susan had been.

Mr Western and his nephew were not known to one another; nor indeed would the former have taken any notice of the latter if he had known him; for, this being a stolen match, and consequently an unnatural one in the opinion of the good squire, he had, from the time of her committing it, abandoned the poor young creature, who was then no more than eighteen, as a monster, and had never since suffered her to be named in his presence.

The kitchen was now a scene of universal confusion, Western enquiring after his daughter, and Fitzpatrick as eagerly after his wife, when Jones entered the room, unfortunately having Sophia's muff in his hand.

As soon as Western saw Jones, he set up the same holla as is used by sportsmen when their game is in view. He then immediately run up and laid hold of Jones, crying, "We have got the dog fox, I warrant the bitch is not far off." The jargon which followed for some minutes, where many spoke different things at the same time, as it would be very difficult to describe, so would it be no less unpleasant to read.

Jones having, at length, shaken Mr Western off, and some of the company having interfered between them, our heroe protested his innocence as to knowing anything of the lady; when Parson Supple stepped up, and said, "It is folly to deny it; for why, the marks of guilt are in thy hands. I will myself asseverate and bind it by an oath, that the muff thou bearest in thy hand belongeth unto Madam Sophia;

for I have frequently observed her, of later days, to bear it about her." "My daughter's muff!" cries the squire in a rage. "Hath he got my daughter's muff? bear witness the goods are found upon him. I'll have him before a justice of peace this instant. Where is my daughter, villain?" "Sir," said Jones, "I beg you would be pacified. The muff, I acknowledge, is the young lady's; but, upon my honour, I have never seen her." At these words Western lost all patience, and grew inarticulate with rage.

Some of the servants had acquainted Fitzpatrick who Mr Western was. The good Irishman, therefore, thinking he had now an opportunity to do an act of service to his uncle, and by that means might possibly obtain his favour, stept up to Jones, and cried out, "Upon my conscience, sir, you may be ashamed of denying your having seen the gentleman's daughter before my face, when you know I found you there upon the bed together." Then, turning to Western, he offered to conduct him immediately to the room where his daughter was; which offer being accepted, he, the squire, the parson, and some others, ascended directly to Mrs Waters's chamber, which they entered with no less violence than Mr Fitzpatrick had done before.

The poor lady started from her sleep with as much amazement as terror, and beheld at her bedside a figure which might very well be supposed to have escaped out of Bedlam. Such wildness and confusion were in the looks of Mr Western; who no sooner saw the lady than he started back, shewing sufficiently by his manner, before he spoke, that this was not the person sought after.

So much more tenderly do women value their reputation than their persons, that, though the latter seemed now in more danger than before, yet, as the former was secure, the lady screamed not with such violence as she had done on the other occasion. However, she no sooner found herself alone than she abandoned all thoughts of further repose; and, as she had sufficient reason to be dissatisfied with her present lodging, she dressed herself with all possible expedition.

Mr Western now proceeded to search the whole house, but to as little purpose as he had disturbed poor Mrs Waters. He then returned disconsolate into the kitchen, where he found Jones in the custody of his servants.

This violent uproar had raised all the people in the house, though it was yet scarcely daylight. Among these was a grave gentleman, who had the honour to be in the commission of the peace for the county of Worcester. Of which Mr Western was no sooner informed than he offered to lay his complaint before him. The justice declined executing his office, as he said he had no clerk present, nor no book about justice business; and that he could not carry all the law in his head about stealing away daughters, and such sort of things.

Here Mr Fitzpatrick offered to lend him his assistance, informing the company that he had been himself bred to the law. (And indeed he had served three years as clerk to an attorney in the north of Ireland, when, chusing a genteeler walk in life, he quitted his master, came over to England, and set up that business which requires no apprenticeship, namely, that of a gentleman, in which he had succeeded, as hath been already partly mentioned.)

Mr Fitzpatrick declared that the law concerning daughters was out of the present case; that stealing a muff was undoubtedly felony, and the goods being found upon the person, were sufficient evidence of the fact.

The magistrate, upon the encouragement of so learned a coadjutor, and upon the violent intercession of the squire, was at length prevailed upon to seat himself in the chair of justice, where being placed, upon viewing the muff which Jones still held in his hand, and upon the parson's swearing it to be the property of Mr Western, he desired Mr Fitzpatrick to draw up a commitment, which he said he would sign.

Jones now desired to be heard, which was at last, with difficulty, granted him. He then produced the evidence of Mr Partridge, as to the finding it; but, what was still more, Susan deposed that Sophia herself had delivered the muff to her, and had ordered her to convey it into the chamber where Mr Jones had found it.

Whether a natural love of justice, or the extraordinary comeliness of Jones, had wrought on Susan to make the discovery, I will not determine; but such were the effects of her evidence, that the magistrate, throwing himself back in his chair, declared that the matter was now altogether as clear on the side of the prisoner as it had before been against him: with which the parson concurred, saying, the Lord forbid he should be instrumental in committing an innocent person to durance. The justice then arose, acquitted the prisoner, and broke up the court.

Mr Western now gave every one present a hearty curse, and, immediately ordering his horses, departed in pursuit of his daughter, without taking the least notice of his nephew Fitzpatrick, or returning any answer to his claim of kindred, notwithstanding all the obligations he had just received from that gentleman. In the violence, moreover, of his hurry, and of his passion, he luckily forgot to demand the muff of Jones: I say luckily; for he would have died on the spot rather than have parted with it.

Jones likewise, with his friend Partridge, set forward the moment he had paid his reckoning, in quest of his lovely Sophia, whom he now resolved never more to abandon the pursuit of. Nor could he bring himself even to take leave of Mrs Waters; of whom he detested the very thoughts, as she had been, though not designedly, the occasion of his missing the happiest interview with Sophia, to whom he now vowed eternal constancy.

As for Mrs Waters, she took the opportunity of the coach which was going to Bath; for which place she set out in company with the two Irish gentlemen, the landlady kindly lending her her cloaths; in return for which she was contented only to receive about double their value, as a recompence for the loan. Upon the road she was perfectly reconciled to Mr Fitzpatrick, who was a very handsome fellow, and indeed did all she could to console him in the absence of his wife.

Thus ended the many odd adventures which Mr Jones encountered at his inn at Upton, where they talk, to this day, of the beauty and lovely behaviour of the charming Sophia, by the name of the Somersetshire angel.

CHAPTER VIII.

In which the history goes backward.

Before we proceed any farther in our history, it may be proper to look a little back, in order to account for the extraordinary appearance of Sophia and her father at the inn at Upton.

The reader may be pleased to remember that, in the ninth chapter of the seventh book of our history, we left Sophia, after a long debate between love and duty, deciding the cause, as it usually, I believe, happens, in favour of the former.

This debate had arisen, as we have there shown, from a visit which her father had just before made her, in order to force her consent to a marriage with Blifil; and which he had understood to be fully implied in her acknowledgment "that she neither must nor could refuse any absolute command of his."

Now from this visit the squire retired to his evening potation, overjoyed at the success he had gained with his daughter; and, as he was of a social disposition, and willing to have partakers in his happiness, the beer was ordered to flow very liberally into the kitchen; so that before eleven in the evening there was not a single person sober in the house except only Mrs Western herself and the charming Sophia.

Early in the morning a messenger was despatched to summon Mr Blifil; for, though the squire imagined that young gentleman had been much less acquainted than he really was with the former aversion of his daughter, as he had not, however, yet received her consent, he longed impatiently to communicate it to him, not doubting but that the intended bride herself would confirm it with her lips. As to the wedding, it had the evening before been fixed, by the male parties, to be celebrated on the next morning save one.

Breakfast was now set forth in the parlour, where Mr Blifil attended, and where the squire and his sister likewise were assembled; and now Sophia was ordered to be called.

O, Shakespear! had I thy pen! O, Hogarth! had I thy pencil! then would I draw the picture of the poor serving-man, who, with pale countenance, staring eyes, chattering teeth, faultering tongue, and trembling limbs,

> (E'en such a man, so faint, so spiritless,
> So dull, so dead in look, so woe-begone,
> Drew Priam's curtains in the dead of night,

And would have told him, half his Troy was burn'd)

entered the room, and declared—That Madam Sophia was not to be found.

"Not to be found!" cries the squire, starting from his chair; "Zounds and d—nation! Blood and fury! Where, when, how, what—Not to be found! Where?"

"La! brother," said Mrs Western, with true political coldness, "you are always throwing yourself into such violent passions for nothing. My niece, I suppose, is only walked out into the garden. I protest you are grown so unreasonable, that it is impossible to live in the house with you."

"Nay, nay," answered the squire, returning as suddenly to himself, as he had gone from himself; "if that be all the matter, it signifies not much; but, upon my soul, my mind misgave me when the fellow said she was not to be found." He then gave orders for the bell to be rung in the garden, and sat himself contentedly down.

No two things could be more the reverse of each other than were the brother and sister in most instances; particularly in this, That as the brother never foresaw anything at a distance, but was most sagacious in immediately seeing everything the moment it had happened; so the sister eternally foresaw at a distance, but was not so quick-sighted to objects before her eyes. Of both these the reader may have observed examples: and, indeed, both their several talents were excessive; for, as the sister often foresaw what never came to pass, so the brother often saw much more than was actually the truth.

This was not however the case at present. The same report was brought from the garden as before had been brought from the chamber, that Madam Sophia was not to be found.

> The squire himself now sallied forth, and began to roar forth the name of Sophia as loudly, and in as hoarse a voice, as whilome did Hercules that of Hylas; and, as the poet tells us that the whole
>
> shore echoed back the name of that beautiful youth, so did the house, the garden, and all the neighbouring fields resound nothing but the name of Sophia, in the hoarse voices of the men, and in the
>
> FIXME(replacing -- with —)-->shrill pipes of the women; while echo seemed so pleased to repeat the beloved sound, that, if there is really such a person, I believe Ovid hath belied her sex. -- Nothing reigned for a long time but confusion; till at last the squire, having sufficiently spent his breath, returned to the parlour, where he found Mrs Western and Mr Blifil, and threw himself, with
>
> the utmost dejection in his countenance, into a great chair.

Here Mrs Western began to apply the following consolation:

"Brother, I am sorry for what hath happened; and that my niece should have behaved herself in a manner so unbecoming her family; but it is all your own doings, and you have nobody to thank but yourself. You know she hath been educated always in a manner directly contrary to my advice, and now you see the consequence. Have I not a thousand times argued with you about giving my niece her own will? But you know I never could prevail upon you; and when I had taken so much pains to eradicate her headstrong opinions, and to rectify your errors in policy, you know she was taken out of my hands; so that I have nothing to answer for. Had I been trusted entirely with the care of her education, no such accident as this had ever befallen you; so that you must comfort yourself by thinking it was all your own doing; and, indeed, what else could be expected from such indulgence?"

"Zounds! sister," answered he, "you are enough to make one mad. Have I indulged her? Have I given her her will?——It was no longer ago than last night that I threatened, if she disobeyed me, to confine her to her chamber upon bread and water as long as she lived.——You would provoke the patience of Job."

"Did ever mortal hear the like?" replied she. "Brother, if I had not the patience of fifty Jobs, you would make me forget all decency and decorum. Why would you interfere? Did I not beg you, did I not intreat you, to leave the whole conduct to me? You have defeated all the operations of the campaign by one false step. Would any man in his senses have provoked a daughter by such threats as these? How often have I told you that English women are not to be treated like Ciracessian[1] slaves. We have the protection of the world; we are to be won by gentle means only, and not to be hectored, and bullied, and beat into compliance. I thank Heaven no Salique law governs here. Brother, you have a roughness in your manner which no woman but myself would bear. I do not wonder my niece was frightened and terrified into taking this measure; and, to speak honestly, I think my niece will be justified to the world for what she hath done. I repeat it to you again, brother, you must comfort yourself by rememb'ring that it is all your own fault. How often have I advised—" Here Western rose hastily from his chair, and, venting two or three horrid imprecations, ran out of the room.

When he was departed, his sister expressed more bitterness (if possible) against him than she had done while he was present; for the truth of which she appealed to Mr Blifil, who, with great complacence, acquiesced entirely in all she said; but excused all the faults of Mr Western, "as they must be considered," he said, "to have proceeded from the too inordinate fondness of a father, which must be allowed the name of an amiable weakness." "So much the more inexcuseable," answered the lady; "for whom doth he ruin by his fondness but his own child?" To which Blifil immediately agreed.

Mrs Western then began to express great confusion on the account of Mr Blifil, and of the usage which he had received from a family to which he intended so much honour. On this subject she treated the folly of her niece with great severity; but concluded with throwing the whole on her brother, who, she said, was inexcuseable to have proceeded so far without better assurances of his daughter's consent: "But he was (says she) always of a violent, headstrong temper; and I can scarce forgive myself for all the advice I have thrown away upon him."

---

[1] Possibly Circassian.

After much of this kind of conversation, which, perhaps, would not greatly entertain the reader, was it here particularly related, Mr Blifil took his leave and returned home, not highly pleased with his disappointment: which, however, the philosophy which he had acquired from Square, and the religion infused into him by Thwackum, together with somewhat else, taught him to bear rather better than more passionate lovers bear these kinds of evils.

CHAPTER IX.

The escape of Sophia.

It is now time to look after Sophia; whom the reader, if he loves her half so well as I do, will rejoice to find escaped from the clutches of her passionate father, and from those of her dispassionate lover.

Twelve times did the iron register of time beat on the sonorous bell-metal, summoning the ghosts to rise and walk their nightly round.——In plainer language, it was twelve o'clock, and all the family, as we have said, lay buried in drink and sleep, except only Mrs Western, who was deeply engaged in reading a political pamphlet, and except our heroine, who now softly stole down-stairs, and, having unbarred and unlocked one of the house-doors, sallied forth, and hastened to the place of appointment.

Notwithstanding the many pretty arts which ladies sometimes practise, to display their fears on every little occasion (almost as many as the other sex uses to conceal theirs), certainly there is a degree of courage which not only becomes a woman, but is often necessary to enable her to discharge her duty. It is, indeed, the idea of fierceness, and not of bravery, which destroys the female character; for who can read the story of the justly celebrated Arria without conceiving as high an opinion of her gentleness and tenderness as of her fortitude? At the same time, perhaps, many a woman who shrieks at a mouse, or a rat, may be capable of poisoning a husband; or, what is worse, of driving him to poison himself.

Sophia, with all the gentleness which a woman can have, had all the spirit which she ought to have. When, therefore, she came to the place of appointment, and, instead of meeting her maid, as was agreed, saw a man ride directly up to her, she neither screamed out nor fainted away: not that her pulse then beat with its usual regularity; for she was, at first, under some surprize and apprehension: but these were relieved almost as soon as raised, when the man, pulling off his hat, asked her, in a very submissive manner, "If her ladyship did not expect to meet another lady?" and then proceeded to inform her that he was sent to conduct her to that lady.

Sophia could have no possible suspicion of any falsehood in this account: she therefore mounted resolutely behind the fellow, who conveyed her safe to a town about five miles distant, where she had the satisfaction of finding the good Mrs Honour: for, as the soul of the waiting-woman was wrapt up in those very habiliments which used to enwrap her body, she could by no means bring herself to trust them out of her sight. Upon these, therefore, she kept guard in person, while she detached the aforesaid fellow after her mistress, having given him all proper instructions.

They now debated what course to take, in order to avoid the pursuit of Mr Western, who they knew would send after them in a few hours. The London road had such charms for Honour, that she was desirous of going on directly; alleging that, as Sophia could not be missed till eight or nine the next morning, her pursuers would not be able to overtake her, even though they knew which way she had gone. But Sophia had too much at stake to venture anything to chance; nor did she dare trust too much to her tender limbs, in a contest which was to be decided only by swiftness. She resolved, therefore, to travel across the country, for at least twenty or thirty miles, and then to take the direct road to London. So, having hired horses to go twenty miles one way, when she intended to go twenty miles the other, she set forward with the same guide behind whom she had ridden from her father's house; the guide having now taken up behind him, in the room of Sophia, a much heavier, as well as much less lovely burden; being, indeed, a huge portmanteau, well stuffed with those outside ornaments, by means of which the fair Honour hoped to gain many conquests, and, finally, to make her fortune in London city.

When they had gone about two hundred paces from the inn on the London road, Sophia rode up to the guide, and, with a voice much fuller of honey than was ever that of Plato, though his mouth is supposed to have been a bee-hive, begged him to take the first turning which led towards Bristol.

Reader, I am not superstitious, nor any great believer of modern miracles. I do not, therefore, deliver the following as a certain truth; for, indeed, I can scarce credit it myself: but the fidelity of an historian obliges me to relate what hath been confidently asserted. The horse, then, on which the guide rode, is reported to have been so charmed by Sophia's voice, that he made a full stop, and expressed an unwillingness to proceed any farther.

Perhaps, however, the fact may be true, and less miraculous than it hath been represented; since the natural cause seems adequate to the effect: for, as the guide at that moment desisted from a constant application of his armed right heel (for, like Hudibras, he wore but one spur), it is more than possible that this omission alone might occasion the beast to stop, especially as this was very frequent with him at other times.

But if the voice of Sophia had really an effect on the horse, it had very little on the rider. He answered somewhat surlily, "That measter had ordered him to go a different way, and that he should lose his place if he went any other than that he was ordered."

Sophia, finding all her persuasions had no effect, began now to add irresistible charms to her voice; charms which, according to the proverb, makes the old mare trot, instead of standing still; charms! to which modern ages have attributed all that irresistible force which the antients imputed to perfect oratory. In a word, she promised she would reward him to his utmost expectation.

The lad was not totally deaf to these promises; but he disliked their being indefinite; for, though perhaps he had never heard that word, yet that, in fact, was his objection. He said, "Gentlevolks did not consider the case of poor volks; that he had like to have been turned away the other day, for riding about the country with a gentleman from Squire Allworthy's, who did not reward him as he should have done."

"With whom?" says Sophia eagerly. "With a gentleman from Squire Allworthy's," repeated the lad; "the squire's son, I think they call 'un."—"Whither? which way did he go?" says Sophia.—"Why, a little o' one side o' Bristol, about twenty miles off," answered the lad.—"Guide me," says Sophia, "to the same place, and I'll give thee a guinea, or two, if one is not sufficient."—"To be certain," said the boy, "it is honestly worth two, when your ladyship considers what a risk I run; but, however, if your ladyship will promise me the two guineas, I'll e'en venture: to be certain it is a sinful thing to ride about my measter's horses; but one comfort is, I can only be turned away, and two guineas will partly make me amends."

The bargain being thus struck, the lad turned aside into the Bristol road, and Sophia set forward in pursuit of Jones, highly contrary to the remonstrances of Mrs Honour, who had much more desire to see London than to see Mr Jones: for indeed she was not his friend with her mistress, as he had been guilty of some neglect in certain pecuniary civilities, which are by custom due to the waiting-gentlewoman in all love affairs, and more especially in those of a clandestine kind. This we impute rather to the carelessness of his temper than to any want of generosity; but perhaps she derived it from the latter motive. Certain it is that she hated him very bitterly on that account, and resolved to take every opportunity of injuring him with her mistress. It was therefore highly unlucky for her, that she had gone to the very same town and inn whence Jones had started, and still more unlucky was she in having stumbled on the same guide, and on this accidental discovery which Sophia had made.

Our travellers arrived at Hambrook[1] at the break of day, where Honour was against her will charged to enquire the route which Mr Jones had taken. Of this, indeed, the guide himself could have informed them; but Sophia, I know not for what reason, never asked him the question.

When Mrs Honour had made her report from the landlord, Sophia, with much difficulty, procured some indifferent horses, which brought her to the inn where Jones had been confined rather by the misfortune of meeting with a surgeon than by having met with a broken head.

Here Honour, being again charged with a commission of enquiry, had no sooner applied herself to the landlady, and had described the person of Mr Jones, than that sagacious woman began, in the vulgar phrase, to smell a rat. When Sophia therefore entered the room, instead of answering the maid, the landlady, addressing herself to the mistress, began the following speech: "Good lack-a-day!

[1] This was the village where Jones met the Quaker.

why there now, who would have thought it? I protest the loveliest couple that ever eye beheld. I-fackins, madam, it is no wonder the squire run on so about your ladyship. He told me indeed you was the finest lady in the world, and to be sure so you be. Mercy on him, poor heart! I bepitied him, so I did, when he used to hug his pillow, and call it his dear Madam Sophia. I did all I could to dissuade him from going to the wars: I told him there were men enow that were good for nothing else but to be killed, that had not the love of such fine ladies." "Sure," says Sophia, "the good woman is distracted." "No, no," cries the landlady, "I am not distracted. What, doth your ladyship think I don't know then? I assure you he told me all." "What saucy fellow," cries Honour, "told you anything of my lady?" "No saucy fellow," answered the landlady, "but the young gentleman you enquired after, and a very pretty young gentleman he is, and he loves Madam Sophia Western to the bottom of his soul." "He love my lady! I'd have you to know, woman, she is meat for his master."—"Nay, Honour," said Sophia, interrupting her, "don't be angry with the good woman; she intends no harm." "No, marry, don't I," answered the landlady, emboldened by the soft accents of Sophia; and then launched into a long narrative too tedious to be here set down, in which some passages dropt that gave a little offence to Sophia, and much more to her waiting-woman, who hence took occasion to abuse poor Jones to her mistress the moment they were alone together, saying, "that he must be a very pitiful fellow, and could have no love for a lady, whose name he would thus prostitute in an ale-house."

Sophia did not see his behaviour in so very disadvantageous a light, and was perhaps more pleased with the violent raptures of his love (which the landlady exaggerated as much as she had done every other circumstance) than she was offended with the rest; and indeed she imputed the whole to the extravagance, or rather ebullience, of his passion, and to the openness of his heart.

This incident, however, being afterwards revived in her mind, and placed in the most odious colours by Honour, served to heighten and give credit to those unlucky occurrences at Upton, and assisted the waiting-woman in her endeavours to make her mistress depart from that inn without seeing Jones.

The landlady finding Sophia intended to stay no longer than till her horses were ready, and that without either eating or drinking, soon withdrew; when Honour began to take her mistress to task (for indeed she used great freedom), and after a long harangue, in which she reminded her of her intention to go to London, and gave frequent hints of the impropriety of pursuing a young fellow, she at last concluded with this serious exhortation: "For heaven's sake, madam, consider what you are about, and whither you are going."

This advice to a lady who had already rode near forty miles, and in no very agreeable season, may seem foolish enough. It may be supposed she had well considered and resolved this already; nay, Mrs Honour, by the hints she threw out, seemed to think so; and this I doubt not is the opinion of many readers, who have, I make no doubt, been long since well convinced of the purpose of our heroine, and have heartily condemned her for it as a wanton baggage.

But in reality this was not the case. Sophia had been lately so distracted between hope and fear, her duty and love to her father, her hatred to Blifil, her compassion, and (why should we not confess the truth?) her love for Jones; which last the behaviour of her father, of her aunt, of every one else, and more particularly of Jones himself, had blown into a flame, that her mind was in that confused state which may be truly said to make us ignorant of what we do, or whither we go, or rather, indeed, indifferent as to the consequence of either.

The prudent and sage advice of her maid produced, however, some cool reflection; and she at length determined to go to Gloucester, and thence to proceed directly to London.

But, unluckily, a few miles before she entered that town, she met the hack-attorney, who, as is before mentioned, had dined there with Mr Jones. This fellow, being well known to Mrs Honour, stopt and spoke to her; of which Sophia at that time took little notice, more than to enquire who he was.

But, having had a more particular account from Honour of this man afterwards at Gloucester, and hearing of the great expedition he usually made in travelling, for which (as hath been before observed) he was particularly famous; recollecting, likewise, that she had overheard Mrs Honour inform him that they were going to Gloucester, she began to fear lest her father might, by this fellow's means, be able to trace her to that city; wherefore, if she should there strike into the London road, she apprehended he would certainly be able to overtake her. She therefore altered her resolution; and, having hired horses to go a week's journey a way which she did not intend to travel, she again set forward after a light refreshment, contrary to the desire and earnest entreaties of her maid, and to the no less vehement remonstrances of Mrs Whitefield, who, from good breeding, or perhaps from good nature (for the poor young lady appeared much fatigued), pressed her very heartily to stay that evening at Gloucester.

Having refreshed herself only with some tea, and with lying about two hours on the bed, while her horses were getting ready, she resolutely left Mrs Whitefield's about eleven at night, and, striking directly into the Worcester road, within less than four hours arrived at that very inn where we last saw her.

Having thus traced our heroine very particularly back from her departure, till her arrival at Upton, we shall in a very few words bring her father to the same place; who, having received the first scent from the post-boy, who conducted his daughter to Hambrook, very easily traced her afterwards to Gloucester; whence he pursued her to Upton, as he had learned Mr Jones had taken that route (for Partridge, to use the squire's expression, left everywhere a strong scent behind him), and he doubted not in the least but Sophia travelled, or, as he phrased it, ran, the same way. He used indeed a very coarse expression, which need not be here inserted; as fox-hunters, who alone will understand it, will easily suggest it to themselves.

BOOK XI.

CONTAINING ABOUT THREE DAYS.

CHAPTER I.

A crust for the critics.

In our last initial chapter we may be supposed to have treated that formidable set of men who are called critics with more freedom than becomes us; since they exact, and indeed generally receive, great condescension from authors. We shall in this, therefore, give the reasons of our conduct to this august body; and here we shall, perhaps, place them in a light in which they have not hitherto been seen.

This word critic is of Greek derivation, and signifies judgment. Hence I presume some persons who have not understood the original, and have seen the English translation of the primitive, have concluded that it meant judgment in the legal sense, in which it is frequently used as equivalent to condemnation.

I am the rather inclined to be of that opinion, as the greatest number of critics hath of late years been found amongst the lawyers. Many of these gentlemen, from despair, perhaps, of ever rising to the bench in Westminster-hall, have placed themselves on the benches at the playhouse, where they have exerted their judicial capacity, and have given judgment, *i.e.*, condemned without mercy.

The gentlemen would, perhaps, be well enough pleased, if we were to leave them thus compared to one of the most important and honourable offices in the commonwealth, and, if we intended to apply to their favour, we would do so; but, as we design to deal very sincerely and plainly too with them, we must remind them of another officer of justice of a much lower rank; to whom, as they not only pronounce, but execute, their own judgment, they bear likewise some remote resemblance.

But in reality there is another light, in which these modern critics may, with great justice and propriety, be seen; and this is that of a common slanderer. If a person who prys into the characters of others, with no other design but to discover their faults, and to publish them to the world, deserves the title of a slanderer of the reputations of men, why should not a critic, who reads with the same malevolent view, be as properly stiled the slanderer of the reputation of books?

Vice hath not, I believe, a more abject slave; society produces not a more odious vermin; nor can the devil receive a guest more worthy of him, nor possibly more welcome to him, than a slanderer. The world, I am afraid, regards not this monster with half the abhorrence which he deserves; and I am more afraid to assign the reason of this criminal lenity shown towards him; yet it is certain that the thief looks innocent in the comparison; nay, the murderer himself can seldom stand in competition with his guilt: for slander is a more cruel weapon than a sword, as the wounds which the former gives are always incurable. One method, indeed, there is of killing, and that the basest and most execrable of all, which bears an exact analogy to the vice here disclaimed against, and that is poison: a means of revenge so base, and yet so horrible, that it was once wisely distinguished by our laws from all other murders, in the peculiar severity of the punishment.

Besides the dreadful mischiefs done by slander, and the baseness of the means by which they are effected, there are other circumstances that highly aggravate its atrocious quality; for it often proceeds from no provocation, and seldom promises itself any reward, unless some black and infernal mind may propose a reward in the thoughts of having procured the ruin and misery of another.

Shakespear hath nobly touched this vice, when he says—

> "Who steals my purse steals trash; 't is something, nothing;
> 'Twas mine, 'tis his, and hath been slave to thousands:
> But he that filches from me my good name
> Robs me of that WHICH NOT ENRICHES HIM,
> BUT MAKES ME POOR INDEED."

With all this my good reader will doubtless agree; but much of it will probably seem too severe, when applied to the slanderer of books. But let it here be considered that both proceed from the same wicked disposition of mind, and are alike void of the excuse of temptation. Nor shall we conclude the injury done this way to be very slight, when we consider a book as the author's offspring, and indeed as the child of his brain.

The reader who hath suffered his muse to continue hitherto in a virgin state can have but a very inadequate idea of this kind of paternal fondness. To such we may parody the tender exclamation of Macduff, "Alas! Thou hast written no book." But the author whose muse hath brought forth will feel the pathetic strain, perhaps will accompany me with tears (especially if his darling be already no more), while I mention the uneasiness with which the big muse bears about her burden, the painful labour with which she produces it, and, lastly, the care, the fondness, with which the tender father nourishes his favourite, till it be brought to maturity, and produced into the world.

Nor is there any paternal fondness which seems less to savour of absolute instinct, and which may so well be reconciled to worldly wisdom, as this. These children may most truly be called the riches of their father; and many of them have with true filial piety fed their parent in his old age: so that not only the affection, but the interest, of the author may be highly injured by these slanderers, whose poisonous breath brings his book to an untimely end.

Lastly, the slander of a book is, in truth, the slander of the author: for, as no one can call another bastard, without calling the mother a whore, so neither can any one give the names of sad stuff, horrid nonsense, &c., to a book, without calling the author a blockhead; which, though in a moral sense it is a preferable appellation to that of villain, is perhaps rather more injurious to his worldly interest.

Now, however ludicrous all this may appear to some, others, I doubt not, will feel and acknowledge the truth of it; nay, may, perhaps, think I have not treated the subject with decent solemnity; but surely a man may speak truth with a smiling countenance. In reality, to depreciate a book maliciously, or even wantonly, is at least a very ill-natured office; and a morose snarling critic may, I believe, be suspected to be a bad man.

I will therefore endeavour, in the remaining part of this chapter, to explain the marks of this character, and to show what criticism I here intend to obviate: for I can never be understood, unless by the very persons here meant, to insinuate that there are no proper judges of writing, or to endeavour to exclude from the commonwealth of literature any of those noble critics to whose labours the learned world are so greatly indebted. Such were Aristotle, Horace, and Longinus, among the antients, Dacier and Bossu among the French, and some perhaps among us; who have certainly been duly authorised to execute at least a judicial authority *in foro literario*.

But without ascertaining all the proper qualifications of a critic, which I have touched on elsewhere, I think I may very boldly object to the censures of any one past upon works which he hath not himself read. Such censurers as these, whether they speak from their own guess or suspicion, or from the report and opinion of others, may properly be said to slander the reputation of the book they condemn.

Such may likewise be suspected of deserving this character, who, without assigning any particular faults, condemn the whole in general defamatory terms; such as vile, dull, d—d stuff, &c., and particularly by the use of the monosyllable low; a word which becomes the mouth of no critic who is not RIGHT HONOURABLE.

Again, though there may be some faults justly assigned in the work, yet, if those are not in the most essential parts, or if they are compensated by greater beauties, it will savour rather of the malice of a slanderer than of the judgment of a true critic to pass a severe sentence upon the whole, merely on account of some vicious part. This is directly contrary to the sentiments of Horace:

Verum ubi plura nitent in carmine, non ego paucis
Offendor maculis, quas aut incuria fudit,
Aut humana parum cavit natura——

But where the beauties, more in number, shine,
I am not angry, when a casual line
(That with some trivial faults unequal flows)
A careless hand or human frailty shows.—MR FRANCIS.

For, as Martial says, *Aliter non fit, Avite, liber*. No book can be otherwise composed. All beauty of character, as well as of countenance, and indeed of everything human, is to be tried in this manner. Cruel indeed would it be if such a work as this history, which hath employed some thousands of hours in the composing, should be liable to be condemned, because some particular chapter, or perhaps chapters, may be obnoxious to very just and sensible objections. And yet nothing is more common than the most rigorous sentence upon books supported by such objections, which, if they were rightly taken (and that they are not always), do by no means go to the merit of the whole. In the theatre especially, a single expression which doth not coincide with the taste of the audience, or with any individual critic of that audience, is sure to be hissed; and one scene which should be disapproved would hazard the whole piece. To write within such severe rules as these is as impossible as to live up to some splenetic opinions: and if we judge according to the sentiments of some critics, and of some Christians, no author will be saved in this world, and no man in the next.

CHAPTER II.

The adventures which Sophia met with after her leaving Upton.

Our history, just before it was obliged to turn about and travel backwards, had mentioned the departure of Sophia and her maid from the inn; we shall now therefore pursue the steps of that lovely creature, and leave her unworthy lover a little longer to bemoan his ill-luck, or rather his ill-conduct.

Sophia having directed her guide to travel through bye-roads, across the country, they now passed the Severn, and had scarce got a mile from the inn, when the young lady, looking behind her, saw several horses coming after on full speed. This greatly alarmed her fears, and she called to the guide to put on as fast as possible.

He immediately obeyed her, and away they rode a full gallop. But the faster they went, the faster were they followed; and as the horses behind were somewhat swifter than those before, so the former were at length overtaken. A happy circumstance for poor Sophia; whose fears, joined to her fatigue, had almost overpowered her spirits; but she was now instantly relieved by a female voice, that greeted her in the softest manner, and with the utmost civility. This greeting Sophia, as soon as she could recover her breath, with like civility, and with the highest satisfaction to herself, returned.

The travellers who joined Sophia, and who had given her such terror, consisted, like her own company, of two females and a guide. The two parties proceeded three full miles together before any one offered again to open their mouths; when our heroine, having pretty well got the better of her fear (but yet being somewhat surprized that the other still continued to attend her, as she pursued no great road, and had already passed through several turnings), accosted the strange lady in a most obliging tone, and said, "She was very happy to find they were both travelling the same way." The other, who, like a ghost, only wanted to be spoke to, readily answered, "That the happiness was entirely hers; that she was a perfect stranger in that country, and was so overjoyed at meeting a companion of her own sex, that she had perhaps been guilty of an impertinence, which required great apology, in keeping pace with her." More civilities passed between these two ladies; for Mrs Honour had now given place to the fine habit of the stranger, and had fallen into the rear. But, though Sophia had great curiosity to know why the other lady continued to travel on through the same bye-roads with herself, nay, though this gave her some uneasiness, yet fear, or modesty, or some other consideration, restrained her from asking the question.

The strange lady now laboured under a difficulty which appears almost below the dignity of history to mention. Her bonnet had been blown from her head not less than five times within the last mile; nor could she come at any ribbon or handkerchief to tie it under her chin. When Sophia was informed of this, she immediately supplied her with a handkerchief for this purpose; which while she was pulling from her pocket, she perhaps too much neglected the management of her horse, for the beast, now unluckily making a false step, fell upon his fore-legs, and threw his fair rider from his back.

Though Sophia came head foremost to the ground, she happily received not the least damage: and the same circumstances which had perhaps contributed to her fall now preserved her from confusion; for the lane which they were then passing was narrow, and very much overgrown with trees, so that the moon could here afford very little light, and was moreover, at present, so obscured in a cloud, that it was almost perfectly dark. By these means the young lady's modesty, which was extremely delicate, escaped as free from injury as her limbs, and she was once more reinstated in her saddle, having received no other harm than a little fright by her fall.

Daylight at length appeared in its full lustre; and now the two ladies, who were riding over a common side by side, looking stedfastly at each other, at the same moment both their eyes became fixed; both their horses stopt, and, both speaking together, with equal joy pronounced, the one the name of Sophia, the other that of Harriet.

This unexpected encounter surprized the ladies much more than I believe it will the sagacious reader, who must have imagined that the strange lady could be no other than Mrs Fitzpatrick, the cousin of Miss Western, whom we before mentioned to have sallied from the inn a few minutes after her.

So great was the surprize and joy which these two cousins conceived at this meeting (for they had formerly been most intimate acquaintance and friends, and had long lived together with their aunt Western), that it is impossible to recount half the congratulations which passed between them, before either asked a very natural question of the other, namely, whither she was going?

This at last, however, came first from Mrs Fitzpatrick; but, easy and natural as the question may seem, Sophia found it difficult to give it a very ready and certain answer. She begged her cousin therefore to suspend all curiosity till they arrived at some inn, "which I suppose," says she, "can hardly be far distant; and, believe me, Harriet, I suspend as much curiosity on my side; for, indeed, I believe our astonishment is pretty equal."

The conversation which passed between these ladies on the road was, I apprehend, little worth relating; and less certainly was that between the two waiting-women; for they likewise began to pay their compliments to each other. As for the guides, they were debarred from the pleasure of discourse, the one being placed in the van, and the other obliged to bring up the rear.

In this posture they travelled many hours, till they came into a wide and well-beaten road, which, as they turned to the right, soon brought them to a very fair promising inn, where they all alighted: but so fatigued was Sophia, that as she had sat her horse during the last five or six miles with great difficulty, so was she now incapable of dismounting from him without assistance. This the landlord, who had hold of her horse, presently perceiving, offered to lift her in his arms from her saddle; and she too readily accepted the tender of his service. Indeed fortune seems to have resolved to put Sophia to the blush that day, and the second malicious attempt succeeded better than the first; for my landlord had no sooner received the young lady in his arms, than his feet, which the gout had lately very severely handled, gave way, and down he tumbled; but, at the same time, with no less dexterity than gallantry, contrived to throw himself under his charming burden, so that he alone received any bruise from the fall; for the great injury which happened to Sophia was a violent shock given to her modesty by an immoderate grin, which, at her rising from the ground, she observed in the countenances of most of the bye-standers. This made her suspect what had really happened, and what we shall not here relate for the indulgence of those readers who are capable of laughing at the offence given to a young lady's delicacy. Accidents of this kind we have never regarded in a comical light; nor will we scruple to say that he must have a very inadequate idea of the modesty of a beautiful young woman, who would wish to sacrifice it to so paltry a satisfaction as can arise from laughter.

This fright and shock, joined to the violent fatigue which both her mind and body had undergone, almost overcame the excellent constitution of Sophia, and she had scarce strength sufficient to totter into the inn, leaning on the arm of her maid. Here she was no sooner seated than she called for a glass of water; but Mrs Honour, very judiciously, in my opinion, changed it into a glass of wine.

Mrs Fitzpatrick, hearing from Mrs Honour that Sophia had not been in bed during the two last nights, and observing her to look very pale and wan with her fatigue, earnestly entreated her to refresh herself with some sleep. She was yet a stranger to her history, or her apprehensions; but, had she known both, she would have given the same advice; for rest was visibly necessary for her; and their long journey through bye-roads so entirely removed all danger of pursuit, that she was herself perfectly easy on that account.

Sophia was easily prevailed on to follow the counsel of her friend, which was heartily seconded by her maid. Mrs Fitzpatrick likewise offered to bear her cousin company, which Sophia, with much complacence, accepted.

The mistress was no sooner in bed than the maid prepared to follow her example. She began to make many apologies to her sister Abigail for leaving her alone in so horrid a place as an inn; but the other stopt her short, being as well inclined to a nap as herself, and desired the honour of being her bedfellow. Sophia's maid agreed to give her a share of her bed, but put in her claim to all the honour. So, after many courtsies and compliments, to bed together went the waiting-women, as their mistresses had done before them.

It was usual with my landlord (as indeed it is with the whole fraternity) to enquire particularly of all coachmen, footmen, postboys, and others, into the names of all his guests; what their estate was, and where it lay. It cannot therefore be wondered at that the many particular circumstances which attended our travellers, and especially their retiring all to sleep at so extraordinary and unusual an hour as ten in the morning, should excite his curiosity. As soon, therefore, as the guides entered the kitchen, he began to examine who the ladies were, and whence they came; but the guides, though they faithfully related all they knew, gave him very little satisfaction. On the contrary, they rather enflamed his curiosity than extinguished it.

This landlord had the character, among all his neighbours, of being a very sagacious fellow. He was thought to see farther and deeper into things than any man in the parish, the parson himself not excepted. Perhaps his look had contributed not a little to procure him this reputation; for there was in this something wonderfully wise and significant, especially when he had a pipe in his mouth; which, indeed, he seldom was without. His behaviour, likewise, greatly assisted in promoting the opinion of his wisdom. In his deportment he was solemn, if not sullen; and when he spoke, which was seldom, he always delivered himself in a slow voice; and, though his sentences were short, they were still interrupted with many hums and ha's, ay ays, and other expletives: so that, though he accompanied his words with certain explanatory gestures, such as shaking or nodding the head, or pointing with his fore-finger, he generally left his hearers to understand more than he expressed; nay, he commonly gave them a hint that he knew much more than he thought proper to disclose. This last circumstance alone may, indeed, very well account for his character of wisdom; since men are strangely inclined to worship what they do not understand. A grand secret, upon which several imposers on mankind have totally relied for the success of their frauds.

This polite person, now taking his wife aside, asked her "what she thought of the ladies lately arrived?" "Think of them?" said the wife, "why, what should I think of them?" "I know," answered he, "what I think. The guides tell strange stories. One pretends to be come from Gloucester, and the other from Upton; and neither of them, for what I can find, can tell whither they are going. But what people ever travel across the country from Upton hither, especially to London? And one of the maid-servants, before she alighted from her horse, asked if this was not the London road? Now I have put all these circumstances together, and whom do you think I have found them out to be?" "Nay," answered she, "you know I never pretend to guess at your discoveries."——"It is a good girl," replied he, chucking her under the chin; "I must own you have always submitted to my knowledge of these matters. Why, then, depend upon it; mind what I say—depend upon it, they are certainly some of the rebel ladies, who, they say, travel with the young Chevalier; and have taken a roundabout way to escape the duke's army."

"Husband," quoth the wife, "you have certainly hit it; for one of them is dressed as fine as any princess; and, to be sure, she looks for all the world like one.——But yet, when I consider one thing"——"When you consider," cries the landlord contemptuously——"Come, pray let's hear what you consider."——"Why, it is," answered the wife, "that she is too humble to be any very great lady: for, while our Betty was warming the bed, she called her nothing but child, and my dear, and sweetheart; and, when Betty offered to pull off her shoes and stockings, she would not suffer her, saying, she would not give her the trouble."

"Pugh!" answered the husband, "that is nothing. Dost think, because you have seen some great ladies rude and uncivil to persons below them, that none of them know how to behave themselves when they come before their inferiors? I think I know people of fashion when I see them—I think I do. Did not she call for a glass of water when she came in? Another sort of women would have called for a dram; you know they would. If she be not a woman of very great quality, sell me for a fool; and, I believe, those who buy me will have a bad bargain. Now, would a woman of her quality travel without a footman, unless upon some such extraordinary occasion?" "Nay, to be sure, husband," cries she, "you know these matters better than I, or most folk." "I think I do know something," said he. "To be sure," answered the wife, "the poor little heart looked so piteous, when she sat down in the chair, I protest I could not help having a compassion for her almost as much as if she had been a poor body. But what's to be done, husband? If an she be a rebel, I suppose you intend to betray her up to the court. Well, she's a sweet-tempered, good-humoured lady, be she what she will, and I shall hardly refrain from crying when I hear she is hanged or beheaded." "Pooh!" answered the husband.——"But, as to what's to be done, it is not so easy a matter to determine. I hope, before she goes away, we shall have the news of a battle; for, if the Chevalier should get the better, she may gain us interest at court, and make our fortunes without betraying her." "Why, that's true," replied the wife; "and I heartily hope she will have it in her power. Certainly she's a sweet good lady; it would go horribly against me to have her come to any harm." "Pooh!" cries the landlord, "women are always so tender-hearted. Why, you would not harbour rebels, would you?" "No, certainly," answered the wife; "and as for betraying her, come what will on't, nobody can blame us. It is what anybody would do in our case."

While our politic landlord, who had not, we see, undeservedly the reputation of great wisdom among his neighbours, was engaged in debating this matter with himself (for he paid little attention to the opinion of his wife), news arrived that the rebels had given the duke the slip, and had got a day's march towards London; and soon after arrived a famous Jacobite squire, who, with great joy in his countenance, shook the landlord by the hand, saying, "All's our own, boy, ten thousand honest Frenchmen are landed in Suffolk. Old England for ever! ten thousand French, my brave lad! I am going to tap away directly."

This news determined the opinion of the wise man, and he resolved to make his court to the young lady when she arose; for he had now (he said) discovered that she was no other than Madam Jenny Cameron herself.

CHAPTER III.

A very short chapter, in which however is a sun, a moon, a star, and an angel.

The sun (for he keeps very good hours at this time of the year) had been some time retired to rest when Sophia arose greatly refreshed by her sleep; which, short as it was, nothing but her extreme fatigue could have occasioned; for, though she had told her maid, and perhaps herself too, that she was perfectly easy when she left Upton, yet it is certain her mind was a little affected with that malady which is attended with all the restless symptoms of a fever, and is perhaps the very distemper which physicians mean (if they mean anything) by the fever on the spirits.

Mrs Fitzpatrick likewise left her bed at the same time; and, having summoned her maid, immediately dressed herself. She was really a very pretty woman, and, had she been in any other company but that of Sophia, might have been thought beautiful; but when Mrs Honour of her own accord attended (for her mistress would not suffer her to be waked), and had equipped our heroine, the charms of Mrs Fitzpatrick, who had performed the office of the morning-star, and had preceded greater glories, shared the fate of that star, and were totally eclipsed the moment those glories shone forth.

Perhaps Sophia never looked more beautiful than she did at this instant. We ought not, therefore, to condemn the maid of the inn for her hyperbole, who, when she descended, after having lighted the fire, declared, and ratified it with an oath, that if ever there was an angel upon earth, she was now above-stairs.

Sophia had acquainted her cousin with her design to go to London; and Mrs Fitzpatrick had agreed to accompany her; for the arrival of her husband at Upton had put an end to her design of going to Bath, or to her aunt Western. They had therefore no sooner finished their tea than Sophia proposed to set out, the moon then shining extremely bright, and as for the frost she defied it; nor had she any of those apprehensions which many young ladies would have felt at travelling by night; for she had, as we have before observed, some little degree of natural courage; and this, her present sensations, which bordered somewhat on despair, greatly encreased. Besides, as she had already travelled twice with safety by the light of the moon, she was the better emboldened to trust to it a third time.

The disposition of Mrs Fitzpatrick was more timorous; for, though the greater terrors had conquered the less, and the presence of her husband had driven her away at so unseasonable an hour from Upton, yet, being now arrived at a place where she thought herself safe from his pursuit, these lesser terrors of I know not what operated so strongly, that she earnestly entreated her cousin to stay till the next morning, and not expose herself to the dangers of travelling by night.

Sophia, who was yielding to an excess, when she could neither laugh nor reason her cousin out of these apprehensions, at last gave way to them. Perhaps, indeed, had she known of her father's arrival at Upton, it might have been more difficult to have persuaded her; for as to Jones, she had, I am afraid, no great horror at the thoughts of being overtaken by him; nay, to confess the truth, I believe she rather wished than feared it; though I might honestly enough have concealed this wish from the reader, as it was one of those secret spontaneous emotions of the soul to which the reason is often a stranger.

When our young ladies had determined to remain all that evening in their inn they were attended by the landlady, who desired to know what their ladyships would be pleased to eat. Such charms were there in the voice, in the manner, and in the affable deportment of Sophia, that she ravished the landlady to the highest degree; and that good woman, concluding that she had attended Jenny Cameron, became in a moment a stanch Jacobite, and wished heartily well to the young Pretender's cause, from the great sweetness and affability with which she had been treated by his supposed mistress.

The two cousins began now to impart to each other their reciprocal curiosity to know what extraordinary accidents on both sides occasioned this so strange and unexpected meeting. At last Mrs Fitzpatrick, having obtained of Sophia a promise of communicating likewise in her turn, began to relate what the reader, if he is desirous to know her history, may read in the ensuing chapter.

CHAPTER IV.

The history of Mrs Fitzpatrick.

Mrs Fitzpatrick, after a silence of a few moments, fetching a deep sigh, thus began:

"It is natural to the unhappy to feel a secret concern in recollecting those periods of their lives which have been most delightful to them. The remembrance of past pleasures affects us with a kind of tender grief, like what we suffer for departed friends; and the ideas of both may be said to haunt our imaginations.

"For this reason, I never reflect without sorrow on those days (the happiest far of my life) which we spent together when both were under the care of my aunt Western. Alas! why are Miss Graveairs and Miss Giddy no more? You remember, I am sure, when we knew each other by no other names. Indeed, you gave the latter appellation with too much cause. I have since experienced how much I deserved it. You, my Sophia, was always my superior in everything, and I heartily hope you will be so in your fortune. I shall never forget the wise and matronly advice you once gave me, when I lamented being disappointed of a ball, though you could not be then fourteen years old.——O my Sophy, how blest must have been my situation, when I could think such a disappointment a misfortune; and when indeed it was the greatest I had ever known!"

"And yet, my dear Harriet," answered Sophia, "it was then a serious matter with you. Comfort yourself therefore with thinking, that whatever you now lament may hereafter appear as trifling and contemptible as a ball would at this time."

"Alas, my Sophia," replied the other lady, "you yourself will think otherwise of my present situation; for greatly must that tender heart be altered if my misfortunes do not draw many a sigh, nay, many a tear, from you. The knowledge of this should perhaps deter me from relating what I am convinced will so much affect you." Here Mrs Fitzpatrick stopt, till, at the repeated entreaties of Sophia, she thus proceeded:

"Though you must have heard much of my marriage; yet, as matters may probably have been misrepresented, I will set out from the very commencement of my unfortunate acquaintance with my present husband; which was at Bath, soon after you left my aunt, and returned home to your father.

"Among the gay young fellows who were at this season at Bath, Mr Fitzpatrick was one. He was handsome, *dégagé,* extremely gallant, and in his dress exceeded most others. In short, my dear, if you was unluckily to see him now, I could describe him no better than by telling you he was the very reverse of everything which he is: for he hath rusticated himself so long, that he is become an absolute wild Irishman. But to proceed in my story: the qualifications which he then possessed so well recommended him, that, though the people of quality at that time lived separate from the rest of the company, and excluded them from all their parties, Mr Fitzpatrick found means to gain admittance. It was perhaps no easy matter to avoid him; for he required very little or no invitation; and as, being handsome and genteel, he found it no very difficult matter to ingratiate himself with the ladies, so, he having frequently drawn his sword, the men did not care publickly to affront him. Had it not been for some such reason, I believe he would have been soon expelled by his own sex; for surely he had no strict title to be preferred to the English gentry; nor did they seem inclined to show him any extraordinary favour. They all abused him behind his back, which might probably proceed from envy; for by the women he was well received, and very particularly distinguished by them.

"My aunt, though no person of quality herself, as she had always lived about the court, was enrolled in that party; for, by whatever means you get into the polite circle, when you are once there, it is sufficient merit for you that you are there. This observation, young as you was, you could scarce avoid making from my aunt, who was free, or reserved, with all people, just as they had more or less of this merit.

"And this merit, I believe, it was, which principally recommended Mr Fitzpatrick to her favour. In which he so well succeeded, that he was always one of her private parties. Nor was he backward in returning such distinction; for he soon grew so very particular in his behaviour to her, that the scandal club first began to take notice of it, and the better-disposed persons made a match between them. For my own part, I confess, I made no doubt but that his designs were strictly honourable, as the phrase is; that is, to rob a lady of her fortune by way of marriage. My aunt was, I conceived, neither young enough nor handsome enough to attract much wicked inclination; but she had matrimonial charms in great abundance.

"I was the more confirmed in this opinion from the extraordinary respect which he showed to myself from the first moment of our acquaintance. This I understood as an attempt to lessen, if possible, that disinclination which my interest might be supposed to give me towards the match; and I know not but in some measure it had that effect; for, as I was well contented with my own fortune, and of all people the least a slave to interested views, so I could not be violently the enemy of a man with whose behaviour to me I was greatly pleased; and the more so, as I was the only object of such respect; for he behaved at the same time to many women of quality without any respect at all.

"Agreeable as this was to me, he soon changed it into another kind of behaviour, which was perhaps more so. He now put on much softness and tenderness, and languished and sighed abundantly. At times, indeed, whether from art or nature I will not determine, he gave his usual loose to gaiety and mirth; but this was always in general company, and with other women; for even in a country-dance, when he was not my partner, he became grave, and put on the softest look imaginable the moment he approached me. Indeed he was in all things so very particuparticular towards me, that I must have been blind not to have discovered it. And, and, and——" "And you was more pleased still, my dear Harriet," cries Sophia; "you need not be ashamed," added she, sighing; "for sure there are irresistible charms in tenderness, which too many men are able to affect." "True," answered her cousin; "men, who in all other instances want common sense, are very Machiavels in the art of loving. I wish I did not know an instance.—Well, scandal now began to be as busy with me as it had before been with my aunt; and some good ladies did not scruple to affirm that Mr Fitzpatrick had an intrigue with us both.

"But, what may seem astonishing, my aunt never saw, nor in the least seemed to suspect, that which was visible enough, I believe, from both our behaviours. One would indeed think that love quite puts out the eyes of an old woman. In fact, they so greedily swallow the addresses which are made to them, that, like an outrageous glutton, they are not at leisure to observe what passes amongst others at the same table. This I have observed in more cases than my own; and this was so strongly verified by my aunt, that, though she often found us together at her return from the pump, the least canting word of his, pretending impatience at her absence, effectually smothered all suspicion. One artifice succeeded with her to admiration. This was his treating me like a little child, and never calling me by any other name in her presence but that of pretty miss. This indeed did him some disservice with your humble servant; but I soon saw through it, especially as in her absence he behaved to me, as I have said, in a different manner. However, if I was not greatly disobliged by a conduct of which I had discovered the design, I smarted very severely for it; for my aunt really conceived me to be what her lover (as she thought him) called me, and treated me in all respects as a perfect infant. To say the truth, I wonder she had not insisted on my again wearing leading-strings.

"At last, my lover (for so he was) thought proper, in a most solemn manner, to disclose a secret which I had known long before. He now placed all the love which he had pretended to my aunt to my account. He lamented, in very pathetic terms, the encouragement she had given him, and made a high merit of the tedious hours in which he had undergone her conversation.—What shall I tell you, my dear Sophia?—Then I will confess the truth. I was pleased with my man. I was pleased with my conquest. To rival my aunt delighted me; to rival so many other women charmed me. In short, I am afraid I did not behave as I should do, even upon the very first declaration—I wish I did not almost give him positive encouragement before we parted.

"The Bath now talked loudly—I might almost say, roared against me. Several young women affected to shun my acquaintance, not so much, perhaps, from any real suspicion, as from a desire of banishing me from a company in which I too much engrossed their favourite man. And here I cannot omit expressing my gratitude to the kindness intended me by Mr Nash, who took me one day aside, and gave me advice, which if I had followed, I had been a happy woman. `Child,' says he, `I am sorry to see the familiarity which subsists between you and a fellow who is altogether unworthy of you, and I am afraid will prove your ruin. As for your old stinking aunt, if it was to be no injury to you and my pretty Sophy Western (I assure you I repeat his words), I should be heartily glad that the fellow was in possession of all that belongs to her. I never advise old women: for, if they take it into their heads to go to the devil, it is no more possible than worth while to keep them from him. Innocence and youth and beauty are worthy a better fate, and I would save them from his clutches. Let me advise you therefore, dear child, never suffer this fellow to be particular with you again.' Many more things he said to me, which I have now forgotten, and indeed I attended very little to them at the time; for inclination contradicted all he said; and, besides, I could not be persuaded that women of quality would condescend to familiarity with such a person as he described.

"But I am afraid, my dear, I shall tire you with a detail of so many minute circumstances. To be concise, therefore, imagine me married; imagine me with my husband, at the feet of my aunt; and then imagine the maddest woman in Bedlam, in a raving fit, and your imagination will suggest to you no more than what really happened.

"The very next day my aunt left the place, partly to avoid seeing Mr Fitzpatrick or myself, and as much perhaps to avoid seeing any one else; for, though I am told she hath since denied everything stoutly, I believe she was then a little confounded at her disappointment. Since that time, I have written to her many letters, but never could obtain an answer, which I must own sits somewhat the heavier, as she herself was, though undesignedly, the occasion of all my sufferings: for, had it not been under the colour of paying his addresses to her, Mr Fitzpatrick would never have found sufficient opportunities to have engaged my heart, which, in other circumstances, I still flatter myself would not have been an easy conquest to such a person. Indeed, I believe I should not have erred so grossly in my choice if I had relied on my own judgment; but I trusted totally to the opinion of others, and very foolishly took the merit of a man for granted whom I saw so universally well received by the women. What is the reason, my dear, that we, who have understandings equal to the wisest and greatest of the other sex, so often make choice of the silliest fellows for companions and favourites? It raises my indignation to the highest pitch to reflect on the numbers of women of sense who have been undone by fools." Here she paused a moment; but, Sophia making no answer, she proceeded as in the next chapter.

CHAPTER V.

In which the history of Mrs Fitzpatrick is continued.

"We remained at Bath no longer than a fortnight after our wedding; for as to any reconciliation with my aunt, there were no hopes; and of my fortune not one farthing could be touched till I was of age, of which I now wanted more than two years. My husband therefore was resolved to set out for Ireland; against which I remonstrated very earnestly, and insisted on a promise which he had made me before our marriage that I should never take this journey against my consent; and indeed I never intended to consent to it; nor will anybody, I believe, blame me for that resolution; but this, however, I never mentioned to my husband, and petitioned only for the reprieve of a month; but he had fixed the day, and to that day he obstinately adhered.

"The evening before our departure, as we were disputing this point with great eagerness on both sides, he started suddenly from his chair, and left me abruptly, saying he was going to the rooms. He was hardly out of the house when I saw a paper lying on the floor, which, I suppose, he had carelessly pulled from his pocket, together with his handkerchief. This paper I took up, and, finding it to be a letter, I made no scruple to open and read it; and indeed I read it so often that I can repeat it to you almost word for word. This then was the letter:

> *'To Mr Brian Fitzpatrick.*
>
> 'SIR,
>
> 'YOURS received, and am surprized you should use me in this manner, as have never seen any of your cash, unless for one linsey-woolsey coat, and your bill now is upwards of £150. Consider, sir, how often you have fobbed me off with your being shortly to be married to this lady and t'other lady; but I can neither live on hopes or promises, nor will my woollen-draper take any such in payment. You tell me you are secure of having either the aunt or the niece, and that you might have married the aunt before this, whose jointure you say is immense, but that you prefer the niece on account of her ready money. Pray, sir, take a fool's advice for once, and marry the first you can get. You will pardon my offering my advice, as you know I sincerely wish you well. Shall draw on you per next post, in favour

of Messieurs John Drugget and company, at fourteen days, which doubt not your honouring, and am,

Sir, your humble servant, 'SAM. COSGRAVE.'

"This was the letter, word for word. Guess, my dear girl—guess how this letter affected me. You prefer the niece on account of her ready money! If every one of these words had been a dagger, I could with pleasure have stabbed them into his heart; but I will not recount my frantic behaviour on the occasion. I had pretty well spent my tears before his return home; but sufficient remains of them appeared in my swollen eyes. He threw himself sullenly into his chair, and for a long time we were both silent. At length, in a haughty tone, he said, `I hope, madam, your servants have packed up all your things; for the coach will be ready by six in the morning.' My patience was totally subdued by this provocation, and I answered, `No, sir, there is a letter still remains unpacked;' and then throwing it on the table I fell to upbraiding him with the most bitter language I could invent.

"Whether guilt, or shame, or prudence, restrained him I cannot say; but, though he is the most passionate of men, he exerted no rage on this occasion. He endeavoured, on the contrary, to pacify me by the most gentle means. He swore the phrase in the letter to which I principally objected was not his, nor had he ever written any such. He owned, indeed, the having mentioned his marriage, and that preference which he had given to myself, but denied with many oaths the having mentioned any such matter at all on account of the straits he was in for money, arising, he said, from his having too long neglected his estate in Ireland. And this, he said, which he could not bear to discover to me, was the only reason of his having so strenuously insisted on our journey. He then used several very endearing expressions, and concluded by a very fond caress, and many violent protestations of love.

"There was one circumstance which, though he did not appeal to it, had much weight with me in his favour, and that was the word jointure in the taylor's letter, whereas my aunt never had been married, and this Mr Fitzpatrick well knew.—— As I imagined, therefore, that the fellow must have inserted this of his own head, or from hearsay, I persuaded myself he might have ventured likewise on that odious line on no better authority. What reasoning was this, my dear? was I not an advocate rather than a judge?—But why do I mention such a circumstance as this, or appeal to it for the justification of my forgiveness?—In short, had he been guilty of twenty times as much, half the tenderness and fondness which he used would have prevailed on me to have forgiven him. I now made no farther objections to our setting out, which we did the next morning, and in a little more than a week arrived at the seat of Mr Fitzpatrick.

"Your curiosity will excuse me from relating any occurrences which past during our journey; for it would indeed be highly disagreeable to travel it over again, and no less so to you to travel it over with me.

"This seat, then, is an ancient mansion-house: if I was in one of those merry humours in which you have so often seen me, I could describe it to you ridiculously enough. It looked as if it had been formerly inhabited by a gentleman. Here was room enough, and not the less room on account of the furniture; for indeed there was very little in it. An old woman, who seemed coeval with the building, and greatly resembled her whom Chamont mentions in the Orphan, received us at the gate, and in a howl scarce human, and to me unintelligible, welcomed her master home. In short, the whole scene was so gloomy and melancholy, that it threw my spirits into the lowest dejection; which my husband discerning, instead of relieving, encreased by two or three malicious observations. `There are good houses, madam,' says he, `as you find, in other places besides England; but perhaps you had rather be in a dirty lodgings at Bath.'

"Happy, my dear, is the woman who, in any state of life, hath a cheerful good-natured companion to support and comfort her! But why do I reflect on happy situations only to aggravate my own misery? my companion, far from clearing up the gloom of solitude, soon convinced me that I must have been wretched with him in any place, and in any condition. In a word, he was a surly fellow, a character perhaps you have never seen; for, indeed, no woman ever sees it exemplified but in a father, a brother, or a husband; and, though you have a father, he is not of that character. This surly fellow had formerly appeared to me the very reverse, and so he did still to every other person. Good heaven! how is it possible for a man to maintain a constant lie in his appearance abroad and in company, and to content himself with shewing disagreeable truth only at home? Here, my dear, they make themselves amends for the uneasy restraint which they put on their tempers in the world; for I have observed, the more merry and gay and good-humoured my husband hath at any time been in company, the more sullen and morose he was sure to become at our next private meeting. How shall I describe his barbarity? To my fondness he was cold and insensible. My little comical ways, which you, my Sophy, and which others, have called so agreeable, he treated with contempt. In my most serious moments he sung and whistled; and whenever I was thoroughly dejected and miserable he was angry, and abused me: for, though he was never pleased with my good-humour, nor ascribed it to my satisfaction in him, yet my low spirits always offended him, and those he imputed to my repentance of having (as he said) married an Irishman.

"You will easily conceive, my dear Graveairs (I ask your pardon, I really forgot myself), that, when a woman makes an imprudent match in the sense of the world, that is, when she is not an arrant prostitute to pecuniary interest, she must necessarily have some inclination and affection for her man. You will as easily believe that this affection may possibly be lessened; nay, I do assure you, contempt will wholly eradicate it. This contempt I now began to entertain for my husband, whom I now discovered to be—I must use the expression—an arrant blockhead. Perhaps you will wonder I did not make this discovery long before; but women will suggest a thousand excuses to themselves for the folly of those they like: besides, give me leave to tell you, it requires a most penetrating eye to discern a fool through the disguises of gaiety and good breeding.

"It will be easily imagined that, when I once despised my husband, as I confess to you I soon did, I must consequently dislike his company; and indeed I had the happiness of being very little troubled with it; for our house was now most elegantly furnished, our cellars well stocked, and dogs and horses provided in great abundance. As my gentleman therefore entertained his neighbours with great hospitality, so his neighbours resorted to him with great alacrity; and sports and drinking consumed so much of his time, that a small part of his conversation, that is to say, of his ill-humours, fell to my share.

"Happy would it have been for me if I could as easily have avoided all other disagreeable company; but, alas! I was confined to some which constantly tormented me; and the more, as I saw no prospect of being relieved from them. These companions were my own racking thoughts, which plagued and in a manner haunted me night and day. In this situation I past through a scene, the horrors of which can neither be painted nor imagined. Think, my dear, figure, if you can, to yourself, what I must have undergone. I became a mother by the man I scorned, hated, and detested. I went through all the agonies and miseries of a lying-in (ten times more painful in such a circumstance than the worst labour can be when one endures it for a man one loves) in a desert, or rather, indeed, a scene of riot and revel, without a friend, without a companion, or without any of those agreeable circumstances which often alleviate, and perhaps sometimes more than compensate, the sufferings of our sex at that season."

CHAPTER VI.

In which the mistake of the landlord throws Sophia into a dreadful consternation.

Mrs Fitzpatrick was proceeding in her narrative when she was interrupted by the entrance of dinner, greatly to the concern of Sophia; for the misfortunes of her friend had raised her anxiety, and left her no appetite but what Mrs Fitzpatrick was to satisfy by her relation.

The landlord now attended with a plate under his arm, and with the same respect in his countenance and address which he would have put on had the ladies arrived in a coach and six. -- The married lady seemed less affected with her own misfortunes than was her cousin; for the former ate very heartily, whereas the latter could hardly swallow a morsel. Sophia likewise showed more concern and sorrow in her countenance than appeared in the other lady; who, having observed these symptoms in her friend, begged her to be comforted, saying, "Perhaps all may yet end better than either you or I expect."

Our landlord thought he had now an opportunity to open his mouth, and was resolved not to omit it. "I am sorry, madam," cries he, "that your ladyship can't eat; for to be sure you must be hungry after so long fasting. I hope your ladyship is not uneasy at anything, for, as madam there says, all may end better than anybody expects. A gentleman who was here just now brought excellent news; and perhaps some folks who have given other folks the slip may get to London before they are overtaken; and if they do, I make no doubt but they will find people who will be very ready to receive them."

All persons under the apprehension of danger convert whatever they see and hear into the objects of that apprehension. Sophia therefore immediately concluded, from the foregoing speech, that she was known, and pursued by her father. She was now struck with the utmost consternation, and for a few minutes deprived of the power of speech; which she no sooner recovered than she desired the landlord to send his servants out of the room, and then, addressing herself to him, said, "I perceive, sir, you know who we are; but I beseech you—nay, I am convinced, if you have any compassion or goodness, you will not betray us."

"I betray your ladyship!" quoth the landlord; "no (and then he swore several very hearty oaths); I would sooner be cut into ten thousand pieces. I hate all treachery. I! I never betrayed any one in my life yet, and I am sure I shall not begin with so sweet a lady as your ladyship. All the world would very much blame me if I should, since it will be in your ladyship's power so shortly to reward me. My wife can witness for me, I knew your ladyship the moment you came into the house: I said it was your honour, before I lifted you from your horse, and I shall carry the bruises I got in your ladyship's service to the grave; but what signified that, as long as I saved your ladyship? To be sure some people this morning would have thought of getting a reward; but no such thought ever entered into my head. I would sooner starve than take any reward for betraying your ladyship."

"I promise you, sir," says Sophia, "if it be ever in my power to reward you, you shall not lose by your generosity."

"Alack-a-day, madam!" answered the landlord; "in your ladyship's power! Heaven put it as much into your will! I am only afraid your honour will forget such a poor man as an innkeeper; but, if your ladyship should not, I hope you will remember what reward I refused—refused! that is, I would have refused, and to be sure it may be called refusing, for I might have had it certainly; and to be sure you might have been in some houses;—but, for my part, would not methinks for the world have your ladyship wrong me so much as to imagine I ever thought of betraying you, even before I heard the good news."

"What news, pray?" says Sophia, something eagerly.

"Hath not your ladyship heard it, then?" cries the landlord; "nay, like enough, for I heard it only a few minutes ago; and if I had never heard it, may the devil fly away with me this instant if I would have betrayed your honour! no, if I would, may I—" Here he subjoined several dreadful imprecations, which Sophia at last interrupted, and begged to know what he meant by the news.—He was going to answer, when Mrs Honour came running into the room, all pale and breathless, and cried out, "Madam, we are all undone, all ruined, they are come, they are come!" These words almost froze up the blood of Sophia; but Mrs Fitzpatrick asked Honour who were come?—"Who?" answered she, "why, the French; several hundred thousands of them are landed, and we shall be all murdered and ravished."

As a miser, who hath, in some well-built city, a cottage, value twenty shillings, when at a distance he is alarmed with the news of a fire, turns pale and trembles at his loss; but when he finds the beautiful palaces only are burnt, and his own cottage remains safe, he comes instantly to himself, and smiles at his good fortunes: or as (for we dislike something in the former simile) the tender mother, when terrified with the apprehension that her darling boy is drowned, is struck senseless and almost dead with consternation; but when she is told that little master is safe, and the Victory only, with twelve hundred brave men, gone to the bottom, life and sense again return, maternal fondness enjoys the sudden relief from all its fears, and the general benevolence which at another time would have deeply felt the dreadful catastrophe, lies fast asleep in her mind;—so Sophia, than whom none was more capable of tenderly feeling the general calamity of her country, found such immediate satisfaction from the relief of those terrors she had of being overtaken by her father, that the arrival of the French scarce made any impression on her. She gently chid her maid for the fright into which she had thrown her, and said "she was glad it was no worse; for that she had feared somebody else was come."

"Ay, ay," quoth the landlord, smiling, "her ladyship knows better things; she knows the French are our very best friends, and come over hither only for our good. They are the people who are to make Old England flourish again. I warrant her honour thought the duke was coming; and that was enough to put her into a fright. I was going to tell your ladyship the news.—His honour's majesty, Heaven bless him, hath given the duke the slip, and is marching as fast as he can to London, and ten thousand French are landed to join him on the road."

Sophia was not greatly pleased with this news, nor with the gentleman who related it; but, as she still imagined he knew her (for she could not possibly have any suspicion of the real truth), she durst not show any dislike. And now the landlord, having removed the cloth from the table, withdrew; but at his departure frequently repeated his hopes of being remembered hereafter.

The mind of Sophia was not at all easy under the supposition of being known at this house; for she still applied to herself many things which the landlord had addressed to Jenny Cameron; she therefore ordered her maid to pump out of him by what means he had become acquainted with her person, and who had offered him the reward for betraying her; she likewise ordered the horses to be in readiness by four in the morning, at which hour Mrs Fitzpatrick promised to bear her company; and then, composing herself as well as she could, she desired that lady to continue her story.

CHAPTER VII.

In which Mrs Fitzpatrick concludes her history.

While Mrs Honour, in pursuance of the commands of her mistress, ordered a bowl of punch, and invited my landlord and landlady to partake of it, Mrs Fitzpatrick thus went on with her relation.

"Most of the officers who were quartered at a town in our neighbourhood were of my husband's acquaintance. Among these there was a lieutenant, a very pretty sort of man, and who was married to a woman, so agreeable both in her temper and conversation, that from our first knowing each other, which was soon after my lying-in, we were almost inseparable companions; for I had the good fortune to make myself equally agreeable to her.

"The lieutenant, who was neither a sot nor a sportsman, was frequently of our parties; indeed he was very little with my husband, and no more than good breeding constrained him to be, as he lived almost constantly at our house. My husband often expressed much dissatisfaction at the lieutenant's preferring my company to his; he was very angry with me on that account, and gave me many a hearty curse for drawing away his companions; saying, `I ought to be d—n'd for having spoiled one of the prettiest fellows in the world, by making a milksop of him.'

"You will be mistaken, my dear Sophia, if you imagine that the anger of my husband arose from my depriving him of a companion; for the lieutenant was not a person with whose society a fool could be pleased; and, if I should admit the possibility of this, so little right had my husband to place the loss of his companion to me, that I am convinced it was my conversation alone which induced him ever to come to the house. No, child, it was envy, the worst and most rancorous kind of envy, the envy of superiority of understanding. The wretch could not bear to see my conversation preferred to his, by a man of whom he could not entertain the least jealousy. O my dear Sophy, you are a woman of sense; if you marry a man, as is most probable you will, of less capacity than yourself, make frequent trials of his temper before marriage, and see whether he can bear to submit to such a superiority.—Promise me, Sophy, you will take this advice; for you will hereafter find its importance." "It is very likely I shall never marry at all," answered Sophia; "I think, at least, I shall never marry a man in whose understanding I see any defects before marriage; and I promise you I would rather give up my own than see any such afterwards." "Give up your understanding!" replied Mrs Fitzpatrick; "oh, fie, child! I will not believe so meanly of you. Everything else I might myself be brought to give up; but never this. Nature would not have allotted this superiority to the wife in so many instances, if she had intended we should all of us have surrendered it to the husband. This, indeed, men of sense never expect of us; of which the lieutenant I have just mentioned was one notable example; for though he had a very good understanding, he always acknowledged (as was really true) that his wife had a better. And this, perhaps, was one reason of the hatred my tyrant bore her.

"Before he would be so governed by a wife, he said, especially such an ugly b— (for, indeed, she was not a regular beauty, but very agreeable and extremely genteel), he would see all the women upon earth at the devil, which was a very usual phrase with him. He said, he wondered what I could see in her to be so charmed with her company: since this woman, says he, hath come among us, there is an end of your beloved reading, which you pretended to like so much, that you could not afford time to return the visits of the ladies in this country; and I must confess I had been guilty of a little rudeness this way; for the ladies there are at least no better than the mere country ladies here; and I think I need make no other excuse to you for declining any intimacy with them.

"This correspondence, however, continued a whole year, even all the while the lieutenant was quartered in that town; for which I was contented to pay the tax of being constantly abused in the manner above mentioned by my husband; I mean when he was at home; for he was frequently absent a month at a time at Dublin, and once made a journey of two months to London: in all which journeys I thought it a very singular happiness that he never once desired my company; nay, by his frequent censures on men who could not travel, as he phrased it, without a wife tied up to their tail, he sufficiently intimated that, had I been never so desirous of accompanying him, my wishes would have been in vain; but, Heaven knows, such wishes were very far from my thoughts.

"At length my friend was removed from me, and I was again left to my solitude, to the tormenting conversation with my own reflections, and to apply to books for my only comfort. I now read almost all day long. How many books do you think I read in three months?" "I can't guess, indeed, cousin," answered Sophia. "Perhaps half a score." "Half a score! half a thousand, child!" answered the other. "I read a good deal in Daniel's English History of France; a great deal in Plutarch's Lives, the Atalantis, Pope's Homer, Dryden's Plays, Chillingworth, the Countess D'Aulnois, and Locke's Human Understanding.

"During this interval I wrote three very supplicating, and, I thought, moving letters to my aunt; but, as I received no answer to any of them, my disdain would not suffer me to continue my application." Here she stopt, and, looking earnestly at Sophia, said, "Methinks, my dear, I read something in your eyes which reproaches me of a neglect in another place, where I should have met with a kinder return." "Indeed, dear Harriet," answered Sophia, "your story is an apology for any neglect; but, indeed, I feel that I have been guilty of a remissness, without so good an excuse.—Yet pray proceed; for I long, though I tremble, to hear the end."

Thus, then, Mrs Fitzpatrick resumed her narrative:—"My husband now took a second journey to England, where he continued upwards of three months; during the greater part of this time I led a life which nothing but having led a worse could make me think tolerable; for perfect solitude can never be reconciled to a social mind, like mine, but when it relieves you from the company of those you hate. What added to my wretchedness was the loss of my little infant: not that I pretend to have had for it that extravagant tenderness of which I believe I might have been capable under other circumstances; but I resolved, in every instance, to discharge the duty of the tenderest mother; and this care prevented me from feeling the weight of that heaviest of all things, when it can be at all said to lie heavy on our hands.

"I had spent full ten weeks almost entirely by myself, having seen nobody all that time, except my servants and a very few visitors, when a young lady, a relation to my husband, came from a distant part of Ireland to visit me. She had staid once before a week at my house, and then I gave her a pressing invitation to return; for she was a very agreeable woman, and had improved good natural parts by a proper education. Indeed, she was to me a welcome guest.

"A few days after her arrival, perceiving me in very low spirits, without enquiring the cause, which, indeed, she very well knew, the young lady fell to compassionating my case. She said, `Though politeness had prevented me from complaining to my husband's relations of his behaviour, yet they all were very sensible of it, and felt great concern upon that account; but none more than herself.' And after some more general discourse on this head, which I own I could not forbear countenancing, at last, after much previous precaution and enjoined concealment, she communicated to me, as a profound secret—that my husband kept a mistress.

"You will certainly imagine I heard this news with the utmost insensibility—Upon my word, if you do, your imagination will mislead you. Contempt had not so kept down my anger to my husband, but that hatred rose again on this occasion. What can be the reason of this? Are we so abominably selfish, that we can be concerned at others having possession even of what we despise? Or are we not rather abominably vain, and is not this the greatest injury done to our vanity? What think you, Sophia?"

"I don't know, indeed," answered Sophia; "I have never troubled myself with any of these deep contemplations; but I think the lady did very ill in communicating to you such a secret."

"And yet, my dear, this conduct is natural," replied Mrs Fitzpatrick; "and, when you have seen and read as much as myself, you will acknowledge it to be so."

"I am sorry to hear it is natural," returned Sophia; "for I want neither reading nor experience to convince me that it is very dishonourable and very ill-natured: nay, it is surely as ill-bred to tell a husband or wife of the faults of each other as to tell them of their own."

"Well," continued Mrs Fitzpatrick, "my husband at last returned; and, if I am thoroughly acquainted with my own thoughts, I hated him now more than ever; but I despised him rather less: for certainly nothing so much weakens our contempt, as an injury done to our pride or our vanity.

"He now assumed a carriage to me so very different from what he had lately worn, and so nearly resembling his behaviour the first week of our marriage, that, had I now had any spark of love remaining, he might, possibly, have rekindled my fondness for him. But, though hatred may succeed to contempt, and may perhaps get the better of it, love, I believe, cannot. The truth is, the passion of love is too restless to remain contented without the gratification which it receives from its object; and one can no more be inclined to love without loving than we can have eyes without seeing. When a husband, therefore, ceases to be the object of this passion, it is most probable some other man—I say, my dear, if your husband grows indifferent to you—if you once come to despise him—I say—that is—if you have the passion of love in you—Lud! I have bewildered myself so—but one is apt, in these abstracted considerations, to lose the concatenation of ideas, as Mr Locke says:—in short, the truth is—in short, I scarce know what it is; but, as I was saying, my husband returned, and his behaviour, at first, greatly surprized me; but he soon acquainted me with the motive, and taught me to account for it. In a word, then, he had spent and lost all the ready money of my fortune; and, as he could mortgage his own estate no deeper, he was now desirous to supply himself with cash for his extravagance, by selling a little estate of mine, which he could not do without my assistance; and to obtain this favour was the whole and sole motive of all the fondness which he now put on.

"With this I peremptorily refused to comply. I told him, and I told him truly, that, had I been possessed of the Indies at our first marriage, he might have commanded it all; for it had been a constant maxim with me, that where a woman disposes of her heart, she should always deposit her fortune; but, as he had been so kind, long ago, to restore the former into my possession, I was resolved likewise to retain what little remained of the latter.

"I will not describe to you the passion into which these words, and the resolute air in which they were spoken, threw him: nor will I trouble you with the whole scene which succeeded between us. Out came, you may be well assured, the story of the mistress; and out it did come, with all the embellishments which anger and disdain could bestow upon it.

"Mr Fitzpatrick seemed a little thunderstruck with this, and more confused than I had seen him, though his ideas are always confused enough, heaven knows. He did not, however, endeavour to exculpate himself; but took a method which almost equally confounded me. What was this but recrimination? He affected to be jealous:—he may, for aught I know, be inclined enough to jealousy in his natural temper; nay, he must have had it from nature, or the devil must have put it into his head; for I defy all the world to cast a just aspersion on my character: nay, the most scandalous tongues have never dared censure my reputation. My fame, I thank heaven, hath been always as spotless as my life; and let falsehood itself accuse that if it dare. No, my dear Graveairs, however provoked, however ill-treated, however injured in my love, I have firmly resolved never to give the least room for censure on this account.—And yet, my dear, there are some people so malicious, some tongues so venomous, that no innocence can escape them. The most undesigned word, the most accidental look, the least familiarity, the most innocent freedom, will be misconstrued, and magnified into I know not what, by some people. But I despise, my dear Graveairs, I despise all such slander. No such malice, I assure you, ever gave me an uneasy moment. No, no, I promise you I am above all that.—But where was I? O let me see, I told you my husband was jealous—And of whom, I pray?—Why, of whom but the lieutenant I mentioned to you before! He was obliged to resort above a year and more back to find any object for this unaccountable passion, if, indeed, he really felt any such, and was not an arrant counterfeit in order to abuse me.

"But I have tired you already with too many particulars. I will now bring my story to a very speedy conclusion. In short, then, after many scenes very unworthy to be repeated, in which my cousin engaged so heartily on my side, that Mr Fitzpatrick at last turned her out of doors; when he found I was neither to be soothed nor bullied into compliance, he took a very violent method indeed. Perhaps you will conclude he beat me; but this, though he hath approached very near to it, he never actually did. He confined me to my room, without suffering me to have either pen, ink, paper, or book: and a servant every day made my bed, and brought me my food.

"When I had remained a week under this imprisonment, he made me a visit, and, with the voice of a schoolmaster, or, what is often much the same, of a tyrant, asked me, `If I would yet comply?' I answered, very stoutly, `That I would die first.' `Then so you shall, and be d—nd!' cries he; `for you shall never go alive out of this room.'

"Here I remained a fortnight longer; and, to say the truth, my constancy was almost subdued, and I began to think of submission; when, one day, in the absence of my husband, who was gone abroad for some short time, by the greatest good fortune in the world, an accident happened.—I—at a time when I began to give way to the utmost despair——everything would be excusable at such a time—at that very time I received——But it would take up an hour to tell you all particulars.—In one word, then (for I will not tire you with circumstances), gold, the common key to all padlocks, opened my door, and set me at liberty.

"I now made haste to Dublin, where I immediately procured a passage to England; and was proceeding to Bath, in order to throw myself into the protection of my aunt, or of your father, or of any relation who would afford it me. My husband overtook me last night at the inn where I lay, and which you left a few minutes before me; but I had the good luck to escape him, and to follow you.

"And thus, my dear, ends my history: a tragical one, I am sure, it is to myself; but, perhaps, I ought rather to apologize to you for its dullness."

Sophia heaved a deep sigh, and answered, "Indeed, Harriet, I pity you from my soul!——But what could you expect? Why, why, would you marry an Irishman?"

"Upon my word," replied her cousin, "your censure is unjust. There are, among the Irish, men of as much worth and honour as any among the English: nay, to speak the truth, generosity of spirit is rather more common among them. I have known some examples there, too, of good husbands; and I believe these are not very plenty in England. Ask me, rather, what I could expect when I married a fool; and I will tell you a solemn truth; I did not know him to be so."—"Can no man," said Sophia, in a very low and altered voice, "do you think, make a bad husband, who is not a fool?" "That," answered the other, "is too general a negative; but none, I believe, is so likely as a fool to prove so. Among my acquaintance, the silliest fellows are the worst husbands; and I will venture to assert, as a fact, that a man of sense rarely behaves very ill to a wife who deserves very well."

CHAPTER VIII.

A dreadful alarm in the inn, with the arrival of an unexpected friend of Mrs Fitzpatrick.

Sophia now, at the desire of her cousin, related—not what follows, but what hath gone before in this history: for which reason the reader will, I suppose, excuse me for not repeating it over again.

One remark, however, I cannot forbear making on her narrative, namely, that she made no more mention of Jones, from the beginning to the end, than if there had been no such person alive. This I will neither endeavour to account for nor to excuse. Indeed, if this may be called a kind of dishonesty, it seems the more inexcusable, from the apparent openness and explicit sincerity of the other lady.—But so it was.

Just as Sophia arrived at the conclusion of her story, there arrived in the room where the two ladies were sitting a noise, not unlike, in loudness, to that of a pack of hounds just let out from their kennel; nor, in shrillness, to cats, when caterwauling; or to screech owls; or, indeed, more like (for what animal can resemble a human voice?) to those sounds which, in the pleasant mansions of that gate which seems to derive its name from a duplicity of tongues, issue from the mouths, and sometimes from the nostrils, of those fair river nymphs, ycleped of old the Naïades; in the vulgar tongue translated oyster-wenches; for when, instead of the antient libations of milk and honey and oil, the rich distillation from the juniper-berry, or, perhaps, from malt, hath, by the early devotion of their votaries, been poured forth in great abundance, should any daring tongue with unhallowed license prophane, *i.e.*, depreciate, the delicate fat Milton oyster, the plaice sound and firm, the flounder as much alive as when in the water, the shrimp as big as a prawn, the fine cod alive but a few hours ago, or any other of the various treasures which those water-deities who fish the sea and rivers have committed to the care of the nymphs, the angry Naïades lift up their immortal voices, and the prophane wretch is struck deaf for his impiety.

Such was the noise which now burst from one of the rooms below; and soon the thunder, which long had rattled at a distance, began to approach nearer and nearer, till, having ascended by degrees upstairs, it at last entered the apartment where the ladies were. In short, to drop all metaphor and figure, Mrs Honour, having scolded violently below-stairs, and continued the same all the way up, came in to her mistress in a most outrageous passion, crying out, "What doth your ladyship think? Would you imagine that this impudent villain, the master of this house, hath had the impudence to tell me, nay, to stand it out to my face, that your ladyship is that nasty, stinking wh—re (Jenny Cameron they call her), that runs about the country with the Pretender? Nay, the lying, saucy villain had the assurance to tell me that your ladyship had owned yourself to be so; but I have clawed the rascal; I have left the marks of my nails in his impudent face. My lady! says I, you saucy scoundrel; my lady is meat for no pretenders. She is a young lady of as good fashion, and family, and fortune, as any in Somersetshire. Did you never hear of the great Squire Western, sirrah? She is his only daughter; she is——, and heiress to all his great estate. My lady to be called a nasty Scotch wh—re by such a varlet!—To be sure I wish I had knocked his brains out with the punch-bowl."

The principal uneasiness with which Sophia was affected on this occasion Honour had herself caused, by having in her passion discovered who she was. However, as this mistake of the landlord sufficiently accounted for those passages which Sophia had before mistaken, she acquired some ease on that account; nor could she, upon the whole, forbear smiling. This enraged Honour, and she cried, "Indeed, madam, I did not think your ladyship would have made a laughing matter of it. To be called whore by such an impudent low rascal. Your ladyship may be angry with me, for aught I know, for taking your part, since proffered service, they say, stinks; but to be sure I could never bear to hear a lady of mine called whore.—Nor will I bear it. I am sure your ladyship is as virtuous a lady as ever sat foot on English ground, and I will claw any villain's eyes out who dares for to offer to presume for to say the least word to the contrary. Nobody ever could say the least ill of the character of any lady that ever I waited upon."

Hinc illae lachrymae; in plain truth, Honour had as much love for her mistress as most servants have, that is to say—But besides this, her pride obliged her to support the character of the lady she waited on; for she thought her own was in a very close manner connected with it. In proportion as the character of her mistress was raised, hers likewise, as she conceived, was raised with it; and, on the contrary, she thought the one could not be lowered without the other.

On this subject, reader, I must stop a moment, to tell thee a story. "The famous Nell Gwynn, stepping one day, from a house where she had made a short visit, into her coach, saw a great mob assembled, and her footman all bloody and dirty; the fellow, being asked by his mistress the reason of his being in that condition, answered, `I have been fighting, madam, with an impudent rascal who called your ladyship a wh—re.' `You blockhead,' replied Mrs Gwynn, `at this rate you must fight every day of your life; why, you fool, all the world knows it.' `Do they?' cries the fellow, in a muttering voice, after he had shut the coach-door, `they shan't call me a whore's footman for all that.'"

Thus the passion of Mrs Honour appears natural enough, even if it were to be no otherwise accounted for; but, in reality, there was another cause of her anger; for which we must beg leave to remind our reader of a circumstance mentioned in the above simile. There are indeed certain liquors, which, being applied to our passions, or to fire, produce effects the very reverse of those produced by water, as they serve to kindle and inflame, rather than to extinguish. Among these, the generous liquor called punch is one. It was not, therefore, without reason, that the learned Dr Cheney used to call drinking punch pouring liquid fire down your throat.

Now, Mrs Honour had unluckily poured so much of this liquid fire down her throat, that the smoke of it began to ascend into her pericranium and blinded the eyes of Reason, which is there supposed to keep her residence, while the fire itself from the stomach easily reached the heart, and there inflamed the noble passion of pride. So that, upon the whole, we shall cease to wonder at the violent rage of the waiting-woman; though at first sight we must confess the cause seems inadequate to the effect.

Sophia and her cousin both did all in their power to extinguish these flames which had roared so loudly all over the house. They at length prevailed; or, to carry the metaphor one step farther, the fire, having consumed all the fuel which the language affords, to wit, every reproachful term in it, at last went out of its own accord.

But, though tranquillity was restored above-stairs, it was not so below; where my landlady, highly resenting the injury done to the beauty of her husband by the flesh-spades of Mrs Honour, called aloud for revenge and justice. As to the poor man, who had principally suffered in the engagement, he was perfectly quiet. Perhaps the blood which he lost might have cooled his anger: for the enemy had not only applied her nails to his cheeks, but likewise her fist to his nostrils, which lamented the blow with tears of blood in great abundance. To this we may add reflections on his mistake; but indeed nothing so effectually silenced his resentment as the manner in which he now discovered his error; for as to the behaviour of Mrs Honour, it had the more confirmed him in his opinion; but he was now assured by a person of great figure, and who was attended by a great equipage, that one of the ladies was a woman of fashion, and his intimate acquaintance.

By the orders of this person, the landlord now ascended, and acquainted our fair travellers that a great gentleman below desired to do them the honour of waiting on them. Sophia turned pale and trembled at this message, though the reader will conclude it was too civil, notwithstanding the landlord's blunder, to have come from her father; but fear hath the common fault of a justice of peace, and is apt to conclude hastily from every slight circumstance, without examining the evidence on both sides.

To ease the reader's curiosity, therefore, rather than his apprehensions, we proceed to inform him that an Irish peer had arrived very late that evening at the inn, in his way to London. This nobleman, having sallied from his supper at the hurricane before commemorated, had seen the attendant of Mrs Fitzpatrick, and upon a short enquiry, was informed that her lady, with whom he was very particularly acquainted, was above. This information he had no sooner received than he addressed himself to the landlord, pacified him, and sent him upstairs with compliments rather civiller than those which were delivered.

It may perhaps be wondered at that the waiting-woman herself was not the messenger employed on this occasion; but we are sorry to say she was not at present qualified for that, or indeed for any other office. The rum (for so the landlord chose to call the distillation from malt) had basely taken the advantage of the fatigue which the poor woman had undergone, and had made terrible depredations on her noble faculties, at a time when they were very unable to resist the attack.

We shall not describe this tragical scene too fully; but we thought ourselves obliged, by that historic integrity which we profess, shortly to hint a matter which we would otherwise have been glad to have spared. Many historians, indeed, for want of this integrity, or of diligence, to say no worse, often leave the reader to find out these little circumstances in the dark, and sometimes to his great confusion and perplexity.

Sophia was very soon eased of her causeless fright by the entry of the noble peer, who was not only an intimate acquaintance of Mrs Fitzpatrick, but in reality a very particular friend of that lady. To say truth, it was by his assistance that she had been enabled to escape from her husband; for this nobleman had the same gallant disposition with those renowned knights of whom we read in heroic story, and had delivered many an imprisoned nymph from durance. He was indeed as bitter an enemy to the savage authority too often exercised by husbands and fathers, over the young and lovely of the other sex, as ever knight-errant was to the barbarous power of enchanters; nay, to say truth, I have often suspected that those very enchanters with which romance everywhere abounds were in reality no other than the husbands of those days; and matrimony itself was, perhaps, the enchanted castle in which the nymphs were said to be confined.

This nobleman had an estate in the neighbourhood of Fitzpatrick, and had been for some time acquainted with the lady. No sooner, therefore, did he hear of her confinement, than he earnestly applied himself to procure her liberty; which he presently effected, not by storming the castle, according to the example of antient heroes, but by corrupting the governor, in conformity with the modern art of war, in which craft is held to be preferable to valour, and gold is found to be more irresistible than either lead or steel.

This circumstance, however, as the lady did not think it material enough to relate to her friend, we would not at that time impart it to the reader. We rather chose to leave him a while under a supposition that she had found, or coined, or by some very extraordinary, perhaps supernatural means, had possessed herself of the money with which she had bribed her keeper, than to interrupt her narrative by giving a hint of what seemed to her of too little importance to be mentioned.

The peer, after a short conversation, could not forbear expressing some surprize at meeting the lady in that place; nor could he refrain from telling her he imagined she had been gone to Bath. Mrs Fitzpatrick very freely answered, "That she had been prevented in her purpose by the arrival of a person she need not mention. In short," says she, "I was overtaken by my husband (for I need not affect to conceal what the world knows too well already). I had the good fortune to escape in a most surprizing manner, and am now going to London with this young lady, who is a near relation of mine, and who hath escaped from as great a tyrant as my own."

His lordship, concluding that this tyrant was likewise a husband, made a speech full of compliments to both the ladies, and as full of invectives against his own sex; nor indeed did he avoid some oblique glances at the matrimonial institution itself, and at the unjust powers given by it to man over the more sensible and more meritorious part of the species. He ended his oration with an offer of his protection, and of his coach and six, which was instantly accepted by Mrs Fitzpatrick, and at last, upon her persuasions, by Sophia.

Matters being thus adjusted, his lordship took his leave, and the ladies retired to rest, where Mrs Fitzpatrick entertained her cousin with many high encomiums on the character of the noble peer, and enlarged very particularly on his great fondness for his wife; saying, she believed he was almost the only person of high rank who was entirely constant to the marriage bed. "Indeed," added she, "my dear Sophy, that is a very rare virtue amongst men of condition. Never expect it when you marry; for, believe me, if you do, you will certainly be deceived."

A gentle sigh stole from Sophia at these words, which perhaps contributed to form a dream of no very pleasant kind; but, as she never revealed this dream to any one, so the reader cannot expect to see it related here.

CHAPTER IX.

The morning introduced in some pretty writing. A stagecoach. The civility of chambermaids. The heroic temper of Sophia. Her generosity. The return to it. The departure of the company, and their

arrival at London; with some remarks for the use of travellers.

Those members of society who are born to furnish the blessings of life now began to light their candles, in order to pursue their daily labours for the use of those who are born to enjoy these blessings. The sturdy hind now attends the levee of his fellow-labourer the ox; the cunning artificer, the diligent mechanic, spring from their hard mattress; and now the bonny housemaid begins to repair the disordered drum-room, while the riotous authors of that disorder, in broken interrupted slumbers, tumble and toss, as if the hardness of down disquieted their repose.

In simple phrase, the clock had no sooner struck seven than the ladies were ready for their journey; and, at their desire, his lordship and his equipage were prepared to attend them.

And now a matter of some difficulty arose; and this was how his lordship himself should be conveyed; for though in stage-coaches, where passengers are properly considered as so much luggage, the ingenious coachman stows half a dozen with perfect ease into the place of four; for well he contrives that the fat hostess, or well-fed alderman, may take up no more room than the slim miss, or taper master; it being the nature of guts, when well squeezed, to give way, and to lie in a narrow compass; yet in these vehicles, which are called, for distinction's sake, gentlemen's coaches, though they are often larger than the others, this method of packing is never attempted.

His lordship would have put a short end to the difficulty, by very gallantly desiring to mount his horse; but Mrs Fitzpatrick would by no means consent to it. It was therefore concluded that the Abigails should, by turns, relieve each other on one of his lordship's horses, which was presently equipped with a side-saddle for that purpose.

Everything being settled at the inn, the ladies discharged their former guides, and Sophia made a present to the landlord, partly to repair the bruise which he had received under herself, and partly on account of what he had suffered under the hands of her enraged waiting-woman. And now Sophia first discovered a loss which gave her some uneasiness; and this was of the hundred-pound bank-bill which her father had given her at their last meeting; and which, within a very inconsiderable trifle, was all the treasure she was at present worth. She searched everywhere, and shook and tumbled all her things to no purpose, the bill was not to be found: and she was at last fully persuaded that she had lost it from her pocket when she had the misfortune of tumbling from her horse in the dark lane, as before recorded: a fact that seemed the more probable, as she now recollected some discomposure in her pockets which had happened at that time, and the great difficulty with which she had drawn forth her handkerchief the very instant before her fall, in order to relieve the distress of Mrs Fitzpatrick.

Misfortunes of this kind, whatever inconveniencies they may be attended with, are incapable of subduing a mind in which there is any strength, without the assistance of avarice. Sophia, therefore, though nothing could be worse timed than this accident at such a season, immediately got the better of her concern, and, with her wonted serenity and cheerfulness of countenance, returned to her company. His lordship conducted the ladies into the vehicle, as he did likewise Mrs Honour, who, after many civilities, and more dear madams, at last yielded to the well-bred importunities of her sister Abigail, and submitted to be complimented with the first ride in the coach; in which indeed she would afterwards have been contented to have pursued her whole journey, had not her mistress, after several fruitless intimations, at length forced her to take her turn on horseback.

The coach, now having received its company, began to move forwards, attended by many servants, and led by two captains, who had before rode with his lordship, and who would have been dismissed from the vehicle upon a much less worthy occasion than was this of accommodating two ladies. In this they acted only as gentlemen; but they were ready at any time to have performed the office of a footman, or indeed would have condescended lower, for the honour of his lordship's company, and for the convenience of his table.

My landlord was so pleased with the present he had received from Sophia, that he rather rejoiced in than regretted his bruise or his scratches. The reader will perhaps be curious to know the *quantum* of this present; but we cannot satisfy his curiosity. Whatever it was, it satisfied the landlord for his bodily hurt; but he lamented he had not known before how little the lady valued her money; "For to be sure," says he, "one might have charged every article double, and she would have made no cavil at the reckoning."

His wife, however, was far from drawing this conclusion; whether she really felt any injury done to her husband more than he did himself, I will not say: certain it is, she was much less satisfied with the generosity of Sophia. "Indeed," cries she, "my dear, the lady knows better how to dispose of her money than you imagine. She might very well think we should not put up such a business without some satisfaction, and the law would have cost her an infinite deal more than this poor little matter, which I wonder you would take." "You are always so bloodily wise," quoth the husband: "it would have cost her more, would it? dost fancy I don't know that as well as thee? but would any of that more, or so much, have come into our pockets? Indeed, if son Tom the lawyer had been alive, I could have been glad to have put such a pretty business into his hands. He would have got a good picking out of it; but I have no relation now who is a lawyer, and why should I go to law for the benefit of strangers?" "Nay, to be sure," answered she, "you must know best." "I believe I do," replied he. "I fancy, when money is to be got, I can smell it out as well as another. Everybody, let me tell you, would not have talked people out of this. Mind that, I say; everybody would not have cajoled this out of her, mind that." The wife then joined in the applause of her husband's sagacity; and thus ended the short dialogue between them on this occasion.

We will therefore take our leave of these good people, and attend his lordship and his fair companions, who made such good expedition that they performed a journey of ninety miles in two days, and on the second evening arrived in London, without having encountered any one adventure on the road worthy the dignity of this history to relate. Our pen, therefore, shall imitate the expedition which it describes, and our history shall keep pace with the travellers who are its subject. Good writers will, indeed, do well to imitate the ingenious traveller in this instance, who always proportions his stay at any place to the beauties, elegancies, and curiosities which it affords. At Eshur, at Stowe, at Wilton, at Eastbury, and at Prior's Park, days are too short for the ravished imagination; while we admire the wondrous power of art in improving nature. In some of these, art chiefly engages our admiration; in others, nature and art contend for our applause; but, in the last, the former seems to triumph. Here Nature appears in her richest attire, and Art, dressed with the modestest simplicity, attends her benignant mistress. Here Nature indeed pours forth the choicest treasures which she hath lavished on this world; and here human nature presents you with an object which can be exceeded only in the other.

The same taste, the same imagination, which luxuriously riots in these elegant scenes, can be amused with objects of far inferior note. The woods, the rivers, the lawns of Devon and of Dorset, attract the eye of the ingenious traveller, and retard his pace, which delay he afterwards compensates by swiftly scouring over the gloomy heath of Bagshot, or that pleasant plain which extends itself westward from Stockbridge, where no other object than one single tree only in sixteen miles presents itself to the view, unless the clouds, in compassion to our tired spirits, kindly open their variegated mansions to our prospect.

Not so travels the money-meditating tradesman, the sagacious justice, the dignified doctor, the warm-clad grazier, with all the numerous offspring of wealth and dulness. On they jog, with equal pace, through the verdant meadows or over the barren heath, their horses measuring four miles and a half per hour with the utmost exactness; the eyes of the beast and of his master being alike directed forwards, and employed in contemplating the same objects in the same manner. With equal rapture the good rider surveys the proudest boasts of the architect, and those fair buildings with which some unknown name hath adorned the rich cloathing town; where heaps of bricks are piled up as a kind of monument to show that heaps of money have been piled there before.

And now, reader, as we are in haste to attend our heroine, we will leave to thy sagacity to apply all this to the Boeotian writers, and to those authors who are their opposites. This thou wilt be abundantly able to perform without our aid. Bestir thyself therefore on this occasion; for, though we will always lend thee proper assistance in difficult places, as we do not, like some others, expect thee to use the arts of divination to discover our meaning, yet we shall not indulge thy laziness where nothing but thy own attention is required; for thou art highly mistaken if thou dost imagine that we intended, when we began this great work, to leave thy sagacity nothing to do; or that, without sometimes exercising this talent, thou wilt be able to travel through our pages with any pleasure or profit to thyself.

CHAPTER X.

Containing a hint or two concerning virtue, and a few more concerning suspicion.

Our company, being arrived at London, were set down at his lordship's house, where, while they refreshed themselves after the fatigue of their journey, servants were despatched to provide a lodging for the two ladies; for, as her ladyship was not then in town, Mrs Fitzpatrick would by no means consent to accept a bed in the mansion of the peer.

Some readers will, perhaps, condemn this extraordinary delicacy, as I may call it, of virtue, as too nice and scrupulous; but we must make allowances for her situation, which must be owned to have been very ticklish; and, when we consider the malice of censorious tongues, we must allow, if it was a fault, the fault was an excess on the right side, and which every woman who is in the self-same situation will do well to imitate. The most formal appearance of virtue, when it is only an appearance, may, perhaps, in very abstracted considerations, seem to be rather less commendable than virtue itself without this formality; but it will, however, be always more commended; and this, I believe, will be granted by all, that it is necessary, unless in some very particular cases, for every woman to support either the one or the other.

A lodging being prepared, Sophia accompanied her cousin for that evening; but resolved early in the morning to enquire after the lady into whose protection, as we have formerly mentioned, she had determined to throw herself when she quitted her father's house. And this she was the more eager in doing from some observations she had made during her journey in the coach.

Now, as we would by no means fix the odious character of suspicion on Sophia, we are almost afraid to open to our reader the conceits which filled her mind concerning Mrs Fitzpatrick; of whom she certainly entertained at present some doubts; which, as they are very apt to enter into the bosoms of the worst of people, we think proper not to mention more plainly till we have first suggested a word or two to our reader touching suspicion in general.

Of this there have always appeared to me to be two degrees. The first of these I chuse to derive from the heart, as the extreme velocity of its discernment seems to denote some previous inward impulse, and the rather as this superlative degree often forms its own objects; sees what is not, and always more than really exists. This is that quick-sighted penetration whose hawk's eyes no symptom of evil can escape; which observes not only upon the actions, but upon the words and looks, of men; and, as it proceeds from the heart of the observer, so it dives into the heart of the observed, and there espies evil, as it were, in the first embryo; nay, sometimes before it can be said to be conceived. An admirable faculty, if it were infallible; but, as this degree of perfection is not even claimed by more than one mortal being; so from the fallibility of such acute discernment have arisen many sad mischiefs and most grievous heart-aches to innocence and virtue. I cannot help, therefore, regarding this vast quick-sightedness into evil as a vicious excess, and as a very pernicious evil in itself. And I am the more inclined to this opinion, as I am afraid it always proceeds from a bad heart, for the reasons I have above mentioned, and for one more, namely, because I never knew it the property of a good one. Now, from this degree of suspicion I entirely and absolutely acquit Sophia.

A second degree of this quality seems to arise from the head. This is, indeed, no other than the faculty of seeing what is before your eyes, and of drawing conclusions from what you see. The former of these is unavoidable by those who have any eyes, and the latter is perhaps no less certain and necessary a consequence of our having any brains. This is altogether as bitter an enemy to guilt as the former is to innocence: nor can I see it in an unamiable light, even though, through human fallibility, it should be sometimes mistaken. For instance, if a husband should accidentally surprize his wife in the lap or in the embraces of some of those pretty young gentlemen who profess the art of cuckold-making, I should not highly, I think, blame him for concluding something more than what he saw, from the familiarities which he really had seen, and which we are at least favourable enough to when we call them innocent freedoms. The reader will easily suggest great plenty of instances to himself; I shall add but one more, which, however unchristian it may be thought by some, I cannot help esteeming to be strictly justifiable; and this is a suspicion that a man is capable of doing what he hath done already, and that it is possible for one who hath been a villain once to act the same part again. And, to confess the truth, of this degree of suspicion I believe Sophia was guilty. From this degree of suspicion she had, in fact, conceived an opinion that her cousin was really not better than she should be.

The case, it seems, was this: Mrs Fitzpatrick wisely considered that the virtue of a young lady is, in the world, in the same situation with a poor hare, which is certain, whenever it ventures abroad, to meet its enemies; for it can hardly meet any other. No sooner therefore was she determined to take the first opportunity of quitting the protection of her husband, than she resolved to cast herself under the protection of some other man; and whom could she so properly choose to be her guardian as a person of quality, of fortune, of honour; and who, besides a gallant disposition which inclines men to knight-errantry, that is, to be the champions of ladies in distress, had often declared a violent attachment to herself, and had already given her all the instances of it in his power?

But, as the law hath foolishly omitted this office of vice-husband, or guardian to an eloped lady, and as malice is apt to denominate him by a more disagreeable appellation, it was concluded that his lordship should perform all such kind offices to the lady in secret, and without publickly assuming the character of her protector. Nay, to prevent any other person from seeing him in this light, it was agreed that the lady should proceed directly to Bath, and that his lordship should first go to London, and thence should go down to that place by the advice of his physicians.

Now all this Sophia very plainly understood, not from the lips or behaviour of Mrs Fitzpatrick, but from the peer, who was infinitely less expert at retaining a secret than was the good lady; and perhaps the exact secrecy which Mrs Fitzpatrick had observed on this head in her narrative served not a little to heighten those suspicions which were now risen in the mind of her cousin.

Sophia very easily found out the lady she sought; for indeed there was not a chairman in town to whom her house was not perfectly well known; and, as she received, in return of her first message, a most pressing invitation, she immediately accepted it. Mrs Fitzpatrick, indeed, did not desire her cousin to stay with her with more earnestness than civility required. Whether she had discerned and resented the suspicion above-mentioned, or from what other motive it arose, I cannot say; but certain it is, she was full as desirous of parting with Sophia as Sophia herself could be of going.

The young lady, when she came to take leave of her cousin, could not avoid giving her a short hint of advice. She begged her, for heaven's sake, to take care of herself, and to consider in how dangerous a situation she stood; adding, she hoped some method would be found of reconciling her to her husband. "You must remember, my dear," says she, "the maxim which my aunt Western hath so often repeated to us both; That whenever the matrimonial alliance is broke, and war declared between husband and wife, she can hardly make a disadvantageous peace for herself on any conditions. These are my aunt's very words, and she hath had a great deal of experience in the world." Mrs Fitzpatrick answered, with a contemptuous smile, "Never fear me, child, take care of yourself; for you are younger than I. I will come and visit you in a few days; but, dear Sophy, let me give you one piece of advice: leave the character of Graveairs in the country, for, believe me, it will sit very awkwardly upon you in this town."

Thus the two cousins parted, and Sophia repaired directly to Lady Bellaston, where she found a most hearty, as well as a most polite, welcome. The lady had taken a great fancy to her when she had seen her formerly with her aunt Western. She was indeed extremely glad to see her, and was no sooner acquainted with the reasons which induced her to leave the squire and to fly to London than she highly applauded her sense and resolution; and after expressing the highest satisfaction in the opinion which Sophia had declared she entertained of her ladyship, by chusing her house for an asylum, she promised her all the protection which it was in her power to give.

As we have now brought Sophia into safe hands, the reader will, I apprehend, be contented to deposit her there a while, and to look a little after other personages, and particularly poor Jones, whom we have left long enough to do penance for his past offences, which, as is the nature of vice, brought sufficient punishment upon him themselves.

BOOK XII.

CONTAINING THE SAME INDIVIDUAL TIME WITH THE FORMER.

CHAPTER I.

Showing what is to be deemed plagiarism in a modern author, and what is to be considered as lawful prize.

The learned reader must have observed that in the course of this mighty work, I have often translated passages out of the best antient authors, without quoting the original, or without taking the least notice of the book from whence they were borrowed.

This conduct in writing is placed in a very proper light by the ingenious Abbé Bannier, in his preface to his Mythology, a work of great erudition and of equal judgment. "It will be easy," says he, "for the reader to observe that I have frequently had greater regard to him than to my own reputation: for an author certainly pays him a considerable compliment, when, for his sake, he suppresses learned quotations that come in his way, and which would have cost him but the bare trouble of transcribing."

To fill up a work with these scraps may, indeed, be considered as a downright cheat on the learned world, who are by such means imposed upon to buy a second time, in fragments and by retail, what they have already in gross, if not in their memories, upon their shelves; and it is still more cruel upon the illiterate, who are drawn in to pay for what is of no manner of use to them. A writer who intermixes great quantity of Greek and Latin with his works, deals by the ladies and fine gentlemen in the same paultry manner with which they are treated by the auctioneers, who often endeavour so to confound and mix up their lots, that, in order to purchase the commodity you want, you are obliged at the same time to purchase that which will do you no service.

And yet, as there is no conduct so fair and disinterested but that it may be misunderstood by ignorance, and misrepresented by malice, I have been sometimes tempted to preserve my own reputation at the expense of my reader, and to transcribe the original, or at least to quote chapter and verse, whenever I have made use either of the thought or expression of another. I am, indeed, in some doubt that I have often suffered by the contrary method; and that, by suppressing the original author's name, I have been rather suspected of plagiarism than reputed to act from the amiable motive assigned by that justly celebrated Frenchman.

Now, to obviate all such imputations for the future, I do here confess and justify the fact. The antients may be considered as a rich common, where every person who hath the smallest tenement in Parnassus hath a free right to fatten his muse.

Or, to place it in a clearer light, we moderns are to the antients what the poor are to the rich. By the poor here I mean that large and venerable body which, in English, we call the mob. Now, whoever hath had the honour to be admitted to any degree of intimacy with this mob, must well know that it is one of their established maxims to plunder and pillage their rich neighbours without any reluctance; and that this is held to be neither sin nor shame among them. And so constantly do they abide and act by this maxim, that, in every parish almost in the kingdom, there is a kind of confederacy ever carrying on against a certain person of opulence called the squire, whose property is considered as free-booty by all his poor neighbours; who, as they conclude that there is no manner of guilt in such depredations, look upon it as a point of honour and moral obligation to conceal, and to preserve each other from punishment on all such occasions.

In like manner are the antients, such as Homer, Virgil, Horace, Cicero, and the rest, to be esteemed among us writers, as so many wealthy squires, from whom we, the poor of Parnassus, claim an immemorial custom of taking whatever we can come at. This liberty I demand, and this I am as ready to allow again to my poor neighbours in their turn. All I profess, and all I require of my brethren, is to maintain the same strict honesty among ourselves which the mob show to one another. To steal from one another is indeed highly criminal and indecent; for this may be strictly stiled defrauding the poor (sometimes perhaps those who are poorer than ourselves), or, to set it under the most opprobrious colours, robbing the spittal.

Since, therefore, upon the strictest examination, my own conscience cannot lay any such pitiful theft to my charge, I am contented to plead guilty to the former accusation; nor shall I ever scruple to take to myself any passage which I shall find in an antient author to my purpose, without setting down the name of the author from whence it was taken. Nay, I absolutely claim a property in all such sentiments the moment they are transcribed into my writings, and I expect all readers henceforwards to regard them as purely and entirely my own. This claim, however, I desire to be allowed me only on condition that I preserve strict honesty towards my poor brethren, from whom, if ever I borrow any of that little of which they are possessed, I shall never fail to put their mark upon it, that it may be at all times ready to be restored to the right owner.

The omission of this was highly blameable in one Mr Moore, who, having formerly borrowed some lines of Pope and company, took the liberty to transcribe six of them into his play of the Rival Modes. Mr Pope, however, very luckily found them in the said play, and, laying violent hands on his own property, transferred it back again into his own works; and, for a further punishment, imprisoned the said Moore in the loathsome dungeon of the Dunciad, where his unhappy memory now remains, and eternally will remain, as a proper punishment for such his unjust dealings in the poetical trade.

CHAPTER II.

In which, though the squire doth not find his daughter, something is found which puts an end to his pursuit.

The history now returns to the inn at Upton, whence we shall first trace the footsteps of Squire Western; for, as he will soon arrive at an end of his journey, we shall have then full leisure to attend our heroe.

The reader may be pleased to remember that the said squire departed from the inn in great fury, and in that fury he pursued his daughter. The hostler having informed him that she had crossed the Severn, he likewise past that river with his equipage, and rode full speed, vowing the utmost vengeance against poor Sophia, if he should but overtake her.

He had not gone far before he arrived at a crossway. Here he called a short council of war, in which, after hearing different opinions, he at last gave the direction of his pursuit to fortune, and struck directly into the Worcester road.

In this road he proceeded about two miles, when he began to bemoan himself most bitterly, frequently crying out, "What pity is it! Sure never was so unlucky a dog as myself!" And then burst forth a volley of oaths and execrations.

The parson attempted to administer comfort to him on this occasion. "Sorrow not, sir," says he, "like those without hope. Howbeit we have not yet been able to overtake young madam, we may account it some good fortune that we have hitherto traced her course aright. Peradventure she will soon be fatigated with her journey, and will tarry in some inn, in order to renovate her corporeal functions; and in that case, in all moral certainty, you will very briefly be *compos voti*."

"Pogh! d—n the slut!" answered the squire, "I am lamenting the loss of so fine a morning for hunting. It is confounded hard to lose one of the best scenting days, in all appearance, which hath been this season, and especially after so long a frost."

Whether Fortune, who now and then shows some compassion in her wantonest tricks, might not take pity of the squire; and, as she had determined not to let him overtake his daughter, might not resolve to make him amends some other way, I will not assert; but he had hardly uttered the words just before commemorated, and two or three oaths at their heels, when a pack of hounds began to open their melodious throats at a small distance from them, which the squire's horse and his rider both perceiving, both immediately pricked up their ears, and the squire, crying, "She's gone, she's gone! Damn me if she is not gone!" instantly clapped spurs to the beast, who little needed it, having indeed the same inclination with his master; and now the whole company, crossing into a corn-field, rode directly towards the hounds, with much hallowing and whooping, while the poor parson, blessing himself, brought up the rear.

Thus fable reports that the fair Grimalkin, whom Venus, at the desire of a passionate lover, converted from a cat into a fine woman, no sooner perceived a mouse than, mindful of her former sport, and still retaining her pristine nature, she leaped from the bed of her husband to pursue the little animal.

What are we to understand by this? Not that the bride was displeased with the embraces of her amorous bridegroom; for, though some have remarked that cats are subject to ingratitude, yet women and cats too will be pleased and purr on certain occasions. The truth is, as the sagacious Sir Roger L'Estrange observes, in his deep reflections, that, "if we shut Nature out at the door, she will come in at the window; and that puss, though a madam, will be a mouser still." In the same manner we are not to arraign the squire of any want of love for his daughter; for in reality he had a great deal; we are only to consider that he was a squire and a sportsman, and then we may apply the fable to him, and the judicious reflections likewise.

The hounds ran very hard, as it is called, and the squire pursued over hedge and ditch, with all his usual vociferation and alacrity, and with all his usual pleasure; nor did the thoughts of Sophia ever once intrude themselves to allay the satisfaction he enjoyed in the chace, which, he said, was one of the finest he ever saw, and which he swore was very well worth going fifty miles for. As the squire forgot his daughter, the servants, we may easily believe, forgot their mistress; and the parson, after having expressed much astonishment, in Latin, to himself, at length likewise abandoned all farther thoughts of the young lady, and, jogging on at a distance behind, began to meditate a portion of doctrine for the ensuing Sunday.

The squire who owned the hounds was highly pleased with the arrival of his brother squire and sportsman; for all men approve merit in their own way, and no man was more expert in the field than Mr Western, nor did any other better know how to encourage the dogs with his voice, and to animate the hunt with his holla.

Sportsmen, in the warmth of a chace, are too much engaged to attend to any manner of ceremony, nay, even to the offices of humanity: for, if any of them meet with an accident by tumbling into a ditch, or into a river, the rest pass on regardless, and generally leave him to his fate: during this time, therefore, the two squires, though often close to each other, interchanged not a single word. The master of the hunt, however, often saw and approved the great judgment of the stranger in drawing the dogs when they were at a fault, and hence conceived a very high opinion of his understanding, as the number of his attendants inspired no small reverence to his quality. As soon, therefore, as the sport was ended by the death of the little animal which had occasioned it, the two squires met, and in all squire-like greeting saluted each other.

The conversation was entertaining enough, and what we may perhaps relate in an appendix, or on some other occasion; but as it nowise concerns this history, we cannot prevail on ourselves to give it a place here. It concluded with a second chace, and that with an invitation to dinner. This being accepted, was followed by a hearty bout of drinking, which ended in as hearty a nap on the part of Squire Western.

Our squire was by no means a match either for his host, or for parson Supple, at his cups that evening; for which the violent fatigue of mind as well as body that he had undergone, may very well account, without the least derogation from his honour. He was indeed, according to the vulgar phrase, whistle drunk; for before he had swallowed the third bottle, he became so entirely overpowered that though he was not carried off to bed till long after, the parson considered him as absent, and having acquainted the other squire with all relating to Sophia, he obtained his promise of seconding those arguments which he intended to urge the next morning for Mr Western's return.

No sooner, therefore, had the good squire shaken off his evening, and began to call for his morning draught, and to summon his horses in order to renew his pursuit, than Mr Supple began his dissuasives, which the host so strongly seconded, that they at length prevailed, and Mr Western agreed to return home; being principally moved by one argument, viz., that he knew not which way to go, and might probably be riding farther from his daughter instead of towards her. He then took leave of his brother sportsman, and expressing great joy that the frost was broken (which might perhaps be no small motive to his hastening home), set forwards, or rather backwards, for Somersetshire; but not before he had first despatched part of his retinue in quest of his daughter, after whom he likewise sent a volley of the most bitter execrations which he could invent.

CHAPTER III.

The departure of Jones from Upton, with what passed between him and Partridge on the road.

At length we are once more come to our heroe; and, to say truth, we have been obliged to part with him so long, that, considering the condition in which we left him, I apprehend many of our readers have concluded we intended to abandon him for ever; he being at present in that situation in which prudent people usually desist from enquiring any farther after their friends, lest they should be shocked by hearing such friends had hanged themselves.

But, in reality, if we have not all the virtues, I will boldly say, neither have we all the vices of a prudent character; and though it is not easy to conceive circumstances much more miserable than those of poor Jones at present, we shall return to him, and attend upon him with the same diligence as if he was wantoning in the brightest beams of fortune.

Mr Jones, then, and his companion Partridge, left the inn a few minutes after the departure of Squire Western, and pursued the same road on foot, for the hostler told them that no horses were by any means to be at that time procured at Upton. On they marched with heavy hearts; for though their disquiet proceeded from very different reasons, yet displeased they were both; and if Jones sighed bitterly, Partridge grunted altogether as sadly at every step.

When they came to the cross-roads where the squire had stopt to take counsel, Jones stopt likewise, and turning to Partridge, asked his opinion which track they should pursue. "Ah, sir," answered Partridge, "I wish your honour would follow my advice." "Why should I not?" replied Jones; "for it is now indifferent to me whither I go, or what becomes of me." "My advice, then," said Partridge, "is, that you immediately face about and return home; for who that hath such a home to return to as your honour, would travel thus about the country like a vagabond? I ask pardon, *sed vox ea sola reperta est.*"

"Alas!" cries Jones, "I have no home to return to;—but if my friend, my father, would receive me, could I bear the country from which Sophia is flown? Cruel Sophia! Cruel! No; let me blame myself!—No; let me blame thee. D—nation seize thee—fool—blockhead! thou hast undone me, and I will tear thy soul from thy body."—At which words he laid violent hands on the collar of poor Partridge, and shook him more heartily than an ague-fit, or his own fears had ever done before.

Partridge fell trembling on his knees, and begged for mercy, vowing he had meant no harm—when Jones, after staring wildly on him for a moment, quitted his hold, and discharged a rage on himself, that, had it fallen on the other, would certainly have put an end to his being, which indeed the very apprehension of it had almost effected.

We would bestow some pains here in minutely describing all the mad pranks which Jones played on this occasion, could we be well assured that the reader would take the same pains in perusing them; but as we are apprehensive that, after all the labour which we should employ in painting this scene, the said reader would be very apt to skip it entirely over, we have saved ourselves that trouble. To say the truth, we have, from this reason alone, often done great violence to the luxuriance of our genius, and have left many excellent descriptions out of our work, which would otherwise have been in it. And this suspicion, to be honest, arises, as is generally the case, from our own wicked heart; for we have, ourselves, been very often most horridly given to jumping, as we have run through the pages of voluminous historians.

Suffice it then simply to say, that Jones, after having played the part of a madman for many minutes, came, by degrees, to himself; which no sooner happened, than, turning to Partridge, he very earnestly begged his pardon for the attack he had made on him in the violence of his passion; but concluded, by desiring him never to mention his return again; for he was resolved never to see that country any more.

Partridge easily forgave, and faithfully promised to obey the injunction now laid upon him. And then Jones very briskly cried out, "Since it is absolutely impossible for me to pursue any farther the steps of my angel—I will pursue those of glory. Come on, my brave lad, now for the army:—it is a glorious cause, and I would willingly sacrifice my life in it, even though it was worth my preserving." And so saying, he immediately struck into the different road from that which the squire had taken, and, by mere chance, pursued the very same through which Sophia had before passed.

Our travellers now marched a full mile, without speaking a syllable to each other, though Jones, indeed, muttered many things to himself. As to Partridge, he was profoundly silent; for he was not, perhaps, perfectly recovered from his former fright; besides, he had apprehensions of provoking his friend to a second fit of wrath, especially as he now began to entertain a conceit, which may not, perhaps, create any great wonder in the reader. In short, he began now to suspect that Jones was absolutely out of his senses.

At length, Jones, being weary of soliloquy, addressed himself to his companion, and blamed him for his taciturnity; for which the poor man very honestly accounted, from his fear of giving offence. And now this fear being pretty well removed, by the most absolute promises of indemnity, Partridge again took the bridle from his tongue; which, perhaps, rejoiced no less at regaining its liberty, than a young colt, when the bridle is slipt from his neck, and he is turned loose into the pastures.

As Partridge was inhibited from that topic which would have first suggested itself, he fell upon that which was next uppermost in his mind, namely, the Man of the Hill. "Certainly, sir," says he, "that could never be a man, who dresses himself and lives after such a strange manner, and so unlike other folks. Besides, his diet, as the old woman told me, is chiefly upon herbs, which is a fitter food for a horse than a Christian: nay, landlord at Upton says that the neighbours thereabouts have very fearful notions about him. It runs strangely in my head that it must have been some spirit, who, perhaps, might be sent to forewarn us: and who knows but all that matter which he told us, of his going to fight, and of his being taken prisoner, and of the great danger he was in of being hanged, might be intended as a warning to us, considering what we are going about? besides, I dreamt of nothing all last night but of fighting; and methought the blood ran out of my nose, as liquor out of a tap. Indeed, sir, *infandum, regina, jubes renovare dolorem*."

"Thy story, Partridge," answered Jones, "is almost as ill applied as thy Latin. Nothing can be more likely to happen than death to men who go into battle. Perhaps we shall both fall in it—and what then?" "What then?" replied Partridge; "why then there is an end of us, is there not? when I am gone, all is over with me. What matters the cause to me, or who gets the victory, if I am killed? I shall never enjoy any advantage from it. What are all the ringing of bells, and bonfires, to one that is six foot under ground? there will be an end of poor Partridge." "And an end of poor Partridge," cries Jones, "there must be, one time or other. If you love Latin, I will repeat you some fine lines out of Horace, which would inspire courage into a coward.

`Dulce et decorum est pro patria mori
Mors et fugacem persequitur virum
Nec parcit imbellis juventae
Poplitibus, timidoque tergo.'"

"I wish you would construe them," cries Partridge; "for Horace is a hard author, and I cannot understand as you repeat them."

"I will repeat you a bad imitation, or rather paraphrase, of my own," said Jones; "for I am but an indifferent poet:

`Who would not die in his dear country's cause? Since, if base fear his dastard step withdraws, From death he cannot fly:—One common grave Receives, at last, the coward and the brave.'"

"That's very certain," cries Partridge. "Ay, sure, *Mors omnibus communis:* but there is a great difference between dying in one's bed a great many years hence, like a good Christian, with all our friends crying about us, and being shot to-day or to-morrow, like a mad dog; or, perhaps, hacked in twenty pieces with the sword, and that too before we have repented of all our sins. O Lord, have mercy upon us! to be sure the soldiers are a wicked kind of people. I never loved to have anything to do with them. I could hardly bring myself ever to look upon them as Christians. There is nothing but cursing and swearing among them. I wish your honour would repent: I heartily wish you would repent before it is too late; and not think of going among them.—Evil communication corrupts good manners.

That is my principal reason. For as for that matter, I am no more afraid than another man, not I; as to matter of that. I know all human flesh must die; but yet a man may live many years, for all that. Why, I am a middle-aged man now, and yet I may live a great number of years. I have read of several who have lived to be above a hundred, and some a great deal above a hundred. Not that I hope, I mean that I promise myself, to live to any such age as that, neither.—But if it be only to eighty or ninety. Heaven be praised, that is a great ways off yet; and I am not afraid of dying then, no more than another man; but, surely, to tempt death before a man's time is come seems to me downright wickedness and presumption. Besides, if it was to do any good indeed; but, let the cause be what it will, what mighty matter of good can two people do? and, for my part, I understand nothing of it. I never fired off a gun above ten times in my life; and then it was not charged with bullets. And for the sword, I never learned to fence, and know nothing of the matter. And then there are those cannons, which certainly it must be thought the highest presumption to go in the way of; and nobody but a madman—I ask pardon; upon my soul I meant no harm; I beg I may not throw your honour into another passion."

"Be under no apprehension, Partridge," cries Jones; "I am now so well convinced of thy cowardice, that thou couldst not provoke me on any account." "Your honour," answered he, "may call me coward, or anything else you please. If loving to sleep in a whole skin makes a man a coward, *non immunes ab illis malis sumus*. I never read in my grammar that a man can't be a good man without fighting. *Vir bonus est quis? Qui consulta patrum, qui leges juraque servat*. Not a word of fighting; and I am sure the scripture is so much against it, that a man shall never persuade me he is a good Christian while he sheds Christian blood."

CHAPTER IV.

The adventure of a beggar-man.

Just as Partridge had uttered that good and pious doctrine, with which the last chapter concluded, they arrived at another cross-way, when a lame fellow in rags asked them for alms; upon which Partridge gave him a severe rebuke, saying, "Every parish ought to keep their own poor." Jones then fell a-laughing, and asked Partridge, "if he was not ashamed, with so much charity in his mouth, to have no charity in his heart. Your religion," says he, "serves you only for an excuse for your faults, but is no incentive to your virtue. Can any man who is really a Christian abstain from relieving one of his brethren in such a miserable condition?" And at the same time, putting his hand in his pocket, he gave the poor object a shilling.

"Master," cries the fellow, after thanking him, "I have a curious thing here in my pocket, which I found about two miles off, if your worship will please to buy it. I should not venture to pull it out to every one; but, as you are so good a gentleman, and so kind to the poor, you won't suspect a man of being a thief only because he is poor." He then pulled out a little gilt pocket-book, and delivered it into the hands of Jones.

Jones presently opened it, and (guess, reader, what he felt) saw in the first page the words Sophia Western, written by her own fair hand. He no sooner read the name than he prest it close to his lips; nor could he avoid falling into some very frantic raptures, notwithstanding his company; but, perhaps, these very raptures made him forget he was not alone.

While Jones was kissing and mumbling the book, as if he had an excellent brown buttered crust in his mouth or as if he had really been a book-worm, or an author who had nothing to eat but his own works, a piece of paper fell from its leaves to the ground, which Partridge took up, and delivered to Jones, who presently perceived it to be a bank-bill. It was, indeed, the very bill which Western had given his daughter the night before her departure; and a Jew would have jumped to purchase it at five shillings less than £100.

The eyes of Partridge sparkled at this news, which Jones now proclaimed aloud; and so did (though with somewhat a different aspect) those of the poor fellow who had found the book; and who (I hope from a principle of honesty) had never opened it: but we should not deal honestly by the reader if we omitted to inform him of a circumstance which may be here a little material, viz. that the fellow could not read.

Jones, who had felt nothing but pure joy and transport from the finding the book, was affected with a mixture of concern at this new discovery; for his imagination instantly suggested to him that the owner of the bill might possibly want it before he should be able to convey it to her. He then acquainted the finder that he knew the lady to whom the book belonged, and would endeavour to find her out as soon as possible, and return it her.

The pocket-book was a late present from Mrs Western to her niece; it had cost five-and-twenty shillings, having been bought of a celebrated toyman; but the real value of the silver which it contained in its clasp was about eighteen-pence; and that price the said toyman, as it was altogether as good as when it first issued from his shop, would now have given for it. A prudent person would, however, have taken proper advantage of the ignorance of this fellow, and would not have offered more than a shilling, or perhaps sixpence, for it; nay, some perhaps would have given nothing, and left the fellow to his action of trover, which some learned serjeants may doubt whether he could, under these circumstances, have maintained.

Jones, on the contrary, whose character was on the outside of generosity, and may perhaps not very unjustly have been suspected of extravagance, without any hesitation gave a guinea in exchange for the book. The poor man, who had not for a long time before been possessed of so much treasure, gave Mr Jones a thousand thanks, and discovered little less of transport in his muscles than Jones had before shown when he had first read the name of Sophia Western.

The fellow very readily agreed to attend our travellers to the place where he had found the pocket-book. Together, therefore, they proceeded directly thither; but not so fast as Mr Jones desired; for his guide unfortunately happened to be lame, and could not possibly travel faster than a mile an hour. As this place, therefore, was at above three miles' distance, though the fellow had said otherwise, the reader need not be acquainted how long they were in walking it.

Jones opened the book a hundred times during their walk, kissed it as often, talked much to himself, and very little to his companions. At all which the guide exprest some signs of astonishment to Partridge; who more than once shook his head, and cryed, Poor gentleman! *orandum est ut sit mens sana in corpore sano.*

At length they arrived at the very spot where Sophia unhappily dropt the pocket-book, and where the fellow had as happily found it. Here Jones offered to take leave of his guide, and to improve his pace; but the fellow, in whom that violent surprize and joy which the first receipt of the guinea had occasioned was now considerably abated, and who had now had sufficient time to recollect himself, put on a discontented look, and, scratching his head, said, "He hoped his worship would give him something more. Your worship," said he, "will, I hope, take it into your consideration that if I had not been honest I might have kept the whole." And, indeed, this the reader must confess to have been true. "If the paper there," said he, "be worth £100, I am sure the finding it deserves more than a guinea. Besides, suppose your worship should never see the lady, nor give it her—and, though your worship looks and talks very much like a gentleman, yet I have only your worship's bare word; and, certainly, if the right owner ben't to be found, it all belongs to the first finder. I hope your worship will consider of all these matters: I am but a poor man, and therefore don't desire to have all; but it is but reasonable I should have my share. Your worship looks like a good man, and, I hope, will consider my honesty; for I might have kept every farthing, and nobody ever the wiser." "I promise thee, upon my honour," cries Jones, "that I know the right owner, and will restore it her." "Nay, your worship," answered the fellow, "may do as you please as to that; if you will but give me my share, that is, one-half of the money, your honour may keep the rest yourself if you please;" and concluded with swearing, by a very vehement oath, "that he would never mention a syllable of it to any man living."

"Lookee, friend," cries Jones, "the right owner shall certainly have again all that she lost; and as for any farther gratuity, I really cannot give it you at present; but let me know your name, and where you live, and it is more than possible you may hereafter have further reason to rejoice at this morning's adventure."

"I don't know what you mean by venture," cries the fellow; "it seems I must venture whether you will return the lady her money or no; but I hope your worship will consider—" "Come, come," said Partridge, "tell his honour your name, and where you may be found; I warrant you will never repent having put the money into his hands." The fellow, seeing no hopes of recovering the possession of the pocket-book, at last complied in giving in his name and place of abode, which Jones writ upon a piece of paper with the pencil of Sophia; and then, placing the paper in the same page where she had writ her name, he cried out, "There, friend, you are the happiest man alive; I have joined your name to that of an angel." "I don't know anything about angels," answered the fellow; "but I wish you would give me a little more money, or else return me the pocket-book." Partridge now waxed wrath: he called the poor cripple by several vile and opprobrious names, and was absolutely proceeding to beat him, but Jones would not suffer any such thing: and now, telling the fellow he would certainly find some opportunity of serving him, Mr Jones departed as fast as his heels would carry him; and Partridge, into whom the thoughts of the hundred pound had infused new spirits, followed his leader; while the man, who was obliged to stay behind, fell to cursing them both, as well as his parents; "for had they," says he, "sent me to charity-school to learn to write and read and cast accounts, I should have known the value of these matters as well as other people."

CHAPTER V.

Containing more adventures which Mr Jones and his companion met on the road.

Our travellers now walked so fast, that they had very little time or breath for conversation; Jones meditating all the way on Sophia, and Partridge on the bank-bill, which, though it gave him some pleasure, caused him at the same time to repine at fortune, which, in all his walks, had never given him such an opportunity of showing his honesty. They had proceeded above three miles, when Partridge, being unable any longer to keep up with Jones, called to him, and begged him a little to slacken his pace: with this he was the more ready to comply, as he had for some time lost the footsteps of the horses, which the thaw had enabled him to trace for several miles, and he was now upon a wide common, where were several roads.

He here therefore stopt to consider which of these roads he should pursue; when on a sudden they heard the noise of a drum, that seemed at no great distance. This sound presently alarmed the fears of Partridge, and he cried out, "Lord have mercy upon us all; they are certainly a coming!" "Who is coming?" cries Jones; for fear had long since given place to softer ideas in his mind; and since his adventure with the lame man, he had been totally intent on pursuing Sophia, without entertaining one thought of an enemy. "Who?" cries Partridge, "why, the rebels: but why should I call them rebels? they may be very honest gentlemen, for anything I know to the contrary. The devil take him that affronts them, I say; I am sure, if they have nothing to say to me, I will have nothing to say to them, but in a civil way. For Heaven's sake, sir, don't affront them if they should come, and perhaps they may do us no harm; but would it not be the wiser way to creep into some of yonder bushes, till they are gone by? What can two unarmed men do perhaps against fifty thousand? Certainly nobody but a madman; I hope your honour is not offended; but certainly no man who hath *mens sana in corpore sano*——" Here Jones interrupted this torrent of eloquence, which fear had inspired, saying, "That by the drum he perceived they were near some town." He then made directly towards the place whence the noise proceeded, bidding Partridge "take courage, for that he would lead him into no danger;" and adding, "it was impossible the rebels should be so near."

Partridge was a little comforted with this last assurance; and though he would more gladly have gone the contrary way, he followed his leader, his heart beating time, but not after the manner of heroes, to the music of the drum, which ceased not till they had traversed the common, and were come into a narrow lane.

And now Partridge, who kept even pace with Jones, discovered something painted flying in the air, a very few yards before him, which fancying to be the colours of the enemy, he fell a bellowing, "Oh Lord, sir, here they are; there is the crown and coffin. Oh Lord! I never saw anything so terrible; and we are within gun-shot of them already."

Jones no sooner looked up, than he plainly perceived what it was which Partridge had thus mistaken. "Partridge," says he, "I fancy you will be able to engage this whole army yourself; for by the colours I guess what the drum was which we heard before, and which beats up for recruits to a puppet-show."

"A puppet-show!" answered Partridge, with most eager transport. "And is it really no more than that? I love a puppet-show of all the pastimes upon earth. Do, good sir, let us tarry and see it. Besides, I am quite famished to death; for it is now almost dark, and I have not eat a morsel since three o'clock in the morning."

They now arrived at an inn, or indeed an ale-house, where Jones was prevailed upon to stop, the rather as he had no longer any assurance of being in the road he desired. They walked both directly into the kitchen, where Jones began to enquire if no ladies had passed that way in the morning, and Partridge as eagerly examined into the state of their provisions; and indeed his enquiry met with the better success; for Jones could not hear news of Sophia; but Partridge, to his great satisfaction, found good reason to expect very shortly the agreeable sight of an excellent smoaking dish of eggs and bacon.

In strong and healthy constitutions love hath a very different effect from what it causes in the puny part of the species. In the latter it generally destroys all that appetite which tends towards the conservation of the individual; but in the former, though it often induces forgetfulness, and a neglect of food, as well as of everything else; yet place a good piece of well-powdered buttock before a hungry lover, and he seldom fails very handsomely to play his part. Thus it happened in the present case; for though Jones perhaps wanted a prompter, and might have travelled much farther, had he been alone, with an empty stomach; yet no sooner did he sit down to the bacon and eggs, than he fell to as heartily and voraciously as Partridge himself.

Before our travellers had finished their dinner, night came on, and as the moon was now past the full, it was extremely dark. Partridge therefore prevailed on Jones to stay and see the puppet-show, which was just going to begin, and to which they were very eagerly invited by the master of the said show, who declared that his figures were the finest which the world had ever produced, and that they had given great satisfaction to all the quality in every town in England.

The puppet-show was performed with great regularity and decency. It was called the fine and serious part of the Provoked Husband; and it was indeed a very grave and solemn entertainment, without any low wit or humour, or jests; or, to do it no more than justice, without anything which could provoke a laugh. The audience were all highly pleased. A grave matron told the master she would bring her two daughters the next night, as he did not show any stuff; and an attorney's clerk and an exciseman both declared, that the characters of Lord and Lady Townley were well preserved, and highly in nature. Partridge likewise concurred with this opinion.

The master was so highly elated with these encomiums, that he could not refrain from adding some more of his own. He said, "The present age was not improved in anything so much as in their puppet-shows; which, by throwing out Punch and his wife Joan, and such idle trumpery, were at last brought to be a rational entertainment. I remember," said he, "when I first took to the business, there was a great deal of low stuff that did very well to make folks laugh; but was never calculated to improve the morals of young people, which certainly ought to be principally aimed at in every puppet-show: for why may not good and instructive lessons be conveyed this way, as well as any other? My figures are as big as the life, and they represent the life in every particular; and I question not but people rise from my little drama as much improved as they do from the great." "I would by no means degrade the ingenuity of your profession," answered Jones, "but I should have been glad to have seen my old acquaintance master Punch, for all that; and so far from improving, I think, by leaving out him and his merry wife Joan, you have spoiled your puppet-show."

The dancer of wires conceived an immediate and high contempt for Jones, from these words. And with much disdain in his countenance, he replied, "Very probably, sir, that may be your opinion; but I have the satisfaction to know the best judges differ from you, and it is impossible to please every taste. I confess, indeed, some of the quality at Bath, two or three years ago, wanted mightily to bring Punch again upon the stage. I believe I lost some money for not agreeing to it; but let others do as they will; a little matter shall never bribe me to degrade my own profession, nor will I ever willingly consent to the spoiling the decency and regularity of my stage, by introducing any such low stuff upon it."

"Right, friend," cries the clerk, "you are very right. Always avoid what is low. There are several of my acquaintance in London, who are resolved to drive everything which is low from the stage." "Nothing can be more proper," cries the exciseman, pulling his pipe from his mouth. "I remember," added he, "(for I then lived with my lord) I was in the footman's gallery, the night when this play of the Provoked Husband was acted first. There was a great deal of low stuff in it about a country gentleman come up to town to stand for parliament-man; and there they brought a parcel of his servants upon the stage, his coachman I remember particularly; but the gentlemen in our gallery could not bear anything so low, and they damned it. I observe, friend, you have left all that matter out, and you are to be commended for it."

"Nay, gentlemen," cries Jones, "I can never maintain my opinion against so many; indeed, if the generality of his audience dislike him, the learned gentleman who conducts the show might have done very right in dismissing Punch from his service."

The master of the show then began a second harangue, and said much of the great force of example, and how much the inferior part of mankind would be deterred from vice, by observing how odious it was in their superiors; when he was unluckily interrupted by an incident, which, though perhaps we might have omitted it at another time, we cannot help relating at present, but not in this chapter.

CHAPTER VI.

From which it may be inferred that the best things are liable to be misunderstood and misinterpreted.

A violent uproar now arose in the entry, where my landlady was well cuffing her maid both with her fist and tongue. She had indeed missed the wench from her employment, and, after a little search, had found her on the puppet-show stage in company with the Merry Andrew, and in a situation not very proper to be described.

Though Grace (for that was her name) had forfeited all title to modesty; yet had she not impudence enough to deny a fact in which she was actually surprized; she, therefore, took another turn, and attempted to mitigate the offence. "Why do you beat me in this manner, mistress?" cries the wench. "If you don't like my doings, you may turn me away. If I am a w—e" (for the other had liberally bestowed that appellation on her), "my betters are so as well as I. What was the fine lady in the puppet-show just now? I suppose she did not lie all night out from her husband for nothing."

The landlady now burst into the kitchen, and fell foul on both her husband and the poor puppet-mover. "Here, husband," says she, "you see the consequence of harbouring these people in your house. If one doth draw a little drink the more for them, one is hardly made amends for the litter they make; and then to have one's house made a bawdy-house of by such lousy vermin. In short, I desire you would be gone to-morrow morning; for I will tolerate no more such doings. It is only the way to teach our servants idleness and nonsense; for to be sure nothing better can be learned by such idle shows as these. I remember when puppet-shows were made of good scripture stories, as Jephthah's Rash Vow, and such good things, and when wicked people were carried away by the devil. There was some sense in those matters; but as the parson told us last Sunday, nobody believes in the devil now-a-days; and here you bring about a parcel of puppets drest up like lords and ladies, only to turn the heads of poor country wenches; and when their heads are once turned topsy-turvy, no wonder everything else is so."

Virgil, I think, tells us, that when the mob are assembled in a riotous and tumultuous manner, and all sorts of missile weapons fly about, if a man of gravity and authority appears amongst them, the tumult is presently appeased, and the mob, which when collected into one body, may be well compared to an ass, erect their long ears at the grave man's discourse.

On the contrary, when a set of grave men and philosophers are disputing; when wisdom herself may in a manner be considered as present, and administering arguments to the disputants; should a tumult arise among the mob, or should one scold, who is herself equal in noise to a mighty mob, appear among the said philosophers; their disputes cease in a moment, wisdom no longer performs her ministerial office, and the attention of every one is immediately attracted by the scold alone.

Thus the uproar aforesaid, and the arrival of the landlady, silenced the master of the puppet-show, and put a speedy and final end to that grave and solemn harangue, of which we have given the reader a sufficient taste already. Nothing indeed could have happened so very inopportune as this accident; the most wanton malice of fortune could not have contrived such another stratagem to confound the poor fellow, while he was so triumphantly descanting on the good morals inculcated by his exhibitions. His mouth was now as effectually stopt, as that of quack must be, if, in the midst of a declamation on the great virtues of his pills and powders, the corpse of one of his martyrs should be brought forth, and deposited before the stage, as a testimony of his skill.

Instead, therefore, of answering my landlady, the puppet-show man ran out to punish his Merry Andrew; and now the moon beginning to put forth her silver light, as the poets call it (though she looked at that time more like a piece of copper), Jones called for his reckoning, and ordered Partridge, whom my landlady had just awaked from a profound nap, to prepare for his journey; but Partridge, having lately carried two points, as my reader hath seen before, was emboldened to attempt a third, which was to prevail with Jones to take up a lodging that evening in the house where he then was. He introduced this with an affected surprize at the intention which Mr Jones declared of removing; and, after urging many excellent arguments against it, he at last insisted strongly that it could be to no manner of purpose whatever; for that, unless Jones knew which way the lady was gone, every step he took might very possibly lead him the farther from her; "for you find, sir," said he, "by all the people in the house, that she is not gone this way. How much better, therefore, would it be to stay till the morning, when we may expect to meet with somebody to enquire of?"

This last argument had indeed some effect on Jones, and while he was weighing it the landlord threw all the rhetoric of which he was master into the same scale. "Sure, sir," said he, "your servant gives you most excellent advice; for who would travel by night at this time of the year?" He then began in the usual stile to trumpet forth the excellent accommodation which his house afforded; and my landlady likewise opened on the occasion——But, not to detain the reader with what is common to every host and hostess, it is sufficient to tell him Jones was at last prevailed on to stay and refresh himself with a few hours' rest, which indeed he very much wanted; for he had hardly shut his eyes since he had left the inn where the accident of the broken head had happened.

As soon as Jones had taken a resolution to proceed no farther that night, he presently retired to rest, with his two bedfellows, the pocket-book and the muff;

but Partridge, who at several times had refreshed himself with several naps, was more inclined to eating than to sleeping, and more to drinking than to either.

And now the storm which Grace had raised being at an end, and my landlady being again reconciled to the puppet-man, who on his side forgave the indecent reflections which the good woman in her passion had cast on his performances, a face of perfect peace and tranquillity reigned in the kitchen; where sat assembled round the fire the landlord and landlady of the house, the master of the puppet-show, the attorney's clerk, the exciseman, and the ingenious Mr Partridge; in which company past the agreeable conversation which will be found in the next chapter.

CHAPTER VII.

Containing a remark or two of our own and many more of the good company assembled in the kitchen.

Though the pride of Partridge did not submit to acknowledge himself a servant, yet he condescended in most particulars to imitate the manners of that rank. One instance of this was, his greatly magnifying the fortune of his companion, as he called Jones: such is a general custom with all servants among strangers, as none of them would willingly be thought the attendant on a beggar: for, the higher the situation of the master is, the higher consequently is that of the man in his own opinion; the truth of which observation appears from the behaviour of all the footmen of the nobility.

But, though title and fortune communicate a splendor all around them, and the footmen of men of quality and of estate think themselves entitled to a part of that respect which is paid to the quality and estate of their masters, it is clearly otherwise with regard to virtue and understanding. These advantages are strictly personal, and swallow themselves all the respect which is paid to them. To say the truth, this is so very little, that they cannot well afford to let any others partake with them. As these therefore reflect no honour on the domestic, so neither is he at all dishonoured by the most deplorable want of both in his master. Indeed it is otherwise in the want of what is called virtue in a mistress, the consequence of which we have before seen: for in this dishonour there is a kind of contagion, which, like that of poverty, communicates itself to all who approach it.

Now for these reasons we are not to wonder that servants (I mean among the men only) should have so great regard for the reputation of the wealth of their masters, and little or none at all for their character in other points, and that, though they would be ashamed to be the footman of a beggar, they are not so to attend upon a rogue or a blockhead; and do consequently make no scruple to spread the fame of the iniquities and follies of their said masters as far as possible, and this often with great humour and merriment. In reality, a footman is often a wit as well as a beau, at the expence of the gentleman whose livery he wears.

After Partridge, therefore, had enlarged greatly on the vast fortune to which Mr Jones was heir, he very freely communicated an apprehension, which he had begun to conceive the day before, and for which, as we hinted at that very time, the behaviour of Jones seemed to have furnished a sufficient foundation. In short, he was now pretty well confirmed in an opinion that his master was out of his wits, with which opinion he very bluntly acquainted the good company round the fire.

With this sentiment the puppet-show man immediately coincided. "I own," said he, "the gentleman surprized me very much, when he talked so absurdly about puppet-shows. It is indeed hardly to be conceived that any man in his senses should be so much mistaken; what you say now accounts very well for all his monstrous notions. Poor gentleman! I am heartily concerned for him; indeed he hath a strange wildness about his eyes, which I took notice of before, though I did not mention it."

The landlord agreed with this last assertion, and likewise claimed the sagacity of having observed it. "And certainly," added he, "it must be so; for no one but a madman would have thought of leaving so good a house to ramble about the country at that time of night."

The exciseman, pulling his pipe from his mouth, said, "He thought the gentleman looked and talked a little wildly;" and then turning to Partridge, "if he be a madman," says he, "he should not be suffered to travel thus about the country; for possibly he may do some mischief. It is a pity he was not secured and sent home to his relations."

Now some conceits of this kind were likewise lurking in the mind of Partridge; for, as he was now persuaded that Jones had run away from Mr Allworthy, he promised himself the highest rewards if he could by any means convey him back. But fear of Jones, of whose fierceness and strength he had seen, and indeed felt, some instances, had however represented any such scheme as impossible to be executed, and had discouraged him from applying himself to form any regular plan for the purpose. But no sooner did he hear the sentiments of the exciseman than he embraced that opportunity of declaring his own, and expressed a hearty wish that such a matter could be brought about.

"Could be brought about!" says the exciseman: "why, there is nothing easier."

"Ah! sir," answered Partridge, "you don't know what a devil of a fellow he is. He can take me up with one hand, and throw me out at window; and he would, too, if he did but imagine—"

"Pogh!" says the exciseman, "I believe I am as good a man as he. Besides, here are five of us."

"I don't know what five," cries the landlady, "my husband shall have nothing to do in it. Nor shall any violent hands be laid upon anybody in my house. The young gentleman is as pretty a young gentleman as ever I saw in my life, and I believe he is no more mad than any of us. What do you tell of his having a wild look with his eyes? they are the prettiest eyes I ever saw, and he hath the prettiest look with them; and a very modest civil young man he is. I am sure I have bepitied him heartily ever since the gentleman there in the corner told us he was crost in love. Certainly that is enough to make any man, especially such a sweet young gentleman as he is, to look a little otherwise than he did before. Lady, indeed! what the devil would the lady have better than such a handsome man with a great estate? I suppose she is one of your quality folks, one of your Townly ladies that we saw last night in the puppet-show, who don't know what they would be at."

The attorney's clerk likewise declared he would have no concern in the business without the advice of counsel. "Suppose," says he, "an action of false imprisonment should be brought against us, what defence could we make? Who knows what may be sufficient evidence of madness to a jury? But I only speak upon my own account; for it don't look well for a lawyer to be concerned in these matters, unless it be as a lawyer. Juries are always less favourable to us than to other people. I don't therefore dissuade you, Mr Thomson (to the exciseman), nor the gentleman, nor anybody else."

The exciseman shook his head at this speech, and the puppet-show man said, "Madness was sometimes a difficult matter for a jury to decide: for I remember," says he, "I was once present at a tryal of madness, where twenty witnesses swore that the person was as mad as a March hare; and twenty others, that he was as much in his senses as any man in England.—And indeed it was the opinion of most people, that it was only a trick of his relations to rob the poor man of his right."

"Very likely!" cries the landlady. "I myself knew a poor gentleman who was kept in a mad-house all his life by his family, and they enjoyed his estate, but it did them no good; for though the law gave it them, it was the right of another."

"Pogh!" cries the clerk, with great contempt, "who hath any right but what the law gives them? If the law gave me the best estate in the country, I should never trouble myself much who had the right."

"If it be so," says Partridge, "*Felix quem faciunt aliena pericula cautum.*"

My landlord, who had been called out by the arrival of a horseman at the gate, now returned into the kitchen, and with an affrighted countenance cried out, "What do you think, gentlemen? The rebels have given the duke the slip, and are got almost to London. It is certainly true, for a man on horseback just now told me so."

"I am glad of it with all my heart," cries Partridge; "then there will be no fighting in these parts."

"I am glad," cries the clerk, "for a better reason; for I would always have right take place."

"Ay, but," answered the landlord, "I have heard some people say this man hath no right."

"I will prove the contrary in a moment," cries the clerk: "if my father dies seized of a right; do you mind me, seized of a right, I say; doth not that right descend to his son; and doth not one right descend as well as another?"

"But how can he have any right to make us papishes?" says the landlord.

"Never fear that," cries Partridge. "As to the matter of right, the gentleman there hath proved it as clear as the sun; and as to the matter of religion, it is quite out of the case. The papists themselves don't expect any such thing. A popish priest, whom I know very well, and who is a very honest man, told me upon his word and honour they had no such design."

"And another priest, of my acquaintance," said the landlady, "hath told me the same thing; but my husband is always so afraid of papishes. I know a great many papishes that are very honest sort of people, and spend their money very freely; and it is always a maxim with me, that one man's money is as good as another's."

"Very true, mistress," said the puppet-show man, "I don't care what religion comes; provided the Presbyterians are not uppermost; for they are enemies to puppet-shows."

"And so you would sacrifice your religion to your interest," cries the exciseman; "and are desirous to see popery brought in, are you?"

"Not I, truly," answered the other; "I hate popery as much as any man; but yet it is a comfort to one, that one should be able to live under it, which I could not do among Presbyterians. To be sure, every man values his livelihood first; that must be granted; and I warrant, if you would confess the truth, you are more afraid of losing your place than anything else; but never fear, friend, there will be an excise under another government as well as under this."

"Why, certainly," replied the exciseman, "I should be a very ill man if I did not honour the king, whose bread I eat. That is no more than natural, as a man may say: for what signifies it to me that there would be an excise-office under another government, since my friends would be out, and I could expect no better than to follow them? No, no, friend, I shall never be bubbled out of my religion in hopes only of keeping my place under another government; for I should certainly be no better, and very probably might be worse."

"Why, that is what I say," cries the landlord, "whenever folks say who knows what may happen! Odsooks! should not I be a blockhead to lend my money to I know not who, because mayhap he may return it again? I am sure it is safe in my own bureau, and there I will keep it."

The attorney's clerk had taken a great fancy to the sagacity of Partridge. Whether this proceeded from the great discernment which the former had into men, as well as things, or whether it arose from the sympathy between their minds; for they were both truly Jacobites in principle; they now shook hands heartily, and drank bumpers of strong beer to healths which we think proper to bury in oblivion.

These healths were afterwards pledged by all present, and even by my landlord himself, though reluctantly; but he could not withstand the menaces of the clerk, who swore he would never set his foot within his house again, if he refused. The bumpers which were swallowed on this occasion soon put an end to the conversation. Here, therefore, we will put an end to the chapter.

CHAPTER VIII.

In which fortune seems to have been in a better humour with Jones than we have hitherto seen her.

As there is no wholesomer, so perhaps there are few stronger, sleeping potions than fatigue. Of this Jones might be said to have taken a very large dose, and it operated very forcibly upon him. He had already slept nine hours, and might perhaps have slept longer, had he not been awakened by a most violent noise at his chamber-door, where the sound of many heavy blows was accompanied with many exclamations of murder. Jones presently leapt from his bed, where he found the master of the puppet-show belabouring the back and ribs of his poor Merry-Andrew, without either mercy or moderation.

Jones instantly interposed on behalf of the suffering party, and pinned the insulting conqueror up to the wall: for the puppet-show man was no more able to contend with Jones than the poor party-coloured jester had been to contend with this puppet-man.

But though the Merry-Andrew was a little fellow, and not very strong, he had nevertheless some choler about him. He therefore no sooner found himself delivered from the enemy, than he began to attack him with the only weapon at which he was his equal. From this he first discharged a volley of general abusive words, and thence proceeded to some particular accusations—"D—n your bl—d, you rascal," says he, "I have not only supported you (for to me you owe all the money you get), but I have saved you from the gallows. Did you not want to rob the lady of her fine riding-habit, no longer ago than yesterday, in the back-lane here? Can you deny that you wished to have her alone in a wood to strip her—to strip one of the prettiest ladies that ever was seen in the world? and here you have fallen upon me, and have almost murdered me, for doing no harm to a girl as willing as myself, only because she likes me better than you."

Jones no sooner heard this than he quitted the master, laying on him at the same time the most violent injunctions of forbearance from any further insult on the Merry-Andrew; and then taking the poor wretch with him into his own apartment, he soon learned tidings of his Sophia, whom the fellow, as he was attending his master with his drum the day before, had seen pass by. He easily prevailed with the lad to show him the exact place, and then having summoned Partridge, he departed with the utmost expedition.

It was almost eight of the clock before all matters could be got ready for his departure: for Partridge was not in any haste, nor could the reckoning be presently adjusted; and when both these were settled and over, Jones would not quit the place before he had perfectly reconciled all differences between the master and the man.

When this was happily accomplished, he set forwards, and was by the trusty Merry-Andrew conducted to the spot by which Sophia had past; and then having handsomely rewarded his conductor, he again pushed on with the utmost eagerness, being highly delighted with the extraordinary manner in which he received his intelligence. Of this Partridge was no sooner acquainted, than he, with great earnestness, began to prophesy, and assured Jones that he would certainly have good success in the end: for, he said, "two such accidents could never have happened to direct him after his mistress, if Providence had not designed to bring them together at last." And this was the first time that Jones lent any attention to the superstitious doctrines of his companion.

They had not gone above two miles when a violent storm of rain overtook them; and, as they happened to be at the same time in sight of an ale-house, Partridge, with much earnest entreaty, prevailed with Jones to enter, and weather the storm. Hunger is an enemy (if indeed it may be called one) which partakes more of the English than of the French disposition; for, though you subdue this never so often, it will always rally again in time; and so it did with Partridge, who was no sooner arrived within the kitchen, than he began to ask the same questions which he had asked the night before. The consequence of this was an excellent cold chine being produced upon the table, upon which not only Partridge, but Jones himself, made a very hearty breakfast, though the latter began to grow again uneasy, as the people of the house could give him no fresh information concerning Sophia.

Their meal being over, Jones was again preparing to sally, notwithstanding the violence of the storm still continued; but Partridge begged heartily for another mug; and at last casting his eyes on a lad at the fire, who had entered into the kitchen, and who at that instant was looking as earnestly at him, he turned suddenly to Jones, and cried, "Master, give me your hand, a single mug shan't serve the turn this bout. Why, here's more news of Madam Sophia come to town. The boy there standing by the fire is the very lad that rode before her. I can swear to my own plaister on his face."—"Heavens bless you, sir," cries the boy, "it is your own plaister sure enough; I shall have always reason to remember your goodness; for it hath almost cured me."

At these words Jones started from his chair, and, bidding the boy follow him immediately, departed from the kitchen into a private apartment; for, so delicate was he with regard to Sophia, that he never willingly mentioned her name in the presence of many people; and, though he had, as it were, from the overflowings of his heart, given Sophia as a toast among the officers, where he thought it was impossible she should be known; yet, even there, the reader may remember how difficultly he was prevailed upon to mention her surname.

Hard therefore was it, and perhaps, in the opinion of many sagacious readers, very absurd and monstrous, that he should principally owe his present misfortune to the supposed want of that delicacy with which he so abounded; for, in reality, Sophia was much more offended at the freedoms which she thought (and not without good reason) he had taken with her name and character, than at any freedoms, in which, under his present circumstances, he had indulged himself with the person of another woman; and to say truth, I believe Honour could never have prevailed on her to leave Upton without her seeing Jones, had it not been for those two strong instances of a levity in his behaviour, so void of respect, and indeed so highly inconsistent with any degree of love and tenderness in great and delicate minds.

But so matters fell out, and so I must relate them; and if any reader is shocked at their appearing unnatural, I cannot help it. I must remind such persons that I am not writing a system, but a history, and I am not obliged to reconcile every matter to the received notions concerning truth and nature. But if this was never so easy to do, perhaps it might be more prudent in me to avoid it. For instance, as the fact at present before us now stands, without any comment of mine upon it, though it may at first sight offend some readers, yet, upon more mature consideration, it must please all; for wise and good men may consider what happened to Jones at Upton as a just punishment for his wickedness with regard to women, of which it was indeed the immediate consequence; and silly and bad persons may comfort themselves in their vices by flattering their own hearts that the characters of men are rather owing to accident than to virtue. Now, perhaps the reflections which we should be here inclined to draw would alike contradict both these conclusions, and would show that these incidents contribute only to confirm the great, useful, and uncommon doctrine, which it is the purpose of this whole work to inculcate, and which we must not fill up our pages by frequently repeating, as an ordinary parson fills his sermon by repeating his text at the end of every paragraph.

We are contented that it must appear, however unhappily Sophia had erred in her opinion of Jones, she had sufficient reason for her opinion; since, I believe, every other young lady would, in her situation, have erred in the same manner. Nay, had she followed her lover at this very time, and had entered this very alehouse the moment he was departed from it, she would have found the landlord as well acquainted with her name and person as the wench at Upton had appeared to be. For while Jones was examining his boy in whispers in an inner room, Partridge, who had no such delicacy in his disposition, was in the kitchen very openly catechising the other guide who had attended Mrs Fitzpatrick; by which means the landlord, whose ears were open on all such occasions, became perfectly well acquainted with the tumble of Sophia from her horse, &c., with the mistake concerning Jenny Cameron, with the many consequences of the punch, and, in short, with almost everything which had happened at the inn whence we despatched our ladies in a coach-and-six when we last took our leaves of them.

CHAPTER IX.

Containing little more than a few odd observations.

Jones had been absent a full half-hour, when he returned into the kitchen in a hurry, desiring the landlord to let him know that instant what was to pay. And now the concern which Partridge felt at being obliged to quit the warm chimney-corner, and a cup of excellent liquor, was somewhat compensated by hearing that he was to proceed no farther on foot, for Jones, by golden arguments, had prevailed with the boy to attend him back to the inn whither he had before conducted Sophia; but to this however the lad consented, upon condition that the other guide would wait for him at the alehouse; because, as the landlord at Upton was an intimate acquaintance of the landlord at Gloucester, it might some time or other come to the ears of the latter that his horses had been let to more than one person; and so the boy might be brought to account for money which he wisely intended to put in his own pocket.

We were obliged to mention this circumstance, trifling as it may seem, since it retarded Mr Jones a considerable time in his setting out; for the honesty of this latter boy was somewhat high—that is, somewhat high-priced, and would indeed have cost Jones very dear, had not Partridge, who, as we have said, was a very cunning fellow, artfully thrown in half-a-crown to be spent at that very alehouse, while the boy was waiting for his companion. This half-crown the landlord no sooner got scent of, than he opened after it with such vehement and persuasive outcry, that the boy was soon overcome, and consented to take half-a-crown more for his stay. Here we cannot help observing, that as there is so much of policy in the lowest life, great men often overvalue themselves on those refinements in imposture, in which they are frequently excelled by some of the lowest of the human species.

The horses being now produced, Jones directly leapt into the side-saddle, on which his dear Sophia had rid. The lad, indeed, very civilly offered him the use of his; but he chose the side-saddle, probably because it was softer. Partridge, however, though full as effeminate as Jones, could not bear the thoughts of degrading his manhood; he therefore accepted the boy's offer: and now, Jones being mounted on the side-saddle of his Sophia, the boy on that of Mrs Honour, and Partridge bestriding the third horse, they set forwards on their journey, and within four hours arrived at the inn where the reader hath already spent so much time. Partridge was in very high spirits during the whole way, and often mentioned to

Jones the many good omens of his future success which had lately befriended him; and which the reader, without being the least superstitious, must allow to have been particularly fortunate. Partridge was moreover better pleased with the present pursuit of his companion than he had been with his pursuit of glory; and from these very omens, which assured the pedagogue of success, he likewise first acquired a clear idea of the amour between Jones and Sophia; to which he had before given very little attention, as he had originally taken a wrong scent concerning the reasons of Jones's departure; and as to what happened at Upton, he was too much frightened just before and after his leaving that place to draw any other conclusions from thence than that poor Jones was a downright madman: a conceit which was not at all disagreeable to the opinion he before had of his extraordinary wildness, of which, he thought, his behaviour on their quitting Gloucester so well justified all the accounts he had formerly received. He was now, however, pretty well satisfied with his present expedition, and henceforth began to conceive much worthier sentiments of his friend's understanding.

The clock had just struck three when they arrived, and Jones immediately bespoke post-horses; but unluckily there was not a horse to be procured in the whole place; which the reader will not wonder at when he considers the hurry in which the whole nation, and especially this part of it, was at this time engaged, when expresses were passing and repassing every hour of the day and night.

Jones endeavoured all he could to prevail with his former guide to escorte him to Coventry; but he was inexorable. While he was arguing with the boy in the inn-yard, a person came up to him, and saluting him by his name, enquired how all the good family did in Somersetshire; and now Jones casting his eyes upon this person, presently discovered him to be Mr Dowling, the lawyer, with whom he had dined at Gloucester, and with much courtesy returned the salutation.

Dowling very earnestly pressed Mr Jones to go no further that night; and backed his solicitations with many unanswerable arguments, such as, that it was almost dark, that the roads were very dirty, and that he would be able to travel much better by day-light, with many others equally good, some of which Jones had probably suggested to himself before; but as they were then ineffectual, so they were still: and he continued resolute in his design, even though he should be obliged to set out on foot.

When the good attorney found he could not prevail on Jones to stay, he as strenuously applied himself to persuade the guide to accompany him. He urged many motives to induce him to undertake this short journey, and at last concluded with saying, "Do you think the gentleman won't very well reward you for your trouble?"

Two to one are odds at every other thing as well as at foot-ball. But the advantage which this united force hath in persuasion or entreaty must have been visible to a curious observer; for he must have often seen, that when a father, a master, a wife, or any other person in authority, have stoutly adhered to a denial against all the reasons which a single man could produce, they have afterwards yielded to the repetition of the same sentiments by a second or third person, who hath undertaken the cause, without attempting to advance anything new in its behalf. And hence, perhaps, proceeds the phrase of seconding an argument or a motion, and the great consequence this is of in all assemblies of public debate. Hence, likewise, probably it is, that in our courts of law we often hear a learned gentleman (generally a serjeant) repeating for an hour together what another learned gentleman, who spoke just before him, had been saying.

Instead of accounting for this, we shall proceed in our usual manner to exemplify it in the conduct of the lad above mentioned, who submitted to the persuasions of Mr Dowling, and promised once more to admit Jones into his side-saddle; but insisted on first giving the poor creatures a good bait, saying, they had travelled a great way, and been rid very hard. Indeed this caution of the boy was needless; for Jones, notwithstanding his hurry and impatience, would have ordered this of himself; for he by no means agreed with the opinion of those who consider animals as mere machines, and when they bury their spurs in the belly of their horse, imagine the spur and the horse to have an equal capacity of feeling pain.

While the beasts were eating their corn, or rather were supposed to eat it (for, as the boy was taking care of himself in the kitchen, the ostler took great care that his corn should not be consumed in the stable), Mr Jones, at the earnest desire of Mr Dowling, accompanied that gentleman into his room, where they sat down together over a bottle of wine.

CHAPTER X.

In which Mr Jones and Mr Dowling drink a bottle together.

Mr Dowling, pouring out a glass of wine, named the health of the good Squire Allworthy; adding, "If you please, sir, we will likewise remember his nephew and heir, the young squire: Come, sir, here's Mr Blifil to you, a very pretty young gentleman; and who, I dare swear, will hereafter make a very considerable figure in his country. I have a borough for him myself in my eye."

"Sir," answered Jones, "I am convinced you don't intend to affront me, so I shall not resent it; but I promise you, you have joined two persons very improperly together; for one is the glory of the human species, and the other is a rascal who dishonours the name of man."

Dowling stared at this. He said, "He thought both the gentlemen had a very unexceptionable character. As for Squire Allworthy himself," says he, "I never had the happiness to see him; but all the world talks of his goodness. And, indeed, as to the young gentleman, I never saw him but once, when I carried him the news of the loss of his mother; and then I was so hurried, and drove, and tore with the multiplicity of business, that I had hardly time to converse with him; but he looked so like a very honest gentleman, and behaved himself so prettily, that I protest I never was more delighted with any gentleman since I was born."

"I don't wonder," answered Jones, "that he should impose upon you in so short an acquaintance; for he hath the cunning of the devil himself, and you may live with him many years, without discovering him. I was bred up with him from my infancy, and we were hardly ever asunder; but it is very lately only that I have discovered half the villany which is in him. I own I never greatly liked him. I thought he wanted that generosity of spirit, which is the sure foundation of all that is great and noble in human nature. I saw a selfishness in him long ago which I despised; but it is lately, very lately, that I have found him capable of the basest and blackest designs; for, indeed, I have at last found out, that he hath taken an advantage of the openness of my own temper, and hath concerted the deepest project, by a long train of wicked artifice, to work my ruin, which at last he hath effected."

"Ay! ay!" cries Dowling; "I protest, then, it is a pity such a person should inherit the great estate of your uncle Allworthy."

"Alas, sir," cries Jones, "you do me an honour to which I have no title. It is true, indeed, his goodness once allowed me the liberty of calling him by a much nearer name; but as this was only a voluntary act of goodness, I can complain of no injustice when he thinks proper to deprive me of this honour; since the loss cannot be more unmerited than the gift originally was. I assure you, sir, I am no relation of Mr Allworthy; and if the world, who are incapable of setting a true value on his virtue, should think, in his behaviour to me, he hath dealt hardly by a relation, they do an injustice to the best of men: for I—but I ask your pardon, I shall trouble you with no particulars relating to myself; only as you seemed to think me a relation of Mr Allworthy, I thought proper to set you right in a matter that might draw some censures upon him, which I promise you I would rather lose my life than give occasion to."

"I protest, sir," cried Dowling, "you talk very much like a man of honour; but instead of giving me any trouble, I protest it would give me great pleasure to know how you came to be thought a relation of Mr Allworthy's, if you are not. Your horses won't be ready this half-hour, and as you have sufficient opportunity, I wish you would tell me how all that happened; for I protest it seems very surprizing that you should pass for a relation of a gentleman, without being so."

Jones, who in the compliance of his disposition (though not in his prudence) a little resembled his lovely Sophia, was easily prevailed on to satisfy Mr Dowling's curiosity, by relating the history of his birth and education, which he did, like Othello.

———Even from his boyish years,
To th' very moment he was bad to tell:

the which to hear, Dowling, like Desdemona, did seriously incline;

He swore 'twas strange, 'twas passing strange;
'Twas pitiful, 'twas wondcrous pitiful.

Mr Dowling was indeed very greatly affected with this relation; for he had not divested himself of humanity by being an attorney. Indeed, nothing is more unjust than to carry our prejudices against a profession into private life, and to borrow our idea of a man from our opinion of his calling. Habit, it is true, lessens the horror of those actions which the profession makes necessary, and consequently habitual; but in all other instances, Nature works in men of all professions alike; nay, perhaps, even more strongly with those who give her, as it were, a holiday, when they are following their ordinary business. A butcher, I make no doubt, would feel compunction at the slaughter of a fine horse; and though a surgeon can feel no pain in cutting off a limb, I have known him compassionate a man in a fit of the gout. The common hangman, who hath stretched the necks of hundreds, is known to have trembled at his first operation on a head: and the very professors of human blood-shedding, who, in their trade of war, butcher thousands, not only of their fellow-professors, but often of women and children, without remorse; even these, I say, in times of peace, when drums and trumpets are laid aside, often lay aside all their ferocity, and become very gentle members of civil society. In the same manner an attorney may feel all the miseries and distresses of his fellow-creatures, provided he happens not to be concerned against them.

Jones, as the reader knows, was yet unacquainted with the very black colours in which he had been represented to Mr Allworthy; and as to other matters, he did not shew them in the most disadvantageous light; for though he was unwilling to cast any blame on his former friend and patron; yet he was not very desirous of heaping too much upon himself. Dowling therefore observed, and not without reason, that very ill offices must have been done him by somebody: "For certainly," cries he, "the squire would never have disinherited you only for a few faults, which any young gentleman might have committed. Indeed, I cannot properly say disinherited: for to be sure by law you cannot claim as heir. That's certain; that nobody need go to counsel for. Yet when a gentleman had in a manner adopted you thus as his own son, you might reasonably have expected some very considerable part, if not the whole; nay, if you had expected the whole, I should not have blamed you: for certainly all men are for getting as much as they can, and they are not to be blamed on that account."

"Indeed you wrong me," said Jones; "I should have been contented with very little: I never had any view upon Mr Allworthy's fortune; nay, I believe I may truly say, I never once considered what he could or might give me. This I solemnly declare, if he had done a prejudice to his nephew in my favour, I would have undone it again. I had rather enjoy my own mind than the fortune of another man. What is the poor pride arising from a magnificent house, a numerous equipage, a splendid table, and from all the other advantages or appearances of fortune, compared to the warm, solid content, the swelling satisfaction, the thrilling transports, and the exulting triumphs, which a good mind enjoys, in the contemplation of a generous, virtuous, noble, benevolent action? I envy not Blifil in the prospect of his wealth; nor shall I envy him in the possession of it. I would not think myself a rascal half an hour, to exchange situations. I believe, indeed, Mr Blifil suspected me of the views you mention; and I suppose these suspicions, as they arose from the baseness of his own heart, so they occasioned his baseness to me. But, I thank Heaven, I know, I feel—I feel my innocence, my friend; and I would not part with that feeling for the world. For as long as I know I have never done, nor even designed, an injury to any being whatever,

Pone me pigris ubi nulla campis
Arbor aestiva recreatur aura,
Quod latus mundi nebulae, malusque
Jupiter urget.

Pone sub curru nimium propinqui
Solis in terra dominibus negata;
Dulce ridentem Lalagen amabo,
Dulce loquentem.[1]

---

[1] Place me where never summer breeze
Unbinds the glebe, or warms the trees:

He then filled a bumper of wine, and drunk it off to the health of his dear Lalage; and, filling Dowling's glass likewise up to the brim, insisted on his pledging him. "Why, then, here's Miss Lalage's health with all my heart," cries Dowling. "I have heard her toasted often, I protest, though I never saw her; but they say she's extremely handsome."

Though the Latin was not the only part of this speech which Dowling did not perfectly understand; yet there was somewhat in it that made a very strong impression upon him. And though he endeavoured by winking, nodding, sneering, and grinning, to hide the impression from Jones (for we are as often ashamed of thinking right as of thinking wrong), it is certain he secretly approved as much of his sentiments as he understood, and really felt a very strong impulse of compassion for him. But we may possibly take some other opportunity of commenting upon this, especially if we should happen to meet Mr Dowling any more in the course of our history. At present we are obliged to take our leave of that gentleman a little abruptly, in imitation of Mr Jones; who was no sooner informed, by Partridge, that his horses were ready, than he deposited his reckoning, wished his companion a good night, mounted, and set forward towards Coventry, though the night was dark, and it just then began to rain very hard.

Where ever-lowering clouds appear,
And angry Jove deforms th' inclement year.

Place me beneath the burning ray,
Where rolls the rapid car of day;
Love and the nymph shall charm my toils,
The nymph who sweetly speaks, and sweetly smiles.
MR FRANCIS.

CHAPTER XI.

The disasters which befel Jones on his departure for Coventry; with the sage remarks of Partridge.

No road can be plainer than that from the place where they now were to Coventry; and though neither Jones, nor Partridge, nor the guide, had ever travelled it before, it would have been almost impossible to have missed their way, had it not been for the two reasons mentioned in the conclusion of the last chapter.

These two circumstances, however, happening both unfortunately to intervene, our travellers deviated into a much less frequented track; and after riding full six miles, instead of arriving at the stately spires of Coventry, they found themselves still in a very dirty lane, where they saw no symptoms of approaching the suburbs of a large city.

Jones now declared that they must certainly have lost their way; but this the guide insisted upon was impossible; a word which, in common conversation, is often used to signify not only improbable, but often what is really very likely, and, sometimes, what hath certainly happened; an hyperbolical violence like that which is so frequently offered to the words infinite and eternal; by the former of which it is usual to express a distance of half a yard, and by the latter, a duration of five minutes. And thus it is as usual to assert the impossibility of losing what is already actually lost. This was, in fact, the case at present; for, notwithstanding all the confident assertions of the lad to the contrary, it is certain they were no more in the right road to Coventry, than the fraudulent, griping, cruel, canting miser is in the right road to heaven.

It is not, perhaps, easy for a reader, who hath never been in those circumstances, to imagine the horror with which darkness, rain, and wind, fill persons who have lost their way in the night; and who, consequently, have not the pleasant prospect of warm fires, dry cloaths, and other refreshments, to support their minds in struggling with the inclemencies of the weather. A very imperfect idea of this horror will, however, serve sufficiently to account for the conceits which now filled the head of Partridge, and which we shall presently be obliged to open.

Jones grew more and more positive that they were out of their road; and the boy himself at last acknowledged he believed they were not in the right road to Coventry; though he affirmed, at the same time, it was impossible they should have mist the way. But Partridge was of a different opinion. He said, "When they first set out he imagined some mischief or other would happen.—Did not you observe, sir," said he to Jones, "that old woman who stood at the door just as you was taking horse? I wish you had given her a small matter, with all my heart; for she said then you might repent it; and at that very instant it began to rain, and the wind hath continued rising ever since. Whatever some people may think, I am very certain it is in the power of witches to raise the wind whenever they please. I have seen it happen very often in my time: and if ever I saw a witch in all my life, that old woman was certainly one. I thought so to myself at that very time; and if I had had any halfpence in my pocket, I would have given her some; for to be sure it is always good to be charitable to those sort of people, for fear what may happen; and many a person hath lost his cattle by saving a halfpenny."

Jones, though he was horridly vexed at the delay which this mistake was likely to occasion in his journey, could not help smiling at the superstition of his friend, whom an accident now greatly confirmed in his opinion. This was a tumble from his horse; by which, however, he received no other injury than what the dirt conferred on his cloaths.

Partridge had no sooner recovered his legs, than he appealed to his fall, as conclusive evidence of all he had asserted; but Jones finding he was unhurt, answered with a smile: "This witch of yours, Partridge, is a most ungrateful jade, and doth not, I find, distinguish her friends from others in her resentment. If the old lady had been angry with me for neglecting her, I don't see why she should tumble you from your horse, after all the respect you have expressed for her."

"It is ill jesting," cries Partridge, "with people who have power to do these things; for they are often very malicious. I remember a farrier, who provoked one of them, by asking her when the time she had bargained with the devil for would be out; and within three months from that very day one of his best cows was drowned. Nor was she satisfied with that; for a little time afterwards he lost a barrel of best-drink: for the old witch pulled out the spigot, and let it run all over the cellar, the very first evening he had tapped it to make merry with some of his neighbours. In short, nothing ever thrived with him afterwards; for she worried the poor man so, that he took to drinking; and in a year or two his stock was seized, and he and his family are now come to the parish."

The guide, and perhaps his horse too, were both so attentive to this discourse, that, either through want of care, or by the malice of the witch, they were now both sprawling in the dirt.

Partridge entirely imputed this fall, as he had done his own, to the same cause. He told Mr Jones, "It would certainly be his turn next; and earnestly entreated him to return back, and find out the old woman, and pacify her. We shall very soon," added he, "reach the inn; for though we have seemed to go forward, I am very certain we are in the identical place in which we were an hour ago; and I dare swear, if it was daylight, we might now see the inn we set out from."

Instead of returning any answer to this sage advice, Jones was entirely attentive to what had happened to the boy, who received no other hurt than what had before befallen Partridge, and which his cloaths very easily bore, as they had been for many years inured to the like. He soon regained his side-saddle, and by the hearty curses and blows which he bestowed on his horse, quickly satisfied Mr Jones that no harm was done.

CHAPTER XII.

Relates that Mr Jones continued his journey, contrary to the advice of Partridge, with what happened on that occasion.

They now discovered a light at some distance, to the great pleasure of Jones, and to the no small terror of Partridge, who firmly believed himself to be bewitched, and that this light was a Jack-with-a-lantern, or somewhat more mischievous.

But how were these fears increased, when, as they approached nearer to this light (or lights as they now appeared), they heard a confused sound of human voices; of singing, laughing, and hallowing, together with a strange noise that seemed to proceed from some instruments; but could hardly be allowed the name of music! indeed, to favour a little the opinion of Partridge, it might very well be called music bewitched.

It is impossible to conceive a much greater degree of horror than what now seized on Partridge; the contagion of which had reached the post-boy, who had been very attentive to many things that the other had uttered. He now, therefore, joined in petitioning Jones to return; saying he firmly believed what Partridge had just before said, that though the horses seemed to go on, they had not moved a step forwards during at least the last half-hour.

Jones could not help smiling in the midst of his vexation, at the fears of these poor fellows. "Either we advance," says he, "towards the lights, or the lights have advanced towards us; for we are now at a very little distance from them; but how can either of you be afraid of a set of people who appear only to be merry-making?"

"Merry-making, sir!" cries Partridge; "who could be merry-making at this time of night, and in such a place, and such weather? They can be nothing but ghosts or witches, or some evil spirits or other, that's certain."

"Let them be what they will," cries Jones, "I am resolved to go up to them, and enquire the way to Coventry. All witches, Partridge, are not such ill-natured hags as that we had the misfortune to meet with last."

"O Lord, sir," cries Partridge, "there is no knowing what humour they will be in; to be sure it is always best to be civil to them; but what if we should meet with something worse than witches, with evil spirits themselves?——Pray, sir, be advised; pray, sir, do. If you had read so many terrible accounts as I have of these matters, you would not be so fool-hardy.——The Lord knows whither we have got already, or whither we are going; for sure such darkness was never seen upon earth, and I question whether it can be darker in the other world."

Jones put forwards as fast as he could, notwithstanding all these hints and cautions, and poor Partridge was obliged to follow; for though he hardly dared to advance, he dared still less to stay behind by himself.

At length they arrived at the place whence the lights and different noises had issued. This Jones perceived to be no other than a barn, where a great number of men and women were assembled, and diverting themselves with much apparent jollity.

Jones no sooner appeared before the great doors of the barn, which were open, than a masculine and very rough voice from within demanded, who was there?—To which Jones gently answered, a friend; and immediately asked the road to Coventry.

"If you are a friend," cries another of the men in the barn, "you had better alight till the storm is over" (for indeed it was now more violent than ever;) "you are very welcome to put up your horse; for there is sufficient room for him at the end of the barn."

"You are very obliging," returned Jones; "and I will accept your offer for a few minutes, whilst the rain continues; and here are two more who will be glad of the same favour." This was accorded with more good-will than it was accepted: for Partridge would rather have submitted to the utmost inclemency of the weather than have trusted to the clemency of those whom he took for hobgoblins; and the poor post-boy was now infected with the same apprehensions; but they were both obliged to follow the example of Jones; the one because he durst not leave his horse, and the other because he feared nothing so much as being left by himself.

Had this history been writ in the days of superstition, I should have had too much compassion for the reader to have left him so long in suspense, whether Beelzebub or Satan was about actually to appear in person, with all his hellish retinue; but as these doctrines are at present very unfortunate, and have but few, if any believers, I have not been much aware of conveying any such terrors. To say truth, the whole furniture of the infernal regions hath long been appropriated by the managers of playhouses, who seem lately to have laid them by as rubbish, capable only of affecting the upper gallery; a place in which few of our readers ever sit.

However, though we do not suspect raising any great terror on this occasion, we have reason to fear some other apprehensions may here arise in our reader, into which we would not willingly betray him; I mean that we are going to take a voyage into fairy-land, and introduce a set of beings into our history, which scarce any one was ever childish enough to believe, though many have been foolish enough to spend their time in writing and reading their adventures.

To prevent, therefore, any such suspicions, so prejudicial to the credit of an historian, who professes to draw his materials from nature only, we shall now proceed to acquaint the reader who these people were, whose sudden appearance had struck such terrors into Partridge, had more than half frightened the post-boy, and had a little surprized even Mr Jones himself.

The people then assembled in this barn were no other than a company of Egyptians, or, as they are vulgarly called, gypsies, and they were now celebrating the wedding of one of their society.

It is impossible to conceive a happier set of people than appeared here to be met together. The utmost mirth, indeed, shewed itself in every countenance; nor was their ball totally void of all order and decorum. Perhaps it had more than a country assembly is sometimes conducted with: for these people are subject to a formal government and laws of their own, and all pay obedience to one great magistrate, whom they call their king.

Greater plenty, likewise, was nowhere to be seen than what flourished in this barn. Here was indeed no nicety nor elegance, nor did the keen appetite of the guests require any. Here was good store of bacon, fowls, and mutton, to which every one present provided better sauce himself than the best and dearest French cook can prepare.

Aeneas is not described under more consternation in the temple of Juno,

Dum stupet obtutuque haeret defixus in uno,

than was our heroe at what he saw in this barn. While he was looking everywhere round him with astonishment, a venerable person approached him with many friendly salutations, rather of too hearty a kind to be called courtly. This was no other than the king of the gypsies himself. He was very little distinguished in dress from his subjects, nor had he any regalia of majesty to support his dignity; and yet there seemed (as Mr Jones said) to be somewhat in his air which denoted authority, and inspired the beholders with an idea of awe and respect; though all this was perhaps imaginary in Jones; and the truth may be, that such ideas are incident to power, and almost inseparable from it.

There was somewhat in the open countenance and courteous behaviour of Jones which, being accompanied with much comeliness of person, greatly recommended him at first sight to every beholder. These were, perhaps, a little heightened in the present instance, by that profound respect which he paid to the king of the gypsies, the moment he was acquainted with his dignity, and which was the sweeter to his gypseian majesty, as he was not used to receive such homage from any but his own subjects.

The king ordered a table to be spread with the choicest of their provisions for his accommodation; and, having placed himself at his right hand, his majesty began to discourse with our heroe in the following manner:—

"Me doubt not, sir, but you have often seen some of my people, who are what you call de parties detache: for dey go about everywhere; but me fancy you imagine not we be so considrable body as we be; and may be you will be surprize more when you hear de gypsy be as orderly and well govern people as any upon face of de earth.

"Me have honour, as me say, to be deir king, and no monarch can do boast of more dutiful subject, ne no more affectionate. How far me deserve deir good-will, me no say; but dis me can say, dat me never design anyting but to do dem good. Me sall no do boast of dat neider: for what can me do oderwise dan consider of de good of dose poor people who go about all day to give me always de best of what dey get. Dey love and honour me darefore, because me do love and take care of dem; dat is all, me know no oder reason.

"About a tousand or two tousand year ago, me cannot tell to a year or two, as can neider write nor read, dere was a great what you call—a volution among de gypsy; for dere was de lord gypsy in dose days; and dese lord did quarrel vid one anoder about de place; but de king of de gypsy did demolish dem all, and made all his subject equal vid each oder; and since dat time dey have agree very well; for dey no tink of being king, and may be it be better for dem as dey be; for me assure you it be ver troublesome ting to be king, and always to do justice; me have often wish to be de private gypsy when me have been forced to punish my dear friend and relation; for dough we never put to death, our punishments be ver severe. Dey make de gypsy ashamed of demselves, and dat be ver terrible punishment; me ave scarce ever known de gypsy so punish do harm any more."

The king then proceeded to express some wonder that there was no such punishment as shame in other governments. Upon which Jones assured him to the contrary; for that there were many crimes for which shame was inflicted by the English laws, and that it was indeed one consequence of all punishment. "Dat be ver strange," said the king; "for me know and hears good deal of your people, dough me no live among dem; and me have often hear dat sham is de consequence and de cause too of many of your rewards. Are your rewards and punishments den de same ting?"

While his majesty was thus discoursing with Jones, a sudden uproar arose in the barn, and as it seems upon this occasion:—the courtesy of these people had by degrees removed all the apprehensions of Partridge, and he was prevailed upon not only to stuff himself with their food, but to taste some of their liquors, which by degrees entirely expelled all fear from his composition, and in its stead introduced much more agreeable sensations.

A young female gypsy, more remarkable for her wit than her beauty, had decoyed the honest fellow aside, pretending to tell his fortune. Now, when they were alone together in a remote part of the barn, whether it proceeded from the strong liquor, which is never so apt to inflame inordinate desire as after moderate fatigue; or whether the fair gypsy herself threw aside the delicacy and decency of her sex, and tempted the youth Partridge with express solicitations; but they were discovered in a very improper manner by the husband of the gypsy, who, from jealousy it seems, had kept a watchful eye over his wife, and had dogged her to the place, where he found her in the arms of her gallant.

To the great confusion of Jones, Partridge was now hurried before the king; who heard the accusation, and likewise the culprit's defence, which was indeed very trifling; for the poor fellow was confounded by the plain evidence which appeared against him, and had very little to say for himself. His majesty, then turning towards Jones, said, "Sir, you have hear what dey say; what punishment do you tink your man deserve?"

Jones answered, "He was sorry for what had happened, and that Partridge should make the husband all the amends in his power: he said, he had very little money about him at that time;" and, putting his hand into his pocket, offered the fellow a guinea. To which he immediately answered, "He hoped his honour would not think of giving him less than five."

This sum, after some altercation, was reduced to two; and Jones, having stipulated for the full forgiveness of both Partridge and the wife, was going to pay the money; when his majesty, restraining his hand, turned to the witness and asked him, "At what time he had discovered the criminals?" To which he answered, "That he had been desired by the husband to watch the motions of his wife from her first speaking to the stranger, and that he had never lost sight of her afterwards till the crime had been committed." The king then asked, "if the husband was with him all that time in his lurking-place?" To which he answered in the affirmative. His Egyptian majesty then addressed himself to the husband as follows: "Me be sorry to see any gypsy dat have no more honour dan to sell de honour of his wife for money. If you had de love for your wife, you would have prevented dis matter, and not endeavour to make her de whore dat you might discover her. Me do order dat you have no money given you, for you deserve punishment, not reward; me do order derefore, dat you be de infamous gypsy, and do wear pair of horns upon your forehead for one month, and dat your wife be called de whore, and pointed at all dat time; for you be de infamous gypsy, but she be no less de infamous whore."

The gypsies immediately proceeded to execute the sentence, and left Jones and Partridge alone with his majesty.

Jones greatly applauded the justice of the sentence: upon which the king, turning to him, said, "Me believe you be surprize: for me suppose you have ver bad opinion of my people; me suppose you tink us all de tieves."

"I must confess, sir," said Jones, "I have not heard so favourable an account of them as they seem to deserve."

"Me vil tell you," said the king, "how the difference is between you and us. My people rob your people, and your people rob one anoder."

Jones afterwards proceeded very gravely to sing forth the happiness of those subjects who live under such a magistrate.

Indeed their happiness appears to have been so compleat, that we are aware lest some advocate for arbitrary power should hereafter quote the case of those people, as an instance of the great advantages which attend that government above all others.

> And here we will make a concession, which would not perhaps have been expected from us, that no limited form of government is capable of rising to the same degree of perfection, or of producing the

> same benefits to society, with this. Mankind have never been so happy, as when the greatest part of the then known world was under the dominion of a single master; and this state of their felicity continued during the reigns of five successive princes.[1] This was the true aera of the golden age, and the only golden age which ever had any existence, unless in the warm imaginations of the poets, from the expulsion from Eden down to this day.

Now if an absolute monarch, with all these great and rare qualifications, should be allowed capable of conferring the greatest good on society; it must be surely granted, on the contrary, that absolute power, vested in the hands of one who is deficient in them all, is likely to be attended with no less a degree of evil.

In short, our own religion furnishes us with adequate ideas of the blessing, as well as curse, which may attend absolute power. The pictures of heaven and of hell will place a very lively image of both before our eyes; for though the prince of the latter can have no power but what he originally derives from the omnipotent Sovereign in the former, yet it plainly appears from Scripture that absolute power in his infernal dominions is granted to their diabolical ruler. This is indeed the only absolute power which can by Scripture be derived from heaven. If, therefore, the several tyrannies upon earth can prove any title to a Divine authority, it must be derived from this original grant to the prince of darkness; and these subordinate deputations must consequently come immediately from him whose stamp they so expressly bear.

To conclude, as the examples of all ages shew us that mankind in general desire power only to do harm, and, when they obtain it, use it for no other purpose; it is not consonant with even the least degree of prudence to hazard an alteration, where our hopes are poorly kept in countenance by only two or three exceptions out of a thousand instances to alarm our fears. In this case it will be much wiser to submit to a few inconveniencies arising from the dispassionate deafness of laws, than to remedy them by applying to the passionate open ears of a tyrant.

Nor can the example of the gypsies, though possibly they may have long been happy under this form of government, be here urged; since we must remember the very material respect in which they differ from all other people, and to which perhaps this their happiness is entirely owing, namely, that they have no false

---

[1] Nerva, Trajan, Adrian, and the two Antonini. -- In reality, I know but of one solid objection to absolute monarchy. The only defect in which excellent constitution seems to be, the difficulty of finding any man adequate to the office of an absolute monarch: for this indispensably requires three qualities very difficult, as it appears from history, to be found in princely natures: first, a sufficient quantity of moderation in the prince, to be contented with all the power which is possible for him to have. 2ndly, Enough of wisdom to know his own happiness. And, 3rdly, Goodness sufficient to support the happiness of others, when not only compatible with, but instrumental to his own.

honours among them, and that they look on shame as the most grievous punishment in the world.

CHAPTER XIII.

A dialogue between Jones and Partridge.

The honest lovers of liberty will, we doubt not, pardon that long digression into which we were led at the close of the last chapter, to prevent our history from being applied to the use of the most pernicious doctrine which priestcraft had ever the wickedness or the impudence to preach.

We will now proceed with Mr Jones, who, when the storm was over, took leave of his Egyptian majesty, after many thanks for his courteous behaviour and kind entertainment, and set out for Coventry; to which place (for it was still dark) a gypsy was ordered to conduct him.

Jones having, by reason of his deviation, travelled eleven miles instead of six, and most of those through very execrable roads, where no expedition could have been made in quest of a midwife, did not arrive at Coventry till near twelve. Nor could he possibly get again into the saddle till past two; for post-horses were now not easy to get; nor were the hostler or post-boy in half so great a hurry as himself, but chose rather to imitate the tranquil disposition of Partridge; who, being denied the nourishment of sleep, took all opportunities to supply its place with every other kind of nourishment, and was never better pleased than when he arrived at an inn, nor ever more dissatisfied than when he was again forced to leave it.

Jones now travelled post; we will follow him, therefore, according to our custom, and to the rules of Longinus, in the same manner. From Coventry he arrived at Daventry, from Daventry at Stratford, and from Stratford at Dunstable, whither he came the next day a little after noon, and within a few hours after Sophia had left it; and though he was obliged to stay here longer than he wished, while a smith, with great deliberation, shoed the post-horse he was to ride, he doubted not but to overtake his Sophia before she should set out from St Albans; at which place he concluded, and very reasonably, that his lordship would stop and dine.

And had he been right in this conjecture, he most probably would have overtaken his angel at the aforesaid place; but unluckily my lord had appointed a dinner to be prepared for him at his own house in London, and, in order to enable him to reach that place in proper time, he had ordered a relay of horses to meet him at St Albans. When Jones therefore arrived there, he was informed that the coach-and-six had set out two hours before.

If fresh post-horses had been now ready, as they were not, it seemed so apparently impossible to overtake the coach before it reached London, that Partridge thought he had now a proper opportunity to remind his friend of a matter which he seemed entirely to have forgotten; what this was the reader will guess, when we inform him that Jones had eat nothing more than one poached egg since he had left the alehouse where he had first met the guide returning from Sophia; for with the gypsies he had feasted only his understanding.

The landlord so entirely agreed with the opinion of Mr Partridge, that he no sooner heard the latter desire his friend to stay and dine, than he very readily put in his word, and retracting his promise before given of furnishing the horses immediately, he assured Mr Jones he would lose no time in bespeaking a dinner, which, he said, could be got ready sooner than it was possible to get the horses up from grass, and to prepare them for their journey by a feed of corn.

Jones was at length prevailed on, chiefly by the latter argument of the landlord; and now a joint of mutton was put down to the fire. While this was preparing, Partridge, being admitted into the same apartment with his friend or master, began to harangue in the following manner.

"Certainly, sir, if ever man deserved a young lady, you deserve young Madam Western; for what a vast quantity of love must a man have, to be able to live upon it without any other food, as you do? I am positive I have eat thirty times as much within these last twenty-four hours as your honour, and yet I am almost famished; for nothing makes a man so hungry as travelling, especially in this cold raw weather. And yet I can't tell how it is, but your honour is seemingly in perfect good health, and you never looked better nor fresher in your life. It must be certainly love that you live upon."

"And a very rich diet too, Partridge," answered Jones. "But did not fortune send me an excellent dainty yesterday? Dost thou imagine I cannot live more than twenty-four hours on this dear pocket-book?"

"Undoubtedly," cries Partridge, "there is enough in that pocket-book to purchase many a good meal. Fortune sent it to your honour very opportunely for present use, as your honour's money must be almost out by this time."

"What do you mean?" answered Jones; "I hope you don't imagine that I should be dishonest enough, even if it belonged to any other person, besides Miss Western——"

"Dishonest!" replied Partridge, "heaven forbid I should wrong your honour so much! but where's the dishonesty in borrowing a little for present spending, since you will be so well able to pay the lady hereafter? No, indeed, I would have your honour pay it again, as soon as it is convenient, by all means; but where can be the harm in making use of it now you want it? Indeed, if it belonged to a poor body, it would be another thing; but so great a lady, to be sure, can never want it, especially now as she is along with a lord, who, it can't be doubted, will let her have whatever she hath need of. Besides, if she should want a little, she can't want the whole, therefore I would give her a little; but I would be hanged before I mentioned the having found it at first, and before I got some money of my own; for

London, I have heard, is the very worst of places to be in without money. Indeed, if I had not known to whom it belonged, I might have thought it was the devil's money, and have been afraid to use it; but as you know otherwise, and came honestly by it, it would be an affront to fortune to part with it all again, at the very time when you want it most; you can hardly expect she should ever do you such another good turn; for *fortuna nunquam perpetuo est bona*. You will do as you please, notwithstanding all I say; but for my part, I would be hanged before I mentioned a word of the matter."

"By what I can see, Partridge," cries Jones, "hanging is a matter *non longe alienum a Scaevolae studiis*." "You should say *alienus*," says Partridge,—"I remember the passage; it is an example under *communis, alienus, immunis, variis casibus serviunt*." "If you do remember it," cries Jones, "I find you don't understand it; but I tell thee, friend, in plain English, that he who finds another's property, and wilfully detains it from the known owner, deserves, *in foro conscientiae*, to be hanged, no less than if he had stolen it. And as for this very identical bill, which is the property of my angel, and was once in her dear possession, I will not deliver it into any hands but her own, upon any consideration whatever, no, though I was as hungry as thou art, and had no other means to satisfy my craving appetite; this I hope to do before I sleep; but if it should happen otherwise, I charge thee, if thou would'st not incur my displeasure for ever, not to shock me any more by the bare mention of such detestable baseness."

"I should not have mentioned it now," cries Partridge, "if it had appeared so to me; for I'm sure I scorn any wickedness as much as another; but perhaps you know better; and yet I might have imagined that I should not have lived so many years, and have taught school so long, without being able to distinguish between *fas et nefas*; but it seems we are all to live and learn. I remember my old schoolmaster, who was a prodigious great scholar, used often to say, *Polly matete cry town is my daskalon*. The English of which, he told us, was, That a child may sometimes teach his grandmother to suck eggs. I have lived to a fine purpose, truly, if I am to be taught my grammar at this time of day. Perhaps, young gentleman, you may change your opinion, if you live to my years: for I remember I thought myself as wise when I was a stripling of one or two and twenty as I am now. I am sure I always taught *alienus*, and my master read it so before me."

There were not many instances in which Partridge could provoke Jones, nor were there many in which Partridge himself could have been hurried out of his respect. Unluckily, however, they had both hit on one of these. We have already seen Partridge could not bear to have his learning attacked, nor could Jones bear some passage or other in the foregoing speech. And now, looking upon his companion with a contemptuous and disdainful air (a thing not usual with him), he cried, "Partridge, I see thou art a conceited old fool, and I wish thou art not likewise an old rogue. Indeed, if I was as well convinced of the latter as I am of the former, thou should'st travel no farther in my company."

The sage pedagogue was contented with the vent which he had already given to his indignation; and, as the vulgar phrase is, immediately drew in his horns. He said, he was sorry he had uttered anything which might give offence, for that he had never intended it; but *Nemo omnibus horis sapit.*

As Jones had the vices of a warm disposition, he was entirely free from those of a cold one; and if his friends must have confest his temper to have been a little too easily ruffled, his enemies must at the same time have confest, that it as soon subsided; nor did it at all resemble the sea, whose swelling is more violent and dangerous after a storm is over than while the storm itself subsists. He instantly accepted the submission of Partridge, shook him by the hand, and with the most benign aspect imaginable, said twenty kind things, and at the same time very severely condemned himself, though not half so severely as he will most probably be condemned by many of our good readers.

Partridge was now highly comforted, as his fears of having offended were at once abolished, and his pride completely satisfied by Jones having owned himself in the wrong, which submission he instantly applied to what had principally nettled him, and repeated in a muttering voice, "To be sure, sir, your knowledge may be superior to mine in some things; but as to the grammar, I think I may challenge any man living. I think, at least, I have that at my finger's end."

If anything could add to the satisfaction which the poor man now enjoyed, he received this addition by the arrival of an excellent shoulder of mutton, that at this instant came smoaking to the table. On which, having both plentifully feasted, they again mounted their horses, and set forward for London.

CHAPTER XIV.

What happened to Mr Jones in his journey from St Albans.

They were got about two miles beyond Barnet, and it was now the dusk of the evening, when a genteel-looking man, but upon a very shabby horse, rode up to Jones, and asked him whether he was going to London; to which Jones answered in the affirmative. The gentleman replied, "I should be obliged to you, sir, if you will accept of my company; for it is very late, and I am a stranger to the road." Jones readily complied with the request; and on they travelled together, holding that sort of discourse which is usual on such occasions.

Of this, indeed, robbery was the principal topic: upon which subject the stranger expressed great apprehensions; but Jones declared he had very little to lose, and consequently as little to fear. Here Partridge could not forbear putting in his word. "Your honour," said he, "may think it a little, but I am sure, if I had a hundred-pound bank-note in my pocket, as you have, I should be very sorry to lose it; but, for my part, I never was less afraid in my life; for we are four of us, and if we all stand by one another, the best man in England can't rob us. Suppose he should have a pistol, he can kill but one of us, and a man can die but once.—That's my comfort, a man can die but once."

Besides the reliance on superior numbers, a kind of valour which hath raised a certain nation among the moderns to a high pitch of glory, there was another reason for the extraordinary courage which Partridge now discovered; for he had at present as much of that quality as was in the power of liquor to bestow.

Our company were now arrived within a mile of Highgate, when the stranger turned short upon Jones, and pulling out a pistol, demanded that little bank-note which Partridge had mentioned.

Jones was at first somewhat shocked at this unexpected demand; however, he presently recollected himself, and told the highwayman, all the money he had in his pocket was entirely at his service; and so saying, he pulled out upwards of three guineas, and offered to deliver it; but the other answered with an oath, That would not do. Jones answered coolly, he was very sorry for it, and returned the money into his pocket.

The highwayman then threatened, if he did not deliver the bank-note that moment, he must shoot him; holding his pistol at the same time very near to his breast. Jones instantly caught hold of the fellow's hand, which trembled so that he could scarce hold the pistol in it, and turned the muzzle from him. A struggle then ensued, in which the former wrested the pistol from the hand of his antagonist, and both came from their horses on the ground together, the highwayman upon his back, and the victorious Jones upon him.

The poor fellow now began to implore mercy of the conqueror: for, to say the truth, he was in strength by no means a match for Jones. "Indeed, sir," says he, "I could have had no intention to shoot you; for you will find the pistol was not loaded. This is the first robbery I ever attempted, and I have been driven by distress to this."

At this instant, at about a hundred and fifty yards' distance, lay another person on the ground, roaring for mercy in a much louder voice than the highwayman. This was no other than Partridge himself, who, endeavouring to make his escape from the engagement, had been thrown from his horse, and lay flat on his face, not daring to look up, and expecting every minute to be shot.

In this posture he lay, till the guide, who was no otherwise concerned than for his horses, having secured the stumbling beast, came up to him, and told him his master had got the better of the highwayman.

Partridge leapt up at this news, and ran back to the place where Jones stood with his sword drawn in his hand to guard the poor fellow; which Partridge no sooner saw than he cried out, "Kill the villain, sir, run him through the body, kill him this instant!"

Luckily, however, for the poor wretch, he had fallen into more merciful hands; for Jones having examined the pistol, and found it to be really unloaded, began to believe all the man had told him, before Partridge came up: namely, that he was a novice in the trade, and that he had been driven to it by the distress he mentioned, the greatest indeed imaginable, that of five hungry children, and a wife lying in of the sixth, in the utmost want and misery. The truth of all which the highwayman most vehemently asserted, and offered to convince Mr Jones of it, if he would take the trouble to go to his house, which was not above two miles off; saying, "That he desired no favour, but upon condition of proving all he had all alledged."

Jones at first pretended that he would take the fellow at his word, and go with him, declaring that his fate should depend entirely on the truth of his story. Upon this the poor fellow immediately expressed so much alacrity, that Jones was perfectly satisfied with his veracity, and began now to entertain sentiments of compassion for him. He returned the fellow his empty pistol, advised him to think of honester means of relieving his distress, and gave him a couple of guineas for the immediate support of his wife and his family; adding, "he wished he had more for his sake, for the hundred pound that had been mentioned was not his own."

Our readers will probably be divided in their opinions concerning this action; some may applaud it perhaps as an act of extraordinary humanity, while those of a more saturnine temper will consider it as a want of regard to that justice which every man owes his country. Partridge certainly saw it in that light; for he testified much dissatisfaction on the occasion, quoted an old proverb, and said, he should not wonder if the rogue attacked them again before they reached London.

The highwayman was full of expressions of thankfulness and gratitude. He actually dropt tears, or pretended so to do. He vowed he would immediately return home, and would never afterwards commit such a transgression: whether he kept his word or no, perhaps may appear hereafter.

Our travellers having remounted their horses, arrived in town without encountering any new mishap. On the road much pleasant discourse passed between Jones and Partridge, on the subject of their last adventure: in which Jones exprest a great compassion for those highwaymen who are, by unavoidable distress, driven, as it were, to such illegal courses, as generally bring them to a shameful death: "I mean," said he, "those only whose highest guilt extends no farther than to robbery, and who are never guilty of cruelty nor insult to any person, which is a circumstance that, I must say, to the honour of our country, distinguishes the robbers of England from those of all other nations; for murder is, amongst those, almost inseparably incident to robbery."

"No doubt," answered Partridge, "it is better to take away one's money than one's life; and yet it is very hard upon honest men, that they can't travel about their business without being in danger of these villains. And to be sure it would be better that all rogues were hanged out of the way, than that one honest man should suffer. For my own part, indeed, I should not care to have the blood of any of them on my own hands; but it is very proper for the law to hang them all. What right hath any man to take sixpence from me, unless I give it him? Is there any honesty in such a man?"

"No, surely," cries Jones, "no more than there is in him who takes the horses out of another man's stable, or who applies to his own use the money which he finds, when he knows the right owner."

These hints stopt the mouth of Partridge; nor did he open it again till Jones, having thrown some sarcastical jokes on his cowardice, he offered to excuse himself on the inequality of fire-arms, saying, "A thousand naked men are nothing to one pistol; for though it is true it will kill but one at a single discharge, yet who can tell but that one may be himself?"

BOOK XIII.

CONTAINING THE SPACE OF TWELVE DAYS.

CHAPTER I.

An Invocation.

Come, bright love of fame, inspire my glowing breast: not thee I will call, who, over swelling tides of blood and tears, dost bear the heroe on to glory, while sighs of millions waft his spreading sails; but thee, fair, gentle maid, whom Mnesis, happy nymph, first on the banks of Hebrus did produce. Thee, whom Maeonia educated, whom Mantua charmed, and who, on that fair hill which overlooks the proud metropolis of Britain, sat'st, with thy Milton, sweetly tuning the heroic lyre; fill my ravished fancy with the hopes of charming ages yet to come. Foretel me that some tender maid, whose grandmother is yet unborn, hereafter, when, under the fictitious name of Sophia, she reads the real worth which once existed in my Charlotte, shall from her sympathetic breast send forth the heaving sigh. Do thou teach me not only to foresee, but to enjoy, nay, even to feed on future praise. Comfort me by a solemn assurance, that when the little parlour in which I sit at this instant shall be reduced to a worse furnished box, I shall be read with honour by those who never knew nor saw me, and whom I shall neither know nor see.

And thou, much plumper dame, whom no airy forms nor phantoms of imagination cloathe; whom the well-seasoned beef, and pudding richly stained with plums, delight: thee I call: of whom in a treckschuyte, in some Dutch canal, the fat ufrow gelt, impregnated by a jolly merchant of Amsterdam, was delivered: in Grub-street school didst thou suck in the elements of thy erudition. Here hast thou, in thy maturer age, taught poetry to tickle not the fancy, but the pride of the patron. Comedy from thee learns a grave and solemn air; while tragedy storms aloud, and rends th' affrighted theatres with its thunders. To soothe thy wearied limbs in slumber, Alderman History tells his tedious tale; and, again, to awaken thee, Monsieur Romance performs his surprizing tricks of dexterity. Nor less thy well-fed bookseller obeys thy influence. By thy advice the heavy, unread, folio lump, which long had dozed on the dusty shelf, piecemealed into numbers, runs nimbly through the nation. Instructed by thee, some books, like quacks, impose on the world by promising wonders; while others turn beaus, and trust all their merits to a gilded outside. Come, thou jolly substance, with thy shining face, keep back thy inspiration, but hold forth thy tempting rewards; thy shining, chinking heap; thy quickly convertible bank-bill, big with unseen riches; thy often-varying stock; the warm, the comfortable house; and, lastly, a fair portion of that bounteous mother, whose flowing breasts yield redundant sustenance for all her numerous offspring, did not some too greedily and wantonly drive their brethren from the teat. Come thou, and if I am too tasteless of thy valuable treasures, warm my heart with the transporting thought of conveying them to others. Tell me, that through thy bounty, the pratling babes, whose innocent play hath often been interrupted by my labours, may one time be amply rewarded for them.

And now, this ill-yoked pair, this lean shadow and this fat substance, have prompted me to write, whose assistance shall I invoke to direct my pen?

First, Genius; thou gift of Heaven; without whose aid in vain we struggle against the stream of nature. Thou who dost sow the generous seeds which art nourishes, and brings to perfection. Do thou kindly take me by the hand, and lead me through all the mazes, the winding labyrinths of nature. Initiate me into all those mysteries which profane eyes never beheld. Teach me, which to thee is no difficult task, to know mankind better than they know themselves. Remove that mist which dims the intellects of mortals, and causes them to adore men for their art, or to detest them for their cunning, in deceiving others, when they are, in reality, the objects only of ridicule, for deceiving themselves. Strip off the thin disguise of wisdom from self-conceit, of plenty from avarice, and of glory from ambition. Come, thou that hast inspired thy Aristophanes, thy Lucian, thy Cervantes, thy Rabelais, thy Molière, thy Shakespear, thy Swift, thy Marivaux, fill my pages with humour; till mankind learn the good-nature to laugh only at the follies of others, and the humility to grieve at their own.

And thou, almost the constant attendant on true genius, Humanity, bring all thy tender sensations. If thou hast already disposed of them all between thy Allen and thy Lyttleton, steal them a little while from their bosoms. Not without these the tender scene is painted. From these alone proceed the noble, disinterested friendship, the melting love, the generous sentiment, the ardent gratitude, the soft compassion, the candid opinion; and all those strong energies of a good mind, which fill the moistened eyes with tears, the glowing cheeks with blood, and swell the heart with tides of grief, joy, and benevolence.

And thou, O Learning! (for without thy assistance nothing pure, nothing correct, can genius produce) do thou guide my pen. Thee in thy favourite fields, where the limpid, gently-rolling Thames washes thy Etonian banks, in early youth I have worshipped. To thee, at thy birchen altar, with true Spartan devotion, I have sacrificed my blood. Come then, and from thy vast, luxuriant stores, in long antiquity piled up, pour forth the rich profusion. Open thy Maeonian and thy Mantuan coffers, with whatever else includes thy philosophic, thy poetic, and thy historical treasures, whether with Greek or Roman characters thou hast chosen to inscribe the ponderous chests: give me a while that key to all thy treasures, which to thy Warburton thou hast entrusted.

Lastly, come Experience, long conversant with the wise, the good, the learned, and the polite. Nor with them only, but with every kind of character, from the minister at his levee, to the bailiff in his spunging-house; from the dutchess at her drum, to the landlady behind her bar. From thee only can the manners of mankind be known; to which the recluse pedant, however great his parts or extensive his learning may be, hath ever been a stranger.

Come all these, and more, if possible; for arduous is the task I have undertaken; and, without all your assistance, will, I find, be too heavy for me to support. But if you all smile on my labours I hope still to bring them to a happy conclusion.

CHAPTER II.

What befel Mr Jones on his arrival in London.

The learned Dr Misaubin used to say, that the proper direction to him was *To Dr* Misaubin, *in the World*; intimating that there were few people in it to whom his great reputation was not known. And, perhaps, upon a very nice examination into the matter, we shall find that this circumstance bears no inconsiderable part among the many blessings of grandeur.

The great happiness of being known to posterity, with the hopes of which we so delighted ourselves in the preceding chapter, is the portion of few. To have the several elements which compose our names, as Sydenham expresses it, repeated a thousand years hence, is a gift beyond the power of title and wealth; and is scarce to be purchased, unless by the sword and the pen. But to avoid the scandalous imputation, while we yet live, of being *one whom nobody knows* (a scandal, by the bye, as old as the days of Homer[1]) will always be the envied portion of those, who have a legal title either to honour or estate.

From that figure, therefore, which the Irish peer, who brought Sophia to town, hath already made in this history, the reader will conclude, doubtless, it must have been an easy matter to have discovered his house in London without knowing the particular street or square which he inhabited, since he must have been one *whom everybody knows*. To say the truth, so it would have been to any of those tradesmen who are accustomed to attend the regions of the great; for the doors of the great are generally no less easy to find than it is difficult to get entrance into them. But Jones, as well as Partridge, was an entire stranger in London; and as he happened to arrive first in a quarter of the town, the inhabitants of which have very little intercourse with the householders of Hanover or Grosvenor-square (for he entered through Gray's-inn-lane), so he rambled about some time before he could even find his way to those happy mansions where fortune segregates from the vulgar those magnanimous heroes, the descendants of antient Britons, Saxons, or Danes, whose ancestors, being born in better days, by sundry kinds of merit, have entailed riches and honour on their posterity.

---

[1] See the 2d Odyssey, ver. 175.

Jones, being at length arrived at those terrestrial Elysian fields, would now soon have discovered his lordship's mansion; but the peer unluckily quitted his former house when he went for Ireland; and as he was just entered into a new one, the fame of his equipage had not yet sufficiently blazed in the neighbourhood; so that, after a successless enquiry till the clock had struck eleven, Jones at last yielded to the advice of Partridge, and retreated to the Bull and Gate in Holborn, that being the inn where he had first alighted, and where he retired to enjoy that kind of repose which usually attends persons in his circumstances.

Early in the morning he again set forth in pursuit of Sophia; and many a weary step he took to no better purpose than before. At last, whether it was that Fortune relented, or whether it was no longer in her power to disappoint him, he came into the very street which was honoured by his lordship's residence; and, being directed to the house, he gave one gentle rap at the door.

The porter, who, from the modesty of the knock, had conceived no high idea of the person approaching, conceived but little better from the appearance of Mr Jones, who was drest in a suit of fustian, and had by his side the weapon formerly purchased of the serjeant; of which, though the blade might be composed of well-tempered steel, the handle was composed only of brass, and that none of the brightest. When Jones, therefore, enquired after the young lady who had come to town with his lordship, this fellow answered surlily, "That there were no ladies there." Jones then desired to see the master of the house; but was informed that his lordship would see nobody that morning. And upon growing more pressing the porter said, "he had positive orders to let no person in; but if you think proper," said he, "to leave your name, I will acquaint his lordship; and if you call another time you shall know when he will see you."

Jones now declared, "that he had very particular business with the young lady, and could not depart without seeing her." Upon which the porter, with no very agreeable voice or aspect, affirmed, "that there was no young lady in that house, and consequently none could he see;" adding, "sure you are the strangest man I ever met with, for you will not take an answer."

I have often thought that, by the particular description of Cerberus, the porter of hell, in the 6th Aeneid, Virgil might possibly intend to satirize the porters of the great men in his time; the picture, at least, resembles those who have the honour to attend at the doors of our great men. The porter in his lodge answers exactly to Cerberus in his den, and, like him, must be appeased by a sop before access can be gained to his master. Perhaps Jones might have seen him in that light, and have recollected the passage where the Sibyl, in order to procure an entrance for Aeneas, presents the keeper of the Stygian avenue with such a sop. Jones, in like manner, now began to offer a bribe to the human Cerberus, which a footman, overhearing, instantly advanced, and declared, "if Mr Jones would give him the sum proposed, he would conduct him to the lady." Jones instantly agreed, and was forthwith conducted to the lodging of Mrs Fitzpatrick by the very fellow who had attended the ladies thither the day before.

Nothing more aggravates ill success than the near approach to good. The gamester, who loses his party at piquet by a single point, laments his bad luck ten times as much as he who never came within a prospect of the game. So in a lottery, the proprietors of the next numbers to that which wins the great prize are apt to account themselves much more unfortunate than their fellow-sufferers. In short, these kind of hairbreadth missings of happiness look like the insults of Fortune, who may be considered as thus playing tricks with us, and wantonly diverting herself at our expense.

Jones, who more than once already had experienced this frolicsome disposition of the heathen goddess, was now again doomed to be tantalized in the like manner; for he arrived at the door of Mrs Fitzpatrick about ten minutes after the departure of Sophia. He now addressed himself to the waiting-woman belonging to Mrs Fitzpatrick; who told him the disagreeable news that the lady was gone, but could not tell him whither; and the same answer he afterwards received from Mrs Fitzpatrick herself. For as that lady made no doubt but that Mr Jones was a person detached from her uncle Western, in pursuit of his daughter, so she was too generous to betray her.

Though Jones had never seen Mrs Fitzpatrick, yet he had heard that a cousin of Sophia was married to a gentleman of that name. This, however, in the present tumult of his mind, never once recurred to his memory; but when the footman, who had conducted him from his lordship's, acquainted him with the great intimacy between the ladies, and with their calling each other cousin, he then recollected the story of the marriage which he had formerly heard; and as he was presently convinced that this was the same woman, he became more surprized at the answer which he had received, and very earnestly desired leave to wait on the lady herself; but she as positively refused him that honour.

Jones, who, though he had never seen a court, was better bred than most who frequent it, was incapable of any rude or abrupt behaviour to a lady. When he had received, therefore, a peremptory denial, he retired for the present, saying to the waiting-woman, "That if this was an improper hour to wait on her lady, he would return in the afternoon; and that he then hoped to have the honour of seeing her." The civility with which he uttered this, added to the great comeliness of his person, made an impression on the waiting-woman, and she could not help answering; "Perhaps, sir, you may;" and, indeed, she afterwards said everything to her mistress, which she thought most likely to prevail on her to admit a visit from the handsome young gentleman; for so she called him.

Jones very shrewdly suspected that Sophia herself was now with her cousin, and was denied to him; which he imputed to her resentment of what had happened at Upton. Having, therefore, dispatched Partridge to procure him lodgings, he remained all day in the street, watching the door where he thought his angel lay concealed; but no person did he see issue forth, except a servant of the house, and in the evening he returned to pay his visit to Mrs Fitzpatrick, which that good lady at last condescended to admit.

There is a certain air of natural gentility, which it is neither in the power of dress to give, nor to conceal. Mr Jones, as hath been before hinted, was possessed of this in a very eminent degree. He met, therefore, with a reception from the lady somewhat different from what his apparel seemed to demand; and after he had paid her his proper respects, was desired to sit down.

The reader will not, I believe, be desirous of knowing all the particulars of this conversation, which ended very little to the satisfaction of poor Jones. For though Mrs Fitzpatrick soon discovered the lover (as all women have the eyes of hawks in those matters), yet she still thought it was such a lover, as a generous friend of the lady should not betray her to. In short, she suspected this was the very Mr Blifil, from whom Sophia had flown; and all the answers which she artfully drew from Jones, concerning Mr Allworthy's family, confirmed her in this opinion. She therefore strictly denied any knowledge concerning the place whither Sophia was gone; nor could Jones obtain more than a permission to wait on her again the next evening.

When Jones was departed Mrs Fitzpatrick communicated her suspicion concerning Mr Blifil to her maid; who answered, "Sure, madam, he is too pretty a man, in my opinion, for any woman in the world to run away from. I had rather fancy it is Mr Jones."—"Mr Jones!" said the lady, "what Jones?" For Sophia had not given the least hint of any such person in all their conversation; but Mrs Honour had been much more communicative, and had acquainted her sister Abigail with the whole history of Jones, which this now again related to her mistress.

Mrs Fitzpatrick no sooner received this information, than she immediately agreed with the opinion of her maid; and, what is very unaccountable, saw charms in the gallant, happy lover, which she had overlooked in the slighted squire. "Betty," says she, "you are certainly in the right: he is a very pretty fellow, and I don't wonder that my cousin's maid should tell you so many women are fond of him. I am sorry now I did not inform him where my cousin was; and yet, if he be so terrible a rake as you tell me, it is a pity she should ever see him any more; for what but her ruin can happen from marrying a rake and a beggar against her father's consent? I protest, if he be such a man as the wench described him to you, it is but an office of charity to keep her from him; and I am sure it would be unpardonable in me to do otherwise, who have tasted so bitterly of the misfortunes attending such marriages."

Here she was interrupted by the arrival of a visitor, which was no other than his lordship; and as nothing passed at this visit either new or extraordinary, or any ways material to this history, we shall here put an end to this chapter.

CHAPTER III.

A project of Mrs Fitzpatrick, and her visit to Lady Bellaston.

When Mrs Fitzpatrick retired to rest, her thoughts were entirely taken up by her cousin Sophia and Mr Jones. She was, indeed, a little offended with the former, for the disingenuity which she now discovered. In which meditation she had not long exercised her imagination before the following conceit suggested itself; that could she possibly become the means of preserving Sophia from this man, and of restoring her to her father, she should, in all human probability, by so great a service to the family, reconcile to herself both her uncle and her aunt Western.

As this was one of her most favourite wishes, so the hope of success seemed so reasonable, that nothing remained but to consider of proper methods to accomplish her scheme. To attempt to reason the case with Sophia did not appear to her one of those methods: for as Betty had reported from Mrs Honour, that Sophia had a violent inclination to Jones, she conceived that to dissuade her from the match was an endeavour of the same kind, as it would be very heartily and earnestly to entreat a moth not to fly into a candle.

If the reader will please to remember that the acquaintance which Sophia had with Lady Bellaston was contracted at the house of Mrs Western, and must have grown at the very time when Mrs Fitzpatrick lived with this latter lady, he will want no information, that Mrs Fitzpatrick must have been acquainted with her likewise. They were, besides, both equally her distant relations.

After much consideration, therefore, she resolved to go early in the morning to that lady, and endeavour to see her, unknown to Sophia, and to acquaint her with the whole affair. For she did not in the least doubt, but that the prudent lady, who had often ridiculed romantic love, and indiscreet marriages, in her conversation, would very readily concur in her sentiments concerning this match, and would lend her utmost assistance to prevent it.

This resolution she accordingly executed; and the next morning before the sun, she huddled on her cloaths, and at a very unfashionable, unseasonable, unvisitable hour, went to Lady Bellaston, to whom she got access, without the least knowledge or suspicion of Sophia, who, though not asleep, lay at that time awake in her bed, with Honour snoring by her side.

Mrs Fitzpatrick made many apologies for an early, abrupt visit, at an hour when, she said, "she should not have thought of disturbing her ladyship, but upon business of the utmost consequence." She then opened the whole affair, told all she had heard from Betty; and did not forget the visit which Jones had paid to herself the preceding evening.

Lady Bellaston answered with a smile, "Then you have seen this terrible man, madam; pray, is he so very fine a figure as he is represented? for Etoff entertained me last night almost two hours with him. The wench I believe is in love with him by reputation." Here the reader will be apt to wonder; but the truth is, that Mrs Etoff, who had the honour to pin and unpin the Lady Bellaston, had received compleat information concerning the said Mr Jones, and had faithfully conveyed the same to her lady last night (or rather that morning) while she was undressing; on which accounts she had been detained in her office above the space of an hour and a half.

The lady indeed, though generally well enough pleased with the narratives of Mrs Etoff at those seasons, gave an extraordinary attention to her account of Jones; for Honour had described him as a very handsome fellow, and Mrs Etoff, in her hurry, added so much to the beauty of his person to her report, that Lady Bellaston began to conceive him to be a kind of miracle in nature.

The curiosity which her woman had inspired was now greatly increased by Mrs Fitzpatrick, who spoke as much in favour of the person of Jones as she had before spoken in dispraise of his birth, character, and fortune.

When Lady Bellaston had heard the whole, she answered gravely, "Indeed, madam, this is a matter of great consequence. Nothing can certainly be more commendable than the part you act; and I shall be very glad to have my share in the preservation of a young lady of so much merit, and for whom I have so much esteem."

"Doth not your ladyship think," says Mrs Fitzpatrick eagerly, "that it would be the best way to write immediately to my uncle, and acquaint him where my cousin is?"

The lady pondered a little upon this, and thus answered—"Why, no, madam, I think not. Di Western hath described her brother to me to be such a brute, that I cannot consent to put any woman under his power who hath escaped from it. I have heard he behaved like a monster to his own wife, for he is one of those wretches who think they have a right to tyrannise over us, and from such I shall ever esteem it the cause of my sex to rescue any woman who is so unfortunate to be under their power.—The business, dear cousin, will be only to keep Miss Western from seeing this young fellow, till the good company, which she will have an opportunity of meeting here, give her a properer turn."

"If he should find her out, madam," answered the other, "your ladyship may be assured he will leave nothing unattempted to come at her."

"But, madam," replied the lady, "it is impossible he should come here—though indeed it is possible he may get some intelligence where she is, and then may lurk about the house—I wish therefore I knew his person.

"Is there no way, madam, by which I could have a sight of him? for, otherwise, you know, cousin, she may contrive to see him here without my knowledge." Mrs Fitzpatrick answered, "That he had threatened her with another visit that afternoon, and that, if her ladyship pleased to do her the honour of calling upon her then, she would hardly fail of seeing him between six and seven; and if he came earlier she would, by some means or other, detain him till her ladyship's arrival."—Lady Bellaston replied, "She would come the moment she could get from dinner, which she supposed would be by seven at farthest; for that it was absolutely necessary she should be acquainted with his person. Upon my word, madam," says she, "it was very good to take this care of Miss Western; but common humanity, as well as regard to our family, requires it of us both; for it would be a dreadful match indeed."

Mrs Fitzpatrick failed not to make a proper return to the compliment which Lady Bellaston had bestowed on her cousin, and, after some little immaterial conversation, withdrew; and, getting as fast as she could into her chair, unseen by Sophia or Honour, returned home.

CHAPTER IV.

Which consists of visiting.

Mr Jones had walked within sight of a certain door during the whole day, which, though one of the shortest, appeared to him to be one of the longest in the whole year. At length, the clock having struck five, he returned to Mrs Fitzpatrick, who, though it was a full hour earlier than the decent time of visiting, received him very civilly; but still persisted in her ignorance concerning Sophia.

Jones, in asking for his angel, had dropped the word cousin, upon which Mrs Fitzpatrick said, "Then, sir, you know we are related: and, as we are, you will permit me the right of enquiring into the particulars of your business with my cousin." Here Jones hesitated a good while, and at last answered, "He had a considerable sum of money of hers in his hands, which he desired to deliver to her." He then produced the pocket-book, and acquainted Mrs Fitzpatrick with the contents, and with the method in which they came into his hands. He had scarce finished his story, when a most violent noise shook the whole house. To attempt to describe this noise to those who have heard it would be in vain; and to aim at giving any idea of it to those who have never heard the like, would be still more vain: for it may be truly said—

—Non acuta
Sic geminant Corybantes aera.

The priests of Cybele do not so rattle their sounding brass.

In short, a footman knocked, or rather thundered, at the door. Jones was a little surprized at the sound, having never heard it before; but Mrs Fitzpatrick very calmly said, that, as some company were coming, she could not make him any answer now; but if he pleased to stay till they were gone, she intimated she had something to say to him.

The door of the room now flew open, and, after pushing in her hoop sideways before her, entered Lady Bellaston, who having first made a very low courtesy to Mrs Fitzpatrick, and as low a one to Mr Jones, was ushered to the upper end of the room.

We mention these minute matters for the sake of some country ladies of our acquaintance, who think it contrary to the rules of modesty to bend their knees to a man.

The company were hardly well settled, before the arrival of the peer lately mentioned, caused a fresh disturbance, and a repetition of ceremonials.

These being over, the conversation began to be (as the phrase is) extremely brilliant. However, as nothing past in it which can be thought material to this history, or, indeed, very material in itself, I shall omit the relation; the rather, as I have known some very fine polite conversation grow extremely dull, when transcribed into books, or repeated on the stage. Indeed, this mental repast is a dainty, of which those who are excluded from polite assemblies must be contented to remain as ignorant as they must of the several dainties of French cookery, which are served only at the tables of the great. To say the truth, as neither of these are adapted to every taste, they might both be often thrown away on the vulgar.

Poor Jones was rather a spectator of this elegant scene, than an actor in it; for though, in the short interval before the peer's arrival, Lady Bellaston first, and afterwards Mrs Fitzpatrick, had addressed some of their discourse to him; yet no sooner was the noble lord entered, than he engrossed the whole attention of the two ladies to himself; and as he took no more notice of Jones than if no such person had been present, unless by now and then staring at him, the ladies followed his example.

The company had now staid so long, that Mrs Fitzpatrick plainly perceived they all designed to stay out each other. She therefore resolved to rid herself of Jones, he being the visitant to whom she thought the least ceremony was due. Taking therefore an opportunity of a cessation of chat, she addressed herself gravely to him, and said, "Sir, I shall not possibly be able to give you an answer to-night as to that business; but if you please to leave word where I may send to you to-morrow—-"

Jones had natural, but not artificial good-breeding. Instead therefore of communicating the secret of his lodgings to a servant, he acquainted the lady herself with it particularly, and soon after very ceremoniously withdrew.

He was no sooner gone than the great personages, who had taken no notice of him present, began to take much notice of him in his absence; but if the reader hath already excused us from relating the more brilliant part of this conversation, he will surely be very ready to excuse the repetition of what may be called vulgar abuse; though, perhaps, it may be material to our history to mention an observation of Lady Bellaston, who took her leave in a few minutes after him, and then said to Mrs Fitzpatrick, at her departure, "I am satisfied on the account of my cousin; she can be in no danger from this fellow."

Our history shall follow the example of Lady Bellaston, and take leave of the present company, which was now reduced to two persons; between whom, as nothing passed, which in the least concerns us or our reader, we shall not suffer ourselves to be diverted by it from matters which must seem of more consequence to all those who are at all interested in the affairs of our heroe.

CHAPTER V.

An adventure which happened to Mr Jones at his lodgings, with some account of a young gentleman who lodged there, and of the mistress of the house, and her two daughters.

The next morning, as early as it was decent, Jones attended at Mrs Fitzpatrick's door, where he was answered that the lady was not at home; an answer which surprized him the more, as he had walked backwards and forwards in the street from break of day; and if she had gone out, he must have seen her. This answer, however, he was obliged to receive, and not only now, but to five several visits which he made her that day.

To be plain with the reader, the noble peer had from some reason or other, perhaps from a regard for the lady's honour, insisted that she should not see Mr Jones, whom he looked on as a scrub, any more; and the lady had complied in making that promise to which we now see her so strictly adhere.

But as our gentle reader may possibly have a better opinion of the young gentleman than her ladyship, and may even have some concern, should it be apprehended that, during this unhappy separation from Sophia, he took up his residence either at an inn, or in the street; we shall now give an account of his lodging, which was indeed in a very reputable house, and in a very good part of the town.

Mr Jones, then, had often heard Mr Allworthy mention the gentlewoman at whose house he used to lodge when he was in town. This person, who, as Jones likewise knew, lived in Bond-street, was the widow of a clergyman, and was left by him, at his decease, in possession of two daughters, and of a compleat set of manuscript sermons.

Of these two daughters, Nancy, the elder, was now arrived at the age of seventeen, and Betty, the younger, at that of ten.

Hither Jones had despatched Partridge, and in this house he was provided with a room for himself in the second floor, and with one for Partridge in the fourth.

The first floor was inhabited by one of those young gentlemen, who, in the last age, were called men of wit and pleasure about town, and properly enough; for as men are usually denominated from their business or profession, so pleasure may be said to have been the only business or profession of those gentlemen to whom fortune had made all useful occupations unnecessary. Playhouses, coffeehouses, and taverns were the scenes of their rendezvous. Wit and humour were the entertainment of their looser hours, and love was the business of their more serious moments. Wine and the muses conspired to kindle the brightest flames in their breasts; nor did they only admire, but some were able to celebrate the beauty they admired, and all to judge of the merit of such compositions.

Such, therefore, were properly called the men of wit and pleasure; but I question whether the same appellation may, with the same propriety, be given to those young gentlemen of our times, who have the same ambition to be distinguished for parts. Wit certainly they have nothing to do with. To give them their due, they soar a step higher than their predecessors, and may be called men of wisdom and vertù (take heed you do not read virtue). Thus at an age when the gentlemen above mentioned employ their time in toasting the charms of a woman, or in making sonnets in her praise; in giving their opinion of a play at the theatre, or of a poem at Will's or Button's; these gentlemen are considering the methods to bribe a corporation, or meditating speeches for the House of Commons, or rather for the magazines. But the science of gaming is that which above all others employs their thoughts. These are the studies of their graver hours, while for their amusements they have the vast circle of connoisseurship, painting, music, statuary, and natural philosophy, or rather *unnatural*, which deals in the wonderful, and knows nothing of Nature, except her monsters and imperfections.

When Jones had spent the whole day in vain enquiries after Mrs Fitzpatrick, he returned at last disconsolate to his apartment. Here, while he was venting his grief in private, he heard a violent uproar below-stairs; and soon after a female voice begged him for heaven's sake to come and prevent murder. Jones, who was never backward on any occasion to help the distressed, immediately ran down-stairs; when stepping into the dining-room, whence all the noise issued, he beheld the young gentleman of wisdom and vertù just before mentioned, pinned close to the wall by his footman, and a young woman standing by, wringing her hands, and crying out, "He will be murdered! he will be murdered!" and, indeed, the poor gentleman seemed in some danger of being choaked, when Jones flew hastily to his assistance, and rescued him, just as he was breathing his last, from the unmerciful clutches of the enemy.

Though the fellow had received several kicks and cuffs from the little gentleman, who had more spirit than strength, he had made it a kind of scruple of conscience to strike his master, and would have contented himself with only choaking him; but towards Jones he bore no such respect; he no sooner therefore found himself a little roughly handled by his new antagonist, than he gave him one of those punches in the guts which, though the spectators at Broughton's amphitheatre have such exquisite delight in seeing them, convey but very little pleasure in the feeling.

The lusty youth had no sooner received this blow, than he meditated a most grateful return; and now ensued a combat between Jones and the footman, which was very fierce, but short; for this fellow was no more able to contend with Jones than his master had before been to contend with him.

And now, Fortune, according to her usual custom, reversed the face of affairs. The former victor lay breathless on the ground, and the vanquished gentleman had recovered breath enough to thank Mr Jones for his seasonable assistance; he received likewise the hearty thanks of the young woman present, who was indeed no other than Miss Nancy, the eldest daughter of the house.

The footman, having now recovered his legs, shook his head at Jones, and, with a sagacious look, cried—"O d—n me, I'll have nothing more to do with you; you have been upon the stage, or I'm d—nably mistaken." And indeed we may forgive this his suspicion; for such was the agility and strength of our heroe, that he was, perhaps, a match for one of the first-rate boxers, and could, with great ease, have beaten all the muffled[1] graduates of Mr Broughton's school.

The master, foaming with wrath, ordered his man immediately to strip, to which the latter very readily agreed, on condition of receiving his wages. This condition was presently complied with, and the fellow was discharged.

And now the young gentleman, whose name was Nightingale, very strenuously insisted that his deliverer should take part of a bottle of wine with him; to which Jones, after much entreaty, consented, though more out of complacence than inclination; for the uneasiness of his mind fitted him very little for conversation at this time. Miss Nancy likewise, who was the only female then in the house, her mamma and sister being both gone to the play, condescended to favour them with her company.

When the bottle and glasses were on the table the gentleman began to relate the occasion of the preceding disturbance.

"I hope, sir," said he to Jones, "you will not from this accident conclude, that I make a custom of striking my servants, for I assure you this is the first time I have been guilty of it in my remembrance, and I have passed by many provoking faults in this very fellow, before he could provoke me to it; but when you hear what hath happened this evening, you will, I believe, think me excusable. I happened to come home several hours before my usual time, when I found four gentlemen of the cloth at whist by my fire;—and my Hoyle, sir—my best Hoyle, which cost me

---

[1] Lest posterity should be puzzled by this epithet, I think proper to explain it by an advertisement which was published Feb. 1, 1747.

N.B.—Mr Broughton proposes, with proper assistance, to open an academy at his house in the Haymarket, for the instruction of those who are willing to be initiated in the mystery of boxing: where the whole theory and practice of that truly British art, with all the various stops, blows, cross-buttocks, &c., incident to combatants, will be fully taught and explained; and that persons of quality and distinction may not be deterred from entering into A course of those lectures, they will be given with the utmost tenderness and regard to the delicacy of the frame and constitution of the pupil, for which reason muffles are provided, that will effectually secure them from the inconveniency of black eyes, broken jaws, and bloody noses.

a guinea, lying open on the table, with a quantity of porter spilt on one of the most material leaves of the whole book. This, you will allow, was provoking; but I said nothing till the rest of the honest company were gone, and then gave the fellow a gentle rebuke, who, instead of expressing any concern, made me a pert answer, `That servants must have their diversions as well as other people; that he was sorry for the accident which had happened to the book, but that several of his acquaintance had bought the same for a shilling, and that I might stop as much in his wages, if I pleased.' I now gave him a severer reprimand than before, when the rascal had the insolence to—-In short, he imputed my early coming home to—— In short, he cast a reflection——He mentioned the name of a young lady, in a manner—in such a manner that incensed me beyond all patience, and, in my passion, I struck him."

Jones answered, "That he believed no person living would blame him; for my part," said he, "I confess I should, on the last-mentioned provocation, have done the same thing."

Our company had not sat long before they were joined by the mother and daughter, at their return from the play. And now they all spent a very chearful evening together; for all but Jones were heartily merry, and even he put on as much constrained mirth as possible. Indeed, half his natural flow of animal spirits, joined to the sweetness of his temper, was sufficient to make a most amiable companion; and notwithstanding the heaviness of his heart, so agreeable did he make himself on the present occasion, that, at their breaking up, the young gentleman earnestly desired his further acquaintance. Miss Nancy was well pleased with him; and the widow, quite charmed with her new lodger, invited him, with the other, next morning to breakfast.

Jones on his part was no less satisfied. As for Miss Nancy, though a very little creature, she was extremely pretty, and the widow had all the charms which can adorn a woman near fifty. As she was one of the most innocent creatures in the world, so she was one of the most chearful. She never thought, nor spoke, nor wished any ill, and had constantly that desire of pleasing, which may be called the happiest of all desires in this, that it scarce ever fails of attaining its ends, when not disgraced by affectation. In short, though her power was very small, she was in her heart one of the warmest friends. She had been a most affectionate wife, and was a most fond and tender mother. As our history doth not, like a newspaper, give great characters to people who never were heard of before, nor will ever be heard of again, the reader may hence conclude, that this excellent woman will hereafter appear to be of some importance in our history.

Nor was Jones a little pleased with the young gentleman himself, whose wine he had been drinking. He thought he discerned in him much good sense, though a little too much tainted with town-foppery; but what recommended him most to Jones were some sentiments of great generosity and humanity, which occasionally dropt from him; and particularly many expressions of the highest disinterestedness in the affair of love. On which subject the young gentleman delivered himself in a language which might have very well become an Arcadian shepherd of old, and which appeared very extraordinary when proceeding from the lips of a modern fine gentleman; but he was only one by imitation, and meant by nature for a much better character.

CHAPTER VI.

What arrived while the company were at breakfast, with some hints concerning the government of daughters.

Our company brought together in the morning the same good inclinations towards each other, with which they had separated the evening before; but poor Jones was extremely disconsolate; for he had just received information from Partridge, that Mrs Fitzpatrick had left her lodging, and that he could not learn whither she was gone. This news highly afflicted him, and his countenance, as well as his behaviour, in defiance of all his endeavours to the contrary, betrayed manifest indications of a disordered mind.

The discourse turned at present, as before, on love; and Mr Nightingale again expressed many of those warm, generous, and disinterested sentiments upon this subject, which wise and sober men call romantic, but which wise and sober women generally regard in a better light. Mrs Miller (for so the mistress of the house was called) greatly approved these sentiments; but when the young gentleman appealed to Miss Nancy, she answered only, "That she believed the gentleman who had spoke the least was capable of feeling most."

This compliment was so apparently directed to Jones, that we should have been sorry had he passed it by unregarded. He made her indeed a very polite answer, and concluded with an oblique hint, that her own silence subjected her to a suspicion of the same kind: for indeed she had scarce opened her lips either now or the last evening.

"I am glad, Nanny," says Mrs Miller, "the gentleman hath made the observation; I protest I am almost of his opinion. What can be the matter with you, child? I never saw such an alteration. What is become of all your gaiety? Would you think, sir, I used to call her my little prattler? She hath not spoke twenty words this week."

Here their conversation was interrupted by the entrance of a maid-servant, who brought a bundle in her hand, which, she said, "was delivered by a porter for Mr Jones." She added, "That the man immediately went away, saying, it required no answer."

Jones expressed some surprize on this occasion, and declared it must be some mistake; but the maid persisting that she was certain of the name, all the women were desirous of having the bundle immediately opened; which operation was at length performed by little Betsy, with the consent of Mr Jones: and the contents were found to be a domino, a mask, and a masquerade ticket.

Jones was now more positive than ever in asserting, that these things must have been delivered by mistake; and Mrs Miller herself expressed some doubt, and said, "She knew not what to think." But when Mr Nightingale was asked, he delivered a very different opinion. "All I can conclude from it, sir," said he, "is, that you are a very happy man; for I make no doubt but these were sent you by some lady whom you will have the happiness of meeting at the masquerade."

Jones had not a sufficient degree of vanity to entertain any such flattering imagination; nor did Mrs Miller herself give much assent to what Mr Nightingale had said, till Miss Nancy having lifted up the domino, a card dropt from the sleeve, in which was written as follows:—

To MR JONES.
The queen of the fairies sends you this;
Use her favours not amiss.

Mrs Miller and Miss Nancy now both agreed with Mr Nightingale; nay, Jones himself was almost persuaded to be of the same opinion. And as no other lady but Mrs Fitzpatrick, he thought, knew his lodging, he began to flatter himself with some hopes, that it came from her, and that he might possibly see his Sophia. These hopes had surely very little foundation; but as the conduct of Mrs Fitzpatrick, in not seeing him according to her promise, and in quitting her lodgings, had been very odd and unaccountable, he conceived some faint hopes, that she (of whom he had formerly heard a very whimsical character) might possibly intend to do him that service in a strange manner, which she declined doing by more ordinary methods. To say the truth, as nothing certain could be concluded from so odd and uncommon an incident, he had the greater latitude to draw what imaginary conclusions from it he pleased. As his temper therefore was naturally sanguine, he indulged it on this occasion, and his imagination worked up a thousand conceits, to favour and support his expectations of meeting his dear Sophia in the evening.

Reader, if thou hast any good wishes towards me, I will fully repay them by wishing thee to be possessed of this sanguine disposition of mind; since, after having read much and considered long on that subject of happiness which hath employed so many great pens, I am almost inclined to fix it in the possession of this temper; which puts us, in a manner, out of the reach of Fortune, and makes us happy without her assistance. Indeed, the sensations of pleasure it gives are much more constant as well as much keener, than those which that blind lady bestows; nature having wisely contrived, that some satiety and languor should be annexed to all our real enjoyments, lest we should be so taken up by them, as to be stopt from further pursuits. I make no manner of doubt but that, in this light, we may see the imaginary future chancellor just called to the bar, the archbishop in crape, and the prime minister at the tail of an opposition, more truly happy than those who are invested with all the power and profit of those respective offices.

Mr Jones having now determined to go to the masquerade that evening, Mr Nightingale offered to conduct him thither. The young gentleman, at the same time, offered tickets to Miss Nancy and her mother; but the good woman would not accept them. She said, "she did not conceive the harm which some people imagined in a masquerade; but that such extravagant diversions were proper only for persons of quality and fortune, and not for young women who were to get their living, and could, at best, hope to be married to a good tradesman."——"A tradesman!" cries Nightingale, "you shan't undervalue my Nancy. There is not a nobleman upon earth above her merit." "O fie! Mr Nightingale," answered Mrs Miller, "you must not fill the girl's head with such fancies: but if it was her good luck" (says the mother with a simper) "to find a gentleman of your generous way of thinking, I hope she would make a better return to his generosity than to give her mind up to extravagant pleasures. Indeed, where young ladies bring great fortunes themselves, they have some right to insist on spending what is their own; and on that account I have heard the gentlemen say, a man has sometimes a better bargain with a poor wife, than with a rich one.——But let my daughters marry whom they will, I shall endeavour to make them blessings to their husbands:——I beg, therefore, I may hear of no more masquerades. Nancy is, I am certain, too good a girl to desire to go; for she must remember when you carried her thither last year, it almost turned her head; and she did not return to herself, or to her needle, in a month afterwards."

Though a gentle sigh, which stole from the bosom of Nancy, seemed to argue some secret disapprobation of these sentiments, she did not dare openly to oppose them. For as this good woman had all the tenderness, so she had preserved all the authority of a parent; and as her indulgence to the desires of her children was restrained only by her fears for their safety and future welfare, so she never suffered those commands which proceeded from such fears to be either disobeyed or disputed. And this the young gentleman, who had lodged two years in the house, knew so well, that he presently acquiesced in the refusal.

Mr Nightingale, who grew every minute fonder of Jones, was very desirous of his company that day to dinner at the tavern, where he offered to introduce him to some of his acquaintance; but Jones begged to be excused, "as his cloaths," he said, "were not yet come to town."

To confess the truth, Mr Jones was now in a situation, which sometimes happens to be the case of young gentlemen of much better figure than himself. In short, he had not one penny in his pocket; a situation in much greater credit among the antient philosophers than among the modern wise men who live in Lombard-street, or those who frequent White's chocolate-house. And, perhaps, the great honours which those philosophers have ascribed to an empty pocket may be one of the reasons of that high contempt in which they are held in the aforesaid street and chocolate-house.

Now if the antient opinion, that men might live very comfortably on virtue only, be, as the modern wise men just above-mentioned pretend to have discovered, a notorious error; no less false is, I apprehend, that position of some writers of romance, that a man can live altogether on love; for however delicious repasts this may afford to some of our senses or appetites, it is most certain it can afford none to others. Those, therefore, who have placed too great a confidence in such writers, have experienced their error when it was too late; and have found that love was no more capable of allaying hunger, than a rose is capable of delighting the ear, or a violin of gratifying the smell.

Notwithstanding, therefore, all the delicacies which love had set before him, namely, the hopes of seeing Sophia at the masquerade; on which, however ill-founded his imagination might be, he had voluptuously feasted during the whole day, the evening no sooner came than Mr Jones began to languish for some food of a grosser kind. Partridge discovered this by intuition, and took the occasion to give some oblique hints concerning the bank-bill; and, when these were rejected with disdain, he collected courage enough once more to mention a return to Mr Allworthy.

"Partridge," cries Jones, "you cannot see my fortune in a more desperate light than I see it myself; and I begin heartily to repent that I suffered you to leave a place where you was settled, and to follow me. However, I insist now on your returning home; and for the expense and trouble which you have so kindly put yourself to on my account, all the cloaths I left behind in your care I desire you would take as your own. I am sorry I can make you no other acknowledgment."

He spoke these words with so pathetic an accent, that Partridge, among whose vices ill-nature or hardness of heart were not numbered, burst into tears; and after swearing he would not quit him in his distress, he began with the most earnest entreaties to urge his return home. "For heaven's sake, sir," says he, "do but consider; what can your honour do?—how is it possible you can live in this town without money? Do what you will, sir, or go wherever you please, I am resolved not to desert you. But pray, sir, consider—do pray, sir, for your own sake, take it into your consideration; and I'm sure," says he, "that your own good sense will bid you return home."

"How often shall I tell thee," answered Jones, "that I have no home to return to? Had I any hopes that Mr Allworthy's doors would be open to receive me, I want no distress to urge me—nay, there is no other cause upon earth, which could detain me a moment from flying to his presence; but, alas! that I am for ever banished from. His last words were—O, Partridge, they still ring in my ears—his last words were, when he gave me a sum of money—what it was I know not, but considerable I'm sure it was—his last words were—`I am resolved from this day forward, on no account to converse with you any more.'"

Here passion stopt the mouth of Jones, as surprize for a moment did that of Partridge; but he soon recovered the use of speech, and after a short preface, in which he declared he had no inquisitiveness in his temper, enquired what Jones meant by a considerable sum—he knew not how much—and what was become of the money.

In both these points he now received full satisfaction; on which he was proceeding to comment, when he was interrupted by a message from Mr Nightingale, who desired his master's company in his apartment.

When the two gentlemen were both attired for the masquerade, and Mr Nightingale had given orders for chairs to be sent for, a circumstance of distress occurred to Jones, which will appear very ridiculous to many of my readers. This was how to procure a shilling; but if such readers will reflect a little on what they have themselves felt from the want of a thousand pounds, or, perhaps, of ten or twenty, to execute a favourite scheme, they will have a perfect idea of what Mr Jones felt on this occasion. For this sum, therefore, he applied to Partridge, which was the first he had permitted him to advance, and was the last he intended that poor fellow should advance in his service. To say the truth, Partridge had lately made no offer of this kind. Whether it was that he desired to see the bank-bill broke in upon, or that distress should prevail on Jones to return home, or from what other motive it proceeded, I will not determine.

CHAPTER VII.

Containing the whole humours of a masquerade.

Our cavaliers now arrived at that temple, where Heydegger, the great Arbiter Deliciarum, the great high-priest of pleasure, presides; and, like other heathen priests, imposes on his votaries by the pretended presence of the deity, when in reality no such deity is there.

Mr Nightingale, having taken a turn or two with his companion, soon left him, and walked off with a female, saying, "Now you are here, sir, you must beat about for your own game."

Jones began to entertain strong hopes that his Sophia was present; and these hopes gave him more spirits than the lights, the music, and the company; though these are pretty strong antidotes against the spleen. He now accosted every woman he saw, whose stature, shape, or air, bore any resemblance to his angel. To all of whom he endeavoured to say something smart, in order to engage an answer, by which he might discover that voice which he thought it impossible he should mistake. Some of these answered by a question, in a squeaking voice, Do you know me? Much the greater number said, I don't know you, sir, and nothing more. Some called him an impertinent fellow; some made him no answer at all; some said, Indeed I don't know your voice, and I shall have nothing to say to you; and many gave him as kind answers as he could wish, but not in the voice he desired to hear.

Whilst he was talking with one of these last (who was in the habit of a shepherdess) a lady in a domino came up to him, and slapping him on the shoulder, whispered him, at the same time, in the ear, "If you talk any longer with that trollop, I will acquaint Miss Western."

Jones no sooner heard that name, than, immediately quitting his former companion, he applied to the domino, begging and entreating her to show him the lady she had mentioned, if she was then in the room.

The mask walked hastily to the upper end of the innermost apartment before she spoke; and then, instead of answering him, sat down, and declared she was tired. Jones sat down by her, and still persisted in his entreaties; at last the lady coldly answered, "I imagined Mr Jones had been a more discerning lover, than to suffer any disguise to conceal his mistress from him." "Is she here, then, madam?" replied Jones, with some vehemence. Upon which the lady cried—"Hush, sir, you will be observed. I promise you, upon my honour, Miss Western is not here."

Jones, now taking the mask by the hand, fell to entreating her in the most earnest manner, to acquaint him where he might find Sophia; and when he could obtain no direct answer, he began to upbraid her gently for having disappointed him the day before; and concluded, saying, "Indeed, my good fairy queen, I know your majesty very well, notwithstanding the affected disguise of your voice. Indeed, Mrs Fitzpatrick, it is a little cruel to divert yourself at the expense of my torments."

The mask answered, "Though you have so ingeniously discovered me, I must still speak in the same voice, lest I should be known by others. And do you think, good sir, that I have no greater regard for my cousin, than to assist in carrying on an affair between you two, which must end in her ruin, as well as your own? Besides, I promise you, my cousin is not mad enough to consent to her own destruction, if you are so much her enemy as to tempt her to it."

"Alas, madam!" said Jones, "you little know my heart, when you call me an enemy of Sophia."

"And yet to ruin any one," cries the other, "you will allow, is the act of an enemy; and when by the same act you must knowingly and certainly bring ruin on yourself, is it not folly or madness, as well as guilt? Now, sir, my cousin hath very little more than her father will please to give her; very little for one of her fashion—you know him, and you know your own situation."

Jones vowed he had no such design on Sophia, "That he would rather suffer the most violent of deaths than sacrifice her interest to his desires." He said, "he knew how unworthy he was of her, every way, that he had long ago resolved to quit all such aspiring thoughts, but that some strange accidents had made him desirous to see her once more, when he promised he would take leave of her for ever. No, madam," concluded he, "my love is not of that base kind which seeks its own satisfaction at the expense of what is most dear to its object. I would sacrifice everything to the possession of my Sophia, but Sophia herself."

Though the reader may have already conceived no very sublime idea of the virtue of the lady in the mask; and though possibly she may hereafter appear not to deserve one of the first characters of her sex; yet, it is certain, these generous sentiments made a strong impression upon her, and greatly added to the affection she had before conceived for our young heroe.

The lady now, after silence of a few moments, said, "She did not see his pretensions to Sophia so much in the light of presumption, as of imprudence. Young fellows," says she, "can never have too aspiring thoughts. I love ambition in a young man, and I would have you cultivate it as much as possible. Perhaps you may succeed with those who are infinitely superior in fortune; nay, I am convinced there are women——but don't you think me a strange creature, Mr Jones, to be thus giving advice to a man with whom I am so little acquainted, and one with whose behaviour to me I have so little reason to be pleased?"

Here Jones began to apologize, and to hope he had not offended in anything he had said of her cousin.—To which the mask answered, "And are you so little versed in the sex, to imagine you can well affront a lady more than by entertaining her with your passion for another woman? If the fairy queen had conceived no better opinion of your gallantry, she would scarce have appointed you to meet her at the masquerade."

Jones had never less inclination to an amour than at present; but gallantry to the ladies was among his principles of honour; and he held it as much incumbent on him to accept a challenge to love, as if it had been a challenge to fight. Nay, his very love to Sophia made it necessary for him to keep well with the lady, as he made no doubt but she was capable of bringing him into the presence of the other.

He began therefore to make a very warm answer to her last speech, when a mask, in the character of an old woman, joined them. This mask was one of those ladies who go to a masquerade only to vent ill-nature, by telling people rude truths, and by endeavouring, as the phrase is, to spoil as much sport as they are able. This good lady, therefore, having observed Jones, and his friend, whom she well knew, in close consultation together in a corner of the room, concluded she could nowhere satisfy her spleen better than by interrupting them. She attacked them, therefore, and soon drove them from their retirement; nor was she contented with this, but pursued them to every place which they shifted to avoid her; till Mr Nightingale, seeing the distress of his friend, at last relieved him, and engaged the old woman in another pursuit.

While Jones and his mask were walking together about the room, to rid themselves of the teazer, he observed his lady speak to several masks, with the same freedom of acquaintance as if they had been barefaced. He could not help expressing his surprize at this; saying, "Sure, madam, you must have infinite discernment, to know people in all disguises." To which the lady answered, "You cannot conceive anything more insipid and childish than a masquerade to the people of fashion, who in general know one another as well here as when they meet in an assembly or a drawing-room; nor will any woman of condition converse with a person with whom she is not acquainted. In short, the generality of persons whom you see here may more properly be said to kill time in this place than in any other; and generally retire from hence more tired than from the longest sermon. To say the truth, I begin to be in that situation myself; and if I have any faculty at guessing, you are not much better pleased. I protest it would be almost charity in me to go home for your sake." "I know but one charity equal to it," cries Jones, "and that is to suffer me to wait on you home." "Sure," answered the lady, "you have a strange opinion of me, to imagine, that upon such an acquaintance, I would let you into my doors at this time of night. I fancy you impute the friendship I have shown my cousin to some other motive. Confess honestly; don't you consider this contrived interview as little better than a downright assignation? Are you used, Mr Jones, to make these sudden conquests?" "I am not used, madam," said Jones, "to submit to such sudden conquests; but as you have taken my heart by surprize, the rest of my body hath a right to follow; so you must pardon me if I resolve to attend you wherever you go." He accompanied these words with some proper actions; upon which the lady, after a gentle rebuke, and saying their familiarity would be observed, told him, "She was going to sup with an acquaintance, whither she hoped he would not follow her; for if you should," said she, "I shall be thought an unaccountable creature, though my friend indeed is not censorious: yet I hope you won't follow me; I protest I shall not know what to say if you do."

The lady presently after quitted the masquerade, and Jones, notwithstanding the severe prohibition he had received, presumed to attend her. He was now reduced to the same dilemma we have mentioned before, namely, the want of a shilling, and could not relieve it by borrowing as before. He therefore walked boldly on after the chair in which his lady rode, pursued by a grand huzza, from all the chairmen present, who wisely take the best care they can to discountenance all walking afoot by their betters. Luckily, however, the gentry who attend at the Opera-house were too busy to quit their stations, and as the lateness of the hour prevented him from meeting many of their brethren in the street, he proceeded without molestation, in a dress, which, at another season, would have certainly raised a mob at his heels.

The lady was set down in a street not far from Hanover-square, where the door being presently opened, she was carried in, and the gentleman, without any ceremony, walked in after her.

Jones and his companion were now together in a very well-furnished and well-warmed room; when the female, still speaking in her masquerade voice, said she was surprized at her friend, who must absolutely have forgot her appointment; at which, after venting much resentment, she suddenly exprest some apprehension from Jones, and asked him what the world would think of their having been alone together in a house at that time of night? But instead of a direct answer to so important a question, Jones began to be very importunate with the lady to unmask; and at length having prevailed, there appeared not Mrs Fitzpatrick, but the Lady Bellaston herself.

It would be tedious to give the particular conversation, which consisted of very common and ordinary occurrences, and which lasted from two till six o'clock in the morning. It is sufficient to mention all of it that is anywise material to this history. And this was a promise that the lady would endeavour to find out Sophia, and in a few days bring him to an interview with her, on condition that he would then take his leave of her. When this was thoroughly settled, and a second meeting in the evening appointed at the same place, they separated; the lady returned to her house, and Jones to his lodgings.

CHAPTER VIII.

Containing a scene of distress, which will appear very extraordinary to most of our readers.

Jones having refreshed himself with a few hours' sleep, summoned Partridge to his presence; and delivering him a bank-note of fifty pounds, ordered him to go and change it. Partridge received this with sparkling eyes, though, when he came to reflect farther, it raised in him some suspicions not very advantageous to the honour of his master: to these the dreadful idea he had of the masquerade, the disguise in which his master had gone out and returned, and his having been abroad all night, contributed. In plain language, the only way he could possibly find to account for the possession of this note, was by robbery: and, to confess the truth, the reader, unless he should suspect it was owing to the generosity of Lady Bellaston, can hardly imagine any other.

To clear, therefore, the honour of Mr Jones, and to do justice to the liberality of the lady, he had really received this present from her, who, though she did not give much into the hackney charities of the age, such as building hospitals, &c., was not, however, entirely void of that Christian virtue; and conceived (very rightly I think) that a young fellow of merit, without a shilling in the world, was no improper object of this virtue.

Mr Jones and Mr Nightingale had been invited to dine this day with Mrs Miller. At the appointed hour, therefore, the two young gentlemen, with the two girls, attended in the parlour, where they waited from three till almost five before the good woman appeared. She had been out of town to visit a relation, of whom, at her return, she gave the following account.

"I hope, gentlemen, you will pardon my making you wait; I am sure if you knew the occasion—I have been to see a cousin of mine, about six miles off, who now lies in.—It should be a warning to all persons (says she, looking at her daughters) how they marry indiscreetly. There is no happiness in this world without a competency. O Nancy! how shall I describe the wretched condition in which I found your poor cousin? she hath scarce lain in a week, and there was she, this dreadful weather, in a cold room, without any curtains to her bed, and not a bushel of coals in her house to supply her with fire; her second son, that sweet little fellow, lies ill of a quinzy in the same bed with his mother; for there is no other bed in the house. Poor little Tommy! I believe, Nancy, you will never see your favourite any more; for he is really very ill. The rest of the children are in pretty good health: but Molly, I am afraid, will do herself an injury: she is but thirteen years old, Mr Nightingale, and yet, in my life, I never saw a better nurse: she tends both her mother and her brother; and, what is wonderful in a creature so young, she shows all the chearfulness in the world to her mother; and yet I saw her—I saw the poor child, Mr Nightingale, turn about, and privately wipe the tears from her eyes." Here Mrs Miller was prevented, by her own tears, from going on, and there was not, I believe, a person present who did not accompany her in them; at length she a little recovered herself, and proceeded thus: "In all this distress the mother supports her spirits in a surprizing manner. The danger of her son sits heaviest upon her, and yet she endeavours as much as possible to conceal even this concern, on her husband's account. Her grief, however, sometimes gets the better of all her endeavours; for she was always extravagantly fond of this boy, and a most sensible, sweet-tempered creature it is. I protest I was never more affected in my life than when I heard the little wretch, who is hardly yet seven years old, while his mother was wetting him with her tears, beg her to be comforted. `Indeed, mamma,' cried the child, `I shan't die; God Almighty, I'm sure, won't take Tommy away; let heaven be ever so fine a place, I had rather stay here and starve with you and my papa than go to it.' Pardon me, gentlemen, I can't help it" (says she, wiping her eyes), "such sensibility and affection in a child.—And yet, perhaps, he is least the object of pity; for a day or two will, most probably, place him beyond the reach of all human evils. The father is, indeed, most worthy of compassion. Poor man, his countenance is the very picture of horror, and he looks like one rather dead than alive. Oh heavens! what a scene did I behold at my first coming into the room! The good creature was lying behind the bolster, supporting at once both his child and his wife. He had nothing on but a thin waistcoat; for his coat was spread over the bed, to supply the want of blankets.—When he rose up at my entrance, I scarce knew him. As comely a man, Mr Jones, within this fortnight, as you ever beheld; Mr Nightingale hath seen him. His eyes sunk, his face pale, with a long beard. His body shivering with cold, and worn with hunger too; for my cousin says she can hardly prevail upon him to eat.—He told me himself in a whisper—he told me—I can't repeat it—he said he could not bear to eat the bread his children wanted. And yet, can you believe it, gentlemen? in all this misery his wife has as good caudle as if she lay in the midst of the greatest affluence; I tasted it, and I scarce ever tasted better.—The means of procuring her this, he said, he believed was sent him by an angel from heaven. I know not what he meant; for I had not spirits enough to ask a single question.

"This was a love-match, as they call it, on both sides; that is, a match between two beggars. I must, indeed, say, I never saw a fonder couple; but what is their fondness good for, but to torment each other?" "Indeed, mamma," cries Nancy, "I have always looked on my cousin Anderson" (for that was her name) "as one of the happiest of women." "I am sure," says Mrs Miller, "the case at present is much otherwise; for any one might have discerned that the tender consideration of each other's sufferings makes the most intolerable part of their calamity, both to the husband and wife. Compared to which, hunger and cold, as they affect their own persons only, are scarce evils. Nay, the very children, the youngest, which is not two years old, excepted, feel in the same manner; for they are a most loving family, and, if they had but a bare competency, would be the happiest people in the world." "I never saw the least sign of misery at her house," replied Nancy; "I am sure my heart bleeds for what you now tell me."—"O child," answered the mother, "she hath always endeavoured to make the best of everything. They have always been in great distress; but, indeed, this absolute ruin hath been brought upon them by others. The poor man was bail for the villain his brother; and about a week ago, the very day before her lying-in, their goods were all carried away, and sold by an execution. He sent a letter to me of it by one of the bailiffs, which the villain never delivered.—What must he think of my suffering a week to pass before he heard of me?"

It was not with dry eyes that Jones heard this narrative; when it was ended he took Mrs Miller apart with him into another room, and, delivering her his purse, in which was the sum of £50, desired her to send as much of it as she thought proper to these poor people. The look which Mrs Miller gave Jones, on this occasion, is not easy to be described. She burst into a kind of agony of transport, and cryed out—"Good heavens! is there such a man in the world?"—But recollecting herself, she said, "Indeed I know one such; but can there be another?" "I hope, madam," cries Jones, "there are many who have common humanity; for to relieve such distresses in our fellow-creatures, can hardly be called more." Mrs Miller then took ten guineas, which were the utmost he could prevail with her to accept, and said, "She would find some means of conveying them early the next morning;" adding, "that she had herself done some little matter for the poor people, and had not left them in quite so much misery as she found them."

They then returned to the parlour, where Nightingale expressed much concern at the dreadful situation of these wretches, whom indeed he knew; for he had seen them more than once at Mrs Miller's. He inveighed against the folly of making oneself liable for the debts of others; vented many bitter execrations against the brother; and concluded with wishing something could be done for the unfortunate family. "Suppose, madam," said he, "you should recommend them to Mr Allworthy? Or what think you of a collection? I will give them a guinea with all my heart."

Mrs Miller made no answer; and Nancy, to whom her mother had whispered the generosity of Jones, turned pale upon the occasion; though, if either of them was angry with Nightingale, it was surely without reason. For the liberality of Jones, if he had known it, was not an example which he had any obligation to follow; and there are thousands who would not have contributed a single halfpenny, as indeed he did not in effect, for he made no tender of anything; and therefore, as the others thought proper to make no demand, he kept his money in his pocket.

I have, in truth, observed, and shall never have a better opportunity than at present to communicate my observation, that the world are in general divided into two opinions concerning charity, which are the very reverse of each other. One party seems to hold, that all acts of this kind are to be esteemed as voluntary gifts, and, however little you give (if indeed no more than your good wishes), you acquire a great degree of merit in so doing. Others, on the contrary, appear to be as firmly persuaded, that beneficence is a positive duty, and that whenever the rich fall greatly short of their ability in relieving the distresses of the poor, their pitiful largesses are so far from being meritorious, that they have only performed their duty by halves, and are in some sense more contemptible than those who have entirely neglected it.

To reconcile these different opinions is not in my power. I shall only add, that the givers are generally of the former sentiment, and the receivers are almost universally inclined to the latter.

CHAPTER IX.

Which treats of matters of a very different kind from those in the preceding chapter.

In the evening Jones met his lady again, and a long conversation again ensued between them: but as it consisted only of the same ordinary occurrences as before, we shall avoid mentioning particulars, which we despair of rendering agreeable to the reader; unless he is one whose devotion to the fair sex, like that of the papists to their saints, wants to be raised by the help of pictures. But I am so far from desiring to exhibit such pictures to the public, that I would wish to draw a curtain over those that have been lately set forth in certain French novels; very bungling copies of which have been presented us here under the name of translations.

Jones grew still more and more impatient to see Sophia; and finding, after repeated interviews with Lady Bellaston, no likelihood of obtaining this by her means (for, on the contrary, the lady began to treat even the mention of the name of Sophia with resentment), he resolved to try some other method. He made no doubt but that Lady Bellaston knew where his angel was, so he thought it most likely that some of her servants should be acquainted with the same secret. Partridge therefore was employed to get acquainted with those servants, in order to fish this secret out of them.

Few situations can be imagined more uneasy than that to which his poor master was at present reduced; for besides the difficulties he met with in discovering Sophia, besides the fears he had of having disobliged her, and the assurances he had received from Lady Bellaston of the resolution which Sophia had taken against him, and of her having purposely concealed herself from him, which he had sufficient reason to believe might be true; he had still a difficulty to combat which it was not in the power of his mistress to remove, however kind her inclination might have been. This was the exposing of her to be disinherited of all her father's estate, the almost inevitable consequence of their coming together without a consent, which he had no hopes of ever obtaining.

Add to all these the many obligations which Lady Bellaston, whose violent fondness we can no longer conceal, had heaped upon him; so that by her means he was now become one of the best-dressed men about town; and was not only relieved from those ridiculous distresses we have before mentioned, but was actually raised to a state of affluence beyond what he had ever known.

Now, though there are many gentlemen who very well reconcile it to their consciences to possess themselves of the whole fortune of a woman, without making her any kind of return; yet to a mind, the proprietor of which doth not deserved to be hanged, nothing is, I believe, more irksome than to support love with gratitude only; especially where inclination pulls the heart a contrary way. Such was the unhappy case of Jones; for though the virtuous love he bore to Sophia, and which left very little affection for any other woman, had been entirely out of the question, he could never have been able to have made any adequate return to the generous passion of this lady, who had indeed been once an object of desire, but was now entered at least into the autumn of life, though she wore all the gaiety of youth, both in her dress and manner; nay, she contrived still to maintain the roses in her cheeks; but these, like flowers forced out of season by art, had none of that lively blooming freshness with which Nature, at the proper time, bedecks her own productions. She had, besides, a certain imperfection, which renders some flowers, though very beautiful to the eye, very improper to be placed in a wilderness of sweets, and what above all others is most disagreeable to the breath of love.

Though Jones saw all these discouragements on the one side, he felt his obligations full as strongly on the other; nor did he less plainly discern the ardent passion whence those obligations proceeded, the extreme violence of which if he failed to equal, he well knew the lady would think him ungrateful; and, what is worse, he would have thought himself so. He knew the tacit consideration upon which all her favours were conferred; and as his necessity obliged him to accept them, so his honour, he concluded, forced him to pay the price. This therefore he resolved to do, whatever misery it cost him, and to devote himself to her, from that great principle of justice, by which the laws of some countries oblige a debtor, who is no otherwise capable of discharging his debt, to become the slave of his creditor.

While he was meditating on these matters, he received the following note from the lady:—

> "A very foolish, but a very perverse accident hath happened since our last meeting, which makes it improper I should see you any more at the usual place. I will, if possible, contrive some other place by to-morrow. In the meantime, adieu."

This disappointment, perhaps, the reader may conclude was not very great; but if it was, he was quickly relieved; for in less than an hour afterwards another note was brought him from the same hand, which contained as follows:—

> "I have altered my mind since I wrote; a change which, if you are no stranger to the tenderest of all passions, you will not wonder at. I am now resolved to see you this evening at my own house, whatever may be the consequence. Come to me exactly at seven; I dine abroad, but will be at home by that time. A day, I find, to those that sincerely love, seems longer than I imagined.

"If you should accidentally be a few moments before me, bid them show you into the drawing-room."

To confess the truth, Jones was less pleased with this last epistle than he had been with the former, as he was prevented by it from complying with the earnest entreaties of Mr Nightingale, with whom he had now contracted much intimacy and friendship. These entreaties were to go with that young gentleman and his company to a new play, which was to be acted that evening, and which a very large party had agreed to damn, from some dislike they had taken to the author, who was a friend to one of Mr Nightingale's acquaintance. And this sort of fun, our heroe, we are ashamed to confess, would willingly have preferred to the above kind appointment; but his honour got the better of his inclination.

Before we attend him to this intended interview with the lady, we think proper to account for both the preceding notes, as the reader may possibly be not a little surprized at the imprudence of Lady Bellaston, in bringing her lover to the very house where her rival was lodged.

First, then, the mistress of the house where these lovers had hitherto met, and who had been for some years a pensioner to that lady, was now become a methodist, and had that very morning waited upon her ladyship, and after rebuking her very severely for her past life, had positively declared that she would, on no account, be instrumental in carrying on any of her affairs for the future.

The hurry of spirits into which this accident threw the lady made her despair of possibly finding any other convenience to meet Jones that evening; but as she began a little to recover from her uneasiness at the disappointment, she set her thoughts to work, when luckily it came into her head to propose to Sophia to go to the play, which was immediately consented to, and a proper lady provided for her companion. Mrs Honour was likewise despatched with Mrs Etoff on the same errand of pleasure; and thus her own house was left free for the safe reception of Mr Jones, with whom she promised herself two or three hours of uninterrupted conversation after her return from the place where she dined, which was at a friend's house in a pretty distant part of the town, near her old place of assignation, where she had engaged herself before she was well apprized of the revolution that had happened in the mind and morals of her late confidante.

CHAPTER X.

A chapter which, though short, may draw tears from some eyes.

Mr Jones was just dressed to wait on Lady Bellaston, when Mrs Miller rapped at his door; and, being admitted, very earnestly desired his company below-stairs, to drink tea in the parlour.

Upon his entrance into the room, she presently introduced a person to him, saying, "This, sir, is my cousin, who hath been so greatly beholden to your goodness, for which he begs to return you his sincerest thanks."

The man had scarce entered upon that speech which Mrs Miller had so kindly prefaced, when both Jones and he, looking stedfastly at each other, showed at once the utmost tokens of surprize. The voice of the latter began instantly to faulter; and, instead of finishing his speech, he sunk down into a chair, crying, "It is so, I am convinced it is so!"

"Bless me! what's the meaning of this?" cries Mrs Miller; "you are not ill, I hope, cousin? Some water, a dram this instant."

"Be not frighted, madam," cries Jones, "I have almost as much need of a dram as your cousin. We are equally surprized at this unexpected meeting. Your cousin is an acquaintance of mine, Mrs Miller."

"An acquaintance!" cries the man.—"Oh, heaven!"

"Ay, an acquaintance," repeated Jones, "and an honoured acquaintance too. When I do not love and honour the man who dares venture everything to preserve his wife and children from instant destruction, may I have a friend capable of disowning me in adversity!"

"Oh, you are an excellent young man," cries Mrs Miller:—"Yes, indeed, poor creature! he hath ventured everything.—If he had not had one of the best of constitutions, it must have killed him."

"Cousin," cries the man, who had now pretty well recovered himself, "this is the angel from heaven whom I meant. This is he to whom, before I saw you, I owed the preservation of my Peggy. He it was to whose generosity every comfort, every support which I have procured for her, was owing. He is, indeed, the worthiest, bravest, noblest; of all human beings. O cousin, I have obligations to this gentleman of such a nature!"

"Mention nothing of obligations," cries Jones eagerly; "not a word, I insist upon it, not a word" (meaning, I suppose, that he would not have him betray the affair of the robbery to any person). "If, by the trifle you have received from me, I have preserved a whole family, sure pleasure was never bought so cheap."

"Oh, sir!" cries the man, "I wish you could this instant see my house. If any person had ever a right to the pleasure you mention, I am convinced it is yourself. My cousin tells me she acquainted you with the distress in which she found us. That, sir, is all greatly removed, and chiefly by your goodness.——My children have now a bed to lie on——and they have——they have——eternal blessings reward you for it!——they have bread to eat. My little boy is recovered; my wife is out of danger, and I am happy. All, all owing to you, sir, and to my cousin here, one of the best of women. Indeed, sir, I must see you at my house.—Indeed my wife must see you, and thank you.—My children too must express their gratitude.——Indeed, sir, they are not without a sense of their obligation; but what is my feeling when I reflect to whom I owe that they are now capable of expressing their gratitude.——Oh, sir, the little hearts which you have warmed had now been cold as ice without your assistance."

Here Jones attempted to prevent the poor man from proceeding; but indeed the overflowing of his own heart would of itself have stopped his words. And now Mrs Miller likewise began to pour forth thanksgivings, as well in her own name, as in that of her cousin, and concluded with saying, "She doubted not but such goodness would meet a glorious reward."

Jones answered, "He had been sufficiently rewarded already. Your cousin's account, madam," said he, "hath given me a sensation more pleasing than I have ever known. He must be a wretch who is unmoved at hearing such a story; how transporting then must be the thought of having happily acted a part in this scene! If there are men who cannot feel the delight of giving happiness to others, I sincerely pity them, as they are incapable of tasting what is, in my opinion, a greater honour, a higher interest, and a sweeter pleasure than the ambitious, the avaricious, or the voluptuous man can ever obtain."

The hour of appointment being now come, Jones was forced to take a hasty leave, but not before he had heartily shaken his friend by the hand, and desired to see him again as soon as possible; promising that he would himself take the first opportunity of visiting him at his own house. He then stept into his chair, and proceeded to Lady Bellaston's, greatly exulting in the happiness which he had procured to this poor family; nor could he forbear reflecting, without horror, on the dreadful consequences which must have attended them, had he listened rather to the voice of strict justice than to that of mercy, when he was attacked on the high road.

Mrs Miller sung forth the praises of Jones during the whole evening, in which Mr Anderson, while he stayed, so passionately accompanied her, that he was often on the very point of mentioning the circumstance of the robbery. However, he luckily recollected himself, and avoided an indiscretion which would have been so much the greater, as he knew Mrs Miller to be extremely strict and nice in her principles. He was likewise well apprized of the loquacity of this lady; and yet such was his gratitude, that it had almost got the better both of discretion and shame, and made him publish that which would have defamed his own character, rather than omit any circumstances which might do the fullest honour to his benefactor.

CHAPTER XI.

In which the reader will be surprized.

Mr Jones was rather earlier than the time appointed, and earlier than the lady; whose arrival was hindered, not only by the distance of the place where she dined, but by some other cross accidents very vexatious to one in her situation of mind. He was accordingly shown into the drawing-room, where he had not been many minutes before the door opened, and in came——no other than Sophia herself, who had left the play before the end of the first act; for this, as we have already said, being, a new play, at which two large parties met, the one to damn, and the other to applaud, a violent uproar, and an engagement between the two parties, had so terrified our heroine, that she was glad to put herself under the protection of a young gentleman who safely conveyed her to her chair.

As Lady Bellaston had acquainted her that she should not be at home till late, Sophia, expecting to find no one in the room, came hastily in, and went directly to a glass which almost fronted her, without once looking towards the upper end of the room, where the statue of Jones now stood motionless.—-In this glass it was, after contemplating her own lovely face, that she first discovered the said statue; when, instantly turning about, she perceived the reality of the vision: upon which she gave a violent scream, and scarce preserved herself from fainting, till Jones was able to move to her, and support her in his arms.

To paint the looks or thoughts of either of these lovers, is beyond my power. As their sensations, from their mutual silence, may be judged to have been too big for their own utterance, it cannot be supposed that I should be able to express them: and the misfortune is, that few of my readers have been enough in love to feel by their own hearts what past at this time in theirs.

After a short pause, Jones, with faultering accents, said—"I see, madam, you are surprized."—"Surprized!" answered she; "Oh heavens! Indeed, I am surprized. I almost doubt whether you are the person you seem."—"Indeed," cries he, "my Sophia, pardon me, madam, for this once calling you so, I am that very wretched Jones, whom fortune, after so many disappointments, hath, at last, kindly conducted to you. Oh! my Sophia, did you know the thousand torments I have suffered in this long, fruitless pursuit."—"Pursuit of whom?" said Sophia, a little recollecting herself, and assuming a reserved air.—"Can you be so cruel to ask that question?" cries Jones; "Need I say, of you?" "Of me!" answered Sophia: "Hath Mr Jones, then, any such important business with me?"—"To some, madam," cries Jones, "this might seem an important business" (giving her the pocket-book). "I hope, madam, you will find it of the same value as when it was lost." Sophia took the pocket-book, and was going to speak, when he interrupted her thus:—"Let us not, I beseech you, lose one of these precious moments which fortune hath so kindly sent us. O, my Sophia! I have business of a much superior kind. Thus, on my knees, let me ask your pardon."—"My pardon!" cries she; "Sure, sir, after what is past, you cannot expect, after what I have heard."—"I scarce know what I say," answered Jones. "By heavens! I scarce wish you should pardon me. O my Sophia! henceforth never cast away a thought on such a wretch as I am. If any remembrance of me should ever intrude to give a moment's uneasiness to that tender bosom, think of my unworthiness; and let the remembrance of what passed at Upton blot me for ever from your mind."

Sophia stood trembling all this while. Her face was whiter than snow, and her heart was throbbing through her stays. But, at the mention of Upton, a blush arose in her cheeks, and her eyes, which before she had scarce lifted up, were turned upon Jones with a glance of disdain. He understood this silent reproach, and replied to it thus: "O my Sophia! my only love! you cannot hate or despise me more for what happened there than I do myself; but yet do me the justice to think that my heart was never unfaithful to you. That had no share in the folly I was guilty of; it was even then unalterably yours. Though I despaired of possessing you, nay, almost of ever seeing you more, I doated still on your charming idea, and could seriously love no other woman. But if my heart had not been engaged, she, into whose company I accidently fell at that cursed place, was not an object of serious love. Believe me, my angel, I never have seen her from that day to this; and never intend or desire to see her again." Sophia, in her heart, was very glad to hear this; but forcing into her face an air of more coldness than she had yet assumed, "Why," said she, "Mr Jones, do you take the trouble to make a defence where you are not accused? If I thought it worth while to accuse you, I have a charge of unpardonable nature indeed."—"What is it, for heaven's sake?" answered Jones, trembling and pale, expecting to hear of his amour with Lady Bellaston. "Oh," said she, "how is it possible! can everything noble and everything base be lodged together in the same bosom?" Lady Bellaston, and the ignominious circumstance of having been kept, rose again in his mind, and stopt his mouth from any reply. "Could I have expected," proceeded Sophia, "such treatment from you? Nay, from any gentleman, from any man of honour? To have my name traduced in public; in inns, among the meanest vulgar! to have any little favours that my unguarded heart may have too lightly betrayed me to grant, boasted of there! nay, even to hear that you had been forced to fly from my love!"

Nothing could equal Jones's surprize at these words of Sophia; but yet, not being guilty, he was much less embarrassed how to defend himself than if she had touched that tender string at which his conscience had been alarmed. By some examination he presently found, that her supposing him guilty of so shocking an outrage against his love, and her reputation, was entirely owing to Partridge's talk at the inns before landlords and servants; for Sophia confessed to him it was from them that she received her intelligence. He had no very great difficulty to make her believe that he was entirely innocent of an offence so foreign to his character; but she had a great deal to hinder him from going instantly home, and putting Partridge to death, which he more than once swore he would do. This point being cleared up, they soon found themselves so well pleased with each other, that Jones quite forgot he had begun the conversation with conjuring her to give up all thoughts of him; and she was in a temper to have given ear to a petition of a very different nature; for before they were aware they had both gone so far, that he let fall some words that sounded like a proposal of marriage. To which she replied, "That, did not her duty to her father forbid her to follow her own inclinations, ruin with him would be more welcome to her than the most affluent fortune with another man." At the mention of the word ruin, he started, let drop her hand, which he had held for some time, and striking his breast with his own, cried out, "Oh, Sophia! can I then ruin thee? No; by heavens, no! I never will act so base a part. Dearest Sophia, whatever it costs me, I will renounce you; I will give you up; I will tear all such hopes from my heart as are inconsistent with your real good. My love I will ever retain, but it shall be in silence; it shall be at a distance from you; it shall be in some foreign land; from whence no voice, no sigh of my despair, shall ever reach and disturb your ears. And when I am dead"—He would have gone on, but was stopt by a flood of tears which Sophia let fall in his bosom, upon which she leaned, without being able to speak one word. He kissed them off, which, for some moments, she allowed him to do without any resistance; but then recollecting herself, gently withdrew out of his arms; and, to turn the discourse from a subject too tender, and which she found she could not support, bethought herself to ask him a question she never had time to put to him before, "How he came into that room?" He began to stammer, and would, in all probability, have raised her suspicions by the answer he was going to give, when, at once, the door opened, and in came Lady Bellaston.

Having advanced a few steps, and seeing Jones and Sophia together, she suddenly stopt; when, after a pause of a few moments, recollecting herself with admirable presence of mind, she said—though with sufficient indications of surprize both in voice and countenance—"I thought, Miss Western, you had been at the play?"

Though Sophia had no opportunity of learning of Jones by what means he had discovered her, yet, as she had not the least suspicion of the real truth, or that Jones and Lady Bellaston were acquainted, so she was very little confounded; and the less, as the lady had, in all their conversations on the subject, entirely taken her side against her father. With very little hesitation, therefore, she went through the whole story of what had happened at the play-house, and the cause of her hasty return.

The length of this narrative gave Lady Bellaston an opportunity of rallying her spirits, and of considering in what manner to act. And as the behaviour of Sophia gave her hopes that Jones had not betrayed her, she put on an air of good humour, and said, "I should not have broke in so abruptly upon you, Miss Western, if I had known you had company."

Lady Bellaston fixed her eyes on Sophia whilst she spoke these words. To which that poor young lady, having her face overspread with blushes and confusion, answered, in a stammering voice, "I am sure, madam, I shall always think the honour of your ladyship's company——" "I hope, at least," cries Lady Bellaston, "I interrupt no business."—"No, madam," answered Sophia, "our business was at an end. Your ladyship may be pleased to remember I have often mentioned the loss of my pocket-book, which this gentleman, having very luckily found, was so kind to return it to me with the bill in it."

Jones, ever since the arrival of Lady Bellaston, had been ready to sink with fear. He sat kicking his heels, playing with his fingers, and looking more like a fool, if it be possible, than a young booby squire, when he is first introduced into a polite assembly. He began, however, now to recover himself; and taking a hint from the behaviour of Lady Bellaston, who he saw did not intend to claim any acquaintance with him, he resolved as entirely to affect the stranger on his part. He said, "Ever since he had the pocket-book in his possession, he had used great diligence in enquiring out the lady whose name was writ in it; but never till that day could be so fortunate to discover her."

Sophia had indeed mentioned the loss of her pocket-book to Lady Bellaston; but as Jones, for some reason or other, had never once hinted to her that it was in his possession, she believed not one syllable of what Sophia now said, and wonderfully admired the extreme quickness of the young lady in inventing such an excuse. The reason of Sophia's leaving the playhouse met with no better credit; and though she could not account for the meeting between these two lovers, she was firmly persuaded it was not accidental.

With an affected smile, therefore, she said, "Indeed, Miss Western, you have had very good luck in recovering your money. Not only as it fell into the hands of a gentleman of honour, but as he happened to discover to whom it belonged. I think you would not consent to have it advertised.—It was great good fortune, sir, that you found out to whom the note belonged."

"Oh, madam," cries Jones, "it was enclosed in a pocket-book, in which the young lady's name was written."

"That was very fortunate, indeed," cries the lady:—"And it was no less so, that you heard Miss Western was at my house; for she is very little known."

Jones had at length perfectly recovered his spirits; and as he conceived he had now an opportunity of satisfying Sophia as to the question she had asked him just before Lady Bellaston came in, he proceeded thus: "Why, madam," answered he, "it was by the luckiest chance imaginable I made this discovery. I was mentioning what I had found, and the name of the owner, the other night to a lady at the masquerade, who told me she believed she knew where I might see Miss Western; and if I would come to her house the next morning she would inform me, I went according to her appointment, but she was not at home; nor could I ever meet with her till this morning, when she directed me to your ladyship's house. I came accordingly, and did myself the honour to ask for your ladyship; and upon my saying that I had very particular business, a servant showed me into this room; where I had not been long before the young lady returned from the play."

Upon his mentioning the masquerade, he looked very slily at Lady Bellaston, without any fear of being remarked by Sophia; for she was visibly too much confounded to make any observations. This hint a little alarmed the lady, and she was silent; when Jones, who saw the agitation of Sophia's mind, resolved to take the only method of relieving her, which was by retiring; but, before he did this, he said, "I believe, madam, it is customary to give some reward on these occasions;—I must insist on a very high one for my honesty;—it is, madam, no less than the honour of being permitted to pay another visit here."

"Sir," replied the lady, "I make no doubt that you are a gentleman, and my doors are never shut to people of fashion."

Jones then, after proper ceremonials, departed, highly to his own satisfaction, and no less to that of Sophia; who was terribly alarmed lest Lady Bellaston should discover what she knew already but too well.

Upon the stairs Jones met his old acquaintance, Mrs Honour, who, notwithstanding all she had said against him, was now so well bred to behave with great civility. This meeting proved indeed a lucky circumstance, as he communicated to her the house where he lodged, with which Sophia was unacquainted.

CHAPTER XII.

In which the thirteenth book is concluded.

The elegant Lord Shaftesbury somewhere objects to telling too much truth: by which it may be fairly inferred, that, in some cases, to lie is not only excusable but commendable.

And surely there are no persons who may so properly challenge a right to this commendable deviation from truth, as young women in the affair of love; for which they may plead precept, education, and above all, the sanction, nay, I may say the necessity of custom, by which they are restrained, not from submitting to the honest impulses of nature (for that would be a foolish prohibition), but from owning them.

We are not, therefore, ashamed to say, that our heroine now pursued the dictates of the above-mentioned right honourable philosopher. As she was perfectly satisfied then, that Lady Bellaston was ignorant of the person of Jones, so she determined to keep her in that ignorance, though at the expense of a little fibbing.

Jones had not been long gone, before Lady Bellaston cryed, "Upon my word, a good pretty young fellow; I wonder who he is; for I don't remember ever to have seen his face before."

"Nor I neither, madam," cries Sophia. "I must say he behaved very handsomely in relation to my note."

"Yes; and he is a very handsome fellow," said the lady: "don't you think so?"

"I did not take much notice of him," answered Sophia, "but I thought he seemed rather awkward, and ungenteel than otherwise."

"You are extremely right," cries Lady Bellaston: "you may see, by his manner, that he hath not kept good company. Nay, notwithstanding his returning your note, and refusing the reward, I almost question whether he is a gentleman.——I have always observed there is a something in persons well born, which others can never acquire.——I think I will give orders not to be at home to him."

"Nay, sure, madam," answered Sophia, "one can't suspect after what he hath done;—besides, if your ladyship observed him, there was an elegance in his discourse, a delicacy, a prettiness of expression that, that——"

"I confess," said Lady Bellaston, "the fellow hath words——And indeed, Sophia, you must forgive me, indeed you must."

"I forgive your ladyship!" said Sophia.

"Yes, indeed you must," answered she, laughing; "for I had a horrible suspicion when I first came into the room——I vow you must forgive it; but I suspected it was Mr Jones himself."

"Did your ladyship, indeed?" cries Sophia, blushing, and affecting a laugh.

"Yes, I vow I did," answered she. "I can't imagine what put it into my head: for, give the fellow his due, he was genteely drest; which, I think, dear Sophy, is not commonly the case with your friend."

"This raillery," cries Sophia, "is a little cruel, Lady Bellaston, after my promise to your ladyship."

"Not at all, child," said the lady;——"It would have been cruel before; but after you have promised me never to marry without your father's consent, in which you know is implied your giving up Jones, sure you can bear a little raillery on a passion which was pardonable enough in a young girl in the country, and of which you tell me you have so entirely got the better. What must I think, my dear Sophy, if you cannot bear a little ridicule even on his dress? I shall begin to fear you are very far gone indeed; and almost question whether you have dealt ingenuously with me."

"Indeed, madam," cries Sophia, "your ladyship mistakes me, if you imagine I had any concern on his account."

"On his account!" answered the lady: "You must have mistaken me; I went no farther than his dress;——for I would not injure your taste by any other comparison—I don't imagine, my dear Sophy, if your Mr Jones had been such a fellow as this—"

"I thought," says Sophia, "your ladyship had allowed him to be handsome"——

"Whom, pray?" cried the lady hastily.

"Mr Jones," answered Sophia;—and immediately recollecting herself, "Mr Jones!—no, no; I ask your pardon;—I mean the gentleman who was just now here."

"O Sophy! Sophy!" cries the lady; "this Mr Jones, I am afraid, still runs in your head."

"Then, upon my honour, madam," said Sophia, "Mr Jones is as entirely indifferent to me, as the gentleman who just now left us."

"Upon my honour," said Lady Bellaston, "I believe it. Forgive me, therefore, a little innocent raillery; but I promise you I will never mention his name any more."

And now the two ladies separated, infinitely more to the delight of Sophia than of Lady Bellaston, who would willingly have tormented her rival a little longer, had not business of more importance called her away. As for Sophia, her mind was not perfectly easy under this first practice of deceit; upon which, when she retired to her chamber, she reflected with the highest uneasiness and conscious shame. Nor could the peculiar hardship of her situation, and the necessity of the case, at all reconcile her mind to her conduct; for the frame of her mind was too delicate to bear the thought of having been guilty of a falsehood, however qualified by circumstances. Nor did this thought once suffer her to close her eyes during the whole succeeding night.

BOOK XIV.

CONTAINING TWO DAYS.

CHAPTER I.

An essay to prove that an author will write the better for having some knowledge of the subject on which he writes.

As several gentlemen in these times, by the wonderful force of genius only, without the least assistance of learning, perhaps, without being well able to read, have made a considerable figure in the republic of letters; the modern critics, I am told, have lately begun to assert, that all kind of learning is entirely useless to a writer; and, indeed, no other than a kind of fetters on the natural sprightliness and activity of the imagination, which is thus weighed down, and prevented from soaring to those high flights which otherwise it would be able to reach.

This doctrine, I am afraid, is at present carried much too far: for why should writing differ so much from all other arts? The nimbleness of a dancing-master is not at all prejudiced by being taught to move; nor doth any mechanic, I believe, exercise his tools the worse by having learnt to use them. For my own part, I cannot conceive that Homer or Virgil would have writ with more fire, if instead of being masters of all the learning of their times, they had been as ignorant as most of the authors of the present age. Nor do I believe that all the imagination, fire, and judgment of Pitt, could have produced those orations that have made the senate of England, in these our times, a rival in eloquence to Greece and Rome, if he had not been so well read in the writings of Demosthenes and Cicero, as to have transferred their whole spirit into his speeches, and, with their spirit, their knowledge too.

I would not here be understood to insist on the same fund of learning in any of my brethren, as Cicero persuades us is necessary to the composition of an orator. On the contrary, very little reading is, I conceive, necessary to the poet, less to the critic, and the least of all to the politician. For the first, perhaps, Byshe's Art of Poetry, and a few of our modern poets, may suffice; for the second, a moderate heap of plays; and, for the last, an indifferent collection of political journals.

To say the truth, I require no more than that a man should have some little knowledge of the subject on which he treats, according to the old maxim of law, *Quam quisque nôrit artem in eâ se exerceat.* With this alone a writer may sometimes do tolerably well; and, indeed, without this, all the other learning in the world will stand him in little stead.

For instance, let us suppose that Homer and Virgil, Aristotle and Cicero, Thucydides and Livy, could have met all together, and have clubbed their several talents to have composed a treatise on the art of dancing: I believe it will be readily agreed they could not have equalled the excellent treatise which Mr Essex hath given us on that subject, entitled, The Rudiments of Genteel Education. And, indeed, should the excellent Mr Broughton be prevailed on to set fist to paper, and to complete the above-said rudiments, by delivering down the true principles of athletics, I question whether the world will have any cause to lament, that none of the great writers, either antient or modern, have ever treated about that noble and useful art.

To avoid a multiplicity of examples in so plain a case, and to come at once to my point, I am apt to conceive, that one reason why many English writers have totally failed in describing the manners of upper life, may possibly be, that in reality they know nothing of it.

This is a knowledge unhappily not in the power of many authors to arrive at. Books will give us a very imperfect idea of it; nor will the stage a much better: the fine gentleman formed upon reading the former will almost always turn out a pedant, and he who forms himself upon the latter, a coxcomb.

Nor are the characters drawn from these models better supported. Vanbrugh and Congreve copied nature; but they who copy them draw as unlike the present age as Hogarth would do if he was to paint a rout or a drum in the dresses of Titian and of Vandyke. In short, imitation here will not do the business. The picture must be after Nature herself. A true knowledge of the world is gained only by conversation, and the manners of every rank must be seen in order to be known.

Now it happens that this higher order of mortals is not to be seen, like all the rest of the human species, for nothing, in the streets, shops, and coffee-houses; nor are they shown, like the upper rank of animals, for so much a-piece. In short, this is a sight to which no persons are admitted without one or other of these qualifications, viz., either birth or fortune, or, what is equivalent to both, the honourable profession of a gamester. And, very unluckily for the world, persons so qualified very seldom care to take upon themselves the bad trade of writing; which is generally entered upon by the lower and poorer sort, as it is a trade which many think requires no kind of stock to set up with.

Hence those strange monsters in lace and embroidery, in silks and brocades, with vast wigs and hoops; which, under the name of lords and ladies, strut the stage, to the great delight of attorneys and their clerks in the pit, and of the citizens and their apprentices in the galleries; and which are no more to be found in real life than the centaur, the chimera, or any other creature of mere fiction. But to let my reader into a secret, this knowledge of upper life, though very necessary for preventing mistakes, is no very great resource to a writer whose province is comedy, or that kind of novels which, like this I am writing, is of the comic class.

What Mr Pope says of women is very applicable to most in this station, who are, indeed, so entirely made up of form and affectation, that they have no character at all, at least none which appears. I will venture to say the highest life is much the dullest, and affords very little humour or entertainment. The various callings in lower spheres produce the great variety of humorous characters; whereas here, except among the few who are engaged in the pursuit of ambition, and the fewer still who have a relish for pleasure, all is vanity and servile imitation. Dressing and cards, eating and drinking, bowing and courtesying, make up the business of their lives.

Some there are, however, of this rank upon whom passion exercises its tyranny, and hurries them far beyond the bounds which decorum prescribes; of these the ladies are as much distinguished by their noble intrepidity, and a certain superior contempt of reputation, from the frail ones of meaner degree, as a virtuous woman of quality is by the elegance and delicacy of her sentiments from the honest wife of a yeoman and shopkeeper. Lady Bellaston was of this intrepid character; but let not my country readers conclude from her, that this is the general conduct of women of fashion, or that we mean to represent them as such. They might as well suppose that every clergyman was represented by Thwackum, or every soldier by ensign Northerton.

There is not, indeed, a greater error than that which universally prevails among the vulgar, who, borrowing their opinion from some ignorant satirists, have affixed the character of lewdness to these times. On the contrary, I am convinced there never was less of love intrigue carried on among persons of condition than now. Our present women have been taught by their mothers to fix their thoughts only on ambition and vanity, and to despise the pleasures of love as unworthy their regard; and being afterwards, by the care of such mothers, married without having husbands, they seem pretty well confirmed in the justness of those sentiments; whence they content themselves, for the dull remainder of life, with the pursuit of more innocent, but I am afraid more childish amusements, the bare mention of which would ill suit with the dignity of this history. In my humble opinion, the true characteristic of the present beau monde is rather folly than vice, and the only epithet which it deserves is that of frivolous.

CHAPTER II.

Containing letters and other matters which attend amours.

Jones had not been long at home before he received the following letter:—

> "I was never more surprized than when I found you was gone. When you left the room I little imagined you intended to have left the house without seeing me again. Your behaviour is all of a piece, and convinces me how much I ought to despise a heart which can doat upon an idiot; though I know not whether I should not admire her cunning more than her simplicity: wonderful both! For though she understood not a word of what passed between us, yet she had the skill, the assurance, the——what shall I call it? to deny to my face that she knows you, or ever saw you before.——Was this a scheme laid between you, and have you been base enough to betray me?——O how I despise her, you, and all the world, but chiefly myself! for——I dare not write what I should afterwards run mad to read; but remember, I can detest as violently as I have loved."

Jones had but little time given him to reflect on this letter, before a second was brought him from the same hand; and this, likewise, we shall set down in the precise words.

> "When you consider the hurry of spirits in which I must have writ, you cannot be surprized at any expressions in my former note.—Yet, perhaps, on reflection, they were rather too warm. At least I would, if possible, think all owing to the odious playhouse, and to the impertinence of a fool, which detained me beyond my appointment.——How easy is it to think well of those we love!——Perhaps you desire I should think so. I have resolved to see you to-night; so come to me immediately.
>
> "*P.S.*—I have ordered to be at home to none but yourself.
>
> "*P.S.*—Mr Jones will imagine I shall assist him in his defence; for I believe he cannot desire to impose on me more than I desire to impose on myself.
>
> "*P.S.*—Come immediately."

To the men of intrigue I refer the determination, whether the angry or the tender letter gave the greatest uneasiness to Jones. Certain it is, he had no violent inclination to pay any more visits that evening, unless to one single person. However, he thought his honour engaged, and had not this been motive sufficient, he would not have ventured to blow the temper of Lady Bellaston into that flame of which he had reason to think it susceptible, and of which he feared the consequence might be a discovery to Sophia, which he dreaded. After some discontented walks therefore about the room, he was preparing to depart, when the lady kindly prevented him, not by another letter, but by her own presence. She entered the room very disordered in her dress, and very discomposed in her looks, and threw herself into a chair, where, having recovered her breath, she said—"You see, sir, when women have gone one length too far, they will stop at none. If any person would have sworn this to me a week ago, I would not have believed it of myself." "I hope, madam," said Jones, "my charming Lady Bellaston will be as difficult to believe anything against one who is so sensible of the many obligations she hath conferred upon him." "Indeed!" says she, "sensible of obligations! Did I expect to hear such cold language from Mr Jones?" "Pardon me, my dear angel," said he, "if, after the letters I have received, the terrors of your anger, though I know not how I have deserved it."—"And have I then," says she, with a smile, "so angry a countenance?—Have I really brought a chiding face with me?"—"If there be honour in man," said he, "I have done nothing to merit your anger.—You remember the appointment you sent me; I went in pursuance."—"I beseech you," cried she, "do not run through the odious recital.—Answer me but one question, and I shall be easy. Have you not betrayed my honour to her?"—Jones fell upon his knees, and began to utter the most violent protestations, when Partridge came dancing and capering into the room, like one drunk with joy, crying out, "She's found! she's found!—Here, sir, here, she's here—Mrs Honour is upon the stairs." "Stop her a moment," cries Jones—"Here, madam, step behind the bed, I have no other room nor closet, nor place on earth to hide you in; sure never was so damned an accident."—"D—n'd indeed!" said the lady, as she went to her place of concealment; and presently afterwards in came Mrs Honour. "Heyday!" says she, "Mr Jones, what's the matter?—That impudent rascal your servant would scarce let me come upstairs. I hope he hath not the same reason to keep me from you as he had at Upton.—I suppose you hardly expected to see me; but you have certainly bewitched my lady. Poor dear young lady! To be sure, I loves her as tenderly as if she was my own sister. Lord have mercy upon you, if you don't make her a good husband! and to be sure, if you do not, nothing can be bad enough for you." Jones begged her only to whisper, for that there was a lady dying in the next room. "A lady!" cries she; "ay, I suppose one of your ladies.—O Mr Jones, there are too many of them in the world; I believe we are got into the house of one, for my Lady Bellaston I darst to say is no better than she should be."—"Hush! hush!" cries Jones, "every word is overheard in the next room." "I don't care a farthing," cries Honour, "I speaks no scandal of any one; but to be sure the servants make no scruple of saying as how her ladyship meets men at another place—where the house goes under the name of a poor gentlewoman; but her ladyship pays the rent, and many's the good thing besides, they say, she hath of her."—Here Jones, after expressing the utmost uneasiness, offered to stop her mouth:—"Hey-day! why sure, Mr Jones, you will let me speak; I speaks no scandal, for I only says what I heard from others—and thinks I to myself, much good may it do the gentlewoman with her riches, if she comes by it in such a wicked manner. To be sure it is better to be poor and honest." "The servants are villains," cries Jones, "and abuse their lady unjustly."—"Ay, to be sure, servants are always villains, and so my lady says, and won't hear a word of it."—"No, I am convinced," says Jones, "my Sophia is above listening to such base scandal." "Nay, I believe it is no scandal, neither," cries Honour, "for why should she meet men at another house?—It can never be for any good: for if she had a lawful design of being courted, as to be sure any lady may lawfully give her company to men upon that account: why, where can be the sense?"—"I protest," cries Jones, "I can't hear all this of a lady of such honour, and a relation of Sophia; besides, you will distract the poor lady in the next room.—Let me entreat you to walk with me down stairs."—"Nay, sir, if you won't let me speak, I have done.—Here, sir, is a letter from my young lady—what would some men give to have this? But, Mr Jones, I think you are not over and above generous, and yet I have heard some servants say——but I am sure you will do me the justice to own I never saw the colour of your money." Here Jones hastily took the letter, and presently after slipped five pieces into her hand. He then returned a thousand thanks to his dear Sophia in a whisper, and begged her to leave him to read her letter: she presently departed, not without expressing much grateful sense of his generosity.

Lady Bellaston now came from behind the curtain. How shall I describe her rage? Her tongue was at first incapable of utterance; but streams of fire darted from her eyes, and well indeed they might, for her heart was all in a flame. And now as soon as her voice found way, instead of expressing any indignation against Honour or her own servants, she began to attack poor Jones. "You see," said she, "what I have sacrificed to you; my reputation, my honour—gone for ever! And what return have I found? Neglected, slighted for a country girl, for an idiot."—"What neglect, madam, or what slight," cries Jones, "have I been guilty of?"—"Mr Jones," said she, "it is in vain to dissemble; if you will make me easy, you must entirely give her up; and as a proof of your intention, show me the letter."—"What letter, madam?" said Jones. "Nay, surely," said she, "you cannot have the confidence to deny your having received a letter by the hands of that trollop."—"And can your ladyship," cries he, "ask of me what I must part with my honour before I grant? Have I acted in such a manner by your ladyship? Could I be guilty of betraying this poor innocent girl to you, what security could you have that I should not act the same part by yourself? A moment's reflection will, I am sure, convince you that a man with whom the secrets of a lady are not safe must be the most contemptible of wretches."—"Very well," said she—"I need not insist on your becoming this contemptible wretch in your own opinion; for the inside of the letter could inform me of nothing more than I know already. I see the footing you are upon."—Here ensued a long conversation, which the reader, who is not too curious, will thank me for not inserting at length. It shall suffice, therefore, to inform him, that Lady Bellaston grew more and more pacified, and at length believed, or affected to believe, his protestations, that his meeting with Sophia that evening was merely accidental, and every other matter which the reader already knows, and which, as Jones set before her in the strongest light, it is plain that she had in reality no reason to be angry with him.

She was not, however, in her heart perfectly satisfied with his refusal to show her the letter; so deaf are we to the clearest reason, when it argues against our prevailing passions. She was, indeed, well convinced that Sophia possessed the first place in Jones's affections; and yet, haughty and amorous as this lady was, she submitted at last to bear the second place; or, to express it more properly in a legal phrase, was contented with the possession of that of which another woman had the reversion.

It was at length agreed that Jones should for the future visit at the house: for that Sophia, her maid, and all the servants, would place these visits to the account of Sophia; and that she herself would be considered as the person imposed upon.

This scheme was contrived by the lady, and highly relished by Jones, who was indeed glad to have a prospect of seeing his Sophia at any rate; and the lady herself was not a little pleased with the imposition on Sophia, which Jones, she thought, could not possibly discover to her for his own sake.

The next day was appointed for the first visit, and then, after proper ceremonials, the Lady Bellaston returned home.

CHAPTER III.

Containing various matters.

Jones was no sooner alone than he eagerly broke open his letter, and read as follows:—

> "Sir, it is impossible to express what I have suffered since you left this house; and as I have reason to think you intend coming here again, I have sent Honour, though so late at night, as she tells me she knows your lodgings, to prevent you. I charge you, by all the regard you have for me, not to think of visiting here; for it will certainly be discovered; nay, I almost doubt, from some things which have dropt from her ladyship, that she is not already without some suspicion. Something favourable perhaps may happen; we must wait with patience; but I once more entreat you, if you have any concern for my ease, do not think of returning hither."

This letter administered the same kind of consolation to poor Jones, which Job formerly received from his friends. Besides disappointing all the hopes which he promised to himself from seeing Sophia, he was reduced to an unhappy dilemma, with regard to Lady Bellaston; for there are some certain engagements, which, as he well knew, do very difficultly admit of any excuse for the failure; and to go, after the strict prohibition from Sophia, he was not to be forced by any human power. At length, after much deliberation, which during that night supplied the place of sleep, he determined to feign himself sick: for this suggested itself as the only means of failing the appointed visit, without incensing Lady Bellaston, which he had more than one reason of desiring to avoid.

The first thing, however, which he did in the morning, was, to write an answer to Sophia, which he inclosed in one to Honour. He then despatched another to Lady Bellaston, containing the above-mentioned excuse; and to this he soon received the following answer:—

> "I am vexed that I cannot see you here this afternoon, but more concerned for the occasion; take great care of yourself, and have the best advice, and I hope there will be no danger.—I am so tormented all this morning with fools, that I have scarce a moment's time to write to you. Adieu.

"*P.S.*—I will endeavour to call on you this evening, at nine.—Be sure to be alone."

Mr Jones now received a visit from Mrs Miller, who, after some formal introduction, began the following speech:—"I am very sorry, sir, to wait upon you on such an occasion; but I hope you will consider the ill consequence which it must be to the reputation of my poor girls, if my house should once be talked of as a house of ill-fame. I hope you won't think me, therefore, guilty of impertinence, if I beg you not to bring any more ladies in at that time of night. The clock had struck two before one of them went away."—"I do assure you, madam," said Jones, "the lady who was here last night, and who staid the latest (for the other only brought me a letter), is a woman of very great fashion, and my near relation."—"I don't know what fashion she is of," answered Mrs Miller; "but I am sure no woman of virtue, unless a very near relation indeed, would visit a young gentleman at ten at night, and stay four hours in his room with him alone; besides, sir, the behaviour of her chairmen shows what she was; for they did nothing but make jests all the evening in the entry, and asked Mr Partridge, in the hearing of my own maid, if madam intended to stay with his master all night; with a great deal of stuff not proper to be repeated. I have really a great respect for you, Mr Jones, upon your own account; nay, I have a very high obligation to you for your generosity to my cousin. Indeed, I did not know how very good you had been till lately. Little did I imagine to what dreadful courses the poor man's distress had driven him. Little did I think, when you gave me the ten guineas, that you had given them to a highwayman! O heavens! what goodness have you shown! How have you preserved this family!—The character which Mr Allworthy hath formerly given me of you was, I find, strictly true.—And indeed, if I had no obligation to you, my obligations to him are such, that, on his account, I should shew you the utmost respect in my power.—Nay, believe me, dear Mr Jones, if my daughters' and my own reputation were out of the case, I should, for your own sake, be sorry that so pretty a young gentleman should converse with these women; but if you are resolved to do it, I must beg you to take another lodging; for I do not myself like to have such things carried on under my roof; but more especially upon the account of my girls, who have little, heaven knows, besides their characters, to recommend them." Jones started and changed colour at the name of Allworthy. "Indeed, Mrs Miller," answered he, a little warmly, "I do not take this at all kind. I will never bring any slander on your house; but I must insist on seeing what company I please in my own room; and if that gives you any offence, I shall, as soon as I am able, look for another lodging."—"I am sorry we must part then, sir," said she; "but I am convinced Mr Allworthy himself would never come within my doors, if he had the least suspicion of my keeping an ill house."—"Very well, madam," said Jones.—"I hope, sir," said she, "you are not angry; for I would not for the world offend any of Mr Allworthy's family. I have not slept a wink all night about this matter."—"I am sorry I have disturbed your rest, madam," said Jones, "but I beg you will send Partridge up to me immediately;" which she promised to do, and then with a very low courtesy retired.

As soon as Partridge arrived, Jones fell upon him in the most outrageous manner. "How often," said he, "am I to suffer for your folly, or rather for my own in keeping you? is that tongue of yours resolved upon my destruction?" "What have I done, sir?" answered affrighted Partridge. "Who was it gave you authority to mention the story of the robbery, or that the man you saw here was the person?" "I, sir?" cries Partridge. "Now don't be guilty of a falsehood in denying it," said Jones. "If I did mention such a matter," answers Partridge, "I am sure I thought no harm; for I should not have opened my lips, if it had not been to his own friends and relations, who, I imagined, would have let it go no farther." "But I have a much heavier charge against you," cries Jones, "than this. How durst you, after all the precautions I gave you, mention the name of Mr Allworthy in this house?" Partridge denied that he ever had, with many oaths. "How else," said Jones, "should Mrs Miller be acquainted that there was any connexion between him and me? And it is but this moment she told me she respected me on his account." "O Lord, sir," said Partridge, "I desire only to be heard out; and to be sure, never was anything so unfortunate: hear me but out, and you will own how wrongfully you have accused me. When Mrs Honour came downstairs last night she met me in the entry, and asked me when my master had heard from Mr Allworthy; and to be sure Mrs Miller heard the very words; and the moment Madam Honour was gone, she called me into the parlour to her. `Mr Partridge,' says she, `what Mr Allworthy is it that the gentlewoman mentioned? is it the great Mr Allworthy of Somersetshire?' `Upon my word, madam,' says I, `I know nothing of the matter.' `Sure,' says she, `your master is not the Mr Jones I have heard Mr Allworthy talk of?' `Upon my word, madam,' says I, `I know nothing of the matter.' `Then,' says she, turning to her daughter Nancy, says she, `as sure as tenpence this is the very young gentleman, and he agrees exactly with the squire's description.' The Lord above knows who it was told her: for I am the arrantest villain that ever walked upon two legs if ever it came out of my mouth. I promise you, sir, I can keep a secret when I am desired. Nay, sir, so far was I from telling her anything about Mr Allworthy, that I told her the very direct contrary; for, though I did not contradict it at that moment, yet, as second thoughts, they say, are best, so when I came to consider that somebody must have informed her, thinks I to myself, I will put an end to the story; and so I went back again into the parlour some time afterwards, and says I, upon my word, says I, whoever, says I, told you that this gentleman was Mr Jones; that is, says I, that this Mr Jones was that Mr Jones, told you a confounded lie: and I beg, says I, you will never mention any such matter, says I; for my master, says I, will think I must have told you so; and I defy anybody in the house ever to say I mentioned any such word. To be certain, sir, it is a wonderful thing, and I have been thinking with myself ever since, how it was she came to know it; not but I saw an old woman here t'other day a begging at the door, who looked as like her we saw in Warwickshire, that caused all that mischief to us. To be sure it is never good to pass by an old woman without giving her something, especially if she looks at you; for all the world shall never persuade me but that they have a great power to do mischief, and to be sure I shall never see an old woman again, but I shall think to myself, *Infandum, regina, jubes renovare dolorem.*"

The simplicity of Partridge set Jones a laughing, and put a final end to his anger, which had indeed seldom any long duration in his mind; and, instead of commenting on his defence, he told him he intended presently to leave those lodgings, and ordered him to go and endeavour to get him others.

CHAPTER IV.

Which we hope will be very attentively perused by young people of both sexes.

Partridge had no sooner left Mr Jones than Mr Nightingale, with whom he had now contracted a great intimacy, came to him, and, after a short salutation, said, "So, Tom, I hear you had company very late last night. Upon my soul you are a happy fellow, who have not been in town above a fortnight, and can keep chairs waiting at your door till two in the morning." He then ran on with much commonplace raillery of the same kind, till Jones at last interrupted him, saying, "I suppose you have received all this information from Mrs Miller, who hath been up here a little while ago to give me warning. The good woman is afraid, it seems, of the reputation of her daughters." "Oh! she is wonderfully nice," says Nightingale, "upon that account; if you remember, she would not let Nancy go with us to the masquerade." "Nay, upon my honour, I think she's in the right of it," says Jones: "however, I have taken her at her word, and have sent Partridge to look for another lodging." "If you will," says Nightingale, "we may, I believe, be again together; for, to tell you a secret, which I desire you won't mention in the family, I intend to quit the house to-day." "What, hath Mrs Miller given you warning too, my friend?" cries Jones. "No," answered the other; "but the rooms are not convenient enough. Besides, I am grown weary of this part of the town. I want to be nearer the places of diversion; so I am going to Pall-mall." "And do you intend to make a secret of your going away?" said Jones. "I promise you," answered Nightingale, "I don't intend to bilk my lodgings; but I have a private reason for not taking a formal leave." "Not so private," answered Jones; "I promise you, I have seen it ever since the second day of my coming to the house. Here will be some wet eyes on your departure. Poor Nancy, I pity her, faith! Indeed, Jack, you have played the fool with that girl. You have given her a longing, which I am afraid nothing will ever cure her of." Nightingale answered, "What the devil would you have me do? would you have me marry her to cure her?" "No," answered Jones, "I would not have had you make love to her, as you have often done in my presence. I have been astonished at the blindness of her mother in never seeing it." "Pugh, see it!" cries Nightingale. "What, the devil should she see?" "Why, see," said Jones, "that you have made her daughter distractedly in love with you. The poor girl cannot conceal it a moment; her eyes are never off from you, and she always colours every time you come into the room. Indeed, I pity her heartily; for she seems to be one of the best-natured and honestest of human creatures." "And so," answered Nightingale, "according to your doctrine, one must not amuse oneself by any common gallantries with women, for fear they should fall in love with us." "Indeed, Jack," said Jones, "you wilfully misunderstand me; I do not fancy women are so apt to fall in love; but you have gone far beyond common gallantries." "What, do you suppose," says Nightingale, "that we have been a-bed together?" "No, upon my honour," answered Jones, very seriously, "I do not suppose so ill of you; nay, I will go farther, I do not imagine you have laid a regular premeditated scheme for the destruction of the quiet of a poor little creature, or have even foreseen the consequence: for I am sure thou art a very good-natured fellow; and such a one can never be guilty of a cruelty of that kind; but at the same time you have pleased your own vanity, without considering that this poor girl was made a sacrifice to it; and while you have had no design but of amusing an idle hour, you have actually given her reason to flatter herself that you had the most serious designs in her favour. Prithee, Jack, answer me honestly; to what have tended all those elegant and luscious descriptions of happiness arising from violent and mutual fondness? all those warm professions of tenderness, and generous disinterested love? Did you imagine she would not apply them? or, speak ingenuously, did not you intend she should?" "Upon my soul, Tom," cries Nightingale, "I did not think this was in thee. Thou wilt make an admirable parson. So I suppose you would not go to bed to Nancy now, if she would let you?" "No," cries Jones, "may I be d—n'd if I would." "Tom, Tom," answered Nightingale, "last night; remember last night——

When every eye was closed, and the pale moon,
And silent stars, shone conscious of the theft."

"Lookee, Mr Nightingale," said Jones, "I am no canting hypocrite, nor do I pretend to the gift of chastity, more than my neighbours. I have been guilty with women, I own it; but am not conscious that I have ever injured any.—Nor would I, to procure pleasure to myself, be knowingly the cause of misery to any human being."

"Well, well," said Nightingale, "I believe you, and I am convinced you acquit me of any such thing."

"I do, from my heart," answered Jones, "of having debauched the girl, but not from having gained her affections."

"If I have," said Nightingale, "I am sorry for it; but time and absence will soon wear off such impressions. It is a receipt I must take myself; for, to confess the truth to you—I never liked any girl half so much in my whole life; but I must let you into the whole secret, Tom. My father hath provided a match for me with a woman I never saw; and she is now coming to town, in order for me to make my addresses to her."

At these words Jones burst into a loud fit of laughter; when Nightingale cried—"Nay, prithee, don't turn me into ridicule. The devil take me if I am not half mad about this matter! my poor Nancy! Oh! Jones, Jones, I wish I had a fortune in my own possession."

"I heartily wish you had," cries Jones; "for, if this be the case, I sincerely pity you both; but surely you don't intend to go away without taking your leave of her?"

"I would not," answered Nightingale, "undergo the pain of taking leave, for ten thousand pounds; besides, I am convinced, instead of answering any good purpose, it would only serve to inflame my poor Nancy the more. I beg, therefore, you would not mention a word of it to-day, and in the evening, or to-morrow morning, I intend to depart."

Jones promised he would not; and said, upon reflection, he thought, as he had determined and was obliged to leave her, he took the most prudent method. He then told Nightingale he should be very glad to lodge in the same house with him; and it was accordingly agreed between them, that Nightingale should procure him either the ground floor, or the two pair of stairs; for the young gentleman himself was to occupy that which was between them.

This Nightingale, of whom we shall be presently obliged to say a little more, was in the ordinary transactions of life a man of strict honour, and, what is more rare among young gentlemen of the town, one of strict honesty too; yet in affairs of love he was somewhat loose in his morals; not that he was even here as void of principle as gentlemen sometimes are, and oftener affect to be; but it is certain he had been guilty of some indefensible treachery to women, and had, in a certain mystery, called making love, practised many deceits, which, if he had used in trade, he would have been counted the greatest villain upon earth.

But as the world, I know not well for what reason, agree to see this treachery in a better light, he was so far from being ashamed of his iniquities of this kind, that he gloried in them, and would often boast of his skill in gaining of women, and his triumphs over their hearts, for which he had before this time received some rebukes from Jones, who always exprest great bitterness against any misbehaviour to the fair part of the species, who, if considered, he said, as they ought to be, in the light of the dearest friends, were to be cultivated, honoured, and caressed with the utmost love and tenderness; but, if regarded as enemies, were a conquest of which a man ought rather to be ashamed than to value himself upon it.

CHAPTER V.

A short account of the history of Mrs Miller.

Jones this day eat a pretty good dinner for a sick man, that is to say, the larger half of a shoulder of mutton. In the afternoon he received an invitation from Mrs Miller to drink tea; for that good woman, having learnt, either by means of Partridge, or by some other means natural or supernatural, that he had a connexion with Mr Allworthy, could not endure the thoughts of parting with him in an angry manner.

Jones accepted the invitation; and no sooner was the tea-kettle removed, and the girls sent out of the room, than the widow, without much preface, began as follows: "Well, there are very surprizing things happen in this world; but certainly it is a wonderful business that I should have a relation of Mr Allworthy in my house, and never know anything of the matter. Alas! sir, you little imagine what a friend that best of gentlemen hath been to me and mine. Yes, sir, I am not ashamed to own it; it is owing to his goodness that I did not long since perish for want, and leave my poor little wretches, two destitute, helpless, friendless orphans, to the care, or rather to the cruelty, of the world.

"You must know, sir, though I am now reduced to get my living by letting lodgings, I was born and bred a gentlewoman. My father was an officer of the army, and died in a considerable rank: but he lived up to his pay; and, as that expired with him, his family, at his death, became beggars. We were three sisters. One of us had the good luck to die soon after of the small-pox; a lady was so kind as to take the second out of charity, as she said, to wait upon her. The mother of this lady had been a servant to my grand-mother; and, having inherited a vast fortune from her father, which he had got by pawnbroking, was married to a gentleman of great estate and fashion. She used my sister so barbarously, often upbraiding her with her birth and poverty, calling her in derision a gentlewoman, that I believe she at length broke the heart of the poor girl. In short, she likewise died within a twelvemonth after my father. Fortune thought proper to provide better for me, and within a month from his decease I was married to a clergyman, who had been my lover a long time before, and who had been very ill used by my father on that account: for though my poor father could not give any of us a shilling, yet he bred us up as delicately, considered us, and would have had us consider ourselves, as highly as if we had been the richest heiresses. But my dear husband forgot all this usage, and the moment we were become fatherless he immediately renewed his addresses to me so warmly, that I, who always liked, and now more than ever esteemed him, soon complied. Five years did I live in a state of perfect happiness with that best of men, till at last—Oh! cruel! cruel fortune, that ever separated us, that deprived me of the kindest of husbands and my poor girls of the tenderest parent.—O my poor girls! you never knew the blessing which ye lost.—I am ashamed, Mr Jones, of this womanish weakness; but I shall never mention him without tears." "I ought rather, madam," said Jones, "to be ashamed that I do not accompany you." "Well, sir," continued she, "I was now left a second time in a much worse condition than before; besides the terrible affliction I was to encounter, I had now two children to provide for; and was, if possipossible, more pennyless than ever; when that great, that good, that glorious man, Mr Allworthy, who had some little acquaintance with my husband, accidentally heard of my distress, and immediately writ this letter to me. Here, sir, here it is; I put it into my pocket to shew it you. This is the letter, sir; I must and will read it to you.

> "'Madam,
>
> "'I heartily condole with you on your late grievous loss, which your own good sense, and the excellent lessons you must have learnt from the worthiest of men, will better enable you to bear than any advice which I am capable of giving. Nor have I any doubt that you, whom I have heard to be the tenderest of mothers, will suffer any immoderate indulgence of grief to prevent you from discharging your duty to those poor infants, who now alone stand in need of your tenderness.
>
> "`However, as you must be supposed at present to be incapable of much worldly consideration, you will pardon my having ordered a person to wait on you, and to pay you twenty guineas, which I beg you will accept till I have the pleasure of seeing you, and believe me to be, madam, &c.'

"This letter, sir, I received within a fortnight after the irreparable loss I have mentioned; and within a fortnight afterwards, Mr Allworthy—the blessed Mr Allworthy, came to pay me a visit, when he placed me in the house where you now see me, gave me a large sum of money to furnish it, and settled an annuity of £50 a-year upon me, which I have constantly received ever since. Judge, then, Mr Jones, in what regard I must hold a benefactor, to whom I owe the preservation of my life, and of those dear children, for whose sake alone my life is valuable. Do not, therefore, think me impertinent, Mr Jones (since I must esteem one for whom I know Mr Allworthy hath so much value), if I beg you not to converse with these wicked women. You are a young gentleman, and do not know half their artful wiles. Do not be angry with me, sir, for what I said upon account of my house; you must be sensible it would be the ruin of my poor dear girls. Besides, sir, you cannot but be acquainted that Mr Allworthy himself would never forgive my conniving at such matters, and particularly with you."

"Upon my word, madam," said Jones, "you need make no farther apology; nor do I in the least take anything ill you have said; but give me leave, as no one can have more value than myself for Mr Allworthy, to deliver you from one mistake, which, perhaps, would not be altogether for his honour; I do assure you, I am no relation of his."

"Alas! sir," answered she, "I know you are not, I know very well who you are; for Mr Allworthy hath told me all; but I do assure you, had you been twenty times his son, he could not have expressed more regard for you than he hath often expressed in my presence. You need not be ashamed, sir, of what you are; I promise you no good person will esteem you the less on that account. No, Mr Jones, the words `dishonourable birth' are nonsense, as my dear, dear husband used to say, unless the word `dishonourable' be applied to the parents; for the children can derive no real dishonour from an act of which they are intirely innocent."

Here Jones heaved a deep sigh, and then said, "Since I perceive, madam, you really do know me, and Mr Allworthy hath thought proper to mention my name to you; and since you have been so explicit with me as to your own affairs, I will acquaint you with some more circumstances concerning myself." And these Mrs Miller having expressed great desire and curiosity to hear, he began and related to her his whole history, without once mentioning the name of Sophia.

There is a kind of sympathy in honest minds, by means of which they give an easy credit to each other. Mrs Miller believed all which Jones told her to be true, and exprest much pity and concern for him. She was beginning to comment on the story, but Jones interrupted her; for, as the hour of assignation now drew nigh, he began to stipulate for a second interview with the lady that evening, which he promised should be the last at her house; swearing, at the same time, that she was one of great distinction, and that nothing but what was intirely innocent was to pass between them; and I do firmly believe he intended to keep his word.

Mrs Miller was at length prevailed on, and Jones departed to his chamber, where he sat alone till twelve o'clock, but no Lady Bellaston appeared.

As we have said that this lady had a great affection for Jones, and as it must have appeared that she really had so, the reader may perhaps wonder at the first failure of her appointment, as she apprehended him to be confined by sickness, a season when friendship seems most to require such visits. This behaviour, therefore, in the lady, may, by some, be condemned as unnatural; but that is not our fault, for our business is only to record truth.

CHAPTER VI.

Containing a scene which we doubt not will affect all our readers.

Mr Jones closed not his eyes during all the former part of the night; not owing to any uneasiness which he conceived at being disappointed by Lady Bellaston; nor was Sophia herself, though most of his waking hours were justly to be charged to her account, the present cause of dispelling his slumbers. In fact, poor Jones was one of the best-natured fellows alive, and had all that weakness which is called compassion, and which distinguishes this imperfect character from that noble firmness of mind, which rolls a man, as it were, within himself, and like a polished bowl, enables him to run through the world without being once stopped by the calamities which happen to others. He could not help, therefore, compassionating the situation of poor Nancy, whose love for Mr Nightingale seemed to him so apparent, that he was astonished at the blindness of her mother, who had more than once, the preceding evening, remarked to him the great change in the temper of her daughter, "who from being," she said, "one of the liveliest, merriest girls in the world, was, on a sudden, become all gloom and melancholy."

Sleep, however, at length got the better of all resistance; and now, as if he had already been a deity, as the antients imagined, and an offended one too, he seemed to enjoy his dear-bought conquest.—To speak simply, and without any metaphor, Mr Jones slept till eleven the next morning, and would, perhaps, have continued in the same quiet situation much longer, had not a violent uproar awakened him.

Partridge was now summoned, who, being asked what was the matter, answered, "That there was a dreadful hurricane below-stairs; that Miss Nancy was in fits; and that the other sister, and the mother, were both crying and lamenting over her." Jones expressed much concern at this news; which Partridge endeavoured to relieve, by saying, with a smile, "he fancied the young lady was in no danger of death; for that Susan" (which was the name of the maid) "had given him to understand, it was nothing more than a common affair. In short," said he, "Miss Nancy hath had a mind to be as wise as her mother; that's all; she was a little hungry, it seems, and so sat down to dinner before grace was said; and so there is a child coming for the Foundling Hospital."——"Prithee, leave thy stupid jesting," cries Jones. "Is the misery of these poor wretches a subject of mirth? Go immediately to Mrs Miller, and tell her I beg leave—Stay, you will make some blunder; I will go myself; for she desired me to breakfast with her." He then rose and dressed himself as fast as he could; and while he was dressing, Partridge, notwithstanding many severe rebukes, could not avoid throwing forth certain pieces of brutality, commonly called jests, on this occasion. Jones was no sooner dressed than he walked downstairs, and knocking at the door, was presently admitted by the maid, into the outward parlour, which was as empty of company as it was of any apparatus for eating. Mrs Miller was in the inner room with her daughter, whence the maid presently brought a message to Mr Jones, "That her mistress hoped he would excuse the disappointment, but an accident had happened, which made it impossible for her to have the pleasure of his company at breakfast that day; and begged his pardon for not sending him up notice sooner." Jones desired, "She would give herself no trouble about anything so trifling as his disappointment; that he was heartily sorry for the occasion; and that if he could be of any service to her, she might command him."

He had scarce spoke these words, when Mrs Miller, who heard them all, suddenly threw open the door, and coming out to him, in a flood of tears, said, "O Mr Jones! you are certainly one of the best young men alive. I give you a thousand thanks for your kind offer of your service; but, alas! sir, it is out of your power to preserve my poor girl.—O my child! my child! she is undone, she is ruined for ever!" "I hope, madam," said Jones, "no villain"——"O Mr Jones!" said she, "that villain who yesterday left my lodgings, hath betrayed my poor girl; hath destroyed her.—I know you are a man of honour. You have a good—a noble heart, Mr Jones. The actions to which I have been myself a witness, could proceed from no other. I will tell you all: nay, indeed, it is impossible, after what hath happened, to keep it a secret. That Nightingale, that barbarous villain, hath undone my daughter. She is—she is—oh! Mr Jones, my girl is with child by him; and in that condition he hath deserted her. Here! here, sir, is his cruel letter: read it, Mr Jones, and tell me if such another monster lives."

The letter was as follows:

> "DEAR NANCY,
>
> "As I found it impossible to mention to you what, I am afraid, will be no less shocking to you, than it is to me, I have taken this method to inform you, that my father insists upon my immediately paying my addresses to a young lady of fortune, whom he hath provided for my—I need not write the detested word. Your own good understanding will make you sensible, how entirely I am obliged to an obedience, by which I shall be for ever excluded from your dear arms. The fondness of your mother may encourage you to trust her with the unhappy consequence of our love, which may be easily kept a secret from the world, and for which I will take care to provide, as I will for you. I wish you may feel less on this account than I have suffered; but summon all your fortitude to your assistance, and forgive and forget the man, whom nothing but the prospect of certain ruin could have forced to write this letter. I bid you forget me, I mean on-

ly as a lover; but the best of friends you shall ever find in your faithful, though unhappy,

"J. N."

When Jones had read this letter, they both stood silent during a minute, looking at each other; at last he began thus: "I cannot express, madam, how much I am shocked at what I have read; yet let me beg you, in one particular, to take the writer's advice. Consider the reputation of your daughter."——"It is gone, it is lost, Mr Jones," cryed she, "as well as her innocence. She received the letter in a room full of company, and immediately swooning away upon opening it, the contents were known to every one present. But the loss of her reputation, bad as it is, is not the worst; I shall lose my child; she hath attempted twice to destroy herself already; and though she hath been hitherto prevented, vows she will not outlive it; nor could I myself outlive any accident of that nature.—What then will become of my little Betsy, a helpless infant orphan? and the poor little wretch will, I believe, break her heart at the miseries with which she sees her sister and myself distracted, while she is ignorant of the cause. O 'tis the most sensible, and best-natured little thing! The barbarous, cruel——hath destroyed us all. O my poor children! Is this the reward of all my cares? Is this the fruit of all my prospects? Have I so chearfully undergone all the labours and duties of a mother? Have I been so tender of their infancy, so careful of their education? Have I been toiling so many years, denying myself even the conveniences of life, to provide some little sustenance for them, to lose one or both in such a manner?" "Indeed, madam," said Jones, with tears in his eyes, "I pity you from my soul."—"O! Mr Jones," answered she, "even you, though I know the goodness of your heart, can have no idea of what I feel. The best, the kindest, the most dutiful of children! O my poor Nancy, the darling of my soul! the delight of my eyes! the pride of my heart! too much, indeed, my pride; for to those foolish, ambitious hopes, arising from her beauty, I owe her ruin. Alas! I saw with pleasure the liking which this young man had for her. I thought it an honourable affection; and flattered my foolish vanity with the thoughts of seeing her married to one so much her superior. And a thousand times in my presence, nay, often in yours, he hath endeavoured to soothe and encourage these hopes by the most generous expressions of disinterested love, which he hath always directed to my poor girl, and which I, as well as she, believed to be real. Could I have believed that these were only snares laid to betray the innocence of my child, and for the ruin of us all?"—At these words little Betsy came running into the room, crying, "Dear mamma, for heaven's sake come to my sister; for she is in another fit, and my cousin can't hold her." Mrs Miller immediately obeyed the summons; but first ordered Betsy to stay with Mr Jones, and begged him to entertain her a few minutes, saying, in the most pathetic voice, "Good heaven! let me preserve one of my children at least."

Jones, in compliance with this request, did all he could to comfort the little girl, though he was, in reality, himself very highly affected with Mrs Miller's story. He told her "Her sister would be soon very well again; that by taking on in that manner she would not only make her sister worse, but make her mother ill too."

"Indeed, sir," says she, "I would not do anything to hurt them for the world. I would burst my heart rather than they should see me cry.—But my poor sister can't see me cry.—I am afraid she will never be able to see me cry any more. Indeed, I can't part with her; indeed, I can't.—And then poor mamma too, what will become of her?—She says she will die too, and leave me: but I am resolved I won't be left behind." "And are you not afraid to die, my little Betsy?" said Jones. "Yes," answered she, "I was always afraid to die; because I must have left my mamma, and my sister; but I am not afraid of going anywhere with those I love."

Jones was so pleased with this answer, that he eagerly kissed the child; and soon after Mrs Miller returned, saying, "She thanked heaven Nancy was now come to herself. And now, Betsy," says she, "you may go in, for your sister is better, and longs to see you." She then turned to Jones, and began to renew her apologies for having disappointed him of his breakfast.

"I hope, madam," said Jones, "I shall have a more exquisite repast than any you could have provided for me. This, I assure you, will be the case, if I can do any service to this little family of love. But whatever success may attend my endeavours, I am resolved to attempt it. I am very much deceived in Mr Nightingale, if, notwithstanding what hath happened, he hath not much goodness of heart at the bottom, as well as a very violent affection for your daughter. If this be the case, I think the picture which I shall lay before him will affect him. Endeavour, madam, to comfort yourself, and Miss Nancy, as well as you can. I will go instantly in quest of Mr Nightingale; and I hope to bring you good news."

Mrs Miller fell upon her knees and invoked all the blessings of heaven upon Mr Jones; to which she afterwards added the most passionate expressions of gratitude. He then departed to find Mr Nightingale, and the good woman returned to comfort her daughter, who was somewhat cheared at what her mother told her; and both joined in resounding the praises of Mr Jones.

CHAPTER VII.

The interview between Mr Jones and Mr Nightingale.

The good or evil we confer on others very often, I believe, recoils on ourselves. For as men of a benign disposition enjoy their own acts of beneficence equally with those to whom they are done, so there are scarce any natures so entirely diabolical, as to be capable of doing injuries, without paying themselves some pangs for the ruin which they bring on their fellow-creatures.

Mr Nightingale, at least, was not such a person. On the contrary, Jones found him in his new lodgings, sitting melancholy by the fire, and silently lamenting the unhappy situation in which he had placed poor Nancy. He no sooner saw his friend appear than he arose hastily to meet him; and after much congratulation said, "Nothing could be more opportune than this kind visit; for I was never more in the spleen in my life."

"I am sorry," answered Jones, "that I bring news very unlikely to relieve you: nay, what I am convinced must, of all other, shock you the most. However, it is necessary you should know it. Without further preface, then, I come to you, Mr Nightingale, from a worthy family, which you have involved in misery and ruin." Mr Nightingale changed colour at these words; but Jones, without regarding it, proceeded, in the liveliest manner, to paint the tragical story with which the reader was acquainted in the last chapter.

Nightingale never once interrupted the narration, though he discovered violent emotions at many parts of it. But when it was concluded, after fetching a deep sigh, he said, "What you tell me, my friend, affects me in the tenderest manner. Sure there never was so cursed an accident as the poor girl's betraying my letter. Her reputation might otherwise have been safe, and the affair might have remained a profound secret; and then the girl might have gone off never the worse; for many such things happen in this town: and if the husband should suspect a little, when it is too late, it will be his wiser conduct to conceal his suspicion both from his wife and the world."

"Indeed, my friend," answered Jones, "this could not have been the case with your poor Nancy. You have so entirely gained her affections, that it is the loss of you, and not of her reputation, which afflicts her, and will end in the destruction of her and her family." "Nay, for that matter, I promise you," cries Nightingale, "she hath my affections so absolutely, that my wife, whoever she is to be, will have very little share in them." "And is it possible then," said Jones, "you can think of deserting her?" "Why, what can I do?" answered the other. "Ask Miss Nancy," replied Jones warmly. "In the condition to which you have reduced her, I sincerely think she ought to determine what reparation you shall make her. Her interest alone, and not yours, ought to be your sole consideration. But if you ask me what you shall do, what can you do less," cries Jones, "than fulfil the expectations of her family, and her own? Nay, I sincerely tell you, they were mine too, ever since I first saw you together. You will pardon me if I presume on the friendship you have favoured me with, moved as I am with compassion for those poor creatures. But your own heart will best suggest to you, whether you have never intended, by your conduct, to persuade the mother, as well as the daughter, into an opinion, that you designed honourably: and if so, though there may have been no direct promise of marriage in the case, I will leave to your own good understanding, how far you are bound to proceed."

"Nay, I must not only confess what you have hinted," said Nightingale; "but I am afraid even that very promise you mention I have given." "And can you, after owning that," said Jones, "hesitate a moment?" "Consider, my friend," answered the other; "I know you are a man of honour, and would advise no one to act contrary to its rules; if there were no other objection, can I, after this publication of her disgrace, think of such an alliance with honour?" "Undoubtedly," replied Jones, "and the very best and truest honour, which is goodness, requires it of you. As you mention a scruple of this kind, you will give me leave to examine it. Can you with honour be guilty of having under false pretences deceived a young woman and her family, and of having by these means treacherously robbed her of her innocence? Can you, with honour, be the knowing, the wilful occasion, nay, the artful contriver of the ruin of a human being? Can you, with honour, destroy the fame, the peace, nay, probably, both the life and soul too, of this creature? Can honour bear the thought, that this creature is a tender, helpless, defenceless, young woman? A young woman, who loves, who doats on you, who dies for you; who hath placed the utmost confidence in your promises; and to that confidence hath sacrificed everything which is dear to her? Can honour support such contemplations as these a moment?"

"Common sense, indeed," said Nightingale, "warrants all you say; but yet you well know the opinion of the world is so contrary to it, that, was I to marry a whore, though my own, I should be ashamed of ever showing my face again."

"Fie upon it, Mr Nightingale!" said Jones, "do not call her by so ungenerous a name: when you promised to marry her she became your wife; and she hath sinned more against prudence than virtue. And what is this world which you would be ashamed to face but the vile, the foolish, and the profligate? Forgive me if I say such a shame must proceed from false modesty, which always attends false honour as its shadow.—But I am well assured there is not a man of real sense and goodness in the world who would not honour and applaud the action. But, admit no other would, would not your own heart, my friend, applaud it? And do not the warm, rapturous sensations, which we feel from the consciousness of an honest, noble, generous, benevolent action, convey more delight to the mind than the undeserved praise of millions? Set the alternative fairly before your eyes. On the one side, see this poor, unhappy, tender, believing girl, in the arms of her wretched mother, breathing her last. Hear her breaking heart in agonies, sighing out your name; and lamenting, rather than accusing, the cruelty which weighs her down to destruction. Paint to your imagination the circumstances of her fond despairing parent, driven to madness, or, perhaps, to death, by the loss of her lovely daughter. View the poor, helpless, orphan infant; and when your mind hath dwelt a moment only on such ideas, consider yourself as the cause of all the ruin of this poor, little, worthy, defenceless family. On the other side, consider yourself as relieving them from their temporary sufferings. Think with what joy, with what transports that lovely creature will fly to your arms. See her blood returning to her pale cheeks, her fire to her languid eyes, and raptures to her tortured breast. Consider the exultations of her mother, the happiness of all. Think of this little family made by one act of yours completely happy. Think of this alternative, and sure I am mistaken in my friend if it requires any long deliberation whether he will sink these wretches down for ever, or, by one generous, noble resolution, raise them all from the brink of misery and despair to the highest pitch of human happiness. Add to this but one consideration more; the consideration that it is your duty so to do—That the misery from which you will relieve these poor people is the misery which you yourself have wilfully brought upon them."

"O, my dear friend!" cries Nightingale, "I wanted not your eloquence to rouse me. I pity poor Nancy from my soul, and would willingly give anything in my power that no familiarities had ever passed between us. Nay, believe me, I had many struggles with my passion before I could prevail with myself to write that cruel letter, which hath caused all the misery in that unhappy family. If I had no inclinations to consult but my own, I would marry her to-morrow morning: I would, by heaven! but you will easily imagine how impossible it would be to prevail on my father to consent to such a match; besides, he hath provided another for me; and to-morrow, by his express command, I am to wait on the lady."

"I have not the honour to know your father," said Jones; "but, suppose he could be persuaded, would you yourself consent to the only means of preserving these poor people?" "As eagerly as I would pursue my happiness," answered Nightingale: "for I never shall find it in any other woman.—O, my dear friend! could you imagine what I have felt within these twelve hours for my poor girl, I am convinced she would not engross all your pity. Passion leads me only to her; and, if I had any foolish scruples of honour, you have fully satisfied them: could my father be induced to comply with my desires, nothing would be wanting to compleat my own happiness or that of my Nancy."

"Then I am resolved to undertake it," said Jones. "You must not be angry with me, in whatever light it may be necessary to set this affair, which, you may depend on it, could not otherwise be long hid from him: for things of this nature make a quick progress when once they get abroad, as this unhappily hath already. Besides, should any fatal accident follow, as upon my soul I am afraid will, unless immediately prevented, the public would ring of your name in a manner which, if your father hath common humanity, must offend him. If you will therefore tell me where I may find the old gentleman, I will not lose a moment in the business; which, while I pursue, you cannot do a more generous action than by paying a visit to the poor girl. You will find I have not exaggerated in the account I have given of the wretchedness of the family."

Nightingale immediately consented to the proposal; and now, having acquainted Jones with his father's lodging, and the coffee-house where he would most probably find him, he hesitated a moment, and then said, "My dear Tom, you are going to undertake an impossibility. If you knew my father you would never think of obtaining his consent.——Stay, there is one way—suppose you told him I was already married, it might be easier to reconcile him to the fact after it was done; and, upon my honour, I am so affected with what you have said, and I love my Nancy so passionately, I almost wish it was done, whatever might be the consequence."

Jones greatly approved the hint, and promised to pursue it. They then separated, Nightingale to visit his Nancy, and Jones in quest of the old gentleman.

CHAPTER VIII.

What passed between Jones and old Mr Nightingale; with the arrival of a person not yet mentioned in this history.

Notwithstanding the sentiment of the Roman satirist, which denies the divinity of fortune, and the opinion of Seneca to the same purpose; Cicero, who was, I believe, a wiser man than either of them, expressly holds the contrary; and certain it is, there are some incidents in life so very strange and unaccountable, that it seems to require more than human skill and foresight in producing them.

Of this kind was what now happened to Jones, who found Mr Nightingale the elder in so critical a minute, that Fortune, if she was really worthy all the worship she received at Rome, could not have contrived such another. In short, the old gentleman, and the father of the young lady whom he intended for his son, had been hard at it for many hours; and the latter was just now gone, and had left the former delighted with the thoughts that he had succeeded in a long contention, which had been between the two fathers of the future bride and bridegroom; in which both endeavoured to overreach the other, and, as it not rarely happens in such cases, both had retreated fully satisfied of having obtained the victory.

This gentleman, whom Mr Jones now visited, was what they call a man of the world; that is to say, a man who directs his conduct in this world as one who, being fully persuaded there is no other, is resolved to make the most of this. In his early years he had been bred to trade; but, having acquired a very good fortune, he had lately declined his business; or, to speak more properly, had changed it from dealing in goods, to dealing only in money, of which he had always a plentiful fund at command, and of which he knew very well how to make a very plentiful advantage, sometimes of the necessities of private men, and sometimes of those of the public. He had indeed conversed so entirely with money, that it may be almost doubted whether he imagined there was any other thing really existing in the world; this at least may be certainly averred, that he firmly believed nothing else to have any real value.

The reader will, I fancy, allow that Fortune could not have culled out a more improper person for Mr Jones to attack with any probability of success; nor could the whimsical lady have directed this attack at a more unseasonable time.

As money then was always uppermost in this gentleman's thoughts, so the moment he saw a stranger within his doors it immediately occurred to his imagination, that such stranger was either come to bring him money, or to fetch it from him. And according as one or other of these thoughts prevailed, he conceived a favourable or unfavourable idea of the person who approached him.

Unluckily for Jones, the latter of these was the ascendant at present; for as a young gentleman had visited him the day before, with a bill from his son for a play debt, he apprehended, at the first sight of Jones, that he was come on such another errand. Jones therefore had no sooner told him that he was come on his son's account than the old gentleman, being confirmed in his suspicion, burst forth into an exclamation, "That he would lose his labour." "Is it then possible, sir," answered Jones, "that you can guess my business?" "If I do guess it," replied the other, "I repeat again to you, you will lose your labour. What, I suppose you are one of those sparks who lead my son into all those scenes of riot and debauchery, which will be his destruction? but I shall pay no more of his bills, I promise you. I expect he will quit all such company for the future. If I had imagined otherwise, I should not have provided a wife for him; for I would be instrumental in the ruin of nobody." "How, sir," said Jones, "and was this lady of your providing?" "Pray, sir," answered the old gentleman, "how comes it to be any concern of yours?"— "Nay, dear sir," replied Jones, "be not offended that I interest myself in what regards your son's happiness, for whom I have so great an honour and value. It was upon that very account I came to wait upon you. I can't express the satisfaction you have given me by what you say; for I do assure you your son is a person for whom I have the highest honour.—Nay, sir, it is not easy to express the esteem I have for you; who could be so generous, so good, so kind, so indulgent to provide such a match for your son; a woman, who, I dare swear, will make him one of the happiest men upon earth."

There is scarce anything which so happily introduces men to our good liking, as having conceived some alarm at their first appearance; when once those apprehensions begin to vanish we soon forget the fears which they occasioned, and look on ourselves as indebted for our present ease to those very persons who at first raised our fears.

Thus it happened to Nightingale, who no sooner found that Jones had no demand on him, as he suspected, than he began to be pleased with his presence. "Pray, good sir," said he, "be pleased to sit down. I do not remember to have ever had the pleasure of seeing you before; but if you are a friend of my son, and have anything to say concerning this young lady, I shall be glad to hear you. As to her making him happy, it will be his own fault if she doth not. I have discharged my duty, in taking care of the main article. She will bring him a fortune capable of making any reasonable, prudent, sober man, happy." "Undoubtedly," cries Jones, "for she is in herself a fortune; so beautiful, so genteel, so sweet-tempered, and so well-educated; she is indeed a most accomplished young lady; sings admirably well, and hath a most delicate hand at the harpsichord." "I did not know any of these matters," answered the old gentleman, "for I never saw the lady: but I do not like her the worse for what you tell me; and I am the better pleased with her father for not laying any stress on these qualifications in our bargain. I shall always think it a proof of his understanding. A silly fellow would have brought in these articles as an addition to her fortune; but, to give him his due, he never mentioned any such matter; though to be sure they are no disparagements to a woman." "I do assure you, sir," cries Jones, "she hath them all in the most eminent degree: for my part, I own I was afraid you might have been a little backward, a little less inclined to the match; for your son told me you had never seen the lady; therefore I came, sir, in that case, to entreat you, to conjure you, as you value the happiness of your son, not to be averse to his match with a woman who hath not only all the good qualities I have mentioned, but many more."—"If that was your business, sir," said the old gentleman, "we are both obliged to you; and you may be perfectly easy; for I give you my word I was very well satisfied with her fortune." "Sir," answered Jones, "I honour you every moment more and more. To be so easily satisfied, so very moderate on that account, is a proof of the soundness of your understanding, as well as the nobleness of your mind."——"Not so very moderate, young gentleman, not so very moderate," answered the father.—"Still more and more noble," replied Jones; "and give me leave to add, sensible: for sure it is little less than madness to consider money as the sole foundation of happiness. Such a woman as this with her little, her nothing of a fortune"—"I find," cries the old gentleman, "you have a pretty just opinion of money, my friend, or else you are better acquainted with the person of the lady than with her circumstances. Why, pray, what fortune do you imagine this lady to have?" "What fortune?" cries Jones, "why, too contemptible a one to be named for your son."—"Well, well, well," said the other, "perhaps he might have done better."—"That I deny," said Jones, "for she is one of the best of women."—"Ay, ay, but in point of fortune I mean," answered the other. "And yet, as to that now, how much do you imagine your friend is to have?"—"How much?" cries Jones, "how much? Why, at the utmost, perhaps £200." "Do you mean to banter me, young gentleman?" said the father, a little angry. "No, upon my soul," answered Jones, "I am in earnest: nay, I believe I have gone to the utmost farthing. If I do the lady an injury, I ask her pardon." "Indeed you do," cries the father; "I am certain she hath fifty times that sum, and she shall produce fifty to that before I consent that she shall marry my son." "Nay," said Jones, "it is too late to talk of consent now; if she had not fifty farthings your son is married."—"My son married!" answered the old gentleman, with surprize. "Nay," said Jones, "I thought you was unacquainted with it." "My son married to Miss Harris!" answered he again. "To Miss Harris!" said Jones; "no, sir; to Miss Nancy Miller, the daughter of Mrs Miller, at whose house he lodged; a young lady, who, though her mother is reduced to let lodgings—"—"Are you bantering, or are you in earnest?" cries the father, with a most solemn voice. "Indeed, sir," answered Jones, "I scorn the character of a banterer. I came to you in most serious earnest, imagining, as I find true, that your son had never dared acquaint you with a match so much inferior to him in point of fortune, though the reputation of the lady will suffer it no longer to remain a secret."

While the father stood like one struck suddenly dumb at this news, a gentleman came into the room, and saluted him by the name of brother.

But though these two were in consanguinity so nearly related, they were in their dispositions almost the opposites to each other. The brother who now arrived had likewise been bred to trade, in which he no sooner saw himself worth £6000 than he purchased a small estate with the greatest part of it, and retired into the country; where he married the daughter of an unbeneficed clergyman; a young lady, who, though she had neither beauty nor fortune, had recommended herself to his choice entirely by her good humour, of which she possessed a very large share.

With this woman he had, during twenty-five years, lived a life more resembling the model which certain poets ascribe to the golden age, than any of those patterns which are furnished by the present times. By her he had four children, but none of them arrived at maturity, except only one daughter, whom, in vulgar language, he and his wife had spoiled; that is, had educated with the utmost tenderness and fondness, which she returned to such a degree, that she had actually refused a very extraordinary match with a gentleman a little turned of forty, because she could not bring herself to part with her parents.

The young lady whom Mr Nightingale had intended for his son was a near neighbour of his brother, and an acquaintance of his niece; and in reality it was upon the account of his projected match that he was now come to town; not, indeed, to forward, but to dissuade his brother from a purpose which he conceived would inevitably ruin his nephew; for he foresaw no other event from a union with Miss Harris, notwithstanding the largeness of her fortune, as neither her person nor mind seemed to him to promise any kind of matrimonial felicity: for she was very tall, very thin, very ugly, very affected, very silly, and very ill-natured.

His brother, therefore, no sooner mentioned the marriage of his nephew with Miss Miller, than he exprest the utmost satisfaction; and when the father had very bitterly reviled his son, and pronounced sentence of beggary upon him, the uncle began in the following manner:

"If you was a little cooler, brother, I would ask you whether you love your son for his sake or for your own. You would answer, I suppose, and so I suppose you think, for his sake; and doubtless it is his happiness which you intended in the marriage you proposed for him.

"Now, brother, to prescribe rules of happiness to others hath always appeared to me very absurd, and to insist on doing this, very tyrannical. It is a vulgar error, I know; but it is, nevertheless, an error. And if this be absurd in other things, it is mostly so in the affair of marriage, the happiness of which depends entirely on the affection which subsists between the parties.

"I have therefore always thought it unreasonable in parents to desire to chuse for their children on this occasion; since to force affection is an impossible attempt; nay, so much doth love abhor force, that I know not whether, through an unfortunate but uncurable perverseness in our natures, it may not be even impatient of persuasion.

"It is, however, true that, though a parent will not, I think, wisely prescribe, he ought to be consulted on this occasion; and, in strictness, perhaps, should at least have a negative voice. My nephew, therefore, I own, in marrying, without asking your advice, hath been guilty of a fault. But, honestly speaking, brother, have you not a little promoted this fault? Have not your frequent declarations on this subject given him a moral certainty of your refusal, where there was any deficiency in point of fortune? Nay, doth not your present anger arise solely from that deficiency? And if he hath failed in his duty here, did you not as much exceed that authority when you absolutely bargained with him for a woman, without his knowledge, whom you yourself never saw, and whom, if you had seen and known as well as I, it must have been madness in you to have ever thought of bringing her into your family?

"Still I own my nephew in a fault; but surely it is not an unpardonable fault. He hath acted indeed without your consent, in a matter in which he ought to have asked it, but it is in a matter in which his interest is principally concerned; you yourself must and will acknowledge that you consulted his interest only, and if he unfortunately differed from you, and hath been mistaken in his notion of happiness, will you, brother, if you love your son, carry him still wider from the point? Will you increase the ill consequences of his simple choice? Will you endeavour to make an event certain misery to him, which may accidentally prove so? In a word, brother, because he hath put it out of your power to make his circumstances as affluent as you would, will you distress them as much as you can?"

By the force of the true Catholic faith St Anthony won upon the fishes. Orpheus and Amphion went a little farther, and by the charms of music enchanted things merely inanimate. Wonderful, both! but neither history nor fable have ever yet ventured to record an instance of any one, who, by force of argument and reason, hath triumphed over habitual avarice.

Mr Nightingale, the father, instead of attempting to answer his brother, contented himself with only observing, that they had always differed in their sentiments concerning the education of their children. "I wish," said he, "brother, you would have confined your care to your own daughter, and never have troubled yourself with my son, who hath, I believe, as little profited by your precepts, as by your example." For young Nightingale was his uncle's godson, and had lived more with him than with his father. So that the uncle had often declared he loved his nephew almost equally with his own child.

Jones fell into raptures with this good gentleman; and when, after much persuasion, they found the father grew still more and more irritated, instead of appeased, Jones conducted the uncle to his nephew at the house of Mrs Miller.

CHAPTER IX.

Containing strange matters.

At his return to his lodgings, Jones found the situation of affairs greatly altered from what they had been in at his departure. The mother, the two daughters, and young Mr Nightingale, were now sat down to supper together, when the uncle was, at his own desire, introduced without any ceremony into the company, to all of whom he was well known; for he had several times visited his nephew at that house.

The old gentleman immediately walked up to Miss Nancy, saluted and wished her joy, as he did afterwards the mother and the other sister; and lastly, he paid the proper compliments to his nephew, with the same good humour and courtesy, as if his nephew had married his equal or superior in fortune, with all the previous requisites first performed.

Miss Nancy and her supposed husband both turned pale, and looked rather foolish than otherwise upon the occasion; but Mrs Miller took the first opportunity of withdrawing; and, having sent for Jones into the dining-room, she threw herself at his feet, and in a most passionate flood of tears, called him her good angel, the preserver of her poor little family, with many other respectful and endearing appellations, and made him every acknowledgment which the highest benefit can extract from the most grateful heart.

After the first gust of her passion was a little over, which she declared, if she had not vented, would have burst her, she proceeded to inform Mr Jones that all matters were settled between Mr Nightingale and her daughter, and that they were to be married the next morning; at which Mr Jones having expressed much pleasure, the poor woman fell again into a fit of joy and thanksgiving, which he at length with difficulty silenced, and prevailed on her to return with him back to the company, whom they found in the same good humour in which they had left them.

This little society now past two or three very agreeable hours together, in which the uncle, who was a very great lover of his bottle, had so well plyed his nephew, that this latter, though not drunk, began to be somewhat flustered; and now Mr Nightingale, taking the old gentleman with him upstairs into the apartment he had lately occupied, unbosomed himself as follows:—

"As you have been always the best and kindest of uncles to me, and as you have shown such unparalleled goodness in forgiving this match, which to be sure may be thought a little improvident, I should never forgive myself if I attempted to deceive you in anything." He then confessed the truth, and opened the whole affair.

"How, Jack?" said the old gentleman, "and are you really then not married to this young woman?" "No, upon my honour," answered Nightingale, "I have told you the simple truth." "My dear boy," cries the uncle, kissing him, "I am heartily glad to hear it. I never was better pleased in my life. If you had been married I should have assisted you as much as was in my power to have made the best of a bad matter; but there is a great difference between considering a thing which is already done and irrecoverable, and that which is yet to do. Let your reason have fair play, Jack, and you will see this match in so foolish and preposterous a light, that there will be no need of any dissuasive arguments." "How, sir?" replies young Nightingale, "is there this difference between having already done an act, and being in honour engaged to do it?" "Pugh!" said the uncle, "honour is a creature of the world's making, and the world hath the power of a creator over it, and may govern and direct it as they please. Now you well know how trivial these breaches of contract are thought; even the grossest make but the wonder and conversation of a day. Is there a man who afterwards will be more backward in giving you his sister, or daughter? or is there any sister or daughter who would be more backward to receive you? Honour is not concerned in these engagements." "Pardon me, dear sir," cries Nightingale, "I can never think so; and not only honour, but conscience and humanity, are concerned. I am well satisfied, that, was I now to disappoint the young creature, her death would be the consequence, and I should look upon myself as her murderer; nay, as her murderer by the cruellest of all methods, by breaking her heart." "Break her heart, indeed! no, no, Jack," cries the uncle, "the hearts of women are not so soon broke; they are tough, boy, they are tough." "But, sir," answered Nightingale, "my own affections are engaged, and I never could be happy with any other woman. How often have I heard you say, that children should be always suffered to chuse for themselves, and that you would let my cousin Harriet do so?" "Why, ay," replied the old gentleman, "so I would have them; but then I would have them chuse wisely.—Indeed, Jack, you must and shall leave the girl."——"Indeed, uncle," cries the other, "I must and will have her." "You will, young gentleman;" said the uncle; "I did not expect such a word from you. I should not wonder if you had used such language to your father, who hath always treated you like a dog, and kept you at the distance which a tyrant preserves over his subjects; but I, who have lived with you upon an equal footing, might surely expect better usage: but I know how to account for it all: it is all owing to your preposterous education, in which I have had too little share. There is my daughter, now, whom I have brought up as my friend, never doth anything without my advice, nor ever refuses to take it when I give it her." "You have never yet given her advice in an affair of this kind," said Nightingale; "for I am greatly mistaken in my cousin, if she would be very ready to obey even your most positive commands in abandoning her inclinations." "Don't abuse my girl," answered the old gentleman with some emotion; "don't abuse my Harriet. I have brought her up to have no inclinations contrary to my own. By suffering her to do whatever she pleases, I have enured her to a habit of being pleased to do whatever I like." "Pardon, me, sir," said Nightingale, "I have not the least design to reflect on my cousin, for whom I have the greatest esteem; and indeed I am convinced you will never put her to so severe a tryal, or lay such hard commands on her as you would do on me.—But, dear sir, let us return to the company; for they will begin to be uneasy at our long absence. I must beg one favour of my dear uncle, which is that he would not say anything to shock the poor girl or her mother." "Oh! you need not fear me," answered he, "I understand myself too well to affront women; so I will readily grant you that favour; and in return I must expect another of you." "There are but few of your commands, sir," said Nightingale, "which I shall not very chearfully obey." "Nay, sir, I ask nothing," said the uncle, "but the honour of your company home to my lodging, that I may reason the case a little more fully with you; for I would, if possible, have the satisfaction of preserving my family, notwithstanding the headstrong folly of my brother, who, in his own opinion, is the wisest man in the world."

Nightingale, who well knew his uncle to be as headstrong as his father, submitted to attend him home, and then they both returned back into the room, where the old gentleman promised to carry himself with the same decorum which he had before maintained.

CHAPTER X.

A short chapter, which concludes the book.

The long absence of the uncle and nephew had occasioned some disquiet in the minds of all whom they had left behind them; and the more, as, during the preceding dialogue, the uncle had more than once elevated his voice, so as to be heard downstairs; which, though they could not distinguish what he said, had caused some evil foreboding in Nancy and her mother, and, indeed, even in Jones himself.

When the good company, therefore, again assembled, there was a visible alteration in all their faces; and the good-humour which, at their last meeting, universally shone forth in every countenance, was now changed into a much less agreeable aspect. It was a change, indeed, common enough to the weather in this climate, from sunshine to clouds, from June to December.

This alteration was not, however, greatly remarked by any present; for as they were all now endeavouring to conceal their own thoughts, and to act a part, they became all too busily engaged in the scene to be spectators of it. Thus neither the uncle nor nephew saw any symptoms of suspicion in the mother or daughter; nor did the mother or daughter remark the overacted complacence of the old man, nor the counterfeit satisfaction which grinned in the features of the young one.

Something like this, I believe, frequently happens, where the whole attention of two friends being engaged in the part which each is to act, in order to impose on the other, neither sees nor suspects the arts practised against himself; and thus the thrust of both (to borrow no improper metaphor on the occasion) alike takes place.

From the same reason it is no unusual thing for both parties to be overreached in a bargain, though the one must be always the greater loser; as was he who sold a blind horse, and received a bad note in payment.

Our company in about half an hour broke up, and the uncle carried off his nephew; but not before the latter had assured Miss Nancy, in a whisper, that he would attend her early in the morning, and fulfil all his engagements.

Jones, who was the least concerned in this scene, saw the most. He did indeed suspect the very fact; for, besides observing the great alteration in the behaviour of the uncle, the distance he assumed, and his overstrained civility to Miss Nancy; the carrying off a bridegroom from his bride at that time of night was so extraordinary a proceeding that it could be accounted for only by imagining that young

Nightingale had revealed the whole truth, which the apparent openness of his temper, and his being flustered with liquor, made too probable.

While he was reasoning with himself, whether he should acquaint these poor people with his suspicion, the maid of the house informed him that a gentlewoman desired to speak with him.——He went immediately out, and, taking the candle from the maid, ushered his visitant upstairs, who, in the person of Mrs Honour, acquainted him with such dreadful news concerning his Sophia, that he immediately lost all consideration for every other person; and his whole stock of compassion was entirely swallowed up in reflections on his own misery, and on that of his unfortunate angel.

What this dreadful matter was, the reader will be informed, after we have first related the many preceding steps which produced it, and those will be the subject of the following book.

BOOK XV.

IN WHICH THE HISTORY ADVANCES ABOUT TWO DAYS.

CHAPTER I.

Too short to need a preface.

There are a set of religious, or rather moral writers, who teach that virtue is the certain road to happiness, and vice to misery, in this world. A very wholesome and comfortable doctrine, and to which we have but one objection, namely, that it is not true.

Indeed, if by virtue these writers mean the exercise of those cardinal virtues, which like good housewives stay at home, and mind only the business of their own family, I shall very readily concede the point; for so surely do all these contribute and lead to happiness, that I could almost wish, in violation of all the antient and modern sages, to call them rather by the name of wisdom, than by that of virtue; for, with regard to this life, no system, I conceive, was ever wiser than that of the antient Epicureans, who held this wisdom to constitute the chief good; nor foolisher than that of their opposites, those modern epicures, who place all felicity in the abundant gratification of every sensual appetite.

But if by virtue is meant (as I almost think it ought) a certain relative quality, which is always busying itself without-doors, and seems as much interested in pursuing the good of others as its own; I cannot so easily agree that this is the surest way to human happiness; because I am afraid we must then include poverty and contempt, with all the mischiefs which backbiting, envy, and ingratitude, can bring on mankind, in our idea of happiness; nay, sometimes perhaps we shall be obliged to wait upon the said happiness to a jail; since many by the above virtue have brought themselves thither.

I have not now leisure to enter upon so large a field of speculation, as here seems opening upon me; my design was to wipe off a doctrine that lay in my way; since, while Mr Jones was acting the most virtuous part imaginable in labouring to preserve his fellow-creatures from destruction, the devil, or some other evil spirit, one perhaps cloathed in human flesh, was hard at work to make him completely miserable in the ruin of his Sophia.

This therefore would seem an exception to the above rule, if indeed it was a rule; but as we have in our voyage through life seen so many other exceptions to it, we chuse to dispute the doctrine on which it is founded, which we don't apprehend to be Christian, which we are convinced is not true, and which is indeed destructive of one of the noblest arguments that reason alone can furnish for the belief of immortality.

But as the reader's curiosity (if he hath any) must be now awake, and hungry, we shall provide to feed it as fast as we can.

CHAPTER II.

In which is opened a very black design against Sophia.

I remember a wise old gentleman who used to say, "When children are doing nothing, they are doing mischief." I will not enlarge this quaint saying to the most beautiful part of the creation in general; but so far I may be allowed, that when the effects of female jealousy do not appear openly in their proper colours of rage and fury, we may suspect that mischievous passion to be at work privately, and attempting to undermine, what it doth not attack above-ground.

This was exemplified in the conduct of Lady Bellaston, who, under all the smiles which she wore in her countenance, concealed much indignation against Sophia; and as she plainly saw that this young lady stood between her and the full indulgence of her desires, she resolved to get rid of her by some means or other; nor was it long before a very favourable opportunity of accomplishing this presented itself to her.

The reader may be pleased to remember, that when Sophia was thrown into that consternation at the playhouse, by the wit and humour of a set of young gentlemen who call themselves the town, we informed him, that she had put herself under the protection of a young nobleman, who had very safely conducted her to her chair.

This nobleman, who frequently visited Lady Bellaston, had more than once seen Sophia there, since her arrival in town, and had conceived a very great liking to her; which liking, as beauty never looks more amiable than in distress, Sophia had in this fright so encreased, that he might now, without any great impropriety, be said to be actually in love with her.

It may easily be believed, that he would not suffer so handsome an occasion of improving his acquaintance with the beloved object as now offered itself to elapse, when even good breeding alone might have prompted him to pay her a visit.

The next morning therefore, after this accident, he waited on Sophia, with the usual compliments, and hopes that she had received no harm from her last night's adventure.

As love, like fire, when once thoroughly kindled, is soon blown into a flame, Sophia in a very short time compleated her conquest. Time now flew away unperceived, and the noble lord had been two hours in company with the lady, before it entered into his head that he had made too long a visit. Though this circumstance alone would have alarmed Sophia, who was somewhat more a mistress of computation at present; she had indeed much more pregnant evidence from the eyes of her lover of what past within his bosom; nay, though he did not make any open declaration of his passion, yet many of his expressions were rather too warm, and too tender, to have been imputed to complacence, even in the age when such complacence was in fashion; the very reverse of which is well known to be the reigning mode at present.

Lady Bellaston had been apprized of his lordship's visit at his first arrival; and the length of it very well satisfied her, that things went as she wished, and as indeed she had suspected the second time she saw this young couple together. This business, she rightly I think concluded, that she should by no means forward by mixing in the company while they were together; she therefore ordered her servants, that when my lord was going, they should tell him she desired to speak with him; and employed the intermediate time in meditating how best to accomplish a scheme, which she made no doubt but his lordship would very readily embrace the execution of.

Lord Fellamar (for that was the title of this young nobleman) was no sooner introduced to her ladyship, than she attacked him in the following strain: "Bless me, my lord, are you here yet? I thought my servants had made a mistake, and let you go away; and I wanted to see you about an affair of some importance."——"Indeed, Lady Bellaston," said he, "I don't wonder you are astonished at the length of my visit; for I have staid above two hours, and I did not think I had staid above half-a-one."——"What am I to conclude from thence, my lord?" said she. "The company must be very agreeable which can make time slide away so very deceitfully."——"Upon my honour," said he, "the most agreeable I ever saw. Pray tell me, Lady Bellaston, who is this blazing star which you have produced among us all of a sudden?"——"What blazing star, my lord?" said she, affecting a surprize. "I mean," said he, "the lady I saw here the other day, whom I had last night in my arms at the playhouse, and to whom I have been making that unreasonable visit."——"O, my cousin Western!" said she; "why, that blazing star, my lord, is the daughter of a country booby squire, and hath been in town about a fortnight, for the first time."——"Upon my soul," said he, "I should swear she had been bred up in a court; for besides her beauty, I never saw anything so genteel, so sensible, so polite."——"O brave!" cries the lady, "my cousin hath you, I find."——"Upon my honour," answered he, "I wish she had; for I am in love with her to distraction."——"Nay, my lord," said she, "it is not wishing yourself very ill neither, for she is a very great fortune: I assure you she is an only child, and her father's estate is a good £3000 a-year." "Then I can assure you, madam," answered the lord, "I think her the best match in England." "Indeed, my lord," replied she, "if you like her, I heartily wish you had her." "If you think so kindly of me, madam," said he, "as she is a relation of yours, will you do me the honour to propose it to her father?" "And are you really then in earnest?" cries the lady, with an affected gravity. "I hope, madam," answered he, "you have a better opinion of me, than to imagine I would jest with your ladyship in an affair of this kind." "Indeed, then," said the lady, "I will most readily propose your lordship to her father; and I can, I believe, assure you of his joyful acceptance of the proposal; but there is a bar, which I am almost ashamed to mention; and yet it is one you will never be able to conquer. You have a rival, my lord, and a rival who, though I blush to name him, neither you, nor all the world, will ever be able to conquer." "Upon my word, Lady Bellaston," cries he, "you have struck a damp to my heart, which hath almost deprived me of being." "Fie, my lord," said she, "I should rather hope I had struck fire into you. A lover, and talk of damps in your heart! I rather imagined you would have asked your rival's name, that you might have immediately entered the lists with him." "I promise you, madam," answered he, "there are very few things I would not undertake for your charming cousin; but pray, who is this happy man?"—"Why, he is," said she, "what I am sorry to say most happy men with us are, one of the lowest fellows in the world. He is a beggar, a bastard, a foundling, a fellow in meaner circumstances than one of your lordship's footmen." "And is it possible," cried he, "that a young creature with such perfections should think of bestowing herself so unworthily?" "Alas! my lord," answered she, "consider the country—the bane of all young women is the country. There they learn a set of romantic notions of love, and I know not what folly, which this town and good company can scarce eradicate in a whole winter." "Indeed, madam," replied my lord, "your cousin is of too immense a value to be thrown away; such ruin as this must be prevented." "Alas!" cries she, "my lord, how can it be prevented? The family have already done all in their power; but the girl is, I think, intoxicated, and nothing less than ruin will content her. And to deal more openly with you, I expect every day to hear she is run away with him." "What you tell me, Lady Bellaston," answered his lordship, "affects me most tenderly, and only raises my compassion, instead of lessening my adoration of your cousin. Some means must be found to preserve so inestimable a jewel. Hath your ladyship endeavoured to reason with her?" Here the lady affected a laugh, and cried, "My dear lord, sure you know us better than to talk of reasoning a young woman out of her inclinations? These inestimable jewels are as deaf as the jewels they wear: time, my lord, time is the only medicine to cure their folly; but this is a medicine which I am certain she will not take; nay, I live in hourly horrors on her account. In short, nothing but violent methods will do." "What is to be done?" cries my lord; "what methods are to be taken?—Is there any method upon earth?—Oh! Lady Bellaston! there is nothing which I would not undertake for such a reward."——"I really know not," answered the lady, after a pause; and then pausing again, she cried out—"Upon my soul, I am at my wit's end on this girl's account.—If she can be preserved, something must be done immediately; and, as I say, nothing but violent methods will do.——If your lordship hath really this attachment to my cousin (and to do her justice, except in this silly inclination, of which she will soon see her folly, she is every way deserving), I think there may be one way, indeed, it is a very disagreeable one, and what I am almost afraid to think of.—It requires a great spirit, I promise you." "I am not conscious, madam," said he, "of any defect there; nor am I, I hope, suspected of any such. It must be an egregious defect indeed, which could make me backward on this occasion." "Nay, my lord," answered she, "I am so far from doubting you, I am much more inclined to doubt my own courage; for I must run a monstrous risque. In short, I must place such a confidence in your honour as a wise woman will scarce ever place in a man on any consideration." In this point likewise my lord very well satisfied her; for his reputation was extremely clear, and common fame did him no more than justice, in speaking well of him. "Well, then," said she, "my lord,—I—I vow, I can't bear the apprehension of it.—No, it must not be.——At least every other method shall be tried. Can you get rid of your engagements, and dine here to-day? Your lordship will have an opportunity of seeing a little more of Miss Western.—I promise you we have no time to lose. Here will be nobody but Lady Betty, and Miss Eagle, and Colonel Hampsted, and Tom Edwards; they will all go soon—and I shall be at home to nobody. Then your lordship may be a little more explicit. Nay, I will contrive some method to convince you of her attachment to this fellow." My lord made proper compliments, accepted the invitation, and then they parted to dress, it being now past three in the morning, or to reckon by the old style, in the afternoon.

CHAPTER III.

A further explanation of the foregoing design.

Though the reader may have long since concluded Lady Bellaston to be a member (and no inconsiderable one) of the great world; she was in reality a very considerable member of the little world; by which appellation was distinguished a very worthy and honourable society which not long since flourished in this kingdom.

Among other good principles upon which this society was founded, there was one very remarkable; for, as it was a rule of an honourable club of heroes, who assembled at the close of the late war, that all the members should every day fight once at least; so 'twas in this, that every member should, within the twenty-four hours, tell at least one merry fib, which was to be propagated by all the brethren and sisterhood.

Many idle stories were told about this society, which from a certain quality may be, perhaps not unjustly, supposed to have come from the society themselves. As, that the devil was the president; and that he sat in person in an elbow-chair at the upper end of the table; but, upon very strict enquiry, I find there is not the least truth in any of those tales, and that the assembly consisted in reality of a set of very good sort of people, and the fibs which they propagated were of a harmless kind, and tended only to produce mirth and good humour.

Edwards was likewise a member of this comical society. To him therefore Lady Bellaston applied as a proper instrument for her purpose, and furnished him with a fib, which he was to vent whenever the lady gave him her cue; and this was not to be till the evening, when all the company but Lord Fellamar and himself were gone, and while they were engaged in a rubber at whist.

To this time then, which was between seven and eight in the evening, we will convey our reader; when Lady Bellaston, Lord Fellamar, Miss Western, and Tom, being engaged at whist, and in the last game of their rubbers, Tom received his cue from Lady Bellaston, which was, "I protest, Tom, you are grown intolerable lately; you used to tell us all the news of the town, and now you know no more of the world than if you lived out of it."

Mr Edwards then began as follows: "The fault is not mine, madam: it lies in the dulness of the age, that doth nothing worth talking of.——O la! though now I think on't there hath a terrible accident befallen poor Colonel Wilcox.——Poor

Ned.——You know him, my lord, everybody knows him; faith! I am very much concerned for him."

"What is it, pray?" says Lady Bellaston.

"Why, he hath killed a man this morning in a duel, that's all."

His lordship, who was not in the secret, asked gravely, whom he had killed? To which Edwards answered, "A young fellow we none of us know; a Somersetshire lad just came to town, one Jones his name is; a near relation of one Mr Allworthy, of whom your lordship I believe hath heard. I saw the lad lie dead in a coffee-house.—Upon my soul, he is one of the finest corpses I ever saw in my life!"

Sophia, who had just began to deal as Tom had mentioned that a man was killed, stopt her hand, and listened with attention (for all stories of that kind affected her), but no sooner had he arrived at the latter part of the story than she began to deal again; and having dealt three cards to one, and seven to another, and ten to a third, at last dropt the rest from her hand, and fell back in her chair.

The company behaved as usually on these occasions. The usual disturbance ensued, the usual assistance was summoned, and Sophia at last, as it is usual, returned again to life, and was soon after, at her earnest desire, led to her own apartment; where, at my lord's request, Lady Bellaston acquainted her with the truth, attempted to carry it off as a jest of her own, and comforted her with repeated assurances, that neither his lordship nor Tom, though she had taught him the story, were in the true secret of the affair.

There was no farther evidence necessary to convince Lord Fellamar how justly the case had been represented to him by Lady Bellaston; and now, at her return into the room, a scheme was laid between these two noble persons, which, though it appeared in no very heinous light to his lordship (as he faithfully promised, and faithfully resolved too, to make the lady all the subsequent amends in his power by marriage), yet many of our readers, we doubt not, will see with just detestation.

The next evening at seven was appointed for the fatal purpose, when Lady Bellaston undertook that Sophia should be alone, and his lordship should be introduced to her. The whole family were to be regulated for the purpose, most of the servants despatched out of the house; and for Mrs Honour, who, to prevent suspicion, was to be left with her mistress till his lordship's arrival, Lady Bellaston herself was to engage her in an apartment as distant as possible from the scene of the intended mischief, and out of the hearing of Sophia.

Matters being thus agreed on, his lordship took his leave, and her ladyship retired to rest, highly pleased with a project, of which she had no reason to doubt the success, and which promised so effectually to remove Sophia from being any further obstruction to her amour with Jones, by a means of which she should never appear to be guilty, even if the fact appeared to the world; but this she made no doubt of preventing by huddling up a marriage, to which she thought the ravished Sophia would easily be brought to consent, and at which all the rest of her family would rejoice.

But affairs were not in so quiet a situation in the bosom of the other conspirator; his mind was tost in all the distracting anxiety so nobly described by Shakespear—

> "Between the acting of a dreadful thing,
> And the first motion, all the interim is
> Like a phantasma, or a hideous dream;
> The genius and the mortal instruments
> Are then in council; and the state of man,
> Like to a little kingdom, suffers then
> The nature of an insurrection."——

Though the violence of his passion had made him eagerly embrace the first hint of this design, especially as it came from a relation of the lady, yet when that friend to reflection, a pillow, had placed the action itself in all its natural black colours before his eyes, with all the consequences which must, and those which might probably attend it, his resolution began to abate, or rather indeed to go over to the other side; and after a long conflict, which lasted a whole night, between honour and appetite, the former at length prevailed, and he determined to wait on Lady Bellaston, and to relinquish the design.

Lady Bellaston was in bed, though very late in the morning, and Sophia sitting by her bed-side, when the servant acquainted her that Lord Fellamar was below in the parlour; upon which her ladyship desired him to stay, and that she would see him presently; but the servant was no sooner departed than poor Sophia began to intreat her cousin not to encourage the visits of that odious lord (so she called him, though a little unjustly) upon her account. "I see his design," said she; "for he made downright love to me yesterday morning; but as I am resolved never to admit it, I beg your ladyship not to leave us alone together any more, and to order the servants that, if he enquires for me, I may be always denied to him."

"La! child," says Lady Bellaston, "you country girls have nothing but sweethearts in your head; you fancy every man who is civil to you is making love. He is one of the most gallant young fellows about town, and I am convinced means no more than a little gallantry. Make love to you indeed! I wish with all my heart he would, and you must be an arrant mad woman to refuse him."

"But as I shall certainly be that mad woman," cries Sophia, "I hope his visits shall not be intruded upon me."

"O child!" said Lady Bellaston, "you need not be so fearful; if you resolve to run away with that Jones, I know no person who can hinder you."

"Upon my honour, madam," cries Sophia, "your ladyship injures me. I will never run away with any man; nor will I ever marry contrary to my father's inclinations."

"Well, Miss Western," said the lady, "if you are not in a humour to see company this morning, you may retire to your own apartment; for I am not frightened at his lordship, and must send for him up into my dressing-room."

Sophia thanked her ladyship, and withdrew; and presently afterwards Fellamar was admitted upstairs.

CHAPTER IV.

By which it will appear how dangerous an advocate a lady is when she applies her eloquence to an ill purpose.

When Lady Bellaston heard the young lord's scruples, she treated them with the same disdain with which one of those sages of the law, called Newgate solicitors, treats the qualms of conscience in a young witness. "My dear lord," said she, "you certainly want a cordial. I must send to Lady Edgely for one of her best drams. Fie upon it! have more resolution. Are you frightened by the word rape? Or are you apprehensive——? Well! if the story of Helen was modern, I should think it unnatural. I mean the behaviour of Paris, not the fondness of the lady; for all women love a man of spirit. There is another story of the Sabine ladies—and that too, I thank heaven, is very antient. Your lordship, perhaps, will admire my reading; but I think Mr Hook tells us, they made tolerable good wives afterwards. I fancy few of my married acquaintance were ravished by their husbands." "Nay, dear Lady Bellaston," cried he, "don't ridicule me in this manner." "Why, my good lord," answered she, "do you think any woman in England would not laugh at you in her heart, whatever prudery she might wear in her countenance?——You force me to use a strange kind of language, and to betray my sex most abominably; but I am contented with knowing my intentions are good, and that I am endeavouring to serve my cousin; for I think you will make her a husband notwithstanding this; or, upon my soul, I would not even persuade her to fling herself away upon an empty title. She should not upbraid me hereafter with having lost a man of spirit; for that his enemies allow this poor young fellow to be."

Let those who have had the satisfaction of hearing reflections of this kind from a wife or a mistress, declare whether they are at all sweetened by coming from a female tongue. Certain it is, they sunk deeper into his lordship than anything which Demosthenes or Cicero could have said on the occasion.

Lady Bellaston, perceiving she had fired the young lord's pride, began now, like a true orator, to rouse other passions to its assistance. "My lord," says she, in a graver voice, "you will be pleased to remember, you mentioned this matter to me first; for I would not appear to you in the light of one who is endeavouring to put off my cousin upon you. Fourscore thousand pounds do not stand in need of an advocate to recommend them." "Nor doth Miss Western," said he, "require any recommendation from her fortune; for, in my opinion, no woman ever had half her charms." "Yes, yes, my lord," replied the lady, looking in the glass, "there have been women with more than half her charms, I assure you; not that I need lessen her on that account: she is a most delicious girl, that's certain; and within these few hours she will be in the arms of one, who surely doth not deserve her, though I will give him his due, I believe he is truly a man of spirit."

"I hope so, madam," said my lord; "though I must own he doth not deserve her; for, unless heaven or your ladyship disappoint me, she shall within that time be in mine."

"Well spoken, my lord," answered the lady; "I promise you no disappointment shall happen from my side; and within this week I am convinced I shall call your lordship my cousin in public."

The remainder of this scene consisted entirely of raptures, excuses, and compliments, very pleasant to have heard from the parties; but rather dull when related at second hand. Here, therefore, we shall put an end to this dialogue, and hasten to the fatal hour when everything was prepared for the destruction of poor Sophia.

But this being the most tragical matter in our whole history, we shall treat it in a chapter by itself.

CHAPTER V.

Containing some matters which may affect, and others which may surprize, the reader.

The clock had now struck seven, and poor Sophia, alone and melancholy, sat reading a tragedy. It was the Fatal Marriage; and she was now come to that part where the poor distrest Isabella disposes of her wedding-ring.

Here the book dropt from her hand, and a shower of tears ran down into her bosom. In this situation she had continued a minute, when the door opened, and in came Lord Fellamar. Sophia started from her chair at his entrance; and his lordship advancing forwards, and making a low bow, said, "I am afraid, Miss Western, I break in upon you abruptly." "Indeed, my lord," says she, "I must own myself a little surprized at this unexpected visit." "If this visit be unexpected, madam," answered Lord Fellamar, "my eyes must have been very faithless interpreters of my heart, when last I had the honour of seeing you; for surely you could not otherwise have hoped to detain my heart in your possession, without receiving a visit from its owner." Sophia, confused as she was, answered this bombast (and very properly I think) with a look of inconceivable disdain. My lord then made another and a longer speech of the same sort. Upon which Sophia, trembling, said, "Am I really to conceive your lordship to be out of your senses? Sure, my lord, there is no other excuse for such behaviour." "I am, indeed, madam, in the situation you suppose," cries his lordship; "and sure you will pardon the effects of a frenzy which you yourself have occasioned; for love hath so totally deprived me of reason, that I am scarce accountable for any of my actions." "Upon my word, my lord," said Sophia, "I neither understand your words nor your behaviour." "Suffer me then, madam," cries he, "at your feet to explain both, by laying open my soul to you, and declaring that I doat on you to the highest degree of distraction. O most adorable, most divine creature! what language can express the sentiments of my heart?" "I do assure you, my lord," said Sophia, "I shall not stay to hear any more of this." "Do not," cries he, "think of leaving me thus cruelly; could you know half the torments which I feel, that tender bosom must pity what those eyes have caused." Then fetching a deep sigh, and laying hold of her hand, he ran on for some minutes in a strain which would be little more pleasing to the reader than it was to the lady; and at last concluded with a declaration, "That if he was master of the world, he would lay it at her feet." Sophia then, forcibly pulling away her hand from his, answered with much spirit, "I promise you, sir, your world and its master I should spurn from me with equal contempt." She then offered to go; and Lord Fellamar, again laying hold of her hand, said, "Pardon me, my beloved angel, freedoms which nothing but despair could have tempted me to take.——Believe me, could I have had any hope that my title and fortune, neither of them inconsiderable, unless when compared with your worth, would have been accepted, I had, in the humblest manner, presented them to your acceptance.——But I cannot lose you.—By heaven, I will sooner part with my soul!—You are, you must, you shall be only mine." "My lord," says she, "I intreat you to desist from a vain pursuit; for, upon my honour, I will never hear you on this subject. Let go my hand, my lord; for I am resolved to go from you this moment; nor will I ever see you more." "Then, madam," cries his lordship, "I must make the best use of this moment; for I cannot live, nor will I live without you."——"What do you mean, my lord?" said Sophia; "I will raise the family." "I have no fear, madam," answered he, "but of losing you, and that I am resolved to prevent, the only way which despair points to me."—He then caught her in his arms: upon which she screamed so loud, that she must have alarmed some one to her assistance, had not Lady Bellaston taken care to remove all ears.

But a more lucky circumstance happened for poor Sophia; another noise now broke forth, which almost drowned her cries; for now the whole house rang with, "Where is she? D—n me, I'll unkennel her this instant. Show me her chamber, I say. Where is my daughter? I know she's in the house, and I'll see her if she's above-ground. Show me where she is."—At which last words the door flew open, and in came Squire Western, with his parson and a set of myrmidons at his heels.

How miserable must have been the condition of poor Sophia, when the enraged voice of her father was welcome to her ears! Welcome indeed it was, and luckily did he come; for it was the only accident upon earth which could have preserved the peace of her mind from being for ever destroyed.

Sophia, notwithstanding her fright, presently knew her father's voice; and his lordship, notwithstanding his passion, knew the voice of reason, which peremptorily assured him, it was not now a time for the perpetration of his villany. Hearing, therefore, the voice approach, and hearing likewise whose it was (for as the squire more than once roared forth the word daughter, so Sophia, in the midst of her struggling, cried out upon her father), he thought proper to relinquish his prey, having only disordered her handkerchief, and with his rude lips committed violence on her lovely neck.

If the reader's imagination doth not assist me, I shall never be able to describe the situation of these two persons when Western came into the room. Sophia tottered into a chair, where she sat disordered, pale, breathless, bursting with indignation at Lord Fellamar; affrighted, and yet more rejoiced, at the arrival of her father.

His lordship sat down near her, with the bag of his wig hanging over one of his shoulders, the rest of his dress being somewhat disordered, and rather a greater proportion of linen than is usual appearing at his bosom. As to the rest, he was amazed, affrighted, vexed, and ashamed.

As to Squire Western, he happened at this time to be overtaken by an enemy, which very frequently pursues, and seldom fails to overtake, most of the country gentlemen in this kingdom. He was, literally speaking, drunk; which circumstance, together with his natural impetuosity, could produce no other effect than his running immediately up to his daughter, upon whom he fell foul with his tongue in the most inveterate manner; nay, he had probably committed violence with his hands, had not the parson interposed, saying, "For heaven's sake, sir, animadvert that you are in the house of a great lady. Let me beg you to mitigate your wrath; it should minister a fulness of satisfaction that you have found your daughter; for as to revenge, it belongeth not unto us. I discern great contrition in the countenance of the young lady. I stand assured, if you will forgive her, she will repent her of all past offences, and return unto her duty."

The strength of the parson's arms had at first been of more service than the strength of his rhetoric. However, his last words wrought some effect, and the squire answered, "I'll forgee her if she wull ha un. If wot ha un, Sophy, I'll forgee thee all. Why dost unt speak? Shat ha un! d—n me, shat ha un! Why dost unt answer? Was ever such a stubborn tuoad?"

"Let me intreat you, sir, to be a little more moderate," said the parson; "you frighten the young lady so, that you deprive her of all power of utterance."

"Power of mine a—," answered the squire. "You take her part then, you do? A pretty parson, truly, to side with an undutiful child! Yes, yes, I will gee you a living with a pox. I'll gee un to the devil sooner."

"I humbly crave your pardon," said the parson; "I assure your worship I meant no such matter."

My Lady Bellaston now entered the room, and came up to the squire, who no sooner saw her, than, resolving to follow the instructions of his sister, he made her a very civil bow, in the rural manner, and paid her some of his best compliments. He then immediately proceeded to his complaints, and said, "There, my lady cousin; there stands the most undutiful child in the world; she hankers after a beggarly rascal, and won't marry one of the greatest matches in all England, that we have provided for her."

"Indeed, cousin Western," answered the lady, "I am persuaded you wrong my cousin. I am sure she hath a better understanding. I am convinced she will not refuse what she must be sensible is so much to her advantage."

This was a wilful mistake in Lady Bellaston, for she well knew whom Mr Western meant; though perhaps she thought he would easily be reconciled to his lordship's proposals.

"Do you hear there," quoth the squire, "what her ladyship says? All your family are for the match. Come, Sophy, be a good girl, and be dutiful, and make your father happy."

"If my death will make you happy, sir," answered Sophia, "you will shortly be so."

"It's a lye, Sophy; it's a d—n'd lye, and you know it," said the squire.

"Indeed, Miss Western," said Lady Bellaston, "you injure your father; he hath nothing in view but your interest in this match; and I and all your friends must acknowledge the highest honour done to your family in the proposal."

"Ay, all of us," quoth the squire; "nay, it was no proposal of mine. She knows it was her aunt proposed it to me first.—Come, Sophy, once more let me beg you to be a good girl, and gee me your consent before your cousin."

"Let me give him your hand, cousin," said the lady. "It is the fashion now-a-days to dispense with time and long courtships."

"Pugh!" said the squire, "what signifies time; won't they have time enough to court afterwards? People may court very well after they have been a-bed together."

As Lord Fellamar was very well assured that he was meant by Lady Bellaston, so, never having heard nor suspected a word of Blifil, he made no doubt of his being meant by the father. Coming up, therefore, to the squire, he said, "Though I have not the honour, sir, of being personally known to you, yet, as I find I have the happiness to have my proposals accepted, let me intercede, sir, in behalf of the young lady, that she may not be more solicited at this time."

"You intercede, sir!" said the squire; "why, who the devil are you?"

"Sir, I am Lord Fellamar," answered he, "and am the happy man whom I hope you have done the honour of accepting for a son-in-law."

"You are a son of a b——," replied the squire, "for all your laced coat. You my son-in-law, and be d—n'd to you!"

"I shall take more from you, sir, than from any man," answered the lord; "but I must inform you that I am not used to hear such language without resentment."

"Resent my a—," quoth the squire. "Don't think I am afraid of such a fellow as thee art! because hast got a spit there dangling at thy side. Lay by your spit, and I'll give thee enough of meddling with what doth not belong to thee. I'll teach you to father-in-law me. I'll lick thy jacket."

"It's very well, sir," said my lord, "I shall make no disturbance before the ladies. I am very well satisfied. Your humble servant, sir; Lady Bellaston, your most obedient."

His lordship was no sooner gone, than Lady Bellaston, coming up to Mr Western, said, "Bless me, sir, what have you done? You know not whom you have affronted; he is a nobleman of the first rank and fortune, and yesterday made proposals to your daughter; and such as I am sure you must accept with the highest pleasure."

"Answer for yourself, lady cousin," said the squire, "I will have nothing to do with any of your lords. My daughter shall have an honest country gentleman; I have pitched upon one for her—and she shall ha' un.—I am sorry for the trouble she hath given your ladyship with all my heart." Lady Bellaston made a civil speech upon the word trouble; to which the squire answered—"Why, that's kind—and I would do as much for your ladyship. To be sure relations should do for one another. So I wish your ladyship a good night.—Come, madam, you must go along with me by fair means, or I'll have you carried down to the coach."

Sophia said she would attend him without force; but begged to go in a chair, for she said she should not be able to ride any other way.

"Prithee," cries the squire, "wout unt persuade me canst not ride in a coach, wouldst? That's a pretty thing surely! No, no, I'll never let thee out of my sight any more till art married, that I promise thee." Sophia told him, she saw he was resolved to break her heart. "O break thy heart and be d—n'd," quoth he, "if a good husband will break it. I don't value a brass varden, not a halfpenny, of any undutiful b— upon earth." He then took violent hold of her hand; upon which the parson once more interfered, begging him to use gentle methods. At that the squire thundered out a curse, and bid the parson hold his tongue, saying, "At'nt in pulpit now? when art a got up there I never mind what dost say; but I won't be priest-ridden, nor taught how to behave myself by thee. I wish your ladyship a good-night. Come along, Sophy; be a good girl, and all shall be well. Shat ha' un, d—n me, shat ha' un!"

Mrs Honour appeared below-stairs, and with a low curtesy to the squire offered to attend her mistress; but he pushed her away, saying, "Hold, madam, hold, you come no more near my house." "And will you take my maid away from me?" said Sophia. "Yes, indeed, madam, will I," cries the squire: "you need not fear being without a servant; I will get you another maid, and a better maid than this, who, I'd lay five pounds to a crown, is no more a maid than my grannum. No, no, Sophy, she shall contrive no more escapes, I promise you." He then packed up his daughter and the parson into the hackney coach, after which he mounted himself, and ordered it to drive to his lodgings. In the way thither he suffered Sophia to be quiet, and entertained himself with reading a lecture to the parson on good manners, and a proper behaviour to his betters.

It is possible he might not so easily have carried off his daughter from Lady Bellaston, had that good lady desired to have detained her; but, in reality, she was not a little pleased with the confinement into which Sophia was going; and as her project with Lord Fellamar had failed of success, she was well contented that other violent methods were now going to be used in favour of another man.

CHAPTER VI.

By what means the squire came to discover his daughter.

Though the reader, in many histories, is obliged to digest much more unaccountable appearances than this of Mr Western, without any satisfaction at all; yet, as we dearly love to oblige him whenever it is in our power, we shall now proceed to shew by what method the squire discovered where his daughter was.

In the third chapter, then, of the preceding book, we gave a hint (for it is not our custom to unfold at any time more than is necessary for the occasion) that Mrs Fitzpatrick, who was very desirous of reconciling her uncle and aunt Western, thought she had a probable opportunity, by the service of preserving Sophia from committing the same crime which had drawn on herself the anger of her family. After much deliberation, therefore, she resolved to inform her aunt Western where her cousin was, and accordingly she writ the following letter, which we shall give the reader at length, for more reasons than one.

> "HONOURED MADAM,
>
> "The occasion of my writing this will perhaps make a letter of mine agreeable to my dear aunt, for the sake of one of her nieces, though I have little reason to hope it will be so on the account of another.
>
> "Without more apology, as I was coming to throw my unhappy self at your feet, I met, by the strangest accident in the world, my cousin Sophy, whose history you are better acquainted with than myself, though, alas! I know infinitely too much; enough indeed to satisfy me, that unless she is immediately prevented, she is in danger of running into the same fatal mischief, which, by foolishly and ignorantly refusing your most wise and prudent advice, I have unfortunately brought on myself.
>
> "In short, I have seen the man, nay, I was most part of yesterday in his company, and a charming young fellow I promise you he is. By what accident he came acquainted with me is too tedious to tell you now; but I have this morning changed my lodgings to avoid him, lest he should by my means discover my cousin; for he doth not yet know where she is, and it is adviseable he should not, till my uncle hath secured her.——No time therefore is to be lost; and I need only

inform you, that she is now with Lady Bellaston, whom I have seen, and who hath, I find, a design of concealing her from her family. You know, madam, she is a strange woman; but nothing could misbecome me more than to presume to give any hint to one of your great understanding and great knowledge of the world, besides barely informing you of the matter of fact.

"I hope, madam, the care which I have shewn on this occasion for the good of my family will recommend me again to the favour of a lady who hath always exerted so much zeal for the honour and true interest of us all; and that it may be a means of restoring me to your friendship, which hath made so great a part of my former, and is so necessary to my future happiness.

"I am, with the utmost respect, honoured madam, your most dutiful obliged niece, and most obedient humble servant, HARRIET FITZPATRICK."

Mrs Western was now at her brother's house, where she had resided ever since the flight of Sophia, in order to administer comfort to the poor squire in his affliction. Of this comfort, which she doled out to him in daily portions, we have formerly given a specimen.

She was now standing with her back to the fire, and, with a pinch of snuff in her hand, was dealing forth this daily allowance of comfort to the squire, while he smoaked his afternoon pipe, when she received the above letter; which she had no sooner read than she delivered it to him, saying, "There, sir, there is an account of your lost sheep. Fortune hath again restored her to you, and if you will be governed by my advice, it is possible you may yet preserve her."

The squire had no sooner read the letter than he leaped from his chair, threw his pipe into the fire, and gave a loud huzza for joy. He then summoned his servants, called for his boots, and ordered the Chevalier and several other horses to be saddled, and that parson Supple should be immediately sent for. Having done this, he turned to his sister, caught her in his arms, and gave her a close embrace, saying, "Zounds! you don't seem pleased; one would imagine you was sorry I have found the girl."

"Brother," answered she, "the deepest politicians, who see to the bottom, discover often a very different aspect of affairs, from what swims on the surface. It is true, indeed, things do look rather less desperate than they did formerly in Holland, when Lewis the Fourteenth was at the gates of Amsterdam; but there is a delicacy required in this matter, which you will pardon me, brother, if I suspect you want. There is a decorum to be used with a woman of figure, such as Lady Bellaston, brother, which requires a knowledge of the world, superior, I am afraid, to yours."

"Sister," cries the squire, "I know you have no opinion of my parts; but I'll shew you on this occasion who is a fool. Knowledge, quotha! I have not been in the country so long without having some knowledge of warrants and the law of the land. I know I may take my own wherever I can find it. Shew me my own daughter, and if I don't know how to come at her, I'll suffer you to call me a fool as long as I live. There be justices of peace in London, as well as in other places."

"I protest," cries she, "you make me tremble for the event of this matter, which, if you will proceed by my advice, you may bring to so good an issue. Do you really imagine, brother, that the house of a woman of figure is to be attacked by warrants and brutal justices of the peace? I will inform you how to proceed. As soon as you arrive in town, and have got yourself into a decent dress (for indeed, brother, you have none at present fit to appear in), you must send your compliments to Lady Bellaston, and desire leave to wait on her. When you are admitted to her presence, as you certainly will be, and have told her your story, and have made proper use of my name (for I think you just know one another only by sight, though you are relations), I am confident she will withdraw her protection from my niece, who hath certainly imposed upon her. This is the only method.—Justices of peace, indeed! do you imagine any such event can arrive to a woman of figure in a civilised nation?"

"D—n their figures," cries the squire; "a pretty civilised nation, truly, where women are above the law. And what must I stand sending a parcel of compliments to a confounded whore, that keeps away a daughter from her own natural father? I tell you, sister, I am not so ignorant as you think me——I know you would have women above the law, but it is all a lye; I heard his lordship say at size, that no one is above the law. But this of yours is Hanover law, I suppose."

"Mr Western," said she, "I think you daily improve in ignorance.——I protest you are grown an arrant bear."

"No more a bear than yourself, sister Western," said the squire.—"Pox! you may talk of your civility an you will, I am sure you never shew any to me. I am no bear, no, nor no dog neither, though I know somebody, that is something that begins with a b; but pox! I will show you I have got more good manners than some folks."

"Mr Western," answered the lady, "you may say what you please, *je vous mesprise de tout mon coeur.* I shall not therefore be angry.——Besides, as my cousin, with that odious Irish name, justly says, I have that regard for the honour and true interest of my family, and that concern for my niece, who is a part of it, that I have resolved to go to town myself upon this occasion; for indeed, indeed, brother, you are not a fit minister to be employed at a polite court.—Greenland—Greenland should always be the scene of the tramontane negociation."

"I thank Heaven," cries the squire, "I don't understand you now. You are got to your Hanoverian linguo. However, I'll shew you I scorn to be behind-hand in civility with you; and as you are not angry for what I have said, so I am not angry for what you have said. Indeed I have always thought it a folly for relations to quarrel; and if they do now and then give a hasty word, why, people should give and take; for my part, I never bear malice; and I take it very kind of you to go up to London; for I never was there but twice in my life, and then I did not stay above a fortnight at a time, and to be sure I can't be expected to know much of the streets and the folks in that time. I never denied that you know'd all these matters better than I. For me to dispute that would be all as one as for you to dispute the management of a pack of dogs, or the finding a hare sitting, with me."—"Which I promise you," says she, "I never will."—"Well, and I promise you," returned he, "that I never will dispute the t'other."

Here then a league was struck (to borrow a phrase from the lady) between the contending parties; and now the parson arriving, and the horses being ready, the squire departed, having promised his sister to follow her advice, and she prepared to follow him the next day.

But having communicated these matters to the parson on the road, they both agreed that the prescribed formalities might very well be dispensed with; and the squire, having changed his mind, proceeded in the manner we have already seen.

CHAPTER VII.

In which various misfortunes befel poor Jones.

Affairs were in the aforesaid situation when Mrs Honour arrived at Mrs Miller's, and called Jones out from the company, as we have before seen, with whom, when she found herself alone, she began as follows:—

"O, my dear sir! how shall I get spirits to tell you; you are undone, sir, and my poor lady's undone, and I am undone." "Hath anything happened to Sophia?" cries Jones, staring like a madman. "All that is bad," cries Honour: "Oh, I shall never get such another lady! Oh that I should ever live to see this day!" At these words Jones turned pale as ashes, trembled, and stammered; but Honour went on—"O! Mr Jones, I have lost my lady for ever." "How? what! for Heaven's sake, tell me. O, my dear Sophia!" "You may well call her so," said Honour; "she was the dearest lady to me. I shall never have such another place."——"D—n your place!" cries Jones; "where is—what—what is become of my Sophia?" "Ay, to be sure," cries she, "servants may be d—n'd. It signifies nothing what becomes of them, though they are turned away, and ruined ever so much. To be sure they are not flesh and blood like other people. No, to be sure, it signifies nothing what becomes of them." "If you have any pity, any compassion," cries Jones, "I beg you will instantly tell me what hath happened to Sophia?" "To be sure, I have more pity for you than you have for me," answered Honour; "I don't d—n you because you have lost the sweetest lady in the world. To be sure you are worthy to be pitied, and I am worthy to be pitied too: for, to be sure, if ever there was a good mistress——" "What hath happened?" cries Jones, in almost a raving fit. "What?—What?" said Honour: "Why, the worst that could have happened both for you and for me.—Her father is come to town, and hath carried her away from us both." Here Jones fell on his knees in thanksgiving that it was no worse. "No worse!" repeated Honour; "what could be worse for either of us? He carried her off, swearing she should marry Mr Blifil; that's for your comfort; and, for poor me, I am turned out of doors." "Indeed, Mrs Honour," answered Jones, "you frightened me out of my wits. I imagined some most dreadful sudden accident had happened to Sophia; something, compared to which, even seeing her married to Blifil would be a trifle; but while there is life there are hopes, my dear Honour. Women in this land of liberty, cannot be married by actual brutal force." "To be sure, sir," said she, "that's true. There may be some hopes for you; but alack-a-day! what hopes are there for poor me? And to be sure, sir, you must be sensible I suffer all this upon your account. All the quarrel the squire hath to me is for taking your part, as I have done, against Mr Blifil." "Indeed, Mrs Honour," answered he, "I am sensible of my obligations to you, and will leave nothing in my power undone to make you amends." "Alas! sir," said she, "what can make a servant amends for the loss of one place but the getting another altogether as good?" "Do not despair, Mrs Honour," said Jones, "I hope to reinstate you again in the same." "Alack-a-day, sir," said she, "how can I flatter myself with such hopes when I know it is a thing impossible? for the squire is so set against me: and yet, if you should ever have my lady, as to be sure I now hopes heartily you will; for you are a generous, good-natured gentleman; and I am sure you loves her, and to be sure she loves you as dearly as her own soul; it is a matter in vain to deny it; because as why, everybody, that is in the least acquainted with my lady, must see it; for, poor dear lady, she can't dissemble: and if two people who loves one another a'n't happy, why who should be so? Happiness don't always depend upon what people has; besides, my lady has enough for both. To be sure, therefore, as one may say, it would be all the pity in the world to keep two such loviers asunder; nay, I am convinced, for my part, you will meet together at last; for, if it is to be, there is no preventing it. If a marriage is made in heaven, all the justices of peace upon earth can't break it off. To be sure I wishes that parson Supple had but a little more spirit, to tell the squire of his wickedness in endeavouring to force his daughter contrary to her liking; but then his whole dependance is on the squire; and so the poor gentleman, though he is a very religious good sort of man, and talks of the badness of such doings behind the squire's back, yet he dares not say his soul is his own to his face. To be sure I never saw him make so bold as just now; I was afeard the squire would have struck him. I would not have your honour be melancholy, sir, nor despair; things may go better, as long as you are sure of my lady, and that I am certain you may be; for she never will be brought to consent to marry any other man. Indeed I am terribly afeared the squire will do her a mischief in his passion, for he is a prodigious passionate gentleman; and I am afeared too the poor lady will be brought to break her heart, for she is as tender-hearted as a chicken. It is pity, methinks, she had not a little of my courage. If I was in love with a young man, and my father offered to lock me up, I'd tear his eyes out but I'd come at him; but then there's a great fortune in the case, which it is in her father's power either to give her or not; that, to be sure, may make some difference."

Whether Jones gave strict attention to all the foregoing harangue, or whether it was for want of any vacancy in the discourse, I cannot determine; but he never once attempted to answer, nor did she once stop till Partridge came running into the room, and informed him that the great lady was upon the stairs.

Nothing could equal the dilemma to which Jones was now reduced. Honour knew nothing of any acquaintance that subsisted between him and Lady Bellaston, and she was almost the last person in the world to whom he would have communicated it. In this hurry and distress, he took (as is common enough) the worst course, and, instead of exposing her to the lady, which would have been of little consequence, he chose to expose the lady to her; he therefore resolved to hide Honour, whom he had but just time to convey behind the bed, and to draw the curtains.

The hurry in which Jones had been all day engaged on account of his poor landlady and her family, the terrors occasioned by Mrs Honour, and the confusion into which he was thrown by the sudden arrival of Lady Bellaston, had altogether driven former thoughts out of his head; so that it never once occurred to his memory to act the part of a sick man; which, indeed, neither the gaiety of his dress, nor the freshness of his countenance, would have at all supported.

He received her ladyship therefore rather agreeably to her desires than to her expectations, with all the good humour he could muster in his countenance, and without any real or affected appearance of the least disorder.

Lady Bellaston no sooner entered the room, than she squatted herself down on the bed: "So, my dear Jones," said she, "you find nothing can detain me long from you. Perhaps I ought to be angry with you, that I have neither seen nor heard from you all day; for I perceive your distemper would have suffered you to come abroad: nay, I suppose you have not sat in your chamber all day drest up like a fine lady to see company after a lying-in; but, however, don't think I intend to scold you; for I never will give you an excuse for the cold behaviour of a husband, by putting on the ill-humour of a wife."

"Nay, Lady Bellaston," said Jones, "I am sure your ladyship will not upbraid me with neglect of duty, when I only waited for orders. Who, my dear creature, hath reason to complain? Who missed an appointment last night, and left an unhappy man to expect, and wish, and sigh, and languish?"

"Do not mention it, my dear Mr Jones," cried she. "If you knew the occasion, you would pity me. In short, it is impossible to conceive what women of condition are obliged to suffer from the impertinence of fools, in order to keep up the farce of the world. I am glad, however, all your languishing and wishing have done you no harm; for you never looked better in your life. Upon my faith! Jones, you might at this instant sit for the picture of Adonis."

There are certain words of provocation which men of honour hold can properly be answered only by a blow. Among lovers possibly there may be some expressions which can be answered only by a kiss. Now the compliment which Lady Bellaston now made Jones seems to be of this kind, especially as it was attended with a look, in which the lady conveyed more soft ideas than it was possible to express with her tongue.

Jones was certainly at this instant in one of the most disagreeable and distressed situations imaginable; for, to carry on the comparison we made use of before, though the provocation was given by the lady, Jones could not receive satisfaction, nor so much as offer to ask it, in the presence of a third person; seconds in this kind of duels not being according to the law of arms. As this objection did not occur to Lady Bellaston, who was ignorant of any other woman being there but herself, she waited some time in great astonishment for an answer from Jones, who, conscious of the ridiculous figure he made, stood at a distance, and, not daring to give the proper answer, gave none at all. Nothing can be imagined more comic, nor yet more tragical, than this scene would have been if it had lasted much longer. The lady had already changed colour two or three times; had got up from the bed and sat down again, while Jones was wishing the ground to sink under him, or the house to fall on his head, when an odd accident freed him from an embarrassment out of which neither the eloquence of a Cicero, nor the politics of a Machiavel, could have delivered him, without utter disgrace.

This was no other than the arrival of young Nightingale, dead drunk; or rather in that state of drunkenness which deprives men of the use of their reason without depriving them of the use of their limbs.

Mrs Miller and her daughters were in bed, and Partridge was smoaking his pipe by the kitchen fire; so that he arrived at Mr Jones's chamber-door without any interruption. This he burst open, and was entering without any ceremony, when Jones started from his seat and ran to oppose him, which he did so effectually, that Nightingale never came far enough within the door to see who was sitting on the bed.

Nightingale had in reality mistaken Jones's apartment for that in which himself had lodged; he therefore strongly insisted on coming in, often swearing that he would not be kept from his own bed. Jones, however, prevailed over him, and delivered him into the hands of Partridge, whom the noise on the stairs soon summoned to his master's assistance.

And now Jones was unwillingly obliged to return to his own apartment, where at the very instant of his entrance he heard Lady Bellaston venting an exclamation, though not a very loud one; and at the same time saw her flinging herself into a chair in a vast agitation, which in a lady of a tender constitution would have been an hysteric fit.

In reality the lady, frightened with the struggle between the two men, of which she did not know what would be the issue, as she heard Nightingale swear many oaths he would come to his own bed, attempted to retire to her known place of hiding, which to her great confusion she found already occupied by another.

"Is this usage to be borne, Mr Jones?" cries the lady.—"Basest of men?——What wretch is this to whom you have exposed me?" "Wretch!" cries Honour, bursting in a violent rage from her place of concealment—"Marry come up!——Wretch forsooth?——as poor a wretch as I am, I am honest; this is more than some folks who are richer can say."

Jones, instead of applying himself directly to take off the edge of Mrs Honour's resentment, as a more experienced gallant would have done, fell to cursing his stars, and lamenting himself as the most unfortunate man in the world; and presently after, addressing himself to Lady Bellaston, he fell to some very absurd protestations of innocence. By this time the lady, having recovered the use of her reason, which she had as ready as any woman in the world, especially on such occasions, calmly replied: "Sir, you need make no apologies, I see now who the person is; I did not at first know Mrs Honour: but now I do, I can suspect nothing wrong between her and you; and I am sure she is a woman of too good sense to put any wrong constructions upon my visit to you; I have been always her friend, and it may be in my power to be much more hereafter."

Mrs Honour was altogether as placable as she was passionate. Hearing, therefore, Lady Bellaston assume the soft tone, she likewise softened hers.——"I'm sure, madam," says she, "I have been always ready to acknowledge your ladyship's friendships to me; sure I never had so good a friend as your ladyship and to be sure, now I see it is your ladyship that I spoke to, I could almost bite my tongue off for very mad.—I constructions upon your ladyship—to be sure it doth not become a servant as I am to think about such a great lady—I mean I was a servant: for indeed I am nobody's servant now, the more miserable wretch is me.—I have lost the best mistress——" Here Honour thought fit to produce a shower of tears.—"Don't cry, child," says the good lady; "ways perhaps may be found to make you amends. Come to me to-morrow morning." She then took up her fan which lay on the ground, and without even looking at Jones walked very majestically out of the room; there being a kind of dignity in the impudence of women of quality, which their inferiors vainly aspire to attain to in circumstances of this nature.

Jones followed her downstairs, often offering her his hand, which she absolutely refused him, and got into her chair without taking any notice of him as he stood bowing before her.

At his return upstairs, a long dialogue past between him and Mrs Honour, while she was adjusting herself after the discomposure she had undergone. The subject of this was his infidelity to her young lady; on which she enlarged with great bitterness; but Jones at last found means to reconcile her, and not only so, but to obtain a promise of most inviolable secrecy, and that she would the next morning endeavour to find out Sophia, and bring him a further account of the proceedings of the squire.

Thus ended this unfortunate adventure to the satisfaction only of Mrs Honour; for a secret (as some of my readers will perhaps acknowledge from experience) is often a very valuable possession: and that not only to those who faithfully keep it, but sometimes to such as whisper it about till it come to the ears of every one except the ignorant person who pays for the supposed concealing of what is publickly known.

CHAPTER VIII.

Short and sweet.

Notwithstanding all the obligations she had received from Jones, Mrs Miller could not forbear in the morning some gentle remonstrances for the hurricane which had happened the preceding night in his chamber. These were, however, so gentle and so friendly, professing, and indeed truly, to aim at nothing more than the real good of Mr Jones himself, that he, far from being offended, thankfully received the admonition of the good woman, expressed much concern for what had past, excused it as well as he could, and promised never more to bring the same disturbances into the house.

But though Mrs Miller did not refrain from a short expostulation in private at their first meeting, yet the occasion of his being summoned downstairs that morning was of a much more agreeable kind, being indeed to perform the office of a father to Miss Nancy, and to give her in wedlock to Mr Nightingale, who was now ready drest, and full as sober as many of my readers will think a man ought to be who receives a wife in so imprudent a manner.

And here perhaps it may be proper to account for the escape which this young gentleman had made from his uncle, and for his appearance in the condition in which we have seen him the night before.

Now when the uncle had arrived at his lodgings with his nephew, partly to indulge his own inclinations (for he dearly loved his bottle), and partly to disqualify his nephew from the immediate execution of his purpose, he ordered wine to be set on the table; with which he so briskly plyed the young gentleman, that this latter, who, though not much used to drinking, did not detest it so as to be guilty of disobedience or want of complacence by refusing, was soon completely finished.

Just as the uncle had obtained this victory, and was preparing a bed for his nephew, a messenger arrived with a piece of news, which so entirely disconcerted and shocked him, that he in a moment lost all consideration for his nephew, and his whole mind became entirely taken up with his own concerns.

This sudden and afflicting news was no less than that his daughter had taken the opportunity of almost the first moment of his absence, and had gone off with a neighbouring young clergyman; against whom, though her father could have had but one objection, namely, that he was worth nothing, yet she had never thought proper to communicate her amour even to that father; and so artfully had she managed, that it had never been once suspected by any, till now that it was consummated.

Old Mr Nightingale no sooner received this account, than in the utmost confusion he ordered a post-chaise to be instantly got ready, and, having recommended his nephew to the care of a servant, he directly left the house, scarce knowing what he did, nor whither he went.

The uncle thus departed, when the servant came to attend the nephew to bed, had waked him for that purpose, and had at last made him sensible that his uncle was gone, he, instead of accepting the kind offices tendered him, insisted on a chair being called; with this the servant, who had received no strict orders to the contrary, readily complied; and, thus being conducted back to the house of Mrs Miller, he had staggered up to Mr Jones's chamber, as hath been before recounted.

This bar of the uncle being now removed (though young Nightingale knew not as yet in what manner), and all parties being quickly ready, the mother, Mr Jones, Mr Nightingale, and his love, stept into a hackney-coach, which conveyed them to Doctors' Commons; where Miss Nancy was, in vulgar language, soon made an honest woman, and the poor mother became, in the purest sense of the word, one of the happiest of all human beings.

And now Mr Jones, having seen his good offices to that poor woman and her family brought to a happy conclusion, began to apply himself to his own concerns; but here, lest many of my readers should censure his folly for thus troubling himself with the affairs of others, and lest some few should think he acted more disinterestedly than indeed he did, we think proper to assure our reader, that he was so far from being unconcerned in this matter, that he had indeed a very considerable interest in bringing it to that final consummation.

To explain this seeming paradox at once, he was one who could truly say with him in Terence, *Homo sum: humani nihil a me alienum puto.* He was never an indifferent spectator of the misery or happiness of any one; and he felt either the one or the other in great proportion as he himself contributed to either. He could not, therefore, be the instrument of raising a whole family from the lowest state of wretchedness to the highest pitch of joy without conveying great felicity to himself; more perhaps than worldly men often purchase to themselves by undergoing the most severe labour, and often by wading through the deepest iniquity.

Those readers who are of the same complexion with him will perhaps think this short chapter contains abundance of matter; while others may probably wish, short as it is, that it had been totally spared as impertinent to the main design, which I suppose they conclude is to bring Mr Jones to the gallows, or, if possible, to a more deplorable catastrophe.

CHAPTER IX.

Containing love-letters of several sorts.

Mr Jones, at his return home, found the following letters lying on his table, which he luckily opened in the order they were sent.

LETTER I.

"Surely I am under some strange infatuation; I cannot keep my resolutions a moment, however strongly made or justly founded. Last night I resolved never to see you more; this morning I am willing to hear if you can, as you say, clear up this affair. And yet I know that to be impossible. I have said everything to myself which you can invent.——Perhaps not. Perhaps your invention is stronger. Come to me, therefore, the moment you receive this. If you can forge an excuse I almost promise you to believe it. Betrayed too——I will think no more.——Come to me directly.——This is the third letter I have writ, the two former are burnt——I am almost inclined to burn this too——I wish I may preserve my senses.——Come to me presently."

LETTER II.

"If you ever expect to be forgiven, or even suffered within my doors, come to me this instant."

LETTER III.

"I now find you was not at home when my notes came to your lodgings. The moment you receive this let me see you;—I shall not stir out; nor shall anybody be let in but yourself. Sure nothing can detain you long."

Jones had just read over these three billets when Mr Nightingale came into the room. "Well, Tom," said he, "any news from Lady Bellaston, after last night's adventure?" (for it was now no secret to any one in that house who the lady was). "The Lady Bellaston?" answered Jones very gravely.——"Nay, dear Tom," cries Nightingale, "don't be so reserved to your friends. Though I was too drunk to see her last night, I saw her at the masquerade. Do you think I am ignorant who the queen of the fairies is?" "And did you really then know the lady at the masquerade?" said Jones. "Yes, upon my soul, did I," said Nightingale, "and have given you twenty hints of it since, though you seemed always so tender on that point, that I would not speak plainly. I fancy, my friend, by your extreme nicety in this matter, you are not so well acquainted with the character of the lady as with her person. Don't be angry, Tom, but upon my honour, you are not the first young fellow she hath debauched. Her reputation is in no danger, believe me."

Though Jones had no reason to imagine the lady to have been of the vestal kind when his amour began; yet, as he was thoroughly ignorant of the town, and had very little acquaintance in it, he had no knowledge of that character which is vulgarly called a demirep; that is to say, a woman who intrigues with every man she likes, under the name and appearance of virtue; and who, though some over-nice ladies will not be seen with her, is visited (as they term it) by the whole town, in short, whom everybody knows to be what nobody calls her.

When he found, therefore, that Nightingale was perfectly acquainted with his intrigue, and began to suspect that so scrupulous a delicacy as he had hitherto observed was not quite necessary on the occasion, he gave a latitude to his friend's tongue, and desired him to speak plainly what he knew, or had ever heard of the lady.

Nightingale, who, in many other instances, was rather too effeminate in his disposition, had a pretty strong inclination to tittle-tattle. He had no sooner, therefore, received a full liberty of speaking from Jones, than he entered upon a long narrative concerning the lady; which, as it contained many particulars highly to her dishonour, we have too great a tenderness for all women of condition to repeat. We would cautiously avoid giving an opportunity to the future commentators on our works, of making any malicious application and of forcing us to be, against our will, the author of scandal, which never entered into our head.

Jones, having very attentively heard all that Nightingale had to say, fetched a deep sigh; which the other, observing, cried, "Heyday! why, thou art not in love, I hope! Had I imagined my stories would have affected you, I promise you should never have heard them." "O my dear friend!" cries Jones, "I am so entangled with this woman, that I know not how to extricate myself. In love, indeed! no, my friend, but I am under obligations to her, and very great ones. Since you know so much, I will be very explicit with you. It is owing, perhaps, solely to her, that I have not, before this, wanted a bit of bread. How can I possibly desert such a woman? and yet I must desert her, or be guilty of the blackest treachery to one who deserves infinitely better of me than she can; a woman, my Nightingale, for whom I have a passion which few can have an idea of. I am half distracted with doubts how to act." "And is this other, pray, an honourable mistress?" cries Nightingale. "Honourable!" answered Jones; "no breath ever yet durst sully her reputation. The sweetest air is not purer, the limpid stream not clearer, than her honour. She is all over, both in mind and body, consummate perfection. She is the most beautiful creature in the universe: and yet she is mistress of such noble elevated qualities, that, though she is never from my thoughts, I scarce ever think of her beauty but when I see it."—"And can you, my good friend," cries Nightingale, "with such an engagement as this upon your hands, hesitate a moment about quitting such a—" "Hold," said Jones, "no more abuse of her: I detest the thought of ingratitude." "Pooh!" answered the other, "you are not the first upon whom she hath conferred obligations of this kind. She is remarkably liberal where she likes; though, let me tell you, her favours are so prudently bestowed, that they should rather raise a man's vanity than his gratitude." In short, Nightingale proceeded so far on this head, and told his friend so many stories of the lady, which he swore to the truth of, that he entirely removed all esteem for her from the breast of Jones; and his gratitude was lessened in proportion. Indeed, he began to look on all the favours he had received rather as wages than benefits, which depreciated not only her, but himself too in his own conceit, and put him quite out of humour with both. From this disgust, his mind, by a natural transition, turned towards Sophia; her virtue, her purity, her love to him, her sufferings on his account, filled all his thoughts, and made his commerce with Lady Bellaston appear still more odious. The result of all was, that, though his turning himself out of her service, in which light he now saw his affair with her, would be the loss of his bread; yet he determined to quit her, if he could but find a handsome pretence: which being communicated to his friend, Nightingale considered a little, and then said, "I have it, my boy! I have found out a sure method; propose marriage to her, and I would venture hanging upon the success." "Marriage?" cries Jones. "Ay, propose marriage," answered Nightingale, "and she will declare off in a moment. I knew a young fellow whom she kept formerly, who made the offer to her in earnest, and was presently turned off for his pains."

Jones declared he could not venture the experiment. "Perhaps," said he, "she may be less shocked at this proposal from one man than from another. And if she should take me at my word, where am I then? caught, in my own trap, and undone for ever." "No;" answered Nightingale, "not if I can give you an expedient by which you may at any time get out of the trap."——"What expedient can that be?" replied Jones. "This," answered Nightingale. "The young fellow I mentioned, who is one of the most intimate acquaintances I have in the world, is so angry with her for some ill offices she hath since done him, that I am sure he would, without any difficulty, give you a sight of her letters; upon which you may decently break with her; and declare off before the knot is tyed, if she should really be willing to tie it, which I am convinced she will not."

After some hesitation, Jones, upon the strength of this assurance, consented; but, as he swore he wanted the confidence to propose the matter to her face, he wrote the following letter, which Nightingale dictated:—

> "MADAM,
>
> "I am extremely concerned, that, by an unfortunate engagement abroad, I should have missed receiving the honour of your ladyship's commands the moment they came; and the delay which I must now suffer of vindicating myself to your ladyship greatly adds to this misfortune. O, Lady Bellaston! what a terror have I been in for fear your

reputation should be exposed by these perverse accidents! There is one only way to secure it. I need not name what that is. Only permit me to say, that as your honour is as dear to me as my own, so my sole ambition is to have the glory of laying my liberty at your feet; and believe me when I assure you, I can never be made completely happy without you generously bestow on me a legal right of calling you mine for ever.—I am,

madam, with most profound respect, your ladyship's most obliged, obedient, humble servant, THOMAS JONES."

To this she presently returned the following answer:

"SIR,

"When I read over your serious epistle, I could, from its coldness and formality, have sworn that you already had the legal right you mention; nay, that we had for many years composed that monstrous animal a husband and wife. Do you really then imagine me a fool? or do you fancy yourself capable of so entirely persuading me out of my senses, that I should deliver my whole fortune into your power, in order to enable you to support your pleasures at my expense? Are these the proofs of love which I expected? Is this the return for—? but I scorn to upbraid you, and am in great admiration of your profound respect.

"P.S. I am prevented from revising:——Perhaps I have said more than I meant.——Come to me at eight this evening."

Jones, by the advice of his privy-council, replied:

"MADAM,

"It is impossible to express how much I am shocked at the suspicion you entertain of me. Can Lady Bellaston have conferred favours on a man whom she could believe capable of so base a design? or can she treat the most solemn tie of love with contempt? Can you imagine, madam, that if the violence of my passion, in an unguarded moment, overcame the tenderness which I have for your honour, I would think of indulging myself in the continuance of an intercourse which could not possibly escape long the notice of the world; and which, when discovered, must prove so fatal to your reputation? If such be your opinion of me, I must pray for a sudden opportunity of returning those pecuniary obligations, which I have been so unfortunate to receive at your hands; and for those of a more tender kind, I shall ever remain, &c." And so concluded in the very words with which he had concluded the former letter.

The lady answered as follows:

"I see you are a villain! and I despise you from my soul. If you come here I shall not be at home."

Though Jones was well satisfied with his deliverance from a thraldom which those who have ever experienced it will, I apprehend, allow to be none of the lightest, he was not, however, perfectly easy in his mind. There was in this scheme too much of fallacy to satisfy one who utterly detested every species of falshood or dishonesty: nor would he, indeed, have submitted to put it in practice, had he not been involved in a distressful situation, where he was obliged to be guilty of some dishonour, either to the one lady or the other; and surely the reader will allow, that every good principle, as well as love, pleaded strongly in favour of Sophia.

Nightingale highly exulted in the success of his stratagem, upon which he received many thanks and much applause from his friend. He answered, "Dear Tom, we have conferred very different obligations on each other. To me you owe the regaining your liberty; to you I owe the loss of mine. But if you are as happy in the one instance as I am in the other, I promise you we are the two happiest fellows in England."

The two gentlemen were now summoned down to dinner, where Mrs Miller, who performed herself the office of cook, had exerted her best talents to celebrate the wedding of her daughter. This joyful circumstance she ascribed principally to the friendly behaviour of Jones, her whole soul was fired with gratitude towards him, and all her looks, words, and actions, were so busied in expressing it, that her daughter, and even her new son-in-law, were very little objects of her consideration.

Dinner was just ended when Mrs Miller received a letter; but as we have had letters enow in this chapter, we shall communicate its contents in our next.

CHAPTER X.

Consisting partly of facts, and partly of observations upon them.

The letter then which arrived at the end of the preceding chapter was from Mr Allworthy, and the purport of it was, his intention to come immediately to town, with his nephew Blifil, and a desire to be accommodated with his usual lodgings, which were the first floor for himself, and the second for his nephew.

The chearfulness which had before displayed itself in the countenance of the poor woman was a little clouded on this occasion. This news did indeed a good deal disconcert her. To requite so disinterested a match with her daughter, by presently turning her new son-in-law out of doors, appeared to her very unjustifiable on the one hand; and on the other, she could scarce bear the thoughts of making any excuse to Mr Allworthy, after all the obligations received from him, for depriving him of lodgings which were indeed strictly his due; for that gentleman, in conferring all his numberless benefits on others, acted by a rule diametrically opposite to what is practised by most generous people. He contrived, on all occasions, to hide his beneficencc, not only from the world, but even from the object of it. He constantly used the words Lend and Pay, instead of Give; and by every other method he could invent, always lessened with his tongue the favours he conferred, while he was heaping them with both his hands. When he settled the annuity of £50 a year therefore on Mrs Miller, he told her, "it was in consideration of always having her first-floor when he was in town (which he scarce ever intended to be), but that she might let it at any other time, for that he would always send her a month's warning." He was now, however, hurried to town so suddenly, that he had no opportunity of giving such notice; and this hurry probably prevented him, when he wrote for his lodgings, adding, if they were then empty; for he would most certainly have been well satisfied to have relinquished them, on a less sufficient excuse than what Mrs Miller could now have made.

But there are a sort of persons, who, as Prior excellently well remarks, direct their conduct by something

> Beyond the fix'd and settled rules
> Of vice and virtue in the schools,
> Beyond the letter of the law.

To these it is so far from being sufficient that their defence would acquit them at the Old Bailey, that they are not even contented, though conscience, the severest of all judges, should discharge them. Nothing short of the fair and honourable will satisfy the delicacy of their minds; and if any of their actions fall short of this mark, they mope and pine, are as uneasy and restless as a murderer, who is afraid of a ghost, or of the hangman.

Mrs Miller was one of these. She could not conceal her uneasiness at this letter; with the contents of which she had no sooner acquainted the company, and given some hints of her distress, than Jones, her good angel, presently relieved her anxiety. "As for myself, madam," said he, "my lodging is at your service at a moment's warning; and Mr Nightingale, I am sure, as he cannot yet prepare a house fit to receive his lady, will consent to return to his new lodging, whither Mrs Nightingale will certainly consent to go." With which proposal both husband and wife instantly agreed.

The reader will easily believe, that the cheeks of Mrs Miller began again to glow with additional gratitude to Jones; but, perhaps, it may be more difficult to persuade him, that Mr Jones having in his last speech called her daughter Mrs Nightingale (it being the first time that agreeable sound had ever reached her ears), gave the fond mother more satisfaction, and warmed her heart more towards Jones, than his having dissipated her present anxiety.

The next day was then appointed for the removal of the new-married couple, and of Mr Jones, who was likewise to be provided for in the same house with his friend. And now the serenity of the company was again restored, and they past the day in the utmost chearfulness, all except Jones, who, though he outwardly accompanied the rest in their mirth, felt many a bitter pang on the account of his Sophia, which were not a little heightened by the news of Mr Blifil's coming to town (for he clearly saw the intention of his journey); and what greatly aggravated his concern was, that Mrs Honour, who had promised to inquire after Sophia, and to make her report to him early the next evening, had disappointed him.

In the situation that he and his mistress were in at this time, there were scarce any grounds for him to hope that he should hear any good news; yet he was as impatient to see Mrs Honour as if he had expected she would bring him a letter with an assignation in it from Sophia, and bore the disappointment as ill. Whether this impatience arose from that natural weakness of the human mind, which makes it desirous to know the worst, and renders uncertainty the most intolerable of pains; or whether he still flattered himself with some secret hopes, we will not determine. But that it might be the last, whoever has loved cannot but know. For of all the powers exercised by this passion over our minds, one of the most wonderful is that of supporting hope in the midst of despair. Difficulties, improbabilities, nay, impossibilities, are quite overlooked by it; so that to any man extremely in love, may be applied what Addison says of Caesar,

"The Alps, and Pyrenaeans, sink before him!"

Yet it is equally true, that the same passion will sometimes make mountains of molehills, and produce despair in the midst of hope; but these cold fits last not long in good constitutions. Which temper Jones was now in, we leave the reader to guess, having no exact information about it; but this is certain, that he had spent two hours in expectation, when, being unable any longer to conceal his uneasiness, he retired to his room; where his anxiety had almost made him frantick, when the following letter was brought him from Mrs Honour, with which we shall present the reader *verbatim et literatim.*

> "SIR,
>
> "I shud sartenly haf kaled on you a cordin too mi prommiss haddunt itt bin that hur lashipp prevent mee; for to bee sur, Sir, you nose very well that evere persun must luk furst at ome, and sartenly such anuther offar mite not have ever hapned, so as I shud ave bin justly to blam, had I not excepted of it when her lashipp was so veri kind as to offar to mak mee hur one uman without mi ever askin any such thing, to be sur shee is won of thee best ladis in thee wurld, and pepil who sase to the kontrari must bee veri wiket pepil in thare harts. To bee sur if ever I ave sad any thing of that kine it as bin thru ignorens, and I am hartili sorri for it. I nose your onur to be a genteelman of more onur and onesty, if I ever said ani such thing, to repete it to hurt a pore servant that as alwais add thee gratest respect in thee wurld for ure onur. To be sur won shud kepe wons tung within wons teeth, for no boddi nose what may hapen; and to bee sur if ani boddi ad tolde mee yesterday, that I shud haf bin in so gud a plase to day, I shud not haf beleeved it; for to be sur I never was a dremd of any such thing, nor shud I ever have soft after ani other bodi's plase; but as her lashipp wass so kine of her one a cord too give it mee without askin, to be sur Mrs Etoff herself, nor no other boddi can blam mee for exceptin such a thing when it fals in mi waye. I beg ure Onur not to menshion ani thing of what I haf sad, for I wish ure Onur all thee gud luk in the wurld; and I don't cuestion butt thatt u will haf Madam Sofia in the end; butt ass to miself ure onur nose I kant bee of ani farder sarvis to u in that matar, nou bein under thee cumand off anuther parson, and nott mi one mistress, I begg ure Onur to say nothing of what past, and belive me to be, sir, ure Onur's umble servant to cumand till deth,
>
> "HONOUR BLACKMORE."

Various were the conjectures which Jones entertained on this step of Lady Bellaston; who, in reality, had little farther design than to secure within her own house the repository of a secret, which she chose should make no farther progress than it had made already; but mostly, she desired to keep it from the ears of Sophia; for though that young lady was almost the only one who would never have repeated it again, her ladyship could not persuade herself of this; since, as she now hated poor Sophia with most implacable hatred, she conceived a reciprocal hatred to herself to be lodged in the tender breast of our heroine, where no such passion had ever yet found an entrance.

While Jones was terrifying himself with the apprehension of a thousand dreadful machinations, and deep political designs, which he imagined to be at the bottom of the promotion of Honour, Fortune, who hitherto seems to have been an utter enemy to his match with Sophia, tried a new method to put a final end to it, by throwing a temptation in his way, which in his present desperate situation it seemed unlikely he should be able to resist.

CHAPTER XI.

Containing curious, but not unprecedented matter.

There was a lady, one Mrs Hunt, who had often seen Jones at the house where he lodged, being intimately acquainted with the women there, and indeed a very great friend to Mrs Miller. Her age was about thirty, for she owned six-and-twenty; her face and person very good, only inclining a little too much to be fat. She had been married young by her relations to an old Turkey merchant, who, having got a great fortune, had left off trade. With him she lived without reproach, but not without pain, in a state of great self-denial, for about twelve years; and her virtue was rewarded by his dying and leaving her very rich. The first year of her widowhood was just at an end, and she had past it in a good deal of retirement, seeing only a few particular friends, and dividing her time between her devotions and novels, of which she was always extremely fond. Very good health, a very warm constitution, and a good deal of religion, made it absolutely necessary for her to marry again; and she resolved to please herself in her second husband, as she had done her friends in the first. From her the following billet was brought to Jones:—

"SIR,

"From the first day I saw you, I doubt my eyes have told you too plainly that you were not indifferent to me; but neither my tongue nor my hand should have ever avowed it, had not the ladies of the family where you are lodged given me such a character of you, and told me such proofs of your virtue and goodness, as convince me you are not only the most agreeable, but the most worthy of men. I have also the satisfaction to hear from them, that neither my person, understanding, or character, are disagreeable to you. I have a fortune sufficient to make us both happy, but which cannot make me so without you. In thus disposing of myself, I know I shall incur the censure of the world; but if I did not love you more than I fear the world, I should not be worthy of you. One only difficulty stops me: I am informed you are engaged in a commerce of gallantry with a woman of fashion. If you think it worth while to sacrifice that to the possession of me, I am yours; if not, forget my weakness, and let this remain an eternal secret between you and

"ARABELLA HUNT."

At the reading of this, Jones was put into a violent flutter. His fortune was then at a very low ebb, the source being stopt from which hitherto he had been supplied. Of all he had received from Lady Bellaston, not above five guineas remained; and that very morning he had been dunned by a tradesman for twice that sum. His honourable mistress was in the hands of her father, and he had scarce any hopes ever to get her out of them again. To be subsisted at her expense, from that little fortune she had independent of her father, went much against the delicacy both of his pride and his love. This lady's fortune would have been exceeding convenient to him, and he could have no objection to her in any respect. On the contrary, he liked her as well as he did any woman except Sophia. But to abandon Sophia, and marry another, that was impossible; he could not think of it upon any account, Yet why should he not, since it was plain she could not be his? Would it not be kinder to her, than to continue her longer engaged in a hopeless passion for him? Ought he not to do so in friendship to her? This notion prevailed some moments, and he had almost determined to be false to her from a high point of honour: but that refinement was not able to stand very long against the voice of nature, which cried in his heart that such friendship was treason to love. At last he called for pen, ink, and paper, and writ as follows to Mrs Hunt:—

"MADAM,

"It would be but a poor return to the favour you have done me to sacrifice any gallantry to the possession of you, and I would certainly do it, though I were not disengaged, as at present I am, from any affair of that kind. But I should not be the honest man you think me, if I did not tell you that my affections are engaged to another, who is a woman of virtue, and one that I never can leave, though it is probable I shall never possess her. God forbid that, in return of your kindness to me, I should do you such an injury as to give you my hand when I cannot give my heart. No; I had much rather starve than be guilty of that. Even though my mistress were married to another, I would not marry you unless my heart had entirely effaced all impressions of her. Be assured that your secret was not more safe in your own breast, than in that of your most obliged, and grateful humble servant,

"T. JONES."

When our heroe had finished and sent this letter, he went to his scrutore, took out Miss Western's muff, kissed it several times, and then strutted some turns about his room, with more satisfaction of mind than ever any Irishman felt in carrying off a fortune of fifty thousand pounds.

CHAPTER XII.

A discovery made by Partridge.

While Jones was exulting in the consciousness of his integrity, Partridge came capering into the room, as was his custom when he brought, or fancied he brought, any good tidings. He had been despatched that morning by his master, with orders to endeavour, by the servants of Lady Bellaston, or by any other means, to discover whither Sophia had been conveyed; and he now returned, and with a joyful countenance told our heroe that he had found the lost bird. "I have seen, sir," says he, "Black George, the gamekeeper, who is one of the servants whom the squire hath brought with him to town. I knew him presently, though I have not seen him these several years; but you know, sir, he is a very remarkable man, or, to use a purer phrase, he hath a most remarkable beard, the largest and blackest I ever saw. It was some time, however, before Black George could recollect me." "Well, but what is your good news?" cries Jones; "what do you know of my Sophia?" "You shall know presently, sir," answered Partridge, "I am coming to it as fast as I can. You are so impatient, sir, you would come at the infinitive mood before you can get to the imperative. As I was saying, sir, it was some time before he recollected my face."—"Confound your face!" cries Jones, "what of my Sophia?" "Nay, sir," answered Partridge, "I know nothing more of Madam Sophia than what I am going to tell you; and I should have told you all before this if you had not interrupted me; but if you look so angry at me you will frighten all of it out of my head, or, to use a purer phrase, out of my memory. I never saw you look so angry since the day we left Upton, which I shall remember if I was to live a thousand years."—"Well, pray go on your own way," said Jones: "you are resolved to make me mad I find." "Not for the world," answered Partridge, "I have suffered enough for that already; which, as I said, I shall bear in my remembrance the longest day I have to live." "Well, but Black George?" cries Jones. "Well, sir, as I was saying, it was a long time before he could recollect me; for, indeed, I am very much altered since I saw him. *Non sum qualis eram.* I have had troubles in the world, and nothing alters a man so much as grief. I have heard it will change the colour of a man's hair in a night. However, at last, know me he did, that's sure enough; for we are both of an age, and were at the same charity school. George was a great dunce, but no matter for that; all men do not thrive in the world according to their learning. I am sure I have reason to say so; but it will be all one a thousand years hence. Well, sir, where was I?—O—well, we no sooner knew each other, than, after many hearty shakes by the hand, we agreed to go to an alehouse and take a pot, and by good luck the beer was some of the best I have met with since I have been in town. Now, sir, I am coming to the point; for no sooner did I name you, and told him that you and I came to town together, and had lived together ever since, than he called for another pot, and swore he would drink to your health; and indeed he drank your health so heartily that I was overjoyed to see there was so much gratitude left in the world; and after we had emptied that pot I said I would buy my pot too, and so we drank another to your health; and then I made haste home to tell you the news."

"What news?" cries Jones, "you have not mentioned a word of my Sophia!" "Bless me! I had like to have forgot that. Indeed, we mentioned a great deal about young Madam Western, and George told me all; that Mr Blifil is coming to town in order to be married to her. He had best make haste then, says I, or somebody will have her before he comes; and, indeed, says I, Mr Seagrim, it is a thousand pities somebody should not have her; for he certainly loves her above all the women in the world. I would have both you and she know, that it is not for her fortune he follows her; for I can assure you, as to matter of that, there is another lady, one of much greater quality and fortune than she can pretend to, who is so fond of somebody that she comes after him day and night."

Here Jones fell into a passion with Partridge, for having, as he said, betrayed him; but the poor fellow answered, he had mentioned no name: "Besides, sir," said he, "I can assure you George is sincerely your friend, and wished Mr Blifil at the devil more than once; nay, he said he would do anything in his power upon earth to serve you; and so I am convinced he will. Betray you, indeed! why, I question whether you have a better friend than George upon earth, except myself, or one that would go farther to serve you."

"Well," says Jones, a little pacified, "you say this fellow, who, I believe, indeed, is enough inclined to be my friend, lives in the same house with Sophia?"

"In the same house!" answered Partridge; "why, sir, he is one of the servants of the family, and very well drest I promise you he is; if it was not for his black beard you would hardly know him."

"One service then at least he may do me," says Jones: "sure he can certainly convey a letter to my Sophia."

"You have hit the nail *ad unguem*" cries Partridge; "how came I not to think of it? I will engage he shall do it upon the very first mentioning."

"Well, then," said Jones, "do you leave me at present, and I will write a letter, which you shall deliver to him to-morrow morning; for I suppose you know where to find him."

"O yes, sir," answered Partridge, "I shall certainly find him again; there is no fear of that. The liquor is too good for him to stay away long. I make no doubt but he will be there every day he stays in town."

"So you don't know the street then where my Sophia is lodged?" cries Jones.

"Indeed, sir, I do," says Partridge.

"What is the name of the street?" cries Jones.

"The name, sir? why, here, sir, just by," answered Partridge, "not above a street or two off. I don't, indeed, know the very name; for, as he never told me, if I had asked, you know, it might have put some suspicion into his head. No, no, sir, let me alone for that. I am too cunning for that, I promise you."

"Thou art most wonderfully cunning, indeed," replied Jones; "however, I will write to my charmer, since I believe you will be cunning enough to find him to-morrow at the alehouse."

And now, having dismissed the sagacious Partridge, Mr Jones sat himself down to write, in which employment we shall leave him for a time. And here we put an end to the fifteenth book.

BOOK XVI.

CONTAINING THE SPACE OF FIVE DAYS.

CHAPTER I.

Of prologues.

I have heard of a dramatic writer who used to say, he would rather write a play than a prologue; in like manner, I think, I can with less pains write one of the books of this history than the prefatory chapter to each of them.

To say the truth, I believe many a hearty curse hath been devoted on the head of that author who first instituted the method of prefixing to his play that portion of matter which is called the prologue; and which at first was part of the piece itself, but of latter years hath had usually so little connexion with the drama before which it stands, that the prologue to one play might as well serve for any other. Those indeed of more modern date, seem all to be written on the same three topics, viz., an abuse of the taste of the town, a condemnation of all contemporary authors, and an eulogium on the performance just about to be represented. The sentiments in all these are very little varied, nor is it possible they should; and indeed I have often wondered at the great invention of authors, who have been capable of finding such various phrases to express the same thing.

In like manner I apprehend, some future historian (if any one shall do me the honour of imitating my manner) will, after much scratching his pate, bestow some good wishes on my memory, for having first established these several initial chapters; most of which, like modern prologues, may as properly be prefixed to any other book in this history as to that which they introduce, or indeed to any other history as to this.

But however authors may suffer by either of these inventions, the reader will find sufficient emolument in the one as the spectator hath long found in the other.

First, it is well known that the prologue serves the critic for an opportunity to try his faculty of hissing, and to tune his cat-call to the best advantage; by which means, I have known those musical instruments so well prepared, that they have been able to play in full concert at the first rising of the curtain.

The same advantages may be drawn from these chapters, in which the critic will be always sure of meeting with something that may serve as a whetstone to his noble spirit; so that he may fall with a more hungry appetite for censure on the history itself. And here his sagacity must make it needless to observe how artfully these chapters are calculated for that excellent purpose; for in these we have always taken care to intersperse somewhat of the sour or acid kind, in order to sharpen and stimulate the said spirit of criticism.

Again, the indolent reader, as well as spectator, finds great advantage from both these; for, as they are not obliged either to see the one or read the others, and both the play and the book are thus protracted, by the former they have a quarter of an hour longer allowed them to sit at dinner, and by the latter they have the advantage of beginning to read at the fourth or fifth page instead of the first, a matter by no means of trivial consequence to persons who read books with no other view than to say they have read them, a more general motive to reading than is commonly imagined; and from which not only law books, and good books, but the pages of Homer and Virgil, of Swift and Cervantes, have been often turned over.

Many other are the emoluments which arise from both these, but they are for the most part so obvious, that we shall not at present stay to enumerate them; especially since it occurs to us that the principal merit of both the prologue and the preface is that they be short.

CHAPTER II.

A whimsical adventure which befel the squire, with the distressed situation of Sophia.

We must now convey the reader to Mr Western's lodgings, which were in Piccadilly, where he was placed by the recommendation of the landlord at the Hercules Pillars at Hyde Park Corner; for at the inn, which was the first he saw on his arrival in town, he placed his horses, and in those lodgings, which were the first he heard of, he deposited himself.

Here, when Sophia alighted from the hackney-coach, which brought her from the house of Lady Bellaston, she desired to retire to the apartment provided for her; to which her father very readily agreed, and whither he attended her himself. A short dialogue, neither very material nor pleasant to relate minutely, then passed between them, in which he pressed her vehemently to give her consent to the marriage with Blifil, who, as he acquainted her, was to be in town in a few days; but, instead of complying, she gave a more peremptory and resolute refusal than she had ever done before. This so incensed her father, that after many bitter vows, that he would force her to have him whether she would or no, he departed from her with many hard words and curses, locked the door, and put the key into his pocket.

While Sophia was left with no other company than what attend the closest state prisoner, namely, fire and candle, the squire sat down to regale himself over a bottle of wine, with his parson and the landlord of the Hercules Pillars, who, as the squire said, would make an excellent third man, and could inform them of the news of the town, and how affairs went; for to be sure, says he, he knows a great deal, since the horses of many of the quality stand at his house.

In this agreeable society Mr Western past that evening and great part of the succeeding day, during which period nothing happened of sufficient consequence to find a place in this history. All this time Sophia past by herself; for her father swore she should never come out of her chamber alive, unless she first consented to marry Blifil; nor did he ever suffer the door to be unlocked, unless to convey her food, on which occasions he always attended himself.

The second morning after his arrival, while he and the parson were at breakfast together on a toast and tankard, he was informed that a gentleman was below to wait on him.

"A gentleman!" quoth the squire, "who the devil can he be? Do, doctor, go down and see who 'tis. Mr Blifil can hardly be come to town yet.—Go down, do, and know what his business is."

The doctor returned with an account that it was a very well-drest man, and by the ribbon in his hat he took him for an officer of the army; that he said he had some particular business, which he could deliver to none but Mr Western himself.

"An officer!" cries the squire; "what can any such fellow have to do with me? If he wants an order for baggage-waggons, I am no justice of peace here, nor can I grant a warrant.—Let un come up then, if he must speak to me."

A very genteel man now entered the room; who, having made his compliments to the squire, and desired the favour of being alone with him, delivered himself as follows:—

"Sir, I come to wait upon you by the command of my Lord Fellamar; but with a very different message from what I suppose you expect, after what past the other night."

"My lord who?" cries the squire; "I never heard the name o'un."

"His lordship," said the gentleman, "is willing to impute everything to the effect of liquor, and the most trifling acknowledgment of that kind will set everything right; for as he hath the most violent attachment to your daughter, you, sir, are the last person upon earth from whom he would resent an affront; and happy is it for you both that he hath given such public demonstrations of his courage as to be able to put up an affair of this kind without danger of any imputation on his honour. All he desires, therefore, is, that you will before me make some acknowledgment; the slightest in the world will be sufficient; and he intends this afternoon to pay his respects to you, in order to obtain your leave of visiting the young lady on the footing of a lover."

"I don't understand much of what you say, sir," said the squire; "but I suppose, by what you talk about my daughter, that this is the lord which my cousin, Lady Bellaston, mentioned to me, and said something about his courting my daughter. If so be that how that be the case—you may give my service to his lordship, and tell un the girl is disposed of already."

"Perhaps, sir," said the gentleman, "you are not sufficiently apprized of the greatness of this offer. I believe such a person, title, and fortune would be nowhere refused."

"Lookee, sir," answered the squire; "to be very plain, my daughter is bespoke already; but if she was not, I would not marry her to a lord upon any account; I hate all lords; they are a parcel of courtiers and Hanoverians, and I will have nothing to do with them."

"Well, sir," said the gentleman, "if that is your resolution, the message I am to deliver to you is that my lord desires the favour of your company this morning in Hyde Park."

"You may tell my lord," answered the squire, "that I am busy and cannot come. I have enough to look after at home, and can't stir abroad on any account."

"I am sure, sir," quoth the other, "you are too much a gentleman to send such a message; you will not, I am convinced, have it said of you, that, after having affronted a noble peer, you refuse him satisfaction. His lordship would have been willing, from his great regard to the young lady, to have made up matters in another way; but unless he is to look on you as a father, his honour will not suffer his putting up such an indignity as you must be sensible you offered him."

"I offered him!" cries the squire; "it is a d—n'd lie! I never offered him anything."

Upon these words the gentleman returned a very short verbal rebuke, and this he accompanied at the same time with some manual remonstrances, which no sooner reached the ears of Mr Western, than that worthy squire began to caper very briskly about the room, bellowing at the same time with all his might, as if desirous to summon a greater number of spectators to behold his agility.

The parson, who had left great part of the tankard unfinished, was not retired far; he immediately attended therefore on the squire's vociferation, crying, "Bless me! sir, what's the matter?"—"Matter!" quoth the squire, "here's a highwayman, I believe, who wants to rob and murder me—for he hath fallen upon me with that stick there in his hand, when I wish I may be d—n'd if I gid un the least provocation."

"How, sir," said the captain, "did you not tell me I lyed?"

"No, as I hope to be saved," answered the squire, "—I believe I might say, 'Twas a lie that I had offered any affront to my lord—but I never said the word, `you lie.'—I understand myself better, and you might have understood yourself better than to fall upon a naked man. If I had a stick in my hand, you would not have dared strike me. I'd have knocked thy lantern jaws about thy ears. Come down into yard this minute, and I'll take a bout with thee at single stick for a broken head, that I will; or I will go into naked room and box thee for a belly-full. At unt half a man, at unt, I'm sure."

The captain, with some indignation, replied, "I see, sir, you are below my notice, and I shall inform his lordship you are below his. I am sorry I have dirtied my fingers with you." At which words he withdrew, the parson interposing to prevent the squire from stopping him, in which he easily prevailed, as the other, though he made some efforts for the purpose, did not seem very violently bent on success. However, when the captain was departed, the squire sent many curses and some menaces after him; but as these did not set out from his lips till the officer was at the bottom of the stairs, and grew louder and louder as he was more and more remote, they did not reach his ears, or at least did not retard his departure.

Poor Sophia, however, who, in her prison, heard all her father's outcries from first to last, began now first to thunder with her foot, and afterwards to scream as loudly as the old gentleman himself had done before, though in a much sweeter voice. These screams soon silenced the squire, and turned all his consideration towards his daughter, whom he loved so tenderly, that the least apprehension of any harm happening to her, threw him presently into agonies; for, except in that single instance in which the whole future happiness of her life was concerned, she was sovereign mistress of his inclinations.

Having ended his rage against the captain, with swearing he would take the law of him, the squire now mounted upstairs to Sophia, whom, as soon as he had unlocked and opened the door, he found all pale and breathless. The moment, however, that she saw her father, she collected all her spirits, and, catching him hold by the hand, she cryed passionately, "O my dear sir, I am almost frightened to death! I hope to heaven no harm hath happened to you." "No, no," cries the squire, "no great harm. The rascal hath not hurt me much, but rat me if I don't ha the la o' un." "Pray, dear sir," says she, "tell me what's the matter; who is it that hath insulted you?" "I don't know the name o' un," answered Western; "some officer fellow, I suppose, that we are to pay for beating us; but I'll make him pay this bout, if the rascal hath got anything, which I suppose he hath not. For thof he was drest out so vine, I question whether he had got a voot of land in the world." "But, dear sir," cries she, "what was the occasion of your quarrel?" "What should it be, Sophy," answered the squire, "but about you, Sophy? All my misfortunes are about you; you will be the death of your poor father at last. Here's a varlet of a lord, the Lord knows who, forsooth! who hath a taan a liking to you, and because I would not gi un my consent, he sent me a kallenge. Come, do be a good girl, Sophy, and put an end to all your father's troubles; come, do consent to ha un; he will be in town within this day or two; do but promise me to marry un as soon as he comes, and you will make me the happiest man in the world, and I will make you the happiest woman; you shall have the finest cloaths in London, and the finest jewels, and a coach and six at your command. I promised Allworthy already to give up half my estate—od rabbet it! I should hardly stick at giving up the whole." "Will my papa be so kind," says she, "as to hear me speak?"—"Why wout ask, Sophy?" cries he, "when dost know I had rather hear thy voice than the musick of the best pack of dogs in England.—Hear thee, my dear little girl! I hope I shall hear thee as long as I live; for if I was ever to lose that pleasure, I would not gee a brass varden to live a moment longer. Indeed, Sophy, you do not know how I love you, indeed you don't, or you never could have run away and left your poor father, who hath no other joy, no other comfort upon earth, but his little Sophy." At these words the tears stood in his eyes; and Sophia (with the tears streaming from hers) answered, "Indeed, my dear papa, I know you have loved me tenderly, and heaven is my witness how sincerely I have returned your affection; nor could anything but an apprehension of being forced into the arms of this man have driven me to run from a father whom I love so passionately, that I would, with pleasure, sacrifice my life to his happiness; nay, I have endeavoured to reason myself into doing more, and had almost worked up a resolution to endure the most miserable of all lives, to comply with your inclination. It was that resolution alone to which I could not force my mind; nor can I ever." Here the squire began to look wild, and the foam appeared at his lips, which Sophia, observing, begged to be heard out, and then proceeded: "If my father's life, his health, or any real happiness of his was at stake, here stands your resolved daughter; may heaven blast me if there is a misery I would not suffer to preserve you!—No, that most detested, most loathsome of all lots would I embrace. I would give my hand to Blifil for your sake."—"I tell thee, it will preserve me," answers the father; "it will give me health, happiness, life, everything.—Upon my soul I shall die if dost refuse me; I shall break my heart, I shall, upon my soul."—"Is it possible," says she, "you can have such a desire to make me miserable?"—"I tell thee noa," answered he loudly, "d—n me if there is a thing upon earth I would not do to see thee happy."—"And will not my dear papa allow me to have the least knowledge of what will make me so? If it be true that happiness consists in opinion, what must be my condition, when I shall think myself the most miserable of all the wretches upon earth?" "Better think yourself so," said he, "than know it by being married to a poor bastardly vagabond." "If it will content you, sir," said Sophia, "I will give you the most solemn promise never to marry him, nor any other, while my papa lives, without his consent. Let me dedicate my whole life to your service; let me be again your poor Sophy, and my whole business and pleasure be, as it hath been, to please and divert you." "Lookee, Sophy," answered the squire, "I am not to be choused in this manner. Your aunt Western would then have reason to think me the fool she doth. No, no, Sophy, I'd have you to know I have a got more wisdom, and know more of the world, than to take the word of a woman in a matter where a man is concerned." "How, sir, have I deserved this want of confidence?" said she; "have I ever broke a single promise to you? or have I ever been found guilty of a falsehood from my cradle?" "Lookee, Sophy," cries he; "that's neither here nor there. I am determined upon this match, and have him you shall, d—n me if shat unt. D—n me if shat unt, though dost hang thyself the next morning." At repeating which words he clinched his fist, knit his brows, bit his lips, and thundered so loud, that the poor afflicted, terrified Sophia sunk trembling into her chair, and, had not a flood of tears come immediately to her relief, perhaps worse had followed.

Western beheld the deplorable condition of his daughter with no more contrition or remorse than the turnkey of Newgate feels at viewing the agonies of a tender wife, when taking her last farewel of her condemned husband; or rather he looked down on her with the same emotions which arise in an honest fair tradesman, who sees his debtor dragged to prison for £10, which, though a just debt, the wretch is wickedly unable to pay. Or, to hit the case still more nearly, he felt the same compunction with a bawd, when some poor innocent, whom she hath ensnared into her hands, falls into fits at the first proposal of what is called seeing company. Indeed this resemblance would be exact, was it not that the bawd hath an interest in what she doth, and the father, though perhaps he may blindly think otherwise, can, in reality, have none in urging his daughter to almost an equal prostitution.

In this condition he left his poor Sophia, and, departing with a very vulgar observation on the effect of tears, he locked the room, and returned to the parson, who said everything he durst in behalf of the young lady, which, though perhaps it was not quite so much as his duty required, yet was it sufficient to throw the squire into a violent rage, and into many indecent reflections on the whole body of the clergy, which we have too great an honour for that sacred function to commit to paper.

CHAPTER III.

What happened to Sophia during her confinement.

The landlady of the house where the squire lodged had begun very early to entertain a strange opinion of her guests. However, as she was informed that the squire was a man of vast fortune, and as she had taken care to exact a very extraordinary price for her rooms, she did not think proper to give any offence; for, though she was not without some concern for the confinement of poor Sophia, of whose great sweetness of temper and affability the maid of the house had made so favourable a report, which was confirmed by all the squire's servants, yet she had much more concern for her own interest than to provoke one, whom, as she said, she perceived to be a very hastish kind of a gentleman.

Though Sophia eat but little, yet she was regularly served with her meals; indeed, I believe, if she had liked any one rarity, that the squire, however angry, would have spared neither pains nor cost to have procured it for her; since, however strange it may appear to some of my readers, he really doated on his daughter, and to give her any kind of pleasure was the highest satisfaction of his life.

The dinner-hour being arrived, Black George carried her up a pullet, the squire himself (for he had sworn not to part with the key) attending the door. As George deposited the dish, some compliments passed between him and Sophia (for he had not seen her since she left the country, and she treated every servant with more respect than some persons shew to those who are in a very slight degree their inferiors). Sophia would have had him take the pullet back, saying, she could not eat; but George begged her to try, and particularly recommended to her the eggs, of which he said it was full.

All this time the squire was waiting at the door; but George was a great favourite with his master, as his employment was in concerns of the highest nature, namely, about the game, and was accustomed to take many liberties. He had officiously carried up the dinner, being, as he said, very desirous to see his young lady; he made therefore no scruple of keeping his master standing above ten minutes, while civilities were passing between him and Sophia, for which he received only a good-humoured rebuke at the door when he returned.

The eggs of pullets, partridges, pheasants, &c., were, as George well knew, the most favourite dainties of Sophia. It was therefore no wonder that he, who was a very good-natured fellow, should take care to supply her with this kind of delicacy, at a time when all the servants in the house were afraid she would be starved; for she had scarce swallowed a single morsel in the last forty hours.

Though vexation hath not the same effect on all persons as it usually hath on a widow, whose appetite it often renders sharper than it can be rendered by the air on Bansted Downs, or Salisbury Plain; yet the sublimest grief, notwithstanding what some people may say to the contrary, will eat at last. And Sophia, herself, after some little consideration, began to dissect the fowl, which she found to be as full of eggs as George had reported it.

But, if she was pleased with these, it contained something which would have delighted the Royal Society much more; for if a fowl with three legs be so invaluable a curiosity, when perhaps time hath produced a thousand such, at what price shall we esteem a bird which so totally contradicts all the laws of animal oeconomy, as to contain a letter in its belly? Ovid tells us of a flower into which Hyacinthus was metamorphosed, that bears letters on its leaves, which Virgil recommended as a miracle to the Royal Society of his day; but no age nor nation hath ever recorded a bird with a letter in its maw.

But though a miracle of this kind might have engaged all the *Académies des Sciences* in Europe, and perhaps in a fruitless enquiry; yet the reader, by barely recollecting the last dialogue which passed between Messieurs Jones and Partridge, will be very easily satisfied from whence this letter came, and how it found its passage into the fowl.

Sophia, notwithstanding her long fast, and notwithstanding her favourite dish was there before her, no sooner saw the letter than she immediately snatched it up, tore it open, and read as follows:—

> "MADAM,
>
> "Was I not sensible to whom I have the honour of writing, I should endeavour, however difficult, to paint the horrors of my mind at the account brought me by Mrs Honour; but as tenderness alone can have any true idea of the pangs which tenderness is capable of feeling, so can this most amiable quality, which my Sophia possesses in the most eminent degree, sufficiently inform her what her Jones must have suffered on this melancholy occasion. Is there a circumstance in the world which can heighten my agonies, when I hear of any misfortune which hath befallen you? Surely there is one only, and with that I am accursed. It is, my Sophia, the dreadful consideration that I am myself the wretched cause. Perhaps I here do myself too much honour, but none will envy me an honour which costs me so extremely dear. Pardon me this presumption, and pardon me a greater still, if I ask you, whether my advice, my assistance, my presence, my absence, my death, or my tortures can bring you any relief? Can the most perfect admiration, the most watchful observance, the most ardent love, the most melting tenderness, the most resigned submission to your will, make you amends for what you are to sacrifice to my happiness? If they can, fly, my lovely angel, to those arms

which are ever open to receive and protect you; and to which, whether you bring yourself alone, or the riches of the world with you, is, in my opinion, an alternative not worth regarding. If, on the contrary, wisdom shall predominate, and, on the most mature reflection, inform you, that the sacrifice is too great; and if there be no way left to reconcile your father, and restore the peace of your dear mind, but by abandoning me, I conjure you drive me for ever from your thoughts, exert your resolution, and let no compassion for my sufferings bear the least weight in that tender bosom. Believe me, madam, I so sincerely love you better than myself, that my great and principal end is your happiness. My first wish (why would not fortune indulge me in it?) was, and pardon me if I say, still is, to see you every moment the happiest of women; my second wish is, to hear you are so; but no misery on earth can equal mine, while I think you owe an uneasy moment to him who is,

Madam, in every sense, and to every purpose, your devoted, THOMAS JONES."

What Sophia said, or did, or thought, upon this letter, how often she read it, or whether more than once, shall all be left to our reader's imagination. The answer to it he may perhaps see hereafter, but not at present: for this reason, among others, that she did not now write any, and that for several good causes, one of which was this, she had no paper, pen, nor ink.

In the evening, while Sophia was meditating on the letter she had received, or on something else, a violent noise from below disturbed her meditations. This noise was no other than a round bout at altercation between two persons. One of the combatants, by his voice, she immediately distinguished to be her father; but she did not so soon discover the shriller pipes to belong to the organ of her aunt Western, who was just arrived in town, where having, by means of one of her servants, who stopt at the Hercules Pillars, learned where her brother lodged, she drove directly to his lodgings.

We shall therefore take our leave at present of Sophia, and, with our usual good-breeding, attend her ladyship.

CHAPTER IV.

In which Sophia is delivered from her confinement.

The squire and the parson (for the landlord was now otherwise engaged) were smoaking their pipes together, when the arrival of the lady was first signified. The squire no sooner heard her name, than he immediately ran down to usher her upstairs; for he was a great observer of such ceremonials, especially to his sister, of whom he stood more in awe than of any other human creature, though he never would own this, nor did he perhaps know it himself.

Mrs Western, on her arrival in the dining-room, having flung herself into a chair, began thus to harangue: "Well, surely, no one ever had such an intolerable journey. I think the roads, since so many turnpike acts, are grown worse than ever. La, brother, how could you get into this odious place? no person of condition, I dare swear, ever set foot here before." "I don't know," cries the squire, "I think they do well enough; it was landlord recommended them. I thought, as he knew most of the quality, he could best shew me where to get among um." "Well, and where's my niece?" says the lady; "have you been to wait upon Lady Bellaston yet?" "Ay, ay," cries the squire, "your niece is safe enough; she is upstairs in chamber." "How!" answered the lady, "is my niece in this house, and does she not know of my being here?" "No, nobody can well get to her," says the squire, "for she is under lock and key. I have her safe; I vetched her from my lady cousin the first night I came to town, and I have taken care o' her ever since; she is as secure as a fox in a bag, I promise you." "Good heaven!" returned Mrs Western, "what do I hear? I thought what a fine piece of work would be the consequence of my consent to your coming to town yourself; nay, it was indeed your own headstrong will, nor can I charge myself with having ever consented to it. Did not you promise me, brother, that you would take none of these headstrong measures? Was it not by these headstrong measures that you forced my niece to run away from you in the country? Have you a mind to oblige her to take such another step?" "Z—ds and the devil!" cries the squire, dashing his pipe on the ground; "did ever mortal hear the like? when I expected you would have commended me for all I have done, to be fallen upon in this manner!" "How, brother!" said the lady, "have I ever given you the least reason to imagine I should commend you for locking up your daughter? Have I not often told you that women in a free country are not to be treated with such arbitrary power? Wc are as free as the men, and I heartily wish I could not say we deserve that freedom better. If you expect I should stay a moment longer in this wretched house, or that I should ever own you again as my relation, or that I should ever trouble myself again with the affairs of your family, I insist upon it that my niece be set at liberty this instant." This she spoke with so commanding an air, standing with her back to the fire, with one hand behind her, and a pinch of snuff in the other, that I question whether Thalestris, at the head of her Amazons, ever made a more tremendous figure. It is no wonder, therefore, that the poor squire was not proof against the awe which she inspired. "There," he cried, throwing down the key, "there it is, do whatever you please. I intended only to have kept her up till Blifil came to town, which can't be long; and now if any harm happens in the mean time, remember who is to be blamed for it."

"I will answer it with my life," cried Mrs Western, "but I shall not intermeddle at all, unless upon one condition, and that is, that you will commit the whole entirely to my care, without taking any one measure yourself, unless I shall eventually appoint you to act. If you ratify these preliminaries, brother, I yet will endeavour to preserve the honour of your family; if not, I shall continue in a neutral state."

"I pray you, good sir," said the parson, "permit yourself this once to be admonished by her ladyship: peradventure, by communing with young Madam Sophia, she will effect more than you have been able to perpetrate by more rigorous measures."

"What, dost thee open upon me?" cries the squire: "if thee dost begin to babble, I shall whip thee in presently."

"Fie, brother," answered the lady, "is this language to a clergyman? Mr Supple is a man of sense, and gives you the best advice; and the whole world, I believe, will concur in his opinion; but I must tell you I expect an immediate answer to my categorical proposals. Either cede your daughter to my disposal, or take her wholly to your own surprizing discretion, and then I here, before Mr Supple, evacuate the garrison, and renounce you and your family for ever."

"I pray you let me be a mediator," cries the parson, "let me supplicate you."

"Why, there lies the key on the table," cries the squire. "She may take un up, if she pleases: who hinders her?"

"No, brother," answered the lady, "I insist on the formality of its being delivered me, with a full ratification of all the concessions stipulated."

"Why then I will deliver it to you.—There 'tis," cries the squire. "I am sure, sister, you can't accuse me of ever denying to trust my daughter to you. She hath a-lived wi' you a whole year and muore to a time, without my ever zeeing her."

"And it would have been happy for her," answered the lady, "if she had always lived with me. Nothing of this kind would have happened under my eye."

"Ay, certainly," cries he, "I only am to blame."

"Why, you are to blame, brother," answered she. "I have been often obliged to tell you so, and shall always be obliged to tell you so. However, I hope you will now amend, and gather so much experience from past errors, as not to defeat my wisest machinations by your blunders. Indeed, brother, you are not qualified for these negociations. All your whole scheme of politics is wrong. I once more, therefore, insist, that you do not intermeddle. Remember only what is past."——

"Z—ds and bl—d, sister," cries the squire, "what would you have me say? You are enough to provoke the devil."

"There, now," said she, "just according to the old custom. I see, brother, there is no talking to you. I will appeal to Mr Supple, who is a man of sense, if I said anything which could put any human creature into a passion; but you are so wrongheaded every way."

"Let me beg you, madam," said the parson, "not to irritate his worship."

"Irritate him?" said the lady; "sure, you are as great a fool as himself. Well, brother, since you have promised not to interfere, I will once more undertake the management of my niece. Lord have mercy upon all affairs which are under the directions of men! The head of one woman is worth a thousand of yours." And now having summoned a servant to show her to Sophia, she departed, bearing the key with her.

She was no sooner gone, than the squire (having first shut the door) ejaculated twenty bitches, and as many hearty curses against her, not sparing himself for having ever thought of her estate; but added, "Now one hath been a slave so long, it would be pity to lose it at last, for want of holding out a little longer. The bitch can't live for ever, and I know I am down for it upon the will."

The parson greatly commended this resolution: and now the squire having ordered in another bottle, which was his usual method when anything either pleased or vexed him, did, by drinking plentifully of this medicinal julap, so totally wash away his choler, that his temper was become perfectly placid and serene, when Mrs Western returned with Sophia into the room. The young lady had on her hat and capuchin, and the aunt acquainted Mr Western, "that she intended to take her niece with her to her own lodgings; for, indeed, brother," says she, "these rooms are not fit to receive a Christian soul in."

"Very well, madam," quoth Western, "whatever you please. The girl can never be in better hands than yours; and the parson here can do me the justice to say, that I have said fifty times behind your back, that you was one of the most sensible women in the world."

"To this," cries the parson, "I am ready to bear testimony."

"Nay, brother," says Mrs Western, "I have always, I'm sure, given you as favourable a character. You must own you have a little too much hastiness in your temper; but when you will allow yourself time to reflect I never knew a man more reasonable."

"Why then, sister, if you think so," said the squire, "here's your good health with all my heart. I am a little passionate sometimes, but I scorn to bear any malice. Sophy, do you be a good girl, and do everything your aunt orders you."

"I have not the least doubt of her," answered Mrs Western. "She hath had already an example before her eyes in the behaviour of that wretch her cousin Harriet, who ruined herself by neglecting my advice. O brother, what think you? You was hardly gone out of hearing, when you set out for London, when who should arrive but that impudent fellow with the odious Irish name—that Fitzpatrick. He broke in abruptly upon me without notice, or I would not have seen him. He ran on a long, unintelligible story about his wife, to which he forced me to give him a hearing; but I made him very little answer, and delivered him the letter from his wife, which I bid him answer himself. I suppose the wretch will endeavour to find us out, but I beg you will not see her, for I am determined I will not."

"I zee her!" answered the squire; "you need not fear me. I'll ge no encouragement to such undutiful wenches. It is well for the fellow, her husband, I was not at huome. Od rabbit it, he should have taken a dance thru the horse-pond, I promise un. You zee, Sophy, what undutifulness brings volks to. You have an example in your own family."

"Brother," cries the aunt, "you need not shock my niece by such odious repetitions. Why will you not leave everything entirely to me?" "Well, well, I wull, I wull," said the squire.

And now Mrs Western, luckily for Sophia, put an end to the conversation by ordering chairs to be called. I say luckily, for had it continued much longer, fresh matter of dissension would, most probably, have arisen between the brother and sister; between whom education and sex made the only difference; for both were equally violent and equally positive: they had both a vast affection for Sophia, and both a sovereign contempt for each other.

CHAPTER V.

In which Jones receives a letter from Sophia, and goes to a play with Mrs Miller and Partridge.

The arrival of Black George in town, and the good offices which that grateful fellow had promised to do for his old benefactor, greatly comforted Jones in the midst of all the anxiety and uneasiness which he had suffered on the account of Sophia; from whom, by the means of the said George, he received the following answer to his letter, which Sophia, to whom the use of pen, ink, and paper was restored with her liberty, wrote the very evening when she departed from her confinement:

> "Sir,
>
> "As I do not doubt your sincerity in what you write, you will be pleased to hear that some of my afflictions are at an end, by the arrival of my aunt Western, with whom I am at present, and with whom I enjoy all the liberty I can desire. One promise my aunt hath insisted on my making, which is, that I will not see or converse with any person without her knowledge and consent. This promise I have most solemnly given, and shall most inviolably keep: and though she hath not expressly forbidden me writing, yet that must be an omission from forgetfulness; or this, perhaps, is included in the word conversing. However, as I cannot but consider this as a breach of her generous confidence in my honour, you cannot expect that I shall, after this, continue to write myself or to receive letters, without her knowledge. A promise is with me a very sacred thing, and to be extended to everything understood from it, as well as to what is expressed by it; and this consideration may, perhaps, on reflection, afford you some comfort. But why should I mention a comfort to you of this kind; for though there is one thing in which I can never comply with the best of fathers, yet am I firmly resolved never to act in defiance of him, or to take any step of consequence without his consent. A firm persuasion of this must teach you to divert your thoughts from what fortune hath (perhaps) made impossible. This your own interest persuades you. This may reconcile, I hope, Mr Allworthy to you; and if it will, you have my injunctions to pursue it. Accidents

> have laid some obligations on me, and your good intentions probably more. Fortune may, perhaps, be some time kinder to us both than at present. Believe this, that I shall always think of you as I think you deserve, and am,
>
> Sir, your obliged humble servant, Sophia Western.
>
> "I charge you write to me no more—at present at least; and accept this, which is now of no service to me, which I know you must want, and think you owe the trifle only to that fortune by which you found it."[1]

A child who hath just learnt his letters would have spelt this letter out in less time than Jones took in reading it. The sensations it occasioned were a mixture of joy and grief; somewhat like what divide the mind of a good man when he peruses the will of his deceased friend, in which a large legacy, which his distresses make the more welcome, is bequeathed to him. Upon the whole, however, he was more pleased than displeased; and, indeed, the reader may probably wonder that he was displeased at all; but the reader is not quite so much in love as was poor Jones; and love is a disease which, though it may, in some instances, resemble a consumption (which it sometimes causes), in others proceeds in direct opposition to it, and particularly in this, that it never flatters itself, or sees any one symptom in a favourable light.

One thing gave him complete satisfaction, which was, that his mistress had regained her liberty, and was now with a lady where she might at least assure herself of a decent treatment. Another comfortable circumstance was the reference which she made to her promise of never marrying any other man; for however disinterested he might imagine his passion, and notwithstanding all the generous overtures made in his letter, I very much question whether he could have heard a more afflicting piece of news than that Sophia was married to another, though the match had been never so great, and never so likely to end in making her completely happy. That refined degree of Platonic affection which is absolutely detached from the flesh, and is, indeed, entirely and purely spiritual, is a gift confined to the female part of the creation; many of whom I have heard declare (and, doubtless, with great truth), that they would, with the utmost readiness, resign a lover to a rival, when such resignation was proved to be necessary for the temporal interest of such lover. Hence, therefore, I conclude that this affection is in nature, though I cannot pretend to say I have ever seen an instance of it.

Mr Jones having spent three hours in reading and kissing the aforesaid letter, and being, at last, in a state of good spirits, from the last-mentioned considerations, he agreed to carry an appointment, which he had before made, into execution. This was, to attend Mrs Miller, and her younger daughter, into the gallery at the play-house, and to admit Mr Partridge as one of the company. For as

[1] Meaning, perhaps, the bank-bill for £100.

Jones had really that taste for humour which many affect, he expected to enjoy much entertainment in the criticisms of Partridge, from whom he expected the simple dictates of nature, unimproved, indeed, but likewise unadulterated, by art.

In the first row then of the first gallery did Mr Jones, Mrs Miller, her youngest daughter, and Partridge, take their places. Partridge immediately declared it was the finest place he had ever been in. When the first music was played, he said, "It was a wonder how so many fiddlers could play at one time, without putting one another out." While the fellow was lighting the upper candles, he cried out to Mrs Miller, "Look, look, madam, the very picture of the man in the end of the common-prayer book before the gunpowder-treason service." Nor could he help observing, with a sigh, when all the candles were lighted, "That here were candles enough burnt in one night, to keep an honest poor family for a whole twelvemonth."

As soon as the play, which was Hamlet, Prince of Denmark, began, Partridge was all attention, nor did he break silence till the entrance of the ghost; upon which he asked Jones, "What man that was in the strange dress; something," said he, "like what I have seen in a picture. Sure it is not armour, is it?" Jones answered, "That is the ghost." To which Partridge replied with a smile, "Persuade me to that, sir, if you can. Though I can't say I ever actually saw a ghost in my life, yet I am certain I should know one, if I saw him, better than that comes to. No, no, sir, ghosts don't appear in such dresses as that, neither." In this mistake, which caused much laughter in the neighbourhood of Partridge, he was suffered to continue, till the scene between the ghost and Hamlet, when Partridge gave that credit to Mr Garrick, which he had denied to Jones, and fell into so violent a trembling, that his knees knocked against each other. Jones asked him what was the matter, and whether he was afraid of the warrior upon the stage? "O la! sir," said he, "I perceive now it is what you told me. I am not afraid of anything; for I know it is but a play. And if it was really a ghost, it could do one no harm at such a distance, and in so much company; and yet if I was frightened, I am not the only person." "Why, who," cries Jones, "dost thou take to be such a coward here besides thyself?" "Nay, you may call me coward if you will; but if that little man there upon the stage is not frightened, I never saw any man frightened in my life. Ay, ay: go along with you: Ay, to be sure! Who's fool then? Will you? Lud have mercy upon such fool-hardiness!—Whatever happens, it is good enough for you.——Follow you? I'd follow the devil as soon. Nay, perhaps it is the devil——for they say he can put on what likeness he pleases.—Oh! here he is again.——No farther! No, you have gone far enough already; farther than I'd have gone for all the king's dominions." Jones offered to speak, but Partridge cried "Hush, hush! dear sir, don't you hear him?" And during the whole speech of the ghost, he sat with his eyes fixed partly on the ghost and partly on Hamlet, and with his mouth open; the same passions which succeeded each other in Hamlet, succeeding likewise in him.

When the scene was over Jones said, "Why, Partridge, you exceed my expectations. You enjoy the play more than I conceived possible." "Nay, sir," answered

Partridge, "if you are not afraid of the devil, I can't help it; but to be sure, it is natural to be surprized at such things, though I know there is nothing in them: not that it was the ghost that surprized me, neither; for I should have known that to have been only a man in a strange dress; but when I saw the little man so frightened himself, it was that which took hold of me." "And dost thou imagine, then, Partridge," cries Jones, "that he was really frightened?" "Nay, sir," said Partridge, "did not you yourself observe afterwards, when he found it was his own father's spirit, and how he was murdered in the garden, how his fear forsook him by degrees, and he was struck dumb with sorrow, as it were, just as I should have been, had it been my own case?—But hush! O la! what noise is that? There he is again.——Well, to be certain, though I know there is nothing at all in it, I am glad I am not down yonder, where those men are." Then turning his eyes again upon Hamlet, "Ay, you may draw your sword; what signifies a sword against the power of the devil?"

During the second act, Partridge made very few remarks. He greatly admired the fineness of the dresses; nor could he help observing upon the king's countenance. "Well," said he, "how people may be deceived by faces! *Nulla fides fronti* is, I find, a true saying. Who would think, by looking in the king's face, that he had ever committed a murder?" He then enquired after the ghost; but Jones, who intended he should be surprized, gave him no other satisfaction, than, "that he might possibly see him again soon, and in a flash of fire."

Partridge sat in a fearful expectation of this; and now, when the ghost made his next appearance, Partridge cried out, "There, sir, now; what say you now? is he frightened now or no? As much frightened as you think me, and, to be sure, nobody can help some fears. I would not be in so bad a condition as what's his name, squire Hamlet, is there, for all the world. Bless me! what's become of the spirit? As I am a living soul, I thought I saw him sink into the earth." "Indeed, you saw right," answered Jones. "Well, well," cries Partridge, "I know it is only a play: and besides, if there was anything in all this, Madam Miller would not laugh so; for as to you, sir, you would not be afraid, I believe, if the devil was here in person.—There, there—Ay, no wonder you are in such a passion, shake the vile wicked wretch to pieces. If she was my own mother, I would serve her so. To be sure all duty to a mother is forfeited by such wicked doings.——Ay, go about your business, I hate the sight of you."

Our critic was now pretty silent till the play, which Hamlet introduces before the king. This he did not at first understand, till Jones explained it to him; but he no sooner entered into the spirit of it, than he began to bless himself that he had never committed murder. Then turning to Mrs Miller, he asked her, "If she did not imagine the king looked as if he was touched; though he is," said he, "a good actor, and doth all he can to hide it. Well, I would not have so much to answer for, as that wicked man there hath, to sit upon a much higher chair than he sits upon. No wonder he ran away; for your sake I'll never trust an innocent face again."

The grave-digging scene next engaged the attention of Partridge, who expressed much surprize at the number of skulls thrown upon the stage. To which

Jones answered, "That it was one of the most famous burial-places about town." "No wonder then," cries Partridge, "that the place is haunted. But I never saw in my life a worse grave-digger. I had a sexton, when I was clerk, that should have dug three graves while he is digging one. The fellow handles a spade as if it was the first time he had ever had one in his hand. Ay, ay, you may sing. You had rather sing than work, I believe."—Upon Hamlet's taking up the skull, he cried out, "Well! it is strange to see how fearless some men are: I never could bring myself to touch anything belonging to a dead man, on any account.—He seemed frightened enough too at the ghost, I thought. *Nemo omnibus horis sapit.*"

Little more worth remembering occurred during the play, at the end of which Jones asked him, "Which of the players he had liked best?" To this he answered, with some appearance of indignation at the question, "The king, without doubt." "Indeed, Mr Partridge," says Mrs Miller, "you are not of the same opinion with the town; for they are all agreed, that Hamlet is acted by the best player who ever was on the stage." "He the best player!" cries Partridge, with a contemptuous sneer, "why, I could act as well as he myself. I am sure, if I had seen a ghost, I should have looked in the very same manner, and done just as he did. And then, to be sure, in that scene, as you called it, between him and his mother, where you told me he acted so fine, why, Lord help me, any man, that is, any good man, that had such a mother, would have done exactly the same. I know you are only joking with me; but indeed, madam, though I was never at a play in London, yet I have seen acting before in the country; and the king for my money; he speaks all his words distinctly, half as loud again as the other.—Anybody may see he is an actor."

While Mrs Miller was thus engaged in conversation with Partridge, a lady came up to Mr Jones, whom he immediately knew to be Mrs Fitzpatrick. She said, she had seen him from the other part of the gallery, and had taken that opportunity of speaking to him, as she had something to say, which might be of great service to himself. She then acquainted him with her lodgings, and made him an appointment the next day in the morning; which, upon recollection, she presently changed to the afternoon; at which time Jones promised to attend her.

Thus ended the adventure at the playhouse; where Partridge had afforded great mirth, not only to Jones and Mrs Miller, but to all who sat within hearing, who were more attentive to what he said, than to anything that passed on the stage.

He durst not go to bed all that night, for fear of the ghost; and for many nights after sweated two or three hours before he went to sleep, with the same apprehensions, and waked several times in great horrors, crying out, "Lord have mercy upon us! there it is."

CHAPTER VI.

In which the history is obliged to look back.

It is almost impossible for the best parent to observe an exact impartiality to his children, even though no superior merit should bias his affection; but sure a parent can hardly be blamed, when that superiority determines his preference.

As I regard all the personages of this history in the light of my children; so I must confess the same inclination of partiality to Sophia; and for that I hope the reader will allow me the same excuse, from the superiority of her character.

This extraordinary tenderness which I have for my heroine never suffers me to quit her any long time without the utmost reluctance. I could now, therefore, return impatiently to enquire what hath happened to this lovely creature since her departure from her father's, but that I am obliged first to pay a short visit to Mr Blifil.

Mr Western, in the first confusion into which his mind was cast upon the sudden news he received of his daughter, and in the first hurry to go after her, had not once thought of sending any account of the discovery to Blifil. He had not gone far, however, before he recollected himself, and accordingly stopt at the very first inn he came to, and dispatched away a messenger to acquaint Blifil with his having found Sophia, and with his firm resolution to marry her to him immediately, if he would come up after him to town.

As the love which Blifil had for Sophia was of that violent kind, which nothing but the loss of her fortune, or some such accident, could lessen, his inclination to the match was not at all altered by her having run away, though he was obliged to lay this to his own account. He very readily, therefore, embraced this offer. Indeed, he now proposed the gratification of a very strong passion besides avarice, by marrying this young lady, and this was hatred; for he concluded that matrimony afforded an equal opportunity of satisfying either hatred or love; and this opinion is very probably verified by much experience. To say the truth, if we are to judge by the ordinary behaviour of married persons to each other, we shall perhaps be apt to conclude that the generality seek the indulgence of the former passion only, in their union of everything but of hearts.

There was one difficulty, however, in his way, and this arose from Mr Allworthy. That good man, when he found by the departure of Sophia (for neither that, nor the cause of it, could be concealed from him), the great aversion which she had for his nephew, began to be seriously concerned that he had been deceived into carrying matters so far. He by no means concurred with the opinion of those parents, who think it as immaterial to consult the inclinations of their children in the affair of marriage, as to solicit the good pleasure of their servants when they intend to take a journey; and who are by law, or decency at least, withheld often from using absolute force. On the contrary, as he esteemed the institution to be of the most sacred kind, he thought every preparatory caution necessary to preserve it holy and inviolate; and very wisely concluded, that the surest way to effect this was by laying the foundation in previous affection.

Blifil indeed soon cured his uncle of all anger on the score of deceit, by many vows and protestations that he had been deceived himself, with which the many declarations of Western very well tallied; but now to persuade Allworthy to consent to the renewing his addresses was a matter of such apparent difficulty, that the very appearance was sufficient to have deterred a less enterprizing genius; but this young gentleman so well knew his own talents, that nothing within the province of cunning seemed to him hard to be achieved.

Here then he represented the violence of his own affection, and the hopes of subduing aversion in the lady by perseverance. He begged that, in an affair on which depended all his future repose, he might at least be at liberty to try all fair means for success. Heaven forbid, he said, that he should ever think of prevailing by any other than the most gentle methods! "Besides, sir," said he, "if they fail, you may then (which will be surely time enough) deny your consent." He urged the great and eager desire which Mr Western had for the match; and lastly, he made great use of the name of Jones, to whom he imputed all that had happened; and from whom, he said, to preserve so valuable a young lady was even an act of charity.

All these arguments were well seconded by Thwackum, who dwelt a little stronger on the authority of parents than Mr Blifil himself had done. He ascribed the measures which Mr Blifil was desirous to take to Christian motives; "and though," says he, "the good young gentleman hath mentioned charity last, I am almost convinced it is his first and principal consideration."

Square, possibly, had he been present, would have sung to the same tune, though in a different key, and would have discovered much moral fitness in the proceeding: but he was now gone to Bath for the recovery of his health.

Allworthy, though not without reluctance, at last yielded to the desires of his nephew. He said he would accompany him to London, where he might be at liberty to use every honest endeavour to gain the lady: "But I declare," said he, "I will never give my consent to any absolute force being put on her inclinations, nor shall you ever have her, unless she can be brought freely to compliance."

Thus did the affection of Allworthy for his nephew betray the superior understanding to be triumphed over by the inferior; and thus is the prudence of the best of heads often defeated by the tenderness of the best of hearts.

Blifil, having obtained this unhoped-for acquiescence in his uncle, rested not till he carried his purpose into execution. And as no immediate business required Mr Allworthy's presence in the country, and little preparation is necessary to men for a journey, they set out the very next day, and arrived in town that evening, when Mr Jones, as we have seen, was diverting himself with Partridge at the play.

The morning after his arrival Mr Blifil waited on Mr Western, by whom he was most kindly and graciously received, and from whom he had every possible assurance (perhaps more than was possible) that he should very shortly be as happy as Sophia could make him; nor would the squire suffer the young gentleman to return to his uncle till he had, almost against his will, carried him to his sister.

CHAPTER VII.

In which Mr Western pays a visit to his sister, in company with Mr Blifil.

Mrs Western was reading a lecture on prudence, and matrimonial politics, to her niece, when her brother and Blifil broke in with less ceremony than the laws of visiting require. Sophia no sooner saw Blifil than she turned pale, and almost lost the use of all her faculties; but her aunt, on the contrary, waxed red, and, having all her faculties at command, began to exert her tongue on the squire.

"Brother," said she, "I am astonished at your behaviour; will you never learn any regard to decorum? Will you still look upon every apartment as your own, or as belonging to one of your country tenants? Do you think yourself at liberty to invade the privacies of women of condition, without the least decency or notice?"——"Why, what a pox is the matter now?" quoth the squire; "one would think I had caught you at—"—"None of your brutality, sir, I beseech you," answered she.——"You have surprized my poor niece so, that she can hardly, I see, support herself.——Go, my dear, retire, and endeavour to recruit your spirits; for I see you have occasion." At which words Sophia, who never received a more welcome command, hastily withdrew.

"To be sure, sister," cries the squire, "you are mad, when I have brought Mr Blifil here to court her, to force her away."

"Sure, brother," says she, "you are worse than mad, when you know in what situation affairs are, to——I am sure I ask Mr Blifil's pardon, but he knows very well to whom to impute so disagreeable a reception. For my own part, I am sure I shall always be very glad to see Mr Blifil; but his own good sense would not have suffered him to proceed so abruptly, had you not compelled him to it."

Blifil bowed and stammered, and looked like a fool; but Western, without giving him time to form a speech for the purpose, answered, "Well, well, I am to blame, if you will, I always am, certainly; but come, let the girl be fetched back again, or let Mr Blifil go to her.——He's come up on purpose, and there is no time to be lost."

"Brother," cries Mrs Western, "Mr Blifil, I am confident, understands himself better than to think of seeing my niece any more this morning, after what hath happened. Women are of a nice contexture; and our spirits, when disordered, are not to be recomposed in a moment. Had you suffered Mr Blifil to have sent his compliments to my niece, and to have desired the favour of waiting on her in the afternoon, I should possibly have prevailed on her to have seen him; but now I despair of bringing about any such matter."

"I am very sorry, madam," cried Blifil, "that Mr Western's extraordinary kindness to me, which I can never enough acknowledge, should have occasioned—" "Indeed, sir," said she, interrupting him, "you need make no apologies, we all know my brother so well."

"I don't care what anybody knows of me," answered the squire;——"but when must he come to see her? for, consider, I tell you, he is come up on purpose, and so is Allworthy."—"Brother," said she, "whatever message Mr Blifil thinks proper to send to my niece shall be delivered to her; and I suppose she will want no instructions to make a proper answer. I am convinced she will not refuse to see Mr Blifil at a proper time."—"The devil she won't!" answered the squire.—"Odsbud!—Don't we know—I say nothing, but some volk are wiser than all the world.——If I might have had my will, she had not run away before: and now I expect to hear every moment she is guone again. For as great a fool as some volk think me, I know very well she hates——" "No matter, brother," replied Mrs Western, "I will not hear my niece abused. It is a reflection on my family. She is an honour to it; and she will be an honour to it, I promise you. I will pawn my whole reputation in the world on her conduct.——I shall be glad to see you, brother, in the afternoon; for I have somewhat of importance to mention to you.—At present, Mr Blifil, as well as you, must excuse me; for I am in haste to dress." "Well, but," said the squire, "do appoint a time." "Indeed," said she, "I can appoint no time. I tell you I will see you in the afternoon."—"What the devil would you have me do?" cries the squire, turning to Blifil; "I can no more turn her, than a beagle can turn an old hare. Perhaps she will be in a better humour in the afternoon."—"I am condemned, I see, sir, to misfortune," answered Blifil; "but I shall always own my obligations to you." He then took a ceremonious leave of Mrs Western, who was altogether as ceremonious on her part; and then they departed, the squire muttering to himself with an oath, that Blifil should see his daughter in the afternoon.

If Mr Western was little pleased with this interview, Blifil was less. As to the former, he imputed the whole behaviour of his sister to her humour only, and to her dissatisfaction at the omission of ceremony in the visit; but Blifil saw a little deeper into things. He suspected somewhat of more consequence, from two or three words which dropt from the lady; and, to say the truth, he suspected right, as will appear when I have unfolded the several matters which will be contained in the following chapter.

CHAPTER VIII.

Schemes of Lady Bellaston for the ruin of Jones.

Love had taken too deep a root in the mind of Lord Fellamar to be plucked up by the rude hands of Mr Western. In the heat of resentment he had, indeed, given a commission to Captain Egglane, which the captain had far exceeded in the execution; nor had it been executed at all, had his lordship been able to find the captain after he had seen Lady Bellaston, which was in the afternoon of the day after he had received the affront; but so industrious was the captain in the discharge of his duty, that, having after long enquiry found out the squire's lodgings very late in the evening, he sat up all night at a tavern, that he might not miss the squire in the morning, and by that means missed the revocation which my lord had sent to his lodgings.

In the afternoon then next after the intended rape of Sophia, his lordship, as we have said, made a visit to Lady Bellaston, who laid open so much of the character of the squire, that his lordship plainly saw the absurdity he had been guilty of in taking any offence at his words, especially as he had those honourable designs on his daughter. He then unbosomed the violence of his passion to Lady Bellaston, who readily undertook the cause, and encouraged him with certain assurance of a most favourable reception from all the elders of the family, and from the father himself when he should be sober, and should be made acquainted with the nature of the offer made to his daughter. The only danger, she said, lay in the fellow she had formerly mentioned, who, though a beggar and a vagabond, had, by some means or other, she knew not what, procured himself tolerable cloaths, and past for a gentleman. "Now," says she, "as I have, for the sake of my cousin, made it my business to enquire after this fellow, I have luckily found out his lodgings;" with which she then acquainted his lordship. "I am thinking, my lord," added she "(for this fellow is too mean for your personal resentment), whether it would not be possible for your lordship to contrive some method of having him pressed and sent on board a ship. Neither law nor conscience forbid this project: for the fellow, I promise you, however well drest, is but a vagabond, and as proper as any fellow in the streets to be pressed into the service; and as for the conscientious part, surely the preservation of a young lady from such ruin is a most meritorious act; nay, with regard to the fellow himself, unless he could succeed (which Heaven forbid) with my cousin, it may probably be the means of preserving him from the gallows, and perhaps may make his fortune in an honest way."

Lord Fellamar very heartily thanked her ladyship for the part which she was pleased to take in the affair, upon the success of which his whole future happiness entirely depended. He said, he saw at present no objection to the pressing scheme, and would consider of putting it in execution. He then most earnestly recommended to her ladyship to do him the honour of immediately mentioning his proposals to the family; to whom he said he offered a *carte blanche*, and would settle his fortune in almost any manner they should require. And after uttering many ecstasies and raptures concerning Sophia, he took his leave and departed, but not before he had received the strongest charge to beware of Jones, and to lose no time in securing his person, where he should no longer be in a capacity of making any attempts to the ruin of the young lady.

The moment Mrs Western was arrived at her lodgings, a card was despatched with her compliments to Lady Bellaston; who no sooner received it than, with the impatience of a lover, she flew to her cousin, rejoiced at this fair opportunity, which beyond her hopes offered itself, for she was much better pleased with the prospect of making the proposals to a woman of sense, and who knew the world, than to a gentleman whom she honoured with the appellation of Hottentot; though, indeed, from him she apprehended no danger of a refusal.

The two ladies being met, after very short previous ceremonials, fell to business, which was indeed almost as soon concluded as begun; for Mrs Western no sooner heard the name of Lord Fellamar than her cheeks glowed with pleasure; but when she was acquainted with the eagerness of his passion, the earnestness of his proposals, and the generosity of his offer, she declared her full satisfaction in the most explicit terms.

In the progress of their conversation their discourse turned to Jones, and both cousins very pathetically lamented the unfortunate attachment which both agreed Sophia had to that young fellow; and Mrs Western entirely attributed it to the folly of her brother's management. She concluded, however, at last, with declaring her confidence in the good understanding of her niece, who, though she would not give up her affection in favour of Blifil, will, I doubt not, says she, soon be prevailed upon to sacrifice a simple inclination to the addresses of a fine gentleman, who brings her both a title and a large estate: "For, indeed," added she, "I must do Sophy the justice to confess this Blifil is but a hideous kind of fellow, as you know, Bellaston, all country gentlemen are, and hath nothing but his fortune to recommend him."

"Nay," said Lady Bellaston, "I don't then so much wonder at my cousin; for I promise you this Jones is a very agreeable fellow, and hath one virtue, which the men say is a great recommendation to us. What do you think, Mrs Western—I shall certainly make you laugh; nay, I can hardly tell you myself for laughing—will you believe that the fellow hath had the assurance to make love to me? But if you should be inclined to disbelieve it, here is evidence enough, his own handwriting, I assure you." She then delivered her cousin the letter with the proposals of marriage, which, if the reader hath a desire to see, he will find already on record in the XVth book of this history.

"Upon my word I am astonished," said Mrs Western; "this is, indeed, a masterpiece of assurance. With your leave I may possibly make some use of this letter." "You have my full liberty," cries Lady Bellaston, "to apply it to what purpose you please. However, I would not have it shewn to any but Miss Western, nor to her unless you find occasion." "Well, and how did you use the fellow?" returned Mrs Western. "Not as a husband," said the lady; "I am not married, I promise you, my dear. You know, Bell, I have tried the comforts once already; and once, I think, is enough for any reasonable woman."

This letter Lady Bellaston thought would certainly turn the balance against Jones in the mind of Sophia, and she was emboldened to give it up, partly by her hopes of having him instantly dispatched out of the way, and partly by having secured the evidence of Honour, who, upon sounding her, she saw sufficient reason to imagine was prepared to testify whatever she pleased.

But perhaps the reader may wonder why Lady Bellaston, who in her heart hated Sophia, should be so desirous of promoting a match which was so much to the interest of the young lady. Now, I would desire such readers to look carefully into human nature, page almost the last, and there he will find, in scarce legible characters, that women, notwithstanding the preposterous behaviour of mothers, aunts, &c., in matrimonial matters, do in reality think it so great a misfortune to have their inclinations in love thwarted, that they imagine they ought never to carry enmity higher than upon these disappointments; again, he will find it written much about the same place, that a woman who hath once been pleased with the possession of a man, will go above halfway to the devil, to prevent any other woman from enjoying the same.

If he will not be contented with these reasons, I freely confess I see no other motive to the actions of that lady, unless we will conceive she was bribed by Lord Fellamar, which for my own part I see no cause to suspect.

Now this was the affair which Mrs Western was preparing to introduce to Sophia, by some prefatory discourse on the folly of love, and on the wisdom of legal prostitution for hire, when her brother and Blifil broke abruptly in upon her; and hence arose all that coldness in her behaviour to Blifil, which, though the squire, as was usual with him, imputed to a wrong cause, infused into Blifil himself (he being a much more cunning man) a suspicion of the real truth.

CHAPTER IX.

In which Jones pays a visit to Mrs Fitzpatrick.

The reader may now, perhaps, be pleased to return with us to Mr Jones, who, at the appointed hour, attended on Mrs Fitzpatrick; but before we relate the conversation which now past it may be proper, according to our method, to return a little back, and to account for so great an alteration of behaviour in this lady, that from changing her lodging principally to avoid Mr Jones, she had now industriously, as hath been seen, sought this interview.

And here we shall need only to resort to what happened the preceding day, when, hearing from Lady Bellaston that Mr Western was arrived in town, she went to pay her duty to him, at his lodgings at Piccadilly, where she was received with many scurvy compellations too coarse to be repeated, and was even threatened to be kicked out of doors. From hence, an old servant of her aunt Western, with whom she was well acquainted, conducted her to the lodgings of that lady, who treated her not more kindly, but more politely; or, to say the truth, with rudeness in another way. In short, she returned from both, plainly convinced, not only that her scheme of reconciliation had proved abortive, but that she must for ever give over all thoughts of bringing it about by any means whatever. From this moment desire of revenge only filled her mind; and in this temper meeting Jones at the play, an opportunity seemed to her to occur of effecting this purpose.

The reader must remember that he was acquainted by Mrs Fitzpatrick, in the account she gave of her own story, with the fondness Mrs Western had formerly shewn for Mr Fitzpatrick at Bath, from the disappointment of which Mrs Fitzpatrick derived the great bitterness her aunt had expressed toward her. She had, therefore, no doubt but that the good lady would as easily listen to the addresses of Mr Jones as she had before done to the other; for the superiority of charms was clearly on the side of Mr Jones; and the advance which her aunt had since made in age, she concluded (how justly I will not say), was an argument rather in favour of her project than against it.

Therefore, when Jones attended, after a previous declaration of her desire of serving him, arising, as she said, from a firm assurance how much she should by so doing oblige Sophia; and after some excuses for her former disappointment, and after acquainting Mr Jones in whose custody his mistress was, of which she thought him ignorant; she very explicitly mentioned her scheme to him, and advised him to make sham addresses to the older lady, in order to procure an easy access to the younger, informing him at the same time of the success which Mr Fitzpatrick had formerly owed to the very same stratagem.

Mr Jones expressed great gratitude to the lady for the kind intentions towards him which she had expressed, and indeed testified, by this proposal; but, besides intimating some diffidence of success from the lady's knowledge of his love to her niece, which had not been her case in regard to Mr Fitzpatrick, he said, he was afraid Miss Western would never agree to an imposition of this kind, as well from her utter detestation of all fallacy as from her avowed duty to her aunt.

Mrs Fitzpatrick was a little nettled at this; and indeed, if it may not be called a lapse of the tongue, it was a small deviation from politeness in Jones, and into which he scarce would have fallen, had not the delight he felt in praising Sophia hurried him out of all reflection; for this commendation of one cousin was more than a tacit rebuke on the other.

"Indeed, sir," answered the lady, with some warmth, "I cannot think there is anything easier than to cheat an old woman with a profession of love, when her complexion is amorous; and, though she is my aunt, I must say there never was a more liquorish one than her ladyship. Can't you pretend that the despair of possessing her niece, from her being promised to Blifil, has made you turn your thoughts towards her? As to my cousin Sophia, I can't imagine her to be such a simpleton as to have the least scruple on such an account, or to conceive any harm in punishing one of these haggs for the many mischiefs they bring upon families by their tragi-comic passions; for which I think it is a pity they are not punishable by law. I had no such scruple myself; and yet I hope my cousin Sophia will not think it an affront when I say she cannot detest every real species of falsehood more than her cousin Fitzpatrick. To my aunt, indeed, I pretend no duty, nor doth she deserve any. However, sir, I have given you my advice; and if you decline pursuing it, I shall have the less opinion of your understanding—that's all."

Jones now clearly saw the error he had committed, and exerted his utmost power to rectify it; but he only faultered and stuttered into nonsense and contradiction. To say the truth, it is often safer to abide by the consequences of the first blunder than to endeavour to rectify it; for by such endeavours we generally plunge deeper instead of extricating ourselves; and few persons will on such occasions have the good-nature which Mrs Fitzpatrick displayed to Jones, by saying, with a smile, "You need attempt no more excuses; for I can easily forgive a real lover, whatever is the effect of fondness for his mistress."

She then renewed her proposal, and very fervently recommended it, omitting no argument which her invention could suggest on the subject; for she was so violently incensed against her aunt, that scarce anything was capable of affording her equal pleasure with exposing her; and, like a true woman, she would see no difficulties in the execution of a favourite scheme.

Jones, however, persisted in declining the undertaking, which had not, indeed, the least probability of success. He easily perceived the motives which induced Mrs Fitzpatrick to be so eager in pressing her advice. He said he would not deny the tender and passionate regard he had for Sophia; but was so conscious of the inequality of their situations, that he could never flatter himself so far as to hope that so divine a young lady would condescend to think on so unworthy a man; nay, he protested, he could scarce bring himself to wish she should. He concluded with a profession of generous sentiments, which we have not at present leisure to insert.

There are some fine women (for I dare not here speak in too general terms) with whom self is so predominant, that they never detach it from any subject; and, as vanity is with them a ruling principle, they are apt to lay hold of whatever praise they meet with; and, though the property of others, convey it to their own use. In the company of these ladies it is impossible to say anything handsome of another woman which they will not apply to themselves; nay, they often improve the praise they seize; as, for instance, if her beauty, her wit, her gentility, her good humour deserve so much commendation, what do I deserve, who possess those qualities in so much more eminent a degree?

To these ladies a man often recommends himself while he is commending another woman; and, while he is expressing ardour and generous sentiments for his mistress, they are considering what a charming lover this man would make to them, who can feel all this tenderness for an inferior degree of merit. Of this, strange as it may seem, I have seen many instances besides Mrs Fitzpatrick, to whom all this really happened, and who now began to feel a somewhat for Mr Jones, the symptoms of which she much sooner understood than poor Sophia had formerly done.

To say the truth, perfect beauty in both sexes is a more irresistible object than it is generally thought; for, notwithstanding some of us are contented with more homely lots, and learn by rote (as children to repeat what gives them no idea) to despise outside, and to value more solid charms; yet I have always observed, at the approach of consummate beauty, that these more solid charms only shine with that kind of lustre which the stars have after the rising of the sun.

When Jones had finished his exclamations, many of which would have become the mouth of Oroöndates himself, Mrs Fitzpatrick heaved a deep sigh, and, taking her eyes off from Jones, on whom they had been some time fixed, and dropping them on the ground, she cried, "Indeed, Mr Jones, I pity you; but it is the curse of such tenderness to be thrown away on those who are insensible of it. I know my cousin better than you, Mr Jones, and I must say, any woman who makes no return to such a passion, and such a person, is unworthy of both."

"Sure, madam," said Jones, "you can't mean——" "Mean!" cries Mrs Fitzpatrick, "I know not what I mean; there is something, I think, in true tenderness bewitching; few women ever meet with it in men, and fewer still know how to value it when they do. I never heard such truly noble sentiments, and I can't tell how it is, but you force one to believe you. Sure she must be the most contemptible of women who can overlook such merit."

The manner and look with which all this was spoke infused a suspicion into Jones which we don't care to convey in direct words to the reader. Instead of making any answer, he said, "I am afraid, madam, I have made too tiresome a visit;" and offered to take his leave.

"Not at all, sir," answered Mrs Fitzpatrick.—"Indeed I pity you, Mr Jones; indeed I do: but if you are going, consider of the scheme I have mentioned—I am convinced you will approve it—and let me see you again as soon as you can.—To-morrow morning if you will, or at least some time to-morrow. I shall be at home all day."

Jones, then, after many expressions of thanks, very respectfully retired; nor could Mrs Fitzpatrick forbear making him a present of a look at parting, by which if he had understood nothing, he must have had no understanding in the language of the eyes. In reality, it confirmed his resolution of returning to her no more; for, faulty as he hath hitherto appeared in this history, his whole thoughts were now so confined to his Sophia, that I believe no woman upon earth could have now drawn him into an act of inconstancy.

Fortune, however, who was not his friend, resolved, as he intended to give her no second opportunity, to make the best of this; and accordingly produced the tragical incident which we are now in sorrowful notes to record.

CHAPTER X.

The consequence of the preceding visit.

Mr Fitzpatrick having received the letter before mentioned from Mrs Western, and being by that means acquainted with the place to which his wife was retired, returned directly to Bath, and thence the day after set forward to London.

The reader hath been already often informed of the jealous temper of this gentleman. He may likewise be pleased to remember the suspicion which he had conceived of Jones at Upton, upon his finding him in the room with Mrs Waters; and, though sufficient reasons had afterwards appeared entirely to clear up that suspicion, yet now the reading so handsome a character of Mr Jones from his wife, caused him to reflect that she likewise was in the inn at the same time, and jumbled together such a confusion of circumstances in a head which was naturally none of the clearest, that the whole produced that green-eyed monster mentioned by Shakespear in his tragedy of Othello.

And now, as he was enquiring in the street after his wife, and had just received directions to the door, unfortunately Mr Jones was issuing from it.

Fitzpatrick did not yet recollect the face of Jones; however, seeing a young well-dressed fellow coming from his wife, he made directly up to him, and asked him what he had been doing in that house? "for I am sure," said he, "you must have been in it, as I saw you come out of it."

Jones answered very modestly, "That he had been visiting a lady there." To which Fitzpatrick replied, "What business have you with the lady?" Upon which Jones, who now perfectly remembered the voice, features, and indeed coat, of the gentleman, cried out——"Ha, my good friend! give me your hand; I hope there is no ill blood remaining between us, upon a small mistake which happened so long ago."

"Upon my soul, sir," said Fitzpatrick, "I don't know your name nor your face." "Indeed, sir," said Jones, "neither have I the pleasure of knowing your name, but your face I very well remember to have seen before at Upton, where a foolish quarrel happened between us, which, if it is not made up yet, we will now make up over a bottle."

"At Upton!" cried the other;——"Ha! upon my soul, I believe your name is Jones?" "Indeed," answered he, "it is."—"O! upon my soul," cries Fitzpatrick, "you are the very man I wanted to meet.—Upon my soul I will drink a bottle with you presently; but first I will give you a great knock over the pate. There is for you, you rascal. Upon my soul, if you do not give me satisfaction for that blow, I will give you another." And then, drawing his sword, put himself in a posture of defence, which was the only science he understood.

Jones was a little staggered by the blow, which came somewhat unexpectedly; but presently recovering himself he also drew, and though he understood nothing of fencing, prest on so boldly upon Fitzpatrick, that he beat down his guard, and sheathed one half of his sword in the body of the said gentleman, who had no sooner received it than he stept backwards, dropped the point of his sword, and leaning upon it, cried, "I have satisfaction enough: I am a dead man."

"I hope not," cries Jones, "but whatever be the consequence, you must be sensible you have drawn it upon yourself." At this instant a number of fellows rushed in and seized Jones, who told them he should make no resistance, and begged some of them at least would take care of the wounded gentleman.

"Ay," cries one of the fellows, "the wounded gentleman will be taken care enough of; for I suppose he hath not many hours to live. As for you, sir, you have a month at least good yet." "D—n me, Jack," said another, "he hath prevented his voyage; he's bound to another port now;" and many other such jests was our poor Jones made the subject of by these fellows, who were indeed the gang employed by Lord Fellamar, and had dogged him into the house of Mrs Fitzpatrick, waiting for him at the corner of the street when this unfortunate accident happened.

The officer who commanded this gang very wisely concluded that his business was now to deliver his prisoner into the hands of the civil magistrate. He ordered him, therefore, to be carried to a public-house, where, having sent for a constable, he delivered him to his custody.

The constable, seeing Mr Jones very well drest, and hearing that the accident had happened in a duel, treated his prisoner with great civility, and at his request dispatched a messenger to enquire after the wounded gentleman, who was now at a tavern under the surgeon's hands. The report brought back was, that the wound was certainly mortal, and there were no hopes of life. Upon which the constable informed Jones that he must go before a justice. He answered, "Wherever you please; I am indifferent as to what happens to me; for though I am convinced I am not guilty of murder in the eye of the law, yet the weight of blood I find intolerable upon my mind."

Jones was now conducted before the justice, where the surgeon who dressed Mr Fitzpatrick appeared, and deposed that he believed the wound to be mortal; upon which the prisoner was committed to the Gatehouse. It was very late at night, so that Jones would not send for Partridge till the next morning; and, as he never shut his eyes till seven, so it was near twelve before the poor fellow, who was greatly frightened at not hearing from his master so long, received a message which almost deprived him of his being when he heard it.

He went to the Gatehouse with trembling knees and a beating heart, and was no sooner arrived in the presence of Jones than he lamented the misfortune that had befallen him with many tears, looking all the while frequently about him in great terror; for as the news now arrived that Mr Fitzpatrick was dead, the poor fellow apprehended every minute that his ghost would enter the room. At last he delivered him a letter, which he had like to have forgot, and which came from Sophia by the hands of Black George.

Jones presently dispatched every one out of the room, and, having eagerly broke open the letter, read as follows:—

> "You owe the hearing from me again to an accident which I own surprizes me. My aunt hath just now shown me a letter from you to Lady Bellaston, which contains a proposal of marriage. I am convinced it is your own hand; and what more surprizes me is, that it is dated at the very time when you would have me imagine you was under such concern on my account.—I leave you to comment on this fact. All I desire is, that your name may never more be mentioned to
>
> "S. W."

Of the present situation of Mr Jones's mind, and of the pangs with which he was now tormented, we cannot give the reader a better idea than by saying, his misery was such that even Thwackum would almost have pitied him. But, bad as it is, we shall at present leave him in it, as his good genius (if he really had any) seems to have done. And here we put an end to the sixteenth book of our history.

BOOK XVII.

CONTAINING THREE DAYS.

CHAPTER I.

Containing a portion of introductory writing.

When a comic writer hath made his principal characters as happy as he can, or when a tragic writer hath brought them to the highest pitch of human misery, they both conclude their business to be done, and that their work is come to a period.

Had we been of the tragic complexion, the reader must now allow we were very nearly arrived at this period, since it would be difficult for the devil, or any of his representatives on earth, to have contrived much greater torments for poor Jones than those in which we left him in the last chapter; and as for Sophia, a good-natured woman would hardly wish more uneasiness to a rival than what she must at present be supposed to feel. What then remains to complete the tragedy but a murder or two and a few moral sentences!

But to bring our favourites out of their present anguish and distress, and to land them at last on the shore of happiness, seems a much harder task; a task indeed so hard that we do not undertake to execute it. In regard to Sophia, it is more than probable that we shall somewhere or other provide a good husband for her in the end—either Blifil, or my lord, or somebody else; but as to poor Jones, such are the calamities in which he is at present involved, owing to his imprudence, by which if a man doth not become felon to the world, he is at least a *felo de se*; so destitute is he now of friends, and so persecuted by enemies, that we almost despair of bringing him to any good; and if our reader delights in seeing executions, I think he ought not to lose any time in taking a first row at Tyburn.

This I faithfully promise, that, notwithstanding any affection which we may be supposed to have for this rogue, whom we have unfortunately made our heroe, we will lend him none of that supernatural assistance with which we are entrusted, upon condition that we use it only on very important occasions. If he doth not therefore find some natural means of fairly extricating himself from all his distresses, we will do no violence to the truth and dignity of history for his sake; for we had rather relate that he was hanged at Tyburn (which may very probably be the case) than forfeit our integrity, or shock the faith of our reader.

In this the antients had a great advantage over the moderns. Their mythology, which was at that time more firmly believed by the vulgar than any religion is at present, gave them always an opportunity of delivering a favourite heroe. Their deities were always ready at the writer's elbow, to execute any of his purposes; and the more extraordinary the invention was, the greater was the surprize and delight of the credulous reader. Those writers could with greater ease have conveyed a heroe from one country to another, nay from one world to another, and have brought him back again, than a poor circumscribed modern can deliver him from a jail.

The Arabians and Persians had an equal advantage in writing their tales from the genii and fairies, which they believe in as an article of their faith, upon the authority of the Koran itself. But we have none of these helps. To natural means alone we are confined; let us try therefore what, by these means, may be done for poor Jones; though to confess the truth, something whispers me in the ear that he doth not yet know the worst of his fortune; and that a more shocking piece of news than any he hath yet heard remains for him in the unopened leaves of fate.

CHAPTER II.

The generous and grateful behaviour of Mrs Miller.

Mr Allworthy and Mrs Miller were just sat down to breakfast, when Blifil, who had gone out very early that morning, returned to make one of the company.

He had not been long seated before he began as follows: "Good Lord! my dear uncle, what do you think hath happened? I vow I am afraid of telling it you, for fear of shocking you with the remembrance of ever having shewn any kindness to such a villain." "What is the matter, child?" said the uncle. "I fear I have shewn kindness in my life to the unworthy more than once. But charity doth not adopt the vices of its objects." "O, sir!" returned Blifil, "it is not without the secret direction of Providence that you mention the word adoption. Your adopted son, sir, that Jones, that wretch whom you nourished in your bosom, hath proved one of the greatest villains upon earth." "By all that's sacred 'tis false," cries Mrs Miller. "Mr Jones is no villain. He is one of the worthiest creatures breathing; and if any other person had called him villain, I would have thrown all this boiling water in his face." Mr Allworthy looked very much amazed at this behaviour. But she did not give him leave to speak, before, turning to him, she cried, "I hope you will not be angry with me; I would not offend you, sir, for the world; but, indeed, I could not bear to hear him called so." "I must own, madam," said Allworthy, very gravely, "I am a little surprized to hear you so warmly defend a fellow you do not know." "O! I do know him, Mr Allworthy," said she, "indeed I do; I should be the most ungrateful of all wretches if I denied it. O! he hath preserved me and my little family; we have all reason to bless him while we live.—And I pray Heaven to bless him, and turn the hearts of his malicious enemies. I know, I find, I see, he hath such." "You surprize me, madam, still more," said Allworthy; "sure you must mean some other. It is impossible you should have any such obligations to the man my nephew mentions." "Too surely," answered she, "I have obligations to him of the greatest and tenderest kind. He hath been the preserver of me and mine. Believe me, sir, he hath been abused, grossly abused to you; I know he hath, or you, whom I know to be all goodness and honour, would not, after the many kind and tender things I have heard you say of this poor helpless child, have so disdainfully called him fellow.—Indeed, my best of friends, he deserves a kinder appellation from you, had you heard the good, the kind, the grateful things which I have heard him utter of you. He never mentions your name but with a sort of adoration. In this very room I have seen him on his knees, imploring all the blessings of heaven upon your head. I do not love that child there better than he loves you."

"I see, sir, now," said Blifil, with one of those grinning sneers with which the devil marks his best beloved, "Mrs Miller really doth know him. I suppose you will find she is not the only one of your acquaintance to whom he hath exposed you. As for my character, I perceive, by some hints she hath thrown out, he hath been very free with it, but I forgive him." "And the Lord forgive you, sir!" said Mrs Miller; "we have all sins enough to stand in need of his forgiveness."

"Upon my word, Mrs Miller," said Allworthy, "I do not take this behaviour of yours to my nephew kindly; and I do assure you, as any reflections which you cast upon him must come only from that wickedest of men, they would only serve, if that were possible, to heighten my resentment against him: for I must tell you, Mrs Miller, the young man who now stands before you hath ever been the warmest advocate for the ungrateful wretch whose cause you espouse. This, I think, when you hear it from my own mouth, will make you wonder at so much baseness and ingratitude."

"You are deceived, sir," answered Mrs Miller; "if they were the last words which were to issue from my lips, I would say you were deceived; and I once more repeat it, the Lord forgive those who have deceived you! I do not pretend to say the young man is without faults; but they are all the faults of wildness and of youth; faults which he may, nay, which I am certain he will, relinquish, and, if he should not, they are vastly overbalanced by one of the most humane, tender, honest hearts that ever man was blest with."

"Indeed, Mrs Miller," said Allworthy, "had this been related of you, I should not have believed it." "Indeed, sir," answered she, "you will believe everything I have said, I am sure you will: and when you have heard the story which I shall tell you (for I will tell you all), you will be so far from being offended, that you will own (I know your justice so well), that I must have been the most despicable and most ungrateful of wretches if I had acted any other part than I have."

"Well, madam," said Allworthy, "I shall be very glad to hear any good excuse for a behaviour which, I must confess, I think wants an excuse. And now, madam, will you be pleased to let my nephew proceed in his story without interruption. He would not have introduced a matter of slight consequence with such a preface. Perhaps even this story will cure you of your mistake."

Mrs Miller gave tokens of submission, and then Mr Blifil began thus: "I am sure, sir, if you don't think proper to resent the ill-usage of Mrs Miller, I shall easily forgive what affects me only. I think your goodness hath not deserved this indignity at her hands." "Well, child," said Allworthy, "but what is this new instance? What hath he done of late?" "What," cries Blifil, "notwithstanding all Mrs Miller hath said, I am very sorry to relate, and what you should never have heard from me, had it not been a matter impossible to conceal from the whole world. In short he hath killed a man; I will not say murdered—for perhaps it may not be so construed in law, and I hope the best for his sake."

Allworthy looked shocked, and blessed himself; and then, turning to Mrs Miller, he cried, "Well, madam, what say you now?"

"Why, I say, sir," answered she, "that I never was more concerned at anything in my life; but, if the fact be true, I am convinced the man, whoever he is, was in fault. Heaven knows there are many villains in this town who make it their business to provoke young gentlemen. Nothing but the greatest provocation could have tempted him; for of all the gentlemen I ever had in my house, I never saw one so gentle or so sweet-tempered. He was beloved by every one in the house, and every one who came near it."

While she was thus running on, a violent knocking at the door interrupted their conversation, and prevented her from proceeding further, or from receiving any answer; for, as she concluded this was a visitor to Mr Allworthy, she hastily retired, taking with her her little girl, whose eyes were all over blubbered at the melancholy news she heard of Jones, who used to call her his little wife, and not only gave her many playthings, but spent whole hours in playing with her himself.

Some readers may, perhaps, be pleased with these minute circumstances, in relating of which we follow the example of Plutarch, one of the best of our brother historians; and others, to whom they may appear trivial, will, we hope, at least pardon them, as we are never prolix on such occasions.

CHAPTER III.

The arrival of Mr Western, with some matters concerning the paternal authority.

Mrs Miller had not long left the room when Mr Western entered; but not before a small wrangling bout had passed between him and his chairmen; for the fellows, who had taken up their burden at the Hercules Pillars, had conceived no hopes of having any future good customer in the squire; and they were moreover farther encouraged by his generosity (for he had given them of his own accord sixpence more than their fare); they therefore very boldly demanded another shilling, which so provoked the squire, that he not only bestowed many hearty curses on them at the door, but retained his anger after he came into the room; swearing that all the Londoners were like the court, and thought of nothing but plundering country gentlemen. "D—n me," says he, "if I won't walk in the rain rather than get into one of their hand-barrows again. They have jolted me more in a mile than Brown Bess would in a long fox-chase."

When his wrath on this occasion was a little appeased, he resumed the same passionate tone on another. "There," says he, "there is fine business forwards now. The hounds have changed at last; and when we imagined we had a fox to deal with, od-rat it, it turns out to be a badger at last!"

"Pray, my good neighbour," said Allworthy, "drop your metaphors, and speak a little plainer." "Why, then," says the squire, "to tell you plainly, we have been all this time afraid of a son of a whore of a bastard of somebody's, I don't know whose, not I. And now here's a confounded son of a whore of a lord, who may be a bastard too for what I know or care, for he shall never have a daughter of mine by my consent. They have beggared the nation, but they shall never beggar me. My land shall never be sent over to Hanover."

"You surprize me much, my good friend," said Allworthy. "Why, zounds! I am surprized myself," answered the squire. "I went to zee sister Western last night, according to her own appointment, and there I was had into a whole room full of women. There was my lady cousin Bellaston, and my Lady Betty, and my Lady Catherine, and my lady I don't know who; d—n me, if ever you catch me among such a kennel of hoop-petticoat b—s! D—n me, I'd rather be run by my own dogs, as one Acton was, that the story-book says was turned into a hare, and his own dogs killed un and eat un. Od-rabbit it, no mortal was ever run in such a manner; if I dodged one way, one had me; if I offered to clap back, another snapped me.

`O! certainly one of the greatest matches in England,' says one cousin (here he attempted to mimic them); `A very advantageous offer indeed,' cries another cousin (for you must know they be all my cousins, thof I never zeed half o' um before). `Surely,' says that fat a—se b—, my Lady Bellaston, `cousin, you must be out of your wits to think of refusing such an offer.'"

"Now I begin to understand," says Allworthy; "some person hath made proposals to Miss Western, which the ladies of the family approve, but is not to your liking."

"My liking!" said Western, "how the devil should it? I tell you it is a lord, and those are always volks whom you know I always resolved to have nothing to do with. Did unt I refuse a matter of vorty years' purchase now for a bit of land, which one o' um had a mind to put into a park, only because I would have no dealings with lords, and dost think I would marry my daughter zu? Besides, ben't I engaged to you, and did I ever go off any bargain when I had promised?"

"As to that point, neighbour," said Allworthy, "I entirely release you from any engagement. No contract can be binding between parties who have not a full power to make it at the time, nor ever afterwards acquire the power of fulfilling it."

"Slud! then," answered Western, "I tell you I have power, and I will fulfil it. Come along with me directly to Doctors' Commons, I will get a licence; and I will go to sister and take away the wench by force, and she shall ha un, or I will lock her up, and keep her upon bread and water as long as she lives."

"Mr Western," said Allworthy, "shall I beg you will hear my full sentiments on this matter?"—"Hear thee; ay, to be sure I will," answered he. "Why, then, sir," cries Allworthy, "I can truly say, without a compliment either to you or the young lady, that when this match was proposed, I embraced it very readily and heartily, from my regard to you both. An alliance between two families so nearly neighbours, and between whom there had always existed so mutual an intercourse and good harmony, I thought a most desirable event; and with regard to the young lady, not only the concurrent opinion of all who knew her, but my own observation assured me that she would be an inestimable treasure to a good husband. I shall say nothing of her personal qualifications, which certainly are admirable; her good nature, her charitable disposition, her modesty, are too well known to need any panegyric: but she hath one quality which existed in a high degree in that best of women, who is now one of the first of angels, which, as it is not of a glaring kind, more commonly escapes observation; so little indeed is it remarked, that I want a word to express it. I must use negatives on this occasion. I never heard anything of pertness, or what is called repartee, out of her mouth; no pretence to wit, much less to that kind of wisdom which is the result only of great learning and experience, the affectation of which, in a young woman, is as absurd as any of the affectations of an ape. No dictatorial sentiments, no judicial opinions, no profound criticisms. Whenever I have seen her in the company of men, she hath been all attention, with the modesty of a learner, not the forwardness of a teacher. You'll pardon me for it, but I once, to try her only, desired her opinion on a point which was controverted between Mr Thwackum and Mr Square. To which she answered, with much sweetness, `You will pardon me, good Mr Allworthy; I am sure you cannot in earnest think me capable of deciding any point in which two such gentlemen disagree.' Thwackum and Square, who both alike thought themselves sure of a favourable decision, seconded my request. She answered with the same good humour, `I must absolutely be excused: for I will affront neither so much as to give my judgment on his side.' Indeed, she always shewed the highest deference to the understandings of men; a quality absolutely essential to the making a good wife. I shall only add, that as she is most apparently void of all affectation, this deference must be certainly real."

Here Blifil sighed bitterly; upon which Western, whose eyes were full of tears at the praise of Sophia, blubbered out, "Don't be chicken-hearted, for shat ha her, d—n me, shat ha her, if she was twenty times as good."

"Remember your promise, sir," cried Allworthy, "I was not to be interrupted." "Well, shat unt," answered the squire; "I won't speak another word."

"Now, my good friend," continued Allworthy, "I have dwelt so long on the merit of this young lady, partly as I really am in love with her character, and partly that fortune (for the match in that light is really advantageous on my nephew's side) might not be imagined to be my principal view in having so eagerly embraced the proposal. Indeed, I heartily wished to receive so great a jewel into my family; but though I may wish for many good things, I would not, therefore, steal them, or be guilty of any violence or injustice to possess myself of them. Now to force a woman into a marriage contrary to her consent or approbation, is an act of such injustice and oppression, that I wish the laws of our country could restrain it; but a good conscience is never lawless in the worst regulated state, and will provide those laws for itself, which the neglect of legislators hath forgotten to supply. This is surely a case of that kind; for, is it not cruel, nay, impious, to force a woman into that state against her will; for her behaviour in which she is to be accountable to the highest and most dreadful court of judicature, and to answer at the peril of her soul? To discharge the matrimonial duties in an adequate manner is no easy task; and shall we lay this burthen upon a woman, while we at the same time deprive her of all that assistance which may enable her to undergo it? Shall we tear her very heart from her, while we enjoin her duties to which a whole heart is scarce equal? I must speak very plainly here. I think parents who act in this manner are accessories to all the guilt which their children afterwards incur, and of course must, before a just judge, expect to partake of their punishment; but if they could avoid this, good heaven! is there a soul who can bear the thought of having contributed to the damnation of his child?

"For these reasons, my best neighbour, as I see the inclinations of this young lady are most unhappily averse to my nephew, I must decline any further thoughts of the honour you intended him, though I assure you I shall always retain the most grateful sense of it."

"Well, sir," said Western (the froth bursting forth from his lips the moment they were uncorked), "you cannot say but I have heard you out, and now I expect you'll hear me; and if I don't answer every word on't, why then I'll consent to gee the matter up. First then, I desire you to answer me one question—Did not I beget her? did not I beget her? answer me that. They say, indeed, it is a wise father that knows his own child; but I am sure I have the best title to her, for I bred her up. But I believe you will allow me to be her father, and if I be, am I not to govern my own child? I ask you that, am I not to govern my own child? and if I am to govern her in other matters, surely I am to govern her in this, which concerns her most. And what am I desiring all this while? Am I desiring her to do anything for me? to give me anything?—Zu much on t'other side, that I am only desiring her to take away half my estate now, and t'other half when I die. Well, and what is it all vor? Why, is unt it to make her happy? It's enough to make one mad to hear volks talk; if I was going to marry myself, then she would ha reason to cry and to blubber; but, on the contrary, han't I offered to bind down my land in such a manner, that I could not marry if I would, seeing as narro' woman upon earth would ha me. What the devil in hell can I do more? I contribute to her damnation!—Zounds! I'd zee all the world d—n'd bevore her little vinger should be hurt. Indeed, Mr Allworthy, you must excuse me, but I am surprized to hear you talk in zuch a manner, and I must say, take it how you will, that I thought you had more sense."

Allworthy resented this reflection only with a smile; nor could he, if he would have endeavoured it, have conveyed into that smile any mixture of malice or contempt. His smiles at folly were indeed such as we may suppose the angels bestow on the absurdities of mankind.

Blifil now desired to be permitted to speak a few words. "As to using any violence on the young lady, I am sure I shall never consent to it. My conscience will not permit me to use violence on any one, much less on a lady for whom, however cruel she is to me, I shall always preserve the purest and sincerest affection; but yet I have read that women are seldom proof against perseverance. Why may I not hope then by such perseverance at last to gain those inclinations, in which for the future I shall, perhaps, have no rival; for as for this lord, Mr Western is so kind to prefer me to him; and sure, sir, you will not deny but that a parent hath at least a negative voice in these matters; nay, I have heard this very young lady herself say so more than once, and declare that she thought children inexcusable who married in direct opposition to the will of their parents. Besides, though the other ladies of the family seem to favour the pretensions of my lord, I do not find the lady herself is inclined to give him any countenance; alas! I am too well assured she is not; I am too sensible that wickedest of men remains uppermost in her heart."

"Ay, ay, so he does," cries Western.

"But surely," says Blifil, "when she hears of this murder which he hath committed, if the law should spare his life——"

"What's that?" cries Western. "Murder! hath he committed a murder, and is there any hopes of seeing him hanged?—Tol de rol, tol lol de rol." Here he fell a singing and capering about the room.

"Child," says Allworthy, "this unhappy passion of yours distresses me beyond measure. I heartily pity you, and would do every fair thing to promote your success."

"I desire no more," cries Blifil; "I am convinced my dear uncle hath a better opinion of me than to think that I myself would accept of more."

"Lookee," says Allworthy, "you have my leave to write, to visit, if she will permit it—but I insist on no thoughts of violence. I will have no confinement, nothing of that kind attempted."

"Well, well," cries the squire, "nothing of that kind shall be attempted; we will try a little longer what fair means will effect; and if this fellow be but hanged out of the way—Tol lol de rol! I never heard better news in my life—I warrant everything goes to my mind.—Do, prithee, dear Allworthy, come and dine with me at the Hercules Pillars: I have bespoke a shoulder of mutton roasted, and a spare-rib of pork, and a fowl and egg-sauce. There will be nobody but ourselves, unless we have a mind to have the landlord; for I have sent Parson Supple down to Basingstoke after my tobacco-box, which I left at an inn there, and I would not lose it for the world; for it is an old acquaintance of above twenty years' standing. I can tell you landlord is a vast comical bitch, you will like un hugely."

Mr Allworthy at last agreed to this invitation, and soon after the squire went off, singing and capering at the hopes of seeing the speedy tragical end of poor Jones.

When he was gone, Mr Allworthy resumed the aforesaid subject with much gravity. He told his nephew, "He wished with all his heart he would endeavour to conquer a passion, in which I cannot," says he, "flatter you with any hopes of succeeding. It is certainly a vulgar error, that aversion in a woman may be conquered by perseverance. Indifference may, perhaps, sometimes yield to it; but the usual triumphs gained by perseverance in a lover are over caprice, prudence, affectation, and often an exorbitant degree of levity, which excites women not overwarm in their constitutions to indulge their vanity by prolonging the time of courtship, even when they are well enough pleased with the object, and resolve (if they ever resolve at all) to make him a very pitiful amends in the end. But a fixed dislike, as I am afraid this is, will rather gather strength than be conquered by time. Besides, my dear, I have another apprehension which you must excuse. I am afraid this passion which you have for this fine young creature hath her beautiful person too much for its object, and is unworthy of the name of that love which is the only foundation of matrimonial felicity. To admire, to like, and to long for the possession of a beautiful woman, without any regard to her sentiments towards us, is, I am afraid, too natural; but love, I believe, is the child of love only; at least, I am pretty confident that to love the creature who we are assured hates us is not in human nature. Examine your heart, therefore, thoroughly, my good boy, and if, upon examination, you have but the least suspicion of this kind, I am sure your own virtue and religion will impel you to drive so vicious a passion from your heart, and your good sense will soon enable you to do it without pain."

BOOK XVII. CHAPTER III.

The reader may pretty well guess Blifil's answer; but, if he should be at a loss, we are not at present at leisure to satisfy him, as our history now hastens on to matters of higher importance, and we can no longer bear to be absent from Sophia.

CHAPTER IV.

An extraordinary scene between Sophia and her aunt.

The lowing heifer and the bleating ewe, in herds and flocks, may ramble safe and unregarded through the pastures. These are, indeed, hereafter doomed to be the prey of man; yet many years are they suffered to enjoy their liberty undisturbed. But if a plump doe be discovered to have escaped from the forest, and to repose herself in some field or grove, the whole parish is presently alarmed, every man is ready to set his dogs after her; and, if she is preserved from the rest by the good squire, it is only that he may secure her for his own eating.

I have often considered a very fine young woman of fortune and fashion, when first found strayed from the pale of her nursery, to be in pretty much the same situation with this doe. The town is immediately in an uproar; she is hunted from park to play, from court to assembly, from assembly to her own chamber, and rarely escapes a single season from the jaws of some devourer or other; for, if her friends protect her from some, it is only to deliver her over to one of their own chusing, often more disagreeable to her than any of the rest; while whole herds or flocks of other women securely, and scarce regarded, traverse the park, the play, the opera, and the assembly; and though, for the most part at least, they are at last devoured, yet for a long time do they wanton in liberty, without disturbance or controul.

Of all these paragons none ever tasted more of this persecution than poor Sophia. Her ill stars were not contented with all that she had suffered on account of Blifil, they now raised her another pursuer, who seemed likely to torment her no less than the other had done. For though her aunt was less violent, she was no less assiduous in teizing her, than her father had been before.

The servants were no sooner departed after dinner than Mrs Western, who had opened the matter to Sophia, informed her, "That she expected his lordship that very afternoon, and intended to take the first opportunity of leaving her alone with him." "If you do, madam," answered Sophia, with some spirit, "I shall take the first opportunity of leaving him by himself." "How! madam!" cries the aunt; "is this the return you make me for my kindness in relieving you from your confinement at your father's?" "You know, madam," said Sophia, "the cause of that confinement was a refusal to comply with my father in accepting a man I detested; and will my dear aunt, who hath relieved me from that distress, involve me in another equally bad?" "And do you think then, madam," answered Mrs Western, "that there is no difference between my Lord Fellamar and Mr Blifil?" "Very little, in my opinion," cries Sophia; "and, if I must be condemned to one, I would certainly have the merit of sacrificing myself to my father's pleasure." "Then my pleasure, I find," said the aunt, "hath very little weight with you; but that consideration shall not move me. I act from nobler motives. The view of aggrandizing my family, of ennobling yourself, is what I proceed upon. Have you no sense of ambition? Are there no charms in the thoughts of having a coronet on your coach?" "None, upon my honour," said Sophia. "A pincushion upon my coach would please me just as well." "Never mention honour," cries the aunt. "It becomes not the mouth of such a wretch. I am sorry, niece, you force me to use these words, but I cannot bear your groveling temper; you have none of the blood of the Westerns in you. But, however mean and base your own ideas are, you shall bring no imputation on mine. I will never suffer the world to say of me that I encouraged you in refusing one of the best matches in England; a match which, besides its advantage in fortune, would do honour to almost any family, and hath, indeed, in title, the advantage of ours." "Surely," says Sophia, "I am born deficient, and have not the senses with which other people are blessed; there must be certainly some sense which can relish the delights of sound and show, which I have not; for surely mankind would not labour so much, nor sacrifice so much for the obtaining, nor would they be so elate and proud with possessing, what appeared to them, as it doth to me, the most insignificant of all trifles."

"No, no, miss," cries the aunt; "you are born with as many senses as other people; but I assure you you are not born with a sufficient understanding to make a fool of me, or to expose my conduct to the world; so I declare this to you, upon my word, and you know, I believe, how fixed my resolutions are, unless you agree to see his lordship this afternoon, I will, with my own hands, deliver you to-morrow morning to my brother, and will never henceforth interfere with you, nor see your face again." Sophia stood a few moments silent after this speech, which was uttered in a most angry and peremptory tone; and then, bursting into tears, she cryed, "Do with me, madam, whatever you please; I am the most miserable undone wretch upon earth; if my dear aunt forsakes me where shall I look for a protector?" "My dear niece," cries she, "you will have a very good protector in his lordship; a protector whom nothing but a hankering after that vile fellow Jones can make you decline." "Indeed, madam," said Sophia, "you wrong me. How can you imagine, after what you have shewn me, if I had ever any such thoughts, that I should not banish them for ever? If it will satisfy you, I will receive the sacrament upon it never to see his face again." "But, child, dear child," said the aunt, "be reasonable; can you invent a single objection?" "I have already, I think, told you a sufficient objection," answered Sophia. "What?" cries the aunt; "I remember none." "Sure, madam," said Sophia, "I told you he had used me in the rudest and vilest manner." "Indeed, child," answered she, "I never heard you, or did not understand you:—but what do you mean by this rude, vile manner?" "Indeed, madam," said Sophia, "I am almost ashamed to tell you. He caught me in his arms, pulled me down upon the settee, and thrust his hand into my bosom, and kissed it with such violence that I have the mark upon my left breast at this moment." "Indeed!" said Mrs Western. "Yes, indeed, madam," answered Sophia; "my father luckily came in at that instant, or Heaven knows what rudeness he intended to have proceeded to." "I am astonished and confounded," cries the aunt. "No woman of the name of Western hath been ever treated so since we were a family. I would have torn the eyes of a prince out, if he had attempted such freedoms with me. It is impossible! sure, Sophia, you must invent this to raise my indignation against him." "I hope, madam," said Sophia, "you have too good an opinion of me to imagine me capable of telling an untruth. Upon my soul it is true." "I should have stabbed him to the heart, had I been present," returned the aunt. "Yet surely he could have no dishonourable design; it is impossible! he durst not: besides, his proposals shew he hath not; for they are not only honourable, but generous. I don't know; the age allows too great freedoms. A distant salute is all I would have allowed before the ceremony. I have had lovers formerly, not so long ago neither; several lovers, though I never would consent to marriage, and I never encouraged the least freedom. It is a foolish custom, and what I never would agree to. No man kissed more of me than my cheek. It is as much as one can bring oneself to give lips up to a husband; and, indeed, could I ever have been persuaded to marry, I believe I should not have soon been brought to endure so much." "You will pardon me, dear madam," said Sophia, "if I make one observation: you own you have had many lovers, and the world knows it, even if you should deny it. You refused them all, and, I am convinced, one coronet at least among them." "You say true, dear Sophy," answered she; "I had once the offer of a title." "Why, then," said Sophia, "will you not suffer me to refuse this once?" "It is true, child," said she, "I have refused the offer of a title; but it was not so good an offer; that is, not so very, very good an offer."—"Yes, madam," said Sophia; "but you have had very great proposals from men of vast fortunes. It was not the first, nor the second, nor the third advantageous match that offered itself." "I own it was not," said she. "Well, madam," continued Sophia, "and why may not I expect to have a second, perhaps, better than this? You are now but a young woman, and I am convinced would not promise to yield to the first lover of fortune, nay, or of title too. I am a very young woman, and sure I need not despair." "Well, my dear, dear Sophy," cries the aunt, "what would you have me say?" "Why, I only beg that I may not be left alone, at least this evening; grant me that, and I will submit, if you think, after what is past, I ought to see him in your company." "Well, I will grant it," cries the aunt. "Sophy, you know I love you, and can deny you nothing. You know the easiness of my nature; I have not always been so easy. I have been formerly thought cruel; by the men, I mean. I was called the cruel Parthenissa. I have broke many a window that has had verses to the cruel Parthenissa in it. Sophy, I was never so handsome as you, and yet I had something of you formerly. I am a little altered. Kingdoms and states, as Tully Cicero says in his epistles, undergo alterations, and so must the human form." Thus run she on for near half an hour upon herself, and her conquests, and her cruelty, till the arrival of my lord, who, after a most tedious visit, during which Mrs Western never once offered to leave the room, retired, not much more satisfied with the aunt than with the niece; for Sophia had brought her aunt into so excellent a temper, that she consented to almost everything her niece said; and agreed that a little distant behaviour might not be improper to so forward a lover.

Thus Sophia, by a little well-directed flattery, for which surely none will blame her, obtained a little ease for herself, and, at least, put off the evil day. And now we have seen our heroine in a better situation than she hath been for a long time before, we will look a little after Mr Jones, whom we left in the most deplorable situation that can be well imagined.

CHAPTER V.

Mrs Miller and Mr Nightingale visit Jones in the prison.

When Mr Allworthy and his nephew went to meet Mr Western, Mrs Miller set forwards to her son-in-law's lodgings, in order to acquaint him with the accident which had befallen his friend Jones; but he had known it long before from Partridge (for Jones, when he left Mrs Miller, had been furnished with a room in the same house with Mr Nightingale). The good woman found her daughter under great affliction on account of Mr Jones, whom having comforted as well as she could, she set forwards to the Gatehouse, where she heard he was, and where Mr Nightingale was arrived before her.

The firmness and constancy of a true friend is a circumstance so extremely delightful to persons in any kind of distress, that the distress itself, if it be only temporary, and admits of relief, is more than compensated by bringing this comfort with it. Nor are instances of this kind so rare as some superficial and inaccurate observers have reported. To say the truth, want of compassion is not to be numbered among our general faults. The black ingredient which fouls our disposition is envy. Hence our eye is seldom, I am afraid, turned upward to those who are manifestly greater, better, wiser, or happier than ourselves, without some degree of malignity; while we commonly look downwards on the mean and miserable with sufficient benevolence and pity. In fact, I have remarked, that most of the defects which have discovered themselves in the friendships within my observation have arisen from envy only: a hellish vice; and yet one from which I have known very few absolutely exempt. But enough of a subject which, if pursued, would lead me too far.

Whether it was that Fortune was apprehensive lest Jones should sink under the weight of his adversity, and that she might thus lose any future opportunity of tormenting him, or whether she really abated somewhat of her severity towards him, she seemed a little to relax her persecution, by sending him the company of two such faithful friends, and what is perhaps more rare, a faithful servant. For Partridge, though he had many imperfections, wanted not fidelity; and though fear would not suffer him to be hanged for his master, yet the world, I believe, could not have bribed him to desert his cause.

While Jones was expressing great satisfaction in the presence of his friends, Partridge brought an account that Mr Fitzpatrick was still alive, though the surgeon declared that he had very little hopes. Upon which, Jones fetching a deep sigh, Nightingale said to him, "My dear Tom, why should you afflict yourself so upon an accident, which, whatever be the consequence, can be attended with no danger to you, and in which your conscience cannot accuse you of having been the least to blame? If the fellow should die, what have you done more than taken away the life of a ruffian in your own defence? So will the coroner's inquest certainly find it; and then you will be easily admitted to bail, and, though you must undergo the form of a trial, yet it is a trial which many men would stand for you for a shilling." "Come, come, Mr Jones," says Mrs Miller, "chear yourself up. I knew you could not be the aggressor, and so I told Mr Allworthy, and so he shall acknowledge too, before I have done with him."

Jones gravely answered, "That whatever might be his fate, he should always lament the having shed the blood of one of his fellow-creatures, as one of the highest misfortunes which could have befallen him. But I have another misfortune of the tenderest kind——O! Mrs Miller, I have lost what I held most dear upon earth." "That must be a mistress," said Mrs Miller; "but come, come; I know more than you imagine" (for indeed Partridge had blabbed all); "and I have heard more than you know. Matters go better, I promise you, than you think; and I would not give Blifil sixpence for all the chance which he hath of the lady."

"Indeed, my dear friend, indeed," answered Jones, "you are an entire stranger to the cause of my grief. If you was acquainted with the story, you would allow my case admitted of no comfort. I apprehend no danger from Blifil. I have undone myself." "Don't despair," replied Mrs Miller; "you know not what a woman can do; and if anything be in my power, I promise you I will do it to serve you. It is my duty. My son, my dear Mr Nightingale, who is so kind to tell me he hath obligations to you on the same account, knows it is my duty. Shall I go to the lady myself? I will say anything to her you would have me say."

"Thou best of women," cries Jones, taking her by the hand, "talk not of obligations to me;—but as you have been so kind to mention it, there is a favour which, perhaps, may be in your power. I see you are acquainted with the lady (how you came by your information I know not), who sits, indeed, very near my heart. If you could contrive to deliver this (giving her a paper from his pocket), I shall for ever acknowledge your goodness."

"Give it me," said Mrs Miller. "If I see it not in her own possession before I sleep, may my next sleep be my last! Comfort yourself, my good young man! be wise enough to take warning from past follies, and I warrant all shall be well, and I shall yet see you happy with the most charming young lady in the world; for I so hear from every one she is."

"Believe me, madam," said he, "I do not speak the common cant of one in my unhappy situation. Before this dreadful accident happened, I had resolved to quit a life of which I was become sensible of the wickedness as well as folly. I do assure you, notwithstanding the disturbances I have unfortunately occasioned in your house, for which I heartily ask your pardon, I am not an abandoned profligate. Though I have been hurried into vices, I do not approve a vicious character, nor will I ever, from this moment, deserve it."

Mrs Miller expressed great satisfaction in these declarations, in the sincerity of which she averred she had an entire faith; and now the remainder of the conversation past in the joint attempts of that good woman and Mr Nightingale to cheer the dejected spirits of Mr Jones, in which they so far succeeded as to leave him much better comforted and satisfied than they found him; to which happy alteration nothing so much contributed as the kind undertaking of Mrs Miller to deliver his letter to Sophia, which he despaired of finding any means to accomplish; for when Black George produced the last from Sophia, he informed Partridge that she had strictly charged him, on pain of having it communicated to her father, not to bring her any answer. He was, moreover, not a little pleased to find he had so warm an advocate to Mr Allworthy himself in this good woman, who was, in reality, one of the worthiest creatures in the world.

After about an hour's visit from the lady (for Nightingale had been with him much longer), they both took their leave, promising to return to him soon; during which Mrs Miller said she hoped to bring him some good news from his mistress, and Mr Nightingale promised to enquire into the state of Mr Fitzpatrick's wound, and likewise to find out some of the persons who were present at the rencounter.

The former of these went directly in quest of Sophia, whither we likewise shall now attend her.

CHAPTER VI.

In which Mrs Miller pays a visit to Sophia.

Access to the young lady was by no means difficult; for, as she lived now on a perfect friendly footing with her aunt, she was at full liberty to receive what visitants she pleased.

Sophia was dressing when she was acquainted that there was a gentlewoman below to wait on her. As she was neither afraid, nor ashamed, to see any of her own sex, Mrs Miller was immediately admitted.

Curtsies and the usual ceremonials between women who are strangers to each other, being past, Sophia said, "I have not the pleasure to know you, madam." "No, madam," answered Mrs Miller, "and I must beg pardon for intruding upon you. But when you know what has induced me to give you this trouble, I hope——" "Pray, what is your business, madam?" said Sophia, with a little emotion. "Madam, we are not alone," replied Mrs Miller, in a low voice. "Go out, Betty," said Sophia.

When Betty was departed, Mrs Miller said, "I was desired, madam, by a very unhappy young gentleman, to deliver you this letter." Sophia changed colour when she saw the direction, well knowing the hand, and after some hesitation, said—"I could not conceive, madam, from your appearance, that your business had been of such a nature.—Whomever you brought this letter from, I shall not open it. I should be sorry to entertain an unjust suspicion of any one; but you are an utter stranger to me."

"If you will have patience, madam," answered Mrs Miller, "I will acquaint you who I am, and how I came by that letter." "I have no curiosity, madam, to know anything," cries Sophia; "but I must insist on your delivering that letter back to the person who gave it you."

Mrs Miller then fell upon her knees, and in the most passionate terms implored her compassion; to which Sophia answered: "Sure, madam, it is surprizing you should be so very strongly interested in the behalf of this person. I would not think, madam"—"No, madam," says Mrs Miller, "you shall not think anything but the truth. I will tell you all, and you will not wonder that I am interested. He is the best-natured creature that ever was born."—She then began and related the story of Mr Anderson.—After this she cried, "This, madam, this is his goodness; but I have much more tender obligations to him. He hath preserved my child."—Here, after shedding some tears, she related everything concerning that fact, suppressing only those circumstances which would have most reflected on her daughter, and concluded with saying, "Now, madam, you shall judge whether I can ever do enough for so kind, so good, so generous a young man; and sure he is the best and worthiest of all human beings."

The alterations in the countenance of Sophia had hitherto been chiefly to her disadvantage, and had inclined her complexion to too great paleness; but she now waxed redder, if possible, than vermilion, and cried, "I know not what to say; certainly what arises from gratitude cannot be blamed—But what service can my reading this letter do your friend, since I am resolved never——" Mrs Miller fell again to her entreaties, and begged to be forgiven, but she could not, she said, carry it back. "Well, madam," says Sophia, "I cannot help it, if you will force it upon me.—Certainly you may leave it whether I will or no." What Sophia meant, or whether she meant anything, I will not presume to determine; but Mrs Miller actually understood this as a hint, and presently laying the letter down on the table, took her leave, having first begged permission to wait again on Sophia; which request had neither assent nor denial.

The letter lay upon the table no longer than till Mrs Miller was out of sight; for then Sophia opened and read it.

This letter did very little service to his cause; for it consisted of little more than confessions of his own unworthiness, and bitter lamentations of despair, together with the most solemn protestations of his unalterable fidelity to Sophia, of which, he said, he hoped to convince her, if he had ever more the honour of being admitted to her presence; and that he could account for the letter to Lady Bellaston in such a manner, that, though it would not entitle him to her forgiveness, he hoped at least to obtain it from her mercy. And concluded with vowing that nothing was ever less in his thoughts than to marry Lady Bellaston.

Though Sophia read the letter twice over with great attention, his meaning still remained a riddle to her; nor could her invention suggest to her any means to excuse Jones. She certainly remained very angry with him, though indeed Lady Bellaston took up so much of her resentment, that her gentle mind had but little left to bestow on any other person.

That lady was most unluckily to dine this very day with her aunt Western, and in the afternoon they were all three, by appointment, to go together to the opera, and thence to Lady Thomas Hatchet's drum. Sophia would have gladly been excused from all, but would not disoblige her aunt; and as to the arts of counterfeiting illness, she was so entirely a stranger to them, that it never once entered into her head. When she was drest, therefore, down she went, resolved to encounter all the horrors of the day, and a most disagreeable one it proved; for Lady Bellaston took every opportunity very civilly and slily to insult her; to all which her dejection of spirits disabled her from making any return; and, indeed, to confess the truth, she was at the very best but an indifferent mistress of repartee.

Another misfortune which befel poor Sophia was the company of Lord Fellamar, whom she met at the opera, and who attended her to the drum. And though both places were too publick to admit of any particularities, and she was farther relieved by the musick at the one place, and by the cards at the other, she could not, however, enjoy herself in his company; for there is something of delicacy in women, which will not suffer them to be even easy in the presence of a man whom they know to have pretensions to them which they are disinclined to favour.

Having in this chapter twice mentioned a drum, a word which our posterity, it is hoped, will not understand in the sense it is here applied, we shall, notwithstanding our present haste, stop a moment to describe the entertainment here meant, and the rather as we can in a moment describe it.

A drum, then, is an assembly of well-dressed persons of both sexes, most of whom play at cards, and the rest do nothing at all; while the mistress of the house performs the part of the landlady at an inn, and like the landlady of an inn prides herself in the number of her guests, though she doth not always, like her, get anything by it.

No wonder then, as so much spirits must be required to support any vivacity in these scenes of dulness, that we hear persons of fashion eternally complaining of the want of them; a complaint confined entirely to upper life. How insupportable must we imagine this round of impertinence to have been to Sophia at this time; how difficult must she have found it to force the appearance of gaiety into her looks, when her mind dictated nothing but the tenderest sorrow, and when every thought was charged with tormenting ideas!

Night, however, at last restored her to her pillow, where we will leave her to soothe her melancholy at least, though incapable we fear of rest, and shall pursue our history, which, something whispers us, is now arrived at the eve of some great event.

CHAPTER VII.

A pathetic scene between Mr Allworthy and Mrs Miller.

Mrs Miller had a long discourse with Mr Allworthy, at his return from dinner, in which she acquainted him with Jones's having unfortunately lost all which he was pleased to bestow on him at their separation; and with the distresses to which that loss had subjected him; of all which she had received a full account from the faithful retailer Partridge. She then explained the obligations she had to Jones; not that she was entirely explicit with regard to her daughter; for though she had the utmost confidence in Mr Allworthy, and though there could be no hopes of keeping an affair secret which was unhappily known to more than half a dozen, yet she could not prevail with herself to mention those circumstances which reflected most on the chastity of poor Nancy, but smothered that part of her evidence as cautiously as if she had been before a judge, and the girl was now on her trial for the murder of a bastard.

Allworthy said, there were few characters so absolutely vicious as not to have the least mixture of good in them. "However," says he, "I cannot deny but that you have some obligations to the fellow, bad as he is, and I shall therefore excuse what hath past already, but must insist you never mention his name to me more; for, I promise you, it was upon the fullest and plainest evidence that I resolved to take the measures I have taken." "Well, sir," says she, "I make not the least doubt but time will shew all matters in their true and natural colours, and that you will be convinced this poor young man deserves better of you than some other folks that shall be nameless."

"Madam," cries Allworthy, a little ruffled, "I will not hear any reflections on my nephew; and if ever you say a word more of that kind, I will depart from your house that instant. He is the worthiest and best of men; and I once more repeat it to you, he hath carried his friendship to this man to a blameable length, by too long concealing facts of the blackest die. The ingratitude of the wretch to this good young man is what I most resent; for, madam, I have the greatest reason to imagine he had laid a plot to supplant my nephew in my favour, and to have disinherited him."

"I am sure, sir," answered Mrs Miller, a little frightened (for, though Mr Allworthy had the utmost sweetness and benevolence in his smiles, he had great terror in his frowns), "I shall never speak against any gentleman you are pleased to think well of. I am sure, sir, such behaviour would very little become me, especially when the gentleman is your nearest relation; but, sir, you must not be angry with me, you must not indeed, for my good wishes to this poor wretch. Sure I may call him so now, though once you would have been angry with me if I had spoke of him with the least disrespect. How often have I heard you call him your son? How often have you prattled to me of him with all the fondness of a parent? Nay, sir, I cannot forget the many tender expressions, the many good things you have told me of his beauty, and his parts, and his virtues; of his good-nature and generosity. I am sure, sir, I cannot forget them, for I find them all true. I have experienced them in my own cause. They have preserved my family. You must pardon my tears, sir, indeed you must. When I consider the cruel reverse of fortune which this poor youth, to whom I am so much obliged, hath suffered; when I consider the loss of your favour, which I know he valued more than his life, I must, I must lament him. If you had a dagger in your hand, ready to plunge into my heart, I must lament the misery of one whom you have loved, and I shall ever love."

Allworthy was pretty much moved with this speech, but it seemed not to be with anger; for, after a short silence, taking Mrs Miller by the hand, he said very affectionately to her, "Come, madam, let us consider a little about your daughter. I cannot blame you for rejoicing in a match which promises to be advantageous to her, but you know this advantage, in a great measure, depends on the father's reconciliation. I know Mr Nightingale very well, and have formerly had concerns with him; I will make him a visit, and endeavour to serve you in this matter. I believe he is a worldly man; but as this is an only son, and the thing is now irretrievable, perhaps he may in time be brought to reason. I promise you I will do all I can for you."

Many were the acknowledgments which the poor woman made to Allworthy for this kind and generous offer, nor could she refrain from taking this occasion again to express her gratitude towards Jones, "to whom," said she, "I owe the opportunity of giving you, sir, this present trouble." Allworthy gently stopped her; but he was too good a man to be really offended with the effects of so noble a principle as now actuated Mrs Miller; and indeed, had not this new affair inflamed his former anger against Jones, it is possible he might have been a little softened towards him, by the report of an action which malice itself could not have derived from an evil motive.

Mr Allworthy and Mrs Miller had been above an hour together, when their conversation was put an end to by the arrival of Blifil and another person, which other person was no less than Mr Dowling, the attorney, who was now become a great favourite with Mr Blifil, and whom Mr Allworthy, at the desire of his nephew, had made his steward; and had likewise recommended him to Mr Western, from whom the attorney received a promise of being promoted to the same office upon the first vacancy; and, in the meantime, was employed in transacting some affairs which the squire then had in London in relation to a mortgage.

This was the principal affair which then brought Mr Dowling to town; therefore he took the same opportunity to charge himself with some money for Mr

Allworthy, and to make a report to him of some other business; in all which, as it was of much too dull a nature to find any place in this history, we will leave the uncle, nephew, and their lawyer concerned, and resort to other matters.

CHAPTER VIII.

Containing various matters.

Before we return to Mr Jones, we will take one more view of Sophia.

Though that young lady had brought her aunt into great good humour by those soothing methods which we have before related, she had not brought her in the least to abate of her zeal for the match with Lord Fellamar. This zeal was now inflamed by Lady Bellaston, who had told her the preceding evening, that she was well satisfied from the conduct of Sophia, and from her carriage to his lordship, that all delays would be dangerous, and that the only way to succeed was to press the match forward with such rapidity that the young lady should have no time to reflect, and be obliged to consent while she scarce knew what she did; in which manner, she said, one-half of the marriages among people of condition were brought about. A fact very probably true, and to which, I suppose, is owing the mutual tenderness which afterwards exists among so many happy couples.

A hint of the same kind was given by the same lady to Lord Fellamar; and both these so readily embraced the advice that the very next day was, at his lordship's request, appointed by Mrs Western for a private interview between the young parties. This was communicated to Sophia by her aunt, and insisted upon in such high terms, that, after having urged everything she possibly could invent against it without the least effect, she at last agreed to give the highest instance of complacence which any young lady can give, and consented to see his lordship.

As conversations of this kind afford no great entertainment, we shall be excused from reciting the whole that past at this interview; in which, after his lordship had made many declarations of the most pure and ardent passion to the silent blushing Sophia, she at last collected all the spirits she could raise, and with a trembling low voice said, "My lord, you must be yourself conscious whether your former behaviour to me hath been consistent with the professions you now make." "Is there," answered he, "no way by which I can atone for madness? what I did I am afraid must have too plainly convinced you, that the violence of love had deprived me of my senses." "Indeed, my lord," said she, "it is in your power to give me a proof of an affection which I much rather wish to encourage, and to which I should think myself more beholden." "Name it, madam," said my lord, very warmly. "My lord," says she, looking down upon her fan, "I know you must be sensible how uneasy this pretended passion of yours hath made me." "Can you be so cruel to call it pretended?" says he. "Yes, my lord," answered Sophia, "all professions of love to those whom we persecute are most insulting pretences. This pursuit of yours is to me a most cruel persecution: nay, it is taking a most ungenerous advantage of my unhappy situation." "Most lovely, most adorable charmer, do not accuse me," cries he, "of taking an ungenerous advantage, while I have no thoughts but what are directed to your honour and interest, and while I have no view, no hope, no ambition, but to throw myself, honour, fortune, everything at your feet." "My lord," says she, "it is that fortune and those honours which gave you the advantage of which I complain. These are the charms which have seduced my relations, but to me they are things indifferent. If your lordship will merit my gratitude, there is but one way." "Pardon me, divine creature," said he, "there can be none. All I can do for you is so much your due, and will give me so much pleasure, that there is no room for your gratitude." "Indeed, my lord," answered she, "you may obtain my gratitude, my good opinion, every kind thought and wish which it is in my power to bestow; nay, you may obtain them with ease, for sure to a generous mind it must be easy to grant my request. Let me beseech you, then, to cease a pursuit in which you can never have any success. For your own sake as well as mine I entreat this favour; for sure you are too noble to have any pleasure in tormenting an unhappy creature. What can your lordship propose but uneasiness to yourself, by a perseverance, which, upon my honour, upon my soul, cannot, shall not prevail with me, whatever distresses you may drive me to." Here my lord fetched a deep sigh, and then said—"Is it then, madam, that I am so unhappy to be the object of your dislike and scorn; or will you pardon me if I suspect there is some other?" Here he hesitated, and Sophia answered with some spirit, "My lord, I shall not be accountable to you for the reasons of my conduct. I am obliged to your lordship for the generous offer you have made; I own it is beyond either my deserts or expectations; yet I hope, my lord, you will not insist on my reasons, when I declare I cannot accept it." Lord Fellamar returned much to this, which we do not perfectly understand, and perhaps it could not all be strictly reconciled either to sense or grammar; but he concluded his ranting speech with saying, "That if she had pre-engaged herself to any gentleman, however unhappy it would make him, he should think himself bound in honour to desist." Perhaps my lord laid too much emphasis on the word gentleman; for we cannot else well account for the indignation with which he inspired Sophia, who, in her answer, seemed greatly to resent some affront he had given her.

While she was speaking, with her voice more raised than usual, Mrs Western came into the room, the fire glaring in her cheeks, and the flames bursting from her eyes. "I am ashamed," says she, "my lord, of the reception which you have met with. I assure your lordship we are all sensible of the honour done us; and I must tell you, Miss Western, the family expect a different behaviour from you." Here my lord interfered on behalf of the young lady, but to no purpose; the aunt proceeded till Sophia pulled out her handkerchief, threw herself into a chair, and burst into a violent fit of tears.

The remainder of the conversation between Mrs Western and his lordship, till the latter withdrew, consisted of bitter lamentations on his side, and on hers of the strongest assurances that her niece should and would consent to all he wished. "Indeed, my lord," says she, "the girl hath had a foolish education, neither adapted to her fortune nor her family. Her father, I am sorry to say it, is to blame for everything. The girl hath silly country notions of bashfulness. Nothing else, my lord, upon my honour; I am convinced she hath a good understanding at the bottom, and will be brought to reason."

This last speech was made in the absence of Sophia; for she had some time before left the room, with more appearance of passion than she had ever shown on any occasion; and now his lordship, after many expressions of thanks to Mrs Western, many ardent professions of passion which nothing could conquer, and many assurances of perseverance, which Mrs Western highly encouraged, took his leave for this time.

Before we relate what now passed between Mrs Western and Sophia, it may be proper to mention an unfortunate accident which had happened, and which had occasioned the return of Mrs Western with so much fury, as we have seen.

The reader then must know that the maid who at present attended on Sophia was recommended by Lady Bellaston, with whom she had lived for some time in the capacity of a comb-brush: she was a very sensible girl, and had received the strictest instructions to watch her young lady very carefully. These instructions, we are sorry to say, were communicated to her by Mrs Honour, into whose favour Lady Bellaston had now so ingratiated herself, that the violent affection which the good waiting-woman had formerly borne to Sophia was entirely obliterated by that great attachment which she had to her new mistress.

Now, when Mrs Miller was departed, Betty (for that was the name of the girl), returning to her young lady, found her very attentively engaged in reading a long letter, and the visible emotions which she betrayed on that occasion might have well accounted for some suspicions which the girl entertained; but indeed they had yet a stronger foundation, for she had overheard the whole scene which passed between Sophia and Mrs Miller.

Mrs Western was acquainted with all this matter by Betty, who, after receiving many commendations and some rewards for her fidelity, was ordered, that, if the woman who brought the letter came again, she should introduce her to Mrs Western herself.

Unluckily, Mrs Miller returned at the very time when Sophia was engaged with his lordship. Betty, according to order, sent her directly to the aunt; who, being mistress of so many circumstances relating to what had past the day before, easily imposed upon the poor woman to believe that Sophia had communicated the whole affair; and so pumped everything out of her which she knew relating to the letter and relating to Jones.

This poor creature might, indeed, be called simplicity itself. She was one of that order of mortals who are apt to believe everything which is said to them; to whom nature hath neither indulged the offensive nor defensive weapons of deceit, and who are consequently liable to be imposed upon by any one who will only be at the expense of a little falshood for that purpose. Mrs Western, having drained

Mrs Miller of all she knew, which, indeed, was but little, but which was sufficient to make the aunt suspect a great deal, dismissed her with assurances that Sophia would not see her, that she would send no answer to the letter, nor ever receive another; nor did she suffer her to depart without a handsome lecture on the merits of an office to which she could afford no better name than that of procuress.—This discovery had greatly discomposed her temper, when, coming into the apartment next to that in which the lovers were, she overheard Sophia very warmly protesting against his lordship's addresses. At which the rage already kindled burst forth, and she rushed in upon her niece in a most furious manner, as we have already described, together with what past at that time till his lordship's departure.

No sooner was Lord Fellamar gone than Mrs Western returned to Sophia, whom she upbraided in the most bitter terms for the ill use she had made of the confidence reposed in her; and for her treachery in conversing with a man with whom she had offered but the day before to bind herself in the most solemn oath never more to have any conversation. Sophia protested she had maintained no such conversation. "How, how! Miss Western," said the aunt; "will you deny your receiving a letter from him yesterday?" "A letter, madam!" answered Sophia, somewhat surprized. "It is not very well bred, miss," replies the aunt, "to repeat my words. I say a letter, and I insist upon your showing it me immediately." "I scorn a lie, madam," said Sophia; "I did receive a letter, but it was without my desire, and, indeed, I may say, against my consent." "Indeed, indeed, miss," cries the aunt, "you ought to be ashamed of owning you had received it at all; but where is the letter? for I will see it."

To this peremptory demand, Sophia paused some time before she returned an answer; and at last only excused herself by declaring she had not the letter in her pocket, which was, indeed, true; upon which her aunt, losing all manner of patience, asked her niece this short question, whether she would resolve to marry Lord Fellamar, or no? to which she received the strongest negative. Mrs Western then replied with an oath, or something very like one, that she would early the next morning deliver her back into her father's hand.

Sophia then began to reason with her aunt in the following manner:—"Why, madam, must I of necessity be forced to marry at all? Consider how cruel you would have thought it in your own case, and how much kinder your parents were in leaving you to your liberty. What have I done to forfeit this liberty? I will never marry contrary to my father's consent, nor without asking yours——And when I ask the consent of either improperly, it will be then time enough to force some other marriage upon me." "Can I bear to hear this," cries Mrs Western, "from a girl who hath now a letter from a murderer in her pocket?" "I have no such letter, I promise you," answered Sophia; "and, if he be a murderer, he will soon be in no condition to give you any further disturbance." "How, Miss Western!" said the aunt, "have you the assurance to speak of him in this manner; to own your affection for such a villain to my face?" "Sure, madam," said Sophia, "you put a very strange construction on my words." "Indeed, Miss Western," cries the lady, "I shall not bear this usage; you have learnt of your father this manner of treating me; he hath taught you to give me the lie. He hath totally ruined you by this false system of education; and, please heaven, he shall have the comfort of its fruits; for once more I declare to you, that to-morrow morning I will carry you back. I will withdraw all my forces from the field, and remain henceforth, like the wise king of Prussia, in a state of perfect neutrality. You are both too wise to be regulated by my measures; so prepare yourself, for to-morrow morning you shall evacuate this house."

Sophia remonstrated all she could; but her aunt was deaf to all she said. In this resolution therefore we must at present leave her, as there seems to be no hopes of bringing her to change it.

CHAPTER IX.

What happened to Mr Jones in the prison.

Mr Jones passed about twenty-four melancholy hours by himself, unless when relieved by the company of Partridge, before Mr Nightingale returned; not that this worthy young man had deserted or forgot his friend; for, indeed, he had been much the greatest part of the time employed in his service.

He had heard, upon enquiry, that the only persons who had seen the beginning of the unfortunate rencounter were a crew belonging to a man-of-war which then lay at Deptford. To Deptford therefore he went in search of this crew, where he was informed that the men he sought after were all gone ashore. He then traced them from place to place, till at last he found two of them drinking together, with a third person, at a hedge-tavern near Aldersgate.

Nightingale desired to speak with Jones by himself (for Partridge was in the room when he came in). As soon as they were alone, Nightingale, taking Jones by the hand, cried, "Come, my brave friend, be not too much dejected at what I am going to tell you——I am sorry I am the messenger of bad news; but I think it my duty to tell you." "I guess already what that bad news is," cries Jones. "The poor gentleman then is dead."—"I hope not," answered Nightingale. "He was alive this morning; though I will not flatter you; I fear, from the accounts I could get, that his wound is mortal. But if the affair be exactly as you told it, your own remorse would be all you would have reason to apprehend, let what would happen; but forgive me, my dear Tom, if I entreat you to make the worst of your story to your friends. If you disguise anything to us, you will only be an enemy to yourself."

"What reason, my dear Jack, have I ever given you," said Jones, "to stab me with so cruel a suspicion?" "Have patience," cries Nightingale, "and I will tell you all. After the most diligent enquiry I could make, I at last met with two of the fellows who were present at this unhappy accident, and I am sorry to say, they do not relate the story so much in your favour as you yourself have told it." "Why, what do they say?" cries Jones. "Indeed what I am sorry to repeat, as I am afraid of the consequence of it to you. They say that they were at too great a distance to overhear any words that passed between you: but they both agree that the first blow was given by you." "Then, upon my soul," answered Jones, "they injure me. He not only struck me first, but struck me without the least provocation. What should induce those villains to accuse me falsely?" "Nay, that I cannot guess," said Nightingale, "and if you yourself, and I, who am so heartily your friend, cannot conceive a reason why they should belie you, what reason will an indifferent court of justice be able to assign why they should not believe them? I repeated the question to them several times, and so did another gentleman who was present, who, I believe, is a seafaring man, and who really acted a very friendly part by you; for he begged them often to consider that there was the life of a man in the case; and asked them over and over, if they were certain; to which they both answered, that they were, and would abide by their evidence upon oath. For heaven's sake, my dear friend, recollect yourself; for, if this should appear to be the fact, it will be your business to think in time of making the best of your interest. I would not shock you; but you know, I believe, the severity of the law, whatwhatever verbal provocations may have been given you." "Alas! my friend," cries Jones, "what interest hath such a wretch as I? Besides, do you think I would even wish to live with the reputation of a murderer? If I had any friends (as, alas! I have none), could I have the confidence to solicit them to speak in the behalf of a man condemned for the blackest crime in human nature? Believe me, I have no such hope; but I have some reliance on a throne still greatly superior; which will, I am certain, afford me all the protection I merit."

He then concluded with many solemn and vehement protestations of the truth of what he had at first asserted.

The faith of Nightingale was now again staggered, and began to incline to credit his friend, when Mrs Miller appeared, and made a sorrowful report of the success of her embassy; which when Jones had heard, he cried out most heroically, "Well, my friend, I am now indifferent as to what shall happen, at least with regard to my life; and if it be the will of Heaven that I shall make an atonement with that for the blood I have spilt, I hope the Divine Goodness will one day suffer my honour to be cleared, and that the words of a dying man, at least, will be believed, so far as to justify his character."

A very mournful scene now past between the prisoner and his friends, at which, as few readers would have been pleased to be present, so few, I believe, will desire to hear it particularly related. We will, therefore, pass on to the entrance of the turnkey, who acquainted Jones that there was a lady without who desired to speak with him when he was at leisure.

Jones declared his surprize at this message. He said, "He knew no lady in the world whom he could possibly expect to see there." However, as he saw no reason to decline seeing any person, Mrs Miller and Mr Nightingale presently took their leave, and he gave orders to have the lady admitted.

If Jones was surprized at the news of a visit from a lady, how greatly was he astonished when he discovered this lady to be no other than Mrs Waters! In this astonishment then we shall leave him awhile, in order to cure the surprize of the reader, who will likewise, probably, not a little wonder at the arrival of this lady.

Who this Mrs Waters was, the reader pretty well knows; what she was, he must be perfectly satisfied. He will therefore be pleased to remember that this lady departed from Upton in the same coach with Mr Fitzpatrick and the other Irish gentleman, and in their company travelled to Bath.

Now there was a certain office in the gift of Mr Fitzpatrick at that time vacant, namely that of a wife: for the lady who had lately filled that office had resigned, or at least deserted her duty. Mr Fitzpatrick therefore, having thoroughly examined Mrs Waters on the road, found her extremely fit for the place, which, on their arrival at Bath, he presently conferred upon her, and she without any scruple accepted. As husband and wife this gentleman and lady continued together all the time they stayed at Bath, and as husband and wife they arrived together in town.

Whether Mr Fitzpatrick was so wise a man as not to part with one good thing till he had secured another, which he had at present only a prospect of regaining; or whether Mrs Waters had so well discharged her office, that he intended still to retain her as principal, and to make his wife (as is often the case) only her deputy, I will not say; but certain it is, he never mentioned his wife to her, never communicated to her the letter given him by Mrs Western, nor ever once hinted his purpose of repossessing his wife; much less did he ever mention the name of Jones. For, though he intended to fight with him wherever he met him, he did not imitate those prudent persons who think a wife, a mother, a sister, or sometimes a whole family, the safest seconds on these occasions. The first account therefore which she had of all this was delivered to her from his lips, after he was brought home from the tavern where his wound had been drest.

As Mr Fitzpatrick, however, had not the clearest way of telling a story at any time, and was now, perhaps, a little more confused than usual, it was some time before she discovered that the gentleman who had given him this wound was the very same person from whom her heart had received a wound, which, though not of a mortal kind, was yet so deep that it had left a considerable scar behind it. But no sooner was she acquainted that Mr Jones himself was the man who had been committed to the Gatehouse for this supposed murder, than she took the first opportunity of committing Mr Fitzpatrick to the care of his nurse, and hastened away to visit the conqueror.

She now entered the room with an air of gaiety, which received an immediate check from the melancholy aspect of poor Jones, who started and blessed himself when he saw her. Upon which she said, "Nay, I do not wonder at your surprize; I believe you did not expect to see me; for few gentlemen are troubled here with visits from any lady, unless a wife. You see the power you have over me, Mr Jones. Indeed, I little thought, when we parted at Upton, that our next meeting would have been in such a place." "Indeed, madam," says Jones, "I must look upon this visit as kind; few will follow the miserable, especially to such dismal habitations." "I protest, Mr Jones," says she, "I can hardly persuade myself you are the same agreeable fellow I saw at Upton. Why, your face is more miserable than any dungeon in the universe. What can be the matter with you?" "I thought, madam," said Jones, "as you knew of my being here, you knew the unhappy reason." "Pugh!" says she, "you have pinked a man in a duel, that's all." Jones exprest some indignation at this levity, and spoke with the utmost contrition for what had happened. To which she answered, "Well, then, sir, if you take it so much to heart, I will relieve you; the gentleman is not dead, and, I am pretty confident, is in no danger of dying. The surgeon, indeed, who first dressed him was a young fellow, and seemed desirous of representing his case to be as bad as possible, that he might have the more honour from curing him: but the king's surgeon hath seen him since, and says, unless from a fever, of which there are at present no symptoms, he apprehends not the least danger of life." Jones shewed great satisfaction in his countenance at this report; upon which she affirmed the truth of it, adding, "By the most extraordinary accident in the world I lodge at the same house; and have seen the gentleman, and I promise you he doth you justice, and says, whatever be the consequence, that he was entirely the aggressor, and that you was not in the least to blame."

Jones expressed the utmost satisfaction at the account which Mrs Waters brought him. He then informed her of many things which she well knew before, as who Mr Fitzpatrick was, the occasion of his resentment, &c. He likewise told her several facts of which she was ignorant, as the adventure of the muff, and other particulars, concealing only the name of Sophia. He then lamented the follies and vices of which he had been guilty; every one of which, he said, had been attended with such ill consequences, that he should be unpardonable if he did not take warning, and quit those vicious courses for the future. He lastly concluded with assuring her of his resolution to sin no more, lest a worse thing should happen to him.

Mrs Waters with great pleasantry ridiculed all this, as the effects of low spirits and confinement. She repeated some witticisms about the devil when he was sick, and told him, "She doubted not but shortly to see him at liberty, and as lively a fellow as ever; and then," says she, "I don't question but your conscience will be safely delivered of all these qualms that it is now so sick in breeding."

Many more things of this kind she uttered, some of which it would do her no great honour, in the opinion of some readers, to remember; nor are we quite certain but that the answers made by Jones would be treated with ridicule by others. We shall therefore suppress the rest of this conversation, and only observe that it ended at last with perfect innocence, and much more to the satisfaction of Jones than of the lady; for the former was greatly transported with the news she had brought him; but the latter was not altogether so pleased with the penitential behaviour of a man whom she had, at her first interview, conceived a very different opinion of from what she now entertained of him.

Thus the melancholy occasioned by the report of Mr Nightingale was pretty well effaced; but the dejection into which Mrs Miller had thrown him still continued. The account she gave so well tallied with the words of Sophia herself in her letter, that he made not the least doubt but that she had disclosed his letter to her aunt, and had taken a fixed resolution to abandon him. The torments this thought gave him were to be equalled only by a piece of news which fortune had yet in store for him, and which we shall communicate in the second chapter of the ensuing book.

BOOK XVIII.

CONTAINING ABOUT SIX DAYS.

CHAPTER I.

A farewel to the reader.

We are now, reader, arrived at the last stage of our long journey. As we have, therefore, travelled together through so many pages, let us behave to one another like fellow-travellers in a stage coach, who have passed several days in the company of each other; and who, notwithstanding any bickerings or little animosities which may have occurred on the road, generally make all up at last, and mount, for the last time, into their vehicle with chearfulness and good humour; since after this one stage, it may possibly happen to us, as it commonly happens to them, never to meet more.

As I have here taken up this simile, give me leave to carry it a little farther. I intend, then, in this last book, to imitate the good company I have mentioned in their last journey. Now, it is well known that all jokes and raillery are at this time laid aside; whatever characters any of the passengers have for the jest-sake personated on the road are now thrown off, and the conversation is usually plain and serious.

In the same manner, if I have now and then, in the course of this work, indulged any pleasantry for thy entertainment, I shall here lay it down. The variety of matter, indeed, which I shall be obliged to cram into this book, will afford no room for any of those ludicrous observations which I have elsewhere made, and which may sometimes, perhaps, have prevented thee from taking a nap when it was beginning to steal upon thee. In this last book thou wilt find nothing (or at most very little) of that nature. All will be plain narrative only; and, indeed, when thou hast perused the many great events which this book will produce, thou wilt think the number of pages contained in it scarce sufficient to tell the story.

And now, my friend, I take this opportunity (as I shall have no other) of heartily wishing thee well. If I have been an entertaining companion to thee, I promise thee it is what I have desired. If in anything I have offended, it was really without any intention. Some things, perhaps, here said, may have hit thee or thy friends; but I do most solemnly declare they were not pointed at thee or them. I question not but thou hast been told, among other stories of me, that thou wast to travel with a very scurrilous fellow; but whoever told thee so did me an injury. No man detests and despises scurrility more than myself; nor hath any man more reason; for none hath ever been treated with more; and what is a very severe fate, I have had some of the abusive writings of those very men fathered upon me, who, in other of their works, have abused me themselves with the utmost virulence.

All these works, however, I am well convinced, will be dead long before this page shall offer itself to thy perusal; for however short the period may be of my own performances, they will most probably outlive their own infirm author, and the weakly productions of his abusive contemporaries.

CHAPTER II.

Containing a very tragical incident.

While Jones was employed in those unpleasant meditations, with which we left him tormenting himself, Partridge came stumbling into the room with his face paler than ashes, his eyes fixed in his head, his hair standing an end, and every limb trembling. In short, he looked as he would have done had he seen a spectre, or had he, indeed, been a spectre himself.

Jones, who was little subject to fear, could not avoid being somewhat shocked at this sudden appearance. He did, indeed, himself change colour, and his voice a little faultered while he asked him, What was the matter?

"I hope, sir," said Partridge, "you will not be angry with me. Indeed I did not listen, but I was obliged to stay in the outward room. I am sure I wish I had been a hundred miles off, rather than have heard what I have heard." "Why, what is the matter?" said Jones. "The matter, sir? O good Heaven!" answered Partridge, "was that woman who is just gone out the woman who was with you at Upton?" "She was, Partridge," cried Jones. "And did you really, sir, go to bed with that woman?" said he, trembling.—"I am afraid what past between us is no secret," said Jones.—"Nay, but pray, sir, for Heaven's sake, sir, answer me," cries Partridge. "You know I did," cries Jones. "Why then, the Lord have mercy upon your soul, and forgive you," cries Partridge; "but as sure as I stand here alive, you have been a-bed with your own mother."

Upon these words Jones became in a moment a greater picture of horror than Partridge himself. He was, indeed, for some time struck dumb with amazement, and both stood staring wildly at each other. At last his words found way, and in an interrupted voice he said, "How! how! what's this you tell me?" "Nay, sir," cries Partridge, "I have not breath enough left to tell you now, but what I have said is most certainly true.—That woman who now went out is your own mother. How unlucky was it for you, sir, that I did not happen to see her at that time, to have prevented it! Sure the devil himself must have contrived to bring about this wickedness."

"Sure," cries Jones, "Fortune will never have done with me till she hath driven me to distraction. But why do I blame Fortune? I am myself the cause of all my misery. All the dreadful mischiefs which have befallen me are the consequences only of my own folly and vice. What thou hast told me, Partridge, hath almost deprived me of my senses! And was Mrs Waters, then—but why do I ask? for thou must certainly know her—If thou hast any affection for me, nay, if thou hast any pity, let me beseech thee to fetch this miserable woman back again to me. O good Heavens! incest——with a mother! To what am I reserved!" He then fell into the most violent and frantic agonies of grief and despair, in which Partridge declared he would not leave him; but at last, having vented the first torrent of passion, he came a little to himself; and then, having acquainted Partridge that he would find this wretched woman in the same house where the wounded gentleman was lodged, he despatched him in quest of her.

If the reader will please to refresh his memory, by turning to the scene at Upton, in the ninth book, he will be apt to admire the many strange accidents which unfortunately prevented any interview between Partridge and Mrs Waters, when she spent a whole day there with Mr Jones. Instances of this kind we may frequently observe in life, where the greatest events are produced by a nice train of little circumstances; and more than one example of this may be discovered by the accurate eye, in this our history.

After a fruitless search of two or three hours, Partridge returned back to his master, without having seen Mrs Waters. Jones, who was in a state of desperation at his delay, was almost raving mad when he brought him his account. He was not long, however, in this condition before he received the following letter:

> "SIR,
>
> "Since I left you I have seen a gentleman, from whom I have learned something concerning you which greatly surprizes and affects me; but as I have not at present leisure to communicate a matter of such high importance, you must suspend your curiosity till our next meeting, which shall be the first moment I am able to see you. O, Mr Jones, little did I think, when I past that happy day at Upton, the reflection upon which is like to embitter all my future life, who it was to whom I owed such perfect happiness. Believe me to be ever sincerely your unfortunate
>
> "J. WATERS."
>
> "P.S. I would have you comfort yourself as much as possible, for Mr Fitzpatrick is in no manner of danger; so that whatever other grievous crimes you may have to repent of, the guilt of blood is not among the number."

Jones having read the letter, let it drop (for he was unable to hold it, and indeed had scarce the use of any one of his faculties). Partridge took it up, and having received consent by silence, read it likewise; nor had it upon him a less sensible effect. The pencil, and not the pen, should describe the horrors which appeared in both their countenances. While they both remained speechless the turnkey entered the room, and, without taking any notice of what sufficiently discovered itself in the faces of them both, acquainted Jones that a man without desired to speak with him. This person was presently introduced, and was no other than Black George.

As sights of horror were not so usual to George as they were to the turnkey, he instantly saw the great disorder which appeared in the face of Jones. This he imputed to the accident that had happened, which was reported in the very worst light in Mr Western's family; he concluded, therefore, that the gentleman was dead, and that Mr Jones was in a fair way of coming to a shameful end. A thought which gave him much uneasiness; for George was of a compassionate disposition, and notwithstanding a small breach of friendship which he had been over-tempted to commit, was, in the main, not insensible of the obligations he had formerly received from Mr Jones.

The poor fellow, therefore, scarce refrained from a tear at the present sight. He told Jones he was heartily sorry for his misfortunes, and begged him to consider if he could be of any manner of service. "Perhaps, sir," said he, "you may want a little matter of money upon this occasion; if you do, sir, what little I have is heartily at your service."

Jones shook him very heartily by the hand, and gave him many thanks for the kind offer he had made; but answered, "He had not the least want of that kind." Upon which George began to press his services more eagerly than before. Jones again thanked him, with assurances that he wanted nothing which was in the power of any man living to give. "Come, come, my good master," answered George, "do not take the matter so much to heart. Things may end better than you imagine; to be sure you an't the first gentleman who hath killed a man, and yet come off." "You are wide of the matter, George," said Partridge, "the gentleman is not dead, nor like to die. Don't disturb my master, at present, for he is troubled about a matter in which it is not in your power to do him any good." "You don't know what I may be able to do, Mr Partridge," answered George; "if his concern is about my young lady, I have some news to tell my master." "What do you say, Mr George?" cried Jones. "Hath anything lately happened in which my Sophia is concerned? My Sophia! how dares such a wretch as I mention her so profanely." "I hope she will be yours yet," answered George. "Why yes, sir, I have something to tell you about her. Madam Western hath just brought Madam Sophia home, and there hath been a terrible to do. I could not possibly learn the very right of it; but my master he hath been in a vast big passion, and so was Madam Western, and I heard her say, as she went out of doors into her chair, that she would never set her foot in master's house again. I don't know what's the matter, not I, but everything was very quiet when I came out; but Robin, who waited at supper, said he had never seen the squire for a long while in such good humour with young madam; that he kissed her several times, and swore she should be her own mistress, and he never would think of confining her any more. I thought this news would please you, and so I slipped out, though it was so late, to inform you of it." Mr Jones assured George that it did greatly please him; for though he should never more presume to lift his eyes toward that incomparable creature, nothing could so much relieve his misery as the satisfaction he should always have in hearing of her welfare.

The rest of the conversation which passed at the visit is not important enough to be here related. The reader will, therefore, forgive us this abrupt breaking off, and be pleased to hear how this great good-will of the squire towards his daughter was brought about.

Mrs Western, on her first arrival at her brother's lodging, began to set forth the great honours and advantages which would accrue to the family by the match with Lord Fellamar, which her niece had absolutely refused; in which refusal, when the squire took the part of his daughter, she fell immediately into the most violent passion, and so irritated and provoked the squire, that neither his patience nor his prudence could bear it any longer; upon which there ensued between them both so warm a bout at altercation, that perhaps the regions of Billingsgate never equalled it. In the heat of this scolding Mrs Western departed, and had consequently no leisure to acquaint her brother with the letter which Sophia received, which might have possibly produced ill effects; but, to say truth, I believe it never once occurred to her memory at this time.

When Mrs Western was gone, Sophia, who had been hitherto silent, as well indeed from necessity as inclination, began to return the compliment which her father had made her, in taking her part against her aunt, by taking his likewise against the lady. This was the first time of her so doing, and it was in the highest degree acceptable to the squire. Again, he remembered that Mr Allworthy had insisted on an entire relinquishment of all violent means; and, indeed, as he made no doubt but that Jones would be hanged, he did not in the least question succeeding with his daughter by fair means; he now, therefore, once more gave a loose to his natural fondness for her, which had such an effect on the dutiful, grateful, tender, and affectionate heart of Sophia, that had her honour, given to Jones, and something else, perhaps, in which he was concerned, been removed, I much doubt whether she would not have sacrificed herself to a man she did not like, to have obliged her father. She promised him she would make it the whole business of her life to oblige him, and would never marry any man against his consent; which brought the old man so near to his highest happiness, that he was resolved to take the other step, and went to bed completely drunk.

CHAPTER III.

Allworthy visits old Nightingale; with a strange discovery that he made on that occasion.

The morning after these things had happened, Mr Allworthy went, according to his promise, to visit old Nightingale, with whom his authority was so great, that, after having sat with him three hours, he at last prevailed with him to consent to see his son.

Here an accident happened of a very extraordinary kind; one indeed of those strange chances whence very good and grave men have concluded that Providence often interposes in the discovery of the most secret villany, in order to caution men from quitting the paths of honesty, however warily they tread in those of vice.

Mr Allworthy, at his entrance into Mr Nightingale's, saw Black George; he took no notice of him, nor did Black George imagine he had perceived him.

However, when their conversation on the principal point was over, Allworthy asked Nightingale, Whether he knew one George Scagrim, and upon what business he came to his house? "Yes," answered Nightingale, "I know him very well, and a most extraordinary fellow he is, who, in these days, hath been able to hoard up £500 from renting a very small estate of £30 a year." "And is this the story which he hath told you?" cries Allworthy. "Nay, it is true, I promise you," said Nightingale, "for I have the money now in my own hands, in five bank-bills, which I am to lay out either in a mortgage, or in some purchase in the north of England." The bank-bills were no sooner produced at Allworthy's desire than he blessed himself at the strangeness of the discovery. He presently told Nightingale that these bank-bills were formerly his, and then acquainted him with the whole affair. As there are no men who complain more of the frauds of business than highwaymen, gamesters, and other thieves of that kind, so there are none who so bitterly exclaim against the frauds of gamesters, &c., as usurers, brokers, and other thieves of this kind; whether it be that the one way of cheating is a discountenance or reflection upon the other, or that money, which is the common mistress of all cheats, makes them regard each other in the light of rivals; but Nightingale no sooner heard the story than he exclaimed against the fellow in terms much severer than the justice and honesty of Allworthy had bestowed on him.

Allworthy desired Nightingale to retain both the money and the secret till he should hear farther from him; and, if he should in the meantime see the fellow, that he would not take the least notice to him of the discovery which he had made. He then returned to his lodgings, where he found Mrs Miller in a very dejected condition, on account of the information she had received from her son-in-law. Mr Allworthy, with great chearfulness, told her that he had much good news to communicate; and, with little further preface, acquainted her that he had brought Mr Nightingale to consent to see his son, and did not in the least doubt to effect a perfect reconciliation between them; though he found the father more sowered by another accident of the same kind which had happened in his family. He then mentioned the running away of the uncle's daughter, which he had been told by the old gentleman, and which Mrs Miller and her son-in-law did not yet know.

The reader may suppose Mrs Miller received this account with great thankfulness, and no less pleasure; but so uncommon was her friendship to Jones, that I am not certain whether the uneasiness she suffered for his sake did not overbalance her satisfaction at hearing a piece of news tending so much to the happiness of her own family; nor whether even this very news, as it reminded her of the obligations she had to Jones, did not hurt as well as please her; when her grateful heart said to her, "While my own family is happy, how miserable is the poor creature to whose generosity we owe the beginning of all this happiness!"

Allworthy, having left her a little while to chew the cud (if I may use that expression) on these first tidings, told her he had still something more to impart, which he believed would give her pleasure. "I think," said he, "I have discovered a pretty considerable treasure belonging to the young gentleman, your friend; but perhaps, indeed, his present situation may be such that it will be of no service to him." The latter part of the speech gave Mrs Miller to understand who was meant, and she answered with a sigh, "I hope not, sir." "I hope so too," cries Allworthy, "with all my heart; but my nephew told me this morning he had heard a very bad account of the affair."——"Good Heaven! sir," said she—"Well, I must not speak, and yet it is certainly very hard to be obliged to hold one's tongue when one hears."—"Madam," said Allworthy, "you may say whatever you please, you know me too well to think I have a prejudice against any one; and as for that young man, I assure you I should be heartily pleased to find he could acquit himself of everything, and particularly of this sad affair. You can testify the affection I have formerly borne him. The world, I know, censured me for loving him so much. I did not withdraw that affection from him without thinking I had the justest cause. Believe me, Mrs Miller, I should be glad to find I have been mistaken." Mrs Miller was going eagerly to reply, when a servant acquainted her that a gentleman without desired to speak with her immediately. Allworthy then enquired for his nephew, and was told that he had been for some time in his room with the gentleman who used to come to him, and whom Mr Allworthy guessing rightly to be Mr Dowling, he desired presently to speak with him.

When Dowling attended, Allworthy put the case of the bank-notes to him, without mentioning any name, and asked in what manner such a person might be punished. To which Dowling answered, "He thought he might be indicted on the Black Act; but said, as it was a matter of some nicety, it would be proper to go to counsel. He said he was to attend counsel presently upon an affair of Mr Western's, and if Mr Allworthy pleased he would lay the case before them." This was agreed to; and then Mrs Miller, opening the door, cried, "I ask pardon, I did not know you had company;" but Allworthy desired her to come in, saying he had finished his business. Upon which Mr Dowling withdrew, and Mrs Miller introduced Mr Nightingale the younger, to return thanks for the great kindness done him by Allworthy: but she had scarce patience to let the young gentleman finish his speech before she interrupted him, saying, "O sir! Mr Nightingale brings great news about poor Mr Jones: he hath been to see the wounded gentleman, who is out of all danger of death, and, what is more, declares he fell upon poor Mr Jones himself, and beat him. I am sure, sir, you would not have Mr Jones be a coward. If I was a man myself, I am sure, if any man was to strike me, I should draw my sword. Do pray, my dear, tell Mr Allworthy, tell him all yourself." Nightingale then confirmed what Mrs Miller had said; and concluded with many handsome things of Jones, who was, he said, one of the best-natured fellows in the world, and not in the least inclined to be quarrelsome. Here Nightingale was going to cease, when Mrs Miller again begged him to relate all the many dutiful expressions he had heard him make use of towards Mr Allworthy. "To say the utmost good of Mr Allworthy," cries Nightingale, "is doing no more than strict justice, and can have no merit in it: but indeed, I must say, no man can be more sensible of the obligations he hath to so good a man than is poor Jones. Indeed, sir, I am convinced the weight of your displeasure is the heaviest burthen he lies under. He hath often lamented it to me, and hath as often protested in the most solemn manner he hath never been intentionally guilty of any offence towards you; nay, he hath sworn he would rather die a thousand deaths than he would have his conscience upbraid him with one disrespectful, ungrateful, or undutiful thought towards you. But I ask pardon, sir, I am afraid I presume to intermeddle too far in so tender a point." "You have spoke no more than what a Christian ought," cries Mrs Miller. "Indeed, Mr Nightingale," answered Allworthy, "I applaud your generous friendship, and I wish he may merit it of you. I confess I am glad to hear the report you bring from this unfortunate gentleman; and, if that matter should turn out to be as you represent it (and, indeed, I doubt nothing of what you say), I may, perhaps, in time, be brought to think better than lately I have of this young man; for this good gentlewoman here, nay, all who know me, can witness that I loved him as dearly as if he had been my own son. Indeed, I have considered him as a child sent by fortune to my care. I still remember the innocent, the helpless situation in which I found him. I feel the tender pressure of his little hands at this moment. He was my darling, indeed he was." At which words he ceased, and the tears stood in his eyes.

As the answer which Mrs Miller made may lead us into fresh matters, we will here stop to account for the visible alteration in Mr Allworthy's mind, and the abatement of his anger to Jones. Revolutions of this kind, it is true, do frequently occur in histories and dramatic writers, for no other reason than because the history or play draws to a conclusion, and are justified by authority of authors; yet, though we insist upon as much authority as any author whatever, we shall use this power very sparingly, and never but when we are driven to it by necessity, which we do not at present foresee will happen in this work.

This alteration then in the mind of Mr Allworthy was occasioned by a letter he had just received from Mr Square, and which we shall give the reader in the beginning of the next chapter.

CHAPTER IV.

Containing two letters in very different stiles.

"MY WORTHY FRIEND,—I informed you in my last that I was forbidden the use of the waters, as they were found by experience rather to increase than lessen the symptoms of my distemper. I must now acquaint you with a piece of news, which, I believe, will afflict my friends more than it hath afflicted me. Dr Harrington and Dr Brewster have informed me that there is no hopes of my recovery.

"I have somewhere read, that the great use of philosophy is to learn to die. I will not therefore so far disgrace mine as to shew any surprize at receiving a lesson which I must be thought to have so long studied. Yet, to say the truth, one page of the Gospel teaches this lesson better than all the volumes of antient or modern philosophers. The assurance it gives us of another life is a much stronger support to a good mind than all the consolations that are drawn from the necessity of nature, the emptiness or satiety of our enjoyments here, or any other topic of those declamations which are sometimes capable of arming our minds with a stubborn patience in bearing the thoughts of death, but never of raising them to a real contempt of it, and much less of making us think it is a real good. I would not here be understood to throw the horrid censure of atheism, or even the absolute denial of immortality, on all who are called philosophers. Many of that sect, as well antient as modern, have, from the light of reason, discovered some hopes of a future state; but in reality, that light was so faint and glimmering, and the hopes were so incertain and precarious, that it may be justly doubted on which side their belief turned. Plato himself concludes his Phaedon with declaring that his best arguments amount only to raise a probability; and Cicero himself seems rather to profess an inclination to believe, than any actual belief in the doctrines of immortality. As to myself, to be very sincere with you, I never was much in earnest in this faith till I was in earnest a Christian.

"You will perhaps wonder at the latter expression; but I assure you it hath not been till very lately that I could, with truth, call myself so. The pride of philosophy had intoxicated my reason, and the sublimest of all wisdom appeared to me, as it did to the Greeks of old, to be foolishness. God hath, however, been so gracious to shew me my error in time, and to bring me into the way of truth, before I sunk into utter darkness forever.

"I find myself beginning to grow weak, I shall therefore hasten to the main purpose of this letter.

"When I reflect on the actions of my past life, I know of nothing which sits heavier upon my conscience than the injustice I have been guilty of to that poor wretch your adopted son. I have, indeed, not only connived at the villany of others, but been myself active in injustice towards him. Believe me, my dear friend, when I tell you, on the word of a dying man, he hath been basely injured. As to the principal fact, upon the misrepresentation of which you discarded him, I solemnly assure you he is innocent. When you lay upon your supposed deathbed, he was the only person in the house who testified any real concern; and what happened afterwards arose from the wildness of his joy on your recovery; and, I am sorry to say it, from the baseness of another person (but it is my desire to justify the innocent, and to accuse none). Believe me, my friend, this young man hath the noblest generosity of heart, the most perfect capacity for friendship, the highest integrity, and indeed every virtue which can ennoble a man. He hath some faults, but among them is not to be numbered the least want of duty or gratitude towards you. On the contrary, I am satisfied, when you dismissed him from your house, his heart bled for you more than for himself.

"Worldly motives were the wicked and base reasons of my concealing this from you so long; to reveal it now I can have no inducement but the desire of serving the cause of truth, of doing right to the innocent, and of making all the amends in my power for a past offence. I hope this declaration, therefore, will have the effect desired, and will restore this deserving young man to your favour; the hearing of which, while I am yet alive, will afford the utmost consolation to,

Sir, Your most obliged, obedient humble servant, THOMAS SQUARE."

The reader will, after this, scarce wonder at the revolution so visibly appearing in Mr Allworthy, notwithstanding he received from Thwackum, by the same post, another letter of a very different kind, which we shall here add, as it may possibly be the last time we shall have occasion to mention the name of that gentleman.

"SIR,

"I am not at all surprized at hearing from your worthy nephew a fresh instance of the villany of Mr Square the atheist's young pupil. I shall not wonder at any murders he may commit; and I heartily pray that your own blood may not seal up his final commitment to the place of wailing and gnashing of teeth.

"Though you cannot want sufficient calls to repentance for the many unwarrantable weaknesses exemplified in your behaviour to this wretch, so much to the prejudice of your own lawful family, and of your character; I say, though these may sufficiently be supposed to prick and goad your conscience at this season, I should yet be wanting to my duty, if I spared to give you some admonition in order to bring you to a due sense of your errors. I therefore pray you seriously to consider the judgment which is likely to overtake this wicked villain; and let it serve at least as a warning to you, that you may not for the future despise the advice of one who is so indefatigable in his prayers for your welfare.

"Had not my hand been withheld from due correction, I had scourged much of this diabolical spirit out of a boy, of whom from his infancy I discovered the devil had taken such entire possession. But reflections of this kind now come too late.

"I am sorry you have given away the living of Westerton so hastily. I should have applied on that occasion earlier, had I thought you would not have acquainted me previous to the disposition.——Your objection to pluralities is being righteous over-much. If there were any crime in the practice, so many godly men would not agree to it. If the vicar of Aldergrove should die (as we hear he is in a declining way), I hope you will think of me, since I am certain you must be convinced of my most sincere attachment to your highest welfare—a welfare to which all worldly considerations are as trifling as the small tithes mentioned in Scripture are, when compared to the weighty matters of the law.

I am, sir, Your faithful humble servant, ROGER THWACKUM."

This was the first time Thwackum ever wrote in this authoritative stile to Allworthy, and of this he had afterwards sufficient reason to repent, as in the case of those who mistake the highest degree of goodness for the lowest degree of weakness. Allworthy had indeed never liked this man. He knew him to be proud and ill-natured; he also knew that his divinity itself was tinctured with his temper, and such as in many respects he himself did by no means approve; but he was at the same time an excellent scholar, and most indefatigable in teaching the two lads. Add to this, the strict severity of his life and manners, an unimpeached honesty, and a most devout attachment to religion. So that, upon the whole, though Allworthy did not esteem nor love the man, yet he could never bring himself to part with a tutor to the boys, who was, both by learning and industry, extremely well qualified for his office; and he hoped, that as they were bred up in his own house, and under his own eye, he should be able to correct whatever was wrong in Thwackum's instructions.

CHAPTER V.

In which the history is continued.

Mr Allworthy, in his last speech, had recollected some tender ideas concerning Jones, which had brought tears into the good man's eyes. This Mrs Miller observing, said, "Yes, yes, sir, your goodness to this poor young man is known, notwithstanding all your care to conceal it; but there is not a single syllable of truth in what those villains said. Mr Nightingale hath now discovered the whole matter. It seems these fellows were employed by a lord, who is a rival of poor Mr Jones, to have pressed him on board a ship.—I assure them I don't know who they will press next. Mr Nightingale here hath seen the officer himself, who is a very pretty gentleman, and hath told him all, and is very sorry for what he undertook, which he would never have done, had he known Mr Jones to have been a gentleman; but he was told that he was a common strolling vagabond."

Allworthy stared at all this, and declared he was a stranger to every word she said. "Yes, sir," answered she, "I believe you are.——It is a very different story, I believe, from what those fellows told this lawyer."

"What lawyer, madam? what is it you mean?" said Allworthy. "Nay, nay," said she, "this is so like you to deny your own goodness: but Mr Nightingale here saw him." "Saw whom, madam?" answered he. "Why, your lawyer, sir," said she, "that you so kindly sent to enquire into the affair." "I am still in the dark, upon my honour," said Allworthy. "Why then do you tell him, my dear sir," cries she. "Indeed, sir," said Nightingale, "I did see that very lawyer who went from you when I came into the room, at an alehouse in Aldersgate, in company with two of the fellows who were employed by Lord Fellamar to press Mr Jones, and who were by that means present at the unhappy rencounter between him and Mr Fitzpatrick." "I own, sir," said Mrs Miller, "when I saw this gentleman come into the room to you, I told Mr Nightingale that I apprehended you had sent him thither to inquire into the affair." Allworthy shewed marks of astonishment in his countenance at this news, and was indeed for two or three minutes struck dumb by it. At last, addressing himself to Mr Nightingale, he said, "I must confess myself, sir, more surprized at what you tell me than I have ever been before at anything in my whole life. Are you certain this was the gentleman?" "I am most certain," answered Nightingale. "At Aldersgate?" cries Allworthy. "And was you in company with this lawyer and the two fellows?"—"I was, sir," said the other, "very near half an hour." "Well, sir," said Allworthy, "and in what manner did the lawyer behave? did you hear all that past between him and the fellows?" "No, sir," answered Nightingale, "they had been together before I came.—In my presence the lawyer said little; but, after I had several times examined the fellows, who persisted in a story directly contrary to what I had heard from Mr Jones, and which I find by Mr Fitzpatrick was a rank falshood, the lawyer then desired the fellows to say nothing but what was the truth, and seemed to speak so much in favour of Mr Jones, that, when I saw the same person with you, I concluded your goodness had prompted you to send him thither."—"And did you not send him thither?" says Mrs Miller.—"Indeed I did not," answered Allworthy; "nor did I know he had gone on such an errand till this moment."—"I see it all!" said Mrs Miller, "upon my soul, I see it all! No wonder they have been closeted so close lately. Son Nightingale, let me beg you run for these fellows immediately——find them out if they are above-ground. I will go myself"—"Dear madam," said Allworthy, "be patient, and do me the favour to send a servant upstairs to call Mr Dowling hither, if he be in the house, or, if not, Mr Blifil." Mrs Miller went out muttering something to herself, and presently returned with an answer, "That Mr Dowling was gone; but that the t'other," as she called him, "was coming."

Allworthy was of a cooler disposition than the good woman, whose spirits were all up in arms in the cause of her friend. He was not however without some suspicions which were near akin to hers. When Blifil came into the room, he asked him with a very serious countenance, and with a less friendly look than he had ever before given him, "Whether he knew anything of Mr Dowling's having seen any of the persons who were present at the duel between Jones and another gentleman?"

There is nothing so dangerous as a question which comes by surprize on a man whose business it is to conceal truth, or to defend falshood. For which reason those worthy personages, whose noble office it is to save the lives of their fellow-creatures at the Old Bailey, take the utmost care, by frequent previous examination, to divine every question which may be asked their clients on the day of tryal, that they may be supplyed with proper and ready answers, which the most fertile invention cannot supply in an instant. Besides, the sudden and violent impulse on the blood, occasioned by these surprizes, causes frequently such an alteration in the countenance, that the man is obliged to give evidence against himself. And such indeed were the alterations which the countenance of Blifil underwent from this sudden question, that we can scarce blame the eagerness of Mrs Miller, who immediately cryed out, "Guilty, upon my honour! guilty, upon my soul!"

Mr Allworthy sharply rebuked her for this impetuosity; and then turning to Blifil, who seemed sinking into the earth, he said, "Why do you hesitate, sir, at giving me an answer? You certainly must have employed him; for he would not, of his own accord, I believe, have undertaken such an errand, and especially without acquainting me."

Blifil then answered, "I own, sir, I have been guilty of an offence, yet may I hope your pardon?"—"My pardon," said Allworthy, very angrily.—"Nay, sir," answered Blifil, "I knew you would be offended; yet surely my dear uncle will forgive the effects of the most amiable of human weaknesses. Compassion for those who do not deserve it, I own is a crime; and yet it is a crime from which you yourself are not entirely free. I know I have been guilty of it in more than one instance to this very person; and I will own I did send Mr Dowling, not on a vain and fruitless enquiry, but to discover the witnesses, and to endeavour to soften their evidence. This, sir, is the truth; which, though I intended to conceal from you, I will not deny."

"I confess," said Nightingale, "this is the light in which it appeared to me from the gentleman's behaviour."

"Now, madam," said Allworthy, "I believe you will once in your life own you have entertained a wrong suspicion, and are not so angry with my nephew as you was."

Mrs Miller was silent; for, though she could not so hastily be pleased with Blifil, whom she looked upon to have been the ruin of Jones, yet in this particular instance he had imposed upon her as well as upon the rest; so entirely had the devil stood his friend. And, indeed, I look upon the vulgar observation, "That the devil often deserts his friends, and leaves them in the lurch," to be a great abuse on that gentleman's character. Perhaps he may sometimes desert those who are only his cup acquaintance; or who, at most, are but half his; but he generally stands by those who are thoroughly his servants, and helps them off in all extremities, till their bargain expires.

As a conquered rebellion strengthens a government, or as health is more perfectly established by recovery from some diseases; so anger, when removed, often gives new life to affection. This was the case of Mr Allworthy; for Blifil having wiped off the greater suspicion, the lesser, which had been raised by Square's letter, sunk of course, and was forgotten; and Thwackum, with whom he was greatly offended, bore alone all the reflections which Square had cast on the enemies of Jones.

As for that young man, the resentment of Mr Allworthy began more and more to abate towards him. He told Blifil, "He did not only forgive the extraordinary efforts of his good-nature, but would give him the pleasure of following his example." Then, turning to Mrs Miller with a smile which would have become an angel, he cryed, "What say you, madam? shall we take a hackney-coach, and all of us together pay a visit to your friend? I promise you it is not the first visit I have made in a prison."

Every reader, I believe, will be able to answer for the worthy woman; but they must have a great deal of good-nature, and be well acquainted with friendship, who can feel what she felt on this occasion. Few, I hope, are capable of feeling what now passed in the mind of Blifil; but those who are will acknowledge that it was impossible for him to raise any objection to this visit. Fortune, however, or the gentleman lately mentioned above, stood his friend, and prevented his undergoing so great a shock; for at the very instant when the coach was sent for, Partridge arrived, and, having called Mrs Miller from the company, acquainted her with the dreadful accident lately come to light; and hearing Mr Allworthy's intention, begged her to find some means of stopping him: "For," says he, "the matter must at all hazards be kept a secret from him; and if he should now go, he will find Mr Jones and his mother, who arrived just as I left him, lamenting over one another the horrid crime they have ignorantly committed."

The poor woman, who was almost deprived of her senses at his dreadful news, was never less capable of invention than at present. However, as women are much readier at this than men, she bethought herself of an excuse, and, returning to Allworthy, said, "I am sure, sir, you will be surprized at hearing any objection from me to the kind proposal you just now made; and yet I am afraid of the consequence of it, if carried immediately into execution. You must imagine, sir, that all the calamities which have lately befallen this poor young fellow must have thrown him into the lowest dejection of spirits; and now, sir, should we all on a sudden fling him into such a violent fit of joy, as I know your presence will occasion, it may, I am afraid, produce some fatal mischief, especially as his servant, who is without, tells me he is very far from being well."

"Is his servant without?" cries Allworthy; "pray call him hither. I will ask him some questions concerning his master."

Partridge was at first afraid to appear before Mr Allworthy; but was at length persuaded, after Mrs Miller, who had often heard his whole story from his own mouth, had promised to introduce him.

Allworthy recollected Partridge the moment he came into the room, though many years had passed since he had seen him. Mrs Miller, therefore, might have spared here a formal oration, in which, indeed, she was something prolix; for the reader, I believe, may have observed already that the good woman, among other things, had a tongue always ready for the service of her friends.

"And are you," said Allworthy to Partridge, "the servant of Mr Jones?" "I can't say, sir," answered he, "that I am regularly a servant, but I live with him, an't please your honour, at present. *Non sum qualis eram*, as your honour very well knows."

Mr Allworthy then asked him many questions concerning Jones, as to his health, and other matters; to all which Partridge answered, without having the least regard to what was, but considered only what he would have things appear; for a strict adherence to truth was not among the articles of this honest fellow's morality or his religion.

During this dialogue Mr Nightingale took his leave, and presently after Mrs Miller left the room, when Allworthy likewise despatched Blifil; for he imagined that Partridge when alone with him would be more explicit than before company. They were no sooner left in private together than Allworthy began, as in the following chapter.

CHAPTER VI.

In which the history is farther continued

"Sure, friend," said the good man, "you are the strangest of all human beings. Not only to have suffered as you have formerly for obstinately persisting in a falshood, but to persist in it thus to the last, and to pass thus upon the world for a servant of your own son! What interest can you have in all this? What can be your motive?"

"I see, sir," said Partridge, falling down upon his knees, "that your honour is prepossessed against me, and resolved not to believe anything I say, and, therefore, what signifies my protestations? but yet there is one above who knows that I am not the father of this young man."

"How!" said Allworthy, "will you yet deny what you was formerly convicted of upon such unanswerable, such manifest evidence? Nay, what a confirmation is your being now found with this very man, of all which twenty years ago appeared against you! I thought you had left the country! nay, I thought you had been long since dead.—In what manner did you know anything of this young man? Where did you meet with him, unless you had kept some correspondence together? Do not deny this; for I promise you it will greatly raise your son in my opinion, to find that he hath such a sense of filial duty as privately to support his father for so many years."

"If your honour will have patience to hear me," said Partridge, "I will tell you all."—Being bid go on, he proceeded thus: "When your honour conceived that displeasure against me, it ended in my ruin soon after; for I lost my little school; and the minister, thinking I suppose it would be agreeable to your honour, turned me out from the office of clerk; so that I had nothing to trust to but the barber's shop, which, in a country place like that, is a poor livelihood; and when my wife died (for till that time I received a pension of £12 a year from an unknown hand, which indeed I believe was your honour's own, for nobody that ever I heard of doth these things besides)—but, as I was saying, when she died, this pension forsook me; so that now, as I owed two or three small debts, which began to be troublesome to me, particularly one[1] which an attorney brought up by law-charges

---

[1] This is a fact which I knew happen to a poor clergyman in Dorsetshire, by the villany of an attorney who, not contented with the exorbitant costs to which the poor man was put by

from 15s. to near £30, and as I found all my usual means of living had forsook me, I packed up my little all as well as I could, and went off.

"The first place I came to was Salisbury, where I got into the service of a gentleman belonging to the law, and one of the best gentlemen that ever I knew, for he was not only good to me, but I know a thousand good and charitable acts which he did while I staid with him; and I have known him often refuse business because it was paultry and oppressive." "You need not be so particular," said Allworthy; "I know this gentleman, and a very worthy man he is, and an honour to his profession."—"Well, sir," continued Partridge, "from hence I removed to Lymington, where I was above three years in the service of another lawyer, who was likewise a very good sort of a man, and to be sure one of the merriest gentlemen in England. Well, sir, at the end of the three years I set up a little school, and was likely to do well again, had it not been for a most unlucky accident. Here I kept a pig; and one day, as ill fortune would have it, this pig broke out, and did a trespass, I think they call it, in a garden belonging to one of my neighbours, who was a proud, revengeful man, and employed a lawyer, one—one—I can't think of his name; but he sent for a writ against me, and had me to size. When I came there, Lord have mercy upon me—to hear what the counsellors said! There was one that told my lord a parcel of the confoundedest lies about me; he said that I used to drive my hogs into other folk's gardens, and a great deal more; and at last he said, he hoped I had at last brought my hogs to a fair market. To be sure, one would have thought that, instead of being owner only of one poor little pig, I had been the greatest hog-merchant in England. Well—" "Pray," said Allworthy, "do not be so particular, I have heard nothing of your son yet." "O it was a great many years," answered Partridge, "before I saw my son, as you are pleased to call him.——I went over to Ireland after this, and taught school at Cork (for that one suit ruined me again, and I lay seven years in Winchester jail)."—"Well," said Allworthy, "pass that over till your return to England."—"Then, sir," said he, "it was about half a year ago that I landed at Bristol, where I staid some time, and not finding it do there, and hearing of a place between that and Gloucester where the barber was just dead, I went thither, and there I had been about two months when Mr Jones came thither." He then gave Allworthy a very particular account of their first meeting, and of everything, as well as he could remember, which had happened from that day to this; frequently interlarding his story with panegyrics on Jones, and not forgetting to insinuate the great love and respect which he had for Allworthy. He concluded with saying, "Now, sir, I have told your honour the whole truth." And then repeated a most solemn protestation, "That he was no

---

a single action, brought afterwards another action on the judgment, as it was called. A method frequently used to oppress the poor, and bring money into the pockets of attorneys, to the great scandal of the law, of the nation, of Christianity, and even of human nature itself.

more the father of Jones than of the Pope of Rome;" and imprecated the most bitter curses on his head, if he did not speak truth.

"What am I to think of this matter?" cries Allworthy. "For what purpose should you so strongly deny a fact which I think it would be rather your interest to own?" "Nay, sir," answered Partridge (for he could hold no longer), "if your honour will not believe me, you are like soon to have satisfaction enough. I wish you had mistaken the mother of this young man, as well as you have his father."—And now being asked what he meant, with all the symptoms of horror, both in his voice and countenance, he told Allworthy the whole story, which he had a little before expressed such desire to Mrs Miller to conceal from him.

Allworthy was almost as much shocked at this discovery as Partridge himself had been while he related it. "Good heavens!" says he, "in what miserable distresses do vice and imprudence involve men! How much beyond our designs are the effects of wickedness sometimes carried!" He had scarce uttered these words, when Mrs Waters came hastily and abruptly into the room. Partridge no sooner saw her than he cried, "Here, sir, here is the very woman herself. This is the unfortunate mother of Mr Jones. I am sure she will acquit me before your honour. Pray, madam——"

Mrs Waters, without paying any regard to what Partridge said, and almost without taking any notice of him, advanced to Mr Allworthy. "I believe, sir, it is so long since I had the honour of seeing you, that you do not recollect me." "Indeed," answered Allworthy, "you are so very much altered, on many accounts, that had not this man already acquainted me who you are, I should not have immediately called you to my remembrance. Have you, madam, any particular business which brings you to me?" Allworthy spoke this with great reserve; for the reader may easily believe he was not well pleased with the conduct of this lady; neither with what he had formerly heard, nor with what Partridge had now delivered.

Mrs Waters answered—"Indeed, sir, I have very particular business with you; and it is such as I can impart only to yourself. I must desire, therefore, the favour of a word with you alone: for I assure you what I have to tell you is of the utmost importance."

Partridge was then ordered to withdraw, but before he went, he begged the lady to satisfy Mr Allworthy that he was perfectly innocent. To which she answered, "You need be under no apprehension, sir; I shall satisfy Mr Allworthy very perfectly of that matter."

Then Partridge withdrew, and that past between Mr Allworthy and Mrs Waters which is written in the next chapter.

CHAPTER VII.

Continuation of the history.

Mrs Waters remaining a few moments silent, Mr Allworthy could not refrain from saying, "I am sorry, madam, to perceive, by what I have since heard, that you have made so very ill a use——" "Mr Allworthy," says she, interrupting him, "I know I have faults, but ingratitude to you is not one of them. I never can nor shall forget your goodness, which I own I have very little deserved; but be pleased to wave all upbraiding me at present, as I have so important an affair to communicate to you concerning this young man, to whom you have given my maiden name of Jones."

"Have I then," said Allworthy, "ignorantly punished an innocent man, in the person of him who hath just left us? Was he not the father of the child?" "Indeed he was not," said Mrs Waters. "You may be pleased to remember, sir, I formerly told you, you should one day know; and I acknowledge myself to have been guilty of a cruel neglect, in not having discovered it to you before. Indeed, I little knew how necessary it was." "Well, madam," said Allworthy, "be pleased to proceed." "You must remember, sir," said she, "a young fellow, whose name was Summer." "Very well," cries Allworthy, "he was the son of a clergyman of great learning and virtue, for whom I had the highest friendship." "So it appeared, sir," answered she; "for I believe you bred the young man up, and maintained him at the university; where, I think, he had finished his studies, when he came to reside at your house; a finer man, I must say, the sun never shone upon; for, besides the handsomest person I ever saw, he was so genteel, and had so much wit and good breeding." "Poor gentleman," said Allworthy, "he was indeed untimely snatched away; and little did I think he had any sins of this kind to answer for; for I plainly perceive you are going to tell me he was the father of your child."

"Indeed, sir," answered she, "he was not." "How!" said Allworthy, "to what then tends all this preface?" "To a story," said she, "which I am concerned falls to my lot to unfold to you. O, sir! prepare to hear something which will surprize you, will grieve you." "Speak," said Allworthy, "I am conscious of no crime, and cannot be afraid to hear." "Sir," said she, "that Mr Summer, the son of your friend, educated at your expense, who, after living a year in the house as if he had been your own son, died there of the small-pox, was tenderly lamented by you, and buried as if he had been your own; that Summer, sir, was the father of this child." "How!" said Allworthy; "you contradict yourself." "That I do not," answered she;

"he was indeed the father of this child, but not by me." "Take care, madam," said Allworthy, "do not, to shun the imputation of any crime, be guilty of falshood. Remember there is One from whom you can conceal nothing, and before whose tribunal falshood will only aggravate your guilt." "Indeed, sir," says she, "I am not his mother; nor would I now think myself so for the world." "I know your reason," said Allworthy, "and shall rejoice as much as you to find it otherwise; yet you must remember, you yourself confest it before me." "So far what I confest," said she, "was true, that these hands conveyed the infant to your bed; conveyed it thither at the command of its mother; at her commands I afterwards owned it, and thought myself, by her generosity, nobly rewarded, both for my secrecy and my shame." "Who could this woman be?" said Allworthy. "Indeed, I tremble to name her," answered Mrs Waters. "By all this preparation I am to guess that she was a relation of mine," cried he. "Indeed she was a near one." At which words Allworthy started, and she continued—"You had a sister, sir." "A sister!" repeated he, looking aghast.—"As there is truth in heaven," cries she, "your sister was the mother of that child you found between your sheets." "Can it be possible?" cries he, "Good heavens!" "Have patience, sir," said Mrs Waters, "and I will unfold to you the whole story. Just after your departure for London, Miss Bridget came one day to the house of my mother. She was pleased to say she had heard an extraordinary character of me, for my learning and superior understanding to all the young women there, so she was pleased to say. She then bid me come to her to the great house; where, when I attended, she employed me to read to her. She expressed great satisfaction in my reading, shewed great kindness to me, and made me many presents. At last she began to catechise me on the subject of secrecy, to which I gave her such satisfactory answers, that, at last, having locked the door of her room, she took me into her closet, and then locking that door likewise, she said she should convince me of the vast reliance she had on my integrity, by communicating a secret in which her honour, and consequently her life, was concerned. She then stopt, and after a silence of a few minutes, during which she often wiped her eyes, she enquired of me if I thought my mother might safely be confided in. I answered, I would stake my life on her fidelity. She then imparted to me the great secret which laboured in her breast, and which, I believe, was delivered with more pains than she afterwards suffered in child-birth. It was then contrived that my mother and myself only should attend at the time, and that Mrs Wilkins should be sent out of the way, as she accordingly was, to the very furthest part of Dorsetshire, to enquire the character of a servant; for the lady had turned away her own maid near three months before; during all which time I officiated about her person upon trial, as she said, though, as she afterwards declared, I was not sufficiently handy for the place. This, and many other such things which she used to say of me, were all thrown out to prevent any suspicion which Wilkins might hereafter have, when I was to own the child; for she thought it could never be believed she would venture to hurt a young woman with whom she had intrusted such a secret. You may be assured, sir, I was well paid for all these affronts, which, together with being informed with the occasion of them, very well contented me. Indeed, the lady had a greater suspicion of Mrs Wilkins than of any other person; not that she had the least aversion to the gentlewoman, but she thought her incapable of keeping a secret, especially from you, sir; for I have often heard Miss Bridget say, that, if Mrs Wilkins had committed a murder, she believed she would acquaint you with it. At last the expected day came, and Mrs Wilkins, who had been kept a week in readiness, and put off from time to time, upon some pretence or other, that she might not return too soon, was dispatched. Then the child was born, in the presence only of myself and my mother, and was by my mother conveyed to her own house, where it was privately kept by her till the evening of your return, when I, by the command of Miss Bridget, conveyed it into the bed where you found it. And all suspicions were afterwards laid asleep by the artful conduct of your sister, in pretending ill-will to the boy, and that any regard she shewed him was out of meer complacence to you."

Mrs Waters then made many protestations of the truth of this story, and concluded by saying, "Thus, sir, you have at last discovered your nephew; for so I am sure you will hereafter think him, and I question not but he will be both an honour and a comfort to you under that appellation."

"I need not, madam," said Allworthy, "express my astonishment at what you have told me; and yet surely you would not, and could not, have put together so many circumstances to evidence an untruth. I confess I recollect some passages relating to that Summer, which formerly gave me a conceit that my sister had some liking to him. I mentioned it to her; for I had such a regard to the young man, as well on his own account as on his father's, that I should willingly have consented to a match between them; but she exprest the highest disdain of my unkind suspicion, as she called it; so that I never spoke more on the subject. Good heavens! Well! the Lord disposeth all things.—Yet sure it was a most unjustifiable conduct in my sister to carry this secret with her out of the world." "I promise you, sir," said Mrs Waters, "she always profest a contrary intention, and frequently told me she intended one day to communicate it to you. She said, indeed, she was highly rejoiced that her plot had succeeded so well, and that you had of your own accord taken such a fancy to the child, that it was yet unnecessary to make any express declaration. Oh! sir, had that lady lived to have seen this poor young man turned like a vagabond from your house: nay, sir, could she have lived to hear that you had yourself employed a lawyer to prosecute him for a murder of which he was not guilty——Forgive me, Mr Allworthy, I must say it was unkind.—Indeed, you have been abused, he never deserved it of you." "Indeed, madam," said Allworthy, "I have been abused by the person, whoever he was, that told you so." "Nay, sir," said she, "I would not be mistaken, I did not presume to say you were guilty of any wrong. The gentleman who came to me proposed no such matter; he only said, taking me for Mr Fitzpatrick's wife, that, if Mr Jones had murdered my husband, I should be assisted with any money I wanted to carry on the prosecution, by a very worthy gentleman, who, he said, was well apprized what a villain I had to deal with. It was by this man I found out who Mr Jones was; and this man, whose name is Dowling, Mr Jones tells me is your steward. I discovered his name by a very odd accident; for he himself refused to tell it me; but Partridge, who met him at my lodgings the second time he came, knew him formerly at Salisbury."

"And did this Mr Dowling," says Allworthy, with great astonishment in his countenance, "tell you that I would assist in the prosecution?"—"No, sir," answered she, "I will not charge him wrongfully. He said I should be assisted, but he mentioned no name. Yet you must pardon me, sir, if from circumstances I thought it could be no other."—"Indeed, madam," says Allworthy, "from circumstances I am too well convinced it was another. Good Heaven! by what wonderful means is the blackest and deepest villany sometimes discovered!—Shall I beg you, madam, to stay till the person you have mentioned comes, for I expect him every minute? nay, he may be, perhaps, already in the house."

Allworthy then stept to the door, in order to call a servant, when in came, not Mr Dowling, but the gentleman who will be seen in the next chapter.

CHAPTER VIII.

Further continuation.

The gentleman who now arrived was no other than Mr Western. He no sooner saw Allworthy, than, without considering in the least the presence of Mrs Waters, he began to vociferate in the following manner: "Fine doings at my house! A rare kettle of fish I have discovered at last! who the devil would be plagued with a daughter?" "What's the matter, neighbour?" said Allworthy. "Matter enough," answered Western: "when I thought she was just a coming to; nay, when she had in a manner promised me to do as I would ha her, and when I was a hoped to have had nothing more to do than to have sent for the lawyer, and finished all; what do you think I have found out? that the little b— hath bin playing tricks with me all the while, and carrying on a correspondence with that bastard of yours. Sister Western, whom I have quarrelled with upon her account, sent me word o't, and I ordered her pockets to be searched when she was asleep, and here I have got un signed with the son of a whore's own name. I have not had patience to read half o't, for 'tis longer than one of parson Supple's sermons; but I find plainly it is all about love; and indeed what should it be else? I have packed her up in chamber again, and to-morrow morning down she goes into the country, unless she consents to be married directly, and there she shall live in a garret upon bread and water all her days; and the sooner such a b— breaks her heart the better, though, d—n her, that I believe is too tough. She will live long enough to plague me." "Mr Western," answered Allworthy, "you know I have always protested against force, and you yourself consented that none should be used." "Ay," cries he, "that was only upon condition that she would consent without. What the devil and doctor Faustus! shan't I do what I will with my own daughter, especially when I desire nothing but her own good?" "Well, neighbour," answered Allworthy, "if you will give me leave, I will undertake once to argue with the young lady." "Will you?" said Western; "why that is kind now, and neighbourly, and mayhap you will do more than I have been able to do with her; for I promise you she hath a very good opinion of you." "Well, sir," said Allworthy, "if you will go home, and release the young lady from her captivity, I will wait upon her within this half-hour." "But suppose," said Western, "she should run away with un in the meantime? For lawyer Dowling tells me there is no hopes of hanging the fellow at last; for that the man is alive, and like to do well, and that he thinks Jones will be out of prison again presently." "How!" said Allworthy; "what, did you employ him then to enquire or to do anything in that matter?" "Not I," answered Western, "he mentioned it to me just now of his own accord." "Just now!" cries Allworthy, "why, where did you see him then? I want much to see Mr Dowling." "Why, you may see un an you will presently at my lodgings; for there is to be a meeting of lawyers there this morning about a mortgage. 'Icod! I shall lose two or dree thousand pounds, I believe, by that honest gentleman, Mr Nightingale." "Well, sir," said Allworthy, "I will be with you within the half-hour." "And do for once," cries the squire, "take a fool's advice; never think of dealing with her by gentle methods, take my word for it those will never do. I have tried 'um long enough. She must be frightened into it, there is no other way. Tell her I'm her father; and of the horrid sin of disobedience, and of the dreadful punishment of it in t'other world, and then tell her about being locked up all her life in a garret in this, and being kept only on bread and water." "I will do all I can," said Allworthy; "for I promise you there is nothing I wish for more than an alliance with this amiable creature." "Nay, the girl is well enough for matter o' that," cries the squire; "a man may go farther and meet with worse meat; that I may declare o'her, thof she be my own daughter. And if she will but be obedient to me, there is narrow a father within a hundred miles o' the place, that loves a daughter better than I do; but I see you are busy with the lady here, so I will go huome and expect you; and so your humble servant."

As soon as Mr Western was gone Mrs Waters said, "I see, sir, the squire hath not the least remembrance of my face. I believe, Mr Allworthy, you would not have known me neither. I am very considerably altered since that day when you so kindly gave me that advice, which I had been happy had I followed." "Indeed, madam," cries Allworthy, "it gave me great concern when I first heard the contrary." "Indeed, sir," says she, "I was ruined by a very deep scheme of villany, which if you knew, though I pretend not to think it would justify me in your opinion, it would at least mitigate my offence, and induce you to pity me: you are not now at leisure to hear my whole story; but this I assure you, I was betrayed by the most solemn promises of marriage; nay, in the eye of heaven I was married to him; for, after much reading on the subject, I am convinced that particular ceremonies are only requisite to give a legal sanction to marriage, and have only a worldly use in giving a woman the privileges of a wife; but that she who lives constant to one man, after a solemn private affiance, whatever the world may call her, hath little to charge on her own conscience." "I am sorry, madam," said Allworthy, "you made so ill a use of your learning. Indeed, it would have been well that you had been possessed of much more, or had remained in a state of ignorance. And yet, madam, I am afraid you have more than this sin to answer for." "During his life," answered she, "which was above a dozen years, I most solemnly assure you I had not. And consider, sir, on my behalf, what is in the power of a woman stript of her reputation and left destitute; whether the good-natured world will suffer such a stray sheep to return to the road of virtue, even if she was never so desirous. I protest, then, I would have chose it had it been in my power; but necessity drove me into the arms of Captain Waters, with whom, though still unmarried, I lived as a wife for many years, and went by his name. I parted with this gentleman at Worcester, on his march against the rebels, and it was then I accidentally met with Mr Jones, who rescued me from the hands of a villain. Indeed, he is the worthiest of men. No young gentleman of his age is, I believe, freer from vice, and few have the twentieth part of his virtues; nay, whatever vices he hath had, I am firmly persuaded he hath now taken a resolution to abandon them." "I hope he hath," cries Allworthy, "and I hope he will preserve that resolution. I must say, I have still the same hopes with regard to yourself. The world, I do agree, are apt to be too unmerciful on these occasions; yet time and perseverance will get the better of this their disinclination, as I may call it, to pity; for though they are not, like heaven, ready to receive a penitent sinner; yet a continued repentance will at length obtain mercy even with the world. This you may be assured of, Mrs Waters, that whenever I find you are sincere in such good intentions, you shall want no assistance in my power to make them effectual."

Mrs Waters fell now upon her knees before him, and, in a flood of tears, made him many most passionate acknowledgments of his goodness, which, as she truly said, savoured more of the divine than human nature.

Allworthy raised her up, and spoke in the most tender manner, making use of every expression which his invention could suggest to comfort her, when he was interrupted by the arrival of Mr Dowling, who, upon his first entrance, seeing Mrs Waters, started, and appeared in some confusion; from which he soon recovered himself as well as he could, and then said he was in the utmost haste to attend counsel at Mr Western's lodgings; but, however, thought it his duty to call and acquaint him with the opinion of counsel upon the case which he had before told him, which was that the conversion of the moneys in that case could not be questioned in a criminal cause, but that an action of trover might be brought, and if it appeared to the jury to be the moneys of plaintiff, that plaintiff would recover a verdict for the value.

Allworthy, without making any answer to this, bolted the door, and then, advancing with a stern look to Dowling, he said, "Whatever be your haste, sir, I must first receive an answer to some questions. Do you know this lady?"—"That lady, sir!" answered Dowling, with great hesitation. Allworthy then, with the most solemn voice, said, "Look you, Mr Dowling, as you value my favour, or your continuance a moment longer in my service, do not hesitate nor prevaricate; but answer faithfully and truly to every question I ask.——Do you know this lady?"—"Yes, sir," said Dowling, "I have seen the lady." "Where, sir?" "At her own lodgings."—"Upon what business did you go thither, sir; and who sent you?" "I went, sir, to enquire, sir, about Mr Jones." "And who sent you to enquire about him?" "Who, sir? why, sir, Mr Blifil sent me." "And what did you say to the lady concerning that matter?" "Nay, sir, it is impossible to recollect every word." "Will you please, madam, to assist the gentleman's memory?" "He told me, sir," said Mrs Waters, "that if Mr Jones had murdered my husband, I should be assisted by any money I wanted to carry on the prosecution, by a very worthy gentleman, who was well apprized what a villain I had to deal with. These, I can safely swear, were the very words he spoke."—"Were these the words, sir?" said Allworthy. "I cannot charge my memory exactly," cries Dowling, "but I believe I did speak to that purpose."—"And did Mr Blifil order you to say so?" "I am sure, sir, I should not have gone on my own accord, nor have willingly exceeded my authority in matters of this kind. If I said so, I must have so understood Mr Blifil's instructions." "Look you, Mr Dowling," said Allworthy; "I promise you before this lady, that whatever you have done in this affair by Mr Blifil's order I will forgive, provided you now tell me strictly the truth; for I believe what you say, that you would not have acted of your own accord and without authority in this matter.——Mr Blifil then likewise sent you to examine the two fellows at Aldersgate?"—"He did, sir." "Well, and what instructions did he then give you? Recollect as well as you can, and tell me, as near as possible, the very words he used."—"Why, sir, Mr Blifil sent me to find out the persons who were eye-witnesses of this fight. He said, he feared they might be tampered with by Mr Jones, or some of his friends. He said, blood required blood; and that not only all who concealed a murderer, but those who omitted anything in their power to bring him to justice, were sharers in his guilt. He said, he found you was very desirous of having the villain brought to justice, though it was not proper you should appear in it." "He did so?" says Allworthy.—"Yes, sir," cries Dowling; "I should not, I am sure, have proceeded such lengths for the sake of any other person living but your worship."—"What lengths, sir?" said Allworthy.—"Nay, sir," cries Dowling, "I would not have your worship think I would, on any account, be guilty of subornation of perjury; but there are two ways of delivering evidence. I told them, therefore, that if any offers should be made them on the other side, they should refuse them, and that they might be assured they should lose nothing by being honest men, and telling the truth. I said, we were told that Mr Jones had assaulted the gentleman first, and that, if that was the truth, they should declare it; and I did give them some hints that they should be no losers."—"I think you went lengths indeed," cries Allworthy.—"Nay, sir," answered Dowling, "I am sure I did not desire them to tell an untruth;——nor should I have said what I did, unless it had been to oblige you."—"You would not have thought, I believe," says Allworthy, "to have obliged me, had you known that this Mr Jones was my own nephew."—"I am sure, sir," answered he, "it did not become me to take any notice of what I thought you desired to conceal."—"How!" cries Allworthy, "and did you know it then?"—"Nay, sir," answered Dowling, "if your worship bids me speak the truth, I am sure I shall do it.—Indeed, sir, I did know it; for they were almost the last words which Madam Blifil ever spoke, which she mentioned to me as I stood alone by her bedside, when she delivered me the letter I brought your worship from her."—"What letter?" cries Allworthy.—"The letter, sir," answered Dowling, "which I brought from Salisbury, and which I delivered into the hands of Mr Blifil."—"O heavens!" cries Allworthy: "Well, and what were the words? What did my sister say to you?"—"She took me by the hand," answered he, "and, as she delivered me the letter, said, `I scarce know what I have written. Tell my brother, Mr Jones is his nephew—He is my son.—Bless him,' says she, and then fell backward, as if dying away. I presently called in the people, and she never spoke more to me, and died within a few minutes afterwards."—Allworthy stood a minute silent, lifting up his eyes; and then, turning to Dowling, said, "How came you, sir, not to deliver me this message?" "Your worship," answered he, "must remember that you was at that time ill in bed; and, being in a violent hurry, as indeed I always am, I delivered the letter and message to Mr Blifil, who told me he would carry them both to you, which he hath since told me he did, and that your worship, partly out of friendship to Mr Jones, and partly out of regard to your sister, would never have it mentioned, and did intend to conceal it from the world; and therefore, sir, if you had not mentioned it to me first, I am certain I should never have thought it belonged to me to say anything of the matter, either to your worship or any other person."

We have remarked somewhere already, that it is possible for a man to convey a lie in the words of truth; this was the case at present; for Blifil had, in fact, told Dowling what he now related, but had not imposed upon him, nor indeed had imagined he was able so to do. In reality, the promises which Blifil had made to Dowling were the motives which had induced him to secrecy; and, as he now very plainly saw Blifil would not be able to keep them, he thought proper now to make this confession, which the promises of forgiveness, joined to the threats, the voice, the looks of Allworthy, and the discoveries he had made before, extorted from him, who was besides taken unawares, and had no time to consider of evasions.

Allworthy appeared well satisfied with this relation, and, having enjoined on Dowling strict silence as to what had past, conducted that gentleman himself to the door, lest he should see Blifil, who was returned to his chamber, where he exulted in the thoughts of his last deceit on his uncle, and little suspected what had since passed below-stairs.

As Allworthy was returning to his room he met Mrs Miller in the entry, who, with a face all pale and full of terror, said to him, "O! sir, I find this wicked woman hath been with you, and you know all; yet do not on this account abandon the poor young man. Consider, sir, he was ignorant it was his own mother; and the discovery itself will most probably break his heart, without your unkindness."

"Madam," says Allworthy, "I am under such an astonishment at what I have heard, that I am really unable to satisfy you; but come with me into my room. Indeed, Mrs Miller, I have made surprizing discoveries, and you shall soon know them."

The poor woman followed him trembling; and now Allworthy, going up to Mrs Waters, took her by the hand, and then, turning to Mrs Miller, said, "What reward shall I bestow upon this gentlewoman, for the services she hath done me?—O! Mrs Miller, you have a thousand times heard me call the young man to whom you are so faithful a friend, my son. Little did I then think he was indeed related to me at all.—Your friend, madam, is my nephew; he is the brother of that wicked viper which I have so long nourished in my bosom.—She will herself tell you the whole story, and how the youth came to pass for her son. Indeed, Mrs

Miller, I am convinced that he hath been wronged, and that I have been abused; abused by one whom you too justly suspected of being a villain. He is, in truth, the worst of villains."

The joy which Mrs Miller now felt bereft her of the power of speech, and might perhaps have deprived her of her senses, if not of life, had not a friendly shower of tears come seasonably to her relief. At length, recovering so far from her transport as to be able to speak, she cried, "And is my dear Mr Jones then your nephew, sir, and not the son of this lady? And are your eyes opened to him at last? And shall I live to see him as happy as he deserves?" "He certainly is my nephew," says Allworthy, "and I hope all the rest."—"And is this the dear good woman, the person," cries she, "to whom all this discovery is owing?"—"She is indeed," says Allworthy.—"Why, then," cried Mrs Miller, upon her knees, "may Heaven shower down its choicest blessings upon her head, and for this one good action forgive her all her sins, be they never so many!"

Mrs Waters then informed them that she believed Jones would very shortly be released; for that the surgeon was gone, in company with a nobleman, to the justice who committed him, in order to certify that Mr Fitzpatrick was out of all manner of danger, and to procure his prisoner his liberty.

Allworthy said he should be glad to find his nephew there at his return home; but that he was then obliged to go on some business of consequence. He then called to a servant to fetch him a chair, and presently left the two ladies together.

Mr Blifil, hearing the chair ordered, came downstairs to attend upon his uncle; for he never was deficient in such acts of duty. He asked his uncle if he was going out, which is a civil way of asking a man whither he is going: to which the other making no answer, he again desired to know when he would be pleased to return?—Allworthy made no answer to this neither, till he was just going into his chair, and then, turning about, he said—"Harkee, sir, do you find out, before my return, the letter which your mother sent me on her death-bed." Allworthy then departed, and left Blifil in a situation to be envied only by a man who is just going to be hanged.

CHAPTER IX.

A further continuation.

Allworthy took an opportunity, whilst he was in the chair, of reading the letter from Jones to Sophia, which Western delivered him; and there were some expressions in it concerning himself which drew tears from his eyes. At length he arrived at Mr Western's, and was introduced to Sophia.

When the first ceremonies were past, and the gentleman and lady had taken their chairs, a silence of some minutes ensued; during which the latter, who had been prepared for the visit by her father, sat playing with her fan, and had every mark of confusion both in her countenance and behaviour. At length Allworthy, who was himself a little disconcerted, began thus: "I am afraid, Miss Western, my family hath been the occasion of giving you some uneasiness; to which, I fear, I have innocently become more instrumental than I intended. Be assured, madam, had I at first known how disagreeable the proposals had been, I should not have suffered you to have been so long persecuted. I hope, therefore, you will not think the design of this visit is to trouble you with any further solicitations of that kind, but entirely to relieve you from them."

"Sir," said Sophia, with a little modest hesitation, "this behaviour is most kind and generous, and such as I could expect only from Mr Allworthy; but as you have been so kind to mention this matter, you will pardon me for saying it hath, indeed, given me great uneasiness, and hath been the occasion of my suffering much cruel treatment from a father who was, till that unhappy affair, the tenderest and fondest of all parents. I am convinced, sir, you are too good and generous to resent my refusal of your nephew. Our inclinations are not in our own power; and whatever may be his merit, I cannot force them in his favour." "I assure you, most amiable young lady," said Allworthy, "I am capable of no such resentment, had the person been my own son, and had I entertained the highest esteem for him. For you say truly, madam, we cannot force our inclinations, much less can they be directed by another." "Oh! sir," answered Sophia, "every word you speak proves you deserve that good, that great, that benevolent character the whole world allows you. I assure you, sir, nothing less than the certain prospect of future misery could have made me resist the commands of my father." "I sincerely believe you, madam," replied Allworthy, "and I heartily congratulate you on your prudent foresight, since by so justifiable a resistance you have avoided misery indeed!" "You speak now, Mr Allworthy," cries she, "with a delicacy which few men are capable of feeling! but surely, in my opinion, to lead our lives with one to whom we are indifferent must be a state of wretchedness.——Perhaps that wretchedness would be even increased by a sense of the merits of an object to whom we cannot give our affections. If I had married Mr Blifil—" "Pardon my interrupting you, madam," answered Allworthy, "but I cannot bear the supposition.—Believe me, Miss Western, I rejoice from my heart, I rejoice in your escape.—I have discovered the wretch for whom you have suffered all this cruel violence from your father to be a villain." "How, sir!" cries Sophia—"you must believe this surprizes me."—"It hath surprized me, madam," answered Allworthy, "and so it will the world.——But I have acquainted you with the real truth." "Nothing but truth," says Sophia, "can, I am convinced, come from the lips of Mr Allworthy.——Yet, sir, such sudden, such unexpected news.——Discovered, you say——may villany be ever so!"—"You will soon enough hear the story," cries Allworthy;—"at present let us not mention so detested a name.—I have another matter of a very serious nature to propose.—O! Miss Western, I know your vast worth, nor can I so easily part with the ambition of being allied to it.—I have a near relation, madam, a young man whose character is, I am convinced, the very opposite to that of this wretch, and whose fortune I will make equal to what his was to have been. Could I, madam, hope you would admit a visit from him?" Sophia, after a minute's silence, answered, "I will deal with the utmost sincerity with Mr Allworthy. His character, and the obligation I have just received from him, demand it. I have determined at present to listen to no such proposals from any person. My only desire is to be restored to the affection of my father, and to be again the mistress of his family. This, sir, I hope to owe to your good offices. Let me beseech you, let me conjure you, by all the goodness which I, and all who know you, have experienced, do not, the very moment when you have released me from one persecution, do not engage me in another as miserable and as fruitless." "Indeed, Miss Western," replied Allworthy, "I am capable of no such conduct; and if this be your resolution, he must submit to the disappointment, whatever torments he may suffer under it." "I must smile now, Mr Allworthy," answered Sophia, "when you mention the torments of a man whom I do not know, and who can consequently have so little acquaintance with me." "Pardon me, dear young lady," cries Allworthy, "I begin now to be afraid he hath had too much acquaintance for the repose of his future days; since, if ever man was capable of a sincere, violent, and noble passion, such, I am convinced, is my unhappy nephew's for Miss Western." "A nephew of your's, Mr Allworthy!" answered Sophia. "It is surely strange. I never heard of him before." "Indeed, madam," cries Allworthy, "it is only the circumstance of his being my nephew to which you are a stranger, and which, till this day, was a secret to me.—Mr Jones, who has long loved you, he! he is my nephew!" "Mr Jones your nephew, sir!" cries Sophia, "can it be possible?"—"He is, indeed, madam," answered Allworthy; "he is my own sister's son—as such I shall always own him; nor am I ashamed of owning him. I am much more ashamed of my past behaviour to him; but I was as ignorant of his merit as of his birth. Indeed, Miss Western, I have used him cruelly——Indeed I have."—Here the good man wiped his eyes, and after a short pause proceeded—"I never shall be able to reward him for his sufferings without your assistance.——Believe me, most amiable young lady, I must have a great esteem of that offering which I make to your worth. I know he hath been guilty of faults; but there is great goodness of heart at the bottom. Believe me, madam, there is." Here he stopped, seeming to expect an answer, which he presently received from Sophia, after she had a little recovered herself from the hurry of spirits into which so strange and sudden information had thrown her: "I sincerely wish you joy, sir, of a discovery in which you seem to have such satisfaction. I doubt not but you will have all the comfort you can promise yourself from it. The young gentleman hath certainly a thousand good qualities, which makes it impossible he should not behave well to such an uncle."—"I hope, madam," said Allworthy, "he hath those good qualities which must make him a good husband.—He must, I am sure, be of all men the most abandoned, if a lady of your merit should condescend—" "You must pardon me, Mr Allworthy," answered Sophia; "I cannot listen to a proposal of this kind. Mr Jones, I am convinced, hath much merit; but I shall never receive Mr Jones as one who is to be my husband—Upon my honour I never will."—"Pardon me, madam," cries Allworthy, "if I am a little surprized, after what I have heard from Mr Western—I hope the unhappy young man hath done nothing to forfeit your good opinion, if he had ever the honour to enjoy it.—Perhaps, he may have been misrepresented to you, as he was to me. The same villany may have injured him everywhere.—He is no murderer, I assure you; as he hath been called."—"Mr Allworthy," answered Sophia, "I have told you my resolution. I wonder not at what my father hath told you; but, whatever his apprehensions or fears have been, if I know my heart, I have given no occasion for them; since it hath always been a fixed principle with me, never to have married without his consent. This is, I think, the duty of a child to a parent; and this, I hope, nothing could ever have prevailed with me to swerve from. I do not indeed conceive that the authority of any parent can oblige us to marry in direct opposition to our inclinations. To avoid a force of this kind, which I had reason to suspect, I left my father's house, and sought protection elsewhere. This is the truth of my story; and if the world, or my father, carry my intentions any farther, my own conscience will acquit me." "I hear you, Miss Western," cries Allworthy, "with admiration. I admire the justness of your sentiments; but surely there is more in this. I am cautious of offending you, young lady; but am I to look on all which I have hitherto heard or seen as a dream only? And have you suffered so much cruelty from your father on the account of a man to whom you have been always absolutely indifferent?" "I beg, Mr Allworthy," answered Sophia, "you will not insist on my reasons;—yes, I have suffered indeed; I will not, Mr Allworthy, conceal——I will be very sincere with you—I own I had a great opinion of Mr Jones—I believe—I know I have suffered for my opinion—I have been treated cruelly by my aunt, as well as by my father; but that is now past—I beg I may not be farther pressed; for, whatever hath been, my resolution is now fixed. Your nephew, sir, hath many virtues—he hath great virtues, Mr Allworthy. I question not but he will do you honour in the world, and make you happy."—"I wish I could make him so, madam," replied Allworthy; "but that I am convinced is only in your power. It is that conviction which hath made me so earnest a solicitor in his favour." "You are deceived indeed, sir; you are deceived," said Sophia. "I hope not by him. It is sufficient to have deceived me. Mr Allworthy, I must insist on being pressed no farther on this subject. I should be sorry—nay, I will not injure him in your favour. I wish Mr Jones very well. I sincerely wish him well; and I repeat it again to you, whatever demerit he may have to me, I am certain he hath many good qualities. I do not disown my former thoughts; but nothing can ever recal them. At present there is not a man upon earth whom I would more resolutely reject than Mr Jones; nor would the addresses of Mr Blifil himself be less agreeable to me."

Western had been long impatient for the event of this conference, and was just now arrived at the door to listen; when, having heard the last sentiments of his daughter's heart, he lost all temper, and, bursting open the door in a rage, cried out—"It is a lie! It is a d—n'd lie! It is all owing to that d—n'd rascal Jones; and if she could get at un, she'd ha un any hour of the day." Here Allworthy interposed, and addressing himself to the squire with some anger in his look, he said, "Mr Western, you have not kept your word with me. You promised to abstain from all violence."—"Why, so I did," cries Western, "as long as it was possible; but to hear a wench telling such confounded lies——Zounds! doth she think, if she can make vools of other volk, she can make one of me?—No, no, I know her better than thee dost." "I am sorry to tell you, sir," answered Allworthy, "it doth not appear, by your behaviour to this young lady, that you know her at all. I ask pardon for what I say: but I think our intimacy, your own desires, and the occasion justify me. She is your daughter, Mr Western, and I think she doth honour to your name. If I was capable of envy, I should sooner envy you on this account than any other man whatever."—"Odrabbit it!" cries the squire, "I wish she was thine, with all my heart—wouldst soon be glad to be rid of the trouble o' her." "Indeed, my good friend," answered Allworthy, "you yourself are the cause of all the trouble you complain of. Place that confidence in the young lady which she so well deserves, and I am certain you will be the happiest father on earth."—"I confidence in her?" cries the squire. "'Sblood! what confidence can I place in her, when she won't do as I would ha' her? Let her gi' but her consent to marry as I would ha' her, and I'll place as much confidence in her as wouldst ha' me."—"You have no right, neighbour," answered Allworthy, "to insist on any such consent. A negative voice your daughter allows you, and God and nature have thought proper to allow you no more."—"A negative voice!" cries the squire, "Ay! ay! I'll show you what a negative voice I ha.—Go along, go into your chamber, go, you stubborn——." "Indeed, Mr Western," said Allworthy, "indeed you use her cruelly—I cannot bear to see this—you shall, you must behave to her in a kinder manner. She deserves the best of treatment." "Yes, yes," said the squire, "I know what she deserves: now she's gone, I'll shew you what she deserves. See here, sir, here is a letter from my cousin, my Lady Bellaston, in which she is so kind to gi' me to understand that the fellow is got out of prison again; and here she advises me to take all the care I can o' the wench. Odzookers! neighbour Allworthy, you don't know what it is to govern a daughter."

The squire ended his speech with some compliments to his own sagacity; and then Allworthy, after a formal preface, acquainted him with the whole discovery which he had made concerning Jones, with his anger to Blifil, and with every particular which hath been disclosed to the reader in the preceding chapters.

Men over-violent in their dispositions are, for the most part, as changeable in them. No sooner then was Western informed of Mr Allworthy's intention to make Jones his heir, than he joined heartily with the uncle in every commendation of the nephew, and became as eager for her marriage with Jones as he had before been to couple her to Blifil.

Here Mr Allworthy was again forced to interpose, and to relate what had passed between him and Sophia, at which he testified great surprize.

The squire was silent a moment, and looked wild with astonishment at this account.—At last he cried out, "Why, what can be the meaning of this, neighbour Allworthy? Vond o'un she was, that I'll be sworn to.——Odzookers! I have hit o't. As sure as a gun I have hit o' the very right o't. It's all along o' zister. The girl hath got a hankering after this son of a whore of a lord. I vound 'em together at my cousin my Lady Bellaston's. He hath turned the head o' her, that's certain—but d—n me if he shall ha her—I'll ha no lords nor courtiers in my vamily."

Allworthy now made a long speech, in which he repeated his resolution to avoid all violent measures, and very earnestly recommended gentle methods to Mr Western, as those by which he might be assured of succeeding best with his daughter. He then took his leave, and returned back to Mrs Miller, but was forced to comply with the earnest entreaties of the squire, in promising to bring Mr Jones to visit him that afternoon, that he might, as he said, "make all matters up with the young gentleman." At Mr Allworthy's departure, Western promised to follow his advice in his behaviour to Sophia, saying, "I don't know how 'tis, but d—n me, Allworthy, if you don't make me always do just as you please; and yet I have as good an estate as you, and am in the commission of the peace as well as yourself."

CHAPTER X.

Wherein the history begins to draw towards a conclusion.

When Allworthy returned to his lodgings, he heard Mr Jones was just arrived before him. He hurried therefore instantly into an empty chamber, whither he ordered Mr Jones to be brought to him alone.

It is impossible to conceive a more tender or moving scene than the meeting between the uncle and nephew (for Mrs Waters, as the reader may well suppose, had at her last visit discovered to him the secret of his birth). The first agonies of joy which were felt on both sides are indeed beyond my power to describe: I shall not therefore attempt it. After Allworthy had raised Jones from his feet, where he had prostrated himself, and received him into his arms, "O my child!" he cried, "how have I been to blame! how have I injured you! What amends can I ever make you for those unkind, those unjust suspicions which I have entertained, and for all the sufferings they have occasioned to you?" "Am I not now made amends?" cries Jones. "Would not my sufferings, if they had been ten times greater, have been now richly repaid? O my dear uncle, this goodness, this tenderness overpowers, unmans, destroys me. I cannot bear the transports which flow so fast upon me. To be again restored to your presence, to your favour; to be once more thus kindly received by my great, my noble, my generous benefactor."—"Indeed, child," cries Allworthy, "I have used you cruelly."——He then explained to him all the treachery of Blifil, and again repeated expressions of the utmost concern, for having been induced by that treachery to use him so ill. "O, talk not so!" answered Jones; "indeed, sir, you have used me nobly. The wisest man might be deceived as you were; and, under such a deception, the best must have acted just as you did. Your goodness displayed itself in the midst of your anger, just as it then seemed. I owe everything to that goodness, of which I have been most unworthy. Do not put me on self-accusation, by carrying your generous sentiments too far. Alas! sir, I have not been punished more than I have deserved; and it shall be the whole business of my future life to deserve that happiness you now bestow on me; for, believe me, my dear uncle, my punishment hath not been thrown away upon me: though I have been a great, I am not a hardened sinner; I thank Heaven, I have had time to reflect on my past life, where, though I cannot charge myself with any gross villany, yet I can discern follies and vices more than enough to repent and to be ashamed of; follies which have been attended with dreadful consequences to myself, and have brought me to the brink of destruction." "I am rejoiced, my dear child," answered Allworthy, "to hear you talk thus sensibly; for as I am convinced hypocrisy (good Heaven! how have I been imposed on by it in others!) was never among your faults, so I can readily believe all you say. You now see, Tom, to what dangers imprudence alone may subject virtue (for virtue, I am now convinced, you love in a great degree). Prudence is indeed the duty which we owe to ourselves; and if we will be so much our own enemies as to neglect it, we are not to wonder if the world is deficient in discharging their duty to us; for when a man lays the foundation of his own ruin, others will, I am afraid, be too apt to build upon it. You say, however, you have seen your errors, and will reform them. I firmly believe you, my dear child; and therefore, from this moment, you shall never be reminded of them by me. Remember them only yourself so far as for the future to teach you the better to avoid them; but still remember, for your comfort, that there is this great difference between those faults which candor may construe into imprudence, and those which can be deduced from villany only. The former, perhaps, are even more apt to subject a man to ruin; but if he reform, his character will, at length, be totally retrieved; the world, though not immediately, will in time be reconciled to him; and he may reflect, not without some mixture of pleasure, on the dangers he hath escaped; but villany, my boy, when once discovered is irretrievable; the stains which this leaves behind, no time will wash away. The censures of mankind will pursue the wretch, their scorn will abash him in publick; and if shame drives him into retirement, he will go to it with all those terrors with which a weary child, who is afraid of hobgoblins, retreats from company to go to bed alone. Here his murdered conscience will haunt him.—Repose, like a false friend, will fly from him. Wherever he turns his eyes, horror presents itself; if he looks backward, unavailable repentance treads on his heels; if forward, incurable despair stares him in the face, till, like a condemned prisoner confined in a dungeon, he detests his present condition, and yet dreads the consequence of that hour which is to relieve him from it. Comfort yourself, I say, my child, that this is not your case; and rejoice with thankfulness to him who hath suffered you to see your errors, before they have brought on you that destruction to which a persistance in even those errors must have led you. You have deserted them; and the prospect now before you is such, that happiness seems in your own power." At these words Jones fetched a deep sigh; upon which, when Allworthy remonstrated, he said, "Sir, I will conceal nothing from you: I fear there is one consequence of my vices I shall never be able to retrieve. O, my dear uncle! I have lost a treasure." "You need say no more," answered Allworthy; "I will be explicit with you; I know what you lament; I have seen the young lady, and have discoursed with her concerning you. This I must insist on, as an earnest of your sincerity in all you have said, and of the stedfastness of your resolution, that you obey me in one instance. To abide intirely by the determination of the young lady, whether it shall be in your favour or no. She hath already suffered enough from solicitations which I hate to think of; she shall owe no further constraint to my family: I know her father will be as ready to torment her now on your account as he hath formerly been on another's; but I am determined she shall suffer no more confinement, no more violence, no more uneasy hours." "O, my dear uncle!" answered Jones, "lay, I beseech you, some command on me, in which I shall have some merit in obedience. Believe me, sir, the only instance in which I could disobey you would be to give an uneasy moment to my Sophia. No, sir, if I am so miserable to have incurred her displeasure beyond all hope of forgiveness, that alone, with the dreadful reflection of causing her misery, will be sufficient to overpower me. To call Sophia mine is the greatest, and now the only additional blessing which heaven can bestow; but it is a blessing which I must owe to her alone." "I will not flatter you, child," cries Allworthy; "I fear your case is desperate: I never saw stronger marks of an unalterable resolution in any person than appeared in her vehement declarations against receiving your addresses; for which, perhaps, you can account better than myself." "Oh, sir! I can account too well," answered Jones; "I have sinned against her beyond all hope of pardon; and guilty as I am, my guilt unfortunately appears to her in ten times blacker than the real colours. O, my dear uncle! I find my follies are irretrievable; and all your goodness cannot save me from perdition."

A servant now acquainted them that Mr Western was below-stairs; for his eagerness to see Jones could not wait till the afternoon. Upon which Jones, whose eyes were full of tears, begged his uncle to entertain Western a few minutes, till he a little recovered himself; to which the good man consented, and, having ordered Mr Western to be shewn into a parlour, went down to him.

Mrs Miller no sooner heard that Jones was alone (for she had not yet seen him since his release from prison) than she came eagerly into the room, and, advancing towards Jones, wished him heartily joy of his new-found uncle and his happy reconciliation; adding, "I wish I could give you joy on another account, my dear child; but anything so inexorable I never saw."

Jones, with some appearance of surprize, asked her what she meant. "Why then," says she, "I have been with your young lady, and have explained all matters to her, as they were told to me by my son Nightingale. She can have no longer any doubt about the letter; of that I am certain; for I told her my son Nightingale was ready to take his oath, if she pleased, that it was all his own invention, and the letter of his inditing. I told her the very reason of sending the letter ought to recommend you to her the more, as it was all upon her account, and a plain proof that you was resolved to quit all your profligacy for the future; that you had never been guilty of a single instance of infidelity to her since your seeing her in town: I am afraid I went too far there; but Heaven forgive me! I hope your future behaviour will be my justification. I am sure I have said all I can; but all to no purpose. She remains inflexible. She says, she had forgiven many faults on account of youth; but expressed such detestation of the character of a libertine, that she absolutely silenced me. I often attempted to excuse you; but the justness of her accusation flew in my face. Upon my honour, she is a lovely woman, and one of the sweetest and most sensible creatures I ever saw. I could have almost kissed her for one expression she made use of. It was a sentiment worthy of Seneca, or of a bishop. `I once fancied madam.' and she, `I had discovered great goodness of heart in Mr Jones; and for that I own I had a sincere esteem; but an entire profligacy of manners will corrupt the best heart in the world; and all which a good-natured libertine can expect is, that we should mix some grains of pity with our contempt and abhorrence.' She is an angelic creature, that is the truth on't." "O, Mrs Miller!" answered Jones, "can I bear to think that I have lost such an angel?" "Lost! no," cries Mrs Miller; "I hope you have not lost her yet. Resolvc to leave such vicious courses, and you may yet have hopes, nay, if she would remain inexorable, there is another young lady, a sweet pretty young lady, and a swinging fortune, who is absolutely dying for love of you. I heard of it this very morning, and I told it to Miss Western; nay, I went a little beyond the truth again; for I told her you had refused her; but indeed I knew you would refuse her. And here I must give you a little comfort; when I mentioned the young lady's name, who is no other than the pretty widow Hunt, I thought she turned pale; but when I said you had refused her, I will be sworn her face was all over scarlet in an instant; and these were her very words: `I will not deny but that I believe he has some affection for me.'"

Here the conversation was interrupted by the arrival of Western, who could no longer be kept out of the room even by the authority of Allworthy himself; though this, as we have often seen, had a wonderful power over him.

Western immediately went up to Jones, crying out, "My old friend Tom, I am glad to see thee with all my heart! all past must be forgotten; I could not intend any affront to thee, because, as Allworthy here knows, nay, dost know it thyself, I took thee for another person; and where a body means no harm, what signifies a hasty word or two? One Christian must forget and forgive another." "I hope, sir," said Jones, "I shall never forget the many obligations I have had to you; but as for any offence towards me, I declare I am an utter stranger." "A't," says Western, "then give me thy fist; a't as hearty an honest cock as any in the kingdom. Come along with me; I'll carry thee to thy mistress this moment." Here Allworthy interposed; and the squire being unable to prevail either with the uncle or nephew, was, after some litigation, obliged to consent to delay introducing Jones to Sophia till the afternoon; at which time Allworthy, as well in compassion to Jones as in compliance with the eager desires of Western, was prevailed upon to promise to attend at the tea-table.

The conversation which now ensued was pleasant enough; and with which, had it happened earlier in our history, we would have entertained our reader; but as we have now leisure only to attend to what is very material, it shall suffice to say that matters being entirely adjusted as to the afternoon visit Mr Western again returned home.

CHAPTER XI.

The history draws nearer to a conclusion.

When Mr Western was departed, Jones began to inform Mr Allworthy and Mrs Miller that his liberty had been procured by two noble lords, who, together with two surgeons and a friend of Mr Nightingale's, had attended the magistrate by whom he had been committed, and by whom, on the surgeons' oaths, that the wounded person was out of all manner of danger from his wound, he was discharged.

One only of these lords, he said, he had ever seen before, and that no more than once; but the other had greatly surprized him by asking his pardon for an offence he had been guilty of towards him, occasioned, he said, entirely by his ignorance who he was.

Now the reality of the case, with which Jones was not acquainted till afterwards, was this:—The lieutenant whom Lord Fellamar had employed, according to the advice of Lady Bellaston, to press Jones as a vagabond into the sea-service, when he came to report to his lordship the event which we have before seen, spoke very favourably of the behaviour of Mr Jones on all accounts, and strongly assured that lord that he must have mistaken the person, for that Jones was certainly a gentleman; insomuch that his lordship, who was strictly a man of honour, and would by no means have been guilty of an action which the world in general would have condemned, began to be much concerned for the advice which he had taken.

Within a day or two after this, Lord Fellamar happened to dine with the Irish peer, who, in a conversation upon the duel, acquainted his company with the character of Fitzpatrick; to which, indeed, he did not do strict justice, especially in what related to his lady. He said she was the most innocent, the most injured woman alive, and that from compassion alone he had undertaken her cause. He then declared an intention of going the next morning to Fitzpatrick's lodgings, in order to prevail with him, if possible, to consent to a separation from his wife, who, the peer said, was in apprehensions for her life, if she should ever return to be under the power of her husband. Lord Fellamar agreed to go with him, that he might satisfy himself more concerning Jones and the circumstances of the duel; for he was by no means easy concerning the part he had acted. The moment his lordship gave a hint of his readiness to assist in the delivery of the lady, it was eagerly embraced by the other nobleman, who depended much on the authority of

Lord Fellamar, as he thought it would greatly contribute to awe Fitzpatrick into a compliance; and perhaps he was in the right; for the poor Irishman no sooner saw these noble peers had undertaken the cause of his wife than he submitted, and articles of separation were soon drawn up and signed between the parties.

Fitzpatrick, who had been so well satisfied by Mrs Waters concerning the innocence of his wife with Jones at Upton, or perhaps, from some other reasons, was now become so indifferent to that matter, that he spoke highly in favour of Jones to Lord Fellamar, took all the blame upon himself, and said the other had behaved very much like a gentleman and a man of honour; and upon that lord's further enquiry concerning Mr Jones, Fitzpatrick told him he was nephew to a gentleman of very great fashion and fortune, which was the account he had just received from Mrs Waters after her interview with Dowling.

Lord Fellamar now thought it behoved him to do everything in his power to make satisfaction to a gentleman whom he had so grossly injured, and without any consideration of rivalship (for he had now given over all thoughts of Sophia), determined to procure Mr Jones's liberty, being satisfied, as well from Fitzpatrick as his surgeon, that the wound was not mortal. He therefore prevailed with the Irish peer to accompany him to the place where Jones was confined, to whom he behaved as we have already related.

When Allworthy returned to his lodgings, he immediately carried Jones into his room, and then acquainted him with the whole matter, as well what he had heard from Mrs Waters as what he had discovered from Mr Dowling.

Jones expressed great astonishment and no less concern at this account, but without making any comment or observation upon it. And now a message was brought from Mr Blifil, desiring to know if his uncle was at leisure that he might wait upon him. Allworthy started and turned pale, and then in a more passionate tone than I believe he had ever used before, bid the servant tell Blifil he knew him not. "Consider, dear sir," cries Jones, in a trembling voice. "I have considered," answered Allworthy, "and you yourself shall carry my message to the villain. No one can carry him the sentence of his own ruin so properly as the man whose ruin he hath so villanously contrived." "Pardon me, dear sir," said Jones; "a moment's reflection will, I am sure, convince you of the contrary. What might perhaps be but justice from another tongue, would from mine be insult; and to whom?—my own brother and your nephew. Nor did he use me so barbarously—indeed, that would have been more inexcusable than anything he hath done. Fortune may tempt men of no very bad dispositions to injustice; but insults proceed only from black and rancorous minds, and have no temptations to excuse them. Let me beseech you, sir, to do nothing by him in the present height of your anger. Consider, my dear uncle, I was not myself condemned unheard." Allworthy stood silent a moment, and then, embracing Jones, he said, with tears gushing from his eyes, "O my child! to what goodness have I been so long blind!"

Mrs Miller entering the room at that moment, after a gentle rap which was not perceived, and seeing Jones in the arms of his uncle, the poor woman in an agony of joy fell upon her knees, and burst forth into the most ecstatic thanksgivings to heaven for what had happened; then, running to Jones, she embraced him eagerly, crying, "My dearest friend, I wish you joy a thousand and a thousand times of this blest day." And next Mr Allworthy himself received the same congratulations. To which he answered, "Indeed, indeed, Mrs Miller, I am beyond expression happy." Some few more raptures having passed on all sides, Mrs Miller desired them both to walk down to dinner in the parlour, where she said there were a very happy set of people assembled—being indeed no other than Mr Nightingale and his bride, and his cousin Harriet with her bridegroom.

Allworthy excused himself from dining with the company, saying he had ordered some little thing for him and his nephew in his own apartment, for that they had much private business to discourse of; but would not resist promising the good woman that both he and Jones would make part of her society at supper.

Mrs Miller then asked what was to be done with Blifil? "for indeed," says she, "I cannot be easy while such a villain is in my house."—Allworthy answered, "He was as uneasy as herself on the same account." "Oh!" cries she, "if that be the case, leave the matter to me, I'll soon show him the outside out of my doors, I warrant you. Here are two or three lusty fellows below-stairs." "There will be no need of any violence," cries Allworthy; "if you will carry him a message from me, he will, I am convinced, depart of his own accord." "Will I?" said Mrs Miller; "I never did anything in my life with a better will." Here Jones interfered, and said, "He had considered the matter better, and would, if Mr Allworthy pleased, be himself the messenger. I know," says he, "already enough of your pleasure, sir, and I beg leave to acquaint him with it by my own words. Let me beseech you, sir," added he, "to reflect on the dreadful consequences of driving him to violent and sudden despair. How unfit, alas! is this poor man to die in his present situation." This suggestion had not the least effect on Mrs Miller. She left the room, crying, "You are too good, Mr Jones, infinitely too good to live in this world." But it made a deeper impression on Allworthy. "My good child," said he, "I am equally astonished at the goodness of your heart, and the quickness of your understanding. Heaven indeed forbid that this wretch should be deprived of any means or time for repentance! That would be a shocking consideration indeed. Go to him, therefore, and use your own discretion; yet do not flatter him with any hopes of my forgiveness; for I shall never forgive villany farther than my religion obliges me, and that extends not either to our bounty or our conversation."

Jones went up to Blifil's room, whom he found in a situation which moved his pity, though it would have raised a less amiable passion in many beholders. He cast himself on his bed, where he lay abandoning himself to despair, and drowned in tears; not in such tears as flow from contrition, and wash away guilt from minds which have been seduced or surprized into it unawares, against the bent of their natural dispositions, as will sometimes happen from human frailty, even to the good; no, these tears were such as the frighted thief sheds in his cart, and are indeed the effects of that concern which the most savage natures are seldom deficient in feeling for themselves.

It would be unpleasant and tedious to paint this scene in full length. Let it suffice to say, that the behaviour of Jones was kind to excess. He omitted nothing which his invention could supply, to raise and comfort the drooping spirits of Blifil, before he communicated to him the resolution of his uncle that he must quit the house that evening. He offered to furnish him with any money he wanted, assured him of his hearty forgiveness of all he had done against him, that he would endeavour to live with him hereafter as a brother, and would leave nothing unattempted to effectuate a reconciliation with his uncle.

Blifil was at first sullen and silent, balancing in his mind whether he should yet deny all; but, finding at last the evidence too strong against him, he betook himself at last to confession. He then asked pardon of his brother in the most vehement manner, prostrated himself on the ground, and kissed his feet; in short he was now as remarkably mean as he had been before remarkably wicked.

Jones could not so far check his disdain, but that it a little discovered itself in his countenance at this extreme servility. He raised his brother the moment he could from the ground, and advised him to bear his afflictions more like a man; repeating, at the same time, his promises, that he would do all in his power to lessen them; for which Blifil, making many professions of his unworthiness, poured forth a profusion of thanks; and then, he having declared he would immediately depart to another lodging, Jones returned to his uncle.

Among other matters, Allworthy now acquainted Jones with the discovery which he had made concerning the £500 bank-notes. "I have," said he, "already consulted a lawyer, who tells me, to my great astonishment, that there is no punishment for a fraud of this kind. Indeed, when I consider the black ingratitude of this fellow toward you, I think a highwayman, compared to him, is an innocent person."

"Good Heaven!" says Jones, "is it possible?—I am shocked beyond measure at this news. I thought there was not an honester fellow in the world.——The temptation of such a sum was too great for him to withstand; for smaller matters have come safe to me through his hand. Indeed, my dear uncle, you must suffer me to call it weakness rather than ingratitude; for I am convinced the poor fellow loves me, and hath done me some kindnesses, which I can never forget; nay, I believe he hath repented of this very act; for it is not above a day or two ago, when my affairs seemed in the most desperate situation, that he visited me in my confinement, and offered me any money I wanted. Consider, sir, what a temptation to a man who hath tasted such bitter distress, it must be, to have a sum in his possession which must put him and his family beyond any future possibility of suffering the like."

"Child," cries Allworthy, "you carry this forgiving temper too far. Such mistaken mercy is not only weakness, but borders on injustice, and is very pernicious to society, as it encourages vice. The dishonesty of this fellow I might, perhaps, have pardoned, but never his ingratitude. And give me leave to say, when we suffer any temptation to atone for dishonesty itself, we are as candid and merciful as we ought to be; and so far I confess I have gone; for I have often pitied the fate of a highwayman, when I have been on the grand jury; and have more than once applied to the judge on the behalf of such as have had any mitigating circumstances in their case; but when dishonesty is attended with any blacker crime, such as cruelty, murder, ingratitude, or the like, compassion and forgiveness then become faults. I am convinced the fellow is a villain, and he shall be punished; at least as far as I can punish him."

This was spoken with so stern a voice, that Jones did not think proper to make any reply; besides, the hour appointed by Mr Western now drew so near, that he had barely time left to dress himself. Here therefore ended the present dialogue, and Jones retired to another room, where Partridge attended, according to order, with his cloaths.

Partridge had scarce seen his master since the happy discovery. The poor fellow was unable either to contain or express his transports. He behaved like one frantic, and made almost as many mistakes while he was dressing Jones as I have seen made by Harlequin in dressing himself on the stage.

His memory, however, was not in the least deficient. He recollected now many omens and presages of this happy event, some of which he had remarked at the time, but many more he now remembered; nor did he omit the dreams he had dreamt the evening before his meeting with Jones; and concluded with saying, "I always told your honour something boded in my mind that you would one time or other have it in your power to make my fortune." Jones assured him that this boding should as certainly be verified with regard to him as all the other omens had been to himself; which did not a little add to all the raptures which the poor fellow had already conceived on account of his master.

CHAPTER XII.

Approaching still nearer to the end.

Jones, being now completely dressed, attended his uncle to Mr Western's. He was, indeed, one of the finest figures ever beheld, and his person alone would have charmed the greater part of womankind; but we hope it hath already appeared in this history that Nature, when she formed him, did not totally rely, as she sometimes doth, on this merit only, to recommend her work.

Sophia, who, angry as she was, was likewise set forth to the best advantage, for which I leave my female readers to account, appeared so extremely beautiful, that even Allworthy, when he saw her, could not forbear whispering Western, that he believed she was the finest creature in the world. To which Western answered, in a whisper, overheard by all present, "So much the better for Tom;—for d—n me if he shan't ha the tousling her." Sophia was all over scarlet at these words, while Tom's countenance was altogether as pale, and he was almost ready to sink from his chair.

The tea-table was scarce removed before Western lugged Allworthy out of the room, telling him he had business of consequence to impart, and must speak to him that instant in private, before he forgot it.

The lovers were now alone, and it will, I question not, appear strange to many readers, that those who had so much to say to one another when danger and difficulty attended their conversation, and who seemed so eager to rush into each other's arms when so many bars lay in their way, now that with safety they were at liberty to say or do whatever they pleased, should both remain for some time silent and motionless; insomuch that a stranger of moderate sagacity might have well concluded they were mutually indifferent; but so it was, however strange it may seem; both sat with their eyes cast downwards on the ground, and for some minutes continued in perfect silence.

Mr Jones during this interval attempted once or twice to speak, but was absolutely incapable, muttering only, or rather sighing out, some broken words; when Sophia at length, partly out of pity to him, and partly to turn the discourse from the subject which she knew well enough he was endeavouring to open, said—

"Sure, sir, you are the most fortunate man in the world in this discovery." "And can you really, madam, think me so fortunate," said Jones, sighing, "while I have incurred your displeasure?"—"Nay, sir," says she, "as to that you best know whether you have deserved it." "Indeed, madam," answered he, "you yourself are as well apprized of all my demerits. Mrs Miller hath acquainted you with the whole truth. O! my Sophia, am I never to hope for forgiveness?"—"I think, Mr Jones," said she, "I may almost depend on your own justice, and leave it to yourself to pass sentence on your own conduct."—"Alas! madam," answered he, "it is mercy, and not justice, which I implore at your hands. Justice I know must condemn me.—Yet not for the letter I sent to Lady Bellaston. Of that I most solemnly declare you have had a true account." He then insisted much on the security given him by Nightingale of a fair pretence for breaking off, if, contrary to their expectations, her ladyship should have accepted his offer; but confest that he had been guilty of a great indiscretion to put such a letter as that into her power, "which," said he, "I have dearly paid for, in the effect it has upon you." "I do not, I cannot," says she, "believe otherwise of that letter than you would have me. My conduct, I think, shews you clearly I do not believe there is much in that. And yet, Mr Jones, have I not enough to resent? After what past at Upton, so soon to engage in a new amour with another woman, while I fancied, and you pretended, your heart was bleeding for me? Indeed, you have acted strangely. Can I believe the passion you have profest to me to be sincere? Or, if I can, what happiness can I assure myself of with a man capable of so much inconstancy?" "O! my Sophia," cries he, "do not doubt the sincerity of the purest passion that ever inflamed a human breast. Think, most adorable creature, of my unhappy situation, of my despair. Could I, my Sophia, have flattered myself with the most distant hopes of being ever permitted to throw myself at your feet in the manner I do now, it would not have been in the power of any other woman to have inspired a thought which the severest chastity could have condemned. Inconstancy to you! O Sophia! if you can have goodness enough to pardon what is past, do not let any cruel future apprehensions shut your mercy against me. No repentance was ever more sincere. O! let it reconcile me to my heaven in this dear bosom." "Sincere repentance, Mr Jones," answered she, "will obtain the pardon of a sinner, but it is from one who is a perfect judge of that sincerity. A human mind may be imposed on; nor is there any infallible method to prevent it. You must expect, however, that if I can be prevailed on by your repentance to pardon you, I will at least insist on the strongest proof of its sincerity." "Name any proof in my power," answered Jones eagerly. "Time," replied she; "time alone, Mr Jones, can convince me that you are a true penitent, and have resolved to abandon these vicious courses, which I should detest you for, if I imagined you capable of persevering in them." "Do not imagine it," cries Jones. "On my knees I intreat, I implore your confidence, a confidence which it shall be the business of my life to deserve." "Let it then," said she, "be the business of some part of your life to shew me you deserve it. I think I have been explicit enough in assuring you, that, when I see you merit my confidence, you will obtain it. After what is past, sir, can you expect I should take you upon your word?"

He replied, "Don't believe me upon my word; I have a better security, a pledge for my constancy, which it is impossible to see and to doubt." "What is that?" said Sophia, a little surprized. "I will show you, my charming angel," cried Jones, seizing her hand and carrying her to the glass. "There, behold it there in that lovely figure, in that face, that shape, those eyes, that mind which shines through these eyes; can the man who shall be in possession of these be inconstant? Impossible! my Sophia; they would fix a Dorimant, a Lord Rochester. You could not doubt it, if you could see yourself with any eyes but your own." Sophia blushed and half smiled; but, forcing again her brow into a frown—"If I am to judge," said she, "of the future by the past, my image will no more remain in your heart when I am out of your sight, than it will in this glass when I am out of the room." "By heaven, by all that is sacred!" said Jones, "it never was out of my heart. The delicacy of your sex cannot conceive the grossness of ours, nor how little one sort of amour has to do with the heart." "I will never marry a man," replied Sophia, very gravely, "who shall not learn refinement enough to be as incapable as I am myself of making such a distinction." "I will learn it," said Jones. "I have learnt it already. The first moment of hope that my Sophia might be my wife taught it me at once; and all the rest of her sex from that moment became as little the objects of desire to my sense as of passion to my heart." "Well," says Sophia, "the proof of this must be from time. Your situation, Mr Jones, is now altered, and I assure you I have great satisfaction in the alteration. You will now want no opportunity of being near me, and convincing me that your mind is altered too." "O! my angel," cries Jones, "how shall I thank thy goodness! And are you so good to own that you have a satisfaction in my prosperity?——Believe me, believe me, madam, it is you alone have given a relish to that prosperity, since I owe to it the dear hope——O! my Sophia, let it not be a distant one.—I will be all obedience to your commands. I will not dare to press anything further than you permit me. Yet let me intreat you to appoint a short trial. O! tell me when I may expect you will be convinced of what is most solemnly true." "When I have gone voluntarily thus far, Mr Jones," said she, "I expect not to be pressed. Nay, I will not."—"O! don't look unkindly thus, my Sophia," cries he. "I do not, I dare not press you.—Yet permit me at least once more to beg you would fix the period. O! consider the impatience of love."—"A twelvemonth, perhaps," said she. "O! my Sophia," cries he, "you have named an eternity."—"Perhaps it may be something sooner," says she; "I will not be teazed. If your passion for me be what I would have it, I think you may now be easy."—"Easy! Sophia, call not such an exulting happiness as mine by so cold a name.——O! transporting thought! am I not assured that the blessed day will come, when I shall call you mine; when fears shall be no more; when I shall have that dear, that vast, that exquisite, ecstatic delight of making my Sophia happy?"—"Indeed, sir," said she, "that day is in your own power."—"O! my dear, my divine angel," cried he, "these words have made me mad with joy.——But I must, I will thank those dear lips which have so sweetly pronounced my bliss." He then caught her in his arms, and kissed her with an ardour he had never ventured before.

At this instant Western, who had stood some time listening, burst into the room, and, with his hunting voice and phrase, cried out, "To her, boy, to her, go to her.——That's it, little honeys, O that's it! Well! what, is it all over? Hath she appointed the day, boy? What, shall it be to-morrow or next day? It shan't be put off a minute longer than next day, I am resolved." "Let me beseech you, sir," says Jones, "don't let me be the occasion"——"Beseech mine a——," cries Western. "I thought thou hadst been a lad of higher mettle than to give way to a parcel of maidenish tricks.——I tell thee 'tis all flimflam. Zoodikers! she'd have the wedding to-night with all her heart. Would'st not, Sophy? Come, confess, and be an honest girl for once. What, art dumb? Why dost not speak?" "Why should I confess, sir," says Sophia, "since it seems you are so well acquainted with my thoughts?"——"That's a good girl," cries he, "and dost consent then?" "No, indeed, sir," says Sophia, "I have given no such consent."—-"And wunt not ha un then to-morrow, nor next day?" says Western.—"Indeed, sir," says she, "I have no such intention." "But I can tell thee," replied he, "why hast nut; only because thou dost love to be disobedient, and to plague and vex thy father." "Pray, sir," said Jones, interfering——"I tell thee thou art a puppy," cries he. "When I vorbid her, then it was all nothing but sighing and whining, and languishing and writing; now I am vor thee, she is against thee. All the spirit of contrary, that's all. She is above being guided and governed by her father, that is the whole truth on't. It is only to disoblige and contradict me." "What would my papa have me do?" cries Sophia. "What would I ha thee do?" says he, "why, gi' un thy hand this moment."—"Well, sir," says Sophia, "I will obey you.—There is my hand, Mr Jones." "Well, and will you consent to ha un to-morrow morning?" says Western.—"I will be obedient to you, sir," cries she.—"Why then to-morrow morning be the day," cries he. "Why then to-morrow morning shall be the day, papa, since you will have it so," says Sophia. Jones then fell upon his knees, and kissed her hand in an agony of joy, while Western began to caper and dance about the room, presently crying out—"Where the devil is Allworthy? He is without now, a talking with that d—d lawyer Dowling, when he should be minding other matters." He then sallied out in quest of him, and very opportunely left the lovers to enjoy a few tender minutes alone.

But he soon returned with Allworthy, saying, "If you won't believe me, you may ask her yourself. Hast nut gin thy consent, Sophy, to be married to-morrow?" "Such are your commands, sir," cries Sophia, "and I dare not be guilty of disobedience." "I hope, madam," cries Allworthy, "my nephew will merit so much goodness, and will be always as sensible as myself of the great honour you have done my family. An alliance with so charming and so excellent a young lady would indeed be an honour to the greatest in England." "Yes," cries Western, "but if I had suffered her to stand shill I shall I, dilly dally, you might not have had that honour yet a while; I was forced to use a little fatherly authority to bring her to." "I hope not, sir," cries Allworthy, "I hope there is not the least constraint." "Why, there," cries Western, "you may bid her unsay all again if you will. Dost repent heartily of thy promise, dost not, Sophia?" "Indeed, papa," cries she, "I do not repent, nor do I believe I ever shall, of any promise in favour of Mr Jones." "Then, nephew," cries Allworthy, "I felicitate you most heartily; for I think you are the happiest of men. And, madam, you will give me leave to congratulate you on this joyful occasion: indeed, I am convinced you have bestowed yourself on one who will be sensible of your great merit, and who will at least use his best endeavours to deserve it." "His best endeavours!" cries Western, "that he will, I warrant un.——Harkee, Allworthy, I'll bet thee five pounds to a crown we have a boy to-morrow nine months; but prithee tell me what wut ha! Wut ha Burgundy, Champaigne, or what? for, please Jupiter, we'll make a night on't." "Indeed, sir," said Allworthy, "you must excuse me; both my nephew and I were engaged before I suspected this near approach of his happiness."—"Engaged!" quoth the squire, "never tell me.—I won't part with thee to-night upon any occasion. Shalt sup here, please the lord Harry." "You must pardon me, my dear neighbour!" answered Allworthy; "I have given a solemn promise, and that you know I never break." "Why, prithee, who art engaged to?" cries the squire.——Allworthy then informed him, as likewise of the company.——"Odzookers!" answered the squire, "I will go with thee, and so shall Sophy! for I won't part with thee to-night; and it would be barbarous to part Tom and the girl." This offer was presently embraced by Allworthy, and Sophia consented, having first obtained a private promise from her father that he would not mention a syllable concerning her marriage.

CHAPTER THE LAST.

In which the history is concluded.

Young Nightingale had been that afternoon, by appointment, to wait on his father, who received him much more kindly than he expected. There likewise he met his uncle, who was returned to town in quest of his new-married daughter.

This marriage was the luckiest incident which could have happened to the young gentleman; for these brothers lived in a constant state of contention about the government of their children, both heartily despising the method which each other took. Each of them therefore now endeavoured, as much as he could, to palliate the offence which his own child had committed, and to aggravate the match of the other. This desire of triumphing over his brother, added to the many arguments which Allworthy had used, so strongly operated on the old gentleman that he met his son with a smiling countenance, and actually agreed to sup with him that evening at Mrs Miller's.

As for the other, who really loved his daughter with the most immoderate affection, there was little difficulty in inclining him to a reconciliation. He was no sooner informed by his nephew where his daughter and her husband were, than he declared he would instantly go to her. And when he arrived there he scarce suffered her to fall upon her knees before he took her up, and embraced her with a tenderness which affected all who saw him; and in less than a quarter of an hour was as well reconciled to both her and her husband as if he had himself joined their hands.

In this situation were affairs when Mr Allworthy and his company arrived to complete the happiness of Mrs Miller, who no sooner saw Sophia than she guessed everything that had happened; and so great was her friendship to Jones, that it added not a few transports to those she felt on the happiness of her own daughter.

There have not, I believe, been many instances of a number of people met together, where every one was so perfectly happy as in this company. Amongst whom the father of young Nightingale enjoyed the least perfect content; for, notwithstanding his affection for his son, notwithstanding the authority and the arguments of Allworthy, together with the other motive mentioned before, he could not so entirely be satisfied with his son's choice; and, perhaps, the presence of Sophia herself tended a little to aggravate and heighten his concern, as a thought now and then suggested itself that his son might have had that lady, or some other such. Not that any of the charms which adorned either the person or mind of Sophia created the uneasiness; it was the contents of her father's coffers which set his heart a longing. These were the charms which he could not bear to think his son had sacrificed to the daughter of Mrs Miller.

The brides were both very pretty women; but so totally were they eclipsed by the beauty of Sophia, that, had they not been two of the best-tempered girls in the world, it would have raised some envy in their breasts; for neither of their husbands could long keep his eyes from Sophia, who sat at the table like a queen receiving homage, or, rather, like a superior being receiving adoration from all around her. But it was an adoration which they gave, not which she exacted; for she was as much distinguished by her modesty and affability as by all her other perfections.

The evening was spent in much true mirth. All were happy, but those the most who had been most unhappy before. Their former sufferings and fears gave such a relish to their felicity as even love and fortune, in their fullest flow, could not have given without the advantage of such a comparison. Yet, as great joy, especially after a sudden change and revolution of circumstances, is apt to be silent, and dwells rather in the heart than on the tongue, Jones and Sophia appeared the least merry of the whole company; which Western observed with great impatience, often crying out to them, "Why dost not talk, boy? Why dost look so grave? Hast lost thy tongue, girl? Drink another glass of wine; sha't drink another glass." And, the more to enliven her, he would sometimes sing a merry song, which bore some relation to matrimony and the loss of a maidenhead. Nay, he would have proceeded so far on that topic as to have driven her out of the room, if Mr Allworthy had not checkt him, sometimes by looks, and once or twice by a "Fie! Mr Western!" He began, indeed, once to debate the matter, and assert his right to talk to his own daughter as he thought fit; but, as nobody seconded him, he was soon reduced to order.

Notwithstanding this little restraint, he was so pleased with the chearfulness and good-humour of the company, that he insisted on their meeting the next day at his lodgings. They all did so; and the lovely Sophia, who was now in private become a bride too, officiated as the mistress of the ceremonies, or, in the polite phrase, did the honours of the table. She had that morning given her hand to Jones, in the chapel at Doctors'-Commons, where Mr Allworthy, Mr Western, and Mrs Miller, were the only persons present.

Sophia had earnestly desired her father that no others of the company, who were that day to dine with him, should be acquainted with her marriage. The same secrecy was enjoined to Mrs Miller, and Jones undertook for Allworthy. This somewhat reconciled the delicacy of Sophia to the public entertainment which, in compliance with her father's will, she was obliged to go to, greatly against her own inclinations. In confidence of this secrecy she went through the day pretty well, till the squire, who was now advanced into the second bottle, could contain his joy no longer, but, filling out a bumper, drank a health to the bride. The health was immediately pledged by all present, to the great confusion of our poor blushing Sophia, and the great concern of Jones upon her account. To say truth, there was not a person present made wiser by this discovery; for Mrs Miller had whispered it to her daughter, her daughter to her husband, her husband to his sister, and she to all the rest.

Sophia now took the first opportunity of withdrawing with the ladies, and the squire sat in to his cups, in which he was, by degrees, deserted by all the company except the uncle of young Nightingale, who loved his bottle as well as Western himself. These two, therefore, sat stoutly to it during the whole evening, and long after that happy hour which had surrendered the charming Sophia to the eager arms of her enraptured Jones.

Thus, reader, we have at length brought our history to a conclusion, in which, to our great pleasure, though contrary, perhaps, to thy expectation, Mr Jones appears to be the happiest of all humankind; for what happiness this world affords equal to the possession of such a woman as Sophia, I sincerely own I have never yet discovered.

As to the other persons who have made any considerable figure in this history, as some may desire to know a little more concerning them, we will proceed, in as few words as possible, to satisfy their curiosity.

Allworthy hath never yet been prevailed upon to see Blifil, but he hath yielded to the importunity of Jones, backed by Sophia, to settle £200 a-year upon him; to which Jones hath privately added a third. Upon this income he lives in one of the northern counties, about 200 miles distant from London, and lays up £200 a-year out of it, in order to purchase a seat in the next parliament from a neighbouring borough, which he has bargained for with an attourney there. He is also lately turned Methodist, in hopes of marrying a very rich widow of that sect, whose estate lies in that part of the kingdom.

Square died soon after he writ the before-mentioned letter; and as to Thwackum, he continues at his vicarage. He hath made many fruitless attempts to regain the confidence of Allworthy, or to ingratiate himself with Jones, both of whom he flatters to their faces, and abuses behind their backs. But in his stead, Mr Allworthy hath lately taken Mr Abraham Adams into his house, of whom Sophia is grown immoderately fond, and declares he shall have the tuition of her children.

Mrs Fitzpatrick is separated from her husband, and retains the little remains of her fortune. She lives in reputation at the polite end of the town, and is so good an economist, that she spends three times the income of her fortune, without running into debt. She maintains a perfect intimacy with the lady of the Irish peer; and in acts of friendship to her repays all obligations she owes her husband.

Mrs Western was soon reconciled to her niece Sophia, and hath spent two months together with her in the country. Lady Bellaston made the latter a formal visit at her return to town, where she behaved to Jones as a perfect stranger, and, with great civility, wished him joy on his marriage.

Mr Nightingale hath purchased an estate for his son in the neighbourhood of Jones, where the young gentleman, his lady, Mrs Miller, and her little daughter reside, and the most agreeable intercourse subsists between the two families.

As to those of lower account, Mrs Waters returned into the country, had a pension of £60 a-year settled upon her by Mr Allworthy, and is married to Parson Supple, on whom, at the instance of Sophia, Western hath bestowed a considerable living.

Black George, hearing the discovery that had been made, ran away, and was never since heard of; and Jones bestowed the money on his family, but not in equal proportions, for Molly had much the greatest share.

As for Partridge, Jones hath settled £50 a-year on him; and he hath again set up a school, in which he meets with much better encouragement than formerly, and there is now a treaty of marriage on foot between him and Miss Molly Seagrim, which, through the mediation of Sophia, is likely to take effect.

We now return to take leave of Mr Jones and Sophia, who, within two days after their marriage, attended Mr Western and Mr Allworthy into the country. Western hath resigned his family seat, and the greater part of his estate, to his son-in-law, and hath retired to a lesser house of his in another part of the country, which is better for hunting. Indeed, he is often as a visitant with Mr Jones, who, as well as his daughter, hath an infinite delight in doing everything in their power to please him. And this desire of theirs is attended with such success, that the old gentleman declares he was never happy in his life till now. He hath here a parlour and ante-chamber to himself, where he gets drunk with whom he pleases: and his daughter is still as ready as formerly to play to him whenever he desires it; for Jones hath assured her that, as, next to pleasing her, one of his highest satisfactions is to contribute to the happiness of the old man; so, the great duty which she expresses and performs to her father, renders her almost equally dear to him with the love which she bestows on himself.

Sophia hath already produced him two fine children, a boy and a girl, of whom the old gentleman is so fond, that he spends much of his time in the nursery, where he declares the tattling of his little grand-daughter, who is above a year and a half old, is sweeter music than the finest cry of dogs in England.

Allworthy was likewise greatly liberal to Jones on the marriage, and hath omitted no instance of shewing his affection to him and his lady, who love him as a father. Whatever in the nature of Jones had a tendency to vice, has been corrected by continual conversation with this good man, and by his union with the lovely and virtuous Sophia. He hath also, by reflection on his past follies, acquired a discretion and prudence very uncommon in one of his lively parts.

To conclude, as there are not to be found a worthier man and woman, than this fond couple, so neither can any be imagined more happy. They preserve the purest and tenderest affection for each other, an affection daily encreased and confirmed by mutual endearments and mutual esteem. Nor is their conduct towards their relations and friends less amiable than towards one another. And such is their condescension, their indulgence, and their beneficence to those below them, that there is not a neighbour, a tenant, or a servant, who doth not most gratefully bless the day when Mr Jones was married to his Sophia.

FINIS.

THE HISTORY OF THE ADVENTURES OF JOSEPH ANDREWS AND HIS FRIEND MR ABRAHAM ADAMS

GENERAL INTRODUCTION.

There are few amusements more dangerous for an author than the indulgence in ironic descriptions of his own work. If the irony is depreciatory, posterity is but too likely to say, "Many a true word is spoken in jest;" if it is encomiastic, the same ruthless and ungrateful critic is but too likely to take it as an involuntary confession of folly and vanity. But when Fielding, in one of his serio-comic introductions to *Tom Jones*, described it as "this prodigious work," he all unintentionally (for he was the least pretentious of men) anticipated the verdict which posterity almost at once, and with ever-increasing suffrage of the best judges as time went on, was about to pass not merely upon this particular book, but upon his whole genius and his whole production as a novelist. His work in other kinds is of a very different order of excellence. It is sufficiently interesting at times in itself; and always more than sufficiently interesting as his; for which reasons, as well as for the further one that it is comparatively little known, a considerable selection from it is offered to the reader in the last two volumes of this edition. Until the present occasion (which made it necessary that I should acquaint myself with it) I own that my own knowledge of these miscellaneous writings was by no means thorough. It is now pretty complete; but the idea which I previously had of them at first and second hand, though a little improved, has not very materially altered. Though in all this hack-work Fielding displayed, partially and at intervals, the same qualities which he displayed eminently and constantly in the four great books here given, he was not, as the French idiom expresses it, *dans son assiette*, in his own natural and impregnable disposition and situation of character and ability, when he was occupied on it. The novel was for him that *assiette*; and all his novels are here.

Although Henry Fielding lived in quite modern times, although by family and connections he was of a higher rank than most men of letters, and although his genius was at once recognised by his contemporaries so soon as it displayed itself in its proper sphere, his biography until very recently was by no means full; and the most recent researches, including those of Mr Austin Dobson—a critic unsurpassed for combination of literary faculty and knowledge of the eighteenth century—have not altogether sufficed to fill up the gaps. His family, said to have descended from a member of the great house of Hapsburg who came to England in the reign of Henry II., distinguished itself in the Wars of the Roses, and in the seventeenth century was advanced to the peerages of Denbigh in England and (later) of Desmond in Ireland. The novelist was the grandson of John Fielding,

Canon of Salisbury, the fifth son of the first Earl of Desmond of this creation. The canon's third son, Edmond, entered the army, served under Marlborough, and married Sarah Gold or Gould, daughter of a judge of the King's Bench. Their eldest son was Henry, who was born on April 22, 1707, and had an uncertain number of brothers and sisters of the whole blood. After his first wife's death, General Fielding (for he attained that rank) married again. The most remarkable offspring of the first marriage, next to Henry, was his sister Sarah, also a novelist, who wrote David Simple; of the second, John, afterwards Sir John Fielding, who, though blind, succeeded his half-brother as a Bow Street magistrate, and in that office combined an equally honourable record with a longer tenure.

Fielding was born at Sharpham Park in Somersetshire, the seat of his maternal grandfather; but most of his early youth was spent at East Stour in Dorsetshire, to which his father removed after the judge's death. He is said to have received his first education under a parson of the neighbourhood named Oliver, in whom a very uncomplimentary tradition sees the original of Parson Trulliber. He was then certainly sent to Eton, where he did not waste his time as regards learning, and made several valuable friends. But the dates of his entering and leaving school are alike unknown; and his subsequent sojourn at Leyden for two years—though there is no reason to doubt it—depends even less upon any positive documentary evidence. This famous University still had a great repute as a training school in law, for which profession he was intended; but the reason why he did not receive the even then far more usual completion of a public school education by a sojourn at Oxford or Cambridge may be suspected to be different. It may even have had something to do with a curious escapade of his about which not very much is known—an attempt to carry off a pretty heiress of Lyme, named Sarah Andrew.

Even at Leyden, however, General Fielding seems to have been unable or unwilling to pay his son's expenses, which must have been far less there than at an English University; and Henry's return to London in 1728-29 is said to have been due to sheer impecuniosity. When he returned to England, his father was good enough to make him an allowance of L200 nominal, which appears to have been equivalent to L0 actual. And as practically nothing is known of him for the next six or seven years, except the fact of his having worked industriously enough at a large number of not very good plays of the lighter kind, with a few poems and miscellanies, it is reasonably enough supposed that he lived by his pen. The only product of this period which has kept (or indeed which ever received) competent applause is *Tom Thumb, or the Tragedy of Tragedies*, a following of course of the *Rehearsal*, but full of humour and spirit. The most successful of his other dramatic works were the *Mock Doctor* and the *Miser*, adaptations of Moliere's famous pieces. His undoubted connection with the stage, and the fact of the contemporary existence of a certain Timothy Fielding, helped suggestions of less dignified occupations as actor, booth-keeper, and so forth; but these have long been discredited and indeed disproved.

In or about 1735, when Fielding was twenty-eight, we find him in a new, a more brilliant and agreeable, but even a more transient phase. He had married (we do not know when or where) Miss Charlotte Cradock, one of three sisters who lived at Salisbury (it is to be observed that Fielding's entire connections, both in life and letters, are with the Western Counties and London), who were certainly of competent means, and for whose alleged illegitimacy there is no evidence but an unsupported fling of that old maid of genius, Richardson. The descriptions both of Sophia and of Amelia are said to have been taken from this lady; her good looks and her amiability are as well established as anything of the kind can be in the absence of photographs and affidavits; and it is certain that her husband was passionately attached to her, during their too short married life. His method, however, of showing his affection smacked in some ways too much of the foibles which he has attributed to Captain Booth, and of those which we must suspect Mr Thomas Jones would also have exhibited, if he had not been adopted as Mr Allworthy's heir, and had not had Mr Western's fortune to share and look forward to. It is true that grave breaches have been made by recent criticism in the very picturesque and circumstantial story told on the subject by Murphy, the first of Fielding's biographers. This legend was that Fielding, having succeeded by the death of his mother to a small estate at East Stour, worth about L200 a year, and having received L1500 in ready money as his wife's fortune, got through the whole in three years by keeping open house, with a large retinue in "costly yellow liveries," and so forth. In details, this story has been simply riddled. His mother had died long before; he was certainly not away from London three years, or anything like it; and so forth. At the same time, the best and soberest judges agree that there is an intrinsic probability, a consensus (if a vague one) of tradition, and a chain of almost unmistakably personal references in the novels, which plead for a certain amount of truth, at the bottom of a much embellished legend. At any rate, if Fielding established himself in the country, it was not long before he returned to town; for early in 1736 we find him back again, and not merely a playwright, but lessee of the "Little Theatre" in the Haymarket. The plays which he produced here—satirico-political pieces, such as *Pasquin* and the *Historical Register*—were popular enough, but offended the Government; and in 1737 a new bill regulating theatrical performances, and instituting the Lord Chamberlain's control, was passed. This measure put an end directly to the "Great Mogul's Company," as Fielding had called his troop, and indirectly to its manager's career as a playwright. He did indeed write a few pieces in future years, but they were of the smallest importance.

After this check he turned at last to a serious profession, entered himself of the Middle Temple in November of the same year, and was called three years later; but during these years, and indeed for some time afterwards, our information about him is still of the vaguest character. Nobody doubts that he had a large share in the *Champion*, an essay-periodical on the usual eighteenth-century model, which began to appear in 1739, and which is still occasionally consulted for the work that is certainly or probably his. He went the Western Circuit, and attended the Wiltshire Sessions, after he was called, giving up his contributions to periodicals soon after that event. But he soon returned to literature proper, or rather made his *debut* in it, with the immortal book now republished. The *History of the Adventures of Joseph Andrews, and his Friend Mr Abraham Adams*, appeared in February 1742, and its author received from Andrew Millar, the publisher, the sum of L183, 11s. Even greater works have fetched much smaller sums; but it will be admitted that *Joseph Andrews* was not dear.

The advantage, however, of presenting a survey of an author's life uninterrupted by criticism is so clear, that what has to be said about *Joseph* may be conveniently postponed for the moment. Immediately after its publication the author fell back upon miscellaneous writing, and in the next year (1743) collected and issued three volumes of *Miscellanies*. In the two first volumes the only thing of much interest is the unfinished and unequal, but in part powerful, *Journey from this World to the Next*, an attempt of a kind which Fontenelle and others, following Lucian, had made very popular with the time. But the third volume of the *Miscellanies* deserved a less modest and gregarious appearance, for it contained, and is wholly occupied by, the wonderful and terrible satire of *Jonathan Wild*, the greatest piece of pure irony in English out of Swift. Soon after the publication of the book, a great calamity came on Fielding. His wife had been very ill when he wrote the preface; soon afterwards she was dead. They had taken the chance, had made the choice, that the more prudent and less wise student-hero and heroine of Mr Browning's *Youth and Art* had shunned; they had no doubt "sighed deep, laughed free, Starved, feasted, despaired," and we need not question, that they had also "been happy."

Except this sad event and its rather incongruous sequel, Fielding's marriage to his wife's maid Mary Daniel—a marriage, however, which did not take place till full four years later, and which by all accounts supplied him with a faithful and excellent companion and nurse, and his children with a kind stepmother—little or nothing is again known of this elusive man of genius between the publication of the *Miscellanies* in 1743, and that of *Tom Jones* in 1749. The second marriage itself in November 1747; an interview which Joseph Warton had with him rather more than a year earlier (one of the very few direct interviews we have); the publication of two anti-Jacobite newspapers (Fielding was always a strong Whig and Hanoverian), called the *True Patriot* and the *Jacobite's Journal* in 1745 and the following years; some indistinct traditions about residences at Twickenham and elsewhere, and some, more precise but not much more authenticated, respecting patronage by the Duke of Bedford, Mr Lyttelton, Mr Allen, and others, pretty well sum up the whole.

Tom Jones was published in February (a favourite month with Fielding or his publisher Millar) 1749; and as it brought him the, for those days, very considerable sum of L600 to which Millar added another hundred later, the novelist must have been, for a time at any rate, relieved from his chronic penury. But he had already, by Lyttelton's interest, secured his first and last piece of preferment, being made Justice of the Peace for Westminster, an office on which he entered with characteristic vigour. He was qualified for it not merely by a solid knowledge of the law, and by great natural abilities, but by his thorough kindness of heart; and, perhaps, it may also be added, by his long years of queer experience on (as Mr Carlyle would have said) the "burning marl" of the London Bohemia. Very shortly afterwards he was chosen Chairman of Quarter Sessions, and established him-himself in Bow Street. The Bow Street magistrate of that time occupied a most singular position, and was more like a French Prefect of Police or even a Minister of Public Safety than a mere justice. Yet he was ill paid. Fielding says that the emoluments, which before his accession had but been L500 a year of "dirty" money, were by his own action but L300 of clean; and the work, if properly performed, was very severe.

That he performed it properly all competent evidence shows, a foolish, inconclusive, and I fear it must be said emphatically snobbish story of Walpole's notwithstanding. In particular, he broke up a gang of cut-throat thieves, which had been the terror of London. But his tenure of the post was short enough, and scarcely extended to five years. His health had long been broken, and he was now constantly attacked by gout, so that he had frequently to retreat on Bath from Bow Street, or his suburban cottage of Fordhook, Ealing. But he did not relax his literary work. His pen was active with pamphlets concerning his office; *Amelia*, his last novel, appeared towards the close of 1751; and next year saw the beginning of a new paper, the *Covent Garden Journal*, which appeared twice a week, ran for the greater part of the year, and died in November. Its great author did not see that month twice again. In the spring of 1753 he grew worse; and after a year's struggle with ill health, hard work, and hard weather, lesser measures being pronounced useless, was persuaded to try the "Portugal Voyage," of which he has left so charming a record in the *Journey to Lisbon*. He left Fordhook on June 26, 1754, reached Lisbon in August, and, dying there on the 8th of October, was buried in the cemetery of the Estrella.

Of not many writers perhaps does a clearer notion, as far as their personality goes, exist in the general mind that interests itself at all in literature than of Fielding. Yet more than once a warning has been sounded, especially by his best and most recent biographer, to the effect that this idea is founded upon very little warranty of scripture. The truth is, that as the foregoing record—which, brief as it is, is a sufficiently faithful summary—will have shown, we know very little about Fielding. We have hardly any letters of his, and so lack the best by far and the most revealing of all character-portraits; we have but one important autobiographic fragment, and though that is of the highest interest and value, it was written far in the valley of the shadow of death, it is not in the least retrospective, and it affords but dim and inferential light on his younger, healthier, and happier days and ways. He came, moreover, just short of one set of men of letters, of whom we have a great deal of personal knowledge, and just beyond another. He was neither of those about Addison, nor of those about Johnson. No intimate friend of his has left us anything elaborate about him. On the other hand, we have a far from inconsiderable body of documentary evidence, of a kind often by no means trustworthy. The best part of it is contained in the letters of his cousin, Lady Mary Wortley Montagu, and the reminiscences or family traditions of her grand-daughter, Lady Louisa Stuart. But Lady Mary, vivacious and agreeable as she is, had with all her talent a very considerable knack of writing for effect, of drawing strong contrasts and the like; and it is not quite certain that she saw very much of Fielding in the last and most interesting third of his life. Another witness, Horace Walpole, to less knowledge and equally dubious accuracy, added decided ill-will, which may have been due partly to the shrinking of a dilettante and a fop from a burly Bohemian; but I fear is also consequent upon the fact that Horace could not afford to despise Fielding's birth, and knew him to be vastly his own superior in genius. We hear something of him again from Richardson; and Richardson hated him with the hatred of dissimilar genius, of inferior social position, and, lastly, of the cat for the dog who touzles and worries her. Johnson partly inherited or shared Richardson's aversion, partly was blinded to Fielding's genius by his aggressive Whiggery. I fear, too, that he was incapable of appreciating it for reasons other than political. It is certain that Johnson, sane and robust as he was, was never quite at ease before genius of the gigantic kind, either in dead or living. Whether he did not like to have to look up too much, or was actually unable to do so, it is certain that Shakespeare, Milton, Swift, and Fielding, those four Atlantes of English verse and prose, all affected him with lukewarm admiration, or with positive dislike, for which it is vain to attempt to assign any uniform secondary cause, political or other. It may be permitted to hint another reason. All Johnson's most sharp-sighted critics have noticed, though most have discreetly refrained from insisting on, his "thorn-in-the-flesh," the combination in him of very strong physical passions with the deepest sense of the moral and religious duty of abstinence. It is perhaps impossible to imagine anything more distasteful to a man so buffeted, than the extreme indulgence with which Fielding regards, and the easy freedom, not to say gusto, with which he depicts, those who succumb to similar temptation. Only by supposing the workings of some subtle influence of this kind is it possible to explain, even in so capricious a humour as Johnson's, the famous and absurd application of the term "barren rascal" to a writer who, dying almost young, after having for many years lived a life of pleasure, and then for four or five one of laborious official duty, has left work anything but small in actual bulk, and fertile with the most luxuriant growth of intellectual originality.

Partly on the *obiter dicta* of persons like these, partly on the still more tempting and still more treacherous ground of indications drawn from his works, a Fielding of fantasy has been constructed, which in Thackeray's admirable sketch attains real life and immortality as a creature of art, but which possesses rather dubious claims as a historical character. It is astonishing how this Fielding of fantasy sinks and shrivels when we begin to apply the horrid tests of criticism to his component parts. The *eidolon*, with inked ruffles and a towel round his head, sits in the Temple and dashes off articles for the *Covent Garden Journal*; then comes Criticism, hellish maid, and reminds us that when the *Covent Garden Journal* appeared, Fielding's wild oats, if ever sown at all, had been sown long ago; that he was a busy magistrate and householder in Bow Street; and that, if he had towels round his head, it was probably less because he had exceeded in liquor than because his Grace of Newcastle had given him a headache by wanting elaborate plans and schemes prepared at an hour's notice. Lady Mary, apparently with some envy, tells us that he could "feel rapture with his cook-maid." "Which many has," as Mr Ridley remarks, from Xanthias Phoceus downwards; but when we remember the historic fact that he married this maid (not a "cook-maid" at all), and that though he always speaks of her with warm affection and hearty respect, such "raptures" as we have of his clearly refer to a very different woman, who was both a lady and a beautiful one, we begin a little to shake our heads. Horace Walpole at second-hand draws us a Fielding, pigging with low companions in a house kept like a hedge tavern; Fielding himself, within a year or two, shows us more than half-undesignedly in the *Voyage to Lisbon* that he was very careful about the appointments and decency of his table, that he stood rather upon ceremony in regard to his own treatment of his family, and the treatment of them and himself by others, and that he was altogether a person orderly, correct, and even a little finikin. Nor is there the slightest reasonable reason to regard this as a piece of hypocrisy, a vice as alien from the Fielding of fancy as from the Fielding of fact, and one the particular manifestation of which, in this particular place, would have been equally unlikely and unintelligible.

It may be asked whether I propose to substitute for the traditional Fielding a quite different person, of regular habits and methodical economy. Certainly not. The traditional estimate of great men is rarely wrong altogether, but it constantly has a habit of exaggerating and dramatising their characteristics. For some things in Fielding's career we have positive evidence of document, and evidence hardly less certain of probability. Although I believe the best judges are now of opinion that his impecuniosity has been overcharged, he certainly had experiences which did not often fall to the lot of even a cadet of good family in the eighteenth century. There can be no reasonable doubt that he was a man who had a leaning towards pretty girls and bottles of good wine; and I should suppose that if the girl were kind and fairly winsome, he would not have insisted that she should possess Helen's beauty, that if the bottle of good wine were not forthcoming, he would have been very tolerant of a mug of good ale. He may very possibly have drunk more than he should, and lost more than he could conveniently pay. It may be put down as morally ascertained that towards all these weaknesses of humanity, and others like unto them, he held an attitude which was less that of the unassailable philosopher than that of the sympathiser, indulgent and excusing. In regard more especially to what are commonly called moral delinquencies, this attitude was so decided as to shock some people even in those days, and many in these. Just when the first sheets of this edition were passing through the press, a violent attack was made in a newspaper correspondence on the morality of *Tom Jones* by certain notorious advocates of Purity, as some say, of Pruriency and Prudery combined, according to less complimentary estimates. Even midway between the two periods we find the admirable Miss Ferrier, a sister of Fielding's own craft, who sometimes had touches of nature and satire not far inferior to his own, expressing by the mouth of one of her characters with whom she seems partly to agree, the sentiment that his works are "vanishing like noxious exhalations." Towards any misdoing by persons of the one sex towards persons of the other, when it involved brutality or treachery, Fielding was pitiless; but when treachery and brutality were not concerned, he was, to say the least, facile. So, too, he probably knew by experience—he certainly knew by native shrewdness and acquired observation—that to look too much on the wine when it is red, or on the cards when they are particoloured, is ruinous to health and fortune; but he thought not over badly of any man who did these things. Still it is possible to admit this in him, and to stop short of that idea of a careless and reckless *viveur* which has so often been put forward. In particular, Lady Mary's view of his childlike enjoyment of the moment has been, I think, much exaggerated by posterity, and was probably not a little mistaken by the lady herself. There are two moods in which the motto is *Carpe diem*, one a mood of simply childish hurry, the other one where behind the enjoyment of the moment lurks, and in which the enjoyment of the moment is not a little heightened by, that vast ironic consciousness of the before and after, which I at least see everywhere in the background of Fielding's work.

The man, however, of whom we know so little, concerns us much less than the author of the works, of which it only rests with ourselves to know everything. I have above classed Fielding as one of the four Atlantes of English verse and prose, and I doubt not that both the phrase and the application of it to him will meet with question and demur. I have only to interject, as the critic so often has to interject, a request to the court to take what I say in the sense in which I say it. I do not mean that Shakespeare, Milton, Swift, and Fielding are in all or even in most respects on a level. I do not mean that the three last are in all respects of the greatest names in English literature. I only mean that, in a certain quality, which for want of a better word I have chosen to call Atlantean, they stand alone. Each of them, for the metaphor is applicable either way, carries a whole world on his shoulders, or looks down on a whole world from his natural altitude. The worlds are different, but they are worlds; and though the attitude of the giants is different also, it agrees in all of them on the points of competence and strength. Take whomsoever else we may among our men of letters, and we shall find this characteristic to be in comparison wanting. These four carry their world, and are not carried by it; and if it, in the language so dear to Fielding himself, were to crash and shatter, the inquiry, "*Que vous reste-t-il?*" could be answered by each, "*Moi!*"

The appearance which Fielding makes is no doubt the most modest of the four. He has not Shakespeare's absolute universality, and in fact not merely the poet's tongue, but the poet's thought seems to have been denied him. His sphere is not the ideal like Milton's. His irony, splendid as it is, falls a little short of that diabolical magnificence which exalts Swift to the point whence, in his own way, he surveys all the kingdoms of the world, and the glory or vainglory of them. All Fielding's critics have noted the manner, in a certain sense modest, in another ostentatious, in which he seems to confine himself to the presentation of things English. They might have added to the presentation of things English—as they appear in London, and on the Western Circuit, and on the Bath Road.

But this apparent parochialism has never deceived good judges. It did not deceive Lady Mary, who had seen the men and manners of very many climes; it did not deceive Gibbon, who was not especially prone to overvalue things English, and who could look down from twenty centuries on things ephemeral. It deceives, indeed, I am told, some excellent persons at the present day, who think Fielding's microcosm a "toylike world," and imagine that Russian Nihilists and French Naturalists have gone beyond it. It will deceive no one who has lived for some competent space of time a life during which he has tried to regard his fellow-creatures and himself, as nearly as a mortal may, *sub specie aeternitatis.*

As this is in the main an introduction to a complete reprint of Fielding's four great novels, the justification in detail of the estimate just made or hinted of the novelist's genius will be best and most fitly made by a brief successive discussion of the four as they are here presented, with some subsequent remarks on the *Miscellanies* here selected. And, indeed, it is not fanciful to perceive in each book a somewhat different presentment of the author's genius; though in no one of the four is any one of his masterly qualities absent. There is tenderness even in *Jonathan Wild*; there are touches in *Joseph Andrews* of that irony of the Preacher, the last echo of which is heard amid the kindly resignation of the *Journey to Lisbon*, in the sentence, "Whereas envy of all things most exposes us to danger from others, so contempt of all things best secures us from them." But on the whole it is safe to say that *Joseph Andrews* best presents Fielding's mischievous and playful wit; *Jonathan Wild* his half-Lucianic half-Swiftian irony; *Tom Jones* his unerring knowledge of human nature, and his constructive faculty; *Amelia* his tenderness, his *mitis sapientia*, his observation of the details of life. And first of the first.

The History of the Adventures of Joseph Andrews and his friend Mr Abraham Adams was, as has been said above, published in February 1742. A facsimile of the agreement between author and publisher will be given in the second volume of this series; and it is not uninteresting to observe that the witness, William Young, is none other than the asserted original of the immortal Mr Adams himself. He might, on Balzac's plea in a tolerably well-known anecdote, have demanded half of the L183, 11s. Of the other origins of the book we have a pretty full account, partly documentary. That it is "writ in the manner of Cervantes," and is intended as a kind of comic epic, is the author's own statement—no doubt as near the actual truth as is consistent with comic-epic theory. That there are resemblances to Scarron, to Le Sage, and to other practitioners of the Picaresque novel is certain; and it was inevitable that there should be. Of directer and more immediate models or starting-points one is undoubted; the other, though less generally admitted, not much less indubitable to my mind. The parody of Richardson's *Pamela*, which was little more than a year earlier (Nov. 1740), is avowed, open, flagrant; nor do I think that the author was so soon carried away by the greater and larger tide of his own invention as some critics seem to hold. He is always more or less returning to the ironic charge; and the multiplicity of the assailants of Joseph's virtue only disguises the resemblance to the long-drawn dangers of Pamela from a single ravisher. But Fielding was also well acquainted with Marivaux's

Paysan Parvenu, and the resemblances between that book and *Joseph Andrews* are much stronger than Fielding's admirers have always been willing to admit. This recalcitrance has, I think, been mainly due to the erroneous conception of Marivaux as, if not a mere fribble, yet a Dresden-Shepherdess kind of writer, good at "preciousness" and patch-and-powder manners, but nothing more.

There was, in fact, a very strong satiric and ironic touch in the author of *Marianne*, and I do not think that I was too rash when some years ago I ventured to speak of him as "playing Fielding to his own Richardson" in the *Paysan Parvenu*.

Origins, however, and indebtedness and the like, are, when great work is concerned, questions for the study and the lecture-room, for the literary historian and the professional critic, rather than for the reader, however intelligent and alert, who wishes to enjoy a masterpiece, and is content simply to enjoy it. It does not really matter how close to anything else something which possesses independent goodness is; the very utmost technical originality, the most spotless purity from the faintest taint of suggestion, will not suffice to confer merit on what does not otherwise possess it. Whether, as I rather think, Fielding pursued the plan he had formed *ab incepto*, or whether he cavalierly neglected it, or whether the current of his own genius carried him off his legs and landed him, half against his will, on the shore of originality, are questions for the Schools, and, as I venture to think, not for the higher forms in them. We have *Joseph Andrews* as it is; and we may be abundantly thankful for it. The contents of it, as of all Fielding's work in this kind, include certain things for which the moderns are scantly grateful. Of late years, and not of late years only, there has grown up a singular and perhaps an ignorant impatience of digressions, of episodes, of tales within a tale. The example of this which has been most maltreated is the "Man of the Hill" episode in *Tom Jones*; but the stories of the "Unfortunate Jilt" and of Mr Wilson in our present subject, do not appear to me to be much less obnoxious to the censure; and *Amelia* contains more than one or two things of the same kind. Me they do not greatly disturb; and I see many defences for them besides the obvious, and at a pinch sufficient one, that divagations of this kind existed in all Fielding's Spanish and French models, that the public of the day expected them, and so forth. This defence is enough, but it is easy to amplify and reintrench it. It is not by any means the fact that the Picaresque novel of adventure is the only or the chief form of fiction which prescribes or admits these episodic excursions. All the classical epics have them; many eastern and other stories present them; they are common, if not invariable, in the abundant mediaeval literature of prose and verse romance; they are not unknown by any means in the modern novel; and you will very rarely hear a story told orally at the dinner-table or in the smoking-room without something of the kind. There must, therefore, be something in them corresponding to an inseparable accident of that most unchanging of all things, human nature. And I do not think the special form with which we are here concerned by any means the worst that they have taken. It has the grand and prominent virtue of being at once and easily skippable. There is about Cervantes and Le Sage, about Fielding and Smollett, none of the treachery of the modern novelist, who induces the conscientious reader to drag through pages, chapters, and sometimes volumes which have nothing to do with the action, for fear he should miss something that has to do with it. These great men have a fearless frankness, and almost tell you in so many words when and what you may skip. Therefore, if the "Curious Impertinent," and the "Baneful Marriage," and the "Man of the Hill," and the "Lady of Quality," get in the way, when you desire to "read for the story," you have nothing to do but turn the page till *finis* comes. The defence has already been made by an illustrious hand for Fielding's inter-chapters and exordiums. It appears to me to be almost more applicable to his insertions.

And so we need not trouble ourselves any more either about the insertions or about the exordiums. They both please me; the second class has pleased persons much better worth pleasing than I can pretend to be; but the making or marring of the book lies elsewhere. I do not think that it lies in the construction, though Fielding's following of the ancients, both sincere and satiric, has imposed a false air of regularity upon that. The Odyssey of Joseph, of Fanny, and of their ghostly mentor and bodily guard is, in truth, a little haphazard, and might have been longer or shorter without any discreet man approving it the more or the less therefor. The real merits lie partly in the abounding humour and satire of the artist's criticism, but even more in the marvellous vivacity and fertility of his creation. For the very first time in English prose fiction every character is alive, every incident is capable of having happened. There are lively touches in the Elizabethan romances; but they are buried in verbiage, swathed in stage costume, choked and fettered by their authors' want of art. The quality of Bunyan's knowledge of men was not much inferior to Shakespeare's, or at least to Fielding's; but the range and the results of it were cramped by his single theological purpose, and his unvaried allegoric or typical form. Why Defoe did not discover the New World of Fiction, I at least have never been able to put into any brief critical formula that satisfies me, and I have never seen it put by any one else. He had not only seen it afar off, he had made landings and descents on it; he had carried off and exhibited in triumph natives such as Robinson Crusoe, as Man Friday, as Moll Flanders, as William the Quaker; but he had conquered, subdued, and settled no province therein. I like *Pamela*; I like it better than some persons who admire Richardson on the whole more than I do, seem to like it. But, as in all its author's work, the handling seems to me academic—the working out on paper of an ingeniously conceived problem rather than the observation or evolution of actual or possible life. I should not greatly fear to push the comparison even into foreign countries; but it is well to observe limits. Let us be content with holding that in England at least, without prejudice to anything further, Fielding was the first to display the qualities of the perfect novelist as distinguished from the romancer.

What are those qualities, as shown in *Joseph Andrews*? The faculty of arranging a probable and interesting course of action is one, of course, and Fielding showed it here. But I do not think that it is at any time the greatest one; and nobody denies that he made great advances in this direction later. The faculty of lively dialogue is another; and that he has not often been refused; but much the same may be said of it. The interspersing of appropriate description is another; but here also we shall not find him exactly a paragon. It is in character—the chief *differentia* of the novel as distinguished not merely from its elder sister the romance, and its cousin the drama, but still more from every other kind of literature—that Fielding stands even here pre-eminent. No one that I can think of, except his greatest successor in the present century, has the same unfailing gift of breathing life into every character he creates or borrows; and even Thackeray draws, if I may use the phrase, his characters more in the flat and less in the round than Fielding. Whether in Blifil he once failed, we must discuss hereafter; he has failed nowhere in *Joseph Andrews*. Some of his sketches may require the caution that they are eighteenth-century men and women; some the warning that they are obviously caricatured, or set in designed profile, or merely sketched. But they are all alive. The finical estimate of Gray (it is a horrid joy to think how perfectly capable Fielding was of having joined in that practical joke of the young gentlemen of Cambridge, which made Gray change his college), while dismissing these light things with patronage, had to admit that "parson Adams is perfectly well, so is Mrs Slipslop." "They *were*, Mr Gray," said some one once, "they were more perfectly well, and in a higher kind, than anything you ever did; though you were a pretty workman too."

Yes, parson Adams is perfectly well, and so is Mrs Slipslop. But so are they all. Even the hero and heroine, tied and bound as they are by the necessity under which their maker lay of preserving Joseph's Joseph-hood, and of making Fanny the example of a franker and less interested virtue than her sister-in-law that might have been, are surprisingly human where most writers would have made them sticks. And the rest require no allowance. Lady Booby, few as are the strokes given to her, is not much less alive than Lady Bellaston. Mr Trulliber, monster and not at all delicate monster as he is, is also a man, and when he lays it down that no one even in his own house shall drink when he "caaled vurst," one can but pay his maker the tribute of that silent shudder of admiration which hails the addition of one more everlasting entity to the world of thought and fancy. And Mr Tow-wouse is real, and Mrs Tow-wouse is more real still, and Betty is real; and the coachman, and Miss Grave-airs, and all the wonderful crew from first to last. The dresses they wear, the manners they exhibit, the laws they live under, the very foods and drinks they live upon, are "past like the shadows on glasses"—to the comfort and rejoicing of some, to the greater or less sorrow of others. But *they* are there—alive, full of blood, full of breath as we are, and, in truth, I fear a little more so. For some purposes a century is a gap harder to cross and more estranging than a couple of millenniums. But in their case the gap is nothing; and it is not too much to say that as they have stood the harder test, they will stand the easier. There are very striking differences between Nausicaa and Mrs Slipslop; there are differences not less striking between Mrs Slipslop and Beatrice. But their likeness is a stranger and more wonderful thing than any of their unlikenesses. It is that they are all women, that they are all live citizenesses of the Land of Matters Un-forgot, the fashion whereof passeth not away, and the franchise whereof, once acquired, assures immortality.

NOTE TO GENERAL INTRODUCTION.

The text of this issue in the main follows that of the standard or first collected edition of 1762. The variants which the author introduced in successive editions during his lifetime are not inconsiderable; but for the purposes of the present issue it did not seem necessary or indeed desirable to take account of them. In the case of prose fiction, more than in any other department of literature, it is desirable that work should be read in the form which represents the completest intention and execution of the author. Nor have any notes been attempted; for again such things, in the case of prose fiction, are of very doubtful use, and supply pretty certain stumbling-blocks to enjoyment; while in the particular case of Fielding, the annotation, unless extremely capricious, would have to be disgustingly full. Far be it at any rate from the present editor to bury these delightful creations under an ugly crust of parallel passages and miscellaneous erudition. The sheets, however, have been carefully read in order to prevent the casual errors which are wont to creep into frequently reprinted texts; and the editor hopes that if any such have escaped him, the escape will not be attributed to wilful negligence. A few obvious errors, in spelling of proper names, &c., which occur in the 1762 version have been corrected: but wherever the readings of that version are possible they have been preferred. The embellishments of the edition are partly fanciful and partly "documentary;" so that it is hoped both classes of taste may have something to feed upon.

AUTHOR'S PREFACE.

As it is possible the mere English reader may have a different idea of romance from the author of these little [1] volumes, and may consequently expect a kind of entertainment not to be found, nor which was even intended, in the following pages, it may not be improper to premise a few words concerning this kind of writing, which I do not remember to have seen hitherto attempted in our language.

The EPIC, as well as the DRAMA, is divided into tragedy and comedy. HOMER, who was the father of this species of poetry, gave us a pattern of both these, though that of the latter kind is entirely lost; which Aristotle tells us, bore the same relation to comedy which his Iliad bears to tragedy. And perhaps, that we have no more instances of it among the writers of antiquity, is owing to the loss of this great pattern, which, had it survived, would have found its imitators equally with the other poems of this great original.

And farther, as this poetry may be tragic or comic, I will not scruple to say it may be likewise either in verse or prose: for though it wants one particular, which the critic enumerates in the constituent parts of an epic poem, namely metre; yet, when any kind of writing contains all its other parts, such as fable, action, characters, sentiments, and diction, and is deficient in metre only, it seems, I think, reasonable to refer it to the epic; at least, as no critic hath thought proper to range it under any other head, or to assign it a particular name to itself.

Thus the Telemachus of the archbishop of Cambray appears to me of the epic kind, as well as the Odyssey of Homer; indeed, it is much fairer and more reasonable to give it a name common with that species from which it differs only in a single instance, than to confound it with those which it resembles in no other. Such are those voluminous works, commonly called Romances, namely, Clelia, Cleopatra, Astraea, Cassandra, the Grand Cyrus, and innumerable others, which contain, as I apprehend, very little instruction or entertainment.

Now, a comic romance is a comic epic poem in prose; differing from comedy, as the serious epic from tragedy: its action being more extended and comprehensive; containing a much larger circle of incidents, and introducing a greater variety of characters. It differs from the serious romance in its fable and action, in this; that as in the one these are grave and solemn, so in the other they are light and ridiculous: it differs in its characters by introducing persons of inferior rank,

---

[1] Joseph Andrews was originally published in 2 vols. duodecimo.

and consequently, of inferior manners, whereas the grave romance sets the highest before us: lastly, in its sentiments and diction; by preserving the ludicrous instead of the sublime. In the diction, I think, burlesque itself may be sometimes admitted; of which many instances will occur in this work, as in the description of the battles, and some other places, not necessary to be pointed out to the classical reader, for whose entertainment those parodies or burlesque imitations are chiefly calculated.

But though we have sometimes admitted this in our diction, we have carefully excluded it from our sentiments and characters; for there it is never properly introduced, unless in writings of the burlesque kind, which this is not intended to be. Indeed, no two species of writing can differ more widely than the comic and the burlesque; for as the latter is ever the exhibition of what is monstrous and unnatural, and where our delight, if we examine it, arises from the surprizing absurdity, as in appropriating the manners of the highest to the lowest, or *e converso*; so in the former we should ever confine ourselves strictly to nature, from the just imitation of which will flow all the pleasure we can this way convey to a sensible reader. And perhaps there is one reason why a comic writer should of all others be the least excused for deviating from nature, since it may not be always so easy for a serious poet to meet with the great and the admirable; but life everywhere furnishes an accurate observer with the ridiculous.

I have hinted this little concerning burlesque, because I have often heard that name given to performances which have been truly of the comic kind, from the author's having sometimes admitted it in his diction only; which, as it is the dress of poetry, doth, like the dress of men, establish characters (the one of the whole poem, and the other of the whole man), in vulgar opinion, beyond any of their greater excellences: but surely, a certain drollery in stile, where characters and sentiments are perfectly natural, no more constitutes the burlesque, than an empty pomp and dignity of words, where everything else is mean and low, can entitle any performance to the appellation of the true sublime.

And I apprehend my Lord Shaftesbury's opinion of mere burlesque agrees with mine, when he asserts, There is no such thing to be found in the writings of the ancients. But perhaps I have less abhorrence than he professes for it; and that, not because I have had some little success on the stage this way, but rather as it contributes more to exquisite mirth and laughter than any other; and these are probably more wholesome physic for the mind, and conduce better to purge away spleen, melancholy, and ill affections, than is generally imagined. Nay, I will appeal to common observation, whether the same companies are not found more full of good-humour and benevolence, after they have been sweetened for two or three hours with entertainments of this kind, than when soured by a tragedy or a grave lecture.

But to illustrate all this by another science, in which, perhaps, we shall see the distinction more clearly and plainly, let us examine the works of a comic history painter, with those performances which the Italians call Caricatura, where we shall find the true excellence of the former to consist in the exactest copying of nature; insomuch that a judicious eye instantly rejects anything *outre*, any liberty which the painter hath taken with the features of that *alma mater*; whereas in the Caricatura we allow all licence—its aim is to exhibit monsters, not men; and all distortions and exaggerations whatever are within its proper province.

Now, what Caricatura is in painting, Burlesque is in writing; and in the same manner the comic writer and painter correlate to each other. And here I shall observe, that, as in the former the painter seems to have the advantage; so it is in the latter infinitely on the side of the writer; for the Monstrous is much easier to paint than describe, and the Ridiculous to describe than paint.

And though perhaps this latter species doth not in either science so strongly affect and agitate the muscles as the other; yet it will be owned, I believe, that a more rational and useful pleasure arises to us from it. He who should call the ingenious Hogarth a burlesque painter, would, in my opinion, do him very little honour; for sure it is much easier, much less the subject of admiration, to paint a man with a nose, or any other feature, of a preposterous size, or to expose him in some absurd or monstrous attitude, than to express the affections of men on canvas. It hath been thought a vast commendation of a painter to say his figures seem to breathe; but surely it is a much greater and nobler applause, that they appear to think.

But to return. The Ridiculous only, as I have before said, falls within my province in the present work. Nor will some explanation of this word be thought impertinent by the reader, if he considers how wonderfully it hath been mistaken, even by writers who have professed it: for to what but such a mistake can we attribute the many attempts to ridicule the blackest villanies, and, what is yet worse, the most dreadful calamities? What could exceed the absurdity of an author, who should write the comedy of Nero, with the merry incident of ripping up his mother's belly? or what would give a greater shock to humanity than an attempt to expose the miseries of poverty and distress to ridicule? And yet the reader will not want much learning to suggest such instances to himself.

Besides, it may seem remarkable, that Aristotle, who is so fond and free of definitions, hath not thought proper to define the Ridiculous. Indeed, where he tells us it is proper to comedy, he hath remarked that villany is not its object: but he hath not, as I remember, positively asserted what is. Nor doth the Abbe Bellegarde, who hath written a treatise on this subject, though he shows us many species of it, once trace it to its fountain.

The only source of the true Ridiculous (as it appears to me) is affectation. But though it arises from one spring only, when we consider the infinite streams into which this one branches, we shall presently cease to admire at the copious field it affords to an observer. Now, affectation proceeds from one of these two causes, vanity or hypocrisy: for as vanity puts us on affecting false characters, in order to purchase applause; so hypocrisy sets us on an endeavour to avoid censure, by concealing our vices under an appearance of their opposite virtues. And though these two causes are often confounded (for there is some difficulty in distinguishing them), yet, as they proceed from very different motives, so they are as clearly distinct in their operations: for indeed, the affectation which arises from vanity is nearer to truth than the other, as it hath not that violent repugnancy of nature to struggle with, which that of the hypocrite hath. It may be likewise noted, that affectation doth not imply an absolute negation of those qualities which are affected; and, therefore, though, when it proceeds from hypocrisy, it be nearly allied to deceit; yet when it comes from vanity only, it partakes of the nature of ostentation: for instance, the affectation of liberality in a vain man differs visibly from the same affectation in the avaricious; for though the vain man is not what he would appear, or hath not the virtue he affects, to the degree he would be thought to have it; yet it sits less awkwardly on him than on the avaricious man, who is the very reverse of what he would seem to be.

From the discovery of this affectation arises the Ridiculous, which always strikes the reader with surprize and pleasure; and that in a higher and stronger degree when the affectation arises from hypocrisy, than when from vanity; for to discover any one to be the exact reverse of what he affects, is more surprizing, and consequently more ridiculous, than to find him a little deficient in the quality he desires the reputation of. I might observe that our Ben Jonson, who of all men understood the Ridiculous the best, hath chiefly used the hypocritical affectation.

Now, from affectation only, the misfortunes and calamities of life, or the imperfections of nature, may become the objects of ridicule. Surely he hath a very ill-framed mind who can look on ugliness, infirmity, or poverty, as ridiculous in themselves: nor do I believe any man living, who meets a dirty fellow riding through the streets in a cart, is struck with an idea of the Ridiculous from it; but if he should see the same figure descend from his coach and six, or bolt from his chair with his hat under his arm, he would then begin to laugh, and with justice. In the same manner, were we to enter a poor house and behold a wretched family shivering with cold and languishing with hunger, it would not incline us to laughter (at least we must have very diabolical natures if it would); but should we discover there a grate, instead of coals, adorned with flowers, empty plate or china dishes on the sideboard, or any other affectation of riches and finery, either on their persons or in their furniture, we might then indeed be excused for ridiculing so fantastical an appearance. Much less are natural imperfections the object of derision; but when ugliness aims at the applause of beauty, or lameness endeavours to display agility, it is then that these unfortunate circumstances, which at first moved our compassion, tend only to raise our mirth.

The poet carries this very far:—

> None are for being what they are in fault,
> But for not being what they would be thought.

Where if the metre would suffer the word Ridiculous to close the first line, the thought would be rather more proper. Great vices are the proper objects of our detestation, smaller faults, of our pity; but affectation appears to me the only true source of the Ridiculous.

But perhaps it may be objected to me, that I have against my own rules introduced vices, and of a very black kind, into this work. To which I shall answer:

first, that it is very difficult to pursue a series of human actions, and keep clear from them. Secondly, that the vices to be found here are rather the accidental consequences of some human frailty or foible, than causes habitually existing in the mind. Thirdly, that they are never set forth as the objects of ridicule, but detestation. Fourthly, that they are never the principal figure at that time on the scene: and, lastly, they never produce the intended evil.

Having thus distinguished Joseph Andrews from the productions of romance writers on the one hand and burlesque writers on the other, and given some few very short hints (for I intended no more) of this species of writing, which I have affirmed to be hitherto unattempted in our language; I shall leave to my good-natured reader to apply my piece to my observations, and will detain him no longer than with a word concerning the characters in this work.

And here I solemnly protest I have no intention to vilify or asperse any one; for though everything is copied from the book of nature, and scarce a character or action produced which I have not taken from my I own observations and experience; yet I have used the utmost care to obscure the persons by such different circumstances, degrees, and colours, that it will be impossible to guess at them with any degree of certainty; and if it ever happens otherwise, it is only where the failure characterized is so minute, that it is a foible only which the party himself may laugh at as well as any other.

As to the character of Adams, as it is the most glaring in the whole, so I conceive it is not to be found in any book now extant. It is designed a character of perfect simplicity; and as the goodness of his heart will recommend him to the good-natured, so I hope it will excuse me to the gentlemen of his cloth; for whom, while they are worthy of their sacred order, no man can possibly have a greater respect. They will therefore excuse me, notwithstanding the low adventures in which he is engaged, that I have made him a clergyman; since no other office could have given him so many opportunities of displaying his worthy inclinations.

BOOK I.

CHAPTER I.

Of writing lives in general, and particularly of Pamela; with a word by the bye of Colley Cibber and others.

It is a trite but true observation, that examples work more forcibly on the mind than precepts: and if this be just in what is odious and blameable, it is more strongly so in what is amiable and praiseworthy. Here emulation most effectually operates upon us, and inspires our imitation in an irresistible manner. A good man therefore is a standing lesson to all his acquaintance, and of far greater use in that narrow circle than a good book.

But as it often happens that the best men are but little known, and consequently cannot extend the usefulness of their examples a great way; the writer may be called in aid to spread their history farther, and to present the amiable pictures to those who have not the happiness of knowing the originals; and so, by communicating such valuable patterns to the world, he may perhaps do a more extensive service to mankind than the person whose life originally afforded the pattern.

In this light I have always regarded those biographers who have recorded the actions of great and worthy persons of both sexes. Not to mention those antient writers which of late days are little read, being written in obsolete, and as they are generally thought, unintelligible languages, such as Plutarch, Nepos, and others which I heard of in my youth; our own language affords many of excellent use and instruction, finely calculated to sow the seeds of virtue in youth, and very easy to be comprehended by persons of moderate capacity. Such as the history of John the Great, who, by his brave and heroic actions against men of large and athletic bodies, obtained the glorious appellation of the Giant-killer; that of an Earl of Warwick, whose Christian name was Guy; the lives of Argalus and Parthenia; and above all, the history of those seven worthy personages, the Champions of Christendom. In all these delight is mixed with instruction, and the reader is almost as much improved as entertained.

But I pass by these and many others to mention two books lately published, which represent an admirable pattern of the amiable in either sex. The former of these, which deals in male virtue, was written by the great person himself, who lived the life he hath recorded, and is by many thought to have lived such a life only in order to write it. The other is communicated to us by an historian who borrows his lights, as the common method is, from authentic papers and records. The reader, I believe, already conjectures, I mean the lives of Mr Colley Cibber and of

Mrs Pamela Andrews. How artfully doth the former, by insinuating that he escaped being promoted to the highest stations in Church and State, teach us a contempt of worldly grandeur! how strongly doth he inculcate an absolute submission to our superiors! Lastly, how completely doth he arm us against so uneasy, so wretched a passion as the fear of shame! how clearly doth he expose the emptiness and vanity of that phantom, reputation!

What the female readers are taught by the memoirs of Mrs Andrews is so well set forth in the excellent essays or letters prefixed to the second and subsequent editions of that work, that it would be here a needless repetition. The authentic history with which I now present the public is an instance of the great good that book is likely to do, and of the prevalence of example which I have just observed: since it will appear that it was by keeping the excellent pattern of his sister's virtues before his eyes, that Mr Joseph Andrews was chiefly enabled to preserve his purity in the midst of such great temptations. I shall only add that this character of male chastity, though doubtless as desirable and becoming in one part of the human species as in the other, is almost the only virtue which the great apologist hath not given himself for the sake of giving the example to his readers.

CHAPTER II.

Of Mr Joseph Andrews, his birth, parentage, education, and great endowments; with a word or two concerning ancestors.

Mr Joseph Andrews, the hero of our ensuing history, was esteemed to be the only son of Gaffar and Gammer Andrews, and brother to the illustrious Pamela, whose virtue is at present so famous. As to his ancestors, we have searched with great diligence, but little success; being unable to trace them farther than his great-grandfather, who, as an elderly person in the parish remembers to have heard his father say, was an excellent cudgel-player. Whether he had any ancestors before this, we must leave to the opinion of our curious reader, finding nothing of sufficient certainty to rely on. However, we cannot omit inserting an epitaph which an ingenious friend of ours hath communicated:—

Stay, traveller, for underneath this pew
Lies fast asleep that merry man Andrew:
When the last day's great sun shall gild the skies,
Then he shall from his tomb get up and rise.
Be merry while thou canst: for surely thou
Shalt shortly be as sad as he is now.

The words are almost out of the stone with antiquity. But it is needless to observe that Andrew here is writ without an *s*, and is, besides, a Christian name. My friend, moreover, conjectures this to have been the founder of that sect of laughing philosophers since called Merry-andrews.

To waive, therefore, a circumstance which, though mentioned in conformity to the exact rules of biography, is not greatly material, I proceed to things of more consequence. Indeed, it is sufficiently certain that he had as many ancestors as the best man living, and, perhaps, if we look five or six hundred years backwards, might be related to some persons of very great figure at present, whose ancestors within half the last century are buried in as great obscurity. But suppose, for argument's sake, we should admit that he had no ancestors at all, but had sprung up, according to the modern phrase, out of a dunghill, as the Athenians pretended they themselves did from the earth, would not this autokopros [1] have been justly

[1] In English, sprung from a dunghill.

entitled to all the praise arising from his own virtues? Would it not be hard that a man who hath no ancestors should therefore be rendered incapable of acquiring honour; when we see so many who have no virtues enjoying the honour of their forefathers? At ten years old (by which time his education was advanced to writing and reading) he was bound an apprentice, according to the statute, to Sir Thomas Booby, an uncle of Mr Booby's by the father's side. Sir Thomas having then an estate in his own hands, the young Andrews was at first employed in what in the country they call keeping birds. His office was to perform the part the ancients assigned to the god Priapus, which deity the moderns call by the name of Jack o' Lent; but his voice being so extremely musical, that it rather allured the birds than terrified them, he was soon transplanted from the fields into the dog-kennel, where he was placed under the huntsman, and made what the sportsmen term whipper-in. For this place likewise the sweetness of his voice disqualified him; the dogs preferring the melody of his chiding to all the alluring notes of the huntsman, who soon became so incensed at it, that he desired Sir Thomas to provide otherwise for him, and constantly laid every fault the dogs were at to the account of the poor boy, who was now transplanted to the stable. Here he soon gave proofs of strength and agility beyond his years, and constantly rode the most spirited and vicious horses to water, with an intrepidity which surprized every one. While he was in this station, he rode several races for Sir Thomas, and this with such expertness and success, that the neighbouring gentlemen frequently solicited the knight to permit little Joey (for so he was called) to ride their matches. The best gamesters, before they laid their money, always inquired which horse little Joey was to ride; and the bets were rather proportioned by the rider than by the horse himself; especially after he had scornfully refused a considerable bribe to play booty on such an occasion. This extremely raised his character, and so pleased the Lady Booby, that she desired to have him (being now seventeen years of age) for her own footboy.

Joey was now preferred from the stable to attend on his lady, to go on her errands, stand behind her chair, wait at her tea-table, and carry her prayer-book to church; at which place his voice gave him an opportunity of distinguishing himself by singing psalms: he behaved likewise in every other respect so well at Divine service, that it recommended him to the notice of Mr Abraham Adams, the curate, who took an opportunity one day, as he was drinking a cup of ale in Sir Thomas's kitchen, to ask the young man several questions concerning religion; with his answers to which he was wonderfully pleased.

CHAPTER III.

Of Mr Abraham Adams the curate, Mrs Slipslop the chambermaid, and others.

Mr Abraham Adams was an excellent scholar. He was a perfect master of the Greek and Latin languages; to which he added a great share of knowledge in the Oriental tongues; and could read and translate French, Italian, and Spanish. He had applied many years to the most severe study, and had treasured up a fund of learning rarely to be met with in a university. He was, besides, a man of good sense, good parts, and good nature; but was at the same time as entirely ignorant of the ways of this world as an infant just entered into it could possibly be. As he had never any intention to deceive, so he never suspected such a design in others. He was generous, friendly, and brave to an excess; but simplicity was his characteristick: he did, no more than Mr Colley Cibber, apprehend any such passions as malice and envy to exist in mankind; which was indeed less remarkable in a country parson than in a gentleman who hath passed his life behind the scenes,—a place which hath been seldom thought the school of innocence, and where a very little observation would have convinced the great apologist that those passions have a real existence in the human mind.

His virtue, and his other qualifications, as they rendered him equal to his office, so they made him an agreeable and valuable companion, and had so much endeared and well recommended him to a bishop, that at the age of fifty he was provided with a handsome income of twenty-three pounds a year; which, however, he could not make any great figure with, because he lived in a dear country, and was a little encumbered with a wife and six children.

It was this gentleman, who having, as I have said, observed the singular devotion of young Andrews, had found means to question him concerning several particulars; as, how many books there were in the New Testament? which were they? how many chapters they contained? and such like: to all which, Mr Adams privately said, he answered much better than Sir Thomas, or two other neighbouring justices of the peace could probably have done.

Mr Adams was wonderfully solicitous to know at what time, and by what opportunity, the youth became acquainted with these matters: Joey told him that he had very early learnt to read and write by the goodness of his father, who, though he had not interest enough to get him into a charity school, because a cousin of his father's landlord did not vote on the right side for a churchwarden in a borough town, yet had been himself at the expense of sixpence a week for his learning. He told him likewise, that ever since he was in Sir Thomas's family he had employed all his hours of leisure in reading good books; that he had read the Bible, the Whole Duty of Man, and Thomas a Kempis; and that as often as he could, without being perceived, he had studied a great good book which lay open in the hall window, where he had read, "as how the devil carried away half a church in sermon-time, without hurting one of the congregation; and as how a field of corn ran away down a hill with all the trees upon it, and covered another man's meadow." This sufficiently assured Mr Adams that the good book meant could be no other than Baker's Chronicle.

The curate, surprized to find such instances of industry and application in a young man who had never met with the least encouragement, asked him, If he did not extremely regret the want of a liberal education, and the not having been born of parents who might have indulged his talents and desire of knowledge? To which he answered, "He hoped he had profited somewhat better from the books he had read than to lament his condition in this world. That, for his part, he was perfectly content with the state to which he was called; that he should endeavour to improve his talent, which was all required of him; but not repine at his own lot, nor envy those of his betters." "Well said, my lad," replied the curate; "and I wish some who have read many more good books, nay, and some who have written good books themselves, had profited so much by them."

Adams had no nearer access to Sir Thomas or my lady than through the waiting-gentlewoman; for Sir Thomas was too apt to estimate men merely by their dress or fortune; and my lady was a woman of gaiety, who had been blest with a town education, and never spoke of any of her country neighbours by any other appellation than that of the brutes. They both regarded the curate as a kind of domestic only, belonging to the parson of the parish, who was at this time at variance with the knight; for the parson had for many years lived in a constant state of civil war, or, which is perhaps as bad, of civil law, with Sir Thomas himself and the tenants of his manor. The foundation of this quarrel was a modus, by setting which aside an advantage of several shillings *per annum* would have accrued to the rector; but he had not yet been able to accomplish his purpose, and had reaped hitherto nothing better from the suits than the pleasure (which he used indeed frequently to say was no small one) of reflecting that he had utterly undone many of the poor tenants, though he had at the same time greatly impoverished himself.

Mrs Slipslop, the waiting-gentlewoman, being herself the daughter of a curate, preserved some respect for Adams: she professed great regard for his learning, and would frequently dispute with him on points of theology; but always insisted on a deference to be paid to her understanding, as she had been frequently at London, and knew more of the world than a country parson could pretend to.

She had in these disputes a particular advantage over Adams: for she was a mighty affecter of hard words, which she used in such a manner that the parson, who durst not offend her by calling her words in question, was frequently at some loss to guess her meaning, and would have been much less puzzled by an Arabian manuscript.

Adams therefore took an opportunity one day, after a pretty long discourse with her on the essence (or, as she pleased to term it, the incence) of matter, to mention the case of young Andrews; desiring her to recommend him to her lady as a youth very susceptible of learning, and one whose instruction in Latin he would himself undertake; by which means he might be qualified for a higher station than that of a footman; and added, she knew it was in his master's power easily to provide for him in a better manner. He therefore desired that the boy might be left behind under his care.

"La! Mr Adams," said Mrs Slipslop, "do you think my lady will suffer any preambles about any such matter? She is going to London very concisely, and I am confidous would not leave Joey behind her on any account; for he is one of the genteelest young fellows you may see in a summer's day; and I am confidous she would as soon think of parting with a pair of her grey mares, for she values herself as much on one as the other." Adams would have interrupted, but she proceeded: "And why is Latin more necessitous for a footman than a gentleman? It is very proper that you clergymen must learn it, because you can't preach without it: but I have heard gentlemen say in London, that it is fit for nobody else. I am confidous my lady would be angry with me for mentioning it; and I shall draw myself into no such delemy." At which words her lady's bell rung, and Mr Adams was forced to retire; nor could he gain a second opportunity with her before their London journey, which happened a few days afterwards. However, Andrews behaved very thankfully and gratefully to him for his intended kindness, which he told him he never would forget, and at the same time received from the good man many admonitions concerning the regulation of his future conduct, and his perseverance in innocence and industry.

CHAPTER IV.

What happened after their journey to London.

No sooner was young Andrews arrived at London than he began to scrape an acquaintance with his party-coloured brethren, who endeavoured to make him despise his former course of life. His hair was cut after the newest fashion, and became his chief care; he went abroad with it all the morning in papers, and drest it out in the afternoon. They could not, however, teach him to game, swear, drink, nor any other genteel vice the town abounded with. He applied most of his leisure hours to music, in which he greatly improved himself; and became so perfect a connoisseur in that art, that he led the opinion of all the other footmen at an opera, and they never condemned or applauded a single song contrary to his approbation or dislike. He was a little too forward in riots at the play-houses and assemblies; and when he attended his lady at church (which was but seldom) he behaved with less seeming devotion than formerly: however, if he was outwardly a pretty fellow, his morals remained entirely uncorrupted, though he was at the same time smarter and genteeler than any of the beaus in town, either in or out of livery.

His lady, who had often said of him that Joey was the handsomest and genteelest footman in the kingdom, but that it was pity he wanted spirit, began now to find that fault no longer; on the contrary, she was frequently heard to cry out, "Ay, there is some life in this fellow." She plainly saw the effects which the town air hath on the soberest constitutions. She would now walk out with him into Hyde Park in a morning, and when tired, which happened almost every minute, would lean on his arm, and converse with him in great familiarity. Whenever she stept out of her coach, she would take him by the hand, and sometimes, for fear of stumbling, press it very hard; she admitted him to deliver messages at her bedside in a morning, leered at him at table, and indulged him in all those innocent freedoms which women of figure may permit without the least sully of their virtue.

But though their virtue remains unsullied, yet now and then some small arrows will glance on the shadow of it, their reputation; and so it fell out to Lady Booby, who happened to be walking arm-in-arm with Joey one morning in Hyde Park, when Lady Tittle and Lady Tattle came accidentally by in their coach. "Bless me," says Lady Tittle, "can I believe my eyes? Is that Lady Booby?"—"Surely," says Tattle. "But what makes you surprized?"—"Why, is not that her footman?" replied Tittle. At which Tattle laughed, and cried, "An old business, I assure you: is it possible you should not have heard it? The whole town hath known it this half-year." The consequence of this interview was a whisper through a hundred visits, which were separately performed by the two ladies[1] the same afternoon, and might have had a mischievous effect, had it not been stopt by two fresh reputations which were published the day afterwards, and engrossed the whole talk of the town.

But, whatever opinion or suspicion the scandalous inclination of defamers might entertain of Lady Booby's innocent freedoms, it is certain they made no impression on young Andrews, who never offered to encroach beyond the liberties which his lady allowed him,—a behaviour which she imputed to the violent respect he preserved for her, and which served only to heighten a something she began to conceive, and which the next chapter will open a little farther.

---

[1] It may seem an absurdity that Tattle should visit, as she actually did, to spread a known scandal: but the reader may reconcile this by supposing, with me, that, notwithstanding what she says, this was her first acquaintance with it.

CHAPTER V.

The death of Sir Thomas Booby, with the affectionate and mournful behaviour of his widow, and the great purity of Joseph Andrews.

At this time an accident happened which put a stop to those agreeable walks, which probably would have soon puffed up the cheeks of Fame, and caused her to blow her brazen trumpet through the town; and this was no other than the death of Sir Thomas Booby, who, departing this life, left his disconsolate lady confined to her house, as closely as if she herself had been attacked by some violent disease. During the first six days the poor lady admitted none but Mrs. Slipslop, and three female friends, who made a party at cards: but on the seventh she ordered Joey, whom, for a good reason, we shall hereafter call JOSEPH, to bring up her tea-kettle. The lady being in bed, called Joseph to her, bade him sit down, and, having accidentally laid her hand on his, she asked him if he had ever been in love. Joseph answered, with some confusion, it was time enough for one so young as himself to think on such things. "As young as you are," replied the lady, "I am convinced you are no stranger to that passion. Come, Joey," says she, "tell me truly, who is the happy girl whose eyes have made a conquest of you?" Joseph returned, that all the women he had ever seen were equally indifferent to him. "Oh then," said the lady, "you are a general lover. Indeed, you handsome fellows, like handsome women, are very long and difficult in fixing; but yet you shall never persuade me that your heart is so insusceptible of affection; I rather impute what you say to your secrecy, a very commendable quality, and what I am far from being angry with you for. Nothing can be more unworthy in a young man, than to betray any intimacies with the ladies." "Ladies! madam," said Joseph, "I am sure I never had the impudence to think of any that deserve that name." "Don't pretend to too much modesty," said she, "for that sometimes may be impertinent: but pray answer me this question. Suppose a lady should happen to like you; suppose she should prefer you to all your sex, and admit you to the same familiarities as you might have hoped for if you had been born her equal, are you certain that no vanity could tempt you to discover her? Answer me honestly, Joseph; have you so much more sense and so much more virtue than you handsome young fellows generally have, who make no scruple of sacrificing our dear reputation to your pride, without considering the great obligation we lay on you by our condescension and confidence? Can you keep a secret, my Joey?" "Madam," says he, "I hope your ladyship can't tax me with ever betraying the secrets of the family; and

I hope, if you was to turn me away, I might have that character of you." "I don't intend to turn you away, Joey," said she, and sighed; "I am afraid it is not in my power." She then raised herself a little in her bed, and discovered one of the whitest necks that ever was seen; at which Joseph blushed. "La!" says she, in an affected surprize, "what am I doing? I have trusted myself with a man alone, naked in bed; suppose you should have any wicked intentions upon my honour, how should I defend myself?" Joseph protested that he never had the least evil design against her. "No," says she, "perhaps you may not call your designs wicked; and perhaps they are not so."—He swore they were not. "You misunderstand me," says she; "I mean if they were against my honour, they may not be wicked; but the world calls them so. But then, say you, the world will never know anything of the matter; yet would not that be trusting to your secrecy? Must not my reputation be then in your power? Would you not then be my master?" Joseph begged her ladyship to be comforted; for that he would never imagine the least wicked thing against her, and that he had rather die a thousand deaths than give her any reason to suspect him. "Yes," said she, "I must have reason to suspect you. Are you not a man? and, without vanity, I may pretend to some charms. But perhaps you may fear I should prosecute you; indeed I hope you do; and yet Heaven knows I should never have the confidence to appear before a court of justice; and you know, Joey, I am of a forgiving temper. Tell me, Joey, don't you think I should forgive you?"—"Indeed, madam," says Joseph, "I will never do anything to disoblige your ladyship."—"How," says she, "do you think it would not disoblige me then? Do you think I would willingly suffer you?"—"I don't understand you, madam," says Joseph.—"Don't you?" said she, "then you are either a fool, or pretend to be so; I find I was mistaken in you. So get you downstairs, and never let me see your face again; your pretended innocence cannot impose on me."—"Madam," said Joseph, "I would not have your ladyship think any evil of me. I have always endeavoured to be a dutiful servant both to you and my master."—"O thou villain!" answered my lady; "why didst thou mention the name of that dear man, unless to torment me, to bring his precious memory to my mind?" (and then she burst into a fit of tears.) "Get thee from my sight! I shall never endure thee more." At which words she turned away from him; and Joseph retreated from the room in a most disconsolate condition, and writ that letter which the reader will find in the next chapter.

CHAPTER VI.

How Joseph Andrews writ a letter to his sister Pamela.

"To MRS PAMELA ANDREWS, LIVING WITH SQUIRE BOOBY.

"DEAR SISTER,—Since I received your letter of your good lady's death, we have had a misfortune of the same kind in our family. My worthy master Sir Thomas died about four days ago; and, what is worse, my poor lady is certainly gone distracted. None of the servants expected her to take it so to heart, because they quarrelled almost every day of their lives: but no more of that, because you know, Pamela, I never loved to tell the secrets of my master's family; but to be sure you must have known they never loved one another; and I have heard her ladyship wish his honour dead above a thousand times; but nobody knows what it is to lose a friend till they have lost him.

"Don't tell anybody what I write, because I should not care to have folks say I discover what passes in our family; but if it had not been so great a lady, I should have thought she had had a mind to me. Dear Pamela, don't tell anybody; but she ordered me to sit down by her bedside, when she was naked in bed; and she held my hand, and talked exactly as a lady does to her sweetheart in a stage-play, which I have seen in Covent Garden, while she wanted him to be no better than he should be.

"If madam be mad, I shall not care for staying long in the family; so I heartily wish you could get me a place, either at the squire's, or some other neighbouring gentleman's, unless it be true that you are going to be married to parson Williams, as folks talk, and then I should be very willing to be his clerk; for which you know I am qualified, being able to read and to set a psalm.

"I fancy I shall be discharged very soon; and the moment I am, unless I hear from you, I shall return to my old master's country-seat, if it be only to see parson Adams, who is the best man in the world. London is a bad place, and there is so little good fellowship, that the next-door neighbours don't know one another. Pray give my service to all friends that inquire for me. So I rest

"Your loving brother,

"JOSEPH ANDREWS."

As soon as Joseph had sealed and directed this letter he walked downstairs, where he met Mrs. Slipslop, with whom we shall take this opportunity to bring the reader a little better acquainted. She was a maiden gentlewoman of about forty-five years of age, who, having made a small slip in her youth, had continued a good maid ever since. She was not at this time remarkably handsome; being very short, and rather too corpulent in body, and somewhat red, with the addition of pimples in the face. Her nose was likewise rather too large, and her eyes too little; nor did she resemble a cow so much in her breath as in two brown globes which she carried before her; one of her legs was also a little shorter than the other, which occasioned her to limp as she walked. This fair creature had long cast the eyes of affection on Joseph, in which she had not met with quite so good success as she probably wished, though, besides the allurements of her native charms, she had given him tea, sweetmeats, wine, and many other delicacies, of which, by keeping the keys, she had the absolute command. Joseph, however, had not returned the least gratitude to all these favours, not even so much as a kiss; though I would not insinuate she was so easily to be satisfied; for surely then he would have been highly blameable. The truth is, she was arrived at an age when she thought she might indulge herself in any liberties with a man, without the danger of bringing a third person into the world to betray them. She imagined that by so long a self-denial she had not only made amends for the small slip of her youth above hinted at, but had likewise laid up a quantity of merit to excuse any future failings. In a word, she resolved to give a loose to her amorous inclinations, and to pay off the debt of pleasure which she found she owed herself, as fast as possible.

With these charms of person, and in this disposition of mind, she encountered poor Joseph at the bottom of the stairs, and asked him if he would drink a glass of something good this morning. Joseph, whose spirits were not a little cast down, very readily and thankfully accepted the offer; and together they went into a closet, where, having delivered him a full glass of ratafia, and desired him to sit down, Mrs. Slipslop thus began:—

"Sure nothing can be a more simple contract in a woman than to place her affections on a boy. If I had ever thought it would have been my fate, I should have wished to die a thousand deaths rather than live to see that day. If we like a man, the lightest hint sophisticates. Whereas a boy proposes upon us to break through all the regulations of modesty, before we can make any oppression upon him." Joseph, who did not understand a word she said, answered, "Yes, madam."—"Yes, madam!" replied Mrs. Slipslop with some warmth, "Do you intend to result my passion? Is it not enough, ungrateful as you are, to make no return to all the favours I have done you; but you must treat me with ironing? Barbarous monster! how have I deserved that my passion should be resulted and treated with ironing?" "Madam," answered Joseph, "I don't understand your hard words; but I am certain you have no occasion to call me ungrateful, for, so far from intending you any wrong, I have always loved you as well as if you had been my own mother." "How, sirrah!" says Mrs. Slipslop in a rage; "your own mother? Do you assinuate that I am old enough to be your mother? I don't know what a stripling may think, but I believe a man would refer me to any green-sickness silly girl whatsomdever: but I ought to despise you rather than be angry with you, for referring the conversation of girls to that of a woman of sense."—"Madam," says Joseph, "I am sure I have always valued the honour you did me by your conversation, for I know you are a woman of learning."—"Yes, but, Joseph," said she, a little softened by the compliment to her learning, "if you had a value for me, you certainly would have found some method of showing it me; for I am convicted you must see the value I have for you. Yes, Joseph, my eyes, whether I would or no, must have declared a passion I cannot conquer.—Oh! Joseph!"

As when a hungry tigress, who long has traversed the woods in fruitless search, sees within the reach of her claws a lamb, she prepares to leap on her prey; or as a voracious pike, of immense size, surveys through the liquid element a roach or gudgeon, which cannot escape her jaws, opens them wide to swallow the little fish; so did Mrs. Slipslop prepare to lay her violent amorous hands on the poor Joseph, when luckily her mistress's bell rung, and delivered the intended martyr from her clutches. She was obliged to leave him abruptly, and to defer the execution of her purpose till some other time. We shall therefore return to the Lady Booby, and give our reader some account of her behaviour, after she was left by Joseph in a temper of mind not greatly different from that of the inflamed Slipslop.

CHAPTER VII.

Sayings of wise men. A dialogue between the lady and her maid; and a panegyric, or rather satire, on the passion of love, in the sublime style.

It is the observation of some antient sage, whose name I have forgot, that passions operate differently on the human mind, as diseases on the body, in proportion to the strength or weakness, soundness or rottenness, of the one and the other.

We hope, therefore, a judicious reader will give himself some pains to observe, what we have so greatly laboured to describe, the different operations of this passion of love in the gentle and cultivated mind of the Lady Booby, from those which it effected in the less polished and coarser disposition of Mrs Slipslop.

Another philosopher, whose name also at present escapes my memory, hath somewhere said, that resolutions taken in the absence of the beloved object are very apt to vanish in its presence; on both which wise sayings the following chapter may serve as a comment.

No sooner had Joseph left the room in the manner we have before related than the lady, enraged at her disappointment, began to reflect with severity on her conduct. Her love was now changed to disdain, which pride assisted to torment her. She despised herself for the meanness of her passion, and Joseph for its ill success. However, she had now got the better of it in her own opinion, and determined immediately to dismiss the object. After much tossing and turning in her bed, and many soliloquies, which if we had no better matter for our reader we would give him, she at last rung the bell as above mentioned, and was presently attended by Mrs Slipslop, who was not much better pleased with Joseph than the lady herself.

"Slipslop," said Lady Booby, "when did you see Joseph?" The poor woman was so surprized at the unexpected sound of his name at so critical a time, that she had the greatest difficulty to conceal the confusion she was under from her mistress; whom she answered, nevertheless, with pretty good confidence, though not entirely void of fear of suspicion, that she had not seen him that morning. "I am afraid," said Lady Booby, "he is a wild young fellow."—"That he is," said Slipslop, "and a wicked one too. To my knowledge he games, drinks, swears, and fights eternally; besides, he is horribly indicted to wenching."—"Ay!" said the lady, "I never heard that of him."—"O madam!" answered the other, "he is so lewd a rascal, that if your ladyship keeps him much longer, you will not have one virgin in your house except myself. And yet I can't conceive what the wenches see in him, to be so foolishly fond as they are; in my eyes, he is as ugly a scarecrow as I ever upheld."—"Nay," said the lady, "the boy is well enough."—"La! ma'am," cries Slipslop, "I think him the ragmaticallest fellow in the family."—"Sure, Slipslop," says she, "you are mistaken: but which of the women do you most suspect?"—"Madam," says Slipslop, "there is Betty the chambermaid, I am almost convicted, is with child by him."—"Ay!" says the lady, "then pray pay her her wages instantly. I will keep no such sluts in my family. And as for Joseph, you may discard him too."—"Would your ladyship have him paid off immediately?" cries Slipslop, "for perhaps, when Betty is gone he may mend: and really the boy is a good servant, and a strong healthy luscious boy enough."—"This morning," answered the lady with some vehemence. "I wish, madam," cries Slipslop, "your ladyship would be so good as to try him a little longer."—"I will not have my commands disputed," said the lady; "sure you are not fond of him yourself?"—"I, madam!" cries Slipslop, reddening, if not blushing, "I should be sorry to think your ladyship had any reason to respect me of fondness for a fellow; and if it be your pleasure, I shall fulfil it with as much reluctance as possible."—"As little, I suppose you mean," said the lady; "and so about it instantly." Mrs. Slipslop went out, and the lady had scarce taken two turns before she fell to knocking and ringing with great violence. Slipslop, who did not travel post haste, soon returned, and was countermanded as to Joseph, but ordered to send Betty about her business without delay. She went out a second time with much greater alacrity than before; when the lady began immediately to accuse herself of want of resolution, and to apprehend the return of her affection, with its pernicious consequences; she therefore applied herself again to the bell, and re-summoned Mrs. Slipslop into her presence; who again returned, and was told by her mistress that she had considered better of the matter, and was absolutely resolved to turn away Joseph; which she ordered her to do immediately. Slipslop, who knew the violence of her lady's temper, and would not venture her place for any Adonis or Hercules in the universe, left her a third time; which she had no sooner done, than the little god Cupid, fearing he had not yet done the lady's business, took a fresh arrow with the sharpest point out of his quiver, and shot it directly into her heart; in other and plainer language, the lady's passion got the better of her reason. She called back Slipslop once more, and told her she had resolved to see the boy, and examine him herself; therefore bid her send him up. This wavering in her mistress's temper probably put something into the waiting-gentlewoman's head not necessary to mention to the sagacious reader.

Lady Booby was going to call her back again, but could not prevail with herself. The next consideration therefore was, how she should behave to Joseph when he came in. She resolved to preserve all the dignity of the woman of fashion to her servant, and to indulge herself in this last view of Joseph (for that she was most certainly resolved it should be) at his own expense, by first insulting and then discarding him.

O Love, what monstrous tricks dost thou play with thy votaries of both sexes! How dost thou deceive them, and make them deceive themselves! Their follies are thy delight! Their sighs make thee laugh, and their pangs are thy merriment!

Not the great Rich, who turns men into monkeys, wheel-barrows, and whatever else best humours his fancy, hath so strangely metamorphosed the human shape; nor the great Cibber, who confounds all number, gender, and breaks through every rule of grammar at his will, hath so distorted the English language as thou dost metamorphose and distort the human senses.

Thou puttest out our eyes, stoppest up our ears, and takest away the power of our nostrils; so that we can neither see the largest object, hear the loudest noise, nor smell the most poignant perfume. Again, when thou pleasest, thou canst make a molehill appear as a mountain, a Jew's-harp sound like a trumpet, and a daisy smell like a violet. Thou canst make cowardice brave, avarice generous, pride humble, and cruelty tender-hearted. In short, thou turnest the heart of man inside out, as a juggler doth a petticoat, and bringest whatsoever pleaseth thee out from it. If there be any one who doubts all this, let him read the next chapter.

CHAPTER VIII.

In which, after some very fine writing, the history goes on, and relates the interview between the lady and Joseph; where the latter hath set an example which we despair of seeing followed by his sex in this vicious age.

Now the rake Hesperus had called for his breeches, and, having well rubbed his drowsy eyes, prepared to dress himself for all night; by whose example his brother rakes on earth likewise leave those beds in which they had slept away the day. Now Thetis, the good housewife, began to put on the pot, in order to regale the good man Phoebus after his daily labours were over. In vulgar language, it was in the evening when Joseph attended his lady's orders.

But as it becomes us to preserve the character of this lady, who is the heroine of our tale; and as we have naturally a wonderful tenderness for that beautiful part of the human species called the fair sex; before we discover too much of her frailty to our reader, it will be proper to give him a lively idea of the vast temptation, which overcame all the efforts of a modest and virtuous mind; and then we humbly hope his good nature will rather pity than condemn the imperfection of human virtue.

Nay, the ladies themselves will, we hope, be induced, by considering the uncommon variety of charms which united in this young man's person, to bridle their rampant passion for chastity, and be at least as mild as their violent modesty and virtue will permit them, in censuring the conduct of a woman who, perhaps, was in her own disposition as chaste as those pure and sanctified virgins who, after a life innocently spent in the gaieties of the town, begin about fifty to attend twice *per diem* at the polite churches and chapels, to return thanks for the grace which preserved them formerly amongst beaus from temptations perhaps less powerful than what now attacked the Lady Booby.

Mr Joseph Andrews was now in the one-and-twentieth year of his age. He was of the highest degree of middle stature; his limbs were put together with great elegance, and no less strength; his legs and thighs were formed in the exactest proportion; his shoulders were broad and brawny, but yet his arm hung so easily, that he had all the symptoms of strength without the least clumsiness. His hair was of a nut-brown colour, and was displayed in wanton ringlets down his back; his forehead was high, his eyes dark, and as full of sweetness as of fire; his nose a little inclined to the Roman; his teeth white and even; his lips full, red, and soft;

his beard was only rough on his chin and upper lip; but his cheeks, in which his blood glowed, were overspread with a thick down; his countenance had a tenderness joined with a sensibility inexpressible. Add to this the most perfect neatness in his dress, and an air which, to those who have not seen many noblemen, would give an idea of nobility.

"Joseph, I am sorry to hear such complaints against you." Such was the person who now appeared before the lady. She viewed him some time in silence, and twice or thrice before she spake changed her mind as to the manner in which she should begin. At length she said to him, "Joseph, I am sorry to hear such complaints against you: I am told you behave so rudely to the maids, that they cannot do their business in quiet; I mean those who are not wicked enough to hearken to your solicitations. As to others, they may, perhaps, not call you rude; for there are wicked sluts who make one ashamed of one's own sex, and are as ready to admit any nauseous familiarity as fellows to offer it: nay, there are such in my family, but they shall not stay in it; that impudent trollop who is with child by you is discharged by this time."

As a person who is struck through the heart with a thunderbolt looks extremely surprised, nay, and perhaps is so too—thus the poor Joseph received the false accusation of his mistress; he blushed and looked confounded, which she misinterpreted to be symptoms of his guilt, and thus went on:—

"Come hither, Joseph: another mistress might discard you for these offences; but I have a compassion for your youth, and if I could be certain you would be no more guilty—Consider, child," laying her hand carelessly upon his, "you are a handsome young fellow, and might do better; you might make your fortune." "Madam," said Joseph, "I do assure your ladyship I don't know whether any maid in the house is man or woman." "Oh fie! Joseph," answered the lady, "don't commit another crime in denying the truth. I could pardon the first; but I hate a lyar." "Madam," cries Joseph, "I hope your ladyship will not be offended at my asserting my innocence; for, by all that is sacred, I have never offered more than kissing." "Kissing!" said the lady, with great discomposure of countenance, and more redness in her cheeks than anger in her eyes; "do you call that no crime? Kissing, Joseph, is as a prologue to a play. Can I believe a young fellow of your age and complexion will be content with kissing? No, Joseph, there is no woman who grants that but will grant more; and I am deceived greatly in you if you would not put her closely to it. What would you think, Joseph, if I admitted you to kiss me?" Joseph replied he would sooner die than have any such thought. "And yet, Joseph," returned she, "ladies have admitted their footmen to such familiarities; and footmen, I confess to you, much less deserving them; fellows without half your charms—for such might almost excuse the crime. Tell me therefore, Joseph, if I should admit you to such freedom, what would you think of me?—tell me freely." "Madam," said Joseph, "I should think your ladyship condescended a great deal below yourself." "Pugh!" said she; "that I am to answer to myself: but would not you insist on more? Would you be contented with a kiss? Would not your inclinations be all on fire rather by such a favour?" "Madam," said Joseph, "if they were, I hope I should be able to controul them, without suffering them to get the better of my virtue." You have heard, reader, poets talk of the statue of Surprize; you have heard likewise, or else you have heard very little, how Surprize made one of the sons of Croesus speak, though he was dumb. You have seen the faces, in the eighteen-penny gallery, when, through the trap-door, to soft or no music, Mr. Bridgewater, Mr. William Mills, or some other of ghostly appearance, hath ascended, with a face all pale with powder, and a shirt all bloody with ribbons;—but from none of these, nor from Phidias or Praxiteles, if they should return to life—no, not from the inimitable pencil of my friend Hogarth, could you receive such an idea of surprize as would have entered in at your eyes had they beheld the Lady Booby when those last words issued out from the lips of Joseph. "Your virtue!" said the lady, recovering after a silence of two minutes; "I shall never survive it. Your virtue!—intolerable confidence! Have you the assurance to pretend, that when a lady demeans herself to throw aside the rules of decency, in order to honour you with the highest favour in her power, your virtue should resist her inclination? that, when she had conquered her own virtue, she should find an obstruction in yours?" "Madam," said Joseph, "I can't see why her having no virtue should be a reason against my having any; or why, because I am a man, or because I am poor, my virtue must be subservient to her pleasures." "I am out of patience," cries the lady: "did ever mortal hear of a man's virtue? Did ever the greatest or the gravest men pretend to any of this kind? Will magistrates who punish lewdness, or parsons who preach against it, make any scruple of committing it? And can a boy, a stripling, have the confidence to talk of his virtue?" "Madam," says Joseph, "that boy is the brother of Pamela, and would be ashamed that the chastity of his family, which is preserved in her, should be stained in him. If there are such men as your ladyship mentions, I am sorry for it; and I wish they had an opportunity of reading over those letters which my father hath sent me of my sister Pamela's; nor do I doubt but such an example would amend them." "You impudent villain!" cries the lady in a rage; "do you insult me with the follies of my relation, who hath exposed himself all over the country upon your sister's account? a little vixen, whom I have always wondered my late Lady Booby ever kept in her house. Sirrah! get out of my sight, and prepare to set out this night; for I will order you your wages immediately, and you shall be stripped and turned away." "Madam," says Joseph, "I am sorry I have offended your ladyship, I am sure I never intended it." "Yes, sirrah," cries she, "you have had the vanity to misconstrue the little innocent freedom I took, in order to try whether what I had heard was true. O' my conscience, you have had the assurance to imagine I was fond of you myself." Joseph answered, he had only spoke out of tenderness for his virtue; at which words she flew into a violent passion, and refusing to hear more, ordered him instantly to leave the room.

He was no sooner gone than she burst forth into the following exclamation:—"Whither doth this violent passion hurry us? What meannesses do we submit to from its impulse! Wisely we resist its first and least approaches; for it is then only we can assure ourselves the victory. No woman could ever safely say, so far only will I go. Have I not exposed myself to the refusal of my footman? I cannot bear the reflection." Upon which she applied herself to the bell, and rung it with infinite more violence than was necessary—the faithful Slipslop attending near at hand: to say the truth, she had conceived a suspicion at her last interview with her mistress, and had waited ever since in the antechamber, having carefully applied her ears to the keyhole during the whole time that the preceding conversation passed between Joseph and the lady.

CHAPTER IX.

What passed between the lady and Mrs Slipslop; in which we prophesy there are some strokes which every one will not truly comprehend at the first reading.

"Slipslop," said the lady, "I find too much reason to believe all thou hast told me of this wicked Joseph; I have determined to part with him instantly; so go you to the steward, and bid him pay his wages." Slipslop, who had preserved hitherto a distance to her lady—rather out of necessity than inclination—and who thought the knowledge of this secret had thrown down all distinction between them, answered her mistress very pertly—"She wished she knew her own mind; and that she was certain she would call her back again before she was got half-way downstairs." The lady replied, she had taken a resolution, and was resolved to keep it. "I am sorry for it," cries Slipslop, "and, if I had known you would have punished the poor lad so severely, you should never have heard a particle of the matter. Here's a fuss indeed about nothing!" "Nothing!" returned my lady; "do you think I will countenance lewdness in my house?" "If you will turn away every footman," said Slipslop, "that is a lover of the sport, you must soon open the coach door yourself, or get a set of mophrodites to wait upon you; and I am sure I hated the sight of them even singing in an opera." "Do as I bid you," says my lady, "and don't shock my ears with your beastly language." "Marry-come-up," cries Slipslop, "people's ears are sometimes the nicest part about them."

The lady, who began to admire the new style in which her waiting-gentlewoman delivered herself, and by the conclusion of her speech suspected somewhat of the truth, called her back, and desired to know what she meant by the extraordinary degree of freedom in which she thought proper to indulge her tongue. "Freedom!" says Slipslop; "I don't know what you call freedom, madam; servants have tongues as well as their mistresses." "Yes, and saucy ones too," answered the lady; "but I assure you I shall bear no such impertinence." "Impertinence! I don't know that I am impertinent," says Slipslop. "Yes, indeed you are," cries my lady, "and, unless you mend your manners, this house is no place for you." "Manners!" cries Slipslop; "I never was thought to want manners nor modesty neither; and for places, there are more places than one; and I know what I know." "What do you know, mistress?" answered the lady. "I am not obliged to tell that to everybody," says Slipslop, "any more than I am obliged to keep it a secret." "I desire you would provide yourself," answered the lady. "With all my heart," replied the waiting-gentlewoman; and so departed in a passion, and slapped the door after her.

The lady too plainly perceived that her waiting-gentlewoman knew more than she would willingly have had her acquainted with; and this she imputed to Joseph's having discovered to her what passed at the first interview. This, therefore, blew up her rage against him, and confirmed her in a resolution of parting with him.

But the dismissing Mrs Slipslop was a point not so easily to be resolved upon. She had the utmost tenderness for her reputation, as she knew on that depended many of the most valuable blessings of life; particularly cards, making curtsies in public places, and, above all, the pleasure of demolishing the reputations of others, in which innocent amusement she had an extraordinary delight. She therefore determined to submit to any insult from a servant, rather than run a risque of losing the title to so many great privileges.

She therefore sent for her steward, Mr Peter Pounce, and ordered him to pay Joseph his wages, to strip off his livery, and to turn him out of the house that evening.

She then called Slipslop up, and, after refreshing her spirits with a small cordial, which she kept in her corset, she began in the following manner:—

"Slipslop, why will you, who know my passionate temper, attempt to provoke me by your answers? I am convinced you are an honest servant, and should be very unwilling to part with you. I believe, likewise, you have found me an indulgent mistress on many occasions, and have as little reason on your side to desire a change. I can't help being surprized, therefore, that you will take the surest method to offend me—I mean, repeating my words, which you know I have always detested."

The prudent waiting-gentlewoman had duly weighed the whole matter, and found, on mature deliberation, that a good place in possession was better than one in expectation. As she found her mistress, therefore, inclined to relent, she thought proper also to put on some small condescension, which was as readily accepted; and so the affair was reconciled, all offences forgiven, and a present of a gown and petticoat made her, as an instance of her lady's future favour.

She offered once or twice to speak in favour of Joseph; but found her lady's heart so obdurate, that she prudently dropt all such efforts. She considered there were more footmen in the house, and some as stout fellows, though not quite so handsome, as Joseph; besides, the reader hath already seen her tender advances had not met with the encouragement she might have reasonable expected. She thought she had thrown away a great deal of sack and sweetmeats on an ungrateful rascal; and, being a little inclined to the opinion of that female sect, who hold one lusty young fellow to be nearly as good as another lusty young fellow, she at last gave up Joseph and his cause, and, with a triumph over her passion highly commendable, walked off with her present, and with great tranquillity paid a visit to a stone-bottle, which is of sovereign use to a philosophical temper.

She left not her mistress so easy. The poor lady could not reflect without agony that her dear reputation was in the power of her servants. All her comfort as to Joseph was, that she hoped he did not understand her meaning; at least she could say for herself, she had not plainly expressed anything to him; and as to Mrs Slipslop, she imagines she could bribe her to secrecy.

But what hurt her most was, that in reality she had not so entirely conquered her passion; the little god lay lurking in her heart, though anger and distain so hood-winked her, that she could not see him. She was a thousand times on the very brink of revoking the sentence she had passed against the poor youth. Love became his advocate, and whispered many things in his favour. Honour likewise endeavoured to vindicate his crime, and Pity to mitigate his punishment. On the other side, Pride and Revenge spoke as loudly against him. And thus the poor lady was tortured with perplexity, opposite passions distracting and tearing her mind different ways.

So have I seen, in the hall of Westminster, where Serjeant Bramble hath been retained on the right side, and Serjeant Puzzle on the left, the balance of opinion (so equal were their fees) alternately incline to either scale. Now Bramble throws in an argument, and Puzzle's scale strikes the beam; again Bramble shares the like fate, overpowered by the weight of Puzzle. Here Bramble hits, there Puzzle strikes; here one has you, there t'other has you; till at last all becomes one scene of confusion in the tortured minds of the hearers; equal wagers are laid on the success, and neither judge nor jury can possibly make anything of the matter; all things are so enveloped by the careful serjeants in doubt and obscurity.

Or, as it happens in the conscience, where honour and honesty pull one way, and a bribe and necessity another.—If it was our present business only to make similes, we could produce many more to this purpose; but a simile (as well as a word) to the wise.—We shall therefore see a little after our hero, for whom the reader is doubtless in some pain.

CHAPTER X.

Joseph writes another letter: his transactions with Mr Peter Pounce, &c., with his departure from Lady Booby.

The disconsolate Joseph would not have had an understanding sufficient for the principal subject of such a book as this, if he had any longer misunderstood the drift of his mistress; and indeed, that he did not discern it sooner, the reader will be pleased to impute to an unwillingness in him to discover what he must condemn in her as a fault. Having therefore quitted her presence, he retired into his own garret, and entered himself into an ejaculation on the numberless calamities which attended beauty, and the misfortune it was to be handsomer than one's neighbours.

He then sat down, and addressed himself to his sister Pamela in the following words:—

"Dear Sister Pamela,—Hoping you are well, what news have I to tell you! O Pamela! my mistress is fallen in love with me-that is, what great folks call falling in love-she has a mind to ruin me; but I hope I shall have more resolution and more grace than to part with my virtue to any lady upon earth.

"Mr Adams hath often told me, that chastity is as great a virtue in a man as in a woman. He says he never knew any more than his wife, and I shall endeavour to follow his example. Indeed, it is owing entirely to his excellent sermons and advice, together with your letters, that I have been able to resist a temptation, which, he says, no man complies with, but he repents in this world, or is damned for it in the next; and why should I trust to repentance on my deathbed, since I may die in my sleep? What fine things are good advice and good examples! But I am glad she turned me out of the chamber as she did: for I had once almost forgotten every word parson Adams had ever said to me.

"I don't doubt, dear sister, but you will have grace to preserve your virtue against all trials; and I beg you earnestly to pray I may be enabled to preserve mine; for truly it is very severely attacked by more than one; but I hope I shall copy your example, and that of Joseph my namesake, and maintain my virtue against all temptations."

Joseph had not finished his letter, when he was summoned downstairs by Mr Peter Pounce, to receive his wages; for, besides that out of eight pounds a year he allowed his father and mother four, he had been obliged, in order to furnish himself with musical instruments, to apply to the generosity of the aforesaid Peter, who, on urgent occasions, used to advance the servants their wages: not before they were due, but before they were payable; that is, perhaps, half a year after they were due; and this at the moderate premium of fifty per cent, or a little more: by which charitable methods, together with lending money to other people, and even to his own master and mistress, the honest man had, from nothing, in a few years amassed a small sum of twenty thousand pounds or thereabouts.

Joseph having received his little remainder of wages, and having stript off his livery, was forced to borrow a frock and breeches of one of the servants (for he was so beloved in the family, that they would all have lent him anything): and, being told by Peter that he must not stay a moment longer in the house than was necessary to pack up his linen, which he easily did in a very narrow compass, he took a melancholy leave of his fellow-servants, and set out at seven in the evening.

He had proceeded the length of two or three streets, before he absolutely determined with himself whether he should leave the town that night, or, procuring a lodging, wait till the morning. At last, the moon shining very bright helped him to come to a resolution of beginning his journey immediately, to which likewise he had some other inducements; which the reader, without being a conjurer, cannot possibly guess, till we have given him those hints which it may be now proper to open.

CHAPTER XI.

Of several new matters not expected.

It is an observation sometimes made, that to indicate our idea of a simple fellow, we say, he is easily to be seen through: nor do I believe it a more improper denotation of a simple book. Instead of applying this to any particular performance, we chuse rather to remark the contrary in this history, where the scene opens itself by small degrees; and he is a sagacious reader who can see two chapters before him.

For this reason, we have not hitherto hinted a matter which now seems necessary to be explained; since it may be wondered at, first, that Joseph made such extraordinary haste out of town, which hath been already shewn; and secondly, which will be now shewn, that, instead of proceeding to the habitation of his father and mother, or to his beloved sister Pamela, he chose rather to set out full speed to the Lady Booby's country-seat, which he had left on his journey to London.

Be it known, then, that in the same parish where this seat stood there lived a young girl whom Joseph (though the best of sons and brothers) longed more impatiently to see than his parents or his sister. She was a poor girl, who had formerly been bred up in Sir John's family; whence, a little before the journey to London, she had been discarded by Mrs Slipslop, on account of her extraordinary beauty: for I never could find any other reason.

This young creature (who now lived with a farmer in the parish) had been always beloved by Joseph, and returned his affection. She was two years only younger than our hero. They had been acquainted from their infancy, and had conceived a very early liking for each other; which had grown to such a degree of affection, that Mr Adams had with much ado prevented them from marrying, and persuaded them to wait till a few years' service and thrift had a little improved their experience, and enabled them to live comfortably together.

They followed this good man's advice, as indeed his word was little less than a law in his parish; for as he had shown his parishioners, by an uniform behaviour of thirty-five years' duration, that he had their good entirely at heart, so they consulted him on every occasion, and very seldom acted contrary to his opinion.

Nothing can be imagined more tender than was the parting between these two lovers. A thousand sighs heaved the bosom of Joseph, a thousand tears distilled from the lovely eyes of Fanny (for that was her name). Though her modesty would only suffer her to admit his eager kisses, her violent love made her more than passive in his embraces; and she often pulled him to her breast with a soft pressure, which though perhaps it would not have squeezed an insect to death, caused more emotion in the heart of Joseph than the closest Cornish hug could have done.

The reader may perhaps wonder that so fond a pair should, during a twelve-month's absence, never converse with one another: indeed, there was but one reason which did or could have prevented them; and this was, that poor Fanny could neither write nor read: nor could she be prevailed upon to transmit the delicacies of her tender and chaste passion by the hands of an amanuensis.

They contented themselves therefore with frequent inquiries after each other's health, with a mutual confidence in each other's fidelity, and the prospect of their future happiness.

Having explained these matters to our reader, and, as far as possible, satisfied all his doubts, we return to honest Joseph, whom we left just set out on his travels by the light of the moon.

Those who have read any romance or poetry, antient or modern, must have been informed that love hath wings: by which they are not to understand, as some young ladies by mistake have done, that a lover can fly; the writers, by this ingenious allegory, intending to insinuate no more than that lovers do not march like horse-guards; in short, that they put the best leg foremost; which our lusty youth, who could walk with any man, did so heartily on this occasion, that within four hours he reached a famous house of hospitality well known to the western traveller. It presents you a lion on the sign-post: and the master, who was christened Timotheus, is commonly called plain Tim. Some have conceived that he hath particularly chosen the lion for his sign, as he doth in countenance greatly resemble that magnanimous beast, though his disposition savours more of the sweetness of the lamb. He is a person well received among all sorts of men, being qualified to render himself agreeable to any; as he is well versed in history and politics, hath a smattering in law and divinity, cracks a good jest, and plays wonderfully well on the French horn.

A violent storm of hail forced Joseph to take shelter in this inn, where he remembered Sir Thomas had dined in his way to town. Joseph had no sooner seated himself by the kitchen fire than Timotheus, observing his livery, began to condole the loss of his late master; who was, he said, his very particular and intimate acquaintance, with whom he had cracked many a merry bottle, ay many a dozen, in his time. He then remarked, that all these things were over now, all passed, and just as if they had never been; and concluded with an excellent observation on the certainty of death, which his wife said was indeed very true. A fellow now arrived at the same inn with two horses, one of which he was leading farther down into the country to meet his master; these he put into the stable, and came and took his place by Joseph's side, who immediately knew him to be the servant of a neighbouring gentleman, who used to visit at their house.

This fellow was likewise forced in by the storm; for he had orders to go twenty miles farther that evening, and luckily on the same road which Joseph himself intended to take. He, therefore, embraced this opportunity of complimenting his friend with his master's horse (notwithstanding he had received express commands to the contrary), which was readily accepted; and so, after they had drank a loving pot, and the storm was over, they set out together.

CHAPTER XII.

Containing many surprizing adventures which Joseph Andrews met with on the road, scarce credible to those who have never travelled in a stage-coach.

Nothing remarkable happened on the road till their arrival at the inn to which the horses were ordered; whither they came about two in the morning. The moon then shone very bright; and Joseph, making his friend a present of a pint of wine, and thanking him for the favour of his horse, notwithstanding all entreaties to the contrary, proceeded on his journey on foot.

He had not gone above two miles, charmed with the hope of shortly seeing his beloved Fanny, when he was met by two fellows in a narrow lane, and ordered to stand and deliver. He readily gave them all the money he had, which was somewhat less than two pounds; and told them he hoped they would be so generous as to return him a few shillings, to defray his charges on his way home.

One of the ruffians answered with an oath, "Yes, we'll give you something presently: but first strip and be d—n'd to you."—"Strip," cried the other, "or I'll blow your brains to the devil." Joseph, remembering that he had borrowed his coat and breeches of a friend, and that he should be ashamed of making any excuse for not returning them, replied, he hoped they would not insist on his clothes, which were not worth much, but consider the coldness of the night. "You are cold, are you, you rascal?" said one of the robbers: "I'll warm you with a vengeance;" and, damning his eyes, snapped a pistol at his head; which he had no sooner done than the other levelled a blow at him with his stick, which Joseph, who was expert at cudgel-playing, caught with his, and returned the favour so successfully on his adversary, that he laid him sprawling at his feet, and at the same instant received a blow from behind, with the butt end of a pistol, from the other villain, which felled him to the ground, and totally deprived him of his senses.

The thief who had been knocked down had now recovered himself; and both together fell to belabouring poor Joseph with their sticks, till they were convinced they had put an end to his miserable being: they then stripped him entirely naked, threw him into a ditch, and departed with their booty.

The poor wretch, who lay motionless a long time, just began to recover his senses as a stage-coach came by. The postillion, hearing a man's groans, stopt his horses, and told the coachman he was certain there was a dead man lying in the ditch, for he heard him groan. "Go on, sirrah," says the coachman; "we are confounded late, and have no time to look after dead men." A lady, who heard what the postillion said, and likewise heard the groan, called eagerly to the coachman to stop and see what was the matter. Upon which he bid the postillion alight, and look into the ditch. He did so, and returned, "that there was a man sitting upright, as naked as ever he was born."—"O J—sus!" cried the lady; "a naked man! Dear coachman, drive on and leave him." Upon this the gentlemen got out of the coach; and Joseph begged them to have mercy upon him: for that he had been robbed and almost beaten to death. "Robbed!" cries an old gentleman: "let us make all the haste imaginable, or we shall be robbed too." A young man who belonged to the law answered, "He wished they had passed by without taking any notice; but that now they might be proved to have been last in his company; if he should die they might be called to some account for his murder. He therefore thought it advisable to save the poor creature's life, for their own sakes, if possible; at least, if he died, to prevent the jury's finding that they fled for it. He was therefore of opinion to take the man into the coach, and carry him to the next inn." The lady insisted, "That he should not come into the coach. That if they lifted him in, she would herself alight: for she had rather stay in that place to all eternity than ride with a naked man." The coachman objected, "That he could not suffer him to be taken in unless somebody would pay a shilling for his carriage the four miles." Which the two gentlemen refused to do. But the lawyer, who was afraid of some mischief happening to himself, if the wretch was left behind in that condition, saying no man could be too cautious in these matters, and that he remembered very extraordinary cases in the books, threatened the coachman, and bid him deny taking him up at his peril; for that, if he died, he should be indicted for his murder; and if he lived, and brought an action against him, he would willingly take a brief in it. These words had a sensible effect on the coachman, who was well acquainted with the person who spoke them; and the old gentleman above mentioned, thinking the naked man would afford him frequent opportunities of showing his wit to the lady, offered to join with the company in giving a mug of beer for his fare; till, partly alarmed by the threats of the one, and partly by the promises of the other, and being perhaps a little moved with compassion at the poor creature's condition, who stood bleeding and shivering with the cold, he at length agreed; and Joseph was now advancing to the coach, where, seeing the lady, who held the sticks of her fan before her eyes, he absolutely refused, miserable as he was, to enter, unless he was furnished with sufficient covering to prevent giving the least offence to decency—so perfectly modest was this young man; such mighty effects had the spotless example of the amiable Pamela, and the excellent sermons of Mr Adams, wrought upon him.

Though there were several greatcoats about the coach, it was not easy to get over this difficulty which Joseph had started. The two gentlemen complained they were cold, and could not spare a rag; the man of wit saying, with a laugh, that charity began at home; and the coachman, who had two greatcoats spread under him, refused to lend either, lest they should be made bloody: the lady's footman desired to be excused for the same reason, which the lady herself, notwithstanding her abhorrence of a naked man, approved: and it is more than probable poor Joseph, who obstinately adhered to his modest resolution, must have perished, unless the postillion (a lad who hath been since transported for robbing a hen-roost) had voluntarily stript off a greatcoat, his only garment, at the same time swearing a great oath (for which he was rebuked by the passengers), "that he would rather ride in his shirt all his life than suffer a fellow-creature to lie in so miserable a condition."

Joseph, having put on the greatcoat, was lifted into the coach, which now proceeded on its journey. He declared himself almost dead with the cold, which gave the man of wit an occasion to ask the lady if she could not accommodate him with a dram. She answered, with some resentment, "She wondered at his asking her such a question; but assured him she never tasted any such thing."

The lawyer was inquiring into the circumstances of the robbery, when the coach stopt, and one of the ruffians, putting a pistol in, demanded their money of the passengers, who readily gave it them; and the lady, in her fright, delivered up a little silver bottle, of about a half-pint size, which the rogue, clapping it to his mouth, and drinking her health, declared, held some of the best Nantes he had ever tasted: this the lady afterwards assured the company was the mistake of her maid, for that she had ordered her to fill the bottle with Hungary-water.

As soon as the fellows were departed, the lawyer, who had, it seems, a case of pistols in the seat of the coach, informed the company, that if it had been daylight, and he could have come at his pistols, he would not have submitted to the robbery: he likewise set forth that he had often met highwaymen when he travelled on horseback, but none ever durst attack him; concluding that, if he had not been more afraid for the lady than for himself, he should not have now parted with his money so easily.

As wit is generally observed to love to reside in empty pockets, so the gentleman whose ingenuity we have above remarked, as soon as he had parted with his money, began to grow wonderfully facetious. He made frequent allusions to Adam and Eve, and said many excellent things on figs and fig-leaves; which perhaps gave more offence to Joseph than to any other in the company.

The lawyer likewise made several very pretty jests without departing from his profession. He said, "If Joseph and the lady were alone, he would be more capable of making a conveyance to her, as his affairs were not fettered with any incumbrance; he'd warrant he soon suffered a recovery by a writ of entry, which was the proper way to create heirs in tail; that, for his own part, he would engage to make so firm a settlement in a coach, that there should be no danger of an ejectment," with an inundation of the like gibberish, which he continued to vent till the coach arrived at an inn, where one servant-maid only was up, in readiness to attend the coachman, and furnish him with cold meat and a dram. Joseph desired to alight, and that he might have a bed prepared for him, which the maid readily promised to perform; and, being a good-natured wench, and not so squeamish as the lady had been, she clapt a large fagot on the fire, and, furnishing Joseph with a greatcoat belonging to one of the hostlers, desired him to sit down and warm himself whilst she made his bed. The coachman, in the meantime, took an opportunity to call up a surgeon, who lived within a few doors; after which, he reminded his passengers how late they were, and, after they had taken leave of Joseph, hurried them off as fast as he could.

The wench soon got Joseph to bed, and promised to use her interest to borrow him a shirt; but imagining, as she afterwards said, by his being so bloody, that he must be a dead man, she ran with all speed to hasten the surgeon, who was more than half drest, apprehending that the coach had been overturned, and some gentleman or lady hurt. As soon as the wench had informed him at his window that it was a poor foot-passenger who had been stripped of all he had, and almost murdered, he chid her for disturbing him so early, slipped off his clothes again, and very quietly returned to bed and to sleep.

Aurora now began to shew her blooming cheeks over the hills, whilst ten millions of feathered songsters, in jocund chorus, repeated odes a thousand times sweeter than those of our laureat, and sung both the day and the song; when the master of the inn, Mr Tow-wouse, arose, and learning from his maid an account of the robbery, and the situation of his poor naked guest, he shook his head, and cried, "good-lack-a-day!" and then ordered the girl to carry him one of his own shirts.

Mrs Tow-wouse was just awake, and had stretched out her arms in vain to fold her departed husband, when the maid entered the room. "Who's there? Betty?"—"Yes, madam."—"Where's your master?"—"He's without, madam; he hath sent me for a shirt to lend a poor naked man, who hath been robbed and murdered."—"Touch one if you dare, you slut," said Mrs Tow-wouse: "your master is a pretty sort of a man, to take in naked vagabonds, and clothe them with his own clothes. I shall have no such doings. If you offer to touch anything, I'll throw the chamber-pot at your head. Go, send your master to me."—"Yes, madam," answered Betty. As soon as he came in, she thus began: "What the devil do you mean by this, Mr Tow-wouse? Am I to buy shirts to lend to a set of scabby rascals?"—"My dear," said Mr Tow-wouse, "this is a poor wretch."—"Yes," says she, "I know it is a poor wretch; but what the devil have we to do with poor wretches? The law makes us provide for too many already. We shall have thirty or forty poor wretches in red coats shortly."—"My dear," cries Tow-wouse, "this man hath been robbed of all he hath."—"Well then," said she, "where's his money to pay his reckoning? Why doth not such a fellow go to an alehouse? I shall send him packing as soon as I am up, I assure you."—"My dear," said he, "common charity won't suffer you to do that."—"Common charity, a f—t!" says she, "common charity teaches us to provide for ourselves and our families; and I and mine won't be ruined by your charity, I assure you."—"Well," says he, "my dear, do as you will, when you are up; you know I never contradict you."—"No," says she; "if the devil was to contradict me, I would make the house too hot to hold him."

With such like discourses they consumed near half-an-hour, whilst Betty provided a shirt from the hostler, who was one of her sweethearts, and put it on poor Joseph. The surgeon had likewise at last visited him, and washed and drest his wounds, and was now come to acquaint Mr Tow-wouse that his guest was in such extreme danger of his life, that he scarce saw any hopes of his recovery. "Here's a pretty kettle of fish," cries Mrs Tow-wouse, "you have brought upon us! We are like to have a funeral at our own expense." Tow-wouse (who, notwithstanding his charity, would have given his vote as freely as ever he did at an election, that any other house in the kingdom should have quiet possession of his guest) answered, "My dear, I am not to blame; he was brought hither by the stage-coach, and Betty had put him to bed before I was stirring."—"I'll Betty her," says she.—At which, with half her garments on, the other half under her arm, she sallied out in quest of the unfortunate Betty, whilst Tow-wouse and the surgeon went to pay a visit to poor Joseph, and inquire into the circumstances of this melancholy affair.

CHAPTER XIII.

What happened to Joseph during his sickness at the inn, with the curious discourse between him and Mr Barnabas, the parson of the parish.

As soon as Joseph had communicated a particular history of the robbery, together with a short account of himself, and his intended journey, he asked the surgeon if he apprehended him to be in any danger: to which the surgeon very honestly answered, "He feared he was; for that his pulse was very exalted and feverish, and, if his fever should prove more than symptomatic, it would be impossible to save him." Joseph, fetching a deep sigh, cried, "Poor Fanny, I would I could have lived to see thee! but God's will be done."

The surgeon then advised him, if he had any worldly affairs to settle, that he would do it as soon as possible; for, though he hoped he might recover, yet he thought himself obliged to acquaint him he was in great danger; and if the malign concoction of his humours should cause a suscitation of his fever, he might soon grow delirious and incapable to make his will. Joseph answered, "That it was impossible for any creature in the universe to be in a poorer condition than himself; for since the robbery he had not one thing of any kind whatever which he could call his own." "I had," said he, "a poor little piece of gold, which they took away, that would have been a comfort to me in all my afflictions; but surely, Fanny, I want nothing to remind me of thee. I have thy dear image in my heart, and no villain can ever tear it thence."

Joseph desired paper and pens, to write a letter, but they were refused him; and he was advised to use all his endeavours to compose himself. They then left him; and Mr Tow-wouse sent to a clergyman to come and administer his good offices to the soul of poor Joseph, since the surgeon despaired of making any successful applications to his body.

Mr Barnabas (for that was the clergyman's name) came as soon as sent for; and, having first drank a dish of tea with the landlady, and afterwards a bowl of punch with the landlord, he walked up to the room where Joseph lay; but, finding him asleep, returned to take the other sneaker; which when he had finished, he again crept softly up to the chamber-door, and, having opened it, heard the sick man talking to himself in the following manner:—

"O most adorable Pamela! most virtuous sister! whose example could alone enable me to withstand all the temptations of riches and beauty, and to preserve my virtue pure and chaste for the arms of my dear Fanny, if it had pleased Heaven that I should ever have come unto them. What riches, or honours, or pleasures, can make us amends for the loss of innocence? Doth not that alone afford us more consolation than all worldly acquisitions? What but innocence and virtue could give any comfort to such a miserable wretch as I am? Yet these can make me prefer this sick and painful bed to all the pleasures I should have found in my lady's. These can make me face death without fear; and though I love my Fanny more than ever man loved a woman, these can teach me to resign myself to the Divine will without repining. O thou delightful charming creature! if Heaven had indulged thee to my arms, the poorest, humblest state would have been a paradise; I could have lived with thee in the lowest cottage without envying the palaces, the dainties, or the riches of any man breathing. But I must leave thee, leave thee for ever, my dearest angel! I must think of another world; and I heartily pray thou may'st meet comfort in this."—Barnabas thought he had heard enough, so downstairs he went, and told Tow-wouse he could do his guest no service; for that he was very light-headed, and had uttered nothing but a rhapsody of nonsense all the time he stayed in the room.

The surgeon returned in the afternoon, and found his patient in a higher fever, as he said, than when he left him, though not delirious; for, notwithstanding Mr Barnabas's opinion, he had not been once out of his senses since his arrival at the inn.

Mr Barnabas was again sent for, and with much difficulty prevailed on to make another visit. As soon as he entered the room he told Joseph "He was come to pray by him, and to prepare him for another world: in the first place, therefore, he hoped he had repented of all his sins." Joseph answered, "He hoped he had; but there was one thing which he knew not whether he should call a sin; if it was, he feared he should die in the commission of it; and that was, the regret of parting with a young woman whom he loved as tenderly as he did his heart-strings." Barnabas bad him be assured "that any repining at the Divine will was one of the greatest sins he could commit; that he ought to forget all carnal affections, and think of better things." Joseph said, "That neither in this world nor the next he could forget his Fanny; and that the thought, however grievous, of parting from her for ever, was not half so tormenting as the fear of what she would suffer when she knew his misfortune." Barnabas said, "That such fears argued a diffidence and despondence very criminal; that he must divest himself of all human passions, and fix his heart above." Joseph answered, "That was what he desired to do, and should be obliged to him if he would enable him to accomplish it." Barnabas replied, "That must be done by grace." Joseph besought him to discover how he might attain it. Barnabas answered, "By prayer and faith." He then questioned him concerning his forgiveness of the thieves. Joseph answered, "He feared that was more than he could do; for nothing would give him more pleasure than to hear they were taken."—"That," cries Barnabas, "is for the sake of justice."—"Yes," said Joseph, "but if I was to meet them again, I am afraid I should attack them, and kill them too, if I could."—"Doubtless," answered Barnabas, "it is lawful to kill a thief; but can you say you forgive them as a Christian ought?" Joseph desired to know what that forgiveness was. "That is," answered Barnabas, "to forgive them as—as—it is to forgive them as—in short, it is to forgive them as a Christian."—Joseph replied, "He forgave them as much as he could."—"Well, well," said Barnabas, "that will do." He then demanded of him, "If he remembered any more sins unrepented of; and if he did, he desired him to make haste and repent of them as fast as he could, that they might repeat over a few prayers together." Joseph answered, "He could not recollect any great crimes he had been guilty of, and that those he had committed he was sincerely sorry for." Barnabas said that was enough, and then proceeded to prayer with all the expedition he was master of, some company then waiting for him below in the parlour, where the ingredients for punch were all in readiness; but no one would squeeze the oranges till he came.

Joseph complained he was dry, and desired a little tea; which Barnabas reported to Mrs Tow-wouse, who answered, "She had just done drinking it, and could not be slopping all day;" but ordered Betty to carry him up some small beer.

Betty obeyed her mistress's commands; but Joseph, as soon as he had tasted it, said, he feared it would increase his fever, and that he longed very much for tea; to which the good-natured Betty answered, he should have tea, if there was any in the land; she accordingly went and bought him some herself, and attended him with it; where we will leave her and Joseph together for some time, to entertain the reader with other matters.

CHAPTER XIV.

Being very full of adventures which succeeded each other at the inn.

It was now the dusk of the evening, when a grave person rode into the inn, and, committing his horse to the hostler, went directly into the kitchen, and, having called for a pipe of tobacco, took his place by the fireside, where several other persons were likewise assembled.

The discourse ran altogether on the robbery which was committed the night before, and on the poor wretch who lay above in the dreadful condition in which we have already seen him. Mrs Tow-wouse said, "She wondered what the devil Tom Whipwell meant by bringing such guests to her house, when there were so many alehouses on the road proper for their reception. But she assured him, if he died, the parish should be at the expense of the funeral." She added, "Nothing would serve the fellow's turn but tea, she would assure him." Betty, who was just returned from her charitable office, answered, she believed he was a gentleman, for she never saw a finer skin in her life. "Pox on his skin!" replied Mrs Tow-wouse, "I suppose that is all we are like to have for the reckoning. I desire no such gentlemen should ever call at the Dragon" (which it seems was the sign of the inn).

The gentleman lately arrived discovered a great deal of emotion at the distress of this poor creature, whom he observed to be fallen not into the most compassionate hands. And indeed, if Mrs Tow-wouse had given no utterance to the sweetness of her temper, nature had taken such pains in her countenance, that Hogarth himself never gave more expression to a picture.

Her person was short, thin, and crooked. Her forehead projected in the middle, and thence descended in a declivity to the top of her nose, which was sharp and red, and would have hung over her lips, had not nature turned up the end of it. Her lips were two bits of skin, which, whenever she spoke, she drew together in a purse. Her chin was peaked; and at the upper end of that skin which composed her cheeks, stood two bones, that almost hid a pair of small red eyes. Add to this a voice most wonderfully adapted to the sentiments it was to convey, being both loud and hoarse.

It is not easy to say whether the gentleman had conceived a greater dislike for his landlady or compassion for her unhappy guest. He inquired very earnestly of the surgeon, who was now come into the kitchen, whether he had any hopes of his recovery? He begged him to use all possible means towards it, telling him, "it was the duty of men of all professions to apply their skill gratis for the relief of the poor and necessitous." The surgeon answered, "He should take proper care; but he defied all the surgeons in London to do him any good."—"Pray, sir," said the gentleman, "what are his wounds?"—"Why, do you know anything of wounds?" says the surgeon (winking upon Mrs Tow-wouse).—"Sir, I have a small smattering in surgery," answered the gentleman.—"A smattering—ho, ho, ho!" said the surgeon; "I believe it is a smattering indeed."

The company were all attentive, expecting to hear the doctor, who was what they call a dry fellow, expose the gentleman.

He began therefore with an air of triumph: "I suppose, sir, you have travelled?"—"No, really, sir," said the gentleman.—"Ho! then you have practised in the hospitals perhaps?"—"No, sir."—"Hum! not that neither? Whence, sir, then, if I may be so bold to inquire, have you got your knowledge in surgery?"—"Sir," answered the gentleman, "I do not pretend to much; but the little I know I have from books."—"Books!" cries the doctor. "What, I suppose you have read Galen and Hippocrates!"—"No, sir," said the gentleman.—"How! you understand surgery," answers the doctor, "and not read Galen and Hippocrates?"—"Sir," cries the other, "I believe there are many surgeons who have never read these authors."—"I believe so too," says the doctor, "more shame for them; but, thanks to my education, I have them by heart, and very seldom go without them both in my pocket."—"They are pretty large books," said the gentleman.—"Aye," said the doctor, "I believe I know how large they are better than you." (At which he fell a winking, and the whole company burst into a laugh.)

The doctor pursuing his triumph, asked the gentleman, "If he did not understand physic as well as surgery." "Rather better," answered the gentleman.—"Aye, like enough," cries the doctor, with a wink. "Why, I know a little of physic too."—"I wish I knew half so much," said Tow-wouse, "I'd never wear an apron again."—"Why, I believe, landlord," cries the doctor, "there are few men, though I say it, within twelve miles of the place, that handle a fever better. *Veniente accurrite morbo*: that is my method. I suppose, brother, you understand *Latin*?"—"A little," says the gentleman.—"Aye, and Greek now, I'll warrant you: *Ton dapomibominos poluflosboio Thalasses*. But I have almost forgot these things: I could have repeated Homer by heart once."—"Ifags! the gentleman has caught a traytor," says Mrs Tow-wouse; at which they all fell a laughing.

The gentleman, who had not the least affection for joking, very contentedly suffered the doctor to enjoy his victory, which he did with no small satisfaction; and, having sufficiently sounded his depth, told him, "He was thoroughly convinced of his great learning and abilities; and that he would be obliged to him if he would let him know his opinion of his patient's case above-stairs."—"Sir," says the doctor, "his case is that of a dead man—the contusion on his head has perforated the internal membrane of the occiput, and divelicated that radical small minute invisible nerve which coheres to the pericranium; and this was attended with a fever at first symptomatic, then pneumatic; and he is at length grown deliriuus, or delirious, as the vulgar express it."

He was proceeding in this learned manner, when a mighty noise interrupted him. Some young fellows in the neighbourhood had taken one of the thieves, and were bringing him into the inn. Betty ran upstairs with this news to Joseph, who begged they might search for a little piece of broken gold, which had a ribband tied to it, and which he could swear to amongst all the hoards of the richest men in the universe.

Notwithstanding the fellow's persisting in his innocence, the mob were very busy in searching him, and presently, among other things, pulled out the piece of gold just mentioned; which Betty no sooner saw than she laid violent hands on it, and conveyed it up to Joseph, who received it with raptures of joy, and, hugging it in his bosom, declared he could now die contented.

Within a few minutes afterwards came in some other fellows, with a bundle which they had found in a ditch, and which was indeed the cloaths which had been stripped off from Joseph, and the other things they had taken from him.

The gentleman no sooner saw the coat than he declared he knew the livery; and, if it had been taken from the poor creature above-stairs, desired he might see him; for that he was very well acquainted with the family to whom that livery belonged.

He was accordingly conducted up by Betty; but what, reader, was the surprize on both sides, when he saw Joseph was the person in bed, and when Joseph discovered the face of his good friend Mr Abraham Adams!

It would be impertinent to insert a discourse which chiefly turned on the relation of matters already well known to the reader; for, as soon as the curate had satisfied Joseph concerning the perfect health of his Fanny, he was on his side very inquisitive into all the particulars which had produced this unfortunate accident.

To return therefore to the kitchen, where a great variety of company were now assembled from all the rooms of the house, as well as the neighbourhood: so much delight do men take in contemplating the countenance of a thief.

Mr Tow-wouse began to rub his hands with pleasure at seeing so large an assembly; who would, he hoped, shortly adjourn into several apartments, in order to discourse over the robbery, and drink a health to all honest men. But Mrs Tow-wouse, whose misfortune it was commonly to see things a little perversely, began to rail at those who brought the fellow into her house; telling her husband, "They were very likely to thrive who kept a house of entertainment for beggars and thieves."

The mob had now finished their search, and could find nothing about the captive likely to prove any evidence; for as to the cloaths, though the mob were very well satisfied with that proof, yet, as the surgeon observed, they could not convict him, because they were not found in his custody; to which Barnabas agreed, and added that these were *bona waviata*, and belonged to the lord of the manor.

"How," says the surgeon, "do you say these goods belong to the lord of the manor?"—"I do," cried Barnabas.—"Then I deny it," says the surgeon: "what can the lord of the manor have to do in the case? Will any one attempt to persuade me that what a man finds is not his own?"—"I have heard," says an old fellow in the corner, "justice Wise-one say, that, if every man had his right, whatever is found belongs to the king of London."—"That may be true," says Barnabas, "in some sense; for the law makes a difference between things stolen and things found; for a thing may be stolen that never is found, and a thing may be found that never was stolen: Now, goods that are both stolen and found are *waviata*; and they belong to the lord of the manor."—"So the lord of the manor is the receiver of stolen goods," says the doctor; at which there was an universal laugh, being first begun by himself.

While the prisoner, by persisting in his innocence, had almost (as there was no evidence against him) brought over Barnabas, the surgeon, Tow-wouse, and several others to his side, Betty informed them that they had overlooked a little piece of gold, which she had carried up to the man in bed, and which he offered to swear to amongst a million, aye, amongst ten thousand. This immediately turned the scale against the prisoner, and every one now concluded him guilty. It was resolved, therefore, to keep him secured that night, and early in the morning to carry him before a justice.

CHAPTER XV.

Showing how Mrs Tow-wouse was a little mollified; and how officious Mr Barnabas and the surgeon were to prosecute the thief: with a dissertation accounting for their zeal, and that of many other persons not mentioned in this history.

Betty told her mistress she believed the man in bed was a greater man than they took him for; for, besides the extreme whiteness of his skin, and the softness of his hands, she observed a very great familiarity between the gentleman and him; and added, she was certain they were intimate acquaintance, if not relations.

This somewhat abated the severity of Mrs Tow-wouse's countenance. She said, "God forbid she should not discharge the duty of a Christian, since the poor gentleman was brought to her house. She had a natural antipathy to vagabonds; but could pity the misfortunes of a Christian as soon as another." Tow-wouse said, "If the traveller be a gentleman, though he hath no money about him now, we shall most likely be paid hereafter; so you may begin to score whenever you will." Mrs Tow-wouse answered, "Hold your simple tongue, and don't instruct me in my business. I am sure I am sorry for the gentleman's misfortune with all my heart; and I hope the villain who hath used him so barbarously will be hanged. Betty, go see what he wants. God forbid he should want anything in my house."

Barnabas and the surgeon went up to Joseph to satisfy themselves concerning the piece of gold; Joseph was with difficulty prevailed upon to show it them, but would by no entreaties be brought to deliver it out of his own possession. He however attested this to be the same which had been taken from him, and Betty was ready to swear to the finding it on the thief.

The only difficulty that remained was, how to produce this gold before the justice; for as to carrying Joseph himself, it seemed impossible; nor was there any great likelihood of obtaining it from him, for he had fastened it with a ribband to his arm, and solemnly vowed that nothing but irresistible force should ever separate them; in which resolution, Mr Adams, clenching a fist rather less than the knuckle of an ox, declared he would support him.

A dispute arose on this occasion concerning evidence not very necessary to be related here; after which the surgeon dressed Mr Joseph's head, still persisting in the imminent danger in which his patient lay, but concluding, with a very important look, "That he began to have some hopes; that he should send him a sanative soporiferous draught, and would see him in the morning." After which Barnabas and he departed, and left Mr Joseph and Mr Adams together.

Adams informed Joseph of the occasion of this journey which he was making to London, namely, to publish three volumes of sermons; being encouraged, as he said, by an advertisement lately set forth by the society of booksellers, who proposed to purchase any copies offered to them, at a price to be settled by two persons; but though he imagined he should get a considerable sum of money on this occasion, which his family were in urgent need of, he protested he would not leave Joseph in his present condition: finally, he told him, "He had nine shillings and threepence halfpenny in his pocket, which he was welcome to use as he pleased."

This goodness of parson Adams brought tears into Joseph's eyes; he declared, "He had now a second reason to desire life, that he might show his gratitude to such a friend." Adams bade him "be cheerful; for that he plainly saw the surgeon, besides his ignorance, desired to make a merit of curing him, though the wounds in his head, he perceived, were by no means dangerous; that he was convinced he had no fever, and doubted not but he would be able to travel in a day or two."

These words infused a spirit into Joseph; he said, "He found himself very sore from the bruises, but had no reason to think any of his bones injured, or that he had received any harm in his inside, unless that he felt something very odd in his stomach; but he knew not whether that might not arise from not having eaten one morsel for above twenty-four hours." Being then asked if he had any inclination to eat, he answered in the affirmative. Then parson Adams desired him to "name what he had the greatest fancy for; whether a poached egg, or chicken-broth." He answered, "He could eat both very well; but that he seemed to have the greatest appetite for a piece of boiled beef and cabbage."

Adams was pleased with so perfect a confirmation that he had not the least fever, but advised him to a lighter diet for that evening. He accordingly ate either a rabbit or a fowl, I never could with any tolerable certainty discover which; after this he was, by Mrs Tow-wouse's order, conveyed into a better bed and equipped with one of her husband's shirts.

In the morning early, Barnabas and the surgeon came to the inn, in order to see the thief conveyed before the justice. They had consumed the whole night in debating what measures they should take to produce the piece of gold in evidence against him; for they were both extremely zealous in the business, though neither of them were in the least interested in the prosecution; neither of them had ever received any private injury from the fellow, nor had either of them ever been suspected of loving the publick well enough to give them a sermon or a dose of physic for nothing.

To help our reader, therefore, as much as possible to account for this zeal, we must inform him that, as this parish was so unfortunate as to have no lawyer in it, there had been a constant contention between the two doctors, spiritual and physical, concerning their abilities in a science, in which, as neither of them professed it, they had equal pretensions to dispute each other's opinions. These disputes were carried on with great contempt on both sides, and had almost divided the parish; Mr Tow-wouse and one half of the neighbours inclining to the surgeon, and Mrs Tow-wouse with the other half to the parson. The surgeon drew his knowledge from those inestimable fountains, called The Attorney's Pocket Companion, and Mr Jacob's Law-Tables; Barnabas trusted entirely to Wood's Institutes. It happened on this occasion, as was pretty frequently the case, that these two learned men differed about the sufficiency of evidence; the doctor being of opinion that the maid's oath would convict the prisoner without producing the gold; the parson, *é contra, totis viribus.* To display their parts, therefore, before the justice and the parish, was the sole motive which we can discover to this zeal which both of them pretended to have for public justice.

O Vanity! how little is thy force acknowledged, or thy operations discerned! How wantonly dost thou deceive mankind under different disguises! Sometimes thou dost wear the face of pity, sometimes of generosity: nay, thou hast the assurance even to put on those glorious ornaments which belong only to heroic virtue. Thou odious, deformed monster! whom priests have railed at, philosophers despised, and poets ridiculed; is there a wretch so abandoned as to own thee for an acquaintance in public?—yet, how few will refuse to enjoy thee in private? nay, thou art the pursuit of most men through their lives. The greatest villainies are daily practised to please thee; nor is the meanest thief below, or the greatest hero above, thy notice. Thy embraces are often the sole aim and sole reward of the private robbery and the plundered province. It is to pamper up thee, thou harlot, that we attempt to withdraw from others what we do not want, or to withhold from them what they do. All our passions are thy slaves. Avarice itself is often no more than thy handmaid, and even Lust thy pimp. The bully Fear, like a coward, flies before thee, and Joy and Grief hide their heads in thy presence.

I know thou wilt think that whilst I abuse thee I court thee, and that thy love hath inspired me to write this sarcastical panegyric on thee; but thou art deceived: I value thee not of a farthing; nor will it give me any pain if thou shouldst prevail on the reader to censure this digression as arrant nonsense; for know, to thy confusion, that I have introduced thee for no other purpose than to lengthen out a short chapter, and so I return to my history.

CHAPTER XVI.

The escape of the thief. Mr Adams's disappointment. The arrival of two very extraordinary personages, and the introduction of parson Adams to parson Barnabas.

Barnabas and the surgeon, being returned, as we have said, to the inn, in order to convey the thief before the justice, were greatly concerned to find a small accident had happened, which somewhat disconcerted them; and this was no other than the thief's escape, who had modestly withdrawn himself by night, declining all ostentation, and not chusing, in imitation of some great men, to distinguish himself at the expense of being pointed at.

When the company had retired the evening before, the thief was detained in a room where the constable, and one of the young fellows who took him, were planted as his guard. About the second watch a general complaint of drought was made, both by the prisoner and his keepers. Among whom it was at last agreed that the constable should remain on duty, and the young fellow call up the tapster; in which disposition the latter apprehended not the least danger, as the constable was well armed, and could besides easily summon him back to his assistance, if the prisoner made the least attempt to gain his liberty.

The young fellow had not long left the room before it came into the constable's head that the prisoner might leap on him by surprize, and, thereby preventing him of the use of his weapons, especially the long staff in which he chiefly confided, might reduce the success of a struggle to a equal chance. He wisely, therefore, to prevent this inconvenience, slipt out of the room himself, and locked the door, waiting without with his staff in his hand, ready lifted to fell the unhappy prisoner, if by ill fortune he should attempt to break out.

But human life, as hath been discovered by some great man or other (for I would by no means be understood to affect the honour of making any such discovery), very much resembles a game at chess; for as in the latter, while a gamester is too attentive to secure himself very strongly on one side the board, he is apt to leave an unguarded opening on the other; so doth it often happen in life, and so did it happen on this occasion; for whilst the cautious constable with such wonderful sagacity had possessed himself of the door, he most unhappily forgot the window.

The thief, who played on the other side, no sooner perceived this opening than he began to move that way; and, finding the passage easy, he took with him the young fellow's hat, and without any ceremony stepped into the street and made the best of his way.

The young fellow, returning with a double mug of strong beer, was a little surprized to find the constable at the door; but much more so when, the door being opened, he perceived the prisoner had made his escape, and which way. He threw down the beer, and, without uttering anything to the constable except a hearty curse or two, he nimbly leapt out of the window, and went again in pursuit of his prey, being very unwilling to lose the reward which he had assured himself of.

The constable hath not been discharged of suspicion on this account; it hath been said that, not being concerned in the taking the thief, he could not have been entitled to any part of the reward if he had been convicted; that the thief had several guineas in his pocket; that it was very unlikely he should have been guilty of such an oversight; that his pretence for leaving the room was absurd; that it was his constant maxim, that a wise man never refused money on any conditions; that at every election he always had sold his vote to both parties, &c.

But, notwithstanding these and many other such allegations, I am sufficiently convinced of his innocence; having been positively assured of it by those who received their informations from his own mouth; which, in the opinion of some moderns, is the best and indeed only evidence.

All the family were now up, and with many others assembled in the kitchen, where Mr Tow-wouse was in some tribulation; the surgeon having declared that by law he was liable to be indicted for the thief's escape, as it was out of his house; he was a little comforted, however, by Mr Barnabas's opinion, that as the escape was by night the indictment would not lie.

Mrs Tow-wouse delivered herself in the following words: "Sure never was such a fool as my husband; would any other person living have left a man in the custody of such a drunken drowsy blockhead as Tom Suckbribe?" (which was the constable's name); "and if he could be indicted without any harm to his wife and children, I should be glad of it." (Then the bell rung in Joseph's room.) "Why Betty, John, Chamberlain, where the devil are you all? Have you no ears, or no conscience, not to tend the sick better? See what the gentleman wants. Why don't you go yourself, Mr Tow-wouse? But any one may die for you; you have no more feeling than a deal board. If a man lived a fortnight in your house without spending a penny, you would never put him in mind of it. See whether he drinks tea or coffee for breakfast." "Yes, my dear," cried Tow-wouse. She then asked the doctor and Mr Barnabas what morning's draught they chose, who answered, they had a pot of cyder-and at the fire; which we will leave them merry over, and return to Joseph.

He had rose pretty early this morning; but, though his wounds were far from threatening any danger, he was so sore with the bruises, that it was impossible for him to think of undertaking a journey yet; Mr Adams, therefore, whose stock was visibly decreased with the expenses of supper and breakfast, and which could not survive that day's scoring, began to consider how it was possible to recruit it. At last he cried, "He had luckily hit on a sure method, and, though it would oblige him to return himself home together with Joseph, it mattered not much." He then sent for Tow-wouse, and, taking him into another room, told him "he wanted to borrow three guineas, for which he would put ample security into his hands." Tow-wouse, who expected a watch, or ring, or something of double the value, answered, "He believed he could furnish him." Upon which Adams, pointing to his saddle-bag, told him, with a face and voice full of solemnity, "that there were in that bag no less than nine volumes of manuscript sermons, as well worth a hundred pounds as a shilling was worth twelve pence, and that he would deposit one of the volumes in his hands by way of pledge; not doubting but that he would have the honesty to return it on his repayment of the money; for otherwise he must be a very great loser, seeing that every volume would at least bring him ten pounds, as he had been informed by a neighbouring clergyman in the country; for," said he, "as to my own part, having never yet dealt in printing, I do not pretend to ascertain the exact value of such things."

Tow-wouse, who was a little surprized at the pawn, said (and not without some truth), "That he was no judge of the price of such kind of goods; and as for money, he really was very short." Adams answered, "Certainly he would not scruple to lend him three guineas on what was undoubtedly worth at least ten." The landlord replied, "He did not believe he had so much money in the house, and besides, he was to make up a sum. He was very confident the books were of much higher value, and heartily sorry it did not suit him." He then cried out, "Coming sir!" though nobody called; and ran downstairs without any fear of breaking his neck.

Poor Adams was extremely dejected at this disappointment, nor knew he what further stratagem to try. He immediately applied to his pipe, his constant friend and comfort in his afflictions; and, leaning over the rails, he devoted himself to meditation, assisted by the inspiring fumes of tobacco.

He had on a nightcap drawn over his wig, and a short greatcoat, which half covered his cassock—a dress which, added to something comical enough in his countenance, composed a figure likely to attract the eyes of those who were not over given to observation.

Whilst he was smoaking his pipe in this posture, a coach and six, with a numerous attendance, drove into the inn. There alighted from the coach a young fellow and a brace of pointers, after which another young fellow leapt from the box, and shook the former by the hand; and both, together with the dogs, were instantly conducted by Mr Tow-wouse into an apartment; whither as they passed, they entertained themselves with the following short facetious dialogue:—

"You are a pretty fellow for a coachman, Jack!" says he from the coach; "you had almost overturned us just now."—"Pox take you!" says the coachman; "if I had only broke your neck, it would have been saving somebody else the trouble; but I should have been sorry for the pointers."—"Why, you son of a b—," answered the other, "if nobody could shoot better than you, the pointers would be of no use."—"D—n me," says the coachman, "I will shoot with you five guineas a shot."—"You be hanged," says the other; "for five guineas you shall shoot at my a—."—"Done," says the coachman; "I'll pepper you better than ever you was peppered by Jenny Bouncer."—"Pepper your grandmother," says the other: "Here's Tow-wouse will let you shoot at him for a shilling a time."—"I know his honour better," cries Tow-wouse; "I never saw a surer shot at a partridge. Every man misses now and then; but if I could shoot half as well as his honour, I would desire no better livelihood than I could get by my gun."—"Pox on you," said the coachman, "you demolish more game now than your head's worth. There's a bitch, Tow-wouse: by G— she never blinked [1] a bird in her life."—"I have a puppy, not a year old, shall hunt with her for a hundred," cries the other gentleman.—"Done," says the coachman: "but you will be pox'd before you make the bett."—"If you have a mind for a bett," cries the coachman, "I will match my spotted dog with your white bitch for a hundred, play or pay."—"Done," says the other: "and I'll run Baldface against Slouch with you for another."—"No," cries he from the box; "but I'll venture Miss Jenny against Baldface, or Hannibal either."—"Go to the devil," cries he from the coach: "I will make every bett your own way, to be sure! I will match Hannibal with Slouch for a thousand, if you dare; and I say done first."

They were now arrived; and the reader will be very contented to leave them, and repair to the kitchen; where Barnabas, the surgeon, and an exciseman were smoaking their pipes over some cyder-and; and where the servants, who attended the two noble gentlemen we have just seen alight, were now arrived.

"Tom," cries one of the footmen, "there's parson Adams smoaking his pipe in the gallery."—"Yes," says Tom; "I pulled off my hat to him, and the parson spoke to me."

"Is the gentleman a clergyman, then?" says Barnabas (for his cassock had been tied up when he arrived). "Yes, sir," answered the footman; "and one there be but few like."—"Aye," said Barnabas; "if I had known it sooner, I should have desired his company; I would always shew a proper respect for the cloth: but what say you, doctor, shall we adjourn into a room, and invite him to take part of a bowl of punch?"

This proposal was immediately agreed to and executed; and parson Adams accepting the invitation, much civility passed between the two clergymen, who both declared the great honour they had for the cloth. They had not been long together before they entered into a discourse on small tithes, which continued a full hour, without the doctor or exciseman's having one opportunity to offer a word.

It was then proposed to begin a general conversation, and the exciseman opened on foreign affairs; but a word unluckily dropping from one of them introduced a dissertation on the hardships suffered by the inferior clergy; which, after a long duration, concluded with bringing the nine volumes of sermons on the carpet.

Barnabas greatly discouraged poor Adams; he said, "The age was so wicked, that nobody read sermons: would you think it, Mr Adams?" said he, "I once intended to print a volume of sermons myself, and they had the approbation of two

[1] To blink is a term used to signify the dog's passing by a bird without pointing at it.

or three bishops; but what do you think a bookseller offered me?"—"Twelve guineas perhaps," cried Adams.—"Not twelve pence, I assure you," answered Barnabas: "nay, the dog refused me a Concordance in exchange. At last I offered to give him the printing them, for the sake of dedicating them to that very gentleman who just now drove his own coach into the inn; and, I assure you, he had the impudence to refuse my offer; by which means I lost a good living, that was afterwards given away in exchange for a pointer, to one who—but I will not say anything against the cloth. So you may guess, Mr Adams, what you are to expect; for if sermons would have gone down, I believe—I will not be vain; but to be concise with you, three bishops said they were the best that ever were writ: but indeed there are a pretty moderate number printed already, and not all sold yet."—"Pray, sir," said Adams, "to what do you think the numbers may amount?"—"Sir," answered Barnabas, "a bookseller told me, he believed five thousand volumes at least."—"Five thousand?" quoth the surgeon: "What can they be writ upon? I remember when I was a boy, I used to read one Tillotson's sermons; and, I am sure, if a man practised half so much as is in one of those sermons, he will go to heaven."—"Doctor," cried Barnabas, "you have a prophane way of talking, for which I must reprove you. A man can never have his duty too frequently inculcated into him. And as for Tillotson, to be sure he was a good writer, and said things very well; but comparisons are odious; another man may write as well as he—I believe there are some of my sermons,"—and then he applied the candle to his pipe.—"And I believe there are some of my discourses," cries Adams, "which the bishops would not think totally unworthy of being printed; and I have been informed I might procure a very large sum (indeed an immense one) on them."—"I doubt that," answered Barnabas: "however, if you desire to make some money of them, perhaps you may sell them by advertising the manuscript sermons of a clergyman lately deceased, all warranted originals, and never printed. And now I think of it, I should be obliged to you, if there be ever a funeral one among them, to lend it me; for I am this very day to preach a funeral sermon, for which I have not penned a line, though I am to have a double price."—Adams answered, "He had but one, which he feared would not serve his purpose, being sacred to the memory of a magistrate, who had exerted himself very singularly in the preservation of the morality of his neighbours, insomuch that he had neither alehouse nor lewd woman in the parish where he lived."—"No," replied Barnabas, "that will not do quite so well; for the deceased, upon whose virtues I am to harangue, was a little too much addicted to liquor, and publickly kept a mistress.—I believe I must take a common sermon, and trust to my memory to introduce something handsome on him."—"To your invention rather," said the doctor: "your memory will be apter to put you out; for no man living remembers anything good of him."

With such kind of spiritual discourse, they emptied the bowl of punch, paid their reckoning, and separated: Adams and the doctor went up to Joseph, parson Barnabas departed to celebrate the aforesaid deceased, and the exciseman descended into the cellar to gauge the vessels.

Joseph was now ready to sit down to a loin of mutton, and waited for Mr Adams, when he and the doctor came in. The doctor, having felt his pulse and examined his wounds, declared him much better, which he imputed to that sanative soporiferous draught, a medicine "whose virtues," he said, "were never to be sufficiently extolled." And great indeed they must be, if Joseph was so much indebted to them as the doctor imagined; since nothing more than those effluvia which escaped the cork could have contributed to his recovery; for the medicine had stood untouched in the window ever since its arrival.

Joseph passed that day, and the three following, with his friend Adams, in which nothing so remarkable happened as the swift progress of his recovery. As he had an excellent habit of body, his wounds were now almost healed; and his bruises gave him so little uneasiness, that he pressed Mr Adams to let him depart; told him he should never be able to return sufficient thanks for all his favours, but begged that he might no longer delay his journey to London.

Adams, notwithstanding the ignorance, as he conceived it, of Mr Tow-wouse, and the envy (for such he thought it) of Mr Barnabas, had great expectations from his sermons: seeing therefore Joseph in so good a way, he told him he would agree to his setting out the next morning in the stage-coach, that he believed he should have sufficient, after the reckoning paid, to procure him one day's conveyance in it, and afterwards he would be able to get on on foot, or might be favoured with a lift in some neighbour's waggon, especially as there was then to be a fair in the town whither the coach would carry him, to which numbers from his parish resorted—And as to himself, he agreed to proceed to the great city.

They were now walking in the inn-yard, when a fat, fair, short person rode in, and, alighting from his horse, went directly up to Barnabas, who was smoaking his pipe on a bench. The parson and the stranger shook one another very lovingly by the hand, and went into a room together.

The evening now coming on, Joseph retired to his chamber, whither the good Adams accompanied him, and took this opportunity to expatiate on the great mercies God had lately shown him, of which he ought not only to have the deepest inward sense, but likewise to express outward thankfulness for them. They therefore fell both on their knees, and spent a considerable time in prayer and thanksgiving.

They had just finished when Betty came in and told Mr Adams Mr Barnabas desired to speak to him on some business of consequence below-stairs. Joseph desired, if it was likely to detain him long, he would let him know it, that he might go to bed, which Adams promised, and in that case they wished one another good-night.

CHAPTER XVII.

A pleasant discourse between the two parsons and the bookseller, 'which was broke off by an unlucky accident happening in the inn, which produced a dialogue between Mrs Tow-wouse and her maid of no gentle kind.

As soon as Adams came into the room, Mr Barnabas introduced him to the stranger, who was, he told him, a bookseller, and would be as likely to deal with him for his sermons as any man whatever. Adams, saluting the stranger, answered Barnabas, that he was very much obliged to him; that nothing could be more convenient, for he had no other business to the great city, and was heartily desirous of returning with the young man, who was just recovered of his misfortune. He then snapt his fingers (as was usual with him), and took two or three turns about the room in an extasy. And to induce the bookseller to be as expeditious as possible, as likewise to offer him a better price for his commodity, he assured them their meeting was extremely lucky to himself; for that he had the most pressing occasion for money at that time, his own being almost spent, and having a friend then in the same inn, who was just recovered from some wounds he had received from robbers, and was in a most indigent condition. "So that nothing," says he, "could be so opportune for the supplying both our necessities as my making an immediate bargain with you."

As soon as he had seated himself, the stranger began in these words: "Sir, I do not care absolutely to deny engaging in what my friend Mr Barnabas recommends; but sermons are mere drugs. The trade is so vastly stocked with them, that really, unless they come out with the name of Whitefield or Wesley, or some other such great man, as a bishop, or those sort of people, I don't care to touch; unless now it was a sermon preached on the 30th of January; or we could say in the title-page, published at the earnest request of the congregation, or the inhabitants; but, truly, for a dry piece of sermons, I had rather be excused; especially as my hands are so full at present. However, sir, as Mr Barnabas mentioned them to me, I will, if you please, take the manuscript with me to town, and send you my opinion of it in a very short time."

"Oh!" said Adams, "if you desire it, I will read two or three discourses as a specimen." This Barnabas, who loved sermons no better than a grocer doth figs, immediately objected to, and advised Adams to let the bookseller have his sermons: telling him, "If he gave him a direction, he might be certain of a speedy answer;" adding, he need not scruple trusting them in his possession. "No," said the bookseller, "if it was a play that had been acted twenty nights together, I believe it would be safe."

Adams did not at all relish the last expression; he said "he was sorry to hear sermons compared to plays." "Not by me, I assure you," cried the bookseller, "though I don't know whether the licensing act may not shortly bring them to the same footing; but I have formerly known a hundred guineas given for a play."—"More shame for those who gave it," cried Barnabas.—"Why so?" said the bookseller, "for they got hundreds by it."—"But is there no difference between conveying good or ill instructions to mankind?" said Adams: "Would not an honest mind rather lose money by the one, than gain it by the other?"—"If you can find any such, I will not be their hindrance," answered the bookseller; "but I think those persons who get by preaching sermons are the properest to lose by printing them: for my part, the copy that sells best will be always the best copy in my opinion; I am no enemy to sermons, but because they don't sell: for I would as soon print one of Whitefield's as any farce whatever."

"Whoever prints such heterodox stuff ought to be hanged," says Barnabas. "Sir," said he, turning to Adams, "this fellow's writings (I know not whether you have seen them) are levelled at the clergy. He would reduce us to the example of the primitive ages, forsooth! and would insinuate to the people that a clergyman ought to be always preaching and praying. He pretends to understand the Scripture literally; and would make mankind believe that the poverty and low estate which was recommended to the Church in its infancy, and was only temporary doctrine adapted to her under persecution, was to be preserved in her flourishing and established state. Sir, the principles of Toland, Woolston, and all the free-thinkers, are not calculated to do half the mischief, as those professed by this fellow and his followers."

"Sir," answered Adams, "if Mr Whitefield had carried his doctrine no farther than you mention, I should have remained, as I once was, his well-wisher. I am, myself, as great an enemy to the luxury and splendour of the clergy as he can be. I do not, more than he, by the flourishing estate of the Church, understand the palaces, equipages, dress, furniture, rich dainties, and vast fortunes, of her ministers. Surely those things, which savour so strongly of this world, become not the servants of one who professed His kingdom was not of it. But when he began to call nonsense and enthusiasm to his aid, and set up the detestable doctrine of faith against good works, I was his friend no longer; for surely that doctrine was coined in hell; and one would think none but the devil himself could have the confidence to preach it. For can anything be more derogatory to the honour of God than for men to imagine that the all-wise Being will hereafter say to the good and virtuous, 'Notwithstanding the purity of thy life, notwithstanding that constant rule of virtue and goodness in which you walked upon earth, still, as thou didst not believe everything in the true orthodox manner, thy want of faith shall condemn thee?' Or, on the other side, can any doctrine have a more pernicious influence on society, than a persuasion that it will be a good plea for the villain at the last day—'Lord, it is true I never obeyed one of thy commandments, yet punish me not, for I believe them all?'"—"I suppose, sir," said the bookseller, "your sermons are of a different kind."—"Aye, sir," said Adams; "the contrary, I thank Heaven, is inculcated in almost every page, or I should belye my own opinion, which hath always been, that a virtuous and good Turk, or heathen, are more acceptable in the sight of their Creator than a vicious and wicked Christian, though his faith was as perfectly orthodox as St Paul's himself."—"I wish you success," says the bookseller, "but must beg to be excused, as my hands are so very full at present; and, indeed, I am afraid you will find a backwardness in the trade to engage in a book which the clergy would be certain to cry down."—"God forbid," says Adams, "any books should be propagated which the clergy would cry down; but if you mean by the clergy, some few designing factious men, who have it at heart to establish some favourite schemes at the price of the liberty of mankind, and the very essence of religion, it is not in the power of such persons to decry any book they please; witness that excellent book called, 'A Plain Account of the Nature and End of the Sacrament;' a book written (if I may venture on the expression) with the pen of an angel, and calculated to restore the true use of Christianity, and of that sacred institution; for what could tend more to the noble purposes of religion than frequent chearful meetings among the members of a society, in which they should, in the presence of one another, and in the service of the Supreme Being, make promises of being good, friendly, and benevolent to each other? Now, this excellent book was attacked by a party, but unsuccessfully." At these words Barnabas fell a-ringing with all the violence imaginable; upon which a servant attending, he bid him "bring a bill immediately; for that he was in company, for aught he knew, with the devil himself; and he expected to hear the Alcoran, the Leviathan, or Woolston commended, if he staid a few minutes longer." Adams desired, "as he was so much moved at his mentioning a book which he did without apprehending any possibility of offence, that he would be so kind to propose any objections he had to it, which he would endeavour to answer."—"I propose objections!" said Barnabas, "I never read a syllable in any such wicked book; I never saw it in my life, I assure you."—Adams was going to answer, when a most hideous uproar began in the inn. Mrs Tow-wouse, Mr Tow-wouse, and Betty, all lifting up their voices together; but Mrs Tow-wouse's voice, like a bass viol in a concert, was clearly and distinctly distinguished among the rest, and was heard to articulate the following sounds:—"O you damn'd villain! is this the return to all the care I have taken of your family? This the reward of my virtue? Is this the manner in which you behave to one who brought you a fortune, and preferred you to so many matches, all your betters? To abuse my bed, my own bed, with my own servant! but I'll maul the slut, I'll tear her nasty eyes out! Was ever such a pitiful dog, to take up with such a mean trollop? If she had been a gentlewoman, like myself, it had been some excuse; but a beggarly, saucy, dirty servant-maid. Get you out of my house, you whore." To which she added another name, which we do not care to stain our paper with. It was a monosyllable beginning with a b—, and indeed was the same as if she had pronounced the words, she-dog. Which term we shall, to avoid offence, use on this occasion, though indeed both the mistress and maid uttered the above-mentioned b—, a word extremely disgustful to females of the lower sort. Betty had borne all hitherto with patience, and had uttered only lamentations; but the last appellation stung her to the quick. "I am a woman as well as yourself," she roared out, "and no she-dog; and if I have been a little naughty, I am not the first; if I have been no better than I should be," cries she, sobbing, "that's no reason you should call me out of my name; my be-betters are wo-rse than me."—"Huzzy, huzzy," says Mrs Tow-wouse, "have you the impudence to answer me? Did I not catch you, you saucy"—and then again repeated the terrible word so odious to female ears. "I can't bear that name," answered Betty: "if I have been wicked, I am to answer for it myself in the other world; but I have done nothing that's unnatural; and I will go out of your house this moment, for I will never be called she-dog by any mistress in England." Mrs Tow-wouse then armed herself with the spit, but was prevented from executing any dreadful purpose by Mr Adams, who confined her arms with the strength of a wrist which Hercules would not have been ashamed of. Mr Tow-wouse, being caught, as our lawyers express it, with the manner, and having no defence to make, very prudently withdrew himself; and Betty committed herself to the protection of the hostler, who, though she could not conceive him pleased with what had happened, was, in her opinion, rather a gentler beast than her mistress.

Mrs Tow-wouse, at the intercession of Mr Adams, and finding the enemy vanished, began to compose herself, and at length recovered the usual serenity of her temper, in which we will leave her, to open to the reader the steps which led to a catastrophe, common enough, and comical enough too perhaps, in modern history, yet often fatal to the repose and well-being of families, and the subject of many tragedies, both in life and on the stage.

CHAPTER XVIII.

The history of Betty the chambermaid, and an account of what occasioned the violent scene in the preceding chapter.

Betty, who was the occasion of all this hurry, had some good qualities. She had good-nature, generosity, and compassion, but unfortunately, her constitution was composed of those warm ingredients which, though the purity of courts or nunneries might have happily controuled them, were by no means able to endure the ticklish situation of a chambermaid at an inn; who is daily liable to the solicitations of lovers of all complexions; to the dangerous addresses of fine gentlemen of the army, who sometimes are obliged to reside with them a whole year together; and, above all, are exposed to the caresses of footmen, stage-coachmen, and drawers; all of whom employ the whole artillery of kissing, flattering, bribing, and every other weapon which is to be found in the whole armoury of love, against them.

Betty, who was but one-and-twenty, had now lived three years in this dangerous situation, during which she had escaped pretty well. An ensign of foot was the first person who made an impression on her heart; he did indeed raise a flame in her which required the care of a surgeon to cool.

While she burnt for him, several others burnt for her. Officers of the army, young gentlemen travelling the western circuit, inoffensive squires, and some of graver character, were set a-fire by her charms!

At length, having perfectly recovered the effects of her first unhappy passion, she seemed to have vowed a state of perpetual chastity. She was long deaf to all the sufferings of her lovers, till one day, at a neighbouring fair, the rhetoric of John the hostler, with a new straw hat and a pint of wine, made a second conquest over her.

She did not, however, feel any of those flames on this occasion which had been the consequence of her former amour; nor, indeed, those other ill effects which prudent young women very justly apprehend from too absolute an indulgence to the pressing endearments of their lovers. This latter, perhaps, was a little owing to her not being entirely constant to John, with whom she permitted Tom Whipwell the stage-coachman, and now and then a handsome young traveller, to share her favours.

Mr Tow-wouse had for some time cast the languishing eyes of affection on this young maiden. He had laid hold on every opportunity of saying tender things to her, squeezing her by the hand, and sometimes kissing her lips; for, as the violence of his passion had considerably abated to Mrs Tow-wouse, so, like water, which is stopt from its usual current in one place, it naturally sought a vent in another. Mrs Tow-wouse is thought to have perceived this abatement, and, probably, it added very little to the natural sweetness of her temper; for though she was as true to her husband as the dial to the sun, she was rather more desirous of being shone on, as being more capable of feeling his warmth.

Ever since Joseph's arrival, Betty had conceived an extraordinary liking to him, which discovered itself more and more as he grew better and better; till that fatal evening, when, as she was warming his bed, her passion grew to such a height, and so perfectly mastered both her modesty and her reason, that, after many fruitless hints and sly insinuations, she at last threw down the warming-pan, and, embracing him with great eagerness, swore he was the handsomest creature she had ever seen.

Joseph, in great confusion, leapt from her, and told her he was sorry to see a young woman cast off all regard to modesty; but she had gone too far to recede, and grew so very indecent, that Joseph was obliged, contrary to his inclination, to use some violence to her; and, taking her in his arms, he shut her out of the room, and locked the door.

How ought man to rejoice that his chastity is always in his own power; that, if he hath sufficient strength of mind, he hath always a competent strength of body to defend himself, and cannot, like a poor weak woman, be ravished against his will!

Betty was in the most violent agitation at this disappointment. Rage and lust pulled her heart, as with two strings, two different ways; one moment she thought of stabbing Joseph; the next, of taking him in her arms, and devouring him with kisses; but the latter passion was far more prevalent. Then she thought of revenging his refusal on herself; but, whilst she was engaged in this meditation, happily death presented himself to her in so many shapes, of drowning, hanging, poisoning, &c., that her distracted mind could resolve on none. In this perturbation of spirit, it accidentally occurred to her memory that her master's bed was not made; she therefore went directly to his room, where he happened at that time to be engaged at his bureau. As soon as she saw him, she attempted to retire; but he called her back, and, taking her by the hand, squeezed her so tenderly, at the same time whispering so many soft things into her ears, and then pressed her so closely with his kisses, that the vanquished fair one, whose passions were already raised, and which were not so whimsically capricious that one man only could lay them, though, perhaps, she would have rather preferred that one—the vanquished fair one quietly submitted, I say, to her master's will, who had just attained the accomplishment of his bliss when Mrs Tow-wouse unexpectedly entered the room, and caused all that confusion which we have before seen, and which it is not necessary, at present, to take any farther notice of; since, without the assistance of a single hint from us, every reader of any speculation or experience, though not married himself, may easily conjecture that it concluded with the discharge of

Betty, the submission of Mr Tow-wouse, with some things to be performed on his side by way of gratitude for his wife's goodness in being reconciled to him, with many hearty promises never to offend any more in the like manner; and, lastly, his quietly and contentedly bearing to be reminded of his transgressions, as a kind of penance, once or twice a day during the residue of his life.

BOOK II.

CHAPTER I.

Of Divisions in Authors.

There are certain mysteries or secrets in all trades, from the highest to the lowest, from that of prime-ministering to this of authoring, which are seldom discovered unless to members of the same calling. Among those used by us gentlemen of the latter occupation, I take this of dividing our works into books and chapters to be none of the least considerable. Now, for want of being truly acquainted with this secret, common readers imagine, that by this art of dividing we mean only to swell our works to a much larger bulk than they would otherwise be extended to. These several places therefore in our paper, which are filled with our books and chapters, are understood as so much buckram, stays, and stay-tape in a taylor's bill, serving only to make up the sum total, commonly found at the bottom of our first page and of his last.

But in reality the case is otherwise, and in this as well as all other instances we consult the advantage of our reader, not our own; and indeed, many notable uses arise to him from this method; for, first, those little spaces between our chapters may be looked upon as an inn or resting-place where he may stop and take a glass or any other refreshment as it pleases him. Nay, our fine readers will, perhaps, be scarce able to travel farther than through one of them in a day. As to those vacant pages which are placed between our books, they are to be regarded as those stages where in long journies the traveller stays some time to repose himself, and consider of what he hath seen in the parts he hath already passed through; a consideration which I take the liberty to recommend a little to the reader; for, however swift his capacity may be, I would not advise him to travel through these pages too fast; for if he doth, he may probably miss the seeing some curious productions of nature, which will be observed by the slower and more accurate reader. A volume without any such places of rest resembles the opening of wilds or seas, which tires the eye and fatigues the spirit when entered upon.

Secondly, what are the contents prefixed to every chapter but so many inscriptions over the gates of inns (to continue the same metaphor), informing the reader what entertainment he is to expect, which if he likes not, he may travel on to the next; for, in biography, as we are not tied down to an exact concatenation equally with other historians, so a chapter or two (for instance, this I am now writing) may be often passed over without any injury to the whole. And in these inscriptions I have been as faithful as possible, not imitating the celebrated Montaigne, who promises you one thing and gives you another; nor some title-page authors, who promise a great deal and produce nothing at all.

There are, besides these more obvious benefits, several others which our readers enjoy from this art of dividing; though perhaps most of them too mysterious to be presently understood by any who are not initiated into the science of authoring. To mention, therefore, but one which is most obvious, it prevents spoiling the beauty of a book by turning down its leaves, a method otherwise necessary to those readers who (though they read with great improvement and advantage) are apt, when they return to their study after half-an-hour's absence, to forget where they left off.

These divisions have the sanction of great antiquity. Homer not only divided his great work into twenty-four books (in compliment perhaps to the twenty-four letters to which he had very particular obligations), but, according to the opinion of some very sagacious critics, hawked them all separately, delivering only one book at a time (probably by subscription). He was the first inventor of the art which hath so long lain dormant, of publishing by numbers; an art now brought to such perfection, that even dictionaries are divided and exhibited piecemeal to the public; nay, one bookseller hath (to encourage learning and ease the public) contrived to give them a dictionary in this divided manner for only fifteen shillings more than it would have cost entire.

Virgil hath given us his poem in twelve books, an argument of his modesty; for by that, doubtless, he would insinuate that he pretends to no more than half the merit of the Greek; for the same reason, our Milton went originally no farther than ten; till, being puffed up by the praise of his friends, he put himself on the same footing with the Roman poet.

I shall not, however, enter so deep into this matter as some very learned criticks have done; who have with infinite labour and acute discernment discovered what books are proper for embellishment, and what require simplicity only, particularly with regard to similes, which I think are now generally agreed to become any book but the first.

I will dismiss this chapter with the following observation: that it becomes an author generally to divide a book, as it does a butcher to joint his meat, for such assistance is of great help to both the reader and the carver. And now, having indulged myself a little, I will endeavour to indulge the curiosity of my reader, who is no doubt impatient to know what he will find in the subsequent chapters of this book.

CHAPTER II.

A surprizing instance of Mr Adams's short memory, with the unfortunate consequences which it brought on Joseph.

Mr Adams and Joseph were now ready to depart different ways, when an accident determined the former to return with his friend, which Tow-wouse, Barnabas, and the bookseller had not been able to do. This accident was, that those sermons, which the parson was travelling to London to publish, were, O my good reader! left behind; what he had mistaken for them in the saddlebags being no other than three shirts, a pair of shoes, and some other necessaries, which Mrs Adams, who thought her husband would want shirts more than sermons on his journey, had carefully provided him.

This discovery was now luckily owing to the presence of Joseph at the opening the saddlebags; who, having heard his friend say he carried with him nine volumes of sermons, and not being of that sect of philosophers who can reduce all the matter of the world into a nutshell, seeing there was no room for them in the bags, where the parson had said they were deposited, had the curiosity to cry out, "Bless me, sir, where are your sermons?" The parson answered, "There, there, child; there they are, under my shirts." Now it happened that he had taken forth his last shirt, and the vehicle remained visibly empty. "Sure, sir," says Joseph, "there is nothing in the bags." Upon which Adams, starting, and testifying some surprize, cried, "Hey! fie, fie upon it! they are not here sure enough. Ay, they are certainly left behind."

Joseph was greatly concerned at the uneasiness which he apprehended his friend must feel from this disappointment; he begged him to pursue his journey, and promised he would himself return with the books to him with the utmost expedition. "No, thank you, child," answered Adams; "it shall not be so. What would it avail me, to tarry in the great city, unless I had my discourses with me, which are *ut ita dicam*, the sole cause, the *aitia monotate* of my peregrination? No, child, as this accident hath happened, I am resolved to return back to my cure, together with you; which indeed my inclination sufficiently leads me to. This disappointment may perhaps be intended for my good." He concluded with a verse out of Theocritus, which signifies no more than that sometimes it rains, and sometimes the sun shines.

Joseph bowed with obedience and thankfulness for the inclination which the parson expressed of returning with him; and now the bill was called for, which, on examination, amounted within a shilling to the sum Mr Adams had in his pocket. Perhaps the reader may wonder how he was able to produce a sufficient sum for so many days: that he may not be surprized, therefore, it cannot be unnecessary to acquaint him that he had borrowed a guinea of a servant belonging to the coach and six, who had been formerly one of his parishioners, and whose master, the owner of the coach, then lived within three miles of him; for so good was the credit of Mr Adams, that even Mr Peter, the Lady Booby's steward, would have lent him a guinea with very little security.

Mr Adams discharged the bill, and they were both setting out, having agreed to ride and tie; a method of travelling much used by persons who have but one horse between them, and is thus performed. The two travellers set out together, one on horseback, the other on foot: now, as it generally happens that he on horseback outgoes him on foot, the custom is, that, when he arrives at the distance agreed on, he is to dismount, tie the horse to some gate, tree, post, or other thing, and then proceed on foot; when the other comes up to the horse he unties him, mounts, and gallops on, till, having passed by his fellow-traveller, he likewise arrives at the place of tying. And this is that method of travelling so much in use among our prudent ancestors, who knew that horses had mouths as well as legs, and that they could not use the latter without being at the expense of suffering the beasts themselves to use the former. This was the method in use in those days when, instead of a coach and six, a member of parliament's lady used to mount a pillion behind her husband; and a grave serjeant at law condescended to amble to Westminster on an easy pad, with his clerk kicking his heels behind him.

The hostler presented him a bill. Adams was now gone some minutes, having insisted on Joseph's beginning the journey on horseback, and Joseph had his foot in the stirrup, when the hostler presented him a bill for the horse's board during his residence at the inn. Joseph said Mr Adams had paid all; but this matter, being referred to Mr Tow-wouse, was by him decided in favour of the hostler, and indeed with truth and justice; for this was a fresh instance of that shortness of memory which did not arise from want of parts, but that continual hurry in which parson Adams was always involved.

Joseph was now reduced to a dilemma which extremely puzzled him. The sum due for horse-meat was twelve shillings (for Adams, who had borrowed the beast of his clerk, had ordered him to be fed as well as they could feed him), and the cash in his pocket amounted to sixpence (for Adams had divided the last shilling with him). Now, though there have been some ingenious persons who have contrived to pay twelve shillings with sixpence, Joseph was not one of them. He had never contracted a debt in his life, and was consequently the less ready at an expedient to extricate himself. Tow-wouse was willing to give him credit till next time, to which Mrs Tow-wouse would probably have consented (for such was Joseph's beauty, that it had made some impression even on that piece of flint which that good woman wore in her bosom by way of heart). Joseph would have found, therefore, very likely the passage free, had he not, when he honestly discovered the nakedness of his pockets, pulled out that little piece of gold which we have mentioned before. This caused Mrs Tow-wouse's eyes to water; she told Joseph she did not conceive a man could want money whilst he had gold in his pocket. Joseph answered he had such a value for that little piece of gold, that he would not part with it for a hundred times the riches which the greatest esquire in the county was worth. "A pretty way, indeed," said Mrs Tow-wouse, "to run in debt, and then refuse to part with your money, because you have a value for it! I never knew any piece of gold of more value than as many shillings as it would change for."—"Not to preserve my life from starving, nor to redeem it from a robber, would I part with this dear piece!" answered Joseph. "What," says Mrs Tow-wouse, "I suppose it was given you by some vile trollop, some miss or other; if it had been the present of a virtuous woman, you would not have had such a value for it. My husband is a fool if he parts with the horse without being paid for him."—"No, no, I can't part with the horse, indeed, till I have the money," cried Tow-wouse. A resolution highly commended by a lawyer then in the yard, who declared Mr Tow-wouse might justify the detainer.

As we cannot therefore at present get Mr Joseph out of the inn, we shall leave him in it, and carry our reader on after parson Adams, who, his mind being perfectly at ease, fell into a contemplation on a passage in Aeschylus, which entertained him for three miles together, without suffering him once to reflect on his fellow-traveller.

At length, having spun out his thread, and being now at the summit of a hill, he cast his eyes backwards, and wondered that he could not see any sign of Joseph. As he left him ready to mount the horse, he could not apprehend any mischief had happened, neither could he suspect that he missed his way, it being so broad and plain; the only reason which presented itself to him was, that he had met with an acquaintance who had prevailed with him to delay some time in discourse.

He therefore resolved to proceed slowly forwards, not doubting but that he should be shortly overtaken; and soon came to a large water, which, filling the whole road, he saw no method of passing unless by wading through, which he accordingly did up to his middle; but was no sooner got to the other side than he perceived, if he had looked over the hedge, he would have found a footpath capable of conducting him without wetting his shoes.

His surprize at Joseph's not coming up grew now very troublesome: he began to fear he knew not what; and as he determined to move no farther, and, if he did not shortly overtake him, to return back, he wished to find a house of public entertainment where he might dry his clothes and refresh himself with a pint; but, seeing no such (for no other reason than because he did not cast his eyes a hundred yards forwards), he sat himself down on a stile, and pulled out his Aeschylus.

A fellow passing presently by, Adams asked him if he could direct him to an alehouse. The fellow, who had just left it, and perceived the house and sign to be within sight, thinking he had jeered him, and being of a morose temper, bade him follow his nose and be d—n'd. Adams told him he was a saucy jackanapes; upon which the fellow turned about angrily; but, perceiving Adams clench his fist, he thought proper to go on without taking any farther notice.

A horseman, following immediately after, and being asked the same question, answered, "Friend, there is one within a stone's throw; I believe you may see it before you." Adams, lifting up his eyes, cried, "I protest, and so there is;" and, thanking his informer, proceeded directly to it.

CHAPTER III.

The opinion of two lawyers concerning the same gentleman, with Mr Adams's inquiry into the religion of his host.

He had just entered the house, and called for his pint, and seated himself, when two horsemen came to the door, and, fastening their horses to the rails, alighted. They said there was a violent shower of rain coming on, which they intended to weather there, and went into a little room by themselves, not perceiving Mr Adams.

One of these immediately asked the other, "If he had seen a more comical adventure a great while?" Upon which the other said, "He doubted whether, by law, the landlord could justify detaining the horse for his corn and hay." But the former answered, "Undoubtedly he can; it is an adjudged case, and I have known it tried."

Adams, who, though he was, as the reader may suspect, a little inclined to forgetfulness, never wanted more than a hint to remind him, overhearing their discourse, immediately suggested to himself that this was his own horse, and that he had forgot to pay for him, which, upon inquiry, he was certified of by the gentlemen; who added, that the horse was likely to have more rest than food, unless he was paid for.

The poor parson resolved to return presently to the inn, though he knew no more than Joseph how to procure his horse his liberty; he was, however, prevailed on to stay under covert, till the shower, which was now very violent, was over.

The three travellers then sat down together over a mug of good beer; when Adams, who had observed a gentleman's house as he passed along the road, inquired to whom it belonged; one of the horsemen had no sooner mentioned the owner's name, than the other began to revile him in the most opprobrious terms. The English language scarce affords a single reproachful word, which he did not vent on this occasion. He charged him likewise with many particular facts. He said, "He no more regarded a field of wheat when he was hunting, than he did the highway; that he had injured several poor farmers by trampling their corn under his horse's heels; and if any of them begged him with the utmost submission to refrain, his horsewhip was always ready to do them justice." He said, "That he was the greatest tyrant to the neighbours in every other instance, and would not suffer a farmer to keep a gun, though he might justify it by law; and in his own family so cruel a master, that he never kept a servant a twelvemonth. In his capacity as a justice," continued he, "he behaves so partially, that he commits or acquits just as he is in the humour, without any regard to truth or evidence; the devil may carry any one before him for me; I would rather be tried before some judges, than be a prosecutor before him: if I had an estate in the neighbourhood, I would sell it for half the value rather than live near him."

Adams shook his head, and said, "He was sorry such men were suffered to proceed with impunity, and that riches could set any man above the law." The reviler, a little after, retiring into the yard, the gentleman who had first mentioned his name to Adams began to assure him "that his companion was a prejudiced person. It is true," says he, "perhaps, that he may have sometimes pursued his game over a field of corn, but he hath always made the party ample satisfaction: that so far from tyrannising over his neighbours, or taking away their guns, he himself knew several farmers not qualified, who not only kept guns, but killed game with them; that he was the best of masters to his servants, and several of them had grown old in his service; that he was the best justice of peace in the kingdom, and, to his certain knowledge, had decided many difficult points, which were referred to him, with the greatest equity and the highest wisdom; and he verily believed, several persons would give a year's purchase more for an estate near him, than under the wings of any other great man." He had just finished his encomium when his companion returned and acquainted him the storm was over. Upon which they presently mounted their horses and departed.

Adams, who was in the utmost anxiety at those different characters of the same person, asked his host if he knew the gentleman: for he began to imagine they had by mistake been speaking of two several gentlemen. "No, no, master," answered the host (a shrewd, cunning fellow); "I know the gentleman very well of whom they have been speaking, as I do the gentlemen who spoke of him. As for riding over other men's corn, to my knowledge he hath not been on horseback these two years. I never heard he did any injury of that kind; and as to making reparation, he is not so free of his money as that comes to neither. Nor did I ever hear of his taking away any man's gun; nay, I know several who have guns in their houses; but as for killing game with them, no man is stricter; and I believe he would ruin any who did. You heard one of the gentlemen say he was the worst master in the world, and the other that he is the best; but for my own part, I know all his servants, and never heard from any of them that he was either one or the other."—"Aye! aye!" says Adams; "and how doth he behave as a justice, pray?"—"Faith, friend," answered the host, "I question whether he is in the commission; the only cause I have heard he hath decided a great while, was one between those very two persons who just went out of this house; and I am sure he determined that justly, for I heard the whole matter."—"Which did He decide it in favour of?" quoth Adams.—"I think I need not answer that question," cried the host, "after the different characters you have heard of him. It is not my business to contradict gentlemen while they are drinking in my house; but I knew neither of them spoke a syllable of truth."—"God forbid!" said Adams, "that men should arrive at such a pitch of wickedness to belye the character of their neighbour from a little private affection, or, what is infinitely worse, a private spite. I rather believe we have mistaken them, and they mean two other persons; for there are many houses on the road."—"Why, prithee, friend," cries the host, "dost thou pretend never to have told a lye in thy life?"—"Never a malicious one, I am certain," answered Adams, "nor with a design to injure the reputation of any man living."—"Pugh! malicious; no, no," replied the host; "not malicious with a design to hang a man, or bring him into trouble; but surely, out of love to oneself, one must speak better of a friend than an enemy."—"Out of love to yourself, you should confine yourself to truth," says Adams, "for by doing otherwise you injure the noblest part of yourself, your immortal soul. I can hardly believe any man such an idiot to risque the loss of that by any trifling gain, and the greatest gain in this world is but dirt in comparison of what shall be revealed hereafter." Upon which the host, taking up the cup, with a smile, drank a health to hereafter; adding, "He was for something present."—"Why," says Adams very gravely, "do not you believe another world?" To which the host answered, "Yes; he was no atheist."—"And you believe you have an immortal soul?" cries Adams. He answered, "God forbid he should not."—"And heaven and hell?" said the parson. The host then bid him "not to profane; for those were things not to be mentioned nor thought of but in church." Adams asked him, "Why he went to church, if what he learned there had no influence on his conduct in life?" "I go to church," answered the host, "to say my prayers and behave godly."—"And dost not thou," cried Adams, "believe what thou hearest at church?"—"Most part of it, master," returned the host. "And dost not thou then tremble," cries Adams, "at the thought of eternal punishment?"—"As for that, master," said he, "I never once thought about it; but what signifies talking about matters so far off? The mug is out, shall I draw another?"

Whilst he was going for that purpose, a stage-coach drove up to the door. The coachman coming into the house was asked by the mistress what passengers he had in his coach? "A parcel of squinny-gut b—s," says he; "I have a good mind to overturn them; you won't prevail upon them to drink anything, I assure you." Adams asked him, "If he had not seen a young man on horseback on the road" (describing Joseph). "Aye," said the coachman, "a gentlewoman in my coach that is his acquaintance redeemed him and his horse; he would have been here before this time, had not the storm driven him to shelter." "God bless her!" said Adams, in a rapture; nor could he delay walking out to satisfy himself who this charitable woman was; but what was his surprize when he saw his old acquaintance, Madam Slipslop? Hers indeed was not so great, because she had been informed by Joseph that he was on the road. Very civil were the salutations on both sides; and Mrs Slipslop rebuked the hostess for denying the gentleman to be there when she asked for him; but indeed the poor woman had not erred designedly; for Mrs Slipslop asked for a clergyman, and she had unhappily mistaken Adams for a person travelling to a neighbouring fair with the thimble and button, or some other such operation; for he marched in a swinging great but short white coat with black buttons, a short wig, and a hat which, so far from having a black hatband, had nothing black about it.

Joseph was now come up, and Mrs Slipslop would have had him quit his horse to the parson, and come himself into the coach; but he absolutely refused, saying, he thanked Heaven he was well enough recovered to be very able to ride; and added, he hoped he knew his duty better than to ride in a coach while Mr Adams was on horseback.

Mrs Slipslop would have persisted longer, had not a lady in the coach put a short end to the dispute, by refusing to suffer a fellow in a livery to ride in the same coach with herself; so it was at length agreed that Adams should fill the vacant place in the coach, and Joseph should proceed on horseback.

They had not proceeded far before Mrs Slipslop, addressing herself to the parson, spoke thus:—"There hath been a strange alteration in our family, Mr Adams, since Sir Thomas's death." "A strange alteration indeed," says Adams, "as I gather from some hints which have dropped from Joseph."—"Aye," says she, "I could never have believed it; but the longer one lives in the world, the more one sees. So Joseph hath given you hints." "But of what nature will always remain a perfect secret with me," cries the parson: "he forced me to promise before he would communicate anything. I am indeed concerned to find her ladyship behave in so unbecoming a manner. I always thought her in the main a good lady, and should never have suspected her of thoughts so unworthy a Christian, and with a young lad her own servant." "These things are no secrets to me, I assure you," cries Slipslop, "and I believe they will be none anywhere shortly; for ever since the boy's departure, she hath behaved more like a mad woman than anything else." "Truly, I am heartily concerned," says Adams, "for she was a good sort of a lady. Indeed, I have often wished she had attended a little more constantly at the service, but she hath done a great deal of good in the parish." "O Mr Adams," says Slipslop, "people that don't see all, often know nothing. Many things have been given away in our family, I do assure you, without her knowledge. I have heard you say in the pulpit we ought not to brag; but indeed I can't avoid saying, if she had kept the keys herself, the poor would have wanted many a cordial which I have let them have. As for my late master, he was as worthy a man as ever lived, and would have done infinite good if he had not been controlled; but he loved a quiet life, Heaven rest his soul! I am confident he is there, and enjoys a quiet life, which some folks would not allow him here."—Adams answered, "He had never heard this before, and was mistaken if she herself (for he remembered she used to commend her mistress and blame her master) had not formerly been of another opinion." "I don't know," replied she, "what I might once think; but now I am confidous matters are as I tell you; the world will shortly see who hath been deceived; for my part, I say nothing, but that it is wondersome how some people can carry all things with a grave face."

Thus Mr Adams and she discoursed, till they came opposite to a great house which stood at some distance from the road: a lady in the coach, spying it, cried, "Yonder lives the unfortunate Leonora, if one can justly call a woman unfortunate whom we must own at the same time guilty and the author of her own calamity." This was abundantly sufficient to awaken the curiosity of Mr Adams, as indeed it did that of the whole company, who jointly solicited the lady to acquaint them with Leonora's history, since it seemed, by what she had said, to contain something remarkable.

The lady, who was perfectly well-bred, did not require many entreaties, and having only wished their entertainment might make amends for the company's attention, she began in the following manner.

CHAPTER IV.

The history of Leonora, or the unfortunate jilt.

Leonora was the daughter of a gentleman of fortune; she was tall and well-shaped, with a sprightliness in her countenance which often attracts beyond more regular features joined with an insipid air: nor is this kind of beauty less apt to deceive than allure; the good humour which it indicates being often mistaken for good nature, and the vivacity for true understanding.

Leonora, who was now at the age of eighteen, lived with an aunt of hers in a town in the north of England. She was an extreme lover of gaiety, and very rarely missed a ball or any other public assembly; where she had frequent opportunities of satisfying a greedy appetite of vanity, with the preference which was given her by the men to almost every other woman present.

Among many young fellows who were particular in their gallantries towards her, Horatio soon distinguished himself in her eyes beyond all his competitors; she danced with more than ordinary gaiety when he happened to be her partner; neither the fairness of the evening, nor the musick of the nightingale, could lengthen her walk like his company. She affected no longer to understand the civilities of others; whilst she inclined so attentive an ear to every compliment of Horatio, that she often smiled even when it was too delicate for her comprehension.

"Pray, madam," says Adams, "who was this squire Horatio?"

Horatio, says the lady, was a young gentleman of a good family, bred to the law, and had been some few years called to the degree of a barrister. His face and person were such as the generality allowed handsome; but he had a dignity in his air very rarely to be seen. His temper was of the saturnine complexion, and without the least taint of moroseness. He had wit and humour, with an inclination to satire, which he indulged rather too much.

This gentleman, who had contracted the most violent passion for Leonora, was the last person who perceived the probability of its success. The whole town had made the match for him before he himself had drawn a confidence from her actions sufficient to mention his passion to her; for it was his opinion (and perhaps he was there in the right) that it is highly impolitick to talk seriously of love to a woman before you have made such a progress in her affections, that she herself expects and desires to hear it.

But whatever diffidence the fears of a lover may create, which are apt to magnify every favour conferred on a rival, and to see the little advances towards themselves through the other end of the perspective, it was impossible that Horatio's passion should so blind his discernment as to prevent his conceiving hopes from the behaviour of Leonora, whose fondness for him was now as visible to an indifferent person in their company as his for her.

"I never knew any of these forward sluts come to good" (says the lady who refused Joseph's entrance into the coach), "nor shall I wonder at anything she doth in the sequel."

The lady proceeded in her story thus: It was in the midst of a gay conversation in the walks one evening, when Horatio whispered Leonora, that he was desirous to take a turn or two with her in private, for that he had something to communicate to her of great consequence. "Are you sure it is of consequence?" said she, smiling. "I hope," answered he, "you will think so too, since the whole future happiness of my life must depend on the event."

Leonora, who very much suspected what was coming, would have deferred it till another time; but Horatio, who had more than half conquered the difficulty of speaking by the first motion, was so very importunate, that she at last yielded, and, leaving the rest of the company, they turned aside into an unfrequented walk.

They had retired far out of the sight of the company, both maintaining a strict silence. At last Horatio made a full stop, and taking Leonora, who stood pale and trembling, gently by the hand, he fetched a deep sigh, and then, looking on her eyes with all the tenderness imaginable, he cried out in a faltering accent, "O Leonora! is it necessary for me to declare to you on what the future happiness of my life must be founded? Must I say there is something belonging to you which is a bar to my happiness, and which unless you will part with, I must be miserable!"—"What can that be?" replied Leonora. "No wonder," said he, "you are surprized that I should make an objection to anything which is yours: yet sure you may guess, since it is the only one which the riches of the world, if they were mine, should purchase for me. Oh, it is that which you must part with to bestow all the rest! Can Leonora, or rather will she, doubt longer? Let me then whisper it in her ears—It is your name, madam. It is by parting with that, by your condescension to be for ever mine, which must at once prevent me from being the most miserable, and will render me the happiest of mankind."

Leonora, covered with blushes, and with as angry a look as she could possibly put on, told him, "That had she suspected what his declaration would have been, he should not have decoyed her from her company, that he had so surprized and frighted her, that she begged him to convey her back as quick as possible;" which he, trembling very near as much as herself, did.

"More fool he," cried Slipslop; "it is a sign he knew very little of our sect."—"Truly, madam," said Adams, "I think you are in the right: I should have insisted to know a piece of her mind, when I had carried matters so far." But Mrs Grave-airs desired the lady to omit all such fulsome stuff in her story, for that it made her sick.

Well then, madam, to be as concise as possible, said the lady, many weeks had not passed after this interview before Horatio and Leonora were what they call on a good footing together. All ceremonies except the last were now over; the writings were now drawn, and everything was in the utmost forwardness preparative to the putting Horatio in possession of all his wishes. I will, if you please, repeat you a letter from each of them, which I have got by heart, and which will give you no small idea of their passion on both sides.

Mrs Grave-airs objected to hearing these letters; but being put to the vote, it was carried against her by all the rest in the coach; parson Adams contending for it with the utmost vehemence.

HORATIO TO LEONORA.

"How vain, most adorable creature, is the pursuit of pleasure in the absence of an object to which the mind is entirely devoted, unless it have some relation to that object! I was last night condemned to the society of men of wit and learning, which, however agreeable it might have formerly been to me, now only gave me a suspicion that they imputed my absence in conversation to the true cause. For which reason, when your engagements forbid me the ecstatic happiness of seeing you, I am always desirous to be alone; since my sentiments for Leonora are so delicate, that I cannot bear the apprehension of another's prying into those delightful endearments with which the warm imagination of a lover will sometimes indulge him, and which I suspect my eyes then betray. To fear this discovery of our thoughts may perhaps appear too ridiculous a nicety to minds not susceptible of all the tendernesses of this delicate passion. And surely we shall suspect there are few such, when we consider that it requires every human virtue to exert itself in its full extent; since the beloved, whose happiness it ultimately respects, may give us charming opportunities of being brave in her defence, generous to her wants, compassionate to her afflictions, grateful to her kindness; and in the same manner, of exercising every other virtue, which he who would not do to any degree, and that with the utmost rapture, can never deserve the name of a lover. It is, therefore, with a view to the delicate modesty of your mind that I cultivate it so purely in my own; and it is that which will sufficiently suggest to you the uneasiness I bear from those liberties, which men to whom the world allow politeness will sometimes give themselves on these occasions.

"Can I tell you with what eagerness I expect the arrival of that blest day, when I shall experience the falsehood of a common assertion, that the greatest human happiness consists in hope? A doctrine which no person had ever stronger reason to believe than myself at present, since none ever tasted such bliss as fires my bosom with the thoughts of spending my future days with such a companion, and that every action of my life will have the glorious satisfaction of conducing to your happiness."

LEONORA TO HORATIO. [1]

"The refinement of your mind has been so evidently proved by every word and action ever since I had the first pleasure of knowing you, that I thought it impossible my good opinion of Horatio could have been heightened to any additional proof of merit. This very thought was my amusement when I received your last letter, which, when I opened, I confess I was surprized to find the delicate sentiments expressed there so far exceeding what I thought could come even from you (although I know all the generous principles human nature is capable of are centred in your breast), that words cannot paint what I feel on the reflection that my happiness shall be the ultimate end of all your actions.

"Oh, Horatio! what a life must that be, where the meanest domestic cares are sweetened by the pleasing consideration that the man on earth who best deserves, and to whom you are most inclined to give your affections, is to reap either profit or pleasure from all you do! In such a case toils must be turned into diversions, and nothing but the unavoidable inconveniences of life can make us remember that we are mortal.

"If the solitary turn of your thoughts, and the desire of keeping them undiscovered, makes even the conversation of men of wit and learning tedious to you, what anxious hours must I spend, who am condemned by custom to the conversation of women, whose natural curiosity leads them to pry into all my thoughts, and whose envy can never suffer Horatio's heart to be possessed by any one, without forcing them into malicious designs against the person who is so happy as to possess it! But, indeed, if ever envy can possibly have any excuse, or even alleviation, it is in this case, where the good is so great, and it must be equally natural to all to wish it for themselves; nor am I ashamed to own it: and to your merit, Horatio, I am obliged, that prevents my being in that most uneasy of all the situations I can figure in my imagination, of being led by inclination to love the person whom my own judgment forces me to condemn."

Matters were in so great forwardness between this fond couple, that the day was fixed for their marriage, and was now within a fortnight, when the sessions chanced to be held for that county in a town about twenty miles' distance from that which is the scene of our story. It seems, it is usual for the young gentlemen of the bar to repair to these sessions, not so much for the sake of profit as to show their parts and learn the law of the justices of peace; for which purpose one of the wisest and gravest of all the justices is appointed speaker, or chairman, as they modestly call it, and he reads them a lecture, and instructs them in the true knowledge of the law.

"You are here guilty of a little mistake," says Adams, "which, if you please, I will correct: I have attended at one of these quarter-sessions, where I observed the counsel taught the justices, instead of learning anything of them."

It is not very material, said the lady. Hither repaired Horatio, who, as he hoped by his profession to advance his fortune, which was not at present very large, for

---

[1] This letter was written by a young lady on reading the former.

the sake of his dear Leonora, he resolved to spare no pains, nor lose any opportunity of improving or advancing himself in it.

The same afternoon in which he left the town, as Leonora stood at her window, a coach and six passed by, which she declared to be the completest, genteelest, prettiest equipage she ever saw; adding these remarkable words, "Oh, I am in love with that equipage!" which, though her friend Florella at that time did not greatly regard, she hath since remembered.

In the evening an assembly was held, which Leonora honoured with her company; but intended to pay her dear Horatio the compliment of refusing to dance in his absence.

Oh, why have not women as good resolution to maintain their vows as they have often good inclinations in making them!

The gentleman who owned the coach and six came to the assembly. His clothes were as remarkably fine as his equipage could be. He soon attracted the eyes of the company; all the smarts, all the silk waistcoats with silver and gold edgings, were eclipsed in an instant.

"Madam," said Adams, "if it be not impertinent, I should be glad to know how this gentleman was drest."

Sir, answered the lady, I have been told he had on a cut velvet coat of a cinnamon colour, lined with a pink satten, embroidered all over with gold; his waistcoat, which was cloth of silver, was embroidered with gold likewise. I cannot be particular as to the rest of his dress; but it was all in the French fashion, for Bellarmine (that was his name) was just arrived from Paris.

This fine figure did not more entirely engage the eyes of every lady in the assembly than Leonora did his. He had scarce beheld her, but he stood motionless and fixed as a statue, or at least would have done so if good breeding had permitted him. However, he carried it so far before he had power to correct himself, that every person in the room easily discovered where his admiration was settled. The other ladies began to single out their former partners, all perceiving who would be Bellarmine's choice; which they however endeavoured, by all possible means, to prevent: many of them saying to Leonora, "O madam! I suppose we shan't have the pleasure of seeing you dance to-night;" and then crying out, in Bellarmine's hearing, "Oh! Leonora will not dance, I assure you: her partner is not here." One maliciously attempted to prevent her, by sending a disagreeable fellow to ask her, that so she might be obliged either to dance with him, or sit down; but this scheme proved abortive.

Leonora saw herself admired by the fine stranger, and envied by every woman present. Her little heart began to flutter within her, and her head was agitated with a convulsive motion: she seemed as if she would speak to several of her acquaintance, but had nothing to say; for, as she would not mention her present triumph, so she could not disengage her thoughts one moment from the contemplation of it. She had never tasted anything like this happiness. She had before known what it was to torment a single woman; but to be hated and secretly cursed by a whole assembly was a joy reserved for this blessed moment. As this vast profusion of ecstasy had confounded her understanding, so there was nothing so foolish as her behaviour: she played a thousand childish tricks, distorted her person into several shapes, and her face into several laughs, without any reason. In a word, her carriage was as absurd as her desires, which were to affect an insensibility of the stranger's admiration, and at the same time a triumph, from that admiration, over every woman in the room.

In this temper of mind, Bellarmine, having inquired who she was, advanced to her, and with a low bow begged the honour of dancing with her, which she, with as low a curtesy, immediately granted. She danced with him all night, and enjoyed, perhaps, the highest pleasure that she was capable of feeling.

At these words, Adams fetched a deep groan, which frighted the ladies, who told him, "They hoped he was not ill." He answered, "He groaned only for the folly of Leonora."

Leonora retired (continued the lady) about six in the morning, but not to rest. She tumbled and tossed in her bed, with very short intervals of sleep, and those entirely filled with dreams of the equipage and fine clothes she had seen, and the balls, operas, and ridottos, which had been the subject of their conversation.

In the afternoon, Bellarmine, in the dear coach and six, came to wait on her. He was indeed charmed with her person, and was, on inquiry, so well pleased with the circumstances of her father (for he himself, notwithstanding all his finery, was not quite so rich as a Croesus or an Attalus).—"Attalus," says Mr. Adams: "but pray how came you acquainted with these names?" The lady smiled at the question, and proceeded. He was so pleased, I say, that he resolved to make his addresses to her directly. He did so accordingly, and that with so much warmth and briskness, that he quickly baffled her weak repulses, and obliged the lady to refer him to her father, who, she knew, would quickly declare in favour of a coach and six.

Thus what Horatio had by sighs and tears, love and tenderness, been so long obtaining, the French-English Bellarmine with gaiety and gallantry possessed himself of in an instant. In other words, what modesty had employed a full year in raising, impudence demolished in twenty-four hours.

Here Adams groaned a second time; but the ladies, who began to smoke him, took no notice.

From the opening of the assembly till the end of Bellarmine's visit, Leonora had scarce once thought of Horatio; but he now began, though an unwelcome guest, to enter into her mind. She wished she had seen the charming Bellarmine and his charming equipage before matters had gone so far. "Yet why," says she, "should I wish to have seen him before; or what signifies it that I have seen him now? Is not Horatio my lover, almost my husband? Is he not as handsome, nay handsomer than Bellarmine? Aye, but Bellarmine is the genteeler, and the finer man; yes, that he must be allowed. Yes, yes, he is that certainly. But did not I, no longer ago than yesterday, love Horatio more than all the world? Aye, but yesterday I had not seen Bellarmine. But doth not Horatio doat on me, and may he not in despair break his heart if I abandon him? Well, and hath not Bellarmine a heart to break too? Yes, but I promised Horatio first; but that was poor Bellarmine's misfortune; if I had seen him first, I should certainly have preferred him. Did not the dear creature prefer me to every woman in the assembly, when every she was laying out for him? When was it in Horatio's power to give me such an instance of affection? Can he give me an equipage, or any of those things which Bellarmine will make me mistress of? How vast is the difference between being the wife of a poor counsellor and the wife of one of Bellarmine's fortune! If I marry Horatio, I shall triumph over no more than one rival; but by marrying Bellarmine, I shall be the envy of all my acquaintance. What happiness! But can I suffer Horatio to die? for he hath sworn he cannot survive my loss: but perhaps he may not die: if he should, can I prevent it? Must I sacrifice myself to him? besides, Bellarmine may be as miserable for me too." She was thus arguing with herself, when some young ladies called her to the walks, and a little relieved her anxiety for the present.

The next morning Bellarmine breakfasted with her in presence of her aunt, whom he sufficiently informed of his passion for Leonora. He was no sooner withdrawn than the old lady began to advise her niece on this occasion. "You see, child," says she, "what fortune hath thrown in your way; and I hope you will not withstand your own preferment." Leonora, sighing, begged her not to mention any such thing, when she knew her engagements to Horatio. "Engagements to a fig!" cried the aunt; "you should thank Heaven on your knees that you have it yet in your power to break them. Will any woman hesitate a moment whether she shall ride in a coach or walk on foot all the days of her life? But Bellarmine drives six, and Horatio not even a pair."—"Yes, but, madam, what will the world say?" answered Leonora: "will not they condemn me?"—"The world is always on the side of prudence," cries the aunt, "and would surely condemn you if you sacrificed your interest to any motive whatever. Oh! I know the world very well; and you shew your ignorance, my dear, by your objection. O' my conscience! the world is wiser. I have lived longer in it than you; and I assure you there is not anything worth our regard besides money; nor did I ever know one person who married from other considerations, who did not afterwards heartily repent it. Besides, if we examine the two men, can you prefer a sneaking fellow, who hath been bred at the university, to a fine gentleman just come from his travels. All the world must allow Bellarmine to be a fine gentleman, positively a fine gentleman, and a handsome man."—"Perhaps, madam, I should not doubt, if I knew how to be handsomely off with the other."—"Oh! leave that to me," says the aunt. "You know your father hath not been acquainted with the affair. Indeed, for my part I thought it might do well enough, not dreaming of such an offer; but I'll disengage you: leave me to give the fellow an answer. I warrant you shall have no farther trouble."

Leonora was at length satisfied with her aunt's reasoning; and Bellarmine supping with her that evening, it was agreed he should the next morning go to her father and propose the match, which she consented should be consummated at his return.

The aunt retired soon after supper; and, the lovers being left together, Bellarmine began in the following manner: "Yes, madam; this coat, I assure you, was made at Paris, and I defy the best English taylor even to imitate it. There is not one of them can cut, madam; they can't cut. If you observe how this skirt is turned, and this sleeve: a clumsy English rascal can do nothing like it. Pray, how do you like my liveries?" Leonora answered, "She thought them very pretty."—"All French," says he, "I assure you, except the greatcoats; I never trust anything more than a greatcoat to an Englishman. You know one must encourage our own people what one can, especially as, before I had a place, I was in the country interest, he, he, he! But for myself, I would see the dirty island at the bottom of the sea, rather than wear a single rag of English work about me: and I am sure, after you have made one tour to Paris, you will be of the same opinion with regard to your own clothes. You can't conceive what an addition a French dress would be to your beauty; I positively assure you, at the first opera I saw since I came over, I mistook the English ladies for chambermaids, he, he, he!"

With such sort of polite discourse did the gay Bellarmine entertain his beloved Leonora, when the door opened on a sudden, and Horatio entered the room. Here 'tis impossible to express the surprize of Leonora.

"Poor woman!" says Mrs Slipslop, "what a terrible quandary she must be in!"—"Not at all," says Mrs Grave-airs; "such sluts can never be confounded."—"She must have then more than Corinthian assurance," said Adams; "aye, more than Lais herself."

A long silence, continued the lady, prevailed in the whole company. If the familiar entrance of Horatio struck the greatest astonishment into Bellarmine, the unexpected presence of Bellarmine no less surprized Horatio. At length Leonora, collecting all the spirit she was mistress of, addressed herself to the latter, and pretended to wonder at the reason of so late a visit. "I should indeed," answered he, "have made some apology for disturbing you at this hour, had not my finding you in company assured me I do not break in upon your repose." Bellarmine rose from his chair, traversed the room in a minuet step, and hummed an opera tune, while Horatio, advancing to Leonora, asked her in a whisper if that gentleman was not a relation of hers; to which she answered with a smile, or rather sneer, "No, he is no relation of mine yet;" adding, "she could not guess the meaning of his question." Horatio told her softly, "It did not arise from jealousy."—"Jealousy! I assure you, it would be very strange in a common acquaintance to give himself any of those airs." These words a little surprized Horatio; but, before he had time to answer, Bellarmine danced up to the lady and told her, "He feared he interrupted some business between her and the gentleman."—"I can have no business," said she, "with the gentleman, nor any other, which need be any secret to you."

"You'll pardon me," said Horatio, "if I desire to know who this gentleman is who is to be entrusted with all our secrets."—"You'll know soon enough," cries Leonora; "but I can't guess what secrets can ever pass between us of such mighty consequence."—"No, madam!" cries Horatio; "I am sure you would not have me understand you in earnest."—"'Tis indifferent to me," says she, "how you understand me; but I think so unseasonable a visit is difficult to be understood at all, at least when people find one engaged: though one's servants do not deny one, one may expect a well-bred person should soon take the hint." "Madam," said Horatio, "I did not imagine any engagement with a stranger, as it seems this gentleman is, would have made my visit impertinent, or that any such ceremonies were to be preserved between persons in our situation." "Sure you are in a dream," says she, "or would persuade me that I am in one. I know no pretensions a common acquaintance can have to lay aside the ceremonies of good breeding." "Sure," said he, "I am in a dream; for it is impossible I should be really esteemed a common acquaintance by Leonora, after what has passed between us?" "Passed between us! Do you intend to affront me before this gentleman?" "D—n me, affront the lady," says Bellarmine, cocking his hat, and strutting up to Horatio: "does any man dare affront this lady before me, d—n me?" "Hark'ee, sir," says Horatio, "I would advise you to lay aside that fierce air; for I am mightily deceived if this lady has not a violent desire to get your worship a good drubbing." "Sir," said Bellarmine, "I have the honour to be her protector; and, d—n me, if I understand your meaning." "Sir," answered Horatio, "she is rather your protectress; but give yourself no more airs, for you see I am prepared for you" (shaking his whip at him). "Oh! *serviteur tres humble*," says Bellarmine: "*Je vous entend parfaitment bien*." At which time the aunt, who had heard of Horatio's visit, entered the room, and soon satisfied all his doubts. She convinced him that he was never more awake in his life, and that nothing more extraordinary had happened in his three days' absence than a small alteration in the affections of Leonora; who now burst into tears, and wondered what reason she had given him to use her in so barbarous a manner. Horatio desired Bellarmine to withdraw with him; but the ladies prevented it by laying violent hands on the latter; upon which the former took his leave without any great ceremony, and departed, leaving the lady with his rival to consult for his safety, which Leonora feared her indiscretion might have endangered; but the aunt comforted her with assurances that Horatio would not venture his person against so accomplished a cavalier as Bellarmine, and that, being a lawyer, he would seek revenge in his own way, and the most they had to apprehend from him was an action.

They at length therefore agreed to permit Bellarmine to retire to his lodgings, having first settled all matters relating to the journey which he was to undertake in the morning, and their preparations for the nuptials at his return.

But, alas! as wise men have observed, the seat of valour is not the countenance; and many a grave and plain man will, on a just provocation, betake himself to that mischievous metal, cold iron; while men of a fiercer brow, and sometimes with that emblem of courage, a cockade, will more prudently decline it.

Leonora was waked in the morning, from a visionary coach and six, with the dismal account that Bellarmine was run through the body by Horatio; that he lay languishing at an inn, and the surgeons had declared the wound mortal. She immediately leaped out of the bed, danced about the room in a frantic manner, tore her hair and beat her breast in all the agonies of despair; in which sad condition her aunt, who likewise arose at the news, found her. The good old lady applied her utmost art to comfort her niece. She told her, "While there was life there was hope; but that if he should die her affliction would be of no service to Bellarmine, and would only expose herself, which might, probably, keep her some time without any future offer; that, as matters had happened, her wisest way would be to think no more of Bellarmine, but to endeavour to regain the affections of Horatio." "Speak not to me," cried the disconsolate Leonora; "is it not owing to me that poor Bellarmine has lost his life? Have not these cursed charms (at which words she looked steadfastly in the glass) been the ruin of the most charming man of this age? Can I ever bear to contemplate my own face again (with her eyes still fixed on the glass)? Am I not the murderess of the finest gentleman? No other woman in the town could have made any impression on him." "Never think of things past," cries the aunt: "think of regaining the affections of Horatio." "What reason," said the niece, "have I to hope he would forgive me? No, I have lost him as well as the other, and it was your wicked advice which was the occasion of all; you seduced me, contrary to my inclinations, to abandon poor Horatio (at which words she burst into tears); you prevailed upon me, whether I would or no, to give up my affections for him; had it not been for you, Bellarmine never would have entered into my thoughts; had not his addresses been backed by your persuasions, they never would have made any impression on me; I should have defied all the fortune and equipage in the world; but it was you, it was you, who got the better of my youth and simplicity, and forced me to lose my dear Horatio for ever."

The aunt was almost borne down with this torrent of words; she, however, rallied all the strength she could, and, drawing her mouth up in a purse, began: "I am not surprized, niece, at this ingratitude. Those who advise young women for their interest, must always expect such a return: I am convinced my brother will thank me for breaking off your match with Horatio, at any rate."—"That may not be in your power yet," answered Leonora, "though it is very ungrateful in you to desire or attempt it, after the presents you have received from him." (For indeed true it is, that many presents, and some pretty valuable ones, had passed from Horatio to the old lady; but as true it is, that Bellarmine, when he breakfasted with her and her niece, had complimented her with a brilliant from his finger, of much greater value than all she had touched of the other.)

The aunt's gall was on float to reply, when a servant brought a letter into the room, which Leonora, hearing it came from Bellarmine, with great eagerness opened, and read as follows:—

"MOST DIVINE CREATURE,—The wound which I fear you have heard I received from my rival is not like to be so fatal as those shot into my heart which have been fired from your eyes, *tout brilliant*. Those are the only cannons by which I am to fall; for my surgeon gives me hopes of being soon able to attend your *ruelle*; till when, unless you would do me an honour which I have scarce the *hardiesse* to think of, your absence will be the greatest anguish which can be felt by,

"Madam,

"*Avec toute le respecte* in the world,
"Your most obedient, most absolute *Devote*,
"BELLARMINE."

As soon as Leonora perceived such hopes of Bellarmine's recovery, and that the gossip Fame had, according to custom, so enlarged his danger, she presently abandoned all further thoughts of Horatio, and was soon reconciled to her aunt, who received her again into favour, with a more Christian forgiveness than we generally meet with. Indeed, it is possible she might be a little alarmed at the hints which her niece had given her concerning the presents. She might apprehend such rumours, should they get abroad, might injure a reputation which, by frequenting church twice a day, and preserving the utmost rigour and strictness in her countenance and behaviour for many years, she had established.

Leonora's passion returned now for Bellarmine with greater force, after its small relaxation, than ever. She proposed to her aunt to make him a visit in his confinement, which the old lady, with great and commendable prudence, advised her to decline: "For," says she, "should any accident intervene to prevent your intended match, too forward a behaviour with this lover may injure you in the eyes of others. Every woman, till she is married, ought to consider of, and provide against, the possibility of the affair's breaking off." Leonora said, "She should be indifferent to whatever might happen in such a case; for she had now so absolutely placed her affections on this dear man (so she called him), that, if it was her misfortune to lose him, she should for ever abandon all thoughts of mankind." She, therefore, resolved to visit him, notwithstanding all the prudent advice of her aunt to the contrary, and that very afternoon executed her resolution.

The lady was proceeding in her story, when the coach drove into the inn where the company were to dine, sorely to the dissatisfaction of Mr Adams, whose ears were the most hungry part about him; he being, as the reader may perhaps guess, of an insatiable curiosity, and heartily desirous of hearing the end of this amour, though he professed he could scarce wish success to a lady of so inconstant a disposition.

CHAPTER V.

A dreadful quarrel which happened at the Inn where the company dined, with its bloody consequences to Mr Adams.

As soon as the passengers had alighted from the coach, Mr Adams, as was his custom, made directly to the kitchen, where he found Joseph sitting by the fire, and the hostess anointing his leg; for the horse which Mr Adams had borrowed of his clerk had so violent a propensity to kneeling, that one would have thought it had been his trade, as well as his master's; nor would he always give any notice of such his intention; he was often found on his knees when the rider least expected it. This foible, however, was of no great inconvenience to the parson, who was accustomed to it; and, as his legs almost touched the ground when he bestrode the beast, had but a little way to fall, and threw himself forward on such occasions with so much dexterity that he never received any mischief; the horse and he frequently rolling many paces' distance, and afterwards both getting up and meeting as good friends as ever.

Poor Joseph, who had not been used to such kind of cattle, though an excellent horseman, did not so happily disengage himself; but, falling with his leg under the beast, received a violent contusion, to which the good woman was, as we have said, applying a warm hand, with some camphorated spirits, just at the time when the parson entered the kitchen.

He had scarce expressed his concern for Joseph's misfortune before the host likewise entered. He was by no means of Mr Tow-wouse's gentle disposition; and was, indeed, perfect master of his house, and everything in it but his guests.

This surly fellow, who always proportioned his respect to the appearance of a traveller, from "God bless your honour," down to plain "Coming presently," observing his wife on her knees to a footman, cried out, without considering his circumstances, "What a pox is the woman about? why don't you mind the company in the coach? Go and ask them what they will have for dinner." "My dear," says she, "you know they can have nothing but what is at the fire, which will be ready presently; and really the poor young man's leg is very much bruised." At which words she fell to chafing more violently than before: the bell then happening to ring, he damn'd his wife, and bid her go in to the company, and not stand rubbing there all day, for he did not believe the young fellow's leg was so bad as he pretended; and if it was, within twenty miles he would find a surgeon to cut it off. Upon these words, Adams fetched two strides across the room; and snapping his fingers over his head, muttered aloud, He would excommunicate such a wretch for a farthing, for he believed the devil had more humanity. These words occasioned a dialogue between Adams and the host, in which there were two or three sharp replies, till Joseph bad the latter know how to behave himself to his betters. At which the host (having first strictly surveyed Adams) scornfully repeating the word "betters," flew into a rage, and, telling Joseph he was as able to walk out of his house as he had been to walk into it, offered to lay violent hands on him; which perceiving, Adams dealt him so sound a compliment over his face with his fist, that the blood immediately gushed out of his nose in a stream. The host, being unwilling to be outdone in courtesy, especially by a person of Adams's figure, returned the favour with so much gratitude, that the parson's nostrils began to look a little redder than usual. Upon which he again assailed his antagonist, and with another stroke laid him sprawling on the floor.

The hostess, who was a better wife than so surly a husband deserved, seeing her husband all bloody and stretched along, hastened presently to his assistance, or rather to revenge the blow, which, to all appearance, was the last he would ever receive; when, lo! a pan full of hog's blood, which unluckily stood on the dresser, presented itself first to her hands. She seized it in her fury, and without any reflection, discharged it into the parson's face; and with so good an aim, that much the greater part first saluted his countenance, and trickled thence in so large a current down to his beard, and over his garments, that a more horrible spectacle was hardly to be seen, or even imagined. All which was perceived by Mrs Slipslop, who entered the kitchen at that instant. This good gentlewoman, not being of a temper so extremely cool and patient as perhaps was required to ask many questions on this occasion, flew with great impetuosity at the hostess's cap, which, together with some of her hair, she plucked from her head in a moment, giving her, at the same time, several hearty cuffs in the face; which by frequent practice on the inferior servants, she had learned an excellent knack of delivering with a good grace. Poor Joseph could hardly rise from his chair; the parson was employed in wiping the blood from his eyes, which had entirely blinded him; and the landlord was but just beginning to stir; whilst Mrs Slipslop, holding down the landlady's face with her left hand, made so dexterous an use of her right, that the poor woman began to roar, in a key which alarmed all the company in the inn.

There happened to be in the inn, at this time, besides the ladies who arrived in the stage-coach, the two gentlemen who were present at Mr Tow-wouse's when Joseph was detained for his horse's meat, and whom we have before mentioned to have stopt at the alehouse with Adams. There was likewise a gentleman just returned from his travels to Italy; all whom the horrid outcry of murder presently brought into the kitchen, where the several combatants were found in the postures already described.

It was now no difficulty to put an end to the fray, the conquerors being satisfied with the vengeance they had taken, and the conquered having no appetite to renew the fight. The principal figure, and which engaged the eyes of all, was Adams, who was all over covered with blood, which the whole company concluded to be his own, and consequently imagined him no longer for this world. But the host, who had now recovered from his blow, and was risen from the ground, soon delivered them from this apprehension, by damning his wife for wasting the hog's puddings, and telling her all would have been very well if she had not intermeddled, like a b—as she was; adding, he was very glad the gentlewoman had paid her, though not half what she deserved. The poor woman had indeed fared much the worst; having, besides the unmerciful cuffs received, lost a quantity of hair, which Mrs Slipslop in triumph held in her left hand.

The traveller, addressing himself to Mrs Grave-airs, desired her not to be frightened; for here had been only a little boxing, which he said, to their *disgracia*, the English were *accustomata* to: adding, it must be, however, a sight somewhat strange to him, who was just come from Italy; the Italians not being addicted to the *cuffardo* but *bastonza*, says he. He then went up to Adams, and telling him he looked like the ghost of Othello, bid him not shake his gory locks at him, for he could not say he did it. Adams very innocently answered, "Sir, I am far from accusing you." He then returned to the lady, and cried, "I find the bloody gentleman is *uno insipido del nullo senso. Dammato di me*, if I have seen such a *spectaculo* in my way from Viterbo."

One of the gentlemen having learnt from the host the occasion of this bustle, and being assured by him that Adams had struck the first blow, whispered in his ear, "He'd warrant he would recover."—"Recover! master," said the host, smiling: "yes, yes, I am not afraid of dying with a blow or two neither; I am not such a chicken as that."—"Pugh!" said the gentleman, "I mean you will recover damages in that action which, undoubtedly, you intend to bring, as soon as a writ can be returned from London; for you look like a man of too much spirit and courage to suffer any one to beat you without bringing your action against him: he must be a scandalous fellow indeed who would put up with a drubbing whilst the law is open to revenge it; besides, he hath drawn blood from you, and spoiled your coat; and the jury will give damages for that too. An excellent new coat upon my word; and now not worth a shilling! I don't care," continued he, "to intermeddle in these cases; but you have a right to my evidence; and if I am sworn, I must speak the truth. I saw you sprawling on the floor, and blood gushing from your nostrils. You may take your own opinion; but was I in your circumstances, every drop of my blood should convey an ounce of gold into my pocket: remember I don't advise you to go to law; but if your jury were Christians, they must give swinging damages. That's all."—"Master," cried the host, scratching his head, "I have no stomach to law, I thank you. I have seen enough of that in the parish, where two of my neighbours have been at law about a house, till they have both lawed themselves into a gaol." At which words he turned about, and began to inquire again after his hog's puddings; nor would it probably have been a sufficient excuse for his wife, that she spilt them in his defence, had not some awe of the company, especially of the Italian traveller, who was a person of great dignity, withheld his rage.

Whilst one of the above-mentioned gentlemen was employed, as we have seen him, on the behalf of the landlord, the other was no less hearty on the side of Mr Adams, whom he advised to bring his action immediately. He said the assault of the wife was in law the assault of the husband, for they were but one person; and he was liable to pay damages, which he said must be considerable, where so bloody a disposition appeared. Adams answered, If it was true that they were but one person, he had assaulted the wife; for he was sorry to own he had struck the husband the first blow. "I am sorry you own it too," cries the gentleman; "for it could not possibly appear to the court; for here was no evidence present but the lame man in the chair, whom I suppose to be your friend, and would consequently say nothing but what made for you."—"How, sir," says Adams, "do you take me for a villain, who would prosecute revenge in cold blood, and use unjustifiable means to obtain it? If you knew me, and my order, I should think you affronted both." At the word order, the gentleman stared (for he was too bloody to be of any modern order of knights); and, turning hastily about, said, "Every man knew his own business."

Matters being now composed, the company retired to their several apartments; the two gentlemen congratulating each other on the success of their good offices in procuring a perfect reconciliation between the contending parties; and the traveller went to his repast, crying, "As the Italian poet says—

'*Je voi* very well *que tutta e pace*,
So send up dinner, good Boniface.'"

The coachman began now to grow importunate with his passengers, whose entrance into the coach was retarded by Miss Grave-airs insisting, against the remonstrance of all the rest, that she would not admit a footman into the coach; for poor Joseph was too lame to mount a horse. A young lady, who was, as it seems, an earl's grand-daughter, begged it with almost tears in her eyes. Mr Adams prayed, and Mrs Slipslop scolded; but all to no purpose. She said, "She would not demean herself to ride with a footman: that there were waggons on the road: that if the master of the coach desired it, she would pay for two places; but would suffer no such fellow to come in."—"Madam," says Slipslop, "I am sure no one can refuse another coming into a stage-coach."—"I don't know, madam," says the lady; "I am not much used to stage-coaches; I seldom travel in them."—"That may be, madam," replied Slipslop; "very good people do; and some people's betters, for aught I know." Miss Grave-airs said, "Some folks might sometimes give their tongues a liberty, to some people that were their betters, which did not become them; for her part, she was not used to converse with servants." Slipslop returned, "Some people kept no servants to converse with; for her part, she thanked Heaven she lived in a family where there were a great many, and had more under her own command than any paultry little gentlewoman in the kingdom." Miss Grave-airs cried, "She believed her mistress would not encourage such sauciness to her betters."—"My betters," says Slipslop, "who is my betters, pray?"—"I am your betters," answered Miss Grave-airs, "and I'll acquaint your mistress."—At which Mrs Slipslop laughed aloud, and told her, "Her lady was one of the great gentry; and such little paultry gentlewomen as some folks, who travelled in stagecoaches, would not easily come at her."

This smart dialogue between some people and some folks was going on at the coach door when a solemn person, riding into the inn, and seeing Miss Grave-airs, immediately accosted her with "Dear child, how do you?" She presently answered, "O papa, I am glad you have overtaken me."—"So am I," answered he; "for one of our coaches is just at hand; and, there being room for you in it, you shall go no farther in the stage unless you desire it."—"How can you imagine I should desire it?" says she; so, bidding Slipslop ride with her fellow, if she pleased, she took her father by the hand, who was just alighted, and walked with him into a room.

Adams instantly asked the coachman, in a whisper, "If he knew who the gentleman was?" The coachman answered, "He was now a gentleman, and kept his horse and man; but times are altered, master," said be; "I remember when he was no better born than myself."—"Ay! ay!" says Adams. "My father drove the squire's coach," answered he, "when that very man rode postillion; but he is now his steward; and a great gentleman." Adams then snapped his fingers, and cried, "He thought she was some such trollop."

Adams made haste to acquaint Mrs Slipslop with this good news, as he imagined it; but it found a reception different from what he expected. The prudent gentlewoman, who despised the anger of Miss Grave-airs whilst she conceived her the daughter of a gentleman of small fortune, now she heard her alliance with the upper servants of a great family in her neighbourhood, began to fear her interest with the mistress. She wished she had not carried the dispute so far, and began to think of endeavouring to reconcile herself to the young lady before she left the inn; when, luckily, the scene at London, which the reader can scarce have forgotten, presented itself to her mind, and comforted her with such assurance, that she no longer apprehended any enemy with her mistress.

Everything being now adjusted, the company entered the coach, which was just on its departure, when one lady recollected she had left her fan, a second her gloves, a third a snuff-box, and a fourth a smelling-bottle behind her; to find all which occasioned some delay and much swearing to the coachman.

As soon as the coach had left the inn, the women all together fell to the character of Miss Grave-airs; whom one of them declared she had suspected to be some low creature, from the beginning of their journey, and another affirmed she had not even the looks of a gentlewoman: a third warranted she was no better than she should be; and, turning to the lady who had related the story in the coach, said, "Did you ever hear, madam, anything so prudish as her remarks? Well, deliver me from the censoriousness of such a prude." The fourth added, "O madam! all these creatures are censorious; but for my part, I wonder where the wretch was bred; indeed, I must own I have seldom conversed with these mean kind of people, so that it may appear stranger to me; but to refuse the general desire of a whole company had something in it so astonishing, that, for my part, I own I should hardly believe it if my own ears had not been witnesses to it."—"Yes, and so handsome a young fellow," cries Slipslop; "the woman must have no compulsion in her: I believe she is more of a Turk than a Christian; I am certain, if she had any Christian woman's blood in her veins, the sight of such a young fellow must have warmed it. Indeed, there are some wretched, miserable old objects, that turn one's stomach; I should not wonder if she had refused such a one; I am as nice as herself, and should have cared no more than herself for the company of stinking old fellows; but, hold up thy head, Joseph, thou art none of those; and she who hath not compulsion for thee is a Myhummetman, and I will maintain it." This conversation made Joseph uneasy as well as the ladies; who, perceiving the spirits which Mrs Slipslop was in (for indeed she was not a cup too low), began to fear the consequence; one of them therefore desired the lady to conclude the story. "Aye, madam," said Slipslop, "I beg your ladyship to give us that story you commensated in the morning;" which request that well-bred woman immediately complied with.

CHAPTER VI.

Conclusion of the unfortunate jilt.

Leonora, having once broke through the bounds which custom and modesty impose on her sex, soon gave an unbridled indulgence to her passion. Her visits to Bellarmine were more constant, as well as longer, than his surgeon's: in a word, she became absolutely his nurse; made his water-gruel, administered him his medicines; and, notwithstanding the prudent advice of her aunt to the contrary, almost intirely resided in her wounded lover's apartment.

The ladies of the town began to take her conduct under consideration: it was the chief topic of discourse at their tea-tables, and was very severely censured by the most part; especially by Lindamira, a lady whose discreet and starch carriage, together with a constant attendance at church three times a day, had utterly defeated many malicious attacks on her own reputation; for such was the envy that Lindamira's virtue had attracted, that, notwithstanding her own strict behaviour and strict enquiry into the lives of others, she had not been able to escape being the mark of some arrows herself, which, however, did her no injury; a blessing, perhaps, owed by her to the clergy, who were her chief male companions, and with two or three of whom she had been barbarously and unjustly calumniated.

"Not so unjustly neither, perhaps," says Slipslop; "for the clergy are men, as well as other folks."

The extreme delicacy of Lindamira's virtue was cruelly hurt by those freedoms which Leonora allowed herself: she said, "It was an affront to her sex; that she did not imagine it consistent with any woman's honour to speak to the creature, or to be seen in her company; and that, for her part, she should always refuse to dance at an assembly with her, for fear of contamination by taking her by the hand."

But to return to my story: as soon as Bellarmine was recovered, which was somewhat within a month from his receiving the wound, he set out, according to agreement, for Leonora's father's, in order to propose the match, and settle all matters with him touching settlements, and the like.

A little before his arrival the old gentleman had received an intimation of the affair by the following letter, which I can repeat verbatim, and which, they say, was written neither by Leonora nor her aunt, though it was in a woman's hand. The letter was in these words:—

"SIR,—I am sorry to acquaint you that your daughter, Leonora, hath acted one of the basest as well as most simple parts with a young gentleman to whom she had engaged herself, and whom she hath (pardon the word) jilted for another of inferior fortune, notwithstanding his superior figure. You may take what measures you please on this occasion; I have performed what I thought my duty; as I have, though unknown to you, a very great respect for your family."

The old gentleman did not give himself the trouble to answer this kind epistle; nor did he take any notice of it, after he had read it, till he saw Bellarmine. He was, to say the truth, one of those fathers who look on children as an unhappy consequence of their youthful pleasures; which, as he would have been delighted not to have had attended them, so was he no less pleased with any opportunity to rid himself of the incumbrance. He passed, in the world's language, as an exceeding good father; being not only so rapacious as to rob and plunder all mankind to the utmost of his power, but even to deny himself the conveniencies, and almost necessaries, of life; which his neighbours attributed to a desire of raising immense fortunes for his children: but in fact it was not so; he heaped up money for its own sake only, and looked on his children as his rivals, who were to enjoy his beloved mistress when he was incapable of possessing her, and which he would have been much more charmed with the power of carrying along with him; nor had his children any other security of being his heirs than that the law would constitute them such without a will, and that he had not affection enough for any one living to take the trouble of writing one.

To this gentleman came Bellarmine, on the errand I have mentioned. His person, his equipage, his family, and his estate, seemed to the father to make him an advantageous match for his daughter: he therefore very readily accepted his proposals: but when Bellarmine imagined the principal affair concluded, and began to open the incidental matters of fortune, the old gentleman presently changed his countenance, saying, "He resolved never to marry his daughter on a Smithfield match; that whoever had love for her to take her would, when he died, find her share of his fortune in his coffers; but he had seen such examples of undutifulness happen from the too early generosity of parents, that he had made a vow never to part with a shilling whilst he lived." He commended the saying of Solomon, "He that spareth the rod spoileth the child;" but added, "he might have likewise asserted, That he that spareth the purse saveth the child." He then ran into a discourse on the extravagance of the youth of the age; whence he launched into a dissertation on horses; and came at length to commend those Bellarmine drove. That fine gentleman, who at another season would have been well enough pleased to dwell a little on that subject, was now very eager to resume the circumstance of fortune. He said, "He had a very high value for the young lady, and would receive her with less than he would any other whatever; but that even his love to her made some regard to worldly matters necessary; for it would be a most distracting sight for him to see her, when he had the honour to be her husband, in less than a coach and six." The old gentleman answered, "Four will do, four will do;" and then took a turn from horses to extravagance and from extravagance to horses, till he came round to the equipage again; whither he was no sooner arrived than Bellarmine brought him back to the point; but all to no purpose; he madc his escape from that subject in a minute; till at last the lover declared, "That in the present situation of his affairs it was impossible for him, though he loved Leonora more than *tout le monde*, to marry her without any fortune." To which the father answered, "He was sorry that his daughter must lose so valuable a match; that, if he had an inclination, at present it was not in his power to advance a shilling: that he had had great losses, and been at great expenses on projects; which, though he had great expectation from them, had yet produced him nothing: that he did not know what might happen hereafter, as on the birth of a son, or such accident; but he would make no promise, or enter into any article, for he would not break his vow for all the daughters in the world."

In short, ladies, to keep you no longer in suspense, Bellarmine, having tried every argument and persuasion which he could invent, and finding them all ineffectual, at length took his leave, but not in order to return to Leonora; he proceeded directly to his own seat, whence, after a few days' stay, he returned to Paris, to the great delight of the French and the honour of the English nation.

But as soon as he arrived at his home he presently despatched a messenger with the following epistle to Leonora:—

"ADORABLE AND CHARMANTE,—I am sorry to have the honour to tell you I am not the *heureux* person destined for your divine arms. Your papa hath told me so with a *politesse* not often seen on this side Paris. You may perhaps guess his manner of refusing me. *Ah, mon Dieu!* You will certainly believe me, madam, incapable myself of delivering this *triste* message, which I intend to try the French air to cure the consequences of. *A jamais! Coeur! Ange! Au diable!* If your papa obliges you to a marriage, I hope we shall see you at Paris; till when, the wind that flows from thence will be the warmest *dans le monde*, for it will consist almost entirely of my sighs. *Adieu, ma princesse! Ah, l'amour!*

"BELLARMINE."

I shall not attempt, ladies, to describe Leonora's condition when she received this letter. It is a picture of horror, which I should have as little pleasure in drawing as you in beholding. She immediately left the place where she was the subject of conversation and ridicule, and retired to that house I showed you when I began the story; where she hath ever since led a disconsolate life, and deserves, perhaps, pity for her misfortunes, more than our censure for a behaviour to which the artifices of her aunt very probably contributed, and to which very young women are often rendered too liable by that blameable levity in the education of our sex.

"If I was inclined to pity her," said a young lady in the coach, "it would be for the loss of Horatio; for I cannot discern any misfortune in her missing such a husband as Bellarmine."

"Why, I must own," says Slipslop, "the gentleman was a little false-hearted; but howsumever, it was hard to have two lovers, and get never a husband at all. But pray, madam, what became of *Our-asho*?"

He remains, said the lady, still unmarried, and hath applied himself so strictly to his business, that he hath raised, I hear, a very considerable fortune. And what is remarkable, they say he never hears the name of Leonora without a sigh, nor hath ever uttered one syllable to charge her with her ill-conduct towards him.

CHAPTER VII.

A very short chapter, in which parson Adams went a great way.

The lady, having finished her story, received the thanks of the company; and now Joseph, putting his head out of the coach, cried out, "Never believe me if yonder be not our parson Adams walking along without his horse!"—"On my word, and so he is," says Slipslop: "and as sure as twopence he hath left him behind at the inn." Indeed, true it is, the parson had exhibited a fresh instance of his absence of mind; for he was so pleased with having got Joseph into the coach, that he never once thought of the beast in the stable; and, finding his legs as nimble as he desired, he sallied out, brandishing a crabstick, and had kept on before the coach, mending and slackening his pace occasionally, so that he had never been much more or less than a quarter of a mile distant from it.

Mrs Slipslop desired the coachman to overtake him, which he attempted, but in vain; for the faster he drove the faster ran the parson, often crying out, "Aye, aye, catch me if you can;" till at length the coachman swore he would as soon attempt to drive after a greyhound, and, giving the parson two or three hearty curses, he cry'd, "Softly, softly, boys," to his horses, which the civil beasts immediately obeyed.

But we will be more courteous to our reader than he was to Mrs Slipslop; and, leaving the coach and its company to pursue their journey, we will carry our reader on after parson Adams, who stretched forwards without once looking behind him, till, having left the coach full three miles in his rear, he came to a place where, by keeping the extremest track to the right, it was just barely possible for a human creature to miss his way. This track, however, did he keep, as indeed he had a wonderful capacity at these kinds of bare possibilities, and, travelling in it about three miles over the plain, he arrived at the summit of a hill, whence looking a great way backwards, and perceiving no coach in sight, he sat himself down on the turf, and, pulling out his Aeschylus, determined to wait here for its arrival.

He had not sat long here before a gun going off very near, a little startled him; he looked up and saw a gentleman within a hundred paces taking up a partridge which he had just shot.

Adams stood up and presented a figure to the gentleman which would have moved laughter in many; for his cassock had just again fallen down below his greatcoat, that is to say, it reached his knees, whereas the skirts of his greatcoat descended no lower than half-way down his thighs; but the gentleman's mirth gave way to his surprize at beholding such a personage in such a place.

Adams, advancing to the gentleman, told him he hoped he had good sport, to which the other answered, "Very little."—"I see, sir," says Adams, "you have smote one partridge;" to which the sportsman made no reply, but proceeded to charge his piece.

Whilst the gun was charging, Adams remained in silence, which he at last broke by observing that it was a delightful evening. The gentleman, who had at first sight conceived a very distasteful opinion of the parson, began, on perceiving a book in his hand and smoaking likewise the information of the cassock, to change his thoughts, and made a small advance to conversation on his side by saying, "Sir, I suppose you are not one of these parts?"

Adams immediately told him, "No; that he was a traveller, and invited by the beauty of the evening and the place to repose a little and amuse himself with reading."—"I may as well repose myself too," said the sportsman, "for I have been out this whole afternoon, and the devil a bird have I seen till I came hither."

"Perhaps then the game is not very plenty hereabouts?" cries Adams. "No, sir," said the gentleman: "the soldiers, who are quartered in the neighbourhood, have killed it all."—"It is very probable," cries Adams, "for shooting is their profession."—"Ay, shooting the game," answered the other; "but I don't see they are so forward to shoot our enemies. I don't like that affair of Carthagena; if I had been there, I believe I should have done other-guess things, d—n me: what's a man's life when his country demands it? a man who won't sacrifice his life for his country deserves to be hanged, d—n me." Which words he spoke with so violent a gesture, so loud a voice, so strong an accent, and so fierce a countenance, that he might have frightened a captain of trained bands at the head of his company; but Mr Adams was not greatly subject to fear; he told him intrepidly that he very much approved his virtue, but disliked his swearing, and begged him not to addict himself to so bad a custom, without which he said he might fight as bravely as Achilles did. Indeed he was charmed with this discourse; he told the gentleman he would willingly have gone many miles to have met a man of his generous way of thinking; that, if he pleased to sit down, he should be greatly delighted to commune with him; for, though he was a clergyman, he would himself be ready, if thereto called, to lay down his life for his country.

The gentleman sat down, and Adams by him; and then the latter began, as in the following chapter, a discourse which we have placed by itself, as it is not only the most curious in this but perhaps in any other book.

CHAPTER VIII.

A notable dissertation by Mr Abraham Adams; wherein that gentleman appears in a political light.

"I do assure you, sir" (says he, taking the gentleman by the hand), "I am heartily glad to meet with a man of your kidney; for, though I am a poor parson, I will be bold to say I am an honest man, and would not do an ill thing to be made a bishop; nay, though it hath not fallen in my way to offer so noble a sacrifice, I have not been without opportunities of suffering for the sake of my conscience, I thank Heaven for them; for I have had relations, though I say it, who made some figure in the world; particularly a nephew, who was a shopkeeper and an alderman of a corporation. He was a good lad, and was under my care when a boy; and I believe would do what I bade him to his dying day. Indeed, it looks like extreme vanity in me to affect being a man of such consequence as to have so great an interest in an alderman; but others have thought so too, as manifestly appeared by the rector, whose curate I formerly was, sending for me on the approach of an election, and telling me, if I expected to continue in his cure, that I must bring my nephew to vote for one Colonel Courtly, a gentleman whom I had never heard tidings of till that instant. I told the rector I had no power over my nephew's vote (God forgive me for such prevarication!); that I supposed he would give it according to his conscience; that I would by no means endeavour to influence him to give it otherwise. He told me it was in vain to equivocate; that he knew I had already spoke to him in favour of esquire Fickle, my neighbour; and, indeed, it was true I had; for it was at a season when the church was in danger, and when all good men expected they knew not what would happen to us all. I then answered boldly, if he thought I had given my promise, he affronted me in proposing any breach of it. Not to be too prolix; I persevered, and so did my nephew, in the esquire's interest, who was chose chiefly through his means; and so I lost my curacy, Well, sir, but do you think the esquire ever mentioned a word of the church? *Ne verbum quidem, ut ita dicam*: within two years he got a place, and hath ever since lived in London; where I have been informed (but God forbid I should believe that,) that he never so much as goeth to church. I remained, sir, a considerable time without any cure, and lived a full month on one funeral sermon, which I preached on the indisposition of a clergyman; but this by the bye. At last, when Mr Fickle got his place, Colonel Courtly stood again; and who should make interest for him but Mr Fickle himself! that very identical Mr Fickle, who had formerly told me the colonel was an enemy to both the church and state, had the confidence to sollicit my nephew for him; and the colonel himself offered me to make me chaplain to his regiment, which I refused in favour of Sir Oliver Hearty, who told us he would sacrifice everything to his country; and I believe he would, except his hunting, which he stuck so close to, that in five years together he went but twice up to parliament; and one of those times, I have been told, never was within sight of the House. However, he was a worthy man, and the best friend I ever had; for, by his interest with a bishop, he got me replaced into my curacy, and gave me eight pounds out of his own pocket to buy me a gown and cassock, and furnish my house. He had our interest while he lived, which was not many years. On his death I had fresh applications made to me; for all the world knew the interest I had with my good nephew, who now was a leading man in the corporation; and Sir Thomas Booby, buying the estate which had been Sir Oliver's, proposed himself a candidate. He was then a young gentleman just come from his travels; and it did me good to hear him discourse on affairs which, for my part, I knew nothing of. If I had been master of a thousand votes he should have had them all. I engaged my nephew in his interest, and he was elected; and a very fine parliament-man he was. They tell me he made speeches of an hour long, and, I have been told, very fine ones; but he could never persuade the parliament to be of his opinion. *Non omnia possumus omnes*. He promised me a living, poor man! and I believe I should have had it, but an accident happened, which was, that my lady had promised it before, unknown to him. This, indeed, I never heard till afterwards; for my nephew, who died about a month before the incumbent, always told me I might be assured of it. Since that time, Sir Thomas, poor man, had always so much business, that he never could find leisure to see me. I believe it was partly my lady's fault too, who did not think my dress good enough for the gentry at her table. However, I must do him the justice to say he never was ungrateful; and I have always found his kitchen, and his cellar too, open to me: many a time, after service on a Sunday—for I preach at four churches—have I recruited my spirits with a glass of his ale. Since my nephew's death, the corporation is in other hands; and I am not a man of that consequence I was formerly. I have now no longer any talents to lay out in the service of my country; and to whom nothing is given, of him can nothing be required. However, on all proper seasons, such as the approach of an election, I throw a suitable dash or two into my sermons; which I have the pleasure to hear is not disagreeable to Sir Thomas and the other honest gentlemen my neighbours, who have all promised me these five years to procure an ordination for a son of mine, who is now near thirty, hath an infinite stock of learning, and is, I thank Heaven, of an unexceptionable life; though, as he was never at an university, the bishop refuses to ordain him. Too much care cannot indeed be taken in admitting any to the sacred office; though I hope he will never act so as to be a disgrace to any order, but will serve his God and his country to the utmost of his power, as I have endeavoured to do before him; nay, and will lay down his life whenever called to that purpose. I am sure I have educated him in those principles; so that I have acquitted my duty, and shall have nothing to answer for on that account. But I do not distrust him, for he is a good boy; and if Providence should throw it in his way to be of as much consequence in a public light as his father once was, I can answer for him he will use his talents as honestly as I have done."

CHAPTER IX.

In which the gentleman discants on bravery and heroic virtue, till an unlucky accident puts an end to the discourse.

The gentleman highly commended Mr Adams for his good resolutions, and told him, "He hoped his son would tread in his steps;" adding, "that if he would not die for his country, he would not be worthy to live in it. I'd make no more of shooting a man that would not die for his country, than—

"Sir," said he, "I have disinherited a nephew, who is in the army, because he would not exchange his commission and go to the West Indies. I believe the rascal is a coward, though he pretends to be in love forsooth. I would have all such fellows hanged, sir; I would have them hanged." Adams answered, "That would be too severe; that men did not make themselves; and if fear had too much ascendance in the mind, the man was rather to be pitied than abhorred; that reason and time might teach him to subdue it." He said, "A man might be a coward at one time, and brave at another. Homer," says he, "who so well understood and copied Nature, hath taught us this lesson; for Paris fights and Hector runs away. Nay, we have a mighty instance of this in the history of later ages, no longer ago than the 705th year of Rome, when the great Pompey, who had won so many battles and been honoured with so many triumphs, and of whose valour several authors, especially Cicero and Paterculus, have formed such elogiums; this very Pompey left the battle of Pharsalia before he had lost it, and retreated to his tent, where he sat like the most pusillanimous rascal in a fit of despair, and yielded a victory, which was to determine the empire of the world, to Caesar. I am not much travelled in the history of modern times, that is to say, these last thousand years; but those who are can, I make no question, furnish you with parallel instances." He concluded, therefore, that, had he taken any such hasty resolutions against his nephew, he hoped he would consider better, and retract them. The gentleman answered with great warmth, and talked much of courage and his country, till, perceiving it grew late, he asked Adams, "What place he intended for that night?" He told him, "He waited there for the stage-coach."—"The stage-coach, sir!" said the gentleman; "they are all passed by long ago. You may see the last yourself almost three miles before us."—"I protest and so they are," cries Adams; "then I must make haste and follow them." The gentleman told him, "he would hardly be able to overtake them; and that, if he did not know his way, he would be in danger of losing himself on the downs, for it would be presently dark; and he might ramble about all night, and perhaps find himself farther from his journey's end in the morning than he was now." He advised him, therefore, "to accompany him to his house, which was very little out of his way," assuring him "that he would find some country fellow in his parish who would conduct him for sixpence to the city where he was going." Adams accepted this proposal, and on they travelled, the gentleman renewing his discourse on courage, and the infamy of not being ready, at all times, to sacrifice our lives to our country. Night overtook them much about the same time as they arrived near some bushes; whence, on a sudden, they heard the most violent shrieks imaginable in a female voice. Adams offered to snatch the gun out of his companion's hand. "What are you doing?" said he. "Doing!" said Adams; "I am hastening to the assistance of the poor creature whom some villains are murdering." "You are not mad enough, I hope," says the gentleman, trembling: "do you consider this gun is only charged with shot, and that the robbers are most probably furnished with pistols loaded with bullets? This is no business of ours; let us make as much haste as possible out of the way, or we may fall into their hands ourselves." The shrieks now increasing, Adams made no answer, but snapt his fingers, and, brandishing his crabstick, made directly to the place whence the voice issued; and the man of courage made as much expedition towards his own home, whither he escaped in a very short time without once looking behind him; where we will leave him, to contemplate his own bravery, and to censure the want of it in others, and return to the good Adams, who, on coming up to the place whence the noise proceeded, found a woman struggling with a man, who had thrown her on the ground, and had almost overpowered her. The great abilities of Mr Adams were not necessary to have formed a right judgment of this affair on the first sight. He did not, therefore, want the entreaties of the poor wretch to assist her; but, lifting up his crabstick, he immediately levelled a blow at that part of the ravisher's head where, according to the opinion of the ancients, the brains of some persons are deposited, and which he had undoubtedly let forth, had not Nature (who, as wise men have observed, equips all creatures with what is most expedient for them) taken a provident care (as she always doth with those she intends for encounters) to make this part of the head three times as thick as those of ordinary men who are designed to exercise talents which are vulgarly called rational, and for whom, as brains are necessary, she is obliged to leave some room for them in the cavity of the skull; whereas, those ingredients being entirely useless to persons of the heroic calling, she hath an opportunity of thickening the bone, so as to make it less subject to any impression, or liable to be cracked or broken: and indeed, in some who are predestined to the command of armies and empires, she is supposed sometimes to make that part perfectly solid.

As a game cock, when engaged in amorous toying with a hen, if perchance he espies another cock at hand, immediately quits his female, and opposes himself to his rival, so did the ravisher, on the information of the crabstick, immediately leap from the woman and hasten to assail the man. He had no weapons but what Nature had furnished him with. However, he clenched his fist, and presently darted it at that part of Adams's breast where the heart is lodged. Adams staggered at the violence of the blow, when, throwing away his staff, he likewise clenched that fist which we have before commemorated, and would have discharged it full in the breast of his antagonist, had he not dexterously caught it with his left hand, at the same time darting his head (which some modern heroes of the lower class use, like the battering-ram of the ancients, for a weapon of offence; another reason to admire the cunningness of Nature, in composing it of those impenetrable materials); dashing his head, I say, into the stomach of Adams, he tumbled him on his back; and, not having any regard to the laws of heroism, which would have restrained him from any farther attack on his enemy till he was again on his legs, he threw himself upon him, and, laying hold on the ground with his left hand, he with his right belaboured the body of Adams till he was weary, and indeed till he concluded (to use the language of fighting) "that he had done his business;" or, in the language of poetry, "that he had sent him to the shades below;" in plain English, "that he was dead."

But Adams, who was no chicken, and could bear a drubbing as well as any boxing champion in the universe, lay still only to watch his opportunity; and now, perceiving his antagonist to pant with his labours, he exerted his utmost force at once, and with such success that he overturned him, and became his superior; when, fixing one of his knees in his breast, he cried out in an exulting voice, "It is my turn now;" and, after a few minutes' constant application, he gave him so dexterous a blow just under his chin that the fellow no longer retained any motion, and Adams began to fear he had struck him once too often; for he often asserted "he should be concerned to have the blood of even the wicked upon him."

Adams got up and called aloud to the young woman. "Be of good cheer, damsel," said he, "you are no longer in danger of your ravisher, who, I am terribly afraid, lies dead at my feet; but God forgive me what I have done in defence of innocence!" The poor wretch, who had been some time in recovering strength enough to rise, and had afterwards, during the engagement, stood trembling, being disabled by fear even from running away, hearing her champion was victorious, came up to him, but not without apprehensions even of her deliverer; which, however, she was soon relieved from by his courteous behaviour and gentle words. They were both standing by the body, which lay motionless on the ground, and which Adams wished to see stir much more than the woman did, when he earnestly begged her to tell him "by what misfortune she came, at such a time of night, into so lonely a place." She acquainted him, "She was travelling towards London, and had accidentally met with the person from whom he had delivered her, who told her he was likewise on his journey to the same place, and would keep her company; an offer which, suspecting no harm, she had accepted; that he told her they were at a small distance from an inn where she might take up her lodging that evening, and he would show her a nearer way to it than by following the road; that if she had suspected him (which she did not, he spoke so kindly to her), being alone on these downs in the dark, she had no human means to avoid him; that, therefore, she put her whole trust in Providence, and walked on, expecting every moment to arrive at the inn; when on a sudden, being come to those bushes, he desired her to stop, and after some rude kisses, which she resisted, and some entreaties, which she rejected, he laid violent hands on her, and was attempting to execute his wicked will, when, she thanked G—, he timely came up and prevented him." Adams encouraged her for saying she had put her whole trust in Providence, and told her, "He doubted not but Providence had sent him to her deliverance, as a reward for that trust. He wished indeed he had not deprived the wicked wretch of life, but G—'s will be done;" said, "He hoped the goodness of his intention would excuse him in the next world, and he trusted in her evidence to acquit him in this." He was then silent, and began to consider with himself whether it would be properer to make his escape, or to deliver himself into the hands of justice; which meditation ended as the reader will see in the next chapter.

CHAPTER X.

Giving an account of the strange catastrophe of the preceding adventure, which drew poor Adams into fresh calamities; and who the woman was who owed the preservation of her chastity to his victorious arm.

The silence of Adams, added to the darkness of the night and loneliness of the place, struck dreadful apprehension into the poor woman's mind; she began to fear as great an enemy in her deliverer as he had delivered her from; and as she had not light enough to discover the age of Adams, and the benevolence visible in his countenance, she suspected he had used her as some very honest men have used their country; and had rescued her out of the hands of one rifler in order to rifle her himself. Such were the suspicions she drew from his silence; but indeed they were ill-grounded. He stood over his vanquished enemy, wisely weighing in his mind the objections which might be made to either of the two methods of proceeding mentioned in the last chapter, his judgment sometimes inclining to the one, and sometimes to the other; for both seemed to him so equally advisable and so equally dangerous, that probably he would have ended his days, at least two or three of them, on that very spot, before he had taken any resolution; at length he lifted up his eyes, and spied a light at a distance, to which he instantly addressed himself with *Heus tu, traveller, heus tu!* He presently heard several voices, and perceived the light approaching toward him. The persons who attended the light began some to laugh, others to sing, and others to hollow, at which the woman testified some fear (for she had concealed her suspicions of the parson himself); but Adams said, "Be of good cheer, damsel, and repose thy trust in the same Providence which hath hitherto protected thee, and never will forsake the innocent." These people, who now approached, were no other, reader, than a set of young fellows, who came to these bushes in pursuit of a diversion which they call bird-batting. This, if you are ignorant of it (as perhaps if thou hast never travelled beyond Kensington, Islington, Hackney, or the Borough, thou mayst be), I will inform thee, is performed by holding a large clap-net before a lanthorn, and at the same time beating the bushes; for the birds, when they are disturbed from their places of rest, or roost, immediately make to the light, and so are inticed within the net. Adams immediately told them what happened, and desired them to hold the lanthorn to the face of the man on the ground, for he feared he had smote him fatally. But indeed his fears were frivolous; for the fellow, though he had been stunned by the last blow he received, had long since recovered his senses, and, finding himself quit of Adams, had listened attentively to the discourse between him and the young woman; for whose departure he had patiently waited, that he might likewise withdraw himself, having no longer hopes of succeeding in his desires, which were moreover almost as well cooled by Mr Adams as they could have been by the young woman herself had he obtained his utmost wish. This fellow, who had a readiness at improving any accident, thought he might now play a better part than that of a dead man; and, accordingly, the moment the candle was held to his face he leapt up, and, laying hold on Adams, cried out, "No, villain, I am not dead, though you and your wicked whore might well think me so, after the barbarous cruelties you have exercised on me. Gentlemen," said he, "you are luckily come to the assistance of a poor traveller, who would otherwise have been robbed and murdered by this vile man and woman, who led me hither out of my way from the high-road, and both falling on me have used me as you see." Adams was going to answer, when one of the young fellows cried, "D—n them, let's carry them both before the justice." The poor woman began to tremble, and Adams lifted up his voice, but in vain. Three or four of them laid hands on him; and one holding the lanthorn to his face, they all agreed he had the most villainous countenance they ever beheld; and an attorney's clerk, who was of the company, declared he was sure he had remembered him at the bar. As to the woman, her hair was dishevelled in the struggle, and her nose had bled; so that they could not perceive whether she was handsome or ugly, but they said her fright plainly discovered her guilt. And searching her pockets, as they did those of Adams, for money, which the fellow said he had lost, they found in her pocket a purse with some gold in it, which abundantly convinced them, especially as the fellow offered to swear to it. Mr Adams was found to have no more than one halfpenny about him. This the clerk said "was a great presumption that he was an old offender, by cunningly giving all the booty to the woman." To which all the rest readily assented.

This accident promising them better sport than what they had proposed, they quitted their intention of catching birds, and unanimously resolved to proceed to the justice with the offenders. Being informed what a desperate fellow Adams was, they tied his hands behind him; and, having hid their nets among the bushes, and the lanthorn being carried before them, they placed the two prisoners in their front, and then began their march; Adams not only submitting patiently to his own fate, but comforting and encouraging his companion under her sufferings.

Whilst they were on their way the clerk informed the rest that this adventure would prove a very beneficial one; for that they would all be entitled to their proportions of £80 for apprehending the robbers. This occasioned a contention concerning the parts which they had severally borne in taking them; one insisting he ought to have the greatest share, for he had first laid his hands on Adams; another claiming a superior part for having first held the lanthorn to the man's face on the ground, by which, he said, "the whole was discovered." The clerk claimed four-fifths of the reward for having proposed to search the prisoners, and likewise the carrying them before the justice: he said, "Indeed, in strict justice, he ought to have the whole." These claims, however, they at last consented to refer to a future decision, but seemed all to agree that the clerk was entitled to a moiety. They then debated what money should be allotted to the young fellow who had been employed only in holding the nets. He very modestly said, "That he did not apprehend any large proportion would fall to his share, but hoped they would allow him something; he desired them to consider that they had assigned their nets to his care, which prevented him from being as forward as any in laying hold of the robbers" (for so those innocent people were called); "that if he had not occupied the nets, some other must;" concluding, however, "that he should be contented with the smallest share imaginable, and should think that rather their bounty than his merit." But they were all unanimous in excluding him from any part whatever, the clerk particularly swearing, "If they gave him a shilling they might do what they pleased with the rest; for he would not concern himself with the affair." This contention was so hot, and so totally engaged the attention of all the parties, that a dexterous nimble thief, had he been in Mr Adams's situation, would have taken care to have given the justice no trouble that evening. Indeed, it required not the art of a Sheppard to escape, especially as the darkness of the night would have so much befriended him; but Adams trusted rather to his innocence than his heels, and, without thinking of flight, which was easy, or resistance (which was impossible, as there were six lusty young fellows, besides the villain himself, present), he walked with perfect resignation the way they thought proper to conduct him.

Adams frequently vented himself in ejaculations during their journey; at last, poor Joseph Andrews occurring to his mind, he could not refrain sighing forth his name, which being heard by his companion in affliction, she cried with some vehemence, "Sure I should know that voice; you cannot certainly, sir, be Mr Abraham Adams?"—"Indeed, damsel," says he, "that is my name; there is something also in your voice which persuades me I have heard it before."—"La! sir," says she, "don't you remember poor Fanny?"—"How, Fanny!" answered Adams: "indeed I very well remember you; what can have brought you hither?"—"I have told you, sir," replied she, "I was travelling towards London; but I thought you mentioned Joseph Andrews; pray what is become of him?"—"I left him, child, this afternoon," said Adams, "in the stage-coach, in his way towards our parish, whither he is going to see you."—"To see me! La, sir," answered Fanny, "sure you jeer me; what should he be going to see me for?"—"Can you ask that?" replied Adams. "I hope, Fanny, you are not inconstant; I assure you he deserves much better of you."—"La! Mr Adams," said she, "what is Mr Joseph to me? I am sure I never had anything to say to him, but as one fellow-servant might to another."—"I am sorry to hear this," said Adams; "a virtuous passion for a young man is what no woman need be ashamed of. You either do not tell me truth, or you are false to a very worthy man." Adams then told her what had happened at the inn, to which she listened very attentively; and a sigh often escaped from her, notwithstanding her utmost endeavours to the contrary; nor could she prevent herself from asking a thousand questions, which would have assured any one but Adams, who never saw farther into people than they desired to let him, of the truth of a passion she endeavoured to conceal. Indeed, the fact was, that this poor girl, having heard of Joseph's misfortune, by some of the servants belonging to the coach which we have formerly mentioned to have stopt at the inn while the poor youth was confined to his bed, that instant abandoned the cow she was milking, and, taking with her a little bundle of clothes under her arm, and all the money she was worth in her own purse, without consulting any one, immediately set forward in pursuit of one whom, notwithstanding her shyness to the parson, she loved with inexpressible violence, though with the purest and most delicate passion. This shyness, therefore, as we trust it will recommend her character to all our female readers, and not greatly surprize such of our males as are well acquainted with the younger part of the other sex, we shall not give ourselves any trouble to vindicate.

CHAPTER XI.

What happened to them while before the justice. A chapter very full of learning.

Their fellow-travellers were so engaged in the hot dispute concerning the division of the reward for apprehending these innocent people, that they attended very little to their discourse. They were now arrived at the justice's house, and had sent one of his servants in to acquaint his worship that they had taken two robbers and brought them before him. The justice, who was just returned from a fox-chase, and had not yet finished his dinner, ordered them to carry the prisoners into the stable, whither they were attended by all the servants in the house, and all the people in the neighbourhood, who flocked together to see them with as much curiosity as if there was something uncommon to be seen, or that a rogue did not look like other people.

The justice, now being in the height of his mirth and his cups, bethought himself of the prisoners; and, telling his company he believed they should have good sport in their examination, he ordered them into his presence. They had no sooner entered the room than he began to revile them, saying, "That robberies on the highway were now grown so frequent, that people could not sleep safely in their beds, and assured them they both should be made examples of at the ensuing assizes." After he had gone on some time in this manner, he was reminded by his clerk, "That it would be proper to take the depositions of the witnesses against them." Which he bid him do, and he would light his pipe in the meantime. Whilst the clerk was employed in writing down the deposition of the fellow who had pretended to be robbed, the justice employed himself in cracking jests on poor Fanny, in which he was seconded by all the company at table. One asked, "Whether she was to be indicted for a highwayman?" Another whispered in her ear, "If she had not provided herself a great belly, he was at her service." A third said, "He warranted she was a relation of Turpin." To which one of the company, a great wit, shaking his head, and then his sides, answered, "He believed she was nearer related to Turpis;" at which there was an universal laugh. They were proceeding thus with the poor girl, when somebody, smoking the cassock peeping forth from under the greatcoat of Adams, cried out, "What have we here, a parson?" "How, sirrah," says the justice, "do you go robbing in the dress of a clergyman? let me tell you your habit will not entitle you to the benefit of the clergy." "Yes," said the witty fellow, "he will have one benefit of clergy, he will be exalted above the heads of the people;" at which there was a second laugh. And now the witty spark, seeing his jokes take, began to rise in spirits; and, turning to Adams, challenged him to cap verses, and, provoking him by giving the first blow, he repeated—

"Molle meum levibus cord est vilebile telis."

Upon which Adams, with a look full of ineffable contempt, told him, "He deserved scourging for his pronunciation." The witty fellow answered, "What do you deserve, doctor, for not being able to answer the first time? Why, I'll give one, you blockhead, with an S.

"'Si licet, ut fulvum spectatur in ignibus haurum.'

"What, canst not with an M neither? Thou art a pretty fellow for a parson! Why didst not steal some of the parson's Latin as well as his gown?" Another at the table then answered, "If he had, you would have been too hard for him; I remember you at the college a very devil at this sport; I have seen you catch a freshman, for nobody that knew you would engage with you." "I have forgot those things now," cried the wit. "I believe I could have done pretty well formerly. Let's see, what did I end with?—an M again—aye—

"'Mars, Bacchus, Apollo, virorum.'

I could have done it once." "Ah! evil betide you, and so you can now," said the other: "nobody in this country will undertake you." Adams could hold no longer: "Friend," said he, "I have a boy not above eight years old who would instruct thee that the last verse runs thus:—

"'Ut sunt Divorum, Mars, Bacchus, Apollo, virorum.'"

"I'll hold thee a guinea of that," said the wit, throwing the money on the table. "And I'll go your halves," cries the other. "Done," answered Adams; but upon applying to his pocket he was forced to retract, and own he had no money about him; which set them all a-laughing, and confirmed the triumph of his adversary, which was not moderate, any more than the approbation he met with from the whole company, who told Adams he must go a little longer to school before he attempted to attack that gentleman in Latin.

The clerk, having finished the depositions, as well of the fellow himself, as of those who apprehended the prisoners, delivered them to the justice; who, having sworn the several witnesses without reading a syllable, ordered his clerk to make the mittimus.

Adams then said, "He hoped he should not be condemned unheard." "No, no," cries the justice, "you will be asked what you have to say for yourself when you come on your trial: we are not trying you now; I shall only commit you to gaol: if you can prove your innocence at size, you will be found ignoramus, and so no harm done." "Is it no punishment, sir, for an innocent man to lie several months in gaol?" cries Adams: "I beg you would at least hear me before you sign the mittimus." "What signifies all you can say?" says the justice: "is it not here in black and white against you? I must tell you you are a very impertinent fellow to take up so much of my time. So make haste with his mittimus."

The clerk now acquainted the justice that among other suspicious things, as a penknife, &c., found in Adams's pocket, they had discovered a book written, as he apprehended, in cyphers; for no one could read a word in it. "Ay," says the justice, "the fellow may be more than a common robber, he may be in a plot against the Government. Produce the book." Upon which the poor manuscript of Aeschylus, which Adams had transcribed with his own hand, was brought forth; and the justice, looking at it, shook his head, and, turning to the prisoner, asked the meaning of those cyphers. "Cyphers?" answered Adams, "it is a manuscript of Aeschylus." "Who? who?" said the justice. Adams repeated, "Aeschylus." "That is an outlandish name," cried the clerk. "A fictitious name rather, I believe," said the justice. One of the company declared it looked very much like Greek. "Greek?" said the justice; "why, 'tis all writing." "No," says the other, "I don't positively say it is so; for it is a very long time since I have seen any Greek." "There's one," says he, turning to the parson of the parish, who was present, "will tell us immediately." The parson, taking up the book, and putting on his spectacles and gravity together, muttered some words to himself, and then pronounced aloud—"Ay, indeed, it is a Greek manuscript; a very fine piece of antiquity. I make no doubt but it was stolen from the same clergyman from whom the rogue took the cassock." "What did the rascal mean by his Aeschylus?" says the justice. "Pooh!" answered the doctor, with a contemptuous grin, "do you think that fellow knows anything of this book? Aeschylus! ho! ho! I see now what it is—a manuscript of one of the fathers. I know a nobleman who would give a great deal of money for such a piece of antiquity. Ay, ay, question and answer. The beginning is the catechism in Greek. Ay, ay, *Pollaki toi*: What's your name?"—"Ay, what's your name?" says the justice to Adams; who answered, "It is Aeschylus, and I will maintain it."—"Oh! it is," says the justice: "make Mr Aeschylus his mittimus. I will teach you to banter me with a false name."

One of the company, having looked steadfastly at Adams, asked him, "If he did not know Lady Booby?" Upon which Adams, presently calling him to mind, answered in a rapture, "O squire! are you there? I believe you will inform his worship I am innocent."—"I can indeed say," replied the squire, "that I am very much surprized to see you in this situation:" and then, addressing himself to the justice, he said, "Sir, I assure you Mr Adams is a clergyman, as he appears, and a gentleman of a very good character. I wish you would enquire a little farther into this affair; for I am convinced of his innocence."—"Nay," says the justice, "if he is a gentleman, and you are sure he is innocent, I don't desire to commit him, not I: I will commit the woman by herself, and take your bail for the gentleman: look into the book, clerk, and see how it is to take bail—come—and make the mittimus for the woman as fast as you can."—"Sir," cries Adams, "I assure you she is as innocent as myself."—"Perhaps," said the squire, "there may be some mistake! pray let us hear Mr Adams's relation."—"With all my heart," answered the justice; "and give the gentleman a glass to wet his whistle before he begins. I know how to behave myself to gentlemen as well as another. Nobody can say I have committed a gentleman since I have been in the commission." Adams then began the narrative, in which, though he was very prolix, he was uninterrupted, unless by several hums and hahs of the justice, and his desire to repeat those parts which seemed to him most material. When he had finished, the justice, who, on what the squire had said, believed every syllable of his story on his bare affirmation, notwithstanding the depositions on oath to the contrary, began to let loose several rogues and rascals against the witness, whom he ordered to stand forth, but in vain; the said witness, long since finding what turn matters were likely to take, had privily withdrawn, without attending the issue. The justice now flew into a violent passion, and was hardly prevailed with not to commit the innocent fellows who had been imposed on as well as himself. He swore, "They had best find out the fellow who was guilty of perjury, and bring him before him within two days, or he would bind them all over to their good behaviour." They all promised to use their best endeavours to that purpose, and were dismissed. Then the justice insisted that Mr Adams should sit down and take a glass with him; and the parson of the parish delivered him back the manuscript without saying a word; nor would Adams, who plainly discerned his ignorance, expose it. As for Fanny, she was, at her own request, recommended to the care of a maid-servant of the house, who helped her to new dress and clean herself.

The company in the parlour had not been long seated before they were alarmed with a horrible uproar from without, where the persons who had apprehended Adams and Fanny had been regaling, according to the custom of the house, with the justice's strong beer. These were all fallen together by the ears, and were cuffing each other without any mercy. The justice himself sallied out, and with the dignity of his presence soon put an end to the fray. On his return into the parlour, he reported, "That the occasion of the quarrel was no other than a dispute to whom, if Adams had been convicted, the greater share of the reward for apprehending him had belonged." All the company laughed at this, except Adams, who, taking his pipe from his mouth, fetched a deep groan, and said, "He was concerned to see so litigious a temper in men. That he remembered a story something like it in one of the parishes where his cure lay:—There was," continued he, "a competition between three young fellows for the place of the clerk, which I disposed of, to the best of my abilities, according to merit; that is, I gave it to him who had the happiest knack at setting a psalm. The clerk was no sooner established in his place than a contention began between the two disappointed candidates concerning their excellence; each contending on whom, had they two been the only competitors, my election would have fallen. This dispute frequently disturbed the congregation, and introduced a discord into the psalmody, till I was forced to silence them both. But, alas! the litigious spirit could not be stifled; and, being no longer able to vent itself in singing, it now broke forth in fighting. It produced many battles (for they were very near a match), and I believe would have ended fatally, had not the death of the clerk given me an opportunity to promote one of them to his place; which presently put an end to the dispute, and entirely reconciled the contending parties." Adams then proceeded to make some philosophical observations on the folly of growing warm in disputes in which neither party is interested. He then applied himself vigorously to smoaking; and a long silence ensued, which was at length broke by the justice, who began to sing forth his own praises, and to value himself exceedingly on his nice discernment in the cause which had lately been before him. He was quickly interrupted by Mr Adams, between whom and his worship a dispute now arose, whether he ought not, in strictness of law, to have committed him, the said Adams; in which the latter maintained he ought to have been committed, and the justice as vehemently held he ought not. This had most probably produced a quarrel (for both were very violent and positive in their opinions), had not Fanny accidentally heard that a young fellow was going from the justice's house to the very inn where the stage-coach in which Joseph was, put up. Upon this news, she immediately sent for the parson out of the parlour. Adams, when he found her resolute to go (though she would not own the reason, but pretended she could not bear to see the faces of those who had suspected her of such a crime), was as fully determined to go with her; he accordingly took leave of the justice and company: and so ended a dispute in which the law seemed shamefully to intend to set a magistrate and a divine together by the ears.

CHAPTER XII.

A very delightful adventure, as well to the persons concerned as to the good-natured reader.

Adams, Fanny, and the guide, set out together about one in the morning, the moon being then just risen. They had not gone above a mile before a most violent storm of rain obliged them to take shelter in an inn, or rather alehouse, where Adams immediately procured himself a good fire, a toast and ale, and a pipe, and began to smoke with great content, utterly forgetting everything that had happened.

Fanny sat likewise down by the fire; but was much more impatient at the storm. She presently engaged the eyes of the host, his wife, the maid of the house, and the young fellow who was their guide; they all conceived they had never seen anything half so handsome; and indeed, reader, if thou art of an amorous hue, I advise thee to skip over the next paragraph; which, to render our history perfect, we are obliged to set down, humbly hoping that we may escape the fate of Pygmalion; for if it should happen to us, or to thee, to be struck with this picture, we should be perhaps in as helpless a condition as Narcissus, and might say to ourselves, *Quod petis est nusquam*. Or, if the finest features in it should set Lady ——'s image before our eyes, we should be still in as bad a situation, and might say to our desires, *Coelum ipsum petimus stultitia*.

Fanny was now in the nineteenth year of her age; she was tall and delicately shaped; but not one of those slender young women who seem rather intended to hang up in the hall of an anatomist than for any other purpose. On the contrary, she was so plump that she seemed bursting through her tight stays, especially in the part which confined her swelling breasts. Nor did her hips want the assistance of a hoop to extend them. The exact shape of her arms denoted the form of those limbs which she concealed; and though they were a little reddened by her labour, yet, if her sleeve slipped above her elbow, or her handkerchief discovered any part of her neck, a whiteness appeared which the finest Italian paint would be unable to reach. Her hair was of a chesnut brown, and nature had been extremely lavish to her of it, which she had cut, and on Sundays used to curl down her neck, in the modern fashion. Her forehead was high, her eyebrows arched, and rather full than otherwise. Her eyes black and sparkling; her nose just inclining to the Roman; her lips red and moist, and her underlip, according to the opinion of the ladies, too pouting. Her teeth were white, but not exactly even. The small-pox had left one only mark on her chin, which was so large, it might have been mistaken for a dimple, had not her left cheek produced one so near a neighbour to it, that the former served only for a foil to the latter. Her complexion was fair, a little injured by the sun, but overspread with such a bloom that the finest ladies would have exchanged all their white for it: add to these a countenance in which, though she was extremely bashful, a sensibility appeared almost incredible; and a sweetness, whenever she smiled, beyond either imitation or description. To conclude all, she had a natural gentility, superior to the acquisition of art, and which surprized all who beheld her.

This lovely creature was sitting by the fire with Adams, when her attention was suddenly engaged by a voice from an inner room, which sung the following song:—

THE SONG.
Say, Chloe, where must the swain stray
  Who is by thy beauties undone?
To wash their remembrance away,
  To what distant Lethe must run?
The wretch who is sentenced to die
  May escape, and leave justice behind;
From his country perhaps he may fly,
  But oh! can he fly from his mind?
O rapture! unthought of before,
  To be thus of Chloe possess'd;
Nor she, nor no tyrant's hard power,
  Her image can tear from my breast.
But felt not Narcissus more joy,
  With his eyes he beheld his loved charms?
Yet what he beheld the fond boy
  More eagerly wish'd in his arms.
How can it thy dear image be
  Which fills thus my bosom with woe?
Can aught bear resemblance to thee
  Which grief and not joy can bestow?
This counterfeit snatch from my heart,
  Ye pow'rs, tho' with torment I rave,
Tho' mortal will prove the fell smart:
  I then shall find rest in my grave.
Ah, see the dear nymph o'er the plain
  Come smiling and tripping along!
A thousand Loves dance in her train,
  The Graces around her all throng.
To meet her soft Zephyrus flies,
  And wafts all the sweets from the flowers,
Ah, rogue I whilst he kisses her eyes,

More sweets from her breath he devours.
My soul, whilst I gaze, is on fire:
But her looks were so tender and kind,
My hope almost reach'd my desire,
And left lame despair far behind.
Transported with madness, I flew,
And eagerly seized on my bliss;
Her bosom but half she withdrew,
But half she refused my fond kiss.
Advances like these made me bold;
I whisper'd her—Love, we're alone.—
The rest let immortals unfold;
No language can tell but their own.
Ah, Chloe, expiring, I cried,
How long I thy cruelty bore!
Ah, Strephon, she blushing replied,
You ne'er was so pressing before.

Adams had been ruminating all this time on a passage in Aeschylus, without attending in the least to the voice, though one of the most melodious that ever was heard, when, casting his eyes on Fanny, he cried out, "Bless us, you look extremely pale!"—"Pale! Mr Adams," says she; "O Jesus!" and fell backwards in her chair. Adams jumped up, flung his Aeschylus into the fire, and fell a-roaring to the people of the house for help. He soon summoned every one into the room, and the songster among the rest; but, O reader! when this nightingale, who was no other than Joseph Andrews himself, saw his beloved Fanny in the situation we have described her, canst thou conceive the agitations of his mind? If thou canst not, waive that meditation to behold his happiness, when, clasping her in his arms, he found life and blood returning into her cheeks: when he saw her open her beloved eyes, and heard her with the softest accent whisper, "Are you Joseph Andrews?"—"Art thou my Fanny?" he answered eagerly: and, pulling her to his heart, he imprinted numberless kisses on her lips, without considering who were present.

If prudes are offended at the lusciousness of this picture, they may take their eyes off from it, and survey parson Adams dancing about the room in a rapture of joy. Some philosophers may perhaps doubt whether he was not the happiest of the three: for the goodness of his heart enjoyed the blessings which were exulting in the breasts of both the other two, together with his own. But we shall leave such disquisitions, as too deep for us, to those who are building some favourite hypothesis, which they will refuse no metaphysical rubbish to erect and support: for our part, we give it clearly on the side of Joseph, whose happiness was not only greater than the parson's, but of longer duration: for as soon as the first tumults of Adams's rapture were over he cast his eyes towards the fire, where Aeschylus lay expiring; and immediately rescued the poor remains, to wit, the sheepskin covering, of his dear friend, which was the work of his own hands, and had been his inseparable companion for upwards of thirty years.

Fanny had no sooner perfectly recovered herself than she began to restrain the impetuosity of her transports; and, reflecting on what she had done and suffered in the presence of so many, she was immediately covered with confusion; and, pushing Joseph gently from her, she begged him to be quiet, nor would admit of either kiss or embrace any longer. Then, seeing Mrs Slipslop, she curtsied, and offered to advance to her; but that high woman would not return her curtsies; but, casting her eyes another way, immediately withdrew into another room, muttering, as she went, she wondered who the creature was.

CHAPTER XIII.

A dissertation concerning high people and low people, with Mrs Slipslop's departure in no very good temper of mind, and the evil plight in which she left Adams and his company.

It will doubtless seem extremely odd to many readers, that Mrs Slipslop, who had lived several years in the same house with Fanny, should, in a short separation, utterly forget her. And indeed the truth is, that she remembered her very well. As we would not willingly, therefore, that anything should appear unnatural in this our history, we will endeavour to explain the reasons of her conduct; nor do we doubt being able to satisfy the most curious reader that Mrs Slipslop did not in the least deviate from the common road in this behaviour; and, indeed, had she done otherwise, she must have descended below herself, and would have very justly been liable to censure.

Be it known then, that the human species are divided into two sorts of people, to wit, high people and low people. As by high people I would not be understood to mean persons literally born higher in their dimensions than the rest of the species, nor metaphorically those of exalted characters or abilities; so by low people I cannot be construed to intend the reverse. High people signify no other than people of fashion, and low people those of no fashion. Now, this word fashion hath by long use lost its original meaning, from which at present it gives us a very different idea; for I am deceived if by persons of fashion we do not generally include a conception of birth and accomplishments superior to the herd of mankind; whereas, in reality, nothing more was originally meant by a person of fashion than a person who drest himself in the fashion of the times; and the word really and truly signifies no more at this day. Now, the world being thus divided into people of fashion and people of no fashion, a fierce contention arose between them; nor would those of one party, to avoid suspicion, be seen publicly to speak to those of the other, though they often held a very good correspondence in private. In this contention it is difficult to say which party succeeded; for, whilst the people of fashion seized several places to their own use, such as courts, assemblies, operas, balls, &c., the people of no fashion, besides one royal place, called his Majesty's Bear-garden, have been in constant possession of all hops, fairs, revels, &c. Two places have been agreed to be divided between them, namely, the church and the playhouse, where they segregate themselves from each other in a remarkable manner; for, as the people of fashion exalt themselves at church over the heads of the people of no fashion, so in the playhouse they abase themselves in the same degree under their feet. This distinction I have never met with any one able to account for: it is sufficient that, so far from looking on each other as brethren in the Christian language, they seem scarce to regard each other as of the same species. This, the terms "strange persons, people one does not know, the creature, wretches, beasts, brutes," and many other appellations evidently demonstrate; which Mrs Slipslop, having often heard her mistress use, thought she had also a right to use in her turn; and perhaps she was not mistaken; for these two parties, especially those bordering nearly on each other, to wit, the lowest of the high, and the highest of the low, often change their parties according to place and time; for those who are people of fashion in one place are often people of no fashion in another. And with regard to time, it may not be unpleasant to survey the picture of dependance like a kind of ladder; as, for instance; early in the morning arises the postillion, or some other boy, which great families, no more than great ships, are without, and falls to brushing the clothes and cleaning the shoes of John the footman; who, being drest himself, applies his hands to the same labours for Mr Second-hand, the squire's gentleman; the gentleman in the like manner, a little later in the day, attends the squire; the squire is no sooner equipped than he attends the levee of my lord; which is no sooner over than my lord himself is seen at the levee of the favourite, who, after the hour of homage is at an end, appears himself to pay homage to the levee of his sovereign. Nor is there, perhaps, in this whole ladder of dependance, any one step at a greater distance from the other than the first from the second; so that to a philosopher the question might only seem, whether you would chuse to be a great man at six in the morning, or at two in the afternoon. And yet there are scarce two of these who do not think the least familiarity with the persons below them a condescension, and, if they were to go one step farther, a degradation.

And now, reader, I hope thou wilt pardon this long digression, which seemed to me necessary to vindicate the great character of Mrs Slipslop from what low people, who have never seen high people, might think an absurdity; but we who know them must have daily found very high persons know us in one place and not in another, to-day and not to-morrow; all which it is difficult to account for otherwise than I have here endeavoured; and perhaps, if the gods, according to the opinion of some, made men only to laugh at them, there is no part of our behaviour which answers the end of our creation better than this.

But to return to our history: Adams, who knew no more of this than the cat which sat on the table, imagining Mrs Slipslop's memory had been much worse than it really was, followed her into the next room, crying out, "Madam Slipslop, here is one of your old acquaintance; do but see what a fine woman she is grown since she left Lady Booby's service."—"I think I reflect something of her," answered she, with great dignity, "but I can't remember all the inferior servants in our family." She then proceeded to satisfy Adams's curiosity, by telling him, "When she arrived at the inn, she found a chaise ready for her; that, her lady being expected very shortly in the country, she was obliged to make the utmost haste;

and, in commensuration of Joseph's lameness, she had taken him with her;" and lastly, "that the excessive virulence of the storm had driven them into the house where he found them." After which, she acquainted Adams with his having left his horse, and exprest some wonder at his having strayed so far out of his way, and at meeting him, as she said, "in the company of that wench, who she feared was no better than she should be."

The horse was no sooner put into Adams's head but he was immediately driven out by this reflection on the character of Fanny. He protested, "He believed there was not a chaster damsel in the universe. I heartily wish, I heartily wish," cried he (snapping his fingers), "that all her betters were as good." He then proceeded to inform her of the accident of their meeting; but when he came to mention the circumstance of delivering her from the rape, she said, "She thought him properer for the army than the clergy; that it did not become a clergyman to lay violent hands on any one; that he should have rather prayed that she might be strengthened." Adams said, "He was very far from being ashamed of what he had done:" she replied, "Want of shame was not the currycuristic of a clergyman." This dialogue might have probably grown warmer, had not Joseph opportunely entered the room, to ask leave of Madam Slipslop to introduce Fanny: but she positively refused to admit any such trollops, and told him, "She would have been burnt before she would have suffered him to get into a chaise with her, if she had once respected him of having his sluts waylaid on the road for him;" adding, "that Mr Adams acted a very pretty part, and she did not doubt but to see him a bishop." He made the best bow he could, and cried out, "I thank you, madam, for that right-reverend appellation, which I shall take all honest means to deserve."-"Very honest means," returned she, with a sneer, "to bring people together." At these words Adams took two or three strides across the room, when the coachman came to inform Mrs Slipslop, "That the storm was over, and the moon shone very bright." She then sent for Joseph, who was sitting without with his Fanny, and would have had him gone with her; but he peremptorily refused to leave Fanny behind, which threw the good woman into a violent rage. She said, "She would inform her lady what doings were carrying on, and did not doubt but she would rid the parish of all such people;" and concluded a long speech, full of bitterness and very hard words, with some reflections on the clergy not decent to repeat; at last, finding Joseph unmoveable, she flung herself into the chaise, casting a look at Fanny as she went, not unlike that which Cleopatra gives Octavia in the play. To say the truth, she was most disagreeably disappointed by the presence of Fanny: she had, from her first seeing Joseph at the inn, conceived hopes of something which might have been accomplished at an alehouse as well as a palace. Indeed, it is probable Mr Adams had rescued more than Fanny from the clanger of a rape that evening.

When the chaise had carried off the enraged Slipslop, Adams, Joseph, and Fanny assembled over the fire, where they had a great deal of innocent chat, pretty enough; but, as possibly it would not be very entertaining to the reader, we shall hasten to the morning; only observing that none of them went to bed that night. Adams, when he had smoaked three pipes, took a comfortable nap in a great chair, and left the lovers, whose eyes were too well employed to permit any desire of shutting them, to enjoy by themselves, during some hours, an happiness which none of my readers who have never been in love are capable of the least conception of, though we had as many tongues as Homer desired, to describe it with, and which all true lovers will represent to their own minds without the least assistance from us.

Joseph thanked her on his knees. Let it suffice then to say, that Fanny, after a thousand entreaties, at last gave up her whole soul to Joseph; and, almost fainting in his arms, with a sigh infinitely softer and sweeter too than any Arabian breeze, she whispered to his lips, which were then close to hers, "O Joseph, you have won me: I will be yours for ever." Joseph, having thanked her on his knees, and embraced her with an eagerness which she now almost returned, leapt up in a rapture, and awakened the parson, earnestly begging him "that he would that instant join their hands together." Adams rebuked him for his request, and told him "He would by no means consent to anything contrary to the forms of the Church; that he had no licence, nor indeed would he advise him to obtain one; that the Church had prescribed a form—namely, the publication of banns—with which all good Christians ought to comply, and to the omission of which he attributed the many miseries which befell great folks in marriage;" concluding, "As many as are joined together otherwise than G—'s word doth allow are not joined together by G—, neither is their matrimony lawful." Fanny agreed with the parson, saying to Joseph, with a blush, "She assured him she would not consent to any such thing, and that she wondered at his offering it." In which resolution she was comforted and commended by Adams; and Joseph was obliged to wait patiently till after the third publication of the banns, which, however, he obtained the consent of Fanny, in the presence of Adams, to put in at their arrival.

The sun had been now risen some hours, when Joseph, finding his leg surprizingly recovered, proposed to walk forwards; but when they were all ready to set out, an accident a little retarded them. This was no other than the reckoning, which amounted to seven shillings; no great sum if we consider the immense quantity of ale which Mr Adams poured in. Indeed, they had no objection to the reasonableness of the bill, but many to the probability of paying it; for the fellow who had taken poor Fanny's purse had unluckily forgot to return it. So that the account stood thus:—

	£ S D
Mr Adams and company, Dr.	0 7 0
In Mr Adams's pocket	0 0 6½
In Mr Joseph's	0 0 0
In Mrs Fanny's	0 0 0
Balance	0 6 5½

They stood silent some few minutes, staring at each other, when Adams whipt out on his toes, and asked the hostess, "If there was no clergyman in that parish?" She answered, "There was."—"Is he wealthy?" replied he; to which she likewise answered in the affirmative. Adams then snapping his fingers returned overjoyed to his companions, crying out, "Heureka, Heureka;" which not being understood, he told them in plain English, "They need give themselves no trouble, for he had a brother in the parish who would defray the reckoning, and that he would just step to his house and fetch the money, and return to them instantly."

CHAPTER XIV.

An interview between parson Adams and parson Trulliber.

Parson Adams came to the house of parson Trulliber, whom he found stript into his waistcoat, with an apron on, and a pail in his hand, just come from serving his hogs; for Mr Trulliber was a parson on Sundays, but all the other six might more properly be called a farmer. He occupied a small piece of land of his own, besides which he rented a considerable deal more. His wife milked his cows, managed his dairy, and followed the markets with butter and eggs. The hogs fell chiefly to his care, which he carefully waited on at home, and attended to fairs; on which occasion he was liable to many jokes, his own size being, with much ale, rendered little inferior to that of the beasts he sold. He was indeed one of the largest men you should see, and could have acted the part of Sir John Falstaff without stuffing. Add to this that the rotundity of his belly was considerably increased by the shortness of his stature, his shadow ascending very near as far in height, when he lay on his back, as when he stood on his legs. His voice was loud and hoarse, and his accents extremely broad. To complete the whole, he had a stateliness in his gait, when he walked, not unlike that of a goose, only he stalked slower.

Mr Trulliber, being informed that somebody wanted to speak with him, immediately slipt off his apron and clothed himself in an old night-gown, being the dress in which he always saw his company at home. His wife, who informed him of Mr Adams's arrival, had made a small mistake; for she had told her husband, "She believed there was a man come for some of his hogs." This supposition made Mr Trulliber hasten with the utmost expedition to attend his guest. He no sooner saw Adams than, not in the least doubting the cause of his errand to be what his wife had imagined, he told him, "He was come in very good time; that he expected a dealer that very afternoon;" and added, "they were all pure and fat, and upwards of twenty score a-piece." Adams answered, "He believed he did not know him." "Yes, yes," cried Trulliber, "I have seen you often at fair; why, we have dealt before now, mun, I warrant you. Yes, yes," cries he, "I remember thy face very well, but won't mention a word more till you have seen them, though I have never sold thee a flitch of such bacon as is now in the stye." Upon which he laid violent hands on Adams, and dragged him into the hog-stye, which was indeed but two steps from his parlour window. They were no sooner arrived there than he cry'd out, "Do but handle them! step in, friend! art welcome to handle them, whether dost buy or no." At which words, opening the gate, he pushed Adams into the pig-stye, insisting on it that he should handle them before he would talk one word with him.

Adams, whose natural complacence was beyond any artificial, was obliged to comply before he was suffered to explain himself; and, laying hold on one of their tails, the unruly beast gave such a sudden spring, that he threw poor Adams all along in the mire. Trulliber, instead of assisting him to get up, burst into a laughter, and, entering the stye, said to Adams, with some contempt, "Why, dost not know how to handle a hog?" and was going to lay hold of one himself, but Adams, who thought he had carried his complacence far enough, was no sooner on his legs than he escaped out of the reach of the animals, and cried out, "*Nihil habeo cum porcis*: I am a clergyman, sir, and am not come to buy hogs." Trulliber answered, "He was sorry for the mistake, but that he must blame his wife," adding, "she was a fool, and always committed blunders." He then desired him to walk in and clean himself, that he would only fasten up the stye and follow him. Adams desired leave to dry his greatcoat, wig, and hat by the fire, which Trulliber granted. Mrs Trulliber would have brought him a basin of water to wash his face, but her husband bid her be quiet like a fool as she was, or she would commit more blunders, and then directed Adams to the pump. While Adams was thus employed, Trulliber, conceiving no great respect for the appearance of his guest, fastened the parlour door, and now conducted him into the kitchen, telling him he believed a cup of drink would do him no harm, and whispered his wife to draw a little of the worst ale. After a short silence Adams said, "I fancy, sir, you already perceive me to be a clergyman."—"Ay, ay," cries Trulliber, grinning, "I perceive you have some cassock; I will not venture to caale it a whole one." Adams answered, "It was indeed none of the best, but he had the misfortune to tear it about ten years ago in passing over a stile." Mrs Trulliber, returning with the drink, told her husband, "She fancied the gentleman was a traveller, and that he would be glad to eat a bit." Trulliber bid her hold her impertinent tongue, and asked her, "If parsons used to travel without horses?" adding, "he supposed the gentleman had none by his having no boots on."—"Yes, sir, yes," says Adams; "I have a horse, but I have left him behind me."—"I am glad to hear you have one," says Trulliber; "for I assure you I don't love to see clergymen on foot; it is not seemly nor suiting the dignity of the cloth." Here Trulliber made a long oration on the dignity of the cloth (or rather gown) not much worth relating, till his wife had spread the table and set a mess of porridge on it for his breakfast. He then said to Adams, "I don't know, friend, how you came to caale on me; however, as you are here, if you think proper to eat a morsel, you may." Adams accepted the invitation, and the two parsons sat down together; Mrs Trulliber waiting behind her husband's chair, as was, it seems, her custom. Trulliber eat heartily, but scarce put anything in his mouth without finding fault with his wife's cookery. All which the poor woman bore patiently. Indeed, she was so absolute an admirer of her husband's greatness and importance, of which she had frequent hints from his own mouth, that she almost carried her adoration to an opinion of his infallibility. To say the truth, the parson had exercised her more ways than one; and the pious woman had so well edified by her husband's sermons, that she had resolved to receive the bad things of this world together with the good. She had indeed been at first a little contentious; but he had long since got the better; partly by her love for this, partly by her fear of that, partly by her religion, partly by the respect he paid himself, and partly by that which he received from the parish. She had, in short, absolutely submitted, and now worshipped her husband, as Sarah did Abraham, calling him (not lord, but) master. Whilst they were at table her husband gave her a fresh example of his greatness; for, as she had just delivered a cup of ale to Adams, he snatched it out of his hand, and, crying out, "I caal'd vurst," swallowed down the ale. Adams denied it; it was referred to the wife, who, though her conscience was on the side of Adams, durst not give it against her husband; upon which he said, "No, sir, no; I should not have been so rude to have taken it from you if you had caal'd vurst, but I'd have you know I'm a better man than to suffer the best he in the kingdom to drink before me in my own house when I caale vurst."

As soon as their breakfast was ended, Adams began in the following manner: "I think, sir, it is high time to inform you of the business of my embassy. I am a traveller, and am passing this way in company with two young people, a lad and a damsel, my parishioners, towards my own cure; we stopt at a house of hospitality in the parish, where they directed me to you as having the cure."—"Though I am but a curate," says Trulliber, "I believe I am as warm as the vicar himself, or perhaps the rector of the next parish too; I believe I could buy them both."—"Sir," cries Adams, "I rejoice thereat. Now, sir, my business is, that we are by various accidents stript of our money, and are not able to pay our reckoning, being seven shillings. I therefore request you to assist me with the loan of those seven shillings, and also seven shillings more, which, peradventure, I shall return to you; but if not, I am convinced you will joyfully embrace such an opportunity of laying up a treasure in a better place than any this world affords."

Suppose a stranger, who entered the chambers of a lawyer, being imagined a client, when the lawyer was preparing his palm for the fee, should pull out a writ against him. Suppose an apothecary, at the door of a chariot containing some great doctor of eminent skill, should, instead of directions to a patient, present him with a potion for himself. Suppose a minister should, instead of a good round sum, treat my lord ——, or sir ——, or esq. —— with a good broomstick. Suppose a civil companion, or a led captain, should, instead of virtue, and honour, and beauty, and parts, and admiration, thunder vice, and infamy, and ugliness, and folly, and contempt, in his patron's ears. Suppose, when a tradesman first carries in his bill, the man of fashion should pay it; or suppose, if he did so, the tradesman should abate what he had overcharged, on the supposition of waiting. In short—suppose what you will, you never can nor will suppose anything equal to the astonishment which seized on Trulliber, as soon as Adams had ended his speech. A while he rolled his eyes in silence; sometimes surveying Adams, then his wife; then casting them on the ground, then lifting them up to heaven. At last he burst forth in the following accents: "Sir, I believe I know where to lay up my little treasure as well as another. I thank G—, if I am not so warm as some, I am content; that is a blessing greater than riches; and he to whom that is given need ask no more. To be content with a little is greater than to possess the world; which a man may possess without being so. Lay up my treasure! what matters where a man's treasure is whose heart is in the Scriptures? there is the treasure of a Christian." At these words the water ran from Adams's eyes; and, catching Trulliber by the hand in a rapture, "Brother," says he, "heavens bless the accident by which I came to see you! I would have walked many a mile to have communed with you; and, believe me, I will shortly pay you a second visit; but my friends, I fancy, by this time, wonder at my stay; so let me have the money immediately." Trulliber then put on a stern look, and cried out, "Thou dost not intend to rob me?" At which the wife, bursting into tears, fell on her knees and roared out, "O dear sir! for Heaven's sake don't rob my master; we are but poor people." "Get up, for a fool as thou art, and go about thy business," said Trulliber; "dost think the man will venture his life? he is a beggar, and no robber." "Very true, indeed," answered Adams. "I wish, with all my heart, the tithing-man was here," cries Trulliber; "I would have thee punished as a vagabond for thy impudence. Fourteen shillings indeed! I won't give thee a farthing. I believe thou art no more a clergyman than the woman there" (pointing to his wife); "but if thou art, dost deserve to have thy gown stript over thy shoulders for running about the country in such a manner." "I forgive your suspicions," says Adams; "but suppose I am not a clergyman, I am nevertheless thy brother; and thou, as a Christian, much more as a clergyman, art obliged to relieve my distress." "Dost preach to me?" replied Trulliber; "dost pretend to instruct me in my duty?" "Ifacks, a good story," cries Mrs Trulliber, "to preach to my master." "Silence, woman," cries Trulliber. "I would have thee know, friend" (addressing himself to Adams), "I shall not learn my duty from such as thee. I know what charity is, better than to give to vagabonds." "Besides, if we were inclined, the poor's rate obliges us to give so much charity," cries the wife. "Pugh! thou art a fool. Poor's reate! Hold thy nonsense," answered Trulliber; and then, turning to Adams, he told him, "he would give him nothing." "I am sorry," answered Adams, "that you do know what charity is, since you practise it no better: I must tell you, if you trust to your knowledge for your justification, you will find yourself deceived, though you should add faith to it, without good works." "Fellow," cries Trulliber, "dost thou speak against faith in my house? Get out of my doors: I will no longer remain under the same roof with a wretch who speaks wantonly of faith and the Scriptures." "Name not the Scriptures," says Adams. "How! not name the Scriptures! Do you disbelieve the Scriptures?" cries Trulliber. "No; but you do," answered Adams, "if I may reason from your practice; for their commands are so explicit, and their rewards and punishments so immense, that it is impossible a man should stedfastly believe without obeying. Now, there is no command more express, no duty more frequently enjoined, than charity. Whoever, therefore, is void of charity, I make no scruple of pronouncing that he is no Christian." "I would not advise thee," says Trulliber, "to say that I am no Christian: I won't take it of you; for I believe I am as good a man as thyself" (and indeed, though he was now rather too corpulent for athletic exercises, he had, in his youth, been one of the best boxers and cudgel-players in the county). His wife, seeing him clench his fist, interposed, and begged him not to fight, but show himself a true Christian, and take the law of him. As nothing could provoke Adams to strike, but an absolute assault on himself or his friend, he smiled at the angry look and gestures of Trulliber; and, telling him he was sorry to see such men in orders, departed without further ceremony.

CHAPTER XV.

An adventure, the consequence of a new instance which parson Adams gave of his forgetfulness.

When he came back to the inn he found Joseph and Fanny sitting together. They were so far from thinking his absence long, as he had feared they would, that they never once missed or thought of him. Indeed, I have been often assured by both, that they spent these hours in a most delightful conversation; but, as I never could prevail on either to relate it, so I cannot communicate it to the reader.

Adams acquainted the lovers with the ill success of his enterprize. They were all greatly confounded, none being able to propose any method of departing, till Joseph at last advised calling in the hostess, and desiring her to trust them; which Fanny said she despaired of her doing, as she was one of the sourest-faced women she had ever beheld.

But she was agreeably disappointed; for the hostess was no sooner asked the question than she readily agreed; and, with a curtsy and smile, wished them a good journey. However, lest Fanny's skill in physiognomy should be called in question, we will venture to assign one reason which might probably incline her to this confidence and good-humour. When Adams said he was going to visit his brother, he had unwittingly imposed on Joseph and Fanny, who both believed he had meant his natural brother, and not his brother in divinity, and had so informed the hostess, on her enquiry after him. Now Mr Trulliber had, by his professions of piety, by his gravity, austerity, reserve, and the opinion of his great wealth, so great an authority in his parish, that they all lived in the utmost fear and apprehension of him. It was therefore no wonder that the hostess, who knew it was in his option whether she should ever sell another mug of drink, did not dare to affront his supposed brother by denying him credit.

They were now just on their departure when Adams recollected he had left his greatcoat and hat at Mr Trulliber's. As he was not desirous of renewing his visit, the hostess herself, having no servant at home, offered to fetch it.

This was an unfortunate expedient; for the hostess was soon undeceived in the opinion she had entertained of Adams, whom Trulliber abused in the grossest terms, especially when he heard he had had the assurance to pretend to be his near relation.

At her return, therefore, she entirely changed her note. She said, "Folks might be ashamed of travelling about, and pretending to be what they were not. That taxes were high, and for her part she was obliged to pay for what she had; she could not therefore possibly, nor would she, trust anybody; no, not her own father. That money was never scarcer, and she wanted to make up a sum. That she expected, therefore, they should pay their reckoning before they left the house."

Adams was now greatly perplexed; but, as he knew that he could easily have borrowed such a sum in his own parish, and as he knew he would have lent it himself to any mortal in distress, so he took fresh courage, and sallied out all round the parish, but to no purpose; he returned as pennyless as he went, groaning and lamenting that it was possible, in a country professing Christianity, for a wretch to starve in the midst of his fellow-creatures who abounded.

Whilst he was gone, the hostess, who stayed as a sort of guard with Joseph and Fanny, entertained them with the goodness of parson Trulliber. And, indeed, he had not only a very good character as to other qualities in the neighbourhood, but was reputed a man of great charity; for, though he never gave a farthing, he had always that word in his mouth.

Adams was no sooner returned the second time than the storm grew exceedingly high, the hostess declaring, among other things, that, if they offered to stir without paying her, she would soon overtake them with a warrant.

Plato and Aristotle, or somebody else, hath said, *that when the most exquisite cunning fails, chance often hits the mark, and that by means the least expected.* Virgil expresses this very boldly:—

> *Turne, quod optanti divum promittere nemo*
> *Auderet, volvenda dies, en! attulit ultro.*

I would quote more great men if I could; but my memory not permitting me, I will proceed to exemplify these observations by the following instance:—

There chanced (for Adams had not cunning enough to contrive it) to be at that time in the alehouse a fellow who had been formerly a drummer in an Irish regiment, and now travelled the country as a pedlar. This man, having attentively listened to the discourse of the hostess, at last took Adams aside, and asked him what the sum was for which they were detained. As soon as he was informed, he sighed, and said, "He was sorry it was so much; for that he had no more than six shillings and sixpence in his pocket, which he would lend them with all his heart." Adams gave a caper, and cry'd out, "It would do; for that he had sixpence himself." And thus these poor people, who could not engage the compassion of riches and piety, were at length delivered out of their distress by the charity of a poor pedlar.

I shall refer it to my reader to make what observations he pleases on this incident: it is sufficient for me to inform him that, after Adams and his companions had returned him a thousand thanks, and told him where he might call to be repaid, they all sallied out of the house without any compliments from their hostess, or indeed without paying her any; Adams declaring he would take particular care never to call there again; and she on her side assuring them she wanted no such guests.

CHAPTER XVI.

A very curious adventure, in which Mr Adams gave a much greater instance of the honest simplicity of his heart, than of his experience in the ways of this world.

Our travellers had walked about two miles from that inn, which they had more reason to have mistaken for a castle than Don Quixote ever had any of those in which he sojourned, seeing they had met with such difficulty in escaping out of its walls, when they came to a parish, and beheld a sign of invitation hanging out. A gentleman sat smoaking a pipe at the door, of whom Adams inquired the road, and received so courteous and obliging an answer, accompanied with so smiling a countenance, that the good parson, whose heart was naturally disposed to love and affection, began to ask several other questions; particularly the name of the parish, and who was the owner of a large house whose front they then had in prospect. The gentleman answered as obligingly as before; and as to the house, acquainted him it was his own. He then proceeded in the following manner: "Sir, I presume by your habit you are a clergyman; and as you are travelling on foot I suppose a glass of good beer will not be disagreeable to you; and I can recommend my landlord's within as some of the best in all this country. What say you, will you halt a little and let us take a pipe together? there is no better tobacco in the kingdom." This proposal was not displeasing to Adams, who had allayed his thirst that day with no better liquor than what Mrs Trulliber's cellar had produced; and which was indeed little superior, either in richness or flavour, to that which distilled from those grains her generous husband bestowed on his hogs. Having, therefore, abundantly thanked the gentleman for his kind invitation, and bid Joseph and Fanny follow him, he entered the alehouse, where a large loaf and cheese and a pitcher of beer, which truly answered the character given of it, being set before them, the three travellers fell to eating, with appetites infinitely more voracious than are to be found at the most exquisite eating-houses in the parish of St. James's.

The gentleman expressed great delight in the hearty and cheerful behaviour of Adams; and particularly in the familiarity with which he conversed with Joseph and Fanny, whom he often called his children; a term he explained to mean no more than his parishioners; saying, "He looked on all those whom God had intrusted to his care to stand to him in that relation." The gentleman, shaking him by the hand, highly applauded those sentiments. "They are, indeed," says he, "the true principles of a Christian divine; and I heartily wish they were universal; but, on the contrary, I am sorry to say the parson of our parish, instead of esteeming his poor parishioners as a part of his family, seems rather to consider them as not of the same species with himself. He seldom speaks to any, unless some few of the richest of us; nay, indeed, he will not move his hat to the others. I often laugh when I behold him on Sundays strutting along the churchyard like a turkey-cock through rows of his parishioners, who bow to him with as much submission, and are as unregarded, as a set of servile courtiers by the proudest prince in Christendom. But if such temporal pride is ridiculous, surely the spiritual is odious and detestable; if such a puffed—up empty human bladder, strutting in princely robes, justly moves one's derision, surely in the habit of a priest it must raise our scorn."

"Doubtless," answered Adams, "your opinion is right; but I hope such examples are rare. The clergy whom I have the honour to know maintain a different behaviour; and you will allow me, sir, that the readiness which too many of the laity show to contemn the order may be one reason of their avoiding too much humility." "Very true, indeed," says the gentleman; "I find, sir, you are a man of excellent sense, and am happy in this opportunity of knowing you; perhaps our accidental meeting may not be disadvantageous to you neither. At present I shall only say to you that the incumbent of this living is old and infirm, and that it is in my gift. Doctor, give me your hand; and assure yourself of it at his decease." Adams told him, "He was never more confounded in his life than at his utter incapacity to make any return to such noble and unmerited generosity." "A mere trifle, sir," cries the gentleman, "scarce worth your acceptance; a little more than three hundred a year. I wish it was double the value for your sake." Adams bowed, and cried from the emotions of his gratitude; when the other asked him, "If he was married, or had any children, besides those in the spiritual sense he had mentioned." "Sir," replied the parson, "I have a wife and six at your service." "That is unlucky," says the gentleman; "for I would otherwise have taken you into my own house as my chaplain; however, I have another in the parish (for the parsonage-house is not good enough), which I will furnish for you. Pray, does your wife understand a dairy?" "I can't profess she does," says Adams. "I am sorry for it," quoth the gentleman; "I would have given you half-a-dozen cows, and very good grounds to have maintained them." "Sir," said Adams, in an ecstasy, "you are too liberal; indeed you are." "Not at all," cries the gentleman: "I esteem riches only as they give me an opportunity of doing good; and I never saw one whom I had a greater inclination to serve." At which words he shook him heartily by the hand, and told him he had sufficient room in his house to entertain him and his friends. Adams begged he might give him no such trouble; that they could be very well accommodated in the house where they were; forgetting they had not a sixpenny piece among them. The gentleman would not be denied; and, informing himself how far they were travelling, he said it was too long a journey to take on foot, and begged that they would favour him by suffering him to lend them a servant and horses; adding, withal, that, if they would do him the pleasure of their company only two days, he would furnish them with his coach and six. Adams, turning to Joseph, said, "How lucky is this gentleman's goodness to you, who I am afraid would be scarce able to hold out on your lame leg!" and then, addressing the person who made him these liberal promises, after much bowing, he cried out, "Blessed be the hour which first introduced me to a man of your charity! you are indeed a Christian of the true primitive kind, and an honour to the country wherein you live. I would willingly have taken a pilgrimage to the Holy Land to have beheld you; for the advantages which we draw from your goodness give me little pleasure, in comparison of what I enjoy for your own sake when I consider the treasures you are by these means laying up for yourself in a country that passeth not away. We will therefore, most generous sir, accept your goodness, as well the entertainment you have so kindly offered us at your house this evening, as the accommodation of your horses to-morrow morning." He then began to search for his hat, as did Joseph for his; and both they and Fanny were in order of departure, when the gentleman, stopping short, and seeming to meditate by himself for the space of about a minute, exclaimed thus: "Sure never anything was so unlucky; I had forgot that my house-keeper was gone abroad, and hath locked up all my rooms; indeed, I would break them open for you, but shall not be able to furnish you with a bed; for she has likewise put away all my linen. I am glad it entered into my head before I had given you the trouble of walking there; besides, I believe you will find better accommodations here than you expected.—Landlord, you can provide good beds for these people, can't you?" "Yes, and please your worship," cries the host, "and such as no lord or justice of the peace in the kingdom need be ashamed to lie in." "I am heartily sorry," says the gentleman, "for this disappointment. I am resolved I will never suffer her to carry away the keys again." "Pray, sir, let it not make you uneasy," cries Adams; "we shall do very well here; and the loan of your horses is a favour we shall be incapable of making any return to." "Ay!" said the squire, "the horses shall attend you here at what hour in the morning you please;" and now, after many civilities too tedious to enumerate, many squeezes by the hand, with most affectionate looks and smiles at each other, and after appointing the horses at seven the next morning, the gentleman took his leave of them, and departed to his own house. Adams and his companions returned to the table, where the parson smoaked another pipe, and then they all retired to rest.

Mr Adams rose very early, and called Joseph out of his bed, between whom a very fierce dispute ensued, whether Fanny should ride behind Joseph, or behind the gentleman's servant; Joseph insisting on it that he was perfectly recovered, and was as capable of taking care of Fanny as any other person could be. But Adams would not agree to it, and declared he would not trust her behind him; for that he was weaker than he imagined himself to be.

This dispute continued a long time, and had begun to be very hot, when a servant arrived from their good friend, to acquaint them that he was unfortunately prevented from lending them any horses; for that his groom had, unknown to him, put his whole stable under a course of physic.

This advice presently struck the two disputants dumb: Adams cried out, "Was ever anything so unlucky as this poor gentleman? I protest I am more sorry on his account than my own. You see, Joseph, how this good-natured man is treated by his servants; one locks up his linen, another physics his horses, and I suppose, by his being at this house last night, the butler had locked up his cellar. Bless us! how good-nature is used in this world! I protest I am more concerned on his account than my own." "So am not I," cries Joseph; "not that I am much troubled about walking on foot; all my concern is, how we shall get out of the house, unless God sends another pedlar to redeem us. But certainly this gentleman has such an affection for you, that he would lend you a larger sum than we owe here, which is not above four or five shillings." "Very true, child," answered Adams; "I will write a letter to him, and will even venture to solicit him for three half-crowns; there will be no harm in having two or three shillings in our pockets; as we have full forty miles to travel, we may possibly have occasion for them."

Fanny being now risen, Joseph paid her a visit, and left Adams to write his letter, which having finished, he despatched a boy with it to the gentleman, and then seated himself by the door, lighted his pipe, and betook himself to meditation.

The boy staying longer than seemed to be necessary, Joseph, who with Fanny was now returned to the parson, expressed some apprehensions that the gentleman's steward had locked up his purse too. To which Adams answered, "It might very possibly be, and he should wonder at no liberties which the devil might put into the head of a wicked servant to take with so worthy a master;" but added, "that, as the sum was so small, so noble a gentleman would be easily able to procure it in the parish, though he had it not in his own pocket. Indeed," says he, "if it was four or five guineas, or any such large quantity of money, it might be a different matter."

They were now sat down to breakfast over some toast and ale, when the boy returned and informed them that the gentleman was not at home. "Very well!" cries Adams; "but why, child, did you not stay till his return? Go back again, my good boy, and wait for his coming home; he cannot be gone far, as his horses are all sick; and besides, he had no intention to go abroad, for he invited us to spend this day and tomorrow at his house. Therefore go back, child, and tarry till his return home." The messenger departed, and was back again with great expedition, bringing an account that the gentleman was gone a long journey, and would not be at home again this month. At these words Adams seemed greatly confounded, saying, "This must be a sudden accident, as the sickness or death of a relation or some such unforeseen misfortune;" and then, turning to Joseph, cried, "I wish you had reminded me to have borrowed this money last night." Joseph, smiling, answered, "He was very much deceived if the gentleman would not have found some excuse to avoid lending it.—I own," says he, "I was never much pleased with his professing so much kindness for you at first sight; for I have heard the gentlemen of our cloth in London tell many such stories of their masters. But when the boy brought the message back of his not being at home, I presently knew what would follow; for, whenever a man of fashion doth not care to fulfil his promises, the custom is to order his servants that he will never be at home to the person so promised. In London they call it denying him. I have myself denied Sir Thomas Booby above a hundred times, and when the man hath danced attendance for about a month or sometimes longer, he is acquainted in the end that the gentleman is gone out of town and could do nothing in the business."—"Good Lord!" says Adams, "what wickedness is there in the Christian world! I profess almost equal to what I have read of the heathens. But surely, Joseph, your suspicions of this gentleman must be unjust, for what a silly fellow must he be who would do the devil's work for nothing! and canst thou tell me any interest he could possibly propose to himself by deceiving us in his professions?"—"It is not for me," answered Joseph, "to give reasons for what men do, to a gentleman of your learning."—"You say right," quoth Adams; "knowledge of men is only to be learned from books; Plato and Seneca for that; and those are authors, I am afraid, child, you never read."—"Not I, sir, truly," answered Joseph; "all I know is, it is a maxim among the gentlemen of our cloth, that those masters who promise the most perform the least; and I have often heard them say they have found the largest vails in those families where they were not promised any. But, sir, instead of considering any farther these matters, it would be our wisest way to contrive some method of getting out of this house; for the generous gentleman, instead of doing us any service, hath left us the whole reckoning to pay." Adams was going to answer, when their host came in, and, with a kind of jeering smile, said, "Well, masters! the squire hath not sent his horses for you yet. Laud help me! how easily some folks make promises!"—"How!" says Adams; "have you ever known him do anything of this kind before?"—"Ay! marry have I," answered the host: "it is no business of mine, you know, sir, to say anything to a gentleman to his face; but now he is not here, I will assure you, he hath not his fellow within the three next market-towns. I own I could not help laughing when I heard him offer you the living, for thereby hangs a good jest. I thought he would have offered you my house next, for one is no more his to dispose of than the other." At these words Adams, blessing himself, declared, "He had never read of such a monster. But what vexes me most," says he, "is, that he hath decoyed us into running up a long debt with you, which we are not able to pay, for we have no money about us, and, what is worse, live at such a distance, that if you should trust us, I am afraid you would lose your money for want of our finding any conveniency of sending it."—"Trust you, master!" says the host, "that I will with all my heart. I honour the clergy too much to deny trusting one of them for such a trifle; besides, I like your fear of never paying me. I have lost many a debt in my lifetime, but was promised to be paid them all in a very short time. I will score this reckoning for the novelty of it. It is the first, I do assure you, of its kind. But what say you, master, shall we have t'other pot before we part? It will waste but a little chalk more, and if you never pay me a shilling the loss will not ruin me." Adams liked the invitation very well, especially as it was delivered with so hearty an accent. He shook his host by the hand, and thanking him, said, "He would tarry another pot rather for the pleasure of such worthy company than for the liquor;" adding, "he was glad to find some Christians left in the kingdom, for that he almost began to suspect that he was sojourning in a country inhabited only by Jews and Turks."

The kind host produced the liquor, and Joseph with Fanny retired into the garden, where, while they solaced themselves with amorous discourse, Adams sat down with his host; and, both filling their glasses, and lighting their pipes, they began that dialogue which the reader will find in the next chapter.

CHAPTER XVII.

A dialogue between Mr Abraham Adams and his host, which, by the disagreement in their opinions, seemed to threaten an unlucky catastrophe, had it not been timely prevented by the return of the lovers.

"Sir," said the host, "I assure you you are not the first to whom our squire hath promised more than he hath performed. He is so famous for this practice, that his word will not be taken for much by those who know him. I remember a young fellow whom he promised his parents to make an exciseman. The poor people, who could ill afford it, bred their son to writing and accounts, and other learning to qualify him for the place; and the boy held up his head above his condition with these hopes; nor would he go to plough, nor to any other kind of work, and went constantly drest as fine as could be, with two clean Holland shirts a week, and this for several years; till at last he followed the squire up to London, thinking there to mind him of his promises; but he could never get sight of him. So that, being out of money and business, he fell into evil company and wicked courses; and in the end came to a sentence of transportation, the news of which brokc thc mother's heart.—I will tell you another true story of him. There was a neighbour of mine, a farmer, who had two sons whom he bred up to the business. Pretty lads they were. Nothing would serve the squire but that the youngest must be made a parson. Upon which he persuaded the father to send him to school, promising that he would afterwards maintain him at the university, and, when he was of a proper age, give him a living. But after the lad had been seven years at school, and his father brought him to the squire, with a letter from his master that he was fit for the university, the squire, instead of minding his promise, or sending him thither at his expense, only told his father that the young man was a fine scholar, and it was pity he could not afford to keep him at Oxford for four or five years more, by which time, if he could get him a curacy, he might have him ordained. The farmer said, 'He was not a man sufficient to do any such thing.'—'Why, then,' answered the squire, 'I am very sorry you have given him so much learning; for, if he cannot get his living by that, it will rather spoil him for anything else; and your other son, who can hardly write his name, will do more at ploughing and sowing, and is in a better condition, than he.' And indeed so it proved; for the poor lad, not finding friends to maintain him in his learning, as he had expected, and being unwilling to work, fell to drinking, though he was a very sober lad before; and in a short time, partly with grief, and partly with good liquor, fell into a consumption, and died.—

Nay, I can tell you more still: there was another, a young woman, and the handsomest in all this neighbourhood, whom he enticed up to London, promising to make her a gentlewoman to one of your women of quality; but, instead of keeping his word, we have since heard, after having a child by her himself, she became a common whore; then kept a coffeehouse in Covent Garden; and a little after died of the French distemper in a gaol.—I could tell you many more stories; but how do you imagine he served me myself? You must know, sir, I was bred a seafaring man, and have been many voyages; till at last I came to be master of a ship myself, and was in a fair way of making a fortune, when I was attacked by one of those cursed guarda-costas who took our ships before the beginning of the war; and after a fight, wherein I lost the greater part of my crew, my rigging being all demolished, and two shots received between wind and water, I was forced to strike. The villains carried off my ship, a brigantine of 150 tons—a pretty creature she was—and put me, a man, and a boy, into a little bad pink, in which, with much ado, we at last made Falmouth; though I believe the Spaniards did not imagine she could possibly live a day at sea. Upon my return hither, where my wife, who was of this country, then lived, the squire told me he was so pleased with the defence I had made against the enemy, that he did not fear getting me promoted to a lieutenancy of a man-of-war, if I would accept of it; which I thankfully assured him I would. Well, sir, two or three years passed, during which I had many repeated promises, not only from the squire, but (as he told me) from the lords of the admiralty. He never returned from London but I was assured I might be satisfied now, for I was certain of the first vacancy; and, what surprizes me still, when I reflect on it, these assurances were given me with no less confidence, after so many disappointments, than at first. At last, sir, growing weary, and somewhat suspicious, after so much delay, I wrote to a friend in London, who I knew had some acquaintance at the best house in the admiralty, and desired him to back the squire's interest; for indeed I feared he had solicited the affair with more coldness than he pretended. And what answer do you think my friend sent me? Truly, sir, he acquainted me that the squire had never mentioned my name at the admiralty in his life; and, unless I had much faithfuller interest, advised me to give over my pretensions; which I immediately did, and, with the concurrence of my wife, resolved to set up an alehouse, where you are heartily welcome; and so my service to you; and may the squire, and all such sneaking rascals, go to the devil together."—"O fie!" says Adams, "O fie! He is indeed a wicked man; but G— will, I hope, turn his heart to repentance. Nay, if he could but once see the meanness of this detestable vice; would he but once reflect that he is one of the most scandalous as well as pernicious lyars; sure he must despise himself to so intolerable a degree, that it would be impossible for him to continue a moment in such a course. And to confess the truth, notwithstanding the baseness of this character, which he hath too well deserved, he hath in his countenance sufficient symptoms of that *bona indoles*, that sweetness of disposition, which furnishes out a good Christian."—"Ah, master! master!" says the host, "if you had travelled as far as I have, and conversed with the many nations where I have traded, you would not give any credit to a man's countenance. Symptoms in his countenance, quotha! I would look there, perhaps, to see whether a man had the small-pox, but for nothing else." He spoke this with so little regard to the parson's observation, that it a good deal nettled him; and, taking the pipe hastily from his mouth, he thus answered: "Master of mine, perhaps I have travelled a great deal farther than you without the assistance of a ship. Do you imagine sailing by different cities or countries is travelling? No.

"Caelum non animum mutant qui trans mare currunt.

"I can go farther in an afternoon than you in a twelvemonth. What, I suppose you have seen the Pillars of Hercules, and perhaps the walls of Carthage. Nay, you may have heard Scylla, and seen Charybdis; you may have entered the closet where Archimedes was found at the taking of Syracuse. I suppose you have sailed among the Cyclades, and passed the famous straits which take their name from the unfortunate Helle, whose fate is sweetly described by Apollonius Rhodius; you have passed the very spot, I conceive, where Daedalus fell into that sea, his waxen wings being melted by the sun; you have traversed the Euxine sea, I make no doubt; nay, you may have been on the banks of the Caspian, and called at Colchis, to see if there is ever another golden fleece." "Not I, truly, master," answered the host: "I never touched at any of these places."—"But I have been at all these," replied Adams. "Then, I suppose," cries the host, "you have been at the East Indies; for there are no such, I will be sworn, either in the West or the Levant."—"Pray where's the Levant?" quoth Adams; "that should be in the East Indies by right." "Oho! you are a pretty traveller," cries the host, "and not know the Levant! My service to you, master; you must not talk of these things with me! you must not tip us the traveller; it won't go here." "Since thou art so dull to misunderstand me still," quoth Adams, "I will inform thee; the travelling I mean is in books, the only way of travelling by which any knowledge is to be acquired. From them I learn what I asserted just now, that nature generally imprints such a portraiture of the mind in the countenance, that a skilful physiognomist will rarely be deceived. I presume you have never read the story of Socrates to this purpose, and therefore I will tell it you. A certain physiognomist asserted of Socrates, that he plainly discovered by his features that he was a rogue in his nature. A character so contrary to the tenour of all this great man's actions, and the generally received opinion concerning him, incensed the boys of Athens so that they threw stones at the physiognomist, and would have demolished him for his ignorance, had not Socrates himself prevented them by confessing the truth of his observations, and acknowledging that, though he corrected his disposition by philosophy, he was indeed naturally as inclined to vice as had been predicated of him. Now, pray resolve me—How should a man know this story if he had not read it?" "Well, master," said the host, "and what signifies it whether a man knows it or no? He who goes abroad, as I have done, will always have opportunities enough of knowing the world without troubling his head with Socrates, or any such fellows." "Friend," cries Adams, "if a man should sail round the world, and anchor in every harbour of it, without learning, he would return home as ignorant as he went out."

"Lord help you!" answered the host; "there was my boatswain, poor fellow! he could scarce either write or read, and yet he would navigate a ship with any master of a man-of-war; and a very pretty knowledge of trade he had too." "Trade," answered Adams, "as Aristotle proves in his first chapter of Politics, is below a philosopher, and unnatural as it is managed now." The host looked stedfastly at Adams, and after a minute's silence asked him, "If he was one of the writers of the Gazetteers? for I have heard," says he, "they are writ by parsons." "Gazetteers!" answered Adams, "what is that?" "It is a dirty newspaper," replied the host, "which hath been given away all over the nation for these many years, to abuse trade and honest men, which I would not suffer to lye on my table, though it hath been offered me for nothing." "Not I truly," said Adams; "I never write anything but sermons; and I assure you I am no enemy to trade, whilst it is consistent with honesty; nay, I have always looked on the tradesman as a very valuable member of society, and, perhaps, inferior to none but the man of learning." "No, I believe he is not, nor to him neither," answered the host. "Of what use would learning be in a country without trade? What would all you parsons do to clothe your backs and feed your bellies? Who fetches you your silks, and your linens, and your wines, and all the other necessaries of life? I speak chiefly with regard to the sailors." "You should say the extravagancies of life," replied the parson; "but admit they were the necessaries, there is something more necessary than life itself, which is provided by learning; I mean the learning of the clergy. Who clothes you with piety, meekness, humility, charity, patience, and all the other Christian virtues? Who feeds your souls with the milk of brotherly love, and diets them with all the dainty food of holiness, which at once cleanses them of all impure carnal affections, and fattens them with the truly rich spirit of grace? Who doth this?" "Ay, who, indeed?" cries the host; "for I do not remember ever to have seen any such clothing or such feeding. And so, in the mean time, master, my service to you." Adams was going to answer with some severity, when Joseph and Fanny returned and pressed his departure so eagerly that he would not refuse them; and so, grasping his crabstick, he took leave of his host (neither of them being so well pleased with each other as they had been at their first sitting down together), and with Joseph and Fanny, who both expressed much impatience, departed, and now all together renewed their journey.

BOOK III.

CHAPTER I.

Matter prefatory in praise of biography.

Notwithstanding the preference which may be vulgarly given to the authority of those romance writers who entitle their books "the History of England, the History of France, of Spain, &c.," it is most certain that truth is to be found only in the works of those who celebrate the lives of great men, and are commonly called biographers, as the others should indeed be termed topographers, or chorographers; words which might well mark the distinction between them; it being the business of the latter chiefly to describe countries and cities, which, with the assistance of maps, they do pretty justly, and may be depended upon; but as to the actions and characters of men, their writings are not quite so authentic, of which there needs no other proof than those eternal contradictions occurring between two topographers who undertake the history of the same country: for instance, between my Lord Clarendon and Mr Whitelocke, between Mr Echard and Rapin, and many others; where, facts being set forth in a different light, every reader believes as he pleases; and, indeed, the more judicious and suspicious very justly esteem the whole as no other than a romance, in which the writer hath indulged a happy and fertile invention. But though these widely differ in the narrative of facts; some ascribing victory to the one, and others to the other party; some representing the same man as a rogue, while others give him a great and honest character; yet all agree in the scene where the fact is supposed to have happened, and where the person, who is both a rogue and an honest man, lived. Now with us biographers the case is different; the facts we deliver may be relied on, though we often mistake the age and country wherein they happened: for, though it may be worth the examination of critics, whether the shepherd Chrysostom, who, as Cervantes informs us, died for love of the fair Marcella, who hated him, was ever in Spain, will any one doubt but that such a silly fellow hath really existed? Is there in the world such a sceptic as to disbelieve the madness of Cardenio, the perfidy of Ferdinand, the impertinent curiosity of Anselmo, the weakness of Camilla, the irresolute friendship of Lothario? though perhaps, as to the time and place where those several persons lived, that good historian may be deplorably deficient. But the most known instance of this kind is in the true history of Gil Blas, where the inimitable biographer hath made a notorious blunder in the country of Dr Sangrado, who used his patients as a vintner doth his wine-vessels, by letting out their blood, and filling them up with water. Doth not every one, who is the least versed in physical history, know that Spain was not the country in which this doctor lived? The same writer hath likewise erred in the country of his archbishop, as well as that of those great personages whose understandings were too sublime to taste anything but tragedy, and in many others. The same mistakes may likewise be observed in Scarron, the Arabian Nights, the History of Marianne and le Paisan Parvenu, and perhaps some few other writers of this class, whom I have not read, or do not at present recollect; for I would by no means be thought to comprehend those persons of surprizing genius, the authors of immense romances, or the modern novel and Atalantis writers; who, without any assistance from nature or history, record persons who never were, or will be, and facts which never did, nor possibly can, happen; whose heroes are of their own creation, and their brains the chaos whence all their materials are selected. Not that such writers deserve no honour; so far otherwise, that perhaps they merit the highest; for what can be nobler than to be as an example of the wonderful extent of human genius? One may apply to them what Balzac says of Aristotle, that they are a second nature (for they have no communication with the first; by which, authors of an inferior class, who cannot stand alone, are obliged to support themselves as with crutches); but these of whom I am now speaking seem to be possessed of those stilts, which the excellent Voltaire tells us, in his letters, "carry the genius far off, but with an regular pace." Indeed, far out of the sight of the reader,

Beyond the realm of Chaos and old Night.

But to return to the former class, who are contented to copy nature, instead of forming originals from the confused heap of matter in their own brains, is not such a book as that which records the achievements of the renowned Don Quixote more worthy the name of a history than even Mariana's: for, whereas the latter is confined to a particular period of time, and to a particular nation, the former is the history of the world in general, at least that part which is polished by laws, arts, and sciences; and of that from the time it was first polished to this day; nay, and forwards as long as it shall so remain?

I shall now proceed to apply these observations to the work before us; for indeed I have set them down principally to obviate some constructions which the good nature of mankind, who are always forward to see their friends' virtues recorded, may put to particular parts. I question not but several of my readers will know the lawyer in the stage-coach the moment they hear his voice. It is likewise odds but the wit and the prude meet with some of their acquaintance, as well as all the rest of my characters. To prevent, therefore, any such malicious applications, I declare here, once for all, I describe not men, but manners; not an individual, but a species. Perhaps it will be answered, Are not the characters then taken from life? To which I answer in the affirmative; nay, I believe I might aver that I have writ little more than I have seen. The lawyer is not only alive, but hath been so these four thousand years; and I hope G— will indulge his life as many yet to come. He hath not indeed confined himself to one profession, one religion, or one country; but when the first mean selfish creature appeared on the human stage, who made self the centre of the whole creation, would give himself no pain, incur

Learn hence, my fair countrywomen, to consider your own weakness, and the many occasions on which the strength of a man may be useful to you; and, duly weighing this, take care that you match not yourselves with the spindle-shanked beaus and *petit-maîtres* of the age, who, instead of being able, like Joseph Andrews, to carry you in lusty arms through the rugged ways and downhill steeps of life, will rather want to support their feeble limbs with your strength and assistance.

Our travellers now moved forwards where the nearest light presented itself; and, having crossed a common field, they came to a meadow, where they seemed to be at a very little distance from the light, when, to their grief, they arrived at the banks of a river. Adams here made a full stop, and declared he could swim, but doubted how it was possible to get Fanny over: to which Joseph answered, "If they walked along its banks, they might be certain of soon finding a bridge, especially as by the number of lights they might be assured a parish was near." "Odso, that's true indeed," said Adams; "I did not think of that."

Accordingly, Joseph's advice being taken, they passed over two meadows, and came to a little orchard, which led them to a house. Fanny begged of Joseph to knock at the door, assuring him "she was so weary that she could hardly stand on her feet." Adams, who was foremost, performed this ceremony; and, the door being immediately opened, a plain kind of man appeared at it: Adams acquainted him "that they had a young woman with them who was so tired with her journey that he should be much obliged to him if he would suffer her to come in and rest herself." The man, who saw Fanny by the light of the candle which he held in his hand, perceiving her innocent and modest look, and having no apprehensions from the civil behaviour of Adams, presently answered, "That the young woman was very welcome to rest herself in his house, and so were her company." He then ushered them into a very decent room, where his wife was sitting at a table: she immediately rose up, and assisted them in setting forth chairs, and desired them to sit down; which they had no sooner done than the man of the house asked them if they would have anything to refresh themselves with? Adams thanked him, and answered he should be obliged to him for a cup of his ale, which was likewise chosen by Joseph and Fanny. Whilst he was gone to fill a very large jug with this liquor, his wife told Fanny she seemed greatly fatigued, and desired her to take something stronger than ale; but she refused with many thanks, saying it was true she was very much tired, but a little rest she hoped would restore her. As soon as the company were all seated, Mr Adams, who had filled himself with ale, and by public permission had lighted his pipe, turned to the master of the house, asking him, "If evil spirits did not use to walk in that neighbourhood?" To which receiving no answer, he began to inform him of the adventure which they met with on the downs; nor had he proceeded far in the story when somebody knocked very hard at the door. The company expressed some amazement, and Fanny and the good woman turned pale: her husband went forth, and whilst he was absent, which was some time, they all remained silent, looking at one another, and heard several voices discoursing pretty loudly. Adams was fully persuaded that spirits were abroad, and began to meditate some exorcisms; Joseph a little inclined to the same opinion; Fanny was more afraid of men; and the good woman herself began to suspect her guests, and imagined those without were rogues belonging to their gang. At length the master of the house returned, and, laughing, told Adams he had discovered his apparition; that the murderers were sheep-stealers, and the twelve persons murdered were no other than twelve sheep; adding, that the shepherds had got the better of them, had secured two, and were proceeding with them to a justice of peace. This account greatly relieved the fears of the whole company; but Adams muttered to himself, "He was convinced of the truth of apparitions for all that."

They now sat chearfully round the fire, till the master of the house, having surveyed his guests, and conceiving that the cassock, which, having fallen down, appeared under Adams's greatcoat, and the shabby livery on Joseph Andrews, did not well suit with the familiarity between them, began to entertain some suspicions not much to their advantage: addressing himself therefore to Adams, he said, "He perceived he was a clergyman by his dress, and supposed that honest man was his footman." "Sir," answered Adams, "I am a clergyman at your service; but as to that young man, whom you have rightly termed honest, he is at present in nobody's service; he never lived in any other family than that of Lady Booby, from whence he was discharged, I assure you, for no crime." Joseph said, "He did not wonder the gentleman was surprized to see one of Mr Adams's character condescend to so much goodness with a poor man."—"Child," said Adams, "I should be ashamed of my cloth if I thought a poor man, who is honest, below my notice or my familiarity. I know not how those who think otherwise can profess themselves followers and servants of Him who made no distinction, unless, peradventure, by preferring the poor to the rich.—Sir," said he, addressing himself to the gentleman, "these two poor young people are my parishioners, and I look on them and love them as my children. There is something singular enough in their history, but I have not now time to recount it." The master of the house, notwithstanding the simplicity which discovered itself in Adams, knew too much of the world to give a hasty belief to professions. He was not yet quite certain that Adams had any more of the clergyman in him than his cassock. To try him therefore further, he asked him, "If Mr Pope had lately published anything new?" Adams answered, "He had heard great commendations of that poet, but that he had never read nor knew any of his works."—"Ho! ho!" says the gentleman to himself, "have I caught you? What!" said he, "have you never seen his Homer?" Adams answered, "he had never read any translation of the classicks." "Why, truly," reply'd the gentleman, "there is a dignity in the Greek language which I think no modern tongue can reach."—"Do you understand Greek, sir?" said Adams hastily. "A little, sir," answered the gentleman. "Do you know, sir," cry'd Adams, "where I can buy an Aeschylus? an unlucky misfortune lately happened to mine." Aeschylus was beyond the gentleman, though he knew him very well by name; he therefore, returning back to Homer, asked Adams, "What part of the Iliad he thought most excellent?" Adams returned, "His question would be properer, What kind of beauty was the chief in poetry? for that Homer was equally excellent in them all. And, indeed," continued he, "what Cicero says of a complete orator may well be applied to a great poet: 'He ought to comprehend all perfections.' Homer did this in the most excellent degree; it is not without reason, therefore, that the philosopher, in the twenty-second chapter of his Poeticks, mentions him by no other appellation than that of the Poet. He was the father of the drama as well as the epic; not of tragedy only, but of comedy also; for his Margites, which is deplorably lost, bore, says Aristotle, the same analogy to comedy as his Odyssey and Iliad to tragedy. To him, therefore, we owe Aristophanes as well as Euripides, Sophocles, and my poor Aeschylus. But if you please we will confine ourselves (at least for the present) to the Iliad, his noblest work; though neither Aristotle nor Horace give it the preference, as I remember, to the Odyssey. First, then, as to his subject, can anything be more simple, and at the same time more noble? He is rightly praised by the first of those judicious critics for not chusing the whole war, which, though he says it hath a complete beginning and end, would have been too great for the understanding to comprehend at one view. I have, therefore, often wondered why so correct a writer as Horace should, in his epistle to Lollius, call him the Trojani Belli Scriptorem. Secondly, his action, termed by Aristotle, Pragmaton Systasis; is it possible for the mind of man to conceive an idea of such perfect unity, and at the same time so replete with greatness? And here I must observe, what I do not remember to have seen noted by any, the Harmotton, that agreement of his action to his subject: for, as the subject is anger, how agreeable is his action, which is war; from which every incident arises and to which every episode immediately relates. Thirdly, his manners, which Aristotle places second in his description of the several parts of tragedy, and which he says are included in the action; I am at a loss whether I should rather admire the exactness of his judgment in the nice distinction or the immensity of his imagination in their variety. For, as to the former of these, how accurately is the sedate, injured resentment of Achilles, distinguished from the hot, insulting passion of Agamemnon! How widely doth the brutal courage of Ajax differ from the amiable bravery of Diomedes; and the wisdom of Nestor, which is the result of long reflection and experience, from the cunning of Ulysses, the effect of art and subtlety only! If we consider their variety, we may cry out, with Aristotle in his 24th chapter, that no part of this divine poem is destitute of manners. Indeed, I might affirm that there is scarce a character in human nature untouched in some part or other. And, as there is no passion which he is not able to describe, so is there none in his reader which he cannot raise. If he hath any superior excellence to the rest, I have been inclined to fancy it is in the pathetic. I am sure I never read with dry eyes the two episodes where Andromache is introduced in the former lamenting the danger, and in the latter the death, of Hector. The images are so extremely tender in these, that I am convinced the poet had the worthiest and best heart imaginable. Nor can I help observing how Sophocles falls short of the beauties of the original, in that imitation of the dissuasive speech of Andromache which he hath put into the mouth of Tecmessa. And yet Sophocles was the greatest genius who ever wrote tragedy; nor have any of his successors in that art, that is to say, neither Euripides nor Seneca the tragedian, been able to come near him. As to his sentiments and diction, I need say nothing; the former are particularly remarkable for the utmost perfection on that head, namely, propriety; and as to the latter, Aristotle, whom doubtless you have read over and over, is very diffuse. I shall mention but one thing more, which that great critic in his division of tragedy calls Opsis, or the scenery; and which is as proper to the epic as to the drama, with this difference, that in the former it falls to the share of the poet, and in the latter to that of the painter. But did ever painter imagine a scene like that in the 13th and 14th Iliads? where the reader sees at one view the prospect of Troy, with the army drawn up before it; the Grecian army, camp, and fleet; Jupiter sitting on Mount Ida, with his head wrapt in a cloud, and a thunderbolt in his hand, looking towards Thrace; Neptune driving through the sea, which divides on each side to permit his passage, and then seating himself on Mount Samos; the heavens opened, and the deities all seated on their thrones. This is sublime! This is poetry!" Adams then rapt out a hundred Greek verses, and with such a voice, emphasis, and action, that he almost frightened the women; and as for the gentleman, he was so far from entertaining any further suspicion of Adams, that he now doubted whether he had not a bishop in his house. He ran into the most extravagant encomiums on his learning; and the goodness of his heart began to dilate to all the strangers. He said he had great compassion for the poor young woman, who looked pale and faint with her journey; and in truth he conceived a much higher opinion of her quality than it deserved. He said he was sorry he could not accommodate them all; but if they were contented with his fireside, he would sit up with the men; and the young woman might, if she pleased, partake his wife's bed, which he advised her to; for that they must walk upwards of a mile to any house of entertainment, and that not very good neither. Adams, who liked his seat, his ale, his tobacco, and his company, persuaded Fanny to accept this kind proposal, in which sollicitation he was seconded by Joseph. Nor was she very difficultly prevailed on; for she had slept little the last night and not at all the preceding; so that love itself was scarce able to keep her eyes open any longer. The offer, therefore, being kindly accepted, the good woman produced everything eatable in her house on the table, and the guests, being heartily invited, as heartily regaled themselves, especially parson Adams. As to the other two, they were examples of the truth of that physical observation, that love, like other sweet things, is no whetter of the stomach.

Supper was no sooner ended, than Fanny at her own request retired, and the good woman bore her company. The man of the house, Adams, and Joseph, who would modestly have withdrawn, had not the gentleman insisted on the contrary, drew round the fireside, where Adams (to use his own words) replenished his pipe, and the gentleman produced a bottle of excellent beer, being the best liquor in his house.

The modest behaviour of Joseph, with the gracefulness of his person, the character which Adams gave of him, and the friendship he seemed to entertain for him, began to work on the gentleman's affections, and raised in him a curiosity to know the singularity which Adams had mentioned in his history. This curiosity Adams was no sooner informed of than, with Joseph's consent, he agreed to gratify it; and accordingly related all he knew, with as much tenderness as was possi-possible for the character of Lady Booby; and concluded with the long, faithful, and mutual passion between him and Fanny, not concealing the meanness of her birth and education. These latter circumstances entirely cured a jealousy which had lately risen in the gentleman's mind, that Fanny was the daughter of some person of fashion, and that Joseph had run away with her, and Adams was concerned in the plot. He was now enamoured of his guests, drank their healths with great chearfulness, and returned many thanks to Adams, who had spent much breath, for he was a circumstantial teller of a story.

Adams told him it was now in his power to return that favour; for his extraordinary goodness, as well as that fund of literature he was master of, [1] which he did not expect to find under such a roof, had raised in him more curiosity than he had ever known. "Therefore," said he, "if it be not too troublesome, sir, your history, if you please."

The gentleman answered, he could not refuse him what he had so much right to insist on; and after some of the common apologies, which are the usual preface to a story, he thus began.

---

[1] The author hath by some been represented to have made a blunder here: for Adams had indeed shown some learning (say they), perhaps all the author had; but the gentleman hath shown none, unless his approbation of Mr Adams be such: but surely it would be preposterous in him to call it so. I have, however, notwithstanding this criticism, which I am told came from the mouth of a great orator in a public coffee-house, left this blunder as it stood in the first edition. I will not have the vanity to apply to anything in this work the observation which M. Dacier makes in her preface to her Aristophanes: Je tiens pour une maxime constante, qu'une beauté mediocré plait plus généralement qu'une beauté sans défaut. Mr Congreve hath made such another blunder in his Love for Love, where Tattle tells Miss Prue, "She should admire him as much for the beauty he commends in her as if he himself was possessed of it."

CHAPTER III.

In which the gentleman relates the history of his life.

Mr. Wilson relates his history. Sir, I am descended of a good family, and was born a gentleman. My education was liberal, and at a public school, in which I proceeded so far as to become master of the Latin, and to be tolerably versed in the Greek language. My father died when I was sixteen, and left me master of myself. He bequeathed me a moderate fortune, which he intended I should not receive till I attained the age of twenty-five: for he constantly asserted that was full early enough to give up any man entirely to the guidance of his own discretion. However, as this intention was so obscurely worded in his will that the lawyers advised me to contest the point with my trustees, I own I paid so little regard to the inclinations of my dead father, which were sufficiently certain to me, that I followed their advice, and soon succeeded, for the trustees did not contest the matter very obstinately on their side. "Sir," said Adams, "may I crave the favour of your name?" The gentleman answered his name was Wilson, and then proceeded.

I stayed a very little while at school after his death; for, being a forward youth, I was extremely impatient to be in the world, for which I thought my parts, knowledge, and manhood thoroughly qualified me. And to this early introduction into life, without a guide, I impute all my future misfortunes; for, besides the obvious mischiefs which attend this, there is one which hath not been so generally observed: the first impression which mankind receives of you will be very difficult to eradicate. How unhappy, therefore, must it be to fix your character in life, before you can possibly know its value, or weigh the consequences of those actions which are to establish your future reputation!

A little under seventeen I left my school, and went to London with no more than six pounds in my pocket; a great sum, as I then conceived; and which I was afterwards surprized to find so soon consumed.

The character I was ambitious of attaining was that of a fine gentleman; the first requisites to which I apprehended were to be supplied by a taylor, a periwig-maker, and some few more tradesmen, who deal in furnishing out the human body. Notwithstanding the lowness of my purse, I found credit with them more easily than I expected, and was soon equipped to my wish. This I own then agreeably surprized me; but I have since learned that it is a maxim among many tradesmen at the polite end of the town to deal as largely as they can, reckon as high as they can, and arrest as soon as they can.

The next qualifications, namely, dancing, fencing, riding the great horse, and music, came into my head: but, as they required expense and time, I comforted myself, with regard to dancing, that I had learned a little in my youth, and could walk a minuet genteelly enough; as to fencing, I thought my good-humour would preserve me from the danger of a quarrel; as to the horse, I hoped it would not be thought of; and for music, I imagined I could easily acquire the reputation of it; for I had heard some of my schoolfellows pretend to knowledge in operas, without being able to sing or play on the fiddle.

Knowledge of the town seemed another ingredient; this I thought I should arrive at by frequenting public places. Accordingly I paid constant attendance to them all; by which means I was soon master of the fashionable phrases, learned to cry up the fashionable diversions, and knew the names and faces of the most fashionable men and women.

Nothing now seemed to remain but an intrigue, which I was resolved to have immediately; I mean the reputation of it; and indeed I was so successful, that in a very short time I had half-a-dozen with the finest women in town.

At these words Adams fetched a deep groan, and then, blessing himself, cried out, "Good Lord! what wicked times these are!"

Not so wicked as you imagine, continued the gentleman; for I assure you they were all vestal virgins for anything which I knew to the contrary. The reputation of intriguing with them was all I sought, and was what I arrived at: and perhaps I only flattered myself even in that; for very probably the persons to whom I showed their billets knew as well as I that they were counterfeits, and that I had written them to myself. "Write letters to yourself!" said Adams, staring. O sir, answered the gentleman, it is the very error of the times. Half our modern plays have one of these characters in them. It is incredible the pains I have taken, and the absurd methods I employed, to traduce the character of women of distinction. When another had spoken in raptures of any one, I have answered, "D—n her, she! We shall have her at H——d's very soon." When he hath replied, "He thought her virtuous," I have answered, "Ay, thou wilt always think a woman virtuous, till she is in the streets; but you and I, Jack or Tom (turning to another in company), know better." At which I have drawn a paper out of my pocket, perhaps a taylor's bill, and kissed it, crying at the same time, "By Gad I was once fond of her."

"Proceed, if you please, but do not swear any more," said Adams.

Sir, said the gentleman, I ask your pardon. Well, sir, in this course of life I continued full three years.—"What course of life?" answered Adams; "I do not remember you have mentioned any."—Your remark is just, said the gentleman, smiling; I should rather have said, in this course of doing nothing. I remember some time afterwards I wrote the journal of one day, which would serve, I believe, as well for any other during the whole time. I will endeavour to repeat it to you.

In the morning I arose, took my great stick, and walked out in my green frock, with my hair in papers (a groan from Adams), and sauntered about till ten. Went to the auction; told lady —— she had a dirty face; laughed heartily at something captain —— said, I can't remember what, for I did not very well hear it; whispered lord ——; bowed to the duke of ——; and was going to bid for a snuff-box, but did not, for fear I should have had it.

From 2 to 4, drest myself. *A groan.*
4 to 6, dined. *A groan.*
6 to 8, coffee-house.
8 to 9, Drury-lane playhouse.
9 to 10, Lincoln's Inn Fields.
10 to 12, Drawing-room. *A great groan.*

At all which places nothing happened worth remark.

At which Adams said, with some vehemence, "Sir, this is below the life of an animal, hardly above vegetation: and I am surprized what could lead a man of your sense into it." What leads us into more follies than you imagine, doctor, answered the gentleman—vanity; for as contemptible a creature as I was, and I assure you, yourself cannot have more contempt for such a wretch than I now have, I then admired myself, and should have despised a person of your present appearance (you will pardon me), with all your learning and those excellent qualities which I have remarked in you. Adams bowed, and begged him to proceed. After I had continued two years in this course of life, said the gentleman, an accident happened which obliged me to change the scene. As I was one day at St James's coffee-house, making very free with the character of a young lady of quality, an officer of the guards, who was present, thought proper to give me the lye. I answered I might possibly be mistaken, but I intended to tell no more than the truth. To which he made no reply but by a scornful sneer. After this I observed a strange coldness in all my acquaintance; none of them spoke to me first, and very few returned me even the civility of a bow. The company I used to dine with left me out, and within a week I found myself in as much solitude at St James's as if I had been in a desart. An honest elderly man, with a great hat and long sword, at last told me he had a compassion for my youth, and therefore advised me to show the world I was not such a rascal as they thought me to be. I did not at first understand him; but he explained himself, and ended with telling me, if I would write a challenge to the captain, he would, out of pure charity, go to him with it. "A very charitable person, truly!" cried Adams. I desired till the next day, continued the gentleman, to consider on it, and, retiring to my lodgings, I weighed the consequences on both sides as fairly as I could. On the one, I saw the risk of this alternative, either losing my own life, or having on my hands the blood of a man with whom I was not in the least angry. I soon determined that the good which appeared on the other was not worth this hazard. I therefore resolved to quit the scene, and presently retired to the Temple, where I took chambers. Here I soon got a fresh set of acquaintance, who knew nothing of what had happened to me. Indeed, they were not greatly to my approbation; for the beaus of the Temple are only the shadows of the others. They are the affectation of affectation. The vanity of these is still more ridiculous, if possible, than of the others. Here I met with smart fellows who drank with lords they did not know, and intrigued with women they never saw. Covent Garden was now the farthest stretch of my ambition; where I shone forth in the balconies at the playhouses, visited whores, made love to orange-wenches, and damned plays. This career was soon put a stop to by my surgeon, who convinced me of the necessity of confining myself to my room for a month. At the end of which, having had leisure to reflect, I resolved to quit all farther conversation with beaus and smarts of every kind, and to avoid, if possible, any occasion of returning to this place of confinement. "I think," said Adams, "the advice of a month's retirement and reflection was very proper; but I should rather have expected it from a divine than a surgeon." The gentleman smiled at Adams's simplicity, and, without explaining himself farther on such an odious subject, went on thus: I was no sooner perfectly restored to health than I found my passion for women, which I was afraid to satisfy as I had done, made me very uneasy; I determined, therefore, to keep a mistress. Nor was I long before I fixed my choice on a young woman, who had before been kept by two gentlemen, and to whom I was recommended by a celebrated bawd. I took her home to my chambers, and made her a settlement during cohabitation. This would, perhaps, have been very ill paid: however, she did not suffer me to be perplexed on that account; for, before quarter-day, I found her at my chambers in too familiar conversation with a young fellow who was drest like an officer, but was indeed a city apprentice. Instead of excusing her inconstancy, she rapped out half-a-dozen oaths, and, snapping her fingers at me, swore she scorned to confine herself to the best man in England. Upon this we parted, and the same bawd presently provided her another keeper. I was not so much concerned at our separation as I found, within a day or two, I had reason to be for our meeting; for I was obliged to pay a second visit to my surgeon. I was now forced to do penance for some weeks, during which time I contracted an acquaintance with a beautiful young girl, the daughter of a gentleman who, after having been forty years in the army, and in all the campaigns under the Duke of Marlborough, died a lieutenant on half-pay, and had left a widow, with this only child, in very distrest circumstances: they had only a small pension from the government, with what little the daughter could add to it by her work, for she had great excellence at her needle. This girl was, at my first acquaintance with her, solicited in marriage by a young fellow in good circumstances. He was apprentice to a linendraper, and had a little fortune, sufficient to set up his trade. The mother was greatly pleased with this match, as indeed she had sufficient reason. However, I soon prevented it. I represented him in so low a light to his mistress, and made so good an use of flattery, promises, and presents, that, not to dwell longer on this subject than is necessary, I prevailed with the poor girl, and conveyed her away from her mother! In a word, I debauched her.— (At which words Adams started up, fetched three strides across the room, and then replaced himself in his chair.) You are not more affected with this part of my story than myself; I assure you it will never be sufficiently repented of in my own opinion: but, if you already detest it, how much more will your indignation be raised when you hear the fatal consequences of this barbarous, this villanous action! If you please, therefore, I will here desist.—"By no means," cries Adams; "go on, I beseech you; and Heaven grant you may sincerely repent of this and many other things you have related!"—I was now, continued the gentleman, as happy as the possession of a fine young creature, who had a good education, and was endued with many agreeable qualities, could make me. We lived some months with vast fondness together, without any company or conversation, more than we found in one another: but this could not continue always; and, though I still preserved great affection for her, I began more and more to want the relief of other company, and consequently to leave her by degrees—at last whole days to herself. She failed not to testify some uneasiness on these occasions, and complained of the melancholy life she led; to remedy which, I introduced her into the acquaintance of some other kept mistresses, with whom she used to play at cards, and frequent plays and other diversions. She had not lived long in this intimacy before I perceived a visible alteration in her behaviour; all her modesty and innocence vanished by degrees, till her mind became thoroughly tainted. She affected the company of rakes, gave herself all manner of airs, was never easy but abroad, or when she had a party at my chambers. She was rapacious of money, extravagant to excess, loose in her conversation; and, if ever I demurred to any of her demands, oaths, tears, and fits were the immediate consequences. As the first raptures of fondness were long since over, this behaviour soon estranged my affections from her; I began to reflect with pleasure that she was not my wife, and to conceive an intention of parting with her; of which, having given her a hint, she took care to prevent me the pains of turning her out of doors, and accordingly departed herself, having first broken open my escrutore, and taken with her all she could find, to the amount of about £200. In the first heat of my resentment I resolved to pursue her with all the vengeance of the law: but, as she had the good luck to escape me during that ferment, my passion afterwards cooled; and, having reflected that I had been the first aggressor, and had done her an injury for which I could make her no reparation, by robbing her of the innocence of her mind; and hearing at the same time that the poor old woman her mother had broke her heart on her daughter's elopement from her, I, concluding myself her murderer ("As you very well might," cries Adams, with a groan), was pleased that God Almighty had taken this method of punishing me, and resolved quietly to submit to the loss. Indeed, I could wish I had never heard more of the poor creature, who became in the end an abandoned profligate; and, after being some years a common prostitute, at last ended her miserable life in Newgate.—Here the gentleman fetched a deep sigh, which Mr Adams echoed very loudly; and both continued silent, looking on each other for some minutes. At last the gentleman proceeded thus: I had been perfectly constant to this girl during the whole time I kept her: but she had scarce departed before I discovered more marks of her infidelity to me than the loss of my money. In short, I was forced to make a third visit to my surgeon, out of whose hands I did not get a hasty discharge.

I now forswore all future dealings with the sex, complained loudly that the pleasure did not compensate the pain, and railed at the beautiful creatures in as gross language as Juvenal himself formerly reviled them in. I looked on all the town harlots with a detestation not easy to be conceived, their persons appeared to me as painted palaces, inhabited by Disease and Death: nor could their beauty make them more desirable objects in my eyes than gilding could make me covet a pill, or golden plates a coffin. But though I was no longer the absolute slave, I found some reasons to own myself still the subject, of love. My hatred for women decreased daily; and I am not positive but time might have betrayed me again to some common harlot, had I not been secured by a passion for the charming Sapphira, which, having once entered upon, made a violent progress in my heart. Sapphira was wife to a man of fashion and gallantry, and one who seemed, I own, every way worthy of her affections; which, however, he had not the reputation of having. She was indeed a coquette *achevée*. "Pray, sir," says Adams, "what is a coquette? I have met with the word in French authors, but never could assign any idea to it. I believe it is the same with *une sotte,* Anglicè, a fool." Sir, answered the gentleman, perhaps you are not much mistaken; but, as it is a particular kind of folly, I will endeavour to describe it. Were all creatures to be ranked in the order of creation according to their usefulness, I know few animals that would not take place of a coquette; nor indeed hath this creature much pretence to anything beyond instinct; for, though sometimes we might imagine it was animated by the passion of vanity, yet far the greater part of its actions fall beneath even that low motive; for instance, several absurd gestures and tricks, infinitely more foolish than what can be observed in the most ridiculous birds and beasts, and which would persuade the beholder that the silly wretch was aiming at our contempt. Indeed its characteristic is affectation, and this led and governed by whim only: for as beauty, wisdom, wit, good-nature, politeness, and health are sometimes affected by this creature, so are ugliness, folly, nonsense, ill-nature, ill-breeding, and sickness likewise put on by it in their turn. Its life is one constant lie; and the only rule by which you can form any judgment of them is, that they are never what they seem. If it was possible for a coquette to love (as it is not, for if ever it attains this passion the coquette ceases instantly), it would wear the face of indifference, if not of hatred, to the beloved object; you may therefore be assured, when they endeavour to persuade you of their liking, that they are indifferent to you at least. And indeed this was the case of my Sapphira, who no sooner saw me in the number of her admirers than she gave me what is commonly called encouragement: she would often look at me, and, when she perceived me meet her eyes, would instantly take them off, discovering at the same time as much surprize and emotion as possible. These arts failed not of the success she intended; and, as I grew more particular to her than the rest of her admirers, she advanced, in proportion, more directly to me than to the others. She affected the low voice, whisper, lisp, sigh, start, laugh, and many other indications of passion which daily deceive thousands. When I played at whist with her, she would look earnestly at me, and at the same time lose deal or revoke; then burst into a ridiculous laugh and cry,

"La! I can't imagine what I was thinking of." To detain you no longer, after I had gone through a sufficient course of gallantry, as I thought, and was thoroughly convinced I had raised a violent passion in my mistress, I sought an opportunity of coming to an eclaircissement with her. She avoided this as much as possible; however, great assiduity at length presented me one. I will not describe all the particulars of this interview; let it suffice that, when she could no longer pretend not to see my drift, she first affected a violent surprize, and immediately after as violent a passion: she wondered what I had seen in her conduct which could induce me to affront her in this manner; and, breaking from me the first moment she could, told me I had no other way to escape the consequence of her resentment than by never seeing, or at least speaking to her more. I was not contented with this answer; I still pursued her, but to no purpose; and was at length convinced that her husband had the sole possession of her person, and that neither he nor any other had made any impression on her heart. I was taken off from following this *ignis fatuus* by some advances which were made me by the wife of a citizen, who, though neither very young nor handsome, was yet too agreeable to be rejected by my amorous constitution. I accordingly soon satisfied her that she had not cast away her hints on a barren or cold soil: on the contrary, they instantly produced her an eager and desiring lover. Nor did she give me any reason to complain; she met the warmth she had raised with equal ardour. I had no longer a coquette to deal with, but one who was wiser than to prostitute the noble passion of love to the ridiculous lust of vanity. We presently understood one another; and, as the pleasures we sought lay in a mutual gratification, we soon found and enjoyed them. I thought myself at first greatly happy in the possession of this new mistress, whose fondness would have quickly surfeited a more sickly appetite; but it had a different effect on mine: she carried my passion higher by it than youth or beauty had been able. But my happiness could not long continue uninterrupted. The apprehensions we lay under from the jealousy of her husband gave us great uneasiness. "Poor wretch! I pity him," cried Adams. He did indeed deserve it, said the gentleman; for he loved his wife with great tenderness; and, I assure you, it is a great satisfaction to me that I was not the man who first seduced her affections from him. These apprehensions appeared also too well grounded, for in the end he discovered us, and procured witnesses of our caresses. He then prosecuted me at law, and recovered £3000 damages, which much distressed my fortune to pay; and, what was worse, his wife, being divorced, came upon my hands. I led a very uneasy life with her; for, besides that my passion was now much abated, her excessive jealousy was very troublesome. At length death rid me of an inconvenience which the consideration of my having been the author of her misfortunes would never suffer me to take any other method of discarding.

I now bad adieu to love, and resolved to pursue other less dangerous and expensive pleasures. I fell into the acquaintance of a set of jolly companions, who slept all day and drank all night; fellows who might rather be said to consume time than to live. Their best conversation was nothing but noise: singing, hollowing, wrangling, drinking, toasting, sp—wing, smoaking were the chief ingredients of our entertainment. And yet, bad as these were, they were more tolerable than our graver scenes, which were either excessive tedious narratives of dull common matters of fact, or hot disputes about trifling matters, which commonly ended in a wager. This way of life the first serious reflection put a period to; and I became member of a club frequented by young men of great abilities. The bottle was now only called in to the assistance of our conversation, which rolled on the deepest points of philosophy. These gentlemen were engaged in a search after truth, in the pursuit of which they threw aside all the prejudices of education, and governed themselves only by the infallible guide of human reason. This great guide, after having shown them the falsehood of that very ancient but simple tenet, that there is such a being as a Deity in the universe, helped them to establish in his stead a certain rule of right, by adhering to which they all arrived at the utmost purity of morals. Reflection made me as much delighted with this society as it had taught me to despise and detest the former. I began now to esteem myself a being of a higher order than I had ever before conceived; and was the more charmed with this rule of right, as I really found in my own nature nothing repugnant to it. I held in utter contempt all persons who wanted any other inducement to virtue besides her intrinsic beauty and excellence; and had so high an opinion of my present companions, with regard to their morality, that I would have trusted them with whatever was nearest and dearest to me. Whilst I was engaged in this delightful dream, two or three accidents happened successively, which at first much surprized me;—for one of our greatest philosophers, or rule-of-right men, withdrew himself from us, taking with him the wife of one of his most intimate friends. Secondly, another of the same society left the club without remembering to take leave of his bail. A third, having borrowed a sum of money of me, for which I received no security, when I asked him to repay it, absolutely denied the loan. These several practices, so inconsistent with our golden rule, made me begin to suspect its infallibility; but when I communicated my thoughts to one of the club, he said, "There was nothing absolutely good or evil in itself; that actions were denominated good or bad by the circumstances of the agent. That possibly the man who ran away with his neighbour's wife might be one of very good inclinations, but over-prevailed on by the violence of an unruly passion; and, in other particulars, might be a very worthy member of society; that if the beauty of any woman created in him an uneasiness, he had a right from nature to relieve himself;"—with many other things, which I then detested so much, that I took leave of the society that very evening and never returned to it again. Being now reduced to a state of solitude which I did not like, I became a great frequenter of the playhouses, which indeed was always my favourite diversion; and most evenings passed away two or three hours behind the scenes, where I met with several poets, with whom I made engagements at the taverns. Some of the players were likewise of our parties. At these meetings we were generally entertained by the poets with reading their performances, and by the players with repeating their parts: upon which occasions, I observed the gentleman who furnished our entertainment was commonly the best pleased of the company; who, though they were pretty civil to him to his face, seldom failed to take the first opportunity of his absence to ridicule him. Now I made some remarks which probably are too obvious to be worth relating. "Sir," says Adams, "your remarks if you please." First then, says he, I concluded that the general observation, that wits are most inclined to vanity, is not true. Men are equally vain of riches, strength, beauty, honours, &c. But these appear of themselves to the eyes of the beholders, whereas the poor wit is obliged to produce his performance to show you his perfection; and on his readiness to do this that vulgar opinion I have before mentioned is grounded; but doth not the person who expends vast sums in the furniture of his house or the ornaments of his person, who consumes much time and employs great pains in dressing himself, or who thinks himself paid for self-denial, labour, or even villany, by a title or a ribbon, sacrifice as much to vanity as the poor wit who is desirous to read you his poem or his play? My second remark was, that vanity is the worst of passions, and more apt to contaminate the mind than any other: for, as selfishness is much more general than we please to allow it, so it is natural to hate and envy those who stand between us and the good we desire. Now, in lust and ambition these are few; and even in avarice we find many who are no obstacles to our pursuits; but the vain man seeks pre-eminence; and everything which is excellent or praiseworthy in another renders him the mark of his antipathy. Adams now began to fumble in his pockets, and soon cried out, "O la! I have it not about me." Upon this, the gentleman asking him what he was searching for, he said he searched after a sermon, which he thought his masterpiece, against vanity. "Fie upon it, fie upon it!" cries he, "why do I ever leave that sermon out of my pocket? I wish it was within five miles; I would willingly fetch it, to read it you." The gentleman answered that there was no need, for he was cured of the passion. "And for that very reason," quoth Adams, "I would read it, for I am confident you would admire it: indeed, I have never been a greater enemy to any passion than that silly one of vanity." The gentleman smiled, and proceeded—From this society I easily passed to that of the gamesters, where nothing remarkable happened but the finishing my fortune, which those gentlemen soon helped me to the end of. This opened scenes of life hitherto unknown; poverty and distress, with their horrid train of duns, attorneys, bailiffs, haunted me day and night. My clothes grew shabby, my credit bad, my friends and acquaintance of all kinds cold. In this situation the strangest thought imaginable came into my head; and what was this but to write a play? for I had sufficient leisure: fear of bailiffs confined me every day to my room: and, having always had a little inclination and something of a genius that way, I set myself to work, and within a few months produced a piece of five acts, which was accepted of at the theatre. I remembered to have formerly taken tickets of other poets for their benefits, long before the appearance of their performances; and, resolving to follow a precedent which was so well suited to my present circumstances, I immediately provided myself with a large number of little papers. Happy indeed would be the state of poetry, would these tickets pass current at the bakehouse, the ale-house, and the chandler's shop: but alas! far otherwise; no taylor will take them in payment for buckram, canvas, stay-tape; nor no bailiff for civility money. They are, indeed, no more than a passport to beg with; a certificate that the owner wants five shillings, which induces well-disposed Christians to charity. I now experienced what is worse than poverty, or rather what is the worst consequence of poverty—I mean attendance and dependance on the great. Many a morning have I waited hours in the cold parlours of men of quality; where, after seeing the lowest rascals in lace and embroidery, the pimps and buffoons in fashion, admitted, I have been sometimes told, on sending in my name, that my lord could not possibly see me this morning; a sufficient assurance that I should never more get entrance into that house. Sometimes I have been at last admitted; and the great man hath thought proper to excuse himself, by telling me he was tied up. "Tied up," says Adams, "pray what's that?" Sir, says the gentleman, the profit which booksellers allowed authors for the best works was so very small, that certain men of birth and fortune some years ago, who were the patrons of wit and learning, thought fit to encourage them farther by entering into voluntary subscriptions for their encouragement. Thus Prior, Rowe, Pope, and some other men of genius, received large sums for their labours from the public. This seemed so easy a method of getting money, that many of the lowest scribblers of the times ventured to publish their works in the same way; and many had the assurance to take in subscriptions for what was not writ, nor ever intended. Subscriptions in this manner growing infinite, and a kind of tax on the publick, some persons, finding it not so easy a task to discern good from bad authors, or to know what genius was worthy encouragement and what was not, to prevent the expense of subscribing to so many, invented a method to excuse themselves from all subscriptions whatever; and this was to receive a small sum of money in consideration of giving a large one if ever they subscribed; which many have done, and many more have pretended to have done, in order to silence all solicitation. The same method was likewise taken with playhouse tickets, which were no less a public grievance; and this is what they call being tied up from subscribing. "I can't say but the term is apt enough, and somewhat typical," said Adams; "for a man of large fortune, who ties himself up, as you call it, from the encouragement of men of merit, ought to be tied up in reality." Well, sir, says the gentleman, to return to my story. Sometimes I have received a guinea from a man of quality, given with as ill a grace as alms are generally to the meanest beggar; and purchased too with as much time spent in attendance as, if it had been spent in honest industry, might have brought me more profit with infinitely more satisfaction. After about two months spent in this disagreeable way, with the utmost mortification, when I was pluming my hopes on the prospect of a plentiful harvest from my play, upon applying to the prompter to know when it came into rehearsal, he informed me he had received orders from the managers to return me the play again, for that they could not possibly act it that season; but, if I would take it and revise it against the next, they would be glad to see it again. I snatched it from him with great indignation, and retired to my room, where I threw myself on the bed in a fit of despair. "You should rather have thrown yourself on your knees," says Adams, "for despair is sinful." As soon, continued the gentleman, as I had indulged the first tumult of my passion, I began to consider coolly what course I should take, in a situation without friends, money, credit, or reputation of any kind. After revolving many things in my mind, I could see no other possibility of furnishing myself with the miserable necessaries of life than to retire to a garret near the Temple, and commence hackney-writer to the lawyers, for which I was well qualified, being an excellent penman. This purpose I resolved on, and immediately put it in execution. I had an acquaintance with an attorney who had formerly transacted affairs for me, and to him I applied; but, instead of furnishing me with any business, he laughed at my undertaking, and told me, "He was afraid I should turn his deeds into plays, and he should expect to see them on the stage." Not to tire you with instances of this kind from others, I found that Plato himself did not hold poets in greater abhorrence than these men of business do. Whenever I durst venture to a coffeehouse, which was on Sundays only, a whisper ran round the room, which was constantly attended with a sneer—That's poet Wilson; for I know not whether you have observed it, but there is a malignity in the nature of man, which, when not weeded out, or at least covered by a good education and politeness, delights in making another uneasy or dissatisfied with himself. This abundantly appears in all assemblies, except those which are filled by people of fashion, and especially among the younger people of both sexes whose birth and fortunes place them just without the polite circles; I mean the lower class of the gentry, and the higher of the mercantile world, who are, in reality, the worst-bred part of mankind. Well, sir, whilst I continued in this miserable state, with scarce sufficient business to keep me from starving, the reputation of a poet being my bane, I accidentally became acquainted with a bookseller, who told me, "It was a pity a man of my learning and genius should be obliged to such a method of getting his livelihood; that he had a compassion for me, and, if I would engage with him, he would undertake to provide handsomely for me." A man in my circumstances, as he very well knew, had no choice. I accordingly accepted his proposal with his conditions, which were none of the most favourable, and fell to translating with all my might. I had no longer reason to lament the want of business; for he furnished me with so much, that in half a year I almost writ myself blind. I likewise contracted a distemper by my sedentary life, in which no part of my body was exercised but my right arm, which rendered me incapable of writing for a long time. This unluckily happening to delay the publication of a work, and my last performance not having sold well, the bookseller declined any further engagement, and aspersed me to his brethren as a careless idle fellow. I had, however, by having half worked and half starved myself to death during the time I was in his service, saved a few guineas, with which I bought a lottery-ticket, resolving to throw myself into Fortune's lap, and try if she would make me amends for the injuries she had done me at the gaming-table. This purchase, being made, left me almost pennyless; when, as if I had not been sufficiently miserable, a bailiff in woman's clothes got admittance to my chamber, whither he was directed by the bookseller. He arrested me at my taylor's suit for thirty-five pounds; a sum for which I could not procure bail; and was therefore conveyed to his house, where I was locked up in an upper chamber. I had now neither health (for I was scarce recovered from my indisposition), liberty, money, or friends; and had abandoned all hopes, and even the desire, of life. "But this could not last long," said Adams; "for doubtless the taylor released you the moment he was truly acquainted with your affairs, and knew that your circumstances would not permit you to pay him." "Oh, sir," answered the gentleman, "he knew that before he arrested me; nay, he knew that nothing but incapacity could prevent me paying my debts; for I had been his customer many years, had spent vast sums of money with him, and had always paid most punctually in my prosperous days; but when I reminded him of this, with assurances that, if he would not molest my endeavours, I would pay him all the money I could by my utmost labour and industry procure, reserving only what was sufficient to preserve me alive, he answered, his patience was worn out; that I had put him off from time to time; that he wanted the money; that he had put it into a lawyer's hands; and if I did not pay him immediately, or find security, I must die in gaol and expect no mercy." "He may expect mercy," cries Adams, starting from his chair, "where he will find none! How can such a wretch repeat the Lord's Prayer; where the word, which is translated, I know not for what reason, trespasses, is in the original, debts? And as surely as we do not forgive others their debts, when they are unable to pay them, so surely shall we ourselves be unforgiven when we are in no condition of paying." He ceased, and the gentleman proceeded. While I was in this deplorable situation, a former acquaintance, to whom I had communicated my lottery-ticket, found me out, and, making me a visit, with great delight in his countenance, shook me heartily by the hand, and wished me joy of my good fortune: for, says he, your ticket is come up a prize of £3000. Adams snapped his fingers at these words in an ecstasy of joy; which, however, did not continue long; for the gentleman thus proceeded:—Alas! sir, this was only a trick of Fortune to sink me the deeper; for I had disposed of this lottery-ticket two days before to a relation, who refused lending me a shilling without it, in order to procure myself bread. As soon as my friend was acquainted with my unfortunate sale he began to revile me and remind me of all the ill-conduct and miscarriages of my life. He said I was one whom Fortune could not save if she would; that I was now ruined without any hopes of retrieval, nor must expect any pity from my friends; that it would be extreme weakness to compassionate the misfortunes of a man who ran headlong to his own destruction. He then painted to me, in as lively colours as he was able, the happiness I should have now enjoyed, had I not foolishly disposed of my ticket. I urged the plea of necessity; but he made no answer to that, and began again to revile me, till I could bear it no longer, and desired him to finish his visit. I soon exchanged the bailiff's house for a prison; where, as I had not money sufficient to procure me a separate apartment, I was crouded in with a great number of miserable wretches, in common with whom I was destitute of every convenience of life, even that which all the brutes enjoy, wholesome air. In these dreadful circumstances I applied by letter to several of my old acquaintance, and such to whom I had formerly lent money without any great prospect of its being returned, for their assistance; but in vain. An excuse, instead of a denial, was the gentlest answer I received. Whilst I languished in a condition too horrible to be described, and which, in a land of humanity, and, what is much more, Christianity, seems a strange punishment for a little inadvertency and indiscretion; whilst I was in this condition, a fellow came into the prison, and, enquiring me out, delivered me the following letter:—

> "SIR,—My father, to whom you sold your ticket in the last lottery, died the same day in which it came up a prize, as you have possibly heard, and left me sole heiress of all his fortune. I am so much touched with your present circumstances, and the uneasiness you must feel at having been driven to dispose of what might have made you happy, that I must desire your acceptance of the enclosed, and am your humble servant,
>
> "HARRIET HEARTY."

And what do you think was enclosed? "I don't know," cried Adams; "not less than a guinea, I hope." Sir, it was a bank-note for £200.—"£200?" says Adams, in a rapture. No less, I assure you, answered the gentleman; a sum I was not half so delighted with as with the dear name of the generous girl that sent it me; and who was not only the best but the handsomest creature in the universe, and for whom I had long had a passion which I never durst disclose to her. I kissed her name a thousand times, my eyes overflowing with tenderness and gratitude; I repeated—But not to detain you with these raptures, I immediately acquired my liberty; and, having paid all my debts, departed, with upwards of fifty pounds in my pocket, to thank my kind deliverer. She happened to be then out of town, a circumstance which, upon reflection, pleased me; for by that means I had an opportunity to appear before her in a more decent dress. At her return to town, within a day or two, I threw myself at her feet with the most ardent acknowledgments, which she rejected with an unfeigned greatness of mind, and told me I could not oblige her more than by never mentioning, or if possible thinking on, a circumstance which must bring to my mind an accident that might be grievous to me to think on. She proceeded thus: "What I have done is in my own eyes a trifle, and perhaps infinitely less than would have become me to do. And if you think of engaging in any business where a larger sum may be serviceable to you, I shall not be over-rigid either as to the security or interest." I endeavoured to express all the gratitude in my power to this profusion of goodness, though perhaps it was my enemy, and began to afflict my mind with more agonies than all the miseries I had underwent; it affected me with severer reflections than poverty, distress, and prisons united had been able to make me feel; for, sir, these acts and professions of kindness, which were sufficient to have raised in a good heart the most violent passion of friendship to one of the same, or to age and ugliness in a different sex, came to me from a woman, a young and beautiful woman; one whose perfections I had long known, and for whom I had long conceived a violent passion, though with a despair which made me endeavour rather to curb and conceal, than to nourish or acquaint her with it. In short, they came upon me united with beauty, softness, and tenderness: such bewitching smiles!—O Mr Adams, in that moment I lost myself, and, forgetting our different situations, nor considering what return I was making to her goodness by desiring her, who had given me so much, to bestow her all, I laid gently hold on her hand, and, conveying it to my lips, I prest it with inconceivable ardour; then, lifting up my swimming eyes, I saw her face and neck overspread with one blush; she offered to withdraw her hand, yet not so as to deliver it from mine, though I held it with the gentlest force. We both stood trembling; her eyes cast on the ground, and mine stedfastly fixed on her. Good G—d, what was then the condition of my soul! burning with love, desire, admiration, gratitude, and every tender passion, all bent on one charming object. Passion at last got the better of both reason and respect, and, softly letting go her hand, I offered madly to clasp her in my arms; when, a little recovering herself, she started from me, asking me, with some show of anger, "If she had any reason to expect this treatment from me." I then fell prostrate before her, and told her, if I had offended, my life was absolutely in her power, which I would in any manner lose for her sake. Nay, madam, said I, you shall not be so ready to punish me as I to suffer. I own my guilt. I detest the reflection that I would have sacrificed your happiness to mine. Believe me, I sincerely repent my ingratitude; yet, believe me too, it was my passion, my unbounded passion for you, which hurried me so far: I have loved you long and tenderly, and the goodness you have shown me hath innocently weighed down a wretch undone before. Acquit me of all mean, mercenary views; and, before I take my leave of you for ever, which I am resolved instantly to do, believe me that Fortune could have raised me to no height to which I could not have gladly lifted you. O, curst be Fortune!—"Do not," says she, interrupting me with the sweetest voice, "do not curse Fortune, since she hath made me happy; and, if she hath put your happiness in my power, I have told you you shall ask nothing in reason which I will refuse." Madam, said I, you mistake me if you imagine, as you seem, my happiness is in the power of Fortune now. You have obliged me too much already; if I have any wish, it is for some blest accident, by which I may contribute with my life to the least augmentation of your felicity. As for myself, the only happiness I can ever have will be hearing of yours; and if Fortune will make that complete, I will forgive her all her wrongs to me. "You may, indeed," answered she, smiling, "for your own happiness must be included in mine. I have long known your worth; nay, I must confess," said she, blushing, "I have long discovered that passion for me you profess, notwithstanding those endeavours, which I am convinced were unaffected, to conceal it; and if all I can give with reason will not suffice, take reason away; and now I believe you cannot ask me what I will deny."—She uttered these words with a sweetness not to be imagined. I immediately started; my blood, which lay freezing at my heart, rushed tumultuously through every vein. I stood for a moment silent; then, flying to her, I caught her in my arms, no longer resisting, and softly told her she must give me then herself. O, sir! can I describe her look? She remained silent, and almost motionless, several minutes. At last, recovering herself a little, she insisted on my leaving her, and in such a manner that I instantly obeyed: you may imagine, however, I soon saw her again.—But I ask pardon: I fear I have detained you too long in relating the particulars of the former interview. "So far otherwise," said Adams, licking his lips, "that I could willingly hear it over again." Well, sir, continued the gentleman, to be as concise as possible, within a week she consented to make me the happiest of mankind. We were married shortly after; and when I came to examine the circumstances of my wife's fortune (which, I do assure you, I was not presently at leisure enough to do), I found it amounted to about six thousand pounds, most part of which lay in effects; for her father had been a wine-merchant, and she seemed willing, if I liked it, that I should carry on the same trade. I readily, and too inconsiderately, undertook it; for, not having been bred up to the secrets of the business, and endeavouring to deal with the utmost honesty and uprightness, I soon found our fortune in a declining way, and my trade decreasing by little and little; for my wines, which I never adulterated after their importation, and were sold as neat as they came over, were universally decried by the vintners, to whom I could not allow them quite as cheap as those who gained double the profit by a less price. I soon began to despair of improving our fortune by these means; nor was I at all easy at the visits and familiarity of many who had been my acquaintance in my prosperity, but had denied and shunned me in my adversity, and now very forwardly renewed their acquaintance with me. In short, I had sufficiently seen that the pleasures of the world are chiefly folly, and the business of it mostly knavery, and both nothing better than vanity; the men of pleasure tearing one another to pieces from the emulation of spending money, and the men of business from envy in getting it. My happiness consisted entirely in my wife, whom I loved with an inexpressible fondness, which was perfectly returned; and my prospects were no other than to provide for our growing family; for she was now big of her second child: I therefore took an opportunity to ask her opinion of entering into a retired life, which, after hearing my reasons and perceiving my affection for it, she readily embraced. We soon put our small fortune, now reduced under three thousand pounds, into money, with part of which we purchased this little place, whither we retired soon after her delivery, from a world full of bustle, noise, hatred, envy, and ingratitude, to ease, quiet, and love. We have here lived almost twenty years, with little other conversation than our own, most of the neighbourhood taking us for very strange people; the squire of the parish representing me as a madman, and the parson as a presbyterian, because I will not hunt with the one nor drink with the other. "Sir," says Adams, "Fortune hath, I think, paid you all her debts in this sweet retirement." Sir, replied the gentleman, I am thankful to the great Author of all things for the blessings I here enjoy. I have the best of wives, and three pretty children, for whom I have the true tenderness of a parent. But no blessings are pure in this world: within three years of my arrival here I lost my eldest son. (Here he sighed bitterly.) "Sir," says Adams, "we must submit to Providence, and consider death as common to all." We must submit, indeed, answered the gentleman; and if he had died I could have borne the loss with patience; but alas! sir, he was stolen away from my door by some wicked travelling people whom they call gipsies; nor could I ever, with the most diligent search, recover him. Poor child! he had the sweetest look—the exact picture of his mother; at which some tears unwittingly dropt from his eyes, as did likewise from those of Adams, who always sympathized with his friends on those occasions. Thus, sir, said the gentleman, I have finished my story, in which if I have been too particular, I ask your pardon; and now, if you please, I will fetch you another bottle: which proposal the parson thankfully accepted.

CHAPTER IV.

A description of Mr Wilson's way of living. The tragical adventure of the dog, and other grave matters.

The gentleman returned with the bottle; and Adams and he sat some time silent, when the former started up, and cried, "No, that won't do." The gentleman inquired into his meaning; he answered, "He had been considering that it was possible the late famous king Theodore might have been that very son whom he had lost;" but added, "that his age could not answer that imagination. However," says he, "G— disposes all things for the best; and very probably he may be some great man, or duke, and may, one day or other, revisit you in that capacity." The gentleman answered, he should know him amongst ten thousand, for he had a mark on his left breast of a strawberry, which his mother had given him by longing for that fruit.

That beautiful young lady the Morning now rose from her bed, and with a countenance blooming with fresh youth and sprightliness, like Miss ——[1], with soft dews hanging on her pouting lips, began to take her early walk over the eastern hills; and presently after, that gallant person the Sun stole softly from his wife's chamber to pay his addresses to her; when the gentleman asked his guest if he would walk forth and survey his little garden, which he readily agreed to, and Joseph at the same time awaking from a sleep in which he had been two hours buried, went with them. No parterres, no fountains, no statues, embellished this little garden. Its only ornament was a short walk, shaded on each side by a filbert-hedge, with a small alcove at one end, whither in hot weather the gentleman and his wife used to retire and divert themselves with their children, who played in the walk before them. But, though vanity had no votary in this little spot, here was variety of fruit and everything useful for the kitchen, which was abundantly sufficient to catch the admiration of Adams, who told the gentleman he had certainly a good gardener. Sir, answered he, that gardener is now before you: whatever you see here is the work solely of my own hands. Whilst I am providing necessaries for my table, I likewise procure myself an appetite for them. In fair seasons I seldom pass less than six hours of the twenty-four in this place, where I am not idle; and by these means I have been able to preserve my health ever since my arrival

---

[1] Whoever the reader pleases.

here, without assistance from physic. Hither I generally repair at the dawn, and exercise myself whilst my wife dresses her children and prepares our breakfast; after which we are seldom asunder during the residue of the day, for, when the weather will not permit them to accompany me here, I am usually within with them; for I am neither ashamed of conversing with my wife nor of playing with my children: to say the truth, I do not perceive that inferiority of understanding which the levity of rakes, the dulness of men of business, or the austerity of the learned, would persuade us of in women. As for my woman, I declare I have found none of my own sex capable of making juster observations on life, or of delivering them more agreeably; nor do I believe any one possessed of a faithfuller or braver friend. And sure as this friendship is sweetened with more delicacy and tenderness, so is it confirmed by dearer pledges than can attend the closest male alliance; for what union can be so fast as our common interest in the fruits of our embraces? Perhaps, sir, you are not yourself a father; if you are not, be assured you cannot conceive the delight I have in my little ones. Would you not despise me if you saw me stretched on the ground, and my children playing round me? "I should reverence the sight," quoth Adams; "I myself am now the father of six, and have been of eleven, and I can say I never scourged a child of my own, unless as his schoolmaster, and then have felt every stroke on my own posteriors. And as to what you say concerning women, I have often lamented my own wife did not understand Greek."—The gentleman smiled, and answered, he would not be apprehended to insinuate that his own had an understanding above the care of her family; on the contrary, says he, my Harriet, I assure you, is a notable housewife, and few gentlemen's housekeepers understand cookery or confectionery better; but these are arts which she hath no great occasion for now: however, the wine you commended so much last night at supper was of her own making, as is indeed all the liquor in my house, except my beer, which falls to my province. "And I assure you it is as excellent," quoth Adams, "as ever I tasted." We formerly kept a maid-servant, but since my girls have been growing up she is unwilling to indulge them in idleness; for as the fortunes I shall give them will be very small, we intend not to breed them above the rank they are likely to fill hereafter, nor to teach them to despise or ruin a plain husband. Indeed, I could wish a man of my own temper, and a retired life, might fall to their lot; for I have experienced that calm serene happiness, which is seated in content, is inconsistent with the hurry and bustle of the world. He was proceeding thus when the little things, being just risen, ran eagerly towards him and asked him blessing. They were shy to the strangers, but the eldest acquainted her father, that her mother and the young gentlewoman were up, and that breakfast was ready. They all went in, where the gentleman was surprized at the beauty of Fanny, who had now recovered herself from her fatigue, and was entirely clean drest; for the rogues who had taken away her purse had left her her bundle. But if he was so much amazed at the beauty of this young creature, his guests were no less charmed at the tenderness which appeared in the behaviour of the husband and wife to each other, and to their children, and at the dutiful and affectionate behaviour of these to their parents. These instances pleased the well-disposed mind of Adams equally with the readiness which they exprest to oblige their guests, and their forwardness to offer them the best of everything in their house; and what delighted him still more was an instance or two of their charity; for whilst they were at breakfast the good woman was called for to assist her sick neighbour, which she did with some cordials made for the public use, and the good man went into his garden at the same time to supply another with something which he wanted thence, for they had nothing which those who wanted it were not welcome to. These good people were in the utmost cheerfulness, when they heard the report of a gun, and immediately afterwards a little dog, the favourite of the eldest daughter, came limping in all bloody and laid himself at his mistress's feet: the poor girl, who was about eleven years old, burst into tears at the sight; and presently one of the neighbours came in and informed them that the young squire, the son of the lord of the manor, had shot him as he past by, swearing at the same time he would prosecute the master of him for keeping a spaniel, for that he had given notice he would not suffer one in the parish. The dog, whom his mistress had taken into her lap, died in a few minutes, licking her hand. She exprest great agony at his loss, and the other children began to cry for their sister's misfortune; nor could Fanny herself refrain. Whilst the father and mother attempted to comfort her, Adams grasped his crabstick and would have sallied out after the squire had not Joseph withheld him. He could not however bridle his tongue—he pronounced the word rascal with great emphasis; said he deserved to be hanged more than a highwayman, and wished he had the scourging him. The mother took her child, lamenting and carrying the dead favourite in her arms, out of the room, when the gentleman said this was the second time this squire had endeavoured to kill the little wretch, and had wounded him smartly once before; adding, he could have no motive but ill-nature, for the little thing, which was not near as big as one's fist, had never been twenty yards from the house in the six years his daughter had had it. He said he had done nothing to deserve this usage, but his father had too great a fortune to contend with: that he was as absolute as any tyrant in the universe, and had killed all the dogs and taken away all the guns in the neighbourhood; and not only that, but he trampled down hedges and rode over corn and gardens, with no more regard than if they were the highway. "I wish I could catch him in my garden," said Adams, "though I would rather forgive him riding through my house than such an ill-natured act as this."

The cheerfulness of their conversation being interrupted by this accident, in which the guests could be of no service to their kind entertainer; and as the mother was taken up in administering consolation to the poor girl, whose disposition was too good hastily to forget the sudden loss of her little favourite, which had been fondling with her a few minutes before; and as Joseph and Fanny were impatient to get home and begin those previous ceremonies to their happiness which Adams had insisted on, they now offered to take their leave. The gentleman importuned them much to stay dinner; but when he found their eagerness to depart he summoned his wife; and accordingly, having performed all the usual ceremonies of bows and curtsies more pleasant to be seen than to be related, they took their leave, the gentleman and his wife heartily wishing them a good journey, and they as heartily thanking them for their kind entertainment. They then departed, Adams declaring that this was the manner in which the people had lived in the golden age.

CHAPTER V.

A disputation on schools held on the road between Mr Abraham Adams and Joseph; and a discovery not unwelcome to them both.

Our travellers, having well refreshed themselves at the gentleman's house, Joseph and Fanny with sleep, and Mr Abraham Adams with ale and tobacco, renewed their journey with great alacrity; and pursuing the road into which they were directed, travelled many miles before they met with any adventure worth relating. In this interval we shall present our readers with a very curious discourse, as we apprehend it, concerning public schools, which passed between Mr Joseph Andrews and Mr Abraham Adams.

They had not gone far before Adams, calling to Joseph, asked him, "If he had attended to the gentleman's story?" He answered, "To all the former part."—"And don't you think," says he, "he was a very unhappy man in his youth?"—"A very unhappy man, indeed," answered the other. "Joseph," cries Adams, screwing up his mouth, "I have found it; I have discovered the cause of all the misfortunes which befel him: a public school, Joseph, was the cause of all the calamities which he afterwards suffered. Public schools are the nurseries of all vice and immorality. All the wicked fellows whom I remember at the university were bred at them.—Ah, Lord! I can remember as well as if it was but yesterday, a knot of them; they called them King's scholars, I forget why—very wicked fellows! Joseph, you may thank the Lord you were not bred at a public school; you would never have preserved your virtue as you have. The first care I always take is of a boy's morals; I had rather he should be a blockhead than an atheist or a presbyterian. What is all the learning in the world compared to his immortal soul? What shall a man take in exchange for his soul? But the masters of great schools trouble themselves about no such thing. I have known a lad of eighteen at the university, who hath not been able to say his catechism; but for my own part, I always scourged a lad sooner for missing that than any other lesson. Believe me, child, all that gentleman's misfortunes arose from his being educated at a public school."

"It doth not become me," answered Joseph, "to dispute anything, sir, with you, especially a matter of this kind; for to be sure you must be allowed by all the world to be the best teacher of a school in all our county." "Yes, that," says Adams, "I believe, is granted me; that I may without much vanity pretend to—nay, I believe I may go to the next county too—but *gloriari non est meum*."— "However, sir, as you are pleased to bid me speak," says Joseph, "you know my late master, Sir Thomas Booby, was bred at a public school, and he was the finest gentleman in all the neighbourhood. And I have often heard him say, if he had a hundred boys he would breed them all at the same place. It was his opinion, and I have often heard him deliver it, that a boy taken from a public school and carried into the world, will learn more in one year there than one of a private education will in five. He used to say the school itself initiated him a great way (I remember that was his very expression), for great schools are little societies, where a boy of any observation may see in epitome what he will afterwards find in the world at large."—"*Hinc illae lachrymae*: for that very reason," quoth Adams, "I prefer a private school, where boys may be kept in innocence and ignorance; for, according to that fine passage in the play of Cato, the only English tragedy I ever read—

> "'If knowledge of the world must make men villains
> May Juba ever live in ignorance!'

"Who would not rather preserve the purity of his child than wish him to attain the whole circle of arts and sciences? which, by the bye, he may learn in the classes of a private school; for I would not be vain, but I esteem myself to be second to none, *nulli secundum*, in teaching these things; so that a lad may have as much learning in a private as in a public education."—"And, with submission," answered Joseph, "he may get as much vice: witness several country gentlemen, who were educated within five miles of their own houses, and are as wicked as if they had known the world from their infancy. I remember when I was in the stable, if a young horse was vicious in his nature, no correction would make him otherwise: I take it to be equally the same among men: if a boy be of a mischievous wicked inclination, no school, though ever so private, will ever make him good: on the contrary, if he be of a righteous temper, you may trust him to London, or wherever else you please—he will be in no danger of being corrupted. Besides, I have often heard my master say that the discipline practised in public schools was much better than that in private."—"You talk like a jackanapes," says Adams, "and so did your master. Discipline indeed! Because one man scourges twenty or thirty boys more in a morning than another, is he therefore a better disciplinarian? I do presume to confer in this point with all who have taught from Chiron's time to this day; and, if I was master of six boys only, I would preserve as good discipline amongst them as the master of the greatest school in the world. I say nothing, young man; remember I say nothing; but if Sir Thomas himself had been educated nearer home, and under the tuition of somebody—remember I name nobody—it might have been better for him:—but his father must institute him in the knowledge of the world. *Nemo mortalium omnibus horis sapit.*" Joseph, seeing him run on in this manner, asked pardon many times, assuring him he had no intention to offend. "I believe you had not, child," said he, "and I am not angry with you; but for maintaining good discipline in a school; for this."—And then he ran on as before, named all the masters who are recorded in old books, and preferred himself to them all. Indeed, if this good man had an enthusiasm, or what the vulgar call a blind side, it was this: he thought a schoolmaster the greatest character in the world, and himself the greatest of all schoolmasters:

neither of which points he would have given up to Alexander the Great at the head of his army.

Adams continued his subject till they came to one of the beautifullest spots of ground in the universe. It was a kind of natural amphitheatre, formed by the winding of a small rivulet, which was planted with thick woods, and the trees rose gradually above each other by the natural ascent of the ground they stood on; which ascent as they hid with their boughs, they seemed to have been disposed by the design of the most skilful planter. The soil was spread with a verdure which no paint could imitate; and the whole place might have raised romantic ideas in elder minds than those of Joseph and Fanny, without the assistance of love.

Here they arrived about noon, and Joseph proposed to Adams that they should rest awhile in this delightful place, and refresh themselves with some provisions which the good-nature of Mrs Wilson had provided them with. Adams made no objection to the proposal; so down they sat, and, pulling out a cold fowl and a bottle of wine, they made a repast with a cheerfulness which might have attracted the envy of more splendid tables. I should not omit that they found among their provision a little paper containing a piece of gold, which Adams imagining had been put there by mistake, would have returned back to restore it; but he was at last convinced by Joseph that Mr Wilson had taken this handsome way of furnishing them with a supply for their journey, on his having related the distress which they had been in, when they were relieved by the generosity of the pedlar. Adams said he was glad to see such an instance of goodness, not so much for the conveniency which it brought them as for the sake of the doer, whose reward would be great in heaven. He likewise comforted himself with a reflection that he should shortly have an opportunity of returning it him; for the gentleman was within a week to make a journey into Somersetshire, to pass through Adams's parish, and had faithfully promised to call on him; a circumstance which we thought too immaterial to mention before; but which those who have as great an affection for that gentleman as ourselves will rejoice at, as it may give them hopes of seeing him again. Then Joseph made a speech on charity, which the reader, if he is so disposed, may see in the next chapter; for we scorn to betray him into any such reading, without first giving him warning.

CHAPTER VI.

Moral reflections by Joseph Andrews; with the hunting adventure, and parson Adams's miraculous escape.

"I have often wondered, sir," said Joseph, "to observe so few instances of charity among mankind; for though the goodness of a man's heart did not incline him to relieve the distresses of his fellow-creatures, methinks the desire of honour should move him to it. What inspires a man to build fine houses, to purchase fine furniture, pictures, clothes, and other things, at a great expense, but an ambition to be respected more than other people? Now, would not one great act of charity, one instance of redeeming a poor family from all the miseries of poverty, restoring an unfortunate tradesman by a sum of money to the means of procuring a livelihood by his industry, discharging an undone debtor from his debts or a gaol, or any suchlike example of goodness, create a man more honour and respect than he could acquire by the finest house, furniture, pictures, or clothes, that were ever beheld? For not only the object himself who was thus relieved, but all who heard the name of such a person, must, I imagine, reverence him infinitely more than the possessor of all those other things; which when we so admire, we rather praise the builder, the workman, the painter, the lace-maker, the taylor, and the rest, by whose ingenuity they are produced, than the person who by his money makes them his own. For my own part, when I have waited behind my lady in a room hung with fine pictures, while I have been looking at them I have never once thought of their owner, nor hath any one else, as I ever observed; for when it hath been asked whose picture that was, it was never once answered the master's of the house; but Ammyconni, Paul Varnish, Hannibal Scratchi, or Hogarthi, which I suppose were the names of the painters; but if it was asked—Who redeemed such a one out of prison? Who lent such a ruined tradesman money to set up? Who clothed that family of poor small children? it is very plain what must be the answer. And besides, these great folks are mistaken if they imagine they get any honour at all by these means; for I do not remember I ever was with my lady at any house where she commended the house or furniture but I have heard her at her return home make sport and jeer at whatever she had before commended; and I have been told by other gentlemen in livery that it is the same in their families: but I defy the wisest man in the world to turn a true good action into ridicule. I defy him to do it. He who should endeavour it would be laughed at himself, instead of making others laugh. Nobody scarce doth any good, yet they all agree in praising those who do. Indeed, it is strange that all men should consent in commending goodness, and no man endeavour to deserve that commendation; whilst, on the contrary, all rail at wickedness, and all are as eager to be what they abuse. This I know not the reason of; but it is as plain as daylight to those who converse in the world, as I have done these three years." "Are all the great folks wicked then?" says Fanny. "To be sure there are some exceptions," answered Joseph. "Some gentlemen of our cloth report charitable actions done by their lords and masters; and I have heard Squire Pope, the great poet, at my lady's table, tell stories of a man that lived at a place called Ross, and another at the Bath, one Al—Al—I forget his name, but it is in the book of verses. This gentleman hath built up a stately house too, which the squire likes very well; but his charity is seen farther than his house, though it stands on a hill,—ay, and brings him more honour too. It was his charity that put him in the book, where the squire says he puts all those who deserve it; and to be sure, as he lives among all the great people, if there were any such, he would know them." This was all of Mr Joseph Andrews's speech which I could get him to recollect, which I have delivered as near as was possible in his own words, with a very small embellishment. But I believe the reader hath not been a little surprized at the long silence of parson Adams, especially as so many occasions offered themselves to exert his curiosity and observation. The truth is, he was fast asleep, and had so been from the beginning of the preceding narrative; and, indeed, if the reader considers that so many hours had passed since he had closed his eyes, he will not wonder at his repose, though even Henley himself, or as great an orator (if any such be), had been in his rostrum or tub before him.

Joseph, who whilst he was speaking had continued in one attitude, with his head reclining on one side, and his eyes cast on the ground, no sooner perceived, on looking up, the position of Adams, who was stretched on his back, and snored louder than the usual braying of the animal with long ears, than he turned towards Fanny, and, taking her by the hand, began a dalliance, which, though consistent with the purest innocence and decency, neither he would have attempted nor she permitted before any witness. Whilst they amused themselves in this harmless and delightful manner they heard a pack of hounds approaching in full cry towards them, and presently afterwards saw a hare pop forth from the wood, and, crossing the water, land within a few yards of them in the meadows. The hare was no sooner on shore than it seated itself on its hinder legs, and listened to the sound of the pursuers. Fanny was wonderfully pleased with the little wretch, and eagerly longed to have it in her arms that she might preserve it from the dangers which seemed to threaten it; but the rational part of the creation do not always aptly distinguish their friends from their foes; what wonder then if this silly creature, the moment it beheld her, fled from the friend who would have protected it, and, traversing the meadows again, passed the little rivulet on the opposite side? It was, however, so spent and weak, that it fell down twice or thrice in its way. This affected the tender heart of Fanny, who exclaimed, with tears in her eyes, against the barbarity of worrying a poor innocent defenceless animal out of its life, and putting it to the extremest torture for diversion. She had not much time to make reflections of this kind, for on a sudden the hounds rushed through the wood, which resounded with their throats and the throats of their retinue, who attended on them on horseback. The dogs now past the rivulet, and pursued the footsteps of the hare; five horsemen attempted to leap over, three of whom succeeded, and two were in the attempt thrown from their saddles into the water; their companions, and their own horses too, proceeded after their sport, and left their friends and riders to invoke the assistance of Fortune, or employ the more active means of strength and agility for their deliverance. Joseph, however, was not so unconcerned on this occasion; he left Fanny for a moment to herself, and ran to the gentlemen, who were immediately on their legs, shaking their ears, and easily, with the help of his hand, obtained the bank (for the rivulet was not at all deep); and, without staying to thank their kind assister, ran dripping across the meadow, calling to their brother sportsmen to stop their horses; but they heard them not.

The hounds were now very little behind their poor reeling, staggering prey, which, fainting almost at every step, crawled through the wood, and had almost got round to the place where Fanny stood, when it was overtaken by its enemies, and being driven out of the covert, was caught, and instantly tore to pieces before Fanny's face, who was unable to assist it with any aid more powerful than pity; nor could she prevail on Joseph, who had been himself a sportsman in his youth, to attempt anything contrary to the laws of hunting in favour of the hare, which he said was killed fairly.

The hare was caught within a yard or two of Adams, who lay asleep at some distance from the lovers; and the hounds, in devouring it, and pulling it backwards and forwards, had drawn it so close to him, that some of them (by mistake perhaps for the hare's skin) laid hold of the skirts of his cassock; others at the same time applying their teeth to his wig, which he had with a handkerchief fastened to his head, began to pull him about; and had not the motion of his body had more effect on him than seemed to be wrought by the noise, they must certainly have tasted his flesh, which delicious flavour might have been fatal to him; but being roused by these tuggings, he instantly awaked, and with a jerk delivering his head from his wig, he with most admirable dexterity recovered his legs, which now seemed the only members he could entrust his safety to. Having, therefore, escaped likewise from at least a third part of his cassock, which he willingly left as his *exuviae* or spoils to the enemy, he fled with the utmost speed he could summon to his assistance. Nor let this be any detraction from the bravery of his character: let the number of the enemies, and the surprize in which he was taken, be considered; and if there be any modern so outrageously brave that he cannot admit of flight in any circumstance whatever, I say (but I whisper that softly, and I solemnly declare without any intention of giving offence to any brave man in the nation), I say, or rather I whisper, that he is an ignorant fellow, and hath never read Homer nor Virgil, nor knows he anything of Hector or Turnus; nay, he is unacquainted with the history of some great men living, who, though as brave as lions, ay, as tigers, have run away, the Lord knows how far, and the Lord knows why, to the surprize of their friends and the entertainment of their enemies. But if persons of such heroic disposition are a little offended at the behaviour of Adams, we assure them they shall be as much pleased with what we shall immediately relate of Joseph Andrews. The master of the pack was just arrived, or, as the sportsmen call it, come in, when Adams set out, as we have before mentioned. This gentleman was generally said to be a great lover of humour; but, not to mince the matter, especially as we are upon this subject, he was a great hunter of men; indeed, he had hitherto followed the sport only with dogs of his own species; for he kept two or three couple of barking curs for that use only. However, as he thought he had now found a man nimble enough, he was willing to indulge himself with other sport, and accordingly, crying out, "Stole away," encouraged the hounds to pursue Mr Adams, swearing it was the largest jack-hare he ever saw; at the same time hallooing and hooping as if a conquered foe was flying before him; in which he was imitated by these two or three couple of human or rather two-legged curs on horseback which we have mentioned before.

Now, thou, whoever thou art, whether a muse, or by what other name soever thou choosest to be called, who presidest over biography, and hast inspired all the writers of lives in these our times: thou who didst infuse such wonderful humour into the pen of immortal Gulliver; who hast carefully guided the judgment whilst thou hast exalted the nervous manly style of thy Mallet: thou who hadst no hand in that dedication and preface, or the translations, which thou wouldst willingly have struck out of the life of Cicero: lastly, thou who, without the assistance of the least spice of literature, and even against his inclination, hast, in some pages of his book, forced Colley Cibber to write English; do thou assist me in what I find myself unequal to. Do thou introduce on the plain the young, the gay, the brave Joseph Andrews, whilst men shall view him with admiration and envy, tender virgins with love and anxious concern for his safety.

No sooner did Joseph Andrews perceive the distress of his friend, when first the quick-scenting dogs attacked him, than he grasped his cudgel in his right hand—a cudgel which his father had of his grandfather, to whom a mighty strong man of Kent had given it for a present in that day when he broke three heads on the stage. It was a cudgel of mighty strength and wonderful art, made by one of Mr Deard's best workmen, whom no other artificer can equal, and who hath made all those sticks which the beaus have lately walked with about the Park in a morning; but this was far his masterpiece. On its head was engraved a nose and chin, which might have been mistaken for a pair of nutcrackers. The learned have imagined it designed to represent the Gorgon; but it was in fact copied from the face of a certain long English baronet, of infinite wit, humour, and gravity. He did intend to have engraved here many histories: as the first night of Captain B——'s play, where you would have seen critics in embroidery transplanted from the boxes to the pit, whose ancient inhabitants were exalted to the galleries, where they played on catcalls. He did intend to have painted an auction room, where Mr Cock would have appeared aloft in his pulpit, trumpeting forth the praises of a china basin, and with astonishment wondering that "Nobody bids more for that fine, that superb—"

He did intend to have engraved many other things, but was forced to leave all out for want of room.

No sooner had Joseph grasped his cudgel in his hands than lightning darted from his eyes; and the heroick youth, swift of foot, ran with the utmost speed to his friend's assistance. He overtook him just as Rockwood had laid hold of the skirt of his cassock, which, being torn, hung to the ground. Reader, we would make a simile on this occasion, but for two reasons: the first is, it would interrupt the description, which should be rapid in this part; but that doth not weigh much, many precedents occurring for such an interruption: the second and much the greater reason is, that we could find no simile adequate to our purpose: for indeed, what instance could we bring to set before our reader's eyes at once the idea of friendship, courage, youth, beauty, strength, and swiftness? all which blazed in the person of Joseph Andrews. Let those, therefore, that describe lions and tigers, and heroes fiercer than both, raise their poems or plays with the simile of Joseph Andrews, who is himself above the reach of any simile.

Now Rockwood had laid fast hold on the parson's skirts, and stopt his flight; which Joseph no sooner perceived than he levelled his cudgel at his head and laid him sprawling. Jowler and Ringwood then fell on his greatcoat, and had undoubtedly brought him to the ground, had not Joseph, collecting all his force, given Jowler such a rap on the back, that, quitting his hold, he ran howling over the plain. A harder fate remained for thee, O Ringwood! Ringwood the best hound that ever pursued a hare, who never threw his tongue but where the scent was undoubtedly true; good at trailing, and sure in a highway; no babler, no overrunner; respected by the whole pack, who, whenever he opened, knew the game was at hand. He fell by the stroke of Joseph. Thunder and Plunder, and Wonder and Blunder, were the next victims of his wrath, and measured their lengths on the ground. Then Fairmaid, a bitch which Mr John Temple had bred up in his house, and fed at his own table, and lately sent the squire fifty miles for a present, ran fiercely at Joseph and bit him by the leg: no dog was ever fiercer than she, being descended from an Amazonian breed, and had worried bulls in her own country, but now waged an unequal fight, and had shared the fate of those we have mentioned before, had not Diana (the reader may believe it or not if he pleases) in that instant interposed, and, in the shape of the huntsman, snatched her favourite up in her arms.

The parson now faced about, and with his crabstick felled many to the earth, and scattered others, till he was attacked by Caesar and pulled to the ground. Then Joseph flew to his rescue, and with such might fell on the victor, that, O eternal blot to his name! Caesar ran yelping away.

The battle now raged with the most dreadful violence, when, lo! the huntsman, a man of years and dignity, lifted his voice, and called his hounds from the fight, telling them, in a language they understood, that it was in vain to contend longer, for that fate had decreed the victory to their enemies.

Thus far the muse hath with her usual dignity related this prodigious battle, a battle we apprehend never equalled by any poet, romance or life writer whatever, and, having brought it to a conclusion, she ceased; we shall therefore proceed in our ordinary style with the continuation of this history. The squire and his companions, whom the figure of Adams and the gallantry of Joseph had at first thrown into a violent fit of laughter, and who had hitherto beheld the engagement with more delight than any chase, shooting-match, race, cock-fighting, bull or bear baiting, had ever given them, began now to apprehend the danger of their hounds, many of which lay sprawling in the fields. The squire, therefore, having first called his friends about him, as guards for safety of his person, rode manfully up to the combatants, and, summoning all the terror he was master of into his countenance, demanded with an authoritative voice of Joseph what he meant by assaulting his dogs in that manner? Joseph answered, with great intrepidity, that they had first fallen on his friend; and if they had belonged to the greatest man in the kingdom, he would have treated them in the same way; for, whilst his veins contained a single drop of blood, he would not stand idle by and see that gentleman (pointing to Adams) abused either by man or beast; and, having so said, both he and Adams brandished their wooden weapons, and put themselves into such a posture, that the squire and his company thought proper to preponderate before they offered to revenge the cause of their four-footed allies.

At this instant Fanny, whom the apprehension of Joseph's danger had alarmed so much that, forgetting her own, she had made the utmost expedition, came up. The squire and all the horsemen were so surprized with her beauty, that they immediately fixed both their eyes and thoughts solely on her, every one declaring he had never seen so charming a creature. Neither mirth nor anger engaged them a moment longer, but all sat in silent amaze. The huntsman only was free from her attraction, who was busy in cutting the ears of the dogs, and endeavouring to recover them to life; in which he succeeded so well, that only two of no great note remained slaughtered on the field of action. Upon this the huntsman declared, "'Twas well it was no worse; for his part he could not blame the gentleman, and wondered his master would encourage the dogs to hunt Christians; that it was the surest way to spoil them, to make them follow vermin instead of sticking to a hare."

The squire, being informed of the little mischief that had been done, and perhaps having more mischief of another kind in his head, accosted Mr Adams with a more favourable aspect than before: he told him he was sorry for what had happened; that he had endeavoured all he could to prevent it the moment he was acquainted with his cloth, and greatly commended the courage of his servant, for so he imagined Joseph to be. He then invited Mr Adams to dinner, and desired the young woman might come with him. Adams refused a long while; but the invitation was repeated with so much earnestness and courtesy, that at length he was forced to accept it. His wig and hat, and other spoils of the field, being gathered together by Joseph (for otherwise probably they would have been forgotten), he put himself into the best order he could; and then the horse and foot moved forward in the same pace towards the squire's house, which stood at a very little distance.

Whilst they were on the road the lovely Fanny attracted the eyes of all: they endeavoured to outvie one another in encomiums on her beauty; which the reader will pardon my not relating, as they had not anything new or uncommon in them: so must he likewise my not setting down the many curious jests which were made on Adams; some of them declaring that parson-hunting was the best sport in the world; others commending his standing at bay, which they said he had done as well as any badger; with such like merriment, which, though it would ill become the dignity of this history, afforded much laughter and diversion to the squire and his facetious companions.

CHAPTER VII.

A scene of roasting, very nicely adapted to the present taste and times.

They arrived at the squire's house just as his dinner was ready. A little dispute arose on the account of Fanny, whom the squire, who was a bachelor, was desirous to place at his own table; but she would not consent, nor would Mr Adams permit her to be parted from Joseph; so that she was at length with him consigned over to the kitchen, where the servants were ordered to make him drunk; a favour which was likewise intended for Adams; which design being executed, the squire thought he should easily accomplish what he had when he first saw her intended to perpetrate with Fanny.

It may not be improper, before we proceed farther, to open a little the character of this gentleman, and that of his friends. The master of this house, then, was a man of a very considerable fortune; a bachelor, as we have said, and about forty years of age: he had been educated (if we may use the expression) in the country, and at his own home, under the care of his mother, and a tutor who had orders never to correct him, nor to compel him to learn more than he liked, which it seems was very little, and that only in his childhood; for from the age of fifteen he addicted himself entirely to hunting and other rural amusements, for which his mother took care to equip him with horses, hounds, and all other necessaries; and his tutor, endeavouring to ingratiate himself with his young pupil, who would, he knew, be able handsomely to provide for him, became his companion, not only at these exercises, but likewise over a bottle, which the young squire had a very early relish for. At the age of twenty his mother began to think she had not fulfilled the duty of a parent; she therefore resolved to persuade her son, if possible, to that which she imagined would well supply all that he might have learned at a public school or university—this is what they commonly call travelling; which, with the help of the tutor, who was fixed on to attend him, she easily succeeded in. He made in three years the tour of Europe, as they term it, and returned home well furnished with French clothes, phrases, and servants, with a hearty contempt for his own country; especially what had any savour of the plain spirit and honesty of our ancestors. His mother greatly applauded herself at his return. And now, being master of his own fortune, he soon procured himself a seat in Parliament, and was in the common opinion one of the finest gentlemen of his age: but what distinguished him chiefly was a strange delight which he took in everything which is ridiculous, odious, and absurd in his own species; so that he never chose a companion without one or more of these ingredients, and those who were marked by nature in the most eminent degree with them were most his favourites. If he ever found a man who either had not, or endeavoured to conceal, these imperfections, he took great pleasure in inventing methods of forcing him into absurdities which were not natural to him, or in drawing forth and exposing those that were; for which purpose he was always provided with a set of fellows, whom we have before called curs, and who did, indeed, no great honour to the canine kind; their business was to hunt out and display everything that had any savour of the abovementioned qualities, and especially in the gravest and best characters; but if they failed in their search, they were to turn even virtue and wisdom themselves into ridicule, for the diversion of their master and feeder. The gentlemen of curlike disposition who were now at his house, and whom he had brought with him from London, were, an old half-pay officer, a player, a dull poet, a quack-doctor, a scraping fiddler, and a lame German dancing-master.

As soon as dinner was served, while Mr Adams was saying grace, the captain conveyed his chair from behind him; so that when he endeavoured to seat himself he fell down on the ground, and this completed joke the first, to the great entertainment of the whole company. The second joke was performed by the poet, who sat next him on the other side, and took an opportunity, while poor Adams was respectfully drinking to the master of the house, to overturn a plate of soup into his breeches; which, with the many apologies he made, and the parson's gentle answers, caused much mirth in the company. Joke the third was served up by one of the waiting-men, who had been ordered to convey a quantity of gin into Mr Adams's ale, which he declaring to be the best liquor he ever drank, but rather too rich of the malt, contributed again to their laughter. Mr Adams, from whom we had most of this relation, could not recollect all the jests of this kind practised on him, which the inoffensive disposition of his own heart made him slow in discovering; and indeed, had it not been for the information which we received from a servant of the family, this part of our history, which we take to be none of the least curious, must have been deplorably imperfect; though we must own it probable that some more jokes were (as they call it) cracked during their dinner; but we have by no means been able to come at the knowledge of them. When dinner was removed, the poet began to repeat some verses, which, he said, were made extempore. The following is a copy of them, procured with the greatest difficulty:—

An extempore Poem on parson Adams.
Did ever mortal such a parson view?
His cassock old, his wig not over-new,
Well might the hounds have him for fox mistaken,
In smell more like to that than rusty bacon [1];

---

[1] All hounds that will hunt fox or other vermin will hunt a piece of rusty bacon trailed on the ground.

But would it not make any mortal stare
To see this parson taken for a hare?
Could Phoebus err thus grossly, even he
For a good player might have taken thee.

At which words the bard whipt off the player's wig, and received the approbation of the company, rather perhaps for the dexterity of his hand than his head. The player, instead of retorting the jest on the poet, began to display his talents on the same subject. He repeated many scraps of wit out of plays, reflecting on the whole body of the clergy, which were received with great acclamations by all present. It was now the dancing-master's turn to exhibit his talents; he therefore, addressing himself to Adams in broken English, told him, "He was a man ver well made for de dance, and he suppose by his walk dat he had learn of some great master." He said, "It was ver pretty quality in clergyman to dance;" and concluded with desiring him to dance a minuet, telling him, "his cassock would serve for petticoats; and that he would himself be his partner." At which words, without waiting for an answer, he pulled out his gloves, and the fiddler was preparing his fiddle. The company all offered the dancing-master wagers that the parson outdanced him, which he refused, saying "he believed so too, for he had never seen any man in his life who looked de dance so well as de gentleman:" he then stepped forwards to take Adams by the hand, which the latter hastily withdrew, and, at the same time clenching his fist, advised him not to carry the jest too far, for he would not endure being put upon. The dancing-master no sooner saw the fist than he prudently retired out of its reach, and stood aloof, mimicking Adams, whose eyes were fixed on him, not guessing what he was at, but to avoid his laying hold on him, which he had once attempted. In the meanwhile, the captain, perceiving an opportunity, pinned a cracker or devil to the cassock, and then lighted it with their little smoking-candle. Adams, being a stranger to this sport, and believing he had been blown up in reality, started from his chair, and jumped about the room, to the infinite joy of the beholders, who declared he was the best dancer in the universe. As soon as the devil had done tormenting him, and he had a little recovered his confusion, he returned to the table, standing up in the posture of one who intended to make a speech. They all cried out, "Hear him, hear him;" and he then spoke in the following manner: "Sir, I am sorry to see one to whom Providence hath been so bountiful in bestowing his favours make so ill and ungrateful a return for them; for, though you have not insulted me yourself, it is visible you have delighted in those that do it, nor have once discouraged the many rudenesses which have been shown towards me; indeed, towards yourself, if you rightly understood them; for I am your guest, and by the laws of hospitality entitled to your protection. One gentleman had thought proper to produce some poetry upon me, of which I shall only say, that I had rather be the subject than the composer. He hath pleased to treat me with disrespect as a parson. I apprehend my order is not the subject of scorn, nor that I can become so, unless by being a disgrace to it, which I hope poverty will never be called. Another gentleman, indeed, hath repeated some sentences, where the order itself is mentioned with contempt. He says they are taken from plays. I am sure such plays are a scandal to the government which permits them, and cursed will be the nation where they are represented. How others have treated me I need not observe; they themselves, when they reflect, must allow the behaviour to be as improper to my years as to my cloth. You found me, sir, travelling with two of my parishioners (I omit your hounds falling on me; for I have quite forgiven it, whether it proceeded from the wantonness or negligence of the huntsman): my appearance might very well persuade you that your invitation was an act of charity, though in reality we were well provided; yes, sir, if we had had an hundred miles to travel, we had sufficient to bear our expenses in a noble manner." (At which words he produced the half-guinea which was found in the basket.) "I do not show you this out of ostentation of riches, but to convince you I speak truth. Your seating me at your table was an honour which I did not ambitiously affect. When I was here, I endeavoured to behave towards you with the utmost respect; if I have failed, it was not with design; nor could I, certainly, so far be guilty as to deserve the insults I have suffered. If they were meant, therefore, either to my order or my poverty (and you see I am not very poor), the shame doth not lie at my door, and I heartily pray that the sin may be averted from yours." He thus finished, and received a general clap from the whole company. Then the gentleman of the house told him, "He was sorry for what had happened; that he could not accuse him of any share in it; that the verses were, as himself had well observed, so bad, that he might easily answer them; and for the serpent, it was undoubtedly a very great affront done him by the dancing-master, for which, if he well thrashed him, as he deserved, he should be very much pleased to see it" (in which, probably, he spoke truth). Adams answered, "Whoever had done it, it was not his profession to punish him that way; but for the person whom he had accused, I am a witness," says he, "of his innocence; for I had my eye on him all the while. Whoever he was, God forgive him, and bestow on him a little more sense as well as humanity." The captain answered with a surly look and accent, "That he hoped he did not mean to reflect upon him; d—n him, he had as much imanity as another, and, if any man said he had not, he would convince him of his mistake by cutting his throat." Adams, smiling, said, "He believed he had spoke right by accident." To which the captain returned, "What do you mean by my speaking right? If you was not a parson, I would not take these words; but your gown protects you. If any man who wears a sword had said so much, I had pulled him by the nose before this." Adams replied, "If he attempted any rudeness to his person, he would not find any protection for himself in his gown;" and, clenching his fist, declared "he had thrashed many a stouter man." The gentleman did all he could to encourage this warlike disposition in Adams, and was in hopes to have produced a battle, but he was disappointed; for the captain made no other answer than, "It is very well you are a parson;" and so, drinking off a bumper to old mother Church, ended the dispute.

Then the doctor, who had hitherto been silent, and who was the gravest but most mischievous dog of all, in a very pompous speech highly applauded what Adams had said, and as much discommended the behaviour to him. He proceeded to encomiums on the Church and poverty; and, lastly, recommended forgiveness of what had passed to Adams, who immediately answered, "That everything was forgiven;" and in the warmth of his goodness he filled a bumper of strong beer (a liquor he preferred to wine), and drank a health to the whole company, shaking the captain and the poet heartily by the hand, and addressing himself with great respect to the doctor; who, indeed, had not laughed outwardly at anything that past, as he had a perfect command of his muscles, and could laugh inwardly without betraying the least symptoms in his countenance. The doctor now began a second formal speech, in which he declaimed against all levity of conversation, and what is usually called mirth. He said, "There were amusements fitted for persons of all ages and degrees, from the rattle to the discussing a point of philosophy; and that men discovered themselves in nothing more than in the choice of their amusements; for," says he, "as it must greatly raise our expectation of the future conduct in life of boys whom in their tender years we perceive, instead of taw or balls, or other childish playthings, to chuse, at their leisure hours, to exercise their genius in contentions of wit, learning, and such like; so must it inspire one with equal contempt of a man, if we should discover him playing at taw or other childish play." Adams highly commended the doctor's opinion, and said, "He had often wondered at some passages in ancient authors, where Scipio, Laelius, and other great men were represented to have passed many hours in amusements of the most trifling kind." The doctor replied, "He had by him an old Greek manuscript where a favourite diversion of Socrates was recorded." "Ay!" says the parson eagerly; "I should be most infinitely obliged to you for the favour of perusing it." The doctor promised to send it him, and farther said, "That he believed he could describe it. I think," says he, "as near as I can remember, it was this: there was a throne erected, on one side of which sat a king and on the other a queen, with their guards and attendants ranged on both sides; to them was introduced an ambassador, which part Socrates always used to perform himself; and when he was led up to the footsteps of the throne he addressed himself to the monarchs in some grave speech, full of virtue, and goodness, and morality, and such like. After which, he was seated between the king and queen, and royally entertained. This I think was the chief part. Perhaps I may have forgot some particulars; for it is long since I read it." Adams said, "It was, indeed, a diversion worthy the relaxation of so great a man; and thought something resembling it should be instituted among our great men, instead of cards and other idle pastime, in which, he was informed, they trifled away too much of their lives." He added, "The Christian religion was a nobler subject for these speeches than any Socrates could have invented." The gentleman of the house approved what Mr Adams said, and declared "he was resolved to perform the ceremony this very evening." To which the doctor objected, as no one was prepared with a speech, "unless," said he (turning to Adams with a gravity of countenance which would have deceived a more knowing man), "you have a sermon about you, doctor." "Sir," said Adams, "I never travel without one, for fear of what may happen." He was easily prevailed on by his worthy friend, as he now called the doctor, to undertake the part of the ambassador; so that the gentleman sent immediate orders to have the throne erected, which was performed before they had drank two bottles; and, perhaps, the reader will hereafter have no great reason to admire the nimbleness of the servants. Indeed, to confess the truth, the throne was no more than this: there was a great tub of water provided, on each side of which were placed two stools raised higher than the surface of the tub, and over the whole was laid a blanket; on these stools were placed the king and queen, namely, the master of the house and the captain. And now the ambassador was introduced between the poet and the doctor; who, having read his sermon, to the great entertainment of all present, was led up to his place and seated between their majesties. They immediately rose up, when the blanket, wanting its supports at either end, gave way, and soused Adams over head and ears in the water. The captain made his escape, but, unluckily, the gentleman himself not being as nimble as he ought, Adams caught hold of him before he descended from his throne, and pulled him in with him, to the entire secret satisfaction of all the company. Adams, after ducking the squire twice or thrice, leapt out of the tub, and looked sharp for the doctor, whom he would certainly have conveyed to the same place of honour; but he had wisely withdrawn: he then searched for his crabstick, and having found that, as well as his fellow travellers, he declared he would not stay a moment longer in such a house. He then departed, without taking leave of his host, whom he had exacted a more severe revenge on than he intended; for, as he did not use sufficient care to dry himself in time, he caught a cold by the accident which threw him into a fever that had like to have cost him his life.

CHAPTER VIII.

Which some readers will think too short and others too long.

Adams, and Joseph, who was no less enraged than his friend at the treatment he met with, went out with their sticks in their hands, and carried off Fanny, notwithstanding the opposition of the servants, who did all, without proceeding to violence, in their power to detain them. They walked as fast as they could, not so much from any apprehension of being pursued as that Mr Adams might, by exercise, prevent any harm from the water. The gentleman, who had given such orders to his servants concerning Fanny that he did not in the least fear her getting away, no sooner heard that she was gone, than he began to rave, and immediately despatched several with orders either to bring her back or never return. The poet, the player, and all but the dancing-master and doctor, went on this errand.

The night was very dark in which our friends began their journey; however, they made such expedition, that they soon arrived at an inn which was at seven miles' distance. Here they unanimously consented to pass the evening, Mr Adams being now as dry as he was before he had set out on his embassy.

This inn, which indeed we might call an ale-house, had not the words, The New Inn, been writ on the sign, afforded them no better provision than bread and cheese and ale; on which, however, they made a very comfortable meal; for hunger is better than a French cook.

They had no sooner supped, than Adams, returning thanks to the Almighty for his food, declared he had eat his homely commons with much greater satisfaction than his splendid dinner; and expressed great contempt for the folly of mankind, who sacrificed their hopes of heaven to the acquisition of vast wealth, since so much comfort was to be found in the humblest state and the lowest provision. "Very true, sir," says a grave man who sat smoaking his pipe by the fire, and who was a traveller as well as himself. "I have often been as much surprized as you are, when I consider the value which mankind in general set on riches, since every day's experience shows us how little is in their power; for what, indeed, truly desirable, can they bestow on us? Can they give beauty to the deformed, strength to the weak, or health to the infirm? Surely if they could we should not see so many ill-favoured faces haunting the assemblies of the great, nor would such numbers of feeble wretches languish in their coaches and palaces. No, not the wealth of a kingdom can purchase any paint to dress pale Ugliness in the bloom of that young maiden, nor any drugs to equip Disease with the vigour of that young man. Do not riches bring us to solicitude instead of rest, envy instead of affection, and danger instead of safety? Can they prolong their own possession, or lengthen his days who enjoys them? So far otherwise, that the sloth, the luxury, the care which attend them, shorten the lives of millions, and bring them with pain and misery to an untimely grave. Where, then, is their value if they can neither embellish nor strengthen our forms, sweeten nor prolong our lives?—Again: Can they adorn the mind more than the body? Do they not rather swell the heart with vanity, puff up the cheeks with pride, shut our ears to every call of virtue, and our bowels to every motive of compassion?" "Give me your hand, brother," said Adams, in a rapture, "for I suppose you are a clergyman."—"No, truly," answered the other (indeed, he was a priest of the Church of Rome; but those who understand our laws will not wonder he was not over-ready to own it).—"Whatever you are," cries Adams, "you have spoken my sentiments: I believe I have preached every syllable of your speech twenty times over; for it hath always appeared to me easier for a cable-rope (which by the way is the true rendering of that word we have translated camel) to go through the eye of a needle than for a rich man to get into the kingdom of heaven."—"That, sir," said the other, "will be easily granted you by divines, and is deplorably true; but as the prospect of our good at a distance doth not so forcibly affect us, it might be of some service to mankind to be made thoroughly sensible—which I think they might be with very little serious attention—that even the blessings of this world are not to be purchased with riches; a doctrine, in my opinion, not only metaphysically, but, if I may so say, mathematically demonstrable; and which I have been always so perfectly convinced of that I have a contempt for nothing so much as for gold." Adams now began a long discourse: but as most which he said occurs among many authors who have treated this subject, I shall omit inserting it. During its continuance Joseph and Fanny retired to rest, and the host likewise left the room. When the English parson had concluded, the Romish resumed the discourse, which he continued with great bitterness and invective; and at last ended by desiring Adams to lend him eighteenpence to pay his reckoning; promising, if he never paid him, he might be assured of his prayers. The good man answered that eighteen-pence would be too little to carry him any very long journey; that he had half a guinea in his pocket, which he would divide with him. He then fell to searching his pockets, but could find no money; for indeed the company with whom he dined had passed one jest upon him which we did not then enumerate, and had picked his pocket of all that treasure which he had so ostentatiously produced.

"Bless me!" cried Adams, "I have certainly lost it; I can never have spent it. Sir, as I am a Christian, I had a whole half-guinea in my pocket this morning, and have not now a single halfpenny of it left. Sure the devil must have taken it from me!"—"Sir," answered the priest, smiling, "you need make no excuses; if you are not willing to lend me the money, I am contented."—"Sir," cries Adams, "if I had the greatest sum in the world—aye, if I had ten pounds about me—I would bestow it all to rescue any Christian from distress. I am more vexed at my loss on your account than my own. Was ever anything so unlucky? Because I have no money in my pocket I shall be suspected to be no Christian."—"I am more unlucky," quoth the other, "if you are as generous as you say; for really a crown would have made me happy, and conveyed me in plenty to the place I am going, which is not above twenty miles off, and where I can arrive by to-morrow night. I assure you I am not accustomed to travel pennyless. I am but just arrived in England; and we were forced by a storm in our passage to throw all we had overboard. I don't suspect but this fellow will take my word for the trifle I owe him; but I hate to appear so mean as to confess myself without a shilling to such people; for these, and indeed too many others, know little difference in their estimation between a beggar and a thief." However, he thought he should deal better with the host that evening than the next morning: he therefore resolved to set out immediately, notwithstanding the darkness; and accordingly, as soon as the host returned, he communicated to him the situation of his affairs; upon which the host, scratching his head, answered, "Why, I do not know, master; if it be so, and you have no money, I must trust, I think, though I had rather always have ready money if I could; but, marry, you look like so honest a gentleman that I don't fear your paying me if it was twenty times as much." The priest made no reply, but, taking leave of him and Adams as fast as he could, not without confusion, and perhaps with some distrust of Adams's sincerity, departed.

He was no sooner gone than the host fell a-shaking his head, and declared, if he had suspected the fellow had no money, he would not have drawn him a single drop of drink, saying he despaired of ever seeing his face again, for that he looked like a confounded rogue.

"Rabbit the fellow," cries he, "I thought, by his talking so much about riches, that he had a hundred pounds at least in his pocket." Adams chid him for his suspicions, which, he said, were not becoming a Christian; and then, without reflecting on his loss, or considering how he himself should depart in the morning, he retired to a very homely bed, as his companions had before; however, health and fatigue gave them a sweeter repose than is often in the power of velvet and down to bestow.

CHAPTER IX.

Containing as surprizing and bloody adventures as can be found in this or perhaps any other authentic history.

It was almost morning when Joseph Andrews, whose eyes the thoughts of his dear Fanny had opened, as he lay fondly meditating on that lovely creature, heard a violent knocking at the door over which he lay. He presently jumped out of bed, and, opening the window, was asked if there were no travellers in the house? and presently, by another voice, if two men and a woman had not taken up there their lodging that night? Though he knew not the voices, he began to entertain a suspicion of the truth—for indeed he had received some information from one of the servants of the squire's house of his design—and answered in the negative. One of the servants, who knew the host well, called out to him by his name just as he had opened another window, and asked him the same question; to which he answered in the affirmative. O ho! said another, have we found you? and ordered the host to come down and open his door. Fanny, who was as wakeful as Joseph, no sooner heard all this than she leaped from her bed, and, hastily putting on her gown and petticoats, ran as fast as possible to Joseph's room, who then was almost drest. He immediately let her in, and, embracing her with the most passionate tenderness, bid her fear nothing, for he would die in her defence. "Is that a reason why I should not fear," says she, "when I should lose what is dearer to me than the whole world?" Joseph, then kissing her hand, said, "He could almost thank the occasion which had extorted from her a tenderness she would never indulge him with before." He then ran and waked his bedfellow Adams, who was yet fast asleep, notwithstanding many calls from Joseph; but was no sooner made sensible of their danger than he leaped from his bed, without considering the presence of Fanny, who hastily turned her face from him, and enjoyed a double benefit from the dark, which, as it would have prevented any offence, to an innocence less pure, or a modesty less delicate, so it concealed even those blushes which were raised in her.

Adams had soon put on all his clothes but his breeches, which, in the hurry, he forgot; however, they were pretty well supplied by the length of his other garments; and now, the house-door being opened, the captain, the poet, the player, and three servants came in. The captain told the host that two fellows, who were in his house, had run away with a young woman, and desired to know in which room she lay. The host, who presently believed the story, directed them, and instantly the captain and poet, justling one another, ran up. The poet, who was the nimblest, entering the chamber first, searched the bed, and every other part, but to no purpose; the bird was flown, as the impatient reader, who might otherwise have been in pain for her, was before advertised. They then enquired where the men lay, and were approaching the chamber, when Joseph roared out, in a loud voice, that he would shoot the first man who offered to attack the door. The captain enquired what fire-arms they had; to which the host answered, he believed they had none; nay, he was almost convinced of it, for he had heard one ask the other in the evening what they should have done if they had been overtaken, when they had no arms; to which the other answered, they would have defended themselves with their sticks as long as they were able, and God would assist a just cause. This satisfied the captain, but not the poet, who prudently retreated downstairs, saying, it was his business to record great actions, and not to do them. The captain was no sooner well satisfied that there were no fire-arms than, bidding defiance to gunpowder, and swearing he loved the smell of it, he ordered the servants to follow him, and, marching boldly up, immediately attempted to force the door, which the servants soon helped him to accomplish. When it was opened, they discovered the enemy drawn up three deep; Adams in the front, and Fanny in the rear. The captain told Adams that if they would go all back to the house again they should be civilly treated; but unless they consented he had orders to carry the young lady with him, whom there was great reason to believe they had stolen from her parents; for, notwithstanding her disguise, her air, which she could not conceal, sufficiently discovered her birth to be infinitely superior to theirs. Fanny, bursting into tears, solemnly assured him he was mistaken; that she was a poor helpless foundling, and had no relation in the world which she knew of; and, throwing herself on her knees, begged that he would not attempt to take her from her friends, who, she was convinced, would die before they would lose her; which Adams confirmed with words not far from amounting to an oath. The captain swore he had no leisure to talk, and, bidding them thank themselves for what happened, he ordered the servants to fall on, at the same time endeavouring to pass by Adams, in order to lay hold on Fanny; but the parson, interrupting him, received a blow from one of them, which, without considering whence it came, he returned to the captain, and gave him so dexterous a knock in that part of the stomach which is vulgarly called the pit, that he staggered some paces backwards. The captain, who was not accustomed to this kind of play, and who wisely apprehended the consequence of such another blow, two of them seeming to him equal to a thrust through the body, drew forth his hanger, as Adams approached him, and was levelling a blow at his head, which would probably have silenced the preacher for ever, had not Joseph in that instant lifted up a certain huge stone pot of the chamber with one hand, which six beaus could not have lifted with both, and discharged it, together with the contents, full in the captain's face. The uplifted hanger dropped from his hand, and he fell prostrated on the floor with a lumpish noise, and his halfpence rattled in his pocket; the red liquor which his veins contained, and the white liquor which the pot contained, ran in one stream down his face and his clothes. Nor had Adams quite escaped, some of the water having in its passage shed its honours on his head, and began to trickle down the wrinkles or rather furrows of his cheeks, when one of the servants, snatching a mop out of a pail of water, which had already done its duty in washing the house, pushed it in the parson's face; yet could not he bear him down, for the parson, wresting the mop from the fellow with one hand, with the other brought his enemy as low as the earth, having given him a stroke over that part of the face where, in some men of pleasure, the natural and artificial noses are conjoined.

Hitherto, Fortune seemed to incline the victory on the travellers' side, when, according to her custom, she began to show the fickleness of her disposition; for now the host, entering the field, or rather chamber of battle, flew directly at Joseph, and, darting his head into his stomach (for he was a stout fellow and an expert boxer), almost staggered him: but Joseph, stepping one leg back, did with his left hand so chuck him under the chin that he reeled. The youth was pursuing his blow with his right hand when he received from one of the servants such a stroke with a cudgel on his temples, that it instantly deprived him of sense, and he measured his length on the ground.

Fanny rent the air with her cries, and Adams was coming to the assistance of Joseph; but the two serving-men and the host now fell on him, and soon subdued him, though he fought like a madman, and looked so black with the impressions he had received from the mop, that Don Quixote would certainly have taken him for an inchanted Moor. But now follows the most tragical part; for the captain was risen again, and, seeing Joseph on the floor, and Adams secured, he instantly laid hold on Fanny, and, with the assistance of the poet and player, who, hearing the battle was over, were now come up, dragged her, crying and tearing her hair, from the sight of her Joseph, and, with a perfect deafness to all her entreaties, carried her downstairs by violence, and fastened her on the player's horse; and the captain, mounting his own, and leading that on which this poor miserable wretch was, departed, without any more consideration of her cries than a butcher hath of those of a lamb; for indeed his thoughts were entertained only with the degree of favour which he promised himself from the squire on the success of this adventure.

The servants, who were ordered to secure Adams and Joseph as safe as possible, that the squire might receive no interruption to his design on poor Fanny, immediately, by the poet's advice, tied Adams to one of the bed-posts, as they did Joseph on the other side, as soon as they could bring him to himself; and then, leaving them together, back to back, and desiring the host not to set them at liberty, nor to go near them, till he had further orders, they departed towards their master; but happened to take a different road from that which the captain had fallen into.

CHAPTER X.

A discourse between the poet and the player; of no other use in this history but to divert the reader.

Before we proceed any farther in this tragedy we shall leave Mr Joseph and Mr Adams to themselves, and imitate the wise conductors of the stage, who in the midst of a grave action entertain you with some excellent piece of satire or humour called a dance. Which piece, indeed, is therefore danced, and not spoke, as it is delivered to the audience by persons whose thinking faculty is by most people held to lie in their heels; and to whom, as well as heroes, who think with their hands, Nature hath only given heads for the sake of conformity, and as they are of use in dancing, to hang their hats on.

The poet, addressing the player, proceeded thus, "As I was saying" (for they had been at this discourse all the time of the engagement above-stairs), "the reason you have no good new plays is evident; it is from your discouragement of authors. Gentlemen will not write, sir, they will not write, without the expectation of fame or profit, or perhaps both. Plays are like trees, which will not grow without nourishment; but like mushrooms, they shoot up spontaneously, as it were, in a rich soil. The muses, like vines, may be pruned, but not with a hatchet. The town, like a peevish child, knows not what it desires, and is always best pleased with a rattle. A farce-writer hath indeed some chance for success: but they have lost all taste for the sublime. Though I believe one reason of their depravity is the badness of the actors. If a man writes like an angel, sir, those fellows know not how to give a sentiment utterance."—"Not so fast," says the player: "the modern actors are as good at least as their authors, nay, they come nearer their illustrious predecessors; and I expect a Booth on the stage again, sooner than a Shakespear or an Otway; and indeed I may turn your observation against you, and with truth say, that the reason no authors are encouraged is because we have no good new plays."—"I have not affirmed the contrary," said the poet; "but I am surprized you grow so warm; you cannot imagine yourself interested in this dispute; I hope you have a better opinion of my taste than to apprehend I squinted at yourself. No, sir, if we had six such actors as you, we should soon rival the Bettertons and Sandfords of former times; for, without a compliment to you, I think it impossible for any one to have excelled you in most of your parts. Nay, it is solemn truth, and I have heard many, and all great judges, express as much; and, you will pardon me if I tell you, I think every time I have seen you lately you have constantly acquired some new excellence, like a snowball. You have deceived me in my estimation of perfection, and have outdone what I thought inimitable."—"You are as little interested," answered the player, "in what I have said of other poets; for d—n me if there are not many strokes, ay, whole scenes, in your last tragedy, which at least equal Shakespear. There is a delicacy of sentiment, a dignity of expression in it, which I will own many of our gentlemen did not do adequate justice to. To confess the truth, they are bad enough, and I pity an author who is present at the murder of his works."—"Nay, it is but seldom that it can happen," returned the poet; "the works of most modern authors, like dead-born children, cannot be murdered. It is such wretched half-begotten, half-writ, lifeless, spiritless, low, grovelling stuff, that I almost pity the actor who is obliged to get it by heart, which must be almost as difficult to remember as words in a language you don't understand."—"I am sure," said the player, "if the sentences have little meaning when they are writ, when they are spoken they have less. I know scarce one who ever lays an emphasis right, and much less adapts his action to his character. I have seen a tender lover in an attitude of fighting with his mistress, and a brave hero suing to his enemy with his sword in his hand. I don't care to abuse my profession, but rot me if in my heart I am not inclined to the poet's side."—"It is rather generous in you than just," said the poet; "and, though I hate to speak ill of any person's production—nay, I never do it, nor will—but yet, to do justice to the actors, what could Booth or Betterton have made of such horrible stuff as Fenton's Mariamne, Frowd's Philotas, or Mallet's Eurydice; or those low, dirty, last-dying-speeches, which a fellow in the city of Wapping, your Dillo or Lillo, what was his name, called tragedies?"—"Very well," says the player; "and pray what do you think of such fellows as Quin and Delane, or that face-making puppy young Cibber, that ill-looked dog Macklin, or that saucy slut Mrs Clive? What work would they make with your Shakespears, Otways, and Lees? How would those harmonious lines of the last come from their tongues?—

"'—No more; for I disdain
All pomp when thou art by: far be the noise
Of kings and crowns from us, whose gentle souls
Our kinder fates have steer'd another way.
Free as the forest birds we'll pair together,
Without rememb'ring who our fathers were:
Fly to the arbors, grots, and flow'ry meads;
There in soft murmurs interchange our souls;
Together drink the crystal of the stream,
Or taste the yellow fruit which autumn yields,
And, when the golden evening calls us home,
Wing to our downy nests, and sleep till morn.'

"Or how would this disdain of Otway—

"'Who'd be that foolish sordid thing call'd man?'"

"Hold! hold! hold!" said the poet: "Do repeat that tender speech in the third act of my play which you made such a figure in."—"I would willingly," said the player, "but I have forgot it."—"Ay, you was not quite perfect in it when you played it," cries the poet, "or you would have had such an applause as was never given on the stage; an applause I was extremely concerned for your losing."—"Sure," says the player, "if I remember, that was hissed more than any passage in the whole play."—"Ay, your speaking it was hissed," said the poet.—"My speaking it!" said the player.—"I mean your not speaking it," said the poet. "You was out, and then they hissed."—"They hissed, and then I was out, if I remember," answered the player; "and I must say this for myself, that the whole audience allowed I did your part justice; so don't lay the damnation of your play to my account."—"I don't know what you mean by damnation," replied the poet.—"Why, you know it was acted but one night," cried the player.—"No," said the poet, "you and the whole town were enemies; the pit were all my enemies, fellows that would cut my throat, if the fear of hanging did not restrain them. All taylors, sir, all taylors."—"Why should the taylors be so angry with you?" cries the player. "I suppose you don't employ so many in making your clothes."—"I admit your jest," answered the poet; "but you remember the affair as well as myself; you know there was a party in the pit and upper gallery that would not suffer it to be given out again; though much, ay infinitely, the majority, all the boxes in particular, were desirous of it; nay, most of the ladies swore they never would come to the house till it was acted again. Indeed, I must own their policy was good in not letting it be given out a second time: for the rascals knew if it had gone a second night it would have run fifty; for if ever there was distress in a tragedy—I am not fond of my own performance; but if I should tell you what the best judges said of it—Nor was it entirely owing to my enemies neither that it did not succeed on the stage as well as it hath since among the polite readers; for you can't say it had justice done it by the performers."—"I think," answered the player, "the performers did the distress of it justice; for I am sure we were in distress enough, who were pelted with oranges all the last act: we all imagined it would have been the last act of our lives."

The poet, whose fury was now raised, had just attempted to answer when they were interrupted, and an end put to their discourse, by an accident, which if the reader is impatient to know, he must skip over the next chapter, which is a sort of counterpart to this, and contains some of the best and gravest matters in the whole book, being a discourse between parson Abraham Adams and Mr Joseph Andrews.

CHAPTER XI.

Containing the exhortations of parson Adams to his friend in affliction; calculated for the instruction and improvement of the reader.

Joseph no sooner came perfectly to himself than, perceiving his mistress gone, he bewailed her loss with groans which would have pierced any heart but those which are possessed by some people, and are made of a certain composition not unlike flint in its hardness and other properties; for you may strike fire from them, which will dart through the eyes, but they can never distil one drop of water the same way. His own, poor youth! was of a softer composition; and at those words, "O my dear Fanny! O my love! shall I never, never see thee more?" his eyes overflowed with tears, which would have become any but a hero. In a word, his despair was more easy to be conceived than related.

Mr Adams, after many groans, sitting with his back to Joseph, began thus in a sorrowful tone: "You cannot imagine, my good child, that I entirely blame these first agonies of your grief; for, when misfortunes attack us by surprize, it must require infinitely more learning than you are master of to resist them; but it is the business of a man and a Christian to summon Reason as quickly as he can to his aid; and she will presently teach him patience and submission. Be comforted, therefore, child; I say be comforted. It is true, you have lost the prettiest, kindest, loveliest, sweetest young woman, one with whom you might have expected to have lived in happiness, virtue, and innocence; by whom you might have promised yourself many little darlings, who would have been the delight of your youth and the comfort of your age. You have not only lost her, but have reason to fear the utmost violence which lust and power can inflict upon her. Now, indeed, you may easily raise ideas of horror, which might drive you to despair."—"O I shall run mad!" cries Joseph. "O that I could but command my hands to tear my eyes out and my flesh off!"—"If you would use them to such purposes, I am glad you can't," answered Adams. "I have stated your misfortune as strong as I possibly can; but, on the other side, you are to consider you are a Christian, that no accident happens to us without the Divine permission, and that it is the duty of a man, and a Christian, to submit. We did not make ourselves; but the same power which made us rules over us, and we are absolutely at his disposal; he may do with us what he pleases, nor have we any right to complain. A second reason against our complaint is our ignorance; for, as we know not future events, so neither can we tell to what purpose any accident tends; and that which at first threatens us with evil may in the end produce our good. I should indeed have said our ignorance is twofold (but I have not at present time to divide properly), for, as we know not to what purpose any event is ultimately directed, so neither can we affirm from what cause it originally sprung. You are a man, and consequently a sinner; and this may be a punishment to you for your sins: indeed in this sense it may be esteemed as a good, yea, as the greatest good, which satisfies the anger of Heaven, and averts that wrath which cannot continue without our destruction. Thirdly, our impotency of relieving ourselves demonstrates the folly and absurdity of our complaints: for whom do we resist, or against whom do we complain, but a power from whose shafts no armour can guard us, no speed can fly?—a power which leaves us no hope but in submission." "O sir!" cried Joseph, "all this is very true, and very fine, and I could hear you all day if I was not so grieved at heart as now I am."—"Would you take physic," says Adams, "when you are well, and refuse it when you are sick? Is not comfort to be administered to the afflicted, and not to those who rejoice or those who are at ease?" "O! you have not spoken one word of comfort to me yet!" returned Joseph. "No!" cries Adams; "what am I then doing? what can I say to comfort you?" "O tell me," cries Joseph, "that Fanny will escape back to my arms, that they shall again enclose that lovely creature, with all her sweetness, all her untainted innocence about her!" "Why, perhaps you may," cries Adams, "but I can't promise you what's to come. You must, with perfect resignation, wait the event: if she be restored to you again, it is your duty to be thankful, and so it is if she be not. Joseph, if you are wise and truly know your own interest, you will peaceably and quietly submit to all the dispensations of Providence, being thoroughly assured that all the misfortunes, how great soever, which happen to the righteous, happen to them for their own good. Nay, it is not your interest only, but your duty, to abstain from immoderate grief; which if you indulge, you are not worthy the name of a Christian." He spoke these last words with an accent a little severer than usual; upon which Joseph begged him not to be angry, saying, he mistook him if he thought he denied it was his duty, for he had known that long ago. "What signifies knowing your duty, if you do not perform it?" answered Adams. "Your knowledge increases your guilt. O Joseph! I never thought you had this stubbornness in your mind." Joseph replied, "He fancied he misunderstood him; which I assure you," says he, "you do, if you imagine I endeavour to grieve; upon my soul I don't." Adams rebuked him for swearing, and then proceeded to enlarge on the folly of grief, telling him, all the wise men and philosophers, even among the heathens, had written against it, quoting several passages from Seneca, and the Consolation, which, though it was not Cicero's, was, he said, as good almost as any of his works; and concluded all by hinting that immoderate grief in this case might incense that power which alone could restore him his Fanny. This reason, or indeed rather the idea which it raised of the restoration of his mistress, had more effect than all which the parson had said before, and for a moment abated his agonies; but, when his fears sufficiently set before his eyes the danger that poor creature was in, his grief returned again with repeated violence, nor could Adams in the least asswage it; though it may be doubted in his behalf whether Socrates himself could have prevailed any better.

They remained some time in silence, and groans and sighs issued from them both; at length Joseph burst out into the following soliloquy:—

> "Yes, I will bear my sorrows like a man,
> But I must also feel them as a man.
> I cannot but remember such things were,
> And were most dear to me."

Adams asked him what stuff that was he repeated? To which he answered, they were some lines he had gotten by heart out of a play. "Ay, there is nothing but heathenism to be learned from plays," replied he. "I never heard of any plays fit for a Christian to read, but Cato and the Conscious Lovers; and, I must own, in the latter there are some things almost solemn enough for a sermon." But we shall now leave them a little, and enquire after the subject of their conversation.

CHAPTER XII.

More adventures, which we hope will as much please as surprize the reader.

Neither the facetious dialogue which passed between the poet and the player, nor the grave and truly solemn discourse of Mr Adams, will, we conceive, make the reader sufficient amends for the anxiety which he must have felt on the account of poor Fanny, whom we left in so deplorable a condition. We shall therefore now proceed to the relation of what happened to that beautiful and innocent virgin, after she fell into the wicked hands of the captain.

The man of war, having conveyed his charming prize out of the inn a little before day, made the utmost expedition in his power towards the squire's house, where this delicate creature was to be offered up a sacrifice to the lust of a ravisher. He was not only deaf to all her bewailings and entreaties on the road, but accosted her ears with impurities which, having been never before accustomed to them, she happily for herself very little understood. At last he changed his note, and attempted to soothe and mollify her, by setting forth the splendor and luxury which would be her fortune with a man who would have the inclination, and power too, to give her whatever her utmost wishes could desire; and told her he doubted not but she would soon look kinder on him, as the instrument of her happiness, and despise that pitiful fellow whom her ignorance only could make her fond of. She answered, she knew not whom he meant; she never was fond of any pitiful fellow. "Are you affronted, madam," says he, "at my calling him so? But what better can be said of one in a livery, notwithstanding your fondness for him?" She returned, that she did not understand him, that the man had been her fellow-servant, and she believed was as honest a creature as any alive; but as for fondness for men—"I warrant ye," cries the captain, "we shall find means to persuade you to be fond; and I advise you to yield to gentle ones, for you may be assured that it is not in your power, by any struggles whatever, to preserve your virginity two hours longer. It will be your interest to consent; for the squire will be much kinder to you if he enjoys you willingly than by force." At which words she began to call aloud for assistance (for it was now open day), but, finding none, she lifted her eyes to heaven, and supplicated the Divine assistance to preserve her innocence. The captain told her, if she persisted in her vociferation, he would find a means of stopping her mouth. And now the poor wretch, perceiving no hopes of succour, abandoned herself to despair, and, sighing out the name of

Joseph! Joseph! a river of tears ran down her lovely cheeks, and wet the handkerchief which covered her bosom. A horseman now appeared in the road, upon which the captain threatened her violently if she complained; however, the moment they approached each other she begged him with the utmost earnestness to relieve a distressed creature who was in the hands of a ravisher. The fellow stopt at those words, but the captain assured him it was his wife, and that he was carrying her home from her adulterer, which so satisfied the fellow, who was an old one (and perhaps a married one too), that he wished him a good journey, and rode on. He was no sooner past than the captain abused her violently for breaking his commands, and threatened to gagg her, when two more horsemen, armed with pistols, came into the road just before them. She again solicited their assistance, and the captain told the same story as before. Upon which one said to the other, "That's a charming wench, Jack; I wish I had been in the fellow's place, whoever he is." But the other, instead of answering him, cried out, "Zounds, I know her;" and then, turning to her, said, "Sure you are not Fanny Goodwill?"—"Indeed, indeed, I am," she cried—"O John, I know you now-Heaven hath sent you to my assistance, to deliver me from this wicked man, who is carrying me away for his vile purposes—O for God's sake rescue me from him!" A fierce dialogue immediately ensued between the captain and these two men, who, being both armed with pistols, and the chariot which they attended being now arrived, the captain saw both force and stratagem were vain, and endeavoured to make his escape, in which however he could not succeed. The gentleman who rode in the chariot ordered it to stop, and with an air of authority examined into the merits of the cause; of which being advertised by Fanny, whose credit was confirmed by the fellow who knew her, he ordered the captain, who was all bloody from his encounter at the inn, to be conveyed as a prisoner behind the chariot, and very gallantly took Fanny into it; for, to say the truth, this gentleman (who was no other than the celebrated Mr Peter Pounce, and who preceded the Lady Booby only a few miles, by setting out earlier in the morning) was a very gallant person, and loved a pretty girl better than anything besides his own money or the money of other people.

The chariot now proceeded towards the inn, which, as Fanny was informed, lay in their way, and where it arrived at that very time while the poet and player were disputing below-stairs, and Adams and Joseph were discoursing back to back above; just at that period to which we brought them both in the two preceding chapters the chariot stopt at the door, and in an instant Fanny, leaping from it, ran up to her Joseph.—O reader! conceive if thou canst the joy which fired the breasts of these lovers on this meeting; and if thy own heart doth not sympathetically assist thee in this conception, I pity thee sincerely from my own; for let the hard-hearted villain know this, that there is a pleasure in a tender sensation beyond any which he is capable of tasting.

Peter, being informed by Fanny of the presence of Adams, stopt to see him, and receive his homage; for, as Peter was an hypocrite, a sort of people whom Mr Adams never saw through, the one paid that respect to his seeming goodness which the other believed to be paid to his riches; hence Mr Adams was so much his favourite, that he once lent him four pounds thirteen shillings and sixpence to prevent his going to gaol, on no greater security than a bond and judgment, which probably he would have made no use of, though the money had not been (as it was) paid exactly at the time.

It is not perhaps easy to describe the figure of Adams; he had risen in such a hurry, that he had on neither breeches, garters, nor stockings; nor had he taken from his head a red spotted handkerchief, which by night bound his wig, turned inside out, around his head. He had on his torn cassock and his greatcoat; but, as the remainder of his cassock hung down below his greatcoat, so did a small stripe of white, or rather whitish, linen appear below that; to which we may add the several colours which appeared on his face, where a long piss-burnt beard served to retain the liquor of the stone-pot, and that of a blacker hue which distilled from the mop.—This figure, which Fanny had delivered from his captivity, was no sooner spied by Peter than it disordered the composed gravity of his muscles; however, he advised him immediately to make himself clean, nor would accept his homage in that pickle.

The poet and player no sooner saw the captain in captivity than they began to consider of their own safety, of which flight presented itself as the only means; they therefore both of them mounted the poet's horse, and made the most expeditious retreat in their power.

The host, who well knew Mr Pounce and Lady Booby's livery, was not a little surprized at this change of the scene; nor was his confusion much helped by his wife, who was now just risen, and, having heard from him the account of what had passed, comforted him with a decent number of fools and blockheads; asked him why he did not consult her, and told him he would never leave following the nonsensical dictates of his own numskull till she and her family were ruined.

Joseph, being informed of the captain's arrival, and seeing his Fanny now in safety, quitted her a moment, and, running downstairs, went directly to him, and stripping off his coat, challenged him to fight; but the captain refused, saying he did not understand boxing. He then grasped a cudgel in one hand, and, catching the captain by the collar with the other, gave him a most severe drubbing, and ended with telling him he had now had some revenge for what his dear Fanny had suffered.

When Mr Pounce had a little regaled himself with some provision which he had in his chariot, and Mr Adams had put on the best appearance his clothes would allow him, Pounce ordered the captain into his presence, for he said he was guilty of felony, and the next justice of peace should commit him; but the servants (whose appetite for revenge is soon satisfied), being sufficiently contented with the drubbing which Joseph had inflicted on him, and which was indeed of no very moderate kind, had suffered him to go off, which he did, threatening a severe revenge against Joseph, which I have never heard he thought proper to take.

The mistress of the house made her voluntary appearance before Mr Pounce, and with a thousand curtsies told him, "She hoped his honour would pardon her husband, who was a very nonsense man, for the sake of his poor family; that indeed if he could be ruined alone, she should be very willing of it; for because as why, his worship very well knew he deserved it; but she had three poor small children, who were not capable to get their own living; and if her husband was sent to gaol, they must all come to the parish; for she was a poor weak woman, continually a-breeding, and had no time to work for them. She therefore hoped his honour would take it into his worship's consideration, and forgive her husband this time; for she was sure he never intended any harm to man, woman, or child; and if it was not for that block-head of his own, the man in some things was well enough; for she had had three children by him in less than three years, and was almost ready to cry out the fourth time." She would have proceeded in this manner much longer, had not Peter stopt her tongue, by telling her he had nothing to say to her husband nor her neither. So, as Adams and the rest had assured her of forgiveness, she cried and curtsied out of the room.

Mr Pounce was desirous that Fanny should continue her journey with him in the chariot; but she absolutely refused, saying she would ride behind Joseph on a horse which one of Lady Booby's servants had equipped him with. But, alas! when the horse appeared, it was found to be no other than that identical beast which Mr Adams had left behind him at the inn, and which these honest fellows, who knew him, had redeemed. Indeed, whatever horse they had provided for Joseph, they would have prevailed with him to mount none, no, not even to ride before his beloved Fanny, till the parson was supplied; much less would he deprive his friend of the beast which belonged to him, and which he knew the moment he saw, though Adams did not; however, when he was reminded of the affair, and told that they had brought the horse with them which he left behind, he answered—Bless me! and so I did.

Adams was very desirous that Joseph and Fanny should mount this horse, and declared he could very easily walk home. "If I walked alone," says he, "I would wage a shilling that the pedestrian outstripped the equestrian travellers; but, as I intend to take the company of a pipe, peradventure I may be an hour later." One of the servants whispered Joseph to take him at his word, and suffer the old put to walk if he would: this proposal was answered with an angry look and a peremptory refusal by Joseph, who, catching Fanny up in his arms, averred he would rather carry her home in that manner, than take away Mr Adams's horse and permit him to walk on foot.

Perhaps, reader, thou hast seen a contest between two gentlemen, or two ladies, quickly decided, though they have both asserted they would not eat such a nice morsel, and each insisted on the other's accepting it; but in reality both were very desirous to swallow it themselves. Do not therefore conclude hence that this dispute would have come to a speedy decision: for here both parties were heartily in earnest, and it is very probable they would have remained in the inn-yard to this day, had not the good Peter Pounce put a stop to it; for, finding he had no longer hopes of satisfying his old appetite with Fanny, and being desirous of having some one to whom he might communicate his grandeur, he told the parson he would convey him home in his chariot. This favour was by Adams, with many bows and acknowledgments, accepted, though he afterwards said, "he ascended the chariot rather that he might not offend than from any desire of riding in it, for that in his heart he preferred the pedestrian even to the vehicular expedition." All matters being now settled, the chariot, in which rode Adams and Pounce, moved forwards; and Joseph having borrowed a pillion from the host, Fanny had just seated herself thereon, and had laid hold of the girdle which her lover wore for that purpose, when the wise beast, who concluded that one at a time was sufficient, that two to one were odds, &c., discovered much uneasiness at his double load, and began to consider his hinder as his fore legs, moving the direct contrary way to that which is called forwards. Nor could Joseph, with all his horsemanship, persuade him to advance; but, without having any regard to the lovely part of the lovely girl which was on his back, he used such agitations, that, had not one of the men come immediately to her assistance, she had, in plain English, tumbled backwards on the ground. This inconvenience was presently remedied by an exchange of horses; and then Fanny being again placed on her pillion, on a better-natured and somewhat a better-fed beast, the parson's horse, finding he had no longer odds to contend with, agreed to march; and the whole procession set forwards for Booby-hall, where they arrived in a few hours without anything remarkable happening on the road, unless it was a curious dialogue between the parson and the steward: which, to use the language of a late Apologist, a pattern to all biographers, "waits for the reader in the next chapter."

CHAPTER XIII.

A curious dialogue which passed between Mr Abraham Adams and Mr Peter Pounce, better worth reading than all the works of Colley Cibber and many others.

The chariot had not proceeded far before Mr Adams observed it was a very fine day. "Ay, and a very fine country too," answered Pounce.—"I should think so more," returned Adams, "if I had not lately travelled over the Downs, which I take to exceed this and all other prospects in the universe."—"A fig for prospects!" answered Pounce; "one acre here is worth ten there; and for my own part, I have no delight in the prospect of any land but my own."—"Sir," said Adams, "you can indulge yourself with many fine prospects of that kind."—"I thank God I have a little," replied the other, "with which I am content, and envy no man: I have a little, Mr Adams, with which I do as much good as I can." Adams answered, "That riches without charity were nothing worth; for that they were a blessing only to him who made them a blessing to others."—"You and I," said Peter, "have different notions of charity. I own, as it is generally used, I do not like the word, nor do I think it becomes one of us gentlemen; it is a mean parson-like quality; though I would not infer many parsons have it neither."—"Sir," said Adams, "my definition of charity is, a generous disposition to relieve the distressed."—"There is something in that definition," answered Peter, "which I like well enough; it is, as you say, a disposition, and does not so much consist in the act as in the disposition to do it. But, alas! Mr Adams, who are meant by the distressed? Believe me, the distresses of mankind are mostly imaginary, and it would be rather folly than goodness to relieve them."—"Sure, sir," replied Adams, "hunger and thirst, cold and nakedness, and other distresses which attend the poor, can never be said to be imaginary evils."—"How can any man complain of hunger," said Peter, "in a country where such excellent salads are to be gathered in almost every field? or of thirst, where every river and stream produces such delicious potations? And as for cold and nakedness, they are evils introduced by luxury and custom. A man naturally wants clothes no more than a horse or any other animal; and there are whole nations who go without them; but these are things perhaps which you, who do not know the world"—"You will pardon me, sir," returned Adams; "I have read of the Gymnosophists."—"A plague of your Jehosaphats!" cried Peter; "the greatest fault in our constitution is the provision made for the poor, except that perhaps made for some others. Sir, I have not an estate which doth not contribute almost as much again to the poor as to the land-tax; and I do assure you I expect to come myself to the parish in the end." To which Adams giving a dissenting smile, Peter thus proceeded: "I fancy, Mr Adams, you are one of those who imagine I am a lump of money; for there are many who, I fancy, believe that not only my pockets, but my whole clothes, are lined with bank-bills; but I assure you, you are all mistaken; I am not the man the world esteems me. If I can hold my head above water it is all I can. I have injured myself by purchasing. I have been too liberal of my money. Indeed, I fear my heir will find my affairs in a worse situation than they are reputed to be. Ah! he will have reason to wish I had loved money more and land less. Pray, my good neighbour, where should I have that quantity of riches the world is so liberal to bestow on me? Where could I possibly, without I had stole it, acquire such a treasure?" "Why, truly," says Adams, "I have been always of your opinion; I have wondered as well as yourself with what confidence they could report such things of you, which have to me appeared as mere impossibilities; for you know, sir, and I have often heard you say it, that your wealth is of your own acquisition; and can it be credible that in your short time you should have amassed such a heap of treasure as these people will have you worth? Indeed, had you inherited an estate like Sir Thomas Booby, which had descended in your family for many generations, they might have had a colour for their assertions." "Why, what do they say I am worth?" cries Peter, with a malicious sneer. "Sir," answered Adams, "I have heard some aver you are not worth less than twenty thousand pounds." At which Peter frowned. "Nay, sir," said Adams, "you ask me only the opinion of others; for my own part, I have always denied it, nor did I ever believe you could possibly be worth half that sum." "However, Mr Adams," said he, squeezing him by the hand, "I would not sell them all I am worth for double that sum; and as to what you believe, or they believe, I care not a fig, no not a fart. I am not poor because you think me so, nor because you attempt to undervalue me in the country. I know the envy of mankind very well; but I thank Heaven I am above them. It is true, my wealth is of my own acquisition. I have not an estate, like Sir Thomas Booby, that has descended in my family through many generations; but I know heirs of such estates who are forced to travel about the country like some people in torn cassocks, and might be glad to accept of a pitiful curacy for what I know. Yes, sir, as shabby fellows as yourself, whom no man of my figure, without that vice of good-nature about him, would suffer to ride in a chariot with him." "Sir," said Adams, "I value not your chariot of a rush; and if I had known you had intended to affront me, I would have walked to the world's end on foot ere I would have accepted a place in it. However, sir, I will soon rid you of that inconvenience;" and, so saying, he opened the chariot door, without calling to the coachman, and leapt out into the highway, forgetting to take his hat along with him; which, however, Mr Pounce threw after him with great violence. Joseph and Fanny stopt to bear him company the rest of the way, which was not above a mile.

BOOK IV.

CHAPTER I.

The arrival of Lady Booby and the rest at Booby-hall.

The coach and six, in which Lady Booby rode, overtook the other travellers as they entered the parish. She no sooner saw Joseph than her cheeks glowed with red, and immediately after became as totally pale. She had in her surprize almost stopt her coach; but recollected herself timely enough to prevent it. She entered the parish amidst the ringing of bells and the acclamations of the poor, who were rejoiced to see their patroness returned after so long an absence, during which time all her rents had been drafted to London, without a shilling being spent among them, which tended not a little to their utter impoverishing; for, if the court would be severely missed in such a city as London, how much more must the absence of a person of great fortune be felt in a little country village, for whose inhabitants such a family finds a constant employment and supply; and with the offals of whose table the infirm, aged, and infant poor are abundantly fed, with a generosity which hath scarce a visible effect on their benefactors' pockets!

But, if their interest inspired so public a joy into every countenance, how much more forcibly did the affection which they bore parson Adams operate upon all who beheld his return! They flocked about him like dutiful children round an indulgent parent, and vyed with each other in demonstrations of duty and love. The parson on his side shook every one by the hand, enquired heartily after the healths of all that were absent, of their children, and relations; and exprest a satisfaction in his face which nothing but benevolence made happy by its objects could infuse.

Nor did Joseph and Fanny want a hearty welcome from all who saw them. In short, no three persons could be more kindly received, as, indeed, none ever more deserved to be universally beloved.

Adams carried his fellow-travellers home to his house, where he insisted on their partaking whatever his wife, whom, with his children, he found in health and joy, could provide:—where we shall leave them enjoying perfect happiness over a homely meal, to view scenes of greater splendour, but infinitely less bliss.

Our more intelligent readers will doubtless suspect, by this second appearance of Lady Booby on the stage, that all was not ended by the dismission of Joseph; and, to be honest with them, they are in the right: the arrow had pierced deeper than she imagined; nor was the wound so easily to be cured. The removal of the object soon cooled her rage, but it had a different effect on her love; that departed with his person, but this remained lurking in her mind with his image. Restless, interrupted slumbers, and confused horrible dreams were her portion the first night. In the morning, fancy painted her a more delicious scene; but to delude, not delight her; for, before she could reach the promised happiness, it vanished, and left her to curse, not bless, the vision.

She started from her sleep, her imagination being all on fire with the phantom, when, her eyes accidentally glancing towards the spot where yesterday the real Joseph had stood, that little circumstance raised his idea in the liveliest colours in her memory. Each look, each word, each gesture rushed back on her mind with charms which all his coldness could not abate. Nay, she imputed that to his youth, his folly, his awe, his religion, to everything but what would instantly have produced contempt, want of passion for the sex, or that which would have roused her hatred, want of liking to her.

Reflection then hurried her farther, and told her she must see this beautiful youth no more; nay, suggested to her that she herself had dismissed him for no other fault than probably that of too violent an awe and respect for herself; and which she ought rather to have esteemed a merit, the effects of which were besides so easily and surely to have been removed; she then blamed, she cursed the hasty rashness of her temper; her fury was vented all on herself, and Joseph appeared innocent in her eyes. Her passion at length grew so violent, that it forced her on seeking relief, and now she thought of recalling him: but pride forbad that; pride, which soon drove all softer passions from her soul, and represented to her the meanness of him she was fond of. That thought soon began to obscure his beauties; contempt succeeded next, and then disdain, which presently introduced her hatred of the creature who had given her so much uneasiness. These enemies of Joseph had no sooner taken possession of her mind than they insinuated to her a thousand things in his disfavour; everything but dislike of her person; a thought which, as it would have been intolerable to bear, she checked the moment it endeavoured to arise. Revenge came now to her assistance; and she considered her dismission of him, stript, and without a character, with the utmost pleasure. She rioted in the several kinds of misery which her imagination suggested to her might be his fate; and, with a smile composed of anger, mirth, and scorn, viewed him in the rags in which her fancy had drest him.

Mrs Slipslop, being summoned, attended her mistress, who had now in her own opinion totally subdued this passion. Whilst she was dressing she asked if that fellow had been turned away according to her orders. Slipslop answered, she had told her ladyship so (as indeed she had).—"And how did he behave?" replied the lady. "Truly, madam," cries Slipslop, "in such a manner that infected everybody who saw him. The poor lad had but little wages to receive; for he constantly allowed his father and mother half his income; so that, when your ladyship's livery was stript off, he had not wherewithal to buy a coat, and must have gone naked if one of the footmen had not incommodated him with one; and whilst he was standing in his shirt (and, to say truth, he was an amorous figure), being told your ladyship would not give him a character, he sighed, and said he had done nothing willingly to offend; that for his part, he should always give your ladyship a good character wherever he went; and he prayed God to bless you; for you was the best of ladies, though his enemies had set you against him. I wish you had not turned him away; for I believe you have not a faithfuller servant in the house."—"How came you then," replied the lady, "to advise me to turn him away?"—"I, madam!" said Slipslop; "I am sure you will do me the justice to say, I did all in my power to prevent it; but I saw your ladyship was angry; and it is not the business of us upper servants to hinterfear on these occasions." "And was it not you, audacious wretch!" cried the lady, "who made me angry? Was it not your tittle-tattle, in which I believe you belyed the poor fellow, which incensed me against him? He may thank you for all that hath happened; and so may I for the loss of a good servant, and one who probably had more merit than all of you. Poor fellow! I am charmed with his goodness to his parents. Why did not you tell me of that, but suffer me to dismiss so good a creature without a character? I see the reason of your whole behaviour now as well as your complaint; you was jealous of the wenches." "I jealous!" said Slipslop; "I assure you, I look upon myself as his betters; I am not meat for a footman, I hope." These words threw the lady into a violent passion, and she sent Slipslop from her presence, who departed, tossing her nose, and crying, "Marry, come up! there are some people more jealous than I, I believe." Her lady affected not to hear the words, though in reality she did, and understood them too. Now ensued a second conflict, so like the former, that it might savour of repetition to relate it minutely. It may suffice to say that Lady Booby found good reason to doubt whether she had so absolutely conquered her passion as she had flattered herself; and, in order to accomplish it quite, took a resolution, more common than wise, to retire immediately into the country. The reader hath long ago seen the arrival of Mrs Slipslop, whom no pertness could make her mistress resolve to part with; lately, that of Mr Pounce, her forerunners; and, lastly, that of the lady herself.

The morning after her arrival being Sunday, she went to church, to the great surprize of everybody, who wondered to see her ladyship, being no very constant church-woman, there so suddenly upon her journey. Joseph was likewise there; and I have heard it was remarked that she fixed her eyes on him much more than on the parson; but this I believe to be only a malicious rumour. When the prayers were ended Mr Adams stood up, and with a loud voice pronounced, "I publish the banns of marriage between Joseph Andrews and Frances Goodwill, both of this parish," &c. Whether this had any effect on Lady Booby or no, who was then in her pew, which the congregation could not see into, I could never discover: but certain it is that in about a quarter of an hour she stood up, and directed her eyes to that part of the church where the women sat, and persisted in looking that way during the remainder of the sermon in so scrutinizing a manner, and with so angry a countenance, that most of the women were afraid she was offended at them. The moment she returned home she sent for Slipslop into her chamber, and told her she wondered what that impudent fellow Joseph did in that parish? Upon which Slipslop gave her an account of her meeting Adams with him on the road, and likewise the adventure with Fanny. At the relation of which the lady often changed her countenance; and when she had heard all, she ordered Mr Adams into her presence, to whom she behaved as the reader will see in the next chapter.

CHAPTER II.

A dialogue between Mr Abraham Adams and the Lady Booby.

Mr Adams was not far off, for he was drinking her ladyship's health below in a cup of her ale. He no sooner came before her than she began in the following manner: "I wonder, sir, after the many great obligations you have had to this family" (with all which the reader hath in the course of this history been minutely acquainted), "that you will ungratefully show any respect to a fellow who hath been turned out of it for his misdeeds. Nor doth it, I can tell you, sir, become a man of your character, to run about the country with an idle fellow and wench. Indeed, as for the girl, I know no harm of her. Slipslop tells me she was formerly bred up in my house, and behaved as she ought, till she hankered after this fellow, and he spoiled her. Nay, she may still, perhaps, do very well, if he will let her alone. You are, therefore, doing a monstrous thing in endeavouring to procure a match between these two people, which will be to the ruin of them both."—"Madam," said Adams, "if your ladyship will but hear me speak, I protest I never heard any harm of Mr Joseph Andrews; if I had, I should have corrected him for it; for I never have, nor will, encourage the faults of those under my care. As for the young woman, I assure your ladyship I have as good an opinion of her as your ladyship yourself or any other can have. She is the sweetest-tempered, honestest, worthiest young creature; indeed, as to her beauty, I do not commend her on that account, though all men allow she is the handsomest woman, gentle or simple, that ever appeared in the parish."—"You are very impertinent," says she, "to talk such fulsome stuff to me. It is mighty becoming truly in a clergyman to trouble himself about handsome women, and you are a delicate judge of beauty, no doubt. A man who hath lived all his life in such a parish as this is a rare judge of beauty! Ridiculous! beauty indeed! a country wench a beauty! I shall be sick whenever I hear beauty mentioned again. And so this wench is to stock the parish with beauties, I hope. But, sir, our poor is numerous enough already; I will have no more vagabonds settled here."—"Madam," says Adams, "your ladyship is offended with me, I protest, without any reason. This couple were desirous to consummate long ago, and I dissuaded them from it; nay, I may venture to say, I believe I was the sole cause of their delaying it."—"Well," says she, "and you did very wisely and honestly too, notwithstanding she is the greatest beauty in the parish."—"And now, madam," continued he, "I only perform my office to Mr Joseph."—"Pray, don't mister such fellows to me," cries the lady. "He," said the parson, "with the consent of Fanny, before my face, put in the banns." "Yes," answered the lady, "I suppose the slut is forward enough; Slipslop tells me how her head runs upon fellows; that is one of her beauties, I suppose. But if they have put in the banns, I desire you will publish them no more without my orders."—"Madam," cries Adams, "if any one puts in a sufficient caution, and assigns a proper reason against them, I am willing to surcease."—"I tell you a reason," says she: "he is a vagabond, and he shall not settle here, and bring a nest of beggars into the parish; it will make us but little amends that they will be beauties."—"Madam," answered Adams, "with the utmost submission to your ladyship, I have been informed by lawyer Scout that any person who serves a year gains a settlement in the parish where he serves."—"Lawyer Scout," replied the lady, "is an impudent coxcomb; I will have no lawyer Scout interfere with me. I repeat to you again, I will have no more incumbrances brought on us: so I desire you will proceed no farther."—"Madam," returned Adams, "I would obey your ladyship in everything that is lawful; but surely the parties being poor is no reason against their marrying. God forbid there should be any such law! The poor have little share enough of this world already; it would be barbarous indeed to deny them the common privileges and innocent enjoyments which nature indulges to the animal creation."—"Since you understand yourself no better," cries the lady, "nor the respect due from such as you to a woman of my distinction, than to affront my ears by such loose discourse, I shall mention but one short word; it is my orders to you that you publish these banns no more; and if you dare, I will recommend it to your master, the doctor, to discard you from his service. I will, sir, notwithstanding your poor family; and then you and the greatest beauty in the parish may go and beg together."—"Madam," answered Adams, "I know not what your ladyship means by the terms master and service. I am in the service of a Master who will never discard me for doing my duty; and if the doctor (for indeed I have never been able to pay for a licence) thinks proper to turn me from my cure, God will provide me, I hope, another. At least, my family, as well as myself, have hands; and he will prosper, I doubt not, our endeavours to get our bread honestly with them. Whilst my conscience is pure, I shall never fear what man can do unto me."—"I condemn my humility," said the lady, "for demeaning myself to converse with you so long. I shall take other measures; for I see you are a confederate with them. But the sooner you leave me the better; and I shall give orders that my doors may no longer be open to you. I will suffer no parsons who run about the country with beauties to be entertained here."—"Madam," said Adams, "I shall enter into no persons' doors against their will; but I am assured, when you have enquired farther into this matter, you will applaud, not blame, my proceeding; and so I humbly take my leave:" which he did with many bows, or at least many attempts at a bow.

CHAPTER III.

What passed between the lady and lawyer Scout.

In the afternoon the lady sent for Mr Scout, whom she attacked most violently for intermeddling with her servants, which he denied, and indeed with truth, for he had only asserted accidentally, and perhaps rightly, that a year's service gained a settlement; and so far he owned he might have formerly informed the parson and believed it was law. "I am resolved," said the lady, "to have no discarded servants of mine settled here; and so, if this be your law, I shall send to another lawyer." Scout said, "If she sent to a hundred lawyers, not one or all of them could alter the law. The utmost that was in the power of a lawyer was to prevent the law's taking effect; and that he himself could do for her ladyship as well as any other; and I believe," says he, "madam, your ladyship, not being conversant in these matters, hath mistaken a difference; for I asserted only that a man who served a year was settled. Now there is a material difference between being settled in law and settled in fact; and as I affirmed generally he was settled, and law is preferable to fact, my settlement must be understood in law and not in fact. And suppose, madam, we admit he was settled in law, what use will they make of it? how doth that relate to fact? He is not settled in fact; and if he be not settled in fact, he is not an inhabitant; and if he is not an inhabitant, he is not of this parish; and then undoubtedly he ought not to be published here; for Mr Adams hath told me your ladyship's pleasure, and the reason, which is a very good one, to prevent burdening us with the poor; we have too many already, and I think we ought to have an act to hang or transport half of them. If we can prove in evidence that he is not settled in fact, it is another matter. What I said to Mr Adams was on a supposition that he was settled in fact; and indeed, if that was the case, I should doubt."—"Don't tell me your facts and your ifs," said the lady; "I don't understand your gibberish; you take too much upon you, and are very impertinent, in pretending to direct in this parish; and you shall be taught better, I assure you, you shall. But as to the wench, I am resolved she shall not settle here; I will not suffer such beauties as these to produce children for us to keep."—"Beauties, indeed! your ladyship is pleased to be merry," answered Scout.—"Mr Adams described her so to me," said the lady. "Pray, what sort of dowdy is it, Mr Scout?"—"The ugliest creature almost I ever beheld; a poor dirty drab, your ladyship never saw such a wretch."—"Well, but, dear Mr Scout, let her be what she will, these ugly women will bring children, you know; so that we must prevent the marriage."—"True, madam," replied Scout, "for the subsequent marriage co-operating with the law will carry law into fact. When a man is married he is settled in fact, and then he is not removable. I will see Mr Adams, and I make no doubt of prevailing with him. His only objection is, doubtless, that he shall lose his fee; but that being once made easy, as it shall be, I am confident no farther objection will remain. No, no, it is impossible; but your ladyship can't discommend his unwillingness to depart from his fee. Every man ought to have a proper value for his fee. As to the matter in question, if your ladyship pleases to employ me in it, I will venture to promise you success. The laws of this land are not so vulgar to permit a mean fellow to contend with one of your ladyship's fortune. We have one sure card, which is, to carry him before Justice Frolick, who, upon hearing your ladyship's name, will commit him without any farther questions. As for the dirty slut, we shall have nothing to do with her; for, if we get rid of the fellow, the ugly jade will—"—"Take what measures you please, good Mr Scout," answered the lady: "but I wish you could rid the parish of both; for Slipslop tells me such stories of this wench, that I abhor the thoughts of her; and, though you say she is such an ugly slut, yet you know, dear Mr Scout, these forward creatures, who run after men, will always find some as forward as themselves; so that, to prevent the increase of beggars, we must get rid of her."—"Your ladyship is very much in the right," answered Scout; "but I am afraid the law is a little deficient in giving us any such power of prevention; however, the justice will stretch it as far as he is able, to oblige your ladyship. To say truth, it is a great blessing to the country that he is in the commission, for he hath taken several poor off our hands that the law would never lay hold on. I know some justices who think as much of committing a man to Bridewell as his lordship at 'size would of hanging him; but it would do a man good to see his worship, our justice, commit a fellow to Bridewell, he takes so much pleasure in it; and when once we ha'um there, we seldom hear any more o'um. He's either starved or eat up by vermin in a month's time."—Here the arrival of a visitor put an end to the conversation, and Mr Scout, having undertaken the cause and promised it success, departed.

This Scout was one of those fellows who, without any knowledge of the law, or being bred to it, take upon them, in defiance of an act of Parliament, to act as lawyers in the country, and are called so. They are the pests of society, and a scandal to a profession, to which indeed they do not belong, and which owes to such kind of rascallions the ill-will which weak persons bear towards it. With this fellow, to whom a little before she would not have condescended to have spoken, did a certain passion for Joseph, and the jealousy and the disdain of poor innocent Fanny, betray the Lady Booby into a familiar discourse, in which she inadvertently confirmed many hints with which Slipslop, whose gallant he was, had preacquainted him; and whence he had taken an opportunity to assert those severe falsehoods of little Fanny which possibly the reader might not have been well able to account for if we had not thought proper to give him this information.

CHAPTER IV.

A short chapter, but very full of matter; particularly the arrival of Mr Booby and his lady.

All that night, and the next day, the Lady Booby past with the utmost anxiety; her mind was distracted and her soul tossed up and down by many turbulent and opposite passions. She loved, hated, pitied, scorned, admired, despised the same person by fits, which changed in a very short interval. On Tuesday morning, which happened to be a holiday, she went to church, where, to her surprize, Mr Adams published the banns again with as audible a voice as before. It was lucky for her that, as there was no sermon, she had an immediate opportunity of returning home to vent her rage, which she could not have concealed from the congregation five minutes; indeed, it was not then very numerous, the assembly consisting of no more than Adams, his clerk, his wife, the lady, and one of her servants. At her return she met Slipslop, who accosted her in these words:—"O meam, what doth your ladyship think? To be sure, lawyer Scout hath carried Joseph and Fanny both before the justice. All the parish are in tears, and say they will certainly be hanged; for nobody knows what it is for"—"I suppose they deserve it," says the lady. "What! dost thou mention such wretches to me?"—"O dear madam," answered Slipslop, "is it not a pity such a graceless young man should die a virulent death? I hope the judge will take commensuration on his youth. As for Fanny, I don't think it signifies much what becomes of her; and if poor Joseph hath done anything, I could venture to swear she traduced him to it: few men ever come to a fragrant punishment, but by those nasty creatures, who are a scandal to our sect." The lady was no more pleased at this news, after a moment's reflection, than Slipslop herself; for, though she wished Fanny far enough, she did not desire the removal of Joseph, especially with her. She was puzzled how to act or what to say on this occasion, when a coach and six drove into the court, and a servant acquainted her with the arrival of her nephew Booby and his lady. She ordered them to be conducted into a drawing-room, whither she presently repaired, having composed her countenance as well as she could, and being a little satisfied that the wedding would by these means be at least interrupted, and that she should have an opportunity to execute any resolution she might take, for which she saw herself provided with an excellent instrument in Scout.

The Lady Booby apprehended her servant had made a mistake when he mentioned Mr Booby's lady; for she had never heard of his marriage: but how great was her surprize when, at her entering the room, her nephew presented his wife to her; saying, "Madam, this is that charming Pamela, of whom I am convinced you have heard so much." The lady received her with more civility than he expected; indeed with the utmost; for she was perfectly polite, nor had any vice inconsistent with good-breeding. They past some little time in ordinary discourse, when a servant came and whispered Mr Booby, who presently told the ladies he must desert them a little on some business of consequence; and, as their discourse during his absence would afford little improvement or entertainment to the reader, we will leave them for a while to attend Mr Booby.

CHAPTER V.

Containing justice business; curious precedents of depositions, and other matters necessary to be perused by all justices of the peace and their clerks.

The young squire and his lady were no sooner alighted from their coach than the servants began to inquire after Mr Joseph, from whom they said their lady had not heard a word, to her great surprize, since he had left Lady Booby's. Upon this they were instantly informed of what had lately happened, with which they hastily acquainted their master, who took an immediate resolution to go himself, and endeavour to restore his Pamela her brother, before she even knew she had lost him.

The justice before whom the criminals were carried, and who lived within a short mile of the lady's house, was luckily Mr Booby's acquaintance, by his having an estate in his neighbourhood. Ordering therefore his horses to his coach, he set out for the judgment-seat, and arrived when the justice had almost finished his business. He was conducted into a hall, where he was acquainted that his worship would wait on him in a moment; for he had only a man and a woman to commit to Bridewell first. As he was now convinced he had not a minute to lose, he insisted on the servant's introducing him directly into the room where the justice was then executing his office, as he called it. Being brought thither, and the first compliments being passed between the squire and his worship, the former asked the latter what crime those two young people had been guilty of? "No great crime," answered the justice; "I have only ordered them to Bridewell for a month." "But what is their crime?" repeated the squire. "Larceny, an't please your honour," said Scout. "Ay," says the justice, "a kind of felonious larcenous thing. I believe I must order them a little correction too, a little stripping and whipping." (Poor Fanny, who had hitherto supported all with the thoughts of Joseph's company, trembled at that sound; but, indeed, without reason, for none but the devil himself would have executed such a sentence on her.) "Still," said the squire, "I am ignorant of the crime—the fact I mean." "Why, there it is in peaper," answered the justice, showing him a deposition which, in the absence of his clerk, he had writ himself, of which we have with great difficulty procured an authentic copy; and here it follows *verbatim et literatim:—*

The depusition of James Scout, layer, and Thomas Trotter, yeoman, taken before mee, one of his magesty's justasses of the piece for

> *Zumersetshire.* "These deponants saith, and first Thomas Trotter for himself saith, that on the — of this instant October, being Sabbath-day, betwin the ours of 2 and 4 in the afternoon, he zeed Joseph Andrews and Francis Goodwill walk akross a certane felde belunging to layer Scout, and out of the path which ledes thru the said felde, and there he zede Joseph Andrews with a nife cut one hassel twig, of the value, as he believes, of three half-pence, or thereabouts; and he saith that the said Francis Goodwill was likewise walking on the grass out of the said path in the said felde, and did receive and karry in her hand the said twig, and so was cumfarting, eading, and abatting to the said Joseph therein. And the said James Scout for himself says that he verily believes the said twig to be his own proper twig," &c.

"Jesu!" said the squire, "would you commit two persons to Bridewell for a twig?" "Yes," said the lawyer, "and with great lenity too; for if we had called it a young tree, they would have been both hanged." "Harkee," says the justice, taking aside the squire; "I should not have been so severe on this occasion, but Lady Booby desires to get them out of the parish; so lawyer Scout will give the constable orders to let them run away, if they please: but it seems they intend to marry together, and the lady hath no other means, as they are legally settled there, to prevent their bringing an incumbrance on her own parish." "Well," said the squire, "I will take care my aunt shall be satisfied in this point; and likewise I promise you, Joseph here shall never be any incumbrance on her. I shall be obliged to you, therefore, if, instead of Bridewell, you will commit them to my custody." "O! to be sure, sir, if you desire it," answered the justice; and without more ado Joseph and Fanny were delivered over to Squire Booby, whom Joseph very well knew, but little guessed how nearly he was related to him. The justice burnt his mittimus, the constable was sent about his business, the lawyer made no complaint for want of justice; and the prisoners, with exulting hearts, gave a thousand thanks to his honour Mr Booby; who did not intend their obligations to him should cease here; for, ordering his man to produce a cloak-bag, which he had caused to be brought from Lady Booby's on purpose, he desired the justice that he might have Joseph with him into a room; where, ordering his servant to take out a suit of his own clothes, with linnen and other necessaries, he left Joseph to dress himself, who, not yet knowing the cause of all this civility, excused his accepting such a favour as long as decently he could. Whilst Joseph was dressing, the squire repaired to the justice, whom he found talking with Fanny; for, during the examination, she had flopped her hat over her eyes, which were also bathed in tears, and had by that means concealed from his worship what might perhaps have rendered the arrival of Mr Booby unnecessary, at least for herself. The justice no sooner saw her countenance cleared up, and her bright eyes shining through her tears, than he secretly cursed himself for having once thought of Bridewell for her. He would willingly have sent his own wife thither, to have had Fanny in her place. And, conceiving almost at the same instant desires and schemes to accomplish them, he employed the minutes whilst the squire was absent with Joseph in assuring her how sorry he was for having treated her so roughly before he knew her merit; and told her, that since Lady Booby was unwilling that she should settle in her parish, she was heartily welcome to his, where he promised her his protection, adding that he would take Joseph and her into his own family, if she liked it; which assurance he confirmed with a squeeze by the hand. She thanked him very kindly, and said, "She would acquaint Joseph with the offer, which he would certainly be glad to accept; for that Lady Booby was angry with them both; though she did not know either had done anything to offend her, but imputed it to Madam Slipslop, who had always been her enemy."

The squire now returned, and prevented any farther continuance of this conversation; and the justice, out of a pretended respect to his guest, but in reality from an apprehension of a rival (for he knew nothing of his marriage), ordered Fanny into the kitchen, whither she gladly retired; nor did the squire, who declined the trouble of explaining the whole matter, oppose it.

It would be unnecessary, if I was able, which indeed I am not, to relate the conversation between these two gentlemen, which rolled, as I have been informed, entirely on the subject of horse-racing. Joseph was soon drest in the plainest dress he could find, which was a blue coat and breeches, with a gold edging, and a red waistcoat with the same: and as this suit, which was rather too large for the squire, exactly fitted him, so he became it so well, and looked so genteel, that no person would have doubted its being as well adapted to his quality as his shape; nor have suspected, as one might, when my Lord ——, or Sir ——, or Mr ——, appear in lace or embroidery, that the taylor's man wore those clothes home on his back which he should have carried under his arm.

The squire now took leave of the justice; and, calling for Fanny, made her and Joseph, against their wills, get into the coach with him, which he then ordered to drive to Lady Booby's. It had moved a few yards only, when the squire asked Joseph if he knew who that man was crossing the field; for, added he, I never saw one take such strides before. Joseph answered eagerly, "O, sir, it is parson Adams!" "O la, indeed, and so it is," said Fanny; "poor man, he is coming to do what he could for us. Well, he is the worthiest, best-natured creature."—"Ay," said Joseph; "God bless him! for there is not such another in the universe." "The best creature living sure," cries Fanny. "Is he?" says the squire; "then I am resolved to have the best creature living in my coach;" and so saying, he ordered it to stop, whilst Joseph, at his request, hallowed to the parson, who, well knowing his voice, made all the haste imaginable, and soon came up with them. He was desired by the master, who could scarce refrain from laughter at his figure, to mount into the coach, which he with many thanks refused, saying he could walk by its side, and he'd warrant he kept up with it; but he was at length over-prevailed on. The squire now acquainted Joseph with his marriage; but he might have spared himself that labour; for his servant, whilst Joseph was dressing, had performed that office before. He continued to express the vast happiness he enjoyed in his sister, and the value he had for all who belonged to her. Joseph made many bows, and exprest as many acknowledgments: and parson Adams, who now first perceived Joseph's new apparel, burst into tears with joy, and fell to rubbing his hands and snapping his fingers as if he had been mad.

They were now arrived at the Lady Booby's, and the squire, desiring them to wait a moment in the court, walked in to his aunt, and calling her out from his wife, acquainted her with Joseph's arrival; saying, "Madam, as I have married a virtuous and worthy woman, I am resolved to own her relations, and show them all a proper respect; I shall think myself therefore infinitely obliged to all mine who will do the same. It is true, her brother hath been your servant, but he is now become my brother; and I have one happiness, that neither his character, his behaviour, or appearance, give me any reason to be ashamed of calling him so. In short, he is now below, dressed like a gentleman, in which light I intend he shall hereafter be seen; and you will oblige me beyond expression if you will admit him to be of our party; for I know it will give great pleasure to my wife, though she will not mention it."

This was a stroke of fortune beyond the Lady Booby's hopes or expectation; she answered him eagerly, "Nephew, you know how easily I am prevailed on to do anything which Joseph Andrews desires—Phoo, I mean which you desire me; and, as he is now your relation, I cannot refuse to entertain him as such." The squire told her he knew his obligation to her for her compliance; and going three steps, returned and told her—he had one more favour, which he believed she would easily grant, as she had accorded him the former. "There is a young woman—"—"Nephew," says she, "don't let my good-nature make you desire, as is too commonly the case, to impose on me. Nor think, because I have with so much condescension agreed to suffer your brother-in-law to come to my table, that I will submit to the company of all my own servants, and all the dirty trollops in the country." "Madam," answered the squire, "I believe you never saw this young creature. I never beheld such sweetness and innocence joined with such beauty, and withal so genteel." "Upon my soul I won't admit her," replied the lady in a passion; "the whole world shan't prevail on me; I resent even the desire as an affront, and—" The squire, who knew her inflexibility, interrupted her, by asking pardon, and promising not to mention it more. He then returned to Joseph, and she to Pamela. He took Joseph aside, and told him he would carry him to his sister, but could not prevail as yet for Fanny. Joseph begged that he might see his sister alone, and then be with his Fanny; but the squire, knowing the pleasure his wife would have in her brother's company, would not admit it, telling Joseph there would be nothing in so short an absence from Fanny, whilst he was assured of her safety; adding, he hoped he could not so easily quit a sister whom he had not seen so long, and who so tenderly loved him. Joseph immediately complied; for indeed no brother could love a sister more; and, recommending Fanny, who rejoiced that she was not to go before Lady Booby, to the care of Mr Adams, he attended the squire upstairs, whilst Fanny repaired with the parson to his house, where she thought herself secure of a kind reception.

CHAPTER VI.

Of which you are desired to read no more than you like.

The meeting between Joseph and Pamela was not without tears of joy on both sides; and their embraces were full of tenderness and affection. They were, however, regarded with much more pleasure by the nephew than by the aunt, to whose flame they were fuel only; and this was increased by the addition of dress, which was indeed not wanted to set off the lively colours in which Nature had drawn health, strength, comeliness, and youth. In the afternoon Joseph, at their request, entertained them with an account of his adventures: nor could Lady Booby conceal her dissatisfaction at those parts in which Fanny was concerned, especially when Mr Booby launched forth into such rapturous praises of her beauty. She said, applying to her niece, that she wondered her nephew, who had pretended to marry for love, should think such a subject proper to amuse his wife with; adding, that, for her part, she should be jealous of a husband who spoke so warmly in praise of another woman. Pamela answered, indeed, she thought she had cause; but it was an instance of Mr Booby's aptness to see more beauty in women than they were mistresses of. At which words both the women fixed their eyes on two looking-glasses; and Lady Booby replied, that men were, in the general, very ill judges of beauty; and then, whilst both contemplated only their own faces, they paid a cross compliment to each other's charms. When the hour of rest approached, which the lady of the house deferred as long as decently she could, she informed Joseph (whom for the future we shall call Mr Joseph, he having as good a title to that appellation as many others—I mean that incontested one of good clothes) that she had ordered a bed to be provided for him. He declined this favour to his utmost; for his heart had long been with his Fanny; but she insisted on his accepting it, alledging that the parish had no proper accommodation for such a person as he was now to esteem himself. The squire and his lady both joining with her, Mr Joseph was at last forced to give over his design of visiting Fanny that evening; who, on her side, as impatiently expected him till midnight, when, in complacence to Mr Adams's family, who had sat up two hours out of respect to her, she retired to bed, but not to sleep; the thoughts of her love kept her waking, and his not returning according to his promise filled her with uneasiness; of which, however, she could not assign any other cause than merely that of being absent from him.

Mr Joseph rose early in the morning, and visited her in whom his soul delighted. She no sooner heard his voice in the parson's parlour than she leapt from her bed, and, dressing herself in a few minutes, went down to him. They passed two hours with inexpressible happiness together; and then, having appointed Monday, by Mr Adams's permission, for their marriage, Mr Joseph returned, according to his promise, to breakfast at the Lady Booby's, with whose behaviour, since the evening, we shall now acquaint the reader.

She was no sooner retired to her chamber than she asked Slipslop "What she thought of this wonderful creature her nephew had married?"—"Madam?" said Slipslop, not yet sufficiently understanding what answer she was to make. "I ask you," answered the lady, "what you think of the dowdy, my niece, I think I am to call her?" Slipslop, wanting no further hint, began to pull her to pieces, and so miserably defaced her, that it would have been impossible for any one to have known the person. The lady gave her all the assistance she could, and ended with saying, "I think, Slipslop, you have done her justice; but yet, bad as she is, she is an angel compared to this Fanny." Slipslop then fell on Fanny, whom she hacked and hewed in the like barbarous manner, concluding with an observation that there was always something in those low-life creatures which must eternally extinguish them from their betters. "Really," said the lady, "I think there is one exception to your rule; I am certain you may guess who I mean."—"Not I, upon my word, madam," said Slipslop. "I mean a young fellow; sure you are the dullest wretch," said the lady. "O la! I am indeed. Yes, truly, madam, he is an accession," answered Slipslop. "Ay, is he not, Slipslop?" returned the lady. "Is he not so genteel that a prince might, without a blush, acknowledge him for his son? His behaviour is such that would not shame the best education. He borrows from his station a condescension in everything to his superiors, yet unattended by that mean servility which is called good behaviour in such persons. Everything he doth hath no mark of the base motive of fear, but visibly shows some respect and gratitude, and carries with it the persuasion of love. And then for his virtues: such piety to his parents, such tender affection to his sister, such integrity in his friendship, such bravery, such goodness, that, if he had been born a gentleman, his wife would have possessed the most invaluable blessing."—"To be sure, ma'am," says Slipslop. "But as he is," answered the lady, "if he had a thousand more good qualities, it must render a woman of fashion contemptible even to be suspected of thinking of him; yes, I should despise myself for such a thought."—"To be sure, ma'am," said Slipslop. "And why to be sure?" replied the lady; "thou art always one's echo. Is he not more worthy of affection than a dirty country clown, though born of a family as old as the flood? or an idle worthless rake, or little puisny beau of quality? And yet these we must condemn ourselves to, in order to avoid the censure of the world; to shun the contempt of others, we must ally ourselves to those we despise; we must prefer birth, title, and fortune, to real merit. It is a tyranny of custom, a tyranny we must comply with; for we people of fashion are the slaves of custom."—"Marry come up!" said Slipslop, who now knew well which party to take. "If I was a woman of your ladyship's fortune and quality, I would be a slave to nobody."—"Me," said the lady; "I am speaking if a young woman of fashion, who had seen nothing of the world, should happen to like such a fellow.—Me, indeed! I hope thou dost not imagine—"—"No, ma'am, to be sure," cries Slipslop. "No! what no?" cried the lady. "Thou art always ready to answer before thou hast heard one. So far I must allow he is a charming fellow. Me, indeed! No, Slipslop, all thoughts of men are over with me. I have lost a husband who—but if I should reflect I should run mad. My future ease must depend upon forgetfulness. Slipslop, let me hear some of thy nonsense, to turn my thoughts another way. What dost thou think of Mr Andrews?"—"Why, I think," says Slipslop, "he is the handsomest, most properest man I ever saw; and if I was a lady of the greatest degree it would be well for some folks. Your ladyship may talk of custom, if you please: but I am confidous there is no more comparison between young Mr Andrews and most of the young gentlemen who come to your ladyship's house in London; a parcel of whipper-snapper sparks: I would sooner marry our old parson Adams. Never tell me what people say, whilst I am happy in the arms of him I love. Some folks rail against other folks because other folks have what some folks would be glad of."—"And so," answered the lady, "if you was a woman of condition, you would really marry Mr Andrews?"—"Yes, I assure your ladyship," replied Slipslop, "if he would have me."—"Fool, idiot!" cries the lady; "if he would have a woman of fashion! is that a question?"—"No, truly, madam," said Slipslop, "I believe it would be none if Fanny was out of the way; and I am confidous, if I was in your ladyship's place, and liked Mr Joseph Andrews, she should not stay in the parish a moment. I am sure lawyer Scout would send her packing if your ladyship would but say the word." This last speech of Slipslop raised a tempest in the mind of her mistress. She feared Scout had betrayed her, or rather that she had betrayed herself. After some silence, and a double change of her complexion, first to pale and then to red, she thus spoke: "I am astonished at the liberty you give your tongue. Would you insinuate that I employed Scout against this wench on account of the fellow?"—"La, ma'am," said Slipslop, frighted out of her wits, "I assassinate such a thing!"—"I think you dare not," answered the lady; "I believe my conduct may defy malice itself to assert so cursed a slander. If I had ever discovered any wantonness, any lightness in my behaviour; if I had followed the example of some whom thou hast, I believe, seen, in allowing myself indecent liberties, even with a husband; but the dear man who is gone" (here she began to sob), "was he alive again" (then she produced tears), "could not upbraid me with any one act of tenderness or passion. No, Slipslop, all the time I cohabited with him he never obtained even a kiss from me without my expressing reluctance in the granting it. I am sure he himself never suspected how much I loved him. Since his death, thou knowest, though it is almost six weeks (it wants but a day) ago, I have not admitted one visitor till this fool my nephew arrived. I have confined myself quite to one party of friends. And can such a conduct as this fear to be arraigned? To be accused, not only of a passion which I have always despised, but of fixing it on such an object, a creature so much beneath my notice!"—"Upon my word, ma'am," says Slipslop, "I do not understand your ladyship; nor know I anything of the matter."—"I believe indeed thou dost not understand me. Those are delicacies which exist only in superior minds; thy coarse ideas cannot comprehend them. Thou art a low creature, of the Andrews breed, a reptile of a lower order, a weed that grows in the common garden of the creation."—"I assure your ladyship," says Slipslop, whose passions were almost of as high an order as her lady's, "I have no more to do with Common Garden than other folks. Really, your ladyship talks of servants as if they were not born of the Christian specious. Servants have flesh and blood as well as quality; and Mr Andrews himself is a proof that they have as good, if not better. And for my own part, I can't perceive my dears [1] are coarser than other people's; and I am sure, if Mr Andrews was a dear of mine, I should not be ashamed of him in company with gentlemen; for whoever hath seen him in his new clothes must confess he looks as much like a gentleman as anybody. Coarse, quotha! I can't bear to hear the poor young fellow run down neither; for I will say this, I never heard him say an ill word of anybody in his life. I am sure his coarseness doth not lie in his heart, for he is the best-natured man in the world; and as for his skin, it is no coarser than other people's, I am sure. His bosom, when a boy, was as white as driven snow; and, where it is not covered with hairs, is so still. Ifakins! if I was Mrs Andrews, with a hundred a year, I should not envy the best she who wears a head. A woman that could not be happy with such a man ought never to be so; for if he can't make a woman happy, I never yet beheld the man who could. I say again, I wish I was a great lady for his sake. I believe, when I had made a gentleman of him, he'd behave so that nobody should deprecate what I had done; and I fancy few would venture to tell him he was no gentleman to his face, nor to mine neither." At which words, taking up the candles, she asked her mistress, who had been some time in her bed, if she had any farther commands? who mildly answered, she had none; and, telling her she was a comical creature, bid her good-night.

---

[1] Meaning perhaps ideas.

CHAPTER VII.

Philosophical reflections, the like not to be found in any light French romance. Mr Booby's grave advice to Joseph, and Fanny's encounter with a beau.

Habit, my good reader, hath so vast a prevalence over the human mind, that there is scarce anything too strange or too strong to be asserted of it. The story of the miser, who, from long accustoming to cheat others, came at last to cheat himself, and with great delight and triumph picked his own pocket of a guinea to convey to his hoard, is not impossible or improbable. In like manner it fares with the practisers of deceit, who, from having long deceived their acquaintance, gain at last a power of deceiving themselves, and acquire that very opinion (however false) of their own abilities, excellencies, and virtues, into which they have for years perhaps endeavoured to betray their neighbours. Now, reader, to apply this observation to my present purpose, thou must know, that as the passion generally called love exercises most of the talents of the female or fair world, so in this they now and then discover a small inclination to deceit; for which thou wilt not be angry with the beautiful creatures when thou hast considered that at the age of seven, or something earlier, miss is instructed by her mother that master is a very monstrous kind of animal, who will, if she suffers him to come too near her, infallibly eat her up and grind her to pieces: that, so far from kissing or toying with him of her own accord, she must not admit him to kiss or toy with her: and, lastly, that she must never have any affection towards him; for if she should, all her friends in petticoats would esteem her a traitress, point at her, and hunt her out of their society. These impressions, being first received, are farther and deeper inculcated by their school-mistresses and companions; so that by the age of ten they have contracted such a dread and abhorrence of the above-named monster, that whenever they see him they fly from him as the innocent hare doth from the greyhound. Hence, to the age of fourteen or fifteen, they entertain a mighty antipathy to master; they resolve, and frequently profess, that they will never have any commerce with him, and entertain fond hopes of passing their lives out of his reach, of the possibility of which they have so visible an example in their good maiden aunt. But when they arrive at this period, and have now passed their second climacteric, when their wisdom, grown riper, begins to see a little farther, and, from almost daily falling in master's way, to apprehend the great difficulty of keeping out of it; and when they observe him look often at them, and sometimes very eagerly and earnestly too (for the monster seldom takes any notice of them till at this age), they then begin to think of their danger; and, as they perceive they cannot easily avoid him, the wiser part bethink themselves of providing by other means for their security. They endeavour, by all methods they can invent, to render themselves so amiable in his eyes, that he may have no inclination to hurt them; in which they generally succeed so well, that his eyes, by frequent languishing, soon lessen their idea of his fierceness, and so far abate their fears, that they venture to parley with him; and when they perceive him so different from what he hath been described, all gentleness, softness, kindness, tenderness, fondness, their dreadful apprehensions vanish in a moment; and now (it being usual with the human mind to skip from one extreme to its opposite, as easily, and almost as suddenly, as a bird from one bough to another) love instantly succeeds to fear: but, as it happens to persons who have in their infancy been thoroughly frightened with certain no-persons called ghosts, that they retain their dread of those beings after they are convinced that there are no such things, so these young ladies, though they no longer apprehend devouring, cannot so entirely shake off all that hath been instilled into them; they still entertain the idea of that censure which was so strongly imprinted on their tender minds, to which the declarations of abhorrence they every day hear from their companions greatly contribute. To avoid this censure, therefore, is now their only care; for which purpose they still pretend the same aversion to the monster: and the more they love him, the more ardently they counterfeit the antipathy. By the continual and constant practice of which deceit on others, they at length impose on themselves, and really believe they hate what they love. Thus, indeed, it happened to Lady Booby, who loved Joseph long before she knew it; and now loved him much more than she suspected. She had indeed, from the time of his sister's arrival in the quality of her niece, and from the instant she viewed him in the dress and character of a gentleman, began to conceive secretly a design which love had concealed from herself till a dream betrayed it to her.

She had no sooner risen than she sent for her nephew. When he came to her, after many compliments on his choice, she told him, "He might perceive, in her condescension to admit her own servant to her table, that she looked on the family of Andrews as his relations, and indeed hers; that, as he had married into such a family, it became him to endeavour by all methods to raise it as much as possible. At length she advised him to use all his heart to dissuade Joseph from his intended match, which would still enlarge their relation to meanness and poverty; concluding that, by a commission in the army, or some other genteel employment, he might soon put young Mr Andrews on the foot of a gentleman; and, that being once done, his accomplishments might quickly gain him an alliance which would not be to their discredit."

Her nephew heartily embraced this proposal, and, finding Mr Joseph with his wife, at his return to her chamber, he immediately began thus: "My love to my dear Pamela, brother, will extend to all her relations; nor shall I show them less respect than if I had married into the family of a duke. I hope I have given you some early testimonies of this, and shall continue to give you daily more. You will excuse me therefore, brother, if my concern for your interest makes me mention what may be, perhaps, disagreeable to you to hear: but I must insist upon it, that, if you have any value for my alliance or my friendship, you will decline any thoughts of engaging farther with a girl who is, as you are a relation of mine, so much beneath you. I know there may be at first some difficulty in your compliance, but that will daily diminish; and you will in the end sincerely thank me for my advice. I own, indeed, the girl is handsome; but beauty alone is a poor ingredient, and will make but an uncomfortable marriage."—"Sir," said Joseph, "I assure you her beauty is her least perfection; nor do I know a virtue which that young creature is not possesst of."—"As to her virtues," answered Mr Booby, "you can be yet but a slender judge of them; but, if she had never so many, you will find her equal in these among her superiors in birth and fortune, which now you are to esteem on a footing with yourself; at least I will take care they shall shortly be so, unless you prevent me by degrading yourself with such a match, a match I have hardly patience to think of, and which would break the hearts of your parents, who now rejoice in the expectation of seeing you make a figure in the world."—"I know not," replied Joseph, "that my parents have any power over my inclinations; nor am I obliged to sacrifice my happiness to their whim or ambition: besides, I shall be very sorry to see that the unexpected advancement of my sister should so suddenly inspire them with this wicked pride, and make them despise their equals. I am resolved on no account to quit my dear Fanny; no, though I could raise her as high above her present station as you have raised my sister."—"Your sister, as well as myself," said Booby, "are greatly obliged to you for the comparison: but, sir, she is not worthy to be compared in beauty to my Pamela; nor hath she half her merit. And besides, sir, as you civilly throw my marriage with your sister in my teeth, I must teach you the wide difference between us: my fortune enabled me to please myself; and it would have been as overgrown a folly in me to have omitted it as in you to do it."—"My fortune enables me to please myself likewise," said Joseph; "for all my pleasure is centered in Fanny; and whilst I have health I shall be able to support her with my labour in that station to which she was born, and with which she is content."—"Brother," said Pamela, "Mr Booby advises you as a friend; and no doubt my papa and mamma will be of his opinion, and will have great reason to be angry with you for destroying what his goodness hath done, and throwing down our family again, after he hath raised it. It would become you better, brother, to pray for the assistance of grace against such a passion than to indulge it."—"Sure, sister, you are not in earnest; I am sure she is your equal, at least."—"She was my equal," answered Pamela; "but I am no longer Pamela Andrews; I am now this gentleman's lady, and, as such, am above her.—I hope I shall never behave with an unbecoming pride: but, at the same time, I shall always endeavour to know myself, and question not the assistance of grace to that purpose." They were now summoned to breakfast, and thus ended their discourse for the present, very little to the satisfaction of any of the parties.

Fanny was now walking in an avenue at some distance from the house, where Joseph had promised to take the first opportunity of coming to her. She had not a shilling in the world, and had subsisted ever since her return entirely on the charity of parson Adams. A young gentleman, attended by many servants, came up to her, and asked her if that was not the Lady Booby's house before him? This, indeed, he well knew; but had framed the question for no other reason than to make her look up, and discover if her face was equal to the delicacy of her shape. He no sooner saw it than he was struck with amazement. He stopt his horse, and swore she was the most beautiful creature he ever beheld. Then, instantly alighting and delivering his horse to his servant, he rapt out half-a-dozen oaths that he would kiss her; to which she at first submitted, begging he would not be rude; but he was not satisfied with the civility of a salute, nor even with the rudest attack he could make on her lips, but caught her in his arms, and endeavoured to kiss her breasts, which with all her strength she resisted, and, as our spark was not of the Herculean race, with some difficulty prevented. The young gentleman, being soon out of breath in the struggle, quitted her, and, remounting his horse, called one of his servants to him, whom he ordered to stay behind with her, and make her any offers whatever to prevail on her to return home with him in the evening; and to assure her he would take her into keeping. He then rode on with his other servants, and arrived at the lady's house, to whom he was a distant relation, and was come to pay a visit.

He ran towards her. The trusty fellow, who was employed in an office he had been long accustomed to, discharged his part with all the fidelity and dexterity imaginable, but to no purpose. She was entirely deaf to his offers, and rejected them with the utmost disdain. At last the pimp, who had perhaps more warm blood about him than his master, began to sollicit for himself; he told her, though he was a servant, he was a man of some fortune, which he would make her mistress of; and this without any insult to her virtue, for that he would marry her. She answered, if his master himself, or the greatest lord in the land, would marry her, she would refuse him. At last, being weary with persuasions, and on fire with charms which would have almost kindled a flame in the bosom of an ancient philosopher or modern divine, he fastened his horse to the ground, and attacked her with much more force than the gentleman had exerted. Poor Fanny would not have been able to resist his rudeness a short time, but the deity who presides over chaste love sent her Joseph to her assistance. He no sooner came within sight, and perceived her struggling with a man, than, like a cannon-ball, or like lightning, or anything that is swifter, if anything be, he ran towards her, and, coming up just as the ravisher had torn her handkerchief from her breast, before his lips had touched that seat of innocence and bliss, he dealt him so lusty a blow in that part of his neck which a rope would have become with the utmost propriety, that the fellow staggered backwards, and, perceiving he had to do with something rougher than the little, tender, trembling hand of Fanny, he quitted her, and, turning about, saw his rival, with fire flashing from his eyes, again ready to assail him; and, indeed, before he could well defend himself, or return the first blow, he received a second, which, had it fallen on that part of the stomach to which it was directed, would have been probably the last he would have had any occasion for; but the ravisher, lifting up his hand, drove the blow upwards to his mouth, whence it dislodged three of his teeth; and now, not conceiving any extraordinary affection for the beauty of Joseph's person, nor being extremely pleased with this method of salutation, he collected all his force, and aimed a blow at Joseph's breast, which he artfully parried with one fist, so that it lost its force entirely in air; and, stepping one foot backward, he darted his fist so fiercely at his enemy, that, had he not caught it in his hand (for he was a boxer of no inferior fame), it must have tumbled him on the ground. And now the ravisher meditated another blow, which he aimed at that part of the breast where the heart is lodged; Joseph did not catch it as before, yet so prevented its aim that it fell directly on his nose, but with abated force. Joseph then, moving both fist and foot forwards at the same time, threw his head so dexterously into the stomach of the ravisher that he fell a lifeless lump on the field, where he lay many minutes breathless and motionless.

When Fanny saw her Joseph receive a blow in his face, and blood running in a stream from him, she began to tear her hair and invoke all human and divine power to his assistance. She was not, however, long under this affliction before Joseph, having conquered his enemy, ran to her, and assured her he was not hurt; she then instantly fell on her knees, and thanked God that he had made Joseph the means of her rescue, and at the same time preserved him from being injured in attempting it. She offered, with her handkerchief, to wipe his blood from his face; but he, seeing his rival attempting to recover his legs, turned to him, and asked him if he had enough? To which the other answered he had; for he believed he had fought with the devil instead of a man; and, loosening his horse, said he should not have attempted the wench if he had known she had been so well provided for.

Fanny now begged Joseph to return with her to parson Adams, and to promise that he would leave her no more. These were propositions so agreeable to Joseph, that, had he heard them, he would have given an immediate assent; but indeed his eyes were now his only sense; for you may remember, reader, that the ravisher had tore her handkerchief from Fanny's neck, by which he had discovered such a sight, that Joseph hath declared all the statues he ever beheld were so much inferior to it in beauty, that it was more capable of converting a man into a statue than of being imitated by the greatest master of that art. This modest creature, whom no warmth in summer could ever induce to expose her charms to the wanton sun, a modesty to which, perhaps, they owed their inconceivable whiteness, had stood many minutes bare-necked in the presence of Joseph before her apprehension of his danger and the horror of seeing his blood would suffer her once to reflect on what concerned herself; till at last, when the cause of her concern had vanished, an admiration at his silence, together with observing the fixed position of his eyes, produced an idea in the lovely maid which brought more blood into her face than had flowed from Joseph's nostrils. The snowy hue of her bosom was likewise changed to vermilion at the instant when she clapped her handkerchief round her neck. Joseph saw the uneasiness she suffered, and immediately removed his eyes from an object, in surveying which he had felt the greatest delight which the organs of sight were capable of conveying to his soul;—so great was his fear of offending her, and so truly did his passion for her deserve the noble name of love.

Fanny, being recovered from her confusion, which was almost equalled by what Joseph had felt from observing it, again mentioned her request; this was instantly and gladly complied with; and together they crossed two or three fields, which brought them to the habitation of Mr Adams.

CHAPTER VIII.

A discourse which happened between Mr Adams, Mrs Adams, Joseph, and Fanny; with some behaviour of Mr Adams which will be called by some few readers very low, absurd, and unnatural.

The parson and his wife had just ended a long dispute when the lovers came to the door. Indeed, this young couple had been the subject of the dispute; for Mrs Adams was one of those prudent people who never do anything to injure their families, or, perhaps, one of those good mothers who would even stretch their conscience to serve their children. She had long entertained hopes of seeing her eldest daughter succeed Mrs Slipslop, and of making her second son an exciseman by Lady Booby's interest. These were expectations she could not endure the thoughts of quitting, and was, therefore, very uneasy to see her husband so resolute to oppose the lady's intention in Fanny's affair. She told him, "It behoved every man to take the first care of his family; that he had a wife and six children, the maintaining and providing for whom would be business enough for him without intermeddling in other folks' affairs; that he had always preached up submission to superiors, and would do ill to give an example of the contrary behaviour in his own conduct; that if Lady Booby did wrong she must answer for it herself, and the sin would not lie at their door; that Fanny had been a servant, and bred up in the lady's own family, and consequently she must have known more of her than they did, and it was very improbable, if she had behaved herself well, that the lady would have been so bitterly her enemy; that perhaps he was too much inclined to think well of her because she was handsome, but handsome women were often no better than they should be; that G— made ugly women as well as handsome ones; and that if a woman had virtue it signified nothing whether she had beauty or no." For all which reasons she concluded he should oblige the lady, and stop the future publication of the banns. But all these excellent arguments had no effect on the parson, who persisted in doing his duty without regarding the consequence it might have on his worldly interest. He endeavoured to answer her as well as he could; to which she had just finished her reply (for she had always the last word everywhere but at church) when Joseph and Fanny entered their kitchen, where the parson and his wife then sat at breakfast over some bacon and cabbage. There was a coldness in the civility of Mrs Adams which persons of accurate speculation might have observed, but escaped her present guests; indeed, it was a good deal covered by the heartiness of Adams, who no sooner heard that Fanny had neither eat nor drank that morning than he presented her a bone of bacon he had just been gnawing, being the only remains of his provision, and then ran nimbly to the tap, and produced a mug of small beer, which he called ale; however, it was the best in his house. Joseph, addressing himself to the parson, told him the discourse which had past between Squire Booby, his sister, and himself concerning Fanny; he then acquainted him with the dangers whence he had rescued her, and communicated some apprehensions on her account. He concluded that he should never have an easy moment till Fanny was absolutely his, and begged that he might be suffered to fetch a licence, saying he could easily borrow the money. The parson answered, That he had already given his sentiments concerning a licence, and that a very few days would make it unnecessary. "Joseph," says he, "I wish this haste doth not arise rather from your impatience than your fear; but, as it certainly springs from one of these causes, I will examine both. Of each of these therefore in their turn; and first for the first of these, namely, impatience. Now, child, I must inform you that, if in your purposed marriage with this young woman you have no intention but the indulgence of carnal appetites, you are guilty of a very heinous sin. Marriage was ordained for nobler purposes, as you will learn when you hear the service provided on that occasion read to you. Nay, perhaps, if you are a good lad, I, child, shall give you a sermon gratis, wherein I shall demonstrate how little regard ought to be had to the flesh on such occasions. The text will be Matthew the 5th, and part of the 28th verse-- *Whosoever looketh on a woman, so as to lust after her*. The latter part I shall omit, as foreign to my purpose. Indeed, all such brutal lusts and affections are to be greatly subdued, if not totally eradicated, before the vessel can be said to be consecrated to honour. To marry with a view of gratifying those inclinations is a prostitution of that holy ceremony, and must entail a curse on all who so lightly undertake it. If, therefore, this haste arises from impatience, you are to correct, and not give way to it. Now, as to the second head which I proposed to speak to, namely, fear: it argues a diffidence, highly criminal, of that Power in which alone we should put our trust, seeing we may be well assured that he is able, not only to defeat the designs of our enemies, but even to turn their hearts. Instead of taking, therefore, any unjustifiable or desperate means to rid ourselves of fear, we should resort to prayer only on these occasions; and we may be then certain of obtaining what is best for us. When any accident threatens us we are not to despair, nor, when it overtakes us, to grieve; we must submit in all things to the will of Providence, and set our affections so much on nothing here that we cannot quit it without reluctance. You are a young man, and can know but little of this world; I am older, and have seen a great deal. All passions are criminal in their excess; and even love itself, if it is not subservient to our duty, may render us blind to it. Had Abraham so loved his son Isaac as to refuse the sacrifice required, is there any of us who would not condemn him? Joseph, I know your many good qualities, and value you for them; but, as I am to render an account of your soul, which is committed to my cure, I cannot see any fault without reminding you of it. You are too much inclined to passion, child, and have set your affections so absolutely on this young woman, that, if G— required her at your hands, I fear you would reluctantly part with her. Now, believe me, no Christian ought so to set his heart on any person or thing in this world, but that, whenever it shall be required or taken from him in any manner by Divine Providence, he may be able, peaceably, quietly, and contentedly to resign it." At which words one came hastily in, and acquainted Mr Adams that his youngest son was drowned. He stood silent a moment, and soon began to stamp about the room and deplore his loss with the bitterest agony. Joseph, who was overwhelmed with concern likewise, recovered himself sufficiently to endeavour to comfort the parson; in which attempt he used many arguments that he had at several times remembered out of his own discourses, both in private and public (for he was a great enemy to the passions, and preached nothing more than the conquest of them by reason and grace), but he was not at leisure now to hearken to his advice. "Child, child," said he, "do not go about impossibilities. Had it been any other of my children I could have borne it with patience; but my little prattler, the darling and comfort of my old age—the little wretch, to be snatched out of life just at his entrance into it; the sweetest, best-tempered boy, who never did a thing to offend me. It was but this morning I gave him his first lesson in *Que Genus*. This was the very book he learnt; poor child! it is of no further use to thee now. He would have made the best scholar, and have been an ornament to the Church;—such parts and such goodness never met in one so young." "And the handsomest lad too," says Mrs Adams, recovering from a swoon in Fanny's arms. "My poor Jacky, shall I never see thee more?" cries the parson. "Yes, surely," says Joseph, "and in a better place; you will meet again, never to part more." I believe the parson did not hear these words, for he paid little regard to them, but went on lamenting, whilst the tears trickled down into his bosom. At last he cried out, "Where is my little darling?" and was sallying out, when to his great surprize and joy, in which I hope the reader will sympathize, he met his son in a wet condition indeed, but alive and running towards him. The person who brought the news of his misfortune had been a little too eager, as people sometimes are, from, I believe, no very good principle, to relate ill news; and, seeing him fall into the river, instead of running to his assistance, directly ran to acquaint his father of a fate which he had concluded to be inevitable, but whence the child was relieved by the same poor pedlar who had relieved his father before from a less distress. The parson's joy was now as extravagant as his grief had been before; he kissed and embraced his son a thousand times, and danced about the room like one frantic; but as soon as he discovered the face of his old friend the pedlar, and heard the fresh obligation he had to him, what were his sensations? not those which two courtiers feel in one another's embraces; not those with which a great man receives the vile treacherous engines of his wicked purposes, not those with which a worthless younger brother wishes his elder joy of a son, or a man congratulates his rival on his obtaining a mistress, a place, or an honour.—No, reader; he felt the ebullition, the overflowings of a full, honest, open heart, towards the person who had conferred a real obligation, and of which, if thou canst not conceive an idea within, I will not vainly endeavour to assist thee.

When these tumults were over, the parson, taking Joseph aside, proceeded thus—"No, Joseph, do not give too much way to thy passions, if thou dost expect happiness." The patience of Joseph, nor perhaps of Job, could bear no longer; he interrupted the parson, saying, "It was easier to give advice than take it; nor did he perceive he could so entirely conquer himself, when he apprehended he had lost his son, or when he found him recovered."—"Boy," replied Adams, raising his voice, "it doth not become green heads to advise grey hairs.—Thou art ignorant of the tenderness of fatherly affection; when thou art a father thou wilt be capable then only of knowing what a father can feel. No man is obliged to impossibilities; and the loss of a child is one of those great trials where our grief may be allowed to become immoderate."—"Well, sir," cries Joseph, "and if I love a mistress as well as you your child, surely her loss would grieve me equally."—"Yes, but such love is foolishness and wrong in itself, and ought to be conquered," answered Adams; "it savours too much of the flesh."—"Sure, sir," says Joseph, "it is not sinful to love my wife, no, not even to doat on her to distraction!"—"Indeed but it is," says Adams. "Every man ought to love his wife, no doubt; we are commanded so to do; but we ought to love her with moderation and discretion."—"I am afraid I shall be guilty of some sin in spite of all my endeavours," says Joseph; "for I shall love without any moderation, I am sure."—"You talk foolishly and childishly," cries Adams.—"Indeed," says Mrs Adams, who had listened to the latter part of their conversation, "you talk more foolishly yourself. I hope, my dear, you will never preach any such doctrine as that husbands can love their wives too well. If I knew you had such a sermon in the house I am sure I would burn it, and I declare, if I had not been convinced you had loved me as well as you could, I can answer for myself, I should have hated and despised you. Marry come up! Fine doctrine, indeed! A wife hath a right to insist on her husband's loving her as much as ever he can; and he is a sinful villain who doth not. Doth he not promise to love her, and to comfort her, and to cherish her, and all that? I am sure I remember it all as well as if I had repeated it over but yesterday, and shall never forget it. Besides, I am certain you do not preach as you practise; for you have been a loving and a cherishing husband to me; that's the truth on't; and why you should endeavour to put such wicked nonsense into this young man's head I cannot devise. Don't hearken to him, Mr Joseph; be as good a husband as you are able, and love your wife with all your body and soul too." Here a violent rap at the door put an end to their discourse, and produced a scene which the reader will find in the next chapter.

CHAPTER IX.

A visit which the polite Lady Booby and her polite friend paid to the parson.

The Lady Booby had no sooner had an account from the gentleman of his meeting a wonderful beauty near her house, and perceived the raptures with which he spoke of her, than, immediately concluding it must be Fanny, she began to meditate a design of bringing them better acquainted; and to entertain hopes that the fine clothes, presents, and promises of this youth, would prevail on her to abandon Joseph: she therefore proposed to her company a walk in the fields before dinner, when she led them towards Mr Adams's house; and, as she approached it, told them if they pleased she would divert them with one of the most ridiculous sights they had ever seen, which was an old foolish parson, who, she said, laughing, kept a wife and six brats on a salary of about twenty pounds a year; adding, that there was not such another ragged family in the parish. They all readily agreed to this visit, and arrived whilst Mrs Adams was declaiming as in the last chapter. Beau Didapper, which was the name of the young gentleman we have seen riding towards Lady Booby's, with his cane mimicked the rap of a London footman at the door. The people within, namely, Adams, his wife and three children, Joseph, Fanny, and the pedlar, were all thrown into confusion by this knock, but Adams went directly to the door, which being opened, the Lady Booby and her company walked in, and were received by the parson with about two hundred bows, and by his wife with as many curtsies; the latter telling the lady "She was ashamed to be seen in such a pickle, and that her house was in such a litter; but that if she had expected such an honour from her ladyship she should have found her in a better manner." The parson made no apologies, though he was in his half-cassock and a flannel nightcap. He said "They were heartily welcome to his poor cottage," and turning to Mr Didapper, cried out, "*Non mea renidet in domo lacunar*." The beau answered, "He did not understand Welsh;" at which the parson stared and made no reply.

Mr Didapper, or beau Didapper, was a young gentleman of about four foot five inches in height. He wore his own hair, though the scarcity of it might have given him sufficient excuse for a periwig. His face was thin and pale; the shape of his body and legs none of the best, for he had very narrow shoulders and no calf; and his gait might more properly be called hopping than walking. The qualifications of his mind were well adapted to his person. We shall handle them first negatively. He was not entirely ignorant; for he could talk a little French and sing two or three Italian songs; he had lived too much in the world to be bashful, and too much at court to be proud: he seemed not much inclined to avarice, for he was profuse in his expenses; nor had he all the features of prodigality, for he never gave a shilling: no hater of women, for he always dangled after them; yet so little subject to lust, that he had, among those who knew him best, the character of great moderation in his pleasures; no drinker of wine; nor so addicted to passion but that a hot word or two from an adversary made him immediately cool.

Now, to give him only a dash or two on the affirmative side: though he was born to an immense fortune, he chose, for the pitiful and dirty consideration of a place of little consequence, to depend entirely on the will of a fellow whom they call a great man; who treated him with the utmost disrespect, and exacted of him a plenary obedience to his commands, which he implicitly submitted to, at the expense of his conscience, his honour, and of his country, in which he had himself so very large a share. And to finish his character; as he was entirely well satisfied with his own person and parts, so he was very apt to ridicule and laugh at any imperfection in another. Such was the little person, or rather thing, that hopped after Lady Booby into Mr Adams's kitchen.

The parson and his company retreated from the chimney-side, where they had been seated, to give room to the lady and hers. Instead of returning any of the curtsies or extraordinary civility of Mrs Adams, the lady, turning to Mr Booby, cried out, "*Quelle Bête! Quel Animal!*" And presently after discovering Fanny (for she did not need the circumstance of her standing by Joseph to assure the identity of her person), she asked the beau "Whether he did not think her a pretty girl?"—"Begad, madam," answered he, "'tis the very same I met." "I did not imagine," replied the lady, "you had so good a taste."—"Because I never liked you, I warrant," cries the beau. "Ridiculous!" said she: "you know you was always my aversion." "I would never mention aversion," answered the beau, "with that face [1]; dear Lady Booby, wash your face before you mention aversion, I beseech you." He then laughed, and turned about to coquet it with Fanny.

Mrs Adams had been all this time begging and praying the ladies to sit down, a favour which she at last obtained. The little boy to whom the accident had happened, still keeping his place by the fire, was chid by his mother for not being more mannerly: but Lady Booby took his part, and, commending his beauty, told the parson he was his very picture. She then, seeing a book in his hand, asked "If he could read?"—"Yes," cried Adams, "a little Latin, madam: he is just got into Quae Genus."—"A fig for quere genius!" answered she; "let me hear him read a little English."—"Lege, Dick, lege," said Adams: but the boy made no answer, till he saw the parson knit his brows, and then cried, "I don't understand you, father."—"How, boy!" says Adams; "what doth lego make in the imperative mood? Legito, doth it not?"—"Yes," answered Dick.—"And what besides ?" says the

---

[1] Lest this should appear unnatural to some readers, we think proper to acquaint them, that it is taken verbatim from very polite conversation.

father. "Lege," quoth the son, after some hesitation. "A good boy," says the father: "and now, child, what is the English of lego?"—To which the boy, after long puzzling, answered, he could not tell. "How!" cries Adams, in a passion;—"what, hath the water washed away your learning? Why, what is Latin for the English verb read? Consider before you speak." The child considered some time, and then the parson cried twice or thrice, "Le—, Le—." Dick answered, "Lego."—"Very well;—and then what is the English," says the parson, "of the verb lego?"—"To read," cried Dick.—"Very well," said the parson; "a good boy: you can do well if you will take pains.—I assure your ladyship he is not much above eight years old, and is out of his Propria quae Maribus already.—Come, Dick, read to her ladyship;"—which she again desiring, in order to give the beau time and opportunity with Fanny, Dick began as in the following chapter.

CHAPTER X.

The history of two friends, which may afford an useful lesson to all those persons who happen to take up their residence in married families.

"Leonard and Paul were two friends."—"Pronounce it Lennard, child," cried the parson.—"Pray, Mr Adams," says Lady Booby, "let your son read without interruption." Dick then proceeded. "Lennard and Paul were two friends, who, having been educated together at the same school, commenced a friendship which they preserved a long time for each other. It was so deeply fixed in both their minds, that a long absence, during which they had maintained no correspondence, did not eradicate nor lessen it: but it revived in all its force at their first meeting, which was not till after fifteen years' absence, most of which time Lennard had spent in the East Indi-es."—"Pronounce it short, Indies," says Adams.—"Pray? sir, be quiet," says the lady.—The boy repeated—"in the East Indies, whilst Paul had served his king and country in the army. In which different services they had found such different success, that Lennard was now married, and retired with a fortune of thirty thousand pounds; and Paul was arrived to the degree of a lieutenant of foot; and was not worth a single shilling.

"The regiment in which Paul was stationed happened to be ordered into quarters within a small distance from the estate which Lennard had purchased, and where he was settled. This latter, who was now become a country gentleman, and a justice of peace, came to attend the quarter sessions in the town where his old friend was quartered, soon after his arrival. Some affair in which a soldier was concerned occasioned Paul to attend the justices. Manhood, and time, and the change of climate had so much altered Lennard, that Paul did not immediately recollect the features of his old acquaintance: but it was otherwise with Lennard. He knew Paul the moment he saw him; nor could he contain himself from quitting the bench, and running hastily to embrace him. Paul stood at first a little surprized; but had soon sufficient information from his friend, whom he no sooner remembered than he returned his embrace with a passion which made many of the spectators laugh, and gave to some few a much higher and more agreeable sensation.

"Not to detain the reader with minute circumstances, Lennard insisted on his friend's returning with him to his house that evening; which request was complied with, and leave for a month's absence for Paul obtained of the commanding officer.

"If it was possible for any circumstance to give any addition to the happiness which Paul proposed in this visit, he received that additional pleasure by finding, on his arrival at his friend's house, that his lady was an old acquaintance which he had formerly contracted at his quarters, and who had always appeared to be of a most agreeable temper; a character she had ever maintained among her intimates, being of that number, every individual of which is called quite the best sort of woman in the world.

"But, good as this lady was, she was still a woman; that is to say, an angel, and not an angel."—"You must mistake, child," cries the parson, "for you read nonsense."—"It is so in the book," answered the son. Mr Adams was then silenced by authority, and Dick proceeded—"For though her person was of that kind to which men attribute the name of angel, yet in her mind she was perfectly woman. Of which a great degree of obstinacy gave the most remarkable and perhaps most pernicious instance.

"A day or two passed after Paul's arrival before any instances of this appeared; but it was impossible to conceal it long. Both she and her husband soon lost all apprehension from their friend's presence, and fell to their disputes with as much vigour as ever. These were still pursued with the utmost ardour and eagerness, however trifling the causes were whence they first arose. Nay, however incredible it may seem, the little consequence of the matter in debate was frequently given as a reason for the fierceness of the contention, as thus: 'If you loved me, sure you would never dispute with me such a trifle as this.' The answer to which is very obvious; for the argument would hold equally on both sides, and was constantly retorted with some addition, as—'I am sure I have much more reason to say so, who am in the right.' During all these disputes, Paul always kept strict silence, and preserved an even countenance, without showing the least visible inclination to either party. One day, however, when madam had left the room in a violent fury, Lennard could not refrain from referring his cause to his friend. Was ever anything so unreasonable, says he, as this woman? What shall I do with her? I doat on her to distraction; nor have I any cause to complain of, more than this obstinacy in her temper; whatever she asserts, she will maintain against all the reason and conviction in the world. Pray give me your advice.—First, says Paul, I will give my opinion, which is, flatly, that you are in the wrong; for, supposing she is in the wrong, was the subject of your contention any ways material? What signified it whether you was married in a red or a yellow waistcoat? for that was your dispute. Now, suppose she was mistaken; as you love her you say so tenderly, and I believe she deserves it, would it not have been wiser to have yielded, though you certainly knew yourself in the right, than to give either her or yourself any uneasiness. For my own part, if ever I marry, I am resolved to enter into an agreement with my wife, that in all disputes (especially about trifles) that party who is most convinced they are right shall always surrender the victory; by which means we shall both be forward to give up the cause. I own, said Lennard, my dear friend, shaking him by the hand, there is great truth and reason in what you say; and I will for the future endeavour to follow your advice. They soon after broke up the conversation, and Lennard, going to his wife, asked her pardon, and told her his friend had convinced him he had been in the wrong. She immediately began a vast encomium on Paul, in which he seconded her, and both agreed he was the worthiest and wisest man upon earth. When next they met, which was at supper, though she had promised not to mention what her husband told her, she could not forbear casting the kindest and most affectionate looks on Paul, and asked him, with the sweetest voice, whether she should help him to some potted woodcock? Potted partridge, my dear, you mean, says the husband. My dear, says she, I ask your friend if he will eat any potted woodcock; and I am sure I must know, who potted it. I think I should know too, who shot them, replied the husband, and I am convinced that I have not seen a woodcock this year; however, though I know I am in the right, I submit, and the potted partridge is potted woodcock if you desire to have it so. It is equal to me, says she, whether it is one or the other; but you would persuade one out of one's senses; to be sure, you are always in the right in your own opinion; but your friend, I believe, knows which he is eating. Paul answered nothing, and the dispute continued, as usual, the greatest part of the evening. The next morning the lady, accidentally meeting Paul, and being convinced he was her friend, and of her side, accosted him thus:—I am certain, sir, you have long since wondered at the unreasonableness of my husband. He is indeed, in other respects, a good sort of man, but so positive, that no woman but one of my complying temper could possibly live with him. Why, last night, now, was ever any creature so unreasonable? I am certain you must condemn him. Pray, answer me, was he not in the wrong? Paul, after a short silence, spoke as follows: I am sorry, madam, that, as good manners obliges me to answer against my will, so an adherence to truth forces me to declare myself of a different opinion. To be plain and honest, you was entirely in the wrong; the cause I own not worth disputing, but the bird was undoubtedly a partridge. O sir! replyed the lady, I cannot possibly help your taste. Madam, returned Paul, that is very little material; for, had it been otherwise, a husband might have expected submission.—Indeed! sir, says she, I assure you!—Yes, madam, cryed he, he might, from a person of your excellent understanding; and pardon me for saying, such a condescension would have shown a superiority of sense even to your husband himself.—But, dear sir, said she, why should I submit when I am in the right?—For that very reason, answered he; it would be the greatest instance of affection imaginable; for can anything be a greater object of our compassion than a person we love in the wrong? Ay, but I should endeavour, said she, to set him right. Pardon me, madam, answered Paul: I will apply to your own experience if you ever found your arguments had that effect. The more our judgments err, the less we are willing to own it: for my own part, I have always observed the persons who maintain the worst side in any contest are the warmest. Why, says she, I must confess there is truth in what you say, and I will endeavour to practise it. The husband then coming in, Paul departed. And Leonard, approaching his wife with an air of good humour, told her he was sorry for their foolish dispute the last night; but he was now convinced of his error. She answered, smiling, she believed she owed his condescension to his complacence; that she was ashamed to think a word had passed on so silly an occasion, especially as she was satisfyed she had been mistaken. A little contention followed, but with the utmost good-will to each other, and was concluded by her asserting that Paul had thoroughly convinced her she had been in the wrong. Upon which they both united in the praises of their common friend.

"Paul now passed his time with great satisfaction, these disputes being much less frequent, as well as shorter than usual; but the devil, or some unlucky accident in which perhaps the devil had no hand, shortly put an end to his happiness. He was now eternally the private referee of every difference; in which, after having perfectly, as he thought, established the doctrine of submission, he never scrupled to assure both privately that they were in the right in every argument, as before he had followed the contrary method. One day a violent litigation happened in his absence, and both parties agreed to refer it to his decision. The husband professing himself sure the decision would be in his favour; the wife answered, he might be mistaken; for she believed his friend was convinced how seldom she was to blame; and that if he knew all—The husband replied, My dear, I have no desire of any retrospect; but I believe, if you knew all too, you would not imagine my friend so entirely on your side. Nay, says she, since you provoke me, I will mention one instance. You may remember our dispute about sending Jackey to school in cold weather, which point I gave up to you from mere compassion, knowing myself to be in the right; and Paul himself told me afterwards he thought me so. My dear, replied the husband, I will not scruple your veracity; but I assure you solemnly, on my applying to him, he gave it absolutely on my side, and said he would have acted in the same manner. They then proceeded to produce numberless other instances, in all which Paul had, on vows of secresy, given his opinion on both sides. In the conclusion, both believing each other, they fell severely on the treachery of Paul, and agreed that he had been the occasion of almost every dispute which had fallen out between them. They then became extremely loving, and so full of condescension on both sides, that they vyed with each other in censuring their own conduct, and jointly vented their indignation on Paul, whom the wife, fearing a bloody consequence, earnestly entreated her husband to suffer quietly to depart the next day, which was the time fixed for his return to quarters, and then drop his acquaintance.

"However ungenerous this behaviour in Lennard may be esteemed, his wife obtained a promise from him (though with difficulty) to follow her advice; but they both expressed such unusual coldness that day to Paul, that he, who was quick of apprehension, taking Lennard aside, pressed him so home, that he at last discovered the secret. Paul acknowledged the truth, but told him the design with which he had done it.—To which the other answered, he would have acted more friendly to have let him into the whole design; for that he might have assured himself of his secresy. Paul replyed, with some indignation, he had given him a sufficient proof how capable he was of concealing a secret from his wife. Lennard returned with some warmth—he had more reason to upbraid him, for that he had caused most of the quarrels between them by his strange conduct, and might (if they had not discovered the affair to each other) have been the occasion of their separation. Paul then said"—But something now happened which put a stop to Dick's reading, and of which we shall treat in the next chapter.

CHAPTER XI.

In which the history is continued.

Joseph Andrews had borne with great uneasiness the impertinence of beau Didapper to Fanny, who had been talking pretty freely to her, and offering her settlements; but the respect to the company had restrained him from interfering whilst the beau confined himself to the use of his tongue only; but the said beau, watching an opportunity whilst the ladies' eyes were disposed another way, offered a rudeness to her with his hands; which Joseph no sooner perceived than he presented him with so sound a box on the ear, that it conveyed him several paces from where he stood. The ladies immediately screamed out, rose from their chairs; and the beau, as soon as he recovered himself, drew his hanger: which Adams observing, snatched up the lid of a pot in his left hand, and, covering himself with it as with a shield, without any weapon of offence in his other hand, stept in before Joseph, and exposed himself to the enraged beau, who threatened such perdition and destruction, that it frighted the women, who were all got in a huddle together, out of their wits, even to hear his denunciations of vengeance. Joseph was of a different complexion, and begged Adams to let his rival come on; for he had a good cudgel in his hand, and did not fear him. Fanny now fainted into Mrs Adams's arms, and the whole room was in confusion, when Mr Booby, passing by Adams, who lay snug under the pot-lid, came up to Didapper, and insisted on his sheathing the hanger, promising he should have satisfaction; which Joseph declared he would give him, and fight him at any weapon whatever. The beau now sheathed his hanger, and taking out a pocket-glass, and vowing vengeance all the time, re-adjusted his hair; the parson deposited his shield; and Joseph, running to Fanny, soon brought her back to life. Lady Booby chid Joseph for his insult on Didapper; but he answered, he would have attacked an army in the same cause. "What cause?" said the lady. "Madam," answered Joseph, "he was rude to that young woman."—"What," says the lady, "I suppose he would have kissed the wench; and is a gentleman to be struck for such an offer? I must tell you, Joseph, these airs do not become you."—"Madam," said Mr Booby, "I saw the whole affair, and I do not commend my brother; for I cannot perceive why he should take upon him to be this girl's champion."—"I can commend him," says Adams: "he is a brave lad; and it becomes any man to be the champion of the innocent; and he must be the basest coward who would not vindicate a woman with whom he is on the brink of marriage."—"Sir," says Mr Booby, "my brother is not a proper match for such a young woman as this."—"No," says Lady Booby; "nor do you, Mr Adams, act in your proper character by encouraging any such doings; and I am very much surprized you should concern yourself in it. I think your wife and family your properer care."—"Indeed, madam, your ladyship says very true," answered Mrs Adams: "he talks a pack of nonsense, that the whole parish are his children. I am sure I don't understand what he means by it; it would make some women suspect he had gone astray, but I acquit him of that; I can read Scripture as well as he, and I never found that the parson was obliged to provide for other folks' children; and besides, he is but a poor curate, and hath little enough, as your ladyship knows, for me and mine."—"You say very well, Mrs Adams," quoth the Lady Booby, who had not spoke a word to her before; "you seem to be a very sensible woman; and I assure you, your husband is acting a very foolish part, and opposing his own interest, seeing my nephew is violently set against this match: and indeed I can't blame him; it is by no means one suitable to our family." In this manner the lady proceeded with Mrs Adams, whilst the beau hopped about the room, shaking his head, partly from pain and partly from anger; and Pamela was chiding Fanny for her assurance in aiming at such a match as her brother. Poor Fanny answered only with her tears, which had long since begun to wet her handkerchief; which Joseph perceiving, took her by the arm, and wrapping it in his carried her off, swearing he would own no relation to any one who was an enemy to her he loved more than all the world. He went out with Fanny under his left arm, brandishing a cudgel in his right, and neither Mr Booby nor the beau thought proper to oppose him. Lady Booby and her company made a very short stay behind him; for the lady's bell now summoned them to dress; for which they had just time before dinner.

Adams seemed now very much dejected, which his wife perceiving, began to apply some matrimonial balsam. She told him he had reason to be concerned, for that he had probably ruined his family with his tricks almost; but perhaps he was grieved for the loss of his two children, Joseph and Fanny. His eldest daughter went on: "Indeed, father, it is very hard to bring strangers here to eat your children's bread out of their mouths. You have kept them ever since they came home; and, for anything I see to the contrary, may keep them a month longer; are you obliged to give her meat, tho'f she was never so handsome? But I don't see she is so much handsomer than other people. If people were to be kept for their beauty, she would scarce fare better than her neighbours, I believe. As for Mr Joseph, I have nothing to say; he is a young man of honest principles, and will pay some time or other for what he hath; but for the girl—why doth she not return to her place she ran away from? I would not give such a vagabond slut a halfpenny though I had a million of money; no, though she was starving." "Indeed but I would," cries little Dick; "and, father, rather than poor Fanny shall be starved, I will give her all this bread and cheese"—(offering what he held in his hand). Adams smiled on the boy, and told him he rejoiced to see he was a Christian; and that if he had a halfpenny in his pocket, he would have given it him; telling him it was his duty to look upon all his neighbours as his brothers and sisters, and love them accordingly. "Yes, papa," says he, "I love her better than my sisters, for she is handsomer than any of them." "Is she so, saucebox?" says the sister, giving him a box on the ear; which the father would probably have resented, had not Joseph, Fanny, and the pedlar at that instant returned together. Adams bid his wife prepare some food for their dinner; she said, "Truly she could not, she had something else to do." Adams rebuked her for disputing his commands, and quoted many texts of Scripture to prove "That the husband is the head of the wife, and she is to submit and obey." The wife answered, "It was blasphemy to talk Scripture out of church; that such things were very proper to be said in the pulpit, but that it was profane to talk them in common discourse." Joseph told Mr Adams "He was not come with any design to give him or Mrs Adams any trouble; but to desire the favour of all their company to the George (an ale-house in the parish), where he had bespoke a piece of bacon and greens for their dinner." Mrs Adams, who was a very good sort of woman, only rather too strict in oeconomies, readily accepted this invitation, as did the parson himself by her example; and away they all walked together, not omitting little Dick, to whom Joseph gave a shilling when he heard of his intended liberality to Fanny.

CHAPTER XII.

Where the good-natured reader will see something which will give him no great pleasure.

The pedlar had been very inquisitive from the time he had first heard that the great house in this parish belonged to the Lady Booby, and had learnt that she was the widow of Sir Thomas, and that Sir Thomas had bought Fanny, at about the age of three or four years, of a travelling woman; and, now their homely but hearty meal was ended, he told Fanny he believed he could acquaint her with her parents. The whole company, especially she herself, started at this offer of the pedlar's. He then proceeded thus, while they all lent their strictest attention:— "Though I am now contented with this humble way of getting my livelihood, I was formerly a gentleman; for so all those of my profession are called. In a word, I was a drummer in an Irish regiment of foot. Whilst I was in this honourable station I attended an officer of our regiment into England a-recruiting. In our march from Bristol to Froome (for since the decay of the woollen trade the clothing towns have furnished the army with a great number of recruits) we overtook on the road a woman, who seemed to be about thirty years old or thereabouts, not very handsome, but well enough for a soldier. As we came up to her, she mended her pace, and falling into discourse with our ladies (for every man of the party, namely, a serjeant, two private men, and a drum, were provided with their woman except myself), she continued to travel on with us. I, perceiving she must fall to my lot, advanced presently to her, made love to her in our military way, and quickly succeeded to my wishes. We struck a bargain within a mile, and lived together as man and wife to her dying day." "I suppose," says Adams, interrupting him, "you were married with a licence; for I don't see how you could contrive to have the banns published while you were marching from place to place." "No, sir," said the pedlar, "we took a licence to go to bed together without any banns." "Ay! ay!" said the parson; "*ex necessitate*, a licence may be allowable enough; but surely, surely, the other is the more regular and eligible way." The pedlar proceeded thus: "She returned with me to our regiment, and removed with us from quarters to quarters, till at last, whilst we lay at Galloway, she fell ill of a fever and died. When she was on her death-bed she called me to her, and, crying bitterly, declared she could not depart this world without discovering a secret to me, which, she said, was the only sin which sat heavy on her heart. She said she had formerly travelled in a company of gypsies, who had made a practice of stealing away children; that for her own part, she had been only once guilty of the crime; which, she said, she lamented more than all the rest of her sins, since probably it might have occasioned the death of the parents; for, added she, it is almost impossible to describe the beauty of the young creature, which was about a year and a half old when I kidnapped it. We kept her (for she was a girl) above two years in our company, when I sold her myself, for three guineas, to Sir Thomas Booby, in Somersetshire. Now, you know whether there are any more of that name in this county." "Yes," says Adams, "there are several Boobys who are squires, but I believe no baronet now alive; besides, it answers so exactly in every point, there is no room for doubt; but you have forgot to tell us the parents from whom the child was stolen." "Their name," answered the pedlar, "was Andrews. They lived about thirty miles from the squire; and she told me that I might be sure to find them out by one circumstance; for that they had a daughter of a very strange name, Pamela, or Pam*e*la; some pronounced it one way, and some the other." Fanny, who had changed colour at the first mention of the name, now fainted away; Joseph turned pale, and poor Dicky began to roar; the parson fell on his knees, and ejaculated many thanksgivings that this discovery had been made before the dreadful sin of incest was committed; and the pedlar was struck with amazement, not being able to account for all this confusion; the cause of which was presently opened by the parson's daughter, who was the only unconcerned person (for the mother was chafing Fanny's temples, and taking the utmost care of her): and, indeed, Fanny was the only creature whom the daughter would not have pitied in her situation; wherein, though we compassionate her ourselves, we shall leave her for a little while, and pay a short visit to Lady Booby.

CHAPTER XIII.

The history, returning to the Lady Booby, gives some account of the terrible conflict in her breast between love and pride; with what happened on the present discovery.

The lady sat down with her company to dinner, but eat nothing. As soon as her cloth was removed she whispered Pamela that she was taken a little ill, and desired her to entertain her husband and beau Didapper. She then went up into her chamber, sent for Slipslop, threw herself on the bed in the agonies of love, rage, and despair; nor could she conceal these boiling passions longer without bursting. Slipslop now approached her bed, and asked how her ladyship did; but, instead of revealing her disorder, as she intended, she entered into a long encomium on the beauty and virtues of Joseph Andrews; ending, at last, with expressing her concern that so much tenderness should be thrown away on so despicable an object as Fanny. Slipslop, well knowing how to humour her mistress's frenzy, proceeded to repeat, with exaggeration, if possible, all her mistress had said, and concluded with a wish that Joseph had been a gentleman, and that she could see her lady in the arms of such a husband. The lady then started from the bed, and, taking a turn or two across the room, cryed out, with a deep sigh, "Sure he would make any woman happy!"—"Your ladyship," says she, "would be the happiest woman in the world with him. A fig for custom and nonsense! What 'vails what people say? Shall I be afraid of eating sweetmeats because people may say I have a sweet tooth? If I had a mind to marry a man, all the world should not hinder me. Your ladyship hath no parents to tutelar your infections; besides, he is of your ladyship's family now, and as good a gentleman as any in the country; and why should not a woman follow her mind as well as man? Why should not your ladyship marry the brother as well as your nephew the sister. I am sure, if it was a fragrant crime, I would not persuade your ladyship to it."—"But, dear Slipslop," answered the lady, "if I could prevail on myself to commit such a weakness, there is that cursed Fanny in the way, whom the idiot—O how I hate and despise him!"—"She! a little ugly mynx," cries Slipslop; "leave her to me. I suppose your ladyship hath heard of Joseph's fitting with one of Mr Didapper's servants about her; and his master hath ordered them to carry her away by force this evening. I'll take care they shall not want assistance. I was talking with this gentleman, who was below, just when your ladyship sent for me."—"Go back," says the Lady Booby, "this instant, for I expect Mr Didapper will soon be going. Do all you can; for I am resolved this wench shall not be in our family: I will endeavour to return to the company; but let me know as soon as she is carried off." Slipslop went away; and her mistress began to arraign her own conduct in the following manner:—

"What am I doing? How do I suffer this passion to creep imperceptibly upon me? How many days are past since I could have submitted to ask myself the question?—Marry a footman! Distraction! Can I afterwards bear the eyes of my acquaintance? But I can retire from them; retire with one in whom I propose more happiness than the world without him can give me! Retire-to feed continually on beauties which my inflamed imagination sickens with eagerly gazing on; to satisfy every appetite, every desire, with their utmost wish. Ha! and do I doat thus on a footman? I despise, I detest my passion.—Yet why? Is he not generous, gentle, kind?—Kind! to whom? to the meanest wretch, a creature below my consideration. Doth he not—yes, he doth prefer her. Curse his beauties, and the little low heart that possesses them; which can basely descend to this despicable wench, and be ungratefully deaf to all the honours I do him. And can I then love this monster? No, I will tear his image from my bosom, tread on him, spurn him. I will have those pitiful charms, which now I despise, mangled in my sight; for I will not suffer the little jade I hate to riot in the beauties I contemn. No; though I despise him myself, though I would spurn him from my feet, was he to languish at them, no other should taste the happiness I scorn. Why do I say happiness? To me it would be misery. To sacrifice my reputation, my character, my rank in life, to the indulgence of a mean and a vile appetite! How I detest the thought! How much more exquisite is the pleasure resulting from the reflection of virtue and prudence than the faint relish of what flows from vice and folly! Whither did I suffer this improper, this mad passion to hurry me, only by neglecting to summon the aids of reason to my assistance? Reason, which hath now set before me my desires in their proper colours, and immediately helped me to expel them. Yes, I thank Heaven and my pride, I have now perfectly conquered this unworthy passion; and if there was no obstacle in its way, my pride would disdain any pleasures which could be the consequence of so base, so mean, so vulgar—" Slipslop returned at this instant in a violent hurry, and with the utmost eagerness cryed out, "O madam! I have strange news. Tom the footman is just come from the George; where, it seems, Joseph and the rest of them are a jinketting; and he says there is a strange man who hath discovered that Fanny and Joseph are brother and sister."—"How, Slipslop?" cries the lady, in a surprize.—"I had not time, madam," cries Slipslop, "to enquire about particles, but Tom says it is most certainly true."

This unexpected account entirely obliterated all those admirable reflections which the supreme power of reason had so wisely made just before. In short, when despair, which had more share in producing the resolutions of hatred we have seen taken, began to retreat, the lady hesitated a moment, and then, forgetting all the purport of her soliloquy, dismissed her woman again, with orders to bid Tom attend her in the parlour, whither she now hastened to acquaint Pamela with the news. Pamela said she could not believe it; for she had never heard that her mother had lost any child, or that she had ever had any more than Joseph and herself. The lady flew into a violent rage with her, and talked of upstarts and disowning relations who had so lately been on a level with her. Pamela made no answer; but her husband, taking up her cause, severely reprimanded his aunt for her behaviour to his wife: he told her, if it had been earlier in the evening she should not have staid a moment longer in her house; that he was convinced, if this young woman could be proved her sister, she would readily embrace her as such, and he himself would do the same. He then desired the fellow might be sent for, and the young woman with him, which Lady Booby immediately ordered; and, thinking proper to make some apology to Pamela for what she had said, it was readily accepted, and all things reconciled.

The pedlar now attended, as did Fanny and Joseph, who would not quit her; the parson likewise was induced, not only by curiosity, of which he had no small portion, but his duty, as he apprehended it, to follow them; for he continued all the way to exhort them, who were now breaking their hearts, to offer up thanksgivings, and be joyful for so miraculous an escape.

When they arrived at Booby-Hall they were presently called into the parlour, where the pedlar repeated the same story he had told before, and insisted on the truth of every circumstance; so that all who heard him were extremely well satisfied of the truth, except Pamela, who imagined, as she had never heard either of her parents mention such an accident, that it must be certainly false; and except the Lady Booby, who suspected the falsehood of the story from her ardent desire that it should be true; and Joseph, who feared its truth, from his earnest wishes that it might prove false.

Mr Booby now desired them all to suspend their curiosity and absolute belief or disbelief till the next morning, when he expected old Mr Andrews and his wife to fetch himself and Pamela home in his coach, and then they might be certain of certainly knowing the truth or falsehood of this relation; in which, he said, as there were many strong circumstances to induce their credit, so he could not perceive any interest the pedlar could have in inventing it, or in endeavouring to impose such a falsehood on them.

The Lady Booby, who was very little used to such company, entertained them all—*viz.* her nephew, his wife, her brother and sister, the beau, and the parson, with great good humour at her own table. As to the pedlar, she ordered him to be made as welcome as possible by her servants. All the company in the parlour, except the disappointed lovers, who sat sullen and silent, were full of mirth; for Mr Booby had prevailed on Joseph to ask Mr Didapper's pardon, with which he was perfectly satisfied. Many jokes passed between the beau and the parson, chiefly on each other's dress; these afforded much diversion to the company. Pamela chid her brother Joseph for the concern which he exprest at discovering a new sister. She said, if he loved Fanny as he ought, with a pure affection, he had no reason to lament being related to her.—Upon which Adams began to discourse on Platonic love; whence he made a quick transition to the joys in the next world, and concluded with strongly asserting that there was no such thing as pleasure in this. At which Pamela and her husband smiled on one another.

BOOK IV. CHAPTER XIII.

This happy pair proposing to retire (for no other person gave the least symptom of desiring rest), they all repaired to several beds provided for them in the same house; nor was Adams himself suffered to go home, it being a stormy night. Fanny indeed often begged she might go home with the parson; but her stay was so strongly insisted on, that she at last, by Joseph's advice, consented.

CHAPTER XIV.

Containing several curious night-adventures, in which Mr Adams fell into many hair-breadth 'scapes, partly owing to his goodness, and partly to his inadvertency.

About an hour after they had all separated (it being now past three in the morning), beau Didapper, whose passion for Fanny permitted him not to close his eyes, but had employed his imagination in contrivances how to satisfy his desires, at last hit on a method by which he hoped to effect it. He had ordered his servant to bring him word where Fanny lay, and had received his information; he therefore arose, put on his breeches and nightgown, and stole softly along the gallery which led to her apartment; and, being come to the door, as he imagined it, he opened it with the least noise possible and entered the chamber. A savour now invaded his nostrils which he did not expect in the room of so sweet a young creature, and which might have probably had no good effect on a cooler lover. However, he groped out the bed with difficulty, for there was not a glimpse of light, and, opening the curtains, he whispered in Joseph's voice (for he was an excellent mimic), "Fanny, my angel! I am come to inform thee that I have discovered the falsehood of the story we last night heard. I am no longer thy brother, but the lover; nor will I be delayed the enjoyment of thee one moment longer. You have sufficient assurances of my constancy not to doubt my marrying you, and it would be want of love to deny me the possession of thy charms."—So saying, he disencumbered himself from the little clothes he had on, and, leaping into bed, embraced his angel, as he conceived her, with great rapture. If he was surprized at receiving no answer, he was no less pleased to find his hug returned with equal ardour. He remained not long in this sweet confusion; for both he and his paramour presently discovered their error. Indeed it was no other than the accomplished Slipslop whom he had engaged; but, though she immediately knew the person whom she had mistaken for Joseph, he was at a loss to guess at the representative of Fanny. He had so little seen or taken notice of this gentlewoman, that light itself would have afforded him no assistance in his conjecture. Beau Didapper no sooner had perceived his mistake than he attempted to escape from the bed with much greater haste than he had made to it; but the watchful Slipslop prevented him. For that prudent woman, being disappointed of those delicious offerings which her fancy had promised her pleasure, resolved to make an immediate sacrifice to her virtue. Indeed she wanted an opportunity to heal some wounds, which her late conduct had, she feared, given her reputation; and, as she had a wonderful presence of mind, she conceived the person of the unfortunate beau to be luckily thrown in her way to restore her lady's opinion of her impregnable chastity. At that instant, therefore, when he offered to leap from the bed, she caught fast hold of his shirt, at the same time roaring out, "O thou villain! who hast attacked my chastity, and, I believe, ruined me in my sleep; I will swear a rape against thee, I will prosecute thee with the utmost vengeance." The beau attempted to get loose, but she held him fast, and when he struggled she cried out "Murder! murder! rape! robbery! ruin!" At which words, parson Adams, who lay in the next chamber, wakeful, and meditating on the pedlar's discovery, jumped out of bed, and, without staying to put a rag of clothes on, hastened into the apartment whence the cries proceeded. He made directly to the bed in the dark, where, laying hold of the beau's skin (for Slipslop had torn his shirt almost off), and finding his skin extremely soft, and hearing him in a low voice begging Slipslop to let him go, he no longer doubted but this was the young woman in danger of ravishing, and immediately falling on the bed, and laying hold on Slipslop's chin, where he found a rough beard, his belief was confirmed; he therefore rescued the beau, who presently made his escape, and then, turning towards Slipslop, received such a cuff on his chops, that, his wrath kindling instantly, he offered to return the favour so stoutly, that had poor Slipslop received the fist, which in the dark passed by her and fell on the pillow, she would most probably have given up the ghost. Adams, missing his blow, fell directly on Slipslop, who cuffed and scratched as well as she could; nor was he behindhand with her in his endeavours, but happily the darkness of the night befriended her. She then cried she was a woman; but Adams answered, she was rather the devil, and if she was he would grapple with him; and, being again irritated by another stroke on his chops, he gave her such a remembrance in the guts, that she began to roar loud enough to be heard all over the house. Adams then, seizing her by the hair (for her double-clout had fallen off in the scuffle), pinned her head down to the bolster, and then both called for lights together. The Lady Booby, who was as wakeful as any of her guests, had been alarmed from the beginning; and, being a woman of a bold spirit, she slipt on a nightgown, petticoat, and slippers, and taking a candle, which always burnt in her chamber, in her hand, she walked undauntedly to Slipslop's room; where she entered just at the instant as Adams had discovered, by the two mountains which Slipslop carried before her, that he was concerned with a female. He then concluded her to be a witch, and said he fancied those breasts gave suck to a legion of devils. Slipslop, seeing Lady Booby enter the room, cried help! or I am ravished, with a most audible voice: and Adams, perceiving the light, turned hastily, and saw the lady (as she did him) just as she came to the feet of the bed; nor did her modesty, when she found the naked condition of Adams, suffer her to approach farther. She then began to revile the parson as the wickedest of all men, and particularly railed at his impudence in chusing her house for the scene of his debaucheries, and her own woman for the object of his bestiality. Poor Adams had before discovered the countenance of his bedfellow, and, now first recollecting he was naked, he was no less confounded than Lady Booby herself, and immediately whipt under the bed-clothes, whence the chaste Slipslop endeavoured in vain to shut him out. Then putting forth his head, on which, by way of ornament, he wore a flannel nightcap, he protested his innocence, and asked ten thousand pardons of Mrs Slipslop for the blows he had struck her, vowing he had mistaken her for a witch. Lady Booby, then casting her eyes on the ground, observed something sparkle with great lustre, which, when she had taken it up, appeared to be a very fine pair of diamond buttons for the sleeves. A little farther she saw lie the sleeve itself of a shirt with laced ruffles. "Heyday!" says she, "what is the meaning of this?" "O, madam," says Slipslop, "I don't know what hath happened, I have been so terrified. Here may have been a dozen men in the room." "To whom belongs this laced shirt and jewels?" says the lady. "Undoubtedly," cries the parson, "to the young gentleman whom I mistook for a woman on coming into the room, whence proceeded all the subsequent mistakes; for if I had suspected him for a man, I would have seized him, had he been another Hercules, though, indeed, he seems rather to resemble Hylas." He then gave an account of the reason of his rising from bed, and the rest, till the lady came into the room; at which, and the figures of Slipslop and her gallant, whose heads only were visible at the opposite corners of the bed, she could not refrain from laughter; nor did Slipslop persist in accusing the parson of any motions towards a rape. The lady therefore desired him to return to his bed as soon as she was departed, and then ordering Slipslop to rise and attend her in her own room, she returned herself thither. When she was gone, Adams renewed his petitions for pardon to Mrs Slipslop, who, with a most Christian temper, not only forgave, but began to move with much courtesy towards him, which he taking as a hint to begin, immediately quitted the bed, and made the best of his way towards his own; but unluckily, instead of turning to the right, he turned to the left, and went to the apartment where Fanny lay, who (as the reader may remember) had not slept a wink the preceding night, and who was so hagged out with what had happened to her in the day, that, notwithstanding all thoughts of her Joseph, she was fallen into so profound a sleep, that all the noise in the adjoining room had not been able to disturb her. Adams groped out the bed, and, turning the clothes down softly, a custom Mrs Adams had long accustomed him to, crept in, and deposited his carcase on the bed-post, a place which that good woman had always assigned him.

As the cat or lap-dog of some lovely nymph, for whom ten thousand lovers languish, lies quietly by the side of the charming maid, and, ignorant of the scene of delight on which they repose, meditates the future capture of a mouse, or surprisal of a plate of bread and butter: so Adams lay by the side of Fanny, ignorant of the paradise to which he was so near; nor could the emanation of sweets which flowed from her breath overpower the fumes of tobacco which played in the parson's nostrils. And now sleep had not overtaken the good man, when Joseph, who had secretly appointed Fanny to come to her at the break of day, rapped softly at the chamber-door, which when he had repeated twice, Adams cryed, "Come in, whoever you are." Joseph thought he had mistaken the door, though she had given him the most exact directions; however, knowing his friend's voice, he opened it, and saw some female vestments lying on a chair. Fanny waking at the same instant, and stretching out her hand on Adams's beard, she cried out,—"O heavens! where am I?" "Bless me! where am I?" said the parson. Then Fanny screamed, Adams leapt out of bed, and Joseph stood, as the tragedians call it, like the statue of Surprize. "How came she into my room?" cryed Adams. "How came you into hers?" cryed Joseph, in an astonishment. "I know nothing of the matter," answered Adams, "but that she is a vestal for me. As I am a Christian, I know not whether she is a man or woman. He is an infidel who doth not believe in witchcraft. They as surely exist now as in the days of Saul. My clothes are bewitched away too, and Fanny's brought into their place." For he still insisted he was in his own apartment; but Fanny denied it vehemently, and said his attempting to persuade Joseph of such a falsehood convinced her of his wicked designs. "How!" said Joseph in a rage, "hath he offered any rudeness to you?" She answered—She could not accuse him of any more than villanously stealing to bed to her, which she thought rudeness sufficient, and what no man would do without a wicked intention.

Joseph's great opinion of Adams was not easily to be staggered, and when he heard from Fanny that no harm had happened he grew a little cooler; yet still he was confounded, and, as he knew the house, and that the women's apartments were on this side Mrs Slipslop's room, and the men's on the other, he was convinced that he was in Fanny's chamber. Assuring Adams therefore of this truth, he begged him to give some account how he came there. Adams then, standing in his shirt, which did not offend Fanny, as the curtains of the bed were drawn, related all that had happened; and when he had ended Joseph told him,—It was plain he had mistaken by turning to the right instead of the left. "Odso!" cries Adams, "that's true: as sure as sixpence, you have hit on the very thing." He then traversed the room, rubbing his hands, and begged Fanny's pardon, assuring her he did not know whether she was man or woman. That innocent creature firmly believing all he said, told him she was no longer angry, and begged Joseph to conduct him into his own apartment, where he should stay himself till she had put her clothes on. Joseph and Adams accordingly departed, and the latter soon was convinced of the mistake he had committed; however, whilst he was dressing himself, he often asserted he believed in the power of witchcraft notwithstanding, and did not see how a Christian could deny it.

CHAPTER XV.

The arrival of Gaffar and Gammar Andrews, with another person not much expected; and a perfect solution of the difficulties raised by the pedlar.

As soon as Fanny was drest Joseph returned to her, and they had a long conversation together, the conclusion of which was, that, if they found themselves to be really brother and sister, they vowed a perpetual celibacy, and to live together all their days, and indulge a Platonic friendship for each other.

The company were all very merry at breakfast, and Joseph and Fanny rather more chearful than the preceding night. The Lady Booby produced the diamond button, which the beau most readily owned, and alledged that he was very subject to walk in his sleep. Indeed, he was far from being ashamed of his amour, and rather endeavoured to insinuate that more than was really true had passed between him and the fair Slipslop.

Their tea was scarce over when news came of the arrival of old Mr Andrews and his wife. They were immediately introduced, and kindly received by the Lady Booby, whose heart went now pit-a-pat, as did those of Joseph and Fanny. They felt, perhaps, little less anxiety in this interval than Oedipus himself, whilst his fate was revealing.

Mr Booby first opened the cause by informing the old gentleman that he had a child in the company more than he knew of, and, taking Fanny by the hand, told him, this was that daughter of his who had been stolen away by gypsies in her infancy. Mr Andrews, after expressing some astonishment, assured his honour that he had never lost a daughter by gypsies, nor ever had any other children than Joseph and Pamela. These words were a cordial to the two lovers; but had a different effect on Lady Booby. She ordered the pedlar to be called, who recounted his story as he had done before.—At the end of which, old Mrs Andrews, running to Fanny, embraced her, crying out, "She is, she is my child!" The company were all amazed at this disagreement between the man and his wife; and the blood had now forsaken the cheeks of the lovers, when the old woman, turning to her husband, who was more surprized than all the rest, and having a little recovered her own spirits, delivered herself as follows: "You may remember, my dear, when you went a serjeant to Gibraltar, you left me big with child; you stayed abroad, you know, upwards of three years. In your absence I was brought to bed, I verily believe, of this daughter, whom I am sure I have reason to remember, for I suckled her at this very breast till the day she was stolen from me. One afternoon, when the child was about a year, or a year and a half old, or thereabouts, two gypsy-women came to the door and offered to tell my fortune. One of them had a child in her lap. I showed them my hand, and desired to know if you was ever to come home again, which I remember as well as if it was but yesterday: they faithfully promised me you should.—I left the girl in the cradle and went to draw them a cup of liquor, the best I had: when I returned with the pot (I am sure I was not absent longer than whilst I am telling it to you) the women were gone. I was afraid they had stolen something, and looked and looked, but to no purpose, and, Heaven knows, I had very little for them to steal. At last, hearing the child cry in the cradle, I went to take it up—but, O the living! how was I surprized to find, instead of my own girl that I had put into the cradle, who was as fine a fat thriving child as you shall see in a summer's day, a poor sickly boy, that did not seem to have an hour to live. I ran out, pulling my hair off and crying like any mad after the women, but never could hear a word of them from that day to this. When I came back the poor infant (which is our Joseph there, as stout as he now stands) lifted up its eyes upon me so piteously, that, to be sure, notwithstanding my passion, I could not find in my heart to do it any mischief. A neighbour of mine, happening to come in at the same time, and hearing the case, advised me to take care of this poor child, and God would perhaps one day restore me my own. Upon which I took the child up, and suckled it to be sure, all the world as if it had been born of my own natural body; and as true as I am alive, in a little time I loved the boy all to nothing as if it had been my own girl.—Well, as I was saying, times growing very hard, I having two children and nothing but my own work, which was little enough, God knows, to maintain them, was obliged to ask relief of the parish; but, instead of giving it me, they removed me, by justices' warrants, fifteen miles, to the place where I now live, where I had not been long settled before you came home. Joseph (for that was the name I gave him myself—the Lord knows whether he was baptized or no, or by what name), Joseph, I say, seemed to me about five years old when you returned; for I believe he is two or three years older than our daughter here (for I am thoroughly convinced she is the same); and when you saw him you said he was a chopping boy, without ever minding his age; and so I, seeing you did not suspect anything of the matter, thought I might e'en as well keep it to myself, for fear you should not love him as well as I did. And all this is veritably true, and I will take my oath of it before any justice in the kingdom."

The pedlar, who had been summoned by the order of Lady Booby, listened with the utmost attention to Gammar Andrews's story; and, when she had finished, asked her if the supposititious child had no mark on its breast? To which she answered, "Yes, he had as fine a strawberry as ever grew in a garden." This Joseph acknowledged, and, unbuttoning his coat, at the intercession of the company, showed to them. "Well," says Gaffar Andrews, who was a comical sly old fellow, and very likely desired to have no more children than he could keep, "you have proved, I think, very plainly, that this boy doth not belong to us; but how are you certain that the girl is ours?" The parson then brought the pedlar forward, and desired him to repeat the story which he had communicated to him the preceding day at the ale-house; which he complied with, and related what the reader, as well as Mr Adams, hath seen before. He then confirmed, from his wife's report, all the circumstances of the exchange, and of the strawberry on Joseph's breast. At the repetition of the word strawberry, Adams, who had seen it without any emotion, started and cried, "Bless me! something comes into my head." But before he had time to bring anything out a servant called him forth. When he was gone the pedlar assured Joseph that his parents were persons of much greater circumstances than those he had hitherto mistaken for such; for that he had been stolen from a gentleman's house by those whom they call gypsies, and had been kept by them during a whole year, when, looking on him as in a dying condition, they had exchanged him for the other healthier child, in the manner before related. He said, As to the name of his father, his wife had either never known or forgot it; but that she had acquainted him he lived about forty miles from the place where the exchange had been made, and which way, promising to spare no pains in endeavouring with him to discover the place.

But Fortune, which seldom doth good or ill, or makes men happy or miserable, by halves, resolved to spare him this labour. The reader may please to recollect that Mr Wilson had intended a journey to the west, in which he was to pass through Mr Adams's parish, and had promised to call on him. He was now arrived at the Lady Booby's gates for that purpose, being directed thither from the parson's house, and had sent in the servant whom we have above seen call Mr Adams forth. This had no sooner mentioned the discovery of a stolen child, and had uttered the word strawberry, than Mr Wilson, with wildness in his looks, and the utmost eagerness in his words, begged to be shewed into the room, where he entered without the least regard to any of the company but Joseph, and, embracing him with a complexion all pale and trembling, desired to see the mark on his breast; the parson followed him capering, rubbing his hands, and crying out, *Hic est quem quaeris; inventus est, &c.* Joseph complied with the request of Mr Wilson, who no sooner saw the mark than, abandoning himself to the most extravagant rapture of passion, he embraced Joseph with inexpressible ecstasy, and cried out in tears of joy, "I have discovered my son, I have him again in my arms!" Joseph was not sufficiently apprized yet to taste the same delight with his father (for so in reality he was); however, he returned some warmth to his embraces: but he no sooner perceived, from his father's account, the agreement of every circumstance, of person, time, and place, than he threw himself at his feet, and, embracing his knees, with tears begged his blessing, which was given with much affection, and received with such respect, mixed with such tenderness on both sides, that it affected all present; but none so much as Lady Booby, who left the room in an agony, which was but too much perceived, and not very charitably accounted for by some of the company.

CHAPTER XVI.

Being the last in which this true history is brought to a happy conclusion.

Fanny was very little behind her Joseph in the duty she exprest towards her parents, and the joy she evidenced in discovering them. Gammar Andrews kissed her, and said, She was heartily glad to see her; but for her part, she could never love any one better than Joseph. Gaffar Andrews testified no remarkable emotion: he blessed and kissed her, but complained bitterly that he wanted his pipe, not having had a whiff that morning.

Mr Booby, who knew nothing of his aunt's fondness, imputed her abrupt departure to her pride, and disdain of the family into which he was married; he was therefore desirous to be gone with the utmost celerity; and now, having congratulated Mr Wilson and Joseph on the discovery, he saluted Fanny, called her sister, and introduced her as such to Pamela, who behaved with great decency on the occasion.

He now sent a message to his aunt, who returned that she wished him a good journey, but was too disordered to see any company: he therefore prepared to set out, having invited Mr Wilson to his house; and Pamela and Joseph both so insisted on his complying, that he at last consented, having first obtained a messenger from Mr Booby to acquaint his wife with the news; which, as he knew it would render her completely happy, he could not prevail on himself to delay a moment in acquainting her with.

The company were ranged in this manner: the two old people, with their two daughters, rode in the coach; the squire, Mr Wilson, Joseph, parson Adams, and the pedlar, proceeded on horseback.

In their way, Joseph informed his father of his intended match with Fanny; to which, though he expressed some reluctance at first, on the eagerness of his son's instances he consented; saying, if she was so good a creature as she appeared, and he described her, he thought the disadvantages of birth and fortune might be compensated. He however insisted on the match being deferred till he had seen his mother; in which, Joseph perceiving him positive, with great duty obeyed him, to the great delight of parson Adams, who by these means saw an opportunity of fulfilling the Church forms, and marrying his parishioners without a licence.

Mr Adams, greatly exulting on this occasion (for such ceremonies were matters of no small moment with him), accidentally gave spurs to his horse, which the generous beast disdaining—for he was of high mettle, and had been used to more expert riders than the gentleman who at present bestrode him, for whose horsemanship he had perhaps some contempt—immediately ran away full speed, and played so many antic tricks that he tumbled the parson from his back; which Joseph perceiving, came to his relief.

This accident afforded infinite merriment to the servants, and no less frighted poor Fanny, who beheld him as he passed by the coach; but the mirth of the one and terror of the other were soon determined, when the parson declared he had received no damage.

The horse having freed himself from his unworthy rider, as he probably thought him, proceeded to make the best of his way; but was stopped by a gentleman and his servants, who were travelling the opposite way, and were now at a little distance from the coach. They soon met; and as one of the servants delivered Adams his horse, his master hailed him, and Adams, looking up, presently recollected he was the justice of peace before whom he and Fanny had made their appearance. The parson presently saluted him very kindly; and the justice informed him that he had found the fellow who attempted to swear against him and the young woman the very next day, and had committed him to Salisbury gaol, where he was charged with many robberies.

Many compliments having passed between the parson and the justice, the latter proceeded on his journey; and the former, having with some disdain refused Joseph's offer of changing horses, and declared he was as able a horseman as any in the kingdom, remounted his beast; and now the company again proceeded, and happily arrived at their journey's end, Mr Adams, by good luck, rather than by good riding, escaping a second fall.

The company, arriving at Mr Booby's house, were all received by him in the most courteous and entertained in the most splendid manner, after the custom of the old English hospitality, which is still preserved in some very few families in the remote parts of England. They all passed that day with the utmost satisfaction; it being perhaps impossible to find any set of people more solidly and sincerely happy. Joseph and Fanny found means to be alone upwards of two hours, which were the shortest but the sweetest imaginable.

In the morning Mr Wilson proposed to his son to make a visit with him to his mother; which, notwithstanding his dutiful inclinations, and a longing desire he had to see her, a little concerned him, as he must be obliged to leave his Fanny; but the goodness of Mr Booby relieved him; for he proposed to send his own coach and six for Mrs Wilson, whom Pamela so very earnestly invited, that Mr Wilson at length agreed with the entreaties of Mr Booby and Joseph, and suffered the coach to go empty for his wife.

On Saturday night the coach returned with Mrs Wilson, who added one more to this happy assembly. The reader may imagine much better and quicker too than I can describe the many embraces and tears of joy which succeeded her arrival. It is sufficient to say she was easily prevailed with to follow her husband's example in consenting to the match.

On Sunday Mr Adams performed the service at the squire's parish church, the curate of which very kindly exchanged duty, and rode twenty miles to the Lady Booby's parish so to do; being particularly charged not to omit publishing the banns, being the third and last time.

At length the happy day arrived which was to put Joseph in the possession of all his wishes. He arose, and drest himself in a neat but plain suit of Mr Booby's, which exactly fitted him; for he refused all finery; as did Fanny likewise, who could be prevailed on by Pamela to attire herself in nothing richer than a white dimity nightgown. Her shift indeed, which Pamela presented her, was of the finest kind, and had an edging of lace round the bosom. She likewise equipped her with a pair of fine white thread stockings, which were all she would accept; for she wore one of her own short round-eared caps, and over it a little straw hat, lined with cherry-coloured silk, and tied with a cherry-coloured ribbon. In this dress she came forth from her chamber, blushing and breathing sweets; and was by Joseph, whose eyes sparkled fire, led to church, the whole family attending, where Mr Adams performed the ceremony; at which nothing was so remarkable as the extraordinary and unaffected modesty of Fanny, unless the true Christian piety of Adams, who publickly rebuked Mr Booby and Pamela for laughing in so sacred a place, and on so solemn an occasion. Our parson would have done no less to the highest prince on earth; for, though he paid all submission and deference to his superiors in other matters, where the least spice of religion intervened he immediately lost all respect of persons. It was his maxim, that he was a servant of the Highest, and could not, without departing from his duty, give up the least article of his honour or of his cause to the greatest earthly potentate. Indeed, he always asserted that Mr Adams at church with his surplice on, and Mr Adams without that ornament in any other place, were two very different persons.

When the church rites were over Joseph led his blooming bride back to Mr Booby's (for the distance was so very little they did not think proper to use a coach); the whole company attended them likewise on foot; and now a most magnificent entertainment was provided, at which parson Adams demonstrated an appetite surprizing as well as surpassing every one present. Indeed the only persons who betrayed any deficiency on this occasion were those on whose account the feast was provided. They pampered their imaginations with the much more exquisite repast which the approach of night promised them; the thoughts of which filled both their minds, though with different sensations; the one all desire, while the other had her wishes tempered with fears.

At length, after a day passed with the utmost merriment, corrected by the strictest decency, in which, however, parson Adams, being well filled with ale and pudding, had given a loose to more facetiousness than was usual to him, the happy, the blest moment arrived when Fanny retired with her mother, her mother-in-law, and her sister.

She was soon undrest; for she had no jewels to deposit in their caskets, nor fine laces to fold with the nicest exactness. Undressing to her was properly discovering, not putting off, ornaments; for, as all her charms were the gifts of nature, she could divest herself of none. How, reader, shall I give thee an adequate idea of this lovely young creature? the bloom of roses and lilies might a little illustrate her complexion, or their smell her sweetness; but to comprehend her entirely, conceive youth, health, bloom, neatness, and innocence, in her bridal bed; conceive all these in their utmost perfection, and you may place the charming Fanny's picture before your eyes.

Joseph no sooner heard she was in bed than he fled with the utmost eagerness to her. A minute carried him into her arms, where we shall leave this happy couple to enjoy the private rewards of their constancy; rewards so great and sweet, that I apprehend Joseph neither envied the noblest duke, nor Fanny the finest duchess, that night.

The third day Mr Wilson and his wife, with their son and daughter, returned home; where they now live together in a state of bliss scarce ever equalled. Mr Booby hath, with unprecedented generosity, given Fanny a fortune of two thousand pounds, which Joseph hath laid out in a little estate in the same parish with his father, which he now occupies (his father having stocked it for him); and Fanny presides with most excellent management in his dairy; where, however, she is not at present very able to bustle much, being, as Mr Wilson informs me in his last letter, extremely big with her first child.

Mr Booby hath presented Mr Adams with a living of one hundred and thirty pounds a year. He at first refused it, resolving not to quit his parishioners, with whom he had lived so long; but, on recollecting he might keep a curate at this living, he hath been lately inducted into it.

The pedlar, besides several handsome presents, both from Mr Wilson and Mr Booby, is, by the latter's interest, made an exciseman; a trust which he discharges with such justice, that he is greatly beloved in his neighbourhood.

As for the Lady Booby, she returned to London in a few days, where a young captain of dragoons, together with eternal parties at cards, soon obliterated the memory of Joseph.

Joseph remains blest with his Fanny, whom he doats on with the utmost tenderness, which is all returned on her side. The happiness of this couple is a perpetual fountain of pleasure to their fond parents; and, what is particularly remarkable, he declares he will imitate them in their retirement, nor will be prevailed on by any booksellers, or their authors, to make his appearance in high life.

THE END.

AN APOLOGY FOR THE LIFE OF MRS. SHAMELA ANDREWS.

In which, the many notorious FALSHOODS and MISREPRSENTATIONS of a Book called

PAMELA,

Are exposed and refuted; and all the matchless ARTS of that young Politician, set in a true and just Light.
Together with

A full Account of all that passed between her and Parson *Arthur Williams*; whose Character is represented in a manner something different from that which he bears in *PAMELA*. The whole being exact Copies of authentick Papers delivered to the Editor.

Necessary to be had in all FAMILIES.
By Mr. *CONNY KEYBER*.

To Miss *Fanny, &c.*

MADAM,

It will be naturally expected, that when I write the Life of *Shamela*, I should dedicate it to some young Lady, whose Wit and Beauty might be the proper Subject of a Comparison with the Heroine of my Piece. This, those, who see I have done it in prefixing your Name to my Work, will much more confirmedly expect me to do; and, indeed, your Character would enable me to run some Length into a Parallel, tho' you, nor any one else, are at all like the matchless *Shamela*.

You see, Madam, I have some Value for your Good-nature, when in a Dedication, which is properly a Panegyrick, I speak against, not for you; but I remember it is a Life which I am presenting you, and why should I expose my Veracity to any Hazard in the Front of the Work, considering what I have done in the Body. Indeed, I wish it was possible to write a Dedication, and get any thing by it, without one Word of Flattery; but since it is not, come on, and I hope to shew my Delicacy at least in the Compliments I intend to pay you.

First, then, Madam, I must tell the World, that you have tickled up and brightned many Strokes in this Work by your Pencil.

Secondly, You have intimately conversed with me, one of the greatest Wits and Scholars of my Age.

Thirdly, You keep very good Hours, and frequently spend an useful Day before others begin to enjoy it. This I will take my Oath on; for I am admitted to your Presence in a Morning before other People's Servants are up; when I have constantly found you reading in good Books; and if ever I have drawn you upon me, I have always felt you very heavy.

Fourthly, You have a Virtue which enables you to rise early and study hard, and that is, forbearing to over-eat yourself, and this in spite of all the luscious Temptations of Puddings and Custards, exciting the Brute (as Dr. *Woodward* calls it) to rebel. This is a Virtue which I can greatly admire, though I much question whether I could imitate it.

Fifthly, A Circumstance greatly to your Honour, that by means of your extraordinary Merit and Beauty; you was carried into the Ball-Room at the *Bath*, by the discerning Mr. *Nash*; before the Age that other young Ladies generally arrived at that Honour, and while your Mamma herself existed in her perfect Bloom. Here you was observed in Dancing to balance your Body exactly, and to weigh every Motion with the exact and equal Measure of Time and Tune; and though you sometimes made a false Step, by leaning too much to one Side; yet every body said you would one time or other, dance perfectly well, and uprightly.

Sixthly, I cannot forbear mentioning those pretty little Sonnets, and sprightly Compositions, which though they came from you with so much Ease, might be mentioned to the Praise of a great or grave Character.

And now, Madam, I have done with you; it only remains to pay my Acknowledgments to an Author, whose Stile I have exactly followed in this Life, it being the properest for Biography. The Reader, I believe, easily guesses, I mean *Euclid's Elements*; it was *Euclid* who taught me to write. It is you, Madam, who pay me for Writing. Therefore I am to both,

A most Obedient, and
obliged humble Servant,
Conny Keyber.

LETTERS TO THE EDITOR.

The EDITOR to *Himself.*

Dear SIR,

However you came by the excellent *Shamela*, out with it, without Fear or Favour, Dedication and all; believe me, it will go through many Editions, be translated into all Languages, read in all Nations and Ages, and to say a bold Word, it will do more good than the *C——y* have done harm in the World,

I am, Sir,
Sincerely your Well-wisher,
Yourself.

JOHN PUFF, *Esq; to the* EDITOR.

SIR,

I have read your *Shamela* through and through, and a most inimitable Performance it is. Who is he, what is he that could write so excellent a Book? he must be doubtless most agreeable to the Age, and to *his Honour* himself; for he is able to draw every thing to Perfection but Virtue. Whoever the Author be, he hath one of the worst and most fashionable Hearts in the World, and I would recommend to him, in his next Performance, to undertake the Life of *his Honour*. For he who drew the Character of Parson *Williams*, is equal to the Task; nay he seems to have little more to do than to pull off the Parson's Gown, and *that* which makes him so agreeable to *Shamela*, and the Cap will fit.

I am, Sir,
Your humble Servant,
JOHN PUFF.

Note, Reader, several other COMMENDATORY LETTERS and COPIES OF VERSES will be prepared against the NEXT EDITION.

AN APOLOGY For the LIFE of Mrs. SHAMELA ANDREWS.
Parson TICKLETEXT *to Parson* OLIVER.

Rev. SIR,

Herewith I transmit you a Copy of sweet, dear, pretty *Pamela*, a little Book which this Winter hath produced, of which, I make no doubt, you have already heard mention from some of your Neighbouring Clergy; for we have made it our common Business here, not only to cry it up, but to preach it up likewise: The Pulpit, as well as the Coffee-house, hath resounded with its Praise, and it is expected shortly, that his L—p will recommend it in a —— Letter to our whole Body.

And this Example, I am confident, will be imitated by all our Cloth in the Country: For besides speaking well of a Brother, in the Character of the Reverend Mr. *Williams*, the useful and truly religious Doctrine of *Grace* is every where inculcated.

This Book is the "SOUL of *Religion*, Good-Breeding, Discretion, Good-Nature, Wit, Fancy, Fine Thought, and Morality. There is an Ease, a natural Air, a dignified Simplicity, and MEASURED FULLNESS in it, that RESEMBLING LIFE, OUT-GLOWS IT. The Author hath reconciled the *pleasing* to the *proper*; the Thought is every where exactly cloathed by the Expression; and becomes its Dress as *roundly* and as close as *Pamela* her Country Habit; or *as she doth her no Habit*, when modest Beauty seeks to hide itself, by casting off the Pride of Ornament, and displays itself without any Covering;" which it frequently doth in this admirable Work, and presents Images to the Reader, which the coldest Zealot cannot read without Emotion.

For my own Part (and, I believe, I may say the same of all the Clergy of my Acquaintance) "I have done nothing but read it to others, and hear others again read it to me, ever since it came into my Hands; and I find I am like to do nothing else, for I know not how long yet to come: because if I lay the Book down *it comes after me*. When it has dwelt all Day long upon the Ear, it takes Possession all Night of the Fancy. It hath Witchcraft in every Page of it.——Oh! I feel an Emotion even while I am relating this: Methinks I see *Pamela* at this Instant, with all the Pride of Ornament cast off.

"Little Book, charming *Pamela*, get thee gone; face the World, in which thou wilt find nothing like thyself." Happy would it be for Mankind, if all other Books were burnt, that we might do nothing but read thee all Day, and dream of thee all Night. Thou alone art sufficient to teach us as much Morality as we want. Dost thou not teach us to pray, to sing Psalms, and to honour the Clergy? Are not these the whole Duty of Man? Forgive me, O Author of *Pamela*, mentioning the Name of a Book so unequal to thine: But, now I think of it, who is the Author, where is he, what is he, that hath hitherto been able to hide such an encircling, all-mastering Spirit, "he possesses every Quality that Art could have charm'd by: yet hath lent it to and concealed it in Nature. The Comprehensiveness of his Imagination must be truly prodigious! It has stretched out this diminutive mere Grain of Mustard-seed (a poor Girl's little, *&c.*) into a Resemblance of that Heaven, which the best of good Books has compared it to."

To be short, this Book will live to the Age of the Patriarchs, and like them will carry on the good Work many hundreds of Years hence, among our Posterity, who will not HESITATE their Esteem with Restraint. If the *Romans* granted Exemptions to Men who begat a *few* Children for the Republick, what Distinction (if

Policy and we should ever be reconciled) should we find to reward this Father of Millions, which are to owe Formation to the future Effect of his Influence.——I feel another Emotion.

As soon as you have read this yourself five or six Times over (which may possibly happen within a Week) I desire you would give it to my little God-Daughter, as a Present from me. This being the only Education we intend henceforth to give our Daughters. And pray let your Servant-Maids read it over, or read it to them. Both your self and the neighbouring Clergy, will supply yourselves for the Pulpit from the Book-sellers, as soon as the fourth Edition is published. I am,

Sir,

Your most humble Servant,

THO. TICKLETEXT.

Parson OLIVER *to Parson* TICKLETEXT.

Rev. SIR,

I Received the Favour of yours with the inclosed Book, and really must own myself sorry, to see the Report I have heard of an epidemical Phrenzy now raging in Town, confirmed in the Person of my Friend.

If I had not known your Hand, I should, from the Sentiments and Stile of the Letter, have imagined it to have come from the Author of the famous Apology, which was sent me last Summer; and on my reading the remarkable Paragraph of *measured Fulness, that resembling Life out-glows it*, to a young Baronet, he cry'd out, *C——ly C——b—r* by G——. But I have since observed, that this, as well as many other Expressions in your Letter, was borrowed from those remarkable Epistles, which the Author, or the Editor hath prefix'd to the second Edition which you send me of his Book.

Is it possible that you or any of your Function can be in earnest, or think the Cause of Religion, or Morality, can want such slender Support? God forbid they should. As for Honour to the Clergy, I am sorry to see them so solicitous about it; for if worldly Honour be meant, it is what their Predecessors in the pure and primitive Age, never had or sought. Indeed the secure Satisfaction of a good Conscience, the Approbation of the Wise and Good, (which, never were or will be the Generality of Mankind) and the extatick Pleasure of contemplating, that their Ways are acceptable to the Great Creator of the Universe, will always attend those, who really deserve these Blessings: But for worldly Honours, they are often the Purchase of Force and Fraud, we sometimes see them in an eminent Degree possessed by Men, who are notorious for Luxury, Pride, Cruelty, Treachery, and the most abandoned Prostitution; Wretches who are ready to invent and maintain Schemes repugnant to the Interest, the Liberty, and the Happiness of Mankind, not to supply their Necessities, or even Conveniencies, but to pamper their Avarice and Ambition. And if this be the Road to worldly Honours, God forbid the Clergy should be even suspected of walking in it.

The History of *Pamela* I was acquainted with long before I received it from you, from my Neighbourhood to the Scene of Action. Indeed I was in hopes that young Woman would have contented herself with the Good-fortune she hath attained; and rather suffered her little Arts to have been forgotten than have revived their Remembrance, and endeavoured by perverting and misrepresenting Facts to be thought to deserve what she now enjoys: for though we do not imagine her the Author of the Narrative itself, yet we must suppose the Instructions were given by her, as well as the Reward, to the Composer. Who that is, though you so earnestly require of me, I shall leave you to guess from that *Ciceronian* Eloquence, with which the Work abounds; and that excellent Knack of making every Character amiable, which he lays his hands on.

But before I send you some Papers relating to this Matter, which will set *Pamela* and some others in a very different Light, than that in which they appear in the printed Book, I must beg leave to make some few Remarks on the Book itself, and its Tendency, (admitting it to be a true Relation,) towards improving Morality, or doing any good, either to the present Age, or Posterity: which when I have done, I shall, I flatter myself, stand excused from delivering it, either into the hands of my Daughter, or my Servant-Maid.

The Instruction which it conveys to Servant-Maids, is, I think, very plainly this, To look out for their Masters as sharp as they can. The Consequences of which will be, besides Neglect of their Business, and the using all manner of Means to come at Ornaments of their Persons, that if the Master is not a Fool, they will be debauched by him; and if he is a Fool, they will marry him. Neither of which, I apprehend, my good Friend, we desire should be the Case of our Sons.

And notwithstanding our Author's Professions of Modesty, which in my Youth I have heard at the Beginning of an Epilogue, I cannot agree that my Daughter should entertain herself with some of his Pictures; which I do not expect to be contemplated without Emotion, unless by one of my Age and Temper, who can see the Girl lie on her Back, with one Arm round Mrs. *Jewkes* and the other round the Squire, naked in Bed, with his Hand on her Breasts, *&c.* with as much Indifference as I read any other Page in the whole Novel. But surely this, and some other Descriptions, will not be put into the hands of his Daughter by any wise Man, though I believe it will be difficult for him to keep them from her; especially if the Clergy in Town have cried and preached it up as you say.

But, my Friend, the whole Narrative is such a Misrepresentation of Facts, such a Perversion of Truth, as you will, I am perswaded, agree, as soon as you have perused the Papers I now inclose to you, that I hope you or some other well-disposed Person, will communicate these Papers to the Publick, that this little Jade may not impose on the World, as she hath on her Master.

The true name of this Wench was SHAMELA, and not *Pamela*, as she stiles herself. Her Father had in his Youth the Misfortune to appear in no good Light at the *Old-Bailey*; he afterwards served in the Capacity of a Drummer in one of the *Scotch* Regiments in the *Dutch* Service; where being drummed out, he came over to *England*, and turned Informer against several Persons on the late Gin-Act; and becoming acquainted with an Hostler at an Inn, where a *Scotch* Gentleman's Horses stood, he hath at last by his Interest obtain'd a pretty snug Place in the

Custom-house. Her Mother sold Oranges in the Play-House; and whether she was married to her Father or no, I never could learn.

After this short Introduction, the rest of her History will appear in the following Letters, which I assure you are authentick.

LETTER I.

SHAMELA ANDREWS *to Mrs.* HENRIETTA MARIA HONORA ANDREWS *at her Lodgings at the* Fan *and* Pepper-Box *in* Drury-Lane.

Dear Mamma,

This comes to acquaint you, that I shall set out in the Waggon on *Monday*, desiring you to commodate me with a Ludgin, as near you as possible, in *Coulstin's-Court*, or *Wild-Street*, or somewhere thereabouts; pray let it be handsome, and not above two Stories high: For Parson *Williams* hath promised to visit me when he comes to Town, and I have got a good many fine Cloaths of the Old Put my Mistress's, who died a wil ago; and I beleve Mrs. *Jervis* will come along with me, for she says she would like to keep a House somewhere about *Short's-Gardens*, or towards *Queen-Street*; and if there was convenience for a *Bannio*, she should like it the better; but that she will settle herself when she comes to Town.——*O! How I long to be in the Balconey at the Old House*——so no more at present from

Your affectionate Daughter,
SHAMELA.

LETTER II.

SHAMELA ANDREWS *to* HENRIETTA MARIA HONORA ANDREWS.

Dear Mamma,

O what News, since I writ my last! the young Squire hath been here, and as sure as a Gun he hath taken a Fancy to me; *Pamela*, says he, (for so I am called here) you was a great Favourite of your late Mistress's; yes, an't please your Honour; says I; and I believe you deserved it, says he; thank your Honour for your good Opinion, says I; and then he took me by the Hand, and I pretended to be shy: Laud, says I, Sir, I hope you don't intend to be rude; no, says he, my Dear, and then he kissed me, 'till he took away my breath——and I pretended to be Angry, and to get away, and then he kissed me again, and breathed very short, and looked very silly; and by Ill-Luck Mrs. *Jervis* came in, and had like to have spoiled Sport.——*How troublesome is such Interruption!* You shall hear now soon, for I shall not come away yet, so I rest,

Your affectionate Daughter,
SHAMELA.

LETTER III.

HENRIETTA MARIA HONORA ANDREWS *to* SHAMELA ANDREWS.

Dear Sham,

Your last Letter hath put me into a great hurry of Spirits, for you have a very difficult Part to act. I hope you will remember your Slip with Parson *Williams*, and not be guilty of any more such Folly. Truly, a Girl who hath once known what is what, is in the highest Degree inexcusable if she respects her *Digressions*; but a Hint of this is sufficient. When Mrs. *Jervis* thinks of coming to Town, I believe I can procure her a good House, and fit for the Business; so I am,

Your affectionate Mother,
HENRIETTA MARIA HONORA ANDREWS.

LETTER IV.

SHAMELA ANDREWS *to* HENRIETTA MARIA HONORA ANDREWS.

Marry come up, good Madam, the Mother had never looked into the Oven for her Daughter, if she had not been there herself. I shall never have done if you upbraid me with having had a small One by *Arthur Williams*, when you yourself—but I say no more. *O! What fine Times when the Kettle calls the Pot.* Let me do what I will, I say my Prayers as often as another, and I read in good Books, as often as I have Leisure; and Parson *William* says, that will make amends.—So no more, but I rest

Your afflicted Daughter,
S——.

LETTER V.

HENRIETTA MARIA HONORA ANDREWS *to* SHAMELA ANDREWS.

Dear Child,

Why will you give such way to your Passion? How could you imagine I should be such a Simpleton, as to upbraid thee with being thy Mother's own Daughter! When I advised you not to be guilty of Folly, I meant no more than that you should take care to be well paid before-hand, and not trust to Promises, which a Man seldom keeps, after he hath had his wicked Will. And seeing you have a rich Fool to deal with, your not making a good Market will be the more inexcusable; indeed, with such Gentlemen as Parson *Williams*, there is more to be said; for they have nothing to give, and are commonly otherwise the best sort of Men. I am glad to hear you read good Books, pray continue so to do. I have inclosed you one of Mr. *Whitefield's* Sermons, and also the Dealings with him, and am

Your affectionate Mother,
HENRIETTA MARIA, *&c.*

LETTER VI.

SHAMELA ANDREWS *to* HENRIETTA MARIA HONORA ANDREWS.

O Madam, I have strange Things to tell you! As I was reading in that charming Book about the Dealings, in comes my Master—to be sure he is a precious One. *Pamela*, says he, what Book is that, I warrant you *Rochester's* Poems.—No, forsooth, says I, as pertly as I could; why how now Saucy Chops, Boldface, says he—Mighty pretty Words, says I, pert again.—Yes (says he) you are a d—d, impudent, stinking, cursed, confounded Jade, and I have a great Mind to kick your A——. You, kiss —— says I. A-gad, says he, and so I will; with that he caught me in his Arms, and kissed me till he made my Face all over Fire. Now this served purely you know, to put upon the Fool for Anger. O! What precious Fools Men are! And so I flung from him in a mighty Rage, and pretended as how I would go out at the Door; but when I came to the End of the Room, I stood still, and my Master cryed out, Hussy, Slut, Saucebox, Boldface, come hither——Yes to be sure, says I; why don't you come, says he; what should I come for says I; if you don't come to me, I'll come to you, says he; I shan't come to you I assure you, says I. Upon which he run up, caught me in his Arms, and flung me upon a Chair, and began to offer to touch my Under-Petticoat. Sir, says I, you had better not offer to be rude; well, says he, no more I won't then; and away he went out of the Room. I was so mad to be sure I could have cry'd.

Oh what a prodigious Vexation it is to a Woman to be made a Fool of.

Mrs. *Jervis* who had been without, harkening, now came to me. She burst into a violent Laugh the Moment she came in. Well, says she, as soon as she could speak, I have Reason to bless myself that I am an Old Woman. Ah Child! if you had known the Jolly Blades of my Age, you would not have been left in the lurch in this manner. Dear Mrs. *Jervis*, says I, don't laugh at one; and to be sure I was a little angry With her.——Come, says she, my dear Honeysuckle, I have one Game to play for you; he shall see you in Bed; he shall, my little Rosebud, he shall see those pretty, little, white, round, panting——and offer'd to pull off my Handkerchief.—Fie, Mrs. *Jervis*, says I, you make me blush, and upon my Fackins, I believe she did: She went on thus. I know the Squire likes you, and notwithstanding the Aukwardness of his Proceeding, I am convinced hath some hot Blood in his Veins, which will not let him rest, 'till he hath communicated some of his Warmth to thee my little Angel; I heard him last Night at our Door, trying if it was open, now to-night I will take care it shall be so; I warrant that he makes the second Trial; which if he doth, he shall find us ready to receive him. I will at first counterfeit Sleep, and after a Swoon; so that he will have you naked in his Possession: and then if you are disappointed, a Plague of all young Squires, say I.——And so, Mrs. *Jervis*, says I, you would have me yield myself to him, would you; you would have me be a second Time a Fool for nothing. Thank you for that, Mrs. *Jervis*. For nothing! marry forbid, says she, you know he hath large Sums of Money, besides abundance of fine Things; and do you think, when you have inflamed him, by giving his Hand a Liberty with that charming Person; and that you know he may easily think he obtains against your Will, he will not give any thing to come at all——. This will not do, Mrs. *Jervis*, answered I. I Have heard my Mamma say, (and so you know, Madam, I have) that in her Youth, Fellows have often taken away in the Morning, what they gave over Night. No, Mrs. *Jervis*, nothing under a regular taking into Keeping, a settled Settlement, for me, and all my Heirs, all my whole Life-time, shall do the Business——or else cross-legged, is the Word, faith, with *Sham*; and then I snapt my Fingers.

Thursday Night, Twelve o'Clock.

Mrs. *Jervis* and I are just in Bed, and the Door unlocked; if my Master should come——Odsbobs! I hear him just coming in at the Door. You see I write in the present Tense, as Parson *Williams* says. Well, he is in Bed between us, we both shamming a Sleep, he steals his Hand into my Bosom, which I, as if in my Sleep, press close to me with mine, and then pretend to awake.—I no sooner see him, but I Scream out to Mrs. *Jervis*, she feigns likewise but just to come to herself; we both begin, she to becall, and I to bescratch very liberally. After having made a pretty free Use of my Fingers, without any great Regard to the Parts I attack'd, I counterfeit a Swoon. Mrs. *Jervis* then cries out, O, Sir, what have you done, you have murthered poor *Pamela*: she is gone, she is gone.——

O what a Difficulty it is to keep one's Countenance, when a violent Laugh desires to burst forth.

The poor Booby frightned out of his Wits, jumped out of Bed, and, in his Shirt, sat down by my Bed-Side, pale and trembling, for the Moon shone, and I kept my Eyes wide open, and pretended to fix them in my Head. Mrs. *Jervis* apply'd Lavender Water, and Hartshorn, and this, for a full half Hour; when thinking I had carried it on long enough, and being likewise unable to continue the Sport any longer, I began by Degrees to come to my self.

The Squire, who had sat all this while speechless, and was almost really in that Condition, which I feigned, the Moment he Saw me give Symptoms of recovering my Senses, fell down on his Knees; and O *Pamela*, cryed he, can you forgive me, my injured Maid? by Heaven, I know not whether you are a Man or a Woman, unless by your swelling Breasts. Will you promise to forgive me: I forgive you! D—n you (says I) and d—n you says he, if you come to that. I wish I had never seen your bold Face, saucy Sow, and so went out of the Room.

O what a silly Fellow is a bashful young Lover!

He was no Sooner out of hearing, as we thought, than we both burst into a violent Laugh. Well, says Mrs. *Jervis*, I never saw any thing better acted than your Part: But I wish you may not have discouraged him from any future Attempt; especially since his Passions are so cool, that you could prevent his Hands going further than your Bosom. Hang him, answered I, he is not quite so cold as that I assure you; our Hands, on neither side, were idle in the Scuffle, nor have left us any Doubt of each other as to that matter.

Friday Morning.

My Master sent for Mrs. *Jervis* as soon as he was up, and bid her give an Account of the Plate and Linnen in her Care; and told her, he was resolved that both she and the little Gipsy (I'll assure him) should set out together. Mrs. *Jervis* made him a saucy Answer; which any Servant of Spirit, you know, would, tho' it should be one's Ruin; and came immediately in Tears to me, crying, she had lost her Place on my Account, and that she should be forced to take to a House, as I mentioned before; and that she hoped I would, at least, make her all the amends in my power, for her Loss on my Account, and come to her House whenever I was sent for. Never fear, says I, I'll warrant we are not so near being turned away, as you imagine; and, i'cod, now it comes into my Head, I have a Fetch for him, and you shall assist me in it. But it being now late, and my Letter pretty long, no more at present from

Your Dutiful Daughter,
SHAMELA.

LETTER VII.

Mrs. LUCRETIA JERVIS *to* HENRIETTA MARIA HONORA ANDREWS.

Madam,

Miss *Sham* being set out in a Hurry for my Master's House in *Lincolnshire*, desired me to acquaint you with the Success of her Stratagem, which was to dress herself in the plain Neatness of a Farmer's Daughter, for she before wore the Cloaths of my late Mistress, and to be introduced by me as a Stranger to her Master. To say the Truth, she became the Dress extremely, and if I was to keep a House a thousand Years, I would never desire a prettier Wench in it.

As soon as my Master saw her, he immediately threw his Arms round her Neck, and smothered her with Kisses (for indeed he hath but very little to say for himself to a Woman.) He swore that *Pamela* was an ugly Slut, (pardon, dear Madam, the Coarseness of the Expression) compared to such divine Excellence. He added, he would turn *Pamela* away immediately, and take this new Girl, whom he thought to be one of his Tenant's Daughters, in her Room.

Miss *Sham* smiled at these Words, and so did your humble Servant, which he perceiving, looked very earnestly at your fair Daughter, and discovered the Cheat.

How, *Pamela*, says he, is it you? I thought, Sir, said Miss, after what had happened, you would have known me in any Dress. No, Hussy, says he, but after what hath happened, I should know thee out of any Dress from all thy Sex. He then was what we Women call rude, when done in the Presence of others; but it seems it is not the first time, and Miss defended herself with great Strength and Spirit.

The Squire, who thinks her a pure Virgin, and who knows nothing of my Character, resolved to send her into *Lincolnshire*, on Pretence of conveying her home; where our old Friend *Nanny Jewkes* is Housekeeper, and where Miss had her small one by Parson *Williams* about a Year ago. This is a Piece of News communicated to us by *Robin* Coachman, who is intrusted by his Master to carry on this Affair privately for him: But we hang together, I believe, as well as any Family of Servants in the Nation.

You will, I believe, Madam, wonder that the Squire, who doth not want Generosity, should never have mentioned a Settlement all this while, I believe it slips his Memory: But it will not be long first, no doubt: For, as I am convinced the young Lady will do nothing unbecoming your Daughter, nor ever admit him to taste her Charms, without something sure and handsome before-hand; so, I am certain, the Squire will never rest till they have danced *Adam* and *Eve's* kissing Dance together. Your Daughter set out Yesterday Morning, and told me, as soon as she arrived, you might depend on hearing from her.

Be pleased to make my Compliments acceptable to Mrs. *Davis* and Mrs. *Silvester*, and Mrs. *Jolly*, and all Friends, and permit me the Honour, Madam, to be with the utmost Sincerity,

Your most Obedient,
Humble Servant,
LUCRETIA JERVIS.

If the Squire should continue his Displeasure against me, so as to insist on the Warning he hath given me, you will see me soon, and I will lodge in the same House with you, if you have room, till I can provide for my self to my Liking.

LETTER VIII.

HENRIETTA MARIA HONORA ANDREWS *to* LUCRETIA JERVIS.

Madam,

I Received the Favour of your Letter, and I find you have not forgot your usual Poluteness, which you learned when you was in keeping with a Lord.

I am very much obliged to you for your Care of my Daughter, am glad to hear she hath taken such good Resolutions, and hope she will have sufficient Grace to maintain them.

All Friends are well, and remember to you. You will excuse the Shortness of this Scroll; for I have Sprained my right Hand, with boxing three new made Officers.—Tho' to my Comfort, I beat them all. I rest,

Your Friend and Servant,
HENRIETTA, *&c.*

LETTER IX.

SHAMELA ANDREWS *to* HENRIETTA MARIA HONORA ANDREWS.

Dear Mamma,

I Suppose Mrs. *Jervis* acquainted you with what past 'till I left *Bedfordshire*; whence I am after a very pleasant Journey arrived in *Lincolnshire*, with your old Acquaintance Mrs. *Jewkes*, who formerly helped Parson *Williams* to me; and now designs I see, to sell me to my Master; thank her for that; she will find two Words go to that Bargain.

The Day after my Arrival here, I received a Letter from Mr. *Williams*, and as you have often desired to see one from him, I have inclosed it to you; it is, I think, the finest I ever received from that charming Man, and full of a great deal of Learning.

O! What a brave Thing it is to be a Schollard, and to be able to talk Latin.

Parson WILLIAMS *to* PAMELA ANDREWS.

Mrs. Pamela,

Having learnt by means of my Clerk, who Yesternight visited the Rev^{d}. Mr. *Peters* with my Commands, that you are returned into this County, I purposed to have saluted your fair Hands this Day towards Even: But am obliged to sojourn this Night at a neighbouring Clergyman's; where we are to pierce a Virgin Barrel of Ale, in a Cup of which I shall not be unmindful to celebrate your Health.

I hope you have remembered your Promise, to bring me a leaden Canister of Tobacco (the Saffron Cut) for in Troth, this Country at present affords nothing worthy the replenishing a Tube with.——Some I tasted, the other Day at an Ale-house, gave me the Heart-Burn, tho' I filled no oftner than five times.

I was greatly concerned to learn, that your late Lady left you nothing, tho' I cannot say the Tidings much surprized me: For I am too intimately acquainted with the Family; (myself, Father, and Grandfather having been successive Incumbents on the same Cure, which you know is in their Gift) I say, I am too well acquainted with them to expect much from their Generosity. They are in Verity, as worthless a Family as any other whatever. The young Gentleman I am informed, is a perfect Reprobate that he hath an *Ingenium Versatile* to every Species of Vice, which, indeed, no one can much wonder at, who animadverts on that want of Respect to the Clergy, which was observable in him when a Child, I remember when he was at the Age of Eleven only, he met my Father without either pulling off his Hat, or riding out of the way. Indeed, a Contempt of the Clergy is the fashionable Vice of the Times; but let such Wretches know, they cannot hate, detest, and despise us, half so much as we do them.

However, I have prevailed on myself to write a civil Letter to your Master, as there is a Probability of his being shortly in a Capacity of rendring me a Piece of Service; my good Friend and Neighbour the Rev[d]. Mr. *Squeeze-Tithe* being, as I am informed by one whom I have employed to attend for that Purpose, very near his Dissolution.

You see, sweet Mrs. *Pamela*, the Confidence with which I dictate these Things to you; whom after those Endearments which have passed between us, I must in some Respects estimate as my Wife: For tho' the Omission of the Service was a Sin; yet, as I have told you, it was a venial One, of which I have truly repented, as I hope you have; and also that you have continued the wholsome Office of reading good Books, and are improved in your Psalmody, of which I shall have a speedy Trial: For I purpose to give you a Sermon next *Sunday*, and shall spend the Evening with you, in Pleasures, which tho' not strictly innocent, are however to be purged away by frequent and sincere Repentance. I am,

Sweet Mrs. Pamela,
Your faithful Servant,
ARTHUR WILLIAMS.

You find, Mamma, what a charming way he hath of Writing, and yet I assure you, that is not the most charming thing belonging to him: For, tho' he doth not put any Dears, and Sweets, and Loves into his Letters, yet he says a thousand of them: For he can be as fond of a Woman, as any Man living.

Sure Women are great Fools, when they prefer a laced Coat to the Clergy, whom it is our Duty to honour and respect.

Well, on *Sunday* Parson *Williams* came, according to his Promise, and an excellent Sermon he preached; his Text was, *Be not Righteous over much*; and, indeed, he handled it in a very fine way; he shewed us that the Bible doth not require too much Goodness of us, and that People very often call things Goodness that are not so. That to go to Church, and to pray, and to sing Psalms, and to honour the Clergy, and to repent, is true Religion; and 'tis not doing good to one another, for that is one of the greatest Sins we can commit, when we don't do it for the sake of Religion. That those People who talk of Vartue and Morality, are the wickedest of all Persons. That 'tis not what we do, but what we believe, that must save us, and a great many other good Things; I wish I could remember them all.

As soon as Church was over, he came to the Squire's House, and drank Tea with Mrs. *Jewkes* and me; after which Mrs. *Jewkes* went out and left us together for an Hour and half—Oh! he is a charming Man.

After Supper he went Home, and then Mrs. *Jewkes* began to catechize me, about my Familiarity with him. I see she wants him herself. Then she proceeded to tell me what an Honour my Master did me in liking me, and that it was both an inexcusable Folly and Pride in me, to pretend to refuse him any Favour. Pray, Madam, says I, consider I am a poor Girl, and have nothing but my Modesty to trust to. If I part with that, what will become of me. Methinks, says she, you are not so mighty modest when you are with Parson *Williams*; I have observed you gloat at one another, in a Manner that hath made me blush. I assure you, I shall let the Squire know what sort of Man he is; you may do your Will, says I, as long as he hath a Vote for Pallamant-Men, the Squire dares do nothing to offend him; and you will only shew that you are jealous of him, and that's all. How now, Mynx, says she; Mynx! No more Mynx than yourself, says I; with that she hit me a Slap on the Shoulder; and I flew at her and scratched her Face, i'cod, 'till she went crying out of the Room; so no more at present, from

Your Dutiful Daughter,
SHAMELA.

LETTER X.

Shamela Andrews *to* Henrietta Maria Honora Andrews.

O Mamma! Rare News! As soon as I was up this Morning, a Letter was brought me from the Squire, of which I send you a Copy.

Squire Booby *to* Pamela.

Dear Creature,

I hope you are not angry with me for the Deceit put upon you, in conveying you to *Lincolnshire*, when you imagined yourself going to *London*. Indeed, my dear *Pamela*, I cannot live without you; and will very shortly come down and convince you, that my Designs are better than you imagine, and such as you may with Honour comply with. I am,

My Dear Creature,
Your doating Lover,
Booby.

Now, Mamma, what think you?——For my own Part, I am convinced he will marry me, and faith so he shall. O! Bless me! I shall be Mrs. *Booby* and be Mistress of a great Estate, and have a dozen Coaches and Six, and a fine House at *London*, and another at *Bath*, and Servants, and Jewels, and Plate, and go to Plays, and Opera's, and Court; and do what I will, and spend what I will. But, poor Parson *Williams*! Well; and can't I see Parson *Williams*, as well after Marriage as before: For I shall never care a Farthing for my Husband. No, I hate and despise him of all Things.

Well, as soon as I had read my Letter, in came Mrs. *Jewkes*. You see, Madam, says she, I carry the Marks of your Passion about me; but I have received order from my Master to be civil to you, and I must obey him: For he is the best Man in the World, notwithstanding your Treatment of him. My Treatment of him, Madam, says I? Yes, says she, your Insensibility to the Honour he intends you, of making you his Mistress. I would have you to know, Madam, I would not be Mistress to the greatest King, no nor Lord in the Universe. I value my Vartue more than I do any thing my Master can give me; and so we talked a full Hour and a half, about my Vartue; and I was afraid at first, she had heard something about the Bantling, but I find she hath not; tho' she is as jealous, and suspicious, as old Scratch.

In the Afternoon, I stole into the Garden to meet Mr. *Williams*; I found him at the Place of his Appointment, and we staid in a kind of Arbour, till it was quite dark. He was very angry when I told him what Mrs. *Jewkes* had threatned——Let him refuse me the Living, says he, if he dares, I will vote for the other Party; and not only so, but will expose him all over the Country. I owe him 150*l.* indeed, but I don't care for that; by that time the Election is past, I shall be able to plead the *Statue* of *Lamentations*.

I could have stayed with the dear Man forever, but when it grew dark, he told me, he was to meet the neighbouring Clergy, to finish the Barrel of Ale they had tapped the other Day, and believed they should not part till three or four in the Morning——So he left me, and I promised to be penitent, and go on with my reading in good Books.

As soon as he was gone, I bethought myself, what Excuse I should make to Mrs. *Jewkes*, and it came into my Head to pretend as how I intended to drown myself; so I stript off one of my Petticoats, and threw it into the Canal; and then I went and hid myself in the Coal-hole, where I lay all Night; and comforted myself with repeating over some Psalms, and other good things, which I had got by heart.

In the Morning Mrs. *Jewkes* and all the Servants were frighted out of their Wits, thinking I had run away; and not devising how they should answer it to their Master. They searched all the likeliest Places they could think of for me, and at last saw my Petticoat floating in the Pond. Then they got a Drag-Net, imagining I was drowned, and intending to drag me out; but at last *Moll* Cook coming for some Coals, discovered me lying all along in no very good Pickle. Bless me! Mrs. *Pamela*, says she, what can be the Meaning of this? I don't know, says I, help me up, and I will go in to Breakfast, for indeed I am very hungry. Mrs. *Jewkes* came in immediately, and was so rejoyced to find me alive, that she asked with great Good-Humour, where I had been? and how my Petticoat came into the Pond. I answered, I believed the Devil had put it into my Head to drown my self; but it was a Fib; for I never saw the Devil in my Life, nor I don't believe he hath any thing to do with me.

So much for this Matter. As soon as I had breakfasted, a Coach and Six came to the Door, and who should be in it but my Master.

I immediately run up into my Room, and stript, and washed, and drest my self as well as I could, and put on my prettiest round-ear'd Cap, and pulled down my Stays, to shew as much as I could of my Bosom, (for Parson *Williams* says that is the most beautiful part of a Woman) and then I practised over all my Airs before the Glass, and then I sat down and read a Chapter in the Whole Duty of Man.

Then Mrs. *Jewkes* came to me and told me, my Master wanted me below, and says she, Don't behave like a Fool; No, thinks I to my self, I believe I shall find Wit enough for my Master and you too.

So down goes me I into the Parlour to him. *Pamela*, says he, the Moment I came in, you see I cannot stay long from you, which I think is a sufficient Proof of the Violence of my Passion. Yes, Sir, says I, I see your Honour intends to ruin me, that nothing but the Destruction of my Vartue will content you.

O what a charming Word that is, rest his Soul who first invented it.

How can you say I would ruin you, answered the Squire, when you shall not ask any thing which I will not grant you. If that be true, says I, good your Honour let me go home to my poor but honest Parents; that is all I have to ask, and do not ruin a poor Maiden, who is resolved to carry her Vartue to the Grave with her.

Hussy, says he, don't provoke me, don't provoke me, I say. You are absolutely in my power, and if you won't let me lie with you by fair Means, I will by Force. O la, Sir, says I, I don't understand your paw Words.——Very pretty Treatment indeed, says he, to say I use paw Words; Hussy, Gipsie, Hypocrite, Saucebox, Boldface, get out of my Sight, or I will lend you such a Kick in the —— I don't care to repeat the Word, but he meant my hinder part. I was offering to go away, for I was half afraid, when he called me back, and took me round the Neck and kissed me, and then bid me go about my Business.

I went directly into my Room, where Mrs. *Jewkes* came to me soon afterwards. So Madam, says she, you have left my Master below in a fine Pet, he hath threshed two or three of his Men already: It is might pretty that all his Servants are to be punished for your Impertinence.

Harkee, Madam, says I, don't you affront me, for if you do, d—n me (I am sure I have repented for using such a Word) if I am not revenged.

How sweet is Revenge: Sure the Sermon Book is in the Right, in calling it the sweetest Morsel the Devil ever dropped into the Mouth of a Sinner.

Mrs. *Jewkes* remembered the Smart of my Nails too well to go farther, and so we sat down and talked about my Vartue till Dinner-time, and then I was sent for to wait on my Master. I took care to be often caught looking at him, and then I always turn'd away my Eyes, and pretended to be ashamed. As soon as the Cloth was removed, he put a Bumper of Champagne into my Hand, and bid me drink——O la I can't name the Health. Parson *Williams* may well say he is a wicked Man.

Mrs. *Jewkes* took a Glass and drank the dear *Monysyllable*; I don't understand that Word, but I believe it is baudy. I then drank towards his Honour's good Pleasure. Ay, Hussy, says he, you can give me Pleasure if you will; Sir, says I, I shall be always glad to do what is in my power, and so I pretended not to know what he meant. Then he took me into his Lap.—O Mamma, I could tell you something if I would—and he kissed me——and I said I won't be slobber'd about so, so I won't; and he bid me get out of the Room for a saucy Baggage, and said he had a good mind to spit in my Face.

Sure no Man over took such a Method to gain a Woman's Heart.

I had not been long in my Chamber before Mrs. *Jewkes* came to me, and told me, my Master would not see me any more that Evening, that is, if he can help it; for, added she, I easily perceive the great Ascendant you have over him, and to confess the Truth, I don't doubt but you will shortly be my Mistress.

What says I, dear Mrs. *Jewkes*, what do you say? Don't flatter a poor Girl, it is impossible his Honour can have any honourable Design upon me. And so we talked of honourable Designs till Supper-time. And Mrs. *Jewkes* and I supped together upon a hot buttered Apple-Pie; and about ten o'Clock we went to Bed.

We had not been a Bed half an Hour, when my Master came pit a pat into the Room in his Shirt as before. I pretended not to hear him, and Mrs. *Jewkes* laid hold of one Arm, and he pulled down the Bed cloaths and came into Bed on the other Side, and took my other Arm and laid it under him, and fell a kissing one of my Breasts as if he would have devoured it; I was then forced to awake, and began to struggle with him, Mrs. *Jewkes* crying why don't you do it? I have one Arm secure, if you can't deal with the rest I am sorry for you. He was as rude as possible to me; but I remembered, Mamma, the Instructions you gave me to avoid being ravished, and followed them, which soon brought him to Terms, and he promised me, on quitting my hold, that he would leave the Bed.

O Parson Williams, *how little are all the Men in the World compared to thee.*

My Master was as good as his Word; upon which Mrs. *Jewkes* said, O Sir, I see you know very little of our *Sect*, by parting so easily from the Blessing when you was so near it. No, Mrs. *Jewkes*, answered he, I am very glad no more hath happened, I would not have injured *Pamela* for the World. And to-morrow Morning perhaps she may hear of something to her Advantage. This she may be certain of, that I will never take her by Force, and then he left the Room.

What think you now, Mrs. *Pamela*, says Mrs. *Jewkes*, are you not yet persuaded my Master hath honourable Designs? I think he hath given no great Proof of them to-night, said I. Your Experience I find is not great, says she, but I am convinced you will shortly be my Mistress, and then what will become of poor me.

With such sort of Discourse we both fell asleep. Next Morning early my Master sent for me, and after kissing me, gave a Paper into my Hand which he bid me read; I did so, and found it to be a Proposal for settling 250*l.* a Year on me, besides several other advantagious Offers, as Presents of Money and other things. Well, *Pamela*, said he, what Answer do you make me to this. Sir, said I, I value my Vartue more than all the World, and I had rather be the poorest Man's Wife, than the richest Man's Whore. You are a Simpleton, said he; That may be, and yet I may have as much Wit as some Folks, cry'd I; meaning me, I suppose, said he, every Man knows himself best, says I. Hussy, says he, get out of the Room, and let me see your saucy Face no more, for I find I am in more Danger than you are, and therefore it shall be my Business to avoid you as much as I can; and it shall be mine, thinks I, at every turn to throw my self in your way. So I went out, and as I parted, I heard him sigh and say he was bewitched.

Mrs. *Jewkes* hath been with me since, and she assures me she is convinced I shall shortly be Mistress of the Family, and she really behaves to me, as if she already thought me so. I am resolved now to aim at it. I thought once of making a little Fortune by my Person. I now intend to make a great one by my Vartue. So asking Pardon for this long Scroll, I am,

Your dutiful Daughter,
SHAMELA.

LETTER XI.

HENRIETTA MARIA HONORA ANDREWS *to* SHAMELA ANDREWS.

Dear Sham,

I Received your last Letter with infinite Pleasure, and am convinced it will be your own Fault if you are not married to your Master, and I would advise you now to take no less Terms. But, my dear Child, I am afraid of one Rock only, That Parson *Williams*, I wish he was out of the Way. A Woman never commits Folly but with such Sort of Men, as by many Hints in the Letters I collect him to be: but, consider my dear Child, you will hereafter have Opportunities sufficient to indulge yourself with Parson *Williams*, or any other you like. My Advice therefore to you is, that you would avoid seeing him any more till the Knot is tied. Remember the first Lesson I taught you, that a married Woman injures only her Husband, but a single Woman herself. I am in hopes of seeing you a great Lady,

Your affectionate Mother,

HENRIETTA MARIA, *&c.*

The following Letter seems to have been written before *Shamela* received the last from her Mother.

LETTER XII.

SHAMELA ANDREWS *to* HENRIETTA MARIA HONORA ANDREWS.

Dear Mamma,

I Little feared when I sent away my last that all my Hopes would be so soon frustrated; but I am certain you will blame Fortune and not me. To proceed then. About two Hours after I had left the Squire, he sent for me into the Parlour. *Pamela*, said he, and takes me gently by the hand, will you walk with me in the Garden; yes, Sir, says I, and pretended to tremble; but I hope your Honour will not be rude. Indeed, says he, you have nothing to fear from me, and I have something to tell you, which if it doth not please you, cannot offend. We walked out together, and he began thus, *Pamela*, will you tell me Truth? Doth the Resistance you make to my Attempts proceed from Vartue only, or have I not some Rival in thy dear Bosom who might be more successful? Sir, says I, I do assure you I never had a thought of any Man in the World. How says he, not of Parson *Williams*! Parson *Williams*, says I, is the last Man upon Earth; and if I was a Dutchess, and your Honour was to make your Addresses to me, you would have no reason to be jealous of any Rival, especially such a Fellow as Parson *Williams*. If ever I had a Liking, I am sure——but I am not worthy of you one Way, and no Riches should ever bribe me the other. My Dear, says he, you are worthy of every Thing, and suppose I should lay aside all Considerations of Fortune, and disregard the Censure of the World, and marry you. O Sir, says I, I am sure you can have no such Thoughts, you cannot demean your self so low. Upon my Soul, I am in earnest, says he,—O Pardon me, Sir, says I, you can't persuade me of this. How Mistress, says he, in a violent Rage, do you give me the Lie? Hussy, I have a great mind to box your saucy Ears, but I am resolved I will never put it in your power to affront me again, and therefore I desire you to prepare your self for your Journey this Instant. You deserve no better Vehicle than a Cart; however, for once you shall have a Chariot, and it shall be ready for you within this half Hour; and so he flung from me in a Fury.

What a foolish Thing it is for a Woman to dally too long with her Lover's Desires; how many have owed their being old Maids to their holding out too long.

Mrs. *Jewkes* came me to presently, and told me, I must make ready with all the Expedition imaginable, for that my Master had ordered the Chariot, and that if I was not prepared to go in it, I should be turned out of Doors, and left to find my way Home on Foot. This startled me a little, yet I resolved, whether in the right or wrong, not to submit nor ask Pardon: For that know you, Mamma, you never could your self bring me to from my Childhood: Besides, I thought he would be no more able to master his Passion for me now, than he had been hitherto; and if he sent two Horses away with me, I concluded he would send four to fetch me back. So, truly, I resolved to brazen it out, and with all the Spirit I could muster up, I told Mrs. *Jewkes* I was vastly pleased with the News she brought me; that no one ever went more readily than I should, from a Place where my Vartue had been in continual Danger. That as for my Master, he might easily get those who were fit for his Purpose; but, for my Part, I preferred my Vartue to all Rakes whatever——And for his Promises, and his Offers to me, I don't value them of a Fig—Not of a Fig, Mrs. *Jewkes*; and then I snapt my Fingers.

Mrs. *Jewkes* went in with me, and helped me to pack up my little All, which was soon done; being no more than two Day-Caps, two Night-Caps, five Shifts, one Sham, a Hoop, a Quilted-Petticoat, two Flannel-Petticoats, two pair of Stockings, one odd one, a pair of lac'd Shoes, a short flowered Apron, a lac'd Neck-Handkerchief, one Clog, and almost another, and some few Books: as, *A full Answer to a plain and true Account*, &c. *The Whole Duty of Man*, with only the Duty to one's Neighbour, torn out. The Third Volume of the *Atalantis*. *Venus in the Cloyster: Or, the Nun in her Smock. God's Dealings with Mr. Whitefield. Orfus and Eurydice.* Some Sermon-Books; and two or three Plays, with their Titles, and Part of the first Act torn off.

So as soon as we had put all this into a Bundle, the Chariot was ready, and I took leave of all the Servants, and particularly Mrs. *Jewkes*, who pretended, I believe, to be more sorry to part with me than she was; and then crying out with an Air of Indifference, my Service to my Master, when he condescends to enquire after me, I flung my self into the Chariot, and bid *Robin* drive on.

We had not gone far, before a Man on Horseback, riding full Speed, overtook us, and coming up to the Side of the Chariot, threw a Letter into the Window, and then departed without uttering a single Syllable.

I immediately knew the Hand of my dear *Williams*, and was somewhat surprised, tho' I did not apprehend the Contents to be so terrible, as by the following exact Copy you will find them.

Parson WILLIAMS *to* PAMELA.

Dear Mrs. PAMELA,

That Disrespect for the Clergy, which I have formerly noted to you in that Villain your Master, hath now broke forth in a manifest Fact. I was proceeding to my Neighbour *Spruce's* Church, where I purposed to preach a Funeral Sermon, on the Death of Mr. *John Gage*, the Exciseman; when I was met by two Persons who are, it seems, Sheriffs Officers, and arrested for the 150*l.* which your Master had lent me; and unless I can find Bail within these few Days, of which I see no likelihood, I shall be carried to Goal. This accounts for my not having visited you these two Days; which you might assure yourself, I should not have fail'd, if the *Potestas* had not been wanting. If you can by any means prevail on your Master to release me, I beseech you so to do, not scrupling any thing for Righteousness sake. I hear he is just arrived in this Country, I have herewith sent him a Letter, of which I transmit you a Copy. So with Prayers for your Success, I Subscribe myself

Your affectionate Friend,
ARTHUR WILLIAMS.

Parson WILLIAMS *to* SQUIRE BOOBY.

Honoured Sir,

I am justly surprized to feel so heavy a Weight of your Displeasure, without being conscious of the least Demerit towards so good and generous a Patron, as I have ever found you: For my own Part, I can truly say,
Nil conscire sibi nullæ pallescere culpæ.

And therefore, as this Proceeding is so contrary to your usual Goodness, which I have often experienced, and more especially in the Loan of this Money for which I am now arrested; I cannot avoid thinking some malicious Persons have insinuated false Suggestions against me; intending thereby, to eradicate those Seeds of Affection which I have hardly travailed to sowe in your Heart, and which promised to produce such excellent Fruit. If I have any ways offended you, Sir, be graciously pleased to let me know it, and likewise to point out to me, the Means whereby I may reinstate myself in your Favour: For next to him, whom the Great themselves must bow down before, I know none to whom I shall bend with more Lowliness than your Honour. Permit me to subscribe myself,

Honoured Sir,
Your most obedient, and most obliged,
And most dutiful humble Servant,
ARTHUR WILLIAMS.

The Fate of poor Mr. *Williams* shocked me more than my own: For, as the *Beggar's Opera* says, *Nothing moves one so much as a great Man in Distress.* And to see a Man of his Learning forced to submit so low, to one whom I have often heard him say, he despises, is, I think, a most affecting Circumstance. I write all this to you, Dear Mamma, at the Inn where I lie this first Night, and as I shall send it immediately, by the Post, it will be in Town a little before me.—— Don't let my coming away vex you: For, as my Master will be in Town in a few Days, I shall have an Opportunity of seeing him; and let the worst come to the worst, I shall be sure of my Settlement at last. Which is all, from

Your dutiful Daughter,
SHAMELA.

P. S. Just as I was going to send this away a Letter is come from my Master, desiring me to return, with a large Number of Promises.—I have him now as sure as a Gun, as you will perceive by the Letter itself, which I have inclosed to you.

This Letter is unhappily lost, as well as the next which *Shamela* wrote, and which contained an Account of all the Proceedings previous to her Marriage. The only remaining one which I could preserve, seems to have been written about a Week after the Ceremony was perform'd, and is as follows:

SHAMELA BOOBY *to* HENRIETTA MARIA HONORA ANDREWS.

Madam,

In my last I left off at our sitting down to Supper on our Wedding Night,[1] where I behaved with as much Bashfulness as the purest Virgin in the World could have done. The most difficult Task for me was to blush; however, by holding my Breath, and Squeezing my Cheeks with my Handkerchief, I did pretty well. My Husband was extreamly eager and impatient to have Supper removed, after which he gave me leave to retire into my Closet for a Quarter of an Hour, which was very agreeable to me; for I employed that time in writing to Mr. *Williams*, who, as I informed you in my last, is released, and presented to the Living, upon the Death of the last Parson. Well, at last I went to Bed, and my Husband soon leap'd in after me; where, I shall only assure you, I acted my Part in such a manner, that no Bridegroom was ever better Satisfied with his Bride's Virginity. And to confess the Truth, I might have been well enough Satisfied too, if I had never been acquainted with Parson *Williams*.

O what regard Men who marry Widows should have to the Qualifications of their former Husbands.

We did not rise the next Morning till eleven, and then we sat down to Breakfast; I eat two Slices of Bread and Butter, and drank three Dishes of Tea, with a good deal of Sugar, and we both look'd very silly. After Breakfast we drest our selves, he in a blue Camblet Coat, very richly lac'd, and Breeches of the same; with a Paduafoy Waistcoat, laced with Silver; and I, in one of my Mistress's Gowns. I will have finer when I come to Town. We then took a Walk in the Garden, and he kissed me several times, and made me a Present of 100 Guineas, which I gave away before Night to the Servants, twenty to one, and ten to another, and so on.

We eat a very hearty Dinner, and about eight in the Evening went to Bed again. He is prodigiously fond of me; but I don't like him half so well as my dear *Williams*. The next Morning we rose earlier, and I asked him for another hundred Guineas, and he gave them me. I sent fifty to Parson *Williams*, and the rest I gave away, two Guineas to a Beggar, and three to a Man riding along the Road, and the rest to other People. I long to be in *London* that I may have an Opportunity of laying some out, as well as giving away. I believe I shall buy every thing I see. What signifies having Money if one doth not spend it.

The next Day, as soon as I was up, I asked him for another Hundred. Why, my Dear, says he, I don't grudge you any thing, but how was it possible for you to lay out the other two Hundred here. La! Sir, says I, I hope I am not obliged to give

---

1 1: This was the Letter which is lost.

you an Account of every Shilling; Troth, that will be being your Servant still. I assure you, I married you with no such view, besides did not you tell me I should be Mistress of your Estate? And I will be too. For tho' I brought no Fortune, I am as much your Wife as if I had brought a Million—yes, but, my Dear, says he, if you had brought a Million, you would spend it all at this rate; besides, what will your Expences be in *London*, if they are so great here. Truly, says I, Sir, I shall live like other Ladies of my Fashion; and if you think, because I was a Servant, that I shall be contented to be governed as you please, I will shew you, you are mistaken. If you had not cared to marry me, you might have let it alone. I did not ask you, nor I did not court you. Madam, says he, I don't value a hundred Guineas to oblige you; but this is a Spirit which I did not expect in you, nor did I ever see any Symptoms of it before. O but Times are altered now, I am your Lady, Sir; yes to my Sorrow, says he, I am afraid—and I am afraid to my Sorrow too: For if you begin to use me in this manner already, I reckon you will beat me before a Month's at an end. I am sure if you did, it would injure me less than this barbarous Treatment; upon which I burst into Tears, and pretended to fall into a Fit. This frighted him out of his wits, and he called up the Servants. Mrs. *Jewkes* immediately came in, and she and another of the Maids fell heartily to rubbing my Temples, and holding Smelling-Bottles to my Nose. Mrs. *Jewkes* told him she fear'd I should never recover, upon which he began to beat his Breasts, and cried out, O my dearest Angel, Curse on my passionate Temper, I have destroy'd her, I have destroy'd her!——would she had spent my whole Estate rather than this had happened. Speak to me, my Love, I will melt myself into Gold for thy Pleasure. At last having pretty well tired my self with counterfeiting, and imagining I had continu'd long enough for my purpose in the sham Fit, I began to move my Eyes, to loosen my Teeth, and to open my Hands, which Mr. *Booby* no sooner perceived than he embraced and kissed me with the eagerest Extacy, asked my Pardon on his Knees for what I had suffered through his Folly and Perverseness, and without more Questions fetched me the Money. I fancy I have effectually prevented any farther Refusals or Inquiry into my Expences. It would be hard indeed, that a Woman who marries a Man only for his Money, should be debarred from spending it.

Well, after all things were quiet, we sat down to Breakfast, yet I resolved not to smile once, nor to say one good-natured, or good-humoured Word on any Account.

Nothing can be more prudent in a Wife, than a sullen Backwardness to Reconciliation; it makes a Husband fearful of offending by the Length of his Punishment.

When we were drest, the Coach was by my Desire ordered for an Airing, which we took in it. A long Silence prevailed on both Sides, tho' he constantly squeezed my Hand, and kissed me, and used other Familiarities, which I peevishly permitted. At last, I opened my Mouth first.—And so, says I, you are sorry you are married;—Pray, my Dear, says he, forget what I said in a Passion. Passion, says I, is apter to discover our Thoughts than to teach us to counterfeit. Well, says he, whether you will believe me or no, I solemnly vow, I would not change thee for the richest Woman in the Universe. No, I warrant you, says I; and yet you could refuse me a nasty hundred Pound. At these very Words, I saw Mr. *Williams* riding as fast as he could across a Field; and I looked out, and saw a Lease of Greyhounds coursing a Hare, which they presently killed, and I saw him alight, and take it from them.

My Husband ordered *Robin* to drive towards him, and looked horribly out of humour, which I presently imputed to Jealousy. So I began with him first; for that is the wisest way. La, Sir, says I; what makes you look so Angry and Grim? Doth the Sight of Mr. *Williams* give you all this Uneasiness? I am sure, I would never have married a Woman of whom I had so bad an Opinion, that I must be uneasy at every Fellow she looks at. My Dear, answer'd he, you injure me extremely, you was not in my Thoughts, nor, indeed, could be, while they were covered by so morose a Countenance; I am justly angry with that Parson, whose Family hath been raised from the Dunghill by ours; and who hath received from me twenty Kindnesses, and yet is not contented to destroy the Game in all other Places, which I freely give him leave to do; but hath the Impudence to pursue a few Hares, which I am desirous to preserve, round about this little Coppice. Look, my Dear, pray look, says he; I believe he is going to turn Higler. To Confess the Truth, he had no less than three ty'd up behind his Horse, and a fourth he held in his Hand.

Pshaw, says I, I wish all the Hares in the Country were d——d (the Parson himself chid me afterwards for using the Word, tho' it was in his Service.) Here's a Fuss, indeed, about a nasty little pitiful Creature, that is not half so useful as a Cat. You shall not persuade me, that a Man of your Understanding, would quarrel with a Clergyman for such a Trifle. No, no, I am the Hare, for whom poor Parson *Williams* is persecuted; and Jealousy is the Motive. If you had married one of your Quality Ladies, she would have had Lovers by dozens, she would so; but because you have taken a Servant-Maid, forsooth! you are jealous if she but looks (and then I began to Water) at a poor P——a——a——rson in his Pu——u——u——lpit, and then out burst a Flood of Tears.

My Dear, said he, for Heaven's sake dry your Eyes, and don't let him be a Witness of your Tears, which I should be sorry to think might be imputed to my Unkindness; I have already given you Some Proofs that I am not jealous of this Parson; I will now give you a very strong one: For I will mount my Horse, and you shall take *Williams* into the Coach. You may be sure, this Motion pleased me, yet I pretended to make as light of it as possible, and told him, I was sorry his Behaviour had made some such glaring Instance, necessary to the perfect clearing my Character.

He soon came up to Mr. *Williams*, who had attempted to ride off, but was prevented by one of our Horsemen, whom my Husband sent to stop him. When we met, my Husband asked him how he did with a very good-humoured Air, and told him he perceived he had found good Sport that Morning. He answered pretty moderate, Sir; for that he had found the three Hares tied on to the Saddle dead in a

Ditch (winking on me at the same time), and added he was sorry there was such a Rot among them.

Well, says Mr. *Booby*, if you please, Mr. *Williams*, you shall come in and ride with my Wife. For my own part, I will mount on Horseback; for it is fine Weather, and besides, it doth not become me to loll in a Chariot, whilst a Clergyman rides on Horseback.

At which Words, Mr. *Booby* leap'd out, and Mr. *Williams* leap'd in, in an Instant, telling my Husband as he mounted, he was glad to see such a Reformation, and that if he continued his Respect to the Clergy, he might assure himself of Blessings from above.

It was now that the Airing began to grow pleasant to me. Mr. *Williams*, who never had but one Fault, *viz.* that he generally smells of Tobacco, was now perfectly sweet; for he had for two Days together enjoined himself as a Penance, not to smoke till he had kissed my Lips. I will loosen you from that Obligation, says I, and observing my Husband looking another way, I gave him a charming Kiss, and then he asked me Questions concerning my Wedding-night; this actually made me blush: I vow I did not think, it had been in him.

As he went along, he began to discourse very learnedly, and told me the Flesh and the Spirit were too distinct Matters, which had not the least relation to each other. That all immaterial Substances (those were his very Words) such as Love, Desire, and so forth, were guided by the Spirit: But fine Houses, large Estates, Coaches, and dainty Entertainments were the Product of the Flesh. Therefore, says he, my Dear, you have two Husbands, one the Object of your Love, and to satisfy your Desire; the other the Object of your Necessity, and to furnish you with those other Conveniences. (I am sure I remember every Word, for he repeated it three Times; O he is very good whenever I desire him to repeat a thing to me three times he always doth it!) as then the Spirit is preferable, to the Flesh, so am I preferable to your other Husband, to whom I am antecedent in Time likewise. I say these things, my Dear, (said he) to satisfie your Conscience. A Fig, for my Conscience, said I, when shall I meet you again in the Garden?

My Husband now rode up to the Chariot, and asked us how we did—I hate the Sight of him. Mr. *Williams* answered very well, at your Service. They then talked of the Weather, and other things, I wished him gone again, every Minute; but all in vain I had no more Opportunity of conversing with Mr. *Williams*.

Well; at Dinner Mr. *Booby* was very civil to Mr. *Williams*, and told him he was sorry for what had happened, and would make him sufficient Amends, if in his power, and desired him to accept of a Note for fifty Pounds; which he was so *good* to receive, notwithstanding all that had past; and told Mr. *Booby*, he hop'd he would be forgiven, and that he would pray for him.

We make a charming Fool of him, i'fackins; Times are finely altered, I have entirely got the better of him, and am resolved never to give him his Humour.

O how foolish it is in a Woman, who hath once got the Reins into her own Hand, ever to quit them again.

After Dinner Mr. *Williams* drank the Church *et cætera*; and smiled on me; when my Husband's Turn came, he drank *et cætera* and the Church; for which he was very severely rebuked by Mr. *Williams*; it being a high Crime, it seems, to name any thing before the Church. I do not know what *Et cetera* is, but I believe it is something concerning chusing Pallament Men; for I asked if it was not a Health to Mr. *Booby's* Borough, and Mr. *Williams* with a hearty Laugh answered, Yes, Yes, it is his Borough we mean.

I slipt out as soon as I could, hoping Mr. *Williams* would finish the Squire, as I have heard him say he could easily do, and come to me; but it happened quite otherwise, for in about half an Hour, *Booby* came to me, and told me he had left Mr. *Williams*, the Mayor of his Borough, and two or three Aldermen heartily at it, and asked me if I would go hear *Williams* sing a Catch, which, added he, he doth to a Miracle.

Every Opportunity of seeing my dear *Williams*, was agreeable to me, which indeed I scarce had at this time; for when we returned, the whole Corporation were got together, and the Room was in a Cloud of Tobacco; Parson *Williams* was at the upper End of the Table, and he hath pure round cherry Cheeks, and his Face look'd all the World to nothing like the Sun in a Fog. If the Sun had a Pipe in his Mouth, there would be no Difference.

I began now to grow uneasy, apprehending I should have no more of Mr. *Williams's* Company that Evening, and not at all caring for my Husband, I advised him to sit down and drink for his Country with the rest of the Company; but he refused, and desired me to give him some Tea; swearing nothing made him so sick, as to hear a Parcel of Scoundrels, roaring forth the Principles of honest Men over their Cups, when, says he, I know most of them are such empty Blockheads, that they don't know their right Hand from their left; and that Fellow there, who hath talked so much of *Shipping*, at the left Side of the Parson, in whom they all place a Confidence, if I don't take care, will sell them to my Adversary.

I don't know why I mention this Stuff to you; for I am sure I know nothing about *Pollitricks*, more than Parson *Williams* tells me; who says that the Court-side are in the right on't, and that every Christian ought to be on the same with the Bishops.

When we had finished our Tea, we walked in the Garden till it was dark, and then my Husband proposed, instead of returning to the Company, (which I desired, that I might see Parson *Williams* again,) to sup in another Room by our selves, which, for fear of making him jealous, and considering too, that Parson *Williams* would be pretty far gone, I was obliged to consent to.

O! what a devilish thing it is, for a Woman to be obliged to go to bed to a spindle-shanked young Squire, she doth not like, when there is a jolly Parson in the same House she is fond of.

In the Morning I grew very peevish, and in the Dumps, notwithstanding all he could say or do to please me. I exclaimed against the Priviledge of Husbands, and vowed I would not be pulled and tumbled about. At last he hit on the only Method, which could have brought me into Humour, and proposed to me a Journey to

London, within a few Days. This you may easily guess pleased me; for besides the Desire which I have of shewing my self forth, of buying fine Cloaths, Jewels, Coaches, Houses, and ten thousand other fine things, Parson *Williams* is, it seems, going thither too, to be *instuted.*

O! what a charming Journey I shall have; for I hope to keep the dear Man in the Chariot with me all the way; and that foolish Booby (for that is the Name Mr. Williams *hath set him) will ride on Horseback.*

So as I shall have an Opportunity of seeing you so shortly, I think I will mention no more Matters to you now. O I had like to have forgot one very material thing; which is that it will look horribly, for a Lady of my Quality and Fashion, to own such a Woman as you for my Mother. Therefore we must meet in private only, and if you will never claim me, nor mention me to any one, I will always allow you what is very handsome. Parson *Williams* hath greatly advised me in this; and says, he thinks I should do very well to lay out twenty Pounds, and set you up in a little Chandler's Shop: but you must remember all my Favours to you will depend on your Secrecy; for I am positively resolved, I will not be known to be your Daughter; and if you tell any one so, I shall deny it with all my Might, which Parson *Williams* says, I may do with a safe Conscience, being now a married Woman. So I rest

Your humble Servant,
SHAMELA.

P. S. The strangest Fancy hath enter'd into my Booby's Head, that can be imagined. He is resolved to have a Book made about him and me; he proposed it to Mr. *Williams*, and offered him a Reward for his Pains; but he says he never writ any thing of that kind, but will recommend my Husband, when he comes to Town, to a Parson *who does that Sort of Business for Folks*, one who can make my Husband, and me, and Parson *Williams*, to be all great People; for he *can make black white*, it seems. Well, but they say my Name is to be altered, Mr. *Williams*, says the first Syllabub hath too comical a Sound, so it is to be changed into *Pamela*; I own I can't imagine what can be said; for to be sure I shan't confess any of my Secrets to them, and so I whispered Parson *Williams* about that, who answered me, I need not give my self any Trouble; for the Gentleman *who writes Lives*, never asked more than a few Names of his Customers, and that he made all the rest out of his own Head; you mistake, Child, said he, if you apprehend any Truths are to be delivered. So far on the contrary, if you had not been acquainted with the Name, you would not have known it to be your own History. I have seen a *Piece of his Performance*, where the Person, whose Life was written, could he have risen from the Dead again, would not have even suspected he had been aimed at, unless by the Title of the Book, which was superscribed with his Name. Well, all these Matters are strange to me, yet I can't help laughing, to think I shall see my self in a printed Book.

So much for Mrs. *Shamela*, or *Pamela*, which I have taken Pains to transcribe from the Originals, sent down by her Mother in a Rage, at the Proposal in her last Letter. The Originals themselves are in my hands, and shall be communicated to you, if you think proper to make them publick; and certainly they will have their Use. The Character of *Shamela*, will make young Gentlemen wary how they take the most fatal Step both to themselves and Families, by youthful, hasty and improper Matches; indeed, they may assure themselves, that all Such Prospects of Happiness are vain and delusive, and that they sacrifice all the solid Comforts of their Lives, to a very transient Satisfaction of a Passion, which how hot so ever it be, will be soon cooled; and when cooled, will afford them nothing but Repentance.

Can any thing be more miserable, than to be despised by the whole World, and that must certainly be the Consequence; to be despised by the Person obliged, which it is more than probable will be the Consequence, and of which, we see an Instance in *Shamela*; and lastly to despise one's self, which must be the Result of any Reflection on so weak and unworthy a Choice.

As to the Character of Parson *Williams*, I am sorry it is a true one. Indeed those who do not know him, will hardly believe it so; but what Scandal doth it throw on the Order to have one bad Member, unless they endeavour to screen and protect him? In him you see a Picture of almost every Vice exposed in nauseous and odious Colours; and if a Clergyman would ask me by what Pattern he should form himself, I would say, Be the reverse of *Williams*: So far therefore he may be of use to the Clergy themselves, and though God forbid there should be many *Williams's* amongst them, you and I are too honest to pretend, that the Body wants no Reformation.

To say the Truth, I think no greater Instance of the contrary can be given than that which appears in your Letter. The confederating to cry up a nonsensical ridiculous Book, (I believe the most extensively so of any ever yet published,) and to be so weak and so wicked as to pretend to make it a Matter of Religion; whereas so far from having any moral Tendency, the Book is by no means innocent: For,

First, There are many lascivious Images in it, very improper to be laid before the Youth of either Sex.

2dly, Young Gentlemen are here taught, that to marry their Mother's Chambermaids, and to indulge the Passion of Lust, at the Expence of Reason and Common Sense, is an Act of Religion, Virtue, and Honour; and, indeed the surest Road to Happiness.

3dly, All Chambermaids are strictly enjoyned to look out after their Masters; they are taught to use little Arts to that purpose: And lastly, are countenanced in Impertinence to their Superiors, and in betraying the Secrets of Families.

4thly, In the Character of Mrs. *Jewkes* Vice is rewarded; whence every Housekeeper may learn the Usefulness of pimping and bawding for her Master.

5thly, In Parson *Williams*, who is represented as a faultless Character, we see a busy Fellow, intermeddling with the private Affairs of his Patron, whom he is very ungratefully forward to expose and condemn on every Occasion.

Many more Objections might, if I had Time or Inclination, be made to this Book; but I apprehend, what hath been said is sufficient to persuade you of the use which may arise from publishing an Antidote to this Poison. I have therefore sent you the Copies of these Papers, and if you have Leisure to communicate them to the Press, I will transmit you the Originals, tho' I assure you, the Copies are exact.

I shall only add, that there is not the least Foundation for any thing which is said of Lady *Davers*, or any of the other Ladies; all that is merely to be imputed to the Invention of the Biographer. I have particularly enquired after Lady *Davers*, and dont hear Mr. *Booby* hath such a Relation, or that there is indeed any such Person existing. I am,

Dear Sir,
Most faithfully and respectfully,
Your humble Servant,
J. OLIVER.

Parson **TICKLETEXT** *to Parson* **OLIVER.**

Dear SIR,

I Have read over the History of *Shamela*, as it appears in those authentick Copies you favour'd me with, and am very much ashamed of the Character, which I was hastily prevailed on to give that Book. I am equally angry with the pert Jade herself, and with the Author of her Life: For I scarce know yet to whom I chiefly owe an Imposition, which hath been so general, that if Numbers could defend me from Shame, I should have no Reason to apprehend it.

As I have your implied Leave to publish, what you so kindly sent me, I shall not wait for the Originals, as you assure me the Copies are exact, and as I am really impatient to do what I think a serviceable Act of Justice to the World.

Finding by the End of her last Letter, that the little Hussy was in Town, I made it pretty much my Business to enquire after her, but with no effect hitherto: As soon as I succeed in this Enquiry, you shall hear what Discoveries I can learn. You will pardon the Shortness of this Letter, as you shall be troubled with a much longer very soon: And believe me,

Dear Sir,
Your most faithful Servant,
THO. TICKLETEXT.

P. S. Since I writ, I have a certain Account that Mr. *Booby* hath caught his Wife in bed with *Williams*; hath turned her off, and is prosecuting him in the spiritual Court.

FINIS

Four Notable Works by Jonathan Swift (Complete and Unabridged), Including: Gulliver's Travels, a Modest Proposal, a Tale of a Tub and the Battle of the Books
Jonathan Swift
Benediction Classics, 2013
456 pages
ISBN: 978-1-78139-383-3

Available from www.amazon.com, www.amazon.co.uk

Jonathan Swift was an Anglo-Irish cleric, Dean of St. Patrick's, Dublin, satirist, essayist and political pamphleteer. Enjoy these four complete and unabridged books in a single volume.

Gulliver's Travels: Gulliver travels to various previously undiscovered and fantastic worlds, enabling Swift to challenge, question, rebuke and poke fun at all manner of political, religious, social, scientific and philosophical groups, ideologies and dogma. Swift is scathing and witty, this work is one of shear caustic genius.

A Modest proposal: This essay is considered by many to be the pinnacle of satire. It was written during the poverty and population crisis in Ireland, where Swift worked as Dean in Dublin, helping the most impoverished. The rich public's only solution was to forget about the poor because they didn't matter, so Swift offered this piece in juxtaposition. He suggested that the children should be sold for food, not only would selling their children solve the poverty crisis, but as they were being eaten by the wealthy that would also solve the over-population issue! Hilarious satire at its best.

A Tale of a Tub: This is Swift's first satirical work and is a commentary on the nature of religion and mankind, as well as taking a particular swipe at authors and their pride. Not an easy read, it has layers of parody and the diversions to the main story get longer and longer until they take over the book. Swift is deliberately asking the reader to ask whether there are deeper meanings within the text or whether it is all meaningless. The plot is based on three brothers: Peter represents the Roman Catholic Church, Jack represents Protestant Churches, and Martin represents the Lutheran church.

The Battle of the Books and Other Short Pieces: More satirical fun. This book starts with a short story called "The Battle of the Books." Based on the disagreement in Swift's day as to which books were of most value - the ancient writers or the moderns, the books literally take up arms and battle each other in a hilarious parody of The Iliad.

Five Novels by Thomas Hardy - Far From The Madding Crowd, The Return of the Native, The Mayor of Casterbridge, Tess of the d'Urbervilles, Jude the Obscure (complete and unabridged)
Thomas Hardy
Benediction Classics, 2013
1114 pages
ISBN: 978-1-78139-356-7

Available from www.amazon.com, www.amazon.co.uk

Thomas Hardy, (1840 - 1928) was an English novelist and poet. He was highly critical of Victorian society and focussed mainly on the declining rural communities.

E M Forster - Collected Works, including A Room with a View, Howards End, The Longest Journey, Where Angels Fear to Tread and The Celestial Omnibus and other Stories
E M Forster
Oxford City Press, 2013
808 pages
ISBN: 978-1-78139-373-4

Available from www.amazon.com, www.amazon.co.uk

Edward Morgan Forster (1879 - 1970) is best known for his beautiful novels - ironic with delicious plots, highlighting the hypocrisy and discrimination in early 20th-century British society.

Also from Benediction Books ...

Wandering Between Two Worlds: Essays on Faith and Art

Anita Mathias

Benediction Books, 2007
152 pages
ISBN: 0955373700
Available from www.amazon.com, www.amazon.co.uk

In these wide-ranging lyrical essays, Anita Mathias writes, in lush, lovely prose, of her naughty Catholic childhood in Jamshedpur, India; her large, eccentric family in Mangalore, a sea-coast town converted by the Portuguese in the sixteenth century; her rebellion and atheism as a teenager in her Himalayan boarding school, run by German missionary nuns, St. Mary's Convent, Nainital; and her abrupt religious conversion after which she entered Mother Teresa's convent in Calcutta as a novice. Later rich, elegant essays explore the dualities of her life as a writer, mother, and Christian in the United States-- Domesticity and Art, Writing and Prayer, and the experience of being "an alien and stranger" as an immigrant in America, sensing the need for roots.

About the Author

Anita Mathias is the author of *Wandering Between Two Worlds: Essays on Faith and Art*. She has a B.A. and M.A. in English from Somerville College, Oxford University, and an M.A. in Creative Writing from the Ohio State University, USA. Anita won a National Endowment of the Arts fellowship in Creative Nonfiction in 1997. She lives in Oxford, England with her husband, Roy, and her daughters, Zoe and Irene.

Anita's website:
http://www.anitamathias.com, and
Anita's blog Dreaming Beneath the Spires:
http://dreamingbeneaththespires.blogspot.com

The Church That Had Too Much
Anita Mathias
Benediction Books, 2010
52 pages
ISBN: 9781849026567
Available from www.amazon.com, www.amazon.co.uk
The Church That Had Too Much was very well-intentioned. She wanted to love God, she wanted to love people, but she was both hampered by her muchness and the abundance of her possessions, and beset by ambition, power struggles and snobbery. Read about the surprising way The Church That Had Too Much began to resolve her problems in this deceptively simple and enchanting fable.

About the Author

Anita Mathias is the author of *Wandering Between Two Worlds: Essays on Faith and Art*. She has a B.A. and M.A. in English from Somerville College, Oxford University, and an M.A. in Creative Writing from the Ohio State University, USA. Anita won a National Endowment of the Arts fellowship in Creative Non-fiction in 1997. She lives in Oxford, England with her husband, Roy, and her daughters, Zoe and Irene.

Anita's website:
    http://www.anitamathias.com, and
Anita's blog Dreaming Beneath the Spires:
    http://dreamingbeneaththespires.blogspot.com

www.ingramcontent.com/pod-product-compliance
Lightning Source LLC
Chambersburg PA
CBHW081130300726
48982CB00005B/909

* 9 7 8 1 7 8 1 3 9 4 7 5 5 *